PENGUIN CLASSICS

# THE MAHĀBHĀRATA

JOHN D. SMITH was born in Nottingham in 1946. He attended Magdalene College, Cambridge, where he read Sanskrit and Hindi. In the early 1970s he held a research fellowship at Christ's College, Cambridge; this was followed by nine years as lecturer in Sanskrit at the School of Oriental and African Studies in the University of London. In 1984 he returned to Cambridge, where he is now emeritus Reader in Sanskrit. He has worked on both Sanskrit and modern Rajasthani, and his publications include *The Vīsaḷadevarāsa: A Restoration of the Text* (Cambridge, 1976) and *The Epic of Pābūjī: A Study, Transcription and Translation* (Cambridge, 1991).

# The Mahābhārata

*An abridged translation by* JOHN D. SMITH

PENGUIN BOOKS

PENGUIN CLASSICS

Published by the Penguin Group
Penguin Books Ltd, 80 Strand, London WC2R ORL, England
Penguin Group (USA) Inc., 375 Hudson Street, New York, New York 10014, USA
Penguin Group (Canada), 90 Eglinton Avenue East, Suite 700, Toronto, Ontario, Canada M4P 2Y3
(a division of Pearson Penguin Canada Inc.)
Penguin Ireland, 25 St Stephen's Green, Dublin 2, Ireland (a division of Penguin Books Ltd)
Penguin Group (Australia), 250 Camberwell Road, Camberwell, Victoria 3124, Australia
(a division of Pearson Australia Group Pty Ltd)
Penguin Books India Pvt Ltd, 11 Community Centre, Panchsheel Park, New Delhi – 110 017, India
Penguin Group (NZ), 67 Apollo Drive, Rosedale, North Shore 0632, New Zealand
(a division of Pearson New Zealand Ltd)
Penguin Books (South Africa) (Pty) Ltd, 24 Sturdee Avenue, Rosebank, Johannesburg 2196, South Africa

Penguin Books Ltd, Registered Offices: 80 Strand, London WC2R ORL, England

www.penguin.com

First published in Penguin Classics 2009
6



Set in 10/12.5 pt PostScript Monotype Bembo
Typeset by Rowland Phototypesetting Ltd, Bury St Edmunds, Suffolk
Printed in England by Clays Ltd, St Ives plc



ISBN: 978-0-140-44681-4

www.greenpenguin.co.uk

Mixed Sources
Product group from well-managed forests and other controlled sources
www.fsc.org Cert no. SA-COC-1592
© 1996 Forest Stewardship Council
FSC

Penguin Books is committed to a sustainable future for our business, our readers and our planet. The book in your hands is made from paper certified by the Forest Stewardship Council.

# Contents

Preface vii
Pronunciation of Sanskrit ix
Introduction xi

The Mahābhārata

1 Beginnings 1
2 The Hall 84
3 The Forest 164
4 Virāṭa 243
5 Perseverance 293
6 Bhīṣma 348
7 Droṇa 413
8 Karṇa 488
9 Śalya 526
10 The Night-raid 563
11 The Women 582
12 Tranquillity 597
13 Instruction 668
14 The Horse Sacrifice 703
15 The Hermitage 734

16 The Clubs 756

17 The Great Journey 771

18 The Ascent to Heaven 779

Variant Readings Adopted 793
Key to Names and Glossary 795
Further Reading 808
Map: The India of the *Mahābhārata* 811
Genealogical Tables 813
Index 817

# Preface

It comes as something of a shock to realize that I have been working on this translation for around one fifth of my entire life; it is also slightly shocking to realize that I have, at last, finished it. The idea of producing a Penguin Classics *Mahābhārata* was initially put to me in 1994. It took some time for me to convince myself of the wisdom of undertaking so enormous a project, to lay to rest other, smaller projects, and to carry out the necessary preparatory tasks, but by 1997 I had begun the job of rendering into English one of the longest texts mankind has ever produced. That work has continued (though not always as smoothly, or as rapidly, as I could have hoped) until now. I wish I could find some elegant epigram to express my feelings at the end of this prolonged and frankly obsessive endeavour, but in fact the most apt words are probably those spoken by Ripley in the third of the *Alien* films, as she prepares to confront the beast: 'You've been in my life so long I can't remember anything else.'

Like all true obsessives, of course, I have revelled in my obsession. The *Mahābhārata* is an endlessly intriguing work, and it has been a privilege to be allowed to explore it at the length and in the detail that even an abridged translation demands. I cannot pretend that I have found it uniformly fascinating, or that I have never become exasperated by its seeming determination to say everything that could possibly be said about every topic that presents itself (and sometimes to say it more than once); however, it has been a truly enriching experience, and I hope that readers of this volume will be able to share something of my sense of enrichment.

Luckily, I never attempted to keep a note of all the many friends and colleagues whom I have approached for help during these years, so I am absolved from attempting to thank them all by name. The translator of a Sanskrit text that tells a long and complex story, and, worse, that explicitly claims to be encyclopedic, requires a great deal of help of many different kinds. Topics on which I have sought help include the interpretation of difficult Sanskrit words and phrases, the identification of plants and animals, the movements of heavenly bodies, the harness of horses, the intricacies of early Indian ritual and theology, the manufacture of weapons, and much else besides, and I am for ever indebted to all those who put so much of their time and effort into answering my questions. I also solicited, and received, much kind assistance with the technical problems of preparing a fairly complex text in computerized form. These necessarily anonymous benefactors know who they are, and they have my heartfelt thanks for assisting me in the long and slow process of getting from there to here.

In two cases I can, and must, name individuals who have played a major role in helping me to complete this work, and to make it as accurate and as readable as possible. My friend and colleague Eivind Kahrs read every word of the entire book, pointing out idiotic typographic errors that had escaped my best efforts at vigilance, alerting me at least twice to cases where I had somehow contrived to say the exact opposite of what I meant, and making innumerable valuable suggestions on issues of interpretation, presentation and phrasing. He also more than once rescued me when I was floundering in the deep waters of Sāṃkhya thought – something which those who have been there will recognize as heroism of a very high order. Then I must also mention my wife Eleanor, who was always on hand to discuss the best way of expressing a difficult idea, to read through passages I was uncertain about and let me know if they 'worked', and generally to keep me at least moderately sane most of the time. To both of these I say: *iṣṭān puṇyakṛtāṃ lokān prāpnuyātaṃ na saṃśayaḥ.*

Pune
February 2008

# Pronunciation of Sanskrit

When written in Roman script, Sanskrit words and names require the use of accented characters to distinguish between certain sounds. Among the vowels, a macron (as in *ā*, *ī*, *ū*) indicates a long vowel: thus *a* is like the *u* in English *sun*, *ā* like the first *a* in *saga*; *i* is like the *i* in *sit*, *ī* like the *ee* in *seem*; *u* is like the *oo* in *soot*, *ū* like the *oo* in *soon*. The vowels *e* and *o* are like the vowels of English *say* and *so* (or, better, like French *é* and *ô*). The diphthongs *ai* and *au* are like the vowels of English *sight* and *sound*. Sanskrit *ṛ* is a vowel, nowadays pronounced in North India as *ri*, further south as *ru*; most Westerners use the North Indian pronunciation, hence *Kṛṣṇa* represents 'Krishna', though in most of peninsular India the name is in fact pronounced 'Krushna'.

Among the consonants, dots below the letters *t*, *d*, *n* and *s* indicate retroflexion: in India these sounds are pronounced with the tongue curled slightly upwards. Few Westerners are able to achieve this convincingly, and for them it is probably best to ignore the dots below *ṭ*, *ḍ* and *ṇ*; however, as in *Kṛṣṇa*, *ṣ* should be pronounced like the *sh* of *ship*, not the *s* of *sip*. An acute accent on an *s* (*ś*) represents a second, slightly different (non-retroflex) *sh*-sound. A dotted *m* (*ṃ*) represents Sanskrit *anusvāra*, a general-purpose nasal which may be pronounced as *m* before labial sounds such as *p*, *b*, *m*, *v*, and as *n* elsewhere. Other accents, such as the dot in *ṅ*, can be safely ignored by the general reader.

Among unaccented characters, note that *c* is always pronounced like the *ch* of English *chip*. The letter *h* is used in combination with many consonants to indicate aspiration; this is another feature that few Westerners can master (the Sanskrit consonant *gh* is *not* like the sequence found in English *hog-house*), and they should probably ignore the *h* in *kh*, *gh*, *ch*, *jh*, *ṭh*, *ḍh*, *th*, *dh*, *ph* and *bh*. Thus *th* and *ph* are not pronounced as in English *thin* and *phone*, but are similar to *t* and *p*.

# Introduction

## THE *MAHĀBHĀRATA*

By the middle of the first millennium BC, the northern part of the Indian subcontinent had largely fallen under the political control of a people who had spread widely over the region from the West, and who were now well advanced in the process of establishing kingdoms centred round major towns. As they spread they carried their language (Sanskrit) and their distinctive culture with them. This was a culture that had already produced a substantial corpus of texts embodying the religion that lay at its core. The Vedas, some parts of which were even then extremely ancient,[1] consisted of large collections of hymns and chants for use in the elaborate rituals with which Brahmin priests sought to maintain order in the kingdom and the cosmos, together with manuals of exegetical and speculative interpretation. Even today these works exude a sense of timelessness: they present a world-view that is self-complete, sophisticated and apparently not subject to change. In reality, however, change of many kinds was already under way, and new world-views were being developed. This was the milieu from which the *Mahābhārata* emerged.

It was, in fact, a period of extraordinary intellectual turbulence, fuelled, no doubt, by dissatisfaction with the idea that Brahmin mediation and Brahmin ritual provided the only ways to religious fulfilment. Major heterodox teachers of the day included Mahāvīra, whose followers today constitute one of the major religions of India

1 The earliest hymns of the Ṛgveda are usually dated to around 1200 BC or even earlier.

(Jainism), and his near contemporary Gautama, founder of one of the major religions of the world (Buddhism). But in addition to these giant figures, it is clear that there were also numerous other dissenters offering a variety of different visions, all of them wholly incompatible with traditional brahmanical teaching. The old order was definitely under threat.

However, the seeming changelessness of Brahmanism was more apparent than real. Already in the later Vedic texts there is a clear shift of emphasis. Esoteric knowledge, which had always been valued, came increasingly to be placed on a par with ritual performance. Religious merit could now be acquired through a life of ascetic renunciation as well as through the undertaking of costly sacrifices. True wisdom now consisted of an understanding of the essential oneness of the human self with everything else in the universe.

Some of these concerns figure prominently in the *Mahābhārata* also; but this was a work very different in kind from anything in the Vedic corpus that had preceded it. To start with, it was not a collection of hymns or an exegetical manual, but a story. The earlier texts had contained numerous briefly told mythological tales, but nothing on the scale of even the shortest imaginable version of the tale of the great war of the Bhāratas.

Second, unlike practically everything that had gone before it, the *Mahābhārata* was not in origin a Brahmin text. The society in which it made its appearance was divided into a hierarchy of four classes, defined by the social roles that members of each class were supposed to play. Below the Brahmin priests and scholars came in turn the Kṣatriyas, who were the designated warriors and rulers, the Vaiśyas, who acted as farmers and merchants, and the Śūdras, whose lot it was to serve the three higher classes. The existence of other social groups was acknowledged: the Sūtas, for example, were charioteers and bards, and are referred to many times in the great tale. However, such groups were explained as springing from the union of people belonging to different primary classes (the Sūtas were said to be the result of the union of a Kṣatriya man with a Brahmin woman).

The *Mahābhārata*, though said to have been narrated by a Sūta who had learnt it from Brahmins, was in fact very much a Kṣatriya text.

Not merely were Kṣatriyas the principal characters in the story it told, but in addition the issues on which it focused were characteristically Kṣatriya issues. Prominent among these was the problem of violence. If doing violence is wrong, leading to bad *karma* and thus more (and worse) rebirths, how is a Kṣatriya to behave, given that – whether as warrior in battle or as punishment-inflicting ruler – doing violence is his role in life? This is a theme to which we shall return, and to which the *Mahābhārata* itself returns again and again, most famously in the section known as *Bhagavadgītā*, the sermon preached by Kṛṣṇa to Arjuna before the start of the great war.

As a large-scale narrative recounting the deeds of warrior heroes, the *Mahābhārata* may appear at first glance to be a martial epic of the sort familiar to Western readers from the *Iliad* and other heroic tales. This is not at all an unreasonable comparison. The story told in the *Mahābhārata* does bear similarities, both large-scale and small-scale, to other epic narratives. The style of the text is reminiscent of other works thought to have originated as orally composed bardic epics. The entire narration is actually said to have come from the lips of a Sūta bard. Even the division of the text into eighteen books (*parvans*) has a certain familiarity, though the *Mahābhārata* in fact subdivides these into relatively short chapters (*adhyāyas*).

However, to think of the *Mahābhārata* as merely one more heroic epic would be a serious over-simplification, for it became much more than that. The story that lies at its core came to be overlaid by numerous additions in the form of narrative digressions, substories and protracted sermons. In the process the character of the work underwent a significant change: the bardic Kṣatriya epic whose early existence we can deduce (but about whose circumstances of performance we can only guess) ended up by becoming a gigantic compendium of chiefly brahmanical lore and a key text in the early development of the Hindu religion.[1]

Nowadays most Hindus would probably identify the *Bhagavadgītā* (the name is often shortened to just *Gītā*) as their most inspirational

1 The ways in which this probably came about are discussed in greater detail below: see pp. lxv–lxvii.

scripture: its popularity was greatly enhanced by Mahatma Gandhi, who studied it devotedly and even published a translation of it, partly composed during one of his periods of imprisonment by the British in Yerawada Gaol, Poona (Pune). The *Mahābhārata* as a whole, however, has fared less consistently well in the land of its creation. This is mainly due to its extraordinarily bloody narrative, and the unmistakable pessimism that underlies it. Not many popular novels boast 1,660,020,000 deaths (see 11.26), and fewer still attribute the slaughter to the will of the gods (see for example 1.58–9). There is also a regional slant: the *Mahābhārata* has largely retained its standing in South India, while in most of the North the parallel story, that of Rāma,[1] has far outstripped it in popularity. Common throughout large parts of India is a superstition that reading the *Mahābhārata* (or at least reading *all* of it) brings misfortune; and the very name of the text is often used in Indian languages to refer to any particularly fierce or unpleasant conflict.

Yet for all people's ambivalence towards the *Mahābhārata*, there can be no mistaking its status even in the rapidly changing India of the late twentieth and twenty-first centuries. It would be hard to find a Hindu who did not know at least the broad outline of the story and the personalities of the chief heroes; well-loved portions of the narrative regularly form the basis for plays and films; more modern retellings have also often appeared, for instance in the form of comic strips. Proof of its enduring hold on the Indian imagination, if any were needed, came in the 1980s when Doordarshan, the Indian state television service, screened a 94-episode serialization of the tale. Not merely was this watched by record numbers of viewers (it later became something of a cult hit in the UK also), but it also saw the very medium of television transformed into something new. The serial brought the gods themselves into viewers' homes, and they responded accordingly, burning incense sticks and sprinkling water before their television sets as they would have done in front of any more traditional shrine; in households all over the land, men and women, young and old, masters

1 See John and Mary Brockington (trans.), *Rāma the Steadfast: An Early Form of the Rāmāyaṇa* (London: Penguin Books, 2006).

and servants joined together to watch the great story unfold with literal devotion.

## THE STORY

In very brief summary, the story told in the *Mahābhārata* is as follows:

(Book I) Bhīṣma, rightful heir to the Kuru throne of central North India, stands aside and swears eternal celibacy to enable his father Śaṃtanu to marry Satyavatī, whose father insists that the kingdom must pass to her heirs. However, the sons born from this marriage in fact die childless, so the seer Vyāsa fathers a son on each of the two widows. Dhṛtarāṣṭra is the elder, but cannot become king because he is born blind. In due course his wife Gāndhārī bears him a hundred sons; these are demons in human form. Dhṛtarāṣṭra's younger brother Pāṇḍu cannot father children because of a curse, but his wife Kuntī is able to give him three sons who are actually fathered by, and are incarnate forms of, various gods; she also helps her co-wife Mādrī to bear two further sons in the same way. The stage is now set for the eternal battle between gods and demons to be played out as a human conflict between the two sets of cousins, the hundred sons of Dhṛtarāṣṭra (Dhārtarāṣṭras or Kauravas) led by the wicked Duryodhana, and the five sons of Pāṇḍu (Pāṇḍavas): the righteous Yudhiṣṭhira, the aggressive Bhīma, the mighty warrior Arjuna and the twins Nakula and Sahadeva.

Before giving birth to the Pāṇḍavas, Kuntī had also secretly borne another divinely fathered boy named Karṇa, who had been brought up by a Sūta and his wife as their adopted son. Like the Kaurava and Pāṇḍava princes, Karṇa has been taught arms by the warrior Brahmin Droṇa. When Duryodhana first encounters him, he is delighted to find a man capable of matching the hated Arjuna's marvellous martial skills, and secures his loyalty for ever by awarding him a kingship. He then plots to murder the five Pāṇḍavas by having them burnt alive, but they escape; not long afterwards all five of them jointly marry the princess Draupadī. Dhṛtarāṣṭra attempts to keep the peace by dividing the kingdom: his son Duryodhana will rule from the city of Hāstinapura, while Pāṇḍu's son Yudhiṣṭhira will be king in Indraprastha.

(Book 2) Some time later, Yudhiṣṭhira performs the magnificent imperial ritual of the royal consecration. Duryodhana, enraged with jealousy, determines to ruin him and his brothers. With the help of his mother's brother Śakuni he engages Yudhiṣṭhira in a rigged dicing game in which he is systematically cheated out of all his wealth and finally his own liberty and that of his brothers and Draupadī. However, Dhṛtarāṣṭra restores to them everything they have lost. At this, Duryodhana demands a second match, to consist of a single throw for a single stake: the losers will have to live in exile in the forest for twelve years and then pass a thirteenth year incognito, with the penalty of a further twelve years in the forest if they are recognized. Yudhiṣṭhira duly loses, and the five brothers and Draupadī set off for the forest.

(Book 3) Years pass as the Pāṇḍavas live out their term of forest exile. The god Indra, Arjuna's real father, disguises himself as a mendicant Brahmin and demands from Karṇa that he give him the earrings and armour with which he had been born, and thus deprive himself of his innate invulnerability against the Pāṇḍavas. Karṇa agrees, but secures from Indra in return a wonderful Spear that will unfailingly kill one mighty enemy in battle.

(Book 4) After completing twelve years in the forest, the Pāṇḍavas now take up various disguises in order to pass the final thirteenth year incognito in the court of King Virāṭa. During this time Draupadī has to endure an attempt at rape by Kīcaka, the commander of the army; he is killed by Bhīma. As the year draws to its close Virāṭa is attacked by Duryodhana and his men; Arjuna, still in his disguise as a eunuch, overcomes them single-handed. The stipulated term of exile ends, and now Arjuna's young son Abhimanyu marries Virāṭa's daughter Uttarā.

(Book 5) The Pāṇḍavas know well that Duryodhana is unlikely to return their half of the kingdom to them. As war between the two sets of cousins comes to seem inevitable, Kṛṣṇa, Vṛṣṇi prince and incarnation of the great god Viṣṇu, announces that he will put his fighting men at Duryodhana's disposal, but that he himself will act as Arjuna's charioteer. Various ambassadors shuttle between the Kauravas and the Pāṇḍavas, and various consultations take place, but Duryodhana is adamant that he will not return a single foot of land to his enemies. Karṇa, who has fallen out with Bhīṣma, vows not to fight as long as

Bhīṣma lives; Kṛṣṇa attempts to persuade him to switch to the Pāṇḍava side, but he refuses. Duryodhana appoints Bhīṣma as his commander; Yudhiṣṭhira likewise appoints Draupadī's brother Dhṛṣṭadyumna.

(Book 6) Before the start of the battle at Kurukṣetra, Arjuna lays down his weapons in despair at the prospect of fighting and killing his kin and his revered elders, and Kṛṣṇa preaches the *Bhagavadgītā* to him. The fighting then begins, and continues for nine bloody days; on the tenth day Arjuna succeeds in killing Bhīṣma. The latter, however, defers the day of his actual death, and remains lying on a bed of arrows throughout the rest of the battle.

(Book 7) Karṇa now prepares to join the fighting. Duryodhana appoints Droṇa to replace Bhīṣma as commander, and the battle resumes. On the thirteenth day Abhimanyu is killed by a group of enemies against whom he has valiantly fought single-handed. The following day, Bhīma's son Ghaṭotkaca is killed by Karṇa, using the Spear he had hoped to reserve for Arjuna. On the fifteenth day the Pāṇḍavas secure the death of Droṇa by means of a devious stratagem.

(Book 8) Karṇa is now appointed as Duryodhana's commander, but on the seventeenth day he is killed by Arjuna. (Book 9) During the eighteenth day the Madra king Śalya acts as commander, before he too dies at Yudhiṣṭhira's hands. Duryodhana's remaining warriors are slaughtered, and he himself takes refuge in a lake. When he is discovered, it is agreed that he will fight a duel with clubs against Bhīma; Bhīma kills him by smashing his thighs with a low blow.

(Book 10) Only three supporters of the Kaurava faction survive. One of them, Droṇa's son Aśvatthāman, dedicates himself to the great god Śiva, penetrates the Pāṇḍava camp at night and massacres everyone in it as they sleep. Pursued and cornered, he releases a powerful weapon that will devastate Pāṇḍava wombs.

(Book 11) The killing is over, and the women mourn the dead. Kuntī reveals to her Pāṇḍava sons that their hated enemy Karṇa was in fact their eldest brother. Yudhiṣṭhira is stunned with grief at this news.

(Book 12) Yudhiṣṭhira re-enters Hāstinapura to assume kingship over the undivided Kurus. He is then taken by Kṛṣṇa to hear a lengthy sermon from Bhīṣma, still lying on his bed of arrows. (Book 13) After completing this sermon, Bhīṣma is at last taken up into heaven.

(Book 14) Thanks to the weapon released by Aśvatthāman, Uttarā, widow of Abhimanyu, gives birth to a stillborn child, Parikṣit, but Kṛṣṇa revives him and thus restores the Kuru lineage. Yudhiṣṭhira performs the great royal horse sacrifice. (Book 15) Dhṛtarāṣṭra, Gāndhārī and Kuntī all retire to a forest hermitage.

(Book 16) The Kurus' Vṛṣṇi allies kill one another in the course of a drunken quarrel, and Kṛṣṇa himself is killed by a hunter named Jarā ('Old Age'). (Book 17) The Pāṇḍavas now resolve to depart from the world. They set out to travel round the entire earth, but as they pass through the great mountains of the North they fall down dead one after another. Only Yudhiṣṭhira remains; he is taken directly to heaven. (Book 18) Here he discovers Duryodhana living in majesty, while his own brothers and kin languish in a grim hell; he resolves that he will remain in hell with them. At this, all signs of hell vanish, and Yudhiṣṭhira learns that he has passed the final test. All the Pāṇḍavas and their allies are now revealed in their rightful places in heaven.

## *DHARMA*

At its simplest, the *Mahābhārata* is thus about the conflict between two sets of cousins: it describes the events that led to war, the eighteen-day war itself, and the long aftermath. But if pressed for a one-word answer as to what the *Mahābhārata* is 'about' at a deeper level, most people would probably reply that it is about *dharma*.

*Dharma* is not a concept that answers directly, or even approximately, to any English term, which is why it has gone untranslated in this book. 'Law', 'duty', 'virtue', 'morality', even 'lot in life', all come moderately close, but none comes close enough. A person's *dharma* is what it is right for that person to do, but one person's *dharma* is different from another's. It may be wrong for you to have sex, but right for me; it may be right for you to take up a life of asceticism in the forest, but wrong for me. A range of factors combines to determine what constitutes *dharma* for any given individual.

To start with, there is the class to which that individual belongs. This is crucial: *dharma* is above all defined in terms of social groupings.

A Brahmin should study the sacred Vedas, but it would be utterly wrong, would be *adharma*, for a Śūdra to do so. The Kṣatriya *dharma* includes fighting, ruling and punishing wrongdoers; the Vaiśya *dharma* excludes these. Only by performing one's own *dharma* can one hope to improve one's station in life at the next rebirth. At *Mahābhārata* 3.198–206 the Brahmin Kauśika is taught a lesson in *dharma* by a wise hunter, whose present degraded status handling slaughtered animals was brought about by a misdeed in a former birth. Kauśika deplores the 'dreadful work' that the hunter does, but the hunter corrects him: it is his *dharma*, and only by performing it properly can he hope to better himself in subsequent births.[1]

In addition to class, however, a person's *dharma* is also affected by his current role in life, something that will change as time passes. What probably started as a set of recognized legitimate roles came to be codified into a sequence of prescribed stages of life, which are said (e.g. at 12.62) to be compulsory for Brahmins, but also open to the other three major classes. In the standard version, there are four stages, which one is expected to pass through in turn. First, a young man should be a student, studying the Vedas – if he is of an appropriate class to do so – and the skills he will need for his life's work (for example, a young Kṣatriya would be likely to study weaponry and martial arts, as the Kaurava and Pāṇḍava princes do at 1.122). Next, in the second stage, he should marry and live as a householder. When his children are grown and independent, he and his wife should retire to the forest to live a holy life: this is the third stage. In the fourth and last stage, he should renounce all worldly things and take up asceticism, living entirely on alms. Naturally, the *dharma* of the same individual differs from one stage of life to the next. As a student, part of his *dharma* is celibacy; as a householder he should beget children. To take up the forest life in the third stage is *dharma*; to do so in the second stage when one has a family to support would be *adharma*.

Finally, *dharma* is not rigid: it may change with external circumstance.

1 It may be worth adding a modern illustration of the same theme. I was once talking to a Hindu villager from the Indian state of Rajasthan when the conversation turned to prostitution. Out of curiosity I asked him what might be the *dharma* of a prostitute; with no hesitation at all, he replied, 'To corrupt and destroy young men.'

The *Mahābhārata* devotes thirty-nine chapters (12.129–67) to '*dharma* in times of trouble', and the topic is touched on at many other points too. Thus at 12.283 we are told that a Brahmin in need may follow the *dharma* of a Kṣatriya or Vaiśya, though the line is drawn at the slave-like status of the Śūdra; and at 12.139 we even learn that the Brahmin seer Viśvāmitra, starving, considered it no breach of *dharma* to steal a piece of dog-meat from a man of the severely degraded Caṇḍāla class.

So *dharma* is not a simple thing; indeed, the *Mahābhārata* repeatedly insists how 'subtle' (*sūkṣma*) it is. This subtlety offers storytellers great opportunities for the development of narratives focusing on personal or existential dilemmas, for situations can arise – or be imagined – in which the demands of a person's *dharma* seem to be mutually contradictory. A simple case is that of the wise hunter mentioned above: killing and butchering animals is condemned in general terms as a violation of *dharma* (see for example 13.115–17), and yet it may be the *dharma* of one's particular class to kill and to butcher. The hunter is apparently at peace with himself, certain that in his case the specific requirement overrides the general one; but things are not so easy for the heroes of the *Mahābhārata*, who find themselves required to kill not animals but humans, and not just any humans but their own close kin and revered elders. The great Pāṇḍava warrior Arjuna famously throws down his weapon as the war at Kurukṣetra is about to begin, and appeals to his charioteer – who happens to be Kṛṣṇa, lord of all creation – for guidance in the impossibly conflicted situation in which he finds himself; it is this appeal that prompts Kṛṣṇa to deliver his celebrated sermon the *Bhagavadgītā*, referred to above.

Yet it is not principally Arjuna whose inner conflict is highlighted in the *Mahābhārata*, but rather his eldest brother Yudhiṣṭhira, for whilst Arjuna may be a Kṣatriya prince and warrior, Yudhiṣṭhira is the king, and the *dharma* of kings is so inherently conflicted that almost a quarter of the *Mahābhārata*'s other great sermon, that delivered chiefly by Bhīṣma on his deathbed, is devoted to expounding it (12.1–128). Here we learn variously that the king's highest *dharma* is to punish wrongdoers (12.70), to protect his subjects (12.72), or to endure both victory and defeat (12.107); elsewhere the highest *dharma* in more general terms is said to be restraint of the senses (12.242), kindness (13.59), lack of greed (13.95), or non-violence (13.115, 14.48–9). However, Bhīṣma also warns Yudhiṣṭhira that the king who pursues his own highest *dharma* commits *adharma* (12.91), for it is his subjects' interests, not his own, that are paramount. Yudhiṣṭhira is constantly torn between a somewhat Brahmin-like inclination towards non-violence and renunciation on the one hand, and the necessarily violent exercise of his Kṣatriya kingship on the other. It is not easy to be a hero in the world of the *Mahābhārata*, for, like *dharma* itself, heroism is not a simple thing.

## HEROES AND VILLAINS

The *Mahābhārata* is famous for its sheer size. It is traditionally said to contain 100,000 verses (most verses consist of two lines each), and this is approximately correct for the traditional 'vulgate' version, the so-called Bombay edition published with Nīlakaṇṭha's commentary. Even the radically pared-down critical edition published in Poona between 1933 and 1966 (on which this translation is based) retains 67,314 verses considered to be authentic. A narrative on such a scale, especially one centred round a war involving the entire known world of the day, inevitably boasts a large cast of characters; thus, to add one more statistic, S. Sörensen's *An Index to the Names in the Mahabharata*[1] runs to 807 two-column pages.

Of the vast number of people who appear at one point or another in this huge text, some are background figures from earlier times whose deeds or sayings are cited to illustrate a particular point; others have nothing to do with the main narrative, figuring rather in substories told during the course of that narrative; yet others are mentioned by name once or twice only, and beyond their names we know nothing at all about them. None the less, there are a substantial number of major characters in the *Mahābhārata*. Some are heroes, some villains; some are heroes who have chosen, or whose situation compels them,

1 Reprinted Delhi: Motilal Banarsidass, 1978.

to side with the villains; some are bellicose, others pacific; most are brave, a few less so. Many of the most central characters are complex, and all are strongly drawn. Each of them incorporates certain characteristics – sometimes in quite striking combinations – and each of them speaks and acts in ways that leave one in no doubt about what those characteristics are. Inconsistencies are rare; when they do occur, as when the normally pugnacious Bhīma argues for peace at 5.72, it may be not merely the reader but other characters in the narrative who are surprised.

Everyone who plays a significant role in the story is either a member of, or closely connected with, the Kuru dynasty that is said to have ruled over a substantial tract of north-west India in an antiquity so remote that it was actually part of a different age of the world (*yuga*).[1] The oldest character to be depicted in detail is Bhīṣma, born two generations before the heroes whose conflict is the *Mahābhārata*'s central theme. In a text rich in very strange lives, Bhīṣma's is one of the strangest lives of all those described. He is the 'revered grandfather' of both sets of warring cousins, but biologically he is no one's grandfather and no one's father, for the defining act of his life is to renounce his right to the kingship and to vow eternal celibacy;[2] he does this to permit his father Śaṃtanu to wed Satyavatī, a girl with whom he has become infatuated. Despite this vow, he then has to act as regent and surrogate father for two generations of Kurus. When the princes who revere him as grandfather – the Pāṇḍava heroes and Kaurava villains – are fully grown, he remains prominent as a highly respected elder, but circumstance makes him a member of the Kaurava court of Duryodhana, not that of the Pāṇḍava king Yudhiṣṭhira; therefore, when war comes, he is appointed as Duryodhana's first commander.[3] In this role he fights with great fierceness for ten days, before allowing himself to be mortally wounded by Arjuna (6.114). But now comes yet another phase in Bhīṣma's extraordinary life. He takes advantage of a boon

**1** See 3.186 ff. The events of the *Mahābhārata* marked the transition from the Dvāpara to the Kali Age.

**2** 1.94. It is this vow that earns him the name Bhīṣma, 'The awesome one'.

**3** 5.153. There is no chronological discrepancy here: in former ages, the human lifespan was much longer than is now the case.

from his father enabling him to choose the hour of his own death, and remains lying on a bed of arrows until and beyond the end of the great battle. He is then appointed by Kṛṣṇa to instruct Yudhiṣṭhira on *dharma*, which he does at enormous length: the two books of the *Mahābhārata* containing his great deathbed sermon[1] add up to over a quarter of the complete text. Finally (13.154) this towering figure – a man who has borne massive responsibilities, but all of whose life has been lived on behalf of others, whether as son, regent, counsellor, military commander or preacher – permits his life to come to an end.

Before marrying Śaṃtanu, Satyavatī had already had a child by the seer Parāśara. Kṛṣṇa Dvaipāyana Vyāsa is an even stranger figure than Bhīṣma, though in his case the strangeness has more of the mysterious about it. We know very little about the course of his life, but he appears in the *Mahābhārata* narrative from time to time, most crucially to father children on the childless widows of Śaṃtanu's son Vicitravīrya, and thus to allow the Kuru line to continue (1.100). His subsequent appearances are mainly brief: he often arrives, gives counsel or grants a boon, and then leaves again. Sometimes, though, he intervenes more directly. He endows Saṃjaya with the divine sight that will allow him to relate the entire course of the war to the blind Dhṛtarāṣṭra (6.2), he oversees Yudhiṣṭhira's great horse sacrifice in Book 14, and he grants the survivors of the war a vision of the fallen warriors (15.36–41). But he also has a quite different, unique role in the *Mahābhārata*: he is its author. Having composed the great tale of the Bhāratas, he taught it to his pupil Vaiśaṃpāyana, who narrated it at Janamejaya's snake sacrifice (1.54–5). Our *Mahābhārata* is that narration as retold by the Sūta Ugraśravas to the holy seers in the Naimiṣa forest (1.1, 1.53).

The generation after Bhīṣma and Vyāsa is that of Vyāsa's biological sons Pāṇḍu, father of the Pāṇḍavas, and Dhṛtarāṣṭra, father of the Kauravas.[2] However, Pāṇḍu dies too early to make much of an impression, and his second wife, Mādrī, follows him into death. Pāṇḍu's first wife Kuntī, by contrast, lives on through all the events of the narrative.

**1** Books 12 and 13, 'Tranquillity' and 'Instruction'.

**2** Or Dhārtarāṣṭras. Strictly speaking, the name Kaurava, which means 'descendant of Kuru', 'member of the Kuru lineage', applies equally to the sons of Pāṇḍu, but in practice it tends to be reserved for Dhṛtarāṣṭra's sons.

She appears first as a naive young girl who inadvertently finds herself giving birth to Karṇa, son of the Sun (1.104), but her role for the greater part of the story is to grieve for the woes that have overwhelmed her family, and in particular for Karṇa, unacknowledged by her as her son until too late (11.27).

Dhṛtarāṣṭra, like Kuntī, survives until long after the war. Born blind, he cannot be king, but he becomes the father of a hundred sons by his wife Gāndhārī. The eldest of these, Duryodhana, is the cause of all the terrible events that threaten to end the entire Kuru lineage, and Dhṛtarāṣṭra is advised again and again to rein him in or even to renounce or kill him. Always his love for his son outweighs every other consideration, and, after perhaps making a vain attempt at persuasion, he always allows Duryodhana to have his way. When Saṃjaya describes the course of the ongoing war to him, he very frequently interrupts to blame fate for the terrible turn that events have taken; almost always, Saṃjaya retorts that the fault is all Dhṛtarāṣṭra's own. Given his clear weakness of judgement, it is striking that three of the epithets most commonly applied to him emphasize the reverse quality: he is called *dhīmat* or *manīṣin*, 'wise', or is said to be *prajñācakṣus*, 'he who sees through his wisdom'. In the aftermath of the war he lives with Yudhiṣṭhira, who treats him with the highest respect and honour, but after fifteen years have passed he reveals that he remains consumed with guilt for having permitted Duryodhana to cause so much destruction, and leaves to take up a holy life in the forest (15.5 ff.). He is accompanied by Kuntī and by his wife Gāndhārī.

Gāndhārī herself is a somewhat stronger figure. She generally takes a more robust line with her errant son, though her efforts to dissuade him from the evil he is plotting are fruitless. Like Bhīṣma and his awesome vow of renunciation and celibacy, as a young bride she makes a dramatically powerful undertaking: discovering that Dhṛtarāṣṭra is blind, she blindfolds herself in perpetuity, determined not to enjoy any advantage over her husband (1.103.12–13). A hint of her inner power[1] comes after the end of the war, when, full of grief and rage, she summons Yudhiṣṭhira. He falls at her feet; her eye falls on his fingertips,

1 And, perhaps, the power of a sense organ denied sensory input for a long period.

visible through the bottom edge of her blindfold, and the nails are scorched (11.15.1–8). The same inner power later allows her to pronounce a curse on Kṛṣṇa, something few mortals would be able to do (11.25).

As well as Dhṛtarāṣṭra and Pāṇḍu, Vyāsa fathers a third son, Vidura. Vidura is not in the direct line of descent, and so cannot become king of the Kurus, but his father grants the blessing that 'he will be righteous, foremost of all the world's wise men' (1.100.26). So he proves to be, constantly giving Dhṛtarāṣṭra excellent advice on which Dhṛtarāṣṭra almost never acts.

Another major figure from this same generation is Droṇa. Aside from his typically bizarre birth (1.121) and the fact that he quarrelled with his friend Drupada (1.122) we know very little about him: why this Brahmin has followed – indeed, excelled at – the Kṣatriya *dharma* of martial arts is unexplained. He has a ruthlessness in pursuing his aims that will be inherited by his son Aśvatthāman. When a Niṣāda prince named Ekalavya outshines his favourite pupil Arjuna as an archer, he demands that Ekalavya sever his right thumb (1.123) to restore Arjuna's supremacy, and it transpires that his chief purpose in training the Kaurava and Pāṇḍava princes in arms is so that they can take vengeance on Drupada on his behalf (1.128). Like Bhīṣma, he is an elder in Duryodhana's court, where he argues in vain for peace. When war comes he is therefore committed to fighting on Duryodhana's behalf, and on Bhīṣma's fall he is appointed as the second Kaurava commander (7.5). He then fights with fury for four more days until he is killed by means of a particularly unpleasant stratagem (7.164–5).

The next generation is that of the Pāṇḍava heroes and Kaurava villains themselves, the two sets of mutually hostile cousins whose dispute will end on the battlefield at Kurukṣetra. As will already have become clear, to refer to the Kauravas as 'villains' is really a gross simplification (though a convenient one): some of those who fight on Duryodhana's side are respected elders, and many others are entirely blameless. But Duryodhana himself is truly villainous, and there is nothing petty about his villainy. From childhood on he hates the Pāṇḍavas with a pure and consistent hatred; he is consumed with jealousy and resentment at their every success. Even as a youth he makes several attempts to murder Bhīma (1.119), and his delight at encountering Karṇa, the one person who can match Arjuna's feats, knows no bounds: to secure his loyalty he awards him a kingship on the spot (1.126–7). Immediately after this he plots unsuccessfully to burn all five Pāṇḍavas and their mother Kuntī alive (1.129–36). Anxious for peace, Dhṛtarāṣṭra proposes a division of the kingdom, which the Pāṇḍavas accept, but when Yudhiṣṭhira performs the great sacrificial rite of the royal consecration, in effect declaring himself emperor, Duryodhana is once again overwhelmed with resentment. With Śakuni's help he stages a rigged gambling match to ruin and enslave his enemies (2.53–8), and when they are released by Dhṛtarāṣṭra he insists on a second match to send them into years of exile (2.67). When they finally return, he refuses to honour the original wager and return their kingdom to them, and he remains obstinately impervious to all arguments for a peaceful settlement, making a war of annihilation inevitable.

But, wicked though he may be, Duryodhana is regally, even majestically wicked, a man without self-delusion, who knows that he is ruled by ambition and desire, and sees nothing shameful in it: 'I have seen Pāṇḍu's son enjoying such dazzling fortune, and I burn with resentment, for I am unused to such sights. I shall enter fire, or swallow poison, or drown myself, for I cannot live so! What man of mettle in this world could bear to see his rivals prosper and himself fail?' (2.43.26–8). His dying *apologia pro vita sua* is worth citing in full:

> I have studied, I have given gifts in the proper manner, I have ruled the earth with all her oceans, I have stood over the heads of my enemies. Who is more blessed than me? The death that is desired by all who call themselves Kṣatriyas and abide by their *dharma*, that death I have now attained. Who is more blessed than me? I have experienced human pleasures worthy of the gods, beyond the reach of other kings, and I have known supreme sovereignty. Who is more blessed than me? Invincible one, I am to go with my friends and my followers to heaven. All of you shall remain here grieving, your purposes frustrated! (9.60.47–50)

Of Dhṛtarāṣṭra's other sons, few merit any comment, for few have distinct personalities. One who does is the second in seniority,

Duḥśāsana. Though lacking Duryodhana's grandeur, he could be said to go some way in compensating for it through sheer nastiness. In the gambling match, Duryodhana may insult the Pāṇḍavas' joint wife Draupadī by exposing his thigh to her (2.63.10–12), but it is left to Duḥśāsana to drag her by her hair and to endeavour to strip her naked in public (2.60.22–5, 2.61.40–41, 2.61.82). Similarly, it is Duḥśāsana who gloatingly jeers at the Pāṇḍavas after their second defeat at dicing (2.68.2–14).

Vikarṇa also stands out among the Kaurava brothers, but for a different reason: he consistently argues in favour of reconciliation and peace, thus earning Duryodhana's contempt. Yuyutsu too distinguishes himself. He is the only man to take up Yudhiṣṭhira's invitation to change sides just before the fighting at Kurukṣetra commences (6.41.89–94); but Yuyutsu is only half-brother to Duryodhana, being Dhṛtarāṣṭra's son by a Vaiśya woman. Neither of these two is strongly characterized.

Duryodhana has many other allies besides his own brothers. Important among these is Śakuni, king of Gāndhāra and brother of Duryodhana's mother Gāndhārī. It is Śakuni to whom Duryodhana expresses his furious resentment of Yudhiṣṭhira's new imperial status (2.43), and it is Śakuni who proposes gambling as a way of ruining Yudhiṣṭhira (2.44). When the match gets under way it is Śakuni whom Duryodhana nominates to play on his behalf (2.53.15). Śakuni is a gambling trickster, the ancient Indian equivalent of a modern card-sharp, and through his trickery he easily defeats the innocent Yudhiṣṭhira in two successive matches (2.53–8, 2.67). He is also able to deploy his illusory skills on the field of battle (7.29). But Śakuni is no mere sleight-of-hand virtuoso. Along with Karṇa he is one of Duryodhana's most trusted advisers, and thus he is co-author of the catastrophe of Kurukṣetra.

Droṇa's son Aśvatthāman is another close ally of Duryodhana. Like his father he is a moderate, repeatedly urging reconciliation and peace; like his father, when war comes anyway, he fights vigorously for Duryodhana. Thus far, there is little to distinguish him from various other Kaurava supporters – Bāhlika, say, or Kṛpa – who act similarly. But on the fifteenth day of fighting something happens that changes him completely: his father Droṇa is killed by means of a deception

(7.164–5), an act of deliberate *adharma* on the part of the highest-ranking Pāṇḍavas. From now on Aśvatthāman's one thought is vengeance, and he fights with renewed ferocity, making free use of powerful celestial weapons and concentrating his attacks on the man who actually wielded the sword, Dhṛṣṭadyumna (7.166–72, 8.41–2). Later, one of only three on the Kaurava side to survive the great battle, he offers himself up to the god Śiva, who enters his body. With this divine protection, he penetrates the Pāṇḍava camp at night and systematically massacres everyone in it as they sleep (10.8). For Dhṛṣṭadyumna and two other Pāñcāla princes, the brothers Uttamaujas and Yudhāmanyu, he reserves a non-military death, killing them like the victims at an animal sacrifice in order to deny them access to the warriors' heaven. When the Pāṇḍavas catch up with him, he is cursed by Kṛṣṇa to live in solitude and sickness for three thousand years (10.16.10–12).

Without question, Duryodhana's most loyal and devoted supporter is Karṇa, the son of the Sun by Kuntī. The bond between the two men is perhaps the strongest of any in the whole *Mahābhārata*; the only competitor would be that between Kṛṣṇa and Arjuna. Duryodhana *needs* Karṇa because he is the only person who can challenge the might of the Pāṇḍavas in general and Arjuna in particular, and he unhesitatingly offers him both friendship and kingship (1.126–7). Karṇa, who is himself a mighty Kṣatriya with divine parentage but the status of a mere Sūta,[1] the butt of Pāṇḍava mockery (1.127.5–7), responds to Duryodhana's overtures with gratitude, devotion and love. Karṇa always supports Duryodhana in his plans to harm the Pāṇḍavas, always urges war when others urge peace; this despite the fact that he knows (5.141) that the Pāṇḍavas are bound to triumph.

His adherence to the Kṣatriya code of honour resembles that of Yudhiṣṭhira, who, unknown to both men, is actually his younger brother. Just as Yudhiṣṭhira 'cannot reject a challenge to gamble with dice at the command of an elder, even though I know the destruction it will bring' (2.67.4), so Karṇa cannot refuse to give a Brahmin the

1 When exactly Karṇa discovers the truth about himself is unclear: see 5.139 and note. However, in a sense this is unimportant, for, even before discovering who he truly is, he is clearly aware that he is no ordinary man.

armour and earrings with which he was born, even though he knows that the Brahmin is really the god Indra, acting to harm Karṇa on behalf of his son, Karṇa's hated enemy Arjuna (3.293–4). His truthfulness too resembles that of Yudhiṣṭhira. Thanks to Karṇa's truthfulness, he does not appear hideous when he cuts off his armour and earrings; thanks to Yudhiṣṭhira's truthfulness, his chariot travels a few inches off the ground. But whereas Yudhiṣṭhira's chariot comes down to earth when he lies to Droṇa about his son Aśvatthāman (7.164.107), Karṇa's honesty remains unblemished.

He is an arrogant man and a boaster, and this leads to a rift with Bhīṣma, so that Karṇa refuses to fight while Bhīṣma lives. But this rift is healed at the end of Book 6 after Bhīṣma's fall, and Karṇa now enters the battle. So great is the threat he poses to the Pāṇḍavas, especially with the Spear he has obtained from Indra in exchange for his armour and earrings, that Kṛṣṇa has to sacrifice the life of a major Pāṇḍava ally, Bhīma's son Ghaṭotkaca; Karṇa finds himself forced to squander the Spear on him, thus preventing him from using it against Arjuna. None the less, on Droṇa's death he is appointed as the third Kaurava commander, and he continues to fight fiercely for Duryodhana, his friend and his lord. By prior agreement with Yudhiṣṭhira, Śalya, acting as Karṇa's charioteer, tries to undermine his confidence (8.26–9), but with little effect. In the end Arjuna succeeds in killing him as he struggles to free the wheel of his chariot, which has become stuck in a rut (8.66.42 ff.).

The Kauravas comprise a hundred brothers, of whom only two (Duryodhana and Duḥśāsana) are really delineated in any detail. The Pāṇḍava brothers are only five in number, but, again, we really get to know only three of them: the youngest two, the twins Nakula and Sahadeva, sons of Mādrī rather than Kuntī, are only lightly sketched. We know that they are incarnations of the twin Aśvin gods and that, like them, they are extremely good-looking. When the Pāṇḍavas act together as a group, they play their parts, as they do throughout the great battle. There is a curious development as the narrative draws towards its end, when it emerges that a previously unsuspected special affection exists between Sahadeva and his stepmother Kuntī (see 15.22 and note). Beyond this, there is little to say about them.

There is also less to say than one might expect about Arjuna, the third eldest of the Pāṇḍava brothers, given that he is the son of the god Indra and the leading warrior in the entire Pāṇḍava army, unmatched by anyone in the world except for Karṇa and the unfortunate Ekalavya (see p. xxv above). This is because he excels so absolutely, and is so free from inner tensions or compulsions: he is the perfect warrior and the perfect prince. Bhīṣma has to live in a world that he has largely renounced; Duryodhana is driven by ambition and resentment; Karṇa has had to find friendship and recognition where he can, and will never betray it; Yudhiṣṭhira and Bhīma, as we shall see, represent opposing attitudes towards existence as a human being. Arjuna rarely displays any such inner complexity. Admittedly, there are one or two points at which he seems to behave in unexpected ways. After insisting, at 1.205, that he will undergo the prescribed penance of twelve years of celibate exile for having disturbed Yudhiṣṭhira when he was lying with the five brothers' joint wife Draupadī, it is striking that 1.206–7 is devoted to the affairs he has with two princesses, followed at 1.211–13 by his abduction of and marriage to Kṛṣṇa's sister Subhadrā. Much later, as the battle rages, he has a terrible quarrel with his older brother Yudhiṣṭhira that seems somewhat out of character for both men (8.46–50). But for most of the time he obeys *dharma* and his brother without wavering.

On the one occasion when he does waver, it forms what many would see as the central, even the defining moment of the entire *Mahābhārata*. At 6.23, when the opposing armies are drawn up and face one another on the field of Kurukṣetra, ready to begin battle, Arjuna asks his charioteer Kṛṣṇa to drive him between the two forces. Observing that the enemy army is full of his kinsmen, he announces that he does not wish to kill them; then he sits down in his chariot and casts aside his weapons. What follows is Kṛṣṇa's celebrated sermon, the *Bhagavadgītā*, in which many of the issues raised by the conflict, and by human life in general, are discussed in religious terms; but even viewed from a purely narrative point of view, Arjuna's sudden access of doubt forms an intensely dramatic moment, emphasizing the enormity of the coming cataclysm by briefly delaying it.

Yudhiṣṭhira, the eldest Pāṇḍava brother, has already been mentioned several times; in particular, I commented (pp. xx–xxi above) on the inherently conflicted *dharma* that he has as a king. Issues of *dharma* have an unusually close bearing on him, for he is the son of *dharma* personified as a deity, the god Dharma.[1] The *dharma* he personally inclines to is one of peace and forbearance (see for example 3.30–32). He specifically condemns the *dharma* of the Kṣatriyas, the class to which he himself belongs, and, in his grief for the killing that has been caused by the battle at Kurukṣetra, even proposes to renounce the kingship and become a forest ascetic (12.7). Others, including his own brothers, his wife Draupadī, and Vyāsa, argue the opposite case: Kṣatriyas *should* engage in military conquest and rule (12.12–13); enemies ought to be killed (12.15) and wrongdoers punished with the rod of force (12.23). Later Bhīṣma elaborates on what they have said in his huge sermon on the *dharma* of kings (12.55–128).

It is not only in his words that Yudhiṣṭhira favours peace, forbearance and the religious life. Though he is the Pāṇḍava king, he often appears more acted upon than acting, particularly during the latter part of Book 2, where he twice accepts a challenge to gamble 'even though I know the destruction it will bring', and where he stands by and watches while his wife is insulted and assaulted (as he does again at 4.15). He employs a large part of his enforced forest exile in a protracted pilgrimage to numerous sacred bathing-places (3.80–153). When, finally, the always inevitable war begins, he takes remarkably little part in the actual fighting until the end, when he suddenly announces that it is his personal mission to kill Śalya (Śalya is in fact the only named warrior of any significance killed by Yudhiṣṭhira during the entire eighteen-day conflict). In brief, one can say that Yudhiṣṭhira favours and embodies the way of disengagement (Sanskrit *nivṛtti*): the almost permanent crisis in which he finds himself results from the fact that, as a Kṣatriya and a king, he ought to follow the way of engagement (*pravṛtti*).

Yudhiṣṭhira's younger brother is Bhīma ('the terrible one'), son of the fierce Wind god, and the contrast between the two could hardly be greater. Where Yudhiṣṭhira is pacific, Bhīma is bellicose; where Yudhiṣṭhira favours forbearance, Bhīma is regularly described as unforbearing;

1 Dharma as a god is not widely referred to outside the *Mahābhārata*.

where Yudhiṣṭhira fights little, Bhīma fights frequently and with extreme violence. He has a giant's strength, which he shows when he rescues his family from Duryodhana's attempt to burn them alive:

Bhīma of terrible speed and valour took up all his brothers and his mother too, and strode forth. That hero, carrying his mother on his shoulder, the twins on his hip, and the two mighty brothers, Kuntī's sons, in his hands, went rapidly on, breaking trees in his speed and splitting open the earth with his feet – the ardent wolf-belly, swift as the wind. (1.136.17–19)

His response to the insults shown to Draupadī by Duryodhana and Duḥśāsana during the two gambling matches is to take two dreadful vows: to break Duryodhana's thigh (2.63.13–15; it was *adharma* for a warrior to land a blow below the waist) and to drink Duḥśāsana's blood (2.61.43–6). Both are duly enacted. His favoured weapon is the club, though he also uses both bow and sword; but sometimes he prefers to kill his enemies with his bare hands, slapping or punching them to death (7.130.21–5). His appetite is ravenous, hence the frequently occurring sobriquet 'wolf-belly'.

Yudhiṣṭhira and Bhīma thus form a sharply contrasting pair. One is all forbearance and peace, the other all anger and violence; one inclines to disengagement, the other extreme engagement. It is clear that, as well as enhancing narrative interest, this contrast embodies in human form the contrast between the two world-views represented by *nivṛtti* and *pravṛtti*: a choice between competing ideologies is on display.[1] But the *Mahābhārata* does not teach any simple lessons, and there is no clear-cut conclusion favouring one over the other. Given the 'subtlety' of *dharma*, and the different *dharmas* proper to different people, this was probably always to be expected.

1 The *Rāmāyaṇa* contains a similar contrast between a disengaged and pacific older brother (Rāma) and a highly engaged and bellicose younger brother (Lakṣmaṇa), and several oral epics current in present-day India also feature comparable contrasting pairs: see my article 'Scapegoats of the gods: the ideology of the Indian epics', in Stuart H. Blackburn, Peter J. Claus, Joyce B. Flueckiger and Susan S. Wadley (eds.), *Oral Epics in India* (Berkeley and London, 1989), pp. 176–94. The human quandary represented by this contrast evidently has deep roots in the culture of India.

Greatly though the Pāṇḍavas suffer at the hands of Duryodhana and his allies, their sufferings are exceeded by those of their joint wife Draupadī. As a woman, she has little say in a strongly male-dominated warrior society; as a woman, she is less able than her husbands to withstand the rigours of thirteen years of exile, twelve of them passed in the forest. Worst, as a woman she is subject to sexual humiliation and assault: she is insulted by Duryodhana (2.63.8–12), she is dragged by the hair and stripped in public by Duḥśāsana (2.61–2), she is abducted by Jayadratha (3.248–56), and she is the victim of an attempted rape by Kīcaka (4.14–15). Kīcaka is killed at once for his offence, but the outrages perpetrated by Jayadratha and, particularly, by Duryodhana and Duḥśāsana, remain constantly in her mind, and she is contemptuous of Yudhiṣṭhira and his – in her view – disastrous disengagement (e.g. 3.13, 3.28–9, 4.16–19); when the question of peace or war arises, she decisively favours war (5.80). Unsurprisingly, then, she has a special closeness to the equally hawkish Bhīma; it is Bhīma to whom she complains about Kīcaka (and, indeed, about Yudhiṣṭhira), and who kills the would-be rapist. It is also Bhīma whom she twice sends to fetch flowers during the term of forest exile (3.146, 3.157).

What stands out most clearly from this rapid survey of some of the main characters appearing in the *Mahābhārata* is the complexity displayed by many of them. Some lead complex lives: Bhīṣma renounces kingship, then has to exercise it on behalf of others; Karṇa is dispossessed of his rightful family and status, and has to find both for himself; Yudhiṣṭhira longs for a life of disengagement, but as a king has to be engaged in doings he finds utterly repugnant. Some are caught up in complex situations: Bhīṣma, Droṇa, Śalya and Kṛpa all find themselves on the wrong side in the great battle, and all four give Yudhiṣṭhira blessings for victory while insisting that they will fight for the Kauravas (6.41); Bhīṣma and Droṇa additionally let it be known how they may be killed, while Śalya works to undermine the confidence of Karṇa, whose chariot he is driving. Some have complex personalities: Duryodhana is a great king but a driven man, unable to tolerate anything other than total domination for himself and total ruin for his enemies; Yudhiṣṭhira and Bhīma between them embody the split between two completely opposing views of how people should lead their lives. These heroes and villains are far from being simple exemplars of good and bad; they are human beings facing real and appalling existential dilemmas, and they speak as clearly and painfully to modern mankind as they did two thousand and more years ago.

## KṚṢṆA

If the characters dealt with so far can be called complex, there is one further character of whom that is doubly true. Kṛṣṇa is every bit as many-faceted a human being as, say, Yudhiṣṭhira or Karṇa, but in addition he is the supreme lord of all, God himself incarnate on earth.[1]

As a man Kṛṣṇa is a prince of the Vṛṣṇis, a people living in the far West of India in what is now the state of Gujarat. He is closely related to the Pāṇḍavas: his father Vasudeva and their mother Kuntī are brother and sister, and to this tie of blood is added alliance by marriage when Arjuna marries his sister Subhadrā (1.213). In the narrative of the first book he plays relatively little part, though already it appears that he has a particularly close relationship with Arjuna. It is at Kṛṣṇa's suggestion that Arjuna secures Subhadrā by abducting her (1.211), and shortly afterwards the two men collaborate to help the Fire god consume the Khāṇḍava forest (1.214–25). However, it is not long before we begin to see more of him at the centre of things as a man whom the Pāṇḍavas trust and, increasingly, rely on. He counsels Yudhiṣṭhira to perform the ritual of the royal consecration, but advises him that first he must kill the wicked king Jarāsaṃdha, an old enemy of the Vṛṣṇis (2.13–14). When the consecration takes place, he takes advantage of a quarrel that arises to kill another old enemy, Śiśupāla (2.42). He is absent during the two disastrous gambling matches, but reappears to visit the Pāṇḍavas several times during their exile in the forest, and he attends the wedding of Arjuna's son Abhimanyu (4.67).

1 It has long been disputed whether Rāma, the parallel figure in the *Rāmāyaṇa*, was a divine incarnation from the start, or whether he was deified sometime after the composition of the earliest form of the text. In the case of Kṛṣṇa, there is no such debate: it is certain that the Kṛṣṇa of the *Mahābhārata* was divine from the beginning.

Book 5, 'Perseverance', opens with Kṛṣṇa leading the Pāṇḍavas' discussion of the policy they should adopt in the face of Duryodhana's intransigence; later (5.70–137) he acts as one of several ambassadors to shuttle backwards and forwards between the two sides, though he entertains no hope of success (5.71), and after this he also attempts to induce Karṇa to shift his allegiance from the Kauravas to the Pāṇḍavas. In between comes an extraordinary scene (5.7). Independently of one another, Arjuna and Duryodhana both visit Kṛṣṇa to ask for his aid in the battle which seems certain to come; they arrive simultaneously. Kṛṣṇa announces that he will give his aid to both: his many fighting men will join one side and he himself the other, though he will not actually fight. The choice is given to Arjuna, who, to Duryodhana's great joy, chooses Kṛṣṇa.

On the battlefield, Kṛṣṇa acts as Arjuna's charioteer and as the Pāṇḍavas' strategic and tactical adviser. His performance in this latter role offers some surprises, to which I shall return later. As agreed, he does not fight in person, though twice (6.55, 6.102.50–70) he seems to be on the point of doing so, and Arjuna has to restrain him. Once the war is over, he continues to figure prominently. He pronounces a terrible curse upon Aśvatthāman, perpetrator of the night-time massacre (10.16.8–15), he is himself cursed by Gāndhārī (11.25), he is among those who counsel Yudhiṣṭhira in his grief, and it is he who arranges for Yudhiṣṭhira to hear Bhīṣma's long deathbed sermon (Books 12–13). In Book 14 he saves the Kuru line from extinction by reviving the stillborn Parikṣit (14.68). Finally, after witnessing a drunken brawl in which all his Vṛṣṇi kinsmen kill one another, he dies when a hunter named Jarā shoots an arrow into the sole of his foot, the one part of his body that is not invulnerable (16.5.16–25).

So much for Kṛṣṇa the man. What of Kṛṣṇa the god, Viṣṇu incarnate?

Gods figure prominently in the *Mahābhārata*, but the gods found there are not entirely the same as those hymned in the Vedas: something much closer to the picture found in modern Hinduism has begun to emerge. The Vedic pantheon had consisted of a large collection of deities, some individual, others referred to only in groups, some associated with natural phenomena such as sun, rain, wind and fire, others more like humans. Many of these are mentioned repeatedly in the later narrative, but there can be no mistaking the fact that they now occupy second place, below two altogether greater deities, each of whom is at different points in the text praised as supreme. The god Śiva, generally aloof and unpredictable, is entirely unknown to the Vedas, though an alternative name used for him, Rudra, is that of a major Vedic deity. Viṣṇu, on the other hand, does figure in a small number of Vedic hymns, but in the *Mahābhārata* he has come to be revered as highest lord, and is shown as intervening in the affairs of men when evil threatens.

Indeed, the entire *Mahābhārata* narrative is the story of one such intervention, and it involves not just Viṣṇu but all the other gods too, though Viṣṇu certainly plays the most important part. The discord and apocalyptic war between the Kaurava and Pāṇḍava cousins is no mere falling-out between mortals. As the first book, 'Beginnings', makes clear (1.58.25 ff.), the human conflict is in fact a transposition to earth of the unending cosmic conflict between gods and demons. Demons have taken birth in royal lineages; the goddess Earth appeals for help to the gods, and they too take human birth to come to her aid. All the major heroes of the *Mahābhārata* are incarnations (*avatāras*, literally 'descents') of deities (1.61), and in the great war at Kurukṣetra they do battle against, and finally defeat, their demonic enemies, before resuming their place in heaven at the close of the narrative (18.5.7–24).

Like the other heroes of the tale, Kṛṣṇa is a god in incarnate form; but whereas the other incarnations are said to be 'partial descents' (*aṃśāvatāras*) of second-rank deities,[1] Kṛṣṇa is an embodiment of the supreme lord Viṣṇu. At various points in the narrative characters speak of him as the highest god: for example, Bhīṣma does so when defending himself for having honoured Kṛṣṇa more highly than Śiśupāla at 2.35.6–29, and Saṃjaya does so when Dhṛtarāṣṭra asks him about Kṛṣṇa at 5.67–8. Bhīṣma's great sermon to Yudhiṣṭhira incorporates a lengthy section (12.321–39) known as the *Nārāyaṇīya* in which Nārāyaṇa[2] is glorified as highest lord, and Kṛṣṇa is named as Nārāyaṇa incarnate.[3] Kṛṣṇa himself makes no secret of his true nature: at 3.186–7 the seer

1 And, in the case of Karṇa and the Pāṇḍavas, the sons of such deities.

2 Generally an alternative name for Viṣṇu; identified by the Pāñcarātra sect with the universal Self.

3 Later in the same sermon (13.14–18) comes a comparable section glorifying Śiva.

Mārkaṇḍeya describes how Kṛṣṇa had shown him the entire world secreted within himself during the universal dissolution. Most remarkable of all, though, is the chapter of the *Bhagavadgītā* (6.33) in which Kṛṣṇa permits Arjuna a sight of his 'supreme godly form'. Arjuna is overwhelmed by what he sees:

> Like numerous river-currents that rush towards the one ocean, those heroes of the world of men enter your flaming mouths; like moths that fly ever faster to destroy themselves in a blazing flame, the worlds hurry ever faster to their destruction in your mouths. With your flaming jaws you lap up complete worlds and devour them whole; your terrible splendours fill the entire universe with fiery energy till it is scorched, O Viṣṇu. (6.33.28–30)

It is no coincidence that it is Arjuna to whom Kṛṣṇa delivers the *Bhagavadgītā* and to whom he reveals his supreme form, for Kṛṣṇa's close relationship with Arjuna is more than a friendship between two men. As well as being identified with the supreme lord Nārāyaṇa, Kṛṣṇa is – somewhat confusingly – also identified with a divine seer of the same name. This Nārāyaṇa is one of a pair, who are most commonly mentioned together: Nara is the primal Man, Nārāyaṇa the Son of Man. Not much is known about these two figures, though we know that they are themselves manifestations of the highest god, and we are told (1.17, 5.48) that they helped the gods win their battle against the demons. This account of their military prowess turns out to be no mere tale of ancient times. In the *Mahābhārata* it is repeatedly stated that Arjuna is Nara and Kṛṣṇa is Nārāyaṇa, and that this renders them invincible (1.219, 5.94, 7.10).

Since Kṛṣṇa is God almighty, he is able to preach to Arjuna with authority about issues of religion in general and *dharma* in particular, and in the *Bhagavadgītā* he does so at length. Like the hunter who teaches the Brahmin Kauśika about *dharma* (3.198–206; see p. xix above), he is insistent that it is one's own *dharma* that one must perform, as for instance at 6.25.35: 'Better one's own *dharma* ill-done than the *dharma* of another well performed. To die in achieving one's own *dharma* is good; the *dharma* of another is dangerous.' He also speaks very clearly of his own purpose in assuming the incarnation of Kṛṣṇa:

I have had many former births, and so have you, Arjuna; I know all of them, but you do not, afflicter of your enemies. Although I am unborn and imperishable, although I am lord of all beings, I assume my own nature and take on existence through my illusory power, for whenever *dharma* lapses and *adharma* increases, heir of Bharata, I create myself; to protect the virtuous, destroy the wicked and restore *dharma* I take on existence in age after age. (6.26.5–7)

Others concur in this view of Kṛṣṇa: it is said that 'Where *dharma* is, there is Kṛṣṇa' (6.41.55), and Vidura tells Dhṛtarāṣṭra that 'Kṛṣṇa here would never commit any blameworthy act; the invincible, highest lord would never deviate from *dharma*' (5.128.22). It is therefore all the more surprising to find that the invincible, highest lord does in fact deviate from *dharma* on numerous occasions. Here I shall cite only three particularly notorious cases.[1]

At 7.117, Duryodhana's ally Bhūriśravas and Sātyaki, ally of the Pāṇḍavas, are doing battle. Having succeeded in destroying each other's weapons, they begin wrestling with one another. At this point Kṛṣṇa urges Arjuna to come to the aid of Sātyaki, who is weary and starting to have the worst of the combat. As Arjuna watches, Bhūriśravas throws Sātyaki to the ground and drags him 'like a lion dragging a mighty elephant in a forest' (verse 59). Arjuna mentally pays Bhūriśravas honour for his achievement; then, 'acting on Kṛṣṇa's instruction, [he] severed with an arrow the arm, complete with sword, of the sacrificer Bhūriśravas'. The mortally injured man not unnaturally upbraids

1 For other examples see 2.21.19–22.4, where he hints to Bhīma to attack and kill a weakened opponent; 7.148, where he has Ghaṭotkaca sent to his death in order to cause Karṇa to squander his Spear on him; and 7.157, where he admits to having sown confusion in Karṇa's mind in order to protect Arjuna. It is probably significant that in every one of these cases Kṛṣṇa's breach of *dharma* comes in the form of words, most typically inciting others to commit acts of *adharma*. To find such an act committed by Kṛṣṇa in person we have to look at a passage whose authenticity was rejected by the editors of the critical edition. In this passage (7, App. I, 16), which occurs in many manuscripts early in 7.121 at a point when Arjuna has sworn to kill Jayadratha before the sun sets, Kṛṣṇa uses his power to hide the sun briefly; this induces Jayadratha to break cover under the impression that the sun has indeed set, and gives Arjuna his chance.

Arjuna for his act of *adharma*: 'This vile act that you have carried out for the sake of Sātyaki the Vṛṣṇi was obviously Kṛṣṇa's idea, and is uncharacteristic of you; for who except a friend of Kṛṣṇa's would inflict such a catastrophe on one who was distracted, engaged in fighting another?' (7.118.13–14). Arjuna seeks to defend his behaviour, referring to a 'great oath' he has taken not to allow any ally to be slain when within bowshot of him, an oath that seems to be mentioned nowhere else. At this point Sātyaki beheads the already dying Bhūriśravas, and Arjuna's deed is forgotten in the condemnation of this new outrage.

Later in Book 7, Droṇa, the current commander of the Kaurava army, is inflicting grave casualties on the Pāṇḍavas' Pāñcāla allies. The Pāṇḍavas know, because he has told them himself (6.41.59–61), that the only way they can kill Droṇa is if he lays down his arms, and that he will only do so if he hears 'terrible ill news' from a man whose word he can trust. Kṛṣṇa now addresses Arjuna. He observes that Droṇa will never be defeated in normal combat, and continues, 'Therefore we must put aside *dharma* and resort to stratagem to conquer him, if Droṇa of the golden chariot is not to kill you all in battle. If [his son] Aśvatthāman were slain, I believe that he would cease to fight; so some person must inform him that his son has been killed on the battlefield' (7.164.68–9). Arjuna will not accept this proposal, but the other Pāṇḍavas do so, Yudhiṣṭhira with some reluctance. Bhīma now kills one of the Pāṇḍavas' own elephants that happens to bear the name Aśvatthāman, and cries out, 'Aśvatthāman is slain!' (7.164.72). But Droṇa is not convinced that the words he has heard are the truth, and continues to fight with undiminished vigour. Kṛṣṇa therefore urges the truthful Yudhiṣṭhira to repeat the untruth: 'A lie would be better than truth, and he that speaks a lie in order to live is not contaminated by it' (7.164.99). Yudhiṣṭhira does so; Droṇa is shaken, but still fights on. Finally, Bhīma not merely repeats the lie a third time, emphasizing that Yudhiṣṭhira lord of *dharma* has vouched for its truth, but also accuses Droṇa, his revered Teacher, of violating *dharma*. Droṇa at last lays down his weapons, and Dhṛṣṭadyumna seizes the opportunity and severs his head.[1]

Three days later, the battle is over. Duryodhana, its instigator, has

1 As had always been destined: see 1.154–5.

left the battlefield and taken refuge in a lake, using his power to solidify its waters. He is discovered and challenged, and after a brief discussion it is settled that he will face Bhīma in a duel with clubs. As the combat begins, Arjuna asks Kṛṣṇa who is more likely to win the encounter. Kṛṣṇa's answer is remarkable: 'Both have received equal instruction . . . but Bhīma is the stronger of the two, while Dhṛtarāṣṭra's son is more practised than the wolf-belly. Now if Bhīma fights according to *dharma*, he will never triumph; but if he fights unfairly he can kill Duryodhana' (9.57.3–4). He reminds Arjuna of Bhīma's vow to break Duryodhana's thigh; then, after a brief digression on Yudhiṣṭhira's lack of wisdom in allowing everything to be staked on the outcome of a single duel, and on Duryodhana's expertise in fighting with clubs, he repeats his main point: 'If that strong-armed hero [Bhīma] will not kill him unfairly, you will have this Kaurava, Dhṛtarāṣṭra's son, for your king!' So Arjuna gestures to Bhīma to remind him of his vow, and Bhīma takes the hint and smashes Duryodhana's thighs with a low blow. As with the death of Bhūriśravas, a further, secondary act of *adharma* then takes place that deflects much of the subsequent debate away from Kṛṣṇa: Bhīma fulfils the second element of his vow (2.68.28) by trampling his fallen enemy's head. Yudhiṣṭhira condemns this act, followed by Kṛṣṇa's brother Balarāma and then by Kṛṣṇa himself. After the fuss over this has died down, Kṛṣṇa proposes to leave. It is left to the dying Duryodhana himself – to the last a great king, as well as a great villain – to get back decisively to the point at issue. Revealing that he is well aware that it was Kṛṣṇa who prompted Bhīma to kill him unfairly, he goes on to list several other instances of deceitful behaviour on Kṛṣṇa's part (including both of those dealt with above), and concludes, 'If you had fought fairly in battle against me and Karṇa and Bhīṣma and Droṇa, be assured that you would not have gained the victory! But I and the other princes who were abiding by our *dharma* have been slain thanks to you and your ignoble, crooked ways' (9.60.37–8). Kṛṣṇa retorts that Duryodhana owes his death to his own misdeeds, leaving Duryodhana's specific accusations unanswered. Later, though, he seeks to reassure the worried Pāṇḍavas about the course on which he has guided them, and in the process he confirms much of what Duryodhana had said:

Duryodhana here with his swift weapons, and those other valiant chariot-fighters, could not have been slain by you on the battlefield in fair fight. That is why I devised these stratagems, lords of men – otherwise the victory of the Pāṇḍavas could never have happened. For not even the world-guardian gods themselves could have killed by fair means those four noble warriors, famed throughout the world. As for Dhṛtarāṣṭra's son here, not even staff-wielding Death could kill him fairly if he stood club in hand and free from weariness. You should not take it to heart that this king has been slain, for, when enemies become too numerous and powerful, they should be slain by deceit and stratagems. This is the path formerly trodden by the gods to slay the demons; and a path trodden by the virtuous may be trodden by all. (9.60.57–62)

## FATE

The question cannot be avoided: why does Kṛṣṇa, the supreme lord of all, who takes on existence in age after age to restore *dharma* whenever it lapses, so consistently favour *adharma* in the conduct of the great battle? The answer is starkly simple. Kṛṣṇa, like the Pāṇḍavas themselves and many of their allies, is in reality a god in temporary human form, and the purpose of the gods is to defeat their eternal enemies the demons, who have taken birth as Duryodhana and the other Kauravas. Indeed, Kṛṣṇa is the greatest of the gods, and therefore has charge of their campaign. Viewed through human eyes, the war at Kurukṣetra is fought to settle the dispute between two sets of royal cousins; from the point of view of Kṛṣṇa and the other gods, the entire world of men is merely the theatre in which their latest battle with their old rivals has to be played out. The gods are not engaging in that battle for our benefit, but for their own, and the niceties of particular human *dharmas* are not high among their priorities.

The Sanskrit term for 'the purpose of the gods' is *daiva*, a derivative from the word *deva*, meaning 'god'. In this translation the word is generally rendered 'fate', since it is not the only term used for the preordained future, but it does clearly indicate who is doing the preordaining. Some of the verses in which it occurs are almost breathtaking in their bland statement of human inconsequentiality in the divine scheme of things, as when the Pāṇḍavas return to face Śakuni in the second gambling match: 'Once again the bull-like chariot-fighters entered that hall, bringing dismay to the hearts of their friends. They sat at their ease to resume the gambling, to destroy the whole world, for they were under fate's oppression' (2.67.6–7).

There is a second, precisely parallel term *pauruṣa*; it is derived from the word for 'man', *puruṣa*, and means 'pertaining to a man', 'the purpose of a man'. In this translation it and its synonym *puruṣakāra* have been variously rendered according to context as 'human effort', 'human aspiration', 'human endeavour', 'human action', etc. The relationship between *daiva* and *pauruṣa*, between divinely ordained fate and human will, is a major theme of the text, and the heroes themselves often comment on it. 'This world is founded upon divine destiny and human aspiration,' says Pāṇḍu (1.114.16); 'but even what is destined only comes to us through timely action.' At 5.75.8–10 Kṛṣṇa tells Bhīma of the subtle interplay between the two forces:

> An action carried out through human effort may be well planned, well performed and properly accomplished, and yet be thwarted by fate. But likewise a fated action, something not carried out by humans, may be frustrated by human effort, heir of Bharata, as happens with cold and heat, rain, hunger and thirst. And a man whose being is constrained by fate may none the less opt to carry out some different action, and fate does not prevent him from doing so; we see the same characteristic here.

And when Kṛpa and Aśvatthāman, two of only three Kauravas to survive Kurukṣetra, debate what should be done in the aftermath of the battle, they express their differing viewpoints in terms of *daiva* and *puruṣakāra* (10.2–3). Aśvatthāman, the advocate of human will, wins the argument, and so his revenge attack on the Pāṇḍava camp takes place that night.

The contrast between the two terms also offers us a second perspective on the contrast between Yudhiṣṭhira's quiescent disengagement from the world and his younger brother Bhīma's aggressive engagement in it (p. xxxii above): Yudhiṣṭhira's nature is to subordinate himself to *daiva*, while Bhīma's is to assert his own *pauruṣa*. Again, no suggestion is made that one of these contrasting attitudes is in itself superior to the other. However, one thing that is said, and is said repeatedly and by different characters, is that fate is supreme and human effort vain. From the humanistic standpoint, the *Mahābhārata* is not an optimistic narrative.

As if their unending conflict with the demons were not enough, there is even a second reason why the gods require the carnage of Kurukṣetra. The story is told at 9.52; the following is Wendy O'Flaherty's account of it.

> Kuru, a great sage, ploughed the fields of Kuru [Kurukṣetra] until Indra came from heaven and asked what he wanted; Kuru replied that he wanted all men who died there to go to heaven. The gods feared that if men dying there gained heaven without sacrifice, the gods would have no share; Indra then offered a more limited boon to Kuru: men who fasted to death there, or who died in battle there, would go to heaven, and Kuru agreed to this.
>
> The shrine is limited in such a way that only a bloody battle will allow the widespread migration so feared by the gods; and when the gods themselves become incarnate as the heroes doomed to die on Kurukṣetra, they preempt many of the free tickets to heaven, simultaneously assuring their own return aloft and the reduction of the number of true mortals who will be able to ascend in this way.[1]

It would be difficult to exaggerate the importance of *daiva* for the narrative: this second, non-human system of motivation and causation is what makes the story what it is. Kṛṣṇa's moments of human *adharma* are perhaps the points where it becomes most startlingly visible, but it is always there. Sometimes we are told explicitly what is going on. At 7.155, while the Pāṇḍavas grieve for Ghaṭotkaca, their fallen ally and Bhīma's son, Kṛṣṇa dances and roars with joy. Asked the reason for his behaviour by a shocked Arjuna, he explains that through this stratagem, the latest in a long sequence of stratagems, he has won a great prize, for the Pāṇḍavas' most dangerous enemy Karṇa is now as good as dead:

1 Wendy Doniger O'Flaherty, *The Origins of Evil in Hindu Mythology* (Berkeley: University of California Press, 1976), p. 261.

he has been forced to use up on Ghaṭotkaca the lethal Spear with which he had intended to kill Arjuna. At other times nothing is said, but it would be a mistake to imagine that nothing is meant. For example, it is necessary that Droṇa should die, and Kṛṣṇa engineers his death by means of a terrible lie (7.164–5). It is not stated explicitly in the text, but it is certainly the case that here too Kṛṣṇa has a motive beyond even the death of the second Kaurava commander. The manner in which he causes Droṇa to be killed fills Droṇa's son Aśvatthāman with an unquenchable thirst for vengeance (see pp. xxvii–xxviii above), and so in Book 10 he carries out his dreadful night-time massacre of the Pāṇḍavas' allies. This completes the slaughter required by the gods.

If a storyteller wants to convey a sense of fate as a powerful force in his narrative, it is not enough for him to describe certain events and then announce that they had always been fated to occur; rather, he must make sure that his listeners or readers know in advance that those events are going to happen. The possibility of surprise is lost, but in its place a feeling of grinding inevitability can be established. The *Mahābhārata* makes extensive use of this technique.

In the first place, the story is told by several narrators, and these narrators frequently anticipate events that still lie in the future. At the outermost level, the form of the story that we read is that narrated by the Sūta Ugraśravas to the seers in the Naimiṣa forest. The very first chapter contains a brief summary of the narrative to come. This is immediately followed by the long lament that Dhṛtarāṣṭra voiced after the great battle, which in effect retells the tale again:

> When I heard that Yudhiṣṭhira, together with his matchless brothers, had been defeated at dice by Śakuni son of Subala and stripped of his kingdom, then, O Saṃjaya, I lost hope of victory. When I heard that Draupadī, wearing a single garment and in the course of her period, had been brought to the assembly, griefstricken and choked with tears, unprotected in the midst of her protectors, then, O Saṃjaya, I lost hope of victory . . . (1.1.105–6)

The second chapter begins with a list of the *Mahābhārata*'s constituent sub-books (*upaparvans*), and then provides another, much longer résumé of the entire story. After further preliminaries, at 1.54 Ugraśravas starts to narrate the *Mahābhārata* as he heard it from Vaiśaṃpāyana at the snake sacrifice of Janamejaya; 1.55 therefore consists of yet another summary, this time in Vaiśaṃpāyana's words.

Other anticipations occur as the tale progresses. For instance, the narrative of the war is placed in the mouth of Saṃjaya, who has been provided by Vyāsa with the divine sight that enables him to see everything that occurs on the battlefield; he describes what he has seen to the blind Dhṛtarāṣṭra. Saṃjaya always starts by informing Dhṛtarāṣṭra of the overall course of events, before narrating them in detail: thus each of the four sections of battle narrative begins with a chapter or two (6.14, 7.6–7, 8.1, 9.1) recounting in brief what is about to happen. So Bhīṣma may not be killed until 6.114, but by the time Arjuna shoots the fatal arrows we have already known of his impending fall for a hundred chapters, and much the same applies to the other great casualties of the war.

But it is not only the various narrators who let us know what is going to happen; many of the characters within the story itself do so too. This is not a matter of foretelling the future, however, but rather of binding it: powerful characters utter powerful words that cannot fail to come true, and the future is now fixed.

There are three particularly common forms for such powerful words to take. If one character is pleased with another, he may offer a *boon*. This is normally the unconditional granting of any wish the beneficiary may express, though occasionally, as with the boon Kuru requests from Indra for all who die at Kurukṣetra to gain heaven (see p. xliii above), the giver may require some modification of the wish before granting it. Boons are given over and over again during the course of the *Mahābhārata* story, and some are of major importance to the course that story takes. For example, the Kāśi princess Ambā, abducted by Bhīṣma along with her two sisters to provide wives for the Kuru prince Vicitravīrya, secures her freedom by revealing that she is already betrothed to another man (5.171). However, that man now jilts her (5.172), and from now on her one aim is to avenge herself on Bhīṣma. At 5.188 her extreme austerities finally win her a boon from Śiva, and she chooses Bhīṣma's downfall; this is granted. We now know who will be the agent of Bhīṣma's ultimate death. Ambā still has more to do before she can achieve her goal, but achieve it she does. She burns herself to death, is reborn as the princess Śikhaṇḍinī, changes sex (thanks to another boon) to become the prince Śikhaṇḍin, and fights on the Pāṇḍava side at Kurukṣetra. Bhīṣma, knowing that Śikhaṇḍin was once a woman, will not fight him, and Arjuna is therefore able to use him as a shield; it is from behind Śikhaṇḍin that he shoots the arrows that, finally, kill his 'revered grandfather'.

A second form for powerful words to take is the *curse*, which works rather like a negative boon. If one character is displeased with another, he may curse him to suffer some unpleasant happening. As with the boon, there may be a brief negotiation over terms, and curses are sometimes mitigated before coming into effect (see for examples 1.11, 3.205–6, 5.193), but once uttered they cannot be revoked, and they too fix the future. At 8.29 Karṇa reveals that he has been cursed twice: once by Rāma Jāmadagnya, that his celestial Weapon of Brahmā will fail him at the hour of greatest need, and once by an unnamed Brahmin, that his chariot-wheel will stick in a rut when he is fighting for his life. We now know how Karṇa will meet his end. At 8.66–7, both curses come to fruition, and he is killed by Arjuna.

The third form of words is the *vow*. If a character makes a serious vow (it has to be admitted that a lot of boastful undertakings are also made that come to nothing), what he vows is bound to happen. At 2.63.8–12 Duryodhana insults Draupadī by exposing his thigh to her; Bhīma vows to break that thigh in battle. We now know the form that Duryodhana's death will take. Nearly a thousand chapters later, at 9.57.44, Bhīma fulfils his word, and Duryodhana lies slain.

All three of these fateful forms of words require the speaker to be a sufficiently powerful person – boons, curses and vows cannot be uttered by just anybody. But if a person does have sufficient power, their words may serve to bind the future in other ways too, sometimes without their even intending it. When the Pāṇḍavas return home from Drupada's capital at 1.182.1, they call out joyfully to their mother that they have won alms; she, without looking up, answers, 'All of you share equally!' What they have won is in fact Drupada's daughter Draupadī, but Kuntī's words cannot be falsified. Thus is brought about the quite extraordinary polyandrous marriage of Draupadī to all five Pāṇḍava brothers.

## BEFORE THE WAR

The *Mahābhārata* divides naturally into three major sections, all of comparable length. The first five books recount the events that led up to the great war at Kurukṣetra; Books 6–10 describe the course of that war and the night-time massacre that followed it; Books 11–18 tell of the war's long aftermath. It will be helpful to look at each of these three sections and to note some of their characteristic features.

The first task of any introductory narrative is to set the scene for what is to follow and to introduce the characters of the story. This the *Mahābhārata* does, but in a somewhat roundabout way. It is not until 1.57 that the narration reaches any of the figures who will be central to the tale (and even then the first such figure to appear is Vyāsa, introduced as the author of the *Mahābhārata* rather than as a character within it). The preceding chapters have been concerned above all with establishing the circumstances of the actual narration of the story. So we begin with the first seven verses of chapter 1, in which we learn of the Sūta Ugraśravas's visit to the holy seers in the Naimiṣa forest. Then come the words 'The Sūta spoke', introducing Ugraśravas's narration. As is normal throughout the text, we also hear from the narrative's audience, in this case the forest seers: they tell the narrator which story they wish to hear, and often interject requests for him to supply this or that information, to repeat what he has said in greater detail, and so forth. Such interjections aside, the whole of what follows is the words spoken by the Sūta – the entire *Mahābhārata* is the narrative as told by him. Thus in verse 44 of 18.5, as the long tale is nearing its end, there appears the phrase 'O Śaunaka': Ugraśravas is addressing the chief of his audience of seers by name.

The headings 'So-and-so spoke' that occur throughout the tale are a distinctive feature of the *Mahābhārata*, one not found in the parallel narrative of the *Rāmāyaṇa*. Naturally enough, they are used to introduce passages of speech, most typically by a narrator or his listener or listeners. In the original Sanskrit text, however, they are also used freely to introduce speech by characters within the story itself, normally in cases where the verse narrative happens not to include a specific 'he said'. Thus a particular chapter may contain a sequence of such headings belonging to different narrative 'levels', some applying to a narrator and others to characters referred to in his narration. In this translation, in the interests of clarity, I have restricted the 'So-and-so spoke' headings to narrators and their listeners only.

Ugraśravas starts his story at 1.3 by telling the first of many tangled tales. This chapter gives the explanation for King Janamejaya's animosity towards the snakes, which will result in his later performing a snake sacrifice: he learns that his father Parikṣit died of snakebite. The reason for this seemingly tangential choice of starting point is that it was at this snake sacrifice that Ugraśravas himself learnt the *Mahābhārata*, when he heard it recited to Janamejaya by Vaiśaṃpāyana, pupil of the tale's author Vyāsa.

Chapters 4–12 appear to be a digression, but in fact lead up to a request for the full story of Janamejaya's sacrifice, which Ugraśravas begins to tell in chapter 14, starting with the ancient myth of the gods' churning of the ocean in search of *amṛta*, the nectar of immortality. Along with the *amṛta* is produced the horse Uccaiḥśravas (1.16); a wager is placed on the colour of its tail, and the snakes are asked to secure the outcome of the bet by acting as black tail-hairs; they refuse, and are therefore cursed to die in a snake sacrifice that will be conducted by Janamejaya (1.18). After more snake-related mythology, chapters 33–4 reveal the way in which some at least of the snakes will be able to survive the sacrifice: a certain child named Āstīka must be born.

Next, rather strangely placed as a flashback in chapters 36–40, comes the actual story of the death of Janamejaya's father Parikṣit.[1] This is followed (1.41–4) by the birth of the saviour of the snakes, Āstīka, and then (1.45–53) by the snake sacrifice itself, which Āstīka does succeed

1 Parikṣit is the link between the generation that fought and died at Kurukṣetra and the new generation for whom the *Mahābhārata* is already an ancient tale: he is the posthumous son of the great warrior hero Abhimanyu, Arjuna's son by Subhadrā. As a result of the narrative's structure, his death is described near the beginning of the text, his birth near the end: see 14.65–9.

in bringing to a premature end. At this point Śaunaka, chief of the Naimiṣa seers, interjects a request to Ugraśravas to recite the *Mahābhārata* as told by Vyāsa at the snake sacrifice. Ugraśravas tells (1.54) how Vyāsa deputed his pupil Vaiśaṃpāyana to tell it in his stead; finally, in chapters 54–5, he introduces Vaiśaṃpāyana's narration. The 'So-and-so spoke' headings now switch from Ugraśravas and the seers comprising his audience to Vaiśaṃpāyana and his audience, the Kuru king Janamejaya. (Of course what we are hearing – or reading – is Ugraśravas's retelling of Vaiśaṃpāyana's narration of Vyāsa's tale.) Aside from a single stray occurrence at 2.46.4, the narration of Ugraśravas the Sūta is not referred to again until the story begins to near its end (15.42–3); then he reappears as narrator in the very last chapter to bring the entire *Mahābhārata* to a conclusion.

However, though Ugraśravas may be distinguished as the outermost narrator and Vaiśaṃpāyana as the chief narrator, these two are far from being the only narrators of the *Mahābhārata*. To start with, the entire battle sequence from 5.157 to 10.9 is narrated by one character within the story (the Sūta Saṃjaya) to another (the blind Dhṛtarāṣṭra), with an appropriate switch in the use of 'So-and-so spoke' headings; the version of this sequence relayed to us is thus Ugraśravas's retelling of Vaiśaṃpāyana's narration of Vyāsa's account of Saṃjaya's battle narrative. And at many other points in the story a character may tell a longer or shorter tale to an audience, or preach a sermon to a prince or a king, and again the 'So-and-so spoke' headings are changed accordingly.

There is nothing particularly unusual in a narrative being placed in the mouth of a named narrator, or even in different narrators' narratives being boxed within one another. What does stand out in the *Mahābhārata* is its extraordinarily roundabout approach to storytelling. The highly simplified account I have just given of the contents of the text's first fifty-five chapters was intended explicitly to point up the narrative's inner logic, and yet even from this it is clear that the story takes some very unexpected turns in simply trying to reach its own starting point. The original Sanskrit text of these first chapters, unabridged and unannotated, is frankly confusing, even bewildering. For example, having concluded 1.2 with some generalized praise for the *Mahābhārata* as a whole,[1] why does Ugraśravas suddenly start 1.3 with a story about a sacrifice being disturbed by a dog? Why, having expressed a desire to hear the tale of the Bhāratas, does Śaunaka ask instead at 1.5 to be told the lineage of the Brahmin descendants of Bhṛgu? When Śaunaka wants to hear the full story of Janamejaya's snake sacrifice at 1.14, is it really necessary for Ugraśravas to begin with an obscure dispute between the mythological mothers of the snakes and the great birds, including several lengthy digressions? In short, allowing that the narrative does always end up on course, why does it so often seem to choose the most meandering route available?

The first hint of an explanation is supplied by the text itself, in a well-known verse that occurs near the beginning (1.56.33) and is then repeated near the end (18.5.38): 'What is found here concerning *dharma*, the proper making of wealth, pleasure and final release, is to be found elsewhere too, O bull-like heir of Bharata; but what is not found here is to be found nowhere.' The *Mahābhārata* itself thus claims to be an encyclopedic work, and the spirit of that claim has been honoured throughout the history of the text's transmission. It has been said, for example, of the version of the text compiled and provided with a commentary by the late seventeenth-century scholar Nīlakaṇṭha that 'Nīlakaṇṭha's guiding principle, on his own admission, was to make the Mahābhārata a *thesaurus of all excellences* (culled no matter from what source)'.[2] The great critical edition published between 1933 and 1966 was the first in which major passages were excised from the work; prior to that, both those who originally assembled the text and those who transmitted it seem to have seen it as their duty to include *everything* that might be of some relevance. As the principal critical editor put it, 'No one in the past found the epic text too long. Far from it. It was perhaps not long enough.'[3]

It is this extreme inclusiveness that has led to the *Mahābhārata*'s colossal size; it is this, too, that has resulted in so many narrative

1 Including an anticipatory occurrence of the verse with which the entire work concludes: see 18.5.54.

2 V. S. Sukthankar, *et al.* (eds.), *The Mahābhārata, for the first time critically edited* (Poona: Bhandarkar Oriental Research Institute, 1933–66), vol. 1, p. lxvii.

3 Ibid., p. lii.

overlaps and backtracks, when two versions of a part of the story are told in immediate succession.[1] And it is because of this that we have to be given the fullest possible version of every piece of narrative background, so that sometimes the text really seems to be losing its way as it proceeds circuitously from one point to another on its already very long route.

The *Mahābhārata*'s willingness to embrace all manner of 'extra' material has also led to the incorporation within it of substories, free-standing narratives that do not form a part of the overall story of the Bhāratas but that are told by one character within that story to another, often to reinforce some point the teller wishes to make. Bhīṣma's great deathbed sermon is one rich source of such substories, but others are scattered throughout the text, wherever there is debate between different characters or instruction of one character by another. However, most of these are fairly small-scale narratives. The larger, more expansively told substories are all gathered together in one place, the long book entitled 'The Forest' (Book 3).

Book 2 ended with the departure of the Pāṇḍavas for their term of exile in the forest, and the whole of the third book is devoted to the time they spend there; it includes numerous stories that are told to them. Of these substories, four stand out, partly because of their scale – these are proper set-piece narratives, not brief accounts – but partly also for their own intrinsic qualities.

At 3.49, Yudhiṣṭhira tells the seer Bṛhadaśva of his ruin through dicing, and adds that no one living is more unfortunate than himself. Bṛhadaśva's response is to tell him the tale of Nala (3.50–77), a king who was also ruined in a gambling match, but whose ruin was even more extreme: he lost his kingdom, his wife, his clothes, even his handsome features, but succeeded in the end in regaining everything.

1 Often, as with Ugraśravas's shorter and longer accounts of the snake sacrifice (1.13, 1.14–44), the repetition is provided with a rationale for its existence: a narrator tells a story in relatively brief form and is then asked by a listener to go into greater detail (note, though, that Ugraśravas's shorter account contains narrative material missing from the longer one). However, there are also many cases where we are simply presented with an unexplained narrative dittography: why, as a single example, does Duḥśāsana have to enter the Pāṇḍavas' living quarters to fetch Draupadī to the assembly hall at 2.60.19 when she has already come there voluntarily at 2.60.15?

After finishing the tale, Bṛhadaśva bestows on Yudhiṣṭhira the gift of skill at gambling (a gift he will put to use in the fourth book). 'Nala' is an attractive story of downfall and regeneration, its two halves hinged round a mysterious forest encounter with a snake who seems to be both friend and foe (3.63). It has remained popular down the ages; it has also often served as a simple text for study by elementary Sanskrit students.

Later, as Yudhiṣṭhira pursues his pilgrimage to the sacred bathing-places, his guide, the seer Lomaśa, tells him the tale of Ṛśyaśṛṅga (3.110–13). A much shorter story, this is particularly remarkable for a scene of almost Shakespearean sexual ambiguity and confusion: the young ascetic Ṛśyaśṛṅga, who has been brought up in the forest and has never seen a human being other than his own father, finds himself the target of a determined effort at seduction by a beautiful young courtesan, and subsequently attempts to tell his father what has happened to him in charming but hilariously naive language.

Somewhat more solemn in tone is the seer Mārkaṇḍeya's tale of Rāma (3.257–75), which, like 'Nala', is prompted by Yudhiṣṭhira's lamenting that he is surely the most unfortunate man on earth. Not so, says Mārkaṇḍeya: Rāma was even more unfortunate. This version of the story is important, as it provides an early point of comparison with the *Rāmāyaṇa*, the canonical account of Rāma's life. It is immediately followed by the tale of Sāvitrī[1] (3.277–83), also told by Mārkaṇḍeya, this time in response to Yudhiṣṭhira's questioning whether any other woman has ever equalled Draupadī's nobility and devotion to her husbands. Sāvitrī's devotion to her own husband Satyavat was so great that she actually succeeded in bringing him back from the dead, as well as in restoring his father's sight and fortune. The story is beautifully told, with its almost formal sequences of parallel utterances (three questions before the problem of Satyavat's impending early death is revealed, five boons before he can be restored to life, eight assurances by the ascetics of the hermitage that all is surely well). Despite being very much an exemplary tale of female virtue and devotion, it remains deeply touching in its depiction of affection between husband and wife.

1 Gustav Holst's short opera *Savitri* is based on this tale.

After the term of forest exile comes the stipulated year of living incognito in a populous place. The Pāṇḍavas choose to do this in the court of the Matsya king, Virāṭa, and the fourth book of the *Mahābhārata* describes their adventures there. The scholar E. Washburn Hopkins, writing over a century ago, was convinced that this entire book was a late addition to the text: he adduced several pieces of evidence for this, one of them being its quality as 'an interlude of pantomime' set in the midst of the otherwise unremittingly bleak narrative.[1] I am not concerned here with the earliness or lateness of particular passages of the great tale,[2] but Hopkins does have a point about the tone of at least some parts of Book 4. Whilst 'Virāṭa' includes events that are dreadful (Kīcaka's attempt to rape Draupadī) and that are momentous (the cattle raid, the marriage of Arjuna's son Abhimanyu to the princess Uttarā), it also repeatedly veers towards the farcical. Each Pāṇḍava has to choose a disguise to maintain for a year. Yudhiṣṭhira, characteristically, elects to be a Brahmin – but a Brahmin who is also, of all things, a skilful gambler, and who is bizarrely named Kaṅka, normally the name of a carrion bird that haunts battlefields (4.6). Arjuna, even more improbably given his strapping physique and his well-founded reputation as a ladies' man (see p. xxx above), opts to be a eunuch, and chooses for himself the name Bṛhannaḍā ('woman with a big penis') (4.10). Even in the book's serious moments a sense of humour is not far from the surface. Bhīma promises Draupadī to kill her would-be rapist Kīcaka; he lies in wait for him in the dark, upon the very bed where Kīcaka expects to find his intended victim, so that when Kīcaka arrives he starts by whispering blandishments, before receiving a very unpleasant surprise (4.21.43 ff.).

These are not isolated moments. When Duryodhana mounts a cattle raid against Virāṭa, Virāṭa's son Uttara boasts of the heroism he would display if only he had a suitable charioteer. Infuriated by a slighting reference he makes to Arjuna in her hearing, Draupadī (who is

1 E. Washburn Hopkins, 'The Bhārata and the Great Bhārata', *American Journal of Philology*, 19. 1 (1898), p. 4.

2 The 'unexpected' shift of mood is in itself not a strong argument for the lateness of the fourth book: one does not have to think hard to find similar shifts in other literary genres.

disguised as a maidservant) persuades Virāṭa that the eunuch Bṛhannaḍā is a wonderful charioteer, and he is instructed to drive for Uttara: 'Pāṇḍu's son began in fun to put on a great act, though really he knew everything he was doing: he tried to put on his armour by tossing it into the air, and the wide-eyed girls burst out laughing when they saw him' (4.35.17–18). Then he drives Uttara on to the battlefield. Not unexpectedly, the young prince is terrified, and makes to run away. But 'Kuntī's son wealth-winner Arjuna too leapt down . . . from the splendid chariot, and ran after the running prince, trailing his long braid and his bright red garments behind him. Some of the soldiers, not recognizing Arjuna, laughed to see him trailing a braid as he ran' (4.36.27–8). This is perhaps the last light-hearted moment in the *Mahābhārata*.

## THE WAR

In 1886 a young English writer published a review of the twenty-fifth fascicle of K. M. Ganguli's monumental translation of the *Mahābhārata*. The tale of the great Bhārata war had clearly failed to impress him. In order to convince his readership of the worthlessness of the 'interminable work', it was to descriptions of battle that he turned for the most damning supporting evidence. In case his own judgement of the text (the general tenor of which emerges from a list of the adjectives he uses – 'monstrous . . . nightmare-like . . . monotonous . . . impossible . . . nebulous') should fail to persuade, he reproduced a short section of battle narrative:[1]

And he soon covered the entire welkin with clusters of blood drinking arrows, and as the infinite rays of the powerful sun entering a small vessel are contracted within it for want of space, so the countless shafts of Arjuna could not find room for their expansion . . . And that hero of inconceivable energy overwhelmed, by means of his celestial weapons, all the great bowmen of the

1 This passage in fact comes, not from any of the four books dealing with the great eighteen-day war at Kurukṣetra, but from the story of the cattle raid that concludes the Pāṇḍavas' long period of exile (4.24–62). The Sanskrit original can be found in the critical edition at 4, App. I, 45.

enemy, although they were possessed of great prowess. And Arjuna then shot three and seventy arrows of sharp points at Drona, and ten at Dussaha, and eight at Drona's son and twelve at Dussasana, and three at Kripa the son of Saradwat. And that slayer of foes pierced Bhishma, the son of Santanu with six arrows and King Duryodhana with a hundred.

The name of the reviewer was Rudyard Kipling.[1] To him it was clear that detailed discussion of such 'profitless' stuff was unnecessary: all he had to do was to assure readers of the *Civil and Military Gazette* that the 'interesting epic' consisted of a sequence of passages 'appealing, exactly as much as this one, to the Western mind'. Such 'fantastic creations', he mused, were 'monstrous, painted in all the crude colours that a barbaric hand can apply; moved by machinery that would be colossal were it not absurd, and placed in all their doings beyond the remotest pale of human sympathy'.

I imagine and hope that readers of a Penguin *Mahābhārata* are likely to be somewhat less certain of their own rightness (and others' wrongness) than was the twenty-year-old Kipling; nevertheless, like Hopkins on the 'pantomime'-like fourth book, he does have a point. The exile and period of living incognito are over, and the long negotiations of Book 5, 'Perseverance', have come to nothing; we have reached the moment to which the entire narrative has been leading up, the beginning of the terrible war which alone can settle the dispute between the two sets of cousins. And at this very point the narration seems to enter a new and slightly disconcerting mode. So far from Homeric realism, the description of the great war of the Bhāratas is both hyperbolical and stylized.

The fighting is described as foreground and background. It consists essentially of a sequence of set-piece encounters between important individual warriors, against a backdrop of endless general clashes between the two sides, in which nameless soldiers routinely perish in mind-numbing numbers, often at the hands of a single great hero:

1 The review appeared in *Civil and Military Gazette* of 24 August 1886; it is reprinted in Thomas Pinney (ed.), *Kipling's India: Uncollected Sketches 1884–88* (London: Papermac, 1987), pp. 175–8. I have silently corrected three typographic errors in the spelling of proper names.

The killer of twenty thousand Pāñcāla chariot-fighters, Droṇa now stood on the battlefield, blazing like a smokeless fire; then Bharadvāja's son of great energy, filled once again with that same fury, severed Vasudāna's head from his body with a broad arrow. And he slew a further five hundred Matsyas, and six thousand Sṛñjayas, and ten thousand elephants, and ten thousand horses also. (7.164.83–5)

Sometimes the anonymous dead are numerous enough to produce grisly special effects:

Then with his torrents of sharp arrows the wearer of the diadem set a dreadful river flowing on that battlefield: its water was blood from the wounds of weapons on men's bodies, its foam human fat; broad in current, it flowed very swiftly, terrible to see and to hear. Corpses of elephants and horses formed its banks, the entrails, marrow and flesh of men its mud. Ghosts and great throngs of demons lined its banks. Its waterweed was hair attached to human skulls, its billows severed pieces of armour, as it bore along thousands of bodies in heaps. Fragments of the bones of men, horses and elephants formed the gravel of that fearful, destructive, hellish river; crows, jackals, vultures and storks, and throngs of carrion beasts and hyenas were approaching its banks from every direction. (6.55.121–5)

Apart from simply contributing to the *Mahābhārata*'s colossal casualty rates, the soldiery at large may be routed:

Broken in that dreadful massacre of Kuru heroes, that fateful annihilation of Kṣatriyas, the entire Kaurava army suddenly took flight, crying. 'Flee, Kurus! All is lost! The very gods led by Indra are slaying us to aid the Pāṇḍavas!' Thus the Kaurava forces perished, as if sinking far from dry land. (7.154.39–41)

After some routs, a compensatory rally may take place. But in general, the lot of the common man fighting at Kurukṣetra is terror and death:

[Bhīṣma] slaughtered their mighty ranks, which broke, great king, so that no two men fled together. Their chariots, elephants and horses were transfixed, their standards and chariot-poles fell; the forces of Pāṇḍu's sons wailed and swooned. Father slew son there, and son slew father; friend slew dear friend in that battle, overpowered by fate. Other Pāṇḍava soldiers were seen tearing off their armour and fleeing, hair dishevelled, heir of Bharata. Yudhiṣṭhira's army, its chariots and elephants stampeding with sounds of distress, seemed then like a stampeding herd of cattle. (6.102.25–9)

Against this backdrop of generalized carnage, the great heroes perform their marvellous feats. Arjuna is the finest of all the warriors, Droṇa's star pupil, an archer who wears two arrow-cases because he can shoot with either hand:

Then the wearer of the diadem blazed with anger, like fire consuming a dry thicket, and he drew his bow back to the ear to pierce Karṇa's vital organs with blazing, death-dealing arrows. Karṇa staggered with pain, but he stood steadfast, for he was a man of extreme steadfastness. Thanks to the anger of the wealth-winner, the cardinal and intermediate points of the horizon became invisible through his torrents of arrows, and so did the brightness of the sun, and Karṇa's chariot, O king, as if the sky were filled with winter fog. There were 2,000 foe-slaying chariot-fighters, excellent men picked at Duryodhana's own choice to protect the wheels of his chariots and the feet of his elephants, and to serve as his vanguard and rearguard; all these Kuru heroes, together with their chariots and horses and drivers, were dispatched in that battle in a moment, O king, by the solitary hero Arjuna, the ambidextrous bull of the Kurus. (8.65.40–43)

Many of the heroes possess special celestial weapons. These are not physical objects, but rather sources of power that can be unleashed through the proper invocation, and their effects vary greatly. At 6.55.110, for example, Arjuna deploys the Weapon of Great Indra, which 'countered all the forces of his enemies, as it poured forth torrents of arrows as bright as purest fire'; eighteen chapters later at 6.73.42, Dhṛṣṭadyumna unlooses the Weapon of Bewilderment at the Kauravas, and 'those heroic men were struck senseless in the battle: the Weapon of Bewilderment stripped them of intelligence and mettle.' To possess and use such weapons demands great power and moral standing, and so only the *Mahābhārata*'s true heroes have them. Naturally, Arjuna has a particularly rich store, acquired on various occasions from a number of different gods: Indra (1.225), Śiva (3.41, 3.163, 7.57), Indra together with the other gods (3.164). Sometimes major heroes engage in what amount to duels with their celestial weapons, as Arjuna and Karṇa do here:

When he heard Vāsudeva speak thus to Karṇa, fierce anger filled Pāṇḍu's son the wealth-winner as he remembered each episode; so great was his rage that fiery flames issued forth from his every orifice, O king, which was a great wonder. When Karṇa saw the wealth-winner looking so, he used the Weapon of Brahmā to shower him with arrows, then tried once again to free his wheel. But Kuntī's son the Pāṇḍava struck down that Weapon with his own, and then released another at Karṇa, his cherished Weapon of Fire, which blazed mightily. Karṇa extinguished that Fire with his Weapon of Varuṇa,[1] blackening the entire horizon with rain-clouds; but the heroic son of Pāṇḍu was undaunted, and before Karṇa's very eyes he blew away those clouds with a Weapon of Wind. (8.67.6–11)

As well as meting out death with weapons both terrestrial and celestial (and occasionally, in Bhīma's case, with his bare hands), the *Mahābhārata* warrior heroes are able to tolerate extraordinary levels of physical suffering:

At this Bhīma, afflicter of his enemies, laughed aloud, and then furiously shot his arrows at Kṛtavarman in that battle. The Sātvata chariot-fighter, skilled in weapons, was pained by these, but he did not tremble, great king, and he attacked Bhīma with his own sharp arrows. Then Bhīma of mighty strength killed his four horses, and felled his charioteer and his gorgeous standard; that slayer of enemy heroes covered him with a hail of various kinds of arrows until, maimed in every limb, he resembled a porcupine. At the death of his horses he went swiftly from his chariot to the chariot of Vṛṣaka your brother-in-law, before the very eyes of your son, great king. (6.78.52–6)

Passages such as those quoted here occur again and again in the four battle books, 'Bhīṣma', 'Droṇa', 'Karṇa' and 'Śalya'. Even the phraseology used does not vary greatly from one occurrence to another.

1 The god of the waters.

For example, when Arjuna pierces Droṇa with 'three and seventy arrows' in the passage quoted by Kipling, he is doing something that happens (not always to Droṇa!) twenty-four times in the course of the battle books; whereas only one person is ever pierced with seventy-two arrows, and no one seems to be pierced with seventy-four. From the diction used at one end of the spectrum to the description of entire sequences of events at the other, the narrative relies heavily on the repetition of certain standard elements.

The stylization of the battle narrative is also reflected in its overall development. The focus on individual 'standard' episodes means that as listeners or readers we gain no sense of progression in the overall war. Day after day a similar sequence of individual occurrences is described. Sometimes, of course, there are narrative high points: the death of a great hero, for instance, is likely to have an impact, causing jubilation to one side and dismay to the other, and sometimes motivating a subsequent revenge attack. However, apart from this, and from Kṛṣṇa's machinations (see pp. xxxviii–xli, xliii–xliv above), these individual occurrences do not interconnect: one thing does not lead to another. The story of the war is anyway stopped dead at each nightfall, to resume the next day as if at a brand new start. As a military campaign, what we are told makes limited sense: no one gains or seeks to gain ground, no army presses home an advantage, tactics are restricted to sending in reinforcements to support a beleaguered hero.

It is clear that the authors of the *Mahābhārata* battle narrative were not attempting to present a realistic description of a military action. The length, repetitiousness and lack of realism of the battle narrative may not appeal greatly to modern Western tastes, but it was clearly very much to Indian tastes of two thousand years ago: textual evidence suggests that the books containing the description of the war are among those most heavily expanded during the text's development into the form we know. And though Kipling's review of Ganguli's translation ended with a claim that India, especially youthful India, had turned against its 'two national epics', and that they were now 'surely dead', the massive popularity of the 1980s television serial of the *Mahābhārata* – which made little or no attempt to abbreviate the battle narrative or to inject Western-style realism into it – proves him to have been utterly wrong: not only the *Mahābhārata* in general, but also its particular way of depicting warfare, retains its appeal in India to the present day. To condemn the *Mahābhārata* for not representing war realistically is to condemn it for failing at something it simply does not attempt to do. The point of its hyperbolical battle narrative is surely to convey, not what battle is like, but what it *ought* to be like, what it was like when true heroes walked the earth, what it would still be like if we earth-dwellers had not been plunged into the fourth-rateness of the present degenerate Age of Kali.

## AFTER THE WAR

The eighteen-day battle is over, and Aśvatthāman has slaughtered most of the survivors in his grim night-raid of Book 10. Now the narrative turns to the aftermath of the conflict. First the fallen heroes have to be mourned and their last rites performed (Book 11). Then, after a proper delay to allow the impurity of death to pass from them, and also to allow Yudhiṣṭhira's anguish at the killing to be allayed, the Pāṇḍavas enter the city of Hāstinapura, capital once more of a reunified Kuru kingdom; Yudhiṣṭhira assumes the kingship (12.1–44). Some time later, he performs the great horse sacrifice (Book 14). After fifteen years have passed, the old, blind Dhṛtarāṣṭra resolves to retire to the forest to live among the ascetics there, and he, Gāndhārī and Kuntī all leave Hāstinapura, ultimately meeting their deaths in a forest fire (Book 15). Twenty-one years later there is a drunken brawl that leads to the complete extermination of the Vṛṣṇis, and Kṛṣṇa too dies at the hands of a hunter named Jarā (Book 16). The Pāṇḍavas understand that their time is past, and prepare to depart from the world. After various trials and tests, the heroes all resume their proper places in heaven (Books 17–18).

The obvious question is: why do the books in which these few events are recounted occupy very nearly one-third of the entire *Mahābhārata*? The answer is that over 80 per cent of their bulk, and over a quarter of the entire text, is taken up by the twelfth and thirteenth books, 'Tranquillity' and 'Instruction', containing Bhīṣma's enormous deathbed sermon.

Bhīṣma's is not the only sermon to occur in the *Mahābhārata*, of course, and Books 12 and 13 are not the only location for sermons. Kṛṣṇa has already preached the *Bhagavadgītā* to Arjuna at the very beginning of the war, in the sixth book, and will later preach the so-called 'subsidiary *gītā*' (*Anugītā*) to him in chapters 16–50 of Book 14; and various shorter instructive discourses are scattered at other points through the text. But 'Tranquillity' and 'Instruction' are by far the longest and most densely didactic sections of the *Mahābhārata*.

Bhīṣma's sermon is divided into four parts, entitled 'The *dharma* of kings', '*Dharma* in times of trouble', 'The *dharma* of final release' and 'The *dharma* of giving'. The first three of these are contained in Book 12, the fourth in Book 13; there is no discontinuity between them, and it has been suggested that 'Instruction' was divided off from 'Tranquillity' as an independent book relatively late in the history of the text's development.[1] The titles give good general indications of the principal topics Bhīṣma deals with, but in fact he ranges much more widely than they suggest. 'The *dharma* of kings', for example, also includes a lengthy discussion (12.60–66) of the *dharmas* of the non-Kṣatriya classes and the four stages of life, as well as numerous shorter digressions; 'The *dharma* of giving' likewise deals additionally with a great variety of other subjects.

Whether the initial incorporation of Bhīṣma's sermon into the *Mahābhārata* was a product of the work's tendency to encyclopedic inclusiveness (see p. l above) cannot be known for sure, but it seems certain that, once it was part of the text, it became a useful receptacle for all manner of didactic and religious material: formal statements on *dharma* and on other topics, animal fables, pious tales, glorifications of the great gods including lists of their thousand names, and much else besides. Presumably Brahmin influence was at work in this particular aspect of the text's development. It may be that it was felt necessary to meet the challenge posed by a work of increasing importance and popularity, but one whose world-view demonstrated a somewhat heterodox pessimism; or it may simply be that the *Mahābhārata* had now come to be regarded as the ideal lodging place for all manner of lore, sacred as well

1 Possibly as part of a more general attempt to raise the number of books to the auspicious number of eighteen at which it now stands; this would be doubly attractive as the great war at Kurukṣetra also lasted eighteen days.

as secular. Either way, the first books of the post-war narrative see the heroic tale of the Kuru warriors positively submerged by a flood of chiefly brahmanical teaching, and contribute significantly to the *Mahābhārata*'s standing as a holy text. Just how high that standing became is attested by the fact that it is often referred to, and indeed refers to itself, as the fifth Veda.[1]

Bhīṣma's great sermon covers many topics. 'The *dharma* of final release', for instance, deals at great length with the twin religio-philosophical systems of Sāṃkhya and Yoga, insisting that it is through asceticism and the mental discipline of Yoga that one may attain oneness with *brahman*, the universal Self, and thus gain release from endless rebirth. It has to be said that Bhīṣma's account of these two systems is not always entirely clear or consistent; however, this is likely at least in part to be a reflection of differences of opinion existing at the time within the two schools of thought. With its usual all-embracing inclusiveness the *Mahābhārata* incorporates the differing views without seeking to reconcile them.

Such self-contradictions can in fact be clear indicators of issues that formed the focus of the great debates of the day. I have already said (p. xi above) that the time in which the *Mahābhārata* first emerged was an intellectually turbulent period, and some of this turbulence is manifested within the text itself. One very contentious issue was animal sacrifice. This lay at the heart of the brahmanical religion codified in the Vedas, and the sanctity of the Vedas remained unquestioned and unquestionable (except by heretics such as Buddhists). However, the mood was clearly turning sharply against the violence involved in such sacrifices,[2] and

1 See 12.314 and note.

2 It has often been suggested that this change of mood resulted from Buddhist influence, and there may be something in this; but one should not forget that in the brahmanical tradition itself there had been a steady increase in emphasis on esoteric knowledge and symbolic sacrifice at the expense of actual ritual killing. Even the form of slaughter used in animal sacrifices indicates a distaste for the violence involved: it was done, not by the ritual priests themselves but by a special slaughterman, and took place behind closed doors away from the central sacrificial area. The animal was throttled, so that it would make no sound. Various euphemisms were used for the act of killing: see 14.91.2 and note. Similarly the word used for 'slaughterman', *śamitṛ*, means literally 'he who makes tranquil'.

the *Mahābhārata*, with magnificent inconsistency, argues passionately on both sides. The first section of 'Tranquillity', 'The *dharma* of kings', speaks approvingly of sacrifice in chapters 8, 15–16, 20, 22, 34, 36, 76, 80 and 127–8. The third section, 'The *dharma* of final release', speaks approvingly of it in chapter 226, and disapprovingly in chapters 169, 255, 257, 260, 264 and 324. There is also (chapter 224) what looks like a promising attempt to bridge the gap between the two views by suggesting that *dharma* has changed: in the Dvāpara Age, the third age of the world that was brought to an end by the war at Kurukṣetra, the paramount *dharma* was indeed sacrifice, but in the Kali Age that succeeded it, the age in which we live now, the paramount *dharma* is the giving of gifts.

Book 14, 'The Horse Sacrifice', displays the same inconsistency even more starkly, if somewhat oddly. After twenty chapters of preparation for Yudhiṣṭhira's great ritual (14.71–90), including the conquest and subordination of all other kings, the sacrifice itself is described in admiring detail in chapter 91. Once it is over, a mysterious mongoose appears and denounces the rite as worthless (chapters 92–3). Taking up the hint, the narrator Vaiśaṃpāyana breaks off from his story to caution the listening Janamejaya – whose snake sacrifice he is attending at the time – against the sacrifice of animals. It may be significant that in both Books 12 and 14, it is the opponents of slaughter who have the last word.

Another seeming discrepancy, but one that had apparently been resolved by the time the *Mahābhārata* came into being, concerns what happens to a person after death. There are basically two accounts. According to the first, if someone has lived virtuously he goes to heaven, whereas if he has lived sinfully he goes to hell; according to the second, if he has accumulated good *karma* (i.e. lived virtuously) he attains a better rebirth, whereas if he has accumulated bad *karma* (lived sinfully) he attains a worse one. Closely connected with the second account is the promise that there is a way to end the otherwise unending sequence of rebirths and to attain final release.

Release (*mokṣa*) is often found as the fourth item in a standard list of the aims of human life, the first three of which are *dharma*, the proper making of wealth (*artha*) and pleasure (*kāma*).[1] More common, however, is a three-member version of the list in which release is omitted,[2] suggesting that it was a relative newcomer; indeed, the concept of rebirth and the 'theory of *karma*' themselves are unknown to the earlier Vedic literature, where the blessed simply attain heaven upon their deaths.

It is obvious that these two accounts of what follows death are, as they stand, irreconcilable. What is more, different parts of the *Mahābhārata* appear to adhere to different accounts: the narrative sections of the text mention heaven much more often than release – it is, for example, repeatedly promised to warriors who perish in battle – but release is spoken of again and again in the *Bhagavadgītā* and *Anugītā*, and in the book of 'Tranquillity'.[3] In fact, however, by the time of the *Mahābhārata* the irreconcilables had been reconciled by means of a small adjustment. Heaven was now temporary: when the merit accumulated through one's good deeds was exhausted, one would fall from heaven back to earth and undergo rebirth. As the *Mahābhārata* nears its conclusion and Yudhiṣṭhira himself finally reaches heaven after a brief but distressing experience of hell, the god Indra adds a little further detail to the picture for him: 'All kings have to see hell – this is inescapable, son. One's merits and demerits form two heaps, bull-like hero. He who first enjoys the merit of his good deeds goes afterwards to hell, whereas he who first endures hell goes afterwards to heaven. The man who goes initially to heaven is the one in whom sin preponderates' (18.3.11–13). But, in the new account, it was only by attaining final release, as Mudgala does in 3.246–7, that the cycle could be broken.

Readers, both Indian and Western, react differently to the *Mahābhārata*'s long didactic sections: for some they are a fascinating resource on religious thought in ancient India, while for others they are simply an unwelcome distraction from the narrative. Here all I shall say is that

1 See for example 1.56.33.

2 See for example 2.22.58. Some of these omissions could be attributed to the exigencies of the metre, but certainly not all.

3 Even here, 'The *dharma* of kings' contains many references to heaven.

the reader who dislikes sermons can take the usual measure to avoid them.

## THE *MAHĀBHĀRATA* AS A TEXT

So what is this *Mahābhārata*, this strange conglomeration of heroic tale, myth, theological tract, free-standing narrative, and much else besides? In India the term most commonly used for it – aside from very general words such as *ākhyāna*, 'story' – is *itihāsa*, 'historical narrative', and it is worth bearing in mind that for believing Hindus the events it describes are real happenings that took place in India's ancient past. By contrast, the *Rāmāyaṇa*, which tells a comparable story in similar metre, language and style, is more normally thought of as a *kāvya*, 'literary composition, poem'; indeed, it is considered to be the *ādikāvya*, the first poem. It is rather striking that two ancient texts with so much in common should traditionally be assigned to different genres, but the reason probably has more to do with the strong perception of Vālmīki, author of the *Rāmāyaṇa*, as the founder of the Sanskrit literary tradition than with any sense that the two works are radically different in character.

Western scholars did not hesitate to use the word 'epic' to refer to both *Mahābhārata* and *Rāmāyaṇa*.[1] It may at first seem dangerously inappropriate to apply a Western genre-term such as 'epic' to texts from a culture that recognizes no comparable genre, and that indeed assigns those texts to other genres; we may appear to be imposing our own exotic categories, when we should be endeavouring to understand and work within indigenous systems of categorization. However, genres are not categories. A category is an impermeable container, and any given item is definitively either in it or out of it. For example, a chemical compound is either organic or inorganic; it cannot be 'rather organic'. A genre, on the other hand, is more like a bundle of typical characteristics, not all of which need apply in every case; thus a narrative

1 This paragraph draws on ideas first explored in my foreword to C. N. Ramachandran and L. N. Bhat (trans.), *Male Madeshwara: A Kannada Oral Epic* (New Delhi: Sahitya Akademi, 2001).

may indeed be 'rather novelistic', or a poem 'rather romantic'. Genre-terms are therefore available for making cross-cultural comparisons, and the question to be asked is not, 'is this the correct genre to assign this text to?', but rather, 'is comparison with other texts within this genre fruitful?'

Use of the term 'epic' (a term that has incidentally come to be widely accepted in India) thus implicitly invites comparison between the *Mahābhārata* and *Rāmāyaṇa* and other large-scale heroic narratives from India and elsewhere in the world, and this can certainly be a fruitful exercise.[1] It has long been recognized that both works, as well as recounting narratives of conflict and heroism, contain clear elements of the style that is known to characterize oral bardic epics from other times and places also: the standard phrases for standard situations, the fixed epithets, the largely end-stopped verse with only occasional enjambment from one verse to another. Our *Mahābhārata* itself claims to be narrated by the Sūta bard Ugraśravas, so there is some agreement here between ancient text and modern scholarship. But clearly something quite unusual happened to turn a bardic heroic narrative about a terrible dynastic war into a comprehensive 100,000-verse compendium of the Hindu lore of the day, a work of which it could be seriously asserted that 'what is not found here is to be found nowhere' (see p. l above). Again, the text itself does not contradict the conclusions reached by modern scholars: it claims to be 'maintained by Brahmins in both longer and shorter forms' (1.1.25), it speaks of the existence of 'various compilations' of itself (1.57.75), and it also refers to a shorter *Bhārata* that did not include the free-standing narratives and consisted of a mere 24,000 verses (1.1.61).

I have suggested that the mechanism which allowed the enormous textual expansion that clearly occurred was the transmitters' perceived duty to include *everything* relevant. Once the text had attained a certain critical mass, its claim to encyclopedic inclusiveness presumably became

1 But one far beyond the scope of this Introduction to investigate in detail. For studies comparing the *Mahābhārata* and *Rāmāyaṇa* to epics from outside India, see John Brockington, *The Sanskrit Epics* (Leiden: Brill, 1998), pp. 50–51, 75–81. For an attempt to examine them in the context of contemporary Indian oral epics, see my article 'Scapegoats of the gods', cited n. 1, p. xxxii above.

self-fulfilling: it must have come to seem natural to incorporate the fullest possible version (sometimes even multiple versions) of each episode, the most detailed narration of background mythology, the most complete theological account. And it must also have come to seem natural to regard the *Mahābhārata* as the proper home for any tale of ancient times, any wise saying – for almost anything, in fact.

How long it took for the text to reach the form known to us is a matter of some debate, but the process is generally thought to have continued for several hundred years. Ancient Indian chronology is almost always problematical to establish, and the period of the *Mahābhārata*'s development is no exception: a plausible estimate is the eight centuries from 400 BC to AD 400. Needless to say, those who added new material did their best to conform to the style of what already existed, with the result that, at the end of this long process, it is extremely difficult (and extremely contentious) to distinguish between earlier and later elements of the text. The problem is not merely one of trying to identify chapters, episodes or entire books that show signs suggestive of a particular dating, for additions were made even at the smallest scale. As Sukthankar rather forlornly remarks in his Prolegomena to the critical edition, the text is 'a mosaic of old and new matter', in any typical chapter of which 'we may read a stanza of the second century B.C. followed by one written in the second century A.D.'[1]

## THIS TRANSLATION

I have now to say a little about the translation presented here. From the start it was a given that this would have to be an abridged *Mahābhārata*; a complete version would require at least another four volumes the size of this one, and would anyway be a duplication of the 'Chicago translation' begun by J. A. B. van Buitenen in the 1970s and now being continued by James L. Fitzgerald and a team of other scholars. A complete rendering would also be a very different undertaking from

1 Sukthankar, *The Mahābhārata*, vol. 1, p. ciii.

this translation, for my aim here has been to produce an English version of the *Mahābhārata* that is as true to the original as I can make it, but of a manageable degree of size and complexity from the point of view of a modern reader. It is not merely the original text's enormous bulk that is likely to daunt such a reader; it is also the highly circuitous narrative form discussed above, leading to digressions within digressions, as well as the repetitious and sometimes frankly tedious detailing of theological doctrines that are nowadays likely to be of little general interest. I have seen it as my task to work through all this material on the reader's behalf, and then to present the whole to the reader in a form that is accurate but digestible. In practice, this has meant reducing large parts of the text to summary form, and translating the remainder in full.

The text translated here is, of course, that of the critical edition; however, I have also regularly consulted the seventeenth-century commentary of Nīlakaṇṭha as published in the old 'Bombay edition', as well as keeping a close eye on more recent English translations. For details of these, see Further Reading.

In terms of pages, about half of this *Mahābhārata* is summary, half translation. Of course this 1 : 1 ratio does not at all reflect the balance of Sanskrit text summarized and Sanskrit text translated, for translation occupies more pages than summary; I have in fact translated just under 11 per cent of the entire text. I have felt it important that the passages translated should normally be long enough for a sense of style and narrative coherence to be established. In choosing what to translate I have tried to be representative; as a single illustration, the index lists sixteen references to rivers of blood, but thirteen of these occur in passages of summary, and only one (the passage quoted on p. lvi above) contains an extended description. I have also, of course, tried to select for full translation passages that, in one way or another, seem likely to make for enjoyable reading, whether because they represent narrative high points, or because they are particularly vividly told, or for whatever other reason. Since I am reliant on my own sense of what is likely to be enjoyable, this has allowed me the luxury of choosing many of my own favourite passages; I hope that as a side effect my own enjoyment of them has helped me produce lively English versions.

Another issue is style. Any ambitions I might have had to translate into 'normal' modern standard English had to be forgotten from day one, for the *Mahābhārata* is not in 'normal' Sanskrit (whatever such a thing might be). It is composed almost entirely in verse, and overwhelmingly (more than 93 per cent) in the simple, easily flowing *anuṣṭubh* metre, but to translate into anything other than English prose would have seemed contrived and over-poetic. Sometimes it is possible to introduce a degree of informal rhythmicality into the English as some small compensation. On the other hand the *Mahābhārata* achieves a very characteristic heightened style through the cumulative impact of the descriptive epithets that occur in verse after verse, and some attempt clearly had to be made to reproduce this deliberately bombastic effect:

When Droṇa, unconquerable and boundlessly powerful, unforbearing and furious, penetrated the Sṛñjaya force, what did you all think? When that immeasurably great warrior spoke as he did to Duryodhana, my undisciplined son, and penetrated the enemy ranks, what counter-measures were taken by Kuntī's son Arjuna? When the brave king of Sindhu was slain, and Bhūriśravas too, and undefeated Droṇa of great ardour attacked the Pāñcālas, what did the unconquerable Pāṇḍava hero think? (7.130.1–4)

A small number of typographic devices need to be mentioned. Passages of translation are printed in normal roman type; passages of summary are italicized, and are in the present tense. In both types of passage, chapter numbers are indicated in square brackets within the text, while in translation the verse numbers appear in the margin. (Occasionally a short passage may be omitted from the translation, resulting in a 'jump' in these marginal numbers.) A long dash is used within summaries to signal that there has been a change of narrative 'level', for example from a discussion between Dhṛtarāṣṭra and Saṃjaya to Saṃjaya's actual narration of the events of the war. The eighteen books (*parvans*) into which the text is divided each appear as a separate major section; within these sections, the much more numerous sub-books (*upaparvans*) are indicated through the use of headings. Occasionally it happens that one sub-book is wholly embedded within another: in such cases, the embedded section is indented slightly at both margins.

*And now, hear the words of Ugraśravas the Sūta, teller of ancient tales, son of Lomaharṣaṇa the Sūta!*

# The Mahābhārata

# BEGINNINGS

## CONTENTS

**[1] Honour first Nārāyaṇa, and Nara, the most excellent of men; honour too Sarasvatī the goddess; then proclaim the Tale of Victory![1]**

Ugraśravas the Sūta, teller of ancient tales, son of Lomaharṣaṇa the Sūta, once approached the Brahmin seers assembled in the Naimiṣa forest to attend the twelve-year sacrifice of Śaunaka their chief, bowing politely to those keepers of keen vows. When he reached their hermitage, he was surrounded by the ascetics who lived in the Naimiṣa, anxious to hear his wonderful stories. He joined his hands together and paid his respects to all the sages, enquiring how their austerities prospered, while those good men greeted him. Then, once all the ascetics were seated, Lomaharṣaṇa's son politely accepted the seat they indicated. Seeing him sitting in comfort and relaxed, one of the seers now asked him, by way of starting the talk, 'Where have you come from, O Sūta? and where have you spent these recent days? Lotus-eyed one, tell all: I wish to know!'

The Sūta spoke:
At the snake sacrifice of noble Janamejaya, the royal seer, and in the very presence of that lord among princes, heir of Parikṣit, splendid stories of

1 See 1.56.19. Nara and Nārāyaṇa are two divine seers with whom the heroes Arjuna and Kṛṣṇa are identified; Sarasvatī is the goddess of learning and eloquence.

every kind, composed by Kṛṣṇa Dvaipāyana Vyāsa, were related in the
10 proper manner by Vaiśaṃpāyana. I heard them there, the wonderful tales
of the *Mahābhārata*. Then, visiting a string of sacred bathing-places and
other sites, I made my way to the holy region named Samantapañcaka,
home to many Brahmins,[1] where, long ago, the war took place of the
Pāṇḍavas and Kauravas, and of all the world's kings. From there I have
come before you here, for I wished to see you: in my eyes, sirs, every
one of you is Brahmā's equal! Noble ones, radiant as sun or fire, I see
that in this sacrifice of yours you have purified yourselves by bathing,
said your prayers, and made the fire-offerings, and now you are sitting at
your ease. What shall I tell you, Brahmins? The splendid tales of ancient
times? Or stories of religion? Or the deeds of lords of men and noble
seers?

The seers spoke:
15 We wish to hear the ancient tale composed by Dvaipāyana, the foremost
of seers, which the very gods and holy Brahmins applauded when they
heard it! It is a most excellent story, splendid in wording and narration,
full of subtle sayings, adorned with Vedic lore. The history of the Bhārata
war, Vyāsa's wonderful composition, forms a sacred canon equal to the
four Vedas; it is holy in word and sense, elegant, and enriched with a
variety of learning. We wish to hear it just as Vaiśaṃpāyana the seer
related it on the instructions of Dvaipāyana at King Janamejaya's sacrifice,
winning acclaim, for it is full of *dharma*, and dispels evil and fear!

The Sūta spoke:
20 First, I bow to the Lord, the primeval being, invoked and praised by
many, the true, one and imperishable, eternal *brahman*, manifest and
unmanifest, existent and non-existent, universal and beyond existence
or non-existence, creator of high and low, ancient, supreme and endless,
Viṣṇu, who confers bliss and is bliss, lovely, pure and immaculate, lord of
the senses, preceptor of the moving and the still, Hari Kṛṣṇa. Now I shall
proclaim, entire, the thought of noble Vyāsa, great seer of boundless
ardour, honoured throughout the earth. Poets have told this history

1 Samantapañcaka is also and more commonly known as Kurukṣetra.

before; others tell it now; yet others shall tell it on earth in times to
come. This great body of knowledge has been set in place in the three 25
worlds. It is maintained by Brahmins in both longer and shorter forms; adorned with fair words and episodes both human and divine, and containing a variety of poetic metres, it is the delight of the learned.

*Now Ugraśravas tells of the origins of the universe, and of the seer Vyāsa who composed the shorter* Bhārata *after the events it describes had occurred. He outlines the story that led up to the great war of destruction; then he repeats the lament voiced by Dhṛtarāṣṭra at the disastrous sequence of events, and Saṃjaya's rejoinder that Dhṛtarāṣṭra's wicked sons do not merit grief at the fate which led them to their death. The great* Mahābhārata *is holy; study of it frees one from sin.*

## LISTINGS OF THE BOOKS

[**2**] *At the seers' request Ugraśravas tells the history of Samantapañcaka and describes the composition of an army. Then he lists the hundred sub-books (*upaparvans*) into which the* Mahābhārata *is divided, and summarizes the contents of each of its eighteen books (*parvans*). All knowledge derives from the* Mahābhārata.

## PAUṢYA

[**3**] *(Now Ugraśravas describes the events leading up to Janamejaya's snake sacrifice, at which he heard the* Mahābhārata *recited.) — Janamejaya and his brothers are in attendance at a sacrifice when a dog approaches. Janamejaya's brothers hit the dog, which goes and complains to its mother, the divine bitch Saramā. Saramā curses Janamejaya to fall victim to an unseen danger; Janamejaya appoints as his household priest Somaśravas, who is capable of countering the ill effects of his wrongdoing. Meanwhile, Uttaṅka, pupil of Veda, visits King Pauṣya to ask for his wife's earrings as a gift for his teacher's wife. On the way back the earrings are seized by Takṣaka, king of the serpents, but he succeeds in recovering them; however, desiring revenge on Takṣaka he goes to Janamejaya*

*and tells him how his father Parikṣit had died has a result of being bitten by the serpent king. Janamejaya is filled with anger against Takṣaka.*

## PULOMAN

[4] — *Ugraśravas now asks the seers what they wish to hear; they leave the choice to Śaunaka, their chief.* [5] *Śaunaka chooses to hear about the Brahmin lineage of Bhṛgu, and Ugraśravas narrates. — The Rākṣasa Puloman calls on Fire to confirm that Bhṛgu's wife Pulomā had previously been betrothed to him, and determines to abduct her.* [6] *When Pulomā is seized by Puloman, the baby Cyavana falls from her womb, whereupon Puloman turns to ash. Bhṛgu is furious at the attempted abduction; when he learns of the part played by Fire, he curses it to feed on all things.* [7] *Angrily, Fire protests: he is the mouth through which the gods and the ancestors receive the oblations offered them; how can their mouth eat all things? He removes himself from the sacrificial rituals. The seers and gods appeal to Brahmā, who assures Fire that only certain of his flames will consume all things, and that his touch will be purificatory; Fire accepts this.*

[8] *Cyavana has a son, Pramati; he has a son, Ruru. Ruru falls in love with the beautiful Pramadvarā, but she is bitten by a snake and dies before their wedding.* [9] *Griefstricken, Ruru learns that Pramadvarā can be restored to life if he gives her half his own lifespan. This he does, and she returns to life; they are married. From then on Ruru kills every snake he sees.*

*One day he sees an old lizard and strikes it with his stick. The lizard remonstrates: he has done Ruru no harm; why did he strike him?* [10] *When Ruru explains his hatred of snakes, the lizard explains that he is not a snake but a lizard. Ruru agrees not to harm him, and asks who he really is: the lizard replies that he was once a seer named Ruru, but was placed under a curse by a Brahmin.* [11] *While still a child, he had frightened a Brahmin with a snake made of straw, and was cursed to become a harmless snake. He had pleaded with the Brahmin, who had then mitigated the curse: it would come to an end when he saw Ruru son of Pramati. This has now occurred. As for Ruru, as a Brahmin he should not perform acts of violence. That is the Kṣatriya way, as when Janamejaya sacrificed the snakes and the Brahmin Āstīka rescued them.*

[12] *The lizard-seer vanishes, and Ruru goes home and asks his father to tell him the story of Janamejaya and the snakes.*

# ĀSTĪKA

[13] — *Now Śaunaka asks Ugraśravas to tell the story of Janamejaya's snake sacrifice and Āstīka. Ugraśravas does so briefly.* [14] *Śaunaka requests the full version of the story, and Ugraśravas agrees to relate it. — Kaśyapa the seer grants each of his two wives a boon; Kadrū requests a thousand snakes for sons, and her sister Vinatā requests two sons of equal might. Kadrū produces a thousand eggs, Vinatā two; after five hundred years Kadrū's eggs hatch into snakes, and Vinatā, impatient, breaks open one of her own eggs to reveal an incompletely formed bird: he is Aruṇa, bird of dawn. Angrily, he curses her to be a slave to Kadrū for five hundred years; his brother will free her if she waits long enough for him to hatch properly. In the course of time the divine bird Garuḍa hatches from the other egg.*

[15] *Kadrū and Vinatā see the horse Uccaiḥśravas, produced from the churning of the ocean. — Śaunaka asks to hear this story, and Ugraśravas narrates it. — The gods wished to obtain* amṛta, *the nectar of immortality. Viṣṇu advised them to churn the ocean.* [16] *Having uprooted Mount Mandara to serve as churning rod, and using the serpent king Vāsuki as rope, the gods and demons churned the ocean. After much labour, the water turned to milk, then to ghee; then the ocean yielded sun and moon, the goddesses Śrī and Surā, the horse Uccaiḥśravas, and Viṣṇu's gem Kaustubha. Finally the* amṛta *appeared; the demons tried to seize it, but Viṣṇu saved it for the gods.* [17] *The gods drank the* amṛta. *The demon Rāhu drank too; before he could swallow it, Viṣṇu, alerted by sun and moon, cut off his head; even today Rāhu's head swallows sun and moon at the eclipse. There was a great battle between the gods, supported by Nara and Nārāyaṇa, and the demons; the gods triumphed.*

[18] *Kadrū and Vinatā now gamble on the colour of the horse Uccaiḥśravas, Vinatā maintaining that it is white, Kadrū that it has a black tail: the loser is to become slave to the winner. Kadrū attempts to persuade her snake sons to turn into black tail-hairs; when they refuse she curses them to be burnt in Janamejaya's snake sacrifice.* [19] *Kadrū and Vinatā now set out to look at Uccaiḥśravas. They see the mighty ocean, and cross it.* [20] *They observe Uccaiḥśravas: its tail contains many black hairs,*[1] *and Vinatā is enslaved. Meanwhile Garuḍa*

1 According to a short chapter interpolated between 19 and 20, the snakes changed their minds and carried out Kadrū's wish.

*has hatched. The gods are alarmed at his fiery form, and offer him praise; he withdraws his heat.*

**[21]** *Garuḍa visits his mother; she is instructed by Kadrū to take her to the island land of snakes. She does so, and at her bidding Garuḍa carries Kadrū's snake sons there. He flies close to the sun, and the snakes are overcome. Kadrū appeals to Indra to shed cooling rain.* **[22]** *Indra pours down rain in abundance, to the joy of the snakes.* **[23]** *When they arrive at the beautiful snake island, the snakes spend some time enjoying themselves; then they demand to be carried elsewhere. When Garuḍa asks his mother why he is at their beck and call, she explains her state of slavery, and he asks the snakes what he can do to free her. They answer that he should bring them* amṛta.

**[24]** *Garuḍa prepares to go in search of* amṛta, *but he is hungry. His mother Vinatā tells him to feed freely on the wild Niṣāda people he will find on his way, but to spare Brahmins. He sets out, and catches and eats thousands of Niṣādas.* **[25]** *However, he releases a Brahmin with a Niṣāda wife whom he had inadvertently swallowed; then he travels on and meets his father Kaśyapa. He tells Kaśyapa of his mission, and adds that he is still hungry. Kaśyapa relates the story of two ascetic brothers who had quarrelled and cursed each other: now one of them lives as a colossal elephant, the other as a colossal turtle; Garuḍa should eat them.*

*He swoops down and seizes them, flies up to heaven and lands on the branch of an enormous banyan tree, which breaks off under his weight.* **[26]** *Garuḍa observes that the diminutive Vālakhilya ascetics are hanging upside-down from the branch, which he carries carefully to avoid hurting them. He again encounters Kaśyapa, who helps him release them to safety, and tells him where he can drop the great branch without harming any Brahmins. This he does; then he eats the elephant and the turtle. Terrible portents now appear to the gods, and Bṛhaspati warns Indra that through his own fault a mighty bird has come to steal the Soma.*[1] *Indra instructs the gods to defend the Soma, and a vast armed host surrounds it.*

**[27]** — *Śaunaka asks to hear how Indra had been at fault and how Garuḍa came to be so powerful, and Ugraśravas relates the story. — Kaśyapa had undertaken a sacrifice to acquire a son, and Indra was fetching for it a load of fuel*

1 i.e. the *amṛta*.

*as big as a mountain, when he saw the Vālakhilyas struggling to carry a single leaf, and mocked them. Furious, they sacrificed and invoked their ascetic power to create a new and superior Indra. But after Kaśyapa had urged moderation, they agreed that the new Indra would be a bird, and would also be the son Kaśyapa desired; and so it happened.*

**[28]** *Garuḍa now does battle with the gods; he withstands their onslaught and routs them, and then seeks the* amṛta. *It is guarded by a tremendous fire; Garuḍa assumes a multitude of mouths and fetches water from rivers, with which he extinguishes it.* **[29]** *Next, he assumes a tiny form in order to dart between the razor-like spokes of a revolving wheel; then he blinds with dust two snakes that turn to ash anyone they see. Now he takes the* amṛta. *As he flies away with it he meets Viṣṇu, and the two exchange boons: Garuḍa will be Viṣṇu's mount, but will also remain above Viṣṇu as the emblem on his standard. Then he is attacked by Indra, whose mighty thunderbolt dislodges a single feather of immeasurable size. Seeing this, Indra seeks his friendship.*

**[30]** *Indra and Garuḍa become friends. Garuḍa explains to Indra that he needs the Soma for a particular purpose, but he agrees not to allow anyone to drink it: as soon as he puts it down Indra can reclaim it. In return, Indra grants him the boon of feeding on snakes. Garuḍa now takes the* amṛta *to the snakes, puts it down on some* kuśa *grass and tells them to take a purificatory bath. Indra takes the* amṛta *away. The snakes lick the grass where it had been, and their tongues become forked; the grass itself becomes purifying from contact with contact with the* amṛta. *Garuḍa's mother Vinatā is freed.*

**[31]** — *Śaunaka asks to hear the names of the chief snakes, and Ugraśravas gives them.* **[32]** *Now Śaunaka asks to hear the further history of the snakes. Ugraśravas begins to narrate. — Śeṣa leaves the other snakes and begins practising austerities in holy places. Questioned by Brahmā, he explains that he is disgusted with his wicked brothers. Brahmā grants him a boon, and he chooses* dharma, *passionlessness and asceticism. Brahmā is pleased with Śeṣa, and appoints him to support the earth.*

**[33]** *Vāsuki discusses with the other snakes how to escape their mother's curse that they will die in Janamejaya's snake sacrifice. Various suggestions are made, some wickeder than others, but Vāsuki rejects them all.* **[34]** *The snake Elāpatra reveals that at the time of the curse he overheard Brahmā tell the other gods that the wicked snakes will perish as a result of it, but that virtuous snakes will* *survive: an ascetic named Jaratkāru will have a son Āstīka, who will stop the snake sacrifice. This son will be born to a woman also called Jaratkāru. Vāsuki has a sister of that name; she should be given to the ascetic.*

**[35]** *Vāsuki visits Brahmā, who confirms that he should give his sister to Jaratkāru the ascetic. Vāsuki gives instructions that he is to be informed at once when Jaratkāru seeks a wife.* **[36]** *However, Jaratkāru has no intention of marrying.*

*Now formerly King Parikṣit had once gone hunting; he had pursued a deer deep into the forest, where he encountered the sage Śamīka. He had asked the sage if he had seen the deer, but Śamīka, under a vow of silence, had said nothing. Angered, Parikṣit had placed a dead snake round his neck and left. Śamīka had a hot-tempered young son named Śṛṅgin; he was taunted by a friend that his father had now turned corpse-carrier.* **[37]** *When Śṛṅgin heard what had happened he instantly cursed Parikṣit to die in seven days' time from the bite of the serpent Takṣaka. Then he told his father what he had done; Śamīka reproved him,* **[38]** *but the curse could not be withdrawn. Śamīka sent a messenger to tell Parikṣit about it; Parikṣit took measures to protect himself. On the seventh day, Kāśyapa the Brahmin came to perform a cure if Parikṣit was bitten; Takṣaka approached him.* **[39]** *Takṣaka asked Kāśyapa to show his power, and bit a tree, which immediately burnt away to ashes; Kāśyapa was able to restore it to life. Seeing this, Takṣaka offered him great riches to induce him to abandon his mission; Kāśyapa accepted, and went away. Takṣaka now had snakes in the guise of ascetics carry gifts of fruit, leaves and water to Parikṣit. As the day ended, Parikṣit noticed a small worm in a piece of fruit, joked with his ministers that its name might be Takṣaka, and invited it to bite him. The worm became Takṣaka, who entwined him in his coils.* **[40]** *Parikṣit died from the snake's venom as if struck by lightning. After the ceremonies had been performed for him, his young son Janamejaya was installed as king. After reigning for some time, he married Vapuṣṭamā, princess of Kāśi.*

**[41]** *Jaratkāru the ascetic wanders the world performing austerities. In a cave he discovers a group of ancestors hanging upside-down from a single strand of grass, at which a rat is slowly gnawing. He offers them his ascetic merit to help them, but they explain that it is asceticism that is the cause of their condition: their one remaining descendant, an ascetic named Jaratkāru, does nothing but perform austerities, instead of marrying and continuing the line.* **[42]** *Jaratkāru identifies himself and agrees to take a wife, provided she bears* *his own name, is offered to him voluntarily, and does not require his support. The snakes learn of his decision and inform Vāsuki, who offers his sister to the ascetic.*

[**43**] *When he learns from Vāsuki that she bears the right name and that he will support her himself, Jaratkāru the ascetic weds Jaratkāru the snake woman; however, he stipulates that he will leave if she ever displeases him in act or word. In the course of time she conceives. Not long afterwards her husband lies sleeping while the sun sinks in the sky; fearing that he will fail to perform the evening rituals she wakes him, after much hesitation. He is angry at being disturbed unnecessarily: the sun does not have sufficient power to set while he is asleep. Despite her pleas he leaves her.* [**44**] *She goes to her brother Vāsuki and tells him that her husband has left; he anxiously asks whether she has conceived the child needed to save the snakes, and she tells him that she has. Later she gives birth to Āstīka: he grows up virtuous and learned in the Veda.*

[**45**] *Janamejaya asks his ministers about his father's life and death; in reply they first praise Parikṣit highly, and then recount the story of his hunting expedition and the encounter with the silent sage.* [**46**] *Janamejaya's ministers tell him of Śṛṅgin's curse, the bribing of Kāśyapa, and Parikṣit's death from Takṣaka's venom. Janamejaya determines to take revenge on Takṣaka.* [**47**] *He questions his priests as to how he can achieve his aim; they prescribe a snake sacrifice. Preparations are made; a portent appears indicating that the sacrifice will be interrupted by a Brahmin. The sacrifice begins: enormous numbers of snakes perish in the flames.*

[**48**] — *Śaunaka asks to hear the names of the officiating priests, and Ugraśravas repeats them. Then he resumes his narrative. — Takṣaka has taken refuge with Indra, who assures him that he is safe. But as the sacrifice continues Vāsuki becomes griefstricken at the death of so many snakes, and he speaks to his sister Jaratkāru: she should tell her son Āstīka to save them.* [**49**] *Jaratkāru relates to Āstīka the story of Kadrū's curse on the snakes, and of his own birth to rescue them. Āstīka promises that he will bring the sacrifice to an end; then he travels to where the ritual is taking place.*

[**50**] *Āstīka praises the sacrifice and Janamejaya himself at length.* [**51**] *Janamejaya proposes to grant Āstīka a boon. The priests tell him to wait until Takṣaka arrives: he has taken refuge with Indra. At Janamejaya's urging the chief priest summons Indra himself, and he arrives with Takṣaka. As the moment approaches when Takṣaka will be sacrificed, the priests tell Janamejaya to offer*

*Āstīka his boon; Āstīka chooses the cessation of the ritual. Janamejaya pleads with him to choose something else, but he refuses.*

**[52]** — *Śaunaka asks to hear the names of all the snakes that were sacrificed. They were too many to repeat in full, replies Ugraśravas, but he lists the chief ones.* **[53]** *Then he continues his narration. — Āstīka even preserves Takṣaka from sacrifice: he calls to him, 'Stay!' and the snake remains suspended in mid-air over the flames. Janamejaya graciously accepts the termination of the sacrifice, and pays his respects to Āstīka, who now returns to his mother and uncle. The snakes are delighted with him and offer him a boon: he chooses that anyone who recites his story shall be invulnerable to snakes. — Now Śaunaka asks Ugraśravas to narrate the tale of the* Mahābhārata *as told by Vyāsa at Janamejaya's snake sacrifice, and Ugraśravas consents.*

## THE EARLIEST LINEAGES

**[54]** — *The great seer Kṛṣṇa Dvaipāyana Vyāsa, grandfather of the Pāṇḍavas and compiler of the Vedas, hears that King Janamejaya is about to undertake a snake sacrifice, and goes to see him. After paying Vyāsa due honour, Janamejaya asks him to tell the story of the Kauravas and the Pāṇḍavas, the events of which he had himself witnessed. Vyāsa instructs his pupil Vaiśaṃpāyana to repeat the tale in full as he had taught it.* **[55]** *Vaiśaṃpāyana briefly recounts the story: the hostility of the Kauravas towards the Pāṇḍavas, and Duryodhana's attempts to harm them; their marriage to Draupadī; the division of the kingdom; Arjuna's exile in the forest; and the gambling match that exiled all the Pāṇḍavas for thirteen years and led to the war in which Duryodhana died.*

Janamejaya spoke:
**[56]** Best of Brahmins, you have told me in short form the whole *Mahābhārata* narrative, the great tale of the Kurus. But as you tell this wonderful story, sinless Brahmin, tremendous curiosity arises in me to hear it at length. So, sir, please tell it again in full, for I am never sated with hearing the great deeds of my forebears. It can have been no trivial cause that led the righteous Pāṇḍavas to slay so many who should not be slain, and to be praised by men for doing so!

Why did those tiger-like heroes, though strong and innocent them- 5
selves, tolerate the anguish inflicted on them by their wicked enemies? How was it that wolf-belly Bhīma, mighty of arm and with the vigour of ten thousand elephants, repressed his fury, best of Brahmins, though suffering torment? How was it that Draupadī, though strong and virtuous, did not burn up the sons of Dhṛtarāṣṭra with her terrible gaze when those wicked men molested her? How was it that Kuntī's sons Bhīma and Arjuna, and Mādrī's twins also, obeyed their brother, the tiger-like Yudhiṣṭhira, and took no notice when his wicked enemies cheated him at dice? How was it that Yudhiṣṭhira himself, best upholder of *dharma*, expert in *dharma*, son of Dharma, tolerated an extreme affliction that
he did not merit? And how was it that Pāṇḍu's son, wealth-winner 10
Arjuna, fighting single-handed with Kṛṣṇa for charioteer, dispatched all the great armies of his foes to the realm of the ancestors? Tell me all as it happened, great ascetic! Tell me everything those mighty chariot-fighters did throughout!

Vaiśaṃpāyana spoke:
I shall proclaim, entire, the thought of noble Vyāsa, great seer of boundless ardour, honoured throughout the three worlds. These hundred thousand verses, composed by Satyavatī's son of boundless power, bring holy rewards: any man of learning who recites them, and any man who hears them, reaches Brahmā's realm and gains equality with the gods.
This ancient tale, praised by the seers, is the greatest of compositions: 15
it is equal to the Vedas; it confers supreme purity; in this most sacred history are expounded in full both *dharma* and the proper making of wealth,[1] and in it may be found the ultimate power of reason. That man of learning will gain wealth who recites this Veda of Kṛṣṇa to men of honour, generosity, truth and belief; and even a most dreadful man who hears this history is freed from his sin – even from the sin of abortion.

This history is named the Tale of Victory; it should be heard by him who desires victory, for he will conquer the entire earth and defeat

1 *Artha*, often mentioned along with *dharma* as two of the three aims of human life. The third is normally *kāma*, pleasure; sometimes *mokṣa*, final release, is added as a fourth. See verses 21 and 33 below.

20 his enemies. This is the best means to secure the birth of a son; this is
the greatest road to prosperity; therefore a senior queen and a prince
regent should listen to it often. Here is excellent instruction on the
proper making of wealth; here is supreme instruction on *dharma*; here is
instruction on release, proclaimed by Vyāsa of boundless understanding.
People tell this tale now; others shall tell it in times to come; through it
sons become obedient and servants well-behaved; the man who hears
this is freed at once from every sin of body, speech and mind. Those who
hear without complaint the great story of the birth of Bharata's heirs
25 need have no fear of sickness, much less of the next world, for Kṛṣṇa
Dvaipāyana Vyāsa, in his benevolence, composed it to confer wealth,
glory, long life, heaven and religious merit by broadcasting throughout
the world the fame of the noble Pāṇḍavas and other Kṣatriyas, rich in
ardour as well as wealth.

The blessed ocean and Mount Himālaya are both considered treasuries
of gems, and the *Bhārata* is reckoned so too. The man of learning who
recites it to Brahmins at the lunar festivals is washed clean of his sin,
conquers the realms of heaven, and becomes one with *brahman*; and the
man who recites as much as a quarter-verse to Brahmins at a *śrāddha*
30 ceremony,[1] that man's *śrāddha* unfailingly reaches his ancestors. Any evil
that a man may do in error as he goes about his daily tasks melts away
as soon as he hears the *Mahābhārata* tale.

It is called *Mahābhārata* because it is the great story of the birth of Bharata's heirs; he who knows this derivation is freed from all his sins. Kṛṣṇa Dvaipāyana Vyāsa, the unwearying sage, composed this excellent *Mahābhārata* tale in the course of three years. What is found here concerning *dharma*, the proper making of wealth, pleasure and final release,[2] is to be found elsewhere too, O bull-like heir of Bharata; but what is not found here is to be found nowhere.

**[57]** There was once a king named Vasu Uparicara, a ruler constant in *dharma* and a keen huntsman; a descendant of Pūru, he conquered the rich and lovely region of Cedi at Indra's instruction. He was living in a hermitage, arms laid aside and rejoicing in austerities, when the god

**1** The ceremony in which offerings of food and water are made to deceased relatives.

**2** See verse 16 and note above.

of the thunderbolt approached that lord of the earth in person. Fearful that the king's asceticism might give him a claim to his own rank, Indra himself talked him out of his ascetic practice.

'Lord of the earth,' said Indra, '*dharma* ought not to be adulterated here on earth. Protect it, for *dharma* maintained maintains the universe! You should devote yourself constantly and attentively to protecting the *dharma* of this world, for if you adhere to *dharma* you will attain to the eternal blessed realms. You are a mortal, I a god, but you have become my dear friend. Lord of men, take for your home that land which is the milk-rich breast of the earth! It is a land full of cattle, a sacred land, well settled, rich in wealth and grain, precious as heaven, temperate, full of the best enjoyments earth can offer; abounding in wealth and jewels beyond all others, this is the land of riches, the land of Vasu! Take Cedi for your home, O king of Cedi! The people there abide by *dharma*; they are happy and virtuous, and indulge in no false gossip even over trivia, much less over serious matters. The menfolk are devoted to their elders' welfare; they do not split up their fathers' property; they do not put cows to the yoke, but fatten them if they are lean. All classes always follow their own *dharma* in Cedi, bestower of honour; and nothing that befalls in the three worlds will be unknown to you!

'In the sky there is a mighty flying chariot, a celestial chariot of crystal, fit for a god: it will be yours, a gift from me. Alone among all mortals you will travel aloft in your wonderful flying chariot, like a god in human form. I give you too a victory garland, formed of lotuses that do not fade, to keep you unwounded by weapons in battle. It shall be your symbol, lord of men, blessed, incomparably mighty, and famed as Indra's Garland!'

Then Indra slayer of Vṛtra gave Vasu a bamboo pole, a most cherished gift, intended for the protection of the learned. When a year had passed, the lord of the earth had it planted in the earth in honour of Indra – and from then on, even to the present day, a pole is planted by every true lord of the earth, in the custom he began, O king. On the second day they raise it up, as he did, all decked with baskets, perfumes, garlands and ornaments; they swathe it properly with wreaths and strings, and there they worship the benevolent lord Indra in the mirthful form that the noble god himself assumed in his affection towards Vasu. For when

great Indra saw this fine worship that Vasu, foremost of kings, had
performed, the mighty one was pleased, and said, 'All men and kings
who shall worship me and joyously observe my festival like King Vasu,
lord of Cedi, they and all their folk shall enjoy fortune and victory, and
25 their people shall prosper and be joyful!' Thus, lord of men, the great
king Vasu was honoured by mighty Indra, the noble, bountiful god,
because he was pleased with him. Men who always observe this festival
of Indra with gifts of land and other gifts, with granting of boons and
mighty sacrifices, are rendered pure through Indra's festival.

After receiving such honour from bountiful Indra, King Vasu, lord of
Cedi, remained then in Cedi, protecting this earth according to *dharma*;
and in his love for the god, he instituted Indra's festival. He had five
heroic sons of boundless power; and he, as paramount lord, consecrated
those sons as kings over different kingdoms. There was Bṛhadratha,
celebrated as a mighty chariot-fighter, who became king of Magadha;
Pratyagraha; Kuśāmba, whom men call Maṇivāhana; Macchila; and the
30 undefeated Kṣatriya Yadu. These sons of Vasu, royal seer of mighty
ardour, settled lands and cities under their own names, O king; thus
there were five Vāsava kings, with five separate dynasties for all time.
As for the noble king Vasu, he lived in the sky in the flying palace of
crystal that Indra had given him, visited by Gandharvas and Apsarases;
and so it was that his name became famous as King Uparicara: he who
travels aloft.

The river Śuktimatī flowed by his city. The story goes that Mount
Kolāhala, a living mountain, had once blocked her way, full of desire for
her; Vasu kicked Mount Kolāhala, and now the river flowed through
the gap caused by his kick. But the mountain had already begotten
twin children on that river; delighted at her release, the river presented
35 them to the king. One was a son: Vasu, truest of royal seers and
bestower of wealth, appointed him his foe-taming general. The other,
a daughter named Girikā, or 'Mountain-girl', the king took for his
beloved wife.

At the due time Vasu's wife Girikā, full of desire for him, bathed so as to be pure for the conceiving of a son, and told him that her seasonal time had come. But that very day his ancestors urged that truest of kings and best of wise men to kill some deer for their *śrāddha*. Unable to disobey his ancestors' command, King Vasu set off to hunt, full of desire, his mind full of nothing but Girikā, supremely lovely like a second Śrī in bodily form; and as he travelled through the beautiful forest, his seed gushed forth. At once the king caught that seed on a leaf from a tree, for he was anxious that it should not be spilt for nought, and that his wife's seasonal time should not pass vainly by. Struck by these thoughts, King Vasu, truest of kings, now reflected over and over: he understood that his seed must not be wasted, and that it was his queen's time for conceiving; and so, in his knowledge of the subtleties of *dharma* and the proper making of wealth, he consecrated that seed with *mantras*. And he addressed a swift-flying hawk that he saw standing by: 'Good sir, for my beloved's sake take this seed quickly to my house, and give it to Girikā, for it is her seasonal time!'

Then the swift hawk took it, and flew rapidly up. The bird was rushing on at its highest speed when another hawk saw it coming and instantly attacked it, thinking that it carried a piece of flesh. The two hawks now started a battle of beaks in the sky, and as they fought King Vasu's seed fell into the waters of the river Yamunā. Now in the Yamunā there lived a beautiful Apsaras named Adrikā,[1] who had been cursed by Brahmā to become a fish; and in her fish-form Adrikā swiftly approached the seed of Vasu that the hawk had dropped from its talons, and swallowed it.

Nine months passed, and then one day fishermen caught that fish, O truest heir of Bharata; and they drew from her belly two human children, male and female. They thought it a great wonder, and informed King Vasu: 'Lord, these two children were born from the body of a fish!' Then King Vasu Uparicara took the boy: he was to become the righteous king Matsya,[2] true to his vows. The Apsaras was immediately released from her curse, for she had previously been told by blessed Brahmā, 'O fair one, when, in your animal form, you give birth to two human children, the end of your curse will come.' Now she had borne them, and when the fisherman cut her open she quit her fish-form and resumed the form of a celestial; and then that beautiful Apsaras returned to the realm

1 Like Girikā, this name also means 'Mountain-girl'.

2 The name means 'fish'.

of the Siddhas, seers and Cāraṇas. As for the daughter born of that fish, she smelt of fish, and the king gave her to the fisherman to be his own daughter. Beautiful, mettlesome and full of every virtue, she was named Satyavatī. Because she mixed with fishermen, the sweet-smiling girl continued for some time to smell of fish.

Obedient to her father, she used to ferry a boat across the river, and so one day the seer Parāśara saw her as he toured the sacred bathing-places. She was supremely lovely, an object of longing even for Siddhas, and as soon as the wise and learned seer saw Vasu's daughter he desired her for her beauty. The bull-like sage then made his purpose plain. Satyavatī said to him, 'See, blessed sir, on both banks of the river seers are standing; how can we lie together under their gaze?' When she spoke so, blessed Parāśara used his power to create a mist which obscured the entire land. The girl was amazed to see the mighty seer create that mist, but she was modest and spirited, and so she said, 'Blessed sir, you should know that I am a virgin and obedient to my father. If I lie with you, sinless one, my virginity will be destroyed; and if my virginity is destroyed, O best of Brahmins, how shall I be able to return home? I should not dare to live at home! Blessed sir, you are wise: give thought to this, and do what you think fit; but do it now!'

In reply, Parāśara, truest of seers, told her affectionately, 'When you have pleasured me you shall remain an intact virgin. And choose a boon, timid lady! Lovely one, choose whatever you wish! No favour granted by me has ever failed, sweet-smiling girl!' When Satyavatī heard this, she chose as her boon that her body should have the finest fragrance, and the blessed Parāśara used his power to grant her heart's desire. Then, pleased by the boon she had obtained, and decked only with the charms of womanhood, she lay with that seer of wonderful deeds. And that is how she became famous on earth by the name Gandhavatī, or 'Fragrant one'; men could smell her fragrance at a league's distance, and so she was also well-known as Yojanagandhā, 'Fragrant at a league'.

Blessed Parāśara now returned to his own home, and Satyavatī, delighted at the unequalled boon she had obtained by lying with him, gave birth that very day. Parāśara's heroic son was born on an island in the Yamunā: his mind fixed on asceticism, he approached his mother

and said, 'Think of me at times of need; I shall appear to you.' Thus Kṛṣṇa Dvaipāyana Vyāsa was born of Satyavatī and Parāśara; the child was named Dvaipāyana, 'Island-born', because of his place of birth. Knowing that *dharma* retreats by one quarter in every age, and seeing too that the lifespan and strength of mortals diminish according to the sequence of the ages, he wished to benefit both *brahman* and Brahmins, and so he compiled the Vedas, and hence is known as Vyāsa, the Compiler. The mighty seer, best granter of boons, now taught the four Vedas, together with the fifth, the *Mahābhārata*, to Sumantu, Jaimini,
Paila, and his own son Śuka; he taught them too to Vaiśaṃpāyana. It was 75
these pupils of his who separately made public the various compilations of the *Bhārata*.

— *After this account of the origin of Vyāsa, Vaiśaṃpāyana goes on to supply brief details of the births of many of the other heroes who figure in the* Mahābhārata *story.*

Janamejaya spoke:
**[58]** O Brahmin, I wish to hear in full of all those heroes, both those that you have mentioned and those that you have not, as well as all the other radiant kings. Please tell me fully, blessed sir, the reason why those godlike chariot-fighters were born on earth!

Vaiśaṃpāyana spoke:
This is truly a mystery even to the gods, or so I have heard; yet, after honouring the self-born Brahmā, I shall relate it to you. Long ago Rāma, Jamadagni's son, wiped out all Kṣatriyas on earth twenty-one times, and then retired to Mount Mahendra to perform austerities.
Now since that heir of Bhṛgu had wiped out all the world's Kṣatriyas, 5
the Kṣatriya women approached Brahmins to give them children, O king. Those Brahmins of keen vows lay with the women, tiger-like hero, each at her due time; not from desire, and never out of season. Thanks to them, the Kṣatriya women conceived in their thousands, and then gave birth to Kṣatriyas renowned for their valour, both boys and girls, to rebuild the Kṣatriya order, O king. Thus that order was fathered on Kṣatriya women by ascetic Brahmins, and it flourished, possessed of

*dharma* and a very long lifespan; so once again four classes existed,[1] with the Brahmins at their head.

Men then approached a woman at her due time, not from desire, and never out of season; and other creatures too, even animals, only approached their mates at the due time, O bull-like heir of Bharata. They throve in *dharma*, living hundreds of thousands of years. At that time people were devoted to *dharma* and performance of vows, protector of the earth, and all men were free of care and disease; the Kṣatriya order once more governed this whole earth, bordered by the ocean, covered with mountains and forests and woods, O lord with the tread of an elephant; and with the return of righteous Kṣatriya rule over this earth, Brahmins and other classes experienced the greatest joy. Kings cast aside the vices that arise from desire and anger, and protected their people, punishing the wicked according to *dharma*; and since the Kṣatriya order was devoted to *dharma*, Indra of a thousand eyes and a hundred sacrifices granted sweet rain where and when it was needed, so that the people flourished. At that time no one ever died in childhood, lord of men, and no one ever knew a woman before he came of age.

Thus this ocean-bounded earth was filled with long-lived people, O bull-like heir of Bharata. Kṣatriyas performed great sacrifices at which many gifts were given to Brahmins, and Brahmins studied the Vedas with their branches and Upaniṣads. At that time, king, no Brahmin sold his *brahman*, or recited the Vedas in the presence of Śūdras. As for the Vaiśyas, they used oxen for their ploughing; they did not put cows to the yoke, but fattened them if they were lean. Men did not milk cows until their calves were weaned. At that time no merchant sold his goods by false measure; people performed their tasks, tiger-like hero, in keeping with *dharma*, for they observed *dharma* and were devoted to *dharma*. Members of every class, O lord of men, busied themselves with their own tasks, so that at that time there was no diminution of *dharma*. Cows gave birth at their due time, O bull-like heir of Bharata, and so did women; trees likewise bore their flowers and fruit in season. Such was life during that excellent Kṛta Age, O king, and the whole earth was completely filled with many living creatures.

1 Brahmins, Kṣatriyas, Vaiśyas (farmers and merchants) and Śūdras (serfs).

Then, when the human world had reached such heights, O bull- 25
like hero, demons were born in royal lineages. At that time they had
suffered many defeats in battle against the gods, and so, stripped of
their sovereignty, they took birth here on earth. Desiring lordship, the
proud demons were born among men, and among many other creatures
on earth, O lord of kings: cattle and horses, asses, camels and buffalo,
carrion creatures, elephants and deer. As they continued to take birth
here, lord of the earth, the earth herself could not support herself.

Some of them, sons of Diti and of Dānu,[1] fallen from heaven, 30
were born as mighty lords of the earth: full of valour but also full
of arrogance, able to change their shapes at will, those foe-crushers
overwhelmed this ocean-bounded earth. They oppressed Brahmins,
Kṣatriyas, Vaiśyas and Śūdras too, and they oppressed other creatures
also in their might; terrifying and slaying many creatures of every
kind, they roamed the whole earth in their hundreds and thousands.
Sometimes those sacrilegious beings, drunk with their power and with
strong drink, even assailed the great seers in their hermitages.

When Earth found herself oppressed in this way by those mighty 35
demons, arrogant in their valour and strength, lord of the earth, she ap-
proached Brahmā for help. Now that she was overwhelmed by demons,
O king, neither wind, nor elephants, nor mountains could support her,
and so, afflicted by the burden she bore and troubled for her safety,
she sought refuge with that god, the grandfather of all beings. She saw
Lord Brahmā, the undying creator of the worlds, surrounded by blessed
gods, Brahmins and mighty seers, and lauded joyfully by Gandharvas
and Apsarases, expert bards all; so she approached, and added her praise
to theirs. Then in her longing for protection, and in the presence of 40
all the world-guardian gods, O heir of Bharata, Earth told him what
had happened. But Earth's purpose was already known to the self-born
supreme lord, O king; how could the creator of the universe not know
all the thoughts of those who inhabit the realms of the gods and demons,
heir of Bharata?

Then, great king, Lord Brahmā Prajāpati, the benevolent, the mighty,
origin of all beings, the lord of Earth, replied to Earth: 'The problem

1 The mothers of two major demon races, the Daityas and Dānavas.

that has brought you to my presence, Lady Earth, is one on which I shall
45 employ all those who live in heaven!' With these words, O king, the
god Brahmā gave Earth leave to depart. Then the creator of creatures
himself addressed all the gods; and he said to them, 'To cast off this
burden from Earth, all of you must use portions of yourselves to take
birth separately on earth to counteract it!' And in just the same way
the blessed one convened the hosts of Gandharvas and Apsarases, and
spoke these excellent words to all of them: 'Use portions of yourselves
to take birth as you please among mortals!' Now Indra and all the other
gods heard what Brahmā, their senior, had said, and they accepted his
words as right, appropriate and beneficial. All of them were impatient
to use portions of themselves to go to earth, and so they approached
50 the foe-slayer Nārāyaṇa in his heaven, Vaikuṇṭha. To that highest lord,
whose hands bear discus and club, whose garments are yellow and whose
complexion is dark, from whose navel sprang a lotus,[1] the slayer of the
enemies of the gods, whose eyes are wide and slanted and lovely, Indra
spoke, in order to cleanse Earth: 'Use a portion of yourself to descend
to earth!' And Hari replied 'I shall do so.'

**[59]** Indra now made an agreement with Nārāyaṇa to descend with
the other gods from heaven to earth in partial form. He gave his
command in person to every one of those who live in heaven, and then
he left Nārāyaṇa's dwelling. So it was that the celestials, to destroy the
enemies of the gods and for the benefit of all the worlds, descended
successively from heaven to this earth, and took birth as they pleased,
tiger-like king, some in the families of Brahmin seers, some in the lines
5 of royal seers; and they slew demons and Rākṣasas, Gandharvas[2] and
serpents, and other man-eating creatures in great numbers. And the
demons and Rākṣasas, Gandharvas and serpents did not slay them, for
they were mighty even as children.

*—Janamejaya now asks to hear the origins of all creatures. Vaiśaṃpāyana lists the classes of beings descended from Dakṣa's thirteen daughters.* **[60]** *Next he*

**1** The lotus from which Brahmā emerged.

**2** Just a few verses above, at 1.58.47, Gandharvas are included among the celestials whom Brahmā requests to come to Earth's aid.

*lists other classes: Brahmā's six sons and their descendants, Sthāṇu's eleven sons the Rudras, Dakṣa's fifty daughters, Prajāpati's eight sons the Vasus and their descendants, and various others.*

**[61]** — *Now Janamejaya asks Vaiśaṃpāyana to detail the births and deeds among men of the gods and demons. Vaiśaṃpāyana lists the many incarnations of the demons, before moving on to those of the gods.*

Vaiśaṃpāyana spoke:
O heir of Bharata, you should know that Bharadvāja's son Droṇa – he whose birth was not from a womb[1] – came into being from a portion of Bṛhaspati, most celebrated seer of the gods. He was born here among mortals, tiger-like king, to hold unrivalled knowledge of weaponry, a
most celebrated hero of great ardour, the glory of his line, with deeds to 65
match Indra's, regarded by experts in the Veda as the foremost among them, both in the Veda itself and in archery.

From a fusion of the great god Śiva and Death, Desire and Anger, O heir of Bharata, there was born Droṇa's son Aśvatthāman, the brave afflicter of his enemies; that mighty hero appeared on earth, lord of men, as a lotus-eyed destroyer of enemy forces.

The eight Vasus were born to Gaṅgā as the sons of Śaṃtanu through Vasiṣṭha's curse and at Indra's command. The youngest of them was Bhīṣma, who brought freedom from fear to the Kurus; wise and elo-
quent, he was expert in the Veda and a destroyer of enemy forces, a hero 70
of great ardour, foremost among the omniscient, who fought against the noble heir of Bhṛgu, Rāma son of Jamadagni.

As for the Brahmin seer who was known on earth as Kṛpa, O king, you should know that that most manly hero was born from the eleven Rudras. And you should know that the foe-crusher Śakuni, who was a king and a mighty chariot-fighter on earth, was an incarnation of Dvāpara.[2]

The Vṛṣṇi foe-crusher Sātyaki, keeper of his word, was born from the group of gods named Maruts, as indeed was the royal seer Drupada,
best of all those who bear arms in this mortal world, O king. You should 75

**1** See 1.121.

**2** The name of the second-worst throw in dice, and of the second-worst of the four ages of the world, personified as a powerful evil being.

know that King Kṛtavarman also shared this origin, that unmatchable
hero, truest of bull-like Kṣatriyas; and the foe-crusher Virāṭa too was
born from the group of Maruts, a royal seer who brought affliction to
the realms of his enemies.

The Gandharva lord well known as Haṃsa son of Ariṣṭā was born in
the Kuru line to increase its glory: he is renowned as Dhṛtarāṣṭra, son of
Kṛṣṇa Dvaipāyana Vyāsa, a long-armed king of great ardour who saw
through his wisdom; he was born blind through his mother's fault and
the anger of his father the seer.

You should know that the blessed Vidura, foremost of fathers and
foremost of the wise, was born in this world as Atri's son.

80 King Duryodhana, the foolish, wicked bringer of disgrace to the
Kurus, was born on earth from a portion of Kali;[1] he was the man of
ill omen, hated throughout the entire universe, who slew the whole
world, the base man who sparked off the terrible enmity which led
to the deaths of so many. All his brothers were Rākṣasas born here
among men. All hundred of them were cruel, Duḥśāsana and the
rest: Durmukha, Duḥsaha and the others I have not named. These
companions of Duryodhana were Rākṣasas.

You should know, O king, that King Yudhiṣṭhira was born as a portion
of Dharma, Bhīma of the Wind, and Arjuna of Indra, king of the gods;
85 and Nakula and Sahadeva, who captured the hearts of the whole world
with their incomparable beauty, were likewise born as portions of the
Aśvins.

The son of the Moon, known as Suvarcas of great energy, became
Arjuna's most celebrated son Abhimanyu. You should know that the
mighty chariot-fighter Dhṛṣṭadyumna was a portion of Fire, and the
man-woman Śikhaṇḍin, O king, was a Rākṣasa; know, too, that the five
sons of Draupadī were the group of the All-gods.[2]

You should know that Karṇa, the mighty chariot-fighter who was
90 born wearing armour, was a matchless portion of the Sun god. As for the

1 The name of the worst throw in dice, and of the worst of the four ages of the world, personified as a powerful evil being.

2 A group of Vedic deities that notionally encompassed all the gods, but in fact had a quite specific membership.

eternal god of gods, Nārāyaṇa, a portion of him came among mortals as Kṛṣṇa Vāsudeva, full of energy. Balarāma of great strength was a portion of the serpent Śeṣa, and you should know that Pradyumna of mighty power was Sanatkumāra.[1]

In the same way, prince of men, many other portions of celestials were born in Vasudeva's line to increase its glory. I have spoken before, O king, of the host of Apsarases: a part of them was born on earth at the command of Indra, and in the world of mortals they became Nārāyaṇa's
harem of sixteen thousand queens, O lord of men. A portion of Śrī was 95
born on earth for men to love: she was the blameless girl Draupadī, born into Drupada's line from the midst of the sacrificial altar. She was neither too short nor too tall; fragrant as a blue lotus, she had long lotus-eyes, fine hips and long, black hair. She possessed the five auspicious marks, and her skin was like beryl; secretly she stirred the hearts of five princes among men. The goddesses Success and Steadfastness were born as the mothers of those five, Kuntī and Mādrī, and Wisdom as Subala's daughter Gāndhārī.

Now, O king, I have told you the partial incarnations of gods and
demons, Gandharvas, Apsarases and Rākṣasas, who were born on earth 100
as kings mad for battle and as nobles in the great line of the Yadus. This account of the partial incarnations, which should be heard without complaint, confers wealth, fame, sons, long life and victory. He who hears of the partial incarnations of the gods, Gandharvas and Rākṣasas comes to understand the beginnings and ends of things; he becomes wise, and does not sink down in times of trouble.

## ORIGINS

## ŚAKUNTALĀ

**[62]** — *Janamejaya requests Vaiśaṃpāyana to recount the origin of the Kuru lineage, and Vaiśaṃpāyana begins to narrate. — Duḥṣanta the*

1 A son of Brahmā.

*descendant of Pūru is a mighty king whose reign brings virtue and well-being to the whole world.* **[63]** *One day he goes out hunting: he kills thousands of creatures in the forest.* **[64]** *Then, in a most beautiful part of the wood, he comes upon a lovely hermitage: it belongs to Kaṇva the seer. Duḥṣanta instructs his companions to wait for him and enters, hoping to meet Kaṇva; inside he sees many Brahmins performing their holy tasks.*

**[65]** *Unable to find Kaṇva, Duḥṣanta calls out, and is greeted by a beautiful girl who welcomes him in the proper manner. She introduces herself as Kaṇva's daughter Śakuntalā. When Duḥṣanta expresses astonishment that the celibate Kaṇva should have a daughter, she tells the story of her birth.*

*— The great seer Viśvāmitra had performed such fierce austerities that Indra feared for his sovereignty, and sent the Apsaras Menakā to seduce him. Menakā reminded Indra of the power of Viśvāmitra's anger, and asked the Wind to blow her skirt apart in his presence.* **[66]** *Menakā appeared before Viśvāmitra, and the Wind did as asked; Viśvāmitra was overcome by desire, and the two of them made love many times. After some time a baby girl was born to Menakā; Menakā now returned to Indra's world, leaving the child under the protection of birds (*śakunta*). Kaṇva saw the child and adopted her, naming her Śakuntalā.*

**[67]** *— Having heard Śakuntalā's story, Duḥṣanta proposes marriage to her by the rite of the Gandharvas, which requires only her own consent. She agrees on condition that the son she bears him shall become prince regent. Duḥṣanta accepts this stipulation, and they make love; then Duḥṣanta sets out homeward, promising to send an escort to fetch her. Kaṇva returns home, and is pleased at her choice; he predicts that her son will be a great ruler.*

**[68]** *Śakuntalā gives birth to a son; he is brought up in the hermitage till the age of six, and is known as Sarvadamana ('All-tamer') for his fearlessness. Kaṇva decides that it is time for the family to be reunited, and for Sarvadamana to become prince regent, and he instructs his followers to take Śakuntalā and the child to Hāstinapura. But when Duḥṣanta sees them he claims to have no recollection of Śakuntalā, and tells her to leave. Śakuntalā upbraids him, emphasizes the joy brought to a man by a wife and son, and reminds him of the story of their meeting; but still he rejects her with harsh words.*

[69] *Again Śakuntalā remonstrates with Duḥṣanta and insists that he must keep his word. She leaves, and now a heavenly voice urges Duḥṣanta not to reject his wife and son. Joyfully he accepts them both, explaining that his earlier rejection was to clear them of the suspicions his people would otherwise have harboured of them. Now the child is installed as prince regent under the name Bharata. He becomes a great monarch, and from him the lineage of the Bhāratas is descended.*

## YAYĀTI

[70] — *Now Vaiśaṃpāyana announces that he will recite the genealogy of the Yādava, Paurava and Bhārata lineages.* — *Kaśyapa marries thirteen of Dakṣa's adopted daughters: of these, Dākṣāyaṇī gives birth to the Ādityas and Vivasvat. Vivasvat's son is Yama, his son Mārtaṇḍa, and his son Manu, the first man. Manu has a child Ilā, who is both male and female, and who gives birth to King Purūravas. Purūravas has six sons by the Apsaras Urvaśī, including Āyus. Āyus too has six sons, including Nahuṣa, and Nahuṣa has six sons including Yayāti. Yayāti has two wives, Devayānī and Śarmiṣṭhā, from whom he gets five sons: Yadu, Pūru, Turvasu, Druhyu and Anu. After a long and virtuous reign he is smitten by old age, and asks for one of his sons to assume his aged body and the kingship, so that he may regain youth and pleasure. All refuse but for Pūru, who takes on the burden while his father enjoys a second youth. After a thousand years, Yayāti installs Pūru as king.*

[71] — *Janamejaya asks to hear how Yayāti came to marry Devayānī, and Vaiśaṃpāyana begins to narrate.* — *During the war between the gods and demons, the demons' household priest Śukra is able to bring fallen demons back to life, but Bṛhaspati, household priest to the gods, does not have this power. In alarm, the gods send Bṛhaspati's son Kaca to pay court to Śukra's daughter Devayānī: this will enable him to acquire the necessary knowledge. Kaca does as he is asked, but after five hundred years of paying court he is killed by demons who discover his identity; they cut his body into tiny pieces and feed them to jackals. Devayānī is distraught, and Śukra revives Kaca, but again he is killed by demons who burn his body and mix the ashes in Śukra's liquor. At Devayānī's urging Śukra again summons*

*Kaca back, but Kaca answers from within his belly. Knowing how dear he is to Devayānī, Śukra gives Kaca his revivifying power, and Kaca bursts out of his belly, then brings him back to life. Śukra proscribes the drinking of liquor by Brahmins, and allows Kaca to return to the gods.*

**[72]** *Before Kaca leaves, Devayānī proposes that they should marry, but Kaca is adamant in his refusal. Devayānī now tells him that the knowledge he has acquired will not work for him; he replies that she will not marry any seer's son, and returns to the gods.*

**[73]** *The gods receive Kaca's knowledge from him. Now one day Indra sees some women bathing: he becomes a breeze and mixes up their clothes. When they emerge, Śarmiṣṭhā, daughter of Vṛṣaparvan the king of the demons, puts on Devayānī's dress, and a quarrel breaks out between them; finally Śarmiṣṭhā hurls Devayānī into a well and leaves her for dead. Yayāti passes by and sees her; he takes her hand and lifts her out. Devayānī goes to her father Śukra and furiously tells him of Śarmiṣṭhā's insults.* **[74]** *Śukra tries to persuade his daughter to calm her anger, but Devayānī insists he take action.* **[75]** *He now goes to Vṛṣaparvan and threatens to abandon the demons; Vṛṣaparvan offers him and Devayānī whatever they want, and Devayānī claims Śarmiṣṭhā as her slave.*

**[76]** *Later, Yayāti is out hunting when he encounters Devayānī and Śarmiṣṭhā. Devayānī proposes that they marry, pointing out that he has once previously taken her hand. He is fearful of the consequences of a Kṣatriya marrying a Brahmin woman. She sends for her father Śukra, who gives the match his blessing, but warns Yayāti not to sleep with Śarmiṣṭhā. Yayāti and Devayānī become man and wife.* **[77]** *In time, Devayānī gives birth to a son. Śarmiṣṭhā, realizing that her youth is passing away, determines that Yayāti must father a child on her too, and asks him to do so. He refuses, reminding her of Śukra's words, but she overcomes his objections. Now Śarmiṣṭhā too gives birth to a son.*

**[78]** *Questioned by Devayānī, Śarmiṣṭhā tells her that the father of her child is an unnamed seer. Devayānī bears Yayāti two sons, Yadu and Turvasu; Śarmiṣṭhā bears him three: Druhyu, Anu and Pūru. One day Devayānī sees Śarmiṣṭhā's three boys: they resemble Yayāti and seem to know him. She learns the truth from Śarmiṣṭhā, and at once announces that she will leave Yayāti. Her father Śukra further curses him to be smitten by old age, but agrees that he may pass the curse on to a son; that son* *will become a great king.* **[79]** *Yayāti approaches his five sons one by one, asking them to take on the burden of his old age and wrongdoing for a thousand years. Each in turn refuses, save for the last, Pūru, who agrees. Yayāti tells Pūru that his lineage will inherit the kingship.*

**[80]** *The rejuvenated Yayāti rules happily and virtuously for a thousand years. Then he restores Pūru's youth to him and proposes to make him king. His subjects query the propriety of passing over the four older sons, but acquiesce when they hear of Pūru's filial devotion. The Yādavas are descended from Yadu, the Yavanas from Turvasu, the Bhojas from Druhyu and the barbarian Mlecchas from Anu; from Pūru are descended the Pauravas, the dynasty of which Janamejaya himself forms a part.*

## THE LATER STORY OF YAYĀTI

**[81]** — *Vaiśaṃpāyana now briefly tells the rest of Yayāti's story. Janamejaya asks to hear it in full, and Vaiśaṃpāyana agrees to narrate it. — After installing Pūru as king and banishing his other sons, Yayāti lives for many years in the forest, sacrificing and performing austerities. Then he goes to heaven,* **[82]** *where he is honoured by the gods. Indra asks him what advice he had given Pūru when he assumed the kingship: Yayāti replies that he had stressed the need to avoid hurtful words.*

**[83]** *Indra now asks him to name his equal in asceticism, and Yayāti answers that he has none among mortals or immortals. To punish him for his pride Indra now casts him out of heaven, but grants his wish that he should fall among good people. As he falls blazing through the sky he is seen by the seer Aṣṭaka, who asks him who he is and assures him that he has arrived among the good.* **[84]** *Yayāti identifies himself and explains his situation. He tells Aṣṭaka that fate brings whatever it brings: the wise person accepts this with equanimity.*

**[85]** *Aṣṭaka questions Yayāti about rebirth, and Yayāti describes the processes by which human beings are reborn as higher or lower creatures, according to the merit of their actions. Only through good deeds may one attain heaven, and pride will undermine even these.* **[86]** *Aṣṭaka asks about the behaviour that is fitting for people in the different stages of life, and about the different kinds of holy sage. Yayāti explains.*

**[87]** *Aṣṭaka now asks whether he possesses any realms within heaven; when Yayāti tells him that he does, he offers them to Yayāti to avert his fall, but Yayāti refuses. Pratardana asks the same question and makes the same offer; again Yayāti declines it.* **[88]** *Vasumanas and Śibi in turn offer Yayāti their heavenly realms, but he continues to refuse their offers. But at this point five gold chariots appear to carry all five of them to heaven. As they go, Yayāti tells Aṣṭaka, Pratardana, Vasumanas and Śibi that he is their mother's father.*

**[89]** — *Janamejaya asks to hear about the kings who succeeded Pūru, and Vaiśaṃpāyana begins to relate their history.* — *In the genealogy of the Paurava dynasty there are six generations from Pūru himself to Duḥṣanta; Duḥṣanta's son by Śakuntalā is Bharata, founder of the Bhārata line. In the fifth generation after Bharata, Saṃvaraṇa becomes king. In his reign there is famine and pestilence, and he is attacked by his Pāñcāla cousins, but after a period spent in exile he wins the favour of the seer Vasiṣṭha and regains his kingdom. Saṃvaraṇa's son is Kuru; in the third or fourth generation*[1] *after Kuru comes Pratīpa, father of Śaṃtanu.* **[90]** — *Janamejaya requests a fuller account of the genealogy, and Vaiśaṃpāyana responds with a complete list from Dakṣa down to Janamejaya himself.*

**[91]** — *(Now Vaiśaṃpāyana begins to narrate the beginning of the central story, starting with Pratīpa.)* — *King Mahābhiṣa is virtuous and a great sacrificer, and so enters heaven. One day the wind chances to lift the dress of Gaṅgā; Mahābhiṣa does not avert his gaze, and is cursed by Brahmā to birth as a mortal before he regains heaven. He chooses to be the son of King Pratīpa. Meanwhile the eight Vasus too have been cursed by Vasiṣṭha to birth as mortals. They request Gaṅgā to become a woman to give birth to them as her sons: their father should be Pratīpa's as yet unborn son Śaṃtanu, and Gaṅgā should drown each child as it is born. She consents on condition that Śaṃtanu is allowed to keep one son.*

Vaiśaṃpāyana spoke:

**[92]** Now King Pratīpa was devoted to the welfare of all beings: he

1 Between verses 51 and 52 of 1.89, notes the editor Sukthankar, 'there appears to have been a palpable lacuna in the original which was filled up, independently, in different ways in the two recensions'.

settled himself for many years on the bank of the Gaṅgā, where he engaged in constant prayer. One day as the royal seer sat deep in study, Gaṅgā herself, lovely as Śrī, full of beauty and virtue, heavenly in form and fair of face, a spirited goddess and supremely desirable, arose from the water and sat upon his right thigh, strong as the trunk of a *śāla* tree. King Pratīpa said to the spirited girl, 'O fair one, what favour may I do that you desire?' She answered, 'O king, I love you! Make love to me, best of Kurus! Rejection of loving women is frowned on by the virtuous.'

Pratīpa now replied, 'Beautiful one, you should know my holy vow: I will not lie with another man's woman, or with a woman of a different class.'

Gaṅgā said, 'I am not ill-favoured! I am not a forbidden woman! I am not an object of any kind of censure! Make love to me, O king, a virgin and a beautiful woman who loves you!'

Pratīpa answered, 'I have refused the favour you are urging me to do you; were I to promise otherwise, my violation of *dharma* would destroy me. You have come to my right thigh to embrace me, timid beauty, but you should know that this is where children and daughters-in-law sit. Lovers sit on the left. But you avoided that, and so I will not lie with you, beautiful lady. Be my daughter-in-law, O fair one! On my son's behalf I accept you, since you came to me on the daughter-in-law's side, girl with fine thighs!'

Gaṅgā replied, 'Be it just so, O king, for you know *dharma*: I shall be united with your son. But understand it is for love of you that I shall give my love to the celebrated line of Bharata! You Bhāratas are the final appeal for all princes upon earth, and I could not complete the story of your virtues, even in hundreds of years, for those who spring from this line of yours show goodness beyond comparison. But your son is not to know my antecedents, nor under any circumstances to enquire into anything that I may do. On these terms I shall live with your son and grant him growing happiness, till, rich in sons, merit and pleasure, he shall attain to heaven.'

After giving her agreement she disappeared before his eyes, O king. But King Pratīpa remembered, and awaited the birth of his son. And so at this time that bull-like Kṣatriya practised austerities with his wife in order to get a son, O heir of Kuru. And when they were both old, their son, Mahābhiṣa, was born; since he was born of a father whose passions were stilled, he was known as Śaṃtanu.[1] Śaṃtanu, aware that the imperishable realms are conquered by means of one's own actions, was a man of strictly virtuous acts, O truest of the Kurus.

When Śaṃtanu had come of age, Pratīpa then informed his son: 'Once, long ago, O Śaṃtanu, a woman approached me for your sake. My son, if that beautiful celestial woman should come to you secretly, full of desire and longing to bear a son, you should not ask her, as is usual, "Lady, who are you, or whose are you?" You should not question her about anything she does, sinless one, but at my command make love to her who loves you!' When King Pratīpa had thus instructed his son Śaṃtanu, he consecrated him as king over his own kingdom and then entered the forest as an ascetic.

Wise King Śaṃtanu was famous throughout the earth as a bowman: in his fondness for the hunt he was always travelling the forests. Alone that truest of kings followed the course of the Gaṅgā, frequented as it is by Siddhas and Cāraṇas, slaying both deer and buffalo. Then one day, great king, he saw a supremely lovely woman blazing with beauty, like Śrī herself in person. She was flawless, with gleaming teeth and decked in heavenly ornaments; she stood alone clad in fine garments, her complexion like the inner petals of a red lotus. When the king saw her, he was astonished by her beauty and felt the hair rise on his body; he drank her in with both eyes, but could not get his fill of her. And as soon as she saw him, a radiant king out travelling, her sensuous heart went out to him in love; she too could not get her fill of him.

Now the king asked her, speaking in soft tones to encourage her, 'Slender-waisted one, are you a goddess, or a demoness, or a Gandharva girl, or an Apsaras? Are you a Yakṣī, or a snake girl? Or are you a mortal woman? Whoever you are, splendid godlike lady, become my wife!'

The faultless girl listened with a soft and lovely smile to the king's words; then, recalling her agreement with the Vasus, she went up to him, and spoke a speech to gladden his heart: 'Lord of the earth, I shall

1 This statement is a *nirvacana*, seeking to explain Śaṃtanu's name through an appeal to the similar word *śānta*, 'stilled'.

become your queen, obedient to your will. But whatever I do, O king, be it for good or ill, you must not stop me or chide me for it. I shall remain with you as long as you follow this course, O king; but if I am stopped or chided I shall leave you, make no doubt!'

King Śaṃtanu assented, and so she was filled with the highest delight, O truest heir of Bharata, at gaining such an incomparable prince. And Śaṃtanu too, having gained her, enjoyed her, giving his desire full rein; but recalling that she was never to be questioned, he took care not to say anything to displease her. The king was delighted with her disposition and her deeds, with her beauty and nobility, and with the services she did him in private. And the goddess Gaṅgā, the divinely lovely river that flows through the three worlds, now in a glorious human form, acted the compliant wife to the lion-like king Śaṃtanu, resplendent as Indra king of the gods, whose good fortune had granted his desire. Skilful at love and its enjoyment, entrancing him with her alluring movements, she made love to her king; and he made love to her.

So rapt was he in love, so taken by her matchless womanly charms, that he had no notion how many years, seasons and months had passed. But as King Śaṃtanu made love with her to his heart's content, he fathered on her eight godlike sons; and one by one, as each was born, O heir of Bharata, she cast them in the water, drowning them in the Gaṅgā's stream while telling them, 'I do this to please you!' It did not please King Śaṃtanu; but he said nothing to her, fearful that she would leave him.

When the eighth was born she seemed full of mirth, and the grieving king, longing for his own son, said to her, 'Do not kill him! Who are you, or whose are you? Why do you harm your sons? Stay, wicked child-killer: do not incur this dreadful sin!'

She answered, 'Best of fathers, longing for a son, I shall not kill your son! But now my time with you has run out, in accordance with the agreement that we made. I am Gaṅgā, daughter of Jahnu, honoured by great seers in their hosts! It was to achieve the purpose of the gods that I lived here with you. These eight sons were the Vasus, blessed gods of mighty power who, through the fault of Vasiṣṭha's curse, took on human form. There is no one on earth but you fit to be their father, and no mortal woman here as fit as I am to give birth to them. Therefore I too

took human form to become their mother; and you fathered the eight Vasus, and in doing so conquered the imperishable realms. But this was the promise that I made to those gods, the Vasus: "I shall free each of you from your human birth as soon as you are born!" And so they were freed from the curse of the noble Vasiṣṭha Āpava. Now fare you well, for I shall go. Look after your son, who will be a keeper of mighty vows.
55 One by one I have brought the Vasus here into your dwelling; know that this my last-born is your son, the gift of Gaṅgā!'

**[93]** *Śaṃtanu asks her what caused Vasiṣṭha to curse the Vasus, and she tells him the story. — Dyaus and the other Vasus were enjoying themselves in the forest near Vasiṣṭha's hermitage. Dyaus's wife persuaded her husband to steal Vasiṣṭha's wish-granting cow in order to confer permanent youth upon a mortal friend of hers; when he came to know this, Vasiṣṭha cursed the Vasus to birth as men. When they pleaded with him, he limited the term of the curse to one year for all but Dyaus himself: he would have a long, virtuous but celibate life as a mortal. — After completing this story, Gaṅgā disappears, taking her child Devavrata with her.* **[94]** *Śaṃtanu now reigns virtuously in Hāstinapura for many years.*

Vaiśaṃpāyana spoke:
Once, as he followed the course of the Gaṅgā after wounding a deer in the hunt, King Śaṃtanu noticed that the river contained little water; and, seeing this, that bull-like hero reflected: 'Why is it that today this best of rivers is not flowing as before?' So the high-minded king sought out the cause, and saw a good-looking boy, handsome and strong, standing wielding a celestial weapon as if he were Indra himself, and damming the entire Gaṅgā with sharp arrows.

25 When he saw the river Gaṅgā dammed by arrows before his eyes, the king was astonished at such a superhuman feat. Now the wise Śaṃtanu had formerly seen his son as a newborn child, and so he could not recognize the boy from memory; but the boy knew Śaṃtanu for his father, and used his magic skill to baffle him by vanishing on the spot. And when King Śaṃtanu saw that marvel happen there he felt sure it was his son, and addressed the Gaṅgā: 'Appear to me!' Then Gaṅgā appeared to him in a supremely lovely form, holding that boy, adorned

with ornaments, by the right hand; and she herself was decked with 30
ornaments and wearing spotless garments. Though he had known her
formerly, Śaṃtanu did not recognize her.

Now Gaṅgā spoke to him. 'Tiger-like king, this is that eighth son
whom you fathered on me long ago. Take him home with you! He
has studied the Vedas with their branches under Vasiṣṭha himself; he
has courage, and has acquired expertise in arms; he is an excellent
bowman, equal in battle to Indra king of the gods; indeed he has won
the approval of the gods, and of the demons too, O heir of Bharata.
Whatever learning is known to Śukra Uśanas, the demons' household
priest, is known to him; and likewise your noble, strong-armed son has
all the learning, complete in every detail, of Aṅgiras's son Bṛhaspati,
household priest of the gods and honoured by gods and demons alike.
As for arms, he knows as much as Jamadagni's son Rāma, the unassailable 35
seer of mighty energy. He is a great bowman, and understands both the
*dharma* of kings and the proper making of wealth. Heroic king, he is
your own heroic son, my gift to you. Take him home!'

So at her bidding Śaṃtanu took his son, blazing like the sun, and returned to his own city. And when he reached his own city, which was like the city of Indra, believing that his fortunes were now prospering in every way he could desire, the Paurava king installed his son as prince regent over the Pauravas.

Śaṃtanu's son won great renown, and delighted the Pauravas, his
own father and the whole land with his conduct, O bull-like heir of
Bharata; and so the king of immeasurable valour passed four years very 40
happily with his son. Then one day, as he visited a forest near to the
river Yamunā, King Śaṃtanu smelt a wonderful fragrance, beyond the
power of words to describe; and when he searched in every direction
for its source, he saw a divinely lovely, dark-eyed fisher girl. At once
he asked her, 'Whose are you, and who are you, timid one? And how
do you like to spend your time?' She answered, 'Bless you, sir, I am a
fisher girl, and it is my duty to ferry a boat across the river, as my father,
the king of the fishermen, has instructed me!'

King Śaṃtanu perceived that this fisher girl was divinely lovely, full 45
of beauty, sweetness and fragrance, and he desired her. He therefore
went straight to her father to ask for her as his wife. But the fisher king

replied to Śaṃtanu lord of the earth, 'My lovely daughter was destined
for a husband from the moment of her birth. However, you must know
what is my heart's desire, lord of men. If you will ask me for her as your
wife, you must give me your word to keep an agreement with me; and
you are true to your word, sinless king! By that agreement I shall give
you this girl, for I will surely never find another husband for her to
match you.'

50 Śaṃtanu answered, 'Fisherman, I shall hear the boon that you request
and then determine my answer, yes or no. If it can be granted, I shall
grant it; if it cannot be granted, I shall refuse.' Then the fisherman spoke
again. 'O king, the son she bears is to be consecrated as king after you:
he and no other is to rule the earth!'

Śaṃtanu would not grant this boon to the fisherman, consumed
though he was by his fierce desire, O heir of Bharata; and so, still
thinking of the fisher girl, the king returned to Hāstinapura, nearly out
of his mind with grief. Some time afterwards, as he continued to grieve
55 and mope, his son Devavrata approached and said to him, 'Father, you
are safe on every side, and all the princes are obedient to you; so why
are you so sad? Why are you always grieving? Why do you seem to
mope, O king, and never speak a word?'

When he heard his son's words, Śaṃtanu replied, 'What you say is
true: I feel despondent. And the reason for my grief, my son, is this:
you are the sole heir in this great line of Bharata, and mortals do not
live for ever. If disaster should somehow befall you, son of Gaṅgā, that
is the end of our line. Now it is true that as my sole son you mean more
to me than a hundred other sons; and I have no desire to marry again
without good reason. But, bless you, I want to prevent the destruction
of our lineage, and those who expound *dharma* equate a single child
60 with sonlessness. The *agnihotra* fire ritual, the three Vedas, sacrifices at
which gifts are given to Brahmins: all of these together are not worth
one sixteenth of a son. So it is among men, and so it is among all
creatures. I have no doubt, wise son, that a son contains within himself
even the eternal triple Veda, ancient and excellent as it is. But you, heir
of Bharata, are a hero, ever unforbearing, always armed, and so, my
sinless son, it is through nothing else but arms that you will meet your
death. That is why I am cast into doubt. How will it be when you are

no more? There: I have told you in full the reason for my grief, my
son.'

When he learnt that this was the reason, whole and in full, Devavrata,
who was an intelligent man, set forth, thinking the matter over. He went 65
straight to an old minister who was well disposed towards his father,
and asked him the reason for his father's grief; and he, when questioned
by the Kuru leader, told him truthfully about the boon requested for
that girl, O bull-like heir of Bharata. Then Devavrata, accompanied by
senior Kṣatriyas, went to the fisher king and asked him in person for his
daughter as wife for his father Śaṃtanu.

The fisherman received him with all proper respect, and, once he was
seated in the royal assembly, he addressed him thus, O heir of Bharata:
'Bull-like hero, you are yourself a lord to match Śaṃtanu: a son who
outranks all fathers! What should I say to you? Who would not suffer 70
torment in rejecting such a desirable, praiseworthy marriage alliance?
Not even Indra himself! The noble from whose seed this child, Satyavatī
of high repute, has sprung, a man equal in virtues to you Bhāratas, has
often praised your father to me, young man, as being the one amongst
all kings worthy to marry her. Once I even turned down the divine seer
Asita, for that truest of seers too was a keen suitor for Satyavatī. But I am
the girl's father, and I have something to say, O bull-like heir of Bharata.
I can see a single, powerful drawback to this match, and that is rivalry.
Anyone who has you for his rival, be he Gandharva or demon, could 75
never live at ease because of your anger, afflicter of your enemies. This
and this alone is the drawback to such a marriage-contract, O prince;
good sir, please understand it!'

In reply, Gaṅgā's son Devavrata spoke fittingly on his father's behalf,
O heir of Bharata, in the hearing of the Kṣatriyas: 'Accept my words
as truth, truest of men! No other man, born or unborn, would dare to
speak such words. I shall do as you have said; the son born to this girl
shall be our king!'

The fisherman now answered him. 'Bull-like heir of Bharata, you 80
have undertaken a difficult deed for the kingdom's sake! You are yourself
a lord to match Śaṃtanu of immeasurable splendour, and your *dharma*
and might confer on you the power to bring about my daughter's
marriage. But, good sir, hear what I say and what else must be done: I

have to speak, O foe-tamer, as the girl's father. The promise you have sworn for Satyavatī's sake in the midst of all the Kṣatriyas is typical of you, for you are dedicated to truth and *dharma*. You will not break it, strong-armed hero: I have no doubt at all of this. But you might have a child, and here the doubts I have are great!'

85 Then, having heard the fisherman's thoughts, and being dedicated to truth and *dharma*, Devavrata spoke his promise, O king, seeking his father's good. 'Hear, O mighty fisher king, these words I speak for my father's sake in the hearing of these Kṣatriyas! I had already renounced the kingship, lord of men; now I make this further resolve concerning children. From today forward, fisherman, I shall practise holy celibacy; and though I shall be sonless, I shall gain imperishable realms in heaven!'

When the fisherman heard Devavrata's words, he felt the hair rise on his body; then, in accord with *dharma*, he made his reply to him:
90 'I give her!' And now the gods in heaven, with the Apsarases and all the hosts of seers, showered Devavrata with flowers, and proclaimed, 'He is Bhīṣma!'[1] Then Bhīṣma addressed Satyavatī of high repute on his father's behalf, and said, 'Mother, mount my chariot, and we shall go home.' With these words he helped the lovely girl into the chariot; and then, returning to Hāstinapura, he presented her to Śaṃtanu. The Kṣatriya lords praised the difficult deed he had done; separately and together, they proclaimed, 'He is Bhīṣma!' And his father Śaṃtanu too, when he learnt of Bhīṣma's mighty deed, was pleased with him, and granted him the boon that he might choose the hour of his death.

**[95]** *Satyavatī bears Śaṃtanu two sons, Citrāṅgada and Vicitravīrya. After Śaṃtanu's death, Bhīṣma installs Citrāṅgada as king, but he perishes in battle with a Gandharva. Bhīṣma now installs Vicitravīrya, who is still a child and acts under Bhīṣma's own instruction.* **[96]** *When the time comes for Vicitravīrya to be married, Bhīṣma attends the* svayaṃvara[2] *of the three daughters of the king of Kāśi. He announces that he is abducting all three, and challenges the*

**1** 'The awesome one'. The name Devavrata too in fact reflects this aspect of Bhīṣma's character, for it means 'the one of godlike vows'.

**2** A ceremony at which a girl chooses her husband from among suitors who come to contend for her.

*Kṣatriyas who are present to try to stop him: they attack him, but he defeats them all and sets off for Hāstinapura. As he goes he is challenged by Śālva, king of Saubha, but after a fierce fight he defeats him too. Preparations are under way for Vicitravīrya's wedding to the three girls when the eldest of them, Ambā, informs Bhīṣma that at the time of her abduction she had already chosen Śālva for her husband; he allows her to leave. The two younger sisters, Ambikā and Ambālikā, are now married to Vicitravīrya, who lives in marital bliss for seven years before dying of consumption.* **[97]** *Satyavatī implores Bhīṣma to carry out his duty to continue the line by fathering children on Ambikā and Ambālikā, but he refuses to break his vow of celibacy: he will tell her the proper Kṣatriya course of action.*

**[98]** *Bhīṣma now tells Satyavatī of the Bhārgava Brahmin Rāma Jāmadagnya, who annihilated the Kṣatriyas: afterwards, Brahmins fathered a new race of Kṣatriyas on Kṣatriya women. Then he relates the story of the seer Dīrghatamas, who was cast out by his own sons but rescued by King Balin, and who at Balin's request fathered the royal seer Aṅga on Queen Sudeṣṇā.* **[99]** *Satyavatī should similarly ask a Brahmin to father children on Ambikā and Ambālikā. She assents, and tells Bhīṣma how, when she was a ferry-woman, the seer Parāśara had seduced her: she gave birth to Kṛṣṇa Dvaipāyana Vyāsa. Bhīṣma agrees that he should be approached to save the line from extinction. Vyāsa is summoned and the task explained to him. He is willing to carry it out, but says that the two young queens must perform an observance for a year to prepare them. Satyavatī urges speed: without a king, the kingdom will fail. Vyāsa agrees to her plea, but warns that in this case the young women's observance must be to tolerate his ugliness and his smell. Satyavatī now informs Ambikā what she must do.*

Vaiśaṃpāyana spoke:

**[100]** Then when the girl's due time came, Satyavatī told her to bathe
and lie in her bed; and quietly she said, 'Ambikā, you have a brother-in-
law, and today he is to come into you. Wait for him; do not fall asleep!
He will come during the night.' When she heard her mother-in-law
say this, she lay in her fine bed, thinking of Bhīṣma and the other
bull-like Kurus. Now Vyāsa the seer had been commissioned to go first
to Ambikā. True to his word, he came into her bed while the lamps
shone bright; and when the princess saw his matted red hair, his blazing 5
eyes and his dark brown beard, she shut her eyes. That night he lay with

her, to please his mother, but the Kāśi princess was too frightened to look at him.

When he left her, his mother came to him and said, 'My son, will she bear a son with princely qualities?' Hearing his mother's words, Vyāsa of unequalled wisdom and extrasensory knowledge was led by fate to pronounce: 'He will have the vigour of ten thousand elephants; he will be learned, a true royal seer; he will be a man of great fortune, great courage and great wisdom; he will have a hundred mighty sons. But because of his mother's fault, he will be completely blind.' When she heard this, his mother replied, 'Great ascetic, a blind man is not a proper king for the Kurus. Please give the Kuru race a second king, to protect our kinsmen and bring glory to the ancestral line!' The mighty ascetic promised to do so, and left. In the course of time, Ambikā gave birth to a blind son.

Now blameless Queen Satyavatī instructed her younger daughter-in-law, and brought the seer to her as she had done before. Vyāsa approached Ambālikā in the selfsame manner and lay with her; but when she saw him she turned pale with distress, O heir of Bharata. Seeing her fearful, pale and distressed, O prince, Satyavatī's son Vyāsa spoke these words: 'Since you have turned pale on seeing my hideous appearance, the son you bear will himself be pale; and Pāṇḍu – the pale one – shall be his name, beautiful lady.' With these words the blessed Vyāsa, truest of seers, left her.

Seeing that he had left her, Satyavatī spoke to her son, and he told her that the child would be born pale. Then his mother once again requested one further son from him, and the great seer gave her his assent. When her time came, the princess gave birth to a boy, pale but bearing auspicious marks, and blazing with good fortune; from him in turn were born those mighty bowmen, the five Pāṇḍavas.

When her elder daughter-in-law's due time came, Satyavatī told her to go to Vyāsa; but, thinking about the appearance and smell of the great seer, the divinely lovely lady was afraid, and did not obey the queen's instruction: the Kāśi princess decked out her maidservant, a girl fair as an Apsaras, with her own ornaments, and sent her to Vyāsa. When the seer came, the maidservant rose and greeted him; she sought his agreement, then lay with him and served him with honour. Vyāsa was delighted by the sexual pleasure she gave him, and the great seer stayed the whole night with her as she made love to him. When he arose, he said to her, 'You shall be a servant no longer! And, fair lady, a glorious child has come into your womb; he will be righteous, foremost of all the world's wise men.' So was the son of Kṛṣṇa Dvaipāyana Vyāsa born, Vidura by name, brother to Dhṛtarāṣṭra and Pāṇḍu, boundless in understanding. Wise in the ways of men, free from desire and anger, he was the god Dharma born in Vidura's form because of the curse of the noble Māṇḍavya.

Vyāsa, having discharged his duty, met his mother once again and told her of the forthcoming birth; then he vanished. Thus, to bring glory to the Kuru line, godlike sons were born of Vyāsa to Vicitravīrya's womenfolk.

[**101**] — *Janamejaya asks to hear how Dharma came to be cursed, and Vaiśaṃpāyana narrates the story. — The seer Māṇḍavya was once performing austerities when fleeing thieves concealed themselves in his hermitage. Pursuing them there, the king's men suspected Māṇḍavya of complicity in their crime, and on the king's order he was impaled on a stake along with them; however, he did not die. Learning that he was a seer, the king freed him, but it proved impossible to pull out the stake, which was cut off and left within him. Māṇḍavya now approached Dharma and asked what sin he had committed to merit such a punishment, and Dharma replied that as a child he had speared insects with reeds. Māṇḍavya decreed that thenceforth guilt should not attach to children younger than fourteen, and cursed Dharma to be born from a Śūdra womb.*

Vaiśaṃpāyana spoke:

[**102**] After the birth of the three princes, the Kurus and their lands, both wild and cultivated, prospered. Corn stood tall on the earth, and the crops were plentiful; rain fell in season, and the trees were rich in flowers and fruit; beasts of burden were happy, birds and wild creatures full of joy; garlands were fragrant, and fruit tasted delicious. Cities were thronged with merchants and craftsmen, and people were brave and learned and virtuous and happy. There were no barbarians, no one took delight in wrongdoing; the Kṛta Age continued in every region of every realm.

The people prospered, for they were given to generosity, religious practice and virtue, promoting sacrifices and observances, and living on terms of affection with each other. They were free from pride and anger, and from greed, and their prosperity was shared, for *dharma* held sway. The teeming city seemed then like a mighty ocean, with its cloud-like gateways, arches and turrets, and its palaces, massed in hundreds like those of the city of great Indra himself. People passed their time pleasantly by rivers and in woods, by ponds and pools and on mountain peaks, and in the lovely forests. The southern Kurus then rivalled their northern kin,[1] associating with Siddhas, seers and Cāraṇas; no one was poor, no women were widows. While Bhīṣma justly ruled over all of that fine kingdom, O king, the Kurus dug many wells and ponds, and built many rest-houses and halls; they built, too, many dwellings for the Brahmins. The land was beautiful to see with all its hundreds of sacred columns, and it prospered, absorbing other realms within itself, while Bhīṣma kept the wheel of *dharma* rolling forward throughout the kingdom.

While the noble young princes performed their duties, the people of town and country held permanent festival, and in the homes of leading Kurus and other citizens, lord of men, cries of 'Take!' and 'Eat!' were always to be heard. From birth onward, Bhīṣma looked after Dhṛtarāṣṭra, Pāṇḍu and sagacious Vidura as though they were his own sons. They passed through their consecration ceremonies, and they undertook religious observance and study; and so, skilled now at work and play, they came to manhood. They had mastered archery, horsemanship, fighting with clubs, and fighting with sword and shield, as well as elephant skills and governance; they studied history and ancient tales, and other disciplines too, O lord, and they understood the teachings of the Vedas with their branches. In valour with the bow, Pāṇḍu outstripped all men, while the strength of the prince Dhṛtarāṣṭra exceeded that of all others; and throughout the three worlds there was no one to equal Vidura for his constancy in *dharma* and his profound knowledge of *dharma*, O king. The line of Śaṃtanu, which had seemed destroyed, was now redeemed. When people saw this, a saying became

1 The mythical land of the northern Kurus was said to resemble heaven on earth.

current throughout every land: 'Among mothers of heroes, the Kāśi princesses; among countries, the land of the Kurus; among experts in *dharma*, Bhīṣma; among cities, Hāstinapura!' However, Dhṛtarāṣṭra could not take on the kingship because of his blindness, and Vidura could not do so because of his mixed parentage; so Pāṇḍu became king.

**[103]** Bhīṣma spoke to the princes: 'This line of ours is famed for the excellence of its virtues and its sovereignty over other kings on earth. Protected by virtuous and noble kings of old, this line of ours has never fallen into decay; now, thanks to myself, Satyavatī, and the noble Kṛṣṇa Vyāsa, it is once again well established, for you are the threads of the lineage. Vidura my son, both I myself, and more especially you, must act so that this line continues to swell like the ocean.

'I have heard of a Yādava princess, one suitable for this line of ours, and also of the daughters of Subala and the Madra king. All of these girls are well-born and beautiful; they are all under their elders' rule; and those bull-like Kṣatriyas too are fit for an alliance with us. It seems to me that, to extend the line, we should make a match with them. You are the wisest of the wise, O Vidura; what do you think?'

Vidura replied, 'You, sir, are our father, you are our mother, you are our most venerated elder; so please decide yourself what will be best for this line, and do it!'

Bhīṣma now learnt from priests that Gāndhārī, Subala's daughter, had worshipped Śiva, the boon-granting god, the blinder of Bhaga; they told him that the lovely Gāndhārī had received the boon of a hundred sons. When Bhīṣma heard that this was so, the grandfather of the Kurus sent word to the king of Gāndhāra. Subala was concerned at Dhṛtarāṣṭra's blindness, but when he gave his mind to thoughts of line, of reputation, and of conduct, he gave the virtuous Gāndhārī to Dhṛtarāṣṭra. When Gāndhārī herself learnt that Dhṛtarāṣṭra was blind, and that her parents wished to marry her to him, O heir of Bharata, the lovely woman took a piece of cloth, folded it repeatedly, and covered her own eyes, O king, for she was intent on serving her husband, and determined to take no precedence over him.

Śakuni, the king of Gāndhāra's son, set out for the Kauravas with his sister, who carried a great fortune; the hero gave his sister to Dhṛtarāṣṭra, together with a fitting retinue, and then returned to his own city after being honoured by Bhīṣma. As for Gāndhārī of the fine hips, she pleased all the Kurus with her demeanour, her good behaviour and her performance of her duties, O heir of Bharata. She won them all over with her conduct; intent on serving her husband and strict in her vows, she would not even speak of other men.

[**104**] The ruler of the Yadus, Vasudeva's father,[1] was named Śūra; he had a daughter named Pṛthā, whose beauty was unrivalled upon earth. That hero had formerly promised his firstborn offspring to Kuntibhoja, son of his father's sister, who was childless and had sought this favour; and since his firstborn was Pṛthā, he gave the girl to him, as friend to noble friend.[2] In her new father's house her duties included serving both gods and guests, and so it happened that she waited on that fierce, terrible Brahmin of keen vows known as Durvāsas, a seer who reserved his moral judgements. She made great efforts to satisfy this fierce man of keen resolve, and the sage, foreseeing troubled times ahead, gave her a magic *mantra*, and told her, 'Whichever god you call on with this *mantra* will graciously bestow on you a son!'

When she heard the priest speak these words, Kuntī, who was still a virgin of unsullied reputation, became curious, and called upon the Sun god. Then that girl of flawless limbs saw approaching her the Sun who gives life to the world, and when she saw this great wonder she was astonished. The maker of light and heat now placed a child in her, and so she gave birth to a hero, best of all those who bear arms. This son of a god, covered with glory, was clad in armour: Kuntī's son was born bearing natural armour, and with earrings illuminating his face. He became famous throughout all the worlds as Karṇa. The great light, best of all gift-givers, restored her virginity, and then returned to heaven.

Then, wishing to conceal the wrong that she had done and fearful of her kin, Kuntī cast her son away in the river, despite his auspicious marks. A Sūta charioteer of good renown and his wife Rādhā adopted the abandoned child as their son; they performed the name-giving ceremony for the boy, saying, 'He was born with riches; let him be

**1** And thus paternal grandfather to Kṛṣṇa Vāsudeva.

**2** Pṛthā is subsequently known as Kuntī, after her adoptive father's name.

Vasuṣeṇa, "Richly armed"!' As this mighty hero grew, he became adept with every weapon, and he paid honour to the Sun until his back was burnt.

Now whenever this hero, true to his vows, was seated at prayer, there was nothing that the noble man would not give to Brahmins. Radiant Indra who gives life to creatures took on the form of a Brahmin beggar and asked him for his earrings and his armour; sadly, Karṇa cut from his body the armour, flowing with blood, and the earrings, and, joining his hands together, offered them to him. Astonished, Indra gave to him a Spear, with the words, 'Whether god, demon or man, whether Gandharva, serpent or Rākṣasa, the one at whom you throw this Spear in anger shall cease to be!' Until that day his name had been Vasuṣeṇa, but from then on, by virtue of that deed, he became Karṇa the Cutter.

[**105**] Kuntibhoja's daughter was beautiful, mettlesome and virtuous; she delighted in *dharma* and kept mighty vows. When her father held her *svayaṃvara*, she chose from amongst the thousands of Kṣatriyas the lion-toothed, elephant-shouldered, bull-eyed, mighty Pāṇḍu; united with Kuntibhoja's daughter, like Indra with Paulomī, Kuru's heir was filled with boundless joy.

Bhīṣma now travelled to the city of the Madras, and there purchased for Pāṇḍu at great cost the daughter of the Madra king, Mādrī, famed throughout the three worlds and celebrated amongst all kings for her beauty, unrivalled upon earth. Then he had noble Pāṇḍu's wedding rites performed. When the guests, men from all round the world, saw the tiger-like Pāṇḍu, lion-chested, elephant-shouldered, bull-eyed, full of spirit, they were astonished.

*Pāṇḍu now sets out on military campaigns against Daśārṇa, Magadha, Mithilā, and the Kāśis, Suhmas and Puṇḍras. Everywhere he triumphs, bringing his enemies under his sway and carrying their wealth back to a jubilant Hāstinapura.*

[**106**] *With Dhṛtarāṣṭra's agreement, Pāṇḍu shares out the wealth he has won. Dhṛtarāṣṭra offers many lavish sacrifices. Pāṇḍu lives in the forest with his two wives, spending his time hunting. Bhīṣma marries Vidura to an illegitimate daughter of King Devaka, who bears him many sons.*

Vaiśaṃpāyana spoke:

[107] Then, O Janamejaya, a hundred sons were born to Dhṛtarāṣṭra from Gāndhārī, and one further son from a Vaiśya woman. And five sons, mighty chariot-fighters, were born to Pāṇḍu from Kuntī and Mādrī; they came from the gods, to extend the line.

Janamejaya spoke:

Truest of Brahmins, how did Gāndhārī bear a hundred sons? How long did it take? How long did they live? And how was one son born to Dhṛtarāṣṭra from a Vaiśya woman? How did Dhṛtarāṣṭra come to be unfaithful to such a virtuous wife as Gāndhārī, when she was so good to him? And how were five sons, mighty chariot-fighters come from the gods, born to Pāṇḍu when he had been cursed by that noble man?[1] Learned ascetic, recount all this in detail as it occurred! I am never sated with tales of my kin.

Vaiśaṃpāyana spoke:

Kṛṣṇa Dvaipāyana Vyāsa once approached Gāndhārī exhausted with hunger and weariness. She ministered to his needs, and in return he granted her a boon. She chose for herself a hundred sons, the equals of her husband, and in the course of time she conceived by Dhṛtarāṣṭra. For two years Gāndhārī carried the embryo within her, but she did not give birth. Then, full of woe, she learnt that Kuntī had born a son, radiant and strong as the morning sun, while her own belly remained hard and unchanged, and she fell to thinking. Unknown to Dhṛtarāṣṭra, Gāndhārī with a mighty effort caused the embryo to fall from her womb, for she was overcome with misery. Then there emerged a dense mass of flesh like a ball of iron, and though she had carried it in her womb for two years, she prepared to cast it away; but Dvaipāyana heard of this and hurried to her. Best of all those who pray, he saw that mass of flesh, and said, 'Daughter of Subala, what is this you are about to do?' She revealed her thoughts truthfully to the mighty seer: 'I learnt that Kuntī had born a son, radiant as the sun, and then, in terrible misery, I caused

1 The story of this curse is not told in full until 1.109, but Vaiśaṃpāyana had earlier related a brief version of it to Janamejaya at 1.90.63–4.

this embryo to fall from my womb. Long ago, you told me that you granted me a hundred sons; and now, in place of a hundred sons, I have born this mass of flesh.'

Vyāsa answered her. 'Daughter of Subala, that is what I said, and it will certainly not prove false! I have never told an untruth even in a trivial case, much less over serious matters. Let a hundred pots filled with ghee be quickly set in place; then sprinkle this ball with cold water.'

When the ball was sprinkled, it separated into a hundred embryos,
each the size of a joint of one's thumb; altogether, as time passed, 20
lord of the peoples, a hundred and one embryos emerged one after
another from that mass of flesh. The blessed Vyāsa then placed the
embryos in the pots and arranged for them to be guarded in well-
protected places; and he instructed Gāndhārī, 'Break open these pots
after a further two years have passed.' After speaking so and making such
arrangements, wise Vyāsa then went to Mount Himālaya to undertake
austerities.

As that time passed, King Duryodhana was born from among them; but in terms of birth, King Yudhiṣṭhira was the eldest.

As soon as his son was born, Dhṛtarāṣṭra convened many priests, and 25
also Bhīṣma and Vidura, and said, 'Yudhiṣṭhira is the eldest prince; he
will bring glory to our line. He has attained the kingship through his
merits, and we have no complaint. But, after him, will this child become
king in turn? Tell me the truth; tell me what is to be!'

As he finished speaking, O heir of Bharata, there came from every
direction the cries of terrible carrion creatures and the ominous howling
of jackals. When they observed all these dreadful portents, O king, the
Brahmins and sagacious Vidura spoke: 'It is plain that this son of yours 30
will bring the line to its end: abandoning him will mean peace, rearing
him great calamity. Be content with ninety-nine sons, O king; and with
this one, act for the welfare of the world and of your line! "Give up
one member for the sake of the family; give up one family for the sake
of the village; give up one village for the sake of the kingdom; give up
the earth for the sake of yourself!" '[1]

1 This saying is cited again at 2.55.10, where it is attributed to Śukra, the demons' household priest, and then again at 5.37.16 and 5.126.48.

This was the advice of Vidura and of all those Brahmins; but the king did not act upon it, for he was filled with love for his son.

Now in the course of a month, O prince, all Dhṛtarāṣṭra's hundred sons were born, and so was one further child, a girl. And it seems that while Gāndhārī was afflicted with her distended belly, a Vaiśya woman used to serve strong-armed Dhṛtarāṣṭra; within the year, O king, she gave birth to his illegitimate son, the wise Yuyutsu of great renown. Thus to wise Dhṛtarāṣṭra were born a hundred sons, heroes and great chariot-fighters all, together with a single daughter, Duḥśalā.

[108] *— Janamejaya asks to hear the names of all the hundred Dhārtarāṣṭras, in order of their birth, and Vaiśaṃpāyana lists them, starting with Duryodhana, Yuyutsu and Duḥśāsana. — All of them are given a full education and, in due time, are married. The daughter Duḥśalā is also married, to Jayadratha king of Sindhu.*

[109] *— Janamejaya now asks to hear of the birth of the Pāṇḍavas, and Vaiśaṃpāyana narrates. — Pāṇḍu is hunting in the forest: he shoots a pair of deer as they mate. The deer are in fact a great ascetic and his wife in animal form; before dying, the male deer remonstrates with Pāṇḍu for his act and curses him to suffer the same fate: when he makes love he will die, and his lover will follow him into death.* [110] *Griefstricken, Pāṇḍu determines on a life of extreme austerities: his wives Kuntī and Mādrī persuade him to allow them to accompany him. Pāṇḍu now returns all his kingly apparel to Hāstinapura, announcing that he will remain in the forest as an ascetic.*

[111] *Living a life of virtue and asceticism in the forest, Pāṇḍu strives to reach heaven and so heads northward, but is advised by ascetics that the way is too hard for his wives to travel. He expresses his despair at his childless state; the ascetics assure him that he will acquire offspring. He now tells Kuntī that she should conceive with the aid of a Brahmin.* [112] *Kuntī demurs, and tells Pāṇḍu the story of King Vyuṣitāśva, who died childless: his widow received from her dead husband the boon of conceiving from his corpse. In the same way she herself can be impregnated by Pāṇḍu mentally, by means of his ascetic power.* [113] *Pāṇḍu remains adamant: for a wife to refuse her husband's wish that she conceive is as sinful as abortion or adultery. As King Kalmāṣapāda's wife conceived with the aid of Vasiṣṭha, as Pāṇḍu himself was conceived with the aid of Vyāsa, so Kuntī must conceive with a Brahmin's aid. Kuntī now tells him of the boon given*

*her by Durvāsas, allowing her to gain a son by any god she chooses to invoke, and Pāṇḍu tells her to invoke the god Dharma, so that she may give birth to a righteous son.*

Vaiśaṃpāyana spoke:
[114] Gāndhārī had been pregnant for a year, O Janamejaya, when Queen Kuntī called upon invincible Dharma to give her a child: she hastened to make an offering to him, and she recited in the proper manner the *mantra* that Durvāsas had previously given her. Kuntī of fine hips lay with Dharma, who assumed bodily form through the power of Yoga, and she conceived a son, best of all living beings, at the midday hour called 'Victory', when the Jyeṣṭhā constellation was in conjunction with the moon, in the bright half of the month, on an auspicious day. In time, Kuntī gave birth to a son of great renown. As soon as that son was born, an incorporeal voice proclaimed: 'This child, Pāṇḍu's firstborn son, will be the best upholder of *dharma*, make no doubt! Known as Yudhiṣṭhira, he will be a famous king, renowned throughout the three worlds for his glory, his ardour and his conduct.'

Having obtained a son through Dharma, Pāṇḍu now spoke again to Kuntī: 'It is said that Kṣatriyas excel in strength; ask now for a son who excels in strength!' When Kuntī heard her husband's words, it was the Wind god Vāyu whom she called upon; and so was born Bhīma, 'the terrible one', a strong-armed hero of terrible valour. When he was born, strong to excess, invincible, the voice spoke once more, O heir of Bharata: 'This newborn child will be the best of all the mighty!' And a miracle occurred as soon as wolf-belly Bhīma was born: he fell from his mother's lap and smashed a mountain to fragments with his limbs. It seems that Kuntī suddenly stood up, troubled by fear of tigers, forgetting that the wolf-belly lay sleeping in her lap; then the child, whose body was dense as adamant, fell on the mountain, and as he fell he smashed it to fragments with his limbs, to the astonishment of the watching Pāṇḍu. On the very day of Bhīma's birth, O truest heir of Bharata, Duryodhana too was born.

After the birth of Bhīma, Pāṇḍu fell again to thinking: 'How may I get an excellent son, the best son in the world? This world is founded upon divine destiny and human aspiration; but even what is destined only comes to us through timely action. Now Indra is said to be king and chief of the gods, immeasurably mighty and determined, heroic, boundless in splendour. I shall win his favour with austerities to obtain from him a very mighty son. The son that Indra gives me will be most excellent; therefore I shall perform great austerities through deeds, thoughts and words.'

Now Kuru's heir, Pāṇḍu of great ardour, consulted mighty seers and told Kuntī to undertake an auspicious vow lasting a year. As for himself, the strong-armed hero remained standing on one foot, and practised fierce asceticism with his mind intensely focused; intent on winning the favour of that god who is lord of the gods, O heir of Bharata, righteous Pāṇḍu pursued his austerities as the sun pursued its course. And after the passage of much time, Indra answered him: 'I shall give you a son who will be famed throughout the three worlds; I shall give you a son, a leader to bring destruction to all his enemies and to accomplish the purposes of gods, Brahmins and his friends!'

Hearing the words of noble Indra, king of the gods, and mindful of them, the righteous Kuru king spoke to Kuntī: 'Lady of fine hips, bear me a son, noble, skilled at governance, radiant and strong as the sun, unconquerable, vigorous, supremely handsome, full of the Kṣatriya ardour! I have won this favour from Indra, lord of the gods; call upon him, sweet-smiling lady!' At his request, that lady of high repute now called on Indra; and the lord of the gods came to her, and fathered Arjuna upon her. As soon as the boy was born, the incorporeal voice proclaimed, making the sky resound with its deep and mighty thunder: 'Kuntī, this child will be courageous as Kārtavīrya, valiant as Śibi, invincible as Indra; he will spread your fame. As Aditi's joy was increased by Viṣṇu, so Arjuna, Viṣṇu's equal, will increase your joy. He will exercise authority over the Madras, the Kurus with the Kekayas, and the Cedis, Kāśis and Karūṣas; he will truly raise the Kuru banner. Through the might of his arm the Fire god will be fully sated with the fat of all the creatures in the Khāṇḍava forest. He will lead his people to victory over the lords of the earth; with his brothers he will perform three horse sacrifices.[1] The equal of Jamadagni's son Rāma, O Kuntī, as valiant as Viṣṇu, best of the brave, this bull-like hero will never suffer defeat; and he will obtain all the celestial weapons, and restore a fortune that was lost.'

Kuntī heard this most wonderful speech spoken at the birth of her son by the wind in the sky. The ascetics living on the hundred-peaked mountain heard the loud proclamation, and they were filled with the greatest joy, and so were the divine seers, and the gods led by Indra. There was a tumultuous sound of drums in the air; a mighty roar arose, while flowers showered down, and all the hosts of the gods came together to honour Kuntī's son, together with serpents, divine birds, Gandharvas and Apsarases, all the lords of creation, and the seven great seers.

But Pāṇḍu of great renown, longing for yet more sons, urged on the lovely Kuntī; she, however, answered, 'The wise do not favour a fourth child, even in times of trouble. After three, they say the woman must be driven by lust; if there is a fifth, she must be a whore. You know that this is *dharma*, and that it makes sense; so how is it that now you act against it, as if through forgetfulness, and ask me for more children?'

**[115]** Now after the birth of Kuntī's sons and those of Dhṛtarāṣṭra, the Madra princess Mādrī spoke to Pāṇḍu in private. 'Afflicter of your enemies, I would not grieve even if you acted ill towards me, and so, sinless king, I do not grieve to remain always lower in rank than the estimable Kuntī; nor did I feel sorrow on hearing of the birth of Gāndhārī's hundred sons, O heir of Kuru. Yet this great sorrow I do bear: both wives were equally sonless, but now my husband has been blessed with offspring from Kuntī. If King Kuntibhoja's daughter were to help me bear children, it would be a kindness to me, and a benefit also to you. Since we are co-wives I feel constraint in speaking of this to Kuntī; but if you are well disposed towards me, urge her yourself in my cause.'

Pāṇḍu replied, 'This matter is always in my thoughts too, O Mādrī, but I have not ventured to speak of it to you, as I was not sure whether

1 In fact the Pāṇḍavas perform a single such sacrifice, but at Vyāsa's bidding it involves three times the normal expenditure on gifts to Brahmins; according to Vyāsa, this makes it equivalent to three sacrifices (14.90.14–15).

you would be pleased or hurt. However, now I know your thoughts I shall do my best. I am sure that when I speak to Kuntī she will accept what I say.'

Next, Pāṇḍu spoke privately to Kuntī. 'Confer offspring on my line, and a benefit on the world! O fair one, do this most excellent deed, both to please me, and to prevent my funeral offerings, and those of my forebears, from destruction. For your own renown, too, carry out this very difficult task! Even after gaining the sovereignty, Indra continued to sacrifice, for he wished for renown; in the same way, lovely one, priests who know the Vedas and have performed the hardest austerities still take instruction from religious elders, for the sake of renown; and royal seers and great ascetic Brahmins too have performed, for renown, many kinds of difficult deeds. Therefore, blameless lady, you should rescue Mādrī from her shipwreck, and win the highest fame by bestowing offspring on her!'

Kuntī heard her husband's request, and then went and spoke to Mādrī: 'Think now of some deity, and, make no doubt, you will receive from him a child like himself!' So Mādrī reflected briefly, and then mentally invoked the two Aśvins; and they came to her, and fathered twin sons on her, Nakula and Sahadeva, whose beauty was incomparable on earth. Then, as before, the incorporeal voice proclaimed those twins: 'These two will far outshine all others in beauty, mettle and virtue, in ardour and in wealth.'

The ascetics living on the hundred-peaked mountain performed the naming ritual for all five boys, lord of the peoples, with love and ceremony and blessings. First they attended to Kuntī's sons, naming the eldest Yudhiṣṭhira, the middle one Bhīma, and the third Arjuna; then the priests affectionately named the sons of Mādrī: the firstborn Nakula, the other Sahadeva. Those truest of Kurus were born a year apart from one another.

Now Pāṇḍu urged Kuntī once again in Mādrī's cause; but when he repeatedly asked her help in private, O king, she answered, 'I spoke to her once: she got two children. In doing so she cheated me! I fear that she may get the better of me, for that is how women act. I was a fool not to realize that a double invocation would bring a double reward. This is why you should not make me act again: please grant me this boon!'

In this way were born Pāṇḍu's five mighty sons, gifts of the gods, famed as the glories of the Kuru line. They possessed the auspicious marks; they were fair to look on as the moon; proud as lions, treading valiantly like lions, lion-necked, those mighty bowmen grew up as princes of men with the valour of gods. And as they grew up on sacred Mount Himālaya they caused amazement to the great seers assembled there, for these five, and their hundred cousins, all glories of the Kuru line, grew swiftly as lotuses in water.

**[116]** *One lovely spring day, Pāṇḍu is overcome by lust for Mādrī; despite her efforts to prevent him, and forgetting his danger, he insists on making love to her, and so dies. Kuntī upbraids Mādrī, and proposes to follow Pāṇḍu into death, but Mādrī insists that this is her duty; she instructs Kuntī to treat the twins like her own sons, and then mounts Pāṇḍu's funeral pile.* **[117]** *The great seers of Himālaya swiftly conduct Kuntī, the five Pāṇḍava boys and Pāṇḍu's body to Hāstinapura. Great crowds greet their arrival. They introduce Pāṇḍu's sons to the Kurus, and tell of his death and that of Mādrī; then they vanish.* **[118]** *At Dhṛtarāṣṭra's command, Vidura has the funeral rites performed. The bodies of Pāṇḍu and Mādrī are taken with all reverence to a wooded spot on the bank of the Gaṅgā, anointed and perfumed, and set ablaze, while all the people lament bitterly. There follow twelve days of mourning.*

**[119]** *The* śrāddha *ceremony is performed for Pāṇḍu, accompanied by feasting and rich gifts to the Brahmins. When it is over, Vyāsa tells his grieving mother Satyavatī that hard times lie ahead, and advises her to retire to the forest. She does so, taking with her Ambikā and Ambālikā: they perform great austerities there, and after some time they die.*

Vaiśampāyana spoke:
Meanwhile, the Pāṇḍavas passed through the consecration ceremonies prescribed by the Veda, and grew up in their father's house, enjoying themselves and playing with the Dhārtarāṣṭras. In all their childish games, the Pāṇḍavas outstripped their cousins. Bhīma wiped the floor with all Dhṛtarāṣṭra's sons at racing and catching, at eating, at scattering dust: as they played hide-and-seek, Pāṇḍu's son would joyously seize them, grab hold of their heads, and force them to fight him; there were a hundred and one of them, princes of great power, but wolf-belly Bhīma had

no difficulty in beating them single-handed. The mighty boy would grab them by the feet, knock them violently down, and drag them shrieking along the ground, grazing their knees and heads and blacking their eyes. When he played in the water, he would seize ten boys in his arms and hold them underwater, releasing them half-dead; and when they climbed a tree to pick its fruit, Bhīma would kick it, and make it shake so hard with the impact of the blow that all the boys would be shaken out of the tree, losing their footing at once and falling headlong with the fruit. The princes struggled to rival the wolf-belly, but they could never get the better of him, whether in fights or races, or other sports. And so in their rivalry Bhīma came to be deeply hated by the Dhārtarāṣṭras, not because he meant them harm, but because of his childish ways.

When Duryodhana of great energy saw all this and understood Bhīma's might, he showed his evil nature. Averse to *dharma* and seeing wickedness everywhere, the foolish prince formed a wicked plan out of greed for power. 'First let me kill the wolf-belly, strongest of the strong, the middle son of Kuntī and Pāṇḍu, by trickery; afterwards I shall triumph over the younger, and over Yudhiṣṭhira the elder too; I shall hold them captive, and rule the earth!' Then, after taking this decision, wicked Duryodhana remained constantly on the watch for a chance to hurt the noble Bhīma.

He set up large, splendid tents for water-sports, O heir of Bharata, at Pramāṇakoṭi on the Gaṅgā. When their games were done, the princes all came ashore, donned clean clothes and fine ornaments, and feasted at their leisure upon food rich with every delicacy they might desire. At the end of the day the Kuru heroes, weary from their sports, slept happily in their tents. Now mighty Bhīma was exhausted, for he had exerted himself more than the rest, giving rides to the other princes as they played in the water. He climbed up on to dry land at Pramāṇakoṭi, and fell asleep for the night in a cool spot he had found, worn out and rather drunk: the Pāṇḍava lay motionless in sleep, O king, as if he were dead. Gently, Duryodhana now bound Bhīma with ropes made of creepers, and then pushed him off the bank into the deep, fierce-flowing river. But Kuntī's son, the best of fighting men, awoke, burst all his bonds, and emerged once more from the water.

When Bhīma fell asleep once more, Duryodhana took deadly, sharp-fanged snakes and set them to bite him furiously in every single limb and vital organ. But though they sank their fangs into his vitals, they could not break the broad-chested hero's skin, so strong was he. Bhīma awoke; he crushed all the snakes, and then killed Duryodhana's much-loved charioteer with a blow of his hand.

Next, Duryodhana took deadliest poison, freshly gathered and horribly virulent, and had it mixed into Bhīma's food. Yuyutsu, Dhṛtarāṣṭra's 40
son by a Vaiśya woman, told Bhīma, for he wished the Pāṇḍavas well. But Bhīma ate it anyway, and digested it without ill effects: the poison was most virulent, yet it had no effect, for Bhīma's strength was so terrible that he could still digest it.

So it was that Duryodhana, with Karṇa and Subala's son Śakuni, attempted to kill the Pāṇḍavas with a variety of tricks. The foe-taming Pāṇḍavas knew all about this, but they mentioned it to no one, in accordance with Vidura's advice.

**[120]** *Now Śaradvat had alarmed Indra by his fierce asceticism and martial supremacy, so he had sent an Apsaras named Jālapadī to break his austerities. When he saw her beautiful half-clothed form his seed gushed forth without his knowledge: it fell into a bed of reeds, where it divided in two and became twin children. Śaṃtanu had come upon the pair when hunting, and brought them up, naming the boy Kṛpa and his sister Kṛpī; later Śaradvat found them, and taught Kṛpa his martial skills.* **[121]** *Similarly, the seer Bharadvāja too had spilled his seed on seeing the Apsaras Ghṛtācī: he placed it in the Soma vessel, from which Droṇa was born. Droṇa grew up to be learned in the Veda and a master of the Fire Weapon; he was a friend of Drupada, son of King Pṛṣata of Pāñcāla. After his father's death he had married Kṛpa's sister Kṛpī, from whom he obtained a son, Aśvatthāman. He had also obtained weapons and the associated knowledge from Rāma Jāmadagnya.*

**[122]** *Droṇa visits his friend Drupada, but Drupada repudiates their friendship. Furious, Droṇa leaves and travels to Hāstinapura; here he impresses the young princes by his skill at shooting reeds. Bhīṣma, who is seeking for a suitable teacher for the young Kuru princes, interviews him and hears that following his rift with Drupada he is looking for suitable pupils. Droṇa takes on the princes, first demanding their promise that when they have mastered weaponry they will* *carry out an undisclosed task for him; the others remain silent, but Arjuna gives his word. Droṇa now teaches them the martial skills. Various other princes also receive instruction from Droṇa, including Karṇa, who looks down on the Pāṇḍavas.* [**123**] *Arjuna becomes an excellent warrior, Droṇa's favourite pupil.*

*A Niṣāda prince named Ekalavya seeks to become Droṇa's pupil, but Droṇa refuses him. Ekalavya goes into the forest and makes an image of Droṇa which he reveres as his teacher, and practises his skills. One day when the Kuru princes are hunting they observe Ekalavya perform an amazing feat of archery. Asked to identify himself, he answers that he is a Niṣāda prince and Droṇa's pupil. Arjuna now mentions to Droṇa that his other pupil Ekalavya is even better at archery than he is himself. Droṇa goes to see Ekalavya, and demands his fee: Ekalavya's right thumb, which Ekalavya happily cuts off and gives him. Now no one can outdo Arjuna. All the princes are excellent warriors, specializing in various forms of fighting, but it is Arjuna who outdoes all the others: he wins the test of concentration that Droṇa sets them all, and rescues Droṇa when he is attacked by a crocodile while bathing. Droṇa rewards him with the Weapon of Brahmā's Head.*

## THE BURNING OF THE HOUSE OF LAC

[**124**] *When he considers that the Kuru princes have completed their studies with him, Droṇa arranges a demonstration of their martial skills. Great crowds turn out to watch. First they display their amazing abilities at archery, then at swordplay. Next, Duryodhana and Bhīma prepare to battle each other with clubs.* [**125**] *The crowd take sides and become unruly; fearing a riot, Droṇa has the match stopped, and introduces Arjuna: there are roars of approval. Arjuna demonstrates the Weapons he has acquired from Droṇa, and shows off his astonishing skills at archery and with other weapons. As the event is about to end, the heroic beating of arm against breast is heard outside the arena.*

Vaiśaṃpāyana spoke:

[**126**] The people fell back, their eyes opened wide in amazement, as Karṇa, the conqueror of enemy fortresses, entered the vast arena like a walking mountain, bearing his natural armour, with his ear-rings illuminating his face, and carrying bow and dagger. Son of the

virgin Kuntī, Karṇa of wide fame and wide eyes was a portion of the keen-rayed Sun god and a slayer of enemy hosts; his courage and valour matched those of mighty lions and bulls and elephants, and in radiance, brilliance and splendour he was like sun, moon or fire. The glorious son of the Sun was as tall as a golden palm tree, a young man of countless virtues and strong as a lion. Strong-armed Karṇa looked all round the circular arena, and bowed to Droṇa and Kṛpa with, as it seemed, no great respect. Transfixed and motionless, the whole crowd was convulsed with curiosity to know who this could be. Then Karṇa, best of all those who speak, spoke in a voice deep as a thundercloud, brother to unknown brother, son of the Sun addressing the son of Indra: 'Son of Kuntī, whatever you have done, I shall outdo it before the eyes of all these men; so do not indulge in self-admiration!'

Before he had finished speaking, O best of all those who speak, the whole crowd leapt to their feet as if propelled by some machine. Duryodhana felt joy, tiger-like hero, but Arjuna was filled at once with shame and anger. Now Karṇa, ever revelling in battle, received Droṇa's assent; and everything that Arjuna had done there, that mighty hero repeated. At this, Duryodhana with his brothers joyfully embraced Karṇa, and he said, 'Welcome, strong-armed hero! We are blessed by your coming, bestower of honour! I, and the Kuru kingdom, are at your disposal to do with as you wish!' Karṇa replied, 'I accept your friendship: nothing else matters to me. But I wish to fight against Kuntī's son in single combat, heir of Bharata!' 'Enjoy the pleasures of life with me,' answered Duryodhana, 'and act to benefit your kin; but place your foot upon the heads of all your enemies, O foe-tamer!'

Arjuna considered that he had been insulted, and so he addressed Karṇa, who stood like a mountain amongst the Dhārtarāṣṭra brothers: 'O Karṇa, yours will be the realms of the uninvited guest and the uninvited prattler, once I have slain you!' Karṇa replied, 'This arena is open to all: what is it to you, Arjuna? Kṣatriyas excel in heroism, and *dharma* defers to strength; why trade in insults, the consolation of the weak? Talk with your arrows, heir of Bharata, till my arrows carry off your head while your teacher looks on!'

Now Arjuna, the conqueror of enemy fortresses, received Droṇa's assent; swiftly he was embraced by his brothers, and then he approached Karṇa to do battle. And for his part, Karṇa was embraced by Duryodhana and all his brothers, and stood ready to fight, grasping bow and arrows. Then clouds covered the sky, with lightning and thunder; rainbows, the bows of Indra, appeared, while lines of cranes shone white. Seeing Indra himself looking down on the arena, the Sun god showed his own affection by burning up any clouds that approached too close.[1] So it was that Pāṇḍu's son Arjuna was seen to be hidden by the shadow of the clouds, while Karṇa was encircled by sunshine.

The sons of Dhṛtarāṣṭra were stationed next to Karṇa; Bharadvāja's son Droṇa, and Kṛpa and Bhīṣma, stood by Arjuna son of Kuntī. The men in the arena took sides, and so did the women; but Kuntibhoja's daughter Kuntī, who understood what was happening, fainted. Vidura, expert in *dharma*, revived her from her faint by sprinkling her with sandal-scented water; then, restored to consciousness, she gazed at her two sons in their armour, and she grieved, but did not try to approach them.

As the two warriors stood brandishing their great bows, Kṛpa son of Śaradvat, who was skilled in the rules of single combat and expert in *dharma*, addressed them: 'Here stands the younger son of Kuntī, son of Pāṇḍu, descendant of Kuru. He will fight you in single combat, sir. Now you too, strong-armed hero, must announce your mother, father and the royal lineage of which you are the glory. Once this is known to Kuntī's son, he will fight you, or he will not.'

When Karṇa heard these words he bowed his head in shame, like a lotus flower that droops when drenched by rain. Duryodhana intervened: 'According to the learned texts, there are three types of king, sir: the one who is of royal line, the one who is a hero, and the one who leads an army. If Arjuna here is unwilling to fight with anyone not a king, then this man will be consecrated by me as king over Aṅga!' And there and then the glorious, mighty chariot-fighter Karṇa was consecrated king of Aṅga by priests who knew the Vedas, with parched grain, flowers and golden pots, while he sat on a golden seat. After the shouts of 'Victory!',

1 The rain god Indra and the Sun are giving support to their respective earthly offspring, Arjuna and Karṇa.

the bull-like king Karṇa, shaded by a royal umbrella, fanned by yak-tail fans, then spoke to the Kaurava king Duryodhana: 'What may I give to you to equal this gift of kingship? Speak, tiger-like king, and I shall do it!' Duryodhana answered, 'I want your friendship for ever!' Karṇa heard these words, and gave his assent. Then with the greatest joy the two men embraced.

**[127]** But now, as if in challenge, the Sūta Adhiratha entered the arena. His upper garment was out of place, and he was sweating and trembling as he supported himself with a stick. When Karṇa saw him, he laid down his bow; driven by respect for his father, he greeted him, bowing a head still wet with the water of his royal consecration. The charioteer made haste to cover his feet with the edge of his garment,[1] and addressed the man who had achieved such great things as 'My son'; he embraced him, and, distracted with love, further moistened with his tears that head still wet from consecration as king of Aṅga.

When Pāṇḍu's son Bhīma saw Adhiratha and realized that Karṇa was a Sūta's son, he burst out laughing, and said, 'Son of a Sūta, you are not entitled to death in battle with Arjuna son of Kuntī! Take up your whip at once, as befits your birth! Nor are you entitled to enjoy the kingship of Aṅga, you lowliest of men, like a dog stealing the sacrificial rice-cake from next to the fire!'

When Karṇa heard these words, his lower lip began to throb; exhaling deeply, he fixed his eye on the sun in the sky. But mighty Duryodhana leapt up in fury from where his brothers were sitting, like a rutting elephant bursting forth from a lotus pool, and he said to Bhīma, the doer of fearful deeds standing before him, 'Wolf-belly, it is not right for you to speak so. For Kṣatriyas, strength is the greatest virtue, and one should agree to fight against anyone calling himself a Kṣatriya; as the saying has it, the source of heroism is as mysterious as the source of rivers. Fire, which pervades the entire world, first sprang from water; the thunderbolt with which the demons were slain was fashioned from a bone of Dadhīca; the blessed god of war is utterly mysterious, for he is said to be the son of Fire, of the Kṛttikā stars, of Śiva, and of Gaṅgā

1 To prevent Karṇa from touching his feet in self-abasement.

too;[1] it is known that the children of Kṣatriya mothers have become Brahmins; Droṇa our Teacher was born from a jar, and the venerable Kṛpa from a bed of reeds.[2] As for your own births, all the kings have heard how they occurred! This man was born with earrings and armour, and bears celestial marks; he resembles the very Sun. How could a doe give birth to such a tiger? Through the valour of his own arm, and my allegiance to him, this lord of men is entitled to kingship over the earth, not merely over Aṅga; and if there is a man who cannot accept what I have done, let him mount his chariot, or stand on foot, and bend his bow!'

At this there was a great uproar throughout the arena, as well as cries of 'Bravo!' Now the sun set, and Duryodhana, taking Karṇa by the hand, O king, left the arena by the light of blazing lamps; the Pāṇḍavas too all returned to their own dwellings, lord of the peoples, as did Droṇa, Kṛpa and Bhīṣma. The spectators went their way, some saying 'Arjuna!', some 'Karṇa!', others 'Duryodhana!'

Now that Kuntī had recognized the king of Aṅga as her son, thanks to the celestial marks he bore, her secret joy increased for love of him. Duryodhana too, O prince, now that he had met Karṇa, rapidly lost his fear of Arjuna. As for heroic Karṇa himself, that most practised warrior always addressed Duryodhana in the friendliest manner. Even Yudhiṣṭhira now believed that there was no bowman upon earth to match Karṇa.

**[128]** *Now Droṇa asks the princes for his fee: they are to capture his enemy Drupada, king of Pāñcāla. This they do, ravaging his city. Droṇa reminds him how he repudiated their earlier friendship and proposes that they become friends again: Drupada will retain the southern half of his former kingdom. Drupada assents, but in his heart he harbours enmity towards Droṇa; he awaits the birth of a son to avenge him.*

**[129]** *Duryodhana becomes aware that the people favour the installation of*

**1** This god, known as Skanda, Kumāra and Kārttikeya (and referred to here as Guha, 'the mysterious one'), was born from Śiva's seed, which had been contained for a while by both Fire and Gaṅgā; he was raised by the Kṛttikās (Pleiades). See further 9.43.

**2** See 1.120–21.

*Yudhiṣṭhira as king. He goes to see Dhṛtarāṣṭra and warns him that his line is in danger of being excluded from the kingship in perpetuity: something must be done.* **[130]** *Dhṛtarāṣṭra remonstrates: Pāṇḍu was a virtuous and popular king, and his son Yudhiṣṭhira resembles him. If Duryodhana and his brothers use force against him, they will be killed by his supporters. Duryodhana suggests that instead the Pāṇḍavas should be sent away to Vāraṇāvata under some harmless pretext; while they are away he will induce the people to change their loyalty with gifts. Once he is secure in the kingship his cousins can return. Again Dhṛtarāṣṭra objects: the elders would be bound to punish such a wicked act. No, replies Duryodhana. Bhīṣma will remain impartial; Droṇa will follow his son Aśvatthāman, who sides with Duryodhana; Kṛpa will take the same side, for Droṇa is married to his sister; and Vidura is financially dependent on the Dhārtarāṣṭras. It is time for action.*

**[131]** *Dhṛtarāṣṭra now has his counsellors sing the praises of Vāraṇāvata, and when the Pāṇḍavas' curiosity is aroused urges them in person to pay a visit there. Yudhiṣṭhira is powerless to oppose Dhṛtarāṣṭra's wish; he goes to see the elders and asks for their blessing, then leaves for Vāraṇāvata with his brothers.*

Vaiśaṃpāyana spoke:

**[132]** Wicked Duryodhana was overjoyed that the king had spoken so to the noble Pāṇḍavas. Now, bull-like heir of Bharata, he led Purocana, one of his aides, into a private room, and, taking him by the right hand, spoke as follows: 'This earth is mine, Purocana, with all its wealth; but as it is mine, so it is yours, and you should protect it! There is no one I trust more than you, no like-minded friend with whom I may discuss my affairs as I do with you. So follow my plans, sir, and wipe out my rivals by means of a cunning trick: act as I shall instruct.

'Dhṛtarāṣṭra has sent the Pāṇḍavas to Vāraṇāvata; at his command they will stay there during the coming festival. So yoke mules to a fast cart and make sure you reach Vāraṇāvata yourself today. When you get there, have a house erected in a well-secluded spot near to the weapon-store. Let it contain four great rooms: spare no expense! Make the builders use whatever materials are inflammable – hemp and resin and so forth – and make them plaster the walls with a clay mixed with ghee, oil and plenty of lac. Then place all over that house hemp, bamboo, ghee, wood, and every other such contrivance; but do it in such a way that the Pāṇḍavas will not suspect you, even if they examine it closely, and other folk too will not realize that it is inflammable, or guess your motive.

'When the house is built there as I have said, you are to give it to the Pāṇḍavas, and Kuntī and her friends, for their dwelling, showing them every honour. Excellent seats, carriages and beds are to be installed there for them, so that my father will be pleased, and everything is to be arranged for them to stay in the city of Vāraṇāvata, free from all suspicion – until the time comes. But then, once you know they are sleeping in utter confidence of their safety, you are to open the door and set fire to the house. In this way the Pāṇḍavas will be burnt alive, but all that their relatives or other folk will say of them is that they died in a fire in their own house.'

Purocana now promised the Kaurava to do as he had said, and set out by mule-cart for the city of Vāraṇāvata. He travelled swiftly, O king, in accordance with Duryodhana's wishes, and did everything just as his prince had bidden him.

[**133**] *The Pāṇḍavas bid farewell to the elders. Some of the Brahmins deplore Dhṛtarāṣṭra's behaviour and propose to follow them, but Yudhiṣṭhira tells them to return home and asks for their blessing. Vidura uses covert language to warn Yudhiṣṭhira of danger from poison and fire. The Pāṇḍavas set out, and arrive in Vāraṇāvata.* [**134**] *The people of Vāraṇāvata greet the Pāṇḍavas with great honour. Purocana attends to their needs and then, after ten days, conducts them to the inflammable house he has had built. Yudhiṣṭhira recognizes it for what it is, but none the less insists that they should stay, so as to avoid alerting Purocana. They must get to know the lie of the land, to aid them when the time comes to flee, and excavate a hiding-place where they will be safe from fire.*

[**135**] *A friend of Vidura arrives, a skilled excavator: he confirms that Purocana plans to burn them all alive. At Yudhiṣṭhira's request he excavates a hiding-place for them under the house: from then on they sleep in it, spending their days travelling from forest to forest under the pretext of hunting.*

Vaiśaṃpāyana spoke:
[**136**] After he had seen them living there happily for a year, and observed their confidence, Purocana was filled with joy. But Kuntī's

son Yudhiṣṭhira, expert in *dharma*, saw how joyful he seemed, and spoke to Bhīma, Arjuna and the twins: 'This wicked Purocana thinks we are utterly confident: we have fooled the cruel wretch. I believe the time for flight has come. We shall fire the weapon-store, burning Purocana too, and flee unobserved, leaving six other people lying here.'

So now, under the pretext of making a gift, Kuntī held a great night- 5
time feast for Brahmins, O king. Women attended it, and enjoyed themselves, eating and drinking their fill, O heir of Bharata; then, late at night, they took leave of their hostess and left for their homes. Now it happened that a Niṣāda[1] woman, urged by fate, had come with her five sons to that feast in search of food. She and her sons drank liquor till they fell into a drunken stupor; then they all passed out, and lay in the Pāṇḍavas' house sleeping as if dead, O king. Then at dead of night, lord, while a violent wind blew, and while folk slept, Bhīma set fire to the place where Purocana was lying.

The blaze caused a mighty heat and noise, which awoke many people. 10
The townsfolk said to one another, 'The wicked fool who carried out Duryodhana's command to have the house built, and then to have it burnt, has brought about his own death! Alas, alas, that Dhṛtarāṣṭra's mind should be so debased that he made his minister burn the pure Pāṇḍava boys alive! At least it is a blessing that the wicked, evil-minded man who burnt those trusting, sinless heroes has now himself been burnt.' The people of Vāraṇāvata stood all round the house that night, grieving in this fashion.

As for the Pāṇḍavas, O king, they escaped with their mother in great 15
distress by means of their underground hiding-place, and went on in secret, unobserved; but, impeded by weariness and fear, those afflicters of their enemies and their mother could not move with haste. Then, lord of kings, Bhīma of terrible speed and valour took up all his brothers and his mother too, and strode forth. That hero, carrying his mother on his shoulder, the twins on his hip, and the two mighty brothers, Kuntī's sons, in his hands, went rapidly on, breaking trees in his speed and splitting open the earth with his feet – the ardent wolf-belly, swift as the wind.

1 The Niṣādas were one of the barbarian tribes.

**[137]** *The people of the town conclude that Purocana has murdered the Pāṇḍavas, and blame Duryodhana and Dhṛtarāṣṭra. They send word of the Pāṇḍavas' death to Dhṛtarāṣṭra, who grieves. Bhīma continues to bear his family towards safety.* **[138]** *He bounds on, carrying Kuntī and the other Pāṇḍavas. When evening comes they rest. Bhīma goes to fetch water: when he returns he weeps to see his noble family reduced to sleeping on the bare ground. He stays awake, watching.*

## THE KILLING OF HIḌIMBA

**[139]** *As the Pāṇḍavas lie sleeping, a Rākṣasa named Hiḍimba who lives nearby smells them; he tells his sister Hiḍimbā to go and kill them so they can feast on human flesh. But when she sees Bhīma she falls in love with him. Assuming the form of a beautiful girl, she attempts to seduce him, but without success.* **[140]** *Hiḍimba, wondering at his sister's delay, follows her. When she sees him coming, Hiḍimbā offers to save Bhīma and his family, but Bhīma assures her that he does not need her help. Hiḍimba realizes her change of heart and attacks her.*

**[141]** *Bhīma jeers at the Rākṣasa and challenges him. They begin a fierce fight: Bhīma repeatedly drags Hiḍimba away to avoid waking his sleeping brothers.* **[142]** *However, the noise of the fight does awaken the Pāṇḍavas. Hiḍimbā explains to them who she is and what is happening. Arjuna taunts Bhīma, offering to help him kill the Rākṣasa: furious, Bhīma slays him at once.*

## THE KILLING OF BAKA

**[143]** *Then he threatens to kill Hiḍimbā too, but Yudhiṣṭhira prevents him. She pleads to be allowed to marry Bhīma: if her wish is granted she will assist the Pāṇḍavas. Yudhiṣṭhira assents, but insists that Bhīma must return to his family each night. Hiḍimbā and Bhīma travel into the mountains and repeatedly make love.*

Vaiśaṃpāyana spoke:
The Rākṣasa woman, who could move as swiftly as thought, made love to Bhīma in place after place, and so she gave birth to Bhīma's mighty

son. His eyes were frightful, his mouth huge, his ears sharp-pointed; he was fearsome and strong, terrible to behold with his copper-coloured lips and his sharp teeth. That foe-tamer was a great bowman, a great hero with great mettle and great arms; he had great speed and a great body, and great powers of illusion. Child of a human but not a human, terrible in speed and mighty in strength, he surpassed Piśācas and other Rākṣasas, as well as human beings. Though a mere child, he had reached what passes among men for manhood, lord of the peoples; brave and strong, he attained excellence with all weapons. Rākṣasa women indeed conceive and give birth on the same day; they can also assume many shapes and change their form at will.

That hairless child and mighty bowman now bowed and touched his parents' feet, and they gave him his name: 'He is as bald as a pot,' said Bhīma to the child's mother, and so his name became Ghaṭotkaca, 'Bald as a pot'. Ghaṭotkaca loved the Pāṇḍavas, and he was always as dear to them as life itself.

Now Hiḍimbā told Bhīma that their time together had run out; with his agreement she went her own way. Ghaṭotkaca, best of Rākṣasas, also bade farewell and set out for the north, promising to return to his father and uncles at time of need. Indeed, noble Indra had created him on account of Karṇa's Spear: his purpose was to destroy the noble Karṇa of incomparable valour.

**[144]** *The Pāṇḍavas travel on, wearing the dress of ascetics, until they meet Vyāsa. He conducts them to the city of Ekacakrā, advising them to live there secretly. Then, after promising that they will attain greatness, he leaves.*

**[145]** *In Ekacakrā the Pāṇḍavas lodge in a Brahmin's house, sharing out the food they beg each day – one half for Bhīma, the other half for the rest of the family. One day Kuntī and Bhīma overhear the Brahmin grieving. He cannot bring himself to abandon his wife and children, who will die without him: better for them all to die together.* **[146]** *The Brahmin's wife proposes to take his place, for his son and daughter will need their father. It is possible that the Rākṣasa will let her live, as she is a woman; anyway she has led a good life.* **[147]** *Next the Brahmin's daughter argues that she is the one who should be sacrificed; then her infant brother babbles that he will kill the Rākṣasa, which brings mirth to the others despite their grief.*

**[148]** *Kuntī asks the cause of their trouble, and is told that a flesh-eating Rākṣasa named Baka demands the daily provision of rice, two buffaloes and one human as his price for protecting the kingdom, which is ruled by a weak king. Now it is the Brahmin's turn, and he intends to take his entire family to Baka so that they may die together.*

**[149]** *Kuntī proposes that one of her sons should go to Baka in place of the Brahmin. He demurs, not wishing to incur the sin of causing the death of a guest whom he believes to be a Brahmin, but Kuntī reassures him: her son is powerful and will escape unharmed. Bhīma is sent to Baka.*

**[150]** *The other Pāṇḍavas return with the alms they have begged. When Yudhiṣṭhira learns what Kuntī has done he is furious: they all depend on Bhīma. But Kuntī convinces him that Bhīma will survive, and that it is right to recompense the Brahmin for his hospitality.*

**[151]** *Bhīma takes the food to Baka. When Baka comes for it he finds Bhīma eating the food himself and ignoring the Rākṣasa. Baka attacks him, first with his hands and then with an uprooted tree, but still Bhīma takes no notice. Finally Bhīma finishes eating and joins in combat with Baka: after a fearful fight, he breaks the Rākṣasa in two.* **[152]** *Bhīma now warns the other Rākṣasas to cease harming humans, and they agree. The townspeople are amazed and delighted by Bhīma's feat.*

## CITRARATHA

**[153]** *The Pāṇḍavas continue living in Ekacakrā. A visiting Brahmin tells them stories of many lands, among them tales of Drupada, king of Pāñcāla. They ask to hear more about Drupada and his children.*

**[154]** *The Brahmin tells of Droṇa's miraculous birth, his friendship with Drupada and his acquisition of weapons from Rāma Jāmadagnya. He tells how Drupada had repudiated their friendship, and how Droṇa, after teaching the Pāṇḍavas martial skills, had instructed them to seize Drupada's kingdom. Though the southern half of the kingdom was returned to him, Drupada continued to harbour enmity towards Droṇa.* **[155]** *Longing for a son capable of avenging him, he encountered two seers, Yāja and Upayāja. Upayāja refused his request for the performance of a ritual to get such a son, but Yāja agreed. When he offered the oblation, a mighty young man emerged from the fire, and a voice* *from the air proclaimed that he was destined to kill Droṇa; then a beautiful, dark girl emerged from the altar, and the voice proclaimed that she was destined to accomplish the purpose of the gods by annihilating the Kṣatriyas. They were named Dhṛṣṭadyumna and Kṛṣṇā (Draupadī).*

[156] *The Pāṇḍavas are greatly disturbed by this story. Kuntī suggests that they travel to Pāñcāla, and her sons agree.* [157] *They are visited by Vyāsa, who tells them the story of a lovelorn girl who had performed austerities to win Śiva's favour: five times she had requested him for a virtuous husband, and he had pronounced that in her next birth she would have five husbands. That girl has been reborn as Draupadī; she is destined to be the Pāṇḍavas' wife.*

[158] *As the Pāṇḍavas continue their journey by night, they inadvertently disturb the Gandharva king Aṅgāraparṇa Citraratha playing with his womenfolk by the Gaṅgā. He is furious, but Arjuna stands up to him, and when Aṅgāraparṇa attacks him he deploys the Fire Weapon which he had received from Droṇa. Aṅgāraparṇa is overcome, but Arjuna spares him; in return, the Gandharva gives up his names and grants Arjuna the power to see everything everywhere. To each Pāṇḍava he further gives a hundred Gandharva horses, and Arjuna gives him the Fire Weapon.* [159] *He asks the Gandharva why he attacked them, and the Gandharva answers that it was because they had with them no fires, no offerings, and, above all, no household priest: no king can succeed without a priest. In the course of his answer he repeatedly refers to Arjuna as 'son of Tapatī'.*

## TAPATĪ

[160] *Arjuna points out that he is the son of Kuntī: who is Tapatī? The Gandharva tells her story. — Tapatī is the daughter of the Sun, of incomparable beauty, and her father is anxiously seeking a husband for her. The Kuru king Saṃvaraṇa is a great devotee of the Sun, who decides that he should marry Tapatī. Once when Saṃvaraṇa is out hunting in the mountains he sees her and falls in love; but when he asks her who she is, she vanishes, and he is unable to find her.* [161] *Saṃvaraṇa falls to the ground, overcome by love, whereupon Tapatī reappears to him. He asks her to marry him according to the rite of the Gandharvas; she replies that*

*she loves him and would like to marry him, but that he must consult her father the Sun.*

[**162**] *Saṃvaraṇa propitiates the Sun and mentally summons his household priest Vasiṣṭha, who arrives on the twelfth day.* [**163**] *Vasiṣṭha intercedes with the Sun on Saṃvaraṇa's behalf, and the Sun grants his wish. Saṃvaraṇa and Tapatī marry there in the mountains: for twelve years they remain there enjoying themselves, while Saṃvaraṇa's kingdom is ravaged by drought and famine. Then Vasiṣṭha brings the king and queen back to their city, and Indra grants rain once more. The son of Saṃvaraṇa and Tapatī is Kuru, Arjuna's ancestor.*

## VASIṢṬHA

[**164**] — *When Arjuna has heard the story of Tapatī, he asks the Gandharva to tell him about Vasiṣṭha, and the Gandharva answers by praising the great seer: Arjuna should seek such a household priest for himself.* [**165**] *Arjuna asks to hear the origin of Vasiṣṭha's dispute with Viśvāmitra, and the Gandharva narrates the story.*

— *Viśvāmitra is king of Kānyakubja. Once when hunting he visits Vasiṣṭha's hermitage, where he is received with great honour, and there he sees Vasiṣṭha's wish-granting cow; he offers Vasiṣṭha his kingdom for her, but Vasiṣṭha refuses. Viśvāmitra with his troops attempts to take her by force, but she creates the various barbarian peoples, who attack and overcome Viśvāmitra's forces. Recognizing that the power of a Brahmin is greater than that of a Kṣatriya, Viśvāmitra determines to become a Brahmin himself; he performs such austerities that he is able to achieve this goal.*

[**166**] *Now King Kalmāṣapāda quarrels with Vasiṣṭha's son Śakti, and strikes him; in return, Śakti curses him to eat human flesh. Viśvāmitra sees this happen, and orders a Rākṣasa to possess Kalmāṣapāda. When a Brahmin requests a dish of meat from the king, he instructs his cook to send human flesh, and is cursed a second time to wander the earth in his craving for this unlawful food. Overcome by the double curse, he now eats Śakti and, at Viśvāmitra's prompting, all Vasiṣṭha's other hundred sons.*

*When he learns what Viśvāmitra has done, Vasiṣṭha attempts suicide, but neither a leap from a mountain, nor fire, nor the sea, will harm him.* **[167]** *He tries to drown himself in a river and to feed himself to crocodiles, but with no better success: he realizes that he cannot die. He is delighted to learn from his son Śakti's widow Adṛśyantī that she is pregnant. Then the two of them are attacked by Kalmāṣapāda.*

**[168]** *Vasiṣṭha releases Kalmāṣapāda from his possession by the Rākṣasa: Kalmāṣapāda agrees henceforth to be respectful to Brahmins, and requests Vasiṣṭha to father a child on his queen. Vasiṣṭha assents. Kalmāṣapāda returns to his city, Ayodhyā, where he is greeted joyfully; Vasiṣṭha lies with the queen, who remains pregnant for twelve years and then splits open her womb with a stone. She gives birth to Aśmaka ('Stone').*

## AURVA

**[169]** *Adṛśyantī gives birth to a son, Parāśara. When he calls Vasiṣṭha 'daddy', his mother tells him not to: his daddy was eaten by a Rākṣasa. Parāśara, who is a great seer, resolves to destroy the entire world. In order to dissuade him, Vasiṣṭha tells him a story.*

*— King Kṛtavīrya is very generous to the Bhṛgu Brahmins, but after his death the Kṣatriyas, discovering that the Bhṛgus have been hoarding wealth, turn on them and kill them. One woman flees after concealing her unborn child in her thigh. She is caught by Kṣatriyas, whereupon the child bursts out of her thigh and blinds them with his brilliance.* **[170]** *They beg the child, who is named Aurva, 'Born from a Thigh', for mercy: he restores their sight and sends them away, but then begins to perform austerities to destroy the entire world. At this his ancestors appears to him to explain that they had deliberately prompted the Kṣatriya attack as a way of bringing their excessively long earthly lives to an end without incurring the penalty for suicide. They ask Aurva to abandon his destructive plan.* **[171]** *Aurva tells them that if he holds back the fire of his anger he himself will be burnt by it; none the less he is willing to do as they wished. They advise him to place the fire in the sea, and he does so: it becomes a great submarine horse's head, spitting fire and drinking water.*

**[172]** *— The young seer Parāśara now decides not to destroy the* *entire world: instead he will kill all Rākṣasas in a sacrifice. Unwilling to break a second vow of his, Vasiṣṭha does not try to stop him, but the seer Pulastya, father of the Rākṣasas, persuades him to break off the sacrifice before its completion. Parāśara now casts away his fire on the northern side of the Himālaya, where it may still be seen consuming Rākṣasas, trees and even stones in season after season.*

[173] — *Now Arjuna asks the Gandharva why Kalmāṣapāda wished Vasiṣṭha to lie with his wife, and why Vasiṣṭha consented. The Gandharva relates the story. — After being cursed by Śakti, Kalmāṣapāda is wandering hungrily in the forest when he comes upon a Brahmin and his wife in sexual union. He catches the Brahmin and, despite his wife's pleas, eats him. The wife now curses him: he too will die if he indulges in sexual union; Vasiṣṭha will lie with his wife, and the child of that coupling will become his heir.*

## DRAUPADĪ'S *SVAYAMVARA*

[174] *Arjuna now asks the Gandharva to recommend a household priest for the Pāṇḍavas. The Gandharva recommends Dhaumya, and receives the Fire Weapon from Arjuna. Dhaumya agrees to be the Pāṇḍavas' priest; encouraged, they set off to attend Draupadī's* svayaṃvara.

[175] *As they travel, still in the guise of Brahmins, they join a party of Brahmins going to the* svayaṃvara *in hopes of rich presents.* [176] *On arriving in Drupada's capital, they lodge at a potter's house. Drupada announces that his daughter will be given in marriage to the man who can string a very strong bow and use it to strike a high target through a small opening, privately hoping that Arjuna may come and claim her. A great crowd gathers in the arena to observe the competition: the Pāṇḍavas sit among the Brahmins. When the time comes, Dhṛṣṭadyumna begins the proceedings.* [177] *He lists the names of all the Kṣatriyas who have come seeking Draupadī's hand.*

Vaiśaṃpāyana spoke:

[178] Decked with earrings and other ornaments, vying together one against the other, each reckoning himself the best for weapons and for

strength, the young men now rushed forward, all full of themselves. They were not short of pride in their looks and valour and high birth, their *dharma* too, and their youthful vigour; the rush of their intoxication was like that of mighty, rutting Himālayan elephants. With their bodies overwhelmed by feelings of love, they vied to stare each other down, and sprang forward from their kingly seats crying 'Draupadī Kṛṣṇā is mine!' The Kṣatriyas assembled in the arena in hopes of winning Drupada's daughter were as splendid as the hosts of the gods when they assembled to contend for Umā, daughter of the mountain king.[1] Their limbs were tormented with the love-god's arrows, and their hearts were given over to Draupadī; those lords of men stepped down into the arena to contend for Drupada's daughter, thinking now of even their friends as enemies.

Now the hosts of the gods arrived in their flying chariots: the Rudras, the Ādityas, the Vasus and the Aśvins, together with the Sādhyas, and all the Maruts too, all headed by Yama and Kubera god of wealth. There were demons, divine birds and mighty serpents, seers, Guhyakas and Cāraṇas, and also the leading Gandharvas Viśvāvasu, Nārada and Parvata,[2] together with the Apsarases. Balarāma the plough-bearer[3] was there, and Kṛṣṇa Keśava, along with the chiefs among the Vṛṣṇis and Andhakas. Those bull-like Yadus watched the events, in accordance with Kṛṣṇa's wishes. The hero of the Yadus himself saw five men resembling mighty, rutting elephants bearing auspicious markings, their limbs covered with ash as if they were fires, and he thought of the Pāṇḍavas. Then to Balarāma he spoke the names of Yudhiṣṭhira, Bhīma, victorious Arjuna, and the two heroic twins; and Balarāma slowly examined those five, and then looked with satisfaction at Kṛṣṇa the stirrer of men.

Other princes, sons and grandsons of many kings, with their eyes, hearts and dispositions given over to Draupadī, strained to see her as she passed, biting their lips, their faces the colour of copper. The strong-armed sons of Kuntī too, and the heroic, noble-minded twins, were all

**1** Umā is a name for Pārvatī, Śiva's wife.

**2** Nārada is a seer, often mentioned together with Parvata, but he is also often linked with the Gandharvas, or even identified as one.

**3** Balarāma is Kṛṣṇa's elder brother; his weapon is a plough.

struck by the love-god's arrows as soon as they set eyes on Draupadī. The sky was thronged with seers and Gandharvas, and with divine birds, serpents, demons and Siddhas; it was filled with a heavenly fragrance and strewn with heavenly garlands; the mighty roar of drums pervaded it, and flying chariots cluttered it on every side, while it resounded with flutes and lutes and cymbals.

Now, one by one, all those hosts of kings displayed their valour in their efforts to win Draupadī Kṛṣṇā. But no matter what force they applied, they could not string that most strong bow: valiant lords of men were thrown down by the spring of that mighty bow till they lay writhing on the ground, crestfallen and seemingly broken in spirit. The strength of the bow reduced the circle of kings to cries of woe; it ground and smashed their armlets and earrings, and turned their hearts away from Draupadī, and left them in affliction. The folk in the crowd were bewildered, and the kings left off their boasting. Now Kuntī's son, the victorious hero Arjuna, made ready to string that bow and fix an arrow to it.

[**179**] After the kings had given up the task of stringing the bow, noble-minded Arjuna rose from amidst the Brahmins. When the leading priests saw Kuntī's son step forward, splendid as a rainbow, they cried out and waved their garments of antelope-skin. Some were displeased, some joyful; others, clever men who earned their living by their intelligence, said to one another, 'O priests, how can a bow that Karṇa, Śalya and other mighty princes of renown could not bend, for all their strength and skill at archery, be strung by a mere Brahmin boy, untrained in weapons and inferior in strength? If, from pride or exuberance or unsteadiness in the Brahmin way, he sets out to stretch that bow, but fails in the task for lack of forethought, Brahmins will become the butt of mockery amongst all the kings. He must be stopped; indeed, he must not go! We will not be mocked; we will not lose our dignity; we will not incur the hatred of the world's kings.'

Yet others said, 'He is a fine young man. His shoulders, arms and thighs are as stout as the trunk of a mighty elephant, and he is as steadfast as Mount Himālaya. His resolve suggests that he is capable of this task. His strength is to be so very resolute: no one would set out on such an undertaking without the strength to carry it out. And there is no task anywhere in the three worlds that is beyond the power of Brahmins among the three classes of men; for priests of firm vows who grow weak through feeding on nothing but water, or air, or fruit, are rendered immensely strong by their brahmanical power. No Brahmin should be looked down on, whether he does right or wrong, and whether the task he faces is pleasant or unpleasant, great or small.'

But even as the priests talked, some saying one thing, some another, Arjuna stood next to the bow, unmoving as a mountain. The afflicter of his enemies walked around it in respectful circumambulation, bowed to it with his head, then took hold of it in joyful excitement. In the time it takes to blink, he strung it; and he took up five arrows and swiftly pierced the target through the opening. It fell to the ground. Then a roar broke out in heaven, and another great roar amongst the crowd in the arena; and Indra rained down celestial flowers upon the head of Kuntī's son, slayer of his enemies. On every side folk waved their garments, or else cried in woe, while flowers rained down all about them from the sky. Musicians blew trumpets in hundreds, and hosts of Sūta and Māgadha bards sang sweet songs of praise.

When Drupada, slayer of his enemies, saw Arjuna's feat, he was delighted, and he made ready to offer him the assistance of his troops. But when that mighty roar began, Yudhiṣṭhira, most excellent upholder of *dharma*, set off quickly for his dwelling with the twins, those highest lords. Meanwhile, Draupadī Kṛṣṇā, seeing that the target had been pierced, and observing that Arjuna resembled Indra himself, took up a splendid white garland and went smilingly up to Kuntī's son. He had won her in the arena; now he accepted her to the applause of the Brahmins. Then, having achieved the unthinkable, he left the arena, and she followed him as his wife.

**[180]** *Drupada is attacked by the Kṣatriyas, who are furious that Draupadī should be given to a Brahmin. Bhīma and Arjuna go to his defence, Bhīma uprooting a tree to serve as a staff. Kṛṣṇa again tells Balarāma that these men must be the Pāṇḍavas.* **[181]** *The Kṣatriyas are led by Karṇa, who does battle against Arjuna. Surprised that a Brahmin should fight so well, Karṇa asks Arjuna whether he is not in fact Indra or Viṣṇu in disguise; when Arjuna assures him that he is really a Brahmin, Karṇa withdraws from the fight. Meanwhile*

*Bhīma fights Śalya,*[1] *whom he hurls to the ground. At this the Kṣatriyas give up and leave; Arjuna and Bhīma now return with Draupadī to where Kuntī has been anxiously awaiting them.*

Vaiśaṃpāyana spoke:
[**182**] When Kuntī's two noble-minded sons reached the potter's workshop where their mother was, those foremost of heroes, full of great joy, told her about Draupadī: 'We have won alms!' But Kuntī was inside the hut; she could not see her sons, and called out, 'All of you share equally!' Only then did she see the girl, and exclaimed, 'Alas for my words!'

Draupadī remained full of great joy, but Kuntī was fearful of breaching *dharma* and ashamed. She took Draupadī by the hand, approached Yudhiṣṭhira, and said, 'My son, my king, here is the daughter of King Drupada. Your younger brothers presented her to me, and I without thinking said, as I so often do, "Share equally!" Bull among Kurus, tell me how my words may not be falsified today, and how the daughter of the king of Pāñcāla may not be touched by an unprecedented breach of *dharma*.'

King Yudhiṣṭhira of mightiest power considered for a moment. Then the hero of the Kurus comforted his mother Kuntī, and spoke as follows to wealth-winner Arjuna: 'Draupadī was won by you, O Pāṇḍava, and in you the princess shall find her happiness. Let fire be lit; let offerings be made; take her hand according to the proper rite!'

But Arjuna answered, 'Lord of men, do not make me party to wrongdoing. This is not that *dharma* to which others adhere. You, sir, should marry first, and then strong-armed Bhīma who achieves the unthinkable; then I myself, and after me Nakula; and finally Sahadeva son of Mādrī. But the wolf-belly and I and the twins, O king, and this girl too, are all subject to you; so you should decide what is to be done in this matter to conform to *dharma* and preserve our good name, and also to please the king of Pāñcāla, and then carry it out. Tell us your decision: we are all under your authority.'

When the brothers saw Draupadī Kṛṣṇā of high repute standing there,

1 The king of the Madras and brother of Pāṇḍu's second wife Mādrī.

they kept looking at each other. All of them took her to their hearts, for as those heroes of boundless power gazed at Draupadī, love made its presence felt and threw their senses into confusion. Indeed, the creator himself had fashioned her lovely form to captivate all creatures as no other woman.

Kuntī's son Yudhiṣṭhira saw their expressions and understood their feelings; and remembering too, bull-like hero, everything that Vyāsa had said, the king now spoke to his brothers, fearful of discord among 15
them: 'Beautiful Draupadī shall be the wife of us all!'

**[183]** *Kṛṣṇa and Balarāma now arrive. Kṛṣṇa congratulates the Pāṇḍavas on their good fortune so far and wishes them well for the future; then he and his brother leave quickly, to avoid giving them away.*

**[184]** *Dhṛṣṭadyumna, unobserved, watches the Pāṇḍavas. He sees that his sister is being properly treated, and hears them tell heroic tales to one another. Then he returns to Drupada, who is anxious to know who it is that has taken his daughter.* **[185]** *Dhṛṣṭadyumna describes what he has seen, and assures his father that the mysterious strangers are indeed the Pāṇḍavas. Delighted, Drupada sends his household priest to them with an invitation to declare themselves openly. Yudhiṣṭhira pays his respects, and answers that Drupada need feel no concern, for Draupadī was properly won. At this point a second messenger arrives from Drupada to announce that the wedding feast is ready.*

**[186]** *The Pāṇḍavas ride to Drupada's palace in the chariots he has provided. Here they find a great range of goods laid out by Drupada in an attempt to discover more about his guests. They eat kingly food and take up weapons, ignoring all the other items. Drupada now comes to pay them his respects.* **[187]** *He asks Yudhiṣṭhira to resolve his doubts by identifying himself and his companions: as soon as he does so, the wedding will proceed. Yudhiṣṭhira now informs him that they are the Pāṇḍavas; Drupada is overcome with joy, and promises Yudhiṣṭhira to restore his kingdom. But when he learns of Yudhiṣṭhira's intention that Draupadī should wed all five Pāṇḍava brothers he is dismayed.*

*At this point Vyāsa arrives.* **[188]** *Drupada asks Vyāsa's advice about the proposed marriage, and Vyāsa asks each person for his view. Drupada himself regards it as improper; his son Dhṛṣṭadyumna is uncertain; Yudhiṣṭhira and Kuntī both maintain that it is perfectly right. Vyāsa agrees with Yudhiṣṭhira, and takes Drupada aside to explain to him how this can be.*

## THE FIVE INDRAS

[189] *Vyāsa tells Drupada how the gods once performed a sacrifice in the Naimiṣa forest. Yama was busy in his sacrificial duties, with the result that creatures no longer died. The gods complained to Brahmā that nothing now distinguished them from men; Brahmā reassured them that once their rite was completed men would start to die again. As the gods returned to their sacrifice, Indra saw a woman weeping into the Gaṅgā: each of her tears became a golden lotus. When he asked her who she was and why she was weeping, she told him to follow her; he did so, and saw a youth playing dice with some young women. The youth ignored him; Indra began to bluster angrily, but at a glance from the youth he found himself paralysed. Next the youth, who was Śiva, told the woman to bring him close so that he could be divested of his pride, and at her touch he collapsed to the ground. Now he was commanded to remove the summit of the mountain and enter, and when he did so he found four other Indras imprisoned there. When Indra begged for his freedom, Śiva told him that all five Indras would return to their own world only after being born as men. However, he agreed to their stipulation that in their human form they must be begotten by deities: Dharma, Wind, Indra and the Aśvins. He also promised that the goddess Śrī would take human form as their wife. Nārāyaṇa agreed to this arrangement, and plucked from his head one white and one black hair: these entered the wombs of Rohiṇī and Devakī, and from them were born Balarāma and Kṛṣṇa. — Vyāsa explains to Drupada that the Pāṇḍavas are the five Indras, and Draupadī is Śrī, and he grants Drupada a sight of their true forms. He also repeats the tale he had earlier told the Pāṇḍavas of the girl who five times asked Śiva for a husband and was granted five husbands in her next birth. Draupadī is both Śrī and the reincarnation of this girl: it is ordained that she should marry the five Pāṇḍavas.*

## THE WEDDING

[190] *Drupada now drops his objections, and the wedding proceeds. Dhaumya marries Draupadī to each of the Pāṇḍava brothers, one on each of five successive*

*days; her virginity is restored each time. Drupada bestows costly presents upon the bridegrooms.* **[191]** *Kuntī gives Draupadī her blessing, and Kṛṣṇa sends the Pāṇḍavas rich gifts.*

## THE COMING OF VIDURA

**[192]** *When word gets about that the Pāṇḍavas are alive and wedded to Drupada's daughter, there is joy among Kṣatriyas in general but gloom among the Dhārtarāṣṭras. Vidura communicates the good news to Dhṛtarāṣṭra, who takes him to mean that Draupadī has chosen Duryodhana for her husband. When he learns that it is the Pāṇḍavas who have married her, and that they have formed many new alliances, he is pleased; but Karṇa and Duryodhana urge that action must swiftly be taken against them.*

**[193]** *Duryodhana proposes guile: by one devious means or another the Pāṇḍavas should be set against one another or killed.* **[194]** *Karṇa disagrees: deceit against the Pāṇḍavas has been attempted before, and has failed; and both the Pāṇḍavas themselves and their new allies the Pāñcālas are firmly committed to one another. Instead, Karṇa suggests an early war against them, before they have had a chance to form further alliances, and in particular before Kṛṣṇa can come to their aid. Dhṛtarāṣṭra is impressed by this argument, but wishes to consult the elders.*

**[195]** *Bhīṣma is strongly opposed to Karṇa's plan, which is contrary to* dharma. *Dhṛtarāṣṭra has already tarnished his name through his earlier attempt to have the Pāṇḍavas killed; the only right course of action now is to give them half the kingdom.*

**[196]** *Droṇa shares Bhīṣma's view: the Pāṇḍavas should be conciliated and welcomed back to receive their rightful due. But Karṇa rounds on Bhīṣma and Droṇa; he tells the story of a worthless king who relied for everything upon his minister. That minister took control of the king's wealth, his womenfolk, and his authority, but, for all he desired it, he was unable to usurp the kingship itself, for kingship is ordained. Dhṛtarāṣṭra should heed all counsel, wicked as well as virtuous. Droṇa rebukes Karṇa, and foresees the destruction of the Kurus if Dhṛtarāṣṭra follows his advice.*

**[197]** *Now Vidura commends the counsel of Bhīṣma and Droṇa to Dhṛtarāṣṭra. He should not favour his own sons over the sons of Pāṇḍu; even if he* *chooses to do so, he will not benefit, for the Pāṇḍavas are invincible. Dhṛtarāṣṭra should seek to restore his good name by pursuing reconciliation.*

[**198**] *Dhṛtarāṣṭra is convinced by the arguments of Bhīṣma, Droṇa and Vidura, and sends Vidura as an ambassador to the Pāṇḍavas to honour them and request their return. Vidura does as he is bidden. Treating Drupada and the Pāṇḍavas with the greatest respect, he urges that the five brothers should return to Hāstinapura with Kuntī and Draupadī.*

## THE GAINING OF THE KINGDOM

Vaiśaṃpāyana spoke:

[**199**] Drupada said, 'It is just as you now tell me, wise Vidura; and I share your great joy, lord, at the forging of this alliance. It is right for these noble princes to return home. However, it would not be right for me to say this to them myself. The Pāṇḍavas should not set out till brave Yudhiṣṭhira, Kuntī's son, thinks fit, and Bhīma and Arjuna too, and the bull-like twins, and also the tiger-like heroes Balarāma and Kṛṣṇa, who know *dharma* and are committed to the princes' welfare.'

Yudhiṣṭhira now addressed Kṛṣṇa, and said, 'O king, I and all who follow me are in your hands. Whatever you are pleased to say, that we shall do.'

Kṛṣṇa Vāsudeva replied, 'I think it right to go; but I defer to the view of King Drupada, who is expert in *dharma*.'

Then Drupada spoke again: 'I completely agree with strong-armed Kṛṣṇa, the heroic prince of Daśārha and highest lord, that the time has come. For, make no doubt, the noble sons of Pāṇḍu are as dear to Vāsudeva as they have now become to me; even Kuntī's son Yudhiṣṭhira, son of Dharma, does not devote as much thought to the princes' welfare as the tiger-like hero Kṛṣṇa Keśava!'

Now that they had noble Drupada's leave to depart, the Pāṇḍavas, with Kṛṣṇa and sagacious Vidura, collected Draupadī Kṛṣṇā and Kuntī of high repute, and travelled pleasantly and at leisure to the City of the Elephant, Hāstinapura. When the Kaurava ruler Dhṛtarāṣṭra learnt that those heroes were approaching, he dispatched his sons to greet the Pāṇḍavas, together with the mighty bowman Vikarṇa,

Citrasena, Droṇa the mightiest of bowmen, and Kṛpa heir of Gotama. Surrounded by this welcoming party, the heroic chariot-fighters now made a stately and resplendent entrance into the city of Hāstinapura.

The city-folk were bursting with curiosity to see those tiger-like heroes, destroyers of grief and affliction, and the Pāṇḍavas heard many kind and heart-warming words uttered by well-wishers: 'Here comes the tiger-like hero Yudhiṣṭhira, expert in *dharma*, returning to protect us through *dharma* as if we were his children! Today is as if the great king Pāṇḍu had returned from the forest he loved in order to work for our welfare, make no doubt! Surely our happiness today is complete, since the brave sons of Kuntī have returned to govern us all. If we have gained any merit through generosity, sacrifice or asceticism, let it serve to keep the Pāṇḍavas in our city for a hundred autumns!'

Now they paid their respects at the feet of Dhṛtarāṣṭra, Bhīṣma, and others deserving of honour; then, after exchanging polite greetings with all the city elders, they entered Dhṛtarāṣṭra's house as he directed.

For some time the mighty, noble Pāṇḍavas rested there; then they were summoned by King Dhṛtarāṣṭra and by Bhīṣma son of Śaṃtanu. Dhṛtarāṣṭra addressed them: 'Son of Kuntī, hear with your brothers what I have to say. Let there be no further discord! You should move to Khāṇḍavaprastha; no one will be able to harm you if you make your dwelling there, for Arjuna will protect you as Indra protects the gods. Receive half of the kingdom, and move to Khāṇḍavaprastha!'

Those bull-like men all accepted the king's words. They bowed to him, and set out for the terrible forest; they received half of the kingdom, and moved to Khāṇḍavaprastha.

When the invincible Pāṇḍavas arrived there, led by Kṛṣṇa, they turned that forest into a town, beautiful as a heaven. At an auspicious place and time the mighty chariot-fighters proclaimed a peace, and then measured out their city under Vyāsa's leadership. They adorned it with moats that seemed like seas, and provided it with a wall standing so high that it enclosed the heavens, like a white cloud, or Mount Himālaya; thus their fine city shone like Bhogavatī, the city of the

serpents. For protection it had fearsome double gates like Garuḍa's
wings, and gateway towers, tall as massed clouds or Mount Mandara
itself, that were filled with weapons of every kind, complete and well
guarded. It was well stocked with spears like fork-tongued snakes,
and watch-towers stood round it at close intervals; the adornments of
that excellent fortress were elephant-goads, hundred-slaying weapons
and many other such instruments of war, including huge discuses of
iron.

Its streets were wide and well laid out to avoid accidents, and a variety
35 of fine white dwellings added to its lustre. And so that city, known
as Indraprastha, shone like Indra's heaven, and grew like a massive
lightning-cloud in the sky. In that lovely place, Yudhiṣṭhira heir of
Kuru set his dwelling, glittering with wealth like the realm of Kubera,
treasurer to the gods. Brahmins, best of all those who know the Veda,
came to Indraprastha, O king, and similarly experts in every language
liked to live there; merchants seeking to trade came to the land from
every direction, and craftsmen of every sort arrived to settle there too.
All round the city were lovely gardens planted with mango trees, plum
40 trees and neems, *aśoka* trees and *campakas*, and many other kinds of
tree, always in blossom and always in fruit, full of many varieties of
birds, and resounding with the intoxicated cries of peacocks and of
cuckoos.

There were houses bright as mirrors; there were many arbours of
creepers; there were entrancing painted houses, pleasure-hills, and many
45 pools filled with purest water; there were lakes of great loveliness, fragrant
with red and blue lotuses and stocked with geese, ducks and *cakravāka*
birds; there were delightful lotus ponds of every kind, surrounded by
trees, as well as huge and beautiful reservoirs. The land was great,
and populated by good folk; living there, great king, the Pāṇḍavas
experienced an ever-increasing joy.

So it was that, after Bhīṣma and King Dhṛtarāṣṭra had reached a just
settlement, the Pāṇḍavas came to dwell in Khāṇḍavaprastha. Ruled by
those five mighty bowmen as if by five Indras, that fine city shone like
50 Bhogavatī, the city of the serpents. Once he had settled them there, O
king, heroic Kṛṣṇa Keśava took his leave of the Pāṇḍavas and returned
with Balarāma to Dvārakā.

## ARJUNA'S EXILE IN THE FOREST

**[200]** — *Janamejaya asks Vaiśampāyana how the Pāṇḍavas avoided disputes over their joint wife Draupadī, and Vaiśampāyana continues his narration. — Yudhiṣṭhira and his brothers rule righteously and in happiness. One day the seer Nārada arrives. He is greeted respectfully, and blesses Draupadī; then he dismisses her, and warns the brothers to avoid falling into dispute over her; it was this that led to the death of the demon brothers Sunda and Upasunda. Yudhiṣṭhira asks to hear this tale in full.*

### SUNDA AND UPASUNDA

**[201]** *Nārada narrates the story. — Sunda and Upasunda, inseparable brothers, have performed such fierce austerities that the gods try to disrupt them, but without success. Finally, Brahmā offers them a boon: they choose mighty strength, the ability to change shape at will, and immortality. When Brahmā rules out immortality, they choose invulnerability except to each other, and rejoin the other demons.* **[202]** *Now they embark on conquering the world. The gods flee to Brahmā's world, and the demon brothers overcome all creatures; taking the forms of fierce animals they slay seers, Brahmins and kings until the earth is laid completely waste. Then they settle in Kurukṣetra.*

**[203]** *The highest divine seers approach Brahmā and tell him what has occurred; after pausing briefly for thought, Brahmā orders Viśvakarman to create a highly desirable woman. Viśvakarman assembles all the loveliest materials in the three worlds and from them forms Tilottamā. At Brahmā's command, Tilottamā agrees to seduce the demon brothers. As she circumambulates the gods before leaving, only Śiva and Indra seem unaffected by her beauty; but three new faces grow on the sides and back of Śiva's head, and eyes grow all over Indra's body.*

**[204]** *Sunda and Upasunda are spending their time in drunken enjoyment when Tilottamā appears before them. Both are instantly infatuated, and in the quarrel that ensues they attack each other with their clubs and kill each other. — After hearing this story from Nārada, the*

*Pāṇḍavas agree that if any brother should set eyes upon another brother with Draupadī, he must be exiled for twelve years of celibate life in the forest.*

**[205]** *One day, a Brahmin whose cattle have been stolen comes to the Pāṇḍavas for assistance. Arjuna knows that the weapon-room is also the room where Yudhiṣṭhira is with Draupadī, but realizing that* dharma *comes before all else he enters and takes up a bow. He slays the robbers, returns the Brahmin's cattle to him, and then prepares to go into exile for twelve years. Yudhiṣṭhira tries to dissuade him, but he insists on strict adherence to* dharma.

**[206]** *Accompanied by many Brahmins, Arjuna travels to Gaṅgādvāra and remains there. Bathing in the Gaṅgā, he is abducted by Ulūpī, daughter of the king of the serpents, who has fallen in love with him. She implores him to lie with her; he explains his vow of celibacy; she argues that the vow applies only to relations with Draupadī, and that even if he incurs a small fault it will be outweighed by the merit of saving her life, for if she cannot have him she will die. Arjuna grants her wish.*

**[207]** *Now he travels eastwards, visiting many sacred places along the way. When he reaches Maṇalūra, he sees Citrāṅgadā, daughter of King Citravāhana, and desires her. The king explains that in his family only one child is born in each generation: Arjuna may have her, so long as he begets on her a son to continue the line. Arjuna agrees, and lives there with her for three years.*

**[208]** *Next Arjuna travels south, where he finds that five of the holy bathing-places are being shunned because of crocodiles. He enters the bathing-place named Saubhadra and is at once attacked by a crocodile; he pulls it out of the water and it turns into a beautiful Apsaras. She explains that she and her four friends had disrupted a Brahmin's austerities, and that he had cursed them to become crocodiles for a hundred years.* **[209]** *She and her friends had begged for mercy, and the Brahmin had conceded that the curse would end when they were pulled out of the water by a man of the highest character. Shortly after leaving the Brahmin they had encountered the seer Nārada, who had advised them to make their way to the southern bathing-places, as Arjuna would soon be visiting them. Having heard this story, Arjuna grants the Apsaras's request and frees her four friends. Then he* *revisits Maṇalūra to see Citrāṅgadā and Babhruvāhana, the son she has born him.*

**[210]** *Now Arjuna travels to the west to visit the sacred places there. In Prabhāsa Kṛṣṇa arrives to meet him, and they pass some time enjoying themselves together there and on Mount Raivataka. Then Arjuna travels with Kṛṣṇa to Dvārakā, where he is greeted with the greatest honour. He stays there with Kṛṣṇa for a long time.*

## THE ABDUCTION OF SUBHADRĀ

**[211]** *At a great festival, Arjuna sees and falls in love with Kṛṣṇa's sister Subhadrā. He asks Kṛṣṇa how he may get her as his wife; Kṛṣṇa replies that, given the uncertain outcome of a* svayaṃvara, *the best course of action would be marriage by abduction. Arjuna sends messengers to Yudhiṣṭhira at Indraprastha to inform him of his plan, and Yudhiṣṭhira agrees to it.* **[212]** *Arjuna now drives in his excellent chariot to Raivataka, where Subhadrā is just completing her worship, seizes her, and makes for Indraprastha. Her drunken kinsmen prepare to pursue him, but Kṛṣṇa remains silent; Balarāma belligerently challenges him to state his mind, for it was he who brought Arjuna among them.*

## THE WEDDING GIFT

**[213]** *Kṛṣṇa persuades his kinsmen that Arjuna has acted properly, and that the match is a worthy one. Arjuna now returns to Dvārakā and weds Subhadrā; after completing his term of exile in Puṣkara, he re-enters Indraprastha. At first Draupadī is jealous of Arjuna's new wife, but when she sees Subhadrā she is won over. Now Kṛṣṇa arrives with Balarāma and all the Vṛṣṇi, Bhoja and Andhaka chiefs. They give great wealth as their wedding gift: chariots, cattle, mares, mules, maidservants, gold, and a thousand elephants. Then they settle down to enjoyment and drinking. In the course of time, Subhadrā gives birth to Abhimanyu, who is greatly loved by Kṛṣṇa and by all the Pāṇḍavas. Draupadī bears five sons: Prativindhya, son of Yudhiṣṭhira; Sutasoma, son of Bhīma; Śrutakarman, son of Arjuna; Śatānīka, son of Nakula; and Śrutasena, son of Sahadeva.*

## THE BURNING OF THE KHĀṆḌAVA FOREST

**[214]** *The Pāṇḍavas live happily in Indraprastha. One hot day, Arjuna suggests a river trip to Kṛṣṇa, and the two of them set out with a group of friends. While they are all enjoying themselves, Arjuna and Kṛṣṇa are approached by a Brahmin with a blazing appearance.* **[215]** *The strange Brahmin requests food for his insatiable appetite; when they ask him what sort of food he eats, he explains that he is Fire. He wishes to devour the Khāṇḍava forest, but Indra always washes it with rain to protect his friend Takṣaka, king of the serpents. Arjuna tells Fire that he is willing to do what he can to overcome Indra, but he and Kṛṣṇa are in need of weapons adequate to the task.*

**[216]** *The Fire now invokes Varuṇa, lord of the waters, and tells him to give to Arjuna the bow Gāṇḍīva with two inexhaustible arrow-cases, and a chariot with a monkey for its emblem, and to Kṛṣṇa a discus. Varuṇa does as asked: Arjuna's new weapons and chariot are glorious and invincible, and Kṛṣṇa's discus will always triumph and always return to his hand. Now that the heroes are prepared, they call on the Fire to begin consuming the forest, and he does so.*

**[217]** *Thousands of creatures perish in the conflagration, and Arjuna and Kṛṣṇa pursue any that attempt to flee. The Fire reaches into the sky and troubles the very gods, who approach Indra and ask him what is happening. Indra rains heavily on the Fire, but the rain is dried up by the heat of the Fire before it can reach the ground. Furious, Indra redoubles his efforts,* **[218]** *but Arjuna covers the forest with his arrows, warding off the rainfall.*

*Takṣaka himself is elsewhere, but his son Aśvasena is unable to escape the Fire, until his mother rescues him by swallowing him and fleeing into the air. However, she is killed by Arjuna's arrows, and Aśvasena is cursed by Arjuna, Kṛṣṇa and the Fire. Arjuna continues to battle against Indra, overcoming his clouds and thunderbolts. Birds, serpents, even the gods and other immortals join in the attack, but Arjuna defeats them, while Kṛṣṇa slaughters demons with his discus. Indra leads a force of gods against the two warriors, but to no avail; finally he breaks off the summit of Mount Mandara and hurls it at Arjuna, but Arjuna shatters it with his arrows.*

**[219]** *The killing continues. A voice from the air announces to Indra that his friend Takṣaka is safe, and that Arjuna and Kṛṣṇa are the invincible Nara and*

*Nārāyaṇa: he should let the forest burn, for this is ordained. Indra withdraws to heaven, and the Fire continues to consume the inhabitants of the forest, while the two warriors kill all who attempt to flee. However, the demon Maya appeals to Arjuna for help and is spared. The only survivors are Aśvasena, Maya, and four* śārṅgaka *birds.*

## THE ŚĀRṄGAKA BIRDS

**[220]** —*Janamejaya asks to hear how the* śārṅgaka *birds survived the Fire, and Vaiśaṃpāyana narrates the story. — The seer Mandapāla performs supreme austerities and reaches the world of the ancestors, but does not receive the reward he expects. The gods' explanation is his lack of a son. Anxious to gain sons without delay, he becomes a* śārṅgaka *bird and mates with the female bird Jaritā, but then abandons her and his four unhatched sons for another female, Lapitā. When he sees the Fire, he praises it and receives a boon in return; he chooses that his sons should be spared.*

**[221]** *When the Fire approaches, Jaritā wonders what to do to save her newly hatched sons. She proposes to cover them with her own body, but they urge her to fly away: she can have further sons, and Mandapāla's intention must not be frustrated. She tells them to hide in a rat-hole; they prefer death by burning to death in the jaws of a rat.* **[222]** *Jaritā tells her sons that the rat has already been killed by a hawk; they prefer to take their chances with the Fire. She attempts to persuade them, but they will not change their minds. Finally, she leaves them and flies to safety.* **[223]** *The four young birds praise the Fire; the Fire assures them that it will honour its promise to their father, and offers them a boon; they request it to burn cats.*

**[224]** *Meanwhile, Mandapāla worries about his sons. When the Fire has passed, Jaritā returns to find them unscathed; then Mandapāla arrives. At first neither Jaritā nor his sons will acknowledge him, but he warns her against jealousy, and is then properly received.* **[225]** *Mandapāla now takes his family and leaves for another place.*

*— The Fire is finally satisfied. Indra offers Arjuna and Kṛṣṇa boons: Arjuna chooses celestial weapons, and Kṛṣṇa chooses Indra's friendship. The Fire grants them leave to depart: Arjuna, Kṛṣṇa and Maya sit down together on the bank of a river.*

# THE HALL

## THE HALL

[1] *The demon Maya, who is a mighty craftsman, wishes to make something for Arjuna by way of thanks for rescuing him. At first Arjuna demurs; then, when Maya insists, he entrusts the choice of gift to Kṛṣṇa. Kṛṣṇa specifies a hall for Yudhiṣṭhira and the Pāṇḍavas. Delighted, Maya carries out his preparations for the task.*

[2] *Now Kṛṣṇa determines to visit his father in Dvārakā. He bids farewell to the Pāṇḍavas and to Kuntī, Subhadrā, Draupadī and Dhaumya. Then he sets out; the Pāṇḍavas accompany him part-way before returning to their own city.*

Vaiśaṃpāyana spoke:

[3] Then Maya addressed Kuntī's son Arjuna, best of victors: 'With your
leave I shall now depart, but I shall soon return. At the time when all
the demons were preparing for a sacrifice near Mount Maināka to the
north of Kailāsa, I left a treasure of jewels by the lovely Lake Bindu,
in the hall of Vṛṣaparvan,[1] keeper of his word. I shall go and fetch it
if it is still there, O heir of Bharata, and then I shall build a hall for
Pāṇḍu's famous son Yudhiṣṭhira. It will be adorned with every kind of
5 gem, and so beautiful as to gladden the heart. And in that same Lake
Bindu, O Kaurava, there is an excellent club that King Yauvanāśva left
there after slaying his enemies in battle. It is decked with gold markings,
massive and strong, capable of withstanding a heavy blow, the equal of
a hundred thousand ordinary clubs, dealing death to all. It is worthy of

1 The king of the demons.

Bhīma, as your bow Gāṇḍīva is worthy of you. There is also Varuṇa's great conch Devadatta, which makes a mighty sound. All this I shall bestow upon you, make no doubt!' With these words to Kuntī's son Arjuna, the demon then set off towards the north-east.

Now near Mount Maināka to the north of Kailāsa is great Hiraṇyaśṛṅga, a holy mountain rich in gems, and lovely Lake Bindu. There King Bhagīratha lived for many years watching the Gaṅgā, known as 'Bhagīratha's river'. There noble Indra, lord of all beings, performed a hundred great sacrifices, heir of Bharata; there he set up sacrificial posts studded with jewels, and altars of gold, to beautify the site, not to set a standard; there the thousand-eyed god, Śacī's husband, attained success through his sacrifice. There the eternal Śiva, lord of beings and creator of all worlds, is worshipped in his fiery energy, surrounded by thousands of spirit beings. There Nara and Nārāyaṇa, Brahmā, Yama and Śiva attend a sacrificial session at the end of every thousand ages. There faithful Kṛṣṇa Vāsudeva sacrificed for the permanent benefit of the virtuous in sessions lasting a thousand years; and there he set up, in thousands and millions, gold-wreathed sacrificial posts and altars of surpassing splendour.

To that place now went Maya. He took the club and conch, O heir of Bharata, and the crystal treasure from Vṛṣaparvan's hall, and with the aid of the Kiṃkara Rākṣasas carried it all back to Indraprastha. Now the demon built a matchless hall, studded with jewels, famed throughout the three worlds for its heavenly beauty. Then he presented that finest of clubs to Bhīma, and gave Kuntī's son Arjuna the incomparable conch Devadatta.

Great king, the very trees in that hall were made of gold! It extended ten thousand cubits in every direction; wonderful in form, it shone with a heavenly light like that of fire, or the sun or moon; indeed, its brilliance seemed to outshine the brilliant splendour of the sun as it blazed forth with a divine radiance. It stood obscuring the sky, like a mountain or a cloud, long and broad and smooth, dispelling sin and weariness. Built of the finest materials, it wore its jewelled walls like a garland; it was rich in gems and in wealth, a masterwork of a master architect. The matchless hall that Maya built was more beautiful than Sudharmā, the divine hall of the Daśārhas, or even that of Brahmā himself. At Maya's command, it was guarded and supported by eight thousand terrible Kiṃkara Rākṣasas, sky-roaming fighters, mighty of body and mighty of strength, with shell-like ears and red or orange eyes.

Within the hall, Maya built an incomparable pool covered with multicoloured lotuses with beryl leaves and jewelled stems, thronged with birds of many kinds, bright with lotus-flowers, full of lovely turtles and fish. A beautiful stairway led down into the clear water of the pool, which never dried up whatever the season, and was shaded by jasmine bushes that trembled in the breeze. It was adorned so richly with jewels that a number of princes who arrived there did not recognize it for what it was, despite the evidence of their eyes, and fell straight in.

All round the hall were great trees of various sorts, always in blossom, and delightful for their dark, cool shade. Everywhere there were fragrant groves, and lotus-pools stocked with geese, ducks and *cakravāka* birds; and the breeze wafted to the Pāṇḍavas the scent of the flowers that grew all round, on land and in water. Such was the hall that Maya built in the space of fourteen months; and then he reported to Yudhiṣṭhira lord of *dharma* that it was complete.

[4] Now King Yudhiṣṭhira took possession of the hall with a feast for ten thousand Brahmins: there were buttered rice, honey, and delicious roots and fruits, as well as brand new clothes and garlands of many kinds; to each one of them the king gave a thousand cattle, till the sound of their benedictions seemed to reach heaven itself, O heir of Bharata. Yudhiṣṭhira, best of Kurus, now worshipped the deities with musical instruments, a variety of songs, and perfumes of various kinds, and installed them in their shrines; after which wrestlers, actors, prizefighters, bards and heralds attended on the noble king for seven nights. After thus honouring the lovely hall, he lived there with his brothers, happy as Indra in his heaven.

*Seers and princes from all over the world attend, and the music is performed by Gandharvas and Apsarases.*

[5] *The great seer Nārada now visits Yudhiṣṭhira, and proceeds to ask him a long series of questions about the manner of his rule over the kingdom. Yudhiṣṭhira promises to abide by the instruction implicit in Nārada's words,* [6] *then replies to him point by point. Next he asks Nārada whether in his travels he has ever*

*seen so fine a hall. Nārada answers that no mortal's hall can compare with it; but he offers to tell of the halls of the world-guardian gods, an offer which is eagerly accepted.*

[7] *Nārada describes Indra's hall, which he built for himself. It is enormous, beautiful, and travels through the air; throngs of divine seers, among them King Hariścandra, attend on Indra there, while Gandharvas and Apsarases make music.*

[8] *In Yama's great hall all human woes are banished, and everything one could desire is to be found; there are all the ancestor kings, including Pāṇḍu, yet despite their great numbers there is no crush.*

[9] *Varuṇa's hall stands in water, and is surrounded by beautiful trees and flowers, while lovely birds fly about inside; in attendance are serpents and demons, oceans, rivers and mountains.*

[10] *Kubera's brilliant white hall floats in the air, and is full of hosts of Apsarases and Gandharvas; Kubera's friend Śiva too is there, with his consort Umā and his ghoulish attendants.*

[11] *Now Nārada relates how once, long ago, the Sun god had visited earth and described to him the wonders of Brahmā's heavenly hall. Nārada expressed a desire to see it, and the Sun conducted him there. It is indescribable, ever-changing in form; it grants ease; high in the heavens, it shines with its own light as if to illuminate the sun. There Brahmā is attended by seers, gods, planets, the Vedas, the seasons: by everything that exists in the three worlds.*

Vaiśaṃpāyana spoke:
Yudhiṣṭhira now once again addressed Nārada: 'As you describe it, best
of all those who speak, the kings are mostly to be found within the
hall of Yama. You said, O lord, that the serpents are in Varuṇa's hall,
together with most of the foremost demons, the rivers and the oceans;
in the hall of Kubera lord of wealth are Yakṣas, Guhyakas, Rākṣasas, 45
Gandharvas and Apsarases, as well as blessed Śiva whose emblem is the
bull; you said that the great seers dwell in Grandfather Brahmā's hall
with all the hosts of the gods and all learning; and in the hall of Indra of
a hundred sacrifices you mentioned by name certain gods, Gandharvas
and great seers. But, mighty sage, you said that, alone among royal seers,
Hariścandra dwells for ever in the hall of noble Indra, lord of the gods.
What deed did he do, or what austerities did he unswervingly perform,

50 that that renowned king should now rival Indra himself? And how, O priest, did you come to meet my father, the blessed Pāṇḍu, in the realm of the ancestors? What did he say, holy sir? I wish to know this; I have the strongest curiosity to hear you tell the whole story!'

Nārada answered, 'Lord of kings, since you ask me about Hariścandra, I shall expound to you the greatness of that wise man. He was a mighty king, an emperor over all the world's kings; all the lords of the earth always acknowledged his authority. Mounted on a single gold-adorned chariot of victory, he conquered the seven continents of the earth with
55 the prowess of his sword, lord of men; and after conquering the whole of the earth with its mountains and forests and groves, he performed the great sacrifice of the royal consecration. At his command all the lords of the earth brought to him their wealth, and waited upon the Brahmins at that sacrifice. And that lord of men gladly bestowed riches upon the sacrificial priests, five times greater than they had asked for; when the time came to enter the sacrificial enclosure, he gratified the Brahmins who had assembled from many quarters with valuable gifts of every kind. Honoured to their heart's content with a variety of foodstuffs, and sated with mounds of gems, those Brahmins proclaimed in delight that he excelled over all other kings in ardour and in renown.

60 'Bull-like son of Kuntī, you should know that this is why Hariścandra of mighty energy now outshines those thousands of kings. When he had completed that great sacrifice he was consecrated in glory as emperor, lord of men; and so too any other king who performs the great sacrifice of the royal consecration dwells in joy with great Indra. Likewise the man who meets his death unfleeing in battle will find joy in Indra's dwelling, O bull-like heir of Bharata, and he who quits his body through keen asceticism will also blaze in glory there forever.

65 'As for your father Pāṇḍu, O son of Kuntī, this is what that heir of Kuru said to you after seeing the astonishing glory of King Hariścandra: "You are capable of conquering the earth, and your brothers are under your authority: perform the most excellent sacrifice, the royal consecration, heir of Bharata!" Tiger-like hero, you should carry out his wishes, and then you will come to share in great Indra's world, together with your forebears.

'It is true, O king, that this great sacrifice is known to be subject to many obstacles, for Brahmin Rākṣasas will search for weak points to destroy the rite. War, too, follows behind it, capable of destroying the earth; indeed, in this case there is a portent of such destruction. Think on this, lord of kings, and then do what is proper. Be always ready and alert to protect the four classes of men; thrive; rejoice; and gratify the Brahmins with your gifts.

'I have told you in full what you asked me. With your leave I shall now depart for the Daśārha city of Dvārakā.'

After speaking thus to the Pāṇḍavas, O Janamejaya, Nārada left amidst the seers with whom he had come. And after his departure, heir of Kuru, Kuntī's son Yudhiṣṭhira discussed that most excellent sacrifice, the royal consecration, with his brothers.

## CONSULTATIONS

Vaiśampāyana spoke:

[12] When Yudhiṣṭhira heard the words of Nārada the seer, he sighed, O heir of Bharata: he could find no peace for worrying over the performance of the royal consecration. Knowing the greatness of noble royal seers, and considering how sacrificers attained the blessed realms through their virtuous deeds, and thinking in particular of the glorious royal seer and sacrificer Hariścandra, he longed to perform the sacrifice of the royal consecration. He paid honour to all his courtiers, and, honoured by them all in return, he turned his thoughts towards the royal consecration; lord among kings, the bull of the Kurus reflected over and over again as he directed his mind towards performing the sacrifice of the royal consecration. Moreover, that king of astonishing power and heroism who maintained purest *dharma* considered what would confer benefit on all people; best of all experts in *dharma*, Yudhiṣṭhira showed kindness to all his subjects and worked for the benefit of all, with no discrimination. So the people flourished under his paternal care, and no one hated him; hence he was known as Ajātaśatru, 'Man without enemies'.

Yudhiṣṭhira, best of all those who speak, summoned his ministers and his brothers, and questioned them repeatedly about the royal consecration. His ministers answered his questions fittingly and with one voice, telling wise Yudhiṣṭhira, who wished to perform the sacrifice, 'A king who is consecrated by that rite attains the status of Varuṇa;[1] one who is already king seeks to gain by that rite the full status of an emperor. Your friends believe that you are worthy of that imperial status, Kuru lord, and that the time has come for your royal consecration. Thanks to your successes as a Kṣatriya, you may choose when to perform that sacrifice, in which Brahmins of keen vows pile up six fires while the Sāmaveda is sung. He who performs the ladled oblations therein accomplishes all sacrifices, and also attains his consecration at the end of the rite; and he is therefore known as a universal conqueror. Strong-armed king, you are capable of this, and we are all obedient to you; so do not hesitate, but fix your mind upon the royal consecration!'

*Yudhiṣṭhira wishes to hear Kṛṣṇa's views, and sends a messenger to Dvārakā to summon him; Kṛṣṇa arrives, and Yudhiṣṭhira asks for his opinion.*

Vaiśampāyana spoke:

**[13]** Kṛṣṇa answered, 'Great king, with all your qualities you are worthy to perform the royal consecration. However, though you know everything, I shall mention something to you, heir of Bharata. They who are known today in this world as Kṣatriyas are descended from those earlier Kṣatriyas who survived the attacks of Rāma son of Jamadagni. You know, bull-like lord of the earth, that they have stated the lines of their descent in authoritative terms: the kings, and the other Kṣatriya lineages on earth, claim origin from the dynasties sprung from Ilā and Ikṣvāku. Kings descended from Ilā and Ikṣvāku number a hundred and one royal lines, bull-like heir of Bharata; but there has also been an extraordinarily wide expansion of the lines of Yayāti and the Bhojas,

**1** In the Vedic period Varuṇa was regarded as sovereign lord (*samrāj*, the same word here translated 'emperor') among the gods. Later he dwindled to become god of the ocean and one of the eight world-guardian deities, ruling over the western quarter; clearly this passage invokes his earlier grandeur.

reaching in every direction, great king, and the Kṣatriyas as a body honour their royal rank equally with the rest.[1]

'But lately the ruler of the central lands, King Jarāsaṃdha Caturyu, to whom the hundred and first royal line has descended, has determined to break away from the rest; and he holds imperial rank by birth. Now, wise king, it seems that King Śiśupāla of great energy supports him fully and has become his general. Vakra the mighty lord of Karūṣa, who fights by illusory power, has joined him like a disciple, great king; and the noble heroes Haṃsa and Ḍibhaka have also both joined the heroic Jarāsaṃdha, along with Dantavakra, Karūṣa, Kalabha and Meghavāhana.

'King Bhagadatta of boundless might, who bears on his head the celestial gem known as the jewel of all creation, who punished the Greek rulers Mura and Naraka, who rules like Varuṇa in the West, your father's old friend, great king – he submits to Jarāsaṃdha in both word and deed, though in his heart he is devoted to you like a father, for he is tied by affection. Only brave King Kuntibhoja Purujit, glory of the Kunti line, afflicter of his enemies, your mother's brother who rules the south-western region of the earth, submits to you in his affection for you.

'Jarāsaṃdha has also been joined by Vāsudeva of Puṇḍra, that villain whom I have not yet killed, who is known as highest lord in Cedi and believes himself the highest lord in this world, thus claiming my own title in his endless folly; he is king over the Vaṅgas, Puṇḍras and Kirātas, and is renowned for his might throughout the three worlds.

'And Bhīṣmaka Caturyu, mighty Bhoja king and friend of Indra, the slayer of enemy heroes who defeated the Pāṇḍyas, Krathas and Kaiśikas through the power of his learning, whose brother Āhṛti is a hero equal in battle to Rāma son of Jamadagni, is devoted to Jarāsaṃdha of Magadha. We are his kin, great king, always respectful to him; we show him kindness and affection, but he has no affection for us and treats us with resolute unkindness. So though he does not recognize his own lineage

1 The mythology of Ila is confused, but some accounts (see 1.70) make him the father of Purūravas, who was the grandson of the moon; Ikṣvāku was directly descended from the sun. The major Kṣatriya dynasties were thus all 'solar' or 'lunar'. For Yayāti and the Bhojas, see 1.80.

or its might, O king, he has seen Jarāsaṃdha's blaze of glory, and has gone over to him.

'Therefore the northern Bhojas and the eighteen junior lines have taken refuge in the West, lord, from fear of Jarāsaṃdha, as have the Śūrasenas, Bhadrakāras, Bodhas, Śālvas and Paṭaccaras, the Sustharas, Sukuṭṭas and the Kuṇindas with the Kuntis, the kings of the Śālveyas with their kinsfolk and followers, the southern Pāñcālas and the eastern Kośalas among the Kuntis. The Matsyas and Saṃnyastapādas have likewise left the northern country in their fear and taken refuge in the South, and in the same way all the Pāñcālas in their fear of Jarāsaṃdha have abandoned their own kingdom and fled in every direction.

'As for Kaṃsa,[1] after oppressing his relatives for some time the fool then took Jarāsaṃdha's two daughters to be his queens: they were named Asti and Prāpti, and were the younger sisters of Sahadeva. Foolish Kaṃsa used the power they brought him to overcome his kinsmen and attain mastery over them. The villain committed dreadful wickedness until, in their affliction at his hands, the seniormost Bhoja Kṣatriyas entered into an alliance with us for the protection of their people. Once I had concluded the marriage of Āhuka's daughter Sutanu to Akrūra, I then took up my kinsmen's cause, together with Balarāma: the two of us slew both Kaṃsa and his brother Sunāman.

'But danger now approached, for Jarāsaṃdha made ready for war. The eighteen junior lines therefore reached a decision, O king: even if we were to strike unceasingly with mighty hundred-slaying weapons, we could not slay his force within three hundred years, for he had two excellent warriors named Haṃsa and Ḍibhaka, mightiest of the mighty, comparable in strength to the gods. In my judgement the three of them – these two heroes together with heroic Jarāsaṃdha – were a match for the three worlds; nor was this my view alone, for all the other princes were of just the same opinion, O foremost of the wise.

'Now as for that great ruler named Haṃsa, as he fought in battle with the eighteen junior lines, O king, someone proclaimed that he had been killed; and on hearing this, heir of Bharata, Ḍibhaka drowned himself in the waters of the Yamunā. Ḍibhaka believed he could not

1 Formerly king of Mathurā and Kṛṣṇa's particular enemy.

bear to live in this world without Haṃsa, and so went to his death. In
the same way when Haṃsa, the conqueror of enemy fortresses, heard
of Ḍibhaka's fate, he too made his way to the Yamunā and drowned
himself there. And when King Jarāsaṃdha learnt that they had both
met their death in the waters of the river, he set out for his own city of
Śūrasena, O bull-like heir of Bharata.

'Enemy-slayer, when that king turned back we all lived joyfully once
more in Mathurā. But when Jarāsaṃdha's daughter, Kaṃsa's lotus-eyed 45
widow, approached her father the king of Magadha, and in her grief at her
husband's loss urged him again and again, "Kill my lord's killer!", then,
great king, we remembered the decision we had previously reached,
and fled in distress: we each gathered up our greatest riches, O king, and
ran headlong with our wealth and our kinsfolk in fear of Jarāsaṃdha.
Our worries led us all to travel to the western region and the lovely
city of Dvārakā, adorned by Mount Raivata. There, O king, we settled 50
once more; and we so perfected our fortifications as to make them
invincible to the very gods. Enemy-slayer, that is where we are now
living in confidence of our safety, for it is a place which even women
could defend, never mind the bull-like Vṛṣṇi heroes! Those heirs of
Madhu are filled with the highest joy, tiger-like Kuru, when they see
the great mountain and the Mādhavī ford.

'Thus we have been wronged by Jarāsaṃdha from the start; and so
kinship prompts us to turn to you. We have great strength: our fort
extends three leagues, with a triple division of men at every league;
at intervals of a league are hundreds of gates, arched and valiantly
manned; and the whole is ringed by Kṣatriyas of the eighteen junior
lines, mad for battle. In our own line there are eighteen thousand troops; 55
Āhuka has a hundred sons, each of whom has three hundred followers.
There is my own son Cārudeṣṇa and his brother Pradyumna, as well
as Cakradeva and Sātyaki, myself and Balarāma, and Sāmba, Balarāma's
equal in battle: these seven are champion warriors. Let me tell you of
others, O king: Kṛtavarman, Anādhṛṣṭi, Samīka, Samitiṃjaya, Kahva,
Śaṅku and Nidānta are seven great chariot-fighters; the two sons of
Andhakabhoja and the old king bring their number to ten. These brave,
mighty heroes, strong as any in the world, live untroubled amongst the
Vṛṣṇis, remembering the central lands where they once dwelt.

60 'Now you, O truest heir of Bharata, have always been endowed with imperial qualities, and it is right for you to establish yourself as emperor over the Kṣatriyas. But my belief is that it will not be possible for you to accomplish the royal consecration while mighty Jarāsaṃdha lives, O king, for in Girivraja his capital he is holding prisoner all the kings whom he defeated, like a lion holding mighty elephants captive in a cave on Mount Himālaya. King Jarāsaṃdha intends to sacrifice those lords of the earth, for it was after worshipping the great god Śiva that he defeated all the princes: every time that he defeated a prince in battle,
65 he brought him, bound, to his fortress and penned him up there. We ourselves, great king, fled Mathurā in fear of Jarāsaṃdha, and travelled to the city of Dvārakā. If you wish to accomplish your ritual, you should strive to rescue those kings and to slay Jarāsaṃdha; otherwise this mission of yours to perform the royal consecration in its entirety cannot be achieved, wisest heir of Kuru! This is my opinion, sinless king. But let it be as you yourself consider; so decide for yourself on the basis of all these considerations, and tell me your decision.'

**[14]** *Yudhiṣṭhira still doubts whether he can achieve success. Bhīma encourages him, and Kṛṣṇa insists that Jarāsaṃdha's wickedness must be stopped: he has eighty-six kings in captivity, and when he has captured fourteen more he will undertake his dreadful sacrifice. The one who defeats him will win both glory and empire.* **[15]** *Yudhiṣṭhira is not persuaded; the risk is too great. Now Arjuna urges him on: as a Kṣatriya he should act decisively against Jarāsaṃdha.* **[16]** *Kṛṣṇa too favours an attack on Jarāsaṃdha, which he is sure will succeed. At Yudhiṣṭhira's request he relates Jarāsaṃdha's story.*

*The mighty king Bṛhadratha of Magadha had married the twin daughters of the king of Kāśi, but no son was born to either of them. Offered a boon by the ascetic Caṇḍakauśika, Bṛhadratha declined it, saying that nothing was of value to a king without heir. Caṇḍakauśika recited a* mantra *over a mango and gave it to him, telling him it would give him what he desired; Bṛhadratha split it in two and gave a half to each of his wives, and both became pregnant. But when their time came, each gave birth to half of a child. The two half-children were abandoned; however, they were rescued by a Rākṣasa woman named Jarā, who put them together so that they became a single, mighty boy. Then she returned the child to the king and his wives.* **[17]** *After explaining to Bṛhadratha* *what had happened, the Rākṣasa woman vanished; Bṛhadratha named his son Jarāsaṃdha, 'Joined by Jarā'. After some time, Caṇḍakauśika returned, and predicted that the boy would become lord over all the earth's kings, and would see Śiva. Bṛhadratha now consecrated his son as king and retired to the forest to practise austerities. Jarāsaṃdha brought all the kings under his sway.*

## THE KILLING OF JARĀSAṂDHA

[**18**] *Now Kṛṣṇa proposes that he himself should accompany Bhīma and Arjuna in an attack on Jarāsaṃdha. Delighted, Yudhiṣṭhira agrees to this, and the three set out, disguised as Brahmins. They travel across country and arrive at the capital of Magadha.*

Vaiśaṃpāyana spoke:

[**19**] 'Son of Kuntī,' said Kṛṣṇa, 'here we are at the great city of Magadha: charming, rich in livestock and well supplied with water, it is a lovely place, healthy and full of fine houses. It has five huge and beautiful hills, sir: Vaihāra, Varāha, Vṛṣabha, Ṛṣigiri and Caitya; and these five mountains, with their great peaks and their cool trees, stand so close together that they seem to combine in protecting the city of Girivraja. Forests of *lodhra* trees – the delightful haunt of lovers – almost hide them from view, with branches thick with perfumed flowers.

'It was here that the noble Gautama, that seer of keen vows, fathered 5
Kākṣīvat and other sons upon the daughter of Uśīnara the Śūdra;
Gautama loved the royal line of Magadha because its kings showed
him such favour in allowing him to live here in this house, and the
mightiest kings, from Aṅga, Vaṅga and elsewhere, used to enjoy staying
in Gautama's dwelling at that time, O Arjuna. See these delightful groves
of *priyāla* trees, son of Kuntī, and these fine *lodhras* growing next to
Gautama's house.

'The serpents Arbuda and Śakravāpin, afflicters of their enemies,
lived here, and the wonderful dwellings of the serpents Svastika and
Maṇi were here also. It is because of Maṇi that this country of Magadha 10
is never shunned by the rain-clouds; and Kauśika and Maṇimat too

showed it great favour. Jarāsaṃdha believes that he has unceasing success in achieving his aims; so let us today lay low his pride in his accomplishments!'

At this the three brothers of mighty power – the two Pāṇḍavas and the Vṛṣṇi – set out for the city of Magadha. And so they came to Girivraja, full of happy and prosperous people of every class, rich in festivals, unassailable. Passing straight by the city gate, they rushed at lofty Mount Caitya, much loved by the people of Magadha, while members of the royal line and ordinary citizens were paying it reverence, as if in their
15 eagerness to slay Jarāsaṃdha they intended to strike at his head. This was where Bṛhadratha had come upon the bull-demon Māṣāda; he killed him, fashioned three kettledrums from his horns and throat, tied hides to them, and set them up in his own city, where those drums resounded whenever divine flowers pounded them.[1]

The mighty peak of Mount Caitya was firm and huge and old, decked with reverential garlands, fixed in its place for ever; those heroes struck it with their powerful arms and broke it off. Only then did they look upon the city of Magadha, and enter it.

20 Now at that moment Jarāsaṃdha's household priests were honouring the king by passing a fire around him as he sat upon an elephant. The heroes entered the city, longing to do battle against Jarāsaṃdha, but in the guise of pious householders, bearing no weapons, armed only with their arms. There they saw the vast, wonderful wealth of the food- and flower-markets, full of all good things, yielding prosperity in every way one might desire. Seeing all that wealth there in the street as they travelled along the royal highway, Kṛṣṇa, Bhīma and wealth-winner Arjuna, those best of mighty men, forcibly seized garlands from a garland-maker. Now, wearing multicoloured clothes, garlands and
25 gleaming earrings, they all entered the dwelling of wise Jarāsaṃdha, like Himālayan lions gazing at a cow-pen. Great king, the arms of those strong-armed heroes, decked with sandal and aloe, shone like pillars of rock. When the people of Magadha saw them, mighty as elephants, tall as the trunk of a *śāla* tree and broad-chested, they were astonished. The mighty bull-like heroes passed straight through three crowded chambers

1 The exact meaning of this very puzzling sentence is uncertain.

and arrogantly approached the king; and Jarāsaṃdha duly rose to greet with hospitality these guests who merited the honour of water for the
feet and a honey drink. 'Welcome to you!' said that lordly king. For 30
this was the vow he had taken, famous throughout the earth, O king: whenever he learnt that pious Brahmin householders had arrived, that king, triumphant in combat, would rise to greet them even in the middle of the night, heir of Bharata.

But now Jarāsaṃdha, truest of kings, saw their extraordinary dress as he approached them, and he was astonished. As soon as those bull-like heroes, enemy-slayers all, saw King Jarāsaṃdha, they said these words, O truest heir of Bharata: 'Welfare and good health, O king!' Then they stood, tiger-like king, looking at the king of Magadha and at one
another. Jarāsaṃdha next addressed the Yādava and the two Pāṇḍavas 35
who were dressed as Brahmins, lord of kings: 'Be seated!' All three bull-like heroes sat down, blazing with good fortune like fires in a great sacrifice.

Now King Jarāsaṃdha, keeper of his word, spoke to them once more, heir of Kuru, reproaching them for the guise in which he saw them: 'As far as I am aware, O priests, nowhere in the world of men do pious Brahmin householders deck their bodies with garlands and perfumes, and yet you are covered with flowers, and your arms show the scars of the bowstring. You display the power of Kṣatriyas while laying claim to that
of Brahmins, and you wear multicoloured clothes and deck your bodies 40
with garlands and perfumes. Speak the truth: who are you? Among kings, truth is an ornament. Why did you break the peak of Mount Caitya? Why did you enter my dwelling through an improper route? Have you no fear of offending a king? This was the deed of someone travelling under false colours. What is your purpose here today? Speak! For the Brahmin, courage lies above all in speech. After approaching me in this fashion, why do you not accept the honour duly offered you? What is your reason for coming to me?'

When high-minded Kṛṣṇa heard these words, he replied with an
eloquent speech in a voice tender yet solemn: 'Pious householders, 45
O king, may be Brahmins or Kṣatriyas or Vaiśyas: the rules for them are both specific and general. A Kṣatriya who always maintains the specific Kṣatriya rules gains good fortune; we have covered ourselves

with flowers because good fortune always attends those who do so. A Kṣatriya's courage lies in his arms, not his speech, and so, O son of Bṛhadratha, his speech is never considered arrogant. The creator placed the Kṣatriya's courage in his arms; if you wish to see it, O king, you shall do so today, make no doubt! We shunned your door because the virtuous always enter a friend's house though the proper door, but an enemy's house improperly. When we come to a house on hostile business we never accept any honour there; you should know that this is our eternal vow.'

[**20**] Jarāsaṃdha answered, 'I do not recall having ever offended you, and even on careful reflection I do not see that I have shown you enmity. Now if there is no enmity, why do you consider me your foe when I have done no wrong? Tell me this, priests, for this is the rule among the virtuous! Even a Kṣatriya who injures an innocent person suffers mental torture for his violation of *dharma*, make no doubt. And so if a man who knows *dharma* and maintains mighty vows goes astray in this world, he goes the way of the wicked and destroys his own fortunes. You are aware that I am foremost among the virtuous of the three worlds for my adherence to the Kṣatriya *dharma*, and that I have done no wrong, and yet you talk such nonsense!'

Kṛṣṇa Vāsudeva said, 'Great king, there is a certain heir to a great line who is carrying out his duty to that line; it is at his command that we three have risen against you. You have gathered up many of the world's Kṣatriyas, O king; how can you consider yourself to have done no wrong after such a cruel and wicked act? Truest of rulers, how could a king harm other virtuous kings? Yet you have seized them to offer them to Śiva! The wrong you have done, son of Bṛhadratha, should come before us, for we practise *dharma* and are strong in *dharma*'s defence. To sacrifice men is something never heard of; how can you wish to sacrifice men to Śiva? You aim to designate your fellow Kṣatriyas as sacrificial victims: is anyone else such a fool as you, Jarāsaṃdha? This is why we have come here to prevent you from destroying our kin, for we wish our kinsmen's welfare and have sought them out in their distress.

'You believe that among all the Kṣatriyas in the world there is none other to equal you. That, O king, is a very grave error of judgement! What Kṣatriya, knowing his own high birth, would fail to enter the incomparable, eternal heaven that is his after death in battle? You should know it is for heaven that Kṣatriyas receive initiation for the battle-sacrifice, ruler of Magadha, and make their offering to all the worlds. Heaven comes from victory, O king, heaven comes from great fame, heaven comes from the pain of battle: this is the unfailing way. This was the source of Indra's triumph; ever intent on this, the god of a hundred sacrifices defeated the demons and now rules over the universe. And for the heaven-bent Kṣatriya, whose enmity could be better than yours, with your vast Magadha armies that glory in their size and strength?

'Do not despise your enemies, O king! Is there not valour in every man, and ardour to equal even yours? Lord of men, it is only while others' valour and ardour remain unknown that you may stake sole claim. And we can match you. That is why, O king, I spoke to you as I did.

'Ruler of Magadha, cast off your arrogant pride towards those who are your equals! Do not set out for the realm of Yama king of the dead with your sons and ministers and troops! The kings Dambhodbhava, Kārtavīrya, Uttara and Bṛhadratha despised their betters, and so perished here with their troops. We do not pretend to be Brahmins; we are here to rescue your captives. I am Kṛṣṇa Vāsudeva lord of the senses, and these two heroic men are Pāṇḍu's sons. We challenge you, king of Magadha: stand firm and fight, or else release all the kings! Do not set out for Yama's realm!'

To this Jarāsaṃdha replied, 'I seize no king whom I have not defeated. Once defeated, who will stand against me? And who is there who has not been defeated by me? This is precisely the mode of life that is said to accord with the Kṣatriya *dharma*, Kṛṣṇa: to act at will, showing valour and gaining mastery over others. And since I observe the vows of a Kṣatriya, how can I now timidly release the kings whom I have procured for the sake of a god? I shall fight you: army against massed army, one against one, or one against two or three, separately or together!'

With these words, King Jarāsaṃdha now ordered the consecration of his son Sahadeva as ruler, for he intended to fight with those heroes of terrible deeds. But as the time of battle drew near, O bull-like heir of Bharata, the king remembered Kauśika and Citrasena, his two generals, who had once been spoken of amongst men as Haṃsa and Ḍibhaka and paid great honour. Great Kṛṣṇa Vāsudeva too recalled that King Jarāsaṃdha was the mightiest of the mighty, with valour to match a tiger, O tiger-like king; but invincible King Kṛṣṇa, keeper of his word, knew too that Jarāsaṃdha of terrible valour was destined to be killed by another. Therefore the slayer of Madhu, Balarāma's younger brother, foremost of self-possessed men, did not himself seek to kill Jarāsaṃdha, but respected Brahmā's command.

**[21]** Now Yadu's heir, the eloquent Kṛṣṇa, spoke to King Jarāsaṃdha, who was determined to fight: 'With which of the three of us does your heart yearn to fight, O king? Which one of us is to prepare for combat?'

When the radiant Jarāsaṃdha of Magadha heard Kṛṣṇa's words, he
chose to do battle with Bhīma, O king. As he stood there ready to fight
he was attended by his household priest, who bore sovereign remedies
5 and treatments for pain and unconsciousness. Learned Jarāsaṃdha had a
blessing performed by a Brahmin of good repute; then, in keeping with
his Kṣatriya vows, he tied on his armour, removed his diadem, combed
his hair, and rose like an ocean in flood. The wise king addressed Bhīma
of terrible valour: 'Bhīma, I shall fight with you: may the better man
win!' And with these words foe-taming Jarāsaṃdha of mighty ardour
attacked Bhīma, like the demon Bali attacking Indra. Mighty Bhīma
had taken counsel with Kṛṣṇa and had had a blessing performed by him;
now in his eagerness to fight he closed with Jarāsaṃdha.

10 Armed only with their arms, the two tiger-like heroes met in battle,
full of the greatest exultation and longing to defeat each other. The
sound of their smashes, arm-locks and neck-locks was most terrible, like
thunderbolts striking a mountain. Both men were full of the greatest
exultation; both men were strong to excess; each longed to defeat the
other, and each sought the other's weak spots. The terrible battle of two
mighty heroes forced people in the vicinity to move out of the way,
like the battle of Indra and Vṛtra. They grappled each other backwards
and forwards, they beat their breasts and threw each other; and as they
15 grappled they struck each other with their knees. Loudly they reviled
each other, and they dealt each other blows that fell like rocks. Both
broad of chest and long of arm, both skilled at close combat, they fought
each other with their arms like iron bars.

The encounter between the two noble heroes began on the first day

of the month of Kārttika, and continued day and night without pause or respite until the thirteenth day. But on the night of the fourteenth, the king of Magadha grew weary and stopped fighting. When Kṛṣṇa the stirrer of men saw how weary King Jarāsaṃdha had become, he spoke
to Bhīma of terrible deeds as if to counsel him: 'Son of Kuntī, it is not 20
permitted to press a weary enemy in battle, for if he is pressed hard he may give up his life – so you should definitely not press the king, son of Kuntī. Now continue to wrestle with him, bull-like heir of Bharata!' Pāṇḍu's son Bhīma, slayer of enemy heroes, heard Kṛṣṇa's words and understood what was Jarāsaṃdha's weak spot; and he determined to kill him. Then Kuru's heir the wolf-belly, mightiest of the mighty, seized the undefeated Jarāsaṃdha in a wrestling hold to defeat him.

[**22**] Now that Bhīma had firmly resolved to kill Jarāsaṃdha, he said to Kṛṣṇa, Yadu's heir, 'It would not be right for me to spare the life of this wicked man, O tiger-like Yadu, now that I have tied my loincloth to do battle!'

Hearing the wolf-belly's words, tiger-like Kṛṣṇa answered him, urging him to haste in his longing for Jarāsaṃdha's death: 'Bhīma, yours is the supreme mettle of the god of Wind: today let us see you swiftly display that mettle against Jarāsaṃdha!'

Then, O king, foe-taming Bhīma of great might tossed mighty 5
Jarāsaṃdha in the air and whirled him round; with his arms he whirled him round a hundred times, O bull-like heir of Bharata, then dashed him down, breaking his back, and roared as he trampled him. The terrible combined cry of the trampled Jarāsaṃdha and the roaring Pāṇḍava struck fear into every living thing: all the people of Magadha were afraid, and women miscarried when they heard the cries of Bhīma and Jarāsaṃdha. Indeed, the sound that Bhīma made convinced the Magadhas that Mount Himālaya had been broken in two, or the earth split open.

Now the foe-taming heroes left the dead king at his palace gate as if 10
he were sleeping there, and set off by night. Kṛṣṇa yoked Jarāsaṃdha's banner-emblazoned chariot, and took the two brothers up into it; then he released his royal kinsmen. When those kings, lords of the earth, saw jewel-worthy Kṛṣṇa, they bestowed jewels upon him, for he had freed them from great danger.

Unwounded, well-armed, triumphant over his enemy, Kṛṣṇa now
mounted that heavenly chariot and set out with the rescued kings from
Girivraja. With Kṛṣṇa for charioteer, and accompanied by his brother
Bhīma, the ambidextrous warrior Arjuna, handsome and skilled at
15 slaying, was invincible to all kings. As for that excellent chariot, with
Bhīma and Arjuna for the warriors within it and Kṛṣṇa for charioteer,
it shone, invincible to all bowmen. This was the very chariot in which
Indra and Viṣṇu had ridden in the battle for Tārā, wife of Bṛhaspati;
now Kṛṣṇa mounted it and rode forth. Bright with refined gold, decked
with clusters of tinkling bells, victory-granting and enemy-slaying, with
its roar like thunderclouds, this was the chariot in which Indra had slain
nine times ninety demons; and the bull-like heroes were delighted to
have won it.

The people of Magadha were astonished to see strong-armed Kṛṣṇa
20 riding in that chariot with the two brothers; and, ridden by Kṛṣṇa, the
chariot – swift as the wind and yoked to heavenly horses – shone all
the brighter. Over that excellent chariot was raised a standard; it had
been made by the gods, and was not attached in any way. Glorious
and rainbow-bright, it could be seen at a distance of a league. Now
Kṛṣṇa thought of Garuḍa, and at once he approached; beneath him, the
standard seemed like a lofty sacred column.[1] Along with other gaping,
roaring creatures that took their places on the standard, Garuḍa the eater
of snakes remained on that excellent chariot, whose wonderful standard
shone with such brilliance that people could hardly bear to look at it, like
25 the thousand-rayed sun at noon. It never caught on trees and was never
harmed by weapons; both gods and men could see that it was divine,
O king. Invincible Kṛṣṇa, the tiger-like hero, mounted that heavenly
chariot with its roar like thunderclouds, and set out with the two Pāṇḍ-
avas. King Vasu had obtained it from Indra,[2] and Bṛhadratha from him,
and in due course it had passed from Bṛhadratha to his son Jarāsaṃdha.

Now strong-armed, lotus-eyed Kṛṣṇa of great renown set out from Girivraja and halted on the plain beyond. There all the townsfolk, led by the Brahmins, came to do him honour in the manner prescribed

1 See 1.29.

2 See 1.57.13–14.

by rule, O king; and the kings whom he had released from bondage 30
also honoured the slayer of Madhu, and addressed him with gratifying words: 'Strong-armed son of Devakī, such protection of *dharma* is no wonder coming from you, with the might of Bhīma and Arjuna to aid you! Today you have rescued us kings as we sank in Jarāsaṃdha's terrible swamp with its mire of grief! We were languishing in Jarāsaṃdha's dreadful mountain fortress, O highest lord Viṣṇu; but – praise be! – you have gained a blaze of glory by freeing us. Tell us kings what we may do for you, tiger-like hero: you should know that, however difficult, it is as good as done!'

High-minded Kṛṣṇa, lord of the senses, answered them soothingly: 35
'Yudhiṣṭhira wishes to perform the sacrifice of the royal consecration. He practises *dharma* and is seeking sovereignty, so all of you should give him aid in accomplishing the rite!'

Then, O bull-like heir of Bharata, those kings rejoiced in their hearts; they gave their assent, and promised what Kṛṣṇa had asked. And those lords of the earth bestowed jewels upon Kṛṣṇa Govinda, prince of Daśārha, who reluctantly accepted out of kindness towards them.

Jarāsaṃdha's son, the mighty chariot-fighter Sahadeva, also came out with a group of his kinsmen and ministers, headed by his household
priest: bowing low he approached Kṛṣṇa Vāsudeva, god among men, 40
with many jewels. To that fearful prince Kṛṣṇa then granted indemnity, and there and then he consecrated Jarāsaṃdha's son as king; then, after swearing friendship with Kṛṣṇa and receiving honour from the two Pāṇḍavas, wise King Sahadeva re-entered Bṛhadratha's city. Lotus-eyed Kṛṣṇa himself, blazing with the greatest glory, took the many jewels he had been given and set forth together with the two sons of Kuntī.

Approaching Indraprastha with the two Pāṇḍava brothers, invincible
Kṛṣṇa met Yudhiṣṭhira lord of *dharma* and joyfully said to him, 'Truest of 45
kings, by good fortune Bhīma has laid low the mighty Jarāsaṃdha, and the kings have been released from their bondage; and by good fortune Bhīma and wealth-winner Arjuna here are well, and have returned unharmed to their city, heir of Bharata.'

Now Yudhiṣṭhira paid due honour to Kṛṣṇa, and joyfully embraced Bhīma and Arjuna; and he and his brothers rejoiced at the death of Jarāsaṃdha and the victory gained for them by the two brothers. Then

Pāṇḍu's son met the rescued kings, and after paying them respect and
50 honour according to age, he gave them leave to depart; and the kings
took their leave and, with joyful hearts, hurried back to their own lands
by various different roads.

Thus did Kṛṣṇa the stirrer of men, the tiger-like hero of mighty
wisdom, bring about the enemy Jarāsaṃdha's death at the hands of the
Pāṇḍavas. Having deliberately brought about his death, the foe-tamer
now took his leave of Yudhiṣṭhira lord of *dharma*, and of Kuntī and
Draupadī, O heir of Bharata, and also from Subhadrā, Bhīma, Arjuna
and the twins; then, after bidding farewell to Dhaumya, he set out for his
own city in that same excellent chariot that Yudhiṣṭhira lord of *dharma*
had bestowed upon him, divine, brilliant as the morning sun, filling the
horizon with its roar.

55 Bull-like heir of Bharata, the Pāṇḍavas headed by Yudhiṣṭhira re-
spectfully circumambulated the unwearying Kṛṣṇa; and when Devakī's
blessed son had left, their mighty victory and gift of indemnity to the
kings rendered them yet more powerful, heir of Bharata. During that
time King Yudhiṣṭhira, who was renowned for his protection of the
kingdom, followed *dharma* and did whatever was proper to promote
*dharma*, the gaining of wealth, and pleasure.[1]

## THE CONQUEST OF THE WORLD

**[23]** *With Yudhiṣṭhira's agreement, Arjuna rides forth to conquer the north; similarly, Bhīma goes to the east, Sahadeva to the south and Nakula to the west.*

*Arjuna defeats numerous peoples, then does battle with Bhagadatta, king of Prāgjyotiṣa; after eight days of fighting, Bhagadatta concedes that Arjuna has the better of him, and agrees to pay tribute to Yudhiṣṭhira.* **[24]** *Next Arjuna travels further north into the mountains, where he makes many conquests, including the Trigartas, Bāhlikas and Kāmbojas.* **[25]** *Further north still, Arjuna defeats the celestial Kiṃpuruṣas and Guhyakas, and at Lake Mānasa he receives tribute of horses from the Gandharvas. Finally he reaches Harivarṣa, the land of the northern Kurus. He is told that, as a mortal, he may not enter; he agrees to*

1 See note to 1.56.16.

*this, but requests tribute for Yudhiṣṭhira, which is duly given. Now he returns to Indraprastha with everything he has won.*

**[26]** *In the East, Bhīma secures the support of the Pāñcālas, and conquers the lands of Gaṇḍakī and Videha. In Daśārṇa he is so impressed by the valour of King Sudharman, who fights him bare-handed, that he appoints him his general. Further east he gains more victories, then approaches Śiśupāla, king of Cedi; Śiśupāla greets him warmly and accedes to Yudhiṣṭhira's wishes. Bhīma stays thirty days with him.* **[27]** *Now Bhīma conquers kingdom after kingdom, including Kosala, Ayodhyā, Kāśi, Matsya, Vatsa, Niṣāda, Videha, Magadha and Vaṅga. Then he returns to Indraprastha with the wealth he has amassed.*

**[28]** *In the South, Sahadeva's conquests include Śūrasena, Matsya and Niṣāda; King Kuntibhoja, Kuntī's adoptive father, also acknowledges his command. He defeats Vinda and Anuvinda of Avanti; then, as he does battle against Nīla of Mahiṣmatī, his army bursts into flame. — Janamejaya asks why this should have happened, and Vaiśaṃpāyana relates. — The god Fire was once caught committing adultery in Mahiṣmatī, and was taken before Nīla. Nīla started to tell him off, but when Fire blazed up in anger he bowed before him, and was rewarded with a boon; Nīla chose security for his army. To the women of Mahiṣmatī, Fire granted the right to act as they pleased. — Sahadeva propitiates the Fire, which agrees not to hinder him; Nīla now welcomes him and pays tribute. Next Sahadeva continues south, conquering Tripura and Surāṣṭra, and many other fabulous realms. Finally he receives the tribute of Vibhīṣaṇa of Laṅkā, and then returns to Indraprastha.*

**[29]** *In the West, Nakula conquers many kingdoms, including Śibi, Trigarta, Ambaṣṭha and Mālava; he also sends an embassy to Kṛṣṇa Vāsudeva, who acknowledges his command. He goes to Madra, whose ruler, Śalya, is the brother of his mother Mādrī; Śalya welcomes him and gives him much wealth. He conquers many barbarian lands in the far West, and returns at last to Indraprastha with ten thousand camels that can barely carry all the treasure he has won.*

## THE ROYAL CONSECRATION

Vaiśaṃpāyana spoke:

**[30]** Yudhiṣṭhira lord of *dharma* afforded protection, maintained truth and destroyed his enemies; thus his subjects engaged happily in their

daily tasks. Taxes were properly collected, and his government was just, and so with generous monsoons the people prospered. Every kind of enterprise fared well – cattle-keeping, agriculture, trade – and all this came about specifically because of the king's actions. No false words were heard, O king; not amongst thieves and deceivers, nor even from
5 the king's favourites. There was neither drought nor flood then, no raging of disease or fire, in the reign of Yudhiṣṭhira constant in *dharma.*

Kings visited Yudhiṣṭhira to perform favours, to wait upon him or to make unsolicited offerings; none of them had any other motive. His treasury grew so great from the just accumulation of wealth that it could not be expended even in hundreds of years; and when Kuntī's son King Yudhiṣṭhira understood the extent of his wealth and his possessions, he determined upon a sacrifice. All his friends, separately and together, told him, 'Now is the time for your sacrifice, lord! Perform it here and now!'

10 They were in the midst of speaking so when Hari Kṛṣṇa arrived, the ancient seer, essence of the Veda, visible to the wise, best of what moves and what stays still, origin and end of all things, lord of past, present and future, Keśava, slayer of the demon Keśin, bulwark of all the Vṛṣṇis, protector in times of trouble, slayer of enemies. He had placed his father Vasudeva Ānakadundubhi in charge of his combined troops, and now, surrounded by a mighty force, the tiger-like hero, heir of Madhu, carried a great mass of wealth of every kind for Yudhiṣṭhira lord of *dharma.* That torrent of wealth was like an ocean of jewels, boundless and inexhaustible, and as he entered the splendid city, the thunder of
15 his chariot seemed to set that ocean roaring. The city of the Bhāratas rejoiced at Kṛṣṇa's arrival, like a sunless place at the coming of the sun or a windless place at the stirring of a breeze.

Yudhiṣṭhira met Kṛṣṇa joyfully and paid him due honour; the bull-like hero gave him a comfortable seat, asked after his welfare, and then, in the company of Bhīma, Arjuna and the twins, and of priests led by Dhaumya and Dvaipāyana Vyāsa, he addressed him: 'Kṛṣṇa, it is thanks to you that the whole earth lies under my authority, and it is through your grace that I have accumulated such great wealth. I wish to devote it all as is proper, son of Devakī, to the foremost Brahmins and
20 the sacrificial fire. Therefore, strong-armed prince of Daśārha, I wish

to perform a sacrifice together with you and my brothers; please give me your assent! Allow yourself, Kṛṣṇa Govinda, to be initiated for the ritual, for if you sacrifice, prince of Daśārha, I shall be freed from sin. Or else permit me, lord, to undertake it with these my brothers: with your permission, Kṛṣṇa, I shall accomplish the highest sacrifice!'

Now Kṛṣṇa replied to him, praising his virtues at length: 'Tiger-like king, you yourself are worthy to be emperor. Accomplish this great sacrifice, and when you have done so, we too shall be blessed with success! Perform the ritual that you desire, while I work for your welfare; if you employ me in this task I shall obey your every word.'

Yudhiṣṭhira said, 'My plans will bear fruit, and success is guaranteed 25
for me, lord of the senses, if you will be at my side as I desire!'

Now with Kṛṣṇa's agreement Pāṇḍu's son Yudhiṣṭhira and his brothers began to put in place the arrangements for the royal consecration. The foe-crushing Pāṇḍava commanded Sahadeva, best of warriors, and all his ministers: 'The sacrificial implements specified by Brahmins for this rite, and all the necessary gear and auspicious items, and the materials for sacrifice that Dhaumya requests: let servants swiftly fetch them in
due order as required. Indrasena, Viśoka, and Arjuna's charioteer Pūru[1] 30
are to be engaged in fetching such food as shall please me: every taste is to be catered for in matters of savour and scent, truest of the Kurus, to gratify and delight the Brahmins.'

Noble Yudhiṣṭhira, lord of *dharma*, had barely finished speaking when Sahadeva, best of warriors, informed him that all his instructions had been carried out. Then, O king, Kṛṣṇa Dvaipāyana Vyāsa fetched ritual priests, blessed Brahmins like visible manifestations of the Vedas. Satyavatī's son himself acted as *brahman*[2] for the rite; the *udgātṛ* was
Susāman, bull of the Dhanaṃjayas; Yājñavalkya, holiest of Brahmins, 35
was appointed a most excellent *adhvaryu*; Vasu's son Paila, aided by Dhaumya, became the *hotṛ*; and their many pupils and sons, all expert in

1 Indrasena and Viśoka are the charioteers of Yudhiṣṭhira and Bhīma respectively.

2 The four chief priests at a Vedic sacrifice are the *hotṛ*, who offers the oblation and recites hymns from the Ṛgveda; the *adhvaryu*, who performs most of the other numerous complex rituals and chants formulae from the Yajurveda; the *udgātṛ*, who sings hymns from the Sāmaveda; and the *brahman*, who oversees the entire event and makes good any ritual errors.

the Vedas and their branches, attended the sacrifice, O bull-like heir of
Bharata. They pronounced a benediction and made arrangements for
the ritual, and then set in order the great sacrificial site as prescribed in
learned texts. There craftsmen were given leave to erect shelters: they
were huge and studded with jewels, like the dwellings of the gods.

At once King Yudhiṣṭhira, truest of Kuru kings, commanded Sahadeva
40 as his minister, 'Make haste to send swift envoys to issue invitations!'
So on the king's instruction Sahadeva now dispatched envoys, telling
them: 'Invite Brahmins and Kṣatriya rulers in every land, and all Vaiśyas
and worthy Śūdras, and bring them here!' At the command of Pāṇḍu's
son they invited all the lords of the earth, while he continued to send
out more and more envoys.

Now, at the chosen moment, the priests initiated Kuntī's son Yu-
dhiṣṭhira for the royal consecration, O heir of Bharata. Once he had
received the initiation, righteous Yudhiṣṭhira, lord of *dharma*, set out
45 for the sacrificial site; surrounded by priests in their thousands, and by
his brothers and kinsmen, his friends and aides, Kṣatriyas from lands
of every sort, and his ministers, that best of kings seemed like Dharma
incarnate, O prince of men. Brahmins too arrived there from every
region, skilled in all fields of learning, expert in the Vedas and their
branches. At the command of Yudhiṣṭhira lord of *dharma*, craftsmen
made thousands of individual dwellings for them and their followers,
well equipped with food and bedding, pleasant in every season; and
those Brahmins, lavishly honoured, settled there, O king, telling many
tales and watching actors and dancers perform. Indeed, the mighty
clamour of noble priests cheerfully eating and conversing could be
50 heard there day and night, as they constantly called out, 'Give, give!',
'Eat, eat!' The lord of *dharma* gave to each of them cows, beds, gold
and women in hundreds of thousands, heir of Bharata.

Thus began the sacrifice of Pāṇḍu's noble son, the one hero on earth as is Indra in his heaven. And now King Yudhiṣṭhira sent Nakula the Pāṇḍava to Hāstinapura, O bull-like heir of Bharata, to invite Bhīṣma, Droṇa, Dhṛtarāṣṭra, Vidura and Kṛpa, and those among all the Kaurava brothers who bore him some affection.

**[31]** Pāṇḍu's son Nakula, triumphant in combat, travelled to Hāstinapura, and invited Bhīṣma and Dhṛtarāṣṭra; and when they heard of the sacrifice of Yudhiṣṭhira lord of *dharma*, they set out for it with joyful hearts, led by Brahmins, for they knew about sacrifices. And others in hundreds were also delighted to come, bull-like hero, for they wished to see the hall and Pāṇḍu's son the lord of *dharma*. All the princes gathered there from every direction, heir of Bharata, carrying many great jewels of every kind. Headed by Droṇa the Teacher, those princes were all welcomed with honour: Dhṛtarāṣṭra, Bhīṣma and sagacious Vidura; all the hundred Kaurava brothers under Duryodhana's leadership; Subala king of Gāndhāra and his mighty son Śakuni; Acala, Vṛṣaka and Karṇa best of chariot-fighters; Ṛta, Śalya king of Madra, and the mighty chariot-fighter Bāhlika; Somadatta the descendant of Kuru; Bhūri, Bhūriśravas and Śala; Aśvatthāman, Kṛpa, Droṇa, and Jayadratha king of Sindhu; Drupada and his son Dhṛṣṭadyumna; Śālva lord of the earth; Bhagadatta of great renown, the king of Prāgjyotiṣa, together with all the barbarian tribes living along the ocean's edge; the kings of the mountain lands, and King Bṛhadbala; Vāsudeva king of Puṇḍra, Vaṅga and Kaliṅga; Ākarṣa and Kuntala, the Vānavāsyas and Andhras; the Tamils and Sinhalas, and the king of Kashmir; Kuntibhoja of great ardour, and mighty Suhma; all the other brave Bāhlika kings; Virāṭa with his sons, and the great chariot-fighter Māцella; and other kings and princes, rulers of many different kingdoms.

Śiśupāla the mighty hero, mad for battle, came with his son to the sacrifice of Pāṇḍu's son, O heir of Bharata; and Balarāma, Aniruddha, Babhru and Sāraṇa all came there, as did Gada, Pradyumna, Sāmba and the brave Cārudeṣṇa; Ulmuka, Niśaṭha and Pradyumna's heroic son; and all the other Vṛṣṇis, mighty chariot-fighters all. These and many other kings, natives of the central lands, came to the great sacrifice of the Pāṇḍava's royal consecration.

At the command of Yudhiṣṭhira lord of *dharma*, they were provided with dwellings, O king, containing many rooms and ornamented with ponds and with trees; the son of Dharma honoured those kings most highly, and they, after receiving his respects, went to the dwellings assigned them. These were tall as the peak of Mount Kailāsa, charming and richly ornamented, and enclosed all round by well-built, high white walls; they had lattices of gold, and were embellished with jewelled floors; their stairs were easy to climb, and their seats and other furnishings large; they were decked with garlands and wreaths, scented with the finest fragrance of aloes, and white as geese; their beauty could be seen a league off; they were spacious, with well-hung doors and many other merits; they contained so much metal that they looked like Himālayan peaks.

When the lords of the earth had taken their rest, they went to see Yudhiṣṭhira lord of *dharma*, so generous to Brahmins, surrounded by many sacrificial priests. The sacrificial enclosure was thronged with princes and noble Brahmins, and it shone like highest heaven thronged with immortals, O king.

[**32**] Yudhiṣṭhira rose and greeted the revered grandfather Bhīṣma, O king, and then spoke these words to Bhīṣma, Droṇa, Kṛpa, Aśvatthāman and Viviṃśati:[1] 'Good sirs, you must all favour me in this sacrifice. Whatever wealth I have here is yours, and so am I myself: act freely as you will to please me, good sirs!'

With these words, Pāṇḍu's firstborn son, already initiated for the ritual, now lost no time in appointing each of them to a fitting duty. King Yudhiṣṭhira put Duḥśāsana in charge of foodstuffs of every kind, and told Aśvatthāman to welcome the Brahmins; he instructed Saṃjaya to honour the kings, and Bhīṣma and Droṇa to determine what should and should not be done, for they were sagacious; he charged Kṛpa with overseeing the gold and jewels and with giving the Brahmins their gifts. Likewise he appointed other tiger-like heroes to various occupations: Bāhlika, Dhṛtarāṣṭra, Somadatta and Jayadratha, brought together by Nakula, lived there like lords, whilst Vidura the chamberlain, being expert in *dharma*, acted as paymaster, and Duryodhana received all the tributary gifts.

The whole world was assembled, longing to gratify Yudhiṣṭhira with the greatest of attainments; longing too to see the hall and the Pāṇḍava lord of *dharma*. No one there brought tribute of less than a thousand, and everyone there showered jewels in profusion upon the lord of *dharma*; the kings vied with each other to bestow their wealth, each hoping that it would be through his gift of jewels that the heir of Kuru brought his sacrifice to completion. The sacrificial enclosure of Kuntī's noble

1 One of the hundred sons of Dhṛtarāṣṭra.

son was resplendent with the assembled kings in all their wealth and glory, with terraced, tower-capped mansions guarded by troops, and with palaces for worldly kings and dwellings for Brahmins that were built in the image of celestial flying chariots, studded with jewels of every kind and furnished in the richest style.

Yudhiṣṭhira, rivalling the god Varuṇa in riches, now performed the 15
sacrifice of the six fires, giving many gifts to Brahmins and satisfying all the people in all their richest desires. The gathering was provided with foodstuffs of every kind, so that everyone was well fed, and it was busy with making offerings of jewels. The very gods were satisfied with the many oblations of milk and butter, accompanied by well-pronounced *mantras*, at that sacrifice performed by great seers. The priests were as satisfied as the gods with the rich gifts and food that they received; indeed, people of all classes were filled with joy at that sacrifice.

## THE PRESENTATION OF THE GUEST-OFFERINGS

Vaiśaṃpāyana spoke:

**[33]** On the day of the consecration, Brahmin seers together with kings entered the sacrificial ground to honour Yudhiṣṭhira. Seated within that ground, the noble Brahmins led by Nārada, and also the royal seers, shone like the gods and divine seers assembled in Brahmā's mansion. Boundlessly powerful, they conversed in the intervals between rituals: 'This is so!' – 'Indeed, it is not so!' – 'It is so, it cannot be
otherwise!' Some gave substance to slender arguments, and whittled 5
down substantial arguments, with reasoning sanctioned by learned texts; some in their wisdom tore apart the arguments established by others like hawks tearing apart a piece of meat in the sky; some, keepers of mighty vows and best of all those who know the Veda, regaled themselves with discourse on *dharma* and the proper making of wealth. Thronged with gods, Brahmins and great seers learned in the Veda, the sacrificial ground seemed like a clear sky thronged with stars. No Śūdra or vow-breaker could approach within that ground in Yudhiṣṭhira's dwelling, O king.

Nārada was delighted to see the glory that the performance of 10

the sacrifice conferred upon the glorious Yudhiṣṭhira, the wise lord
of *dharma*. The sage, seeing all the Kṣatriyas assembled there, fell to
thinking, O lord of men, and he remembered the tale, told long ago in
Brahmā's mansion, concerning the partial incarnations,[1] bull-like heir of
Bharata. So, knowing as he did that this was an assembly of gods, O heir
of Kuru, Nārada directed his thoughts towards lotus-eyed Hari Kṛṣṇa.
The lord Nārāyaṇa, slayer of the foes of the gods, wise conqueror of
enemy fortresses, the creator himself, had taken birth among Kṣatriyas
15 in accordance with his promise; long ago he had told the gods, 'You
will only regain the realms of heaven after killing one another!' And
after instructing all of them so, blessed Nārāyaṇa, the benevolent lord
of the world, had been born on earth in the race of Yadu, in the line of
the Andhakas and Vṛṣṇis, as the best of patriarchs, shining in his great
glory like the moon among the stars. That foe-crusher, the might of
whose arm was venerated by the very gods under Indra, was now living
as Hari Kṛṣṇa, a mortal man.

'Alas! The mighty one, self-born Nārāyaṇa, will take back to heaven
20 the Kṣatriya class that has become so powerful!' – this was the thought of
righteous Nārada, for he knew Hari to be Nārāyaṇa, the lord who merits
worship with sacrifices. Best of experts in *dharma*, Nārada of mighty
wisdom remained respectfully at the great sacrifice of Yudhiṣṭhira, wise
lord of *dharma*.

Now Bhīṣma addressed the lord of *dharma*, O king: 'Let due honour
be shown to the kings, Yudhiṣṭhira heir of Bharata, for it is said that the
six who deserve the guest-offering are a teacher, a priest, a relative, a
pious householder, a friend and a king; they are said to deserve it when
they come to stay for a year. Now these kings have been staying with us
25 for a long time, so let a guest-offering be brought for each one of them,
O king; and let it be brought first for the one among them who is best
and most powerful!'

Yudhiṣṭhira answered him, 'Heir of Kuru, for which one of them do you think it right to bring the guest-offering first? Tell me, grandfather!'

Then Bhīṣma son of Śaṃtanu decided in his mind, O heir of Bharata, and ruled that Kṛṣṇa the Vṛṣṇi was the most deserving man on earth:

1 See 1.61.

'For in the midst of these assembled kings, he blazes with ardour, strength and valour like a sun blazing among stars. Like a sunless place at the coming of the sun or a windless place at the stirring of a breeze, this sacrificial enclosure of ours is brightened and gladdened by Kṛṣṇa.' Now Sahadeva of mighty energy, with Bhīṣma's approval, offered in the proper manner the finest guest-offering to the Vṛṣṇi hero, and Kṛṣṇa accepted it with the rite prescribed in learned texts.

But Śiśupāla could not bear to see Kṛṣṇa Vāsudeva receive such honour. The mighty king of Cedi denounced both Bhīṣma and Yudhiṣṭhira lord of *dharma* in the assembly, and then he reviled Vāsudeva. **[34]** 'This Vṛṣṇi does not merit princely honour as if he were a king, while all these noble lords of the earth are standing here! O Pāṇḍava, your conduct does not befit the noble Pāṇḍavas, for you have shown honour to lotus-eyed Kṛṣṇa because of your partiality towards him! You are mere children, you Pāṇḍavas; you do not understand that *dharma* is subtle. Gaṅgā's son Bhīṣma here so lacks discernment that he has transgressed *dharma*. Bhīṣma, who adheres to *dharma* as you do yourself, now acts to show favour, and in doing so he has earned the utter contempt of virtuous folk throughout the three worlds. How can this man of Daśārha, who is not even a king, so merit honour that you pay him your respects in the midst of all these lords of the earth?

'Perhaps, bull-like heir of Bharata, it is because you regard him as an elder – but while old Vasudeva stands here, how can his son merit this? Or perhaps you think that Kṛṣṇa Vāsudeva is your benevolent supporter – but while Drupada stands here, how can Madhu's heir deserve such honour? Or perhaps, bull-like Kuru, you consider Kṛṣṇa your teacher – but while Droṇa stands here, why pay such respect to the Vṛṣṇi? Or perhaps, heir of Kuru, you regard him as your priest – but while the priest Dvaipāyana stands here, why honour Kṛṣṇa? The slayer of Madhu is not a priest, not a teacher, not a king; why else did you pay him such respect, best of Kurus, except to show favour? Or perhaps Madhu's slayer really deserves your honour – but then why show disrespect to all the kings by bringing them here, heir of Bharata?

'We do not offer our tribute to Kuntī's noble son from fear or greed, or to ingratiate ourselves! We offer him our tribute because he practises *dharma* and is seeking sovereignty; yet he pays us no respect! Why else but to show disrespect to this assembly of kings did you honour with the guest-offering this Kṛṣṇa, who bears none of the marks of royalty? The reputation for *dharma* of Dharma's son Yudhiṣṭhira has suddenly been lost, for who would pay proper honour to a man lapsed from *dharma*, a man born in the Vṛṣṇi line who has already killed a king?[1] Today Yudhiṣṭhira's adherence to *dharma* has been stripped away, and instead he is filled with meanness of spirit, for he presented the guest-offering to Kṛṣṇa.

'If the sons of Kuntī are so frightened, so mean-spirited and wretched, should you yourself not have told them, Kṛṣṇa, just what respect the heir of Madhu merits? And why, stirrer of men, did you accept the honour that the wretches offered you, knowing yourself unworthy of it? What is more, you prize their honour, though it is not rightfully yours, like a dog that grabs a morsel of an oblation to eat in secret. Indeed, no disrespect has been shown to these lords among princes, for it is clearly you yourself whom the Kurus have fooled, you stirrer of men! Bestowing royal honour upon your unroyal self is like marrying a eunuch or showing a blind man a beautiful scene, slayer of Madhu. We have seen King Yudhiṣṭhira for what he is; we have seen Bhīṣma for what he is; and we have also seen Kṛṣṇa Vāsudeva here for what he is: all is now truly known!'

With these words Śiśupāla rose from his splendid throne and left the sacrificial enclosure with the other kings.

**[35]** King Yudhiṣṭhira now hurried to Śiśupāla and addressed him in sweet and conciliatory tones: 'Lord of the earth, it was not right to speak as you have done; it was an extreme breach of *dharma*, and needlessly harsh, for Bhīṣma son of Śaṃtanu certainly understands the highest *dharma*, O prince; do not treat him with unjust disrespect! See, too, these many lords of the earth who are your seniors: they bear with the honour shown to Kṛṣṇa, and you should do likewise. Lord of Cedi, Bhīṣma knows Kṛṣṇa truly and fully: you do not know him as the Kaurava does.'

1 Many manuscripts here insert an extra line identifying the king as Śiśupāla's former ally Jarāsaṃdha (see 2.18–22), and at 2.39 Śiśupāla again denounces Kṛṣṇa for killing Jarāsaṃdha unfairly. But Kṛṣṇa had also previously killed another king, Jarāsaṃdha's son-in-law Kaṃsa (see 2.13.29–33).

But Bhīṣma said, 'This man should receive neither courtesy nor conciliation, for he objects to the honour shown to Kṛṣṇa, who is seniormost in all the world. If a Kṣatriya is so expert a warrior that he defeats another Kṣatriya, and then, after overpowering him, sets him free, then he deserves that man's veneration; and in this assembly of kings I do not see a single lord of the earth who has not been defeated in battle by Kṛṣṇa's ardour! It is not only we who should show great respect to invincible Kṛṣṇa: all the three worlds should respect the stirrer of men! Many bull-like Kṣatriyas have been defeated in battle by Kṛṣṇa, and the whole world is completely founded upon the Vṛṣṇi prince; therefore, even if more senior kings are present, it is Kṛṣṇa and no other whom we honour. You should not speak as you did; you should not think thus!

'O king, I have waited upon many who are senior in learning, and from them as they talked I have heard of the many virtues of virtuous Kṛṣṇa, highly regarded by those assemblies of good men. I have often, too, heard men speak at length of the deeds that this wise man performed from the day of his birth. It is not from mere partiality, king of Cedi, that we honour the stirrer of men, nor because of our friendship for him, or because he has favoured us in any way; he is honoured by good men throughout the earth, and brings every earthly joy, and we pay him honour because we know of his fame, his heroism and his victory.

'We did not overlook anyone here, not even the youngest, and our judgement was that Hari Kṛṣṇa is the most deserving of respect, surpassing the very elders in his virtues. Among Brahmins he is seniormost in learning, among Kṣatriyas greatest in might. These are two settled reasons for Kṛṣṇa Govinda to be honoured, for who but Keśava amongst men in this world is so distinguished for his learning in the Veda and its branches, and likewise his boundless power? Generosity, skill, Vedic learning, heroism, modesty, renown, the highest intelligence, humility, glory, steadfastness, happiness and well-being: all these are contained in invincible Kṛṣṇa; and so all of you should agree to honour him, your most excellent teacher, father and elder, who both deserves and receives honour! Priest, elder, worthy relative by marriage, pious householder, king and friend: Kṛṣṇa lord of the senses is all of these, and therefore the invincible one is honoured. Kṛṣṇa alone is the origin and dissolution of the three worlds; for Kṛṣṇa's sake this whole universe was put in place; sun and moon, stars and planets, the cardinal and minor points of the compass, all is founded upon Kṛṣṇa!

'But the man Śiśupāla here is a mere child, and does not know that Kṛṣṇa is everywhere and always; this is why he speaks as he does. For the wise man who strives after the highest *dharma* will see all according to *dharma*, but not so this Cedi king. Indeed, who among all these noble princes, both young and old, thinks Kṛṣṇa unworthy? Who would not honour him? Yet Śiśupāla has concluded that our honour was wrongly bestowed; in that case let him act to right that wrong!'

[**36**] *Sahadeva in turn threatens to place his foot upon the head of any king who disputes Kṛṣṇa's right to the honour: no one does, and Sahadeva is rewarded with celestial praise and a shower of flowers. But Śiśupāla and his allies are furious, and plan to wreck Yudhiṣṭhira's sacrifice.*

## THE KILLING OF ŚIŚUPĀLA

[**37**] *Seeing that there is going to be trouble, Yudhiṣṭhira asks Bhīṣma for advice, but Bhīṣma is dismissive. He states that for Śiśupāla and his allies to plot against Kṛṣṇa is like a pack of dogs barking at a sleeping lion; the result will be their death.* [**38**] *Śiśupāla replies furiously, insulting Bhīṣma. He belittles Kṛṣṇa's achievements and accuses Bhīṣma of feigning virtue for his own ends.* [**39**] *He concludes by denouncing Kṛṣṇa for wrongdoing in bringing about Jarāsaṃdha's death by underhand means. Hearing all this, Bhīma is enraged: he rises to attack Śiśupāla. Bhīṣma restrains him, but he continues to seethe with anger; Śiśupāla mockingly urges Bhīṣma to let Bhīma go so that he may meet his death.*

[**40**] *Now Bhīṣma tells Bhīma about Śiśupāla: when he was born he had three eyes and four arms, and he brayed like an ass. Appalled, his parents proposed to abandon their son, but a voice told them that they should look after him, and added that his extra eye and arms would vanish when he sat on the lap of the man who was destined to kill him. Many kings came to see the extraordinary child, and he was placed in the lap of each, to no effect; then Kṛṣṇa and Balarāma arrived, and as soon as the boy sat in Kṛṣṇa's lap his extra eye and arms vanished. His griefstricken mother asked Kṛṣṇa for a boon,*

*and, when he agreed, requested that he should forgive her son's sins; Kṛṣṇa promised to do so one hundred times. That, says Bhīṣma, is why Śiśupāla can now make his challenge.* [**41**] *Finally, Bhīṣma suggests that Śiśupāla's actions must be prompted, not by his own volition, but by Kṛṣṇa, who now wishes to reclaim that portion of his own fiery energy that is Śiśupāla.*

*Śiśupāla answers that if Bhīṣma wishes to offer praise, he should offer it to any of the kings and other mighty men who are present; Bhīṣma resembles the* bhūliṅga *bird, which preaches caution but chooses to feed on scraps of meat from the teeth of a lion. To this Bhīṣma replies that the kings of whom Śiśupāla speaks are worth no more than straw. The furious kings gather to attack him, but Bhīṣma defies them and tells them to challenge Kṛṣṇa instead.*

Vaiśampāyana spoke:
[**42**] As soon as the Cedi king, Śiśupāla of mighty valour, heard Bhīṣma's words, he was filled with longing to fight Kṛṣṇa Vāsudeva, and spoke thus to him: 'I challenge you! Do battle with me, you stirrer of men, so that I may today slay you together with the Pāṇḍavas! For the Pāṇḍavas, like you, Kṛṣṇa, thoroughly merit death at my hands, in that they passed over kings to pay honour to your unroyal self. They were childish enough to pay honour to you – an undeserving wicked slave, not a king – as if you deserved it; and so in my judgement, Kṛṣṇa, they merit death!' Having spoken thus, the tiger-like king stood there, roaring angrily.

When he had finished speaking, Kṛṣṇa then softly addressed all the 5
kings, and the Pāṇḍavas who were with them: 'Princes, this man is our greatest enemy. He is the son of a Sātvata woman,[1] and yet in his cruelty he opposes the Sātvatas, though they have done him no harm. When he heard that I had left for the city of Prāgjyotiṣa, lords of men, this vicious man set Dvārakā ablaze, though he is sister's son to my father. Once when the Bhoja Kṣatriyas were at play on Mount Raivataka, he slew many of them, and took all the rest captive back to his own city. At my father's horse sacrifice this malevolent man stole the sacrificial horse that had been released under heavy guard, in order to frustrate

1 The Sātvatas are a Yādava people, of whom Kṛṣṇa himself is one: Śiśupāla is the son of Kṛṣṇa's paternal aunt.

the rite. Against her will the fool abducted the wife of famous Babhru as she travelled hence on business to the Sauvīras. And he resorted to magic disguise to abduct for the king of Karūṣa poor Bhadrā, princess of Viśāla. In everything he injures his mother's brother!

'I have borne this great grief for my father's sister's sake; but today by good fortune this is happening in the presence of all the kings. Sirs, all of you have seen his dreadful offence against me today; bear in mind also the deeds he has done behind my back. I can no longer tolerate this offence of a man whose arrogance before this council of all kings renders him worthy of death. The fool has a death-wish; he once paid suit to Rukmiṇī,[1] though he could no more gain her than a Śūdra could aspire to hear a recitation of the Veda!'

Thus and more spoke Kṛṣṇa Vāsudeva. The assembled lords of men all heard what he had to say, and they reproached the Cedi king; but at Kṛṣṇa's words Śiśupāla of mighty energy burst into peals of mirth, and laughingly said, 'Kṛṣṇa, how can you shamelessly speak of Rukmiṇī, particularly before these assembled princes, when she was formerly mine? Apart from you, slayer of Madhu, what man with any self-regard would ever speak in virtuous company of a wife who formerly belonged to another? Pardon me, Kṛṣṇa, if you wish, or else pardon me not – whether you are angry or well disposed, what have I to fear from you?'

Even as he spoke these words, blessed Kṛṣṇa, the slayer of Madhu, tormentor of his enemies, furiously severed his head with his discus, and that strong-armed hero fell, like a mountain-peak struck by a thunderbolt. And then the kings saw a wonderful fiery energy rise from the lord of Cedi's body, like the sun rising through the sky, great king; it greeted lotus-eyed Kṛṣṇa, honoured by all the world, and then entered him, lord of men. When all the lords of the earth saw this, they thought it a great wonder that that fiery energy should enter strong-armed Kṛṣṇa, the highest lord. Cloudless, the sky poured down rain and blazing thunderbolts, and the earth trembled, when Kṛṣṇa slew the Cedi king. Some kings were speechless, for the time defied speech; they merely stared at Kṛṣṇa. Some wrung their hands in their anger, while others,

1 Kṛṣṇa's wife.

nearly swooning with rage, bit their lips. There were some kings who privately applauded the Vṛṣṇi prince, while others were infuriated, and yet others caught between different emotions. But the great seers were delighted, and approached Kṛṣṇa Keśava to praise him along with noble Brahmins and mighty kings.

Pāṇḍu's son Yudhiṣṭhira now told his brothers to waste no time in performing the observances for brave King Śiśupāla, son of Damaghoṣa, and they carried out their brother's command. Then Yudhiṣṭhira, together with the other lords of the earth, consecrated his son as king and sovereign over the Cedis.

And now, O king, the sacrifice of the Kuru king of mighty power shone forth in all its opulence, to the delight of the young men: under the protection of Kṛṣṇa Keśava, it was free from impediments, properly performed, and rich in wealth, grain and foodstuffs of every kind. Strong-armed Kṛṣṇa, stirrer of men, brought the mighty sacrificial rite of the royal consecration to its conclusion, protecting it with bow, discus and club. Then when Yudhiṣṭhira lord of *dharma* had taken the final ritual bath, he was approached by all the Kṣatriya princes, who addressed him thus: 'We felicitate you on your attainment of imperial rank, righteous lord! You have increased the renown of all your lineage through this rite, prince of kings, and acquired great merit also! Now, tiger-like hero, honoured in every way we could desire, we ask you for leave: please permit us to return to our own lands.'

When Yudhiṣṭhira lord of *dharma* heard the kings' words, he paid them all due honour, and then instructed his brothers: 'Every one of these kings came to me in affection; now, enemy-afflicters all, they have asked for leave and are setting out for their own lands. Therefore, good sirs, accompany these most excellent monarchs to the borders of our domain.' The virtuous Pāṇḍavas obeyed their brother's command and accompanied each of those foremost kings according to merit. Dhṛṣṭadyumna of mighty energy set out at once with Virāṭa, and wealth-winner Arjuna, the great chariot-fighter, with noble Drupada; powerful Bhīma travelled with Bhīṣma and Dhṛtarāṣṭra, and the great chariot-fighter Sahadeva with heroic Droṇa and his son Aśvatthāman; Nakula went with Subala and his son Śakuni, O king, and Draupadī's sons, together with Abhimanyu, went with the kings of the mountain lands. In the same way bull-like Kṣatriyas accompanied each of the other Kṣatriyas; and all the priests were likewise honoured as they departed.

When all those lords among princes had left, O bull-like heir of Bharata, Kṛṣṇa Vāsudeva of great energy then addressed Yudhiṣṭhira: 'I too ask you for leave: I wish to return to Dvārakā, heir of Kuru. I felicitate you on your achievement of the royal consecration, the most excellent of rites!'

At this, the lord of *dharma* replied to Madhu's slayer, 'Kṛṣṇa Govinda, it is through your grace that I have achieved the rite: through your grace all the Kṣatriya princes, obedient to my will, came to me bearing splendid offerings. Without you, O hero, we shall take no pleasure in dwelling here – but of course you must return to the city of Dvārakā.'

Then righteous Hari Kṛṣṇa of wide fame, accompanied by Yudhiṣṭhira, visited Kuntī and happily told her, 'Aunt, today your sons have attained imperial rank; they have achieved their aims and become wealthy. Be glad for them! As for myself, with your permission I must return to Dvārakā.' After this, Keśava also paid his respects to Subhadrā and Draupadī. Then, leaving the women's quarters with Yudhiṣṭhira, he bathed, prayed and had blessings performed by Brahmins. Dāruka[1] now yoked his fine chariot, lovely as a cloud, and brought it to him, O king; and, seeing that his chariot had arrived, with its beautiful Garuḍa banner, high-minded, lotus-eyed Kṛṣṇa respectfully circumambulated it, mounted, and set out for the city of Dvārakā. Glorious Yudhiṣṭhira lord of *dharma* accompanied mighty Vāsudeva on foot, together with his brothers.

Then, halting his wonderful chariot for a moment, lotus-eyed Hari Kṛṣṇa spoke to Kuntī's son Yudhiṣṭhira: 'Lord of the peoples, be constantly alert in the protection of your subjects! And as living creatures depend on the rain-cloud, birds on the mighty tree, and the immortal gods on thousand-eyed Indra, may your kinsmen depend on you.' When they had done conversing, Kṛṣṇa and Pāṇḍu's son Yudhiṣṭhira took leave of each other, and returned to their own homes.

1 Kṛṣṇa's charioteer.

After Kṛṣṇa, best of the Sātvatas, had left for Dvārakā, King Duryodhana and Śakuni son of Subala were the only bull-like heroes left dwelling in Yudhiṣṭhira's heavenly hall.[1] 60

## THE GAMBLING MATCH

Vaiśaṃpāyana spoke:

**[43]** While Duryodhana dwelt in that hall, bull-like heir of Bharata, he slowly examined the whole place with Śakuni; and in it the Kaurava saw schemes of celestial wonder that he had never seen before in Hāstinapura, the City of the Elephant. Once, in the middle of the hall, Dhṛtarāṣṭra's royal son came upon a crystal floor; fooled into thinking it water, King Duryodhana drew up his garments. After this he walked
about the hall with angry heart and averted gaze. Next, seeing a pond 5
of crystalline water adorned with crystal lotuses, he thought it was a floor, and fell, fully clothed, headlong into the water; when the servants saw that he had fallen in the pond, they laughed uproariously, before giving him clean clothes at the king's command. Then mighty Bhīma and Arjuna and the twins saw him in this state, and they too all burst out laughing. Angry Duryodhana could not bear their mirth; maintaining a dignified mien, he avoided their gaze. But now once again he drew up his garments as though for wading, to set foot on what was in fact
dry land, and once again everyone laughed at him; and he bumped his 10
forehead against a door which had seemed to him open, and then halted in front of an open door, believing it closed. Thus King Duryodhana was tricked repeatedly, lord of the peoples, before taking leave of Pāṇḍu's son Yudhiṣṭhira.

It was with a cheerless heart that he returned to the City of the Elephant, for he had seen the amazing wealth displayed at the great rite of the royal consecration; and so King Duryodhana began to think wicked thoughts as he travelled, burning with jealousy of the Pāṇḍavas' fortune, and wearied with brooding. He had seen Kuntī's sons happy, and all the princes obedient to Yudhiṣṭhira's will; he had seen the

1 In verse 43 above, Śakuni was said to have travelled home with his father Subala.

whole world, down to the children, favouring him, heir of Kuru; and he had seen the unsurpassed greatness of the noble Pāṇḍavas. Now Dhṛtarāṣṭra's son Duryodhana grew pale, and he travelled on, distracted with brooding on the hall and the matchless fortune of the wise lord of *dharma*. So preoccupied was Duryodhana then that he said not a word to Subala's son Śakuni, who kept trying to engage him in talk. Finally, perceiving his state of distraction, Śakuni said, 'Duryodhana, why do you sigh as you travel?'

Duryodhana answered him: 'I have seen this whole earth obedient to Yudhiṣṭhira's will, conquered for him by noble Arjuna with the prowess of his weapons; I have seen, uncle, that sacrifice of Kuntī's son which matched the sacrifice of Indra among the gods; and I am so full of resentment that I burn day and night, like a shallow lake drying out at the onset of the hot weather. Observe Śiśupāla slain by the Sātvata chief, and not a man there to support him! The kings were all burning with a Pāṇḍava flame and forgave that crime; yet who could truly forgive it? What Kṛṣṇa Vāsudeva did was a great wrong, and it came about through the might of the noble Pāṇḍavas.

'What is more, all the kings approached Kuntī's son King Yudhiṣṭhira bearing jewels of every kind, like Vaiśyas paying taxes! I have seen Pāṇḍu's son enjoying such dazzling fortune, and I burn with resentment, for I am unused to such sights. I shall enter fire, or swallow poison, or drown myself, for I cannot live so! What man of mettle in this world could bear to see his rivals prosper and himself fail? If today I tolerate this new-found fortune of my rival, then I am neither woman nor non-woman, neither man nor non-man! What man like me would not burn to see such sovereignty over the earth, such wealth, such a sacrifice? But alone I am powerless to gain that kingly fortune for myself, and I see no allies; that is why I contemplate death. It seems to me that fate is supreme and human effort vain,[1] when I see that Kuntī's son has gained such a splendid fortune.

1 The terms translated 'fate' and 'human effort', *daiva* and *pauruṣa*, are parallel formations often contrasted with each other: *daiva* is 'the will of the gods' (*deva*), *pauruṣa* 'the will of a man' (*puruṣa*).

'Once before[1] I strove for his destruction, son of Subala, and yet he
overcame it all, and thrives like a lotus in water. And so it seems to me
that fate is supreme and human effort vain, for Dhṛtarāṣṭra's sons are
failing and the sons of Kuntī always thrive! I have seen their fortune and 35
their splendid hall; I have seen their guards deride me; and I burn as if
with fire. So let me be, uncle, for today I am full of woe. But you may
tell Dhṛtarāṣṭra that resentment has taken possession of me.'

**[44]** Śakuni replied, 'Duryodhana, do not be angry with Yudhiṣṭhira,
for Pāṇḍu's sons always enjoy good fortune. More than once before now
you have taken them captive with a variety of schemes, but through
their good fortune the tiger-like heroes have escaped. They have gained
Draupadī for their wife, and Drupada together with his sons for their
friends; and heroic Kṛṣṇa Vāsudeva is their ally in gaining mastery
over the earth. They inherited unchallenged wealth from their father,
lord of the earth, and have increased it through their ardour. What
grounds for grief in this? Wealth-winner Arjuna satisfied the Fire god, 5
and gained the bow Gāṇḍīva with two inexhaustible arrow-cases, and
celestial weapons also;[2] with that wonderful bow and the prowess of his
own arm he has brought the lords of the earth under his authority. What
grounds for grief in this? That ambidextrous enemy-afflicter freed the
demon Maya from Fire's burning and so brought about the construction
of the hall;[3] at Maya's command, that hall was supported by terrible
Kiṃkara Rākṣasas.[4] What grounds for grief in this?

'As for the lack of allies of which you spoke, heir of Bharata, that is
not so, for these mighty chariot-fighters your brothers are your allies;
and so is the great bowman Droṇa with his wise son Aśvatthāman; and 10
Karṇa the Sūta's son, and the great chariot-fighter Kṛpa heir of Gotama;
and I myself with my brothers, and Somadatta's son Bhūriśravas. Join
together with all these, and conquer the whole earth!'

'Together with you, O king,' said Duryodhana, 'and with these other mighty chariot-fighters, I shall defeat them, if you think it good. And

**1** See 1.129–38.

**2** See 1.214–16, 225.

**3** See 1.219, 2.1.

**4** See 2.3.

once they are defeated, the earth shall be mine, and all the lords of the earth, and that costly hall!'

Śakuni answered, 'Wealth-winner Arjuna, Kṛṣṇa Vāsudeva, Bhīma,
15 Yudhiṣṭhira, Nakula, Sahadeva, Drupada with his sons – these cannot be defeated in battle by force, not even by the hosts of the gods, for they are great chariot-fighters and mighty bowmen, expert in arms and mad for battle. But I know the means by which Yudhiṣṭhira himself may be defeated, O king: listen, and approve it!'

'If they can indeed be defeated without recklessness towards friends and other noble supporters,' replied Duryodhana, 'then tell me, uncle!'

Śakuni said, 'Kuntī's son is fond of gambling, but he does not know how to play. If the lord of kings is challenged, he will not be able to refuse; and I am skilled at playing – I have no equal on earth, none in
20 the three worlds. So challenge Kuntī's son to a match. Thanks to my skill at dice, bull-like king, you may be sure that I shall take for you his kingdom and his splendid fortune! But you must tell the king about all this, Duryodhana; once I have your father's consent, I shall defeat him, make no doubt.'

'Son of Subala,' answered Duryodhana, 'you should tell the Kuru lord Dhṛtarāṣṭra yourself in the proper manner; I cannot talk of this to him.'

**[45]** Śakuni son of Subala had experienced the great rite of King Yudhiṣṭhira's royal consecration in company with Gāndhārī's son Duryodhana; now, wishing to favour Duryodhana, whose opinion he had already learnt and whose words he had listened to, he approached Dhṛtarāṣṭra who saw through his wisdom as the wise lord of men sat before him, and spoke to him: 'Great king, Duryodhana has become pale, wan and thin; you should know that he is downcast and anxious, bull-like
5 heir of Bharata; and yet you do not properly investigate the unbearable grief that an enemy is causing your eldest son! Why do you not find out about it?'

'Duryodhana, my son,' cried Dhṛtarāṣṭra, 'what troubles you so deeply? If it is a matter that would be proper for me to hear, then tell me of it, heir of Kuru! Śakuni here says that you are pale, wan and thin, and yet even when I set my mind to it I can see no cause for you to grieve: all our mighty sovereignty is invested in you, son, and neither your brothers nor your allies act to displease you. You wear fine clothes, you eat meat stews, noble horses bear you: why are you wan and thin? You have costly beds and lovely women, fine houses and every enjoyment you could wish. All this is at your call, as you well know, as though you were a god, and yet one so unconquerable seems downcast. Why are you grieving, son?'

'I eat this and I wear that,' answered Duryodhana, 'like any base-born man; but I harbour a fierce resentment as I endure the reversal of my fortune. The unforbearing man who, to free himself of his enemy's vexations, would destroy his own kingdom if it fell to the enemy – he is truly a man! Contentment destroys good fortune, heir of Bharata, and so do self-regard, compassion and fear; the one whom these affect will attain nothing great. Those pleasures of mine please me no more, for I have seen Kuntī's son Yudhiṣṭhira enjoying such dazzling fortune, and it strikes the colour from my face! I see my rivals prosper and myself fail; I see, though I cannot bear to see, the fortune of Kuntī's son rising before me; and so I am pale and downcast, wan and thin.

'There are eighty-eight thousand pious householders, performers of the domestic rites, whom Yudhiṣṭhira maintains with thirty slave-girls apiece; ten thousand more daily eat the finest food from golden vessels in his dwelling; the king of Kāmboja has sent him skins of *kadalī* deer, black, brown and red, and blankets of the highest quality; she-elephants, cows and horses in their hundreds and thousands roam his lands, as well as three thousand she-camels; and at the start of his splendid rite princes brought masses of jewels of every kind to Kuntī's son, lord of the earth. I have never seen nor even heard of such wealth as came to Pāṇḍu's wise son at his sacrifice! Now that I have seen my enemy receive that boundless torrent of wealth, O king, I find no comfort, for I can think of nothing else.

'Vāṭadhāna Brahmins, rich in cattle, stood in hundreds at his gate, bearing offerings worth thirty billion, but were refused; they gained entrance only when they brought their offerings in the form of lovely golden water-pots. The ocean itself brought for him Varuṇa's drinking-vessel, which even the women of the celestials do not use when they carry mead to Indra; it was cast from a thousand pieces of gold and adorned with many jewels, and when I saw it, I felt as though I were utterly consumed by fever. Bearing that goblet, the Pāṇḍavas now travel to the oceans of the east and south; bearing it, they travel likewise to that of the west; but no one travels to that of the north, father, except for birds.

'And a marvel occurred there: hear me as I tell you of it. Whenever a full hundred thousand Brahmins were being served their food, there was an established signal: a conch was always blown. Heir of Bharata, I heard the glorious sound of that conch sounding again and again, till the hair rose on my body! The hall was filled with numerous princes who had come to watch – and, lord of men, those princes brought with them all manner of jewels – but at the sacrifice of Pāṇḍu's wise son those lords of the earth waited like Vaiśyas on the Brahmins, great king!

'Indra the king of the gods does not have such a fortune; neither does Yama or Varuṇa; not even Kubera, lord of the Guhyakas and god of wealth, has the fortune Yudhiṣṭhira has, O king. Now that I have seen the matchless wealth of Pāṇḍu's son, I have no peace, for my mind is on fire!'

Now Śakuni spoke. 'Hero of true valour, listen while I tell you the way to acquire the wonderful fortune you have seen in the hands of Pāṇḍu's son. I am known throughout the whole earth for my skill at dice, heir of Bharata: I know their inner secrets, I know how to wager, I know the subtleties of the game. Kuntī's son is fond of gambling, but he does not know how to play; if he is challenged, he is sure to come. Challenge him to gamble with you!'

When King Duryodhana heard Śakuni's words he spoke at once to Dhṛtarāṣṭra: 'Here is a skilled gamester, O king, who can get me the fortune of Pāṇḍu's son through gambling: please permit it!'

Dhṛtarāṣṭra replied, 'I act on the counsel of my wise minister, Vidura the chamberlain. I shall decide this matter after consulting him, for he respects *dharma* and is far-sighted; he will announce a decision that secures the greatest good and is proper for both parties.'

'If the chamberlain is consulted,' retorted Duryodhana, 'he will prevent you; and if you are prevented, lord of kings, I shall die, make no doubt! And when I am dead, king, enjoy yourself with Vidura; for you will rule the whole earth – what need will you have of me?'

Dhṛtarāṣṭra listened to Duryodhana's frank and tortured words, and then he spoke to his servants in accordance with his wishes: 'Let craftsmen swiftly build me a great hall, delightful and lovely to see, with thousands of pillars and hundreds of doors! Strew it with jewels; lay out dice everywhere; and when it is properly built, with a fine entrance, come and inform me privately.' Then, after taking this decision in order to calm Duryodhana, Dhṛtarāṣṭra the lord of the earth sent for Vidura, O king; for without asking Vidura he never decided anything. He knew the evils of gambling, and yet he was swayed by love for his son.

When wise Vidura heard what he had done and understood that the 50
gates of Kali[1] were at hand, and that Destruction had shown its face, he
hurried to Dhṛtarāṣṭra. Brother approached noble firstborn brother; he
bowed his head to Dhṛtarāṣṭra's feet and spoke. 'I cannot applaud this
resolve of yours, O king! My lord, act to prevent gambling from causing
discord among your sons.'

'Chamberlain,' answered Dhṛtarāṣṭra, 'my sons will not quarrel with
my sons; the gods in heaven will bestow their favour on us, make no
doubt! Whether it be fair or foul, whether it be good or ill, let this
friendly gambling match proceed, for so it is ordained, make no doubt!
I myself shall be near at hand, and also Bhīṣma, Bharata's bull-like heir, 55
so there will surely be no misconduct even at fate's decree. Mount
your chariot with its horses swift as the wind and go this very day to
Khāṇḍavaprastha; fetch Yudhiṣṭhira here! I tell you this, Vidura: my
resolve cannot be countermanded. It seems to me that fate is supreme,
to bring this about!'

Wise Vidura heard him. Thinking, 'All is lost!' he went in utter misery to the river's son, Bhīṣma of mighty wisdom.

**[46]** — *Janamejaya requests to hear the story again in greater detail, and Vaiśaṃpāyana obliges.* — *Dhṛtarāṣṭra knows that Vidura will oppose the gambling match, and tells Duryodhana to abandon the idea; then he asks him why he is so dissatisfied. Duryodhana answers by describing the tremendous wealth that came in tribute to Yudhiṣṭhira, and the humiliations he himself underwent in Indraprastha.* **[47]** *He lists in detail the wonderful treasures that Yudhiṣṭhira received from all over the world:* **[48]** *in many cases kings were refused*

1 See 1.61.80 and note.

*entrance despite having brought costly gifts. Great numbers of Brahmins were lavishly fed.* [**49**] *Yudhiṣṭhira was waited on by kings, and kings brought him the chariot, armour and other items needed for the royal consecration. The sound of hundreds of conches being blown at the culmination of the ritual was so great that all the kings fainted, save for the Pāṇḍavas themselves and Dhṛṣṭadyumna, Sātyaki and Kṛṣṇa, who all laughed at the sight. Now that he has seen all this, Duryodhana has no peace of mind.*

[**50**] *Dhṛtarāṣṭra appeals to Duryodhana to be satisfied with what he has, and to abide by his* dharma*: this is the only way to find happiness. But Duryodhana counters that a Kṣatriya should further his own interests, whether this involves* dharma *or* adharma*; he wishes to be dissatisfied, for dissatisfaction leads to fortune. He cites the deception by means of which Indra slew Namuci:*[1] *enemies who prosper must be destroyed.*

[**51**] *Śakuni now makes his proposal to divest Yudhiṣṭhira of his fortune by means of gambling, rather than war; Duryodhana supports him; Dhṛtarāṣṭra says that he wishes to consult Vidura. Duryodhana objects: Vidura is not well disposed towards him. Reluctantly, Dhṛtarāṣṭra agrees to the plan. He orders the building of the hall, and instructs Vidura to fetch Yudhiṣṭhira. Vidura disapproves, but Dhṛtarāṣṭra stands firm.*

Vaiśaṃpāyana spoke:

[**52**] Now, with his thoroughbred horses, swift, powerful and well
broken-in, Vidura set forth against his will to meet the wise Pāṇḍavas,
for King Dhṛtarāṣṭra had so commanded him. He raced along the
road towards them, reached King Yudhiṣṭhira's city, and entered, to
be greeted with honour by the Brahmins; arriving at the royal palace,
opulent as the palace of Kubera, righteous Vidura of mighty wisdom
approached Dharma's son Yudhiṣṭhira. Noble Yudhiṣṭhira Ajātaśatru,[2]
the truly steadfast king, welcomed Vidura with all proper honour, and
5 then asked him about Dhṛtarāṣṭra and his sons. 'Chamberlain, your heart
seems empty of joy. I trust that you have come on pleasant business?
and that the old king's sons do his bidding? and that his people too are
obedient to his will?'

1 See 9.42.

2 See 2.12.8.

'The noble king is well, and so are his sons,' replied Vidura; 'he is ever surrounded by his Indra-like kin, and his sons please him with their courteous behaviour. Nothing causes him grief, O king: he has inner strength and contentment. However, the king of the Kurus addresses you thus, having first enquired after your eternal welfare: "Come, son, and see the hall of your Dhārtarāṣṭra brothers, which matches your own hall in loveliness! Come with your brothers, son of Kuntī, and enjoy a friendly gambling match in it. Your arrival would cause us joy, good sir, and all the Kurus are assembled ready!" Noble King Dhṛtarāṣṭra has installed gamesters there, and there you will see them assembled, cheats that they are. It is to tell you this that I have come: grant your approval, king!'

'Chamberlain,' answered Yudhiṣṭhira, 'if we gamble, we shall quarrel; 10
knowing this, who would agree to a match? But what do you consider proper, sir? All of us shall be ruled by your decision.'

Vidura said, 'I know that gambling brings disaster, and I tried to prevent it, but the king sent me to you. You have heard what I say, and you are learned; act for the best.'

'Apart from King Dhṛtarāṣṭra's sons, what other cheating gamblers will play there?' asked Yudhiṣṭhira. 'Tell me what I ask: who are these assembled hundreds against whom I shall have to play?'

'Lord of the peoples, there is Śakuni, king of Gāndhāra,' replied Vidura. 'He plays for the highest stakes; he has skilful hands, and knows the ways of the dice. Also there are Viviṃśati and King Citrasena, as well as Satyavrata, Purumitra and Jaya.'

'The most dangerous cheats are assembled there,' said Yudhiṣṭhira, 'men who gamble under the guise of trickery. But, as people say, this whole world is under the sway of what fate ordains, and today I have no
option but to gamble against cheats. I do not wish, wise sir, to refuse to 15
go to the match, since it is commanded by King Dhṛtarāṣṭra. A father is always dear to a son, and so I shall act as you instruct me, Vidura. I shall not gamble against my will with Śakuni unless he is so bold as to challenge me in that hall; but if I am challenged, I shall never refuse, for such is the eternal vow that I have sworn.'

After speaking thus to Vidura, Yudhiṣṭhira lord of *dharma* commanded all arrangements for the journey to be swiftly made. On the following

day he set out with his followers and companions, together with the
womenfolk, Draupadī chief among them. 'Fate robs us of wisdom as a
sudden glare robs us of sight; man is bound as if by snares, and follows
the dictate of destiny!' With these words King Yudhiṣṭhira set forth with
Vidura the chamberlain, for Kuntī's foe-taming son could not withstand
20 that challenge. Pāṇḍu's son, the slayer of enemy heroes, mounted the
chariot that Bāhlika had given him and travelled surrounded by his
brothers, blazing with royal glory, with Brahmins in the van, for he was
challenged by Dhṛtarāṣṭra and by his compact with fate.

Reaching Hāstinapura, he went to Dhṛtarāṣṭra's dwelling, where the
righteous Pāṇḍava met Dhṛtarāṣṭra; the lord also met Droṇa, Bhīṣma,
Karṇa and Kṛpa, as was proper, as well as Aśvatthāman, Droṇa's son.
Then the strong-armed hero met Somadatta, Duryodhana, Śalya and
25 Śakuni son of Subala, and all the other kings who had already assembled
there, together with Jayadratha and all the Kurus.

Now strong-armed Yudhiṣṭhira, encircled by his brothers, entered
the dwelling of wise King Dhṛtarāṣṭra. There he saw Queen Gāndhārī,
so devoted to her husband, ever surrounded by her daughters-in-law as
the Rohiṇī constellation is surrounded by stars; he paid Gāndhārī his
respects and received her greeting. Next he saw the aged lord, father
Dhṛtarāṣṭra who saw through his wisdom; the king kissed him on the
head, and then kissed the other four Pāṇḍavas, beginning with Bhīma.
30 There was joy among the Kauravas, lord of the peoples, to see the
handsome, tiger-like Pāṇḍavas.

Next, with Dhṛtarāṣṭra's leave, they entered their jewelled quarters,
where visitors came to see Draupadī and the other women; when the
daughters-in-law of Dhṛtarāṣṭra saw the mighty, splendid wealth of
Drupada's daughter they were not well pleased. After conversing with
the ladies, all the tiger-like heroes left to perform their daily exercises and
their toilet; then, their daily tasks completed, they perfumed themselves
with heavenly sandalwood and had blessings spoken by benevolent
35 Brahmins; and after this those heirs of Kuru ate a delicious meal and
retired to their lodgings, where their womenfolk sang them to sleep.
The night passed pleasantly for them in the enjoyment of love, and
when the time came, well rested, they cast off sleep to the strains of
songs in their praise. Thus all of them spent an agreeable night. In the

morning they completed their daily tasks, and then entered the lovely hall, which was thronged with gamblers.

**[53]** Now Śakuni addressed Yudhiṣṭhira. 'The hall has been made ready, king, and everyone here is impatient to play. Let us agree to throw the dice and gamble, Yudhiṣṭhira!'

'Gambling is deceit,' answered Yudhiṣṭhira; 'it is evil, and there is no Kṣatriya valour or moral firmness in it. Why do you praise gambling, O king? No one has praise for the cheating gambler's pride in his deceit! So do not defeat me viciously and dishonestly, Śakuni.'

Śakuni replied, 'The calculating man who knows the ways of deception, whose cunning never falters in his struggles with the dice, and who has the intelligence to understand gambling: he is the man who emerges unscathed from the match. You fear that wagering with dice will ruin you utterly: this is why you say, "It is fate!" Put aside your misgivings and gamble with us, prince; lay your stake, do not delay!'

'Hear the words of Asita Devala,' said Yudhiṣṭhira, 'the truest of sages, who stands always at the gates of heaven. "This deceitful gaming with cheats is evil; honest victory in war is the finest game! Noble men do not utter barbarism or perform deceits; clean, honourable warfare is the rule for men of virtue." We strive to serve venerable Brahmins to the best of our ability; do not deprive us of that wealth, Śakuni, by defeating us utterly at gambling! I have no desire for pleasures or wealth gained through deceit, for the gambler's way of life wins no honour even if he is honest.'

'When a Vedic scholar competes against one without such scholarship,' answered Śakuni, 'or a learned man against men without learning, that is deception, Yudhiṣṭhira, though people do not call it so. If you think it deception to compete with me here, or if you are afraid, then refuse the wager!'

'If I am challenged, I shall not refuse,' said Yudhiṣṭhira, 'for such is the vow that I have sworn. Fate is mighty, O king, and I am under the control of its ordinance. Tell me with whom in this assembly I am to gamble, and also what will be the stake against me; then let the match proceed!'

Duryodhana now spoke: 'I shall stake my wealth and jewels, lord of the peoples, and Śakuni here, my mother's brother, will play for me.'

'For one person to gamble by means of another seems to me unfair,' said Yudhiṣṭhira, 'and with all your learning, you too must know that this is so. But let play proceed nevertheless!'

Now, as the match drew near, all the kings entered the hall, headed by Dhṛtarāṣṭra. Bhīṣma, Droṇa, Kṛpa and sagacious Vidura followed, heir of Bharata; they were not well pleased. In pairs and separately the lion-necked princes of mighty power sat on their many gorgeous lion-thrones, till the hall shone with all the assembled kings as Indra's heaven shines with the blessed gods who gather there. All of those heroes were experts in the Veda, all were radiant as the sun in human form. Now, great king, that friendly gambling match began.

'Here, O king, I have a glorious jewel,' said Yudhiṣṭhira, 'a lovely pearl necklace set in finest gold. It is of great worth, for it arose from the churning of the ocean.[1] This is my stake, king; now, what is your stake against me? Let things be done in due order, brother, and I shall win this game!'

Duryodhana answered, 'I have both jewels and wealth of every kind, but I do not glory in my riches. I shall win this game!'

Then Śakuni, expert dicer, took up the dice; and 'I have won!' said Śakuni to Yudhiṣṭhira.

**[54]** 'It is by cheating me that you won this game from me,' said Yudhiṣṭhira; 'but still let us play, Śakuni, wagering thousands upon thousands! Here I have a hundred jars, each filled with a thousand coins; I have treasure, inexhaustible gold, riches in plenty. This is my stake, king; I wager it against you!'

Thus Yudhiṣṭhira spoke; and 'I have won!' said Śakuni to the king.

'Here is the glorious kingly chariot that carried us here,' said Yudhiṣṭhira; 'it is worth a thousand, decked in tiger-skins, fast-moving with its fine wheels and other gear, adorned with clusters of tinkling bells, roaring like thunderclouds or the ocean, a wonderful, victory-granting chariot drawn by eight fine horses the colour of ospreys that are esteemed throughout the land: all know that neither the chariot nor the

1 See 1.15–17.

horses' hooves so much as touch the ground. This is my stake, king; I wager it against you!'

Hearing this, Śakuni resolved and performed his deceit; and 'I have won!' said Śakuni to Yudhiṣṭhira.

'I have a thousand rutting elephants, son of Subala,' said Yudhiṣṭhira, 'with golden girths and auspicious markings, garlanded with gold; they are mounts fit for kings, well broken-in and capable of withstanding all the din of battle, with tusks like plough-shafts and mighty bodies; each one has eight she-elephants for its mates; fortress-destroyers all, these elephants are as huge as mountains or clouds. This is my stake, king; I wager it against you!'

As he spoke these words, Subala's son burst out laughing; and 'I have won!' said Śakuni to Yudhiṣṭhira.

'I have a hundred thousand slave-girls,' said Yudhiṣṭhira, 'young and lovely, with shell bracelets, medallions and other fair adornments; they are decked with costly garlands and ornaments, well dressed, and sprinkled with sandal-scented water; they bear gold and jewels, and all of them are clad in fine garments. Skilled at singing and dancing, they wait upon householders, ministers and kings at my command. This is my stake, king; I wager it against you!'

Hearing this, Śakuni resolved and performed his deceit; and 'I have won!' said Śakuni to Yudhiṣṭhira.

'I have as many thousands of male slaves,' said Yudhiṣṭhira, 'respectful, obedient, and always dressed in fine clothes; wise, intelligent and skilful, these young men with their gleaming earrings carry dishes to serve my guests food day and night. This is my stake, king; I wager it against you!'

Hearing this, Śakuni resolved and performed his deceit; and 'I have won!' said Śakuni to Yudhiṣṭhira.

'I have as many chariots,' said Yudhiṣṭhira, 'with banners and golden trappings, provided with well-trained horses and chariot-fighters who are expert at many forms of war, each one of whom receives at least a thousand as his stipend, for this is their monthly pay, whether fighting or not. This is my stake, king; I wager it against you!'

Kuntī's son finished speaking; and 'I have won!' said the hateful, wicked Śakuni to Yudhiṣṭhira.

'I have Gandharva horses,' said Yudhiṣṭhira, 'dappled like partridges, garlanded with gold, which Citraratha was pleased to bestow upon Arjuna the bearer of the bow Gāṇḍīva.[1] This is my stake, king; I wager it against you!'

Hearing this, Śakuni resolved and performed his deceit; and 'I have won!' said Śakuni to Yudhiṣṭhira.

'I have tens of thousands of other chariots, carts and horses,' said Yudhiṣṭhira; 'they stand ready yoked, together with draft animals of every kind. And in the same way I have standing ready a full sixty thousand broad-chested men, drinkers of milk and eaters of rice-grain, selected in their thousands from every class. This is my stake, king; I wager it against you!'

Hearing this, Śakuni resolved and performed his deceit; and 'I have won!' said Śakuni to Yudhiṣṭhira.

'I have four hundred treasure-chests, clad in copper and iron,' said Yudhiṣṭhira, 'each one of which contains five hundredweight of purest gold. This is my stake, king; I wager it against you!'

Hearing this, Śakuni resolved and performed his deceit; and 'I have won!' said Śakuni to Yudhiṣṭhira.

**[55]** Now Vidura spoke to Dhṛtarāṣṭra: 'Great king, listen to what I have to say to you, and take it to heart, even though what you hear may be no more palatable to you than medicine to a man bent on death. When, long ago, this wicked-minded Duryodhana was only just born, he howled horribly, like a jackal; and now, employed as fate's instrument, he will be the destroyer of the line of Bharata! In your mind you do not realize that a jackal is living in your house in the shape of Duryodhana; but listen to the words of Śukra.[2] "The honey-gatherer gathers his honey, and does not notice the precipice; he climbs to the top, and then either falls or throws himself to his death."[3] And so Duryodhana, crazed with wagering at dice as if with honey, does not look about him; he ignores a precipice as he antagonizes these mighty chariot-fighters. Great king, you know that even amongst the world's kings the Andhakas, Yādavas and Bhojas jointly abandoned Kaṃsa, regarding him as unfit;

1 See 2.216.

2 The household priest of the demons (see 1.71).

3 This is a reference to the well-known parable of the honey-gatherers: see 5.62.

and when he was killed at their behest by foe-slaying Kṛṣṇa, they, his own kin, rejoiced for a hundred years. Let the ambidextrous warrior Arjuna curb Duryodhana at your behest, and when he is curbed, let the Kurus rejoice at their ease!

'Trade this crow for peacocks, this jackal for tigers! Trade Duryodhana for the Pāṇḍavas, king; do not drown in an ocean of grief! "Give up one member for the sake of the family; give up one family for the sake of the village; give up one village for the sake of the kingdom; give up the earth for the sake of yourself!" – so spoke Śukra, the knower of all, the knower of every man's heart, the terror of every enemy, to the mighty demons when they abandoned Jambha.

'It is said, O king, that a certain man took into his house birds from the forest, whose saliva yielded gold; but then he pressed them too hard instead of enjoying them forever, and so, O afflicter of your enemies, destroyed at once both his present and his future in a blind lust for gold. Do not harm the Pāṇḍavas in your own desires for the present, bull-like heir of Bharata, or like that man who killed the birds you will later rue your foolishness! Like a garland-maker in a garden, lovingly take from the Pāṇḍavas each flower as they produce it, one after another; do not burn the trees complete with their roots like a charcoal-burner! Do not bring humiliation on yourself, your sons, your ministers and your troops; for is there anyone, even Indra himself with the Maruts, that could fight against the assembled sons of Kuntī, heir of Bharata?

**[56]** 'Gambling is the root of dissension; it has for its consequence discord and mighty war. In embarking on it, Dhṛtarāṣṭra's son Duryodhana is starting a fierce feud. Through Duryodhana's fault, the descendants of Pratīpa, Śaṃtanu and Bhīma, and the Bāhlikas, will all come to grief, for in his utter madness Duryodhana is banishing security from the land, like a mad bull that breaks its own horn by force.

'Whether warrior or seer, the man who violates his own judgement to follow another's inclination is like someone who puts to sea in a boat steered by a child: he plunges into terrible disaster, O king. Duryodhana is gambling with Yudhiṣṭhira, and this pleases you, for you believe that he is winning. But from this contest for excessive stakes there will arise a war bringing destruction to all men. This ill-advised fascination of yours will bear heavy fruit; a spell has been spoken, and in your heart it has grown into an obsession. Enjoy the fruit of friendship with Yudhiṣṭhira; placate the mighty bowman Arjuna, so that he gives up his enmity!

'You descendants of Pratīpa and Śaṃtanu, and you too, O king, hear Śukra's word, let it not pass you by! A dreadful, blazing fire is leaping up; extinguish it – do not make war! If Pāṇḍu's son Yudhiṣṭhira Ajātaśatru, overcome through his lack of skill, gives free rein to his fury, and so too do wolf-belly Bhīma, and the ambidextrous warrior Arjuna, and the twins, what refuge will there be for you then in the tumult that will follow? Before this match, great king, you were a mine of as much wealth as your heart could wish. If you now win great riches from the Pāṇḍavas, what do you gain? To win true wealth, win over Kuntī's sons!
10 All of us know Śakuni's skill in gambling: the king of the mountain
lands knows how to cheat at dice. Let him return whence he came, for the mountain king fights through trickery!'

[57] Duryodhana said, 'Always it is our enemies whose glory forms your boast, while you sneer covertly at us sons of Dhṛtarāṣṭra, and despise us like children. We know you, Vidura, and we know whose friend you are. It is easy to recognize the man whose affections lie elsewhere, for he directs his praise and blame accordingly: your tongue betrays your heart and your mind, and proclaims the depth of your hostility. We took you in like a wild creature and cherished you, but like a cat you harm the man who feeds you. It is said that there is nothing more sinful than hurting one's master; how is it, chamberlain, that you do not fear this sin? We have won great rewards by defeating our enemies, and you should not chastise us for it, chamberlain; but always you delight to find common cause with our foes – again and again you oppose us, fool that you are!

5 'The man who speaks enviously has already joined the enemy, and in their friendship for the enemy such men keep their secrets close. How does the shame of that friendship not hold you back? Today you have told us here exactly what you want; you should not despise us, for we know what is in your mind! Go and learn wisdom from the elders! Protect what reputation you have established, Vidura; do not meddle in the affairs of others! You should not despise us on account of your own importance, Vidura; you should not be always chastising us. I do

not ask you what is best for me, so leave well alone, chamberlain, and stop trying our endurance!

'There is but one ruler; there is no other; that ruler rules a man before he is ever born. Ruled by him, like water down a slope, I flow wherever I am directed! If someone breaks a rock with his head, or offers food to a snake, it is the ruler's rule that he carries out. But the man who tries to exert his own rule by force in this world makes enemies for himself. Those who are learned should only tolerate a person who follows the way of friendship; but the man who starts a blazing fire and fails to run in haste from it is left with nothing, heir of Bharata, not even ash.

'One should not shelter a hostile enemy – especially, O chamberlain, a man who does harm. Therefore, Vidura, go where you want to go! Despite every conciliation, the unchaste wife still deserts her husband!'

Vidura replied, 'The friendship of those who would reject a man on such a pretext is like death itself, O king; would you not say so? But the hearts of kings are fickle; first they conciliate, then they slay with bludgeons. Dull-witted prince, you consider yourself a mature man, and me a foolish child; but the true fool is he who makes a man his friend and then turns against him. This dull-witted man is as much a stranger to improvement as is the whore to the house of the Vedic scholar; and constancy appeals no more to this bull-like heir of Bharata than a sixty-year-old husband to a young girl!

'If all you want is sycophancy regardless of whether your acts are good or ill, then go and ask the womenfolk, and the dumb and the lame, and other such fools, O king! A sycophant is easy to find here, heir of Pratīpa; but the man who speaks unwelcome truth is as hard to find as the man who will listen to it. None the less, a king's best companion is the one who, trusting in *dharma* and putting aside his master's likes and dislikes, speaks unwelcome truths. The virtuous will drink, but the wicked refuse, a medicine that is bitter, sharp-tasting, fiery, disreputable, harsh and foul-smelling. Quell your anger, great king, and drink it!

'To Dhṛtarāṣṭra son of Vicitravīrya, and to his sons, I wish eternal wealth and glory; and I wish the same to you, and pay you honour. For myself, let the Brahmins speak a blessing for me. This is what I dutifully tell you, heir of Kuru: a learned man should not stir to anger snakes whose mere gaze is venomous.'

[58] Now Śakuni addressed Yudhiṣṭhira once more. 'You have already lost much of the Pāṇḍavas' wealth, son of Kuntī; declare what wealth you stake now, if any remains unlost!'

'I know that I have incalculable wealth, Śakuni son of Subala,' answered Yudhiṣṭhira; 'why do you question me about my wealth? Let the wager be ten thousand, a million, ten billion and one billion more, a hundred million, a thousand billion, a thousand million, a hundred thousand billion! This is my stake, king; I wager it against you!'

Hearing this, Śakuni resolved and performed his deceit; and 'I have won!' said Śakuni to Yudhiṣṭhira.

5 'I have horses and cows, including many milkers,' said Yudhiṣṭhira; 'I have numberless sheep and goats; and I have all the livestock of every kind to the east of the Sindhu,[1] son of Subala. This is my stake, king; I wager it against you!'

Hearing this, Śakuni resolved and performed his deceit; and 'I have won!' said Śakuni to Yudhiṣṭhira.

'My remaining wealth is my city, my country, my land,' said Yudhiṣṭhira, 'together with all the wealth belonging to non-Brahmins, and the non-Brahmin populace itself. This is my stake, king; I wager it against you!'

Hearing this, Śakuni resolved and performed his deceit; and 'I have won!' said Śakuni to Yudhiṣṭhira.

'The earrings and neck-chains,' said Yudhiṣṭhira, 'and all the bodily adornments that lend lustre to these princes – this is my stake, king; I wager it against you!'

10 Hearing this, Śakuni resolved and performed his deceit; and 'I have won!' said Śakuni to Yudhiṣṭhira.

'My wager is this dark young man Nakula,' said Yudhiṣṭhira, 'with red eyes, lion-like shoulders and strong arms, together with whatever wealth he owns.'

'King Yudhiṣṭhira,' said Śakuni, 'Prince Nakula, so dear to you, has been added to our treasure! What will you wager next?' With these words he took up the dice; and 'I have won!' said Śakuni to Yudhiṣṭhira.

'Sahadeva here expounds the different *dharmas*,' said Yudhiṣṭhira, 'and

1 The Indus river.

has acquired a worldwide reputation as a scholar. I love the prince, and he does not deserve this, but I wager him against you as though I loved him not.'

Hearing this, Śakuni resolved and performed his deceit; and 'I have 15
won!' said Śakuni to Yudhiṣṭhira. 'Mādrī's twin sons are dear to you, O king; now you have lost them to me. But I think that Bhīma and wealth-winner Arjuna mean even more to you!'

'Be sure that you are breaching *dharma*, fool,' said Yudhiṣṭhira, 'in disregarding propriety and seeking to sow dissension among those who wish each other well!'

'The drunk man may fall in a ditch,' replied Śakuni, 'and the absent-minded man may bump into a post; but you are the eldest and best, O king! I pay honour to you, bull-like heir of Bharata! When these cheating gamesters gamble like crazy men, they rave about things never seen, asleep or awake!'

'Prince Arjuna is the world's most spirited hero,' said Yudhiṣṭhira; 20
'like a boat he rescues us in battle and defeats our enemies. He does not deserve this, but I wager him against you, Śakuni.'

Hearing this, Śakuni resolved and performed his deceit; and 'I have won!' said Śakuni to Yudhiṣṭhira. 'I have won from you the bowman of the Pāṇḍavas, the ambidextrous warrior, the son of Pāṇḍu! Now, king, wager your beloved Bhīma, for he is all the stake that you have left!'

'Prince Bhīma is our leader and the leader of our warriors,' said Yudhiṣṭhira, 'like Indra himself, the god of the thunderbolt and enemy of the demons; noble Bhīma with his lion-like shoulders, glaring with knitted brows, ever unforbearing, foe-crusher and foremost of club-wielders, is unmatched in strength by any other man. He does not deserve this, but I wager him against you, O king.'

Hearing this, Śakuni resolved and performed his deceit; and 'I have 25
won!' said Śakuni to Yudhiṣṭhira. 'You have lost much wealth; you have lost your brothers, your horses and elephants, son of Kuntī; declare what wealth you stake now, if any remains unlost!'

'I myself remain,' said Yudhiṣṭhira, 'seniormost of all the brothers, and loved by them. If you win me I shall work for you, for I shall be my own downfall.'

Hearing this, Śakuni resolved and performed his deceit; and 'I have won!' said Śakuni to Yudhiṣṭhira. 'This is a most sinful thing that you have done, to lose your own self; if other wealth remains, O king, loss of oneself is a sin!'

Thus Śakuni, who knew the ways of the dice, won every one of those world-heroes by wagering, throw after throw. Now he spoke again: 'One stake is left to you unlost, your own beloved queen. Wager Draupadī, the Pāñcāla princess; win yourself back with her!'

'I wager her against you,' said Yudhiṣṭhira. 'She is neither short nor tall, neither swarthy nor florid, and her silken garments are dyed red; her eyes are like petals of autumn lotuses, her scent is the scent of autumn lotuses, she decks herself with autumn lotuses, and she is equal in beauty to Śrī. She is a woman such as any man might want who wished for gentleness, who wished for perfect beauty, who wished for perfect disposition. Last to retire to bed and first to rise, she knows everything that has been done or left undone by everybody, even the cowherds and shepherds. Her sweat-flecked face is lovely as a lotus or jasmine flower, her waist slender as a sacrificial altar; her hair is long, her eyes the colour of copper, her body not marred by too much hair. Such is the Pāñcāla princess Draupadī, O king, with her slender waist and her lovely limbs; alas, I wager her against you, son of Subala.'

When Yudhiṣṭhira lord of *dharma* spoke these words, O heir of Bharata, all the elder courtiers were heard to cry, 'Woe! Woe!' The hall was in turmoil; all the kings fell to talking, while Bhīṣma, Droṇa, Kṛpa and the other senior Kurus broke into a sweat. Vidura sat plunged in thought, head in hands, looking like a dead man; staring at the ground, he hissed like a snake. But Dhṛtarāṣṭra was elated, and asked over and over again, 'Has he won? Has he won?', making no attempt to maintain his dignity. Karṇa was overwhelmed with joy, and so were Duḥśāsana and the other Kauravas, while others in the hall wept. As for Subala's crazed son Śakuni, he did not hesitate; and 'I have won!' he said triumphantly as he took up the dice yet again.

**[59]** Now Duryodhana spoke. 'Come, chamberlain,' he said, 'and fetch here Draupadī of great renown, the Pāṇḍavas' beloved wife! She shall sweep the house, and then hurry away to enjoy her life with our other slave-girls!'

'The unthinkable is happening, thanks to you and your kind,' answered

Vidura. 'Fool! You do not see that you are caught in a trap; you do not realize that you are hanging over a precipice; you are like a deer that stupidly provokes tigers to fury! You are carrying on your head snakes of deadly venom, their poison-sacs full; do not enrage them, fool! Do not set out for Yama's realm! In my judgement Draupadī Kṛṣṇā has not fallen into servitude, heir of Bharata, for King Yudhiṣṭhira was not his own master when he wagered her.

'This prince, Dhṛtarāṣṭra's son, is like the bamboo that dies in putting forth fruit: he is ripe, and this is the time for his death, yet he does not understand that gambling leads to the most dangerous of feuds. A man should not act to wound; he should not speak cruelly; he should not snatch the final possession from one who has lost all; he should not utter that hurtful, infernal word which causes another man distress. When bad words leave a person's mouth to bring grief night and day to those they hurt, they never fail to strike the weakest spots; therefore no learned man will direct them at others.

'It is said that once, when men had lost a knife, their goat tore at the ground with its hooves till it dug up another: its throat was cut most horribly. Do not do likewise! Do not dig up a feud with the Pāṇḍavas! Men do not speak ill of a praiseworthy man, whether pious householder, forest-dwelling sage, or learned ascetic; but curs forever bay like you. Son of Dhṛtarāṣṭra, you do not realize that this is the dreadful, crooked gate to hell: many of the Kurus will follow you and Duḥśāsana through it, thanks to your success at gambling! Bottle-gourds may sink and stones may float, boats may forever sail the wrong way on the water, but this foolish prince, Dhṛtarāṣṭra's son, will never listen to my beneficial words. Without doubt he will be the end of the Kurus, a terrible destruction sweeping all away, for the prophetic, beneficial words of his friends are ignored, and only greed flourishes!'

**[60]** 'Curse you, chamberlain!' said the son of Dhṛtarāṣṭra, and in his mad pride he caught the eye of his page and addressed him in the midst of all the nobles in the hall. 'Fetch Draupadī, my page! You have no fear of the Pāṇḍavas, even if the chamberlain here is scared and disputes my order! But, after all, he has never wanted us to prosper!'

The page, a Sūta, received his orders. He set off as soon as he learnt King Duryodhana's command, entered the dwelling as a dog might enter the den of a lion, and approached the Pāṇḍavas' queen. 'Yudhiṣṭhira is overcome by the intoxication of gambling,' he said, 'and so, Draupadī, you have been won by Duryodhana. You must therefore now enter Dhṛtarāṣṭra's household: I shall conduct you to your duties, daughter of Drupada!'

'How can you speak so, page?' replied Draupadī. 'What prince would ever wager his own wife? The foolish king may be overcome by the intoxication of gambling, but had he nothing else to stake?'

'It was when he had nothing else to stake that Pāṇḍu's son Yudhiṣṭhira Ajātaśatru wagered you,' answered the page. 'First the king staked his brothers and, indeed, himself; then, princess, he staked you.'

'Go, son of a Sūta,' said Draupadī; 'go and ask that gambler in the hall: "Heir of Bharata, did you first lose yourself, or me?" Return when you have learnt this, son of a Sūta; then you may conduct me there.'

So he went back to the hall and announced what Draupadī had said. 'These were Draupadī's words to you: "When you lost me, of whom were you master? Did you first lose yourself, or me?"' But Yudhiṣṭhira remained motionless, like a dead man, and made no answer to the Sūta, whether for good or ill.

Now Duryodhana spoke. 'Let the Pāñcāla princess, Draupadī Kṛṣṇā, come here in person to pose this question! Here in this hall let everyone hear what she and this man have to say!'

The Sūta page, obedient to Duryodhana's will, returned to the royal quarters and spoke to Draupadī in evident distress. 'Princess, the courtiers there summon you! I think that the destruction of the Kauravas must be at hand, for if you are to come to the hall, princess, it is clear that Duryodhana, basest of men, cares nothing for our welfare.'

Draupadī answered, 'This, for sure, is what the ordainer ordained. The wise and the foolish are touched alike by both good and ill, but a single *dharma* has been declared paramount in this world which will, if protected, maintain us in peace.'

Now when Yudhiṣṭhira realized what Duryodhana intended to do, he sent to Draupadī a messenger whom she trusted, O bull-like heir of Bharata; and the Pāñcāla princess came to the hall and stood before her father-in-law Dhṛtarāṣṭra, weeping and wearing a single unbelted garment, for she was in the midst of her period. King Duryodhana looked at the faces before him and exultantly addressed the Sūta: 'Bring her right here, page! Let the Kurus speak to her face to face!'

Then the Sūta, who was obedient to his will but fearful of the anger of Drupada's daughter, put aside pride, and appealed once more to the courtiers: 'What should I say to Draupadī Kṛṣṇā?'

'Look, Duḥśāsana,' said Duryodhana, 'this idiot son of a Sūta of mine is frightened of wolf-belly Bhīma! Lay hold of Drupada's daughter yourself, and bring her here. Our rivals are powerless: what can they do?'

Prince Duḥśāsana listened to his brother, then arose, his eyes red with
anger. He entered the quarters of the mighty chariot-fighters, and spoke
to Princess Draupadī. 'Come, Pāñcāla girl, come! You have been won. 20
Put aside modesty, Draupadī, and look upon Duryodhana with your
long lotus-eyes! Now you must transfer your affections to the Kurus,
for they have won you fairly. Come to the hall!'

Then she arose, her heart full of grief, and she wiped her pale face
with her hand. In her distress she ran to the womenfolk of old King
Dhṛtarāṣṭra, the bull-like Kuru; but Duḥśāsana rushed at her, roaring
in fury, and grabbed the wife of the lord of men by her long, dark,
flowing hair. Her hair, which had been sprinkled with water purified
by *mantras* during the ritual bath concluding the great rite of the royal
consecration, was now handled roughly by Dhṛtarāṣṭra's son to slight the
Pāṇḍavas' manhood. Duḥśāsana laid hold of Draupadī Kṛṣṇā with her
deep black hair and led her towards the hall, unprotected in the midst
of her protectors, dragging her as the wind drags at a battered plantain
tree. As she was dragged along, she bowed her slender body low and 25
spoke softly: 'Today I am in the midst of my period, dull-witted prince,
and I am wearing a single garment! You ignoble man, you should not
take me to the hall!'

But he held Draupadī Kṛṣṇā firm by her black hair, and he said to her, 'Call for aid to Arjuna and Kṛṣṇa, to Nara and Nārāyaṇa; I am taking you! You may be in the midst of your period, daughter of Drupada, and you may be wearing a single garment or, indeed, none at all; you have been won at gambling and you have been made our slave! Enjoy your pleasures now amongst our other slave-girls!'

Her hair was dishevelled and her garment fallen half off through

Duḥśāsana's manhandling. But, modest and burning with anger, Drau-
padī Kṛṣṇā softly spoke these words: 'The men here in this hall expound
learned texts and perform the rituals; all of them are warriors like Indra;
all of them are my elders or as good as my elders. I cannot stand before
30 them like this! You are acting cruelly and ignobly. Do not strip my
clothes from me! Do not drag me! The princes could never forgive
what you are doing, even if the very gods with Indra were to take your
side!

'King Yudhiṣṭhira is the son of Dharma and abides by *dharma*, and
*dharma* is subtle, requiring skill to understand it. I would not wish even a
word of mine to deviate from virtue and bring my lord the least atom of
blame. But for you to drag me into the midst of the Kuru heroes in the
midst of my period is ignoble; and nobody here shows me any respect!
Clearly they all approve your way of thinking. A curse upon you! The
*dharma* of the Bhāratas is destroyed, and so is adherence to the Kṣatriya
way, for every one of the Kurus in this hall is watching whilst the limits
of Kuru *dharma* are breached. Droṇa has no mettle, nor Bhīṣma, nor,
for sure, noble King Dhṛtarāṣṭra here, for they, the seniormost of the
Kurus, take no notice of this savage violation of *dharma*!'

35 Thus the slender-waisted lady lamented, and she gazed at her furious
husbands, inflaming the Pāṇḍavas with her glances till they were ready
to burst with anger. Neither the loss of their kingship, nor that of their
wealth or their finest jewels, caused them to grieve as did the angry gaze
that Draupadī Kṛṣṇā directed at them in her distress.

As for Duḥśāsana, when he saw her looking at her wretched husbands,
he shook her roughly till she nearly fainted, and 'Slave!' he said with
a savage laugh. And Karṇa praised his words, laughing aloud in great
glee; and Subala's son, Śakuni king of Gāndhāra, likewise applauded
Duḥśāsana. But apart from these two, and from Duryodhana son of
Dhṛtarāṣṭra, the other courtiers who were present were greatly grieved
to see Draupadī Kṛṣṇā dragged into the hall.

40 'Good lady,' said Bhīṣma, 'it is true that *dharma* is subtle, so that
I cannot properly decide this question of yours; for I recognize that
whilst a man without property cannot wager the property of another,
a woman is always subservient to her husband. Pāṇḍu's son Yudhiṣṭhira
would give up the world and all its wealth, but he would never abandon

truth, and he stated that he had been won; this is why I cannot judge this question of yours. Śakuni is unequalled among men at gambling, but he allowed Yudhiṣṭhira son of Kuntī free choice, and that noble man did not consider that what took place was deceit; this is why I cannot address this question of yours.'

'The king was challenged in this hall by skilled gamblers,' replied
Draupadī, 'by wicked, ignoble deceivers, men who love gambling,
while he had had little practice. How can you say that he was allowed
free choice? Foremost among the Kurus and the Pāṇḍavas, he is pure
by nature and does not understand the ways of deceit; that is why, even
though he had been won by all of them conspiring together, he agreed
to wager me afterwards. Let all the Kurus present in this hall, men with 45
sons and daughters-in-law under their authority, consider what I have
said, and properly decide this question of mine!'

Thus she lamented and wept, gazing over and over again at her husbands, while Duḥśāsana spoke to her words that were harsh and hateful and bitter. Dragged along in the midst of her period, with her garment slipping from her, though she least deserved such treatment – wolf-belly Bhīma looked at her, and then at Yudhiṣṭhira, and in his unbearable distress he gave vent to his fury.

**[61]** 'The gamblers in this land have their whores, Yudhiṣṭhira,' he
said, 'but they do not wager them; indeed, they show them kindness!
The offerings of wealth and other fine goods that the king of Kāśi
brought, the jewels that other kings presented to us, our steeds, our
riches, our armour, our weapons, our kingdom, we ourselves and you
yourself, have all been wagered and won by others, and this has not
angered me, for you are master of all we own. But it seems to me
that in staking Draupadī you went too far. The girl does not deserve 5
this; she has joined herself to the Pāṇḍavas, yet, thanks to you, she is
tormented by base, cruel, deceitful Kauravas! It is for her sake that I
turn my fury on you, king. I shall burn these arms of yours! Fetch fire,
Sahadeva!'

'Bhīma!' said Arjuna. 'Never before have you spoken such words! Our cruel enemies must have destroyed your respect for *dharma*. You should not give those enemies what they desire. Practise highest *dharma*, and do not rebel against your righteous elder brother; for if a king is challenged by others, he should recall his Kṣatriya *dharma* and gamble at their wish: this brings us great glory!'

10 'Wealth-winner Arjuna,' answered Bhīma, 'if I believed that he had acted out of self-indulgence, I would overpower him and burn his two arms in a blazing fire!'

Now when Dhṛtarāṣṭra's son Vikarṇa saw the Pāṇḍavas so distressed, and Draupadī in such torment, he spoke these words: 'Princes, you must decide the matter put to you by Drupada's daughter; if we fail to judge this matter we shall go straight to hell! Bhīṣma and Dhṛtarāṣṭra, the two seniormost of the Kurus, both say nothing, and so does sagacious Vidura; Bharadvāja's son Droṇa, the Teacher of us all, and Kṛpa too, the
15 two truest of Brahmins, do not address this question. But the other lords of the earth who are assembled here from every quarter should put aside personal anger and desire, and speak as they judge. Fair Draupadī has raised this matter repeatedly; consider it, princes, and give your answer: which of you takes which side?'

Many times Vikarṇa addressed all those courtiers thus, but the lords of the earth did not reply to him, whether for good or ill. Then, after speaking so several times to them all, he wrung his hands, exhaled deeply, and said, 'Decide the matter, or decide it not, lords of the earth! Either way, O Kauravas, I shall tell you what I think
20 proper in this case. It is said, O best of men, that kings are subject to four vices: hunting, drinking, dicing and excessive sexual indulgence. The man who is addicted to these lives his life shunning *dharma*, and the world holds the deeds of such an unfit person to be of no account.

'Pāṇḍu's son entered upon the wager of Draupadī when he was utterly given over to one such vice, having been challenged by cheating gamesters; further, this blameless girl is the common wife of all of the Pāṇḍavas, and the wager was made by Yudhiṣṭhira after he himself had been lost; what is more, it was Subala's son Śakuni himself who first named Draupadī Kṛṣṇā when he was seeking a stake. Bearing all this in mind, I consider that she has not been won.'

25 At these words, there arose in the hall a great uproar of voices praising Vikarṇa and condemning Śakuni. When the noise was stilled, Rādhā's son Karṇa, nearly swooning with rage, brandished a handsome arm and

spoke: 'Many perversities are to be seen in Vikarṇa, which, though they spring from him, will destroy him as fire burns the firestick that kindles it. These princes have said not a word, for all the pleading of Draupadī Kṛṣṇā: I think they think Drupada's daughter fairly won! Son of Dhṛtarāṣṭra, it is your own childish folly that tears you apart, so that you, a boy, speak an old man's words in the midst of the assembly. Nor do you truly understand *dharma*, dull-witted younger brother of Duryodhana, if you claim that Draupadī has not been won, when won she was! How can you think Kṛṣṇā not won, son of Dhṛtarāṣṭra, when Pāṇḍu's eldest son staked all his possessions in this hall, and Draupadī was one of those possessions? How can you think Kṛṣṇā not won, bull-like heir of Bharata, when she was fairly won? Draupadī was named aloud, and the Pāṇḍavas assented; so for what reason do you think her not won?

'Or perhaps you think it was not right that she was brought to this hall wearing a single garment; well, hear my superior view of this issue too. The gods ordain one husband for a woman, heir of Kuru, yet she submits to several: thus she is clearly a whore, and in my judgement it is not remarkable that she should be brought to the hall, or that she should be wearing a single garment, or, indeed, none at all! Subala's son Śakuni fairly won all the Pāṇḍavas' wealth: whatever riches they possessed, and this woman, and themselves.

'Duḥśāsana, this Vikarṇa with his wise talk is just a foolish boy. Strip off the Pāṇḍavas' garments, and those of Draupadī too!'

When the Pāṇḍavas heard this, heir of Bharata, they all removed their upper garments and sat down in the hall. Then Duḥśāsana forcibly grabbed Draupadī's garment in the middle of the hall, O king, and began to pull it from her. But, lord of the peoples, as he pulled at Draupadī's garment, another garment just like it appeared, and this happened over and over again. At this, all the lords of the earth gave a dreadful cry as they saw this most wonderful sight in the world.

But Bhīma, wringing his hands, his lower lip throbbing in anger, loudly pronounced a curse in the midst of the kings: 'Kṣatriyas of the world, hear these words of mine that no other man ever spoke before, nor will ever speak again! Lords of the earth, may I not attain the realm of all my ancestors if, having said this, I do not carry it out; if in battle

I do not rip open the breast of this wicked sinner, this bastard Bhārata, and drink his blood!'

His words made the hair rise on everyone's body. Those who heard them did him great honour, and reviled Dhṛtarāṣṭra's son. As for Duḥśāsana, having amassed a pile of garments in the middle of the hall, he sat down, wearied and ashamed. The princes of men present in the hall uttered many a hair-raising cry of 'Alas! Alas!' when they saw the sons
50 of Kuntī; people called out, 'The Kauravas will not decide Draupadī's question!' and they censured Dhṛtarāṣṭra.

Now Vidura, expert in *dharma*, raised his arms to silence the courtiers, and spoke these words: 'Draupadī has posed this question; now she weeps pitifully as though she had no one to protect her, while you will not decide the matter! This is an affront to *dharma*, courtiers! The person who comes before the assembly in distress is like a blazing fire; the courtiers in that assembly extinguish the flames with truth and *dharma*. When such a distressed person poses a question on *dharma* to the courtiers, they should decide that question, putting
55 aside personal anger and desire. Vikarṇa has addressed the question according to his own wisdom, lords of men, and now you too should decide it, and speak as you judge. For if a member of an assembly who understands *dharma* will not decide such a question, half of the guilt of lying is his; and if a member of an assembly who understands *dharma* gives a false answer, the full guilt of lying is his, for sure!'

*To reinforce his point, Vidura now cites the story of Prahlāda, who gave true judgement against his own son;*[1] *but it is to no avail.*

The princes heard what Vidura had to say, but they spoke not a word. Then Karṇa said to Duḥśāsana, 'Take this slave-girl, Draupadī Kṛṣṇā, into the house!' And in the middle of the hall, Duḥśāsana dragged her away, wretched and ashamed, trembling and crying out pitifully to the Pāṇḍavas.

**[62]** 'I have a great duty that I should have performed before, but

1 For this story see 5.35, where the alternative form of name Prahrāda is used.

could not,' said Draupadī, 'because of my distress at being dragged here by force by this mighty man. I greet the elders in this assembly of Kurus! Let me not be blamed for not doing so sooner.' Then the wretched girl fell, partly from his manhandling and partly from grief, and there in the hall she lamented, for she was unused to such treatment.

'Kings once assembled in the arena to see me at my *svayaṃvara*, but otherwise I have never before been seen in public; and today I am brought into this hall! Till now in my own house neither wind nor sun has ever seen me; and today in the middle of this hall, this assembly of Kurus, I am exposed to the view of all! Till now in my own house the Pāṇḍavas would not permit the wind to touch me; and today they allow me to be touched by this wicked man! I think that fate has turned against me, for now these Kurus permit their daughter-in-law, their daughter, to be tormented when she does not deserve it! But worse than this is that I, a virtuous and upright woman, should today have to enter right into the middle of the hall! Where is the *dharma* of the lords of the earth? Formerly righteous women were not brought into the hall, or so we have been told; but this ancient eternal law has lapsed among the Kauravas! How could I – wife of the Pāṇḍavas, sister of Pṛṣata's heir Dhṛṣṭadyumna, friend of Kṛṣṇa Vāsudeva – enter this hall of kings?

'I am the wife of Yudhiṣṭhira lord of *dharma*, and equal to him by birth; tell me, am I slave or free? I shall abide by what you say, O Kauravas! But for this base man, defiler of the Kauravas' good name, to torment me so badly: that I shall not tolerate long! Whether you consider me won or unwon, kings, I want your answer; I shall abide by what you say, O Kauravas!'

Bhīṣma answered her: 'O fair one, I have already said that the way of *dharma* is the highest; not even noble priests can follow it in this world. And in this world whatever a powerful man regards as *dharma* is said by others to be *dharma*, even if it falls within the limits of *adharma*. I cannot judge this question of yours with certainty, because of the subtlety, profundity and seriousness of the issue.

'The end of this Kuru line must be at hand, since the Kurus are all devoted to greed and folly! Those born into such lines, O fair one, do not fall from the path of *dharma*, even when calamity overwhelms them; and you stand here as our daughter-in-law. Your conduct, Pāñcāla princess, is proper and befitting, for though you have met with misfortune, you still maintain your regard for *dharma*. These elders, Droṇa and the others, are experts in *dharma*, but they sit with heads down, as if they were dead men with empty bodies. However, in my judgement it is Yudhiṣṭhira himself who is the authority on this question of yours. He should tell you whether you are won or unwon.'

The lords of the earth saw everything that had happened, and Draupadī shrieking like a stricken osprey, but they spoke not a word, whether for good or ill, for they were frightened of Dhṛtarāṣṭra's son. And Dhṛtarāṣṭra's son saw that those sons and grandsons of princes were silenced, and then with a smile he spoke to the daughter of the king of Pāñcāla. 'Let this question of yours pass to Bhīma of noble mettle, to Arjuna, to Sahadeva, to your husband, to Nakula, O daughter of Drupada; let them address the matter you have raised. Let them decide for your sake, in the midst of these nobles, that Yudhiṣṭhira is not your master, Pāñcāla girl! Let them all make the lord of *dharma* a liar, and you will escape slavery! The noble lord of *dharma*, Indra-like Yudhiṣṭhira, abides by *dharma*: let him tell you this himself – is he your master, or is he not? Then when he has spoken, you must at once declare yourself his or ours. All these Kauravas here in the hall share in your own misery; that is why, when they see your husbands so unfortunate, these heroes of noble mettle cannot decide your case.'

Now all the courtiers present there gave loud applause to the words of the Kuru king: they waved their garments and roared, though cries of woe were also heard. All the princes were delighted, and they did honour to righteous Duryodhana, best of Kurus. All of them regarded Yudhiṣṭhira out of the corners of their eyes, wondering what the expert in *dharma* would say, filled with the greatest curiosity too to know what Arjuna Bībhatsu, the Pāṇḍava undefeated in battle, would say, and Bhīma, and the twins.

When the noise was stilled, Bhīma spoke, brandishing a mighty, well-formed, sandal-scented arm: 'If Yudhiṣṭhira lord of *dharma* were

not our elder and lord of our line, we should not forgive this! If the master of our merits and our austerities, the lord of our lives, considers himself won, we too are won. No mortal who walks the earth would have escaped me alive for laying hands on the hair of the Pāñcāla
princess here! Look at these two long, well-formed arms of mine, like 35
two iron bars! Not even Indra of a hundred sacrifices could escape once he had come between them! Bound as I am by the snares of *dharma*, I start no trouble: respect prevents me, and Arjuna is restraining me. But if the lord of *dharma* lets me loose, with my bare hands for weapons I shall ravage these wicked Dhārtarāṣṭras as a lion ravages lesser creatures!'

But now Bhīṣma, Droṇa and Vidura spoke to him: 'You must show forbearance! With you, anything may happen!'

**[63]** Karṇa said, 'They say that these three may hold no property: the slave, the student and the dependent woman. As the wife of a slave, lady, you are now the property of Duryodhana here, a slave-girl without husband, one of the slaves he owns. So enter our house, and favour us with your attentions: we bid you enter, and we assign you this duty! We Dhārtarāṣṭras are now all your lords, princess, not the sons of Pāṇḍu! Lovely one, quickly choose another husband, one who will not wager you into slavery! Among slaves, as you know, a sensual disposition towards one's masters is never taken amiss: let yours be so!

'Nakula is defeated; so is Bhīma; so are Yudhiṣṭhira, Sahadeva and Arjuna. Enter our house as our slave, daughter of Drupada, for those
who have been defeated are no longer your husbands. What value to 5
himself can Kuntī's son put upon his valour and his manliness, to gamble away in the midst of the assembly this daughter of Drupada, king of Pāñcāla?'

When unforbearing Bhīma heard this, he snorted furiously in his distress; but, loyal to King Yudhiṣṭhira and bound by the snares of *dharma*, he merely turned his angry red eyes upon Karṇa as if to burn him up. 'O king,' he said, 'I am not angry with this son of a Sūta, for in truth this is the *dharma* of slaves, which is now ours. But how would our enemies have resisted me today if you had not wagered this lady, lord of men?'

As for King Duryodhana, when he heard the words of Rādhā's son
Karṇa, he addressed Yudhiṣṭhira who sat silent before him, nearly out of
his mind: 'O king, Bhīma, Arjuna and the twins accept your authority.
Decide the question of whether you consider Draupadī Kṛṣṇā unwon!'
10 Then, after speaking thus to Kuntī's son, he drew apart his garment, and,
looking at the Pāñcāla princess with the smile of a man intoxicated by
absolute power, to amuse Rādhā's son and outrage Bhīma, he exposed
to the gaze of Draupadī – long like a plantain-stem, graced with every
auspicious mark, firm as an elephant's trunk, strong as adamant – his
own left thigh.

Wolf-belly Bhīma saw this. Opening wide his red eyes, he announced
to him in the midst of the kings, as if declaiming it to the entire assembly,
'May the wolf-belly not share his ancestors' realm if in a mighty battle
15 I do not smash that thigh with my club!' So great was his rage that
fiery flames issued forth from his every orifice, as from the hollows of a
burning tree.

'Behold the great danger that you face from Bhīma!' said Vidura.
'Take note of it: it is like the noose of King Varuṇa![1] Be sure that this
terrible disaster that has arisen amongst the Bhāratas was directed from
the first by fate. You sons of Dhṛtarāṣṭra, you have wagered for excessive
stakes, and now you dispute over this woman in the hall. Your security
seems in great danger, for the Kurus are engaging in wicked plots. Learn
quickly your *dharma*! If it is not well understood, the whole assembly
will be befouled!

'If the gambler Yudhiṣṭhira had wagered this woman earlier, before
losing himself, he would have been her master. But, as I judge it,
property wagered by one not its owner is like property won in a dream!
When you hear what Gāndhārī's son Duryodhana has to say, do not
deviate from this *dharma*, Kurus!'

20 'I shall abide by the word of Bhīma,' said Duryodhana; 'likewise that
of Arjuna and of the twins too. If they will declare that Yudhiṣṭhira was
not their master, then Drupada's daughter will escape slavery.'

'When first he staked us,' Arjuna replied, 'King Yudhiṣṭhira, the noble

1 See note to 2.12.11. One of Varuṇa's functions in the Vedic period was the punishment of sinners, whom he bound in fetters.

lord of *dharma*, Kuntī's son, was our master. But whose master was he after losing himself? That is what all of you Kurus must decide!'

And then in the house of King Dhṛtarāṣṭra a jackal howled loudly in the chamber of the sacred fire. Asses gave answer, king, and so did frightful birds all around. Sagacious Vidura heard this dreadful noise, as did Śakuni son of Subala. Bhīṣma, Droṇa and learned Kṛpa heir of Gotama loudly called out blessings. Then Gāndhārī and the learned Vidura in great distress informed the king of the terrible portent they had witnessed, at which the king spoke these words: 'Dull-witted prince Duryodhana, you have brought down destruction upon yourself for speaking discourteously in the assembly to a woman belonging to these bull-like Kurus, and especially to Draupadī, their lawful wife!'

Then wise Dhṛtarāṣṭra, who wished his Pāṇḍava kinsmen well, withdrew; and after wise reflection the sagacious king addressed Drupada's daughter Kṛṣṇā in conciliatory tones: 'Daughter of Drupada, choose from me whatever boon you wish, for among my daughters-in-law you are the most distinguished in your devotion to *dharma*!'

'If you are granting me a boon, bull-like heir of Bharata,' answered Draupadī, 'my choice is that glorious Yudhiṣṭhira, who observes all *dharma*, should be freed from slavery. For I would not have ignorant boys cry out, "Here is the slave's son!" when they see my spirited son Prativindhya coming. Having been once a king's son, and cherished like no other man, he would die, heir of Bharata, if he found he was now the son of a slave.'

'Lady, I give you a second boon,' said Dhṛtarāṣṭra. 'Choose one from me, for my heart grants it. A single boon is not worthy of you!'

'For my second boon,' Draupadī replied, 'I choose Bhīma, wealth-winner Arjuna, Nakula and Sahadeva, with their chariots and their bows.'

'Choose a third from me,' Dhṛtarāṣṭra now said; 'two do not do you sufficient honour, for of all my daughters-in-law you are best in the practice of *dharma*!'

'Blessed sir,' said Draupadī, 'greed destroys *dharma*. I cannot take a third boon from you, for I am not worthy, truest of kings. They say that the Vaiśya receives one boon, the Kṣatriya woman two, while three boons are for the king, prince of kings, and a hundred boons for the Brahmin. These husbands of mine were in terrible straits, but they have been rescued, and they will live to see good fortunes through acts of virtue, O king!'

**[64]** Karṇa said, 'Of all the women whose beauty we hear praised in the world, not one has done such a deed, as far as we have heard. When the sons of Kuntī and of Dhṛtarāṣṭra were filled with extreme rage, this Draupadī Kṛṣṇā became the Pāṇḍavas' deliverance; when they were sinking and drowning in a shifting, shipless ocean, this Pāñcāla princess became the boat that brought the Pāṇḍavas to land!'

When, in the midst of the Kurus, the unforbearing Bhīma heard this – that the Pāṇḍavas had been rescued by a woman – he said, with angry heart, 'According to Devala there are three lights in a man: offspring, deeds and learning. Through these, creatures attain being, for when the body, impure, lifeless and empty, is cast away by one's kin, it is these three that still exist of a man. But one of our lights has been put out, because our wife has been tainted: how, wealth-winner Arjuna, can offspring be born from a tainted woman?'

'Bhāratas never respond to the insults of the base,' answered Arjuna, 'whether these are spoken or unspoken; they remain always the most superior of men. Virtuous folk remember only the kindnesses they have been shown, not the acts of hostility; they have the self-confidence to distinguish between the two.'

'Right here, right now,' said Bhīma to Yudhiṣṭhira, 'I shall slay all these assembled enemies! Step outside, prince of kings, and cut them down, roots and all! Why should we trouble to discuss it? I shall kill them here and now, and you shall rule the earth!' With these words, Bhīma, who was surrounded by his younger brothers like a lion surrounded by deer, began to glance repeatedly towards his club. Kuntī's son Arjuna tirelessly calmed him and cooled him, but the strong-armed hero was sweating with his inner burning. So great was his rage, lord of men, that from his ears and other orifices a fiery flame issued forth, smoking and sparking; his puckered frown contorted his face till he appeared like Death at the time of doomsday.

Yudhiṣṭhira restrained the strong-armed hero with his own arm: 'Do not do this!' he said to him; 'stand easy, heir of Bharata!' Then, when he had restrained mighty Bhīma, whose eyes were red with anger, he joined his hands together and approached his father Dhṛtarāṣṭra.

**[65]** 'O king,' said Yudhiṣṭhira, 'what should we do for you? Command us: you are our lord, and our wish is always to remain under your authority, heir of Bharata!'

'Bless you, Yudhiṣṭhira Ajātaśatru!' replied Dhṛtarāṣṭra. 'You have my leave to go in peace and welfare, with all your wealth. Rule your own kingdom! But give due thought to this, an old man's command which I utter with all my wisdom: it will confer the greatest benefit upon you.

'You know, Yudhiṣṭhira my son, that the way of all the *dharmas* is subtle: you are courteous and wise, and you wait upon your elders. Where there is intelligence there is peace. Attain peace, heir of Bharata! An axe makes no impression on a non-wooden object, but on wood it is wielded to effect; the most superior of men take no heed of acts of hostility, for they see virtues, not faults, and they do not indulge in strife. Base men may utter insults in a dispute, Yudhiṣṭhira, and middling men reply with insults of their own; but the wise never respond to hurtful insults, whether these are spoken or unspoken; they remain always the most superior of men. Virtuous folk remember only the kindnesses they have been shown, not the acts of hostility; they have the self-confidence to distinguish between the two. Your own behaviour in this honourable assembly has been noble; therefore, my son, do not take Duryodhana's insulting behaviour to heart.

'Heir of Bharata, look at your mother Gāndhārī; look too at me, your old blind father who stands here praying for your virtues. I connived at this gambling match for the sake of seeing: I wished to see my friends, and also my sons' strengths and weaknesses.

'With you as ruler, O king, and wise Vidura, learned in every lore, as minister, the Kurus are to be envied! In you is *dharma*, in Arjuna heroism, in Bhīma valour, and in the twins, those foremost of men, are faith and obedience to elders. Bless you, Yudhiṣṭhira Ajātaśatru! Return to Khāṇḍavaprastha. May there be brotherhood with your Dhārtarāṣṭra brothers, and may your heart reflect on *dharma*.'

When Yudhiṣṭhira, best heir of Bharata and lord of *dharma*, heard these words, he gave his full assent in due form and departed with his brothers. They mounted their cloud-like chariots, and together with Draupadī Kṛṣṇā they set forth with hearts full of joy for Indraprastha, best of cities.

## THE SECOND GAMBLING MATCH

Vaiśaṃpāyana spoke:
**[66]** O king, when Duḥśāsana learnt that wise Dhṛtarāṣṭra had given the Pāṇḍavas leave to depart, he went at once to his brother. Best heir of Bharata, he found Duryodhana in the company of his ministers, and in his distress, O bull-like heir of Bharata, he spoke these words to him: 'That old man is throwing away everything that we took such trouble to acquire; he has handed our wealth over to our enemy! Understand this, mighty chariot-fighters!'

Duryodhana, Karṇa and Śakuni son of Subala now plotted together in their pride against the Pāṇḍavas. They hastily approached wise King Dhṛtarāṣṭra son of Vicitravīrya, and addressed him in bland tones.

'Have you not heard, O king,' said Duryodhana, 'what Bṛhaspati, the learned household priest of the gods, said to Indra when he expounded governance to him? "Tormentor of your enemies, enemies should be slain by every means, before they do you harm through war or through force." Now if we were to use the Pāṇḍavas' wealth to pay honour to all the other princes, and then engage the Pāṇḍavas themselves in battle, how could we fail?

'If a man places round his neck and on his back snakes of deadly venom, angry and ready to bite him, how can he cast them off again? The Pāṇḍavas are angry, father; they are armed and mounted in their chariots, and like angry snakes of deadly venom they will destroy us utterly! Arjuna goes about wearing battle-armour, with his two splendid arrow-cases opened; over and over again he takes up his bow Gāṇḍīva and looks about him, hissing. Wolf-belly Bhīma, we have heard, is brandishing his heavy club; he has hastened to yoke his chariot and has set out at speed. Nakula has taken up his sword and his shield decked with eight moons; he and Sahadeva and King Yudhiṣṭhira are making their attitude clear through their gestures. All of them have mounted their chariots, which are full of weapons and other gear; they are whipping up the chariot-teams and riding out to muster their army. They will never forgive us, since they suffered such injury at our hands – and which of them could forgive Draupadī's torment?

'Bless you, bull-like heir of Bharata! We should gamble again with the Pāṇḍavas for a stake of exile in the forest: in this way we shall be able to get them into our power! Whoever is defeated in the match, whether they or we ourselves, must enter the mighty forest for twelve years, clad in antelope-skins,[1] then dwell for a thirteenth year unrecognized in a populous place, and, if recognized, for a further twelve years in the forest.

'Let this wager proceed! Let the Pāṇḍavas throw the dice and gamble 20
again with us! This, bull-like king, is our most pressing duty, for Śakuni here knows in full how to win at dicing. We shall embrace our allies and establish ourselves firmly in the kingship, while we prepare an invincible army, vast and powerful; and then if, in the thirteenth year, they should succeed in completing their observance, we shall defeat them, O king! Give your approval, afflicter of your enemies!'

'By all means bring them back here,' replied Dhṛtarāṣṭra, 'even if they have travelled halfway! Let the Pāṇḍavas return, and let them gamble again!'

Thereupon Droṇa, Somadatta, the great chariot-fighter Bāhlika, 25
Vidura, Droṇa's son Aśvatthāman, Yuyutsu the heroic son of the Vaiśya woman,[2] Bhūriśravas, Bhīṣma son of Śaṃtanu, and the great chariot-fighter Vikarṇa – all of them said, 'Do not gamble again! Let there be peace!' But though all his friends opposed it, since they understood how matters stood, Dhṛtarāṣṭra had the Pāṇḍavas summoned, for he was fond of his son.

Now Gāndhārī, who had grown thin with grief, great king, spoke words of *dharma* to Dhṛtarāṣṭra lord of men, prompted by her love for

**1** As becomes explicit later (2.68.9), the losers are to be made to act out the observances undertaken by those who are about to perform a Vedic sacrifice, which include dressing in antelope-skins – without, of course, receiving the benefit that the ritual itself would bring. (When the hero of the *Rāmāyaṇa* is exiled, he is similarly told to wear the matted hair and bark-cloth garments of an ascetic: *Rāmāyaṇa* 2.16.25.)

**2** See 1.107.35–6.

her son: 'At Duryodhana's birth the sagacious chamberlain said, "He should be dispatched to the other world. He will certainly defile his
30 lineage, for no sooner was he born, heir of Bharata, than he howled like a jackal. It is plain that he will bring the line to its end; take note of this, O Kurus." My lord, you should not lend your approval to the opinions of immature boys! You should not become the cause of this terrible destruction of the line!

'Who would breach a dam once it was built? Who would fan flames that had died down? Kuntī's sons are resolved upon peace; who would stir them to new anger? You remember this, O Kaurava, but let me remind you again: learning teaches nothing to a fool, whether for good or ill! An old man like you, king, should never adopt a boy's opinions; your sons should be guided by you. They should not desert you and go
35 their own ways! Your judgement is founded on peace, *dharma*, and the judgement of another; let it not now turn against you. Wealth that is acquired through cruelty is easily lost, but when it grows gently it passes to sons and grandsons!'

Then the great king answered Gāndhārī, who understood *dharma*: 'By all means let the lineage end! I cannot prevent it. Let it be exactly as they desire; let the Pāṇḍavas return, and let my sons gamble again with the sons of Pāṇḍu!'

**[67]** Yudhiṣṭhira son of Kuntī had travelled halfway when a page addressed him at the command of wise King Dhṛtarāṣṭra. 'These are your father's words to you, heir of Bharata: "The hall has been made ready, king. O Yudhiṣṭhira son of Pāṇḍu, come, throw the dice and gamble!"'

'It is at fate's command that creatures experience good and ill,' replied Yudhiṣṭhira, 'and neither can be prevented if I must gamble again. I cannot reject a challenge to gamble with dice at the command of an elder, even though I know the destruction it will bring.'

5 With these words, Pāṇḍu's son turned back with his brothers; though he knew Śakuni's trickery, the son of Kuntī returned to gamble again. Once again the bull-like chariot-fighters entered that hall, bringing dismay to the hearts of their friends. They sat at their ease to resume the gambling, to destroy the whole world, for they were under fate's oppression.

Śakuni said, 'The old man returned your wealth to you, and I applaud that! But now, bull-like heir of Bharata, listen while I tell you of a single wager for a great stake. If we are defeated in the match by you, we must enter the mighty forest for twelve years, clad in the skins of *ruru* deer, then dwell for a thirteenth year unrecognized in a populous place, and, if recognized, for a further twelve years in the forest. If, on the other hand, you are defeated by us, you must dwell for twelve years in the forest together with Draupadī Kṛṣṇā, clad in antelope-skins. And when the thirteenth year is completed, the kingdom is to be returned again, by us or by yourselves, to its rightful owners. With this resolve, Yudhiṣṭhira heir of Bharata, come, throw the dice, and gamble again with us!'

'Woe and alas!' said the courtiers. 'Their kinsmen are not warning them of their great danger, and the bull-like heirs of Bharata themselves seem unaware that they should beware!'

Kuntī's son, the lord of men, heard many such murmurings, but, in his modesty and adherence to *dharma*, he returned to gamble again. Despite what he knew, the hero of mighty wisdom set the gambling in motion once more, hoping that it would not lead to the destruction of the Kurus. 'How could a king such as I, maintaining my *dharma*,' he said, 'refuse when challenged? Śakuni, I gamble with you!'

'Horses and cows, including many milkers,' said Śakuni; 'limitless sheep and goats; elephants; treasure and gold; slaves and slave-girls – all these are staked in this our single wager for exile in the forest, sons of Pāṇḍu! Whoever is defeated, you or ourselves, must go and dwell in the forest! With this resolve let us gamble, bull-like heir of Bharata, on a single throw for exile in the forest.'

Kuntī's son gave him assent; Subala's son took up the dice; and 'I have won!' said Śakuni to Yudhiṣṭhira.

[**68**] Kuntī's sons, defeated, turned their minds towards exile in the forest; one after another, they took antelope-skins for their upper garments. Then seeing those foe-tamers dressed in antelope-skins, stripped of their kingdom and setting out for the forest, Duḥśāsana said, 'Now the wheel of noble King Duryodhana's rule rolls forward, and the Pāṇḍavas are humiliated and overtaken by utter disaster! Today the gods themselves have stepped forth along their smooth sky-paths, so

5 that we are better and older and greater than our enemies! Kuntī's sons have been plunged into hell, for a long time, for ever! They are stripped of their happiness and of their kingdom; they are lost for endless years! Pāṇḍu's sons, who have always laughed at the sons of Dhṛtarāṣṭra in the intoxication of their might, are now defeated and stripped of their wealth, and they are going to the forest! Let them cast off the bright armour they wore, and these shining, heavenly garments; let them all wear skins of *ruru* deer, for they assented to the wager with Subala's son! Always they fed their minds with the one thought: "In the three worlds there are no other men such as we." Now those same Pāṇḍavas will come to know themselves in adversity, barren as sterile sesame seeds!

'You are men of such spirit, O Kaurava; but do not imagine that these new garments confer any benefit upon you. Behold, the mighty Pāṇḍavas are dressed in sacrificial antelope-skins – but they have undergone no rite of initiation![1]

10 'Wise King Drupada has done an ill deed in giving his daughter, the Pāñcāla princess, to the Pāṇḍavas, for Kuntī's sons are now eunuchs; they are no husbands for Draupadī! When you see them in the forest, daughter of Drupada, stripped of wealth and rank and forced to wear antelope-skins instead of fine clothes, what pleasure will be yours? Choose another husband, whoever you wish! All the Kurus assembled here are patient and forbearing, and they are very wealthy; so choose one of them for your husband! Do not let this reversal of fortune cause you pain! The Pāṇḍavas are barren; they are just like sterile sesame seeds, or leather effigies of animals, or grainless barley plants. Why should you wait upon the fallen sons of Pāṇḍu? It is wasted labour, like tending barren sesame seeds!'

Such were the insults that Dhṛtarāṣṭra's cruel son hurled at the
15 Pāṇḍavas. When unforbearing Bhīma heard them, he reviled him loudly, and angrily checked him; he rushed at him, like a mountain lion at a jackal, and said, 'Vicious man! Your speech may give pleasure to the wicked, but it is not justified by any accomplishment on your part, for in the midst of these kings it is Śakuni's skill of which you boast! Well,

1 See note to 2.66.18. The following verses make it clear that among the elements of the Pāṇḍavas' thirteen-year 'observance' is celibacy.

just as you strike here at our vital organs with the arrows of your words,
so I shall remind you of them when I cut open your vital organs in
battle! And as for your protectors, who follow you because they are in
thrall to desire and greed, I shall dispatch them and their followers to
the realm of Yama!'

As Bhīma spoke these words, clad in antelope-skins and overwhelmed
with grief, but holding to the path of his *dharma*, the shameless Duḥśāsana
danced round him in the midst of the Kurus, calling out 'Cow! Cow!'

'Duḥśāsana,' answered Bhīma, 'your talent is the cruel, the harsh, 20
the vicious. Who but you could boast after acquiring wealth through
deceit? May Kuntī's son, the wolf-belly, not attain the realms of the
virtuous if he does not rip open your breast and drink your blood in
battle! Once I have slain the sons of Dhṛtarāṣṭra before the very eyes of
all their bowmen, then I shall soon find peace: I tell you this truthfully.'

Now, in his joy, foolish King Duryodhana amused himself by imitating
Bhīma's lion-like walk as the Pāṇḍavas left the hall. The wolf-belly turned
half round, and said, 'Fool! You achieve nothing by this, for I shall soon
make my reply to you, and remind you of your deeds, by killing you
and your followers!' Then, though he had seen himself slighted, Bhīma, 25
mighty and proud, restrained his anger, for he was loyal to his king.
In the assembly of the Kauravas, as he was leaving, he spoke these
words: 'I shall slay Duryodhana; wealth-winner Arjuna will slay Karṇa;
and Sahadeva will slay the cheating gamester Śakuni. And in the midst
of this assembly I shall again pronounce my mighty vow – the gods
will make it come true when we engage in combat – I shall kill this
wicked Duryodhana with my club in battle, and trample his head into
the ground with my foot! As for this cruel, wicked Duḥśāsana, this
self-styled hero, like a lion I shall drink his blood!'

'Bhīma,' said Arjuna, 'the resolve of the virtuous is not known 30
through words alone: in the fourteenth year from now, they shall see
what happens! The earth will drink the blood of Duryodhana, Karṇa,
the wicked Śakuni, and Duḥśāsana! At your command, O Bhīma, I shall
slay in battle Karṇa, the speaker of envy, the instigator of wicked people!
Arjuna promises, as a favour to Bhīma: with my feathered arrows I shall
kill Karṇa and his followers in battle!

'As for any other kings who are foolish enough to fight against me,

I shall dispatch them all to the realm of Yama with my sharp arrows. Mount Himālaya will shift position, the sun will grow dim, the moon lose its coolness, if my truth should falter; so if, in the fourteenth year from now, Duryodhana does not return the kingdom with due honour, this will all come true!'

When Arjuna had spoken, Mādrī's glorious son Sahadeva of mighty energy brandished a mighty arm; full of longing to achieve the death of Subala's son Śakuni, he spoke these words, hissing like a snake, his eyes red with rage: 'Fool and defiler of the good name of the Gāndhāras! What you suppose to be dice are not dice; they are sharp arrows, and you have chosen them for yourself in battle! I shall carry out the task Bhīma assigned me regarding you and your kin; you had best complete all your own tasks! I shall attack you and your kin in battle, and swiftly slay you, if, son of Subala, you will stand and fight according to Kṣatriya *dharma*.'

After Sahadeva had spoken, lord of the peoples, Nakula too, the most handsome of men, spoke these words: 'The wicked Dhārtarāṣṭras who, to remain in Duryodhana's favour, insulted Drupada's daughter in this gambling match, are seeking their own deaths, urged on by fate; I shall show many of them Yama's realm! At the command of Yudhiṣṭhira lord of *dharma*, and following Draupadī's path, I shall soon rid the earth of Dhṛtarāṣṭra's sons!'

*The brothers now go to Dhṛtarāṣṭra.* **[69]** *Yudhiṣṭhira bids farewell to the Kauravas. Vidura says that Kuntī shall stay in his house while the Pāṇḍavas are away.*

**[70]** *Draupadī bids Kuntī farewell and goes forth, weeping, still wearing her menstrual garment, her hair unfastened. Kuntī, lamenting bitterly, bids farewell to her sons, who then leave for the forest. Vidura takes Kuntī to his house; then he receives a summons from Dhṛtarāṣṭra, and goes to see him.*

**[71]** *Dhṛtarāṣṭra asks about the manner of the Pāṇḍavas' departure, and Vidura describes how Yudhiṣṭhira covered his eyes to avoid burning those on whom his gaze fell; Bhīma showed the might of his arms; Arjuna sprinkled sand to indicate the numberless arrows he would shoot at his enemies; Nakula and Sahadeva disguised their appearance with mud and dust; Draupadī went stained and dishevelled, in token that in the fourteenth year the wives of her* *enemies would grieve over their slain menfolk; Dhaumya sang the hymns for the dead, in token that the same hymns would later be sung for the Kauravas. There were terrible portents as the Pāṇḍavas left the city. Now Nārada appears, pronounces that in the fourteenth year the Kauravas will perish, and vanishes.*

*Duryodhana, Karṇa and Śakuni appeal to Droṇa for support; he assents, but adds that Drupada's son Dhṛṣṭadyumna, who is to kill him, has sided with the Pāṇḍavas. In the fourteenth year the Kauravas will be slaughtered: better to make peace. Dhṛtarāṣṭra is of the same opinion.*

**[72]** *Saṃjaya tells Dhṛtarāṣṭra that the coming destruction is his fault. Dhṛtarāṣṭra blames fate and the actions of those who insulted Draupadī; Vidura had given him good advice, but, from partiality towards his son, he had not taken it.*

# THE FOREST

## THE FOREST

[1] — *Janamejaya asks Vaiśaṃpāyana to tell how the Pāṇḍavas fared after their defeat at dicing, and Vaiśaṃpāyana begins to narrate. — The Pāṇḍavas, together with Draupadī and a small number of attendants, leave Hāstinapura and head north. The people of the city, reviling the Kauravas, follow them with the intention of sharing their exile, but at Yudhiṣṭhira's entreaty they agree sadly to return to their homes. The Pāṇḍavas travel on, accompanied by a group of Brahmins; they camp for the night on the bank of the Gaṅgā.*

[2] *In the morning, Yudhiṣṭhira attempts to persuade the Brahmins to return: hardships lie ahead, and he will not be able to provide for them. But the Brahmins insist that they wish to remain with him in the forest. One of their number, the wise Śaunaka, instructs Yudhiṣṭhira: love and the passion it arouses are to be shunned; wealth does not bring happiness; sensual pleasures lead to destruction. He advises Yudhiṣṭhira to practise austerities.* [3] *Yudhiṣṭhira approaches Dhaumya, his priest, and asks how he may provide for the Brahmins; Dhaumya advises him to turn to the Sun, source of all nourishment. Yudhiṣṭhira now performs austerities and worships the Sun, invoking him under his hundred and eight names.* [4] *The Sun reveals himself to Yudhiṣṭhira and promises to provide him with food for twelve years; Yudhiṣṭhira now feeds the Brahmins and his brothers. Then they all travel on to the Kāmyaka forest.*

[5] *Meanwhile, Dhṛtarāṣṭra consults Vidura and asks him how the loyalty of the people may be secured. Vidura's advice is to restore the Pāṇḍavas and repudiate Śakuni; otherwise the Kurus will be destroyed. But Dhṛtarāṣṭra rejects this counsel and dismisses Vidura, who sets out to join the Pāṇḍavas.*

[6] *The Pāṇḍavas have reached the Kāmyaka forest and settled there. Vidura*

*arrives; Yudhiṣṭhira is fearful that he brings yet another summons to gamble, but greets him with honour. Vidura explains that Dhṛtarāṣṭra has rejected him for advocating a policy of conciliation; Yudhiṣṭhira replies that he will himself adhere to that policy.*

[7] *Dhṛtarāṣṭra is overcome with grief at his treatment of Vidura, and sends Saṃjaya to find him and bring him back. Saṃjaya travels to the Kāmyaka forest and finds Vidura there with the Pāṇḍavas. Vidura agrees to his request and returns with him to Hāstinapura; he forgives Dhṛtarāṣṭra, and the two are reconciled.*

[8] *When Duryodhana hears the news of the reconciliation between Dhṛtarāṣṭra and Vidura, he is enraged, fearing that the Pāṇḍavas will be restored. Śakuni, Duḥśāsana and Karṇa all agree that this will not happen; but Karṇa then proposes that the four of them should go and kill the Pāṇḍavas, and this is joyfully agreed upon. They set forth in their chariots; but Kṛṣṇa Dvaipāyana Vyāsa, perceiving with his divine insight what they are doing, arrives and stops them. Then he goes to see Dhṛtarāṣṭra,* [9] *and warns him that his son's hatred of the Pāṇḍavas will bring catastrophe. The advice of the elders should be heeded: Dhṛtarāṣṭra should reject Duryodhana and make peace with the Pāṇḍavas.*

[10] *Dhṛtarāṣṭra ascribes the unfolding disaster to fate and his love for his son. Vyāsa agrees that love for a son overcomes everything else, and tells the story of the cow Surabhi, who cried to Indra when a ploughman beat her son, until Indra sent heavy rain to stop the ploughing. The Pāṇḍavas are Vyāsa's own son's sons; therefore he urges Dhṛtarāṣṭra to make peace with them.*

[11] *Now the seer Maitreya arrives. He has met the Pāṇḍavas in the forest, and denounces Dhṛtarāṣṭra for conniving at Duryodhana's wrongdoing; then he addresses Duryodhana directly and tells him to make peace. Duryodhana says nothing. Maitreya now curses him: there will be a great war, in which Bhīma will smash his thigh with his club. Dhṛtarāṣṭra pleads; Maitreya replies that the curse will come to pass unless Duryodhana seeks peace. Then he leaves.*

## THE KILLING OF KIRMĪRA

[12] *Maitreya had mentioned that Bhīma had killed the Rākṣasa Kirmīra; Dhṛtarāṣṭra now asks Vidura to tell the story, and he does so. — When the Pāṇḍavas entered the Kāmyaka, they had encountered a dreadful Rākṣasa, the*

*terror of the forest; he gave his name as Kirmīra, and announced that he would kill and eat Bhīma in revenge for Bhīma's slaying of his brother Baka and his friend Hiḍimba. Bhīma had uprooted a tree and struck Kirmīra with it, but the Rākṣasa replied in kind. A fierce wrestling match then took place, which concluded with Bhīma strangling Kirmīra to death. Thus the forest had been made safe, and the Pāṇḍavas made their dwelling there.*

## THE MAN OF THE MOUNTAINS

[**13**] *The Pāṇḍavas are visited in the forest by their allies: the Bhojas, Vṛṣṇis and Andhakas with Kṛṣṇa, and the lords of the Pāñcālas, Cedis and Kekayas. Kṛṣṇa reviles the Kauravas; to calm him, Arjuna praises his many great deeds, after which Kṛṣṇa declares that Arjuna and he are Nara and Nārāyaṇa, and are one and the same. Now Draupadī comes to Kṛṣṇa and pays him honour. Then she pours out her woes – the terrible treatment she underwent in the hall while her mighty husbands did nothing to protect her, and all the suffering caused by Duryodhana's previous outrages. Weeping, she upbraids all those who have allowed her to suffer so: her husbands, sons, brothers, father and other kin, as well as Kṛṣṇa himself. In reply, Kṛṣṇa swears that the wives of her enemies will weep; Dhṛṣṭadyumna vows that he will kill Droṇa, Śikhaṇḍin will kill Bhīṣma, Bhīma will kill Duryodhana, and Arjuna will kill Karṇa.* [**14**] *Kṛṣṇa assures Draupadī that if he had been in Dvārakā when the gambling match took place he would have attended it and prevented the disaster.*

## THE KILLING OF THE LORD OF SAUBHA

[**15**] *Yudhiṣṭhira asks Kṛṣṇa why he had been absent from Dvārakā, and Kṛṣṇa replies that he had visited the city of Saubha in order to destroy it. Then he tells the story. — When Śālva the demonic lord of Saubha heard that Kṛṣṇa had killed Śiśupāla, he attacked Dvārakā, slaying many young Vṛṣṇi warriors and swearing to kill Kṛṣṇa himself. Then he flew off in his aerial city. After his return, Kṛṣṇa learnt what had happened; he found Śālva and challenged him, and after a long battle destroyed him and his demon forces.*

[**16**] — *Yudhiṣṭhira asks to hear this story in detail, and Kṛṣṇa begins to narrate. — Śālva launches a savage onslaught on Dvārakā, where strong defences are prepared.* [**17**] *The city is besieged and attacked; the Vṛṣṇi princes, Kṛṣṇa's own sons, rally to its defence. Sāmba does battle with Kṣemavṛddhi, Śālva's general, and forces him back; then he fights and kills the demon Vegavat. Cārudeṣṇa does battle with the great demon warrior Vivindhya and kills him. Pradyumna makes ready to attack Śālva himself,* [**18**] *and then attacks him fiercely; Śālva fights back equally fiercely. Śālva is briefly rendered unconscious by one of Pradyumna's arrows, but then recovers; he in turn reduces Pradyumna to unconsciousness, then showers arrows upon him.* [**19**] *Pradyumna's charioteer Dāruki carries him off the field, but Pradyumna, coming round, remonstrates with him and orders him to return.* [**20**] *Dāruki does as he is bidden, and drives Pradyumna back to the battle against Śālva. Pradyumna wards off Śālva's arrows, and overcomes him with arrows of his own. He is about to kill him when he receives a warning from the gods not to do so, as it is ordained that Kṛṣṇa will bring about his death. Śālva flees.*

[**21**] *When Kṛṣṇa himself returns to Dvārakā he finds the city in a sorry state. He sets out for Saubha, promising that he will destroy it and slay Śālva. Śālva sees him coming; he keeps Saubha in mid-air and showers down demonic weapons, but Kṛṣṇa counters them all.* [**22**] *The battle continues. A messenger comes to tell Kṛṣṇa that Śālva has killed his father Vasudeva; Kṛṣṇa reasons that this must mean that the rest of his family must also be dead, and is overcome by grief. But then he pulls himself together, deciding that the message is a trick.* [**23**] *He battles on, while Śālva attacks him with demonic illusions. He is buried under a hail of rocks, but breaks out. Then he launches his discus Sudarśana at Saubha; the city is cut in two, and falls to earth. The discus returns to Kṛṣṇa's hand, and finally he kills Śālva with it. — After telling this story to Yudhiṣṭhira, Kṛṣṇa leaves for Dvārakā. Dhṛṣṭadyumna and the Cedis and Kekayas also depart.*

[**24**] *The Pāṇḍavas continue on their way. The townsfolk accompanying them utter laments and revile Duryodhana; then they return to their homes.* [**25**] *Now the Pāṇḍavas consider where they should spend their exile; they agree on Lake Dvaitavana, and travel there. Reaching the lovely spot, they establish themselves*

*under a mighty tree.* **[26]** *The great seer Mārkaṇḍeya visits the Pāṇḍavas in their new home. He warns Yudhiṣṭhira not to commit* adharma *by resorting to force: he must serve out the full term of his exile.* **[27]** *The Brahmin Dālbhya Baka instructs Yudhiṣṭhira on the benefits for a Kṣatriya of maintaining close contact with Brahmins.*

**[28]** *Draupadī contrasts the Pāṇḍavas' present miserable state with the joy of the Kauravas at their downfall, and with the opulent life they themselves used to live. She censures Yudhiṣṭhira for his passivity in the face of all the hardships that she and his brothers must now endure, and asks how any true Kṣatriya could fail to be moved to anger at their plight.* **[29]** *Now she tells of the mighty demon Prahlāda's conversation with his grandson Bali: Bali had asked whether it was better to exercise forbearance or might, and Prahlāda had answered that different courses of action suit different occasions. In Draupadī's view the time for forbearance is past.*

**[30]** *Yudhiṣṭhira replies that anger leads to evil and should not be indulged; better far is forbearance.* **[31]** *Draupadī counters that Yudhiṣṭhira's adherence to* dharma *has not prevented catastrophe overtaking him. It is God, the ordainer, who commands all human actions, and humans are powerless to withstand his will; Draupadī censures him for causing Yudhiṣṭhira's downfall.* **[32]** *Yudhiṣṭhira remonstrates with Draupadī: he adheres to* dharma *not in hope of gain but because it is right. Proclaimed by wise seers,* dharma *is the only way to attain heaven. The rewards for practising* dharma *may be invisible to mortals, but they are assuredly real.*

**[33]** *Draupadī continues her plaint. All creatures must act; even what is fated by the ordainer results from a person's previous actions. Everything results from chance, fate and human endeavour; actions may succeed or fail, but one should not refrain from acting.*

**[34]** *Now Bhīma joins in the debate, and urges war against the Dhārtarāṣṭras. A* dharma *which brings nothing but harm is a false* dharma*; an excessive regard for* dharma *impedes the acquisition of wealth, and wealth is necessary for the proper practice of* dharma *itself. Yudhiṣṭhira should breach a lesser* dharma *to achieve a greater: he should fight to regain his kingdom.* **[35]** *Yudhiṣṭhira accepts that his actions have done them all great harm, but he insists that, having agreed to the gambling match, he must now accept the consequences. The time for vigorous action is long gone; they must all exercise forbearance.*

**[36]** *Bhīma speaks again. It does not befit a king to wait meekly, and all of*

*Yudhiṣṭhira's brothers long to do battle against those who have wronged them. Anyway, how can such mighty heroes as they go unrecognized for a year, as required by the wager? Instead they should cut short their exile and fight, as is the Kṣatriya's* dharma.

**[37]** *Yudhiṣṭhira warns that wilful, unplanned actions do not bring success. The Kauravas are armed and ready; to defeat them as things stand is impossible. Bhīma accepts that this is so. Kṛṣṇa Dvaipāyana Vyāsa now arrives and tells Yudhiṣṭhira not to fear; he imparts to him special knowledge which will allow Arjuna to overcome their enemies by acquiring celestial weapons. The Pāṇḍavas travel from Dvaitavana to the Kāmyaka forest.*

**[38]** *Yudhiṣṭhira teaches Arjuna the knowledge he received from Vyāsa, and tells him to travel north in search of the god Indra. Bearing his bow Gāṇḍīva, Arjuna receives Draupadī's blessing and sets out. He travels far over the mountains, till an ascetic stops him and attempts to turn him back. Arjuna refuses; the ascetic announces that he is in fact Indra, and grants Arjuna a boon. Arjuna chooses celestial weapons, and Indra replies that he will grant these once Arjuna has met Śiva.*

**[39]** *— Janamejaya asks Vaiśaṃpāyana to narrate the story of how Arjuna acquired the celestial weapons in detail, and Vaiśaṃpāyana agrees to do so. — Arjuna travels to the peak of Himālaya; he settles in a beautiful wood there and performs fierce austerities. The seers visit Śiva to warn him of what Arjuna is doing, but Śiva answers that Arjuna's aim is not one that need alarm them, and that he will grant his wish at once.*

**[40]** *Śiva now assumes the form of a man of the mountains; bearing a bow, he comes to where Arjuna is. Arjuna is on the point of shooting at Mūka, a demon who has taken on the form of a boar to attack him; the mountain man shoots too. Furious, Arjuna threatens to kill him. The mountain man echoes his threats, and they fight, shooting many arrows at each other. Arjuna is astonished to find that his arrows have no effect on his opponent; when he has exhausted his supply he resorts in turn to the bow Gāṇḍīva itself, a sword, and trees and rocks. Finally they wrestle with each other, and Arjuna is overcome. Śiva now praises Arjuna, who recognizes and propitiates the god.* **[41]** *He offers Arjuna a boon, and Arjuna chooses the Pāśupata Weapon, known as the Weapon of Brahmā's Head.*[1] *Śiva agrees, but warns him that, improperly used, the Weapon*

1 Presumably this 'realizes' Droṇa's gift of this Weapon to Arjuna at the end of 1.123.

*will destroy the entire world. After instructing Arjuna in its use, he returns to heaven.*

[**42**] *Now the world-guardian gods appear. Yama predicts that Arjuna will kill Karṇa, and gives him his staff; Varuṇa gives him his noose, and Kubera the Weapon of Disappearance. Indra tells Arjuna that he must visit him in heaven to receive further celestial weapons; he will send his own charioteer, Mātali, to take him there.*

## THE JOURNEY TO INDRA'S WORLD

[**43**] *Mātali arrives with Indra's magnificent chariot and tells Arjuna to mount. After bathing in the Gaṅgā, Arjuna does so. They fly up, and Arjuna sees the stars, which are really warriors who have attained heaven, seers, and other celestial beings. Then they reach Indra's city.* [**44**] *Arjuna looks at the lovely city and the heavenly garden Nandana. He is praised by celestial beings. He meets Indra, who embraces him and shares his throne with him.*

[**45**] *Indra gives Arjuna his thunderbolt; Arjuna remains with Indra for five years, and learns music and dancing from the Gandharva king Citrasena. The seer Lomaśa sees him sharing Indra's throne; Indra explains that Arjuna is his son, and that he and Kṛṣṇa, who are Nara and Nārāyaṇa, will defeat the Nivātakavaca demons, who are threatening the gods themselves from their underworld realm. Lomaśa himself should go to Kāmyaka to explain to Yudhiṣṭhira why Arjuna has been absent for so long, and to guide him on a pilgrimage. Lomaśa agrees to do so, and sets out.*

[**46**] *Meanwhile Dhṛtarāṣṭra, who has learnt from Vyāsa of Arjuna's doings, laments to Saṃjaya: Arjuna is enraged and invincible, and Duryodhana is bound to be defeated. Saṃjaya agrees with him. Dhṛtarāṣṭra adds that his son is a fool and is guided by fools; he cannot withstand Arjuna, Bhīma and Kṛṣṇa.*

[**47**] — *Janamejaya interrupts Vaiśaṃpāyana's narrative to ask what food the Pāṇḍavas had in the forest, and Vaiśaṃpāyana tells him that they and the Brahmins accompanying them lived well on forest produce and the flesh of deer.*

[**48**] — *Dhṛtarāṣṭra resumes his lament: the Pāṇḍava twins, Nakula and Sahadeva, are also mighty warriors, and together with Bhīma, Arjuna, Kṛṣṇa and the Pāṇḍavas' allies they will triumph in any war. Saṃjaya replies that the fault is Dhṛtarāṣṭra's own, for not restraining Duryodhana. He adds that,*

*after the Pāṇḍavas' downfall, Kṛṣṇa had vowed to vowed to reinstate them by destroying their enemies, but Yudhiṣṭhira had insisted that he wait for the term of exile to come to an end before doing so. Dhṛṣṭadyumna's Pāñcālas had likewise promised Draupadī that they would avenge the insult she had suffered.*

**[49]** *During Arjuna's absence in Indra's world, Bhīma turns on Yudhiṣṭhira once more: he is to blame for sending into danger the brother on whom the others all depend, and he is to blame for their exile in the forest. Bhīma once again urges an early attack on the Dhārtarāṣṭras. While Yudhiṣṭhira is attempting to calm him down, the seer Bṛhadaśva arrives. Yudhiṣṭhira greets him respectfully, then tells him how he was cheated in the gambling match; he concludes by saying that no one is more unfortunate than himself. Bṛhadaśva tells him of Nala, who suffered even more as a result of being cheated, and Yudhiṣṭhira asks to hear the story in full.*

## NALA

**[50]** *Bṛhadaśva begins to narrate. — Nala, king of Niṣadha, is a man of the highest virtues and accomplishments. King Bhīma of Vidarbha is similarly possessed of excellences, but has no children until the seer Damana grants him three sons and a lovely daughter, Damayantī. Though Nala and Damayantī have never met, they hear such wonderful things about each other that they fall in love. One day, Nala catches a goose; in return for its freedom the bird promises to win Damayantī over for him. When, in turn, it is caught by Damayantī, it urges her to marry Nala.*

**[51]** *Damayantī now pines; her father Bhīma decides to hold a* svayaṃvara *for her, and invites all the kings to attend. Indra asks the seers Parvata and Nārada, who have come to see him, why no kings are visiting him; they reply that they have all gone to Damayantī's* svayaṃvara. *At this, the world-guardian gods Indra, Yama and Varuṇa, and the Fire god Agni, decide to attend it themselves. On the way they see Nala travelling to the ceremony, and ask him to act as their envoy.* **[52]** *When he learns their purpose, Nala asks to be excused, since his mission is the same as theirs, but the gods insist. Through their power he is able to enter Damayantī's well-guarded dwelling. When he sees Damayantī his love increases, but he controls himself, informs her that four gods have come to seek her hand,*

*and tells her to choose one of them.* **[53]** *Damayantī assures Nala that her love is for him alone. He remonstrates; she proposes that he should attend the* svayaṃvara *together with the gods, and she will then choose him in their presence. Nala returns and tells the gods what has happened.*

**[54]** *The ceremony begins, and Damayantī finds herself confronted by five identical kings; she cannot tell which of them is Nala. She now appeals to the gods to show him to her, and they assume their divine forms. Damayantī recognizes Nala, and chooses him for her husband. The gods now give Nala eight boons. Indra grants sight of himself at sacrifices, and the ability to walk anywhere unobstructed; Agni grants the presence of fire wherever wanted, and immunity to fire; Yama grants excellent taste in food, and strict adherence to* dharma*; Varuṇa grants the presence of water wherever wanted, and a splendid garland. In addition, the gods together bestow on him twin children. They then return to heaven, and Nala lives a life of virtue and happiness with Damayantī.*

**[55]** *Indra now encounters Kali and Dvāpara, who are planning to attend the* svayaṃvara*. When he learns that it has already taken place, and what the outcome was, Kali is furious; he determines to possess Nala and ruin him, and he instructs Dvāpara to enter the dice.*

**[56]** *Kali and Dvāpara await their opportunity. Finally, in the twelfth year, Nala commits a minor ritual fault, and Kali enters him. He also causes Nala's brother Puṣkara to challenge him to a gambling match. Nala gambles obsessively, always losing. Damayantī tries to persuade him to talk to his ministers, but he takes no notice of her.* **[57]** *Unable to prevent Nala from losing everything, she takes the charioteer Vārṣṇeya into her confidence, and asks him to take her children to her relatives in Vidarbha.*

**[58]** *Nala is ruined; Puṣkara taunts him, suggesting he should wager Damayantī. Enraged, Nala leaves with nothing but a single garment. He stays outside the city, where he is joined by Damayantī; she too has only a single garment to wear. The townsfolk, under threat from Puṣkara, offer them no help. After some time the starving Nala sees some gold birds and attempts to catch them with his garment; they fly off with it, for they are the dice, and do not wish him to retain any possessions at all. Nala laments, and suggests that Damayantī should leave him and return to her home in Vidarbha, but she refuses to go without him.* **[59]** *Nala cannot bring himself to visit his father-in-law's house in such a condition. The* *two of them wander about, each covered with half a garment. They come upon a lodge, where Damayantī falls asleep on the ground. But Nala can find no rest, and after much toing and froing he finally decides to leave her and sets off, out of his mind and possessed by Kali.*

**[60]** *When Damayantī awakes to find Nala gone, she is terrified and laments bitterly, cursing the cause of Nala's grief to experience yet greater grief himself. A great constrictor attacks her; she is rescued by a hunter, who then seeks to seduce her. She curses him, and he falls down dead.*

**[61]** *Now Damayantī wanders alone through the great forest, calling on Nala to return to her. She sees a tiger and asks it either to give her news of Nala or to eat her, but it ignores her and goes its own way. She appeals to a mountain, but it remains silent. Next she comes upon a hermitage, and tells the ascetics there her story; they foretell that she will regain Nala, and then vanish. She continues on her way, pausing to ask an* aśoka *tree for news; then she encounters a caravan of merchants bound for Cedi,* **[62]** *and travels on with them. One night when encamped at a pool, the caravan is trampled by a herd of elephants that have come to drink. Damayantī blames herself. She continues her journey with Brahmins who have survived the slaughter and arrives in the city of the Cedis. The queen mother sees her and questions her; Damayantī answers truthfully, but without revealing her identity, and the queen mother engages her as a maidservant.*

**[63]** *Meanwhile, Nala sees a great forest fire and hears cries for help. Entering the fire, he finds the serpent king Karkoṭaka, who promises to help Nala if he rescues him. Karkoṭaka makes himself small, and Nala bears him out of the fire, but then Karkoṭaka insists he continue walking, counting his steps, and at the tenth step he bites him.*[1] *Nala loses his handsome appearance. Karkoṭaka explains that he has done this so that Nala will not be recognized, and assures him that the poison will harm not him but the being who has possessed him. He tells him to take up employment with King Ṛtuparṇa as a charioteer named Bāhuka; from Ṛtuparṇa he will learn the skill of gambling, which will allow him to regain what he has lost. Finally, he gives Nala a pair of garments which will restore his appearance, and vanishes.*

1 The Sanskrit word *daśa*, 'ten', also means 'bite!'

**[64]** *Nala reaches Ṛtuparṇa's city and tells the king that he is a charioteer and cook named Bāhuka; Ṛtuparṇa engages him. Every evening Nala recites a verse lamenting his lost love.*

**[65]** *Damayantī's father Bhīma sends Brahmins out to search for the missing couple; a Brahmin named Sudeva sees Damayantī, recognizes her and introduces himself. Damayantī weeps, and the queen mother asks Sudeva who she is.* **[66]** *Sudeva explains Damayantī's identity; the queen mother realizes that she is her own niece, and arranges for her to return home to Vidarbha.*

**[67]** *Now Bhīma sends the Brahmins out to search for Nala; Damayantī tells them verses to recite wherever they go.* **[68]** *After some time the Brahmin Parṇāda returns: Ṛtuparṇa's charioteer Bāhuka had been greatly moved by the verses, and had replied with verses of his own. Damayantī now sends Sudeva to Ṛtuparṇa to announce that she is holding a second* svayaṃvara, *which will take place the very next day.*

**[69]** *The charioteer Bāhuka is anguished to hear Ṛtuparṇa's reason for wishing to reach Vidarbha at speed, but promises to carry him there in time. At first Ṛtuparṇa questions his choice of horses, but when they begin their journey he is amazed at Bāhuka's skill, and wonders whether he might not really be King Nala.*

**[70]** *As they pass a* vibhītaka *tree, Ṛtuparṇa announces the number of leaves and nuts on it.*[1] *Bāhuka insists on stopping to count them, and finds that the king is right; he is an expert at gambling and counting. Bāhuka requests to be given this skill in exchange for his own skill with horses, and Ṛtuparṇa agrees: at once Kali leaves Nala's body, vomiting Karkoṭaka's poison. Nala is on the point of cursing him, but Kali placates him and enters the* vibhītaka *tree.*

**[71]** *Ṛtuparṇa arrives in Vidarbha; Damayantī hears the noise of the chariot and thinks that it must be driven by Nala. Bhīma welcomes Ṛtuparṇa, but he is puzzled over the reason for his visit, and Ṛtuparṇa is puzzled at the lack of any sign of a* svayaṃvara. **[72]** *Now Damayantī sends her maidservant Keśinī to question Bāhuka. Bāhuka denies all knowledge of the present whereabouts of Nala, but when Keśinī repeats the verses that Damayantī had taught the Brahmins whom*

1 The nuts of the *vibhītaka* were used as dice.

*she sent out in search of Nala,*[1] *he weeps and repeats his own verse response.*

**[73]** *When Damayantī hears of this, she sends Keśinī once more to watch Bāhuka closely. She returns, and reports that narrow places open to let him pass, water and fire come at his call, and flowers crushed in his hands become fresh and sweet-smelling. Almost certain now, Damayantī asks Keśinī to obtain some meat cooked by Bāhuka; when she tastes it she recognizes Nala's cooking. She sends Keśinī back to Bāhuka with her two children: he weeps to see them.*

**[74]** *Damayantī informs her mother of her suspicions, and her parents send for Bāhuka. She confronts him, remonstrating with him for having deserted her. He explains that he had been possessed by Kali; now he is free, and he has returned for her. But then he in turn remonstrates with her: how could she announce a second* svayaṃvara*?* **[75]** *Damayantī explains her actions, and invokes Wind, Sun and Moon to testify that she is innocent; the Wind god proclaims that this indeed so, and calls upon Nala to take her back. Nala puts on the garment given him by Karkoṭaka, resumes his own form, and is reunited with Damayantī.*

**[76]** *Next morning, Bhīma and Nala pay honour to each other; then Nala asks Ṛtuparṇa's forgiveness for deceiving him, to which Ṛtuparṇa replies by asking Nala's forgiveness for any offence he may have done him. Nala gives Ṛtuparṇa his skill with horses, and Ṛtuparṇa leaves for his own city.*

**[77]** *After a month, Nala returns to Niṣadha and challenges Puṣkara either to gamble once again or to do battle. Assuming he will win again, Puṣkara is happy to agree to another gambling match, and infuriates Nala by expressing his desire to win Damayantī. However, Nala now reduces him to ruin him in a single throw; but then he forgives him. Puṣkara stays with him as a guest for a month before returning home.* **[78]** *Now Nala lives happily in Niṣadha with Damayantī. — After finishing the story of Nala, Bṛhadaśva tells Yudhiṣṭhira of the good fortune that comes from hearing it, and bestows on him the skill of gambling with dice. After Bṛhadaśva's departure, Yudhiṣṭhira learns from travelling Brahmins and ascetics that Arjuna is practising fierce austerities.*

1 See 3.67–8.

**[79]** *Draupadī and the three remaining younger Pāṇḍavas complain to Yudhiṣṭhira that in Arjuna's absence they no longer take pleasure in dwelling in the Kāmyaka forest.*

## THE PILGRIMAGE

**[80]** *Nārada arrives and is honoured. Yudhiṣṭhira asks him to explain the rewards of pilgrimage, and Nārada replies by telling him of Bhīṣma's encounter with the seer Pulastya. Bhīṣma had asked the same question, and Pulastya had answered that pilgrimage could bring rewards even greater than those of sacrifices. He began to list the sacred bathing-places which a man ought to visit in sequence, starting with Puṣkara, and expounded to Bhīṣma the particular benefits which each of them would confer;* **[81]** *among them was Kurukṣetra, which he described as exceptionally holy,* **[82]** *as well as many other sacred bathing-places.* **[83]** *He had concluded with Prayāga, where the Gaṅgā and Yamunā rivers flow together, and had urged Bhīṣma to undertake the journey; Bhīṣma had done so. Similarly, Nārada tells Yudhiṣṭhira that he should go on a pilgrimage to the bathing-places: the seer Lomaśa will accompany him. After saying this, he vanishes.*

**[84]** *Now Yudhiṣṭhira speaks to Dhaumya. He tells him how he has sent Arjuna to acquire weapons powerful enough to overcome the might of the Pāṇḍavas' enemies; however, in his absence the remaining brothers and Draupadī now find the Kāmyaka forest a cheerless place, and they wish to travel elsewhere.* **[85]** *In answer, Dhaumya begins his own description of the sacred bathing-places. He starts with those in the East, including the Naimiṣa forest and Prayāga.* **[86]** *Next, he speaks of the bathing-places in the South, such as the river Payoṣṇī, Agastya's hermitage, Surāṣṭra and Dvārakā;* **[87]** *then he praises the bathing-places of Avanti in the West, among them those on the river Narmadā and Puṣkara.* **[88]** *Finally, he describes the bathing-places of the North, in particular the ones situated on the rivers Sarasvatī and Yamunā.*

**[89]** *Lomaśa arrives, and explains that he has been sent by Indra to tell the Pāṇḍavas about Arjuna's doings. Arjuna has succeeded in obtaining celestial weapons, including the awesome Weapon of Brahmā's Head; more than a match for Karṇa, he will soon rejoin his brothers.* **[90]** *Lomaśa tells Yudhiṣṭhira that Arjuna wishes him to undertake a pilgrimage; he, Lomaśa, will accompany and protect him. Yudhiṣṭhira is delighted. He sends most of the Brahmins who are* *accompanying him back to Hāstinapura, where Dhṛtarāṣṭra is happy to receive them.* **[91]** *The remaining Brahmins ask Yudhiṣṭhira to be allowed to accompany him, and he grants their request. As the Pāṇḍavas prepare to set out, Vyāsa, Nārada and Parvata appear and bless them. Then the journey begins.*

**[92]** *Yudhiṣṭhira complains to Lomaśa that he, a virtuous man, has to endure suffering while his wicked enemies thrive. Lomaśa replies that the demons too were wicked, and their wickedness destroyed them; the gods, on the other hand, practised virtue and went on pilgrimage, and so won glory. In the same way Yudhiṣṭhira will triumph and his enemies will fail.*

**[93]** *The travellers reach the Naimiṣa forest and travel on to Prayāga, bathing at the sacred bathing-places and distributing great wealth. At Gayā they perform the seasonal sacrifices.*

## AGASTYA

**[94]** *The Pāṇḍavas travel to Agastya's hermitage, where Yudhiṣṭhira asks Lomaśa to tell him the story of how Agastya killed the demon Vātāpi. Lomaśa begins to narrate. — The demon Ilvala, who is able to bring the dead back to life, is in the habit of feeding his younger brother Vātāpi to Brahmins in the form of goat's meat, and then killing his victims by resuscitating the goat.*

*At this time Agastya sees his ancestors hanging face-down in a cave: they tell him that he must acquire offspring to secure their release. Unable to find a woman adequate to the purpose, he creates Lopāmudrā, who is raised by the king of Vidarbha as his daughter.* **[95]** *When she reaches marriageable age, Agastya takes her for his wife. After their wedding, he demands that she cast away her rich garments and live as an ascetic. This she meekly does, but when he calls her to lie with him she insists on fine linen and ornaments. Agastya goes in search of these.* **[96]** *He visits King Śrutarvan and requests wealth from him, but when he hears the state of Śrutarvan's treasury he withdraws his request. The two of them go together to Vadhryaśva; he is in the same situation. All three now go to Trasadasyu, but he too lacks the necessary resources. Agastya, Śrutarvan, Vadhryaśva and Trasadasyu all now decide to request wealth from Ilvala.*

**[97]** *Ilvala greets his visitors, and then serves them his brother Vātāpi as* *cooked meat. But Agastya consumes and digests Vātāpi, and then requests wealth from Ilvala; Ilvala bestows great riches on Agastya and the three kings. Agastya returns to Lopāmudrā and impregnates her, and Dṛḍhasyu is born after a seven-year pregnancy.*

**[98]** — *Now Yudhiṣṭhira asks to hear more about Agastya, and Lomaśa narrates further.* — *In the first age of the world, the gods are harassed by Vṛtra and the demons. They approach Brahmā for help, and he tells them to ask the seer Dadhīca for his bones; they should make a thunderbolt weapon from these. When the gods visit Dadhīca he is happy to grant their wish, and Tvaṣṭṛ fashions his bones into a thunderbolt.* **[99]** *Armed with the bolt, Indra leads the gods into battle against the demons. At first the demons prevail, but then Viṣṇu places his own fiery energy in Indra, and so do the other gods and the seers; now Indra is able to slay Vṛtra with the thunderbolt. The demons flee and take refuge in the ocean, where they plot the destruction of the world, starting with its ascetics.*

**[100]** *The demons undertake night-time raids and kill many ascetics; the gods seek Viṣṇu's help.* **[101]** *Viṣṇu answers that they must make the ocean dry, and that only Agastya can achieve this for them. The gods go to Agastya and praise him for the help he gave them once before by stopping the Vindhya mountain from growing.*

**[102]** — *Yudhiṣṭhira asks to hear this story, and Lomaśa relates it. Jealous of Mount Meru, which the sun circumambulates at sunrise and sunset, the Vindhya mountain had begun to grow to an enormous size. The gods had requested Agastya's aid, and he told the mountain to stop growing until he returned from a visit to the south; but he never returned.*

— *Now the gods ask Agastya to drink up the ocean, and he agrees to this.* **[103]** *He drinks the ocean dry, and the gods kill the demons who were hiding there. Then they request Agastya to restore the water, but he replies that he has already digested it. So the gods approach Brahmā.* **[104]** *Brahmā assures the gods that in time the ocean will return to normal, thanks to King Bhagīratha's kinsmen.*

— *Yudhiṣṭhira requests this story in full, and Lomaśa narrates it.* — *King Sagara is mighty but has no son from his two wives. He performs austerities and approaches Śiva, who promises him that one of his wives will bear him sixty thousand sons, but that they will all die together; his other wife will bear him a single son who will succeed him. Both queens now become pregnant. One of them gives birth to a gourd, and Sagara hears a voice from the air telling him to keep each of its seeds in a pot of ghee.* **[105]** *From the seeds are born the sixty thousand Sāgaras,*[1] *who are so ferocious that mortals and gods alike seek Brahmā's protection; but Brahmā predicts that soon all the Sāgaras will perish.*

*Later, Sagara is conducting a horse sacrifice when the horse disappears into the empty ocean. Though the Sāgaras search, they cannot find it, but Sagara demands that they continue; they dig out the ocean, causing much suffering to the creatures of the underworld, until they find the horse in the company of the seer Kapila.* **[106]** *The Sāgaras take the horse; Kapila opens his eyes and burns them all to ashes. Nārada sees this happen, and informs Sagara.*

*Sagara has another son, Asamañjas, by his second wife, but he had terrorized the people until Sagara banished him. Sagara now requests Asamañjas's son Aṃśumat to retrieve the missing horse. Aṃśumat enters the ocean and finds the horse with Kapila, to whom he does honour. Kapila grants him boons, and Aṃśumat chooses first the horse, and then water to purify the dead Sāgaras. Kapila answers that Aṃśumat's grandson will bring the Gaṅgā from heaven to provide the purifying water. Sagara concludes his sacrifice, and in time is succeeded by Aṃśumat, followed by Aṃśumat's son Dilīpa and his son Bhagīratha.*

**[107]** *Bhagīratha performs austerities on Mount Himālaya until Gaṅgā offers him a boon; he chooses that she should bring her water to purify the Sāgaras. She agrees, but warns that Śiva will have to bear the force of her fall. Bhagīratha approaches Śiva, who agrees to this.* **[108]** *Gaṅgā now leaps from heaven, and Śiva breaks her fall on his forehead. She purifies the Sāgaras and fills the ocean.*

**[109]** *Now Yudhiṣṭhira and his followers travel on to Mount Hemakūṭa; here any utterance causes rainfall and a hail of stones, and it is impossible to climb the mountain. Lomaśa explains that an ancient ascetic named Ṛṣabha, who hated people talking to him, had caused the rain and the stones; the gods too, seeking privacy for themselves, had made the mountain impassable. The travellers continue to the Kauśikī river.*

1 The word *sāgara* means 'ocean'.

## ṚŚYAŚṚṄGA

Lomaśa spoke:
[**110**] Here, bull-like heir of Bharata, is the Kauśikī, the pure river of the gods, and here you may see Viśvāmitra's lovely hermitage; here too is the holy hermitage of Kaśyapa's noble heir Vibhāṇḍaka, whose son Ṛśyaśṛṅga was a disciplined ascetic. He it was who used the power of his austerities to make Indra grant rain; he it was for fear of whom that slayer of Bala and Vṛtra poured down rain in a time of drought. Vibhāṇḍaka's son of mighty ardour was born to a doe; he it was who performed the great miracle in Lomapāda's
5 kingdom, and to whom King Lomapāda gave his daughter Śāntā in thanks for the return of the crops, as the Sun god gave his daughter Sāvitrī to Brahmā.

Yudhiṣṭhira spoke:
How was Vibhāṇḍaka's son Ṛśyaśṛṅga born of a doe, when such a mixed union is forbidden? How did he become an ascetic? And why was Indra so fearful of this wise young man that the slayer of Bala and Vṛtra poured down rain when a drought was in progress? How beautiful was the princess Śāntā, keeper of her word, to arouse desire in the heart of a deer-like ascetic? And how was it, when the royal seer Lomapāda was well known for his virtue, that
10 Indra granted no rain in his kingdom? Blessed sir, please tell me all in full, just as it happened, for I long to hear the story of Ṛśyaśṛṅga.

Lomaśa spoke:
Hear how Ṛśyaśṛṅga of mighty energy, a child whom the elders honoured for his great ardour, was born at the great lake Mahāhrada as the son of Vibhāṇḍaka, a Brahmin seer perfected by austerities, unfailingly potent and resplendent as Prajāpati.

The heir of Kaśyapa came to Mahāhrada and undertook austerities there; that seer exerted himself for so long that he won the honour of the divine seers. As he bathed in the water, O king, his eye fell on the Apsaras Urvaśī, and his seed gushed forth. A doe then drank it in together with the water, being thirsty; she became pregnant, king, for fate cannot fail and the will of the gods must be. To that doe was born his son, the great seer Ṛśyaśṛṅga, constant in asceticism; he grew up without ever leaving the forest. O king, that noble man bore the horn of a deer on his head, and so he became known as Ṛśyaśṛṅga ('Deer-horn'). He had never seen a human being other than his father, and so, O king, his mind did not swerve from holy celibacy.

At this same time a friend of Daśaratha, a man named Lomapāda, was ruler over Aṅga. That lord of the earth is said to have acted wilfully and falsely towards Brahmins, so the Brahmins then abandoned him; and since it happened that the king had lost his household priest, Indra of a thousand eyes granted no rain, to the affliction of the people. The lord of the earth consulted wise, ascetic Brahmins, experts in the matter of the granting of rain by the lord of the gods. 'How may the god of rain grant rain? Let a way be found,' he urged them, and the wise Brahmins voiced their opinions.

One of their number, a great sage, told the king, 'The Brahmins are angry with you, lord of kings. Perform an expiation, and fetch the sage's son Ṛśyaśṛṅga, O prince! He is a forest-dweller, ignorant of women and devoted to rectitude. If that great ascetic will make an appearance in your kingdom, the god of rain will at once grant rain; of this I have no doubt, O king.'

When Lomapāda heard these words he went and performed an expiation for himself, returning once the Brahmins were conciliated, and the people, seeing their king returned, welcomed him back. Then the lord of Aṅga summoned his aides, men skilled in counsel, and did his best to settle on a plan that would lead to a visit by Ṛśyaśṛṅga. His ministers were learned, well acquainted with worldly affairs, and expert at governance; with their help the invincible Lomapāda arrived at a plan. Then the lord of the earth had brought before him leading courtesans, women with every sort of skill, and he addressed them thus: 'Fair ladies, find some means to bring the seer's son Ṛśyaśṛṅga to my kingdom by arousing his desire and winning his trust!' But those women feared

the seer's curse as much as they feared the king; pale and listless,
they answered that the task was impossible.

One of them, however, an old woman, spoke to Lomapāda:
'Great king, I shall do my best to bring that ascetic here. Please
give your approval to the purposes I wish to pursue; then I shall be
35 able to arouse the desire of the seer's son Ṛśyaśṛṅga!' The prince
approved her every purpose: he gave her much wealth and jewels
of every kind. Then, lord of the earth, she set straight out for the
forest, taking with her certain supremely lovely young women.

[111] O heir of Bharata, to achieve the king's aims she created
a floating hermitage, acting both at the king's command and
according to her own intelligence. She decked it with artificial
trees bearing flowers and fruit of many kinds, together with bushes
and creepers of every sort; the fruit they yielded was as delicious
as one could wish. She made that floating hermitage to be utterly
beautiful, utterly captivating; it was so lovely that it seemed a
miracle. Mooring the vessel not far from Vibhāṇḍaka's hermitage,
5 she sent men to spy out where the sage passed his time. Then that
courtesan, thinking of nothing but the task at hand, saw her chance
against Kaśyapa's heir and sent out her daughter, a girl admired for
her intelligence. The clever girl approached the young man who
was constant in asceticism; reaching the hermitage, she saw the
seer's son.

The courtesan said, 'O sage, I trust that the ascetics are well?
and that you all have plenty of roots and fruit to eat? and that
you yourself, sir, are happy in this hermitage? It is to visit you
that I have come here today.[1] I trust that the ascetics' austerities
are prospering, and that your father's ardour remains undimmed?
I trust, O priest, that he is pleased with you, and that your Vedic
studies are progressing, Ṛśyaśṛṅga?'

Ṛśyaśṛṅga replied, 'Sir, clearly you yourself prosper, for you are
radiant as the sunlight, and I am sure that you merit my respectful
greeting! I shall be happy to give you the water for washing your
10 feet and the fruit and roots, as *dharma* prescribes! Sit at your ease on

1 The courtesan here deliberately refers to herself in the masculine.

this comfortable mat of *kuśa* grass covered with a black antelope-skin. Where is your hermitage? And what is the name of the vow that you observe? You seem like a god, O Brahmin!'

The courtesan said, 'My hermitage, son of Vibhāṇḍaka, is lovely; it lies beyond this three-league mountain range. Our *dharma* there forbids respectful greeting, nor do we use water for washing our feet.'

Ṛśyaśṛṅga replied, 'Then let me give you ripe fruits, cashews and myrobalans, and nuts and berries of various sorts! Here are *priyāla* fruit for you to enjoy!'

But she put them all aside and gave him costly foods; rich-tasting and well presented, they gave Ṛśyaśṛṅga much delight. And she gave him fragrant garlands, bright, many-coloured clothes, and the finest drinks. Then she made merry, and played, and laughed aloud. She amused herself with a ball at his side, bending low like a vine breaking under the weight of its fruit; and, bringing her body up close to his body, she embraced Ṛśyaśṛṅga repeatedly. She pulled down and broke off blossoming sprays of *sarja*, *aśoka* and *tilaka* trees; her intoxication and feigned modesty aroused the desire of the great seer's son. Then, when she saw that Ṛśyaśṛṅga was changed, she pressed his body with her own again and again before slowly departing, still gazing at him, under the pretext of attending an *agnihotra* ritual. She left Ṛśyaśṛṅga mad, out of his mind with love; distracted, unable to think of anything but her, sighing, he was the very picture of affliction.

Not long afterwards there appeared Vibhāṇḍaka, Kaśyapa's heir, his eyes orange as a lion's, his body covered by hair to the tips of his fingers, a Vedic scholar leading a life of virtue and meditation. As he approached, he saw his son seated there alone, plunged in thought and depressed, sighing again and again as he stared into the air. So Vibhāṇḍaka spoke to the downcast boy: 'Son, why are you not piling up logs for fuel? I trust you have offered today's *agnihotra*, and washed the two ritual ladles? I trust you have brought the calf to the oblation cow? You seem different, son, full of care and distraught. Today why are you so sad? I ask you: who was it that came here today?'

**[112]** Ṛśyaśṛṅga answered his father, 'A religious student with
braided hair came here, neither short nor tall, a spirited boy with
a golden complexion and long lotus-eyes, as radiant as the son of a
god. Most beautiful to look on, he blazed like the sun, with black-
and-white eyes fairer than those of *cakora* birds. His braids were
dark, well combed and perfumed; they were fastened with threads
of gold, and very long. Round his throat, like the water-trough
round the base of a tree, was something that shone like lightning
in the sky, and below the throat he had two hairless swellings that
I found most alluring. The waist around his navel was slender, but
he had the fullest hips, and under his garment, as I have this belt,
5 he had one of gleaming gold. On each of his feet shone another
amazingly lovely thing that jingled, and, fastened to his hands, as
I have this rosary, he had bands that also made sounds; when he
moved his limbs, these things resounded like geese making merry
on a lake.

'His clothes were wonderfully beautiful – these ones of mine
are nothing like so fair. His face, too, was amazingly lovely, and his
voice seemed to gladden my heart; when he spoke, he sounded
like the song of the cuckoo, and it perturbed my very soul to hear
him. As a forest in the midst of spring exudes a sweet smell when
the breeze stirs it, so he too sent forth the most excellent fragrance
as the wind played upon him. His braids, which were neatly tied,
were parted evenly in two upon his brow, and on his ears he seemed
10 to have pretty circles of many colours. With his right hand he kept
striking a strange round fruit: over and over again it would reach
the ground and then spring up high in the most marvellous way;
and when he had struck it, he would whirl round, quivering like
a tree caught by the wind. He looked like the son of a god, and
when I saw him, father, I felt the deepest joy; father, I felt love.

'He kept embracing my body, taking hold of my hair, lowering my face to his own, placing his mouth on mine, murmuring to me. It filled me with rapture. He did not think highly of water for washing the feet, or of these fruits which I had fetched for him; "This is my observance!" he said, and gave me other fruits that were new to me. I ate those fruits; these ones of ours do not match them in taste. Unlike these, they had no rind; unlike these, they had no pith. This noble youth also gave to me to drink the most delicious liquids; as soon as I drank them I felt the highest delight, and the very earth seemed to shift beneath me.

'These fragrant and many-coloured garlands, strung with silk, are his: radiant with his austerities, he scattered them here when he left for his own hermitage. Now he has gone, I have become distracted, and my body seems on fire. I want to go straight to him; I want him to come round here every day. I will go to him, father! What is the name of the observance be that he practises? I want to practise it with him, to practise the same austerities as that boy with his fierce discipline!'

[**113**] Vibhāṇḍaka said, 'Son, these are Rākṣasas! They assume that amazingly lovely form to go about, but though matchlessly fair they are utterly terrible, for they think of nothing but obstructing asceticism. Yes, they are beautiful, son, but they are cruel: they use every means to arouse the desire of sages in the forests, and so banish them from both happiness and the heavenly realms. The disciplined sage will have nothing whatever to do with them in his quest for the realms of the virtuous. My innocent child, they are evildoers who delight in obstructing the austerities of ascetics. Those were liquors, son, wicked and not to be drunk; only base men resort to them. As for these garlands, with their bright colours and perfumes, they are not considered fitting for ascetics!'

Vibhāṇḍaka told his son that women were Rākṣasas in order to hold him back; then he went to track the woman down. When, after three days, he failed to find her, he returned to the hermitage. But meanwhile, Ṛśyaśṛṅga had set out to gather fruit, as is the way of ascetics; and that courtesan too set out to arouse the desire of Kaśyapa's ascetic heir. The moment Ṛśyaśṛṅga saw her he became enraptured. Then he hurriedly rushed up to her and said, 'Good sir, let us both leave for your hermitage before my father returns!'

So, O king, they tricked Vibhāṇḍaka's only son into boarding the boat, and they dropped the mooring. Then, using every means to keep his desire aroused, they arrived close to where the king of Aṅga lived. Once that most splendid boat had been brought to

shore, the king had it moored within sight of a hermitage; and when he fetched the boy from the wharf he likewise had a lovely
10 grove constructed named 'Hermitage of the King'. But then he had Vibhāṇḍaka's only son settled in the women's quarters; and at once he saw Indra pour down rain, while the earth filled with water.

Now Lomapāda, his desires fulfilled, gave his daughter Śāntā to Ṛśyaśṛṅga. The king also acted to counter Vibhāṇḍaka's anger: he had oxen plough close by the roads on which the ascetic was approaching, and stationed numerous cattle and brave herdsmen there, commanding them, 'When Vibhāṇḍaka questions you in his fervour to regain his son, you must join your hands together and answer him, "These beasts are your son's, and so is this ploughing. What favour may we do you, mighty seer? We are all your slaves, yours to command!"'

Meanwhile the sage, a man of fierce anger, came with roots and fruits to his hermitage. He searched there for his son, but
15 could not find him, and became deeply enraged. Bursting with anger and suspecting that this was the king's doing, he set out for Campā, intending to put to the torch the king of Aṅga and his realm. Kaśyapa's heir was weary and hungry when he came upon those well-stocked cattle-stations; the herdsmen greeted him with all proper respect, and he spent the night there like a king. He received such honour from them that he asked them, 'Good sirs, who is your master?' Then they all approached and answered, 'This wealth is at your son's disposal.'

Wherever he went he was treated respectfully, and, as he listened to the pleasant words addressed to him, his fury died down and he grew joyful. Then he went to meet the king in his city. He was greeted with honour by that bull-like hero, and he saw his son living there like the god Indra in heaven; there, too, he saw Śāntā,
20 his daughter-in-law, radiant as a flash of lightning. After seeing the villages and cattle-stations, and his son, and Śāntā, his mighty anger was stilled; indeed, lord of men, Vibhāṇḍaka was most gracious towards King Lomapāda. The great seer entrusted his son to him, and told that boy, whose power was like that of Sun or Fire, 'Once

a son is born to you, you must return to the forest after showing this king every favour.'

Ṛśyaśṛṅga obeyed his words and went back to his father's place; and Śāntā served him properly, as Rohiṇī faithfully serves the Moon in the sky,[1] as lovely Arundhatī serves Vasiṣṭha, as Lopāmudrā serves Agastya. And just as Damayantī was obedient to Nala, and Śacī obeys thunderbolt-wielding Indra, and Indrasenā Nāḍāyanī is always obedient to Mudgala, O Yudhiṣṭhira, so Śāntā always
obeyed Ṛśyaśṛṅga, and served him lovingly in the forest. Here you 25
can see the holy hermitage of that celebrated seer, adding to the beauty of Mahāhrada. Bathe here to attain your wishes, king; then, purified, continue your tour of the sacred bathing-places.

**[114]** *Yudhiṣṭhira and his brothers travel from the Kauśikī to Kaliṅga and the Vaitaraṇī river, which Lomaśa tells them is the holy place where Rudra won the best share in the sacrifice from the other gods. They bathe in the river, and Yudhiṣṭhira receives the ability to see and hear all things throughout the world. Then Lomaśa shows him a forest: here Viśvakarman had performed a sacrifice and had paid his priest, Kaśyapa, by giving him the Earth. Earth threatened to descend to the underworld until Kaśyapa conciliated her, when she reappeared in the form of an altar. Yudhiṣṭhira ascends the altar while Lomaśa pronounces a blessing upon him.*

## KĀRTAVĪRYA

**[115]** *Yudhiṣṭhira learns from the ascetic Akṛtavraṇa that Rāma Jāmadagnya is due to arrive next day. At Yudhiṣṭhira's request, Akṛtavraṇa relates Rāma's story. — The Bhārgava Brahmin Ṛcīka marries Satyavatī, daughter of King Gādhi of Kānyakubja. Bhṛgu visits the couple and offers Satyavatī a boon; she chooses for herself and her mother each to bear a son.*

1 The Rohiṇī constellation is said to be the Moon's favourite wife. The other figures mentioned (apart from Nala and Damayantī and the deities Indra and Śacī) are seers and their wives.

*Bhṛgu gives instructions: each woman is to embrace a particular tree. But when they do so, they mix the trees up, and Bhṛgu tells Satyavatī that her son will be a Brahmin who behaves like a Kṣatriya, while her mother's son will be a Kṣatriya who behaves like a Brahmin. At her entreaty, however, he agrees to allow the effect of the error to fall upon her grandson, not her son. She gives birth to Jamadagni, who excels at both Vedic learning and archery.*

**[116]** *Jamadagni marries Reṇukā, daughter of King Prasenajit. She bears him five sons, Rāma being the last but greatest of these. One day she sees King Citraratha and is overcome with desire for him. Jamadagni understands her thought and commands his four eldest sons to kill her; when, dumbfounded, they fail to do so, he curses them to lose their human reason and live like animals. Rāma, on the other hand, unquestioningly beheads his mother; but when his father grants him a boon he chooses that she should return to life, that he himself should be free of the taint of killing, and that his brothers should regain their own natures. Some time afterwards, Jamadagni's hermitage is laid waste by King Kārtavīrya. When Rāma learns of this he attacks and kills Kārtavīrya; Kārtavīrya's sons respond by killing Jamadagni.*

**[117]** *The grieving Rāma performs his father's funeral rites and swears to wipe out the Kṣatriya race; he does so twenty-one times until stopped by Ṛcīka. — The next day, Rāma arrives in person, and Yudhiṣṭhira pays him honour.*

**[118]** *Yudhiṣṭhira resumes his travels, visiting the bathing-places of the river Godāvarī. He reaches Śūrpāraka and then travels on to Prabhāsa, where he performs great austerities. There the Pāṇḍavas are visited by Kṛṣṇa, Balarāma and Sātyaki.* **[119]** *Balarāma laments to see the mighty Pāṇḍavas reduced to such a state while their enemies prosper.* **[120]** *Sātyaki proposes an alliance to overthrow the Kauravas; when they lie slain, Abhimanyu can rule until Yudhiṣṭhira has completed his term in exile. But Kṛṣṇa replies that neither Yudhiṣṭhira nor his brothers will forsake* dharma *in this way, and Yudhiṣṭhira confirms this: one day they will defeat Duryodhana, but not yet. The visitors leave, and Yudhiṣṭhira continues on his way. He reaches the river Payoṣṇī.*

**[121]** *After bathing in the Payoṣṇī, the Pāṇḍavas travel on to the Narmadā. Lomaśa tells them that this is the site where the story of Cyavana took place, and Yudhiṣṭhira asks to hear about the great Bhārgava ascetic.*

## SUKANYĀ

[**122**] *Lomaśa narrates. — Bhṛgu's son Cyavana performs austerities for so long that he becomes an anthill. When Sukanyā, the lovely daughter of King Śaryāti, comes to bathe in the nearby lake, he sees her and desires her; but she, seeing only eyes in an anthill, pricks them with a thorn. Cyavana responds by blocking the bowels and bladders of Śaryāti's men. Śaryāti investigates, learns the truth, and seeks Cyavana's pardon; Cyavana agrees on condition that he marry Sukanyā, and Śaryāti assents gladly.*

[**123**] *One day the twin Aśvins see Sukanyā undressed after her bath, and they seek to persuade her to abandon her decrepit husband in favour of one of them. She refuses, and they suggest instead that they use their healing powers to restore Cyavana's youth, and that she then choose between the three of them. Cyavana agrees to this, and all three bathe in the lake. They emerge youthful, handsome, and identical in appearance; but Sukanyā chooses Cyavana, who is so delighted that he awards the Aśvins the right to drink Soma.*

[**124**] *Śaryāti pays a visit, and Cyavana performs a sacrifice for him. He draws a cup of Soma for the Aśvins, but Indra appears and commands him not to offer it to them, since as healers they do not merit it; if Cyavana disobeys, Indra will strike him with his thunderbolt. Cyavana ignores him and pours the Soma; Indra makes to hurl his bolt; Cyavana paralyses his arm and creates a fearsome demon named Intoxication to attack him.* [**125**] *Terrified, Indra concedes. Cyavana releases him and divides Intoxication up amongst liquor, women, dicing and hunting. — Now Lomaśa continues to describe to Yudhiṣṭhira the sacred bathing-places on their route. They reach the river Yamunā, where Māndhātṛ and Somaka worshipped.*

## MĀNDHĀTṚ

[**126**] *At Yudhiṣṭhira's request, Lomaśa tells the story of Māndhātṛ. — King Yuvanāśva is childless; he entrusts his kingdom to his ministers and takes up residence in the forest. One day he enters Bhṛgu's hermitage and,*

*being thirsty, drinks a jar of water that he finds there. In the morning he learns that the water had been consecrated with* mantras *to allow his own wife to give birth to a mighty son; now he is himself pregnant with that child. A hundred years pass, and Yuvanāśva's side splits open; a boy emerges, and Indra himself suckles him with his forefinger, hence he is named Māndhātṛ (*māṃ dhātā, *'he shall suck me'). He becomes a great ruler and sacrificer.*

## JANTU

[127] *Now Yudhiṣṭhira asks to hear about Somaka, and Lomaśa narrates. — King Somaka has a hundred wives, but only one son, Jantu by name. He seeks for a way to obtain a hundred sons, and his priest tells him that this can be achieved by sacrificing Jantu, who will be reborn to his own mother.*

[128] *Somaka's wives try to prevent the sacrifice, but it goes ahead, and all of them become pregnant. After ten months Jantu is reborn, along with ninety-nine brothers. Later Somaka dies, and discovers his priest burning in hell for performing the sacrifice. Somaka insists on sharing his punishment, and after the term is served they both attain the heavenly realms.*

[129] *Now Lomaśa resumes his description of the bathing-places. Yudhiṣṭhira bathes at Plakṣāvataraṇa; he is freed from sin and receives the ability to see all the worlds. The Pāṇḍavas travel on to the river Sarasvatī.* [130] *Next their journey takes them to Kashmir, Lake Mānasa and Mount Bhṛgutuṅga. Here Lomaśa tells how Indra and Agni once assumed the forms of a hawk and a dove to test King Uśīnara. — The dove seeks refuge with the king.*

## THE HAWK AND THE DOVE

[131] *The hawk remonstrates: Uśīnara is depriving him of his rightful food. The king offers him other food, but the hawk refuses and requests instead a piece of Uśīnara's own flesh equal in weight to the dove. Uśīnara is happy to comply, but however much of his flesh he cuts off it never*

*balances the dove's weight; finally he places his entire maimed body on the scale. Indra praises him highly.*

## AṢṬĀVAKRA

**[132]** *Lomaśa points out the hermitage of Śvetaketu, and narrates his story. — The sage Uddālaka has a favoured pupil, Kahoḍa, to whom he gives his daughter Sujātā in marriage. She becomes pregnant; her child, while still in the womb, slights Kahoḍa's learning and is cursed by his angry father to be crooked in all eight limbs (*aṣṭāvakra*). When the birth is imminent, Kahoḍa goes to King Janaka to seek wealth, but he is worsted in debate by the Sūta Bandin, and is put to death by drowning. Aṣṭāvakra grows up knowing nothing of this: he regards Uddālaka as his father and Uddālaka's son Śvetaketu as his brother, until, at the age of twelve, he learns the truth. Then he and Śvetaketu go to Janaka's court.*

**[133]** *Aṣṭāvakra's eloquence persuades the gatekeeper to admit him to the sacrificial ground, and his skill with riddles persuades the king to allow him to challenge Bandin.* **[134]** *Bandin names things that are unique, and Aṣṭāvakra replies with things that exist in twos; next Bandin lists things in threes, and Aṣṭāvakra answers with things in fours; they proceed in this way until Bandin fails at the number thirteen and Aṣṭāvakra completes his verse for him. Applauded for his feat, he calls for Bandin to be drowned, at which point Bandin reveals that he is the son of Varuṇa, and that he has been sending the Brahmins he drowns to officiate at his father's sacrifice. The lost Brahmins now reappear, among them Kahoḍa, who honours his son for his achievement.*

## YAVAKRĪTA

**[135]** *Lomaśa points out the hermitage of Raibhya, where Yavakrīta died. Yudhiṣṭhira asks to hear this story, and Lomaśa narrates. — The scholar Raibhya and the ascetic Bharadvāja are friends, but Bharadvāja's son Yavakrīta is vexed to see that his father receives less honour than Raibhya, and he undertakes terrible austerities to attain knowledge of the Veda.*

*Repeatedly Indra tries to dissuade him from this course, but in the end he grants him his desire.*

**[136]** *When Yavakrīta tells his father of his achievement, Bharadvāja warns him not to be proud, and tells him the story of Bāladhi and Medhāvin. Bāladhi performed great austerities and gained a son Medhāvin, who was to live as long as the mountains stood; but in his pride Medhāvin insulted the seer Dhanuṣākṣa, who responded by breaking down the mountains, prompting Medhāvin's death. Yavakrīta promises his father that he will treat Raibhya with respect, but in fact he begins to take delight in offending other seers.*

**[137]** *Yavakrīta dishonours Raibhya's daughter-in-law. Raibhya creates a sorceress who exactly resembles her, and also a Rākṣasa, and tells them to kill Yavakrīta. The sorceress seduces Yavakrīta, and then steals his water-pot so that he cannot cleanse himself. Now the Rākṣasa attacks him; he flees, seeking a pool or a river in which to bathe and restore his purity, but all are dry. Finally Yavakrīta tries to enter the room in which his father's sacred fire is kept, but the blind Śūdra guard prevents him, and he is killed by the Rākṣasa.*

**[138]** *When Bharadvāja learns what has happened, he grieves bitterly and announces that he himself will also die, and that Raibhya too will be killed by his eldest son. He burns Yavakrīta's body and enters the flames.*

**[139]** *During a sacrificial session, Raibhya's eldest son, Parāvasu, encounters his father dressed in an antelope-skin at night and kills him, thinking that he is an animal. Arvāvasu, his younger brother, agrees to perform an expiation on Parāvasu's behalf to allow him to complete the ritual. But when Arvāvasu returns after completing the expiation, Parāvasu has him thrown out as a Brahmin-killer. At this point the gods step in and grant Arvāvasu a boon: he chooses that Raibhya, Bharadvāja and Yavakrīta should all return to life, and that Parāvasu should be free from his sin. When Yavakrīta asks how Raibhya had been able to kill him despite his Vedic learning and asceticism, the gods reply that Yavakrīta's learning had been easily acquired, while Raibhya's had been gained with great effort.*

**[140]** *The Pāṇḍavas pursue their journey northwards. Lomaśa warns them that soon they will encounter dangerous Yakṣas and other supernatural beings;*

*Yudhiṣṭhira cautions Bhīma to guard Draupadī carefully.* [**141**] *Then he proposes that he and Nakula should go on with Lomaśa, while Bhīma leads the remainder of the party down to safety, but Bhīma refuses, vowing that he will carry Draupadī if the need arises. Draupadī too insists that she will go on. They arrive in the realm of King Subāhu, who welcomes them. Then after resting for the night they proceed on foot towards Mount Himālaya, longing to see Arjuna.*

[**142**] *Yudhiṣṭhira addresses his wife and brothers: he speaks of his grief at their five years of separation from Arjuna, whose merits he praises highly. Now they will all travel on to Mount Gandhamādana to find him.* [**143**] *They set off for the mountain, but are halted by a violent gale and a dust storm which brings complete darkness. The Pāṇḍavas cling to trees or huddle on the ground. The gale is followed by torrential rain, causing the mountain rivers to overflow.*

[**144**] *When the storm has abated, Nakula observes that Draupadī is fainting from exhaustion. Dismayed, Yudhiṣṭhira blames himself for her plight; Brahmins comfort him while his brothers tend Draupadī. When she has revived, Yudhiṣṭhira raises the question of how she will be able to continue the journey through the mountains. Bhīma suggests enlisting the help of his Rākṣasa son Ghaṭotkaca, and when Yudhiṣṭhira agrees to this he summons him by the power of thought.*

[**145**] *Ghaṭotkaca flies through the air carrying Draupadī, and other Rākṣasas similarly carry the Pāṇḍavas: in this way they are swiftly borne along. They see Mount Kailāsa and soon reach the lovely hermitage of Nara and Nārāyaṇa with its wonderful jujube tree. Welcomed by the seers, they stay here in great delight* [**146**] *for six days. Then Draupadī sees a beautiful, fragrant flower that has been carried in on the breeze, and she implores Bhīma to go in search of more such flowers. He sets off along the mountain paths, enjoying the beauty of the scenery but fearful for Yudhiṣṭhira's welfare in his absence. Attacked by wild animals, he kills them with his bare hands and travels on, roaring, blowing his conch and beating his chest. The great monkey Hanumān hears these sounds and responds by striking the ground thunderously with his tail. Bhīma seeks out the monkey and roars at him, but Hanumān languidly complains at the noise he is making and tells him he can go no further.*

[**147**] *Bhīma demands that the great monkey let him past; Hanumān refuses and invites him to jump over him. Bhīma replies that to do so would be to dishonour the supreme being who resides within him – otherwise he would*

*leap over him as Hanumān, Bhīma's brother,*[1] *once leapt over the ocean. Now Hanumān tells Bhīma to lift his tail and pass under it, but Bhīma finds he does not have the strength to do so. At Bhīma's request Hanumān now identifies himself, and briefly relates the story of Rāma and Sītā in which he had played such an important part long before.*

[**148**] *Delighted, Bhīma bows low and begs to be allowed to see Hanumān in his mighty form, but Hanumān refuses: this is the wrong age of the world for that. At Bhīma's request he describes the four ages: the Kṛta Age in which* dharma *is perfect, and the Tretā, Dvāpara and Kali ages, in each of which it is successively reduced by a quarter.*

[**149**] *Bhīma once again asks to see Hanumān's old form; Hanumān assumes the colossal shape he took on to leap over the ocean. Seeing this, Bhīma praises Hanumān, saying that no one, not even Rāvaṇa, could match him; Hanumān assents to this, but explains that if he had killed Rāvaṇa, Rāma's glory would have been tarnished. Then he tells Bhīma the route to travel to reach the place of fragrant flowers, and urges him to abide by the* dharma *of the Kṣatriyas.* [**150**] *Then he resumes his normal form. The brothers embrace, and Hanumān promises to help the Pāṇḍavas in battle by entering Arjuna's standard*[2] *and roaring terribly; then he disappears. Bhīma continues on his way, and reaches the place of fragrant flowers.*

[**151**] *Bhīma approaches the pool where fragrant lotuses bloom. The Rākṣasas guarding it demand to know who he is.* [**152**] *Bhīma explains who he is and why he has come. The Rākṣasas reply that the pool belongs to Kubera, lord of the Yakṣas; Bhīma must seek his permission to enter. Bhīma ignores them and continues towards the pool, and they attack him; but he overcomes them, killing many of their number. Bhīma now drinks from the pool and plucks its fragrant flowers, while the Rākṣasas flee to Kubera and tell him what has happened. He laughs, and tells them that Bhīma may take as many flowers as he wishes.*

[**153**] *While Bhīma gathers flowers, another mighty gale blows up. Seeing it, Yudhiṣṭhira looks about for his brothers and realizes that Bhīma is missing. When Draupadī explains where he has gone, Yudhiṣṭhira insists that they must go and join him. With the help of Ghaṭotkaca and his Rākṣasa comrades the*

**1** Bhīma and Hanumān are both sons of the Wind god.

**2** Arjuna has the emblem of a monkey on his standard.

*entire Pāṇḍava party travels to Kubera's pool, where Yudhiṣṭhira reproaches Bhīma for killing the guards. Then they settle there for a while.*

## THE KILLING OF JAṬĀSURA

[154] *A Rākṣasa named Jaṭāsura abducts the Pāṇḍavas one day while Bhīma is absent. Sahadeva manages to escape; Yudhiṣṭhira remonstrates with the Rākṣasa and weighs him down so that he cannot travel fast. Sahadeva challenges Jaṭāsura, and then Bhīma arrives and also challenges him. Jaṭāsura drops the other Pāṇḍavas and closes with Bhīma; the two fight with trees and rocks, then wrestle each other. Eventually, seeing the Rākṣasa tiring, Bhīma hurls him to the ground, breaking all his limbs, and severs his head with a blow from his elbow.*

## THE BATTLE AGAINST THE YAKṢAS

[155] *Now Yudhiṣṭhira and the other Pāṇḍavas return to the hermitage of Nārāyaṇa and settle there. One day Yudhiṣṭhira explains that, at the end of his five-year absence, Arjuna will meet them at Mount Śveta, and so they set off there. On the way they stay for some days in the hermitage of the seer Vṛṣaparvan; then they travel on, and reach Mount Śveta and the lovely Mount Gandhamādana. They visit the seer Ārṣṭiṣeṇa in his hermitage.* [156] *Ārṣṭiṣeṇa greets the Pāṇḍavas. He expresses the hope that Yudhiṣṭhira is maintaining* dharma, *and warns him of the danger from the supernatural beings who frequent the mountain. Finally, he invites them all to stay with him.*

[157] — *Janamejaya asks to hear in detail about the Pāṇḍavas' life on Mount Gandhamādana, and Vaiśampāyana obliges. — The Pāṇḍavas pass the remainder of the fifth year of Arjuna's absence in Ārṣṭiṣeṇa's hermitage, where they see many wonderful things. One day beautiful, fragrant flowers are carried in by the breeze, and Draupadī implores Bhīma to rid the mountain of its Rākṣasas so that she may deck herself in flowers and visit its summit. Bhīma climbs to the top of the mountain and does battle single-handed against the Yakṣas and Rākṣasas; many are slain and the rest flee. The Rākṣasa Maṇimat attempts to rally them and engages Bhīma in combat, but Bhīma kills him with his club, and the rout is complete.*

[**158**] *Alarmed at Bhīma's absence, the other Pāṇḍavas seek him out; when Yudhiṣṭhira sees what he has done he castigates him for the slaughter. Meanwhile the surviving Rākṣasas tell the Yakṣa lord Kubera what has happened, and Kubera at once leads a mighty Yakṣa army against the Pāṇḍavas. But when he sees what fine warriors they are he is pleased. He tells Bhīma that his actions have released him from the curse of Agastya: once Maṇimat had spat on Agastya, who had cursed him to die with his troops at the hands of a mortal man; Kubera himself would be freed from his sin on seeing that man.*

[**159**] *Now Kubera warns Yudhiṣṭhira that he should keep Bhīma in check, and adds that Arjuna, who is learning to use celestial weapons in Indra's heaven, will soon rejoin his brothers. Then he returns to his home.*

[**160**] *The next morning, Dhaumya points out the great mountains to Yudhiṣṭhira: Mandara, Asta the western mountain, and Meru, round which sun and moon circle.* [**161**] *In their lovely mountain dwelling the Pāṇḍavas now await Arjuna's arrival. One day they see Indra's chariot approach, driven by Mātali: Arjuna is within it. They greet him with joy, and he tells them that he has mastered the use of the celestial weapons.* [**162**] *Now Indra himself arrives. Yudhiṣṭhira pays him honour and receives his blessing.*

[**163**] *After Indra's departure, Yudhiṣṭhira asks Arjuna to describe his time in heaven, and Arjuna relates his story. — While performing austerities, he is attacked by a man of the mountains who proves to be invulnerable to every weapon. This is in fact Śiva, who now resumes his own form and grants Arjuna a boon. Arjuna chooses the celestial weapons, and Śiva gives him the Pāśupata Weapon.*

[**164**] *The next day, Arjuna is visited by Indra and the other gods, who present him with their weapons. Indra tells him that he is to come and stay with him in heaven to learn the use of the weapons, and vanishes; then Mātali arrives with Indra's chariot and takes him there. There Arjuna stays, sharing Indra's throne and studying the weapons.*

[**165**] *When Arjuna has mastered the celestial weapons, Indra demands his fee: he must kill the Nivātakavaca demons. Arjuna sets out with Mātali in Indra's chariot. The gods bless him and give him the conch Devadatta.*[1] [**166**] *He reaches the ocean and sees the city of the Nivātakavacas. When the*

1 This conch, which Indra gives to Arjuna again in chapter 171 below, had in fact already been presented to him by the demon Maya: see 2.3.18.

*demons hear the sound of the chariot, they arm themselves and close the gates of the city. Arjuna blows his conch Devadatta, and the Nivātakavacas attack him.*

**[167]** *Assailed on all sides, Arjuna slays numerous demons with his arrows, while Mātali steers the chariot so that many others are trampled by the horses. Now Arjuna deploys the Mādhava Weapon. The desperate demons resort to their illusory power.* **[168]** *They produce a hail of rocks, a torrent of water, fire and fierce wind; one after the other, Arjuna uses his knowledge of celestial weapons to overcome them. Now a terrible darkness falls, and even Mātali is afraid; Arjuna pits his own illusory power against it, and for a while darkness and light follow each other in quick succession.*

**[169]** *Though he cannot see them, Arjuna continues to battle fiercely against the Nivātakavacas, till they flee for the safety of their city. Light returns and reveals the massive scale of their losses. But now they take to the air and pile rocks and mountains on Arjuna. Arjuna deploys Indra's Thunderbolt Weapon; it kills the demons and destroys their illusions. Mātali drives Arjuna into the lovely city and explains that it had originally belonged to the gods. The Nivātakavacas had performed fierce austerities and won a boon from Brahmā, and they had chosen to live there and to be invulnerable to the gods; this is why Indra had taught Arjuna the use of the celestial weapons.*

**[170]** *Returning to Indra's heaven, Arjuna observes another splendid city. Mātali tells him of Pulomā and Kālakā, two demon women who won from Brahmā the boon that their descendants should be invulnerable to the gods: this city of Hiraṇyapura is where those descendants live. Arjuna attacks the demons and kills many of them; they make their city fly through the air, but Arjuna shoots it down in ruin. He continues to battle against them single-handed, but cannot overcome them, and so deploys the Weapon of Rudra. Immediately the battlefield is filled with the forms of fierce creatures that set upon the demons and destroy them. Mātali praises Arjuna's feat and drives him back to Indra's heaven, where the gods also heap praise upon him.*

**[171]** *Indra rewards Arjuna with impregnable armour, the conch Devadatta, and a diadem. Arjuna spends five years in Indra's heaven and then returns to his brothers. — After hearing Arjuna's account of his adventures, Yudhiṣṭhira asks to see the celestial weapons, and Arjuna promises to show them the following day.* **[172]** *The next morning, he shows his brothers the celestial weapons. As he is about to use them, the earth trembles, mountains are torn apart and the* *sun ceases to shine. The immortals appear, and Nārada warns Arjuna never to use the weapons unless there is real need.*

## THE CONSTRICTOR

**[173]** *Reunited, the Pāṇḍavas spend a further four years in the forest: ten years of their term of exile have now passed. As the eleventh year passes, Bhīma persuades Yudhiṣṭhira to mount an attack on Duryodhana, and Ghaṭotkaca bears them down from the mountain.*

**[174]** *The Pāṇḍavas return to Vṛṣaparvan's hermitage, where they spend the night before setting out once again for the realm of King Subāhu. Here they are rejoined by their retinue, and Ghaṭotkaca leaves them. They proceed to Mount Yāmuna, where they settle. It is here that Bhīma is rescued from a snake by Yudhiṣṭhira, and it is here that the Pāṇḍavas pass their twelfth year, before moving on to the lake Dvaitavana.*

**[175]** *— Janamejaya asks Vaiśaṃpāyana how it could be that the mighty Bhīma was overcome by a snake, and Vaiśaṃpāyana tells him the story. — As Bhīma roams through the forest hunting deer, he sees an enormous constrictor in a mountain cave. It seizes him, and despite his strength he cannot free himself.* **[176]** *Bhīma wants to know how the snake was able to overcome his might, and the snake agrees to tell him before eating him. Formerly he was King Nahuṣa, but he treated Brahmins with dishonour and Agastya cursed him to become a snake. However, Indra specified that the curse would be lifted when someone gave correct answers to his questions, and sympathetic Brahmins added that he would be able to outmatch the strength of any creature. Bhīma now laments his fate, not for himself but for his family.*

*Meanwhile, Yudhiṣṭhira has seen terrible portents. Discovering that Bhīma is missing, he tracks him down.* **[177]** *When he learns the situation he offers to answer the snake's questions. The snake asks him, 'Who is a Brahmin?', to which Yudhiṣṭhira replies that a Brahmin is someone who lives a virtuous life, rather than someone born in a particular line. At this, the snake releases Bhīma.* **[178]** *Now Yudhiṣṭhira questions the snake about human conduct and its consequences in the afterlife, and about the nature of consciousness. The snake answers wisely, concluding with an account of his own fall; then, freed from his curse, he returns to heaven.*

## THE MEETING WITH MĀRKAṆḌEYA

**[179]** *The rainy season comes and passes, while the Pāṇḍavas travel along the river Sarasvatī; then they return to the Kāmyaka forest.* **[180]** *Kṛṣṇa arrives with his wife Satyabhāmā, and greets them warmly. He brings news of Draupadī's family, and of her children and Abhimanyu. Then he promises Yudhiṣṭhira the support of his people in reclaiming his kingdom. At this point the mighty ascetic Mārkaṇḍeya arrives, as does Nārada.*

**[181]** *Yudhiṣṭhira asks Mārkaṇḍeya about the consequences of human actions: do they pursue a man into the next world? Mārkaṇḍeya replies that men were first created pure and good; they were friends with the gods and lived for thousands of years. But they became corrupted, wicked and short-lived. When a man dies he is reborn instantly, and his former deeds determine his lot.* **[182]** *Now the Pāṇḍavas ask Mārkaṇḍeya about the greatness of Brahmins, and he replies by telling them the story of a Haihaya king who accidentally killed an ascetic while hunting. With his companions he visited Tārkṣya Ariṣṭanemi, the ascetic's father, and confessed what he had done; but then Tārkṣya showed them his son, who had been restored to life through the power of asceticism.*

**[183]** *Next Mārkaṇḍeya tells the story of Atri. Atri planned to retire to the forest, and went to see King Vainya in hopes of receiving wealth to pass on to his sons. But when he offered praise to Vainya he was contradicted by another ascetic, Gautama, and a dispute arose as to whether kings hold supreme power. Sanatkumāra, asked to resolve it, agreed with Atri and declared that kings have been granted supremacy by Brahmins in order to maintain* dharma. *Pleased with this outcome, Vainya rewarded Atri generously.*

**[184]** *Now Mārkaṇḍeya speaks again of Tārkṣya. He asked Sarasvatī for instruction; she told him that the man who knows* brahman *attains heaven, as does the one who gives gifts of cattle. She also gave rules for the performance of the* agnihotra *ritual, from which she herself first arose.*

## THE FISH

**[185]** *Yudhiṣṭhira asks to hear the story of Manu Vaivasvata, and Mārkaṇḍeya narrates. — Manu is engaged in performing austerities when he* *is addressed by a little fish, which asks him to save it from being eaten by bigger fishes. He takes it and keeps it in a jar. When it outgrows the jar, he transfers it to a pond; when it outgrows the pond he transfers it to the Gaṅgā; when it outgrows even the Gaṅgā he releases it into the ocean. The fish warns him that soon a terrible flood will destroy everything on earth: Manu should build a boat and place in it the seeds of all creatures, and then await the fish. Manu does as he has been told, and the fish comes. It tows his boat to the Himālaya and tells him to moor it there. Then it reveals that it is in fact Brahmā, and instructs Manu to create all creatures.*

**[186]** *Yudhiṣṭhira now remarks that Mārkaṇḍeya has, uniquely, experienced the repeated dissolution and re-creation of the world, and asks him to describe it. — Mārkaṇḍeya begins by reverencing Kṛṣṇa, whom he identifies as the creator of all. He then describes the succession of the ages. The Kṛta Age lasts for a total of 4,800 years; it is followed in turn by the Tretā Age (3,600 years), the Dvāpara Age (2,400 years) and the Kali Age (1,200 years), after which comes a new Kṛta Age. A thousand such cycles constitute one day of Brahmā. As each cycle nears its end men become degenerate and nature begins to fail; at the end of the thousandth cycle the world is devastated by famine, fire and flood, till nothing is left but a raging ocean. Mārkaṇḍeya wanders alone through this desolation till he sees a child sitting beneath a banyan tree. The child, who is Kṛṣṇa, bids him enter his mouth; Mārkaṇḍeya does so, and finds within the whole world. Mārkaṇḍeya remains there for a hundred and one years, till a breeze wafts him back through Kṛṣṇa's mouth.*

*Mārkaṇḍeya asks Kṛṣṇa for an explanation of what he has seen.* **[187]** *Kṛṣṇa answers: he is Nārāyaṇa and all the gods, he is the source of all that is sacred. He takes on human form to overcome evil; he is the creator and destroyer of all. He has shown Mārkaṇḍeya the world hidden within himself during the dissolution; when Brahmā awakes he will re-create it. — Mārkaṇḍeya assures Yudhiṣṭhira that the Kṛṣṇa sitting before him is this same greatest of gods; Yudhiṣṭhira should place his trust in him.*

**[188]** *The Pāṇḍavas pay honour to Kṛṣṇa; then Yudhiṣṭhira asks Mārkaṇḍeya to tell him more about the characteristics of the Kali Age. Mārkaṇḍeya describes how the whole world will degenerate into barbarism and ruin; then, at the end* *of the Kali Age, a new Kṛta Age will begin, and a Brahmin named Kalki Viṣṇuyaśas will destroy the barbarians and bring peace.* [**189**] *He will give the world to the twice-born at a great horse sacrifice, and then* dharma *will prosper once more. Mārkaṇḍeya urges Yudhiṣṭhira to observe* dharma, *and Yudhiṣṭhira promises to do so.*

## THE FROG

[**190**] *Again Yudhiṣṭhira asks Mārkaṇḍeya about the greatness of Brahmins, and Mārkaṇḍeya narrates. — The Ikṣvāku king Parikṣit is out hunting when he comes upon a lovely pond. Resting there, he sees an exceedingly beautiful girl and desires her; she agrees to be his on condition that he never lets her see water. He agrees and takes her home, and they live together. One day, tired and thirsty, he comes upon a hidden pond, and suggests she dive in; she does so, and does not reappear. When he has the pond drained he finds nothing but a frog. He now gives orders for all frogs to be killed, until the frog king comes to beg him to stop, and reveals that the 'girl' was in fact a frog: she is his own daughter, who has deceived many kings in this way. Parikṣit still wants her back, and her father hands her over with the pronouncement that her children will be hostile to Brahmins. In time three sons are born to her, named Śala, Dala and Bala. Parikṣit hands the kingdom over to Śala and retires to the forest. Śala learns that the horses of the seer Vāmadeva are exceptionally swift; he borrows them, then refuses to return them, and Vāmadeva has him killed by Rākṣasas. Dala succeeds him; he attempts to shoot Vāmadeva with his arrows, and Vāmadeva first makes him shoot his own son and then paralyses him. Dala's wife intercedes for him, and Vāmadeva frees Dala from his sin.*

## INDRADYUMNA

[**191**] — *Now Mārkaṇḍeya is asked whether there is anyone older than himself, and he replies with the story of Indradyumna, who had fallen from heaven when his fame ran out. Looking for someone who*

*recognized him he had approached Mārkaṇḍeya, who suggested he ask an owl that lived in the mountains. The owl passed him on to a crane that was even older than itself, and the crane to a yet older turtle; the turtle had recognized Indradyumna, who was then able to return to heaven.*

## DHUNDHUMĀRA

**[192]** — *Yudhiṣṭhira asks Mārkaṇḍeya why the Ikṣvāku king Kuvalāśva came to be known as Dhundhumāra, and Mārkaṇḍeya tells the story.* — *The seer Uttaṅka wins a boon from Viṣṇu; when he chooses devotion to* dharma, *Viṣṇu grants the boon and adds that he will also bring about the destruction of the demon Dhundhu by means of King Kuvalāśva.*

**[193]** *Kuvalāśva is the son of Bṛhadaśva, the Ikṣvāku king of Ayodhyā. When Bṛhadaśva retires to the forest, Uttaṅka goes to him and urges him instead to kill Dhundhu, a demon who is performing austerities in an attempt to overthrow the gods.* **[194]** *Bṛhadaśva promises that his son Kuvalāśva will carry out the task.*

— *At this point Yudhiṣṭhira interrupts the story with a request to learn Dhundhu's origin, and Mārkaṇḍeya obliges.* — *Brahmā is born from a lotus that grows from the navel of the sleeping Viṣṇu; he is frightened by two demons, Madhu and Kaiṭabha, and wakes Viṣṇu. Viṣṇu and the demons exchange boons: his boon is that he will kill them, and their boon is that they will become his sons. Viṣṇu now beheads the two with his discus.*

**[195]** *Dhundhu is the son of Madhu and Kaiṭabha. Granted a boon by Brahmā, he chooses to be invulnerable to gods, demigods and demons; he then fiercely assails Viṣṇu and the other gods. It is at this time that Kuvalāśva and his twenty-one thousand sons attack him. They dig him out of his underground lair; when he burns them with his fire, Kuvalāśva dowses the fire with water that streams from his body, and thus becomes known as Dhundhumāra, 'Killer of Dhundhu'. The gods give him boons and blessings. The Ikṣvāku line springs from the three of his sons who survive the encounter with Dhundhu.*

## THE FAITHFUL WIFE

[**196**] — *Now Yudhiṣṭhira questions Mārkaṇḍeya about the greatness of women and their fearsomely difficult* dharma. *Mārkaṇḍeya replies that a woman attains heaven not through any religious practice but through obedience to her husband,* [**197**] *and he relates the tale of the Brahmin Kauśika. — Kauśika curses a female crane when its droppings fall on him, and the bird falls dead. He then begs food from a village woman, but becomes enraged when she tends to her husband first. She maintains that her* dharma *is unqualified obedience to her husband, and tells Kauśika that he should overcome his anger; she advises him to visit a hunter living in Mithilā, who will proclaim* dharma *to him.*

## THE BRAHMIN'S CONVERSATION WITH THE HUNTER

[**198**] *Kauśika travels to the prosperous city of Mithilā, where he finds the hunter selling meat in the slaughterhouse; the hunter takes him home. Kauśika deplores the hunter's occupation, but the hunter explains that it is his hereditary calling, which it would be wrong to turn away from. People should follow their* dharma *and avoid wrongdoing.*

[**199**] *The hunter explains that his terrible profession is a consequence of bad deeds in a previous life, which he is striving to destroy. Meat lawfully eaten does not pollute, and it is right to do perform one's own* dharma *as well as possible, even if the task be an unpleasant one. Whatever may be said about non-violence, life entails killing: merely to walk on the ground results in the death of creatures. But the person who is devoted to his job earns a good name.* [**200**] *There are many disparities between people's merit and their lot in life, and these result from their deeds in a previous birth. Questioned by Kauśika, the hunter tells him that creatures are reborn over and over again; they attain higher or lower births according to their past deeds. Only through* dharma *may one break the chain and reach freedom.*

[**201**] *The hunter describes how the wise man adheres to* dharma *and*

*avoids evil acts. Then he gives a brief account of the constitution of the world according to the Sāṃkhya philosophy.* **[202]** *At Kauśika's request he lists the elements and their properties, and expounds the importance of overcoming the senses.* **[203]** *Then he speaks of the three Sāṃkhya qualities:* tamas, *Darkness, leading to dullness and ignorance,* rajas, *Passion, leading to engagement with the world, and* sattva, *Goodness, leading to wise detachment. Next he discourses on the different vital airs that energize the body, and emphasizes that only through virtue and restraint may final release be won.*

**[204]** *Kauśika praises the hunter's wisdom; the hunter invites him to visit his parents. Then he speaks of the honour in which he holds his parents, and the care which he lavishes upon them.* **[205]** *He chides Kauśika for leaving home without taking his own parents' leave, and urges him to return quickly and do them due honour. Now Kauśika blesses the hunter for saving him from falling into evil, and asks him the reason for his present lowly status. The hunter explains that in his former life he was a Brahmin, but he had shot an ascetic by mistake when hunting. The wounded man had cursed him to be reborn as a hunter.* **[206]** *The hunter had begged forgiveness, and the ascetic mitigated the curse by permitting him to be deeply virtuous in his hunter's birth. Kauśika, having heard all this, returns to his home and honours his parents.*

## AṄGIRAS

**[207]** — *Yudhiṣṭhira asks Mārkaṇḍeya to tell him about Aṅgiras and the many different ritual fires, and about the birth of Skanda the war god. Mārkaṇḍeya narrates. — The god of Fire, Agni, withdraws to the forest to perform austerities, and in his absence the sage Aṅgiras takes on his role. Agni is dismayed, but Aṅgiras persuades him to resume his primacy and to make Aṅgiras his first-born son. Aṅgiras himself now has a son, Bṛhaspati. The various fires are all descendants of Aṅgiras:* **[208]** *his own sons and daughters are all ritual fires,* **[209]** *and many more ritual fires are born in Bṛhaspati's lineage.* **[210]** *The fire of asceticism, Tapas, is born as the result of the austerities performed by mighty sages,* **[211]** *and further fires are born in Tapas's lineage.*

**[212]** *Agni hides in the ocean, but is given away by fish: he curses them to become the food of other creatures. He hides in the earth, then again in the ocean; Aṅgiras brings him back.*

**[213]** — *Having spoken of the origin of the fires, Mārkaṇḍeya now tells of the birth of Skanda.* — *The gods and demons are striving against one another, and the demons have the upper hand. Indra sets out to find a hero who will rally the demoralized army of the gods. He encounters a woman being molested by the demon Keśin, and rescues her. She is Prajāpati's daughter Devasenā ('Army of the gods'), and she tells Indra that her husband will be a mighty hero. Indra decides that only Fire can father such a hero. A ceremony is performed to induce Fire to come forth from the sun. He does so, but is captivated by the wives of the seven seers and chooses to become the household fire so that he may see them every day; after some time, frustrated, he leaves for the forest.*

*Dakṣa's daughter Svāhā, who is in love with him, decides to go to him in the form of the seers' wives.* **[214]** *She visits him, assuming the forms of one after another of the wives of the seers in order to lie with him again and again. She cannot assume the form of Vasiṣṭha's wife Arundhatī, whose ascetic power and faithfulness is too great, so all in all she lies with him six times; each time she then becomes a bird to carry away his seed and deposit it in a lake on Mount Śveta. From the seed is born the six-headed Skanda, who attains full growth in four days; his roars and his might terrify the world. He splits open Mount Krauñca.*

**[215]** *Svāhā claims that Skanda is her own son, and Viśvāmitra establishes that this is the truth, but none the less the six seers leave their wives. The gods appeal to Indra; he sends the Mothers of the World to kill Skanda, but when they see him they adopt him as their son. Fire too comes to visit his child.*

**[216]** *Indra leads an attack on Skanda; Skanda breathes fire and burns the forces of the gods, who defect to him. When Indra's thunderbolt strikes Skanda's side, it produces another terrifying young man, Viśākha. Indra too now takes refuge with Skanda.* **[217]** *The thunderbolt's impact produces yet more male beings: they are to be Skanda's companions. The daughters of the fire named Tapas come to Skanda and ask to become Mothers of the World; he grants their wish.*

**[218]** *The goddess Śrī herself now pays honour to Skanda, and the* *seers appeal to him to replace Indra; even Indra pleads with him, but he refuses, and asks instead to command the army of the gods. After his installation, Rudra honours him; he comes to be known as Rudra's son, since Fire is known as Rudra and permeated by Rudra. Now Indra brings in Devasenā, and Skanda is married to her.* [**219**] *The six seers' wives approach Skanda and ask to be his mothers. He agrees, and they become the constellation of the Kṛttikās. The Mothers of the World ask to replace the earlier Mothers and to devour their children. Skanda appoints them to be the diseases that afflict children up to the age of sixteen.* [**220**] *Svāhā asks to stay always with Agni; Skanda grants this. Then at Brahmā's urging he goes and honours his father Śiva.*

[**221**] *Śiva now sets off in a magnificent procession of the gods. As they go they are attacked by an enormous force of demons. At first Indra's troops are able to withstand them, but then a mighty demon named Mahiṣa joins the assault, brandishing a mountain. The gods flee, but Skanda kills Mahiṣa and the rest of the demons. Indra pays him great honour.*

## DRAUPADĪ'S CONVERSATION WITH SATYABHĀMĀ

[**222**] *Kṛṣṇa's chief queen Satyabhāmā asks Draupadī how she keeps the Pāṇḍavas faithful to her: does she use spells or potions? Draupadī replies that she decries such methods; she waits dutifully upon her five husbands. Before Yudhiṣṭhira's downfall she was responsible for the running of the whole imperial household.* [**223**] *She tells Satyabhāmā that she should similarly devote herself fully to Kṛṣṇa, who will then give her his love.* [**224**] *Kṛṣṇa, who is ready to leave, now summons Satyabhāmā. Before joining him, she assures Draupadī that she and he husbands will regain what they have lost.*

## THE TOUR OF THE CATTLE-STATIONS

[**225**] *One day a Brahmin who has visited the Pāṇḍavas in the forest goes on to see Dhṛtarāṣṭra, and tells him of their circumstances. Dhṛtarāṣṭra is grieved and*

*deeply troubled, for he fears that in time the Pāṇḍavas will seek their revenge and overwhelm the Kauravas.*

**[226]** *Karṇa and Śakuni urge Duryodhana to make the most of his good fortune and the distress of his enemies: he should lead a party to observe the Pāṇḍavas in their forest exile and savour their misery.* **[227]** *Duryodhana likes this plan, but fears that Dhṛtarāṣṭra will not permit him to go. He tells Karṇa and Śakuni to devise a way round the problem; Karṇa proposes a tour of the cattle-stations, and this is agreed on.* **[228]** *The proposal is put to Dhṛtarāṣṭra. He objects that it might lead to an encounter with the Pāṇḍavas, but Śakuni persuades him and he gives his reluctant assent. Duryodhana now travels towards Lake Dvaitavana with a large body of followers.*

**[229]** *Duryodhana completes his inspection of the cattle and continues towards Lake Dvaitavana, hunting and pursuing other enjoyments along the way. But when an advance party reaches the lake they are sent back by the Gandharvas whose king is encamped there.* **[230]** *When Duryodhana learns what has happened he angrily instructs his troops to attack the Gandharvas. A great battle takes place: many Gandharvas are slain, but their king Citrasena uses his illusory weapons against the Kauravas, who flee in large numbers. Karṇa alone withstands the attack, but in time his chariot is destroyed and he is forced to flee.* **[231]** *Duryodhana holds his ground, but is taken prisoner along with a number of his supporters. The rest flee and seek refuge with Yudhiṣṭhira. Bhīma speaks harshly of Duryodhana and his advisers, till Yudhiṣṭhira silences him.*

**[232]** *Yudhiṣṭhira instructs his brothers to free Duryodhana, using as little force as possible.* **[233]** *Cheered on by the Kauravas, the four Pāṇḍavas ride out against the Gandharvas. They try to achieve their aims through light skirmishing and parley, but to no avail. A violent battle begins.* **[234]** *The Pāṇḍava brothers kill huge numbers of Gandharvas, Arjuna using his celestial weapons to great effect. Citrasena, concealing himself, uses his powers of illusion against Arjuna, who battles back fiercely. Overpowered, Citrasena now reveals himself to his old friend*[1] *and the fighting comes to an end.*

**[235]** *Citrasena explains why Duryodhana was taken prisoner; Arjuna none the less demands that he be freed. Yudhiṣṭhira thanks the Gandharvas and gives them leave to depart, and Indra revives their fallen comrades. Yudhiṣṭhira now upbraids Duryodhana for his behaviour and sends him home.*

1 See 3.45.

**[236]** *Duryodhana travels to Hāstinapura in shame. On the way, Karṇa congratulates him on his victory;* **[237]** *Duryodhana explains that his release was not his own doing, and describes to Karṇa the Pāṇḍavas' battle against the Gandharvas.* **[238]** *He reveals the humiliation of his rescue at the hands of those he has wronged, and announces that he intends to fast to death; Duḥśāsana shall rule in his place. Duḥśāsana and Karṇa do their best to dissuade him.* **[239]** *Śakuni too tries to cheer him, but he is adamant; he sits and begins his fast. Meanwhile the demons have learnt of his intention, which will harm their cause. They send a woman named Kṛtyā to fetch him to them in the underworld, and she does so.*

**[240]** *The demons instruct Duryodhana: he was created for them by Śiva and the Goddess, and they will ensure his victory. Kṛtyā returns Duryodhana to the place where he had started his fast. In the morning Karṇa urges him to abandon thoughts of dying, and he arises, full of resolve, and rides in splendour into his city.* **[241]** *Bhīṣma scolds him over his shameful behaviour and advocates making peace with the Pāṇḍavas, but Duryodhana and his followers simply laugh at him and walk away.*

*Now Duryodhana tells his followers that he wishes to perform the royal consecration, but his household priest explains that this cannot be done while Yudhiṣṭhira lives. However, there is an alternative and equal rite, in which the sacrificial enclosure is ploughed with a plough made of gold brought in tribute. Duryodhana orders arrangements to be made for its performance.*

**[242]** *Invitations are sent out to kings and Brahmins, and a messenger is also sent to Dvaitavana to invite the Pāṇḍavas. Yudhiṣṭhira will not attend, as his term of exile is not yet complete. The rite is performed,* **[243]** *and Duryodhana returns home. Karṇa congratulates him and bids him look forward to the day when the Pāṇḍavas are slain and he can perform the royal consecration itself; and he vows to kill Arjuna. News of this vow reaches Yudhiṣṭhira and causes him much anxiety.*

## THE DREAM DEER

**[244]** *Yudhiṣṭhira has a dream in which he is approached by weeping deer. When he asks them what troubles them, they answer that they are the few deer to have survived the Pāṇḍavas' skilful hunting, and they ask him to move elsewhere so* *that their numbers may increase once more. In the morning he and his brothers leave for Kāmyaka.*

## THE BUSHEL OF RICE

[**245**] *Kṛṣṇa Dvaipāyana Vyāsa visits the Pāṇḍavas; seeing their sufferings, he discourses to them on the importance of maintaining equanimity through good and bad fortune. Yudhiṣṭhira asks him whether giving or asceticism carries the greater benefit in the next life; Vyāsa replies that giving is superior,* [**246**] *and tells the story of Mudgala, who lived off grains of rice he gleaned and yet gave food generously to others. He was visited by the seer Durvāsas in the form of a naked madman; Durvāsas ate all of Mudgala's food for six days running, and yet Mudgala continued to give without ill feeling. Durvāsas now praised Mudgala highly and told him that he had earned a place in heaven, but when the gods' messenger arrived to take him there he asked first to know more of the nature of life in heaven.* [**247**] *The messenger was amazed, but described the delights of heaven to Mudgala; he also described how, once the merit that earns a person a place in heaven is exhausted, he falls back to earth to suffer rebirth as a human. Mudgala now declined the offer. Instead he practised total serenity until he attained eternal release. Vyāsa tells Yudhiṣṭhira that he too should not grieve, and assures him that he will regain his lost kingdom. Then he leaves.*

## THE ABDUCTION OF DRAUPADĪ

[**248**] *One day while the Pāṇḍavas are out hunting, King Jayadratha of Sindhu passes by the hermitage where they are staying; he sees Draupadī and desires her. He sends his companion Koṭikāśya to find out who she is.*

[**249**] *Koṭikāśya addresses Draupadī. He praises her beauty, names all the princes who are travelling in his party, and asks her to identify herself.* [**250**] *Draupadī modestly answers him, and explains that her five husbands will soon be home; she invites the travellers to stay and await their return.* [**251**] *Now Jayadratha himself visits her; she greets him courteously. He asks her to abandon her husbands and be his wife. Furious, she refuses.* [**252**] *She*

*warns Jayadratha not to incur the enmity of the Pāṇḍavas, but he drags her into his chariot. Dhaumya follows among the footsoldiers as he carries her off.*

[253] *Meanwhile, the Pāṇḍavas observe bad portents and return from their hunt. They find Draupadī's maidservant in tears; she tells them what has happened and they set out in pursuit. They catch up with Jayadratha's army; Dhaumya calls out to them to attack.*

[254] *Jayadratha asks Draupadī to identify her husbands to him, and she does so. Then the Pāṇḍavas attack.* [255] *Jayadratha's supporters are slaughtered, and he himself flees for the forest. Draupadī is rescued, and Bhīma and Arjuna prepare to pursue Jayadratha, but Yudhiṣṭhira stops them, reminding them that he is married to Dhṛtarāṣṭra's daughter Duḥśalā. However, Draupadī is enraged and insists that they should go. Yudhiṣṭhira now returns with Draupadī and the twins to the hermitage. Bhīma and Arjuna ride after Jayadratha; Arjuna shoots his horses, and he runs away. Bhīma follows him; as he does so, Arjuna cautions him not to kill him.*

[256] *Bhīma catches up with Jayadratha, seizes him by the hair and beats him, kicking him in the head. Arjuna intervenes, and Bhīma contents himself with shaving Jayadratha's head with a crescent-shaped arrow, leaving five tufts of hair, and forcing him to acknowledge himself the Pāṇḍavas' slave. Then he parades him before Yudhiṣṭhira and Draupadī, before releasing him on their instructions. Jayadratha, shamed, performs austerities to secure a boon from Śiva. He asks to be able to defeat all five Pāṇḍavas in battle, but Śiva tells him that is impossible; however, he will be able to check each of them in battle, save for Arjuna, who is under Kṛṣṇa's protection.*

## RĀMA

[257] *Yudhiṣṭhira speaks to Mārkaṇḍeya. He bemoans his fate, and asks whether any other man was ever so unfortunate.* [258] *Mārkaṇḍeya responds with the name of Rāma, who suffered unmatched woe. Yudhiṣṭhira asks to hear about him, and Mārkaṇḍeya relates. — The Ikṣvāku king Daśaratha has four sons by his three queens: Rāma, Lakṣmaṇa, Śatrughna and Bharata. King Janaka of Videha has a daughter Sītā, who is married to Rāma.*

*The Rākṣasa Rāvaṇa is descended from Prajāpati through Pulastya.*

**[259]** *Rāvaṇa has a brother, Kumbhakarṇa, two half-brothers, Vibhīṣaṇa and Khara, and a half-sister, Śūrpaṇakhā. The first three perform fierce austerities until Brahmā grants each of them a boon. Rāvaṇa chooses to be invincible to gods, demons, and other supernatural beings; Kumbhakarṇa chooses to sleep long; Vibhīṣaṇa chooses virtue and the Weapon of Brahmā, to which Brahmā adds immortality. Rāvaṇa now expels his older half-brother, Kubera, from Laṅkā; Vibhīṣaṇa goes with him.*

*Rāvaṇa becomes king of the Rākṣasas, and the gods themselves fear him.* **[260]** *The Fire god, speaking on behalf of the immortals, appeals to Brahmā for help. Brahmā explains that Rāvaṇa is invincible to all but men, and reveals that Viṣṇu has already taken human form to destroy him. He instructs them all to beget sons on bears and monkeys to help Viṣṇu, and they do so. He also instructs a female Gandharva named Dundubhī to take the form of the hunchback Mantharā, and tells her what she must do.*

**[261]** *Daśaratha determines to make Rāma prince regent. Mantharā incites Kaikeyī, mother of Rāma's half-brother Bharata; Kaikeyī goes to Daśaratha and claims a boon he had formerly promised her. She demands that Bharata becomes prince regent instead, and that Rāma is exiled to the forest. Rāma leaves with his brother Lakṣmaṇa and his wife Sītā. After a time, Daśaratha dies and Kaikeyī tells Bharata to take the kingship, but he will not do so. He visits Rāma in his forest exile, and then rules from Nandigrāma with a pair of Rāma's sandals before him.*

*Meanwhile Rāma does battle with Khara in a dispute occasioned by Śūrpaṇakhā; he slays Khara and fourteen thousand Rākṣasas, and Śūrpaṇakhā presents herself to Rāvaṇa with her nose and lips cut off. Rāvaṇa determines on vengeance.* **[262]** *He commands his former minister Mārīca to help him, and Mārīca reluctantly agrees. The two of them travel to Rāma's hermitage, where Rāvaṇa takes the form of an ascetic and Mārīca takes the form of a golden deer.*

*Sītā sees the deer and sends Rāma to catch it, leaving Lakṣmaṇa on guard. After a chase Rāma recognizes the deer as a Rākṣasa and kills it with a an arrow; the dying Mārīca calls out in Rāma's voice. Sītā hears and is fearful; Lakṣmaṇa assures her that all is well, but she insists that he follow Rāma. Now Rāvaṇa enters. Sītā offers him hospitality, but he resumes his own shape and invites her to become his wife. When she scornfully rejects him, he drags her away by the hair and carries her off through the sky. The vulture Jaṭāyu sees Sītā being abducted,* [**263**] *and attacks Rāvaṇa, who cuts off his wings. As she is carried away, Sītā tries to leave a trail of ornaments; she drops her robe into a group of five monkeys.*

*Meanwhile Rāma meets Lakṣmaṇa, and the two of them learn what has happened from the dying Jaṭāyu. Lakṣmaṇa is seized by the Rākṣasa Kabandha, and despairs; Rāma encourages him, and together they kill Kabandha. From the body emerges the Gandharva Viśvāvasu, who had been cursed to be born as a Rākṣasa: he advises the brothers to seek the help of the monkey Sugrīva.*

[**264**] *Rāma and Lakṣmaṇa travel to Lake Pampā; on the nearby Mount Ṛśyamūka they meet Sugrīva, who shows them Sītā's robe. Rāma installs Sugrīva as king of all the monkeys and promises to kill his brother Vālin, while Sugrīva promises to rescue Sītā. They all travel to the Kiṣkindhā forest, where Sugrīva roars in challenge to Vālin. Vālin's wife tries to prevent Vālin from fighting his brother, but he insists. Neither monkey can overcome the other, but, at a signal, Rāma shoots Vālin. Sugrīva takes over his kingdom.*

*In the meantime Rāvaṇa has placed the grieving Sītā in a palace near a grove of* aśoka *trees. Her Rākṣasa guards threaten to eat her, but she replies that she would prefer this to life without Rāma, the only man she will have. The guards go to report her words to Rāvaṇa, and in their absence a Rākṣasa woman named Trijaṭā passes on to her news of Rāma's doings; she assures her that he will soon rescue her and defeat Rāvaṇa.* [**265**] *Rāvaṇa visits Sītā and asks her to become his queen, but she will have nothing to do with him. He promises not to approach her as long as she is unwilling, and leaves.*

[**266**] *Rāma and Lakṣmaṇa continue to stay with Sugrīva, but Rāma is impatient and sends Lakṣmaṇa to Sugrīva to find out what steps he is taking. Sugrīva answers that he has sent monkeys out in every direction to seek for news of Sītā; they are due to return soon. The monkeys that travelled to the north, east and west do return, but without news; however, there is no sign of the party that went south. After two months there is word of them suggesting they have been successful, and soon they arrive, led by Hanumān, who confirms that they have located Sītā, and tells of their doings. They had despaired on reaching the shore of the*

*ocean, but then Jaṭāyu's brother Saṃpāti had appeared and told them the whole story of his brother's death and Rāma's misfortune; he had also spoken of Laṅkā, and said that he was sure Sītā would be found there. Hanumān now leapt the ocean; he found Sītā, and reassured her, and she gave him a jewel as a token. Then he set the city ablaze and returned home.*

**[267]** *Great armies of monkeys now come to aid Rāma. They set out and reach the shore. Rāma warns the ocean that if it does not make way he will use celestial weapons to dry it up. The ocean replies that if it does so for Rāma, it may have to do so for others also; better that the skilled monkey Nala should construct a causeway. Rāma instructs Nala, and the causeway is built. Vibhīṣaṇa arrives; Rāma installs him as king of the Rākṣasas. Then they cross over to Laṅkā.*

*Now Rāma sends the monkey Aṅgada to Rāvaṇa.* **[268]** *Aṅgada visits Rāvaṇa in his fortified stronghold of Laṅkā. He warns him that if he does not release Sītā there will be a massacre of the Rākṣasas. Furious, Rāvaṇa has him seized, but he escapes back to Rāma, who attacks Laṅkā. There is great slaughter on both sides, but it is Rāma who succeeds in destroying the city.*

**[269]** *Rāvaṇa leads his forces against Rāma, and there is a fierce battle.* **[270]** *The Rākṣasa Prahasta attacks Vibhīṣaṇa, and is slain by him. Dhūmrākṣa assails the host of monkeys; Hanumān overcomes him and kills him. When Rāvaṇa hears the news he has the sleeping Kumbhakarṇa woken and sends him out to fight together with Vajravega and Pramāthin.* **[271]** *Kumbhakarṇa laughs at the monkeys' assaults on him and takes Sugrīva captive, but Lakṣmaṇa kills him with the Weapon of Brahmā. Then he turns his attack on Vajravega and Pramāthin, who fight back until they are slain by the monkeys Hanumān and Nīla.*

**[272]** *Hearing of the deaths of his generals, Rāvaṇa now sends his son Indrajit into battle. Indrajit fights fiercely against Lakṣmaṇa and Aṅgada; then, when his chariot and horses are destroyed, he becomes invisible and showers arrows upon Rāma and Lakṣmaṇa, and they fall to the ground.* **[273]** *Vibhīṣaṇa rescues the two brothers and Sugrīva frees their bodies of arrows. Vibhīṣaṇa presents them with water sent by Kubera that allows them to see what is invisible. Now Lakṣmaṇa does battle with Indrajit once more and slays him. When Rāvaṇa sees that Indrajit's chariot is empty* *he determines to kill Sītā, but the wise Rākṣasa Avindhya stops him and urges him to kill Rāma instead.*

**[274]** *Rāvaṇa rides out in his chariot to see his army worsted by the monkeys. He uses his illusory power to create thousands of Rākṣasa warriors, but these are slain by Rāma. Then he creates numerous Rākṣasa doubles of Rāma and Lakṣmaṇa themselves, but once again Rāma kills them. Now Indra's charioteer Mātali arrives in his chariot and urges Rāma to mount it and slay Rāvaṇa. At first doubtful whether this is a further illusion, Rāma is persuaded by Vibhīṣaṇa. Mātali drives him to Rāvaṇa, and the two do battle; Rāma kills Rāvaṇa with the Weapon of Brahmā. Nothing is left of the Rākṣasa's body, not even ash.*

**[275]** *The gods and other celestials pay honour to Rāma, who hands Laṅkā over to Vibhīṣaṇa. Avindhya brings Sītā to Rāma, but he will not take her back, for she has been in another man's hands. She calls on the gods to testify to her innocence, and they do so. Daśaratha too appears and tells Rāma that he should return to Ayodhyā and rule. Rāma now takes Sītā back. Brahmā offers him a boon; he chooses for the fallen monkeys to come back to life. Sītā grants Hanumān that his life shall last as long as Rāma's fame. They all return across the causeway, and Rāma rewards the monkeys and dismisses them. He installs Aṅgada as prince regent in Kiṣkindhā, then receives his own kingship back from his brother Bharata. He performs ten horse sacrifices.*

**[276]** — *Having finished narrating the story of Rāma, Mārkaṇḍeya now warns Yudhiṣṭhira not to grieve. He has the support of his mighty brothers, who rescued Draupadī when she was abducted, whereas Rāma had to face a dreadful Rākṣasa in battle, with only monkeys for his companions.*

## SĀVITRĪ

Yudhiṣṭhira spoke:
**[277]** Great sage, I do not grieve for myself, or for these my brothers, or for the loss of my kingdom, so much as I grieve for Drupada's daughter here. When wicked men tormented us in the gambling match, it was Draupadī who saved us, and then Jayadratha

abducted her from the forest by force. Has anyone before ever seen or heard of such a woman as this daughter of Drupada, so noble and so intent on serving her husbands?

Mārkaṇḍeya spoke:
King Yudhiṣṭhira, hear how the princess Sāvitrī attained all the greatness to which well-born women may aspire.

There was once a king of Madra who was a most righteous man. He supported the Brahmins and granted shelter to those in need; true to his word and highly disciplined, he performed many sacrifices and gave many gifts. He was a skilful ruler, and loved alike by town and country people. This prince was named Aśvapati: he was devoted to the well-being of all creatures, merciful and truthful, but he was childless, and, as his life wore on, grief afflicted him. He performed strict observances to get a child, restricting his eating to certain times, and remaining chaste and disciplined: truest of kings, he offered a hundred thousand oblations accompanied by the Sāvitrī prayer,[1] and ate only in the sixth watch of each day. He maintained these observances for eighteen years, O king; then, at the conclusion of the eighteenth year, the goddess Sāvitrī was satisfied, and showed herself to the king in her own form.

Joyfully arising from the *agnihotra* offering, the boon-granting goddess addressed the prince: 'Prince, I am pleased with your pure chastity, your self-control, your observances, and your whole-hearted devotion to me. Choose whatever boon you desire, King Aśvapati of the Madras! And may you never fail in *dharma*.'

Aśvapati answered, 'It was out of my desire for *dharma* that I undertook this quest for children. O goddess, may I have many sons to further my line! This is the boon that I choose, O goddess, if you are pleased with me, for the Brahmins tell me that offspring is the highest *dharma*.'

'I already knew this purpose of yours, O king,' said Sāvitrī, 'and had requested Brahmā for sons on your behalf; and from the favour that the self-born lord bears towards you here on earth, you will

1 *Ṛgveda Saṃhitā* 10.3.62.

very soon have a resplendent daughter, good sir. Do not make any kind of answer, for I am pleased with you, and I tell you this through Brahmā's generosity.'

The king gave his assent to Sāvitrī's words, beseeching her once more, 'May it be soon!' Then, when Sāvitrī had disappeared, he returned home and lived happily in his kingdom, ruling his subjects according to *dharma*.

Now after some time had passed, that king, keeper of his word, made his virtuous eldest queen pregnant. The child grew within the princess of Mālava, O bull-like heir of Bharata, like the moon in the sky during the bright fortnight, and when her time came, she gave birth to a lotus-eyed daughter. Delighted, the king performed the rites for her, and since she was the gift of Sāvitrī who had been pleased with his offerings, Sāvitrī was the name that he and the priests gave her.

The king's daughter grew like Śrī herself in bodily form, and in time the girl became a young woman. When people saw her with her slender waist and full hips, like a golden image, they thought a young goddess had appeared. Her eyes were like lotus-petals and she blazed with splendour; and yet no one would wed her, for her splendour kept them back.

Now once, on the occasion of the moon's change of phase, she fasted, bathed her head, approached the gods with oblations in the proper manner, and bade the priests recite; then, lovely as Śrī herself, she took the remaining flowers to her noble father. First she paid her respects at her father's feet and presented the flowers to him, and then that lady of fine hips stood at the king's side, joining her hands together. Seeing his daughter, divinely beautiful and of marriageable age, and yet unwooed by suitors, the king grew sad. 'Daughter,' he said, 'it is time for you to be married, but no one has asked me for you; so choose a husband for yourself, a man your equal in virtues. Tell me what man you wish for, and I shall give you to him when I have made enquiries. Choose as you wish, for I have heard this said by priests reciting from the instruction on *dharma*, and you too should hear it, O fair one, as I repeat it: "Blameworthy the father who does not give away his daughter, blameworthy the husband who does not lie with his wife, and blameworthy the son who does not protect his mother after her husband's death."[1] Now you have heard these words of mine, hasten to find a husband: act so that I may not become blameworthy in the eyes of the gods!'

After speaking to his daughter, he appointed aged ministers and urged them to accompany her. Modestly, the spirited girl paid her respects at her father's feet; having heard his command she set out without hesitation. Accompanied by elderly aides, she mounted a golden chariot and set out for the lovely forest hermitages of the royal seers; and there, my son, she visited every hermitage in turn after first paying her respects at the feet of those worthy elders. In this manner the king's daughter travelled to one after another residence of leading Brahmins, distributing wealth in all the sacred bathing-places.

**[278]** The Madra king was seated in his hall engaged in conversation with Nārada, O heir of Bharata, when Sāvitrī and the ministers arrived back at her father's house after visiting every single hermitage. Seeing her father seated with Nārada, the lovely woman paid her respects to both by bowing her head at their feet. Nārada asked, 'Where has your daughter been to, king, and where has she returned from? She is of marriageable age, so why do you not give her to a husband?'

Aśvapati replied, 'This was the very reason I sent her out. She has just now returned, divine seer, so let her say what husband she has chosen.'

Her father urged the lovely woman to tell her tale in full, and she, accepting his command as if it were that of a god, spoke as follows: 'There was in Śālva a righteous Kṣatriya king named Dyumatsena. After some time, he became blind; and once that wise man, whose son was still a child, had lost his sight, a neighbour who was an old enemy saw his opportunity, and seized the kingdom. With his wife and infant son he set out for the forest, and there Dyumatsena of mighty vows practised austerities. His son Satyavat, born in the

1 Cited from *Manusmṛti* 9.4.

city but raised in a forest hermitage, is the one I have chosen in my heart for a husband, for he is suited to me.'

But Nārada said, 'Alas! Sāvitrī has unwittingly done a great wrong, O king, in choosing the virtuous Satyavat! His father speaks truth, his mother speaks truth, and this is why the Brahmins named him Satyavat ('Truthful'). As a child he loved horses, and used to make horses out of clay and draw pictures of horses, and so he is also known as Citrāśva ('Dappled-horse').'

The king asked, 'Is Prince Satyavat, Dyumatsena's joy, now a man of ardour and intelligence? Is he forbearing? Is he brave?'

Nārada answered, 'He has the ardour of the sun, he is Bṛhaspati's equal in intelligence; he is as brave as Indra and as forbearing as the earth.'

Now Aśvapati asked, 'Is Prince Satyavat generous? Does he support the Brahmins? Is he handsome and noble? Is he fair to look on?'

Nārada answered, 'In generosity to the limits of his ability he equals Saṃkṛti's son Rantideva; he supports the Brahmins and speaks the truth like Uśīnara's son Śibi; he is as noble as Yayāti and as fair to look on as the moon; and in beauty Dyumatsena's mighty son is like one of the Aśvins.[1] He is restrained, he is gentle, he is brave; he is truthful and disciplined; he is friendly, he is free of envy; he is modest and steadfast. In short, he is described, both by those who are senior in austerities and those who are senior in good character, as being ever full of uprightness and possessed of firm resolve.'

'Blessed sir,' said Aśvapati, 'as you describe him to me, he is full of every virtue. Tell me also his faults, if he has any.'

'Satyavat has one fault, and no other,' replied Nārada. 'In one year from today, his life will reach its end and he will die.'

'Come, Sāvitrī,' said the king. 'You must go and choose another, lovely woman, for his one fault is so great that it outweighs all his

1 Rantideva was famous for his vast Vedic sacrifices and his munificent gifts to Brahmins; for Śibi and Yayāti see 1.70–88. The Aśvins were celebrated for their beauty (see for example 1.61.85).

virtues: blessed Nārada, whom the very gods honour, has told me that his span of life is short, and that in a year he will die.'

Sāvitrī answered, 'Only once does an inheritance fall due; only once is a girl given in marriage; only once does one say, "I give you this!" These three things happen only once. Whether his span of life is long or short, whether he is full of virtues or of faults, I have chosen him once for my husband, and I shall not choose another. A thing is first decided with the mind, and then announced with the voice; finally it is carried out in actions. The mind is therefore my authority.'

Nārada said, 'Best of men, your daughter Sāvitrī has made her mind up firmly, and there is no way in which she can be deflected from this *dharma*. The virtues possessed by Satyavat are found in no other man, and so I do indeed approve your daughter's marriage to him.'

'Blessed sir,' replied the king, 'the words you have spoken are true, and cannot be questioned. I shall do it as you say, sir, for you are my teacher.'

'Let there be no obstacle to the marriage of your daughter Sāvitrī,' said Nārada. 'Now I must go. My blessings on you all.' And with these words Nārada ascended into the sky and returned to the highest heaven.

Now the king had the arrangements made for his daughter's wedding. **[279]** Paying heed to what had been said about her marriage, he collected together everything needed for the wedding, and then he summoned all the old Brahmins, the sacrificial and household priests. On the auspicious day the king set out with his daughter and went to Dyumatsena's hermitage in the pure forest. With the Brahmins he approached the royal seer on foot, and there he saw the noble blind king, seated on a mat of *kuśa* grass beneath a *śāla* tree. He greeted the royal seer with all the respect he merited, and, keeping his voice low, introduced himself.

Expert in *dharma*, Dyumatsena presented him with the guest-offering, a seat, and a cow; then king asked king the reason for his coming. Aśvapati told him the whole of his purpose and his obligation regarding Satyavat: 'This lovely daughter of mine, royal

seer, is named Sāvitrī. You understand *dharma*: follow your *dharma*
and accept her as your daughter-in-law!'

Dyumatsena said, 'We have lost our kingdom; we live in the forest and practise *dharma* as temperate ascetics. Your daughter does not deserve this. How will she tolerate the hardship of forest life in a hermitage?'

10 Aśvapati answered, 'Since my daughter knows, as I know myself,
that both happiness and unhappiness are ephemeral, such a response is not fitting in my case. I have come to you with my mind made up, O king. Please do not destroy my hopes! Please do not reject me when I have come to you in friendship and affection and love. You are suited to me for a match, and I to you, so accept my daughter as your daughter-in-law and as Satyavat's wife!'

Dyumatsena said, 'Long ago I desired an alliance with you, but now I have lost my kingdom: this is why I hesitated. But let this purpose of yours – which I once longed for too – be fulfilled this very day! I long to have you as my guest.'

15 Then the two kings convened all the Brahmins who lived in
that hermitage, and bade them perform the wedding in the proper manner. And Aśvapati, after giving his daughter and a fitting dowry, returned to his home, filled with the greatest joy. As for Satyavat, he rejoiced at having gained a wife endowed with every virtue, and she rejoiced at having gained the husband her heart desired. Once her father had left, she put aside all her ornaments and took bark garments and a cloak of brown. She pleased everyone with her attentive acts, her virtues, her modesty and self-control, and
20 with her fulfilment of their every wish. Her mother-in-law was
delighted with all the services she performed for her in matters such as dress; her father-in-law with her worship of the gods and her restrained speech; and her husband with her sweet tongue, her skill and her tranquil nature, as well as with her attentions to him in private.

In this fashion these good people passed some time living in that hermitage and practising austerities, heir of Bharata; but whether Sāvitrī was lying down or standing, by day or by night, the words that Nārada had spoken remained in her mind.

[**280**] Much time passed, until one day the time came when Satyavat was to die, O king. As Sāvitrī counted day after day, the words that Nārada had spoken remained constantly in her heart; now, thinking, 'He is to die in four days' time,' the lovely girl began a three-night observance, remaining standing by day and by night.

When the king heard of the young woman's hard vow, he was sorrowful. He arose, and spoke soothing words to Sāvitrī: 'This is a most demanding quest that you have undertaken, princess! Standing for three nights is extremely difficult.'

'Do not be troubled, father,' replied, Sāvitrī; 'I shall accomplish this vow. It is performed with resolve, and resolve attains results.'

Dyumatsena said, 'I certainly cannot tell you to break your vow; a person such as myself should more properly bid you to accomplish it.'

With these words the high-minded king fell silent, and Sāvitrī remained standing, looking as though she had been turned to wood. The day before her husband's death was due, bull-like heir of Bharata, she passed the night standing and grieving. Then when the sun was risen just two yards over the horizon, thinking, 'Today is the day,' she made an offering into the blazing fire, performed the morning rituals, and paid her respects, in order of seniority, to all the aged Brahmins and her parents-in-law, standing intently with her hands joined together. All the ascetics who lived in that forest hermitage pronounced upon her good and kindly blessings that she should not be widowed, and Sāvitrī, deep in contemplation, mentally accepted all that the ascetics said, thinking, 'May it be so!' The princess waited for the time and the moment to come, and thought about what Nārada had said, and she was filled with sorrow.

Then her parents-in-law spoke affectionately to her as she stood by herself: 'You have properly accomplished your vow in the prescribed manner. The time has now come to eat, and you should do so at once.'

But Sāvitrī answered, 'I shall eat when the sun has set and I have achieved my desire: this is the resolve and the compact that I have made in my heart.'

Now while Sāvitrī was speaking thus about taking food, Satyavat started out for the forest with an axe over his shoulder. Sāvitrī said to her husband, 'Please do not go alone! I shall come with you, for I cannot bear to part from you.'

20 Satyavat replied, 'You have never been into the forest before, and the way will be difficult for you, lovely girl. How will you go on foot when you are worn out from your vow to fast?'

'My fast has not exhausted me, and I feel no fatigue,' said Sāvitrī. 'Please do not forbid me to go, for I long to do so!'

Satyavat answered her, 'If you have a longing to go, then I shall do as you wish. But first bid farewell to my parents, so that I incur no fault.'

Then Sāvitrī of mighty vows approached her parents-in-law, and said, 'My husband here is going to the great forest to gather fruit. I ask permission from the lady and from my father-in-law to go
25 out with him, for I cannot bear to be apart from him. Your son is setting out for the forest on account of his parents' *agnihotra* ritual, and so I may not keep him back, as I might if he set out otherwise. But almost a year has past, and I have not left the hermitage; now I have the greatest curiosity to see the forest in bloom.'

'Ever since her father gave Sāvitrī to be my daughter-in-law,' said Dyumatsena, 'I do not remember her saying anything involving a request; so by all means let the young woman attain this desire of hers. But, daughter, do not neglect Satyavat on the way.'

Her parents-in-law both gave her leave, and the lady of high repute set out with her husband. She seemed full of mirth, but her
30 heart was afflicted. Wide-eyed, she saw all round her the lovely woods, delightful and resounding with the cries of peacocks; and Satyavat would sweetly say to Sāvitrī, 'Look at the pure-flowing rivers and the splendid trees in blossom!' But wherever they went, the blameless girl watched her husband, for she remembered the sage's words and thought of him as dead already. She walked with gentle tread behind her husband, her heart torn in two, waiting for the time.

**[281]** With his wife brave Satyavat gathered fruit and filled a dish; then he split logs. As he was splitting a log, he started to sweat, and his head began to ache from his labours. Tormented by fatigue, he went up to his beloved wife and said, 'My head has begun to ache from my labours, Sāvitrī, and I have pain in my limbs and my heart. I feel unwell, lady of measured speech: my head feels as if it is pierced by spikes, and I want to sleep. O fair one, I do not have the strength to stand.'

Now Sāvitrī went to her husband and embraced him; she sat on the ground and took his head in her lap. The poor girl thought over Nārada's words, and knew this day and hour and minute for the fated moment. Then all at once she saw a handsome man dressed in yellow clothes and wearing a crown. He was radiant and strong as the sun; his dark skin shone, and his eyes were red. Noose in hand, a terrifying figure, he stood next to Satyavat and looked straight at him.

As soon as she saw him, she gently laid down her husband's head and arose. Joining her hands together she spoke, heart trembling in her distress: 'I recognize you as a deity, for this is no human form. Lord, tell me, if you will, who you are and what you intend.'

He answered her, 'Sāvitrī, you are intent on serving your husband, and you have also gained ascetic power; therefore I speak with you. Fair lady, know that I am Yama. The life of your husband Prince Satyavat here has reached its end, and I shall bind and take him. This is what I intend.' Then after saying this, the blessed king of the ancestors proceeded as a favour to tell her properly his whole intention: 'This man is righteous and handsome, an ocean of virtues, and it would not be right for him to be taken by my servants; therefore I have come myself.'

Then from Satyavat's body Yama forcibly drew out a person the size of a thumb, bound by his noose and under his control. And with the life removed, that body ceased to breathe and lost its lustre; motionless, it was no longer fair to look on. Then, having bound him, Yama set off southwards; and Sāvitrī too, grieving, followed after Yama, a noble woman, intent on serving her husband and perfect in her vows.

Yama said, 'Turn back, Sāvitrī! Go and perform his funeral rites.

You have discharged your duties towards your husband; you have gone as far as you may go.'

20 'Where my husband is taken,' replied Sāvitrī, 'or where he goes of his own accord, there I too must go: this is eternal *dharma*. And thanks to my austerities, my conduct towards my elders, my love for my husband, my observances, and your own favour towards me, my going is not impeded. Wise men who understand the truth of things declare that he is a friend who walks with one for seven steps, and with this friendship in mind I wish to say something: hear me.[1] Only the self-controlled go to the forest, whether to practise the householder's *dharma*, the student's life or the ascetic's exertions; and in their wisdom it is *dharma* that they proclaim. Therefore the virtuous say that *dharma* is paramount. With a single *dharma* that the virtuous approve, all people can travel that path; I do not seek a second *dharma*, or a third. Therefore the virtuous say that *dharma* is paramount.'

25 Yama said, 'Turn back! But I am pleased with these words you have spoken, every consonant and vowel, every point of your argument. Choose any boon, other than the life of this man! I shall give you what you want in full, blameless lady.'

'My father-in-law has lost his kingdom and his sight,' replied Sāvitrī; 'he lives in the forest, in a hermitage. May the king regain his sight and become as mighty as the blazing sun through your favour.'

Yama said, 'I give you what you want in full, blameless lady: as you have spoken, so it shall be. But I see that you are fatigued by this journey. Turn back! Go, do not weary yourself.'

'How could I be weary when I am near my husband?' asked Sāvitrī. 'My fixed way lies where my husband is, and where you take my husband, there I shall go. Lord of the gods, listen while I speak once more. They say a single meeting with virtuous people is greatly to be desired, but better still is friendship with them; it is never fruitless to meet a virtuous man. Therefore one should live amongst the virtuous.'

1 This speech of Sāvitrī is obscure.

Yama said, 'This most salutary speech that you have spoken to me pleases my heart and enhances the wisdom of the wise. Lovely girl, choose further a second boon, other than the life of this Satyavat!'

'The king, my wise father-in-law, was long ago robbed of his own kingdom,' answered Sāvitrī; 'may he regain it, and may the venerable man never stray from his *dharma*. This is the second boon I ask of you.'

Yama said, 'The king shall soon regain his own kingdom, and he will never stray from his *dharma*. Princess, now that I have granted you this wish, turn back! Go, do not weary yourself.'

'All beings on earth are governed by you and your ordinances,' replied Sāvitrī, 'and it is by ordinance that you bear them away, not from choice; hence, O god, you are known as Yama.[1] Listen to what I have to say. The eternal *dharma* of the virtuous is to do no harm to any creature by deed or thought or word, and to practise kindness and generosity. For the most part the world is like this, and men are as kindly as they can be; but it is only the virtuous who show compassion even to their enemies when they come before them.'

Yama said, 'These words you have spoken are like water to a thirsty man. Choose further whatever boon you wish, fair lady, other than the life of this Satyavat!'

'The king my father has no son,' answered Sāvitrī; 'may he father a hundred sons to extend his line. This is the third boon I ask of you.'

Yama said, 'Your father shall have a hundred radiant sons, fair lady, to extend his line. Princess, now that this wish has been granted, turn back, for you have come far down this road!'

'This is not far when I am near my husband,' replied Sāvitrī, 'for my heart rushes forward yet farther. So as you go along, listen once again as I say these words that come to me. You are Vivasvat's son of mighty energy,[2] so the wise call you Vaivasvata; all beings are

1 The word for 'ordinance' is *niyama*.

2 Vivasvat is a name of the Sun god.

pleased with your peace and *dharma*, so you are known on earth as Dharmarāja.

'People trust the virtuous more even than they trust themselves, and so above all everyone desires the friendship of the virtuous. Indeed, amongst all creatures it is friendship which gives rise to trust, and so above all people trust the virtuous.'

Yama said, 'Fair lady, never before have I heard such words as you have spoken, and I am pleased with them. Choose a fourth boon, other than the life of this man; then go!'

'May there be born to Satyavat and me,' answered Sāvitrī, 'a hundred mighty, heroic sons to continue the line for us both. This is the fourth boon I ask of you.'

45 Yama said, 'A hundred mighty, heroic sons shall be yours, lady, to bring you joy. Now, princess, do not fatigue yourself; turn back, for you have come far down this road!'

'The virtuous always practise eternal *dharma*,' replied Sāvitrī; 'the virtuous never know despair or anguish. The coming together of virtuous people is never fruitless; the virtuous have nothing to fear from the virtuous. Through their truth, the virtuous guide the sun through the sky; through their austerities, the virtuous support the earth. The virtuous are the way of the past and the future, O king; amongst the virtuous, the virtuous are never despondent. The virtuous work for others, expecting no return, for they always know that such behaviour has the approval of noble people. A favour shown to virtuous men is never vain: neither one's wealth nor one's honour will be lost through it. And since among the virtuous this is always, invariably, the case, therefore the virtuous are the protectors of all mankind.'

50 Yama said, 'The more you speak of *dharma* so pleasingly and eloquently, and with such great significance, the more I feel the highest affection for you. Lady, you are a keeper of your word; now choose an incomparable boon!'

Sāvitrī answered, 'This gift of yours does not exclude any prize as did your other boons, bestower of honour. I choose my boon. Let this Satyavat live, for without my husband I am as good as dead. Deprived of my husband, I have no desire for happiness;

deprived of my husband, I have no desire for heaven; deprived of my husband, I have no desire for fortune; I cannot live without my husband. You yourself granted me the boon of a hundred sons, and yet you are taking my husband away. I choose my boon. Let this Satyavat live, and then your own word will come true!'

Now Yama Dharmarāja, Vivasvat's son, gave his assent and untied his noose; full of joy, he spoke these words to Sāvitrī: 'Lady, you are the delight of your family. Here is your husband; I have set him free and restored his health. Take him. He will achieve his aims and live with you a life of four hundred years, and he will gain fame in the world for righteously performing sacrifices. Satyavat shall beget a hundred sons on you, and they will all be Kṣatriya kings. They will father sons and grandsons of their own, and all of them will be for ever known on earth by your name. Your father too shall have a hundred sons by your mother Mālavī, and they and their sons and grandsons will be forever called Mālavas. Your brothers will be godlike Kṣatriyas.'

After granting her the boon in this manner, Yama Dharmarāja of mighty energy sent Sāvitrī back; then he returned to his own home. Once he had left, Sāvitrī, having regained her husband, went to where his lifeless body lay. Seeing her husband on the ground, she went up to him and embraced him; she sat on the ground and took his head on to her lap. Then Satyavat recovered consciousness, and he spoke to Sāvitrī, looking lovingly at her again and again, like someone returned from a journey abroad: 'How long I have slept! Why did you not wake me? And where is that dark man who dragged me away?'

'Indeed, bull-like hero,' answered Sāvitrī, 'you have slept long on my lap. The blessed god Yama who binds all creatures has gone. You are rested, noble prince, and sleep has left you, so arise if you are able. See, night has fallen!'

Now that Satyavat had regained consciousness, he arose as if from a pleasant sleep. Then, seeing that the forest surrounded them on every side, he said, 'Lady of slender waist, I set out with you to gather fruit; then, as I was splitting a log, my head began to hurt. So severe was my headache that I could not stand for

long, and I fell asleep on your lap: all this I remember, fair lady.
You embraced me, and sleep took my mind; then I saw a terrible
70 darkness, and a man of mighty power. If you know, lady of slender
waist, then tell me what this was: was what I saw a dream, or was
it real?'

'Night is setting in,' replied Sāvitrī. 'Tomorrow I shall tell you
everything that happened, prince. For now, good sir, arise, arise;
you are strict in your vows, so consider your parents! Night has
fallen here, and the sun has set; nocturnal creatures are on the
prowl, exultantly uttering their cruel cries, and the leaves are
rustling as beasts roam the forest; in the south-west fierce jackals
are howling horribly, making my heart tremble.'

75 Satyavat said, 'The forest is frightful to see, and it is covered in
dense darkness. You will not recognize the path; you will not be
able to go.'

'Today there was a fire in this part of the forest,' answered Sāvitrī,
'and there is a dry tree still burning; flames appear from time to
time as the wind fans them. I shall fetch fire and make a blaze
all round us. We have these logs here. Do not be troubled if you
cannot go, for I see you are still unwell, and you will not recognize
the path in the dense darkness of the forest. If you agree we shall
set out tomorrow at daybreak, when the forest is light again. Let
us stay here for the night, sinless prince, if you approve.'

80 Satyavat said, 'My headache has stopped, and my limbs feel well.
By your favour, I wish to rejoin my mother and father, for I have
never before returned so late to the hermitage. Before dusk comes
my mother keeps me in, and even when I go out by day both my
parents become anxious, and my father searches for me with the
other residents of the hermitage. Often in the past my mother and
father have been very unhappy and have scolded me for coming
home late; so I wonder what state they are in now on my account.
85 They will suffer much sadness until they see me again. They are
old, and they love me deeply: before now they have told me,
weeping at night in their great unhappiness, "Son, if we lose you,
we shall not live a moment; our lives are assured just as long as you
survive. We are old and blind, and you are our support; the family

line depends on you, and so do our funeral rites, our fame and our descendants."

'And it is true: my mother is old, and my father is old, and I am their support. What state will they be in if they do not see me tonight? I curse that sleep through which my father and my blameless mother have been brought to this distress on my account. And I too am in distress, facing a terrible calamity, for I could not live without my mother and father. Doubtless at this very moment my father, who sees through his wisdom, is distractedly questioning the residents of the hermitage one by one. Fair lady, I do not grieve for myself as I grieve for my father, and for my elderly mother who has followed her husband; today they will both suffer terrible affliction for my sake. I live only if they live. I must support them, and I must do what would please them, for that is why I live.'

With these words the righteous Satyavat, who respected his parents and was loved by them, raised his arms and wept aloud in his unhappiness. Then virtuous Sāvitrī, seeing her husband so racked by grief, wiped the tears from his eyes and said, 'If I have performed austerities, if I have given gifts, if I have made offerings, then let this night be auspicious for my parents-in-law and my husband! I do not remember having ever spoken an untrue word, even in a trivial matter; by this truth let my parents-in-law survive this day!'

Satyavat said, 'I want to see my parents. Sāvitrī, let us go at once! If I now find that some harm has befallen my mother or my father, I shall not live, lady of fine hips; in truth, I shall take my own life. If your mind is set on *dharma*, if you want me to live, if it is your duty to please me, then let us go to the hermitage.'

Then lovely Sāvitrī arose. She tied up her hair and raised her husband to his feet, holding him in her arms. Satyavat stood up; he rubbed his limbs with his hands, looking all round, and cast a glance at the dish. But Sāvitrī said to him, 'Tomorrow you shall fetch these fruits. I shall carry this axe of yours for our safety.' She hung the laden dish from the branch of a tree, took up the axe, and came back to where her husband was. Then that girl with fine thighs laid her husband's arm over her left shoulder, and, putting her own right arm round his waist, gently set out.

105 Satyavat said, 'Timid lady, I come here frequently, and so the paths are known to me, and I can see them by the moonlight showing between the trees. We have reached the path where we gathered fruit. Fair lady, continue along the way by which we came; do not hesitate. And at this thicket of *palāśa* trees the path divides in two; continue by the way that goes north, and make haste! I am well, I am strong, I want to see both my parents.' With these words he hurried forward towards the hermitage.

[**282**] Meanwhile in the great forest Dyumatsena had regained his sight; he rejoiced to see everything with his own eyes. With his wife Śaibyā he visited all the hermitages, bull-like hero, and he became extremely troubled on account of his son. The couple went round hermitages, rivers, forests and lakes, searching in place after place; when they heard any sound they would look up, thinking that it was their son, and hurry forward in the belief that
5 Satyavat and Sāvitrī were coming. Like mad creatures they rushed about, their feet bruised, grazed, and torn till they bled, their bodies pierced by *kuśa* grass and thorns. Then all the Brahmins who lived in those hermitages came and gathered round to calm them, before conducting them to their own hermitage. There aged ascetics stayed with the king and his wife, and soothed them with wonderful tales of the kings of old. But even when the old couple were calm once more, their longing to see their son prompted them to recall with great sadness his childhood doings. Racked with grief, they wept, and again and again they pitifully asked, 'Ah, my son, ah, my good daughter-in-law, where are you, where are you?'

10 Suvarcas the ascetic said, 'As Sāvitrī his wife excels in austerities, self-control and proper conduct, so Satyavat is alive.'

Gautama said, 'I have studied the Vedas with their branches, and I have accumulated great ascetic merit; as a youth I practised holy celibacy, and I satisfied my teachers and the sacrificial fire; I have observed all the vows intently, living on nothing but air, fasting, and whatever else was proper for me; through my austerities I know every person's intentions. Know this for truth: Satyavat still lives.'

His pupil said, 'As these words which have come from my teacher's mouth can never be false, so Satyavat is alive.'

The seers said, 'As Sāvitrī his wife bears all the auspicious marks 15
indicating that she will not be widowed, so Satyavat is alive.'

Bhāradvāja said, 'As Sāvitrī his wife excels in austerities, self-control and proper conduct, so Satyavat is alive.'

Dālbhya said, 'As your sight has returned, and as Sāvitrī kept her vow and left without taking food, so Satyavat is alive.'

Māṇḍavya said, 'As the cries of birds and animals can be heard in an auspicious direction, and as you conduct yourself like a king, so Satyavat is alive.'

Dhaumya said, 'As your son possesses every virtue and is loved by the people, and as he bears marks indicating a long life, so Satyavat is alive.'

With these words the ascetics, who spoke only truth, comforted 20
Dyumatsena; and, thinking over what they had said, he seemed to regain his resolve. Then, a moment later, Sāvitrī and her husband Satyavat reached the hermitage by night, and entered joyfully.

The Brahmins said, 'Today we see you with son and sight restored, and we all wish you well, lord of the earth. You are reunited with your son, you have seen Sāvitrī again, and you have regained your sight; we felicitate you on all three! The words of all of us come true, make no doubt: it will not be long before you prosper even more.'

Now, son of Kuntī, all the Brahmins lit a fire and took their 25
seats next to King Dyumatsena; and Śaibyā, Satyavat and Sāvitrī, who were standing to one side, cast off their grief and sat down with the Brahmins' leave. Then, full of curiosity, all the ascetics who were sitting with the king asked Prince Satyavat, 'Sir, why did you not return sooner with your wife? Why did you come back in the middle of the night? What was your motive? You have given anxiety to your father and mother, and to us too, O prince. We know that there must be a reason: please tell us everything.'

'My father gave me leave to go into the forest with Sāvitrī,' 30 replied Satyavat, 'but as I was splitting logs there I was seized by a headache, and I know that I slept long because of the pain – I have never slept for such a time before. We returned in the middle of the night to allay the anxiety of all of you, and for no other reason.'

Gautama said, 'So you do not know how your father Dyumat-
sena suddenly regained his sight. Sāvitrī must tell us this. Sāvitrī, I
wish to hear it, for you understand causes and effects, and I know,
35 Sāvitrī, that in splendour you are like the goddess Sāvitrī. You
know how this has happened, so let the truth be told; if there is
nothing that you must keep secret, then tell us!'

'It is as you understand it,' answered Sāvitrī, 'and your intention shall not be thwarted; nor is there anything I must keep secret. Hear now the truth of this matter.

'Noble Nārada foretold my husband's death, and today the day
came, so I did not leave his side. As he slept, Yama approached in
person with his servants; he bound him and took him away towards
the region where the ancestors dwell. I praised that mighty god
with truthful words, and he granted me five boons; listen while I
40 tell of them. There were two boons for my father-in-law, his sight
and his kingdom, and I received a hundred sons for my father, and
a hundred for myself. I also received back my husband Satyavat,
who will live a life of four hundred years, for I had resolutely
performed a vow for the sake of my husband's life. I have told you
in truth and in full how this happened, how this great grief of mine
ended in joy.'

The seers said, 'The line of the king was sinking in a lake of darkness, overcome by disasters, when it was saved by you, a virtuous girl well born and well disposed, who had earned merit by practising *dharma*.'

Thus the assembled seers praised and did honour to that most excellent woman. Then they bade farewell to the king and his son, and went at once in peace and joy to their own homes.

**[283]** When that night had passed and the disc of the sun was risen, all the ascetics assembled after performing their morning rituals. The great seers did not weary of discoursing again and again to Dyumatsena on every aspect of the greatness that was

Sāvitrī's. Then, O king, all the counsellors arrived from Śālva to announce that their king had been killed by his own minister. They recounted what had happened: how, on hearing that the minister had killed him together with his associates and kinsmen, the forces of the enemy had fled, and how the people were now of one opinion towards King Dyumatsena – blind or sighted, he was to be their king. 'With this resolve we have been sent here, lord,' they said. 'Here are your chariots, and here your fourfold army. Set forth, O king, and blessings on you! Your victory has already been proclaimed in the city. Long may you hold the office of your ancestors!'

Then when they saw that their king had regained his sight and his bodily vigour, their eyes opened wide in amazement, and they prostrated themselves before him. The king now took his leave of the aged Brahmins who lived in the hermitage, and all of them did him honour. Then he set out for the city. And Śaibyā too set out with Sāvitrī in a brilliant, well-appointed chariot drawn by men and guarded by an army. The household priests joyfully consecrated Dyumatsena king, and consecrated his noble son as prince regent. Much time passed, and then the promised hundred sons were born to Sāvitrī to increase her fame, unretreating heroes all. And likewise a hundred of her own mighty brothers were born to Aśvapati king of Madra and Queen Mālavī.

Thus it happened that Sāvitrī rescued from calamity herself, her father and mother, her parents-in-law, and her husband's whole line; and in just the same way fair Draupadī here, who like Sāvitrī is a high-born woman renowned for her good character, will save you all.

## THE TAKING OF THE EARRINGS

Janamejaya spoke:

**[284]** Great Brahmin, when Lomaśa came at Indra's command to Pāṇḍu's son Yudhiṣṭhira, he said, 'Once ambidextrous Arjuna arrives here, I shall take away the keen fear that you have but never speak of.' Best of learned men, what was that great fear concerning Karṇa of which the virtuous man would speak to no one?

Vaiśaṃpāyana spoke:
Since you ask me, tiger-like king, I shall tell you this story. Listen to
5 my words, best heir of Bharata. The twelfth year had passed and the thirteenth had arrived, when Indra, acting for the Pāṇḍavas' good, prepared to beg from Karṇa. Now the Sun god knew great Indra's purpose concerning Karṇa's earrings, great king, and so he approached Karṇa, speaker of truth and supporter of Brahmins, as the hero lay unsuspecting on a costly bed covered with rich draperies.

The Sun showed himself to him at night at the end of a dream, prince of kings, for he felt the greatest tenderness and love for his son. Assuming through his power the form of a Brahmin, a handsome Vedic scholar,
10 he gently spoke these words to Karṇa to benefit him: 'Karṇa my son, best of all those who maintain truth, listen to what I have to say, for I tell you out of friendship what is for your greatest good, strong-armed hero. Indra will come to you in the guise of a Brahmin, Karṇa; he wants to take your earrings, for he wishes to benefit the Pāṇḍavas. Like the whole world, he knows your character: that when the virtuous beg from you, you always give and never request for yourself; when Brahmins ask you, son, you always give wealth and whatever else they name, and you never refuse. Indra knows that you are like this, so he himself will come
15 to beg for your earrings and your armour. Even though he asks, you must not give the earrings to him; conciliate him as best you can, for this is your highest good. When Indra speaks of your earrings, son, you must persist in putting him off with many reasons and examples, and with gifts of wealth of many other kinds: jewels and women, pleasures and riches of every sort. If you give your lovely natural earrings, Karṇa, your life will be ended and you will come into the power of death. Bestower of honour, as long as you have your armour and your earrings you cannot be killed in battle by your enemies: take heed of what I
20 say. For both these jewelled treasures arose from the *amṛta*;[1] therefore, Karṇa, you should guard them if your life is dear to you.'

1 The elixir of immortality, gained by the gods when they churned the ocean: see 1.15.

'Who are you that speaks to me so,' asked Karṇa, 'showing me such utter friendship? Blessed sir, if you will, tell me who you are, dressed as you are like a Brahmin.'

The Brahmin answered, 'My son, I am the thousand-rayed Sun, and I am instructing you out of friendship. Act as I have said, for this is your greatest good.'

Karṇa said, 'It must indeed be my greatest possible good that the mighty lord of the rays tells me today for my welfare! Now listen to what I have to say: I propitiate you, granter of boons, and I speak from affection for you.

'If I am dear to you, I should not be deflected from this vow of mine.
All the world knows of my vow, O Sun: that I would certainly give my 25
very life to the leading Brahmins. Best of sky-rangers, if Indra comes to me in the guise of a Brahmin to beg from me for the Pāṇḍavas' benefit, I shall give him my earrings and my excellent armour, so that my fame, renowned throughout the three worlds, may not perish. It is not fitting for a person such as myself to save my life at the cost of incurring dishonour; what is fitting, what the world approves, is an honourable death. So if the slayer of Bala and Vṛtra approaches me to beg, and asks
for my earrings for the Pāṇḍavas' benefit, I shall give him both earrings 30
and armour; to do so will bring me fame in the world, and bring him infamy!

'I choose fame in the world, O Sun, even over life itself; for he that has fame gains heaven, whilst he that has none perishes. Like a mother, fame in the world gives men life, while infamy kills them even as they live. Lord of the world, here is an old verse sung by the creator himself, telling how a man's fame is his life: "*Fame is what matters most to a man in the next world; an unsullied fame lengthens his life in this world.*"

'So by giving away these two parts of my body I shall gain eternal 35
fame; and by giving a gift to Brahmins in the proper manner, by offering up my body in the sacrifice of battle, by doing a very difficult deed, and by conquering my enemies on the battlefield, I shall gain fame and nothing but fame. By freeing from fear the fearful who plead for their lives in battle, by releasing from great danger the old, the young and the Brahmins, I shall gain the highest glory in this world, O Slayer of

Rāhu.[1] So I shall give this greatest gift of alms to Indra in his Brahmin guise, O Sun god, and attain the highest rank in this world.'

[**285**] The Sun said, 'Karṇa, do not act to hurt yourself, your friends,
your wives and sons, your mother and father! Living creatures wish
to gain glory and lasting fame in the highest heaven without suffering
bodily harm, O best of living creatures. But since you seek eternal fame
at the cost of your life, it will take your life away, make no doubt. It is for
the living that fathers, mothers and sons exert themselves to fulfil their
duties. The same is true, tiger-like hero, of whatever other kinsmen one
5 may have in the world, and also of kings; remember this. Fame is good
for a living man, radiant prince, but what is the use of fame to a person
who has died and been burnt to ash? A dead man cannot know fame;
fame can be enjoyed only by the living. The fame of a dead man is like
the garland on a corpse.

'I tell you this to benefit you, because you are devoted to me, and
because it is my duty to protect my devotees. When I know that
someone feels the highest devotion towards me, strong-armed hero, I in
turn become devoted to him; so you should do what I say. Furthermore,
there is something very sacred here, something put in place by the gods.
This is why I tell you this; you should act without hesitation. What the
gods have made secret cannot be known by you, bull-like hero, and so I
10 cannot tell this secret to you. In time you will know it. But I will repeat
what I have said: remember it, son of Rādhā. Do not give your earrings
to Indra when he begs for them!

'With your beautiful earrings, radiant hero, you are as lovely to see
as the spotless moon in the sky between the two Viśākhā stars. Fame is
good for a living man; remember this, and refuse Indra your earrings,
son! You can dispel the desire that the king of the gods has for your
earrings, sinless one, by repeating many kinds of arguments and reasons:
thwart this plan of Indra's, O Karṇa, with well-argued words full of
15 sweetness and eloquence. You are forever vying with ambidextrous
Arjuna, tiger-like hero, and heroic Arjuna will meet you in battle.
As long as you have your earrings, Arjuna cannot defeat you on the
battlefield, even if Indra acts as his weapon. So if you wish to defeat

1 See 1.17.

Arjuna in battle, Karṇa, you must not give Indra these lovely earrings of yours!'

**[286]** Karṇa said, 'You know me, blessed lord of the rays: I am not devoted to any other god at all as I am to you with your most fiery beams. Not my wife, not my sons, not my self, not my friends are loved by me with such constant devotion as you, lord of the rays. There is no doubt that noble beings show loving devotion to their beloved devotees; this is well known to you, O Sun. And since your beloved devotee Karṇa recognizes no other deity in heaven, therefore you have spoken for my welfare, blessed sir. But I ask you once more with bended head, conciliating you again and again. I speak as before, lord of the fiery beams: please pardon me.

'I do not fear death as I fear untruth! I would never hesitate to give even my life to any good person, and especially to a Brahmin. As for what you have told me concerning Arjuna Pāṇḍava, O Sun god, cast off the grief of anguish from your mind over Arjuna and me: I shall defeat Arjuna in battle. You know yourself, lord, that I too have mighty strength of arms received from Jamadagni's son Rāma and from noble Droṇa. Permit this vow of mine, O best of gods. If the god of the thunderbolt begs, I shall give my very life.'

The Sun said, 'If, son, you give these lovely earrings to the god of the thunderbolt, you should also speak to him to gain victory, hero of mighty strength. You should give the god of a hundred sacrifices your earrings under a stipulation, for as long as you have those earrings you cannot be killed by any being. It is because Indra seeks your destruction by Arjuna in battle, child, that he wants to take your earrings. So with pleasing words you should again and again propitiate the lord of the gods, who never fails in his purpose, and make your request: "Give me your unfailing Spear to destroy my enemies, and I shall give you, god of a thousand eyes, my earrings and my excellent armour." On this stipulation give Indra your earrings, and with the Spear you will slay your enemies on the field of battle, Karṇa; for the Spear of the king of the gods will not return to your hand without killing foes by hundreds and by thousands, strong-armed hero!'

With these words the Sun of a thousand rays suddenly vanished. Later, after his prayers, Karṇa related his dream to the Sun; he told him in sequence everything that had passed between the two of them that night, as it was seen, as it took place, as it was said. On hearing it, the blessed Sun god, the slayer of Rāhu, said to Karṇa with the hint of a smile, 'Just so!' Then Rādhā's son, the slayer of enemy heroes, knew it to be the truth, and he waited for Indra, longing only for the Spear.

**[287]** —*Janamejaya wishes to know the secret to which the Sun referred, and to know more about Karṇa's earrings and armour. Vaiśaṃpāyana narrates. — A Brahmin ascetic visits Kuntibhoja and asks for hospitality. Kuntibhoja instructs his adopted daughter Kuntī to look after him, impressing on her the need to satisfy his every wish.* **[288]** *Kuntī promises to give the Brahmin excellent care, and Kuntibhoja assigns her to him as his servant.* **[289]** *She discharges her duties so well that, after a year, the Brahmin offers her a boon. When she assures him that it is enough for her to have secured his good opinion, he provides her with a* mantra *with which she can summon any god to do her bidding. Then he vanishes.*

**[290]** *It is the time of Kuntī's period. She sees the sun rise and uses her* mantra *to summon the Sun god. He comes, and asks what she wants; she replies that she only summoned him out of curiosity and asks him to leave. However, he will not do so without first fathering a son on her; if she refuses he will curse her, her father and the Brahmin who gave her the* mantra. **[291]** *Kuntī secures the Sun's agreement that her virginity will be restored and that her son will possess divine earrings and armour, and lies with him.*

**[292]** *In the course of time, a son is born to Kuntī wearing earrings and armour. She places him in a basket and sets him afloat on the river Aśva with her blessings and lamentations. The basket travels downstream to the Gaṅgā.* **[293]** *The childless wife of a Sūta named Adhiratha sees the basket; the couple open it and find the baby within, and adopt him as their son. He grows up under the names Vasuṣeṇa and Vṛṣa; Kuntī learns of his identity through a spy. He becomes a great warrior, an ally of Duryodhana and an enemy of the Pāṇḍavas.*

Vaiśaṃpāyana spoke:
Every midday, when Karṇa would stand in the water with hands joined together and praise the shining sun, O prince of kings, Brahmins would approach him there for wealth, and there was nothing that he would not

give them then. Now Indra became a Brahmin and approached him, saying 'Give alms!' Rādhā's son answered him, 'You are welcome!'

**[294]** When Karṇa saw the king of the gods arrive in the guise of a Brahmin, he welcomed him, not knowing what was in his mind. 'What may I give you?' Adhiratha's son then asked the priest. 'Women wearing golden necklaces? Or villages with many herds of cows?'

'I am not here to seek gifts of women wearing golden necklaces,' replied the Brahmin, 'nor of anything else to increase my pleasure. Let such things be given to those who ask for them. If you are true to your word, sinless hero, then cut off your natural armour and your earrings, and give them to me! This is what I want you to give me; do so at once, afflicter of your enemies! Of all prizes, this is the prize I judge the highest.'

'Land, women, cattle, well-irrigated fields,' said Karṇa, 'these I will give you, priest; but not my armour, not my earrings.' However, though Karṇa pleaded with him with many such words, the Brahmin would not ask for any other boon from him, best heir of Bharata. And though Karṇa conciliated him to the best of his ability, and paid him all due honour, that best of Brahmins wanted no other boon.

When that truest of Brahmins would not choose another boon, Rādhā's son laughed and spoke to him again: 'My natural armour and my earrings arose from the *amṛta*, priest, and because of them I cannot be killed by anyone in the three worlds. So I cannot give them. Bull-like Brahmin, accept from me the excellent gift of the vast kingdom of earth, secure and empty of enemies! If I am deprived of my earrings and my natural armour I shall be vulnerable to my enemies, truest of Brahmins.'

But then, when blessed Indra would still not choose another boon, Karṇa laughed and spoke to him once more: 'Lord of the highest gods, I already knew you, but it would not be proper for me to give a boon to you, O Indra, without gaining anything. For you are the lord of the gods in person, the lord and creator of all other beings, and you should be giving a boon to me! If, lord Indra, I give you my earrings and my armour, I shall become vulnerable and you will become laughable; therefore by all means take my earrings and my excellent armour, but as part of an exchange. I will not give them otherwise.'

Indra said, 'The Sun already knew that I was approaching you; no doubt he told you everything. By all means let it be as you desire, Karṇa. Aside from my thunderbolt, choose whatever you want.'

Then Karṇa joyfully went up to Indra. His aim achieved, he set his mind on the unfailing Spear, and made his choice: 'In exchange for armour and earrings, Indra, give me your unfailing Spear that slays hosts of enemies in the thick of battle!'

Indra seemed to reflect for a moment in his mind; then, lord of the earth, he spoke to Karṇa of the Spear: 'Give me your earrings and your natural armour too, and receive my Spear, Karṇa, on this stipulation. When I slay demons, the unfailing Spear flies from my hand and kills enemies in hundreds before returning to my hand again. When it lies in your hand, Sūta's son, it will kill a single mighty enemy, a roaring, blazing hero; then it will return to me.'

'I only want to kill a single enemy in mighty battle,' answered Karṇa, 'a roaring, blazing hero of whom I am afraid.'

Indra said, 'You shall kill a single mighty, roaring enemy in battle; but the one whom you seek is protected by someone very great. Kṛṣṇa is his protector, whom experts in the Veda call Hari, the invincible Boar, the unfathomable Nārāyaṇa.'

'Even so,' replied Karṇa, 'let the excellent unfailing Spear be mine for the killing of a single hero, blessed lord, so that I may slay my blazing enemy. And I shall cut off and give you my earrings and my armour; but when they have been cut from my body, may I not appear hideous.'

Indra said, 'Because you shun untruth, Karṇa, you will not appear hideous at all, nor will your body bear any wound; you will regain the appearance and the radiance of your father, O best of all those who speak. But if you thoughtlessly release this weapon without need, when you are not in danger and other weapons lie to hand, it will fall upon yourself.'

'I shall release this Spear of Indra', answered Karṇa, 'when I am in severest danger, as you have instructed me: I tell you this truthfully.'

He accepted the blazing Spear, lord of the peoples; then he took a sharp knife and cut the armour from his every limb. When they saw Karṇa cutting himself in this way, gods, men, demons and the hosts of Siddhas all let out a roar, for he showed no sign of pain. Then heavenly drums thundered, and heavenly flowers rained down from on high, as Karṇa, heroic man, was seen still smiling while cutting his own body with a knife. After cutting the heavenly armour from his body he presented it, still wet with blood, to Indra; and in the same way he cut off and presented his earrings. It is for this deed that he is known as Karṇa the Cutter. And Indra, laughing at the deception that had brought Karṇa glory throughout the world, believed he had achieved his purpose for the Pāṇḍavas; so after this he returned directly to heaven.

When the Kauravas learnt of the robbing of Karṇa, they were all 40
dejected and humiliated; but the Pāṇḍavas in the forest were filled with joy to hear that the Sūta's son had been left in such a state.

Janamejaya spoke:
Where were the Pāṇḍava heroes staying, and from whom did they hear the good news? What did they do when the twelfth year had passed? Blessed sir, make all this known to me.

Vaiśaṃpāyana spoke:
After rescuing Draupadī and driving away Jayadratha, and after hearing in full from Mārkaṇḍeya the ancient tales of gods and seers, the heroic men returned with their priests and their chariots and followers, all their cooks and their chamberlains, from their hermitage in the Kāmyaka forest to holy Dvaitavana, for they had completed their whole, dreadful exile in the forest.

## THE FIRESTICKS

**[295]** *Yudhiṣṭhira is approached by a Brahmin whose firesticks have been carried off after becoming tangled in a deer's antlers; he is anxious that his* agnihotra *ritual will be spoilt. The Pāṇḍavas set out in search of the deer, but in vain.*

*Nakula expresses his anger at their plight.* **[296]** *Yudhiṣṭhira ascribes their situation to* dharma, *but the other three Pāṇḍavas blame themselves for not having killed the Kauravas who insulted and cheated them.*

*Yudhiṣṭhira now sends Nakula to look for water. He finds a pool, and is about to drink when a voice from the air warns him not to do so without first answering some questions; he ignores it, drinks, and falls down dead. In turn, Yudhiṣṭhira sends Sahadeva, Arjuna and Bhīma after Nakula, and one by one they all defy the warning, drink and die. Now Yudhiṣṭhira himself approaches the pool.*

**[297]** *Yudhiṣṭhira sees his brothers lying dead, and laments. He enters the water to drink, and hears the warning voice. At Yudhiṣṭhira's request the speaker shows himself as a Yakṣa, who now asks a long sequence of questions; Yudhiṣṭhira answers them correctly, and is allowed to choose one of his brothers to be brought back to life. He chooses Nakula, explaining that it would be wrong to favour his own mother, Kuntī, over Mādrī. The Yakṣa responds by bringing all four of his brothers back to life.*

**[298]** *The Yakṣa now reveals that he is Yudhiṣṭhira's father, Dharma; he wished to see Yudhiṣṭhira and to test him. He grants Yudhiṣṭhira a boon; Yudhiṣṭhira chooses for the Brahmin to regain his firesticks. Dharma grants him a second boon; he chooses for the Pāṇḍavas to remain unrecognized during their thirteenth year of exile. As a third boon he asks for a virtuous character. After granting these boons, Dharma vanishes.*

**[299]** *Now that the year of exile incognito is about to begin, Yudhiṣṭhira takes leave of the ascetics who have remained with the Pāṇḍavas during their stay in the forest. Dhaumya reminds him that the gods themselves have often resorted to disguise. The Brahmins pronounce blessings on the Pāṇḍavas, and they set out.*

# VIRĀṬA

## VIRĀṬA

Janamejaya spoke:
[1] How did my forefathers live incognito in the city of Virāṭa for fear of Duryodhana?

Vaiśaṃpāyana spoke:
Once Yudhiṣṭhira, best upholder of *dharma*, had obtained those boons from Dharma, he went back to the hermitage and related the whole story to the Brahmins; and after telling them everything, he gave the Brahmin back his pair of firesticks. Then Dharma's son, high-minded King Yudhiṣṭhira, called all his younger brothers together, O heir of Bharata, and addressed them:

'We have passed these twelve years in exile from our kingdom; now 5
the thirteenth year has come. It will be very hard to pass. So, Arjuna son of Kuntī, choose well some place where we may go from here to pass all these days unknown to our enemies.'

'Lord of men,' answered Arjuna, 'thanks to the boon of Dharma himself we shall go about unrecognized by men. But, bull-like heir of Bharata, I shall name some delightful, secluded lands for us to live in; choose one of them. All round the territory of the Kurus there are lovely kingdoms with abundant food: Pāñcāla, Cedi and Matsya, Śūrasena,
Paṭaccara, Daśārṇa and Navarāṣṭra, Malla, Śālva and Yugaṃdhara. Which 10
of these pleases you, prince of kings, as the dwelling-place where we shall pass this final year?'

'It is indeed as you say, strong-armed hero,' Yudhiṣṭhira replied. 'What was said by the blessed Dharma, the lord of all beings, cannot fail to come true. None the less, we must certainly all consult together and look for a place to live that is delightful, auspicious, pleasant and safe. Virāṭa, the Matsya king, is mighty: he would harbour the Pāṇḍavas. He is virtuous and generous, an elder of very great wealth. My brother, we shall stay for this year in the city of Virāṭa, working for him. Now, heirs of Kuru, let each one of us state what task he will be able to perform for him!'

'Prince of men,' said Arjuna, 'what work will you do in King Virāṭa's kingdom? What task will you perform to pass your days, good sir? You are kindly and generous, modest and virtuous, a man of true valour; what will you do, Pāṇḍava king, now that you are overcome by disaster? You are not accustomed to such woes as the common people know, so how will you come through this terrible disaster that has befallen you?'

'Hear, heirs of Kuru, what task I shall perform once I have met the bull-like hero King Virāṭa,' answered Yudhiṣṭhira. 'I shall become a courtier of that noble king in the guise of a Brahmin named Kaṅka,[1] a keen gambler who knows the ways of the dice. I shall throw the lovely dice: black dice and red dice; dice of beryl, of gold, of ivory; dice of moonstone! If the king questions me, I shall tell him, "Long ago I was Yudhiṣṭhira's dearest friend!" There: I have told you how I shall spend my time. Wolf-belly Bhīma, what task will you perform to pass your days in the city of Virāṭa?'

[**2**] 'I think I shall approach King Virāṭa claiming to be a master cook named Ballava,'[2] said Bhīma. 'I shall cook him soups, for I am skilful in kitchen work, and I shall delight him by outperforming even the well-trained chefs who have cooked for him before. I shall fetch firewood in huge bundles, and the king will rejoice to see such a grand feat! If mighty elephants or powerful bulls need taming, O king, I shall tame them too; and if there are wrestlers who will wrestle with me in

**1** In the *Mahābhārata*, the word *kaṅka* refers principally to a carrion bird that haunts battlefields, identified by Fitzgerald as the huge and hideous Adjutant Stork ('Some storks and eagles eat carrion; herons and ospreys do not: kaṅkas and kuraras (and baḍas) in the *Mahābhārata*', *Journal of the American Oriental Society*, 118.2 (1998), pp. 257–61.

**2** 'Cowherd'.

the ring, I shall lay them low to make him happier still. (But I shall
certainly not kill those fighters – I shall bring them down in such a way
that they survive.) If I am asked, I shall say I used to be Yudhiṣṭhira's
cook, butcher, soup-maker and wrestler. And I shall guard myself as I
go about, lord of the peoples. This is how I promise to pass my days.'

Yudhiṣṭhira said, 'The best of men, Kṛṣṇa's companion, whom the
Fire god once approached in the guise of a Brahmin when he wished to
burn down the Khāṇḍava forest,[1] the mighty, strong-armed hero, Kuru's 10
unvanquished heir: what task will Kuntī's son, wealth-winner Arjuna,
perform? The finest of warriors, who entered the forest and satiated
the Fire by defeating Indra and slaying the serpents and Rākṣasas from
his single chariot: what shall Arjuna do? Of heat-giving bodies the best
is the sun; of two-legged creatures, the Brahmin; of snakes, the cobra;
of radiant beings, the fire; of weapons the foremost is the thunderbolt;
of cattle, the humped bull; of bodies of water, the ocean; of showers,
the storm; of serpents, Dhṛtarāṣṭra;[2] among elephants the greatest is
Airāvata;[3] of beloved creatures the chief is one's son; of friends the best
is one's wife. Wolf-belly Bhīma, as each of these beings is marked out 15
for distinction in its own class, so among all bowmen young Arjuna
Guḍākeśa is the best!

'So, heir of Bharata, what shall Arjuna Bībhatsu do, he whose bow
is Gāṇḍīva, whose horses are white, who is no lower than Indra or
Kṛṣṇa Vāsudeva? He lived five years in the house of thousand-eyed
Indra, brilliant and godlike in form, and acquired the celestial weapons.
I reckon him a twelfth Rudra, a thirteenth Āditya! His arms are long
and even, the skin scarred by the bowstring on both the left arm and
the right, as an ox's hump is scarred by the yoke. Like Himālaya among
mountains, like the ocean among watercourses, like Indra among the
gods, like the Fire god among the Vasus, like the tiger among beasts, like 20
Garuḍa among birds, Arjuna is finest among those who bear armour;
what shall he do?'

'Lord of the earth,' replied Arjuna, 'I shall claim to be a eunuch.

1 See 1.214 ff.

2 Not the Kaurava monarch, but a serpent king of the same name.

3 Indra's elephant.

My great bowstring-scars will be difficult to hide, O king; but I will deck my ears with earrings that flash like fire, and braid the hair of my head, lord, and my name shall be Bṛhannaḍā![1] In woman's form I shall amuse the king and those who live in the women's quarters by reciting tale after tale; and I shall teach the ladies in Virāṭa's palace singing,
25 wonderful dancing, and musical instruments of every kind. I shall speak much of the proper conduct that people achieve through their deeds, and I shall disguise myself with my illusory appearance, son of Kuntī. If the king asks me, heir of Bharata, I shall say, "I lived as Draupadī's maid in Yudhiṣṭhira's household!" Disguised, like Nala,[2] by means of this artifice, I shall pass my days pleasantly in Virāṭa's palace, prince of kings.'

[**3**] Yudhiṣṭhira said, 'Nakula my brother, you are delicate, brave, handsome and accustomed to comfort; what will you do as you go about there?'

'I shall become King Virāṭa's master of horses,' answered Nakula, 'under the name of Granthika. I am very fond of this work; I am skilled at training horses and at healing them, and horses are always as dear to me as they are to you, king of the Kurus. If people speak to me in the city of Virāṭa, I shall tell them that this is how I shall pass my days!'

5 Yudhiṣṭhira said, 'Sahadeva, how will you pass your days in the king's presence? And what will you do as you go about in disguise, my brother?'

'I shall become King Virāṭa's overseer of cattle,' replied Sahadeva, 'for I am expert at herding, milking and inspecting cattle. Keep it in mind that I shall be known by the name Tantipāla. I shall perform my work skilfully, so dispel any fears in your heart: you yourself always used to employ me with the cattle, and I have skill with them, and know the work well, lord of the peoples. Markings, bodily movements and auspicious features of cows, all this I know well, lord of the earth, and
10 more besides. And I know too which bulls bear favourable marks, so that barren cows will calve after merely scenting their urine. So this is what I shall do, for I always love this work; and be pleased to know that no one shall recognize me, prince!'

**1** 'Woman with a big penis'.

**2** See 3.63.

Yudhiṣṭhira said, 'Here stands our beloved wife, dearer than life itself, deserving the protection due a mother, the honour due an elder sister. What task will Draupadī Kṛṣṇā perform? She does not know how to do the work that other women do. She is a delicate maiden, a princess of high repute, a noble woman intent on serving her husbands: how will she go about? Since the day of her birth, this lovely girl has known nothing but garlands and perfumes, ornaments and clothes of every kind.'

'Maidservants work for others, heir of Bharata,' answered Draupadī, 'but live in the world independently; convention does not permit other women the same freedom to come and go. So I shall claim to be a maidservant, skilled at hairdressing; if you seek after me, this will be how I shall disguise myself. I shall serve Sudeṣṇā, the king's wife of high repute. Once I am with her, she will look after me, so do not be so troubled.'

'You speak well, Draupadī,' said Yudhiṣṭhira, 'as a well-born woman should speak; you know nothing of wickedness, for you stand firm in your vows of womanly virtue.'

**[4]** *Yudhiṣṭhira announces that their household priest Dhaumya and all their servants must leave them and go to Pāñcāla. Before the Pāṇḍavas set out, Dhaumya instructs Yudhiṣṭhira on how to comport himself in the household of a king, and performs auspicious rituals.*

Vaiśaṃpāyana spoke:

**[5]** Armed with daggers and bearing arrow-cases and other weapons, cased in arm-guards and finger-guards, the heroes set out towards the river Yamunā. Those mighty bowmen followed the southern bank on foot, spending their nights in hideaways in the mountains or the forest, and shooting the various species of deer. Passing north of Daśārṇa, south of Pāñcāla, and straight through Yakṛlloma and Śūrasena, the Pāṇḍavas entered the kingdom of Matsya, claiming to be hunters.

As they arrived in that land, Draupadī said to the king, 'Look, there are footpaths and fields of different crops; clearly Virāṭa's capital must be far distant. Let us spend the rest of the night here, for I am deeply weary.'

'Wealth-winner Arjuna,' said Yudhiṣṭhira, 'pick up the Pāñcāla princess and carry her. We shall spend the night in the capital, heir of Bharata, free of this forest!'

So, like an elephant king, Arjuna swiftly took up Draupadī, and did not set her down till they arrived near the city. Once they had reached the capital, Kuntī's son Yudhiṣṭhira said to Arjuna, 'Where shall we stow our weapons before entering the city? If we enter it armed, my brother, we shall cause the people alarm, make no doubt; and we have vowed that if even one of us is recognized, we must return to the forest for a further twelve years.'

'Prince of men,' replied Arjuna, 'here on this peak is a huge, dense *śamī* tree. It has awesome branches, so it is hard to climb, and it stands next to the burning-ground; no one comes here, lord, for it is growing off the path, in forest frequented by beasts and savage creatures. Let us stow our weapons in it and then set out for the city; in this way we shall be able to pass our days here free from worry, heir of Bharata.'

After speaking these words to righteous King Yudhiṣṭhira, he set about storing the weapons, bull-like heir of Bharata. His noble, thundering bow Gāṇḍīva, the slayer of enemy hosts with which the heir of Kuru had triumphed over gods, men and serpents from his single chariot, and conquered other wealthy kingdoms, Kuntī's son Arjuna now unstrung and rendered harmless. Heroic Yudhiṣṭhira released the unbreakable string of the bow with which the afflicter of his enemies had defended Kurukṣetra, the land of the Kurus. With his bow mighty Bhīma had defeated the Pāñcālas in battle, and checked many enemies when fighting alone during the conquest of the world;[1] foes had fled when they heard its roar in battle, like the rending of a mountain or a clap of thunder; with it he had also given a beating to King Jayadratha of Sindhu.[2] Now Bhīma unfastened its string. Brave Nakula, the Pāṇḍava who bellowed in battle, removed the string of the bow with which he had subjugated the western quarter, and then the mighty hero Sahadeva unstrung the weapon with which that amiable prince had subjugated the South.[3]

**1** See 2.26–7.

**2** See 3.256.

**3** See 2.28–9.

Together with their bows they stored their long swords of steel,
their costly arrow-cases and their razor-edged arrows. Nakula himself 25
climbed the tree to place the weapons there: he tied them firmly with strong knots on to parts of the tree he thought looked sturdy, and where he saw that the rain would pass by. And the Pāṇḍavas also tied up the body of a dead man there, so that when people smelt the foul stench they would know that a corpse was tied there, and would stay far away from that *śamī* tree. 'She is our mother, who was aged 180, and we are hanging her in this tree because this is the custom in our family, practised even by our forebears!' – this is what those afflicters of their enemies said to everyone they spoke to, even cowherds and shepherds.

Now the foe-crushing sons of Kuntī approached the city. Yudhiṣṭhira 30
assigned secret names to each of them: Jaya, Jayanta, Vijaya, Jayatsena and Jayadbala. Then, in accordance with their vows, they entered that great city to pass the thirteenth year incognito in the kingdom of Virāṭa.

**[6]** King Yudhiṣṭhira was the first to approach Virāṭa as he sat in his hall. He had placed his dice of gold and beryl under his arm and covered them with his garment. So the famed lord of that kingdom was approached by the lord of men of great renown, the glory of the Kuru line, noble-minded and honoured by kings among men but unassailable as a deadly snake, the bull-like hero excelling in strength and beauty, blazing in form like an immortal, a sun obscured by densely massed clouds, a fire covered over by ash.

When King Virāṭa saw Pāṇḍu's son striding towards him like the moon obscured by clouds, he asked his ministers, Brahmins and Sūtas, and those of the people who sat as members of his council, 'Who is this
that has arrived here and is looking at my hall for the first time? This 5
most excellent of men cannot be a Brahmin. It seems to me that he is a lord of the earth: he has no slave, no chariot, no earrings, and yet close up he shines as bright as Indra himself. Bodily signs declare him to have received the royal consecration on his head, or so I think. He approaches me as free from care as a rutting elephant approaching a lotus pool!'

Then as Virāṭa mused thus, the bull-like hero Yudhiṣṭhira approached him and said, 'My sovereign, know that I am a Brahmin, come here to seek a living after losing all I owned. My wish, sinless lord, is to dwell here with you and do your bidding.'

The king was delighted. 'Welcome!' he said at once. 'Accept what you seek; I am happy to greet you, my son. From what king's realm have you come here? Tell me truly your family and your name, and also whatever occupation is yours.'

10 'I used to be Yudhiṣṭhira's friend,' answered Yudhiṣṭhira, 'and I am a Brahmin, a descendant of Vyāghrapad. I am a gambler, skilled at throwing the dice, and I am known by the name of Kaṅka, O Virāṭa.'

'I shall grant you whatever boon you desire,' said Virāṭa. 'Rule over Matsya: I submit to your authority! I have always been fond of clever gamblers, and you, godlike sir, merit a kingdom!'

'Lord of the peoples,' replied Yudhiṣṭhira, 'I will never dispute with those I have defeated: no one vanquished by me may keep his wealth. Let me obtain this highest of boons through your grace, king of Matsya!'

'If anyone offends you,' said Virāṭa, 'I shall kill him, even if he holds indemnity; if he is a Brahmin, I shall exile him from the kingdom. Let all the citizens hear me: as I am lord over this realm, so is Kaṅka! You shall be my friend, and ride with me in the same carriage; you shall enjoy clothing, food and drink in plenty. You may always see whatever
15 is within and whatever is without: I hold my door open for you! If men grown thin for lack of livelihood petition you, you may always answer them on my authority: I shall give everything you promise, make no doubt. While you are with me, you will have nothing to fear.'

Thus the bull-like hero gained his audience with King Virāṭa, and a boon. From then on he lived there, highly respected and happy; and no one found out what he was doing.

[7] Now there approached a second man, fearful in strength and blazing with glory, but with the graceful tread of a lion. In his hand he bore a spoon, a ladle and an unsheathed sword of purest dark metal. He appeared to be a cook, but in his supreme radiance he was like the sun that illuminates this world. Dressed all in black, as strong as Mount Himālaya, he approached the king of Matsya and stood before him.

When the king saw him arrive he was well pleased, and he addressed all the citizens: 'Who is this bull-like young man that I see, high-shouldered like a lion and extraordinarily handsome? I have never before seen so sun-like a man! No matter how I ponder, I cannot grasp his perfection, nor reach truly into the mind of this bull-like hero.'

Then Pāṇḍu's high-minded son went up to Virāṭa and spoke these words like a man in deep distress: 'Lord of men, I am a cook named Ballava. Employ me, for I prepare excellent sauces!'

'Bestower of honour,' said Virāṭa, 'I cannot believe that you are a cook, for you seem to resemble thousand-eyed Indra himself; and in glory and beauty and valour, my son, you shine out like a leader among men!'

'Lord of men,' replied Bhīma, 'a cook I am, and your servant. Above all I know how to make exceptional soups, O king, all of which were formerly tasted by King Yudhiṣṭhira himself. Also, no one is my equal in strength: I have always been a fighter, and I have been matched against elephants and lions. Sinless prince, I shall ever act to please you!'

Virāṭa said, 'I grant you your boon, and you shall work skilfully in the kitchen as you say. I do not think that this work is worthy of you, for you merit the sea-rimmed earth itself! But it is done as you desire: be the superintendent in my kitchen, appointed by me to be in charge of my servants who are already in place there.'

Thus was Bhīma assigned to the kitchen: he came to be much loved by King Virāṭa. There he dwelt, O king, and neither the common folk nor any of the servants there found him out.

[**8**] Dark-eyed Draupadī's hair was soft and flawless, and curled at the ends; now she tied it up and concealed it at her right side. She put on a single black garment, large and very dirty, and having thus attired herself as a maidservant, she began to wander about as if suffering some affliction. When they saw her rushing about, men and women hurried up to her and asked her, 'Who are you, and what do you want?' She answered that she was a maidservant, lord of men, and that she had come hoping to work for anyone who would feed her. But because of her beauty, her appearance and her soft voice, no one could believe that she was a maidservant come looking for food.

However, Virāṭa's wife Sudeṣṇā, a highly respected Kekaya princess, observed Drupada's daughter as she looked down from the palace roof. When she saw such a lovely woman dressed in a single garment and with no one to protect her, she summoned her and said, 'Lady, who are you, and what do you want?' Draupadī answered that she was a maidservant, lord of men, and that she had come hoping to work for anyone who would feed her.

'People of beauty like yours do not live as you describe, lovely girl,' said Sudeṣṇā; 'they have plenty of such slaves and slave-girls to command! Your ankles are unobtrusive, your thighs firm; you are deep in three ways,[1] high in six,[2] and pink in the five pink places;[3] your voice falters like a goose; you have good hair and breasts, and a lovely complexion; your hips and bosom are full; like a Kashmiri mare you excel in every respect; your eyelashes are curved, your lower lip red as a *bimba* fruit, your waist slender; your neck is marked like a conch-shell; your veins cannot be seen; your face is like the full moon. Tell me, lady, who you are – you cannot possibly be a maidservant! Are you a Yakṣī or a goddess, a Gandharva woman or an Apsaras? Are you Alambusā, Miśrakeśī or Puṇḍarīkā?[4] Are you Mālinī?[5] Are you the consort of Indra or Varuṇa, or of Tvaṣṭṛ or the creator Prajāpati? Of all the goddesses renowned among the gods, which one are you, fair lady?'

'I am no goddess,' replied Draupadī, 'nor a Gandharva or Rākṣasa woman or a demoness. I am a maidservant who works for others: I tell you this truthfully. I know hairdressing, and I am good at grinding unguents; also, I shall thread the loveliest garlands of many colours. I won the good opinion of Satyabhāmā, Kṛṣṇa's beloved queen, and of Draupadī Kṛṣṇā, the wife of the Pāṇḍavas, unmatched for beauty among the Kurus. This is how I go about, earning a very fine living; and I stay wherever I am for as long as I get clothing. Mālinī is the name that the queen herself gave me. Now, Queen Sudeṣṇā, I have arrived at your house.'

Sudeṣṇā said, 'I would give you my own head to dwell on – I have no doubt of this at all – but that the king would then single-mindedly pursue you. See, the women of the royal household and those who live in my own house are gazing intently at you, so what man would you not captivate? And see the trees that grow here round my house; even they

1 According to the commentator Nīlakaṇṭha, voice, intellect and navel.

2 Nose, eyes, ears, nails, breasts and nape of the neck.

3 Soles of feet and hands, corners of eyes, lips, tongue and nails.

4 Names of Apsarases.

5 Name of a female Rākṣasa, mother of the virtuous Vibhīṣaṇa in the story of Rāma (see 3.259–75).

seem to be bowing before you, so what man would you not captivate?
Lady of fine hips, once King Virāṭa sees your more-than-human beauty
he will leave me and single-mindedly pursue you, for whichever man
you gaze at intently with your long eyes will fall into love's clutches,
lady of flawless limbs! And any man who sees you constantly, with your 25
lovely smile and your utterly flawless limbs, will fall into the clutches of
love! The female crab spawns only to die, and so I believe it will be for
me if you dwell here, sweet-smiling girl.'

'I am not to be had by Virāṭa, nor by any other man at all,' answered
Draupadī. 'I have five young Gandharvas for my husbands, fair queen;
they are sons of a certain Gandharva king of great mettle, and they
guard me constantly, so men approach me at their peril. My Gandharva
husbands will be pleased to let me stay anywhere where no one gives
me leftover food or asks me to wash their feet; but if a man should lust 30
after me like other common women, he will enter on his next life that
very night! No man can seduce me, lady, for my Gandharvas are grim,
and they are powerful.'

Sudeṣṇā said, 'In that case, daughter, I give you leave to stay here as you wish; nor will you ever have to touch leftover food, or anyone's feet.'

Thus Virāṭa's wife encouraged Draupadī Kṛṣṇā, O Janamejaya, and no one there knew who she truly was.

**[9]** As for Sahadeva, he approached Virāṭa dressed in the very clothes
worn by cowherds and speaking in their tongue. When the king saw
the blazing bull-like hero coming, he went up to that heir of Kuru and
asked him, 'Whose son are you, where have you come from, and what
do you want, my son? Tell me truly, bull-like hero, for I have never seen
you before.' Sahadeva, the afflicter of his enemies, stood before the king
and spoke in a voice like a monsoon storm: 'I am a Vaiśya, Ariṣṭanemi
by name; I was the overseer of cattle of those bull-like Kurus, the sons
of Kuntī. I wish to live in your household, chief of the peoples, for I 5
no longer know anything of those lion-like kings. I cannot live by any
other profession, and I do not care for any king but you.'

'Whether you are a Brahmin or a Kṣatriya,' replied Virāṭa, 'you are as handsome as the lord of the sea-rimmed earth. Tell me the truth, tormentor of your enemies! Vaiśya work would not be worthy of you. From what king's realm have you come here? Tell me whatever occupation is yours, how you will live permanently in our household, and what your wage here will be.'

Sahadeva said, 'The eldest of Pāṇḍu's five sons was King Yudhiṣṭhira. He had a hundred hundred herds comprising eighty thousand cattle, other herds of ten thousand, and yet others of twice as many. I was their overseer; people knew me as Tantipāla. There is nothing for ten leagues in every direction that I do not know concerning the overseeing of my herds, be it past, present or future. My virtues were well known to that noble man, and King Yudhiṣṭhira of the Kurus was pleased with me. For my cows breed fast, and they are never sick: I know the various means to attain this. These are the skills which I have. And I know too which bulls bear favourable marks, so that barren cows will calve after merely scenting their urine.'

'I have collected a herd of a hundred thousand,' answered Virāṭa; 'chosen according to the qualities of each type of cattle. I hand my beasts and herdsmen over to you; from now on let all my cattle be in your charge!'

So, lord of the peoples, that prince of men lived there pleasantly unknown to the king; nor did anyone else ever find him out. And Virāṭa paid him the wage he requested.

[**10**] Now someone else appeared at the rampart wall, supremely beautiful, a huge, strong-armed man wearing women's ornaments, decked with earrings, long shell bracelets and lovely anklets of gold, tossing his long, thick hair, treading like an elephant in rut, shaking the earth with his steps as he approached Virāṭa in his hall. When the king saw him arrive on the floor of the hall, an enemy-ravager concealed in a disguise, Indra's son shining with supreme radiance and treading like a mighty elephant, he asked all those who were near about him, 'Where does he come from? I have never heard of such a man before!' And when none of those men said they knew him, he then spoke these words in his amazement:

'You are a man in every respect; handsome, dark and young, you are like the lord of an elephant herd. Unfasten your shell bracelets and lovely anklets of gold! Unbraid your hair and take off your earrings! Comb your hair into a proper crest, dress yourself differently, and become a bearer of bow and armour and arrows! Mount a chariot, sir, and race! Be like my sons to me, or like myself! For I am old, and I wish to hand over my duties; become ruler of all Matsya straightway! Men such as you do not resemble eunuchs at all, it seems to me.'

'I sing and I dance,' replied Arjuna, 'and I play instruments. I am a good dancer, I am an expert singer. Give me to your daughter Uttarā, lord of men, and I shall be the queen's dancing-master! As for this appearance of mine: what is the point of speaking of it? It would only increase my great grief. Know me as Bṛhannaḍā, lord of men, a son or daughter without father or mother.'

Virāṭa said, 'I grant you your boon, Bṛhannaḍā: teach my daughter 10
and her friends to dance. But I do not think that this work is worthy of you, for you merit the sea-rimmed earth itself!'

The king of Matsya tested Bṛhannaḍā in dancing and music and other such arts; and having thus learnt that he was indeed no man, he then sent him to the princess's quarters. The lord of men, wealth-winner Arjuna, taught singing and music to Virāṭa's daughter and her friends and attendants, and they grew fond of Pāṇḍu's son. Thus the wealth-winner lived there in disguise, self-possessed and sharing in their enjoyments. No one there, whether inside or outside the household, found him out as he stayed there in this way.

[11] Now another Pāṇḍava lord appeared while King Virāṭa was inspecting his horses. The common folk saw him striding towards them; he looked like the disc of the sun emerging from a cloud. He inspected the horses in every direction, and the enemy-slaying king of Matsya watched him as he did so, and then said to his followers, 'Where does this godlike man come from? He inspects my horses closely – he must surely be a wise expert on horses! Have him brought straight in to me, for this hero blazes like an immortal!'

The enemy-slayer approached the king and said, 'May victory be yours, prince, and blessings on you! I have always been respected for my work with horses, O king; I shall be your skilled master of horses!'

'I shall give you chariots, wealth and a dwelling,' answered Virāṭa, 'for 5
you deserve to be my master of horses. Where are you from? Whose son are you? How did you come here? Tell me this, and also whatever occupation is yours.'

Nakula said, 'The eldest of Pāṇḍu's five sons was King Yudhiṣṭhira. I used to be employed by him among his horses, O tormentor of your enemies. I know the nature of horses, and their whole training, how to correct the vicious ones, and how to cure their every illness. No horse of mine is ever timid; no mare of mine is vicious, never mind the stallions. People call me by the name of Granthika, and so did Pāṇḍu's son Yudhiṣṭhira.'

'Let whatever horses I have be subject to you from this day on,' replied Virāṭa; 'and let whatever grooms I have be in your charge, and
10 all my charioteers! If this is pleasing to you, godlike man, then tell me what payment you have in mind. This work with horses does not seem worthy of you, for to me you seem like a much-respected king! To see you here, so fair to behold, is to me the same as seeing Yudhiṣṭhira himself. But how can Pāṇḍu's blameless son pass his days dwelling in the forest, bereft of servants?'

Thus did the delighted King Virāṭa honour the young Pāṇḍava who resembled a Gandharva lord. Nor did anyone else ever find him out as he went about within the household, acting pleasantly and agreeably to all.

So the Pāṇḍavas of unerring vision lived in Matsya as they had sworn. Lords of the sea-rimmed earth, now much distressed, they concentrated on living incognito.

Janamejaya spoke:
[**12**] O Brahmin, while they lived thus in Matsya's city, what did those mighty heroes the Pāṇḍavas do next?

Vaiśaṃpāyana spoke:
The heirs of Kuru dwelt there thus disguised, and they won the good opinion of the king. Listen to what they did.

As Yudhiṣṭhira attended Virāṭa's court, he became a favourite of the other courtiers, and also of Virāṭa himself and his sons, lord of the peoples, for Pāṇḍu's son knew the inner secrets of the dice, and made everyone play dice-games just as he pleased, as if they were
5 his captive birds. Unknown to Virāṭa, that tiger-like hero, the lord of *dharma*, won wealth which he distributed in due measure among

his brothers. As for Bhīma, he sold for Yudhiṣṭhira the meat dishes and various other foodstuffs that the king of Matsya left uneaten. Arjuna sold worn garments which he obtained within the women's quarters and gave the profit to the Pāṇḍavas. Pāṇḍu's son Sahadeva, dressed in his cowherd's clothes, gave the Pāṇḍavas curd, milk and ghee, and Nakula gave them the wealth he obtained when the king
was pleased with his work among the horses. Poor Draupadī Kṛṣṇā 10
looked after all the brothers, but the lovely girl did so in such a way as to remain unrecognized. Supporting one another in this way and watching over Kṛṣṇā, the mighty chariot-fighters lived in concealment, lord of men.

Now in the fourth month there fell the great festival of Brahmā, which was richly celebrated by the people of Matsya. Wrestlers assembled there by the thousand from every direction, O king, endowed with mighty bodies and great bravery, like the Kālakhañja demons. Glorying in their heroism and priding themselves on their strength, they were greeted with honour by the king. Lion-shouldered, lion-waisted, lion-necked, bodies gleaming, these spirited men had more than once won the prize in the arena while princes watched.

One of them was a huge man who challenged all the other wrestlers, 15
but none of them would go near him as he leapt about the arena; and when all the wrestlers became downcast and dispirited, the king of Matsya commanded the man to fight his cook. Then Bhīma reluctantly assented to his urging, since he could not openly refuse the king; that tiger-like hero with his tiger-soft tread entered the great arena to Virāṭa's delight. Kuntī's son Bhīma tied on his belt while the crowd cheered, and then he challenged that wrestler, who looked like the demon Vṛtra.
Both men were grimly determined, both full of fierce valour, like two 20
mighty sixty-year-old elephants in rut.[1]

Bhīma the roaring enemy-slayer lifted the bellowing wrestler off his feet and dragged him by his arms, like a tiger dragging an elephant; to the utter amazement of the other wrestlers and the people of Matsya, the strong-armed hero held him aloft and spun him round. And when he

1 This is presumably intended to refer to elephants in their prime, but in fact an elephant of sixty would be nearing the end of its life.

had spun him a hundred times, till he swooned and lost consciousness, the strong-armed wolf-belly Bhīma crushed that wrestler on the ground.

When he saw that the world-famous wrestler Jīmūta had been laid low, Virāṭa was overjoyed, and so were his kinsmen. In his joy the high-minded king gave generously to Ballava in the great arena, as Kubera the god of wealth himself might have done. Then Bhīma brought the king of Matsya the highest pleasure by similarly laying low many other wrestlers and men of great might; and when no further men could be found there to match him, the king had him fight tigers, lions and elephants. After that, the wolf-belly was sent by Virāṭa to the women's quarters to fight against mighty, furious lions in the midst of the women there.

Pāṇḍu's son Arjuna Bībhatsu also pleased Virāṭa and all his womenfolk with his singing and fine dancing. Nakula gave pleasure to the king with the swift and well-trained horses that he collected in many places, truest of kings, and Virāṭa, pleased, gave a generous gift to him, and another to Sahadeva, O lord, on seeing his well-tamed bulls. In this way the bull-like heroes lived there in concealment, performing their tasks for King Virāṭa.

## THE KILLING OF KĪCAKA

Vaiśaṃpāyana spoke:

[**13**] Ten months passed by while Kuntī's sons, those mighty chariot-fighters, lived in disguise in Matsya's city; but Draupadī, who deserved to be waited on, lived miserably in the service of Sudeṣṇā, lord of the peoples. Now Virāṭa's general, Kīcaka, saw the lotus-faced Pāñcāla princess as she went about in Sudeṣṇā's house, and as soon as he saw her, in form like a divine maiden, a walking deity, the arrows of the god of love pierced him, and he desired her. Scorched with the flames of desire, the general approached Sudeṣṇā[1] and, laughing a little, spoke these words: 'I have never previously seen this lovely girl here in King Virāṭa's dwelling. She utterly intoxicates me with her beauty, as fresh

1 Sudeṣṇā is said to be Kīcaka's sister; however, as she is a Kekaya Kṣatriya and he a Sūta, this is a little strange.

liquor intoxicates with its smell! Fair lady, who is this divinely beautiful maiden who has captured my heart? Tell me who the lovely one is and where she is from! She has churned up my mind and taken control of me, and from now on I know there is no other medicine for me.

'Ah, this lovely maid of yours pleases me with her fresh beauty. It is not right for her to work for you; let her command me and whatever I own! I have a great house, richly endowed with many elephants, horses and chariots, opulent in its variety of food and drink, entrancing with its bright ornaments of gold – let her shed her radiance upon it!'

Then, bidding Sudeṣṇā depart, Kīcaka approached the princess Draupadī and spoke to her winningly, like a jackal addressing a young lioness in the forest: 'This beauty and this youth of yours are unsurpassed; but unshared, lovely girl, they are as useless as the finest garland unworn! Radiant though you are, beautiful one, you do not shine. I shall give up all my former wives: let them become your slaves, sweet-smiling beauty! And I too stand here as your slave – O fair-faced one, I shall be for ever yours to command!'

'Son of a Sūta,' answered Draupadī, 'You desire that which you should not, for I am a lowly maidservant, a despised hairdresser. I am a married woman, good sir, so these words of yours are not proper. Consider *dharma*: it is their wives that living creatures should hold dear. You should never under any circumstances set your mind on the wife of another, for the rule observed by men of virtue is to shun what should not be done. The wicked man who succumbs to folly and entertains wrong desires falls into terrible infamy and extreme danger.

'Be not aroused, son of a Sūta; do not throw away your life today by desiring me, for I am unattainable, and heroes protect me. You cannot have me! My husbands are Gandharvas, and if you anger them they will slay you. So stop: do not destroy yourself. The road you wish to travel is impassable to men; you are trying to act like a wilful, foolish child who stands on one bank of a river and wants to cross to the other. Whether you sink into the earth, or fly aloft, or flee across the ocean, you will find no escape from my husbands, for they are the sons of gods, and violent. Why do you long for me so much, Kīcaka, like some sick man longing for the night of his death? Why do you set your mind on me, like a child that lies in its mother's lap and wants to hold the moon?'

[14] Rejected by the princess, Kīcaka spoke to Sudeṣṇā, overwhelmed as he was by his dreadful, immoral lust: 'Sudeṣṇā of Kekaya, arrange for me to lie with your maidservant! Try to get her for me, or I shall take my life!'

Again and again he repeated these words, and then Virāṭa's spirited queen, hearing his lamentations, took pity on him. To pursue her goal Sudeṣṇā considered both his purpose and Draupadī's distress, and she said to the Sūta, 'Have liquor and food prepared for the holiday; I will send her to you to fetch liquor for me. And when I have sent her there, and she is alone with you and under no constraint, ingratiate yourself with her: maybe she will make love with you.'

So then Kīcaka went home as his sister had bidden him, and had liquor brought, well filtered and fit for a king; and he had skilled servants prepare excellent goat, lamb and many different kinds of venison, as well as other very fine food and drink. When this was done he informed Queen Sudeṣṇā, and she sent her maidservant to Kīcaka's house: 'My fair maidservant, get up and go to Kīcaka's dwelling to fetch me drink, for thirst is tormenting me!'

'Princess, I cannot go to his dwelling,' replied Draupadī. 'You yourself know how shameless he is, O queen; and while I stay in your house, lovely maiden of flawless limbs, I will not act lustfully and sin against my husbands. You yourself know the stipulation I made, O queen, when I first entered your house. Kīcaka is a fool whose lust makes him arrogant, and when he sees me he will dishonour me. I will not go there, lovely woman with fair tresses! You have many servant-girls at your command, princess; send someone else, good lady, for he will dishonour me.'

'He would never harm you when I have sent you there,' said Sudeṣṇā, and handed her a gold drinking-vessel with a lid.

Draupadī set out for Kīcaka's dwelling to fetch liquor, fearful, weeping and praying for divine protection: 'As I know no man other than the Pāṇḍavas, by this truth let Kīcaka not overpower me when he sees me!' Then she worshipped the Sun for a moment. The Sun learnt the whole tale from the slender-waisted woman, and he commanded a Rākṣasa to give her invisible protection and not to leave the blameless lady under any circumstances.

When the Sūta saw Draupadī Kṛṣṇā arrive like a frightened doe, he stood up joyfully, like a shipwrecked traveller rescued by a boat. [15] 'Welcome, lady of fair tresses!' he cried. 'Night has become day for me now that you have come to be my mistress. Do my pleasure! My servants shall fetch you gold garlands, shell bracelets, earrings, anklets of gold, silk garments and antelope-skins. I have a splendid bed made ready for you: come with me there and drink my honey-wine!'

'The princess has sent me to you to fetch liquor,' answered Draupadī. 'She said, "Fetch me drink quickly, for I am thirsty." '

'Someone else will take filtered liquor to the princess!' said the Sūta's son, and he took hold of her right hand. Shaking at his touch she threw Kīcaka to the floor and fled for protection to the hall where King Yudhiṣṭhira was. But as she fled, Kīcaka laid hold of her by the hair, and before the king's eyes he threw her down and kicked her. Then the Rākṣasa assigned by the Sun swept Kīcaka aside with the speed of the wind; at the force of the Rākṣasa's blow he fell writhing to the ground, and lay motionless as an uprooted tree.

Bhīma and Yudhiṣṭhira were seated there. They saw Kṛṣṇā, and could not bear to see her kicked by Kīcaka. High-minded Bhīma, eager to kill the wicked Kīcaka, ground tooth against tooth in fury; but Yudhiṣṭhira lord of *dharma* squeezed Bhīma's thumb with his own to prevent him, O king, for fear that they would be discovered.

Weeping, Drupada's daughter of fine hips reached the door of the hall. She gazed at her husbands as they sat there wretched at heart, and addressed the Matsya king, protecting their disguise and the pledge they had sworn in accordance with *dharma*, but seeming to blaze with the fierceness of her eye: 'I am the proud wife of men whose enemy can never sleep as long as he lives to set foot on the earth – and the son of a Sūta has kicked me. I am the proud wife of men who are givers, not beggars, who support the Brahmins and speak the truth – and the son of a Sūta has kicked me. I am the proud wife of men whose drums roar and whose bowstrings twang without cease – and the son of a Sūta has kicked me. I am the proud wife of men who are ardent, forbearing, mighty and proud – and the son of a Sūta has kicked me. I am the proud wife of men who could slay this whole world, but who are bound by the fetters of *dharma* – and the son of a Sūta has kicked me.

'They are the refuge of those who approach them seeking refuge, but now they wander the earth in concealment: where are those warriors today? How could those mighty heroes of boundless power bear to see their beloved, virtuous wife kicked by the Sūta's son, as if they were eunuchs? Where is their anger, where their heroism and ardour, that they did not try to protect their wife when she was kicked by a wicked man?

'What can I do when Virāṭa watches while *dharma* is defiled, and tolerates the kicking of an innocent woman? O king, your behaviour towards Kīcaka is not at all kingly! Yours seems to be the *dharma* of barbarians; it does not appear in a good light in the assembly. Kīcaka is in breach of his *dharma*, but so indeed is the Matsya king, and the courtiers too must be ignorant of *dharma* if they choose to wait upon him. I shall not scold you, King Virāṭa, in your own assembly, but it was not right that I should be struck by this man in your presence: let the courtiers behold Kīcaka's transgression!'

'I know nothing of the dispute between the two of you,' said Virāṭa, 'for I was not present; without knowing the truth of the matter, what competence can I have to judge it?'

But then the courtiers, who did know what had happened, praised Draupadī Kṛṣṇā highly, crying, 'Bravo! Bravo!' and denouncing Kīcaka: 'The man who has for his wife this long-eyed woman, beautiful from head to foot, has the highest fortune, and will never have cause for regret!'

Thus the courtiers gazed at Kṛṣṇā and praised her; but Yudhiṣṭhira was so angry that sweat broke out on his forehead. Kuru's heir addressed Princess Draupadī, his own beloved queen: 'Go, maidservant, do not linger here! Go to Sudeṣṇā's dwelling. The wives of heroes suffer for love of their husbands, but they win the heaven of their husbands with their obedient suffering. I think that your husbands do not consider this the occasion for anger; that is why they do not rush to your aid – those Gandharvas radiant as the sun. Maidservant, you have misjudged the occasion, running to and fro like some dancing-girl, and you are interrupting the Matsyas' game of dice here in the royal assembly! Go, maidservant; your Gandharvas will do what you wish.'

'Too kind are those whose lawful wife I am!' retorted Draupadī. 'And yet they may fall victim to anyone in the world, for the eldest of them is a gambler!' With these words Kṛṣṇā of fine hips rushed out to Sudeṣṇā's dwelling, untying her hair, her eyes red with fury. Then she wept ceaselessly, till her face shone as bright as the disc of the moon in the sky when it emerges from a cloud-bank.

Sudeṣṇā said, 'Who has struck you, lady of fine hips? Lovely woman, why do you weep? For what reason are you not happy today? Who has vexed you?'

'Kīcaka struck me when I went there to fetch liquor for you,' replied 40
Draupadī. 'He struck me before the king's eyes in the hall, just as if no one else were there!'

'Lady of fair tresses,' said Sudeṣṇā, 'if you wish it I shall kill this Kīcaka, who in his crazed lust desires an unattainable woman like you.'

'Others will kill him,' answered Draupadī: 'those whom he has wronged. I think that this very day he will surely pass over to the other world!'

**[16]** *During the night, Draupadī goes to Bhīma and wakes him. She urges him to kill Kīcaka, and he asks her to tell him everything that has happened to her.* **[17]** *She pours out her scorn for Yudhiṣṭhira: it is thanks to him that she was molested by Duḥśāsana, then by Jayadratha, and now again by Kīcaka. His disastrous gambling has reduced him from the status of emperor to that of attendant at another's court.* **[18]** *As for Bhīma, he has to cook and to fight with animals; when the queen sees signs of Draupadī's tenderness towards him, she gossips about the love-affair between her cook and her maidservant. Mighty Arjuna has to wear ornaments and braided hair; he spends his time surrounded by girls. Sahadeva has to tend cattle, Nakula horses. Yudhiṣṭhira is responsible for the terrible misfortune into which they have all fallen.* **[19]** *Finally, Draupadī laments for herself: she is a princess, but now she has to do menial work for another; her hands are callused.*

**[20]** *Bhīma tries to calm Draupadī, urging her to be patient for the month-and-a-half that remains. She answers that it is her treatment at the hands of Kīcaka that has brought her to such a state, and insists that she will take poison if he is not killed.*

Vaiśaṃpāyana spoke:
**[21]** 'Timid lady,' said Bhīma, 'I shall do as you say: today I shall slay

Kīcaka with his kinsmen! Make an assignation with him on the evening of this coming night, and cast off your sadness and grief, sweet-smiling Draupadī. The Matsya king has had a dance-hall constructed; girls dance there by day, but at night they go to their homes. There is a bed there, timid one, strong and well-built: there I shall introduce him to his late
5 ancestors! But make sure that no one sees you make your rendezvous with him, O fair one, and that he waits nearby.'

Talking thus and shedding tears, the two of them somehow found heart to bear the remainder of that bitter night. The next morning, when night had passed, Kīcaka arose. He went straight to the royal palace and spoke to Draupadī: 'Before the king's eyes in the hall I threw you down and kicked you, and you got no help, for the stronger man overpowered you. He is named as king of the Matsyas, but that is merely
10 words, for the true king of the Matsyas is his general, I myself! So accept me gladly, timid one; I shall be your slave. I shall give you at once a hundred gold coins, lady of fine hips, and I shall give you a hundred slave-girls, and a hundred male slaves besides, as well as a carriage drawn by she-mules. Timid one, let us unite!'

'Today you must accept one stipulation, Kīcaka,' said Draupadī. 'No one, friend or brother, must know that you are with me, for I am fearful that we may be discovered by my famed Gandharvas. Promise me this, and I am yours.'

'I shall do as you say, lady of fine hips,' replied Kīcaka; 'I shall go
15 all alone to your dwelling to unite with you, so that those Gandharvas radiant as the sun will not discover you. I am crazed with love, lady of fine thighs!'

'The Matsya king has had a dance-hall constructed here,' said Draupadī; 'girls dance there by day, but at night they go to their homes. Go there in the dark: the Gandharvas do not know it, so there we shall escape blame, make no doubt!'

Thus Draupadī Kṛṣṇā spoke of this matter with Kīcaka; for her, O king, the next half of the day passed like a month. But Kīcaka went home utterly overwhelmed by joy, for the fool did not realize that she
20 was his death in the form of a maidservant. He was particularly fond of perfumes, ornaments and garlands, and so, besotted as he was, he made haste to adorn himself; and for him the time seemed to pass slowly as

he performed this task, thinking of nothing but the long-eyed woman. Even more good-looking now, he prepared to give up good looks for ever, like a lamp nearing extinction and starting to burn up its wick. Trustful, besotted Kīcaka did not notice the day passing by as he thought only of his tryst.

Now lovely Draupadī went to the kitchen and approached her husband Bhīma, the heir of Kuru. The lady of fair tresses told him, 'I have made an assignation with Kīcaka in the dance-hall, just as you said, afflicter of your enemies. He will come alone to the dance-hall when it is empty at night. Strong-armed hero, slay this Kīcaka! Lust has made the Sūta's son arrogant, son of Kuntī; go to the dance-hall, O Pāṇḍava, and take his life. In his arrogance he even looks down on the Gandharvas. You are the best of fighting men: take out the Sūta's son like an elephant tearing out a reed! Heir of Bharata, I am overwhelmed with misery, so wipe away my tears, and maintain your own and your family's honour, good sir!'

'Welcome, beautiful lady of fine hips,' answered Bhīma. 'What you tell me pleases me, for I do not want him to have any companion. I have the same pleasure in learning from you of your assignation with Kīcaka that I had when I killed Hiḍimba![1] I swear to you by truth, by my brothers and by *dharma* that I shall slay Kīcaka, as Indra, lord of the gods, slew Vṛtra. Whether in private or in public, I shall crush Kīcaka, and if the Matsyas come to hear of it, I shall surely kill them too; then I shall kill Duryodhana and win back the earth! Let Kuntī's son Yudhiṣṭhira continue to serve the Matsya king if he wishes!'

'My lord and hero,' said Draupadī, 'to keep your word to me you must slay Kīcaka in secret.' 'I shall do it just as you say, timid one!' replied Bhīma. 'Wicked Kīcaka desires an unattainable woman. Tonight, blameless lady, unseen in the dark, I shall crush his head like an elephant trampling a wood-apple!'

That night, Bhīma went first to the dance-hall and sat there concealed, waiting for Kīcaka as a hidden lion waits for a deer. As for Kīcaka, he adorned himself to his liking and approached at the appointed time, hoping for union with the Pāñcāla princess. He entered that hall, his

1 See 1.139–42.

mind on his assignation. Once inside the building, which was huge and
completely dark, the wicked man came upon Bhīma of incomparable
might, who was waiting alone after arriving there earlier: the Sūta laid
hands on his own death, who lay there on the bed blazing with fury at
his assault on Draupadī. Drawing closer, the besotted Kīcaka spoke to
him with a smile, his mind aswirl with excitement: 'I have conferred
boundless wealth of many sorts upon you; I directed that it all be given
45 you, and then came swiftly here. It is not without reason that the women
of my house always praise me, saying, "No other man is as well dressed
and handsome as you!"'

Bhīma answered him, 'My felicitations on your good looks and your
self-esteem; however, you have never experienced any sensation such
as this!' And with these words strong-armed Kuntī's son, Bhīma of
terrible valour, leapt up with a laugh and seized the vile man by his
garlanded, perfumed hair. Finding himself laid hold of in this way,
Kīcaka, mightiest of the mighty, used his strength to free his hair, and
then swiftly seized Bhīma by the arms. Then the two lion-like heroes
wrestled with one another like two mighty elephants fighting in spring
50 for a female. Bhīma tripped slightly, for sheer rage had made him
unsteady on his feet, whereupon mighty Kīcaka kneed him and hurled
him to the ground.

Thrown to the ground by the powerful Kīcaka, Bhīma then swiftly
leapt up again like a snake struck with a stick, and the two rivals, Sūta and
Pāṇḍava, both strong men and both drunk with their strength, harried
each other in the deserted hall at midnight. Then that fine building
trembled over and over again, while the two men roared at each other
in their mighty rage. Bhīma slapped Kīcaka on the chest with the flat of
55 his hands, yet Kīcaka, blazing with fury, did not move even a step. But
after enduring for a little while his enemy's onslaught, which none on
earth could endure, the Sūta then began, despite himself, to fail, for he
was overcome by Bhīma's might; and when mighty Bhīma saw that he
was failing, he hugged him to his chest and shook him unconscious.

Then, exhaling deeply in his anger, wolf-belly Bhīma, the best of victors, once again seized him hard by the hair; catching hold of Kīcaka, mighty Bhīma roared aloud like a hungry tiger that has caught a great deer. He squeezed all his limbs, his hands, feet, head and neck, inside his body, as Śiva, the bearer of the Pināka weapon, did to the sacrificial beast.[1] And when he had mangled him in every limb and reduced him to a ball of flesh, mighty Bhīma showed him to Kṛṣṇā. Pāṇḍu's son of great ardour said to Draupadī, 'Pāñcāla princess, come and see what I have done to this lover!' Then, his anger appeased by having killed Kīcaka in this way, he bade farewell to Draupadī Kṛṣṇā and quickly returned to the kitchen.

As for Draupadī, that best of women rejoiced at having secured Kīcaka's death. Freed from her distress, she now addressed the guards of the hall: 'Kīcaka lies here, slain by my Gandharva husbands for lusting after a married woman. Come and see!' When the guards of the dance-hall heard her words, they came swiftly in their thousands, bearing torches; and when they reached the building they saw Kīcaka lying slain on the ground, doused in blood. 'Where is his neck? Where are his feet? Where his hands and head?' they asked, and then they concluded that he had been killed by a Gandharva.

[**22**] At this point all Kīcaka's kinsmen arrived. When they saw him, they stood round him weeping; at the sight of Kīcaka with all his limbs mangled, like a turtle hauled on to dry land, the hair rose on their bodies and they were frightened, for Bhīma had crushed him as Indra crushes demons. They wished to perform the last rites for him, and so they began to carry him away; and then those assembled sons of Sūtas saw Draupadī Kṛṣṇā of flawless limbs standing nearby, leaning against a pillar. One of Kīcaka's folk among the assembled Sūtas said to them, 'Let us kill this adulteress at once, for Kīcaka was killed on her account! Better still, instead of killing her here, let us burn her together with her lover – we should show the Sūta's son every kindness, even after death!'

Then they addressed Virāṭa: 'Kīcaka was killed on her account, and she should be burnt with him today: please permit it!' And the king, remembering the Sūtas' might, was happy to allow the maidservant to be burnt with the son of a Sūta, lord of the peoples. So Kīcaka's folk returned to lotus-eyed Kṛṣṇā, who was swooning with terror, and seized

1 When Śiva disrupts the sacrifice of Dakṣa, from which he had been excluded, the sacrifice itself flees from him in the form of a deer, but he destroys it (12.274) and, in a passage considered secondary by the editor, beheads it (12, App. I, 28.111).

10 her forcibly. Then they all lifted the slender-waisted lady on to the bier, bound her fast, and bore her away towards the burning-ground.

As blameless Kṛṣṇā was carried off by those Sūtas' sons, O king, she cried out for the protection of her husbands, for she had husbands to protect her. 'Jaya, Jayanta, Vijaya, Jayatsena and Jayadbala, hear my words: the sons of Sūtas are taking me! The terrible twang of the bowstring against your palms, sounding like the roar of a thunderbolt, has been heard in great battles, spirited and famed Gandharvas, and so has the mighty din of your chariots. Hear my words: the sons of Sūtas are taking me!'

15 As soon as Bhīma heard Kṛṣṇā's pitiful words, he leapt from his bed without pause for thought and answered her: 'Maidservant, I hear the words you speak, so you need not fear the Sūtas' sons, timid one!' Then with these words strong-armed Bhīma swelled up in his eagerness to kill; flexing his limbs and donning different clothes, he set forth, leaping the wall rather than using the gate. Swiftly he uprooted a tree from the rampart, and headed towards the burning-ground where Kīcaka's folk had gone. Brandishing this sixty-foot tree, trunk, branches and all,
20 mighty Bhīma rushed at the Sūtas like staff-wielding Death; so swiftly did his thighs carry him that banyans, *aśvatthas* and *kiṃśuka* trees fell to the earth and lay in heaps.

When the Sūtas saw this Gandharva come at them like a raging lion, they were all terrified; they trembled in their misery and fear. Kīcaka's folk saw a Gandharva approaching like Death as they prepared to burn the body of their eldest brother, and, trembling with misery and fear, they said to one another, 'A mighty Gandharva is coming: he is furious, and is brandishing a tree! Quickly release the maidservant, for great danger is upon us!' Gazing at the tree that Bhīma had torn from the ground they let go of Draupadī on the spot and ran headlong for the city.

25 Bhīma saw them running away, and, like Indra the god of the thunderbolt attacking the demons, he dispatched a hundred and five of them to the realm of Yama. Then he released Draupadī Kṛṣṇā, lord of the peoples, and comforted her; and the strong-armed hero, the unconquerable wolf-belly, addressed the Pāñcāla princess as she stood there downcast, her eyes filled with tears: 'This, timid one, is how they

are slain who wrong your innocent self! Go forth to the city, Kṛṣṇā: you are no longer in danger. I shall return to Virāṭa's kitchen by another route.'

Thus a hundred and five lay dead there, heir of Bharata, like a great forest that has been felled, its trees lying tumbled in disorder. A hundred and five of Kīcaka's folk were slain, O king, as was the general himself before: altogether a hundred and six Sūtas. When the men and women of the city came and beheld this great marvel, heir of Bharata, they were utterly astounded and could not speak a word.

**[23]** When the people saw those Sūtas lying slain, they went and informed the king: 'Lord, the Gandharvas have killed more than a hundred sons of Sūtas! They lie on the ground, looking as if the huge peak of a mountain had been split apart and scattered by a thunderbolt. That maidservant has also been freed, and she is returning to your house. Your whole city is in danger, king, for the maidservant is so lovely and the Gandharvas so mighty, and men's favourite indulgence is in sex, make no doubt! You must swiftly establish a strategy to prevent this city of yours from meeting with destruction in the shape of a maidservant, O king.'

When Virāṭa the general heard their words, he gave orders for the last rites to be performed for the Sūtas: 'Let all Kīcaka's folk be quickly cremated on a single well-blazing pyre, with plenty of gems and incense!' And in his alarm the king told Queen Sudeṣṇā, 'When your maidservant gets here, say to her on my authority, "Maidservant, go! Go wherever you will, good lady of fine hips, for the king fears defeat at the hands of your Gandharvas!" I dare not tell her this myself, since she is under the Gandharvas' protection; however, women are blameless, and so I call on you to speak to her.'

Draupadī Kṛṣṇā had been freed from her danger and released by Bhīma, who had wiped out those sons of Sūtas; now the spirited girl washed herself and her garments with water and then set out for the city, like a doe that has been terrified by a tiger. When men saw her, O king, they ran headlong in every direction, and some of them covered their eyes in their terror of the Gandharvas.

Then the Pāñcāla princess saw Bhīma standing at the kitchen door, O king, looking like a mighty elephant in rut. Full of wonder, but speaking softly and using signs, she said to him, 'Honour to the Gandharva king who set me free!' Bhīma answered, 'When men here on earth owe allegiance to a woman, to hear her command releases them from their debt!'

Next she saw wealth-winner Arjuna in the dance-hall, where the strong-armed hero was teaching the king's daughters dancing. The girls left the hall with Arjuna and watched while Draupadī Kṛṣṇā drew close, a woman innocent but wronged. 'What a blessing that you were set free, maidservant,' they said; 'what a blessing that you have returned, and that those Sūtas lie slain who wronged your innocent self!'

'How were you set free, maidservant,' asked Bṛhannaḍā, 'and how were those wicked men slain? I want to hear it all: tell me just as it happened!'

But the maidservant replied, 'Bṛhannaḍā, what concern do you have with a maidservant? You spend all your days in comfort in the girls' quarters, fair one, and know none of the distress that a maidservant experiences; so why do you laughingly question me in my distress?'

'Fair child,' answered Bṛhannaḍā, 'Bṛhannaḍā too suffers extreme distress in this subhuman form of hers; you do not understand her.'

But Draupadī took the girls with her, entered the royal palace, and fearlessly approached Sudeṣṇā. The princess addressed her on Virāṭa's authority: 'Maidservant, go quickly wherever you wish to go! The king, good lady, fears defeat at the hands of your Gandharvas, and you yourself are young and lovely, your beauty incomparable on earth.'

'Let the king grant me just thirteen days' grace, fair queen,' replied Draupadī; 'this will satisfy those Gandharvas, make no doubt, and they will then take me away from here and do whatever you wish. The king and his kinsmen will certainly benefit from this.'

## THE CATTLE RAID

**[24]** *The people of Matsya are delighted at the death of the hated Kīcaka clan. Meanwhile, however, Duryodhana's spies, who have been searching for the Pāṇḍavas, return to Hāstinapura and report that they can find no trace of them in the forest. They also report the death of Kīcaka.*

**[25]** *Duryodhana reflects, and instructs his spies to try again. But Karṇa intervenes, urging him to send cleverer men. Duḥśāsana agrees, though he suspects that the Pāṇḍavas are already dead.* **[26]** *Droṇa warns that such excellent men as the Pāṇḍavas, all of them so devoted to each other, are most unlikely to have met their end. A thorough search should be undertaken.* **[27]** *Bhīṣma supports Droṇa in maintaining that the Pāṇḍavas will still be alive, and adds that intelligence should be deployed to trace them. The land where Yudhiṣṭhira is living will be prosperous and its people will be virtuous and contented.* **[28]** *Kṛpa agrees with Bhīṣma's views on tracing the Pāṇḍavas. In the meantime, Duryodhana's best policy will be to build up his resources and his army, and to strengthen his alliances, in readiness for the day when they return from their exile.*

**[29]** *Now Suśarman, king of Trigarta and an old enemy of Matsya, observes that the death of Kīcaka leaves Virāṭa vulnerable, and proposes to launch an attack on his kingdom. Karṇa strongly supports this suggestion, arguing that the Pāṇḍavas are too weak to pose any threat. Duryodhana approves the plan, and Suśarman sets out for a cattle raid against Matsya.*

**[30]** *At the end of the Pāṇḍavas' thirteenth year of exile, King Virāṭa receives news from a cowherd that Suśarman of Trigarta has attacked and is driving off hundreds of thousands of cattle. At once he rides out at the head of a great army, accompanied by his brothers and his son Śaṅkha; he also gives orders for Kaṅka, Ballava, Tantipāla and Granthika to be equipped to join his force.*

**[31]** *Virāṭa's army catches up with that of Suśarman, and a fierce battle begins. Virāṭa cuts his way through the Trigarta troops until he reaches Suśarman's chariot, and the two kings shower each other with arrows until night falls.*

**[32]** *Darkness brings the battle to a halt, but soon the moon rises and fighting resumes. Suśarman and his brother, supported by a chariot force, succeed in taking Virāṭa prisoner, and the Matsya army begins to flee. Yudhiṣṭhira tells Bhīma to rescue him, but to avoid giving away his identity by using his superhuman strength. All four Pāṇḍavas now battle mightily against the men of Trigarta, and Bhīma rescues Virāṭa and captures Suśarman, whose army is routed. They return the cattle and other treasures to Virāṭa; he rewards them and proposes to make Yudhiṣṭhira king, but Yudhiṣṭhira merely tells him to have his victory proclaimed in the city.*

Vaiśaṃpāyana spoke:

**[33]** While the Matsya king made for Trigarta in hopes of regaining

his livestock, Duryodhana with his ministers attacked the kingdom of Virāṭa. Bhīṣma, Droṇa, Karṇa, Kṛpa the master of weaponry, Droṇa's son Aśvatthāman, Subala's son Śakuni, the lord Duḥśāsana, Viviṃśati, Vikarṇa, heroic Citrasena, Durmukha, Duḥsaha, and the other mighty chariot-fighters: all these attacked King Virāṭa's kingdom of Matsya. Swiftly they put his cattle-stations to flight and took the cattle by force:
5 the Kurus rounded up sixty thousand cows with a great mass of chariots, and drove them off.

As the cowherds in the cattle-stations were slain by the mighty chariot-fighters in that terrible conflict, they let out a loud cry; but their overseer hastily mounted a chariot in his fear, and drove straight for the city, wailing in his affliction. Entering the city of the king, he rode to the royal palace, leapt down from his chariot, and went in to announce the news. There he saw the Matsya king's proud son, Bhūmiṃjaya by name,[1] and he told him all about the plundering of the
10 kingdom's livestock. 'The Kurus are driving off sixty thousand cows! Arise, win back the cattle, the wealth through which the kingdom prospers! Prince, if you wish to do good, set out swiftly yourself, for the Matsya king has left you here in charge of the empty city. The lord of men boasts about you in the midst of the assembly: "My son is like me, brave and the heir to a great line; my son is ever the hero, a warrior skilled with weapons of every sort!" Let the prince of men's words come true indeed: win back the cattle, best of cattle-owners, and turn back the Kurus! Burn their forces with the terrible fiery
15 energy of your arrows! Destroy the enemy troops with the well-planed, gold-shafted arrows that fly from your bow, as the lord of an elephant herd would destroy an enemy herd! In the midst of your enemies, play on the loud-voiced lute that is your bow, with its fastening-knots for tuning-cords, its bowstring for strings, its own staff for neck, and its arrows for notes. Have your silver-white horses yoked to your chariot, and your standard of a golden lion raised, lord; let the gold-shafted, bright-tipped arrows which you shoot so dextrously obscure the sun and cut short the lives of kings! Conquer all the Kurus in battle, as Indra conquered the demons with his thunderbolt; return to this city

1 Bhūmiṃjaya ('Conqueror of the earth') is also known as Uttara.

after winning great renown! You, as the lord of Matsya's son, are the ultimate protector of the kingdom, so let all who live within the realm find protection in you today!'

When these courage-inspiring words were addressed to Prince Uttara in the midst of his womenfolk, he gave his answer, boasting before the people of the women's quarters: **[34]** 'Today, strong bowman that I am, I would follow the trail of the cows, if only I had some charioteer who was skilled with horses! What I lack is a man to drive me: quickly find someone suitable to be my charioteer when I set forth! My own charioteer was finally killed in a great battle that lasted for twenty-eight days, if not a month. But if I could just get another man with skill in controlling the horses, I would set out at speed today with my mighty standard raised; I would force my way through the ranks of my enemies with all their elephants, horses and chariots, defeat the Kurus, overwhelming them with the prowess of my weapons, and fetch back the cows! Bringing terror to Duryodhana, Bhīṣma son of Śaṃtanu, Karṇa the Cutter, Kṛpa, Droṇa and his son Aśvatthāman, and all the other mighty bowmen gathered there, just as Indra terrified the demons in battle with his thunderbolt, I would fetch back the cows in a trice! It is because the Kurus found the country empty that they have been able to make off with our cattle – what could I do when I was not there? But if all those Kurus see my heroism today, they will wonder if they have come under attack from Arjuna son of Kuntī himself!'

Now as he spoke these words again and again amidst his womenfolk, the Pāñcāla princess could not bear his referring to Arjuna Bībhatsu. The poor woman bashfully stepped out towards him from amongst the women and softly said, 'That most handsome youth with the air of a mighty elephant, the one known as Bṛhannaḍā, used to be Arjuna's charioteer. He was that noble man's pupil with the bow, and in no way his inferior: I saw him before, brave sir, when I went to join the Pāṇḍavas. When the Fire god burned down the great Khāṇḍava forest,[1] he was in charge of Arjuna's fine horses; he was the charioteer when Kuntī's son defeated all creatures throughout Khāṇḍavaprastha. There is no driver to match him! Make no doubt, brave sir, he will obey the

1 See 1.214 ff.

command of your younger sister here, the princess of fine hips; and if he were your charioteer you would certainly return with the cows after defeating all the Kurus!'

Hearing the maidservant speak thus to him, he in turn addressed his sister: 'Go, lady of flawless limbs, and fetch this Bṛhannaḍā!' And at her brother's command she hastened to the dance-hall where that strong-armed son of Pāṇḍu was staying under cover of his disguise.

**[35]** When Bṛhannaḍā saw his friend the wide-eyed princess, O king, he laughed and asked her why she had come. She approached the bull-like hero and addressed him affectionately in the midst of her companions: 'Bṛhannaḍā, the cows of this realm are being driven off by the Kurus, and my brother is to set forth, bow in hand, to defeat them. His charioteer was slain in battle not long ago, and there is no
5 Sūta to match that man who might act as his charioteer. However, my maidservant spoke to him of your skill with horses, Bṛhannaḍā, as he was striving to find a charioteer. So, Bṛhannaḍā, you must drive for my brother, and drive well, before our cows are carried off further by the Kurus! If you will not carry out my wishes today, though I have asked you affectionately, I shall give up my life!'

Hearing his friend of the fine hips speak so, Arjuna, afflicter of his enemies, went into the presence of the prince of boundless power, treading rapidly like an elephant in rut, while the wide-eyed young
10 princess followed him like a she-elephant. The prince saw him while he was still far distant, and said, 'With you as charioteer, Kuntī's son Arjuna the wealth-winner satiated the Fire god in the Khāṇḍava forest and conquered the whole earth: the maidservant told me all about you, for she knew the Pāṇḍavas. Take charge of my horses in just the same way, Bṛhannaḍā, as I battle with the Kurus to regain our cattle! I am told that you were once Arjuna's favourite charioteer, and that it was with your help that the bull-like Pāṇḍava conquered the earth!'

To these words of the prince, Bṛhannaḍā replied, 'What power do
15 I have to drive a chariot in the thick of battle? Singing, dancing, or playing musical instruments of various sorts: that I will do, good sir, but how am I to drive a chariot?'

'Bṛhannaḍā,' said Uttara, 'be you singer or dancer, quickly mount my chariot and take charge of my fine horses!'

Then, foe-tamer, in the presence of Princess Uttarā,[1] Pāṇḍu's son began in fun to put on a great act, though really he knew everything he was doing: he tried to put on his armour by tossing it into the air, and the wide-eyed girls burst out laughing when they saw him. But when Prince Uttara saw Bṛhannaḍā acting so foolishly, he personally tied the costly armour on to him; he himself also wore splendid armour that shone like the sun. Raising his standard of a lion, he commanded Bṛhannaḍā to drive his chariot; and then, carrying costly bows and many fine arrows, that hero set forth with Bṛhannaḍā as his charioteer.

Now Uttarā and the girls who were her friends said, 'Bṛhannaḍā, once you have defeated in battle the Kurus under Bhīṣma and Droṇa, bring us some lovely clothes for our dolls – delicate and beautiful ones of every kind!'

Kuntī's son, the son of Pāṇḍu, laughed to hear all the girls speak so, but his reply sounded like thunder or drums: 'If Uttara here defeats the mighty chariot-fighters in battle, I shall fetch you beautiful, heavenly clothes!' Then with these words brave Arjuna Bībhatsu urged on the horses forward towards the many standards and banners of the Kurus.

**[36]** Virāṭa's son Bhūmiṃjaya Uttara set out from the capital. 'Drive on,' he told his charioteer, 'to where those Kurus are! Once I have defeated the assembled Kurus who long for victory, and taken back their cows, I shall swiftly return to my own city.' So Pāṇḍu's son urged on the excellent horses; and, urged on by that tiger-like hero, those horses with their gold trappings seemed to fly like wind through the air.

Wealth-winner Arjuna and the son of the Matsya king had not gone far when the two enemy-slayers saw the mighty Kuru force. They passed near a burning-ground, and then they caught up with the Kurus. Their army was huge, and roared like the ocean; it seemed like a densely wooded forest moving slowly through space, and as it moved, it raised a dust from the earth that robbed creatures of their sight and reached as far as the sky, truest of men. When he saw that great force with all its elephants, horses and chariots, overseen by Karṇa, Duryodhana, Kṛpa, Bhīṣma son of Śaṃtanu, and wise Droṇa the mighty bowman, together with his son Aśvatthāman, Virāṭa's son felt the hair rise on his body,

**1** Uttara's sister.

and in terror he said to Kuntī's son, 'I dare not fight against the Kurus! See, my hair stands on end! I cannot do battle with this boundless Kuru army, so fierce and full of so many heroes; even the gods would find it invincible! I have no hope of penetrating the army of the Bhāratas with its fearful bows, its chariots, elephants and horses, its footsoldiers and its standards. For no sooner do I see my enemies on the battlefield than my soul seems to quake within me – there are Droṇa, Bhīṣma, Kṛpa, Karṇa, Viviṃśati, Aśvatthāman, Vikarṇa, Somadatta and Bāhlika, and there too is brave King Duryodhana, best of chariot-fighters. All are splendid, mighty bowmen, expert in warfare. No sooner do I see these Kurus, warriors arrayed for war, than my hair stands on end and despair seizes me!'

Before the eyes of the bold and cunning Arjuna, the cowardly and stupid prince continued his foolish lament. 'My father has set out for Trigarta, leaving me behind in an empty city: he has taken the whole army with him, and I have no troops here. I am all alone, a mere boy and untrained; I cannot fight against enemies who are numerous and expert in arms. Turn back, Bṛhannaḍā!'

Arjuna said, 'You seem cast down with fear, and a reason for your foes to rejoice; and yet thus far your enemies have done nothing on the field of battle! It was you yourself who said, "Carry me towards the Kauravas!" – so I shall take you to where their standards are most dense. Strong-armed hero, I shall take you into the midst of the Kurus, whose bows are strung to fight for the earth itself, like vultures fighting for flesh! After vowing manly deeds before men and women alike, after setting forth still boasting, why do you now not wish to fight? If you go home without winning back those cows, O hero, men and women together will laugh at you. As for me, I was praised by the maidservant for my skill in this business of driving, so I cannot make for the city without first winning back the cows. What with the maidservant's praise and your own command, how could I not fight all those Kurus? Stand firm!'

'Let the Kurus take most of the Matsyas' wealth, if they so wish,' answered Uttara; 'and let women and men laugh at me!' And with these words the foolish prince, still decked with earrings, leapt in terror down from the chariot and ran headlong, abandoning his pride, his bow and his arrows.

Bṛhannaḍā said, 'Our forefathers did not consider it to be the Kṣatriya's *dharma* to flee like this. Better for you to die in battle than to flee in terror!' And Kuntī's son wealth-winner Arjuna too leapt down with these words from the splendid chariot, and ran after the running prince, trailing his long braid and his bright red garments behind him.

Some of the soldiers, not recognizing Arjuna, laughed to see him trailing a braid as he ran. But seeing how fast he was running, the Kurus began to say, 'Who can this be, disguised by his apparel like a fire concealed under ashes? There is something of the man about him, and something of the woman, and he bears a resemblance to Arjuna, though in eunuch's form. The head and neck are his, and so are those arms like iron bars; the tread is like his. This cannot be anyone but the wealth-winner! As the lord Indra is among the immortals, so is the wealth-winner among men: who but Arjuna in this world would come against us alone? A single son was left behind in Virāṭa's empty city, and it looks as if he has set forth, though through childishness rather than manliness. For surely that is Kuntī's son Arjuna going along under cover of disguise! Uttara must have made him his charioteer before setting out from the city, and now it seems that he is fleeing in fear at the sight of our standards, and the wealth-winner is clearly trying to catch him as he runs!' Thus all the Kurus mused separately amongst themselves when they saw Pāṇḍu's son in disguise, heir of Bharata, but they were unable to reach any firm conclusion.

Wealth-winner Arjuna ran on after the fleeing Uttara, and after a hundred paces he quickly laid hold of him by the hair. Finding himself laid hold of by Arjuna, Virāṭa's son wailed much and wretchedly in his affliction: 'I shall give you a hundred pure gold coins, eight bright beryl gems set in gold, a chariot with a gold flagstaff yoked to excellent steeds, and ten rutting elephants: let me go, Bṛhannaḍā!'

But tiger-like Arjuna laughed at him as he wailed in this manner, almost out of his mind, and he brought him back to the chariot. Then Kuntī's son said to the boy, swooning as he was with terror, 'If, O tormentor of your enemies, you dare not fight your enemies, then come and take charge of the horses for me, and I will fight them! Protected by the might of my arms, drive forth against this terrible chariot-force! It is utterly unassailable, for it is overseen by mighty,

heroic chariot-fighters; but you should not fear, foremost of princes, for you are a Kṣatriya. I shall fight the Kurus, afflicter of your enemies,
45 and win back your beasts! Be my driver, best of men, and penetrate this unassailable, invincible chariot-force; I shall fight the Kurus!'

Arjuna Bībhatsu, who had never suffered defeat, spent some time encouraging Virāṭa's son Uttara with such words. Then Kuntī's son, the best of fighting men, forced the reluctant prince, who was struggling in his terror, to mount the chariot.

**[37]** *The sight of Bṛhannaḍā forcing Uttara on to his chariot makes the Kauravas downcast, and Droṇa forecasts disaster; he is certain the charioteer is Arjuna. But Duryodhana is pleased: if Arjuna has been recognized, the Pāṇḍavas will have to undergo a further twelve years of exile.*

**[38]** *Arjuna instructs Uttara to fetch the Pāṇḍavas' weapons from their hiding-place in the* śamī *tree. Uttara objects that there is a corpse in the tree, but Arjuna insists. When the weapons are unwrapped, Uttara is astonished at their excellence, and asks about each one. Arjuna tells him all about them.* **[39]** *Now Uttara wants to know where the Pāṇḍavas themselves are. Arjuna answers that he is Arjuna, and identifies the others also. To confirm the truth of this claim, Uttara asks Arjuna to list his ten names, and, when he does so, to explain the meaning of each one. Uttara is delighted to be in Arjuna's presence, and his fear leaves him.* **[40]** *He tells Arjuna that he will act as his charioteer, and Arjuna replies that he will do battle with the Kauravas and win back Virāṭa's cattle. Uttara asks how it is that Arjuna became a eunuch; Arjuna tells him that he has observed a vow of celibacy for a year at Yudhiṣṭhira's direction, but that he is not a eunuch. Uttara now makes ready to drive the chariot, and Arjuna casts off his disguise as Bṛhannaḍā.*

**[41]** *The sound of Arjuna's conch and of his bow Gāṇḍīva leaves Uttara stunned. Droṇa too hears it and recognizes it; he perceives bad portents and urges the Kauravas to stand firm.* **[42]** *Duryodhana claims that the thirteenth year is not yet complete, and that the Pāṇḍavas will therefore have to return to the forest for a further twelve years. The Kauravas are there to fight against the army of Matsya in support of Trigarta, and that is what they should do; Droṇa is influenced by his affection for Arjuna.* **[43]** *Karṇa now boasts that he is Arjuna's equal, and will overcome him in battle.* **[44]** *Kṛpa counsels caution. Arjuna has accomplished many great feats; Karṇa, who can claim no such achievements, is* *acting rashly. The Kauravas are in danger from Arjuna and should join forces against him.* [45] *Aśvatthāman too chides Karṇa for his boasting. Arjuna will not forgive the wrongs done to the Pāṇḍavas, and no one can survive his fury; it is foolish to enter into a fight with him.*

[46] *Bhīṣma defends Karṇa: he is obeying the Kṣatriya duty to fight, and Bhīṣma believes that fighting is the right course of action. At Bhīṣma's request, Droṇa pardons Duryodhana and Karṇa for speaking against him; then he asks Bhīṣma to adjudicate on whether the Pāṇḍavas have completed the allotted period of their exile.* [47] *Bhīṣma calculates that the term of exile is indeed complete. The Pāṇḍavas will certainly not give up what is rightfully theirs, so the Kauravas should prepare for war. Duryodhana announces that he will not restore the Pāṇḍavas' kingdom to them. Bhīṣma now orders the disposition of the Kaurava forces: a quarter are to hold the city, a quarter to drive off the cattle, and the remainder to face Arjuna.*

[48] *Arjuna approaches rapidly; Droṇa recognizes him. Arjuna orders Uttara to drive to where Duryodhana is; Droṇa proposes attacking him from the rear. Arjuna scatters the enemy with his arrows and turns the cattle with the sound of his conch and his chariot.*

[49] *Next, Arjuna pushes forward towards Duryodhana. The Kauravas attack him, but he breaks through them and instructs Uttara to drive him to where Karṇa is. Vikarṇa attempts to defend Karṇa, but Arjuna forces him to flee, and then kills numbers of Kaurava warriors including Karṇa's brother Saṃgrāmajit. Karṇa attacks Arjuna, but he cannot withstand him; he too flees.*

[50] *Uttara asks Arjuna which of the Kaurava warriors he wishes to confront next; Arjuna points out in turn Kṛpa, Droṇa, Aśvatthāman, Duryodhana, Karṇa and Bhīṣma. Uttara drives him to Kṛpa.* [51] *At this point Indra and the other gods arrive; they have come to watch Arjuna do battle with his celestial weapons.*

[52] *Arjuna and Kṛpa shower arrows upon each other. Arjuna's arrows make Kṛpa's horses rear, but he allows Kṛpa to recover his balance before severing his bow and cutting off his armour with further arrows. Kṛpa takes up bow after bow, but Arjuna destroys them all; then he kills Kṛpa's horses and his charioteer. Other Kaurava warriors attack Arjuna to support Kṛpa, but Arjuna holds them off; they carry Kṛpa away to safety.*

[53] *Arjuna now tells Uttara to drive him to Droṇa, and Uttara does so. Arjuna greets Droṇa and announces that, since the Pāṇḍavas' term of exile*

*is completed, they have come to avenge themselves on the Kauravas; however, he will not strike at Droṇa till Droṇa has struck at him. Droṇa responds by showering Arjuna with arrows, and the two begin a mighty combat, each shooting huge numbers of arrows at the other, and each countering the other's arrows and celestial weapons. Droṇa is unable to overcome Arjuna, and his son Aśvatthāman enters the fray to give him a chance to retreat.*

[54] *Aśvatthāman is overwhelmed by Arjuna's arrows, but he succeeds in severing his bowstring, earning the applause of the watching gods. Arjuna restrings, and a fierce combat begins; however, in time Aśvatthāman runs out of arrows, while Arjuna continues to shoot shafts from his inexhaustible arrow-cases. At this point Karṇa joins in the battle, and Arjuna turns his attention to him, while Aśvatthāman's allies bring him fresh supplies of arrows.*

[55] *Arjuna challenges Karṇa to make good his boasts, and Karṇa disdainfully and boastfully accepts the challenge. Arjuna sneers at Karṇa for having fled after his brother's death; then the battle between the two begins. Both fight fiercely, but in the end Arjuna kills Karṇa's horses and renders him briefly unconscious. Overcome by pain, he leaves the battlefield while Arjuna taunts him.*

[56] *Arjuna instructs Uttara to drive him to Bhīṣma, whom he swears to overcome. His attack is countered by Duḥśāsana, Vikarṇa, Duḥsaha and Viviṃśati; Duḥśāsana wounds both Arjuna and Uttara, but Arjuna overcomes him and puts him to flight. Vikarṇa takes up the fight, but is immediately pierced by Arjuna's arrows and falls from his chariot. Duḥsaha and Viviṃśati attack Arjuna as they try to rescue Vikarṇa, but Arjuna wounds them both and kills their horses; they are carried away to safety by other warriors.*

[57] *Now all the Kauravas combine together to attack Arjuna, but he slays them in such numbers that a river of blood flows on the battlefield.* [58] *Duryodhana, Karṇa, Duḥśāsana, Viviṃśati, Droṇa, Aśvatthāman and Kṛpa shower arrows upon Arjuna, but he is unscathed, and shoots arrows in such numbers that his enemies all flee.*

[59] *Bhīṣma himself now attacks Arjuna, and there is a fierce battle between them, watched with amazed admiration by the onlookers. First one gains the upper hand, then the other. Citrasena and Indra praise the combatants, and Indra showers them with flowers. Finally Arjuna's arrows reduce Bhīṣma to unconsciousness, and his charioteer bears him away.*

[60] *Duryodhana returns to the attack and pierces Arjuna in the forehead with an arrow. He is joined by Vikarṇa riding an elephant, but Arjuna shoots*

*the beast dead and Vikarṇa has to take refuge on Viviṃśati's chariot. Next Arjuna wounds Duryodhana, who takes flight. Arjuna taunts him for quitting the battle.* **[61]** *Arjuna's words goad Duryodhana into returning to the fray: he is joined by Karṇa, Bhīṣma, Droṇa, Kṛpa, Viviṃśati and Duḥśāsana. Arjuna is surrounded, but he makes use of the Weapon of Bewilderment; the sound of his bow Gāṇḍīva terrifies his enemies, and the blast of his conch renders them unconscious. On Arjuna's instruction, Uttara collects up the clothes of all of them except for Bhīṣma. Bhīṣma shoots once more, but Arjuna kills his horses and charioteer, and pierces him with ten arrows before driving away. When Duryodhana regains consciousness he accuses Bhīṣma of letting Arjuna escape, but in reply Bhīṣma mocks him, and tells him to return home and let Arjuna keep the cattle he has won. Arjuna drives up: he bows to Bhīṣma and Droṇa and salutes Aśvatthāman and Kṛpa with arrows,*[1] *but he breaks Duryodhana's crown. Then with a blast of his conch he leaves, telling Uttara to return to his city.*

**[62]** *Now Arjuna rounds up Virāṭa's herds. When Kaurava soldiers emerge from the forest and ask for his instructions, he tells them to go in peace. Uttara is to wait until all the cattle have been collected together and the horses watered and rested, and is then to have his victory proclaimed in the city.*

## THE WEDDING

Vaiśaṃpāyana spoke:

**[63]** Meanwhile, Virāṭa the general had won back his cattle. Accompanied by the other four Pāṇḍavas, he entered the city in joy: having defeated the Trigartas in battle and regained all of his cows, the great king now shone in glory together with Kuntī's sons. As the hero sat on his throne, to the great happiness of his friends, all the counsellors and Brahmins approached him. The Matsya king, commander of his army, received the homage of counsellors and Brahmins; then he returned their greetings and gave them leave to depart.

Now Virāṭa the general, the king of the Matsyas, asked about Uttara: 5

1 According to the commentator Nīlakaṇṭha, the arrows would be dropped at the feet of the person saluted – presumably a kind of warrior's greeting.

'Where has he gone?' he said. The women and girls of his household, and the other residents of the women's quarters, happily answered him, 'The Kurus plundered our cattle; but Bhūmiṃjaya was enraged, and with the greatest boldness he set forth all alone with Bṛhannaḍā to defeat the six great chariot-fighters who had attacked us: Droṇa, Bhīṣma son of Śaṃtanu, Kṛpa, Karṇa, Duryodhana, and Droṇa's son Aśvatthāman.'

King Virāṭa was deeply grieved to hear that his son had set out, longing to do battle, with a single chariot and with Bṛhannaḍā for his charioteer. He announced to all his chief ministers, 'We can be sure that those Kurus and other kings will never remain near here once they learn that the Trigartas have been defeated. So let those of my troops who were not injured by the Trigartas set out with a mighty force to rescue Uttara!' For his son's sake he quickly dispatched horses and elephants and chariots, together with many brave footsoldiers, all bearing wonderful weapons and ornaments. And the king of the Matsyas, Virāṭa the general, hastened to command his fourfold army: 'Swiftly discover whether the prince is alive or not! I believe that the man who is accompanied by a eunuch as his charioteer will not survive.'

Yudhiṣṭhira lord of *dharma* laughed, and told Virāṭa who was suffering great grief over the Kurus, 'Lord of men, if Bṛhannaḍā is his charioteer, no enemy will be able to plunder your cows today! For, served by that charioteer, your son will be able to conquer in battle all the kings of the earth, the Kurus too, and even the gods, demons, Yakṣas and serpents!'

But now swift-travelling messengers dispatched by Uttara reached the city of Virāṭa to declare his victory. Then the king's minister announced to him this great triumph and the defeat of the Kurus, and told him that Uttara was on his way: 'All the cows have been won back, and the Kurus are defeated; and, O afflicter of your enemies, Uttara and his charioteer are safe!'

'I felicitate you on the winning back of your cows,' said Yudhiṣṭhira in his disguise as Kaṅka, 'and on the defeat of the Kurus; and I felicitate you on the news that your son is alive, bull-like prince! But I do not think it at all remarkable that your son has conquered the Kurus: victory is assured for the man who has Bṛhannaḍā for his charioteer.'

When King Virāṭa heard of the triumph of Prince Uttara of boundless power, he felt the hair rise on his body. He rewarded the messengers with

fine garments, and then urged his ministers, 'Let the royal highways be decked with banners, and all the deities be worshipped with offerings of flowers! Let princes, warrior chiefs, well-adorned courtesans and
musicians of every kind set forth to greet my son! Let a player of bells 25
and cymbals make haste to mount a rutting elephant and proclaim my victory at every crossroads! Let Princess Uttarā too deck herself in alluring clothes and ornaments, and set out with many young girls to greet Bṛhannaḍā!'

Then on hearing the king's command, men bearing auspicious emblems as well as kettledrums, trumpets and conches, and lovely women dressed in the finest clothes, along with Sūta and Māgadha bards with cymbals, trumpets and other musical instruments, all set forth from the city of mighty Virāṭa to greet his son of infinite strength. And after sending out his army, and the girls, and well-adorned courtesans, the most wise Matsya king said in excitement, 'Maidservant, fetch the dice! Let the game proceed, Kaṅka!'

When he said this, Pāṇḍu's son looked at him and answered, 'A 30
gambler should not gamble when he is excited, or so I have heard: I dare not gamble today with you when you are so full of happiness. However, I wish to do what will please you; let it proceed if you think fit.'

Virāṭa said, 'Women, cows, gold and whatever other wealth I own: you cannot keep any of it back for me even if I do not gamble!'

'Prince of kings, bestower of honour,' replied Kaṅka, 'why should you gamble? There are many evils in gambling, and so one should avoid it. You must have seen or heard of Pāṇḍu's son Yudhiṣṭhira: he had a
very great and wealthy kingdom, and godlike brothers, and he gambled 35
them all away! This is why I do not approve of gambling. However, if you think fit, O king, and if it pleases you, then let the two of us gamble.'

Now as the dicing began, the Matsya said to Pāṇḍu's son, 'Just see how such mighty Kurus were defeated by my son!' And then Yudhiṣṭhira lord of *dharma* answered the Matsya king, 'How can the man who has Bṛhannaḍā for his charioteer fail to conquer?'

At these words Virāṭa said to the Pāṇḍava, 'You call yourself a Brahmin, and yet you praise a eunuch equally with my son! You have

no idea of what is proper to say and what improper, and you treat me
with disrespect! Why should he not defeat all the Kurus under Bhīṣma
40 and Droṇa? However, for friendship's sake, Brahmin, I pardon you this
offence; but you should not speak so again if you wish to live.'

'Prince of kings,' replied Yudhiṣṭhira, 'Where Droṇa, Bhīṣma, Droṇa's son Aśvatthāman, Karṇa the Cutter, Kṛpa and Duryodhana are gathered together along with other mighty chariot-fighters, there Indra himself in person, surrounded by the hosts of the Maruts, could battle against them all; but otherwise who could do so but Bṛhannaḍā?'

'Repeatedly I forbade you,' said Virāṭa, 'and yet you do not restrain your tongue. Where no one has restraint, no one practises *dharma*!' Then the furious king struck Yudhiṣṭhira hard in the face with a die, angrily rebuking him: 'Do not speak so!'

45 The violence of the blow drew blood from his nose; Kuntī's son
caught it in his hands before it could reach the ground, and then the
righteous man looked towards Draupadī, who was standing to one side.
The blameless lady understood his intent and, obedient to her husband's
unspoken thought, filled a gold vessel with water and caught in it the
blood that flowed from Pāṇḍu's son.

Now Uttara slowly approached the city, full of joy, showered with fine
perfumes and many and various garlands; town and country men were
honouring him, and so were their women. Reaching the palace gate, he
50 had his arrival announced to his father. The doorkeeper entered, and at
once addressed Virāṭa: 'Your son Uttara, accompanied by Bṛhannaḍā, stands at the gate!' The Matsya king joyfully told his chamberlain, 'Bring them both in at once, for I long to see them!' But Yudhiṣṭhira, the king of the Kurus, whispered into the chamberlain's ear, 'Let Uttara enter alone – do not bring Bṛhannaḍā in! Strong-armed hero, he has sworn a vow that if anyone inflicts a wound on my body or causes my blood to flow except in battle, that man shall surely not live. The moment that he saw me bloodied, fury would get the better of him and he would slay Virāṭa on the spot, together with his ministers, troops and steeds!'

[**64**] Then the king's eldest son, Bhūmiṃjaya Uttara, entered. He paid his respects at his father's feet, and then he saw Yudhiṣṭhira the sinless lord of *dharma*, sitting bloodstained and distracted by himself on

the ground, attended by the maidservant. Uttara hastily asked his father, 'Who struck this man, O king? Who did this wicked deed?'

'I struck this false Brahmin,' answered Virāṭa, 'and it is less than he deserved for praising the eunuch when I was praising your heroism!'

"O king,' said Uttara, 'you have done wrong. Make haste to conciliate him, or his terrible Brahmin venom will destroy you utterly!'

Hearing his son's words, Virāṭa, the enricher of his kingdom, asked pardon of Kuntī's son, who was like a fire concealed under ashes. But as the king asked him for pardon, Pāṇḍu's son replied, 'I pardoned this long ago, O king, and I harbour no anger. Great king, if this blood from my nose had fallen on the ground, you and your kingdom would have perished, make no doubt! But I do not blame you for striking someone blameless, O king, for harshness quickly takes possession of the powerful.'

Once the bleeding stopped, Bṛhannaḍā entered. He greeted both Virāṭa and Kaṅka, and drew close. But now that he had been pardoned by the king of the Kurus, the Matsya king began to praise Uttara, freshly returned from battle, within the hearing of the ambidextrous Arjuna. 'Son of the Kekaya princess,' he said, 'in you I have an heir! No other son of mine has ever matched you, or ever will. How was your encounter with Karṇa, my son, who misses not one mark in a thousand when in action? How was your encounter with Bhīṣma, my son, who is without equal in the whole world of men, immovable as the ocean, unbearable as doomsday fire? How was your encounter with the Brahmin Droṇa, my son, the Teacher of the Vṛṣṇi heroes and the Pāṇḍavas, and of all Kṣatriyas, the best of all those who bear arms? How was your encounter with the man known as Aśvatthāman, the Teacher's son, another hero among bearers of arms? How was your encounter with Kṛpa, my son, the sight of whom in battle makes men despair like ruined merchants? How was your encounter with Duryodhana, my son, the prince who could penetrate a mountain with his powerful arrows?'

Uttara answered, 'It was not I who won back the cows, it was not I who defeated the enemy; that deed was done entirely by a certain son of a god. For I was fleeing in terror when the god's son stopped me, and took up position in the interior of my chariot, a young man and yet Indra-like. It was he who won back the cows, it was he who

defeated the Kurus – the deed was that hero's; I did not do it, father. It was he who with his arrows put to flight Kṛpa son of Śaradvat, Droṇa, Droṇa's son Aśvatthāman, Karṇa the Sūta's son, and Bhīṣma. And in that battle he addressed the prince Duryodhana, mighty as the lord of an elephant-herd, but now fearful in defeat: "Heir of Kuru, I do not think you will be safe in Hāstinapura. Exert yourself if you want to save
25 your life! You will not escape by fleeing, king, so make up your mind to do battle; if you conquer you will enjoy the earth, and if you are killed you will attain heaven!"

'Then tiger-like King Duryodhana turned back. Surrounded by his aides, he stood on his chariot shooting arrows like thunderbolts and hissing like a snake. At that my hair stood on end and my legs were paralysed, father; but then, strong as a lion, that young man blew the Kuru force apart with his arrows as if it were a mass of clouds, and after driving off that chariot-force he laughed at the Kurus, O king, and took away their clothes. Alone that hero rounded up those six chariot-fighters, as an angry tiger in the forest rounds up grazing deer.'

30 'Where is that strong-armed hero,' asked Virāṭa, 'that god's son of great renown, who has won back for me on the battlefield the cattle seized by the Kurus? I wish to see and to pay honour to the mighty son of a god who has saved for me both you and my cows.'

Uttara said, 'Father, that god's son of mighty energy vanished; but I believe that tomorrow or the next day he will reappear.'

Virāṭa did not know that the man being described, Arjuna son of Pāṇḍu, was living under cover of disguise in his own house. With the permission of the noble Virāṭa, Kuntī's son personally presented the
35 Kurus' clothes to Virāṭa's daughter; and the lovely Uttarā was delighted to receive those costly, fine garments of every kind.

Kuntī's son Arjuna had planned with Uttara in secret everything that had to be done regarding King Yudhiṣṭhira; now, bull-like hero, he and the son of the Matsya king joyfully carried it out to the letter. [**65**] Thus it was that, on the third day, the five Pāṇḍava brothers bathed and donned white apparel, for they had completed their vow as agreed. With Yudhiṣṭhira at their head, the mighty chariot-fighters, adorned with every ornament and radiant as elephants bearing auspicious markings,

all now went to Virāṭa's hall and sat on kingly thrones, where they shone
bright as sacrificial fires on their altars.

While they were sitting there, King Virāṭa came to his hall to conduct
all his royal business; when he saw the Pāṇḍavas there, glorious as blazing 5
fires, the Matsya king said to Kaṅka, who had a godlike appearance as if
he were Indra the lord of the gods seated with the hosts of the Maruts,
'I understood you to be a dice-player, and I made you my courtier. So
now how is it that you are richly adorned and sit on a kingly throne?'

O king, when Arjuna heard Virāṭa's jovial words, he smiled, and
answered, 'This is someone worthy to sit on the throne of Indra
himself! He is a supporter of Brahmins, learned in the Veda, munificent,
a sacrificer and firm in his vows. This is that bull of the Kurus, Kuntī's
son Yudhiṣṭhira, whose fame pervades the world like the light of the
rising sun! Like the fiery rays of the risen sun, the rays of his glory spread 10
in all directions.

'Ten thousand spirited elephants used to follow behind him, O king,
when he lived among the Kurus; thirty thousand chariots with gold
trappings and excellent horses always followed him; once eight hundred
Sūta and Māgadha bards with gleaming jewelled earrings used to praise
him as the seers praise Indra! Every day the Kurus and all the other
kings waited on him like servants, O king, as the immortals wait upon
Kubera, and in those days he exacted tribute from all the lords of the 15
earth, feudatory and freeman alike, as if they were mere merchants,
great king.

'Eighty thousand pious Brahmin householders depended on this
king, who observed his vows keenly; he looked after people who were
old, destitute, crippled or lame as if they were his sons, and he protected
his subjects through the exercise of *dharma*, lord. This is a prince who
keeps his word in matters of *dharma*, self-control and anger – he is
gracious, a supporter of Brahmins and a speaker of the truth; but Lord
Duryodhana and his people chafe at his glory and prowess, and so do
Karṇa and Śakuni son of Subala. His virtues cannot be counted, lord 20
of men, for this son of Pāṇḍu is ever devoted to *dharma* and free from
cruelty. So how might a bull-like prince such as this, a great Pāṇḍava
king and lord of the earth, not merit a kingly throne?'

**[66]** Virāṭa said, 'If this is Kuntī's son Yudhiṣṭhira, the king of the

Kurus, then which of you is his brother Arjuna, and which the mighty Bhīma, and Nakula and Sahadeva? Who is Draupadī of high repute? Since the Pāṇḍavas were defeated in the gambling match, nothing has been heard of them.'

'Lord of men,' replied Arjuna, 'the one who calls himself Ballava, your cook, is strong-armed Bhīma of terrible speed and valour. It was he who killed the furious Rākṣasas on Mount Gandhamādana and gathered heavenly, fragrant flowers for Draupadī Kṛṣṇā;[1] he was the Gandharva who slew the wicked Kīcakas, and who killed tigers, bears and boars in the women's quarters of your palace.[2]

'The one who was your master of horses is Nakula, afflicter of his enemies, and your overseer of cattle is Sahadeva; these are the two sons of Mādrī, famed as mighty chariot-fighters, handsome in their alluring clothes, bull-like heroes capable of defeating warriors of every sort in their thousands.

'O king, this maidservant, slender-waisted, sweet-smiling, with eyes like lotus petals, is Draupadī, for whose sake the Kīcakas were slain.

'And I, great king, am Arjuna; you must have heard of me. I am Kuntī's son, younger brother to Bhīma and elder to the twins. In your palace we have lived incognito, as comfortably as babes in the womb, great king!'

Once Arjuna had spoken of the five Pāṇḍavas, Virāṭa's son spoke of Arjuna's own valour. 'This is the man who roamed among the hosts of chariot-fighters in the midst of the enemy like a lion among deer, always killing the best of them; this is the man who shot and killed a mighty, gold-armoured elephant with a single arrow, so that it struck the earth with both tusks as it fell on the battlefield; this is the man who won back the cows and conquered the Kurus in battle, and who has deafened me in both ears with the blast of his conch!'

The Matsya king of mighty energy listened to Uttara's words, and then, aware that he had wronged Yudhiṣṭhira, he answered him: 'I am happy that the time has come for me to beg pardon of the son of Pāṇḍu! And I shall bestow Uttarā upon Kuntī's son Arjuna, if you agree.'

1 See 3.157.

2 See 4.12.26–8.

Uttara said, 'The Pāṇḍavas deserve worship, honour and respect. I agree that the time has come: let us pay them honour, for they are honourable and noble!'

'Yes, I too was rescued by Bhīma when I fell into the hands of the enemy on the battlefield,' said Virāṭa, 'and he won back my cows as well. It is through the valour of the Pāṇḍavas' arms that we have secured victory in battle, good sir. So all of us, together with our ministers, now ask pardon of Kuntī's bull-like son Yudhiṣṭhira and his brothers: whatever we have in our ignorance said to the lord of men, may Pāṇḍu's righteous son here be pleased to forgive it!'

Overjoyed, noble Virāṭa now approached King Yudhiṣṭhira and made a treaty with him; and he presented to him his whole kingdom, including the rod of office, the treasury and the city. And the Matsya king of mighty energy repeatedly congratulated all the Pāṇḍavas, especially wealth-winner Arjuna; again and again he embraced Yudhiṣṭhira and Bhīma and the two sons of Mādrī, and kissed them on the head.[1] Virāṭa the general did not weary of gazing at them, and in his great contentment he said to King Yudhiṣṭhira, 'I felicitate you all on your safe return from the forest, and on completing your difficult task without being discovered by your wicked enemies! As for this kingdom of ours and whatever other wealth we own, let the sons of Kuntī accept it all without hesitation! And let the wealth-winner, the ambidextrous Arjuna, accept Uttarā, for he is the truest of men and will be a fit husband for her.'

Hearing these words, Yudhiṣṭhira lord of *dharma* looked at Kuntī's son the wealth-winner; and Arjuna, seeing his brother look at him, addressed the Matsya king: 'O king, I accept your daughter, but as my daughter-in-law, for it would be fitting to form an alliance between us, the truest of the Matsyas and the truest of the Bhāratas.'

**[67]** Virāṭa said, 'Best of the Pāṇḍavas, I am giving you my daughter; why do you not wish to accept her as your wife?'

'While I lived in the women's quarters,' replied Arjuna, 'I saw your daughter all the time, and both in private and in public she trusted me like a father. She is fond of me and respects me as a dancer and an expert singer, and always thinks of me as her teacher. Since I lived for a year in

1 Literally 'smelt the head', a standard form of affectionate greeting in ancient India.

her company after she reached marriageable age, O king, it would be
5 natural for you or others to harbour suspicion; therefore, pure, highly disciplined and self-controlled as I am, it is for my son that I request you for your daughter, lord of the earth, and thus I establish her purity. I do not see that suspicion can attach to her whether as your daughter or my daughter-in-law, whether as regards my son or my self; thus her purity will be established. O afflicter of your enemies, I fear to make an unsuitable union and I fear impropriety, so I accept your daughter Uttarā as my daughter-in-law.

'Lord of the peoples, my strong-armed son Abhimanyu is sister's son to Kṛṣṇa Vāsudeva. He is himself like the son of a god, and Kṛṣṇa loves him; a mere boy, he is skilled in weapons. He would be a fitting son-in-law for you and husband for your daughter.'

10 Virāṭa said, 'What I have heard befits Kuntī's son the wealth-winner, the best of the Kurus, who is so constant in *dharma* and wise! O Pāṇḍava, let whatever you judge should be done be done at once. All my desires have been brought to fruition if Arjuna is to be my kinsman!'

Even as the prince of kings spoke these words, Kuntī's son Yudhiṣṭhira gave his assent to the union, according to the agreement between the Matsya and the Pāṇḍava; and then he and King Virāṭa sent word to all their friends and to Kṛṣṇa Vāsudeva, O heir of Bharata.

Now that the thirteenth year of their exile was complete, the five
15 Pāṇḍavas prospered in Virāṭa's city of Upaplavya; and while they were dwelling there Arjuna Bībhatsu sent men to fetch Kṛṣṇa the stirrer of men, and Abhimanyu, and many of the Daśārhas, from the country of Ānarta. The kings of Kāśi and Śibi, who were friendly with Yudhiṣṭhira, arrived together with their two armies, lord of the earth, and Drupada of mighty ardour brought another army, along with Draupadī's heroic sons, Śikhaṇḍin, who had never suffered defeat, and the unconquerable Dhṛṣṭadyumna, the best of all those who bear arms. All these army-commanders were sacrificers, and generous to Brahmins; all were skilled with every kind of weapon; all were brave and ready to die in battle.

When the Matsya king, the best upholder of *dharma*, saw them all
20 arrive, he was delighted to be giving his daughter to Abhimanyu. Once the princes had arrived from every direction, Kṛṣṇa Vāsudeva came

there, along with Balarāma the plough-bearer, who was garlanded with forest flowers, Kṛtavarman son of Hṛdika, Sātyaki, Anādhṛṣṭi, Akrūra, Sāmba and Niśaṭha; and those afflicters of their enemies brought with them Abhimanyu and his mother. Indrasena and the other servants all arrived together after spending the year elsewhere,[1] bringing the Pāṇḍavas' well-appointed chariots; numerous Vṛṣṇis, Andhakas and Bhojas of incomparable power followed radiant Kṛṣṇa Vāsudeva, that tiger-like Vṛṣṇi, with ten thousand elephants, a million horses, a hundred million chariots and a billion footsoldiers.

Kṛṣṇa bestowed as wealth upon each of the noble Pāṇḍavas women, 25
jewels and garments. Then the wedding of Matsya and Pāṇḍava was celebrated in the proper manner. Conches, kettledrums, horns and war-drums sounded in the Matsya king's palace to mark his alliance with the Pāṇḍavas; wild animals of many kinds were slain, and so were hundreds of domestic beasts fit for sacrifice; various intoxicating liquors were served; singers, storytellers, actors and heralds attended to praise the guests, along with Sūta and Māgadha bards.

Now the finest women of Matsya arrived, led by Sudeṣṇā. Beautiful
from head to foot, they wore gleaming jewelled earrings; those ladies 30
were fair of complexion, lovely and well adorned, but Draupadī Kṛṣṇā outshone them all in beauty and fame and glory. In their midst was Princess Uttarā, adorned for her wedding; they led her forward as though she were the daughter of great Indra. On behalf of his and Subhadrā's son, Kuntī's son the wealth-winner then accepted Virāṭa's daughter of flawless limbs. The great king Yudhiṣṭhira son of Kuntī too was standing there, as handsome as Indra, and he likewise accepted her as his daughter-in-law.

After accepting her, Kuntī's son Arjuna had noble Abhimanyu's wedding rites performed in the presence of Kṛṣṇa the stirrer of men.
King Virāṭa gave him seven thousand horses swift as the wind and two 35
hundred excellent elephants, together with much other wealth. Then after the wedding, Yudhiṣṭhira lord of *dharma* gave to the Brahmins all the goods that invincible Kṛṣṇa had brought: thousands of cows, jewels, clothes of every kind, fine ornaments, chariots and beds. Bull-like heir

1 See 4.4. Indrasena is Yudhiṣṭhira's charioteer.

of Bharata, the Matsya king's city, thronged with joyful, well-fed folk, shone as if at a great festival.

# PERSEVERANCE

## PERSEVERANCE

[1] *After Abhimanyu's wedding, the Pāṇḍavas and their chief allies assemble. Kṛṣṇa addresses them all; he reminds them that the Pāṇḍavas' exile was achieved by deceit, but states that none the less their only desire is to win back their rightful kingdom. A war between the two factions would cause great destruction. He proposes that an envoy should be sent to Duryodhana to persuade him to return Yudhiṣṭhira's half of the kingdom to him.*

[2] *Kṛṣṇa's brother Balarāma agrees with this plan, but he warns that the envoy must adopt a humble tone: Yudhiṣṭhira chose of his own free will to gamble with Śakuni, an expert at dicing, and Śakuni did nothing wrong in defeating him. Sātyaki is enraged to hear this,* [3] *and announces that Balarāma's words betray his own cowardice. Yudhiṣṭhira was deceived by people he trusted, and the challenge came from them: why should he now show humility? The Kauravas are falsely claiming that the Pāṇḍavas were recognized before completing their period of exile. They deserve death in battle, and this should be their fate if Yudhiṣṭhira does not regain his kingdom at once.*

[4] *Drupada agrees that force is likely to be necessary, and that Duryodhana does not merit a gentle approach. The Pāṇḍavas and their allies should hasten to send envoys to all the other kings to secure their support before Duryodhana can do likewise. Drupada also proposes that his own household priest should be sent as an envoy to Dhṛtarāṣṭra.* [5] *Kṛṣṇa approves this plan, whilst pointing out that good relations should be maintained with the Kauravas until Duryodhana actually refuses to make peace. He then leaves for Dvārakā.*

*Yudhiṣṭhira, Virāṭa and Drupada now prepare for war, summoning many kings to come to their aid, and a large force gathers. When Duryodhana learns of this, he too assembles his supporters. Drupada sends his household priest to the Kauravas,* [6] *giving him careful instructions. Duryodhana will certainly refuse to return Yudhiṣṭhira's kingdom to him, but the priest should seek to convince others of the rightness of his cause: this will lead to dissension among the Kaurava faction, giving the Pāṇḍavas an opportunity to complete their military preparations. The priest sets out.*

Vaiśaṃpāyana spoke:

[7] After Kṛṣṇa and Madhu's heir Balarāma had left for Dvārakā with all the Vṛṣṇis and Andhakas, and with the Bhojas in their hundreds, Dhṛtarāṣṭra's son King Duryodhana kept himself informed about the Pāṇḍavas' doings by means of envoys sent to act as spies. When he learnt that Kṛṣṇa heir of Madhu had left, he set out for the city of Dvārakā with excellent horses swift as the wind, taking only a small force of men. And on the very same day the son of Kuntī and Pāṇḍu, wealth-winner Arjuna, also set out at speed for that lovely city of Ānarta.

5 The two tiger-like heirs of Kuru reached Dvārakā; they approached, and saw Kṛṣṇa lying asleep. Then as Kṛṣṇa Govinda slept, Duryodhana entered there and sat down on a splendid seat at his head. After him high-minded Arjuna, the wearer of the diadem, entered; he stood at Kṛṣṇa's feet, bowing and joining his hands together.

When Kṛṣṇa the Vṛṣṇi awoke, the first person he saw was the wearer
of the diadem. He welcomed the two of them and paid them due
honour; then the slayer of Madhu asked them the reason for their visit.
At this Duryodhana, laughing a little, addressed Kṛṣṇa: 'Sir, be pleased
10 to grant me your help in this coming war! For you bear the same
friendship towards me and towards Arjuna, just as we, heir of Madhu,
share an equal relationship with you. Now I was the first to approach
you today, slayer of Madhu, and the virtuous, observing precedence,
favour the first to arrive. You, O stirrer of men, are by far the best of the
virtuous on earth today, and so are ever honoured: maintain the way of
the virtuous!'

Kṛṣṇa replied, 'I have no doubt, sir, that you approached me here first;
however, it was Kuntī's son the wealth-winner whom first I saw, O king.
Since you were the first to approach, but he was the first to be seen, I
15 shall give help to both of you, Duryodhana. But the saying goes that the

youngest should be asked to choose first, and so Kuntī's son the wealth-winner deserves the first choice. I have a great force of a hundred million cowherds, strong as myself, known as the Nārāyaṇas, battle-hardened warriors all; let these soldiers, unconquerable in warfare, belong to one side, and I myself will join the other, though I shall lay down my weapons and not fight in the battle. So choose one or the other of these, son of Kuntī, whichever you find the more pleasing, for according to *dharma* you have the first choice.'

When Kuntī's son the wealth-winner heard Kṛṣṇa's words, he chose Kṛṣṇa Keśava, though he would not fight in the battle. Duryodhana was delighted to have gained a thousand thousand warriors, and to learn that Kṛṣṇa was excluded from fighting; having acquired an entire army in this way, the prince of fearful strength now went to see mighty Balarāma. He told him in full the reason for his visit; but then Balarāma Vāsudeva spoke these words to Dhṛtarāṣṭra's son: 'Tiger-like hero, you should remember everything I said earlier during Virāṭa's wedding festivities; I spoke to restrain Kṛṣṇa lord of the senses for your sake, heir of Kuru, repeatedly insisting, O king, that we share an equal relationship to both sides. But Kṛṣṇa Keśava did not agree with what I said, and I cannot distance myself from him for so much as a moment; therefore I have determined, in view of Kṛṣṇa's position, that I will help neither the Pāṇḍavas nor Duryodhana. You are born in the lineage of Bharata, which is honoured by all the princes: go and fight according to the Kṣatriya *dharma*, bull-like heir of Bharata!'

Hearing this, King Duryodhana now embraced Balarāma the plough-bearer; knowing that Kṛṣṇa was excluded from fighting, he considered the victory as good as won. Next, Dhṛtarāṣṭra's son went to see Kṛtavarman, and Kṛtavarman gave his army to him. Surrounded on all sides by that terrible army, Kuru's heir returned home, rejoicing himself and bringing joy to his friends.

After Duryodhana's departure, Kṛṣṇa now asked Arjuna the wearer of the diadem, 'What did you have in mind when you chose me though I will not fight?'

Arjuna answered, 'You could kill all of them, sir, there is no doubt of that; and I too can kill them unaided, highest lord. You have fame in this world, sir, and glory will be yours; and I too seek glory. That is why I chose you. I have always hoped that you would be my charioteer – be pleased to grant this long-held wish, sir!'

35 'It befits you, son of Kuntī,' said Kṛṣṇa, 'that you wish to compete with me. Let your wish be fulfilled: I shall be your charioteer!'

Kuntī's son Arjuna was delighted. Along with Kṛṣṇa, he now returned to Yudhiṣṭhira, accompanied by the best men of Daśārha.

**[8]** *King Śalya of Madra, having received Yudhiṣṭhira's envoy, sets out to join him with a vast army. Hearing that he is on his way, Duryodhana hastens to prepare for him wonderful accommodation where he is treated with every honour. Śalya assumes that this is Yudhiṣṭhira's doing; when he learns that Duryodhana is responsible he grants him a boon, and Duryodhana chooses Śalya himself as his general. Śalya now continues on his way to Upaplavya, where the Pāṇḍavas are staying, and tells Yudhiṣṭhira what has happened. Yudhiṣṭhira assures him that he acted properly, but asks one favour of him. When Karṇa and Arjuna meet in battle he will have to serve as Karṇa's charioteer; he should act so as to protect Arjuna by sapping Karṇa's fiery energy. Śalya agrees to do this, and to help Yudhiṣṭhira in any other way he can. He counsels him not to give way to sorrow, and observes that even Indra and his consort had to suffer unhappiness.*

## INDRA'S VICTORY

**[9]** *Yudhiṣṭhira asks to hear the story, and Śalya narrates. — Tvaṣṭṛ hates Indra, and he creates the three-headed Viśvarūpa. One of Viśvarūpa's mouths repeats the Vedas, one drinks liquor, and the third seems to swallow the whole world; he is a mighty ascetic. Indra recognizes Viśvarūpa's austerities as a threat to his own supremacy, and he sends Apsarases to seduce him, but they return in failure. Indra now hurls his thunderbolt at him; Viśvarūpa falls, slain, but his fiery energy remains undiminished. Indra persuades a carpenter to cut off his three heads; he does so, and three species of birds issue from the three mouths.*

*Tvaṣṭṛ is furious to hear of Viśvarūpa's death; he creates the demon Vṛtra to kill Indra. Vṛtra and Indra battle fiercely; Vṛtra swallows Indra, but Indra escapes when he yawns, and the battle resumes. Indra is unable to withstand Vṛtra, and in despair the gods go to Viṣṇu.*

[10] *Hearing the pleas of Indra and the other gods, Viṣṇu tells them to placate Vṛtra and bring about peace between him and Indra; once this has been done, Viṣṇu will enter Indra's weapon, thus allowing Indra to slay Vṛtra. The gods and seers go to Vṛtra and urge peace on him; he agrees, but only on condition that he is not to be killed by Indra or the other gods with anything wet or dry, made of stone or of wood, sword or thunderbolt, by day or by night. After much thought, Indra finds his chance: he hurls a mass of sea-foam at Vṛtra when it is twilight, and Viṣṇu enters the foam and kills Vṛtra. There is great jubilation, but Indra is now burdened by the sin of falsehood in addition to his earlier crime of slaying the Brahmin Viśvarūpa. He hides in the waters; there is drought, and the gods, having lost their king, are seized by fear.*

[11] *The gods decide to make King Nahuṣa their king. When he objects that he lacks sufficient power, they grant him the ability to appropriate the power of any being that he sees. This boon undermines his virtue, and when he sees Indra's wife Śacī he lusts after her. She flees to Bṛhaspati for protection, and he promises to prevent her coming to harm. Nahuṣa hears of this and is furious.* [12] *The gods seek to persuade him to stop pursuing Śacī, but he is unmoved by their words, and they agree to bring her to him. When they arrive at Bṛhaspati's house to fetch her, Bṛhaspati refuses to hand her over. He advises that she should go to Nahuṣa and ask him to allow her more time, and she agrees to this. She visits Nahuṣa.*

[13] *Nahuṣa asks Śacī to become his wife. She replies that she wishes to have time in which to find out what has happened to Indra; after that she will be his. Then she returns to Bṛhaspati's house. The gods now ask Viṣṇu how Indra may be freed from the sin of Brahminicide; Viṣṇu answers that he must sacrifice to him with a horse sacrifice. The gods go to Indra, and the horse sacrifice takes place; Indra's sin is distributed amongst trees, rivers, mountains, the earth and women. Indra returns to his former strength, but, realizing that Nahuṣa is still too powerful for him to overcome, he disappears once more. Śacī appeals for help to Upaśruti, the oracle goddess.*

[14] *Upaśruti promises to take Śacī to Indra. She leads her through forests and mountains to a lake on an island in the ocean: Indra has entered the fibre of a lotus stalk there. Śacī praises him and tells him of Nahuṣa's deeds; she urges him to kill Nahuṣa.* [15] *Indra answers that Nahuṣa cannot be overcome by valour, but that he has a plan: Śacī is to ask Nahuṣa*

*to come to her in a carriage drawn by seers, and then she will be his. She carries out his instruction; delighted, Nahuṣa yokes the seers, while Śacī implores Bṛhaspati to make haste and find Indra.*

*Bṛhaspati offers an oblation and sends the Fire god to search for him. Fire does so, but cannot find him; however, he cannot enter the waters and refuses Bṛhaspati's command to do so.* **[16]** *Bṛhaspati praises Fire and assures him that he may safely enter the waters. Fire does so, and finds Indra hidden in the fibre of a lotus stalk. Now Bṛhaspati goes to Indra, accompanied by the gods, Gandharvas and seers. He praises Indra, who grows in strength and asks what task he is to perform; Bṛhaspati tells him of Nahuṣa's wickedness. Kubera, Yama, Soma, Varuṇa and the Fire god agree to join forces with Indra in return for a share in the sacrifice.*

**[17]** *At this point Agastya appears and announces that Nahuṣa has been overthrown. He had given the wrong answer on a point of Vedic learning, and had also touched Agastya's head with his foot; Agastya therefore cursed him to wander the earth for a thousand years in the form of a great snake.*[1] *All beings now congratulate Indra on his good fortune.*

**[18]** *Indra mounts his elephant Airāvata and returns to the three worlds. Aṅgiras honours him with hymns from the Atharvaveda; Indra gives him the boon that his name Atharvāṅgirasa will be preserved in the Atharvaveda, and that he will have a share in the sacrifice. Then he reigns happily. — Now Śalya assures Yudhiṣṭhira that, like Indra, he will regain his kingdom and see his enemies destroyed. He repeats his promise to help Yudhiṣṭhira by sapping Karṇa's fiery energy.*

**[19]** *The Sātvata warrior Sātyaki joins Yudhiṣṭhira with a mighty army, as do Dhṛṣṭaketu of Cedi, Jayatsena of Magadha, and the Pāṇḍya king. With the forces of Drupada and Virāṭa, Yudhiṣṭhira has seven armies at his disposal. Duryodhana receives the support of Bhagadatta, Bhūriśravas, Śalya, the Bhoja king Kṛtavarman, Jayadratha of Sindhu, Sudakṣiṇa of Kāmboja, Nīla of Māhiṣmatī, Vinda and Anuvinda of Avanti, and the five Kekaya kings; he has control over eleven armies, and Hāstinapura is too small to contain them all.*

**[20]** *Drupada's household priest is received with proper honour by Dhṛtarāṣṭra, Bhīṣma and Vidura. He lists the wrongs done to the Pāṇḍavas. Their inheritance*

1 For the story of Nahuṣa's eventual release from this curse, see 3.175–8.

*went to the Kauravas, who made attempts on their life and then cheated them out of the kingdom they had gained for themselves; then they had to endure exile in the forest and in the city of Virāṭa. All this they have put behind them: their only desire is reconciliation without war, and the return of what is rightfully theirs.*

**[21]** *Bhīṣma supports the priest, but Karṇa angrily interrupts him: the Pāṇḍavas are now ignoring the terms imposed on them after the gambling match, and Duryodhana will not yield a single foot of land to them. But Dhṛtarāṣṭra speaks in praise of Bhīṣma's words and announces that he will send the Sūta Saṃjaya as an envoy to the Pāṇḍavas.*

## SAṂJAYA'S MISSION

**[22]** *Dhṛtarāṣṭra briefs Saṃjaya on his mission. The Pāṇḍavas have no faults and many virtues, and Duryodhana is a fool to hate them as he does. Yudhiṣṭhira is supported by mighty warriors from all over the earth, including the invincible Kṛṣṇa and Arjuna. Saṃjaya is to treat the Pāṇḍavas with all civility and to say whatever will help avert a war.*

**[23]** *Saṃjaya visits the Pāṇḍavas in Upaplavya and conveys to Yudhiṣṭhira Dhṛtarāṣṭra's good wishes for them. Yudhiṣṭhira replies with similar good wishes for the Kauravas, but then he turns to the feud between the two factions, and he asks whether the Kauravas recall the occasions on which the Pāṇḍavas have shown their great might as warriors.* **[24]** *Saṃjaya assures him that Dhṛtarāṣṭra is grieved by the wrongs done to the Pāṇḍavas, and that their military prowess has not been forgotten. He is sure that Yudhiṣṭhira will be able to achieve peace. Then he announces that he bears a message from Dhṛtarāṣṭra.*

**[25]** *The Pāṇḍavas and their allies gather to listen to Dhṛtarāṣṭra's message, and Saṃjaya greets them all. He says that Dhṛtarāṣṭra hopes for peace; the Pāṇḍavas should not start a war, which would cause terrible destruction.*

**[26]** *Yudhiṣṭhira replies. No one wishes for war, but the Pāṇḍavas have a just cause. Dhṛtarāṣṭra is enjoying every luxury and favouring his wicked son; there is no way that both factions can prosper when the Kauravas have taken the Pāṇḍavas' kingdom and aspire to total domination. The Pāṇḍavas are mighty, and they are full of anger; they will not tolerate Duryodhana's continued evildoing. The wrongs of the past are forgiven, but the kingdom must be returned.*

**[27]** *Saṃjaya answers that the evil of war should be avoided at all costs – even the cost of Yudhiṣṭhira's kingdom. He advises Yudhiṣṭhira to practise self-control, and not to give himself up to fulfilling the desire for possessions and sensual pleasure. If he is now going to wage war, what was the point of his years in exile? He could have fought instead of going to the forest: his allies would have backed him, and he would have been in a stronger position than he is now. But in fact Yudhiṣṭhira follows* dharma, *and he should continue to follow it by not fighting now.*

**[28]** *Yudhiṣṭhira agrees that nothing is higher than* dharma, *but he argues that* dharma *in times of trouble*[1] *is different from normal* dharma. *Only the wise can give counsel as to the proper course of action in such cases, and he will abide by the advice of Kṛṣṇa.*

**[29]** *Kṛṣṇa states that action is more important than anything else: it is action that maintains everything in the world. No alternative to war is open to Yudhiṣṭhira, and it is a part of the* dharma *of a king to go to war against those who seize land. The Kauravas' behaviour in the assembly was abominable, especially towards Draupadī. He then announces that he himself will visit the Kauravas and try to negotiate an honourable peace. If he fails, there will certainly be war.*

**[30]** *Saṃjaya now bids farewell to Yudhiṣṭhira. Yudhiṣṭhira lists the members of the Kaurava faction and asks Saṃjaya to greet them individually on his behalf. For Duryodhana there is an additional message: Yudhiṣṭhira's* dharma *will enable him to destroy his enemies. Duryodhana's desire to rule supreme over the Kurus has no justification, and he must either return Indraprastha to Yudhiṣṭhira or fight.* **[31]** *Saṃjaya should appeal to Dhṛtarāṣṭra, Bhīṣma and Vidura to achieve peace, and he should tell Duryodhana that the Pāṇḍavas have forgiven his past wrongs, but now they must have what is rightfully theirs. Indeed, five villages will be sufficient for the five Pāṇḍava brothers; to grant them just that much will avert war.*

**[32]** *Saṃjaya returns to Hāstinapura, where he greets Dhṛtarāṣṭra and conveys Yudhiṣṭhira's greeting to him. Then he upbraids Dhṛtarāṣṭra for the evil that he has done: the Kauravas will be destroyed by it. Dhṛtarāṣṭra has fallen under the sway of his own sons, and has favoured untrustworthy advisers over trustworthy; as a result he will lose his kingdom. Finally, Saṃjaya says that he will deliver Yudhiṣṭhira's message before the assembly in the morning.*

1 *Āpaddharma*, dealt with at length at 12.129–67.

## WAKEFULNESS

**[33]** *Dhṛtarāṣṭra summons Vidura. He tells him that since Saṃjaya's visit he is disturbed and unable to sleep, and he requests Vidura to discourse on* dharma.

*Vidura speaks of wisdom and folly, and of things that are grouped in ones, in twos, and so forth, up to tens. Then he describes the qualities of the virtuous man, concluding with advice that Dhṛtarāṣṭra should repair the damage done to his good name by returning the Pāṇḍavas' kingdom to them.* **[34]** *He describes the behaviour of the wise king, who never acts without considering the consequences, and who takes care to maintain the good opinion of his subjects. He stresses the importance of controlling one's senses and avoiding bad company and abusive talk. Dhṛtarāṣṭra fails to see that his sons' hatred of the Pāṇḍavas has subverted their judgement; it is Yudhiṣṭhira who should inherit the kingship.*

**[35]** *Vidura praises honesty, and tells how the Dānava demon Virocana was once asked by his wife Keśinī whether Dānavas or Brahmins were superior. He maintained the superiority of the Dānavas, but then the Brahmin Sudhanvan arrived and gave the opposite opinion. They agreed to stake their lives on the issue, and, at Sudhanvan's suggestion, they went to Virocana's father Prahrāda for a ruling. Prahrāda ruled in favour of Sudhanvan, who rewarded his honesty by sparing Virocana's life. Dhṛtarāṣṭra should not speak untruth for the sake of land: in the absence of truth, no other virtues can exist. The Pāṇḍavas treat him as their father; he should treat them as his sons.*

**[36]** *Next Vidura quotes the advice once given by Atri's son to the Sādhya gods: one should not speak maliciously or falsely. He adds that there are many ways in which a noble family may be destroyed, and counsels control of the senses. Dhṛtarāṣṭra says that he has treated Yudhiṣṭhira badly, and that Yudhiṣṭhira will now kill all his sons. Vidura replies that peace can only be attained through knowledge and discipline. United, kinsmen support each other; disunited, they meet with destruction. Dhṛtarāṣṭra must bring peace between his sons and the Pāṇḍavas.*

**[37]** *Vidura lists the seventeen kinds of foolish men. A king's true friend is one who gives him good but unwelcome advice. Together, the hundred Kauravas and five Pāṇḍavas can rule the earth, but the Kauravas are like a forest and the Pāṇḍavas like the tigers that live there: there can be no forest without the tigers, and no tigers without the forest.*

**[38]** *Now Vidura speaks words of wisdom on a variety of topics. He concludes by blaming Dhṛtarāṣṭra for forsaking the Pāṇḍavas and entrusting the kingship to Duryodhana: soon he will see him lose it.* **[39]** *Dhṛtarāṣṭra objects that he cannot abandon his son. Vidura replies that the wicked should be avoided, and kinsmen should be supported. Dhṛtarāṣṭra should give the Pāṇḍavas a few villages; with them as allies he will prosper. After more words of wisdom, he warns Dhṛtarāṣṭra to treat Pāṇḍu's sons and his own equally.*

**[40]** *Vidura continues with his wise sayings, ending with the* dharmas *of the four classes of men. Yudhiṣṭhira cannot perform his proper Kṣatriya* dharma, *and Dhṛtarāṣṭra should set him on the right course. Dhṛtarāṣṭra answers that he accepts what Vidura has said, and that in his mind he favours the Pāṇḍava; but whenever he sees Duryodhana his opinion changes back again. Fate is all-powerful, and human effort vain.*

**[41]** *Dhṛtarāṣṭra asks if Vidura has left anything unsaid. Vidura replies that the immortal seer Sanatsujāta will speak to him about profound matters that Vidura, as the son of a Śūdra mother, cannot talk of. He mentally summons Sanatsujāta, who appears.*

## SANATSUJĀTA

**[42]** *Dhṛtarāṣṭra asks Sanatsujāta why he maintains that there is no death. Sanatsujāta answers that distraction is death; one should cease to desire the fruits of one's actions, for death results from passion. He describes the perfect Brahmin: a man free of exertion, accepting no gifts, who makes no display of his religious practices or his learning.*

**[43]** *Sanatsujāta states that asceticism is more effective than Vedic learning in saving a man from evil. He lists the forms of behaviour that damage asceticism, and those that strengthen it. Questioned by Dhṛtarāṣṭra, he says that there are many Vedas, but only one absolute truth; the true Brahmin is he who, firmly based in truth, sees* brahman. **[44]** *He describes the way to attain* brahman *by disciplined study with a teacher.* Brahman *cannot be described: it has no properties, but it is the basis of the entire universe.* **[45]** Brahman *springs from the primeval seed that is perceived as the eternal blessed one by those who are adept at Yoga. The man who sees his own self in all beings does not sorrow.*

## WAR AND PEACE

[**46**] *Dawn comes. The Kauravas and all their allies assemble in the hall. The gatekeeper announces Saṃjaya, who enters, declares that the Pāṇḍavas send their greetings to all, and prepares to deliver their message.*

[**47**] *Saṃjaya reports what was said by Arjuna: if Duryodhana does not return the kingdom to Yudhiṣṭhira, he is asking for war with a mighty army, and when he sees the Pāṇḍavas and their allies ranged against him he will come to regret it. In particular, glorious Kṛṣṇa, victor over men and demons, is giving Arjuna his help; and Arjuna himself is ready to use his weapons to annihilate the Kauravas. Duryodhana is suffering from delusion; he should follow the advice of Bhīṣma, Kṛpa, Droṇa, Aśvatthāman and Vidura.*

[**48**] *Bhīṣma speaks of Nara and Nārāyaṇa, the divine seers with whose help the gods succeeded in defeating the demons: they are Arjuna and Kṛṣṇa, and they cannot be defeated. He accuses Duryodhana of listening only to the base Sūta's son Karṇa, to Śakuni and to Duḥśāsana. When Karṇa objects, Bhīṣma contemptuously points out that, for all his boasts, Karṇa has achieved nothing. Droṇa too argues for negotiation with the Pāṇḍavas. But Dhṛtarāṣṭra ignores the two elders and addresses Saṃjaya. This is the moment at which the Kauravas lose all hope of life.*

[**49**] *Dhṛtarāṣṭra asks Saṃjaya about Yudhiṣṭhira: whose counsel does he listen to? Saṃjaya replies that his rule is absolute. Dhṛtarāṣṭra then asks about his forces; Saṃjaya swoons at the question, but recovers and lists the mighty warriors ranged against the Kauravas.*

[**50**] *Dhṛtarāṣṭra says that he is particularly fearful of Bhīma, and describes his awesome qualities as a fighter. The Dhārtarāṣṭras and their allies stand no chance against him. But he adds that he himself is in thrall to fate, and cannot stop his sons from pursuing the disastrous course they have chosen.* [**51**] *Next he speaks of Arjuna, who has defeated the very gods: with Gāṇḍīva for his bow and Kṛṣṇa for his charioteer he is utterly irresistible.* [**52**] *Finally he praises the valour of Yudhiṣṭhira's allies, and the uncompromising virtue of Yudhiṣṭhira himself. If the Kauravas elect to fight against him, destruction is inevitable.*

[**53**] *Saṃjaya agrees with Dhṛtarāṣṭra's assessment, but retorts that his wisdom has not prevented him from falling under Duryodhana's sway: he has connived in every wrong that his son has done the Pāṇḍavas. Duryodhana must now be*

*restrained; there is no point in Dhṛtarāṣṭra's bemoaning the Pāṇḍavas' strength as though there were nothing he could do.*

[**54**] *Duryodhana speaks: the Kauravas are capable of defeating their enemies. When the Pāṇḍavas went to the forest, they gathered allies round them and spoke of attacking Dhṛtarāṣṭra to regain their kingdom. At that time, the advice of Droṇa, Kṛpa, Bhīṣma and Aśvatthāman was that the Pāṇḍavas did not have the strength to defeat the Kauravas; now they are much weaker, and the Kauravas are completely confident of their ability to beat them. As for Bhīma, Duryodhana himself is more than a match for him. The Kaurava warriors are mighty, and the Pāṇḍavas are outnumbered.*

[**55**] *Now Duryodhana asks Saṃjaya about Yudhiṣṭhira's preparations for war. Saṃjaya answers that all the Pāṇḍavas have made ready, and are sure that they will triumph. At Duryodhana's request he describes the Pāṇḍavas' horses.*

[**56**] *Dhṛtarāṣṭra asks Saṃjaya to list the allies of the Pāṇḍavas, and Saṃjaya does so. Each of the Pāṇḍavas and their supporters has been assigned particular Kaurava warriors to fight and kill, and Saṃjaya lists these also. Dhṛtarāṣṭra laments: in his view no one can withstand the might of the Pāṇḍava forces. Duryodhana asserts that he and his men are quite capable of defeating them, but Dhṛtarāṣṭra retorts that he is speaking like a madman. He asks Saṃjaya who is inspiring the Pāṇḍavas; Saṃjaya answers that it is Dhṛṣṭadyumna, who has sent a message of his own warning the Kauravas to make peace or face death.*

[**57**] *Now Dhṛtarāṣṭra urges Duryodhana to return Yudhiṣṭhira's kingdom to him and to avoid warfare. But Duryodhana is intent on performing the sacrifice of battle, from which he says he will return triumphant; he will not yield a speck of land. Dhṛtarāṣṭra renounces him and predicts that he and his men will be slaughtered by Bhīma.*

[**58**] *At Dhṛtarāṣṭra's request, Saṃjaya describes his meeting with Kṛṣṇa and Arjuna, and relays the message that Kṛṣṇa sent: the Kauravas have no hope against Arjuna.* [**59**] *Dhṛtarāṣṭra tells Duryodhana that in his judgement the Pāṇḍavas will be the victors in a war: they have support amongst the gods, and Arjuna is invincible. Once again he argues for peace.*

[**60**] *Duryodhana, enraged, replies that the gods will not meddle in human affairs, and claims that he himself has powers greater than theirs. He will defeat and destroy all his enemies.*

[**61**] *As Dhṛtarāṣṭra addresses Saṃjaya once more, Karṇa interrupts to boast of his own prowess. Bhīṣma retorts that Arjuna is greatly his superior and will*

*defeat and kill him. Karṇa announces that he will not fight for as long as Bhīṣma lives, and leaves the assembly.*

**[62]** *Duryodhana continues to maintain that he, Karṇa and Duḥśāsana will prevail over the Pāṇḍavas. Vidura responds with two parables. Two birds, caught in a fowler's net, succeeded in escaping by flying away with it, but then they quarrelled with one another and perished; quarrels among kinsmen lead to ruin. And honey-gatherers in the mountains fell to their deaths attempting to gather some particularly wonderful honey; Duryodhana likewise has eyes only for his goal and does not see the impending catastrophe.*

**[63]** *Dhṛtarāṣṭra reminds Duryodhana of the might of the Pāṇḍavas and their allies, and urges him to pay heed to his elders, who all caution against war.* **[64]** *Then he asks Saṃjaya what Arjuna said after Kṛṣṇa had spoken. Saṃjaya answers that he sent his greetings to the Kauravas, but warned that he would kill them if Yudhiṣṭhira's kingdom was not returned to him.*

**[65]** *The assembly now breaks up. Dhṛtarāṣṭra privately asks Saṃjaya for his own estimate of the relative strength of the two sides. Saṃjaya insists that Vyāsa and Gāndhārī must also be present before he will speak.* **[66]** *Then he gives his opinion. Arjuna and Kṛṣṇa have taken their present births out of choice. Kṛṣṇa is the supreme lord of all, and where he is, there is victory.*

**[67]** *At Dhṛtarāṣṭra's request, Saṃjaya speaks further about Kṛṣṇa's divinity and his own devotion to him. Dhṛtarāṣṭra tells Duryodhana that he should take refuge in Kṛṣṇa, but Duryodhana refuses obdurately; Dhṛtarāṣṭra and Gāndhārī both give him up for lost. On Vyāsa's advice, Dhṛtarāṣṭra asks Saṃjaya how to attain ultimate peace through Kṛṣṇa; Saṃjaya preaches the control of the senses.*

**[68]** *Dhṛtarāṣṭra asks to hear the names of Kṛṣṇa and their meanings, and Saṃjaya tells them to him;* **[69]** *Dhṛtarāṣṭra now praises Kṛṣṇa as supreme lord.*

## THE MISSION OF THE BLESSED LORD

**[70]** *Meanwhile, Yudhiṣṭhira turns to Kṛṣṇa for help. He lists the wrongs that have been done to him and his family, and laments their decline into poverty. War will be terrible, but it is the Kṣatriya* dharma*; he wishes neither to give up his kingdom nor to destroy the Kuru line, and he asks Kṛṣṇa's advice. Kṛṣṇa announces that he will travel in person to the Kauravas in an effort at peace.*

*Yudhiṣṭhira attempts to dissuade him, but Kṛṣṇa insists, and Yudhiṣṭhira wishes his mission well.*

[**71**] *Kṛṣṇa says that he is sure the Kauravas will not agree to peace; they have behaved shamefully and deserve to die, especially Duryodhana. He himself will go and attempt to make peace, but he will also observe the Kauravas' preparations for war; he has no doubt that war will come.*

Vaiśampāyana spoke:
[**72**] 'Slayer of Madhu,' said Bhīma, 'you should speak to them in
whatever way may lead to peace among the Kurus. Do not threaten them
with war! Duryodhana is resentful and always in a fury; he is proud, and
hates what would be for his own good, so he should not be addressed
sharply. Deal with him in a spirit of friendship! Wicked-hearted by
nature, he thinks like a thief; he is overcome by the intoxication of
absolute power, and he is conducting a feud against the Pāṇḍavas. He is
shortsighted, and harsh and abusive in his speech; his valour is exercised
cruelly and his anger is long-lasting. He is unbiddable, a wicked man
5 who loves deceit. He would die rather than accept defeat, and he will
never change his mind. I think, Kṛṣṇa, that to achieve peace with such
a man will be supremely difficult!

'He opposes even his friends, for he has abandoned *dharma* in favour
of falsehood: whatever his friends say or think, he acts against it. In
thrall to anger, he follows his own base nature, pursuing wickedness as
naturally as a snake that has been struck with sticks. You know well
Duryodhana's army, his character, his nature, his strength and his valour.
Once the Kauravas and their sons were peaceable, and so were we: we
10 and our kin used to rejoice like the gods! But now the Bhāratas will be
consumed by Duryodhana's anger, slayer of Madhu, as the forests are
consumed by fire at the end of the cold season.

'It is well known that there have been eighteen kings who exterminated their own kin, their friends and their friends' kin. The demons were prosperous and seemed to blaze with fiery energy, but when in time their *dharma* was subverted, then Bali was born. Similarly among the Haihayas was born Udāvarta, among the Nīpas Janamejaya, among the Tālajaṅghas Bahula, among the Kṛmis the haughty Vasu, among the Suvīras Ajabindu, among the Surāṣṭras Kuśarddhika, among the

Balīhas Arjaka, among the Cīnas Dhautamūlaka, among the Videhas Hayagrīva, among the Mahaujases Varapra, among the Sundaravegas Bāhu, among the Dīptākṣas Purūravas, among the Cedis and Matsyas Sahaja, among the Pracetas Bṛhadbala, among the Indravatsas Dhāraṇa, among the Mukuṭas Vigāhana, and among the Nandivegas Śama. These were the base men born at the end of an age of the world to defile their lineage, Kṛṣṇa.

'So too for us Kurus at the end of the age fate has prepared this Duryodhana, this base and wicked man, to put our lineage to the torch. This is why you should speak gently and softly to him in accordance with *dharma* and the proper making of wealth. Let your words agree largely with his own wishes; let them not be fierce, for his own valour is exercised fiercely. Kṛṣṇa, all of us will be subservient to Duryodhana, and follow him humbly, if the Bhāratas may thereby escape destruction! Act, Vāsudeva, so as to bring about a state of neutrality between us and the Kauravas, so that disaster may not befall the Kurus. Say to the aged grandfather Bhīṣma and the other courtiers, "Let there be brotherhood among the brothers! Let Dhṛtarāṣṭra's son be tranquil!"

'This is what I say. The king himself approves it, and Arjuna too has no wish for war, for there is great compassion in Arjuna.'

**[73]** Strong-armed Kṛṣṇa Keśava burst out laughing when he heard Bhīma speak these unprecedentedly mild words: it seemed to him like finding a mountain that weighed little or a fire that was cool. So Balarāma's younger brother Kṛṣṇa Vāsudeva, the bearer of the bow Śārṅga, addressed Bhīma as he sat there brimming with mercy, hoping to inflame him like a wind fanning a fire. 'At other times, Bhīma, it is war that you applaud, and you long to crush the cruel sons of Dhṛtarāṣṭra who revel in killing. You do not sleep, afflicter of your enemies, but lie awake, face down, always speaking terrible, bellicose, hurtful words. Consumed by your own fiery rage, you exhale deeply, Bhīma, troubled at heart like a smoking fire. You lie on your own, roaring like a weak man oppressed by a heavy burden, so that some who do not understand even think you are mad. You run about uprooting and bending trees like an elephant, Bhīma, roaring while you trample the earth with your feet. You take no pleasure in the company here, son of Pāṇḍu; you remain alone, never greeting anyone by

10 day or by night. You sit in solitude, smiling for no reason or seeming to weep, and sometimes you sit for long spells with your head between your knees and your eyes closed. Always you are seen to frown repeatedly and lick your lips, Bhīma. All this is the result of anger.

'You used to say, "As the sun with its rays is seen rising bright in the East, and as it disappears in the West, forever circling, so I tell you this truthfully, and I shall not break my vow: I shall attack the resentful Duryodhana and kill him with my club!" In the midst of your brothers you used to lay your hand on your club and swear this truly; yet today, afflicter of your enemies, your mind is resolved on peace!

15 'Ah! Now that the time of war draws near, you seem to see reasons to oppose war where no such reasons exist – is this fear that you are feeling, Bhīma? Ah! Sleeping and waking you see hostile portents, son of Kuntī, and this is why you seek peace. Ah! Like a eunuch you have no hope of finding any manliness within yourself; you are overwhelmed by despair, and so your mind is altered. Your heart trembles, your mind is depressed and your legs are paralysed; this is why you seek peace. It is said, son of Kuntī, that the mind of a mortal is inconstant and capricious, like the seeds of the kapok tree dispersed by a strong wind,
20 and indeed your mind is now so altered that I feel I am hearing human speech from a cow! This will cause the hearts of the other Pāṇḍavas to sink as though they were shipwrecked.

'This is a great marvel to me – as great as if a mountain should start to move – that you should speak such words, words so unlike Bhīma! Consider your own deeds, heir of Bharata, and the lineage into which you were born; arise, cast off despair, O hero, and be firm! This weariness does not befit you, foe-tamer: a Kṣatriya obtains nothing that he does not seize with might!'

**[74]** When Kṛṣṇa Vāsudeva spoke to him in this manner, Bhīma, ever angry and unforbearing, rushed up to him like a spirited horse and spoke at once: 'Invincible one, you completely misjudge my intention! By disposition I am utterly devoted to war, and my valour is true; you have dwelt with me long, prince of Daśārha, and you know my mettle. Or rather you do not know me: you are like a shipwrecked man swimming in a lake, and that is why you attack me with such unfitting words – for how could anyone who knows me as Bhīma speak as unfittingly of me as you do, heir of Madhu?

'So I shall tell you something, lord of the Vṛṣṇis, of my manliness and unmatched might. To praise oneself is not at all a noble thing, but your intemperate words have wounded me, so I shall speak of my own strength.

'Behold these two worlds, Kṛṣṇa, the heaven and the earth, where all these beings have existed; immovable and infinite, they are the origin and dwelling-place of all. If these two were suddenly to clash together in fury like two rocks, I would use my two arms to hold them apart, together with all their creatures, the moving and the still! Behold this space between my arms like iron bars; I know of no man who could free himself once he was held there. If Mount Himālaya, the ocean and Indra himself, wielder of the thunderbolt and slayer of Bala, were all three to exert their strength together, they could not rescue the man whom I had overpowered! If all the Kṣatriyas were to string their bows to attack the Pāṇḍavas, I should fight them and trample them into the ground with the sole of my foot!

'Invincible one, you cannot fail to recognize my valour: I have conquered kings and brought them into subjection. But if you truly do not know me, O stirrer of men, I who am like the brilliance of the rising sun, then you shall come to know me in the dense press of battle! Why have you been berating me with harsh words, sinless one, as though pricking a wound? I have spoken as I think, but you should know that there is more to me than this, and when the day of slaughter comes, you shall see me in the press of battle putting to flight elephants, chariot-fighters and horsemen; you and all the world shall see me furiously slaying bull-like Kṣatriya heroes and dragging the very best among them! The marrow has not run dry in my bones, and my heart does not tremble; I feel no fear even if the whole world turns on me in fury. But, slayer of Madhu, for friendship and for no other reason I show mercy and endure all these torments, lest otherwise our Bhārata people should perish.'

**[75]** The blessed lord said, 'I spoke as I did from affection and because I wanted to know what was in your mind – not to scold you or to show off my learning, not because of anger or doubt. I know your greatness,

I know the strength that is yours, I know your deeds, and I would not insult you. Son of Pāṇḍu, I see a thousand times more good in you than you see in yourself: with your kinsmen and friends you befit the lineage of your birth, Bhīma, honoured as it is by all the kings.

'But those people who seek to understand[1] the doubtful distinction between fate and human effort, O wolf-belly, can never reach any conclusion, for the very thing that leads to success in a man's doings may also lead to his destruction: human action is by nature doubtful. Actions may be regarded in one way by wise men skilled at foreseeing unwanted outcomes, and yet turn out quite differently, like the currents of the wind. An action carried out through human effort may be well planned, well performed and properly accomplished, and yet be thwarted by fate. But likewise a fated action, something not carried out by humans, may be frustrated by human effort, heir of Bharata, as happens with cold and heat, rain, hunger and thirst. And a man whose being is constrained by fate may none the less opt to carry out some different action, and fate does not prevent him from doing so; we see the same characteristic here.

'Son of Pāṇḍu, there is no course that this world can take other than action. Understanding this, one should continue on one's way; the results will come from a combination of destiny and human effort. He who continues to act with this understanding is neither distressed by failure nor elated by success. This is all I was trying to express, Bhīma: that in war with the Kauravas one should not imagine that success is certain. If misfortune should occur in such a case, one should not fall into utter gloom, and surrender to despair or exhaustion. This is why I spoke to you as I did.

'In the morning, son of Pāṇḍu, I shall approach Dhṛtarāṣṭra and strive to bring peace without abandoning your cause. If they make peace, I shall win boundless fame, your desire will be achieved, and they will attain the highest good fortune. But if the Kauravas remain unmoved and reject my words, there will certainly be war and terrible doings as a result. The burden in this war will be laid upon you, Bhīma; Arjuna must also bear the yoke, and the two of you must carry the others along.

1 Literally 'who wish to know the course of'.

If war comes, I shall be the charioteer of Arjuna Bībhatsu, for this was
his desire – it is not that I do not wish to fight. Wolf-belly, this is why, 20
when I felt doubtful about your thinking, I assailed you with manly
words to kindle your fiery energy.'

**[76]** *Now Arjuna speaks. He tells Kṛṣṇa to act in whatever way he considers fitting.* **[77]** *Kṛṣṇa answers that he will do what he can; but he cannot control fate, and he does not expect peace.*

**[78]** *Nakula's view is that Kṛṣṇa should act as the occasion demands; a gentle approach will be wise, since no one could fail to be intimidated by the threat posed by the Pāṇḍavas and their allies. He is optimistic that Kṛṣṇa will succeed in bringing peace.* **[79]** *Sahadeva, by contrast, favours war, in order to avenge the wrong done to Draupadī in the gambling match. Sātyaki supports him, and there are cries of approval at his call for battle.*

**[80]** *Now Draupadī speaks. She is grieved to hear Yudhiṣṭhira and Bhīma seeking peace, and she applauds Sahadeva and Sātyaki. She maintains that Duryodhana clearly only desires peace if he can retain the Pāṇḍavas' kingdom; Kṛṣṇa's mission is therefore pointless, and war is the right course of action. Her own humiliation at the hands of the Kauravas deserves to be avenged, and if Yudhiṣṭhira and Arjuna will not fight, her sons will. Seeing her weep, Kṛṣṇa assures her that soon she will see the Kaurava women weeping. He will carry out his mission, but if Duryodhana does not concede he and his allies will be destroyed, and the Pāṇḍavas will be restored to their fortunes.*

**[81]** *Kṛṣṇa has his chariot prepared, and he and Sātyaki mount. Good portents appear, and seers honour Kṛṣṇa. He sets off; the Pāṇḍavas and their allies follow him for some distance. Then Yudhiṣṭhira urges Kṛṣṇa to comfort Kuntī and greet the elders, and Arjuna vows that if Duryodhana fails to concede he will kill the Kaurava Kṣatriyas; his words prompt Bhīma to utter mighty roars. Now Kṛṣṇa departs. On the way he meets a party of great seers headed by Rāma Jāmadagnya; they are visiting earth to watch him conduct his mission. Rāma wishes him well and promises to see him again in the assembly.*

**[82]** *Kṛṣṇa travels on, accompanied by a strong force. Wherever he goes, marvels occur. He passes through Śālibhavana and reaches Vṛkasthala, where he spends the night.* **[83]** *Learning that Kṛṣṇa is approaching, Dhṛtarāṣṭra makes ready to greet him with great honour, and he has Duryodhana prepare the finest accommodation at Vṛkasthala; but Kṛṣṇa ignores it.*

**[84]** *Dhṛtarāṣṭra tells Vidura of his plans for honouring Kṛṣṇa. He lists the rich gifts he will give him, and gives orders for Duḥśāsana's house to be made ready for him to stay in.* **[85]** *Vidura replies that Dhṛtarāṣṭra is acting from dishonest motives in treating Kṛṣṇa so lavishly; but he will not succeed in winning his allegiance away from the Pāṇḍavas. Instead, Dhṛtarāṣṭra should offer him what he seeks: a just peace.* **[86]** *Duryodhana agrees that Kṛṣṇa will remain loyal to the Pāṇḍavas, and he opposes giving him any gifts. Bhīṣma urges Dhṛtarāṣṭra to agree to Kṛṣṇa's proposals for peace, but Duryodhana insists that he will never share the kingdom, and speaks of taking Kṛṣṇa captive. Dhṛtarāṣṭra rebukes him, and Bhīṣma utters a furious condemnation and then walks out.*

**[87]** *The next day Kṛṣṇa arrives; he is met by all the townsfolk and all the Kauravas except for Duryodhana. He goes to Dhṛtarāṣṭra's house and exchanges greetings with Dhṛtarāṣṭra and his allies. Then, after spending some time in friendly talk with them, he goes to see Vidura.* **[88]** *Next he visits his father's sister, Kuntī. She asks after the Pāṇḍavas and Draupadī, contrasting their former glory with their present woes and praising them highly; she grieves specially for Draupadī. She blames her father for having her adopted by Kuntibhoja, and gives Kṛṣṇa messages to pass on to all the Pāṇḍavas. Kṛṣṇa comforts her with their greetings and promises that they will soon triumph over their enemies.*

**[89]** *Now Kṛṣṇa visits Duryodhana, whom he finds in company with Duḥśāsana, Karṇa and Śakuni. He is greeted in the proper manner and offered a meal, which he refuses: he will not eat with them until he has succeeded in his mission. He urges Duryodhana to give up his hatred of the Pāṇḍavas, and announces that he will stay with Vidura. The seniormost Kauravas try to persuade him to accept their hospitality, but he will not do so.*

**[90]** *After the evening meal, Vidura tells Kṛṣṇa that his mission is not a wise one, for Duryodhana and his supporters are determined to keep the Pāṇḍavas' kingdom: they will ignore his words.* **[91]** *Kṛṣṇa answers that he knows well what is in the minds of Duryodhana and the others, but he must still do what is right by trying honestly to bring peace.*

**[92]** *In the morning Kṛṣṇa is driven with great ceremony to the assembly. He enters, and is received with due honour. The seers arrive from heaven; they are greeted and given seats. Then Kṛṣṇa sits down, followed by all the assembled rulers. All eyes are on Kṛṣṇa: there is silence.*

Vaiśaṃpāyana spoke:

[93] When all the kings were seated in silence, Kṛṣṇa of the gleaming teeth began to speak in a voice like the sound of a drum. Madhu's heir fixed his eyes upon Dhṛtarāṣṭra as he spoke, but his voice resounded throughout the entire assembly, like a thundercloud at summer's end. 'Heir of Bharata, let there be peace between Kauravas and Pāṇḍavas without putting the warriors to work! This is what I have come to strive for. There are no other words that I can say for your welfare, foe-taming king, for you already know all that is to be known. This Kuru lineage 5
stands today foremost among all the kings, O prince, for it is rich in Vedic learning and virtuous deeds, and excels in every good quality: heir of Bharata, the Kurus are distinguished for their mercy and kindness, their compassion and lack of cruelty, and for their uprightness, forbearance and truth. When such a lineage as this maintains such greatness, king, any unworthy act would be unfitting, especially if occasioned by you – for you, O truest of the Kurus, are chief among those who prevent the Kurus from acting falsely, whether towards friends or strangers.

'But, heir of Kuru, your boorish sons, led by Duryodhana, have turned their backs on *dharma* and the proper making of wealth. Greed has seized their hearts and they have abandoned all rules of behaviour. They are acting with cruelty towards their own leading kinsmen: you 10
know this, bull-like heir of Bharata. This is why this most dreadful disaster has arisen amongst the Kurus; if you take no heed of it, it will destroy the earth. And yet it can be mitigated if you so wish, bull-like heir of Bharata, for I do not think that peace is difficult to achieve in this case. Peace depends on you, lord of the peoples, and on me: restrain your sons, and I shall restrain the others, heir of Kuru. After all, prince of kings, it is for your sons and their followers to obey your command, and it is also greatly to their benefit to abide by your authority. And 15
what benefits you benefits the Pāṇḍavas too, O king, as they await my instructions while I strive to bring peace.

'Examine the matter in all its aspects, lord of the peoples, and then act: let the Bhāratas be united behind you! Practise *dharma* and the proper making of wealth under the protection of the Pāṇḍavas, lord of men, for such heroes cannot be overcome by any hostile effort; if the noble Pāṇḍavas protect you, not even Indra with the other gods could defeat you, never mind mere kings! If you had on your side not only Bhīṣma, Droṇa, Kṛpa, Karṇa, Viviṃśati, Aśvatthāman, Vikarṇa, Somadatta, Bāhlika, the kings of Sindhu and Kaliṅga, and Sudakṣiṇa of Kāmboja, but also Yudhiṣṭhira, Bhīma, the ambidextrous warrior Arjuna, the twins Nakula and Sahadeva, Sātyaki of great ardour, and the mighty chariot-fighter Yuyutsu,[1] then who would be so perverse as to fight against them, bull-like heir of Bharata? With the Kauravas and Pāṇḍavas together, foe-slayer, you will attain sovereignty over the world and, moreover, you will be unassailable by your enemies. And so, lord of the earth, those lords of the earth who are your equals, and even those who are superior to you, will become your allies; and you, protected on all sides by sons, grandsons, brothers, fathers and friends, will be able to live in happiness. If you grant all these Pāṇḍavas esteem and honour as you used to, lord of the earth, you will enjoy the entire earth, for together with them as well as your own people, heir of Bharata, you will defeat all other enemies: this is wholly to your advantage! Afflicter of your enemies, you will enjoy the earth that they themselves will win for you, if, with your sons and ministers, you will just unite with them.

'However, great king, if there is war, great destruction will take place; and if both sides are destroyed, what *dharma* will you see in that? Tell me, bull-like heir of Bharata: what happiness will you gain through the slaughter in battle of the Pāṇḍavas or of your own mighty sons? Both the Pāṇḍavas and your own warriors are all brave, expert in arms and eager to do battle: protect them from this great danger! Let us not see all the heroes on both sides, Pāṇḍavas and Kauravas alike, destroyed in battle and struck down by chariot-fighters from their chariots. O truest of kings, the kings of the earth have assembled; in thrall to anger, they will slay all creatures here! Protect the world, king – let all these creatures not perish! Heir of Kuru, once you return to your natural state deliverance will follow. These rulers are pure, generous, modest, noble, well born and mutually supportive: protect them from this great danger, O king!

1 Yuyutsu is Dhṛtarāṣṭra's illegitimate son (for his birth, see 1.107.35–6): he is well disposed towards the Pāṇḍavas (e.g. 1.119.39–40). When Yudhiṣṭhira gives the warriors an opportunity to change sides before the great battle begins, Yuyutsu is the only one to do so: he transfers his allegiance from Duryodhana to Yudhiṣṭhira (6.41.88–95). However, this has not yet happened, so his inclusion in the second half of Kṛṣṇa's list is rather odd.

'Let these lords of the earth meet together in goodwill, take food and 35
drink together, and then return each to his own home, dressed in fine robes and garlanded, bull-like heir of Bharata; let them do honour to one another and give up their resentments and feuds, O afflicter of your enemies! Your life is drawing towards its end; let that affection which you used to bear towards the Pāṇḍavas be yours once more, today and forever, bull-like heir of Bharata. It was you who raised them when they were fatherless children; now protect them along with your sons, as is proper, for it falls to you to look after them, particularly at times of disaster. Bull-like heir of Bharata, do not ruin both your *dharma* and the proper making of wealth!

'The Pāṇḍavas send you greetings and propitiations, O king, and they 40
say to you, "At your command we and our followers suffered misery: we passed these twelve years in the forest, and a thirteenth year incognito in a populous place. Certain that you, our father, would stand by the agreement, we ourselves did not break it: our Brahmins know this. So, bull-like heir of Bharata, stand by your agreement with us, for we have stood by it, and after our endless torments we wish to regain our share of the kingdom. Please combine *dharma* with the proper making of wealth to help us! We endure these many torments because we recognize you
as our elder, so you should act towards us like a father or mother. The 45
behaviour of both elders and pupils is very important, heir of Bharata, because if we take a wrong path it is for our father to set us right. Set us on our path, O king – and likewise set yourself on your own road!"

'Your sons also speak thus to this assembly, bull-like heir of Bharata: "Among these courtiers who know *dharma*, any unworthy act would be unfitting. Wherever *dharma* is slain by *adharma* and truth by untruth before men's very eyes, the courtiers of that place too are slain. If *dharma* is wounded by *adharma* and seeks refuge in an assembly, and the courtiers there do not cut the dart out from it, they too are wounded; *dharma* brings them down as a river brings down the trees growing on its banks!"

'These are men who hold *dharma* in their thoughts, who sit in silence 50
reflecting on *dharma*, and what they have said is truth, *dharma* and justice, bull-like heir of Bharata. What answer can you give them other than to grant what they ask? Let the lords of the earth who are seated together

here in the assembly first ponder on *dharma* and the proper making of wealth, and then speak if I am telling the truth! Release these Kṣatriyas from the noose of death, bull-like Kṣatriya; make peace, best heir of Bharata, do not fall prey to anger. Give the Pāṇḍavas the share they have inherited, as is right, and then, your aims achieved, enjoy pleasures with your sons, afflicter of your enemies!

'You know that Yudhiṣṭhira Ajātaśatru always abides by the *dharma* of
the virtuous, and you know how he behaves towards you and your sons,
55 lord of men. You tried to burn him, you cast him out, and yet once again
he now turns to you. You and your sons banished him to Indraprastha,
yet while he lived there he gained mastery over all the princes and made
them subject to you, O king – he never infringed your authority. This is
how he was conducting himself when Subala's son Śakuni, who wanted
to rob him of his lands and wealth and grain, committed the worst of
frauds against him; yet even on reaching that state, and seeing Draupadī
Kṛṣṇā dragged into the hall, Yudhiṣṭhira of immeasurable greatness was
unshakable in maintaining the Kṣatriya *dharma*.

'As for me, heir of Bharata, I seek what is best for them and for
you. Do not cut all beings off from *dharma*, happiness and the proper
60 making of wealth, king! Your sons believe what is harmful to them to
be wholesome, and what is wholesome, harmful; in their greed they
have gone too far. Restrain them, lord of the peoples! The foe-taming
sons of Kuntī stand ready to obey you or to fight you; take your own
stand on what will be best for you, O king!'

All the princes applauded this speech in their hearts, but not one of them was prepared to speak a word.

## DAMBHODBHAVA

**[94]** *The kings are reduced to silence by Kṛṣṇa's speech, but Rāma Jāmadagnya speaks: he tells the story of the mighty king Dambhodbhava. — Dambhodbhava boasts that no one can match him in battle, till the Brahmins tell him that Nara and Nārāyaṇa can do so. He visits them on Mount Gandhamādana, where they are performing austerities, and challenges them; they repeatedly assure him that a hermitage is no* *place for a fight, but he insists. Nara then picks a handful of reeds; when Dambhodbhava begins to shower arrows on him he renders them harmless and throws the reeds, which pierce all Dambhodbhava's troops, till Dambhodbhava falls at Nara's feet. — Rāma points out that Arjuna and Kṛṣṇa are Nara and Nārāyaṇa. He advises the Kauravas to make peace with them.*

## MĀTALI

**[95]** *Next Kaṇva addresses Duryodhana. He urges him to make peace, and tells the story of Indra's charioteer Mātali. — Mātali has a daughter Guṇakeśī, for whom he wishes to find a husband. Convinced that there is no one suitable amongst men or immortals, he sets out to search the underworld realm of the serpents.* **[96]** *On the way he is joined by Nārada; the two visit Varuṇa together, and Nārada shows Varuṇa's world to Mātali.*

**[97]** *Nārada shows Mātali the underworld city of Pātāla, inhabited by demons and certain extreme ascetics. He asks whether Mātali approves of anyone there as a husband for his daughter, but he does not.* **[98]** *Next Nārada shows him Hiraṇyapura, the golden city of demons, but Mātali will not marry his daughter to one of the enemies of the gods.*

**[99]** *Nārada shows Mātali the realm of the great birds, enemies of the serpents.* **[100]** *Then he shows him the seventh subterranean region, that of Rasātala; here lives Surabhi, the mother of all cattle and source of the ocean of milk that was churned by the gods and demons.*[1] **[101]** *Finally he shows him the city of Bhogavatī, home of the great serpents. Here Mātali selects the serpent Sumukha, grandson of Āryaka, as a husband for Guṇakeśī.*

**[102]** *When Nārada proposes the match to Āryaka, he is hesitant: Garuḍa has killed Sumukha's father and vowed to kill Sumukha also. But Mātali insists; he takes Sumukha to Indra, who confers long life on him.* **[103]** *When Garuḍa hears of this he remonstrates angrily with Indra and boasts of his own great strength. Viṣṇu asks him to support his right arm; Garuḍa collapses under its weight, and asks pardon for his arrogance. —*

1 See 1.15.

*Kaṇva tells Duryodhana that he too should not take on the superior might of the Pāṇḍavas, but Duryodhana is unmoved.*

## GĀLAVA

**[104]** *Nārada warns Duryodhana against stubbornness, and tells the story of Gālava. — The god Dharma takes the form of Vasiṣṭha and visits Viśvāmitra, who is performing austerities, to ask him for food. Viśvāmitra prepares food, but in the meanwhile Dharma is fed by others; when Viśvāmitra brings food to him, he tells him to wait. Viśvāmitra waits motionless for a hundred years till Dharma returns; pleased, the god raises Viśvāmitra from his Kṣatriya rank to that of Brahmin.*

*Viśvāmitra now gives his student Gālava leave to depart; Gālava annoys Viśvāmitra by repeatedly asking what gift he should give him, and finally Viśvāmitra tells him to bring eight hundred white horses with one black ear each.* **[105]** *Gālava, emaciated with anxiety, wonders how to fulfil his teacher's command. He is deciding to approach Viṣṇu for aid when Garuḍa appears and offers to help him.*

**[106]** *Garuḍa asks Gālava which direction to take him in. He describes the East,* **[107]** *then the South,* **[108]** *the West* **[109]** *and the North.* **[110]** *Gālava asks Garuḍa to take him to the East, but the great bird's speed terrifies him. He blurts out his problem, and Garuḍa promises to help; they will return home after resting for a while on Mount Ṛṣabha.*

**[111]** *On Mount Ṛṣabha they are fed by the Brahmin woman ascetic Śāṇḍilī and fall asleep. When Garuḍa awakes he finds that he has lost his wings: Śāṇḍilī, aware of his idea of carrying her before Prajāpati, has used her power to remove them. He succeeds in placating her, and she restores his wings. Now Garuḍa and Gālava return home; they meet Viśvāmitra, who tells Gālava that he must hurry to fulfil his promise.*

**[112]** *Garuḍa proposes that Gālava should approach King Yayāti for help. He takes Gālava to Pratiṣṭhāna, introduces him to Yayāti, and explains his problem.* **[113]** *Yayāti explains that he is no longer as wealthy as he once was; however, he cannot send a petitioner away empty-handed, and he gives Gālava his daughter Mādhavī, who is destined to found four dynasties: by offering her as a bride to other great kings he will be able to* *obtain what he seeks. Gālava accepts her and offers her to the Ikṣvāku king Haryaśva.*

**[114]** *Haryaśva has only two hundred black-eared white horses, and asks to be allowed to father one son on Mādhavī in return for these. Mādhavī explains that, thanks to a boon, she will become a virgin once more after giving birth. She advises Gālava to give her to Haryaśva and to three other kings: in this way he will gain all the horses he needs and she will bear four sons.*

*Haryaśva's son Vasumanas is born, and Gālava now goes with Mādhavī to King Divodāsa.* **[115]** *Divodāsa is happy to accept Mādhavī on the same terms as Haryaśva: she bears him a son, Pratardana.* **[116]** *Next Gālava visits King Uśīnara and proposes that he father two sons on Mādhavī in return for four hundred horses. But Uśīnara has only two hundred to give, so he restricts himself to one son. Mādhavī gives birth to Śibi.*

**[117]** *Garuḍa congratulates Gālava on his success; when Gālava reminds him that he is still two hundred horses short, Garuḍa tells him of the origin of the black-eared white horses: originally there were a thousand, but only six hundred survive. He recommends Gālava to present his six hundred horses to Viśvāmitra together with Mādhavī. Gālava does so, and Viśvāmitra begets Aṣṭaka on Mādhavī. Now Gālava sends her back to her father Yayāti and bids farewell to Garuḍa.*

**[118]** *Yayāti*[1] *holds a* svayaṃvara *for Mādhavī, but she rejects all the many suitors who attend, and chooses the forest instead; she lives an ascetic life there. Yayāti lives for thousands of years, but then dies and goes to heaven. He looks down on the other celestials, and is punished by ceasing to be recognized.* **[119]** *Condemned to fall from heaven, he requests that he may fall among good people. He arrives in the midst of a sacrifice being performed by Mādhavī's four sons; when he identifies himself and reveals what has happened to him all four offer him their own merit. He refuses, but then Mādhavī herself appears and tells him who they are. He accepts their merit, together with half of hers. Gālava arrives and offers him an eighth of his ascetic power.*

**[120]** *Yayāti's celestial form is renewed. Now Vasumanas bestows on him*

1 Chapters 118–21 tell a variant version of the story found at 1.81–8.

*the fruit of his generosity, forbearance and sacrificial rectitude. Pratardana gives him his martial glory; Śibi gives the rewards of his truthfulness, and Aṣṭaka those of his sacrifices. Yayāti rises from the earth,* **[121]** *and returns to heaven, where he is welcomed with joy. He asks what led to his earlier fall; Brahmā answers that it was his pride. — Nārada concludes by warning Duryodhana against pride and advising him to make peace with the Pāṇḍavas.*

Vaiśampāyana spoke:
**[122]** 'Blessed Nārada,' said Dhṛtarāṣṭra, 'it is exactly as you say, and I too share your desire, but I am powerless!'

Then, heir of Bharata, he addressed Kṛṣṇa: 'Keśava, you have spoken to me of heavenly and earthly considerations, and of questions of *dharma* and justice. But I do not have freedom of action, son. What is being done is not pleasing to me, so, strong-armed Kṛṣṇa, highest lord, do please strive to win over my foolish and undisciplined Duryodhana! This would be the greatest act of friendship on your part, O stirrer of men.'

5 So Kṛṣṇa, expert in *dharma* and the proper making of wealth, turned
to the resentful Duryodhana and spoke sweetly to him. 'Duryodhana,
truest of the Kurus, hear what I have to say: it is particularly apposite
for you and your followers. You are wise and well born, rich in Vedic
learning and virtuous deeds, and excelling in every good quality: you
should act well in this matter. The course you are considering, son, is
one that would be pursued by the wicked and low-born, the cruel and
shameless. In this world we see that the way of the virtuous is consistent
with *dharma* and the proper making of wealth, bull-like heir of Bharata,
10 while that of the wicked runs contrary to both; yet more than once
we have seen you take this contrary path. *Adharma* such as this, and
the consequences it brings, are terrible and will cause great loss of life.
Many times, heir of Bharata, infamous acts have been done at your
instigation. It is by shunning this harmful course that you will achieve
the greatest good for yourself; you will also, O afflicter of your enemies,
free yourself from the wicked and infamous deeds of your brothers,
servants and friends.

'Tiger-like hero, bull-like heir of Bharata, the Pāṇḍavas are wise, brave, resolute, self-possessed and learned in the Veda: make peace with them! This would be beneficial, lord of the peoples, and it would be pleasing to wise Dhṛtarāṣṭra, grandfather Bhīṣma, Droṇa, sagacious Vidura, Kṛpa, Somadatta, wise Bāhlika, Aśvatthāman, Vikarṇa and Saṃjaya, as well as to most of your kinsmen and friends, O afflicter of your enemies. What is more, son, the safety of the entire world resides in peace.

'My son, you are modest and well born, learned and devoid of cruelty; abide by the instruction of your father and mother, bull-like heir of Bharata, for they say that the best course is what a father instructs. When utter disaster strikes, everyone remembers his father's instruction. Reconciliation with the Pāṇḍavas is what your father wishes, and his ministers agree with him; best of Kurus, let his wish be yours also.

'When a man hears his friends' counsel but does not act upon it, its consequence is to burn him as though he had eaten a snake-gourd. If he procrastinates, and fails through folly to act on excellent advice, his undertakings come to nothing and he suffers remorse; but if he acts on excellent advice as soon as he receives it, giving up his own earlier opinion, he thrives happily in this world. The contrary man, who refuses to accept what is said by those who wish him well, and heeds only contrary advice, falls into the power of his enemies. When anyone rejects the opinion of the virtuous and instead adopts that of the wicked, his friends soon find themselves lamenting the calamity that has overtaken him. He who dismisses his best counsellors in favour of inferior ones meets with terrible disaster from which there is no rescue; if anyone consorts with wicked people, behaving wrongly and never listening to his friends, favouring strangers and despising his own folk, the very earth curses that man, heir of Bharata.

'But you have quarrelled with the heroic Pāṇḍavas, and now you seek the help of others who, bull-like hero, are boorish, incapable fools. What man on earth but you would reject his kin, mighty Indra-like chariot-fighters all, in hopes of help from others? From birth you have always abused Kuntī's sons, and yet the Pāṇḍavas have never shown you anger, for they abide by *dharma*; wronged from birth, my strong-armed son, Pāṇḍu's sons of great renown have none the less acted well towards

you. And you too should act in just the same way, bull-like heir of
Bharata, towards your own leading kinsmen: do not fall prey to anger.

'The wise link their undertakings to the three aims of human life.[1]
But if the three aims cannot be achieved together, men follow *dharma*
and the proper making of wealth; and if all three are separated out, the
wise man follows *dharma* and the middling man the proper making of
wealth, while the fool makes the worst choice and follows pleasure. If,
through sensuality and greed, a man abandons *dharma* to seek pleasure
35 and wealth through improper means, that man perishes; anyone seeking
pleasure and wealth should also practise *dharma* from the outset, for
neither wealth nor pleasure is ever found away from *dharma*. Indeed,
lord of the peoples, they say that *dharma* is the one means to achieve
the three aims, because he who uses that means to seek them prospers
as swiftly as fire in a dry thicket. But you, my son, are using improper
means to seek sovereignty, mighty, glorious and renowned amongst all
kings; and a man who treats wrongfully those who act well towards him
40 cuts himself down as one cuts down a forest with an axe, O king. Heir
of Bharata, one should not vex anyone in the three worlds who is ready
to give up his life – not even a rather common person, so how much
less those bull-like sons of Pāṇḍu! But the man in thrall to anger loses
his judgement, for everything that grows great is cut back; see the proof
here, heir of Bharata!

'Alliance with the Pāṇḍavas will be better for you than alliance with
wicked folk, my son, for if you establish friendship with them, you
will achieve all your desires. At present, truest of kings, you enjoy the
earth that Pāṇḍu's sons have conquered, and yet you turn your back on
the Pāṇḍavas themselves and seek help elsewhere. You hope to prosper
by granting power to Duḥśāsana, Durviṣaha,[2] Karṇa and Śakuni son of
45 Subala; but these are not your equals in knowledge, *dharma* and the
proper making of wealth, nor do they equal the Pāṇḍavas in valour,
heir of Bharata. Indeed, you and all these kings together are incapable
of looking at furious Bhīma's face in battle. And this whole princely
force that stands close by, son – Bhīṣma, Droṇa, Karṇa and Kṛpa,

1 *Dharma*, the proper making of wealth, and pleasure: see 1.56.16 and note.

2 One of Dhṛtarāṣṭra's sons.

Somadatta's son Bhūriśravas, Aśvatthāman and Jayadratha – all of these together could not fight against wealth-winner Arjuna, for, once roused to anger, Arjuna cannot be defeated even by all the gods and demons, Gandharvas and men. Do not set your heart on war!

'Show me a single man in this whole princely force who would go 50
home safe and sound after meeting Arjuna in battle – what will you gain by destroying all these people, bull-like heir of Bharata? And let me show you the one man whom you must defeat to gain victory, the one who in Khāṇḍavaprastha defeated gods, Gandharvas, Yakṣas, demons and serpents;[1] what mortal could fight him? You know, too, of the great and marvellous battle between one and many at the city of Virāṭa:[2] that in itself is sufficient demonstration! Arjuna, the mighty hero whom you hope to defeat in this battle, is unconquerable, unassailable, victorious, invincible! And who, including Indra himself, could challenge Kuntī's 55
son when he advances against him with me for his second? The man who could defeat Arjuna in battle would be able to lift the earth with his two arms, to burn all these creatures with the fire of his anger, to hurl the very gods down from heaven!

'Behold your sons, your brothers, your family members and kinsmen: let them not perish on your account, O truest heir of Bharata! Let the Kauravas survive, let the lineage not come to an end; do not become known as the infamous destroyer of the line, lord of men! The mighty Pāṇḍava chariot-fighters will install you yourself as prince regent and your father King Dhṛtarāṣṭra as sovereign. Do not despise the fortune 60
that is ready to come to you, my son: if you give the Pāṇḍavas their half, you will attain great fortune. Make peace with the Pāṇḍavas; follow your friends' advice; if you establish friendship with them as your allies, you will enjoy long prosperity!'

[**123**] Next Bhīṣma son of Śaṃtanu, who had listened to the words of Kṛṣṇa Keśava, addressed the resentful Duryodhana, O bull-like heir of Bharata. 'Kṛṣṇa has spoken to you from his desire for peace between friends. Reflect on what he has said, son: do not fall prey to anger. If you do not do as the noble Keśava says, you will never achieve good

**1** See 1.214 ff.

**2** See 4.48–62.

fortune or happiness or prosperity. The strong-armed hero has told you, my son, of the making of wealth in accordance with *dharma*. Pursue that goal; do not destroy all these creatures, O king! Amongst all kings the fortune of this Bhārata lineage blazes the brightest, and yet you are going to destroy it through your wickedness while Dhṛtarāṣṭra still lives! Rejecting in your malice the truthful and beneficial words of Keśava, your father and wise Vidura, O best heir of Bharata, you will deprive of life yourself, your ministers, your sons, your cattle, your kinsmen and your friends. Do not destroy the line! Do not take the wicked path of the base and evil-minded! Do not hand your aged parents over to grief!'

In thrall to anger, Duryodhana exhaled deeply again and again. Now Droṇa addressed these words to him. 'Keśava has told you, my son, of *dharma* and the proper making of wealth, and so has Bhīṣma son of Śaṃtanu; approve what they say, lord of men! Both men are wise and intelligent, self-controlled and learned in the Veda; both wish you well. What they have said is to your benefit, so accept it, afflicter of your enemies! Have the great wisdom to follow the advice of Kṛṣṇa and Bhīṣma, and not to act on that of fools. These men who are urging you on never act in your interest; they will tie the hostility of others round your neck in battle. Do not slay all the Kurus, and all your own sons and brothers! You should know that any force containing Kṛṣṇa Vāsudeva and Arjuna is invincible. Kṛṣṇa and Bhīṣma are your friends, son, and the words they have said to you here are the truth. If you do not accept them, you will regret it later, heir of Bharata! Arjuna is even greater than Rāma Jāmadagnya has said,[1] and not even the gods could resist Kṛṣṇa son of Devakī. But, bull-like hero, what is the use of speaking to you here of happiness and welfare? You have heard it all: now do as you wish, for I cannot say anything further to you, truest heir of Bharata.'

When Droṇa had finished speaking, Vidura the chamberlain fixed his eyes upon Dhṛtarāṣṭra's resentful son Duryodhana and said, 'Duryodhana, bull-like heir of Bharata, I do not grieve for you. But I do grieve for these two elders, Gāndhārī and your father, who will live unprotected with you, an enemy, for their protector. When their friends and counsellors lie slain they will be as helpless as birds whose wings

1 See 5.94.

have been cut off, and they will travel this earth as beggars, lamenting that they had for their son such a wicked, evil destroyer of his line!'

Now King Dhṛtarāṣṭra addressed Duryodhana as he sat with his
brothers, surrounded by kings. 'Duryodhana, heed the words of noble
Kṛṣṇa and accept them, for they are entirely well-meant and offer you
security for all time. With Kṛṣṇa here for our tireless ally we shall achieve
our most dearly held aims amongst all other kings! In full accord with 25
Keśava, my son, approach Yudhiṣṭhira and bring about total prosperity
and welfare for the Bhāratas! Vāsudeva is your auspicious river-crossing,
son; use him to reach the holy confluence. I think the moment has
arrived: Duryodhana, do not let it pass! If you spurn Keśava when he
seeks peace and argues your cause, there is no way for you to avoid
overwhelming defeat.'

[**124**] When Bhīṣma and Droṇa had heard what Dhṛtarāṣṭra had to say,
they spoke in his support to the disobedient Duryodhana. 'Until Kṛṣṇa
and Arjuna don armour, until the bow Gāṇḍīva stirs into motion, until
Dhaumya[1] offers up this enemy force into the fire of the Pāṇḍava army,
until the mighty bowman, modest Yudhiṣṭhira, gazes in fury at your
army – till then let slaughter pause! Until we see the mighty bowman,
Kuntī's son Bhīma, stationed among his troops – till then let slaughter
pause! Until he delights the soldiery with his manoeuvres, until he 5
severs the heads of elephant-fighters in battle with his hero-slaying club
as though they were the fruits of a tree in the season of ripeness – till
then let slaughter pause! Until those experts in arms Nakula, Sahadeva,
Pṛṣata's heir Dhṛṣṭadyumna, Virāṭa, Śikhaṇḍin and the son of Śiśupāla
arm themselves and shoot so rapidly that they overrun us like crocodiles
overrunning the great ocean – till then let slaughter pause! Until fierce
vulture-feathered shafts fall upon the delicate bodies of kings – till then
let slaughter pause! Until great iron arrows, shot swiftly by far-shooting 10
expert bowmen of note, strike our warriors' breasts, smeared though
they are with sandal and aloe, adorned though they are with pearl
necklaces and medallions – till then let slaughter pause!

'Let Yudhiṣṭhira lord of *dharma* hold you with both arms as you bow your head in greeting; in token of peace, let the elephant-like king, so

1 The Pāṇḍavas' household priest.

generous to Brahmins, lay on your shoulder his right hand, marked with standard, elephant-goad and banner, O bull-like heir of Bharata; as you sit before him, let him massage your back with a hand dyed with red lac and bearing jewels on fingers and palm. Let strong-armed wolf-belly Bhīma, whose shoulders are like the trunks of *śāla* trees, embrace you, bull-like heir of Bharata, and greet you with mild words in token of peace. Receive the greetings of the other three, Arjuna and the twins, and greet them lovingly in turn, prince, kissing them on the head.[1] Let the lords of men shed tears of joy to see you reconciled with your brave Pāṇḍava brothers. Let universal prosperity be proclaimed in the capitals of the kings; enjoy the earth in brotherly affection, and cast off your sickness!'

**[125]** Duryodhana had listened to these unwelcome words in the assembly of the Kurus, and now he replied to strong-armed Kṛṣṇa Vāsudeva of great renown. 'Keśava, please consider before you speak like this. You single me out for harsh denunciation without reason, slayer of Madhu, because of the Pāṇḍavas' expressions of devotion to you; but do you consider the strengths and weaknesses of both cases before your constant censure? You, the chamberlain Vidura, the king, Droṇa the Teacher and grandfather Bhīṣma all denounce me alone among all the princes; and yet I am not aware that I have committed any offence. All you gentlemen hate me, and so do all the kings, and yet, foe-taming Keśava, however hard I think I cannot bring to mind any wrongdoing, neither extreme nor even trifling.

'Slayer of Madhu, the Pāṇḍavas were happy to start gambling, and Śakuni won their kingdom from them: how am I to blame for this? As for the wealth the Pāṇḍavas lost in that match, I agreed its immediate return to them; and it is no fault of mine, best of victors, that the invincible sons of Kuntī were beaten at dice and exiled to the forest. So what crime is alleged that they should have fallen out with us, their foes? Kṛṣṇa, the Pāṇḍavas are weak, and yet they seem to delight in being our enemies. What have we done? For what sin do the Pāṇḍavas and Sṛñjayas wish to kill the sons of Dhṛtarāṣṭra?

'No fierce word or deed can frighten us or cow us here – not even

1 See 4.66.23 and note.

fear of Indra. And I know of no follower of the Kṣatriya *dharma* who could defeat us in battle, foe-crushing Kṛṣṇa. Slayer of Madhu, not even the gods can defeat Bhīṣma, Kṛpa, Droṇa and their troops in battle; how much less Pāṇḍu's sons? If we follow our *dharma* in battle, heir of Madhu, and in due course meet death by the sword, our gain will be heaven itself. And for us Kṣatriyas, O stirrer of men, our chief *dharma* is indeed to lie on the battlefield on a bed of arrows; so if we achieve a hero's bed in battle without bowing before our enemies, that will be no grief for us! Which of these well born men who live by the Kṣatriya *dharma* would ever bow so in fear before anyone, thinking to save his life?

' "One should strive, one should not submit," said Mātaṅga, "for manliness consists in striving; when evil times come, better even to break than to bend before anyone." These words are prized by men who pursue their own welfare. A man such as I should bow only before *dharma* and before Brahmins, with no thought for anyone else, and should behave so as long as he lives. This is the *dharma* of the Kṣatriyas, and this has always been my own opinion. So as long as I live, Keśava, they will never again get their hands on that share of the kingdom that was formerly agreed by my father. And as long as King Dhṛtarāṣṭra survives, either we or they must lay weapons aside and live in subservience, heir of Madhu. My kingdom cannot be given away. If it was formerly given when I was dependent on others, this was done through ignorance or fear, O stirrer of men, and I was a mere child at the time. Never again, lord of the Vṛṣṇis, will the Pāṇḍavas get their hands on it now! From now on, for as long as I survive, strong-armed Keśava, not even as much land as one might pierce with the tip of a sharp needle will be surrendered by us to the Pāṇḍavas!'

[**126**] Kṛṣṇa the prince of Daśārha laughed. Eyes wild with fury, he addressed these words to Duryodhana in the assembly of the Kurus. 'You shall have your hero's bed – rest assured, you shall have it! Stand firm with your ministers: there will be a mighty battle. Since you believe, fool, that you have committed no offence against the Pāṇḍavas, let these lords of the earth hear the whole tale!

'You were consumed with rage at the noble Pāṇḍavas' good fortune, and so you and Śakuni son of Subala undertook this ill-advised gambling

5 match, heir of Bharata – how else could your kinsmen, superior men
who are honoured by good folk and honest in their dealings, have
joined with a crook in such wickedness? Gambling with dice, my wise
son, brings discontent and destruction even to the virtuous; among the
wicked, it leads to discord and disaster. And so you, along with men of
good deeds but evil outcomes, unthinkingly accomplished this terrible
disaster that started with a gambling match.

'Who else but you could insult the wife of a kinsman, and speak
to her as you spoke to Draupadī after bringing her to the hall? The
Pāṇḍavas' queen is well born, endowed with good character, and more
precious to them than their own lives, and you abused her so!

10 'All the Kurus know how Duḥśāsana addressed Kuntī's sons in the
Kuru assembly when those afflicters of their enemies had to go into
exile. What man of virtue could act in so unworthy a fashion towards
his own kin, men of proper conduct, free from greed and constant
in virtue? The words used again and again by Karṇa, Duḥśāsana and
yourself were the words of cruel men, ignoble and harsh.

'You tried your best to burn them with their mother in Vāraṇāvata
when they were boys, but your efforts were not successful. The Pāṇḍavas
then spent a very long time living in hiding with their mother in a
15 Brahmin's house in Ekacakra. You attempted to destroy them using
poison, snakes[1] and every kind of trick, but your efforts were not
successful.

'This is how you have always thought of the Pāṇḍavas and treated
them falsely, sir; how can you be free of fault towards Pāṇḍu's noble
sons? Many times you have cruelly acted towards them as no one should
act, a false and ignoble man, yet today you make yourself out to be quite
the opposite.

'Time and again peace has been urged on you by your mother and
father, Bhīṣma, Droṇa and Vidura, but you do not make peace, prince.
There would be great gain in peace for both you and Kuntī's son, and
yet it does not please you: what can this be but weakness of judgement?
20 If you act against your friends' advice, king, you will find no safety.
What you are doing is wicked and infamous!'

1 Literally 'snake-contrivances' (*sarpabandhaiś*). See 1.119.36–41.

While the Daśārha prince was addressing these words to resentful
Duryodhana, Duḥśāsana spoke in the assembly of the Kurus. 'King,
if you do not make peace with the Pāṇḍavas of your own free will,
it seems to me that the Kauravas will bind you and hand you over to
Kuntī's son. Bhīṣma, Droṇa and your father will hand the three of us
– Karṇa the Cutter, you and myself – over to the Pāṇḍavas, bull-like
hero!'

When Dhṛtarāṣṭra's son Duryodhana heard his brother's words, he
rose and, hissing like a mighty snake, he strode angrily out, ignoring 25
Vidura, Dhṛtarāṣṭra, the great king Bāhlika, Kṛpa, Somadatta, Bhīṣma,
Droṇa and Kṛṣṇa the stirrer of men. All these the evil-minded, shameless
man ignored, boorishly abandoning all rules of behaviour, a proud man
despising those who deserved his respect. And when his brothers saw
the bull-like man stride out, they and their ministers followed him, and
so did all the kings.

Seeing Duryodhana rise in the assembly and stride out angrily with
his brothers, Bhīṣma son of Śaṃtanu spoke. 'When a man abandons
*dharma* and the proper making of wealth in favour of fury, his enemies
soon laugh at his downfall. This wicked Dhārtarāṣṭra prince is ignorant 30
of right procedure; full of false pride of kingship, he is in thrall to
anger and greed. I think that all these Kṣatriyas are now ripe for death,
O stirrer of men, for in their folly all the princes and their ministers
have followed him.'

Hearing Bhīṣma's words, the heroic prince of Daśārha, lotus-eyed
Kṛṣṇa, addressed all those who remained, headed by Bhīṣma and Droṇa.
'Great is the fault of the Kuru elders, that they do not forcibly restrain
this king who exercises his sovereignty so foolishly. O foe-tamers, I think
the time has come for this, and if it is done, all may yet be well! Listen if
you please, sinless Bhāratas, to the beneficial words I shall speak before 35
you because I am well disposed towards you.

'The old king of the Bhojas had a evildoer of a son, a man without
self-control; seizing the sovereignty from his father while he still lived,
he gave himself over to anger. This man, Kaṃsa son of Ugrasena, was
abandoned by his kinsmen. For the welfare of our relatives I cut him
down in a great battle; then we and our relatives paid honour to Āhuka
Ugrasena, and made him king to bring glory to the Bhoja Kṣatriyas. By

abandoning one man, Kaṃsa, for the sake of the line, all the Yādavas, Andhakas and Vṛṣṇis prospered and throve happily, heir of Bharata.

40 'And when arrays were formed and weapons were brandished in the
war of the gods and demons, the supreme lord Prajāpati spoke, O king; when the worlds were riven and on the point of destruction, heir of Bharata, the blessed god of creation, who had brought those worlds into being, said, "The demons, the Daityas and Dānavas, shall be defeated, and the celestials, the Ādityas, Vasus and Rudras, shall prevail. In this war, gods, demons, men, Gandharvas, serpents and Rākṣasas shall contend together and slay one another." Having come to this conclusion, the supreme lord Prajāpati then addressed Dharma: "Bind these Daityas
45 and Dānavas and hand them over to Varuṇa!" Then on the supreme
lord's instruction, Dharma bound all the Daityas and Dānavas and gave them to Varuṇa; and Varuṇa, the lord of the waters, bound them with Dharma's bonds and with his own, and still he carefully guards those demons in the ocean.

'In the same fashion, you should bind Duryodhana, Karṇa, Śakuni son of Subala and Duḥśāsana, and hand them over to the Pāṇḍavas. "Give up one man for the sake of the family; give up one family for the sake of the village; give up one village for the sake of the kingdom; give up the earth for the sake of yourself!"[1] O king, bind Duryodhana and make peace with the Pāṇḍavas, and the Kṣatriyas shall not perish on your account, bull-like Kṣatriya!'

[**127**] After hearing what Kṛṣṇa had to say, King Dhṛtarāṣṭra hastened to speak to Vidura, expert in *dharma*. 'Brother, go and fetch Gāndhārī here! She is wise and far-sighted, and with her I shall win over my evil-minded son. If she can calm the wicked, scheming prince, we may yet follow the advice of our friend Kṛṣṇa; by speaking appositely she may yet show this fool the way, though he is overwhelmed with
5 greed and surrounded by evil companions. She may be able to allay this
huge and dreadful calamity that Duryodhana is causing us, and bring us unfailing welfare for years to come!'

When Vidura heard King Dhṛtarāṣṭra's words, he obeyed his command and fetched far-sighted Gāndhārī. Then Dhṛtarāṣṭra addressed

1 See 1.107.32 and note.

her: 'Gāndhārī, this wicked son of yours disobeys my commands, and in his greed for sovereignty he is likely to forfeit both sovereignty and life! Boorishly abandoning all rules of behaviour, the fool and his wicked associates have left the assembly, rejecting the advice of their friends.'

Princess Gāndhārī of high repute listened to her husband's words; then, seeking the highest good, she answered, 'Speedily bring him here, this sick-minded son of mine who craves a kingdom! Kingdoms cannot be governed by boors who violate *dharma* and the proper making of wealth. But you yourself are greatly to blame here, Dhṛtarāṣṭra, since in your fondness for your son you followed his judgement, despite knowing his wickedness; so it is that now, gripped by desire and anger, he is pursuing the path of delusion, O king, and you cannot turn him away from it however hard you try. Dhṛtarāṣṭra is receiving his reward for conferring kingship on a wicked, puerile, ill-led, greedy fool.

'How could a man of sense connive at division amongst his own kin? Yet you are divided from your kin, and your enemies will overpower you. Great king, when misfortunes can be overcome by treating one's kinsmen with friendship and generosity, who would choose instead to resort to violence against them?'

Now, commanded by both Dhṛtarāṣṭra and Duryodhana's mother, Vidura the chamberlain brought the resentful Duryodhana back to the assembly. He re-entered the hall to hear his mother's words, eyes copper-red in anger, hissing like a snake. Gāndhārī saw him enter there, her son who had set out on a wrong path, and she spoke apposite words of reproach. 'Duryodhana my boy, listen to what I say: I speak for your welfare and that of your followers, and for your happiness in the future.

'If you make peace, you will show honour to Bhīṣma, your father and me, and also to Droṇa and your other friends. My wise son, a kingdom cannot be gained, maintained, or enjoyed merely by the exercise of one's will! Bull-like heir of Bharata, the undisciplined man will not enjoy a kingdom long; it is the self-controlled, intelligent man who can guard a kingdom. Desire and anger distract a man from his purposes: it is by defeating these two enemies that a king conquers the earth. How the wicked seek this great rank of sovereignty over the lords of the earth; yet they are unable to maintain it, for he who seeks what is great must keep his senses under the control of *dharma* and the proper making of wealth. The senses, when controlled, allow intelligence to prosper as fuel does a fire. But when they are untamed, they can even kill, as untamed, unbroken horses may kill an incompetent charioteer upon the road.

'If a man attempts to master his ministers without first mastering himself, he will fail helplessly, the master of neither self nor ministers. But if first of all he conquers the self as though it were a country, his attempts to master his ministers and his enemies will not be in vain. The man who disciplines his senses, who masters his ministers, who punishes offenders, who acts resolutely and after due deliberation: he is the one whom fortune favours most. Like two monstrous fish held in a fine-meshed net, desire and anger within a man's body will tear his wisdom apart; allowed to thrive, desire and anger put the gods in fear of the man who would follow them, and they seal the entrance to heaven against the heaven-bound man. But the king who truly knows how to conquer desire, anger, greed, hypocrisy and pride can claim the earth for his own. If a king seeks *dharma*, the proper making of wealth, and the overthrow of his enemies, he should be constantly engaged in restraining his senses; but if he is overcome by desire or anger and acts falsely towards his own folk or others, he will have no friends.

'The Pāṇḍavas are united and wise; they are foe-crushing heroes. Joined with them, son, you will enjoy the earth in happiness. What was said by Bhīṣma son of Śaṃtanu and the mighty chariot-fighter Droṇa is the truth: Kṛṣṇa and Pāṇḍu's son Arjuna are invincible. Turn for help now to tireless, strong-armed Kṛṣṇa, for if Keśava is well disposed, he will act for the happiness of both sides.

'When a man rejects the counsel of wise and learned friends who wish him well, he gives joy to his enemies. My son, there is no good in war, no *dharma* and no scope for the proper making of wealth; how can it bring happiness? There is not always even victory. Do not set your heart on war! When Bhīṣma, your father and Bāhlika gave the sons of Pāṇḍu their share, O most wise foe-tamer, it was because they feared discord; and today you see the fruit of that gift, in that you enjoy the entire earth, made safe for you by those heroes! Foe-tamer, give Pāṇḍu's sons what is rightly theirs, if you and your ministers wish to enjoy the allegiance of half of the earth's kings. Half the earth is enough for you and your ministers to live; follow the advice of your friends, heir of Bharata, and win fame!

'The Pāṇḍavas are glorious and self-controlled, intelligent and disciplined. If you fight them, son, you will lose great happiness. Rein 45
in the anger of your friends, and rule your kingdom as you should, granting the sons of Pāṇḍu their share, bull-like heir of Bharata. Day by day you have inflicted humiliation on them for thirteen years: enough! End it now, my wise son, for it thrives on desire and anger. Karṇa, this ever-wrathful Sūta's son who seeks your gain, is no match for the sons of Kuntī, and neither is your brother Duḥśāsana. When rage has taken hold of Bhīṣma, Droṇa and Kṛpa, Karṇa and Bhīma, wealth-winner Arjuna and Dhṛṣṭadyumna, all of your subjects will surely be no more. Son, do not give way to resentment and wipe out the Kurus! The whole of the earth will feel the slaughter caused by you and the Pāṇḍavas. And you are a fool to think that Bhīṣma, Droṇa, Kṛpa and the others 50
will fight with all their might: that will not happen now. For to men of such self-control, considerations of kingship, affection and rank apply equally to you and to the Pāṇḍavas, but *dharma* outweighs all of them; and if they were to sacrifice their lives in battle under the constraint of having accepted King Dhṛtarāṣṭra's bread, they would not be able to look King Yudhiṣṭhira in the eye. In this world, son, we do not see men acquiring riches through greed; so give up your greed and be tranquil, bull-like heir of Bharata!'

[**128**] But the Kaurava ignored these significant words spoken by his mother, and furiously returned to the company of his undisciplined friends; he left the hall and consulted King Śakuni son of Subala, who knew the ways of the dice. And this was the plan agreed by Duryodhana, Karṇa, Subala's son and Duḥśāsana: 'Before Kṛṣṇa, this stirrer of men, can act rapidly with King Dhṛtarāṣṭra and Bhīṣma son of Śaṃtanu to take us captive, we ourselves should capture that lord of the senses by force, 5
just as Indra forcibly captured Virocana's tiger-like son Bali![1] When the Pāṇḍavas hear that Kṛṣṇa the Vṛṣṇi has been seized, they will lose their

1 In most versions of this story it was Viṣṇu in his incarnation as the Dwarf, rather than Indra, who overcame Bali and confined him to the underworld, but references also exist to a direct conflict between Bali and Indra. See also 12.216–18.

spirit and their will, like fangless snakes. For this strong-armed hero is the comfort and strength of all of them, and once the boon-granting bull of all the Sātvatas has been seized, the Pāṇḍavas and Somakas will be stripped of their resolve. So we should bind rapid-acting Keśava here and now – let Dhṛtarāṣṭra cry all he will – and make war upon our enemies!'

Now Sātyaki, who was wise and could read gestures and expressions, soon came to know of the wicked plan of these wicked, scheming men, He therefore set out with Hṛdika's son Kṛtavarman, and told him, 'Muster the army with haste, and wait at the gate of the hall, armed and with troops arrayed, till I can inform tireless Kṛṣṇa of this.'

Heroic Sātyaki entered the hall like a lion entering its mountain cave, and told noble Keśava of the plan; and then he spoke to Dhṛtarāṣṭra and Vidura, informing them of it with the hint of a smile: 'These fools want to commit an act far removed from *dharma* and the proper making of wealth, something virtuous men would denounce – but there is no way they can achieve it! Soon these deluded, wicked idiots, overwhelmed by desire and anger, in thrall to rage and greed, will combine together to try to capture lotus-eyed Kṛṣṇa here, like children or dull-witted men trying to catch a blazing fire in a cloth.'

When far-sighted Vidura heard Sātyaki speak these words, he addressed strong-armed Dhṛtarāṣṭra in the Kuru assembly: 'Enemy-afflicting king, time has run out for all these sons of yours who are preparing to commit an act that is both infamous and impossible. We are told that they want to combine together to overpower lotus-eyed Kṛṣṇa by force and take him captive! This tiger-like hero is unassailable and invincible. If they attack him they will be no more, like moths flying into a flame; for if the stirrer of men wishes, he can dispatch all of them to the realm of Yama as they struggle against him, like a furious lion slaying other beasts. But Kṛṣṇa here would never commit any blameworthy act; the invincible, highest lord would never deviate from *dharma*.'

After Vidura had spoken in this fashion, Kṛṣṇa Keśava fixed his eye upon Dhṛtarāṣṭra, and addressed him while his friends all listened together: 'If these raging men seek to restrain me with might, or I them, then allow it, O king. I could curb them all despite their fury, but I would never commit any wicked or blameworthy act. In their greed for the Pāṇḍavas' possessions, your sons will lose their own; if this is what they want, Yudhiṣṭhira's goal is accomplished! Here and now I could subdue them and those who follow them, heir of Bharata, and hand them over to Kuntī's sons – what would be wrong in this? However, here in your presence I shall not undertake any such blameworthy act at the prompting of anger or wicked reasoning, great king. Let it be as Duryodhana desires: I accept all his terms, heir of Bharata.'

When Dhṛtarāṣṭra heard this, he said to Vidura, 'Quickly bring here this wicked Duryodhana who so covets the kingdom, together with his friends and ministers, his brothers and followers! Perhaps I may be able to set him on the right path.' So Vidura the chamberlain brought the reluctant Duryodhana back to the assembly again, accompanied by his brothers and in the midst of all the kings. Then King Dhṛtarāṣṭra spoke to Duryodhana, surrounded as he was by Karṇa, Duḥśāsana and those kings: 'You cruel man, devoted to wickedness and associated with people of base conduct! You have conspired with your wicked associates to attempt a wicked deed, an act both impossible and infamous, that virtuous folk would denounce, something that only a fool such as you would embark on to defile his lineage! I am told that you have conspired with your wicked associates to capture lotus-eyed Kṛṣṇa here, who is unassailable and invincible. Even the gods under Indra could not overpower him, but you are so stupid that you want to seize him, like a child who wants the moon! You do not know Keśava: he cannot be withstood in battle by gods or men, Gandharvas, demons or serpents. You cannot seize the wind with your hand, you cannot touch the moon with your hand, you cannot support the earth on your head, and you cannot seize Keśava by force!'

When Dhṛtarāṣṭra had finished speaking, Vidura the chamberlain fixed his eye upon the king's resentful son Duryodhana, and said, 'The monkey king named Dvivida[1] once covered Keśava with a huge shower of rocks at the gate of Saubha; with every effort he battled to take Madhu's heir captive, but he could not capture him. This is the man you want to seize by force! At Nirmocana, six thousand mighty demons

1 Dvivida was one of the monkeys who took Rāma's side in the *Rāmāyaṇa*; the story of his attempt to capture Kṛṣṇa seems not to appear elsewhere.

bound him with bonds, but they could not capture him. This is the
man you want to seize by force! At Prāgjyotiṣa, Naraka and his Dānavas
could not capture Kṛṣṇa Vāsudeva. This is the man you want to seize
45 by force! In childhood too, the infant Kṛṣṇa slew Pūtanā,[1] and he held
up Mount Govardhana to protect the cows,[2] bull-like heir of Bharata.
He slew Ariṣṭa, Dhenuka and mighty Cāṇūra, Aśvarāja and Kaṃsa the
evildoer, Jarāsaṃdha, Vakra, the heroic Śiśupāla and Bāṇa; many kings
he has slain in battle. He triumphed over King Varuṇa and Agni the
god of Fire, both boundlessly powerful, and he defeated Indra himself
when he stole his coral tree.[3] As he lay upon the one great ocean he
slew Madhu and Kaiṭabha,[4] and in a later birth he also slew Hayagrīva.
50 He is the maker, but he is not made; he is the cause of all human effort.
Whatever Vāsudeva desires he achieves without exertion. You do not
know Kṛṣṇa Govinda, the invincible, terrible in valour like an angry
snake of deadly venom, an unconquered mass of fiery energy! If you
assail tireless, strong-armed Kṛṣṇa, then, like a moth flying into a flame,
you and your ministers will be no more.'

[**129**] After Vidura had spoken, heroic Kṛṣṇa Keśava, the slayer of
enemy hosts, addressed Dhṛtarāṣṭra's son. 'Foolish Duryodhana, you
mistakenly believe that I am alone, and so you hope to overpower me
and take me captive. But here before you are all the Pāṇḍavas, and
the Andhakas and Vṛṣṇis too; here are the Ādityas, Rudras and Vasus,
along with the great seers!' With these words Keśava the slayer of
enemy heroes laughed aloud; and as noble Vāsudeva laughed, the gods
themselves issued forth from his body, fiery, lightning-bright, each no
5 larger than a thumb. On his forehead was Brahmā, on his breast Rudra;
the world-guardian gods appeared on his arms, and Agni emerged from
his mouth; the Ādityas were there, and the Sādhyas, Vasus and Aśvins,
likewise the Maruts with Indra, and the All-gods; Yakṣas, Gandharvas

**1** A female Rākṣasa who tried to kill him by suckling him at her poisoned breast.

**2** Kṛṣṇa held this mountain aloft for seven days with his little finger to shelter the people and cattle of Vṛndāvana from storms sent by Indra.

**3** The *pārijāta* was one of five trees produced at the churning of the ocean of milk (see 1.15–17) and taken by Indra to heaven; Kṛṣṇa stole it from him.

**4** See 3.194.

and Rākṣasas could also be seen. On two of his forearms there appeared Balarāma and the wealth-winner: to the right was Arjuna with his bow, and to the left Balarāma with his plough. At Kṛṣṇa's back were Bhīma, Yudhiṣṭhira and the two sons of Mādrī, while the Andhakas and Vṛṣṇis led by Pradyumna brandished their mighty weapons at his front. In Kṛṣṇa's many hands could be seen all his own weapons, blazing as he brandished them: his conch, discus and club, his spear, bow and plough, and Nandaka his sword. From his eyes, nose and ears fiery flames issued forth in every direction, smoking most fearfully, while rays of light like sunbeams shone from the pores of his skin.

When the kings saw this terrible form of noble Keśava, they closed their eyes in their fear, save for Droṇa, Bhīṣma, sagacious Vidura, noble Saṃjaya and the ascetic seers; to them the blessed stirrer of men had granted divine vision. And at the sight of this great marvel performed by Madhu's heir on the floor of the hall, heavenly drums sounded and a shower of flowers fell; the whole earth shook, and the ocean was convulsed. Heir of Bharata, the princes were utterly astounded.

Then the foe-taming, tiger-like hero withdrew that form of his, that wonderful, brilliant, divine perfection; and taking Sātyaki and Hṛdika's son Kṛtavarman by the hand, the slayer of Madhu took leave of the seers and left. Then in the midst of the uproar that had broken out, Nārada and the other seers also vanished and went their ways, which was a great wonder. The Kauravas and the kings, seeing that Kṛṣṇa had set out, followed the tiger-like hero, as the gods follow Indra of a hundred sacrifices; but Vāsudeva of immeasurable greatness paid no heed to that whole group of kings, and strode forth like a smoking fire.

Now Dāruka appeared with Kṛṣṇa's great chariot: it was bright, decked with small bells, splendid with lavish gold, swift, and loud as thunder; full of fine gear, it was covered by a brilliant tiger-skin and surrounded by a guard-rail, and to it were harnessed Sainya and Sugrīva. The mighty chariot-fighter Kṛtavarman son of Hṛdika, a hero much honoured among the Vṛṣṇis, now likewise appeared mounted on his chariot. Foe-taming Vāsudeva had his chariot ready to leave, when the great king Dhṛtarāṣṭra addressed him one more time. 'You see, stirrer of men, how much power I have over my sons; all is known to you, tormentor of your enemies, nothing is hidden. Please do not harbour suspicions of me; what I desire and strive for is peace among the Kurus, but you have seen the state in which I find myself. I have no evil intentions towards the Pāṇḍavas, Keśava – you heard the words I spoke to Duryodhana. The Kurus and the kings of the earth all know that I have made every effort to strive for peace, heir of Madhu!'

Then strong-armed Kṛṣṇa spoke to King Dhṛtarāṣṭra, Droṇa, grand-
30 father Bhīṣma, the chamberlain, Bāhlika and Kṛpa: 'Gentlemen, you have seen what happened in the Kuru assembly: how a boorish fool repeatedly rose to leave in anger. However, King Dhṛtarāṣṭra declares himself powerless. I beg leave of you all; I shall return to Yudhiṣṭhira.' With these words the bull-like hero Vāsudeva set out on his chariot, followed by mighty bowmen and heroes among the Bhāratas: Bhīṣma, Droṇa, Kṛpa, the chamberlain, Dhṛtarāṣṭra, Bāhlika, Aśvatthāman, Vikarṇa and the mighty chariot-fighter Yuyutsu. And even as the Kurus watched, he left in his great, bright chariot decked with bells to see his father's sister Kuntī.

[130] *Kṛṣṇa tells Kuntī of Duryodhana's refusal to make peace, and asks what word to take to the Pāṇḍavas. In reply, she gives him a message for Yudhiṣṭhira: he should maintain his royal* dharma.

## THE INSTRUCTION OF VIDURĀ'S SON

[131] *Kuntī cites the story of Vidurā and her son. — The Kṣatriya lady Vidurā scolds her son Saṃjaya, who is lying in misery after a defeat by the king of Sindhu. She urges him to get up and show courage,* [132] *telling him to live up to his name ('Victory'). The family has fallen upon hard times; he must follow the Kṣatriya code and slay his enemies.* [133] *Saṃjaya complains at his mother's harsh words; she continues to urge him to do battle and gain victory. He argues that he does not have the resources to fight; she insists that he must act,* [134] *tells him to show no fear, and reveals the existence of hidden wealth. Saṃjaya is stirred to action by her words, and achieves all that she has told him to do.*

**[135]** — *Now Kuntī gives Kṛṣṇa messages for Arjuna, Bhīma, Draupadī and the twins. Kṛṣṇa leaves and sets out in his chariot. Karṇa travels with him for some distance, and the two men have a long discussion.*

**[136]** *Bhīṣma and Droṇa make another attempt to persuade Duryodhana to make peace with the Pāṇḍavas, pointing out that there are many unfavourable portents.* **[137]** *Duryodhana appears downcast, but says nothing. Bhīṣma and Droṇa continue to speak against war.*

## PERSUADING KARṆA

**[138]** *Dhṛtarāṣṭra asks Saṃjaya what Kṛṣṇa said to Karṇa as they rode together in Kṛṣṇa's chariot, and Saṃjaya describes the conversation to him. — Kṛṣṇa tells Karṇa that his birth makes him the eldest of the Pāṇḍavas, and offers him the kingship. His five younger brothers and their sons and supporters will all joyfully acknowledge his sovereignty.*

**[139]** *Karṇa answers that though he is Kuntī's son, and thus a Pāṇḍava, he was abandoned by his mother; his true parents are Adhiratha and Rādhā, who took him in and brought him up.*[1] *Duryodhana too has treated him with favour, and he cannot now change his allegiance. Kṛṣṇa must not let Yudhiṣṭhira know Karṇa's story, since he would then reject the kingship, and Karṇa would hand it to Duryodhana. Instead, Yudhiṣṭhira will triumph; the coming battle will be a great sacrifice of Kṣatriyas officiated over by the Pāṇḍavas, and it is Karṇa's prayer that those who die will gain heaven.*

**[140]** *Kṛṣṇa smiles to hear Karṇa's refusal, and remarks that the Pāṇḍavas are certain of victory. The coming battle will usher in the Kali Age. He tells Karṇa to arrange for it to begin on the coming day of the new moon, and assures him that all who die fighting will reach heaven.* **[141]** *Karṇa says that all portents indicate disaster for the Kauravas, and that he has dreamed of Yudhiṣṭhira's victory. He expects that he will next meet Kṛṣṇa in heaven. The two men embrace and part.*

**[142]** — *After the failure of Kṛṣṇa's mission, Vidura tells Kuntī of his fears*

1 This is strange: Karṇa has never been told the story of his birth, which was previously referred to by the Sun as a secret that he could not yet know (3.285.9, 3.287–92). The encounter with Kuntī in 5.142–4 reads like the expected revelation scene, and the present sequence in which Kṛṣṇa tries to persuade Karṇa seems like a (rather clumsy) later insertion.

*for the future. She agrees that no good can come of the approaching war, and says that she will try to change Karṇa's mind, since she is in fact his mother. She goes to the bank of the Gaṅgā, where Karṇa is praying to the Sun,* **[143]** *and tells him that he is her son, not a Sūta; then she invites him to take up his rightful position as eldest among the Pāṇḍavas.*

**[144]** *The Sun speaks to confirm the truth of Kuntī's words and to urge Karṇa to act as she suggests. But Karṇa will not change sides, for he says that Kuntī has never behaved to him like a mother, and his allegiance is to the Kauravas. He does promise Kuntī that he will not kill Yudhiṣṭhira, Bhīma, Nakula or Sahadeva. However, either he will kill Arjuna or Arjuna will kill him; thus Kuntī will still have five sons.*

**[145]** *Meanwhile Kṛṣṇa returns to the Pāṇḍavas in Upaplavya. He informs them that Duryodhana has rejected his counsel, and Yudhiṣṭhira asks how the senior Kauravas reacted to this. In answer, Kṛṣṇa says that Bhīṣma narrated the recent history of the Kuru line up to Pāṇḍu's succession, emphasizing the validity of the Pāṇḍavas' claims and urging Duryodhana to give them half the kingdom.* **[146]** *Then Droṇa continued Bhīṣma's narrative by describing how Dhṛtarāṣṭra received the kingship from Pāṇḍu; he counselled Duryodhana to follow Bhīṣma's advice. After Droṇa had spoken, Vidura pleaded with Bhīṣma to act to prevent the coming calamity, and Gāndhārī spoke of the justness of Yudhiṣṭhira's cause.*

**[147]** *Kṛṣṇa continues with an account of Dhṛtarāṣṭra's words: he reminded Duryodhana of figures from earlier history who had been disinherited for one reason or another despite being the eldest son, just as happened to himself. Then he appealed to Duryodhana to give half the kingdom to the Pāṇḍavas.*

**[148]** *Kṛṣṇa concludes his report by describing how Duryodhana took no notice of all these pleas, but simply ordered preparations to be made for battle. He tells Yudhiṣṭhira that he himself made further efforts to avert war by conciliation, threat and inducement, but without success. Now the only course of action is to punish the wrongdoers with death on the battlefield.*

## MARCHING TO WAR

**[149]** *Yudhiṣṭhira gives orders for the disposition of his troops. He has seven armies, led by seven great generals, and he asks his brothers which of them* *should be the commander in overall charge. Sahadeva opts for Virāṭa, Nakula for Drupada, Arjuna for Dhṛṣṭadyumna, and Bhīma for Śikhaṇḍin. Yudhiṣṭhira himself decides to leave the choice to Kṛṣṇa. Kṛṣṇa agrees that any one of the generals would be equal the task, and urges that the troops be arrayed for battle: war is inevitable, and victory certain. They march forth, leaving Draupadī in Upaplavya, and encamp in Kurukṣetra.*

[150] *Meanwhile, Duryodhana too gives the command for preparations to be made for war, and announces that they will march the next day.*

[151] *Yudhiṣṭhira questions Kṛṣṇa once again about Duryodhana's response to his mission. Kṛṣṇa answers that Duryodhana heeded neither him nor Bhīṣma and Vidura, listening only to Śakuni, Karṇa and Duḥśāsana. War must follow. Yudhiṣṭhira orders the troops to be arrayed for battle, though he remains deeply unhappy at the prospect of fighting his revered elders.*

[152] *The next morning, Duryodhana orders the disposition of his eleven armies. He has a vast force, splendidly equipped.*

## THE INSTALLATION OF BHĪṢMA

[153] *Duryodhana approaches Bhīṣma and asks him to accept overall command of the Kaurava forces. Bhīṣma agrees to do so on the condition that either he or Karṇa will be the first to fight. Karṇa responds by swearing that he will not fight while Bhīṣma lives. Duryodhana now installs Bhīṣma as commander; there are grim portents. Now the Kauravas march out and encamp in Kurukṣetra.*

[154] *When Yudhiṣṭhira learns that Bhīṣma has been appointed to the command of the Kauravas, he asks Kṛṣṇa to assemble the generals of the various armies fighting for the Pāṇḍavas. They come before him, and he installs Dhṛṣṭadyumna as his commander. Balarāma arrives; he announces that he cannot bear to see the coming destruction, and is therefore going on a pilgrimage to the sacred bathing-places on the river Sarasvatī.*

[155] *Now Rukmin, the mighty Bhoja king and wielder of the bow Vijaya, arrives together with his great army. Still smarting from Kṛṣṇa's abduction of his sister Rukmiṇī and his subsequent defeat at Kṛṣṇa's hands, he offers his assistance to the Pāṇḍavas, claiming that if Arjuna is overcome by fear on the battlefield he will kill his foes for him. Arjuna laughs at him; he then goes to Duryodhana and makes him a similar offer which is similarly rejected.*

[156] *Dhṛtarāṣṭra requests Saṃjaya to tell him everything that happens in the coming conflict. Saṃjaya agrees to do so.*

## ULŪKA'S MISSION

[157] *Saṃjaya begins his narration to Dhṛtarāṣṭra. — Duryodhana sends Śakuni's son Ulūka to the Pāṇḍavas to deliver a taunting message.* [158] *Ulūka comes before the Pāṇḍavas and delivers Duryodhana's taunts;* [159] *the Pāṇḍavas are enraged. Seeing that Bhīma is barely able to contain himself, Kṛṣṇa advises Ulūka to leave quickly and inform Duryodhana that he has carried out his task, and he adds a further message from himself warning Duryodhana that he faces destruction at the hands of the Pāṇḍavas.* [160] *Arjuna adds his own message to Duryodhana: he will slay Bhīṣma. Ulūka returns to Duryodhana and tells him what has been said; Duryodhana orders his troops to be arrayed for battle.*

## THE REVIEW OF THE MAJOR AND MINOR WARRIORS

[161] *At Yudhiṣṭhira's command, Dhṛṣṭadyumna leads the Pāṇḍava forces out. He assigns to each of his own chief warriors a named Kaurava opponent.*

[162] *— Dhṛtarāṣṭra asks Saṃjaya what Bhīṣma did after his installation as commander, and Saṃjaya relates everything to him. — Bhīṣma tells Duryodhana to put aside fear and to trust in his knowledge and experience. Duryodhana asks Bhīṣma to name the major and minor warriors in the Kaurava force. Bhīṣma proceeds to list them, commenting on the merits of each one: Duryodhana and his brothers, Bhīṣma himself, Kṛtavarman, Śalya, Bhūriśravas, Jayadratha;* [163] *Sudakṣiṇa, Nīla, Vinda and Anuvinda, the five Trigarta brothers, Duryodhana's son Lakṣmaṇa and Duḥśāsana's son, Daṇḍadhāra, Bṛhadbala, Kṛpa;* [164] *Śakuni and Aśvatthāman – for all Aśvatthāman's prowess Bhīṣma does not think highly of him – Droṇa, Paurava, Karṇa's son Vṛṣasena, Jalasaṃdha, Bāhlika, the Rākṣasa king Alāyudha, Bhagadatta;* [165] *the brothers Acala and Vṛṣaka, and Karṇa – Bhīṣma says that he considers Karṇa worth no more than half a warrior.*

*Droṇa agrees, and Karṇa is enraged. He urges Duryodhana to rid himself of*

*Bhīṣma, whom he accuses of trying to sow dissent in the army, and vows that he will not fight until Bhīṣma is dead.* [**166**] *Now Bhīṣma becomes furious, and rounds on Karṇa. Duryodhana calms him and asks him now to name the major and minor warriors in the Pāṇḍava force. Bhīṣma speaks of Yudhiṣṭhira, Bhīma, whom he reckons worth eight warriors, and the twins. Then he describes Arjuna's incomparable skills as a fighter. The assembled kings become dejected.*

[**167**] *Bhīṣma continues his review of the Pāṇḍava force: Draupadī's sons, Virāṭa's son Uttara, Abhimanyu, Sātyaki, Uttamaujas, Yudhāmanyu, Virāṭa, Drupada;* [**168**] *Śikhaṇḍin, Dhṛṣṭadyumna, Dhṛṣṭadyumna's son Kṣatradharman, Dhṛṣṭaketu, Śikhaṇḍin's son Kṣatradeva, the Pāñcāla and Kekaya kings, and others of the Pāṇḍavas' allies;* [**169**] *Rocamāna and Purujit, and Bhīma's Rākṣasa son Ghaṭotkaca. Bhīṣma says that he will do battle against all the warriors whom he has named, save for Śikhaṇḍin, who was previously a woman.*

## AMBĀ

[**170**] *Duryodhana asks Bhīṣma to tell the reason why he will not kill Śikhaṇḍin, and Bhīṣma narrates the story. — After the death of his father Śaṃtanu, Bhīṣma consecrates his half-brother Citrāṅgada as king, and when Citrāṅgada dies he consecrates his younger brother Vicitravīrya. Anxious to secure a bride for him, Bhīṣma then attends the* svayaṃvara *of the three princesses of Kāśi, Ambā, Ambikā and Ambālikā. In front of all the assembled kings he abducts the three girls on his chariot, challenging anyone to stop him. He easily beats off their attack, and carries the princesses to Vicitravīrya in Hāstinapura.*

[**171**] *The wedding has been arranged when Ambā, the eldest princess, tells Bhīṣma that she is already betrothed to King Śālva,*[1] *and asks him to release her.* [**172**] *He does so, and she travels to Śālva, but the king rejects her because of her abduction by Bhīṣma. She pleads with him, but he is unyielding. He tells her to return to Bhīṣma.*

[**173**] *Determined to have her revenge on Bhīṣma, Ambā consults some ascetics, requesting them to instruct her in the performance of austerities.* [**174**] *The ascetics advise her to return to her father, but she is not willing to do so. At this point*

1 Not the demonic king of the flying city of Saubha killed by Kṛṣṇa at 3.23, but a human king of the same name ruling a terrestrial city of the same name.

*her grandfather, the royal seer Hotravāhana, arrives; he tells her to visit Rāma Jāmadagnya, who will help her.*

**[175]** *Now Rāma's friend Akṛtavraṇa appears, bearing Rāma's greetings to Hotravāhana. Hotravāhana tells him Ambā's story, and Ambā adds that she intends to take her grievance to Rāma.* **[176]** *Akṛtavraṇa asks whether Ambā's grievance is against Bhīṣma or against Śālva; she asks him to judge which of them is to blame, and he names Bhīṣma. She says that she wants Bhīṣma killed in battle. Rāma arrives, and, when the greetings are done, Ambā is introduced to him. He hears her story and agrees to help her by persuading either Bhīṣma or Śālva to change their conduct, but she insists that what she desires is Bhīṣma's death.*

**[177]** *Rāma says that he will only fight at the request of a Brahmin; Ambā continues to insist that he kill Bhīṣma. Akṛtavraṇa reminds Rāma that he had once sworn to slay any Kṣatriya who defeated all the other Kṣatriyas together; this Bhīṣma has done. Rāma now agrees that if he cannot persuade Bhīṣma he will fight him. He sets off in search of Bhīṣma,* **[178]** *then sends a message to him. Bhīṣma at once travels to see him. Rāma tells Bhīṣma to take Ambā for himself, but Bhīṣma refuses; he agrees to fight Rāma at Kurukṣetra.*

**[179]** *Bhīṣma obtains the blessing of his stepmother Satyavatī and then sets out majestically for Kurukṣetra. Here his mother the river Gaṅgā appears in human form and tries to prevent the fight, but neither combatant will withdraw.*

**[180]** *Bhīṣma tells Rāma that he must fight from a chariot, and Rāma appears in a celestial chariot driven by Akṛtavraṇa. After the initial formalities, battle begins. The two men shower each other with arrows and wound each other badly; Rāma swoons, and Bhīṣma, bitterly regretful at having hurt his teacher, ceases fighting. The sun sets.*

**[181]** *Next morning the battle resumes. Once again Rāma and Bhīṣma shower one another with arrows; then both resort to celestial weapons. Bhīṣma is rendered unconscious, and his charioteer bears him away from the battle, but then he recovers and returns to the fight. He fells Rāma with the Fire Weapon, but Rāma too recovers. The two continue to fight until sunset.*

**[182]** *The fighting continues the next day. Rāma hurls a variety of terrible weapons at Bhīṣma, but Bhīṣma succeeds in warding them off and showers Rāma with arrows. Rāma responds with a celestial weapon that covers Bhīṣma and his chariot with darts; Bhīṣma pierces Rāma with yet more arrows. Both men are badly wounded when sunset brings their combat to an end.*

[**183**] *In the morning Rāma and Bhīṣma resume their fight. Rāma's arrows kill Bhīṣma's charioteer and then fell Bhīṣma himself, to the joy of Rāma and his followers. Bhīṣma is tended by eight Brahmins; he regains consciousness to see that his mother Gaṅgā has taken charge of his chariot. He tells her to go and takes control of it himself, then fells Rāma with an arrow. Bad portents appear, but nightfall ends the day's battle. The next day it resumes, and it continues for twenty-three days.*

[**184**] *At night Bhīṣma prays for the gods to show him how to defeat Rāma. Then in a dream he sees the eight Brahmins who had tended him; they assure him that he is under their protection, and advise him to make use of the Sleepmaking Weapon.*

[**185**] *The battle continues the next morning. After a fierce exchange of arrows, Rāma attacks Bhīṣma with the Weapon of Brahmā; Bhīṣma counteracts it with a second Weapon of Brahmā, and the two Weapons collide, provoking a cataclysmic fire. Bhīṣma now prepares to use the Sleepmaking Weapon,* [**186**] *but Nārada tells him that the gods do not want him to use it, and the eight Brahmins concur. Bhīṣma withdraws the Weapon. Rāma's ancestors now come and urge him to cease the fight, but he refuses; Nārada and a group of ascetics likewise urge Bhīṣma to stop fighting, but he too refuses to do so. In the end, Rāma's ancestors compel him to lay down his Weapon. At the bidding of the eight Brahmins, Bhīṣma approaches Rāma; the two are reconciled. Now Rāma summons Ambā.*

[**187**] *Rāma tells Ambā that he can do no more for her, and advises her to seek Bhīṣma's protection, but she refuses. Rāma leaves, and Bhīṣma returns to the city and tells his mother what has happened. He has spies report on Ambā's doings. What he learns worries him greatly: she resorts to extreme austerities at various sacred places. Gaṅgā visits her and asks what she hopes to achieve, and Ambā replies that she wishes to be reborn in order to destroy Bhīṣma. To protect her son, Gaṅgā curses her: if she is reborn, it will be as an ill-favoured river. But Ambā persists with her austerities. In the course of time she becomes the river Ambā in Vatsabhūmi with one half of her body; but through her ascetic merit she remains a young woman with the other half.*

[**188**] *Ambā continues her austerities until Śiva appears and grants her a boon. She chooses to defeat Bhīṣma, and Śiva tells her that she will kill him after being reborn as a great warrior in King Drupada's line. Ambā now makes a pyre and burns herself on it, vowing Bhīṣma's destruction.*

[**189**] *Meanwhile, Drupada, childless, requests a son from Śiva to avenge*

*himself on Bhīṣma.*[1] *Śiva grants him a daughter who will become a son. His queen gives birth to a girl; they bring her up as a boy named Śikhaṇḍin.*

**[190]** *When Drupada's daughter Śikhaṇḍinī grows up he worries what to do with her; his wife advises him to trust in Śiva's promise and find a wife for the girl. Drupada marries Śikhaṇḍinī to the princess of Daśārṇa; soon the deception comes to light, and the Daśārṇa king, Hiraṇyavarman, sends a furious message to Drupada threatening to kill him and all his family.*

**[191]** *Drupada attempts to conciliate Hiraṇyavarman, and consults his queen, claiming to have acted in ignorance of his child's true sex.* **[192]** *The queen accepts responsibility for the deception. Drupada informs his ministers of the true state of affairs and has the city prepared against attack. Full of shame, Śikhaṇḍinī enters a forest and fasts. The Yakṣa Sthūṇākarṇa offers her a boon; she asks to become a man.*

**[193]** *Sthūṇākarṇa agrees to a temporary exchange of sexes with Śikhaṇḍinī; once the king of Daśārṇa has been appeased they will exchange back again. Śikhaṇḍin now returns to the city with the good news. Hiraṇyavarman's envoy arrives to challenge Drupada to battle; Drupada sends his own envoy back to Hiraṇyavarman inviting him to have Śikhaṇḍin's maleness verified. Hiraṇyavarman sends young women to do so; they report that he is indeed a man, and Hiraṇyavarman joyfully resumes his friendship with Drupada. Meanwhile Kubera*[2] *comes to visit Sthūṇākarṇa, who hides from him; when Kubera learns from his attendants what has happened, he curses him to remain a woman for ever. The other Yakṣas plead with him to mitigate the curse, and he agrees that Sthūṇākarṇa will regain his own sex once Śikhaṇḍin has died in battle. When Śikhaṇḍin comes to honour his agreement with Sthūṇākarṇa, Sthūṇākarṇa tells him of the curse, and he returns home in joy. Under Droṇa's tuition he becomes a great warrior. — Bhīṣma concludes the narrative by repeating that he will not fight Śikhaṇḍin, since he was once a woman.*

**[194]** *Duryodhana asks how long it would take Bhīṣma to wipe out the forces of the Pāṇḍavas, and how long it would take Droṇa, Kṛpa, Karṇa or Aśvatthāman. Bhīṣma answers that he could do it in one month. Droṇa gives*

**1** In his translation, J. A. B. van Buitenen (p. 555) correctly notes that 'as there is no particular reason for Drupada to hate Bhīṣma, this is probably borrowed from Drupada's effort to beget a son to kill Droṇa: [1.128,] 1.155'.

**2** The god of the Yakṣas.

*the same answer. Kṛpa says that he would need two months, Aśvatthāman that he could destroy the Pāṇḍava forces in ten days. Then Karṇa claims to be able to achieve this in five days, and Bhīṣma laughs scornfully at him.*

**[195]** *When Yudhiṣṭhira hears of this exchange he asks Arjuna how long it would take him to wipe out the forces of the Kauravas. Arjuna replies that with his Pāśupata Weapon he could do so instantaneously, but that this would not be proper. However, the Pāṇḍavas and their allies are mighty warriors, and they will prevail.*

**[196]** *The Kaurava forces march forth and encamp in the West of Kurukṣetra.* **[197]** *The Pāṇḍava forces too march out.*

# BHĪṢMA

## THE CREATION OF THE CONTINENT OF JAMBŪ

Janamejaya spoke:
[1] How did those heroes fight, the Kauravas, Pāṇḍavas and Somakas,[1] and the noble princes who had come together from many countries?

Vaiśaṃpāyana spoke:
Hear, lord of the earth, how those heroes, the Kauravas, Pāṇḍavas and Somakas, fought on Kurukṣetra, that place of asceticism. The mighty Pāṇḍavas came to Kurukṣetra with the Somakas and advanced against the Kauravas, for they were eager for victory. Accomplished Vedic scholars all, they revelled in warfare, hoping for victory in combat, but prepared for death on the battlefield.

5 Advancing towards the unconquerable army of Dhṛtarāṣṭra's son Duryodhana, they encamped with their troops on the western side, facing East. Kuntī's son Yudhiṣṭhira had tents by the thousand erected in the proper manner beyond Samantapañcaka. It seemed as if the whole earth had been emptied, stripped of men and horses, chariots and elephants, leaving only the children and the elderly behind; for the force which had assembled was as great as the area of Jambūdvīpa[2] on which the sun shines, truest of princes. Men of every complexion, they overspread an area of many leagues with all its provinces and rivers,

1 Strictly a subgroup of the Pāñcālas, but often used to refer to the Pāñcālas as a whole.
2 One of the great continents of earth: see chapters 6–11 below.

mountains and forests. Bull-like hero, King Yudhiṣṭhira commanded foodstuffs of every kind for them and their beasts, and established for them a variety of passwords to identify the speaker as an ally of the Pāṇḍavas; as the time for battle approached, Kuru's heir also equipped them all with tokens of recognition, both *noms de guerre* and insignia.

When Dhṛtarāṣṭra's high-minded son saw the massed standards of the Pāṇḍavas, he and all the allied kings drew up their array against the Pāṇḍavas. The Pāṇḍava warriors rejoiced to see Duryodhana in the midst of a thousand elephants, surrounded by his brothers and with a white umbrella held over his head. They blew their great conches and beat kettledrums in thousands; and the Pāṇḍavas and brave Kṛṣṇa Vāsudeva were delighted in their hearts to see their troops so full of joy. Then the tiger-like heroes Kṛṣṇa and Arjuna stood on their chariot and blew their divine conches to inspire their troops; but the Kaurava warriors and their beasts pissed and shat themselves when they heard the combined sound of Pāñcajanya and Devadatta. When other creatures hear the sound of a lion roaring, they are filled with fear; so it was with Duryodhana's army at that time.

Dust was stirred up from the ground, until nothing could be made out – the sun itself disappeared, enveloped in the dust of the armies – and rain-clouds poured showers of flesh and blood, drenching all the troops, which was a great wonder. Then a wind arose; close to the ground it was full of small stones with which it pelted the troops, but it dispersed the dust.

The two armies stood prepared on Kurukṣetra then, O king, like two heaving oceans, full of great joy to be going to war; the meeting of those two forces was wonderful, like that of two oceans at doomsday. The whole earth had been emptied by the Kurus' mustering of those armies, leaving only the children and the elderly behind.

Next the Kauravas, Pāṇḍavas and Somakas agreed terms and established rules of engagement, O bull-like heir of Bharata: that on cessation of hostilities mutual goodwill should be duly restored as formerly, with no further resort to guile; that if a verbal attack were made, any counter-attack must also be purely verbal; that one who had withdrawn from the midst of the battle must under no circumstances be killed; that chariot-fighter should be matched against chariot-fighter, elephant-rider against

elephant, horseman against horse, footsoldier against footsoldier only,
30 heir of Bharata; that blows should be struck with regard for propriety, courage, strength and age, and after issuing a challenge, but never against someone unsuspecting or in distress; that if anyone were engaged in fighting another, or were distracted or facing away, or had lost weapon or shield, he must under no circumstances be killed; likewise that heralds, guides, weapon-bearers, drummers and conch-blowers should not be struck under any circumstances. Having agreed these terms, the Kauravas, Pāṇḍavas and Somakas gazed at each other in profound amazement. Then the noble, bull-like heroes took up their places; they and their troops alike were glad at heart and full of joy.

[**2**] Now as the dreadful battle approached, the blessed seer Vyāsa who was watching by dawn and by dusk, Satyavatī's son, best of experts in the Veda, the all-seeing grandfather of the Bhāratas who knew past, present and future, spoke privately to King Dhṛtarāṣṭra son of Vicitravīrya as he grieved in torment and considered his sons' wicked ways:

'O king, time has run out for your sons and the other lords of the
5 earth; they will meet in battle and slay one another. As their time runs out and they perish, heir of Bharata, remember that time will take its course and do not give your heart over to grief. But if you wish to see it come to pass in the battle, lord of the peoples, let me grant you sight; observe this war!'

'Truest of Brahmin seers,' answered Dhṛtarāṣṭra, 'I have no wish to see the killing of my kinsmen. But through your fiery energy may I hear in full about this war.'

Since he did not wish to see the battle but wished to hear about it, generous Vyāsa, lord of boons, granted a boon to Saṃjaya: 'O king, Saṃjaya here will describe this war to you; everything that comes to
10 pass in the battle will be visible to him. And, equipped with this divine sight, O king, Saṃjaya will relate the war to you. He will know it all; overt or covert, occurring by day or by night, Saṃjaya will know everything, even what people are thinking in their hearts. Weapons will not harm him, fatigue will not trouble him; this son of Gavalgaṇa will emerge living from the warfare. O bull-like heir of Bharata, I too shall spread the fame of these Kauravas, and of all the Pāṇḍavas. Do not grieve! This was destined long ago, and you should not grieve

over it: it could not have been prevented. Where *dharma* is, there is victory!'

After speaking these words, the blessed grandfather of the Kurus addressed strong-armed Dhṛtarāṣṭra once more: 'O king, in this war there will be great destruction, for today I see these portents of danger. Hawks, vultures, crows and storks, as well as jungle crows, are flocking in multitudes on the edges of forests; these carrion birds are delighted, for they foresee a savage conflict in which they will feed on the flesh of elephants and horses. With their cry of "Khaṭākhaṭā!", cranes, terrible heralds of danger, are flying high overhead towards the South. Every day, both by dawn and by dusk, heir of Bharata, I see that the sun as it rises and sets is obscured by clouds shaped like headless bodies;[1] three-coloured, with red and white edges and black necks, and flashing with lightning, these bars of cloud cover the sun at twilight. I have seen that the sun, the moon and the stars all blaze by day and by night, so that night cannot be distinguished from day; this betokens destruction. During the full-moon night of the month of Kārttika the light of the moon was so faint that it could not be seen, for it was the colour of fire, and the sky was the same colour.

'Brave princes, kings and the sons of kings, heroes with arms like iron bars, will lie slain, covering the earth! Every day I hear at night a dreadful sound in the sky, as if a hog and a cat were fighting.[2] Images of deities tremble and laugh; they vomit blood from their mouths, sweat, and fall to the ground. Drums sound without being struck, lord of the peoples, and the great chariots of Kṣatriyas roll forward without horses to draw them. Cuckoos, woodpeckers, blue jays, cocks, parrots, cranes and peacocks utter terrible cries; hundreds of swarms of locusts appear at daybreak like mounted warriors bearing arms, insignia and shields. Both dawn and dusk blaze as if the horizon were on fire, and there have been showers of blood and bones, heir of Bharata.

'Even Arundhatī, who is famed and honoured by virtuous folk

1 These clouds are sometimes identified with Rāhu, the demon of the eclipse beheaded by Viṣṇu: see 1.17.

2 The editor of the *Bhīṣmaparvan*, S. K. Belvalkar, points out that these sounds are said to be made by meteors that forebode calamity.

throughout the three worlds, has put Vasiṣṭha in the shade;[1] Saturn is afflicting the Rohiṇī constellation, O king, and the mark on the moon has disappeared. There will be great danger! Thunder can be heard, terrible and unceasing, though the sky is cloudless, and steeds weep and shed teardrops.'

[3] *Vyāsa continues to enumerate portents of doom, and tells Dhṛtarāṣṭra to consider how universal destruction may be avoided.* [4] *Dhṛtarāṣṭra replies that he believes destruction to be destined; the warriors who die in the battle will achieve glory in this world and bliss in the next. Vyāsa responds that it is indeed time that both destroys and re-creates the worlds; however, the killing of kin is a sin, and Dhṛtarāṣṭra should strive for peace. But Dhṛtarāṣṭra explains with regret that his sons will not obey him. At Dhṛtarāṣṭra's request, Vyāsa lists the happy characteristics of those warriors who are assured of victory; but he adds that there can be no military action without loss.*

[5] *Vyāsa now leaves. Dhṛtarāṣṭra observes to Saṃjaya that vast numbers of kings and warriors have assembled at Kurukṣetra to fight for possession of the earth, and asks for a full description of the countries and cities they have come from. Saṃjaya begins to describe the properties of the earth, listing the various kinds of creatures: all arise from the earth and return to it at their deaths. Whoever owns the earth owns everything, and so kings kill each other for it.* [6] *He lists the elements and their properties: earth is the foremost of them. Then he describes the circular cosmic island Sudarśana,* [7] *the different continents it contains and the beings who inhabit them.*

[8] *At Dhṛtarāṣṭra's request Saṃjaya describes the continents to the north and east of Mount Meru. The eastern continent contains an enormous* jambū *tree from which it gains its name;* [9] *Saṃjaya describes the different divisions (*varṣas*) of Jambūdvīpa.*

[10] *Dhṛtarāṣṭra requests a detailed description of Bhāratavarṣa, the division over which the great battle will be fought. Saṃjaya enumerates the mountains, rivers and peoples of Bhāratavarṣa. If Earth is well treated she yields endless riches; therefore the Kauravas and Pāṇḍavas are struggling to possess her.* [11] *He*

1 Arundhatī, wife of the seer Vasiṣṭha, is an exemplar of devotion to her husband. Like the other great seers, Vasiṣṭha is also a star in the Great Bear: he is Mizar, and Arundhatī is the associated minor star Alcor. Now, uncharacteristically, Alcor is outshining Mizar.

*completes his description by telling Dhṛtarāṣṭra of the four ages, Kṛta, Tretā, Dvāpara and Kali, and their characteristics. The Dvāpara Age is drawing to its end, and will soon give way to the degenerate Kali Age.*

## THE EARTH

[12] *Dhṛtarāṣṭra asks Saṃjaya to describe the ocean, the other continents (*dvīpas*), and the heavenly bodies. Saṃjaya agrees, and gives a brief description of the ocean followed by an extensive description of Śākadvīpa.* [13] *Then he describes Kuśadvīpa, Śālmalikadvīpa, Krauñcadvīpa, and the heavenly bodies.*

## THE SERMON OF THE BLESSED LORD

[14] *After witnessing the first phase of the battle, Saṃjaya returns to Dhṛtarāṣṭra to report on what he has seen. He tells him of the death of Bhīṣma, who has been killed by Śikhaṇḍin.*

[15] *Deeply grieved, Dhṛtarāṣṭra asks to hear how the mighty Bhīṣma could have been killed. Who were his protectors on the battlefield? Bhīṣma had defeated even Rāma Jāmadagnya in battle; to have slain such a man, Śikhaṇḍin must be an incomparable warrior. His death is a disaster for the Kauravas. Dhṛtarāṣṭra repeatedly demands to know how it happened.* [16] *Saṃjaya answers that he will tell Dhṛtarāṣṭra everything that he has seen, whether with his own eyes or through the powers given him by Vyāsa. Then he begins his narration.*

*— Duryodhana assigns Duḥśāsana to the task of protecting Bhīṣma, especially against Śikhaṇḍin. The next morning the two vast armies are arrayed for battle; Bhīṣma heads the Kaurava force.*

[17] *Bhīṣma addresses all the kings who are allied to the Kauravas, urging them to carry out their* dharma *as Kṣatriyas by fighting to the death. The fearsome Kaurava army advances.* [18] *The din is overwhelming, and the weapons and other gear flash like lightning or fire. The force that Bhīṣma leads is enormous.*

[19] *Yudhiṣṭhira asks Arjuna to array the Pāṇḍava troops in a suitable formation, and Arjuna chooses the Thunderbolt array. Then he gives the order to advance. The Pāṇḍava force too is huge and magnificent. Grim portents appear.*

[**20**] — *Dhṛtarāṣṭra asks Saṃjaya to describe the two opposing armies in greater detail, and he does so.* — *Both forces are great and fearsome; the Kauravas face west, the Pāṇḍavas east. The Kaurava army is full of mighty heroes and greatly outnumbers the Pāṇḍavas; but the Pāṇḍava army is invincible since it is led by Kṛṣṇa and Arjuna.*

[**21**] *When Yudhiṣṭhira sees the force ranged against him he becomes despondent, but Arjuna reassures him: where* dharma *is, there is victory; where Kṛṣṇa is, there is victory.* [**22**] *Yudhiṣṭhira rides in a splendid chariot attended by Brahmins pronouncing blessings. Arjuna's is covered with bells and gleams with gold; it is driven by Kṛṣṇa. The sight of Bhīma is enough to terrify the Kauravas. The two armies confront each other.*

[**23**] **The *Bhagavadgītā*.**[1] — *Dhṛtarāṣṭra asks Saṃjaya what happened next, and Saṃjaya relates.* — *Duryodhana surveys the two armies and declares that his is the superior force. Bhīṣma roars a lion-roar, and the Kauravas sound their drums and trumpets; the Pāṇḍavas reply with blasts on their conches. Arjuna asks Kṛṣṇa to halt the chariot between the two armies so that he may observe all who are about to fight. When he sees so many of his kinsmen gathered there, he loses his will for battle and sits down, casting aside his weapons.*

[**24**] *Kṛṣṇa upbraids Arjuna for his unseemly weakness, and Arjuna asks him for guidance. Kṛṣṇa answers that he should not grieve, for the life of embodied beings has neither beginning nor end. They simply pass through one existence after another; how then is it possible to kill? Even if Arjuna believes in birth and death, he has no cause for grief, since the born are sure to die and the dead to be reborn. Arjuna should obey his* dharma, *which is to fight. If he does not do so he will achieve ignominy, whereas by fighting he will gain either heaven through death or earth through victory. The way of the Vedas is diffuse and dominated by the pursuit of earthly desires; better to act with detachment, unconcerned for the fruit of the action. The man who frees himself from desires gains peace of mind.*

Saṃjaya spoke:

[**25**] Arjuna said, 'If you consider that intellectual attitude is more important than action, O Kṛṣṇa Keśava, then why do you direct me

1 The *upaparvan* (sub-book) of Kṛṣṇa's sermon starts at chapter 14 and contains not merely the text of the *Bhagavadgītā* but also the context in which it was delivered. The sermon itself extends from chapter 23 to chapter 40.

to perform a terrible action? I feel that you confuse my intellect with words that are contradictory, so tell me decisively one single way for me to attain what is best.'

The blessed lord replied, 'I have long maintained that in this world there are two schools of thought, sinless one: Sāṃkhya philosophers follow the discipline of knowledge, and *yogīs* follow the discipline of action. A man does not achieve freedom from *karma* by not undertaking actions, or attain perfection by mere renunciation; for no one can remain even a moment without performing actions – everyone is forced to perform actions by the three qualities that derive from nature.[1]

'The person who controls the faculties of action,[2] but who continues in his mind to dwell on their objects, is deluded; they call him a fraud. But the person who restrains the sense organs with his mind, Arjuna, and who then undertakes the discipline of action with the faculties of action, is detached; he is the man of distinction. You should perform your regular actions, for action is superior to inaction, and through inaction not even your bodily life can be maintained. Excepting action for sacrificial purposes, action enslaves this world; son of Kuntī, that is the purpose for which you should perform actions, but without attachment to their results.

'Long ago, after creating human beings and the sacrifice, Prajāpati declared, "Through this you shall procreate; let this be your wish-granting cow. Prosper the gods with this, and let the gods prosper you. Prospering each other, you shall attain the highest good; for if you prosper them through sacrifice, the gods will grant you the pleasures you desire, whereas the person who enjoys their gifts without giving in return is no more than a thief. The virtuous eat only sacrificial leftovers; they are freed from all their sins. But the wicked cook for themselves, and what they eat is sin."

'Creatures exist through food; food arises from rain; rain exists through sacrifice; sacrifice arises from action. (You should know that action originates from *brahman*, and *brahman* from the Eternal, so that

**1** A reference to Sāṃkhya philosophy: see 3.203, and chapters 35–6 below.

**2** As opposed to those of cognition. The faculties of cognition are eye, ear, tongue, nose and skin; those of action are hand, foot, anus, genitals and voice.

*brahman* is present in all of these, and is always installed in the sacrifice.) This is how the wheel is set spinning;[1] the one who does not keep it spinning in this world lives in sin, delighting in the senses. Son of Kuntī, his life is worthless. But the person who delights in the self, who finds satisfaction in the self, who is contented with the self alone – there is nothing he needs to do. It matters not to him whether a thing is done or not done in this world, and he has no dependence of interest in any creature.

'So you should always perform with detachment the tasks that have to be done, for by performing actions with detachment a man attains the highest good; it was through action that Janaka[2] and others achieved perfection. You should act, too, with the very maintenance of the world in view. What the good man does, other folk do also: he sets the standard, and the world follows it.

'For myself, son of Kuntī, there is nothing in the three worlds that I have to do, since there is nothing to be attained that has not been attained. I simply engage in action, for if I did not engage tirelessly in action, people would do nothing but follow my path, son of Kuntī. These worlds would collapse if I did not perform actions, and I would be the cause of social disarray – I would slay these human beings. As the ignorant act in their attachment to action, heir of Bharata, so the man of knowledge should do, but with detachment, to achieve the maintenance of the world. He should not cause intellectual confusion in those who are ignorant and attached to action; the man of knowledge should favour all actions, while acting with discipline himself.

'Truly all actions are performed by the three qualities of nature, though the person who is deluded by the sense of "I" thinks that he is the agent. He who truly knows the distribution of the qualities and their actions understands that even the qualities are subject to the qualities, and he remains detached, strong-armed hero; but those who are deluded about the qualities of nature become attached to the actions

1 The circle forming the 'wheel' is closed by the implied final statement, 'Action exists through creatures.'

2 King of Videha and father of Sītā (see the story of Rāma, 3.257–75), Janaka was a model of royal piety.

of those qualities. The one who knows all this should not disturb the slower-witted folk who do not know it.

'Entrust all actions to me, focus your mind on the universal Self, 30
rid yourself of hope and personal concerns, cast off your sickness, and fight. People who always follow this teaching of mine faithfully and uncomplainingly are freed from *karma*; but you should know that those fools who complain and fail to follow my teaching, deluded in every aspect of their knowledge, are lost.

'Even the man who does have knowledge acts in accordance with his own nature, for creatures follow their nature: what is the use of suppressing it? Located in every object of every sense are love and hate. One should not fall into their clutches, for they are one's enemies.

'Better one's own *dharma* ill-done than the *dharma* of another well 35
performed. To die in achieving one's own *dharma* is good; the *dharma* of another is dangerous.'

Now Arjuna asked, 'So what impels a man to commit sin, Vṛṣṇi prince, seeming to force him even against his will?'

The blessed lord replied, 'It is desire, it is anger. It arises from the quality of *rajas*, Passion, and is voracious and very wicked: know it for the enemy here. As a fire is obscured by smoke, a mirror by dust, an embryo by its caul, so this world is obscured by it. The knowledge of the knowledgeable man is obscured by it, for it is his eternal enemy,
an insatiable fire in the shape of desire, son of Kuntī. Its home is said 40
to be the senses, the mind and the intellect, and it uses these to delude the human being by obscuring his knowledge. So first of all, bull-like heir of Bharata, you should control the senses in order to rid yourself of this wicked thing that destroys knowledge of every kind. It is said that the senses are highly developed. But the mind is higher than the senses, and the intellect higher than the mind; that which is higher than the intellect is he.[1] This being so, strong-armed hero, you should think of that which is higher than the intellect, compose yourself, and slay your invincible enemy in the shape of desire.

**[26]** 'Long ago I proclaimed this imperishable discipline to Vivasvat;[2]

1 The self.

2 A name for the Sun god; the great-grandfather of Manu, the first man: see 1.70.

Vivasvat declared it to Manu, and Manu told it to Ikṣvāku, and so, transmitted in succession, it came to be known by the royal seers. But over a long period of time, afflicter of your enemies, this discipline was lost on earth. This is the ancient discipline which I have proclaimed to you today because you are my devotee and my friend, for this is the greatest mystery.'

'Your birth was recent,' said Arjuna, 'and Vivasvat was born long ago; how am I to understand this, that you proclaimed it in the beginning?'

5 The blessed lord replied, 'I have had many former births, and so
have you, Arjuna; I know all of them, but you do not, afflicter of
your enemies. Although I am unborn and imperishable, although I
am lord of all beings, I assume my own nature and take on existence
through my illusory power, for whenever *dharma* lapses and *adharma*
increases, heir of Bharata, I create myself; to protect the virtuous,
destroy the wicked and restore *dharma* I take on existence in age after
age.

'The person who knows this truth about my divine birth and actions
does not find rebirth when he casts off his body, Arjuna; he finds me.
10 Many have put aside passion, fear and anger, filled themselves with
me and taken refuge in me; purified by the austerity of knowledge,
they have attained my own state. As people turn to me, so I accept
them; in every way human beings are following my path, son of
Kuntī.

'Those who want their actions to succeed in this world offer sacrifices
to the deities, for in the world of men success follows action swiftly. The
four classes of society were created by me, according to the distribution
of the qualities and their actions; you should know that this was my act,
and yet I am actionless and imperishable. Actions do not pollute me,
for I have no desire for the fruits of actions; he who recognizes that
15 I am so is not enslaved by his own actions. The ancients who sought
release knew this too, and they performed actions; therefore you too
must perform actions as the ancients did long ago.

'Even the seers are perplexed about what is action and what inaction, so I shall explain action to you; when you know it, you will be freed from evil. It is necessary to know about action, to know about wrong action, and to know about inaction: the way of action is hard to understand.

The one who can see inaction in action and action in inaction[1] is
wise among people; he performs all actions with discipline. If all his
undertakings are empty of desire and will, the wise call him a man
of learning, for his *karma* is burnt away by the fire of his knowledge.
If he gives up all attachment to the fruits of his actions, and is ever 20
satisfied and free from dependence, then even if he engages in action
he in fact does nothing at all. If he rids himself of hope, controls his
mind and gives up all possessions, performing actions only with the
body, he incurs no sin. If he is content with whatever he happens to get,
passing beyond the pairs of opposites,[2] remaining free of jealousy and
retaining equanimity in both success and failure, then even though he
acts he is not enslaved. If he attains detachment and freedom, fixes his
mind on knowledge and acts for the purpose of sacrifice, all his *karma*
is dissolved.

'The offering is *brahman*; the oblation of *brahman* is offered up by
*brahman* into the fire of *brahman*. He who meditates on the ritual as
*brahman* will indeed attain *brahman*. Some *yogīs* undertake sacrifice as an 25
act directed to the gods, while others offer up sacrifice itself, sacrificing
it in the fire of *brahman*. Some offer up hearing and the other senses
into the fires of restraint, and others offer up sound and the other
sense-objects into the fires of the senses. Some offer up all the actions
of their faculties of action and those of their breathing into the fire of
self-control and discipline, kindling it with knowledge; other seekers,
men of keen vows, sacrifice property, asceticism, discipline, or Vedic
study and knowledge. Some who follow the way of breath-control offer
up exhalation into inhalation or inhalation into exhalation, constraining
the course of both; others restrict their eating and offer up exhalation 30
into exhalation. Every one of these understands the sacrifice, and the
sacrifice destroys the sin of all of them. Those who partake of the
nectar of immortality that is the leavings of the sacrifice find the eternal
*brahman*; but he who does not sacrifice loses this world – how much
more the next, truest of Kurus?

1 i.e. the person who understands that not every action affects *karma*, while failure to act may affect it.

2 Happiness and unhappiness, etc.

'Thus sacrifices of many kinds are made into the mouth of *brahman*;[1]
you should know that all of them arise from action, and knowing this
you will be set free. The sacrifice of knowledge is superior to that of
property, afflicter of your enemies; son of Kuntī, all action, without
exception, is brought to completion in knowledge, so you should know
it. If you humbly question them as you attend upon them, the men of
35 knowledge who see truly will teach their knowledge to you. Once you
know it you will not return to delusion, son of Pāṇḍu; through it you
will see all beings within yourself, and then within me.

'Even if you are a worse sinner than all other sinners, the boat of
knowledge will be sufficient to ferry you across all wickedness. As a fire
once kindled reduces its kindling to ash, Arjuna, so the fire of knowledge
reduces to ash all actions,[2] for there is no purifier on earth to match
knowledge. Once perfected by discipline, one finds it in time within
oneself; the man of faith, intent upon it and in control of his senses,
gains knowledge, and once he has gained it he at once achieves supreme
40 peace. But the ignorant unbeliever, full of doubt, perishes; the doubter
loses this world and the next, and his happiness. Wealth-winner Arjuna,
actions do not enslave the self-controlled man with the discipline to
entrust all his actions to me and the knowledge to destroy all his doubts.
So use the sword of knowledge to destroy this doubt that ignorance has
planted in your heart; take up this discipline and arise, heir of Bharata!'

**[27]** *Arjuna asks whether it is better to act or to renounce action. Kṛṣṇa replies that action is the superior course, for renunciation cannot be attained without yogic actions, which lead to* brahman *and do not create* karma. *The learned man is impartial, seeing no distinction between different beings; detached, with his senses controlled, he attains oneness with* brahman.

**[28]** *Kṛṣṇa tells Arjuna that true renunciation is detached action, not non-action. The* yogī *is self-sufficient and full of equanimity; he engages in steady contemplation, and this leads him to oneness with Kṛṣṇa, so that he sees both himself and Kṛṣṇa in everything. Arjuna comments that it is difficult to control*

**1** This probably refers to the fire, through which the offering reaches its intended recipient.

**2** i.e. all *karma*.

*the mind in such a way; Kṛṣṇa insists that none the less it can be done. If a* yogī *does not entirely succeed, he still attains a very high rebirth in which he can strive once more to perfect his Yoga and achieve release.*

**[29]** *Now Kṛṣṇa reveals that as well as a material nature he has another, higher nature which is the basis of the universe; he is the essential property that makes each being what it is, but only his devotees can perceive this truth; all others are lost to illusion. Of devotees, the highest are those with the knowledge, acquired only after many rebirths, that Kṛṣṇa is everything; these few attain him directly. Others worship different deities, unaware that when these grant their wishes it is because Kṛṣṇa ordains it. Such people become true devotees only when they have rid themselves of their bad* karma *and delusion.*

**[30]** *Kṛṣṇa explains that the person who dies thinking of him attains him; Arjuna should therefore fight, keeping him always in mind. Once anyone attains Kṛṣṇa he experiences no further rebirth. The entire universe is subject to cyclic emergence from the unmanifest and reabsorption back into it; but the unmanifest itself undergoes no change. It is where those people go who have escaped from rebirth; it is Kṛṣṇa's own highest dwelling; it is the supreme being.*

**[31]** *Kṛṣṇa now announces to Arjuna the royal mystery which leads to release from rebirth. As supreme being he cyclically creates and reabsorbs all creatures, but he acts with detachment. His devotees worship him with the sacrifice of knowledge which, unlike the Vedic sacrifice, brings an end to rebirth; but even rituals devoted with faith to other deities reach him. Arjuna should perform every act as an offering to him; those who do this attain release, however base their origins.*

**[32]** *Kṛṣṇa tells Arjuna that not even the gods know his origin, since, like all other creatures, they themselves originate from him; those who understand this attain Kṛṣṇa himself. Arjuna asks to hear more, and Kṛṣṇa answers that he is the foremost being in every category, the seed of all beings without which nothing can exist; with a part of himself he supports the entire universe.*

Saṃjaya spoke:

**[33]** 'What you have told me as a kindness to me,' said Arjuna, 'this highest mystery known as the universal Self, has dispelled my delusion. You have told me in full how beings come into existence and how they cease to exist, and you have told me too, lotus-eyed Kṛṣṇa, of your own imperishable greatness. Now I desire to see your godly form, just as you have described yourself, highest lord and supreme god. If you think that I will be capable of looking upon it, lord of Yoga, show me your imperishable self!'

The blessed lord replied, 'Behold my various divine forms, son of Kuntī, in their hundreds and thousands, with all their different colours and shapes! Behold the Ādityas, Vasus and Rudras, the Aśvins and the Maruts;[1] behold many wonders never previously seen, heir of Bharata! Behold here today within my body the entire universe with all its creatures, moving and still; and behold whatever else you wish, Arjuna Guḍākeśa! But you will not be able to look upon me with these your own eyes, so I grant you divine sight. Behold my godly Yoga!'

With these words, O king, Hari Kṛṣṇa the great lord of Yoga revealed to Kuntī's son his supreme godly form, with its many mouths and eyes, its many heavenly ornaments, its many raised weapons and its many other wonderful sights, wearing heavenly clothes and garlands, anointed with heavenly perfumes: god infinite and all-seeing, in whom all marvels reside. If the light of a thousand suns were to rise all at once in the sky, it would be like the light of that great one. Then Pāṇḍu's son beheld in the body of the god of gods the entire universe in all its many subdivisions. The wealth-winner was filled with amazement, and the hair rose on his body; he bowed his head, joined his hands together, and addressed the god.

'I see the gods within your body, O god, and all the distinct classes of beings; I see Lord Brahmā on his lotus seat, and all the seers and divine serpents. I see you everywhere, infinite in form with your many arms and bellies and faces and eyes; I see of you no end, middle or beginning, lord of the universe, universal in form. I see you bearing diadem, club and discus, a mass of fiery energy blazing in all directions. I gaze at you with difficulty, for all around you is the radiance of fire or sun, but measureless.

'You are the Eternal, the supreme knowable entity; you are this universe's ultimate abode; you are imperishable, the protector of perpetual *dharma*; I believe you are the everlasting being. Without beginning or middle or end, infinitely potent and infinitely strong, with sun and

1 Groups of deities.

moon for your eyes and the blazing fire for your mouth, I behold you
scorching this universe with your fiery energy; for this world that lies 20
between heaven and earth, with the whole horizon, is pervaded by you
alone.

'The three worlds are set shaking, great one, to see this wonderful, terrible form of yours, for yonder the hosts of the gods are entering you, some of them fearfully extolling you with hands joined together, while throngs of great seers and Siddhas pronounce benedictions and praise you with mighty praises. Rudras and Ādityas, Vasus and Sādhyas, All-gods, Aśvins and Maruts, ancestors, Gandharvas, Yakṣas and demons in multitudes, all gaze at you amazed. Strong-armed one, seeing this mighty form of yours, with its many mouths and eyes, its many arms and thighs and feet, its many bellies, its many dreadful fangs, the worlds are set shaking, and so am I. When I see you touching the sky, blazing in many colours, jaws gaping, huge eyes ablaze, my very soul quakes,
O Viṣṇu, and I lose all courage and tranquillity; at the mere sight of 25
your mouths, bright as doomsday fire and full of dreadful fangs, I lose my bearings and know no comfort. Show mercy, lord of gods, abode of the universe!

'And there are all Dhṛtarāṣṭra's sons alongside the hosts of their allies, the lords of the earth, and Bhīṣma, and Droṇa, and that Sūta's son Karṇa, and with them our own leading warriors, all rushing into your terrible mouths with their dreadful fangs. I can see some caught between your teeth, their heads smashed. Like numerous river-currents that rush towards the one ocean, those heroes of the world of men enter your flaming mouths; like moths that fly ever faster to destroy themselves in a blazing flame, the worlds hurry ever faster to their destruction in
your mouths. With your flaming jaws you lap up complete worlds and 30
devour them whole; your terrible splendours fill the entire universe with fiery energy till it is scorched, O Viṣṇu. Tell me, who are you with your dreadful form? Honour to you; show mercy, best of gods! I wish to know who you are, O primal being, for I do not understand what you have set out to do.'

The blessed lord replied, 'I am Time, the destroyer of worlds, fully developed, and I have set out here to bring the worlds to their end. Even without your presence in battle, all these warriors arrayed in opposing

ranks will cease to be. So arise and gain glory: conquer your foes and
enjoy your prosperous realm! I myself slew these long ago; be the mere
instrument, ambidextrous warrior. Droṇa and Bhīṣma and Jayadratha
and Karṇa, and the other heroic warriors too, have been killed by me;
kill them! Do not be dismayed. Fight! You will conquer your enemies
in battle.'

35 When he heard Kṛṣṇa Keśava speak these words, Arjuna the wearer
of the diadem trembled; he joined his hands together, paid honour and
bowed, and spoke once again to Kṛṣṇa, stammering in his fear: 'Lord
of the senses, it is right that the singing of your praises delights the
universe and fills it with love; terrified Rākṣasas flee in all directions,
and all the hosts of Siddhas bow before you. And why should they not
bow to you, O great one? You are the first creator, more venerable even
than Brahmā; O infinite lord of the gods, abode of the universe, you
are the Eternal, the existent and the non-existent, and what is beyond
both. You are the primal god, the ancient being; you are this universe's
ultimate abode; you are that which knows and that which is to be
known, the highest resting-place; in your infinite form you pervade the
universe. You are the Wind god, Yama, Fire, Varuṇa, the moon; you are
Prajāpati and Brahmā the great-grandfather. Honour, honour to you
40 a thousand times over, and then honour to you yet again! Honour to
you from before and from behind; honour to you from all sides, O you
who are all. Infinitely potent, immeasurably valiant, you bring all to
completion, and so you are all.

'If, thinking you a friend, I have spoken too strongly through heed-
lessness or affection – "Hey, Kṛṣṇa Yādava, my friend!" – not knowing
of this your greatness; or if in jest I have done you dishonour, invincible
one, when we were amusing ourselves, or lying, or sitting, or eating,
whether alone or in company; then I beg your forgiveness; you are
measureless! You are the father of the entire world, moving and still; you
are its preceptor, revered and venerable. No other is your equal, never
mind your superior, in all the three worlds, for your power is matchless!
So I bow and prostrate myself and beseech your grace, worshipful lord:
please pardon me, O god, as a father his son, a friend his friend, or a lover
45 his beloved. I have seen what was never seen before, and I feel the hair
rise on my body; my mind is shaken with fear. Let me see, O god, that

other form of yours; show mercy, lord of gods, abode of the universe! I wish to see you just as before, bearing diadem, club and discus; O thousand-armed god of universal form, assume that four-armed form of yours!'

The blessed lord replied, 'Because I am well disposed towards you, Arjuna, I have used my own Yoga to show you this supreme form of mine, full of fiery energy, universal, infinite, primal, which no one but you has ever seen before. Not through the Vedas, or sacrifice or study, not through the giving of gifts, not through rituals or fierce austerities could anyone other than you, Kuru hero, see me in such a form in the world of men. Do not be dismayed or bewildered to see this form of mine, awesome as it is; become once more fearless and happy at heart, and behold here that other form of mine!'

With these words to Arjuna, Kṛṣṇa Vāsudeva showed him once more 50
his own normal form; the great one comforted the frightened man by
assuming once again his gentle aspect. Arjuna said, 'Seeing this gentle
human form of yours, stirrer of men, I have come to my senses and am
again myself.'

The blessed lord replied, 'This form of mine which you have seen
is most difficult to see; even the gods constantly long to see this form.
Not through the Vedas, not through austerities, not through the giving
of gifts, not through sacrifice can I be seen as you have seen me. But,
Arjuna, afflicter of your enemies, through undivided devotion I can be
truly known and seen so, and so entered into. The one who performs 55
actions for me, who holds me highest, who is devoted to me; the one
who is free from attachment and bears no enmity towards any creature
– he is the one who comes to me, son of Pāṇḍu.'

**[34]** *Arjuna asks whether devotion to Kṛṣṇa or worship of the unmanifest is the better way. Kṛṣṇa replies that both ways lead to him, but that the way of the unmanifest is the harder. If possible Arjuna should fix his mind on Kṛṣṇa; failing all else, he should at least give up concern for the fruits of his actions. The faithful devotee who achieves this, and who is composed and full of equanimity, is dear to Kṛṣṇa.*

**[35]** *Kṛṣṇa discourses on the Sāṃkhya philosophy, speaking of the body and its properties, knowledge,* brahman, *the individual self and the three* *qualities that derive from nature. The one who sees the supreme lord in everything, and understands the fundamental oneness of diverse reality, attains* brahman.

[36] *Kṛṣṇa continues his discourse.* Brahman *is the womb in which he places the seed from which all beings ultimately spring. The three qualities enslave embodied beings by causing attachment:* sattva, *Goodness, causes attachment to happiness and knowledge,* rajas, *Passion, causes attachment to action, and* tamas, *Darkness, causes attachment to error and sloth. The one who understands that the qualities are the only agents passes beyond them and attains Kṛṣṇa, self-sufficient and full of equanimity.*

[37] *Now Kṛṣṇa likens worldly existence to an* aśvattha *tree with its roots above and its branches below. It is fed by the three qualities and puts forth sensuality as its shoots, and it leads to human action; one should fell it with the axe of detachment and pass on to the place from which no one returns. There are two entities in the world: one which passes away, comprising all beings, and one which does not, the changeless. But there is also a higher entity, the supreme being, and this is Kṛṣṇa.*

[38] *Kṛṣṇa explains that there is a divine and a demonic creation, and describes the characteristics of each. Demonic people are slaves to desire, anger and greed, and undergo repeated demonic rebirths, whereas those who are free of these faults attain the highest state.*

[39] *Kṛṣṇa now describes the way in which each person's faith is shaped by whichever of the three qualities predominates in that person; the same applies to the food he eats, the sacrifices he offers, the austerities he performs, the gifts he gives. The three parts of the utterance* oṃ tat sat, *which means* brahman, *should be used in all acts of sacrifice, austerity and giving.*

[40] *Arjuna asks to hear about renunciation, and Kṛṣṇa replies that what is to be renounced is desire and the fruits of actions; sacrifice, austerities and giving should never be given up, but rather performed with detachment. Renunciation itself is affected by the three qualities, and so are knowledge, action and actor; so too are intelligence, steadfastness and happiness. No creature in heaven or on earth is free from the qualities, which determine the characteristic duties of the four classes of men. Each man should perform his own tasks; it is detachment that releases from* karma. *Attaining oneness with* brahman *leads to the highest devotion towards Kṛṣṇa and final peace. Lastly, Kṛṣṇa urges Arjuna to reflect on what he has heard, and to fix his mind on Kṛṣṇa alone.*

## THE KILLING OF BHĪṢMA

Saṃjaya spoke:

[**41**] The mighty chariot-fighters saw wealth-winner Arjuna once more bearing his bow Gāṇḍīva and his arrows, and they let out a great roar. The Pāṇḍavas and Somakas, together with their followers, were full of joy, and they blew their sea-born conches; then kettledrums and war-drums and rasps and cow-horns were sounded all at once, causing a mighty noise. Lord of men, the gods, the Gandharvas and the ancestors
all came to look, and so did Siddhas and Cāraṇas in throngs; and the 5
blessed seers, led by Indra of a hundred sacrifices, all came together there to see that great war. Then brave Yudhiṣṭhira looked at the two armies, marshalled ready to fight, ever-shifting like the sea, O king, and he took off his armour, laid aside his splendid weapon, and climbed quickly down from his chariot, joining his hands together. Quiet Yudhiṣṭhira, the lord of *dharma*, fixed his eye on grandfather Bhīṣma and set out eastwards on foot, towards the ranks of his enemies.

When wealth-winner Arjuna, Kuntī's son, saw him set out, he too quickly climbed down from his chariot and followed him, and so
did his brothers; and blessed Kṛṣṇa Vāsudeva too followed behind, 10
as did the chief allied kings, for they were anxious. Arjuna asked Yudhiṣṭhira, 'What is your purpose, O king? Why have you left us and set out eastwards on foot, towards the ranks of your enemies?' Bhīma said, 'Lord of kings, where are you going, laying aside armour and weapons, leaving your brothers behind and heading towards armed enemy warriors, O king?' Nakula's words were, 'You are my eldest brother, Bharata's heir. Seeing you behave in this way, fear strikes my heart. Tell me, sir, where are you going?' And Sahadeva too said, 'Here is this dreadful battle-array, against whom we have to fight. Where are
you going, O king, heading towards your enemies?' But though his 15
brothers spoke to him in this way, O heir of Kuru, quiet Yudhiṣṭhira said nothing, and went straight on. High-minded Kṛṣṇa Vāsudeva spoke to them in his wisdom, laughing a little. 'I know his intention. First the king will seek the permission of Bhīṣma, Droṇa, Kṛpa heir of Gotama, Śalya and all the elders; then he will fight his foes. In former days it

was said that he who fails to seek his elders' permission before fighting mighty enemies is sure to incur blame. I believe that one who fights the mighty after seeking permission in the proper manner is certain to triumph in the fight.'

20 As Kṛṣṇa said these words in the presence of the troops of Duryodhana son of Dhṛtarāṣṭra, a great uproar arose among some of them, while others fell silent.

Duryodhana's soldiers saw Yudhiṣṭhira from far off, and they began to converse with each other: 'He is no lord, he is a disgrace to his race! It is plain that King Yudhiṣṭhira is coming here in fear, approaching Bhīṣma with his brothers, to beg for his protection! With wealth-winner Arjuna to look after him, and wolf-belly Bhīma, son of Pāṇḍu, and Nakula and Sahadeva too, why does this Pāṇḍava come in fear? He cannot have been born in the Kṣatriya race, famous throughout the world, for he lacks
25 mettle and fears battle in his heart!' Then all those Kṣatriyas praised the Kauravas, while in joyful excitement all of them waved their garments; and all the soldiers there heaped blame on Yudhiṣṭhira together with his brothers and Kṛṣṇa Keśava. Then after reviling Yudhiṣṭhira, the Kaurava army quickly fell silent once more, O lord of the peoples, wondering, 'What will King Yudhiṣṭhira here say? And how will Bhīṣma answer? What will battle-boasting Bhīma say, and Kṛṣṇa, and Arjuna? What is his intention?' There were grave doubts in both armies concerning Yudhiṣṭhira at that time, O king.

30 He forced his way through the ranks of his enemies, thick with arrows and spears, and, surrounded by his brothers, quickly went straight up to Bhīṣma. King Yudhiṣṭhira son of Pāṇḍu then clasped Bhīṣma's feet in his hands, and he addressed Bhīṣma son of Śaṃtanu, who had come to fight: 'Unconquerable one, I salute you. I shall fight with you, sir! Permit me to do so, and grant me your blessing.' Bhīṣma replied, 'If you had not come to me about the battle in this way, lord of the earth, I should have cursed you, great king and heir of Bharata, to defeat. But, my son, I am pleased with you. Fight and obtain the victory, O Pāṇḍava!
35 May you gain whatever else you desire in the battle. And choose a gift, son of Kuntī: what do you desire from me? Great king, with things as they stand, you cannot be defeated. It is truly said, great king, that man is the slave of money, but money is no man's slave; and I am tied by

money to the Kauravas. So it is that I say to you impotently, heir of Kuru – for I am held fast by money – what, other than my aid in battle, do you wish?'

Yudhiṣṭhira answered him, 'Wise sir, ever my well-wisher, give me your counsel, but fight for the Kaurava cause! This is my choice for ever.' Bhīṣma said, 'King, Kuru's heir, what help can I give you here? Given that I shall fight for the cause of your enemies, tell me what you wish to say!' Yudhiṣṭhira replied, 'How may I in the battle defeat you, sir, who have never suffered defeat? Tell me this to help me, if you think it good.' Bhīṣma answered, 'Son of Kuntī, I know of no man who might defeat me as I fight in the battle, not even Indra of a hundred sacrifices, if he were to appear.' Yudhiṣṭhira said, 'Alas! Then I ask you, grandfather – honour be to you – tell me the way in which you yourself may be defeated by your enemies in the battle!' Bhīṣma replied, 'I know of no enemy, sir, who might defeat me in battle. The time of my death has not yet come. Come to me again later!'

Strong-armed Yudhiṣṭhira respectfully accepted the words of Bhīṣma, O heir of Kuru, and, after paying him honour once more, went on with his brothers towards the chariot of their Teacher Droṇa, through the midst of all the watchful soldiers. He greeted Droṇa, and respectfully circumambulated him; and he spoke aloud to that unconquerable one words uniquely suited to his own interest: 'Blessed sir, I salute you. I shall fight without sin and conquer all my enemies, if you permit me, O Brahmin.' Droṇa said, 'If you had not come to me after making up your mind to fight, I should have cursed you, great king, to utter defeat. But, sinless Yudhiṣṭhira, I am pleased with you and honoured by you. I give you permission: fight and obtain the victory! And let me do what you desire: tell me what it is you want. With things as they stand, great king, what – other than my aid in battle – do you wish? It is truly said, great king, that man is the slave of money, but money is no man's slave; and I am tied by money to the Kauravas. So it is that I say to you impotently: what – other than my aid in battle – do you wish? I shall fight for the Kaurava cause, but I shall pray for your victory.'

Yudhiṣṭhira answered him, 'Pray for my victory, O Brahmin, and give me counsel to help me, but fight for the Kaurava cause! This is the gift I choose.' Droṇa said, 'O king, your victory is assured, since you

have Hari Kṛṣṇa for your counsellor, and I promise you you will defeat
55 your enemies in the battle. Where *dharma* is, there is Kṛṣṇa, and where Kṛṣṇa is, there is victory. Son of Kuntī, go, and fight! And ask me: what shall I tell you?' Yudhiṣṭhira said, 'Best of Brahmins, I ask you – listen to what I wish to say – how I may in the battle defeat you, who have never suffered defeat.' Droṇa replied, 'There is no victory for you as long as I continue to fight in the battle. Strive with your brothers for my speedy death!' Yudhiṣṭhira answered, 'Alas! Then tell me, strong-armed hero, the way in which you may be killed: my Teacher, I fall here before you and ask you this. Honour be to you!' Droṇa said, 'I know of no enemy, sir, who might kill me while I stand in the battle, fighting in fury,
60 pouring forth torrents of arrows like rain. Only when I am prepared for death, O king, my weapon laid down, my mind abstracted, may anyone kill me in this warriors' battle: I tell you this truthfully. And I shall lay down my weapon in the battle when I hear terrible ill news from a man whose word I can trust: I tell you this truthfully.'

Yudhiṣṭhira heard what Bharadvāja's wise son had to say, great king, and then he asked his Teacher's leave and set out to see Kṛpa son of Śaradvat. The king greeted Kṛpa, and respectfully circumambulated him; then he spoke eloquent words to that most unconquerable one: 'I pay you honour, revered sir. I shall fight without sin and conquer all my
65 enemies, if you permit me, sinless one.' Kṛpa said, 'If you had not come to me after making up your mind to fight, I should have cursed you, great king, to utter defeat. It is truly said, great king, that man is the slave of money, but money is no man's slave; and I am tied by money to the Kauravas. I believe that I must fight for their cause. So it is that I say to you impotently: what – other than my aid in battle – do you wish?' Yudhiṣṭhira replied, 'Alas! then I ask you, my teacher – listen to what I say' – then with these words the king, shaken and fainting, fell silent. But Kṛpa heir of Gotama, who knew what he wished to say, answered him. 'I am impossible to kill, lord of the earth. Fight and obtain the
70 victory! I am pleased that you came, and I shall pray for your victory every morning when I rise, lord of men: I tell you this truthfully.'

King Yudhiṣṭhira heard what Gotama's heir had to say, great king, and then he asked Kṛpa's leave and set out towards Śalya, king of Madra. The king greeted Śalya, and respectfully circumambulated him; and he spoke to that unconquerable one words uniquely suited to his own interest: 'I pay you honour, revered sir. I shall fight without sin and conquer my enemies, if you permit me, great king.' Śalya said, 'If you had not come to me after making up your mind to fight, I should have cursed you, great king, to defeat in the battle. But I am pleased with you and honoured by you: may that which you desire be yours. Indeed, I do give you permission: fight and obtain the victory! And tell me further what you need, O hero: what shall I give you? With things as they stand, great king, what – other than my aid in battle – do you wish? It is truly said, great king, that man is the slave of money, but money is no man's slave; and I am tied by money to the Kauravas. I shall do what you wish, sister's son, according to your desire. So it is that I say to you impotently: what – other than my aid in battle – do you wish?'

Yudhiṣṭhira answered him, 'Give me always the best counsel to help me, great king, but by all means fight for the cause of my enemies! This is the gift I choose.' Śalya said, 'Tell me, best of kings, what help I can give you here, given that I shall fight for the cause of your enemies, since my allegiance has been secured with money by the Kauravas.' Yudhiṣṭhira replied, 'My gift is the same one that you promised during the preparations for war:[1] in the battle you should act to destroy the ardour of the Sūta's son Karṇa.' Śalya answered, 'This wish of yours will come to fruition, according to your desire, son of Kuntī. Go, and fight with confidence! I promise you victory.'

Kuntī's son sought leave from his mother's brother, the lord of Madra, and then, surrounded by his brothers, he came out from the great army. Meanwhile Kṛṣṇa Vāsudeva, Gada's elder brother, approached Rādhā's son Karṇa on the battlefield, and spoke to him on behalf of the Pāṇḍavas: 'Karṇa, I have heard that, for hatred of Bhīṣma, you will not fight. Take our side until Bhīṣma is killed! When Bhīṣma is killed, son of Rādhā, you can go to the aid of Dhṛtarāṣṭra's son Duryodhana in the battle, if you view that as fair.' Karṇa replied, 'I shall not act against the wishes of Dhṛtarāṣṭra's son, Kṛṣṇa Keśava, for you should know that I have resolved to give up my life in Duryodhana's service.'

When Kṛṣṇa heard this he turned back, O heir of Bharata, and

1 See 5.8.

rejoined the Pāṇḍavas and their leader Yudhiṣṭhira. The eldest of the
Pāṇḍava brothers now called out in the midst of the army, 'If anyone will
90 take our side, I shall accept him as an ally!' Then Yuyutsu fixed his eye
on the Pāṇḍavas and gladly addressed Kuntī's son Yudhiṣṭhira, the lord
of *dharma*: 'I shall openly fight the sons of Dhṛtarāṣṭra for your cause
in the battle, sinless king, if you will accept me.' Yudhiṣṭhira answered,
'Come, come! We shall all fight your untutored brothers, Yuyutsu: both
Kṛṣṇa Vāsudeva and we Pāṇḍavas all say so. I accept you, strong-armed
hero! Fight for my cause. I see now that Dhṛtarāṣṭra's line depends on
you, and so do his funeral offerings. Accept us, radiant prince, as we
accept you! Dhṛtarāṣṭra's son Duryodhana, angriest of fools, will cease
95 to be!' Then Kuru's heir Yuyutsu left your sons and went over to the
army of the sons of Pāṇḍu, to the beat of a kettledrum.

Now King Yudhiṣṭhira, together with his younger brothers, joyfully
donned once more his shining armour, bright with gold. All those bull-
like heroes took to their chariots, and they arrayed their troops again as
before; and they sounded kettledrums and *puṣkara* drums in hundreds,
and roared their various lion-roars. Dhṛṣṭadyumna and the other princes
all rejoiced greatly once again to see the tiger-like Pāṇḍavas in their
100 chariots. And seeing the dignity of Pāṇḍu's sons, as they paid honour
to the honourable, the lords of the earth assembled there revered them
greatly; kings spoke of the good-heartedness of those noble men, their
mercy when appropriate, and their great kindness to their kinsmen.
Everywhere were heard fair words – 'Bravo! Bravo!' – and praises for
those famous men, delighting mind and heart. Aryan and barbarian
alike, all who were there and saw or heard about the deeds of Pāṇḍu's
sons at that time sobbed and wept. Then they beat great kettledrums
and *puṣkara* drums in hundreds, and in high spirits they joyfully blew
their milk-white conches.

[**42**] *On the first day of the battle, the opposing armies hurl themselves at each other. Bhīma, roaring terrifyingly, leads the Pāṇḍava brothers in their first attack on the Dhārtarāṣṭras, and the earth is filled with the sound and sight of numberless arrows being shot. At first the other kings stand back and watch the encounter; then they too join in the fray.* [**43**] *The noise of the first morning of battle is immense. Thousands of pairs of individual warriors fight each other in*

*single combat, in chariots, on horseback or elephant-back, or on foot. To begin with the conflict is lovely to see, but it soon becomes a raging battle and impossible to make out: it resembles the war between the gods and demons.* **[44]** *Father fights son, kinsman fights kinsman, friend fights friend. Elephants tear at each other and rush in all directions. The cries of dying soldiers are like the wailing of ghosts; others, though terribly wounded, continue to attack their enemies. The battle wears on; the Pāṇḍava army begins to waver as it nears the great Bhīṣma.*

**[45]** *As morning draws to an end, Bhīṣma, supported by Durmukha, Kṛtavarman, Kṛpa, Śalya and Viviṃśati, plunges into the Pāṇḍava armies and slays many. In response, Arjuna's son Abhimanyu launches a furious attack against Bhīṣma and his close supporters; though they savagely counterattack him, they cannot stay his assault, and he even succeeds in cutting down Bhīṣma's standard with his arrows. The Pāṇḍava forces move in to protect Abhimanyu against Bhīṣma's violently renewed attack; Bhīṣma now severs Bhīma's standard with a single arrow. Uttara, son of Virāṭa, attacks Śalya's chariot from elephant-back and kills all four horses, but Śalya kills him and his elephant, and leaps on to Kṛtavarman's chariot. Seeing this, Uttara's brother Śaṅkha advances to attack Śalya; Śalya kills his horses, but he finds safety on Arjuna's chariot. Meanwhile, Bhīṣma causes massive slaughter among the Pāṇḍavas and their allies with his arrows. The sun sets on a rout of the Pāṇḍavas at the end of the first day's battle.*

**[46]** *Yudhiṣṭhira, appalled by the destruction caused by Bhīṣma, discusses his possible courses of action with Kṛṣṇa. Should he abandon his quest for the kingdom? Bhīma is fighting to the utmost of his great power, but he cannot overcome Bhīṣma and Droṇa; only Arjuna could achieve this, and Arjuna is not yet fully engaged in the fight. Kṛṣṇa comforts Yudhiṣṭhira and advises him to rely on Dhṛṣṭadyumna, the commander of his forces. Yudhiṣṭhira appeals to Dhṛṣṭadyumna to exert himself, and Dhṛṣṭadyumna cheers the Pāṇḍavas with his enthusiasm. Yudhiṣṭhira requests him to array his forces in the bird-shaped* Krauñca *formation; next morning, Dhṛṣṭadyumna does so, placing Arjuna at the head of the vast army. Armed and ready, the Pāṇḍava forces await sunrise.* **[47]** *Duryodhana, seeing the forces of his enemies arrayed against him, likewise assembles his allies and assures them that with Bhīṣma for their leader they can overcome their enemies. The Kaurava army takes the field, and both sides sound their war conches ready for the coming battle.*

**[48]** *The second day of fighting commences. Duryodhana instructs his forces to begin the fight, and Bhīṣma resumes his assault on the Pāṇḍava forces, to deadly* *effect. Seeing this, Arjuna instructs Kṛṣṇa to drive his chariot close to Bhīṣma. The Kaurava chiefs shower arrows upon him, but he replies in kind, killing many chariot-fighters, while Dhṛṣṭadyumna advances against Droṇa. Duryodhana, dismayed, urges Bhīṣma to attack Arjuna, and these two now meet in a single combat which wins the admiration of the very immortals; yet despite the vast numbers of arrows shot and the many wounds suffered, neither is able to overcome the other.* **[49]** *Droṇa and Dhṛṣṭadyumna too exchange many arrows, till Droṇa severs Dhṛṣṭadyumna's bow and kills his charioteer and horses. Bhīma intervenes to rescue Dhṛṣṭadyumna and attack Droṇa; in response, Duryodhana sends the forces of the king of Kaliṅga to launch a counterattack against Bhīma.*

**[50]** *Bhīma, supported by the men of Cedi, faces the assault of the Kaliṅgas and Niṣādas. The battle is terrific, and the Cedis retreat, but Bhīma stands firm. Śakradeva, prince of Kaliṅga, kills Bhīma's horses and attacks him with many arrows, but Bhīma kills him with his club; next he kills the prince Bhānumat with his sword; then he strides alone about the battlefield slaying men, elephants and horses. Śrutāyus, the king of Kaliṅga, engages him in single combat; Bhīma kills him with seven arrows, and also the Niṣāda prince Ketumat. The Kaliṅgas surround him, but he kills hundreds of them single-handed and continues his rampage. The Kaliṅgas flee, but then rally again; meanwhile Dhṛṣṭadyumna, together with other Pāṇḍava leaders, goes to Bhīma's support. Blood flows in torrents as they cut down the Kaliṅgas. Bhīṣma approaches, but Sātyaki kills his charioteer and his horses carry him away again; Bhīma completes the destruction of the Kaliṅga forces.*

**[51]** *In the afternoon of the second day various inconclusive combats occur, among them one between Abhimanyu and Duryodhana's son Lakṣmaṇa. Seeing this both Duryodhana and Arjuna hasten to their sons' assistance. The Kaurava leaders take this opportunity to launch an assault on Arjuna, but so fierce is his archery that no one can advance against him: those who attempt to do so perish, and the rest flee. Seeing this, Bhīṣma decides to withdraw his forces for the day as the sun sets.*

**[52]** *At daybreak the next morning both armies are arrayed for the third day of warfare. Bhīṣma forms his army into the* Garuḍa *formation, with himself at its beak and Droṇa and Kṛtavarman for its eyes. Arjuna and Dhṛṣṭadyumna respond by placing the Pāṇḍava forces in a Half-moon formation. The fighting resumes,* **[53]** *but in the tumult of battle neither side can gain the advantage. A thick dust arises, obscuring everything, but as the slaughter continues the dust is* *laid by the spilt blood of the dead warriors, elephants and horses, and visibility returns.* **[54]** *Arjuna is surrounded, but beats back his attackers; similarly, Abhimanyu and Sātyaki are surrounded by Śakuni and his Gāndhāra men, but fight back and kill many of them. Bhīṣma and Droṇa attack Yudhiṣṭhira, but he, together with Nakula and Sahadeva, gains the upper hand. Duryodhana attacks Bhīma and Ghaṭotkaca; Bhīma pierces him with an arrow, and he is driven away unconscious by his charioteer, while his troops flee. There are further Pāṇḍava gains, to the extent that a rout of the Kauravas seems inevitable. Duryodhana himself succeeds in rallying them; then he accuses Bhīṣma of not exerting himself fully in the Kaurava cause. Bhīṣma replies that the Pāṇḍavas are invincible even to the gods, but vows none the less to check them in battle that day. Duryodhana is delighted, and has war conches and drums sounded.*

**[55]** *In the afternoon of the third day Bhīṣma leads the Kaurava forces in a fierce attack on the Pāṇḍavas: he shoots arrows with such swiftness that he seems to be everywhere at once. The Pāṇḍava army sustains massive losses, gives way, and is routed. Kṛṣṇa now urges Arjuna to fulfil his vow to kill Bhīṣma, and drives his chariot towards Bhīṣma's. Seeing this Yudhiṣṭhira's army rallies; but Bhīṣma's ceaseless hail of arrows thwarts Arjuna and continues to inflict great slaughter on his followers. Kṛṣṇa decides that he must slay Bhīṣma himself, leaps down from Arjuna's chariot and rushes at Bhīṣma; but Arjuna stops him, swearing that he will carry out his pledge.*

Saṃjaya spoke:
Then Kṛṣṇa Vāsudeva took up the reins once more. Slayer of his enemies, he laid hold of his conch Pāñcajanya and made the horizon roar with its noise. When the Kuru heroes saw him, with his neck-chain and armlets and earrings awhirl, the curved lashes of his eyes coated with dust, his teeth gleaming as he raised his conch, they shouted out loud. Then the beat of drums and tabors, the din of chariot-wheels and of kettledrums, and the fierce lion-roars of the heroes erupted throughout the Kuru
forces. Arjuna's bow Gāṇḍīva sounded like thunder; the sound reached 105
the heavens and the horizon, as the pure bright arrows shooting from the bow of Pāṇḍu's son flew in every direction.

The Kaurava lord Duryodhana, together with Bhīṣma and Bhūriśravas and a force of men, advanced against him, arrows brandished in his hand, like fire about to consume a dry thicket. Bhūriśravas shot at Arjuna seven golden-shafted broad arrows, Duryodhana hurled a fiercely speeding lance, Śalya a club, and Bhīṣma son of Śaṃtanu a spear. But he countered those seven fine arrows shot by Bhūriśravas with seven of his own, and with a razor-edged arrow he destroyed the lance thrown by Duryodhana's hand; then with two arrows that hero cut down the spear thrown by Śaṃtanu's son as it descended on him, lightning-bright, and the club thrown by the Madra king's arm.

110 Now with the might of his two arms Arjuna drew his lovely bow Gāṇḍīva, immeasurably great, and with the proper rite he sent forth into the heavens the wonderful, the dreadful Weapon of Great Indra. With that most excellent Weapon, the noble Arjuna, the mighty bowman, wearer of the diadem, countered all the forces of his enemies, as it poured forth torrents of arrows as bright as purest fire. The arrows that Kuntī's son Arjuna shot from his bow cut down chariots and standard-crests, bows and the arms that held them, and entered the bodies of enemy princes, mighty elephants and horses. The son of Kuntī filled the entire horizon with his keen-edged, sharp arrows; with the sound of Gāṇḍīva he struck terror into the hearts of his enemies. As this most terrible conflict continued, the sounds of conches and of kettledrums and the fierce roars of war were drowned out by Gāṇḍīva's sound.

115 Now when they recognized the sound of Gāṇḍīva, King Virāṭa and his heroic men, and Drupada, the brave king of Pāñcāla, came there full of mettle; but all your troops, Dhṛtarāṣṭra, were plunged into utter despair whenever they heard the roar of Gāṇḍīva, and not one of them would advance against it.

In that dreadful conflict of kings brave chariot-fighters were slain with their charioteers; and elephants, with their great banners and their girths of pure gold, suffered a rain of iron arrows and fell straight down, deprived of life, their armour and bodies broken by the wearer of the diadem. With his sharp, broad, keen-pointed shafts, feathered and fiercely speeding, Arjuna son of Kuntī struck hard at the mighty standards heading the forces of his enemies, cutting their supports and destroying their posts. And in that battle squadrons of footsoldiers,
120 chariot-fighters, horses and elephants were struck by wealth-winner Arjuna's arrows; deprived at once of life, their bodies stiffened, and they

fell to the ground, their armour and bodies broken in the great battle by that wonderful Weapon of Indra, O king.

Then with his torrents of sharp arrows the wearer of the diadem set a dreadful river flowing on that battlefield: its water was blood from the wounds of weapons on men's bodies, its foam human fat; broad in current, it flowed very swiftly, terrible to see and to hear. Corpses of elephants and horses formed its banks, the entrails, marrow and flesh of men its mud. Ghosts and great throngs of demons lined its banks. Its waterweed was hair attached to human skulls, its billows severed pieces of armour, as it bore along thousands of bodies in heaps. Fragments of the bones of men, horses and elephants formed the gravel of that fearful, destructive, hellish river; crows, jackals, vultures and storks, and
throngs of carrion beasts and hyenas were approaching its banks from 125
every direction.

When they saw the river set in flow by Arjuna's swarms of arrows, with its fearful current of fat, marrow and blood, cruel as mighty Vaitaraṇī, river of the world of the dead, all the men of Cedi and Pāñcāla, Karūṣa and Matsya, and the Pāṇḍavas, together gave a roar, terrifying the army of the enemy generals as a lion might terrify herds of deer; and Arjuna the bearer of Gāṇḍīva, and Kṛṣṇa the stirrer of men both roared with great joy. Then the Kauravas, with Bhīṣma, Droṇa, Duryodhana and Bāhlika, their bodies badly wounded by Arjuna's weapons, saw that the sun had withdrawn its rays; they saw that the dreadful Weapon of Indra had overspread the sky, unbearable, like doomsday; they saw that evening twilight had come, streaked red with the sun's light; and they retreated from the field. Wealth-winner Arjuna too, having triumphed over his enemies and won glory and fame in the world, went with the princes and his brothers to his tent for the night, his task accomplished.

Among the Kauravas there was uproar as night fell, and a terrible
wail went up. 'Arjuna has killed ten thousand chariot-fighters; he has 130
killed seven hundred elephants, and wiped out all the men of the East, all the forces from Sauvīra, and the Kṣudrakas and men of Mālava. The wealth-winner has done a great deed, such as no one else would be able to do. Śrutāyus the king of Ambaṣṭha, Durmarṣaṇa and Citrasena, Droṇa, Kṛpa, the king of Sindhu and Bāhlika, Bhūriśravas, Śalya and Śala, O king, together with Bhīṣma, have all been conquered by the

wearer of the diadem, the greatest chariot-fighter in the world, through the valour of his own arm!' With such words all your forces went to their tents, O heir of Bharata; and by the light of thousands of blazing torches and shining lamps all the soldiers of the Kaurava army encamped for the night in terror of the wearer of the diadem.

**[56]** *On the fourth day of the battle, Bhīṣma leads the attack on Arjuna, who is in the vanguard of the Pāṇḍava forces in an array similar to the previous day's. Drums, trumpets and conches are sounded, and the battle resumes. Bhīṣma and Arjuna face each other in single combat.* **[57]** *Arjuna's son Abhimanyu too causes great bloodshed; Duryodhana sends a great body of Trigartas, Madras and Kekayas to surround him and Arjuna. The Pāṇḍava commander Dhṛṣṭadyumna sees this and leads a large force against the attackers. Śalya engages Dhṛṣṭadyumna in battle,* **[58]** *and showers arrows upon him; Abhimanyu rushes to attack Śalya. Many of the leading Kauravas take up position to defend Śalya; the leading Pāṇḍavas face them.*

Saṃjaya spoke:
Now Bhīma the mighty Pāṇḍava saw Duryodhana, and he took up his club, thinking to bring the battle to an end. O Dhṛtarāṣṭra, when your sons saw strong-armed Bhīma, club raised, looking like Mount Kailāsa with its peak, they ran headlong in fear. But Duryodhana in fury commanded the ruler of Magadha to support him; with a force of ten thousand spirited Magadha elephants in his van he advanced against Bhīma. When wolf-belly Bhīma saw that elephant force descending on him he leapt down from his chariot, club in hand and roaring like a lion; wielding his huge, heavy iron club, he rushed to attack that elephant force, as if he were gaping Death himself. Strong-armed Bhīma, the mighty hero, strode all over the battlefield striking down elephants with his club, like Indra armed with his thunderbolt. And he roared a great roar that shook men's minds and hearts, at which the elephants formed into a dense mass to struggle against him.

But then the sons of Draupadī, and the great chariot-fighter Abhimanyu son of Subhadrā, and Nakula and Sahadeva, and Dhṛṣṭadyumna heir of Pṛṣata, who were guarding Bhīma's rear, rushed to attack those elephants with a shower of arrows, like clouds pouring rain upon mountains. With their razor-edged steel arrows and their shafts of various sorts the Pāṇḍavas severed the elephant-fighters' heads; their heads fell, and arms still bearing bracelets, and hands still grasping elephant-goads, as if it were raining stones. The elephant-fighters riding headless on the backs of their elephants looked like broken trees on the tops of mountains.

We saw other mighty elephants slain by Dhṛṣṭadyumna, O Dhṛtarāṣṭra; they lay dead or fell dying at the hands of Pṛṣata's noble heir. Then the king of Magadha sent an elephant that looked like Indra's own Airāvaṇa against Abhimanyu's chariot in that battle. When he saw that magnificent elephant of Magadha descending upon him, Subhadrā's heroic son, slayer of enemy heroes, killed it with a single arrow; then, after bringing down his elephant, that conqueror of enemy fortresses, Arjuna's son, struck off the king's head with a broad silver-shafted arrow. As for Bhīma son of Pāṇḍu, he forced his way through that elephant troop and strode all over the battlefield smashing elephants as Indra smashed the mountains: we saw elephants slain by Bhīma in that battle with a single blow, like mountains struck by Indra's thunderbolt. Elephants lay slain like mountains, with broken tusks, broken temples, broken legs, broken backs, broken heads; others trumpeted and sat down, refusing to fight; yet others pissed and shat in their terror and pain. Wherever Bhīma went, we saw mountainous, lifeless elephants slain by him, while others trumpeted; still others vomited blood, their heads smashed in; those mighty elephants sank fearfully down to the ground, like mountains on the surface of the earth.

Bhīma's body was smeared with fat and blood; doused in grease and marrow he strode all over the battlefield like staff-wielding Death. Wolf-belly Bhīma, bearing his club drenched in elephant blood, looked as terrible and frightening as Śiva bearing his weapon Pināka, and the remaining elephants, ravaged by him in his fury, suddenly stampeded, crushing your ranks, while mighty bowmen, and chariot-fighters led by Abhimanyu, guarded that hero, as the gods guard Indra when he fights with the thunderbolt. Bearing his club drenched in blood, himself doused in elephant blood, Bhīma looked like the terrible form of Death. We saw him put his club to work in every direction, O heir of Bharata; we saw him dance like the dancing Śiva; great king, we saw his terrible,

heavy, deadly club, looking like the staff of Yama king of the dead, sounding like the thunderbolt of Indra. Plastered with hair and marrow, smeared with blood, it was like Śiva's weapon Pināka when he strikes down creatures in his fury. Bhīma drove that elephant force with his
60 club, as a herdsman might use a stick to drive his herd of beasts, and your elephants, being slain by that club and by arrows, stampeded and crushed their own forces. Scattering those elephants as a great wind scatters the clouds, Bhīma stood there in the battlefield, like the staff-wielding Śiva in a burning-ground.

**[59]** *Seeing the destruction of his elephant force, Duryodhana sends all his troops to attack Bhīma, but Bhīma checks them single-handed with his fearsome club, slaying them in great numbers. Bhīṣma advances on Bhīma in his chariot, but Sātyaki counterattacks him.* **[60]** *Bhīma and Duryodhana exchange many arrows. Fourteen of Dhṛtarāṣṭra's sons face Bhīma; he kills them all with his arrows. Bhīṣma urges his forces to attack Bhīma. Bhagadatta of Prāgjyotiṣa, riding his elephant, pierces Bhīma with an arrow and renders him unconscious, at which Bhīma's son Ghaṭotkaca, wild with rage, assumes a terrifying illusory form and does battle against Bhagadatta. Bhīṣma announces that the Kauravas must rescue Bhagadatta, but changes his mind when he sees and hears Ghaṭotkaca, opting instead to withdraw for the day. Night finds the Kauravas overcome with shame, the Pāṇḍavas full of joy, and Duryodhana grieving for his slain brothers and making his plans.*

**[61]** — *Dhṛtarāṣṭra interrupts Saṃjaya's narrative to lament the terrible course of events and to ask how the Pāṇḍavas are achieving their successes. Saṃjaya retorts that the Pāṇḍavas are simply fighting fairly; the blame lies squarely on Dhṛtarāṣṭra himself, who never accepted the advice of his well-wishers, and on his wicked sons. Then he resumes his report on the conduct of the war. — Duryodhana asks Bhīṣma the same question, and receives much the same answer. Bhīṣma tells him that, with Kṛṣṇa on their side, the Pāṇḍavas are invincible. Long ago, at an assembly of all the gods, Brahmā paid great homage to the Lord of the Universe, and implored him to take birth in the line of Yadu to slay the Daitya and Asura demons.* **[62]** *The Lord agreed, and vanished; the other gods asked Brahmā whom he had praised so highly, and he told them of the greatness of Vāsudeva. It is this same Kṛṣṇa against whom Duryodhana has insisted on fighting.* **[63]** *Duryodhana asks Bhīṣma to tell him more about*

*Vāsudeva, and Bhīṣma does so. Kṛṣṇa protects those who are in great danger, and this is why Yudhiṣṭhira has sought refuge with him.* **[64]** *Bhīṣma continues to speak of Kṛṣṇa, and tells Duryodhana of the great seers' reverence for him. Duryodhana begins to entertain a greater respect for Kṛṣṇa and the Pāṇḍavas. Bhīṣma concludes by reminding Duryodhana that he now knows who Nara and Nārāyaṇa*[1] *are and why they have taken birth, and why the Pāṇḍavas are invincible; he should make peace with them or face destruction. Then both men return to their tents to sleep.*

**[65]** *On the fifth day the sun rises and the battle begins anew. The Dhārtarāṣṭras are in the Crocodile formation, the Pāṇḍavas in the Hawk formation. At Duryodhana's request, Droṇa attacks the Pāṇḍava force; then he himself comes under attack by Bhīma. Bhīṣma comes to his support, but when Śikhaṇḍin joins the fray he avoids him, remembering that he used to be a woman.* **[66]** *The battle continues, with terrible noise and dreadful sights: the earth is strewn with severed heads and limbs, wounded elephants trumpet in their distress and riderless horses run wild in all directions.* **[67]** *Arjuna showers arrows with his bow Gāṇḍīva, and his enemies are overwhelmed. Warriors from the opposing sides engage each other in single combat. Lightning flashes in a cloudless sky, gales blow, the carnage continues.*

**[68]** *Bhīṣma pierces Bhīma with many arrows and severs his bow; Sātyaki attacks Bhīṣma, but Bhīṣma kills his charioteer and his horses bolt. Bhīṣma now begins to kill the Pāṇḍava force like Indra killing the Dānava demons, but they stand firm and mount an attack on Bhīṣma under the leadership of Dhṛṣṭadyumna.* **[69]** *Arjuna and Aśvatthāman battle fiercely, piercing each other with many arrows; but, out of respect for Aśvatthāman's father Droṇa, Arjuna decides to show him mercy, and leaves him alone. Duryodhana and Bhīma also attack each other with their arrows. Abhimanyu successfully fights several simultaneous Dhārtarāṣṭra attackers; seeing this Duryodhana's son Lakṣmaṇa rushes up to do battle with him, but Abhimanyu kills his horses and his charioteer. Kṛpa takes Lakṣmaṇa up into his own chariot and bears him away to safety.* **[70]** *Sātyaki is slaying Kaurava warriors so swiftly with his torrents of arrows that Duryodhana dispatches a force of ten thousand chariot-fighters against him; but Sātyaki slays them too. Bhūriśravas counterattacks him, scattering his followers,*

1 Two divine seers: they represent (and their names signify) Man and the Son of Man; in the *Mahābhārata* they are identified with Arjuna and Kṛṣṇa.

*whereupon Sātyaki's ten sons challenge Bhūriśravas to combat, separately or together. He agrees to fight them all at once, cuts down the numerous arrows they shoot at him, and severs first their bows and then their heads. Enraged, Sātyaki attacks him. The two warriors slay each other's horses, then leap to the ground and fight with sword and shield, till Bhīma takes Sātyaki up into his chariot and Duryodhana takes Bhūriśravas up into his. As the day draws to an end, Arjuna kills twenty-five thousand chariot-fighters sent against him by Duryodhana. The sun sets, and the two armies withdraw to their respective camps.*

**[71]** *On the sixth day, at Yudhiṣṭhira's command, Dhṛṣṭadyumna disposes his troops in the Crocodile formation, while Bhīṣma disposes his in the* Krauñca *formation. The battle resumes: Bhīṣma and Droṇa slay many of the Pāṇḍava forces, while Bhīma and Arjuna cause great destruction among the Kauravas.*

Dhṛtarāṣṭra spoke:

**[72]** Our soldiers are so excellent and of such very varied types; they are arrayed in the proper manner to guarantee success, O Saṃjaya; we look after them extremely well, and so they are always devoted to us. They are modest and free from vice, and their valour is already proved. Neither too old nor too young, neither thin nor fat, they are agile and tall, strong of limb and healthy; they are committed to a life of armour and weapons; well armed, they are skilled at fighting with swords, with fists and with clubs. Lances, spears and darts, iron bludgeons, bolts and javelins and clubs of all sorts, *kampanas*[1] and bows, iron lances, various kinds of slings, and bare-fist fighting: all these they use with skill in time of war. They are forward in learning; they put effort into their training; they are accomplished in all the arts of weapon-handling; they are skilled at mounting and descending, riding and jumping, fighting properly, advancing and retreating. They have been well tested in the handling of elephants, horses and chariots, and after testing they have been awarded the proper pay – uninfluenced by connection, bribery or family tie, or by strength of friendship or considerations of family or marriage. They are prosperous and well-born; their families are pleased with our good treatment of them; they

1 A weapon of unknown type whose name means literally 'shaker'.

have received many benefits from us; they are men of good name and of intelligence.

O Saṃjaya, our army is in the charge of many world-famous leaders, victorious men of prominent deeds, comparable to the world-guardian gods. It is overseen by many Kṣatriyas who are honoured the world over, who have joined us of their own volition, bringing their troops and followers. It resembles a great ocean, filled by the rivers flowing into it on all sides; it is full of elephants, and of chariots like wingless
birds. Our numerous soldiers make up the water of that fearful ocean, 15
their horses and elephants its waves; it is full of slings, swords, clubs, spears, arrows and lances. It is lashed by the wind of rushing horses and elephants, bearing many standards and ornaments, and covered with jewelled cloths, like the mighty, boundless, roaring ocean. It is in the charge of Droṇa and Bhīṣma, and of Kṛtavarman, Kṛpa and Duḥśāsana, Jayadratha and his followers, Bhagadatta and Vikarṇa, Aśvatthāman son of Droṇa, Śakuni son of Subala, and Bāhlika. For such an army, overseen by such noble, mighty world-heroes, to be slain in battle – this must have
been fated to happen. Such preparations for war were never seen on 20
earth before by men, or even by the blessed ancient seers, O Saṃjaya. For such a massive force, skilled with every kind of weapon, to be killed in battle – what else can that be but destiny? Saṃjaya, it seems completely contrary to reason for such a terrible force to fail in battle against the Pāṇḍavas. Most likely the gods, conspiring on the Pāṇḍava side, are fighting my army; and so my men were slain. What Vidura said was well-meant and sound, O Saṃjaya,[1] but my foolish son Duryodhana
would not accept it. I believe that noble, all-knowing man had formed 25
such a view long before, because he foresaw all this. Most likely this had to be so, in every detail, Saṃjaya, for everything must be as the creator first determined; it cannot be otherwise.

Saṃjaya spoke:

**[73]** It is through your own fault, O bull-like king, that you find yourself in such a calamity, for Duryodhana refuses to see the consequences that you foresaw in actions which confound *dharma*. Lord of the peoples,

1 Vidura had repeatedly urged a peaceful settlement during Book 5, 'Perseverance'.

it was through your fault that this gambling match ever took place; it was through your fault that the war with the Pāṇḍavas began; having committed the fault yourself, receive the reward for it yourself today! For each person experiences the consequences of the actions he has done, either here or in the next world, O king; what has happened to you is but fitting. Therefore, my king, though you find yourself in this great calamity, be still and listen while I describe the course of the battle.

5 After brave Bhīma had broken your mighty ranks with his sharp arrows, he next encountered all Duryodhana's younger brothers: Duḥśāsana, Durviṣaha, Duḥsaha, Durmada, Jaya, Jayatsena, Vikarṇa, Citrasena, Sudarśana, Cārucitra, Suvarman, Duṣkarṇa and Karṇa himself.[1] When he saw these and many other sons of Dhṛtarāṣṭra, great chariot-fighters all, full of the fury of war, so near to him, Bhīma of great strength forced his way into your mighty ranks, placed in Bhīṣma's charge during that battle. Then those lords of men called out to one another, 'Here comes
10 wolf-belly Bhīma! Let us take him alive!' Kuntī's son was surrounded by the brothers of Duryodhana, intent on this resolve, as the sun is surrounded by great doom-presaging planets at the time of destruction of all beings. Bhīma son of Pāṇḍu reached the centre of the array, and yet he felt no fear, like great Indra when he encountered the demons in their war against the gods. Then hundreds of thousands of chariot-fighters all covered that lone hero with a hail of terrible arrows, O lord, while he likewise covered them. In that battle he killed the best of those warriors as they sat on horseback or elephant-back or in their chariots, paying no heed to the sons of Dhṛtarāṣṭra; for high-minded Bhīma understood their resolve to capture him, and he had made up his mind to slay every
15 one of them, O king. So Pāṇḍu's son quit his chariot; with his club he attacked the massive force, great as an ocean, of the sons of Dhṛtarāṣṭra.

When Bhīma plunged into that force, Dhṛṣṭadyumna heir of Pṛṣata left his combat with Droṇa, and went quickly to the place where Subala's son Śakuni was. As that bull-like hero proceeded to rend apart your great army, he came upon Bhīma's empty chariot in the midst of the conflict; and seeing Bhīma's charioteer Viśoka there Dhṛṣṭadyumna became almost senseless with grief, great king. Griefstricken, choked

1 Not the major hero Karṇa but a son of Dhṛtarāṣṭra bearing the same name.

with tears and speaking through his sighs, he asked, 'Where is Bhīma, dearer to me than my own life?' Then Viśoka joined his hands together 20
and answered Dhṛṣṭadyumna, 'The mighty Pāṇḍava, Bhīma of great energy, stationed me here and plunged into this Dhārtarāṣṭra force, great as an ocean. As he left he cheerfully addressed these words to me, O tiger-like hero: "Rein in the horses and wait here for a while, charioteer, while I quickly slay those who stand here ready to slay me!" When they saw that hero of mighty strength rushing forward club in hand, every single Pāṇḍava soldier sought to rival him. Then, as that tumultuous, fearful battle continued, O king, your friend broke that mighty array and plunged in.'

When Pṛṣata's heir, Dhṛṣṭadyumna of great strength, heard Viśoka's 25
words, he replied to that charioteer in the middle of the battlefield, 'O charioteer, today I have no use for life if I cast off my love for the Pāṇḍavas and abandon Bhīma in battle. What would the assembled Kṣatriyas say of me if I left the battlefield without Bhīma after being present when he showed such single-minded purpose? The gods with Fire at their head inflict great harm upon the man who abandons his companions to return home unharmed. Bhīma of mighty strength is my friend and my kinsman; that destroyer of enemies is devoted to me, and I to him. So I shall follow where wolf-belly Bhīma has gone. Watch 30
me strike down my enemies as Indra struck down the demons!'

O heir of Bharata, with these words brave Dhṛṣṭadyumna set out into the midst of the enemy army, following Bhīma's track marked out by club-ravaged elephants. Then he saw Bhīma consuming the ranks of his enemies as if with fire, in his might smashing kings in battle, like a wind smashing trees. Chariot-fighters and horsemen, footsoldiers and elephants cried loudly in distress as Bhīma slew them in that battle; and a great uproar arose among your troops, sir, as they perished at the hand of Bhīma, skilful expert at many forms of war.

Then all your skilled bowmen surrounded wolf-belly Bhīma and 35
fearlessly attacked him on all sides with a shower of weapons. When Pṛṣata's heir, mighty Dhṛṣṭadyumna, saw that Pāṇḍu's son Bhīma – the most excellent of all bearers of arms – was assailed on all sides by world-heroes with a terrible force of their allies, he went to his side and ministered to him, while Bhīma, wounded all over his body

with arrows, stood spewing forth the poison of his fury, club in hand, like Death at the time of destruction. Swiftly the noble Dhṛṣṭadyumna removed the arrows from Bhīma's body and took him up into his own chariot; embracing him closely, he ministered to him in the midst of their enemies. Then your son Duryodhana approached his brothers while the great battle continued, and said, 'This wicked son of Drupada has joined forces with Bhīma. Go, all of you, and kill him! Do not give your enemy a chance to seek reinforcements.'

40 At these words the merciless Dhārtarāṣṭras, acting at the command of the eldest among them, descended on Dhṛṣṭadyumna's chariot, weapons raised for the kill, like terrible comets at the end of time. Those heroes, bearing their lovely bows and shaking the earth with the sound of their bowstrings and their chariot-wheels, showered arrows upon Drupada's son Dhṛṣṭadyumna as clouds shower torrents of water on a mountain. But that expert at many forms of war was unshaken in the battle, and cut them down with his own well-sharpened arrows. When the youthful son of Drupada realized that your brave sons, standing round his chariot in the battle, were striving against him, he was fiercely determined to slay them. In his fury that great chariot-fighter shot the Weapon of Bewilderment at your sons, O king, like Indra at battle against the demons. Then those heroic men were struck senseless in the battle: the Weapon of Bewilderment stripped them of intelligence and mettle. And on every side all the Kauravas ran headlong together with their horses and elephants and chariots, when they realized your sons were senseless and unconscious, as though their time had run out.

But at that moment Droṇa, best of all bearers of arms, came upon
45 Drupada and wounded him with three dreadful arrows; then King
Drupada, badly wounded by Droṇa in that battle, and remembering his
ancient feud against him,[1] retreated from the field. After overcoming
Drupada, Droṇa of great energy blew his conch, and all the Somakas,
hearing that sound, were struck with terror. Now the ardent Droṇa,
best of all bearers of arms, heard that your sons had been struck senseless
in the battle by the Weapon of Bewilderment, and in his fervour for

1 Droṇa and Drupada had been childhood friends, but Drupada repudiated their friendship: 1.122.

the princes he hurried there from his battle with Drupada. There that
mighty bowman, Bharadvāja's son of great energy, saw Dhṛṣṭadyumna
and Bhīma striding all over the vast battlefield; and that great chariot-
fighter also saw your sons lying senseless. Then, taking up the Weapon
of Intelligence, he destroyed the Weapon of Bewilderment, and your 50
sons, great chariot-fighters all, were revived and returned to the battle
to fight against Bhīma and Pṛṣata's heir.

Yudhiṣṭhira summoned his warriors and addressed them: 'Let twelve
armed chariot-fighter heroes led by Abhimanyu do their best to follow
the track of Bhīma and Pṛṣata's heir in the battle. Let them get news
of them, for my heart is troubled.' Those valiant warriors, brave and
manly, received this command, assented, and set out all together as the
sun reached its midday point. The Kekayas, the sons of Draupadī, and
brave Dhṛṣṭaketu, foe-tamers all, under Abhimanyu's leadership, and
accompanied by a great army, formed the Needle-point array in that 55
battle and broke the chariot-forces of the Dhārtarāṣṭras. Lord of men,
your army, terrified of Bhīma and struck senseless by Dhṛṣṭadyumna,
could not resist those mighty bowmen as they advanced under Abhi-
manyu's leadership, any more than a woman of the street can resist the
advances of a man in a drunken stupor. Those great bowmen came
on with their gold-embellished standards, and rushed forward to reach
Dhṛṣṭadyumna and wolf-belly Bhīma. When those two saw the mighty
bowmen under Abhimanyu's leadership, they were filled with joy as
they struck down your ranks.

Now the brave prince of Pāñcāla, Pṛṣata's heir, saw Droṇa his Teacher 60
coming swiftly towards him, and he gave up his aim of slaying your
sons. He had the Kekaya king take wolf-belly Bhīma up into his chariot,
and then furiously rushed to attack Droṇa, master of every weapon.
Bharadvāja's son Droṇa of great energy, destroyer of his enemies, in fury
severed his bow with a broad shaft as he launched his attack; and he shot
other arrows in hundreds at Pṛṣata's heir, to benefit Duryodhana, and
mindful of the funeral offerings of his lord.[1] Then the heir of Pṛṣata,
slayer of enemy heroes, took up another bow and pierced Droṇa with

1 If the Kauravas are annihilated there will be no male heir to make the funeral offering (*śrāddha*) for Bhīṣma, who will thus not attain the blessed realm of the ancestors.

65 seventy gold-shafted, stone-whetted arrows. Once again heroic Droṇa, tormentor of his enemies, severed his bow; with four excellent arrows he swiftly sent his four horses to the terrible realm of Yama king of the dead, and with another broad shaft he sent his charioteer to his death. When his horses were killed Dhṛṣṭadyumna, strong-armed, mighty chariot-fighter, leapt quickly down from his own chariot and climbed into Abhimanyu's great chariot. Droṇa shook the Pāṇḍava ranks, with all their horses, elephants and chariots, before the very eyes of Bhīma and Pṛṣata's heir. All the mighty Pāṇḍava chariot-fighters saw their force broken by Droṇa of boundless ardour, and could do nothing to prevent
70 it; and that force, being slain by Droṇa with his sharp arrows, began to heave first one way then the other, like a storm-tossed sea. When they saw that force in such straits, your forces were delighted; and when they saw Droṇa the Teacher furiously consuming the ranks of his enemies as if with fire, your soldiers all shouted, 'Bravo! Bravo!', O heir of Bharata.

**[74]** *The Dhārtarāṣṭras, restored to their senses, return to their attack on Bhīma, who now approaches them in his chariot. He and Duryodhana attack each other with their arrows. Then Yudhiṣṭhira once again sends Abhimanyu with a small force to support Bhīma, at which the Kauravas abandon their fight against him.*

*In the afternoon of the sixth day Duryodhana and the other great chariot-fighters travel to where Abhimanyu, Bhīma and Dhṛṣṭadyumna are inflicting casualties upon the Kaurava army. There is great slaughter on both sides; yet there is not a single man who does not wish to fight.* **[75]** *As the sun grows red, Duryodhana attacks Bhīma, who responds by cataloguing the crimes Duryodhana has committed against the Pāṇḍavas and swearing that he will kill him that very day unless he abandons the fight. Bhīma then showers Duryodhana with arrows, killing his horses and severing his canopy and his standard. Kṛpa takes the badly wounded Duryodhana up into his own chariot. The focus of the conflict now shifts to the remaining Dhārtarāṣṭras and Abhimanyu's force. Abhimanyu severs Vikarṇa's standard, kills his charioteer and horses, and pierces him with many arrows. Durmukha kills the charioteer and horses of Śrutakarman, but Sutasoma takes Śrutakarman into his own chariot. Śrutakīrti attacks Jayatsena, who severs his bow; Śatānīka then fights and slays both Jayatsena and Duṣkarṇa, upon which the Dhārtarāṣṭras and Bhīṣma launch a* *savage assault on the Pāṇḍava forces, killing great numbers. The sun sets, and the combatants withdraw to their camps.*

**[76]** *On the morning of the seventh day Duryodhana speaks to Bhīṣma: despite the excellence of his troops the Pāṇḍavas have enjoyed such successes against them. He asks Bhīṣma to help him secure the victory. Bhīṣma replies that the Pāṇḍava forces are numerous and fierce, and motivated by strong hostility to the Kauravas. None the less he will fight against them to his greatest ability, even at the cost of his life. Duryodhana is cheered.* **[77]** *Bhīṣma now lists the many great warriors who are prepared to fight to the death for Duryodhana's cause; however, the Pāṇḍavas have Kṛṣṇa, whose presence renders them invincible. Then he gives Duryodhana a healing herb that cures his wounds.*

*Bhīṣma places his forces in the Circle formation; Yudhiṣṭhira places his in the Thunderbolt formation, and the battle commences once more. Arjuna vows to Kṛṣṇa that he will that day slay all Dhārtarāṣṭras who face him on the battlefield. He deploys the Weapon of Indra, and the arrows he shoots are so numerous that amongst all the thousands of kings, horses and elephants on the Kaurava side, not one escapes injury.* **[78]** *Duryodhana exhorts his troops to give the strongest support to Bhīṣma; Bhīṣma then rapidly comes to where Arjuna's chariot is. Meanwhile, Virāṭa does battle with Droṇa.*

Saṃjaya spoke:
Bharadvāja's son Droṇa pierced the Matsya king with a feathered shaft in that battle, and with a single arrow he severed both his standard and his bow. Casting aside his severed bow, Virāṭa the general swiftly took up another, heavy and strong, and blazing arrows like venomous snakes. With three he pierced Droṇa, with four his horses, with one he pierced his standard, and with five his charioteer; then with a single arrow he pierced his bow. At that the bull-like Brahmin Droṇa was enraged: with eight well-planed arrows he slew Virāṭa's horses, best heir of Bharata, and with a single feathered shaft his charioteer. At the death of his horses and charioteer, Virāṭa, best of chariot-fighters, leapt down from his chariot and swiftly climbed into the chariot of his son Śaṅkha. Then the two of them, father and son, fighting from a single chariot, strongly countered Bharadvāja's son with a great shower of arrows. Lord of men, in that battle Droṇa in fury quickly shot an arrow like a venomous snake at Śaṅkha; piercing his heart, that arrow drank up his blood on

the battlefield, then fell to earth, brightly smeared with blood. At once he fell from his chariot, slain by the arrow of Bharadvāja's son, dropping his bow and his arrows, before his father's eyes. When Virāṭa saw his son killed, he ran headlong in fear, leaving his conflict with Droṇa, who resembled gaping Death. Then Bharadvāja's son swiftly tore apart the mighty ranks of the Pāṇḍavas, scattering them on the battlefield by hundreds and by thousands.

25 Now Śikhaṇḍin encountered Droṇa's son Aśvatthāman in that battle,
great king, and he struck him between the eyebrows with three speeding
arrows. With those three fastened to his forehead, that tiger-like hero
appeared like Mount Meru with its three lofty peaks of gold. Then,
in half the time it takes to blink, Aśvatthāman furiously took aim with
many arrows at Śikhaṇḍin's charioteer and his standard, his horses and
his weapon, and cut them down, O king. At the death of his horses,
Śikhaṇḍin, best of chariot-fighters, leapt down from his chariot; he took
up his sharp sword and his bright arrow-shield, and strode in fury about
the field afflicting his enemies like a bird of prey. As Śikhaṇḍin ranged
with his sword over the battlefield, great king, Droṇa's son Aśvatthāman
30 saw no opportunity to strike him, which was a great wonder. Then
in his extreme anger Aśvatthāman shot many thousands of arrows at
Śikhaṇḍin in that battle, O bull-like heir of Bharata. Śikhaṇḍin, best of
the mighty, with his sharp-bladed sword cut apart that dreadful shower
of arrows as it descended on him in the battle. At this, Droṇa's son
severed his bright shield, beautifully adorned with a hundred moons,
and reduced his sword to fragments in that battle; and he pierced him
with many sharp feathered arrows, O king. But Śikhaṇḍin whirled the
sword that Aśvatthāman had broken with his arrows, and swiftly hurled
it, blazing like a snake. Droṇa's son, showing his swiftness of hand on
the battlefield, severed that sword as it descended rapidly on him, bright
as doomsday fire; and he pierced Śikhaṇḍin with many iron arrows.
35 O king, Śikhaṇḍin was badly wounded by those sharp arrows, and he
quickly climbed into the chariot of Madhu's heir, the noble Sātyaki.

Now mighty Sātyaki in fury pierced the mighty Rākṣasa, the cruel Alambusa, with his terrible arrows. Then, heir of Bharata, that Rākṣasa prince severed his bow with a half-moon arrow, and pierced him with further arrows in that battle: he used the illusory power of the Rākṣasas

to pour showers of arrows upon him. Then we saw the wonderful valour
of Sātyaki heir of Śini, who was untroubled even as he was struck by
those sharp arrows. That Vṛṣṇi hero, Madhu's famous heir, deployed the
Weapon of Indra which he had obtained from victorious Arjuna. That 40
Weapon reduced the Rākṣasa illusion to ash, O heir of Bharata, and
poured terrible arrows on Alambusa from all sides as a monsoon cloud
might pour torrents of water upon a mountain. Pressed so by Madhu's
noble heir, the Rākṣasa ran headlong in fear, leaving his conflict with
Sātyaki.

Having vanquished the Rākṣasa prince, invincible to even Indra in
battle, before the eyes of your soldiers, Śini's most valiant heir Sātyaki
gave a roar; he struck down your men with many sharp arrows, and they
fled in terror. Now at that moment Drupada's mighty son Dhṛṣṭadyumna
covered your son Duryodhana, lord of men, with a hail of well-planed
arrows in that battle, great king. Though covered with arrows by 45
Dhṛṣṭadyumna, most royal heir of Bharata, the lord of men your son
was unshaken, and he swiftly pierced Dhṛṣṭadyumna with sixty and
thirty arrows in that battle, which was a great wonder. Commander
Dhṛṣṭadyumna, the mighty chariot-fighter, in fury severed his bow, sir,
and quickly slew his four horses; and he swiftly pierced him with seven
well-sharpened arrows. At the death of his horses the mighty, strong-
armed Duryodhana leapt down from his chariot and ran on foot straight
against Pṛṣata's heir Dhṛṣṭadyumna, brandishing his sword. Then Śakuni 50
of great strength, in his fervour for the prince, approached Duryodhana
king of all the world, and took him up into his own chariot. But the
heir of Pṛṣata, slayer of enemy heroes, having defeated the king, struck
down your troops as Indra, thunderbolt in hand, struck down the troops
of the demons.

Meanwhile, Kṛtavarman attacked the mighty chariot-fighter Bhīma,
covering him with arrows as a great cloud covers the sun. At this Bhīma,
afflicter of his enemies, laughed aloud, and then furiously shot his
arrows at Kṛtavarman in that battle. The Sātvata chariot-fighter, skilled
in weapons, was pained by these, but he did not tremble, great king, and
he attacked Bhīma with his own sharp arrows. Then Bhīma of mighty
strength killed his four horses, and felled his charioteer and his gorgeous
standard; that slayer of enemy heroes covered him with a hail of various 55

kinds of arrows until, maimed in every limb, he resembled a porcupine. At the death of his horses he went swiftly from his chariot to the chariot of Vṛṣaka your brother-in-law, before the very eyes of your son, great king. And Bhīma rushed in fury to attack your troops, and slew them in fury, like staff-wielding Death.

**[79]** — *Dhṛtarāṣṭra again comments on the Kauravas' lack of success, and blames fate, but Saṃjaya repeats that his own and his sons' misdeeds are to blame. Then he continues his narration. — Arjuna's son Irāvat does battle with the princes Vinda and Anuvinda of Avanti, who fight from a single chariot after he kills Anuvinda's horses; now he kills Vinda's charioteer, and the horses bolt. Ghaṭotkaca loses his horses to Bhagadatta's arrows, and flees. Nakula loses his horses to Śalya's arrows, but finds refuge in Sahadeva's chariot. Sahadeva and Śalya exchange many arrows, until one arrow of Sahadeva's renders Śalya unconscious, and his charioteer bears him away to safety.*

**[80]** *At noon on the seventh day Yudhiṣṭhira attacks Śrutāyus of Ambaṣṭha. The two exchange many arrows. Yudhiṣṭhira, pierced by Śrutāyus's arrows, is filled with such fury that the very immortals are alarmed, but he restrains himself, and kills Śrutāyus's horses and charioteer; Śrutāyus flees. Cekitāna of the Vṛṣṇis loses his charioteer and horses to Kṛpa's arrows; he leaps to the ground and takes to his club, with which he kills Kṛpa's horses and charioteer. The two now fight on the ground with swords until both fall through exhaustion. Cekitāna's ally Karakarṣa takes him up into his own chariot, and Śakuni does the same for Kṛpa. Dhṛṣṭaketu loses his charioteer and horses to Bhūriśravas's arrows, but finds refuge in Śatānīka's chariot. Abhimanyu meets with success in battle against the Dhārtarāṣṭras Citrasena, Vikarṇa and Durmarṣaṇa, but refrains from killing them so as not to falsify Bhīma's vow to do so. Bhīṣma goes to their rescue, and Arjuna in turn instructs Kṛṣṇa to drive his chariot to that place, where he challenges the warriors supporting Bhīṣma, including Suśarman, king of Trigarta.*

**[81]** *Arjuna slays many of Bhīṣma's supporters and moves to attack Bhīṣma himself; he is joined by all his brothers. Yudhiṣṭhira sees Śikhaṇḍin fleeing after having his weapon severed by Bhīṣma, and angrily upbraids him; Śikhaṇḍin returns to the fight, using the Weapon of Varuṇa to overcome Śalya's attacks on him. Bhīṣma overwhelms Yudhiṣṭhira, and Bhīma rushes to his defence. Most of the Kauravas flee, but Citrasena remains; Bhīma hurls his club at him, but*

*Citrasena leaps to the ground, sword and shield in hand, while the club destroys his chariot.* **[82]** *Vikarṇa takes Citrasena up into his own chariot. Yudhiṣṭhira and the twins advance on Bhīṣma. Bhīṣma and Yudhiṣṭhira exchange vast numbers of arrows, and Bhīṣma kills Yudhiṣṭhira's horses; Yudhiṣṭhira finds refuge in Nakula's chariot. At Yudhiṣṭhira's urging the warriors of the Pāṇḍavas surround Bhīṣma in great numbers, but he destroys them as a forest fire destroys dry grass, severing heads like palm-fruits. The formations of both armies are broken, and confused individual fighting occurs; then Dhṛṣṭadyumna and Sātyaki begin a concerted attack on the Kaurava warriors. Vinda and Anuvinda of Avanti kill Dhṛṣṭadyumna's horses, but he finds refuge in Sātyaki's chariot. Night falls, and the two armies withdraw to their camps, praising each other.*

**[83]** *On the morning of the eighth day, Bhīṣma leads forth the Kaurava army, arrayed in the Oceanic formation; seeing it, Yudhiṣṭhira calls on Dhṛṣṭadyumna to form a counter-array, and he places his forces in the* Śṛṅgāṭaka *formation. The battle is resumed.* **[84]** *Yudhiṣṭhira urges his forces to attack Bhīṣma, but Bhīṣma kills them in great numbers: only Bhīma can stand against him. Various of the Dhārtarāṣṭras attack Bhīma, but he slays them all, whereupon the others flee in fear. Duryodhana is greatly distressed, and laments his evil fate; Bhīṣma replies that death in the battle is inevitable; not even the gods can defeat the Pāṇḍavas in battle.*

**[85]** — *Again Dhṛtarāṣṭra ascribes the slaughter of his sons to fate, but again Saṃjaya tells him that the blame lies with his own failure to control his sons as his well-wishers had advised. Then he resumes his narration. — At noon on the eighth day the Pāṇḍava forces divide into three sections: their chief allies launch a concerted assault on Bhīṣma, while Arjuna leads an attack on the kings under Duryodhana's command, and Abhimanyu, Ghaṭotkaca and Bhīma turn their attack on the remaining Kauravas. There is great slaughter on both sides: in particular, Droṇa kills many of the Sṛñjayas*[1] *and Somakas, while Bhīma slays great numbers of Kauravas. A river of blood flows. Bhīma destroys many enemy elephants, and Nakula and Sahadeva destroy many horses.*

**[86]** *Arjuna's son Irāvat had been born to the widowed daughter of the king of the serpents; when Arjuna was in Indra's world Irāvat had presented himself to his father and vowed to support him in time of battle. He now arrives on the battlefield with a large body of cavalry. In the ensuing clash with the Kaurava*

1 Strictly a subgroup of the Pāñcālas, but often used to refer to the Pāñcālas as a whole.

*cavalry many horses are killed. Then Śakuni's brothers, supported by Śakuni himself, lead a counterattack, but they are no match for Irāvat, who slays them all except for Vṛṣaka.*

Saṃjaya spoke:
When Duryodhana saw that they had all fallen he was afraid, and he spoke
45 furiously to the dreadful-looking Rākṣasa Alambusa son of Ṛśyaśṛṅga,
a mighty bowman, foe-taming master of illusion, and long-standing
enemy of Bhīma on account of the killing of Baka.[1] 'See, O hero, how
this mighty son of Arjuna, this master of illusion, has visited hateful and
terrible destruction on my forces! Now you can travel anywhere at will,
sir, and you are skilled at illusory combat; you are already the enemy
of Kuntī's son; therefore slay Irāvat in battle!' The dreadful-looking
Rākṣasa assented, and went to the place where Arjuna's young son
was, roaring his lion-roar, longing to kill Irāvat of great strength in the
battle, surrounded by his own forces and accompanied by a body of
warrior-heroes, well mounted, skilled at fighting, wielders of bright
50 lances. And the valiant Irāvat too, slayer of his enemies, hastened on in
fury to counter the Rākṣasa who sought his death.

That mightiest of Rākṣasas, seeing Irāvat descending on him, hastened
to deploy his powers of illusion. He fashioned great numbers of illusory
horses, well ridden by terrible Rākṣasas bearing pikes and spears in their
hands. These two thousand warriors advanced in fury to meet Irāvat's
men, and before long they had dispatched each other to the world of the
dead. On the death of that force, the two enemies, mad for battle, met
55 in battle, like Indra and Vṛtra. Seeing the battle-crazed Rākṣasa rushing
towards him, Irāvat of mighty strength furiously counter-charged him.
As the wicked Rākṣasa came up to him, he cut his brilliant bow and
his arrow-case into five pieces with his sword. Alambusa, seeing that
his bow had been severed, ascended rapidly into the sky to trick the
furious Irāvat with his powers of illusion. But Irāvat knew how to find
his enemies' weak spots; he could change form at will, and was difficult
to counter. He too flew into the sky: he tricked the Rākṣasa with his
own illusions, and severed his limbs with his arrows. But though that

1 A Rākṣasa killed by Bhīma: 1.151.

best of Rākṣasas was cut asunder again and again by Irāvat's arrows, his
body became whole, great king, and he regained his youth. For illusion 60
is natural to those creatures, and their age and form are subject to their
own wishes; so it was that that Rākṣasa's body re-grew, though cut in
pieces.

Now Irāvat in fury chopped again and again at that mighty Rākṣasa
with his sharp axe. The heroic Rākṣasa, chopped like a tree by the
mighty Irāvat, roared terribly. The sound was shattering. Wounded by
the axe, the great Rākṣasa bled heavily; and then he became enraged,
and speedily joined battle. Seeing his enemy exerting his power in
that conflict, Ṛśyaśṛṅga's son assumed a terrible, vast form, and tried
to seize him in the midst of the vanguard, before the eyes of all. But 65
when Irāvat saw the noble Rākṣasa employing such an illusion, he
too was enraged, and proceeded to create his own illusion. As that
hero, who never retreated in battle, was overwhelmed with rage, his
mother's serpent kinsfolk came up to him. Completely covered by great
numbers of snakes in that battle, O king, he assumed a vast form like the
serpent Ananta;[1] then he covered that Rākṣasa with snakes of various
kinds. Covered with snakes, that bull-like Rākṣasa reflected, and then
assumed the form of an eagle and devoured those snakes. Seeing his
mother's kinsfolk devoured through illusion, Irāvat was stupefied; and
the Rākṣasa slew him with his sword. Severed by the Rākṣasa, Irāvat's 70
head fell to the ground, still decked with earrings and a diadem, lovely
as a lotus or the moon.

**[87]** *Seeing that Irāvat has been killed, Bhīma's Rākṣasa son Ghaṭotkaca in fury roars so fiercely that the Kauravas are struck with fear. He then assumes a terrible form and attacks, supported by many other Rākṣasas; Duryodhana leads an elephant force against him, and slays a number of his supporters. Furious, Ghaṭotkaca vows to avenge the wrongs Duryodhana has done the Pāṇḍavas if he will face him on the battlefield.*

**[88]** *Ghaṭotkaca and Duryodhana exchange many arrows. Ghaṭotkaca raises a mighty spear to hurl at Duryodhana, but Bhagadatta places himself and his elephant in front of him; Ghaṭotkaca in fury kills the elephant with the*

1 Ananta or Śeṣa is the snake that serves as Viṣṇu's couch.

*spear; Bhagadatta escapes. Duryodhana now faces Ghaṭotkaca. Bhīṣma hears and recognizes the Rākṣasa's roars and urges all the Kaurava chiefs to go to Duryodhana's aid. Ghaṭotkaca and his Rākṣasa forces now do battle against the foremost Kauravas; Ghaṭotkaca beats them back and causes great carnage.* [89] *Then he resumes his attack on Duryodhana, but is in turn attacked by numerous Kaurava chariot-warriors. Yudhiṣṭhira hears and recognizes his great roars, and he dispatches Bhīma at the head of a force to go to his aid. A dreadful battle occurs: red smoke obscures the battlefield, and a river of blood flows. The Kauravas are made to flee.*

[90] *Duryodhana attacks Bhīma and wounds him; in fury, Ghaṭotkaca and his followers turn their attack on Duryodhana. Droṇa urges his leading chariot-warriors to go to his aid, and a great battle occurs. Bhīma wounds Droṇa and is attacked in turn by Duryodhana and Aśvatthāman. Seeing his danger, Abhimanyu and the other Pāṇḍava warriors rush to his aid. Aśvatthāman kills many of Ghaṭotkaca's supporters; in response Ghaṭotkaca creates an illusion in which the Kauravas perceive themselves utterly overcome by their enemies; despite the efforts of Bhīṣma and Droṇa to rally them they flee, routed.* [91] *Duryodhana proposes to Bhīṣma to do battle himself against Ghaṭotkaca, but Bhīṣma tells him he should fight his peers, the Pāṇḍavas and the kings allied to them, and he dispatches Bhagadatta on his elephant against Ghaṭotkaca. A great battle occurs, and the Pāṇḍava forces suffer heavy losses. Ghaṭotkaca and Bhagadatta face each other: each foils the wonderful spears hurled by the other. Bhagadatta showers arrows on Ghaṭotkaca and the other Pāṇḍava leaders; Bhīma joins in the attack with his club, and Arjuna too rides up. As the battle continues, Bhīma tells Arjuna of the death of his son Irāvat.* [92] *Arjuna speaks to Kṛṣṇa about his grief over Irāvat's death and his distaste for the business of battle; none the less he resumes fighting. Warriors from the opposing sides engage each other in single combat. Bhīma, attacked by a number of the Dhārtarāṣṭras, slays them whilst warding off the attacks of Droṇa. The battle is terrific, and both armies suffer greatly. Night falls, and the warriors withdraw to their camps.*

[93] *Duryodhana discusses the situation with Śakuni, Duḥśāsana and Karṇa. The senior warriors Droṇa, Bhīṣma, Kṛpa, Śalya and Bhūriśravas are not offering the Pāṇḍavas sufficient resistance, and the Kauravas are being seriously weakened: what should be done? Karṇa responds that Bhīṣma should be asked to renounce his command, since he is not able or willing to bring the fighting to a successful end, and he, Karṇa, will then wipe out the Pāṇḍavas.*

*Duryodhana and his brothers now ride in procession to Bhīṣma's quarters, where Duryodhana puts the proposal to Bhīṣma: either he should make good his promise to slay all the Pāṇḍavas, or he should allow Karṇa to fight in his stead.* **[94]** *Deeply wounded by Duryodhana's words, Bhīṣma replies by once again stressing Arjuna's invincibility, reminding him of his great feats. In his folly Duryodhana has provoked the Pāṇḍavas into war, and now it is for him to fight them. As for Bhīṣma himself, he will slay all the Somakas and Pāñcālas, save only for Śikhaṇḍin; tomorrow he will fight a battle that will be remembered till the end of the world.*

**[95]** *On the morning of the ninth day, Duryodhana announces Bhīṣma's promise of the night before to his forces; to Duḥśāsana he explains that protection of Bhīṣma is the paramount task, especially against Śikhaṇḍin: the senior warriors must see to this task. So the army moves out with Bhīṣma surrounded by chariot-warriors; seeing this, Arjuna advises Dhṛṣṭadyumna to deploy Śikhaṇḍin where he will face Bhīṣma; Arjuna will protect him. Bhīṣma places his forces in the Foursquare formation, and the Pāṇḍavas too array themselves. The two armies rush at each other, and the dreadful battle is resumed.*

**[96]** *Abhimanyu launches a savage attack on the Kaurava forces, who are unable to withstand his showers of arrows and are routed. Duryodhana dispatches Alambusa against Abhimanyu, and the Pāṇḍava forces, terrified by his roars, suffer heavy losses and are routed in turn. Alambusa turns his attack on the sons of Draupadī: Prativindhya pierces his armour and wounds him, but he recovers and kills the horses and charioteers of all five brothers, and then rushes forward to kill them; but Abhimanyu comes to their rescue and engages Alambusa in battle.* **[97]** *Abhimanyu and Alambusa exchange many arrows. Alambusa creates darkness; Abhimanyu dispels it with the Sun Weapon. Overcome, Alambusa abandons his chariot and flees. Seeing Abhimanyu's success, Bhīṣma and other Kaurava chariot-warriors turn their attack on him. Arjuna comes with other Pāṇḍava warriors to his aid, and a great battle takes place. Sātyaki attacks first Kṛpa then Aśvatthāman, whom he wounds; Droṇa comes to his aid, and Arjuna rushes to attack him.* **[98]** *Droṇa and Arjuna exchange many arrows. Duryodhana sends Suśarman of Trigarta to Droṇa's aid; more arrows are exchanged, and Arjuna's valour overcomes the Trigarta warriors, who flee. Duryodhana now dispatches many of his senior warriors to attack the Pāṇḍavas. Bhagadatta and Śrutāyus with their elephant-warriors attack Bhīma; Bhīma slaughters the elephants, tearing them limb from limb till, smeared* *with their blood, he resembles Rudra. The remaining elephants stampede, and Duryodhana's forces flee the field.*

**[99]** *At noon on the ninth day Bhīṣma begins his attack on the Somakas. A battle develops between Bhīṣma on the one side and Dhṛṣṭadyumna, Śikhaṇḍin, Virāṭa and Drupada on the other. Many arrows are exchanged, though Bhīṣma avoids striking Śikhaṇḍin. Numerous other warriors join in on both sides, and the battle becomes general and terrible. A river of blood flows, and lamentations are heard at Duryodhana's wickedness against the virtuous Pāṇḍavas. Hearing them, Duryodhana urges on his senior warriors, and the battle, fruit either of fate or of Duryodhana's wrongdoing, continues.*

**[100]** *Arjuna kills many men of Trigarta, and Duryodhana, seeing his forces fleeing, joins Bhīṣma in leading his army against Arjuna. The Pāṇḍavas too join in. Citrasena loses his horses and charioteer to Abhimanyu's arrows, but finds refuge in Durmukha's chariot. Bāhlika loses his horses and charioteer to Bhīma's arrows, but finds refuge in Lakṣmaṇa's chariot. Sātyaki attacks Bhīṣma; they exchange many arrows. A general battle gets under way.* **[101]** *Duryodhana tells Duḥśāsana that protection of Bhīṣma is their paramount duty, so that Bhīṣma will be able to wipe out the Pāñcālas and Pāṇḍavas, and Duḥśāsana arranges for Bhīṣma to be covered by a large body of men. Śakuni begins to harry Yudhiṣṭhira, Nakula and Sahadeva, and Duryodhana sends ten thousand cavalry to attack the Pāṇḍava force, but the three brothers slay them with their swords, severing numerous heads. Dismayed, Duryodhana dispatches Śalya with a force of chariot-warriors to reinforce the attack; he and the three Pāṇḍavas exchange many arrows, and Bhīma hurries to join his brothers.*

**[102]** *Bhīṣma now attacks the Pāṇḍavas. They surround him, but he slaughters them in their thousands like a raging forest fire.*

Saṃjaya spoke:
O king, in every direction we saw chariots in their hundreds and thousands, some with broken axles and gear, others with broken wheels.
20 Lord of the peoples, the earth was littered with chariots broken despite their guard-rails, with slain chariot-fighters, with arrows, fine armour lying smashed, and spears, with clubs and bludgeons, daggers and shafts, ballast-blocks and arrow-cases, and broken wheels, human arms, bows, swords, and heads still decked with earrings, with arm-guards and finger-guards, broken standards and bows cut asunder. And elephants

and horses whose riders had been killed, O king, rushed hither and thither at speed there in their hundreds and thousands. Try as they might, the Pāṇḍava heroes could not prevent their great chariot-fighters fleeing, as Bhīṣma's arrows tormented them; brave as great Indra, he slaughtered their mighty ranks, which broke, great king, so that no two men fled together. Their chariots, elephants and horses were transfixed, their standards and chariot-poles fell; the forces of Pāṇḍu's sons wailed and swooned. Father slew son there, and son slew father; friend slew dear friend in that battle, overpowered by fate. Other Pāṇḍava soldiers were seen tearing off their armour and fleeing, hair dishevelled, heir of Bharata. Yudhiṣṭhira's army, its chariots and elephants stampeding with sounds of distress, seemed then like a stampeding herd of cattle.

Then Bhīṣma, best of the Kurus, roaring again and again like a lion, swiftly poured showers of arrows upon the chariot of wealth-winner Arjuna; and in an instant his chariot, with its horses and its charioteer, disappeared completely behind that arrow-shower. But Kṛṣṇa Vāsudeva was untroubled. The Sātvata lord showed his steadfastness, and urged on the horses as Bhīṣma's arrows struck them. Then Kuntī's son Arjuna took up his heavenly, thundering bow, severed Bhīṣma's bow and cut it down with his sharp arrows. When his bow was severed, the Kaurava lord your father[1] had another great bow ready in the time it takes to blink; with his arms he drew that thundering bow – whereupon Arjuna in his fury severed it likewise. Bhīṣma son of Śaṃtanu himself paid tribute to his dexterity: 'Bravo, strong-armed son of Kuntī, bravo!' With these words Bhīṣma laid hold of yet another splendid bow, and shot arrows at the chariot of Kuntī's son in that battle. But Vāsudeva displayed his great power in controlling the horses, and thwarted those arrows by moving in circles.

Bhīṣma and Arjuna, the two tiger-like heroes, were so wounded with arrows that they looked like two furious bulls bearing the marks of each other's horns. But Vāsudeva saw that Kuntī's son was fighting with restraint, while Bhīṣma was firing ceaseless showers of arrows in the battle,[2]

**1** i.e. your respected elder relative.

**2** This passage is very similar to the sequence at 6.55 where Kṛṣṇa attempts to intervene personally in the fighting.

blazing like the sun in his position between the two armies, constantly
striking down Yudhiṣṭhira's best warriors and bringing doomsday de-
struction to his troops. Then Kṛṣṇa, Madhu's strong-armed heir, slayer of
enemy heroes, could not bear it. The mighty lord of Yoga quit Arjuna's
silver-coloured horses, sir; full of fury, he leapt down from the great
chariot and rushed at Bhīṣma to fight him bare-handed. Whip in hand,
the ardent Kṛṣṇa of immeasurable splendour roared again and again like
a lion. The lord of the earth seemed to split the earth open with his feet,
55 as, eyes reddened with anger and intent on Bhīṣma's death, he struck
terror into the hearts of your warriors in the great battle. When they
saw Madhu's heir advancing on Bhīṣma in that battle, the soldiers there
cried 'Bhīṣma is slain! Bhīṣma is slain!', and all ran headlong from fear
of Vāsudeva. The stirrer of men, dressed in yellow silk, his body dark as
sapphire, shone, as he ran towards Bhīṣma, like a rain-cloud wreathed
in lightning. Roaring, the ardent, bull-like lord of the Yādavas rushed
towards him, as a lion towards an elephant, or the leader of a herd
towards a rival bull.

When Bhīṣma saw lotus-eyed Kṛṣṇa Govinda descending on him
in the battle, he calmly drew his great bow and addressed him with
60 untroubled mind: 'Come, come, lotus-eyed god of gods! Honour be
to you! Best of the Sātvatas, slay me today in the great battle! For even
if I am killed by you in combat, sinless god Kṛṣṇa, I shall enjoy the
greatest blessing in both this world and the next. The three worlds have
conferred an honour upon me in the battle today, Govinda.'

Then Kuntī's strong-armed son Arjuna, who had pursued Kṛṣṇa
Keśava closely, threw his arms around him in restraint. But lotus-eyed
Kṛṣṇa, the highest lord, though restrained by Kuntī's son, sped on,
carrying him with him. With all his strength the son of Kuntī, slayer
of enemy heroes, dug in his heels and managed to stop Kṛṣṇa, lord of
65 the senses, at the tenth step. Then Arjuna, slayer of enemy heroes, in
his distress addressed Kṛṣṇa as he hissed like a snake, his eyes wild with
fury: 'Turn back, strong-armed Kṛṣṇa Keśava. You must not break the
word you previously uttered – "I shall not fight!" People will call you
liar, heir of Madhu. No, this whole burden is mine; I shall kill Bhīṣma,
keeper of his word. I swear by our friendship, Madhu's heir, tormentor
of your enemies, and by my own truth and merit, that I shall make an

end of our enemies. Today see unconquerable Bhīṣma of mighty vows effortlessly laid low, like the crescent moon at the end of time!'

The heir of Madhu heard noble Arjuna's words, but he angrily said 70
nothing, and climbed back into the chariot. Then as those two tiger-like heroes returned to their chariot, Bhīṣma son of Śaṃtanu once more covered them with a shower of arrows, as a cloud covers a mountain with rain.

*Bhīṣma continues his terrible work, and the sun sets on the Pāṇḍava forces fleeing before him.* **[103]** *Yudhiṣṭhira orders his suffering troops to withdraw to camp. Then while Bhīṣma receives the felicitations of the Kauravas, the Pāṇḍava chiefs discuss the situation. Yudhiṣṭhira says that Bhīṣma is invincible in battle and proposes to abandon the campaign and retire to the forest. Kṛṣṇa insists that Arjuna, or he himself, is capable of killing Bhīṣma, but Yudhiṣṭhira will not allow him to break his vow not to fight. Instead they will visit Bhīṣma and ask him to advise them how he may be killed.*

Saṃjaya spoke:
After these discussions, O elder brother of Pāṇḍu, the heroic Pāṇḍavas all went together with brave Kṛṣṇa Vāsudeva to Bhīṣma's dwelling, leaving off weapons and armour. They entered, and then they bowed their heads to Bhīṣma; bull-like king, the Pāṇḍavas paid Bhīṣma honour, bowed
their heads to him, and requested his protection. Strong-armed Bhīṣma, 55
grandfather of the Kurus, addressed them: 'Welcome to you, Kṛṣṇa lord of the Vṛṣṇis! Welcome to you, wealth-winner Arjuna! Welcome to Yudhiṣṭhira son of Dharma, and to Bhīma and the twins! What task may I do today to increase your felicity? Even if it be most difficult, I shall do it with all my heart.' As Bhīṣma son of Gaṅgā continued to repeat these affectionate words, Yudhiṣṭhira son of Dharma spoke sadly to him. 'How may we win, knower of *dharma*? How may we get the kingdom? How may there be no further loss of life? Tell me, lord! Tell us yourself the way in which you may be killed – how may we overcome
you in battle, O king? Grandfather of the Kurus, you have no weak spot, 60
however tiny; you are always to be seen in battle with your bow drawn tight in a circle. But when you roar, and aim and draw your bow, we cannot look at you, strong-armed hero, as you stand bright as the sun

in your chariot. O slayer of enemy heroes, destroyer of men and horses,
chariots and elephants, what man would dare to kill you, bull-like heir
of Bharata? You have inflicted destruction on my mighty army, highest
lord, covering them with great showers of arrows. Tell me, grandfather,
how I may conquer you in battle, how the kingdom may be mine, how
there may be peace for my army!'

65 O elder brother of Pāṇḍu, Śaṃtanu's son Bhīṣma then replied to the
Pāṇḍavas. 'Son of Kuntī, you will see no success in battle while I live:
I tell you this truthfully. But when I have been defeated in battle, you
will certainly conquer the Kauravas. Strike swiftly at me if you wish for
victory in battle! I give you permission, sons of Kuntī: strike at me as
you please. I consider it fortunate that I am known to you.'[1]

Yudhiṣṭhira replied, 'Then tell us how we may in the battle defeat
you as you fight in fury, like staff-wielding Death. Indra the wielder
of the thunderbolt can be defeated, and so can Varuṇa and Yama;
but you, sir, are invincible to the very gods and demons under Indra's
70 leadership.' Bhīṣma said, 'Strong-armed Pāṇḍava, what you say is true: I
cannot be defeated in battle, even by the gods and demons under Indra's
leadership, when I take up my weapons and my splendid bow intent
on combat. But, O king, once I lay down my weapons your mighty
chariot-fighters may kill me in battle. It does not please me to fight
against a man who has laid down his weapons, who has fallen, or whose
armour and standard are lost; a man who flees, a fearful man, or one
who has surrendered; a woman, a man with a woman's name, a cripple,
or the father of a single son; or a childless man, or a deformed man. And
listen to the resolve which I made long back, son of Kuntī: under no
75 circumstances will I fight after seeing a warrior of ill omen. This great
chariot-fighter Śikhaṇḍin son of Drupada, O king, who is in your army,
is battle-hungry, brave and triumphant in combat; but you yourselves
know the whole truth about him – how he was originally a woman and
only later attained male sex. Heroic Arjuna should arm himself, place
Śikhaṇḍin before him in battle, and swiftly assail me with his arrows;
under no circumstances would I be willing to take up my arrows to

1 Ganguli takes this to refer to Bhīṣma's invincibility: it is fortunate that the Pāṇḍavas know of this and have therefore taken steps to bring the war to an end.

strike at that warrior of ill omen, especially since he was originally a woman. Wealth-winner Arjuna, Pāṇḍu's son, should seize that chance and swiftly strike me all over with his arrows, bull-like heir of Bharata. I know of no man in the world who might slay me when I am ready for 80
battle, except for blessed Kṛṣṇa, or wealth-winner Arjuna son of Pāṇḍu. For this reason, Arjuna Bībhatsu should place a certain other person before him when he faces me, and then slay me; in this way you will have the victory. Do it as I have said, son of Kuntī, and you will defeat the assembled sons of Dhṛtarāṣṭra in the battle!'

The sons of Kuntī paid their respects to the noble Bhīṣma, grandfather of the Kurus, took their leave, and returned to their own tent.

*Arjuna is deeply unhappy at the thought of killing Bhīṣma, but Kṛṣṇa reminds him of his vow to do so: the gods have settled what is to happen, and it is fated. The Pāṇḍavas now retire to bed.*

[**104**] *At sunrise on the tenth day the two armies are placed in formation, and the battle resumes. Arjuna, with Śikhaṇḍin before him, goes to attack Bhīṣma, while Nakula, Sahadeva and Sātyaki cause great slaughter in the Kaurava army. Bhīṣma counterattacks violently. Śikhaṇḍin pierces Bhīṣma with many arrows; Bhīṣma will not fight back. Arjuna urges Śikhaṇḍin to slay Bhīṣma while he himself deals with the Kaurava forces.* [**105**] *Duryodhana tells Bhīṣma that his army is suffering greatly from the attacks of the Pāṇḍavas, and that only Bhīṣma himself is capable of saving them. Bhīṣma replies that thus far he has fulfilled his vow to kill ten thousand enemy warriors daily; today he will either die himself or slay the Pāṇḍavas. He then begins a ferocious attack on the Pāṇḍava forces, slaying hundreds of thousands.* [**106**] *Arjuna urges Śikhaṇḍin to attack Bhīṣma; he rushes at him, followed by the other warriors. Members of Bhīṣma's protecting force resist the Pāṇḍava attackers. Dhṛṣṭadyumna urges them on again. Duḥśāsana and Arjuna exchange many arrows; Duḥśāsana is wounded, but recovers.*

[**107**] *Alambusa and Sātyaki exchange many arrows; though hit, Sātyaki is unaffected. Bhagadatta attacks Sātyaki, and more arrows are exchanged, but to no better effect. Duryodhana now dispatches a large force of chariot-warriors against Sātyaki. Meanwhile Abhimanyu and Sudakṣiṇa of Kāmboja are also exchanging arrows. There are many encounters between Pāṇḍava warriors seeking to attack Bhīṣma and members of his protecting force resisting them. Though*

*Arjuna too is resisted, he none the less succeeds in forcing Duryodhana back and overcoming his troops; Duḥśāsana resumes his attacks on him.*

[**108**] *Droṇa witnesses numbers of inauspicious portents and fears that Arjuna is going to seek to kill Bhīṣma, making use of Śikhaṇḍin, and he instructs Aśvatthāman to attack the latter.* [**109**] *Numerous Kaurava warriors exchange arrows with Bhīma; Jayadratha of Sindhu loses his horses and charioteer to Bhīma's arrows, but finds refuge in Citrasena's chariot. The Kauravas, joined now by Śalya, resume their exchanges with Bhīma, who fends them all off simultaneously. Arjuna, seeing Bhīma's feats, comes and joins him; the Kauravas despair to see the two brothers fighting together. Duryodhana urges Suśarman to attack them.* [**110**] *Bhīma and Arjuna face their Kaurava enemies and begin to overcome their forces with great slaughter. Śalya and then Droṇa exchange arrows with them; other warriors join in, and the battle becomes more general. The Pāṇḍavas rush to attack Bhīṣma, with Śikhaṇḍin before them.*

Saṃjaya spoke:

[**111**] On the tenth day, in that encounter between Bhīṣma and Arjuna, the dreadful battle-carnage continued unceasingly. Bhīṣma son of Śaṃtanu, afflicter of his enemies and master of weaponry, slew warriors in their tens of thousands and more, O king; their names and families barely known, O prince, all those unretreating heroes were slain there by Bhīṣma.

10 Then, after afflicting the ranks of the Pāṇḍavas for ten days, the
righteous Bhīṣma, afflicter of his enemies, grew weary of living. Desiring
for death to come swiftly upon him in battle, your strong-armed father
Bhīṣma Devavrata decided to kill no more of the best of men who came
upon him in battle; and he spoke to Pāṇḍu's son Yudhiṣṭhira, who was
close to him, O king: 'Most wise Yudhiṣṭhira, learned in every lore,
hear the words I say, which lead to *dharma* and to heaven. My son,
heir of Bharata, I am utterly weary of this body: my time for killing
15 great numbers of the living in war is past. So, if you wish to please me,
place before you Kuntī's son Arjuna, and also the Pāñcālas and Sṛñjayas,
and strive to kill me!' When Pāṇḍu's son of true understanding learnt
Bhīṣma's thought, he became intent on attacking Bhīṣma in that battle
together with the Sṛñjayas.

*The Pāṇḍava force, with Arjuna and Śikhaṇḍin at the head, launches an attack on Bhīṣma. Numerous single combats take place; the Dhārtarāṣṭras seek the death of Arjuna and Śikhaṇḍin. The battle is terrible.* [**112**] *Abhimanyu and Duryodhana exchange many arrows; so do Aśvatthāman and Sātyaki; so also Paurava and Dhṛṣṭaketu, who kill each other's horses and then fight on the ground with swords until both fall and are taken up into the chariots of allies. Citrasena and Suśarman exchange arrows, as do Abhimanyu and Bṛhadbala, and Droṇa and Dhṛṣṭadyumna. Arjuna, keeping Śikhaṇḍin ahead of him, goes to attack Bhīṣma; the Kaurava forces rush at him and a battle takes place. Meanwhile Śikhaṇḍin pierces Bhīṣma with many arrows; Bhīṣma responds with a ferocious attack on the Pāṇḍavas and their supporters in which he slays thousands of warriors. Śikhaṇḍin hits Bhīṣma with many arrows, but Bhīṣma does not respond, something Śikhaṇḍin does not understand. Arjuna urges Śikhaṇḍin on: only he can fight Bhīṣma. So Śikhaṇḍin continues to shoot arrows at Bhīṣma, while Bhīṣma attacks the rest of the Pāṇḍava force and is attacked by them in turn. Duḥśāsana seeks to protect Bhīṣma by fighting all the Pāṇḍavas single-handed: so fiercely does he fight that they cannot resist him. Finally Arjuna overcomes him, and turns his attack on Bhīṣma once more. Śikhaṇḍin is piercing Bhīṣma with many arrows, but they have little effect. Duryodhana urges his warriors to attack Arjuna; Arjuna makes use of celestial weapons to annihilate them, and the Kaurava army is routed. Duḥśāsana loses his horses and charioteer to Arjuna's arrows, as do a number of other great Kaurava fighters. Arjuna causes terrible carnage among the Kauravas.*

[**113**] *There is fierce and indiscriminate fighting. Śalya, Kṛpa, Citrasena, Duḥśāsana and Vikarṇa cause heavy losses in the Pāṇḍava ranks, while Arjuna causes carnage among the Kauravas. Dhṛṣṭadyumna sends a force of Somakas and Sṛñjayas to attack Bhīṣma; Bhīṣma responds by killing thousands of warriors, horses and elephants; he also kills Śatānīka, brother of Virāṭa. Kṛṣṇa urges Arjuna to slay him. Arjuna and Bhīṣma exchange showers of arrows; the greatest of the Pāṇḍavas are overcome by Bhīṣma's arrows, but Arjuna rescues them. Śikhaṇḍin now rushes against Bhīṣma, while Arjuna kills Bhīṣma's followers. Many of the leading allies of the Pāṇḍavas join the attack on Bhīṣma; Bhīṣma slays many of their forces. But Arjuna, with Śikhaṇḍin in front of him, pierces Bhīṣma.* [**114**] *Attacked by all the Pāṇḍavas with Śikhaṇḍin in front of them, Bhīṣma is pierced everywhere, but to little effect: he continues to shoot at his Pāṇḍava opponents.*

Saṃjaya spoke:
Śikhaṇḍin, best of chariot-fighters, guarded by Arjuna the wearer of the
diadem, severed Bhīṣma's bow in that battle and pierced him with ten
arrows, and his charioteer with ten, and severed his standard with one.
Bhīṣma son of Gaṅgā took up another, swifter bow, but Arjuna severed
25 this too with three sharp broad shafts; and in this way the ambidextrous
son of Pāṇḍu, afflicter of his enemies, in fury repeatedly severed every
bow that Bhīṣma took up. When his bow was severed, Bhīṣma licked the
corners of his mouth in fury; in fury he seized his mountain-splitting
spear; in fury he hurled it at Arjuna's chariot. When Pāṇḍu's son saw
it descending on him like a blazing thunderbolt he took up five sharp
broad shafts; and in fury he severed that spear with his five arrows into
five pieces, hurled though it was with the strength of Bhīṣma's arm, best
heir of Bharata. Severed by the furious wearer of the diadem, it fell like
a broken thunderbolt falling from a cloud-mass.

30 When Bhīṣma saw his spear severed he was filled with anger; that
hero, the conqueror of enemy fortresses, thought to himself in that
battle: 'With a single bow I could kill all the Pāṇḍavas if only mighty
Kṛṣṇa Viṣvaksena were not their protector. There are two reasons why
I shall not fight the Pāṇḍavas: their invulnerability, and Śikhaṇḍin's
feminine sex. Long ago when my father married Satyavatī, he was
pleased with me and granted me the ability to die when I choose, and
also invulnerability in battle. So now I consider that the proper time for
my death has come.' When the seers and the Vasus[1] realized the resolve
of Bhīṣma of boundless ardour, they addressed him from the heavens:
35 'What you have resolved, O hero, pleases us greatly! Do it, mighty
bowman! Turn your mind from war!' As these words came to an end a
pleasant breeze began to blow, fragrant and agreeable, and charged with
water-drops; the kettledrums of the gods roared with a great noise, and
a rain of flowers fell upon Bhīṣma, O prince.

*Bhīṣma rushes at Arjuna. Śikhaṇḍin pierces him, as do other Pāṇḍavas, to little effect. Then Arjuna severs his standard and all his bows; Bhīṣma ceases to fight, and tells Duḥśāsana that these painful, destructive arrows are Arjuna's,*

1 A group of gods including Indra.

*not Śikhaṇḍin's. Arjuna continues his attack, and Yudhiṣṭhira sends in all his forces to join in, while all the Dhārtarāṣṭras come to Bhīṣma's aid.*

Saṃjaya spoke:
Bhīṣma had killed ten thousand warriors during that tenth day; now
he stood firm in battle while weapons pierced his vital organs. Then
Kuntī's son, wealth-winner Arjuna, who was standing at the head of
the army, ordered his forces to charge through the midst of the Kuru
ranks. We were afraid of Kuntī's son the wealth-winner with his white 75
horses, and we ran headlong from the great battle, under a hail of
sharp weapons. But the Sauvīras and Kitavas, the peoples of East, West
and North, the Mālavas, the Abhīṣāhas and Śūrasenas, the Śibis and
Vasātis, the people of Śālva, the Trigartas, and the Ambaṣṭhas together
with the Kekayas – these twelve peoples, though they were afflicted
by arrows and wounded, did not abandon Bhīṣma in the battle as he
fought with the wearer of the diadem. Then, however, many warriors
surrounded that one man on all sides; they drove away all the Kurus
and covered him with showers of arrows. 'Lay him low! Capture him!
Pierce him! Overpower him!' – these were the tumultuous sounds
around Bhīṣma's chariot, O king, as they struck him with torrents of 80
arrows in hundreds and thousands, until there was not so much as a
finger's-breadth unwounded upon his body. And so, lord, your father,
cut to pieces in battle by Arjuna with his sharp-pointed arrows, fell
headlong from his chariot, facing the East, as day neared its end, before
the very eyes of your sons.

As Bhīṣma fell from his chariot, there was a tremendous sound
throughout the heavens, as gods and kings uttered lamentations. And
when we saw Bhīṣma our noble grandfather falling, our hearts fell
headlong with him. As the strong-armed hero, foremost of all bowmen,
fell like a toppled Pole of Indra,[1] he made the earth resound. And yet he
did not touch the earth, so covered was he with masses of protruding
arrows. As the mighty bowman, Bharata's bull-like heir, lay on his bed 85
of arrows after falling from his chariot, a divine state took possession of
him; a rain fell, and the earth trembled.

1 A pole erected and decorated in honour of Indra: see 1.57.17–26.

*Bhīṣma will not allow his life to depart yet, for it is the inauspicious time prior to the winter solstice. The Kauravas are dumbstruck at his loss.*

Saṃjaya spoke:
105 When Śaṃtanu's unkillable son was killed, Bhīṣma of mighty power, his
terrible absence was immediately felt by the Kurus, O king: wounded
with sharp arrows, our heroes slain, defeated by the ambidextrous
Arjuna, we did not know what to do. On the other hand the Pāṇḍavas,
heroes with arms like iron bars, who had gained both a victory and high
rank in the other world, all blew their great conches; and the Somakas
and Pāñcālas too were filled with joy, lord of men; and while thousands
of trumpets blew, Bhīma of enormous strength beat his chest fiercely
and danced. When Gaṅgā's son was laid low, heroes from both armies
together laid aside their weapons and gave themselves over to thought.
110 Others cried out and ran headlong, or lost their senses; yet others
condemned the Kṣatriya way, or paid their respects to Bhīṣma. The very
seers and ancestors praised Bhīṣma of mighty vows: the forebears of the
Bhāratas gave him praise. And Śaṃtanu's wise and heroic son, praying
and practising the Yoga of the Great Upaniṣad, remained, awaiting his
time.

[**115**] *At Bhīṣma's fall, both Kauravas and Pāṇḍavas are downcast; the sun is dimmed and the earth wails. The Pāṇḍavas blow conches and trumpets, while the Dhārtarāṣṭras are overcome by grief and bewilderment.*

Saṃjaya spoke:
When he saw that Bhīṣma was fallen, your heroic son Duḥśāsana, who had been stationed close to Bhīṣma, armed and with his own force of men, by his brother,[1] rushed up to Droṇa's forces with the utmost speed. The tiger-like Duḥśāsana urged on his troops and went forth; and when the Kurus saw him coming, they surrounded him, anxious to know what he would say, great king. Then that Kaurava told Droṇa that Bhīṣma was slain, and Droṇa, on hearing the ill news, suddenly fell

1 In chapter 101 Duryodhana instructed Duḥśāsana to make protection of Bhīṣma his first duty.

down from his chariot. When he regained consciousness, Bharadvāja's 25
son of great energy called off his own forces, sir. Seeing that the Kurus had stopped fighting, the Pāṇḍavas too sent messengers on swift horses to make their soldiers observe a ceasefire. When in due course the forces stopped fighting on every side, all the kings stripped off their armour and went up to Bhīṣma; and warriors in their hundreds and thousands, ceasing to fight, approached the noble hero, like gods approaching the creator Prajāpati.

When they reached Bhīṣma, Bharata's bull-like heir, as he lay there, they paid their respects and then stood back, Kauravas and Pāṇḍavas
together. Then the righteous Bhīṣma, son of Śaṃtanu, addressed the 30
Kauravas and Pāṇḍavas as they stood there bowing before him. 'Welcome, blessed ones! Welcome, mighty chariot-fighters! I am pleased to see you, godlike heroes.' After greeting them in this way, with his head hanging unsupported, he said, 'My head is hanging completely unsupported: please give me a headrest.' Then the kings fetched for him the most excellent headrests, delicate and soft; but the grandfather did not want them. And the tiger-like hero spoke laughingly to those
kings: 'These are not fitting for the beds of heroes, O princes!' Then he 35
looked at wealth-winner Arjuna, Pāṇḍu's long-armed son, and he said to that best of men, mightiest bowman in the world, 'Strong-armed wealth-winner Arjuna, my head is hanging unsupported; please give me a headrest you consider suitable.'

Arjuna laid aside his great bow, paid his respects to the grandfather, and said, his eyes filled with tears, 'Best of the Kurus, finest of all bearers of arms, command me! I am your servant, unconquerable one; what am I to do, grandfather?' Śaṃtanu's son replied, 'Son, my head is hanging unsupported. Arjuna, best of the Kurus, fetch me a
headrest; give me swiftly, O hero, one to suit my bed. For you, O 40
son of Kuntī, are a strong-armed hero, the best of all bowmen, one who knows the *dharma* of the Kṣatriyas, intelligent and mettlesome.' Swift in resolve, Arjuna gave his assent, took up his bow Gāṇḍīva and his straight arrows, and consecrated them; then, after requesting permission from the noble Bhīṣma, loftiest of the Bhāratas, he shot three sharp, swift arrows to form a support for his head. The righteous Bhīṣma, best heir of Bharata, expert in *dharma* and the proper making

of wealth, was pleased that the ambidextrous Arjuna had understood his intention.

Now there approached learned physicians skilled at removing arrows,
equipped with all the tools of their trade. When Gaṅgā's son saw them,
he spoke as follows: 'Honour the healers, give them their due, and send
them away. In my present situation I have no need for physicians, for I
have attained the highest state known in the *dharma* of the Kṣatriyas. It
would not be right to treat my wounds, O kings, as I lie on this bed of
55 arrows; and in the end I am to be burnt with these very arrows!' When
your son Duryodhana heard Bhīṣma's words, he paid due honour to the
physicians and sent them away.

*Both sides now withdraw to their camps for the evening. Kṛṣṇa congratulates Yudhiṣṭhira on Bhīṣma's fall; Yudhiṣṭhira ascribes their success to Kṛṣṇa's grace.* **[116]** *The next morning the leaders on both sides go to see Bhīṣma, as do many other folk. Kauravas and Pāṇḍavas lay aside their weapons and form an assembly together in his honour.*

Saṃjaya spoke:

Bhīṣma suppressed his pain with fortitude, O bull-like heir of Bharata;
10 suffering from the arrows, he spoke most joylessly. 'My body suffers
from these arrows; I am fainting with the pain of the arrows; I desire
water,' he said to those kings. Then, O king, all those Kṣatriyas brought
him various foodstuffs and pitchers of cool water. When he saw those
things brought, Bhīṣma son of Śaṃtanu said, 'Today I cannot eat any
mortal foodstuffs from the hands of mortal men. I lie on a bed of arrows,
and remain, awaiting the return of the sun and moon.'[1] After saying this,
heir of Bharata, Śaṃtanu's son, his voice filled with distress, spoke to
15 those princes about strong-armed wealth-winner Arjuna. The strong-
armed one now approached and paid his respects to the grandfather;
with hands joined together, he stood there bowing, and said, 'What
may I do?' Seeing Pāṇḍu's son standing before him paying his respects,

1 i.e. the winter solstice, when the sun will return from its inauspicious course through the southern sky. It is not clear whether the reference to the moon specifies some more detailed astronomical circumstance, or whether it is simply a 'poetic' addition.

O king, the righteous Bhīṣma was pleased, and he said to wealth-winner Arjuna, 'My body burns, and I am pierced all over by these great arrows; my vital organs are consumed by pain, and my mouth is dry. Give me water to ease my body, Arjuna! For you are capable of giving me water in the proper manner, great bowman.'

The heroic Arjuna gave his assent, and, mounting his chariot, strung his mighty bow Gāṇḍīva and drew it. Hearing the twang of the bowstring against his palm, sounding like the roar of a thunderbolt, all creatures were afraid, and so were all the princes. Then that best of chariot-fighters respectfully circumambulated with his chariot the prostrate Bhīṣma, best heir of Bharata and finest of all bearers of arms. Kuntī's son of great renown then fixed a blazing arrow to his bow and consecrated it; while the whole world watched, he shot, and with his Parjanya Weapon he split open the ground to the right side of Bhīṣma. From that place arose a pure, clear torrent of water, cool, ambrosial, and of divine scent and taste. Thus Kuntī's son Arjuna of divine deeds and valour assuaged the thirst of Bhīṣma, bull of the Kurus, with a torrent of cool water. At that deed of Kuntī's son, acting like Indra himself, the lords of the earth were utterly astounded: seeing Arjuna Bībhatsu's extraordinary, superhuman deed, the Kurus began to tremble like cattle afflicted by cold. And in their amazement all the kings waved their garments, and uproar broke out all round, with the sounds of conches and kettledrums. Śaṃtanu's son Bhīṣma, his thirst eased, then spoke to Arjuna Bībhatsu, O king, paying him honour before all the princes and heroes: 'Strong-armed heir of Kuru, this is no wonder coming from you! Nārada spoke of you as an ancient seer of immeasurable splendour. With Kṛṣṇa Vāsudeva for your companion you will accomplish great deeds which even Indra with all the gods would surely not dare do! The wise see in you the end of the entire Kṣatriya race, son of Kuntī. Among bowmen you are the one true bowman; you are the finest of men on earth.'

*Bhīṣma continues: Duryodhana's foolishness will bring his own destruction at Bhīma's hands. Seeing Duryodhana, he appeals to him to end the battle and give half the kingdom to the Pāṇḍavas; but Duryodhana will not agree.*

**[117]** *The warriors return to their camps, and Karṇa comes to see Bhīṣma. He identifies himself to Bhīṣma as a person Bhīṣma has hated greatly; Bhīṣma* *welcomes him and tells him he does not hate him, and appeals for peace. But Karṇa replies that he is Duryodhana's ally, and that the battle is fated to take its course. He asks for Bhīṣma's permission to fight, which Bhīṣma grants. Karṇa returns to Duryodhana's camp.*

# DROṆA

## THE INSTALLATION OF DROṆA

[1] — *Full of grief at the news of Bhīṣma's death, Dhṛtarāṣṭra urges Saṃjaya to continue his narration, and he proceeds to do so. — The Kauravas bid farewell to Bhīṣma, and both sides march out to resume the battle; but without Bhīṣma the Kauravas are much enfeebled, and they suffer greatly from Pāṇḍava attacks. In their distress they remember Karṇa, who has not joined in the battle so far because of his vow not to fight while Bhīṣma lives.* [2] *Karṇa too wants to aid the Kauravas, and he joins them on the battlefield. After praising Bhīṣma, he announces that he will now fight on their side against the Pāṇḍavas, and he calls for armour, weapons, horses and chariot, and rides to where Bhīṣma lies.* [3] *Karṇa addresses Bhīṣma: now that he has fallen, who can overcome the all-powerful Pāṇḍavas? Arjuna, aided by Kṛṣṇa, will slay the Dhārtarāṣṭras; but if Bhīṣma will permit it, he, Karṇa, will fight him.* [4] *Bhīṣma is pleased, and blesses and praises Karṇa. He urges him to fight to protect the Kaurava army, and Karṇa now takes his leave and goes to join the Kauravas, who greet him with shouts of joy.*

[5] *Duryodhana consults Karṇa as to who should be appointed commander in place of Bhīṣma. Karṇa answers that all of the Kaurava warriors are fit to lead, but, since one only can be chosen, it should be Droṇa, whose leadership, warrior skills and wisdom are such that all will follow him. Duryodhana requests Droṇa to assume the command, to shouts of acclamation. Droṇa assents, though he warns that he will not be able to kill Dhṛṣṭadyumna, who is indeed destined to kill him. Then with due ceremony he is installed as commander, to the sound of drums, conches and shouts of joy.*

[6] *Having assumed the command on the eleventh day of fighting, Droṇa*

*now arrays his forces for battle and advances against the Pāṇḍavas in a vast Cart formation containing all the great Kaurava heroes, with Karṇa at the head. Meanwhile Yudhiṣṭhira places his forces in the Crane formation, headed by Arjuna: Arjuna and Karṇa face each other. As Droṇa leads his forces into battle there are portents of destruction: the earth trembles, a shower of flesh, bones and blood falls, beasts and birds of prey appear in great numbers, meteors blaze. The two armies fall on each other, and Droṇa rapidly gains the ascendancy with his arrows and his celestial weapons. Dhṛṣṭadyumna counterattacks, but Droṇa continues to slaughter the terrified forces of the Pāṇḍavas.*

**[7]** *Yudhiṣṭhira gives orders that Droṇa is to be checked, and many of his seniormost followers set about protecting the Pāṇḍava army from his attacks. This enrages Droṇa, who, acting like a young man despite his years, shoots arrows so numerous that nothing else can be seen, inflicting terrible casualties. But after slaying his enemies by the thousand, he is himself killed, to the universal lamentations of his friends and the joy of the Pāṇḍavas.*

**[8]** *— Dhṛtarāṣṭra, appalled at this news, asks Saṃjaya how the mighty Droṇa could possibly have been killed. He extols Droṇa's greatness and asks to hear details of the fighting; it must have been Dhṛṣṭadyumna who overcame him, he believes, but he cannot imagine how.* **[9]** *Griefstricken, Dhṛtarāṣṭra faints and falls to the ground. The women of the royal household tend and fan him, until he comes to. Then he resumes his questioning of Saṃjaya. Who protected Droṇa against Yudhiṣṭhira, against Bhīma, against Arjuna, against the other Pāṇḍava heroes? He believes that the Pāṇḍavas are invincible, aided as they are by Kṛṣṇa Vāsudeva.* **[10]** *He describes the greatness of Vāsudeva, who has overcome demons, enemy kings, and even the gods. The Kauravas cannot defeat Arjuna and Kṛṣṇa, who are Nara and Nārāyaṇa; Yudhiṣṭhira's triumph is inevitable. He repeats his request to Saṃjaya to recount the events of the battle.*

**[11]** *— Saṃjaya resumes his narration. — After his installation as commander, Droṇa asks Duryodhana what he wishes him to do, and Duryodhana asks him to bring Yudhiṣṭhira before him alive. Droṇa wonders why he does not seek Yudhiṣṭhira's death, and Duryodhana explains that to kill Yudhiṣṭhira would cause Arjuna to wipe out the Kauravas; instead, he intends to defeat him at dicing yet again, and so send the Pāṇḍavas back to the forest. Droṇa agrees to this plan, on the stipulation that Arjuna must first be removed from the battle, for not even the gods or the demons could take Yudhiṣṭhira captive in Arjuna's presence.*

[12] *Yudhiṣṭhira comes to hear of Droṇa's plan through spies, and warns Arjuna not to let it succeed; Arjuna assures him that he will not allow him to be captured. The two armies advance against each other, and battle recommences. Droṇa seems to be everywhere at once, and his arrows kill many Pāṇḍava warriors:* [13] *his ferocity causes a river of blood to flow. He is attacked by the Pāṇḍavas led by Yudhiṣṭhira. Many great warriors fight each other in single combat. Abhimanyu overpowers Paurava, and is attacked by Jayadratha; when Jayadratha withdraws after his sword breaks, Abhimanyu is assailed by Śalya, who hurls a spear at him; Abhimanyu catches it and hurls it back at Śalya, killing his charioteer.* [14] *Śalya leaps down from his chariot brandishing a club. Abhimanyu stands ready for him, but Bhīma tells him to step aside. He and Śalya engage each other in a furious fight with clubs; each man falls from the blows of the other, but whereas Śalya has to be helped away by Kṛtavarman, Bhīma is on his feet again in a moment. The Kauravas are discomfited, and the Pāṇḍavas overwhelm them.*

[15] *Karṇa's son Vṛṣasena goes to the aid of the Kaurava army, shooting vast numbers of arrows; he is attacked by Nakula's son Śatānīka and the other sons of Draupadī. Aśvatthāman leads a force of chariot-fighters to his defence, and the Pāṇḍavas join the fray in support of their sons. The Kauravas begin to flee, and Yudhiṣṭhira's soldiers kill many of them. Then Droṇa attacks Yudhiṣṭhira, cutting off his bow and killing Kumāra, guardian of his wheels. Droṇa pierces the Pāṇḍavas with many arrows, and kills their allies Vyāghradatta and Siṃhasena when they attack him. Just as the Kauravas are exulting, Arjuna appears, shooting arrows so dense they cause darkness. The sun sets.*

## THE KILLING OF THE SWORN WARRIORS

[16] *Both armies withdraw to their camps. Droṇa declares to Duryodhana that Arjuna and Kṛṣṇa are invincible: someone must challenge Arjuna and draw him away, and then Droṇa will be able to capture Yudhiṣṭhira. Suśarman, king of Trigarta, replies that his men hate Arjuna deeply for the wrongs he has done them: they will draw him away and kill him. Then many princes of Trigarta and elsewhere come forward with their troops to swear an oath; they give gifts to the Brahmins, light holy fires, and call down on themselves the*

*worst possible punishments if they should turn back without killing Arjuna. Then they challenge Arjuna to fight them in the southern part of the battlefield, and Arjuna tells Yudhiṣṭhira that he cannot turn down their challenge. When Yudhiṣṭhira reminds him of Droṇa's threat, Arjuna replies that Drupada's son Satyajit will protect him, and Yudhiṣṭhira assents to this. Arjuna now sets out to fight the Trigartas, while Duryodhana's forces, delighted at his absence, strive to capture Yudhiṣṭhira.*

**[17]** *On the twelfth day of the battle the Trigarta warriors joyfully greet Arjuna's arrival. Arjuna blows his conch Devadatta; the sound briefly paralyses his enemies, but they rapidly recover, and many arrows are exchanged. Arjuna kills Sudhanvan, causing panic among his followers, who flee; Arjuna attacks all the more savagely. The king of Trigarta rallies his men, reminding them of their vow.* **[18]** *At Arjuna's bidding, Kṛṣṇa drives towards the enemy warriors. Arjuna is surrounded and covered with showers of arrows. Furiously, he shoots the Weapon of Tvaṣṭṛ, whereupon thousands of images of himself and Kṛṣṇa appear; deceived, his enemies strike at these, killing one another, and Arjuna overwhelms them with arrows; but they reply in kind and cover Arjuna and Kṛṣṇa with so many arrows that they cannot be seen. Arjuna responds with the Wind Weapon, so that his enemies are blown away like dry leaves; then he attacks them so savagely that the battlefield resembles the realm of Yama.*

**[19]** *Meanwhile, Droṇa, preparing to take advantage of Arjuna's absence, places his forces in the* Garuḍa *formation; seeing that mighty array, Yudhiṣṭhira warns Dhṛṣṭadyumna not to allow him to be taken captive, whereupon Dhṛṣṭadyumna launches a powerful attack upon Droṇa. Durmukha counterattacks him, and while these two fight Droṇa slays and scatters the Pāṇḍava army. The fighting becomes general. Many elephants attack one another, until their bodies are so numerous that the earth seems covered with hills. Empty chariots and riderless horses and elephants rush in every direction; everything is covered in blood. In the midst of this tumult, Droṇa attacks Yudhiṣṭhira.*

**[20]** *To defend Yudhiṣṭhira, Satyajit launches an assault on Droṇa. The two of them fight fiercely, but in the end Droṇa cuts off Satyajit's head; Yudhiṣṭhira, fearful of Droṇa, withdraws. Droṇa is attacked by many of Yudhiṣṭhira's supporters, but he kills and defeats them. Such is the slaughter that a river of blood flows. Beating back Yudhiṣṭhira's defenders, Droṇa approaches Yudhiṣṭhira himself; Yudhiṣṭhira once again flees from him. Droṇa continues to crush the Pāṇḍavas and their allies.* **[21]** *Seeing the rout of their enemies, the Kauravas* *join in the attack. Delighted, Duryodhana remarks to Karṇa that even Bhīma is utterly overwhelmed by Droṇa, but Karṇa warns him that Bhīma is far from beaten: he will lead a force against Droṇa, who will need protecting. Hearing this, Duryodhana and his brothers hasten to Droṇa, and find him facing a Pāṇḍava attack.* **[22]** *Many heroes of the Pāṇḍava army, with excellent horses of many different colours and splendid standards, join in single combat with their Kaurava enemies.*

**[23]** — *Dhṛtarāṣṭra laments the fate that has brought him and Duryodhana to their present state; now that both Bhīṣma and Droṇa are dead, there is no future for them. He asks Saṃjaya to continue his description of the battle.* **[24]** *Saṃjaya takes up the story again. — The Pāṇḍava assault on Droṇa is fierce, and numerous further single combats take place.* **[25]** *Duryodhana attacks Bhīma with a force of elephants; Bhīma kills great numbers of them. He and Duryodhana exchange many arrows, and Duryodhana's bow and standard are both severed. The Aṅga lord comes to Duryodhana's defence; he is killed by Bhīma. Bhagadatta the king of Prāgjyotiṣa attacks Bhīma with his mighty elephant, and the cry goes up that it has killed him, though in fact he has escaped; thinking Bhīma dead, Yudhiṣṭhira leads an attack on Bhagadatta, but his terrible elephant puts the Pāṇḍava forces to flight. Bhīma returns to the attack, but his horses are terrified and carry him away, and Bhagadatta and his elephant continue to rout the Pāṇḍavas.*

**[26]** *Arjuna asks Kṛṣṇa to drive him to where Bhagadatta is, but as he approaches the place he is challenged by the warriors who have sworn to kill him. Initially uncertain whether to go on to Yudhiṣṭhira's aid or to take up this challenge, he opts for the latter course, and is at once attacked with thousands of arrows; he responds with the Weapon of Brahmā and a hail of his own arrows, and slaughters his enemies in great numbers, to universal acclaim. Then he tells Kṛṣṇa once more to take him to Bhagadatta.* **[27]** *He is followed by the king of Trigarta and his brothers, and turns back briefly to defeat them, before finally reaching Bhagadatta. Ten thousand warriors surround him, but he overcomes them. The battle with Bhagadatta begins.*

**[28]** *Bhagadatta attacks with weapon after weapon, but Arjuna fends them off, and with his arrows cuts off the Prāgjyotiṣa elephant's armour and pierces Bhagadatta many times. In fury Bhagadatta releases the Weapon of Viṣṇu at him, but Kṛṣṇa receives it on the breast, where it turns into a garland of victory. Arjuna remonstrates with him for intervening in the battle, but Kṛṣṇa explains:*

*in his form as Viṣṇu, he himself had long ago given this Weapon to the demon Naraka at the request of Naraka's mother, the Earth; not even the gods would be able to survive it. Now that Bhagadatta has lost it, Arjuna should slay him. Arjuna now kills Bhagadatta's elephant with one arrow, and pierces Bhagadatta in the heart with another.*

[**29**] *Two princes of Gāndhāra now attack Arjuna fiercely, but he kills them with a single arrow. At this, Śakuni resorts to his powers of illusion: weapons of every description fall on Arjuna, and fierce animals assail him, but he dispels them with his arrows; darkness descends, but he counteracts it with the Weapon of Light; floods of water appear, but he dries them out with the Sun Weapon. Śakuni, seeing the laughing Arjuna destroy his wiles, flees, leaving Arjuna to rout the Kaurava forces.*

[**30**] *There is terrible fighting. Nīla, king of Mahiṣmatī, engages Aśvatthāman in single combat, but Aśvatthāman kills him. The Pāṇḍavas are troubled: how can Arjuna come to their aid when he is busy elsewhere on the battlefield?* [**31**] *Bhīma does battle with several of the leading Kauravas at once; Yudhiṣṭhira sends Nakula, Sahadeva and Sātyaki with a force to his aid. The fighting becomes general, and there is great carnage. The Pāṇḍavas mount an attack on Droṇa; he responds by slaying great numbers with his arrows. Now Arjuna appears and likewise slaughters the Kauravas, including Karṇa's three brothers. Karṇa attacks him, and is in turn attacked by Bhīma, Dhṛṣṭadyumna and Sātyaki. Duryodhana comes to his aid, and there is fierce fighting. The sun sets, and the maimed and bloody warriors on both sides withdraw to their camps.*

## THE KILLING OF ABHIMANYU

[**32**] *On the thirteenth day, after a miserable night, Duryodhana accuses Droṇa of failing to keep his promise to capture Yudhiṣṭhira; Droṇa replies that no one can overcome the joint force of Arjuna and Kṛṣṇa. Then, however, he makes a new oath which he swears to keep: today he will kill one of the chief Pāṇḍava heroes. Duryodhana is to keep Arjuna occupied elsewhere. So a force of warriors sworn to kill Arjuna once more engages him in battle, whilst his young son Abhimanyu does battle against the magnificent Wheel formation in which Droṇa has arrayed his troops. After performing wonderful feats, and slaying his enemies by the thousand, Abhimanyu is killed. — Dhṛtarāṣṭra requests Saṃjaya to tell*

*him how this happened, and Saṃjaya promises to do so.* **[33]** *He begins by praising Abhimanyu: the five Pāṇḍavas separately possess many great virtues, but Abhimanyu combines them all, together with those of Kṛṣṇa.*

Saṃjaya spoke:
Great king, Droṇa the Teacher drew up the Wheel formation, and all the kings, mighty as Indra, took their places in it. All the princes were assembled there, all under oath, all bearing gold-decked standards, all in red-dyed garments, all wearing red ornaments, all with red banners, all garlanded with gold. There were ten thousand of them, strong bowmen owing allegiance to your handsome grandson Lakṣmaṇa; they shared each other's woes and each other's courage; they vied with each other and strove for each other's good.

Duryodhana the king was surrounded by the great chariot-fighters Karṇa, Duḥśāsana and Kṛpa. Shaded by a white umbrella, fanned by yak-tail fans, he was as glorious as the king of the gods or the rising sun. Droṇa took up the commander's position at the head of the army, and Jayadratha king of Sindhu too stood there, glorious as Mount Meru. Thirty of your sons, led by Aśvatthāman, flanked Jayadratha; great king, they looked like the gods themselves. Also flanking the king of Sindhu were illustrious chariot-fighters: Śakuni the gambler, prince of Gāndhāra, and Śalya, and Bhūriśravas.

**[34]** Under Bhīma's leadership, the Pāṇḍavas attacked that unassailable army guarded by Bharadvāja's son Droṇa. Sātyaki and Cekitāna, Dhṛṣṭadyumna heir of Pṛṣata, valiant Kuntibhoja and Drupada the great chariot-fighter; Abhimanyu son of Arjuna, Kṣatradharman and brave Bṛhatkṣatra, Dhṛṣṭaketu king of Cedi, Mādrī's sons Nakula and Sahadeva, and Ghaṭotkaca; valiant Yudhāmanyu and undefeated Śikhaṇḍin, unconquerable Uttamaujas and mighty chariot-fighter Virāṭa; the furious sons of Draupadī, the brave son of Śiśupāla, the heroic Kekayas and the Sṛñjayas in their thousands – these and hordes of others, skilled bowmen mad for battle, suddenly rushed to attack Bharadvāja's son Droṇa in their eagerness for the fight. But brave Droṇa, untroubled, countered all of them together with a great torrent of arrows. Like a flood of water meeting an unbreakable mountain, or an ocean reaching the shore, they could not assail Droṇa; tormented by the arrows flying from his bow, the Pāṇḍavas could not remain before Bharadvāja's son, O king. Thus we saw the wonderful strength of Droṇa's arms: the Pāñcālas and Sṛñjayas together were unable to assail him.

When Yudhiṣṭhira saw Droṇa advancing in fury, he considered many ways of countering him; but, concluding that no one else was capable, he placed the intolerably heavy burden upon Arjuna's son Abhimanyu. He spoke these words to that slayer of enemy heroes, no less eminent than Kṛṣṇa Vāsudeva, no less mighty than Arjuna: 'My son, act in such a way that when Arjuna returns he will not censure me! I do not know the way to break open the Wheel formation. You, or Arjuna or Kṛṣṇa, or indeed Pradyumna, might break open the Wheel; strong-armed hero, there is no fifth person! Abhimanyu my son, please grant this request, which is made by your father's and your mother's kin, and by all these soldiers: swiftly take up arms and destroy Droṇa's army, otherwise Arjuna will censure me when he returns from his battle.'

Abhimanyu answered, 'As I desire victory for my kin, I shall force my way in battle into Droṇa's fine, strong, steadfast army, and break it open, for my father has taught me how to break open such an army. But I do not know how to get out if any danger should arise.'

Yudhiṣṭhira replied, 'Battle to break the army open, excellent man, and grant us passage! We shall follow you wherever you go, my son. You are the equal in battle of wealth-winner Arjuna, son; we shall make you our leader and follow you, protecting you on every side.' Bhīma added, 'I shall follow you, and so will Dhṛṣṭadyumna and Sātyaki, and the Pāñcālas, the Kekayas, the Matsyas and all the Prabhadrakas. Once you have broken open the formation – in this place and that, just a few times – we shall lay it waste and slay all its finest warriors.'

Abhimanyu said, 'I shall enter this unassailable army of Droṇa, as a furious moth might enter a blazing fire. The deed I do today will benefit both my families, and bring joy to my mother's brother[1] and my father. Today all creatures will see the throngs of enemy soldiers driven in battle by me, a single boy!'

Yudhiṣṭhira said, 'Son of Subhadrā, may your strength increase for speaking so! You dare to break open Droṇa's unbreakable army despite

1 Kṛṣṇa.

the tiger-like heroes who guard it, mighty bowmen and fighters equal in valour to the hosts of the immortals!'

**[35]** Subhadrā's son heard the words of the wise Yudhiṣṭhira, the lord of *dharma*, and urged his driver Sumitra on towards Droṇa's army, O heir of Bharata. But the charioteer, urged repeatedly to go, answered Abhimanyu with these words, O king: 'My lord, this is an extreme burden that the Pāṇḍavas have laid upon you! Please give thought to your capabilities before fighting. Droṇa the Teacher has laboured to gain expertise with the ultimate in weapons, whereas you have been raised in the greatest comfort: what experience have you of war?' Then Abhimanyu replied laughingly, 'Charioteer, who exactly is this Droṇa? and who are all these Kṣatriyas? If it were Indra himself on his elephant Airāvata, accompanied by the hosts of immortals, I would fight him at the forefront of the battle; so these Kṣatriyas cause me no alarm. This enemy army is not worth one sixteenth part of me! Son of a Sūta, even if in battle I encounter my mother's brother, world-conquering Viṣṇu himself, together with my own father Arjuna, I shall feel no fear.'

When Abhimanyu had finished ridiculing the words of his charioteer, he again instructed him to drive without delay towards Droṇa's army. Then the charioteer, greatly saddened, urged on the three-year-old horses with their golden trappings. Driven by Sumitra towards Droṇa's army, the horses rushed swiftly and valiantly forward against Droṇa, O king. When they saw Abhimanyu coming, all the Kauravas under Droṇa's leadership attacked him, while the Pāṇḍavas followed behind him. Arjuna's son excelled Arjuna himself; in his golden armour, and with his tall standard displaying a lovely *karṇikāra* tree, he fought pugnaciously against those great chariot-fighters headed by Droṇa, like a lion-cub fighting against elephants. At a distance of twenty paces the warriors strove to strike one another, so that for a while the battlefield seemed an ocean swirling like the Gaṅgā. Then, O king, a most dreadful, tumultuous battle began between heroes battling to kill each other.

As that frightful battle progressed, Arjuna's son Abhimanyu broke open the Kaurava array before Droṇa's very eyes, and entered within. As soon as the mighty hero had entered in the enemy's midst and started slaying his foes, he was surrounded by throngs of infantrymen, and warriors on horseback and elephant-back and in chariots, their weapons upraised. The sounds of various sorts of musical instruments were heard, and shouts, bellows and roars, yells of defiance, lion-roars, calls of 'Stand! Stand!', dreadful cries of 'Do not go! Stand! Come to me!' Calling out over and over again, 'Here I am!', and making the earth resound with their elephants' trumpeting, their armour's chinking, their laughter, and the sound of their horses' hooves and their chariots' wheels, the Kaurava warriors rushed against Arjuna's son.

20 As they descended upon him in speed and strength, that hero of swift weapons slew whole companies of them with his body-splitting arrows, for he knew how to find their weak spots. And even as they died from his sharp arrows of various shapes, they continued to fall upon him in that battle, like moths falling into a flame. Like a priest scattering *kuśa* grass on the altar at a sacrifice, Abhimanyu rapidly scattered the earth with their bodies and with individual limbs. The muscular arms of your warriors, cased in arm-guards and finger-guards, bearing arrow-shields and bows, swords, shields, elephant-goads and bridles, lances and axes, throwing-balls, iron-tipped arrows and spears of various sorts, bolts and
25 bludgeons, fine javelins and *kampanas*, whips and great conches, iron lances and goads, hammers and slings, nooses and rocks, decked in bracelets and armlets, anointed with sweet-smelling ointments, were severed by Arjuna's son in their thousands; great king, as they lay twitching, doused in blood, they seemed like five-headed snakes cut down by Garuḍa. Many enemy heads, with fine noses, faces and hair, free from wounds, decked with lovely earrings, their lower lips bitten in rage, flowing with much blood, covered with beautiful garlands, diadems and turbans, resplendent with diamonds and jewels, seeming
30 like stemless lotuses, or the sun or moon, well-perfumed heads that once spoke kind words to friends, were scattered by Arjuna's son upon the earth.

Chariots as grand as celestial cities, properly equipped, lost their poles and their pole-joints, their banner-staffs and their drivers' seats, lost their yoke-joints, axle-trees and axles, the rims and spokes of their wheels, lost the wheels themselves, lost all their gear and their interiors; all their parts were broken; all their parts were cut to pieces, and the warriors in them slain by the thousand, as Abhimanyu shattered them with his arrows in every direction. As for his enemies' elephants and

their riders, with their banners and goads and standards, he cut them
down with his sharp-bladed, sharp-pointed arrows, together with their
arrow-cases and their armour, their girths and neck-chains and blankets,
their bells, their trunks and tusks, and those forming the rearguard to 35
protect them. Horses from Vanāyu and the mountains, from Kāmboja
and Āraṭṭa and Bāhlika, with firm tails, ears and eyes, swift and riding
well, well ridden by accomplished warriors fighting with spears, lances
and darts, had their yak-tail crests and horse-cloths destroyed, their
ornaments scattered, their tongues and eyes cut out, all their entrails and
livers cast about, their riders killed, their harness broken; they brought
joy to carrion creatures as they lay bathed in their own shit and piss
and blood, with their armour cut off. Thus Abhimanyu took delight in
slaughtering your steeds.

Achieving unthinkably difficult deeds alone, like Viṣṇu himself in 40
former times, he smashed all three divisions of your mighty army, and
even killed masses of your footsoldiers. When they saw Subhadrā's son
fiercely slaying that army single-handed, like the god of war slaying
the army of the demons, your soldiers and your sons stared all around,
mouths dry, eyes a-quiver, bodies sweating, hair standing on end. Full
of the will to flee, but without the will to conquer their enemies, they
called out to each other by family name, hoping to escape alive; then,
abandoning the slain – sons and fathers, friends and kin – they fled away,
urging their horses and elephants to go at speed.

**[36]** *Furious at the rout, Duryodhana himself attacks Abhimanyu; Droṇa sends great warriors to his aid. They shoot numberless arrows at Abhimanyu, but he returns yet more at them, slaying many and wounding even Karṇa. Śalya is so badly hurt that he sinks down unconscious, and at this sight the Kaurava forces flee like deer fleeing a lion.* **[37]** *Śalya's younger brother attacks Abhimanyu, who swiftly slays him; his followers take flight. Others of his supporters assail Abhimanyu in great numbers, but Abhimanyu, fighting first gently and then fiercely, overwhelms them with his arrows and they retreat.*

**[38]** *Abhimanyu's arrows pierce many of the greatest Kaurava warriors. Droṇa observes to Kṛpa that he has no equal as an archer: if he wished, he could slay the entire Kaurava army, but for some reason he does not wish to. Hearing Droṇa speak so approvingly of the young enemy, Duryodhana addresses his* *chief warriors, accusing Droṇa of being a self-regarding fool intent on protecting Abhimanyu out of affection for his father Arjuna; and he urges them to destroy Abhimanyu. Duḥśāsana answers: he vows to kill Abhimanyu, and advances against him.*

[39] *Abhimanyu smilingly addresses Duḥśāsana, upbraiding him as cruel and vicious. Then he showers him with arrows until Duḥśāsana sinks down unconscious; his charioteer bears him away. The Pāṇḍavas roar with delight at Abhimanyu's deed and rush to attack Droṇa's forces. Duryodhana tells Karṇa what has happened, and he launches a powerful assault on Abhimanyu. Though struck by many arrows, Abhimanyu is untroubled: he counterattacks fiercely and overcomes him. Seeing this, Karṇa's younger brother attacks Abhimanyu, while the Pāṇḍavas roar their praise of him.* [40] *Abhimanyu responds to the arrows of Karṇa's brother with a single arrow which cuts off his head; Karṇa, full of pain and grief, retreats. Abhimanyu now puts the Kaurava army to rout, consuming them as a fire consumes dry grass.*

[41] *The other Pāṇḍavas follow behind Abhimanyu, putting the Kauravas to flight; but Jayadratha of Sindhu single-handedly checks them. After being defeated by Bhīma following his abduction of Draupadī, he had performed great asceticism until Śiva appeared and granted him the boon of being able to check all the Pāṇḍavas save for Arjuna.* [42] *Jayadratha's arrows pierce all the great Pāṇḍava heroes: he destroys Bhīma's standard, bow and horses, and Bhīma has to take refuge in Sātyaki's chariot, to the great applause of the Kauravas. The Pāṇḍavas are prevented from taking the path opened up by Abhimanyu; try as they may, they cannot overcome Jayadratha.*

[43] *Meanwhile, Abhimanyu continues his single-handed battle against the Kauravas, killing numerous great heroes.* [44] *Many Kaurava warriors approach him to do battle, but, like rivers approaching the ocean, none return. Śalya's son Rukmaratha engages him in single combat, but is swiftly killed. Rukmaratha's followers surround him and cover him with showers of arrows from every side, so that he can no longer be seen; but Abhimanyu deploys the illusory Gandharva Weapon. His form appears replicated by hundreds and thousands, like a weapon-wielding firebrand, and his enemies are cut to pieces. Seeing this, Duryodhana himself attacks Abhimanyu, but after the briefest battle he is forced to retreat.*

[45] *While most of the Kauravas flee, Duryodhana's son Lakṣmaṇa rides against Abhimanyu; seeing this, Duryodhana follows him, and other warriors follow Duryodhana. The two grandsons of Dhṛtarāṣṭra, Abhimanyu and*

*Lakṣmaṇa, exchange many arrows; then Abhimanyu cuts off Lakṣmaṇa's head with a single arrow. Duryodhana is enraged, and shouts, 'Kill him!'; but when six mighty warriors surround him, Abhimanyu beats them back and attacks Jayadratha's forces. His enemies retreat before his assault.*

[46] *The fighting continues. Again Abhimanyu is surrounded by the leading Kauravas, and many arrows are exchanged. Abhimanyu slays Bṛhadbala, king of Kosala.*

Saṃjaya spoke:

[47] Arjuna's son now struck Karṇa in the ear with a barbed arrow,[1] and pierced him with fifty further arrows, enraging him mightily; Rādhā's son Karṇa replied by piercing Abhimanyu with that same number, so that, covered with arrows in every limb, he looked most splendid, O heir of Bharata. Then in fury he turned Karṇa into a flowing spring of blood, and heroic Karṇa too became a splendid sight, bathed in blood and bristling with arrows. Doused in blood and with limbs bristling with arrows, those two noble warriors appeared like *kiṃśuka* trees in bloom. Now Subhadrā's son Abhimanyu laid low Karṇa's six brave aides, expert at many forms of war, together with their horses and charioteers, their standards and their chariots; and, untroubled, he pierced all the other great bowmen with ten arrows apiece, which was a great wonder. Then he slew the son of the king of Magadha with six straight-flying arrows: he felled the young Aśvaketu with his horses and his charioteer. With a razor-edged arrow he killed the Bhoja ruler of Mṛttikāvatī, with his banner displaying an elephant, and roared as he shot off his arrows.

The son of Duḥśāsana now pierced Abhimanyu's four horses with four arrows each; he pierced his charioteer with one arrow, and Arjuna's son himself with ten. Then Arjuna's son pierced the son of Duḥśāsana with seven swift-flying arrows; eyes red with rage, he spoke in a loud voice: 'Your father quit the battle and fled like a coward. At least you know how to fight: bravo! But today you will not escape.' With these words he shot at him an iron arrow, polished by the smith – but Droṇa's son Aśvatthāman cut it down with three shafts. Arjuna's son

1 The text plays on words: Karṇa's name means 'ear', and the word for 'barbed' literally means 'having ears'.

severed his standard, then struck Śalya with three arrows, and Śalya struck him with nine vulture-feathered arrows. Severing his standard in turn, Abhimanyu pierced his paired charioteers with six iron arrows, and Śalya made off to find another chariot.

15 Now Abhimanyu slew the five warriors Śatruṃjaya, Candraketu, Meghavega, Suvarcas and Sūryabhāsa, and pierced Śakuni son of Subala. Śakuni in turn pierced him with three arrows, and then said to Duryodhana, 'Let us all work to crush him, before he kills us one by one!' And manly Karṇa the Cutter then said to Droṇa, 'Quickly command his death at our hands, before he kills us all!' Then the mighty bowman Droṇa spoke in reply to them all: 'Is there a single one of you who can see any flaw in the young man?[1] See the swiftness with which the lion-like Pāṇḍava is travelling all over the battlefield today, just as his
20 father does! Where his chariot passes, all we can see is his bow drawn tight in a circle while he rapidly fixes arrows and shoots them. I am dumbfounded by his arrows, as if he had mortally injured me – and yet Subhadrā's son, slayer of enemy heroes, also affords me great joy! He gives me the highest delight as he travels over the battlefield, offering no flaw to the enraged chariot-fighters of the Kauravas! As he shoots his arrows with such lightness of touch in all directions, I see no distinction in battle between him and Arjuna, bearer of the bow Gāṇḍīva.'

Then Karṇa, who was suffering from the arrows of Arjuna's son, spoke further to Droṇa. 'It is only because of my duty to stay that I
25 am staying, so severely afflicted am I by Abhimanyu. The arrows of that ardent young man are dreadful beyond anything; today I feel them destroying my heart with their terrible fiery energy!' Droṇa the Teacher answered Karṇa with a quiet laugh: 'His armour is impenetrable, and he is young and quick to valour. I taught his father the skill of wearing armour, and this conqueror of enemy fortresses clearly knows it all! It is possible to sever his bow and his bowstring with well-aimed arrows, and to destroy his horses with their bridles, and his paired charioteers.

1 Literally 'any opening in him' (*'syāntaram*): some characteristic offering his enemies a 'way in' to him. (An *antara* need not always be a flaw: at 6.103.79 Bhīṣma uses the word to refer to his own refusal to fight Śikhaṇḍin, who was originally a woman: this offers the Pāṇḍavas a chance to kill him.)

Do this if you can, great bowman, son of Rādhā; then when you have made him turn away from the battle, strike him from behind![1] Even the gods and demons could not defeat him as long as he bears his bow; if you wish to achieve this, rid him of chariot and bow.'

When Karṇa the Cutter heard Droṇa's words he swiftly severed Abhimanyu's bow as he shot his arrows with such lightness of touch. Then Kṛtavarman killed his horses, and Kṛpa heir of Gotama his paired charioteers, while others poured showers of arrows upon him as he stood with bow severed: hastening to act at this time for haste, six mighty chariot-fighters mercilessly poured showers of arrows upon the boy who stood alone and chariotless. His bow severed, chariotless, Abhimanyu none the less maintained the warrior's *dharma*. Bearing sword and shield he leapt gloriously into the air: following the ways of the Kaiśikas[2] and others, and with his own lightness and strength, Arjuna's son ranged about the sky, in might like Garuḍa lord of birds. The Kauravas' great bowmen stared upwards, fearing he might fall upon them with his sword, and pierced him with their shafts in that battle, looking for a weak spot. Then Droṇa severed his sword at its jewelled hilt, and with his arrows Rādhā's son Karṇa destroyed his fine shield. Abhimanyu, deprived of sword and shield but physically still whole, returned from sky to earth, and rushed against Droṇa, brandishing a chariot-wheel.

His body shone with the dust of chariot-wheels, and as he bore the wheel high in his hands Abhimanyu, glorious in battle, looked for a moment exactly as if he were imitating Kṛṣṇa with his discus. His face stained a uniform colour with the blood that flowed, his brow twisted in a frown, roaring loud lion-roars, Abhimanyu, lord of measureless strength in battle, outshone the mighty kings surrounding him.

[**48**] The son of Viṣṇu's sister, adorned with Viṣṇu's weapon, the chariot-fighter Abhimanyu shone in the battle like a second Kṛṣṇa. When the kings of the earth saw his beauty, which even the gods could

**1** The word *paścāt*, as well as 'from behind', may mean simply 'afterwards', but the reference to 'turning away' suggests the interpretation given here.

**2** Not known. At a later similar reference (9.56.46) the editor has preferred *kauśika-* to *kaiśika-*, but this is no clearer.

hardly bear to see, with his hair tossed up by the wind, brandishing a fine wheel as a weapon, they were seriously alarmed, and they cut that wheel to pieces. Then Arjuna's son, great chariot-fighter that he was, seized a mighty club. Deprived of bow, chariot and sword, and now deprived by his enemies of his wheel, Abhimanyu, club in hand, rushed to attack
5 Aśvatthāman. When he saw that club being brandished like a blazing thunderbolt, the bull-like Aśvatthāman left his chariot and took three paces away. Subhadrā's son slew his horses and his paired charioteers with that club, but his body was so covered with arrows that he resembled a porcupine. He killed Kālakeya son of Subala, and seventy-seven of his followers from Gāndhāra; then he killed ten Brahma-Vasātīya chariot-fighters, destroyed seven Kekaya chariots and ten elephants, and with his club smashed the chariot of Duḥśāsana's son together with its horses. Then, sir, Duḥśāsana's son, furious, brandished a club of his own and
10 rushed to attack Subhadrā's son, calling out, 'Stand! Stand!' Wielding their clubs, those two enemy heroes struck at each other in their desire to kill one another, like Śiva and the demon Andhaka long ago. Each of those two enemy-afflicters hit the other with the head of his club; each fell to the ground in the midst of the battlefield like a toppled Pole of Indra. Then Duḥśāsana's son arose, and increased the glory of the Kurus by striking the son of Subhadrā on the head with his club as he attempted to rise. Subhadrā's son, the slayer of enemy heroes, fainting from the impact of that club and from his own exertions, fell lifeless to the ground. Thus, O king, was one slain by many in the battle.

The hero who had laid waste the entire Kuru army, like an elephant in a lotus pond, now lay resplendent in death, like a wild elephant
15 slain by hunters. Your warriors surrounded the fallen hero, now still, like a spring fire that has consumed a forest, or a wind that has died down after battering the treetops, or the sun when it sinks in the West after scorching the troops of the Bhāratas, or the moon in eclipse, or a dried-up ocean. His face was like the full moon, his hair covered his eyes; when your mighty chariot-fighters saw him lying on the ground they were filled with the greatest joy, and repeatedly roared lion-roars. Lord of the peoples, your warriors' rejoicing knew no bounds, while
20 tears fell from the eyes of the enemy heroes. Celestial beings cried out when they saw that hero fall, like the moon falling from the sky: 'This

single warrior lies here, slain by six great Dhārtarāṣṭra chariot-fighters led by Droṇa and Karṇa. This is not *dharma*, we maintain!'

But at brave Abhimanyu's death the earth was most splendid to see, like a full-moon sky wreathed in stars, for it was flooded with pools of blood, and strewn with gold-shafted arrows and with the heads of heroes, still gleaming with their earrings. Many-coloured elephant-cloths, banners, yak-tail fans, fine garments cast away, the glittering ornaments of chariots and horses, men and elephants, sharp steel swords like newly sloughed snakes, bows, broken arrows, spears, lances, darts and *kampanas*, and other weapons of every kind – covered with all these, the earth was splendid to see. All the horses, cut down together with their riders by Subhadrā's son, lying sleeping the sleep of death, doused in blood, rendered the ground impassable. Mountainous elephants, lying slain by arrows, with their goads and drivers, their armour and weapons and banners; fine chariots, without horses, charioteers or fighters, scattered over the earth like despoiled lakes where the elephants have been killed; throngs of footsoldiers lying slain, with all their various weapons and ornaments – these made the earth dreadful to behold, terrifying the faint-hearted.

When they saw Abhimanyu lying fallen on the ground, radiant as the sun or moon, your warriors experienced the greatest joy, and the Pāṇḍavas the greatest woe. When he was killed, O king – a child not yet attained to manhood – the entire Pāṇḍava army ran headlong before the very eyes of Yudhiṣṭhira lord of *dharma*. Seeing his army falling asunder at the death of Subhadrā's son, Yudhiṣṭhira addressed his brave followers: 'He has gone to heaven, a fallen hero who never turned away from battle. Stand firm! Do not fear! We shall conquer our enemies in battle!' With these words the lord of *dharma*, radiant Yudhiṣṭhira of great ardour, best of fighters, drove away grief from the grieving. 'First he killed many snake-like enemy princes in battle, and then Arjuna's son followed them into death. He killed ten thousand warriors, and he killed the king of Kosala; Arjuna's son, the equal of Kṛṣṇa and Arjuna themselves, has certainly attained Indra's heaven. He destroyed chariots and horses, men and elephants by the thousand, yet he was not sated with battle. He should not be mourned, for he performed deeds of merit!'

For ourselves, having killed a leading Pāṇḍava warrior, and suffering
from Pāṇḍava arrows, we returned to our camp in the evening, doused
40 in blood. Both we and our enemies gazed long at the battlefield as we
left it, O king, exhausted and barely conscious. Then came that strange
ill-omened time between day and night. Jackals howled, while the
sun, looking like a garland of lotuses, slowly sank towards the western
mountain. Removing the lustre of fine swords, spears, lances, guard-
rails, armour and ornaments, and bringing sky and earth together, the sun
took on his favourite form of fire.[1] Heaped with many slain elephants,
like cloud-covered mountain-peaks smashed by thunderbolts, complete
with their banners and goads, their armour and drivers, the earth seemed
to groan. But it was splendid to see, with all the huge broken chariots
looking, lord of men, like fortresses sacked by enemies, their lords and
foot-followers, horses and charioteers slain, their gear destroyed, their
45 flags and banners lost. The battlefield was a dreadful sight, with its masses
of chariot-horses of every kind, lying killed together with their chari-
oteers, harness and insignia cast aside, tongues, teeth, entrails and eyes all
put out. Heroes bearing the finest weapons, their armour and insignia
cast aside, men who had formed the rearguard for elephants, horses and
chariots that were now all destroyed, who were accustomed to sleeping
in the costliest of beds, now lay friendless upon the earth in death.

On the battlefield, overjoyed, dogs and jackals, crows, jungle crows
and eagles, wolves and hyenas, blood-drinking birds, hordes of Rākṣasas
and terrible gangs of Piśācas tore open the skins of the fallen to drink
their fat and blood, and eat their marrow and flesh. As they tore out
the entrails they laughed and sang, dragging corpses away by the score.
With blood for its water, massed bodies for its current, chariots for
rafts, elephants for its rocky straits, men's heads for its pebbles, flesh
50 for its mud, decked with discarded weapons of various sorts, a river of
blood flowed from the slaughter of the great warriors, impassable and
dangerous as the underworld river itself. It flowed strongly through the
middle of the battlefield, carrying fear, carrying the living and the dead.
Round it, throngs of hideous fearsome Piśācas ate and drank their fill,
while dogs, jackals and carrion-birds joyfully shared their food, to the

1 The sun 'enters' fire during the hours of darkness.

terror of the living. Gazing long at the battlefield, ghastly at nightfall like the realm of Yama king of the dead, the survivors then went on their way, while headless bodies rose up in throngs. And people could see Abhimanyu lying in the field, with all his costly ornaments scattered about. A mighty chariot-fighter, the equal of Indra himself, he lay dead like a sacrificial fire unfed with offerings.

**[49]** *Yudhiṣṭhira and the other Pāṇḍavas grieve for Abhimanyu. Yudhiṣṭhira praises his heroism and berates himself for having sent him to his death. In his desire for victory he has done a great wrong to both Abhimanyu and the mighty Arjuna, who in his fury will surely wipe out the Kauravas.*

**[50]** *After sunset, Arjuna returns. He has won a great victory over the warriors sworn to kill him, but he is full of foreboding. When he and Kṛṣṇa reach the camp they find it joyless and dark, and Abhimanyu is not to be seen. Arjuna quickly realizes what has happened, for he has heard of Droṇa's deployment of the Wheel formation that Abhimanyu knew how to enter but not how to leave. He is griefstricken, and laments his young son's death. Kṛṣṇa endeavours to console him: Abhimanyu has followed the way of the true hero. But Arjuna now asks his brothers how Abhimanyu came to be killed when they were present in the field, and accuses them of cowardice in failing to protect him.* **[51]** *Yudhiṣṭhira describes to Arjuna how at the Pāṇḍavas' urging Abhimanyu had agreed to enter the Wheel, and how the Pāṇḍavas themselves had been checked by Jayadratha, thanks to his boon from Śiva, allowing Abhimanyu to be unhorsed by six Kaurava warriors and finally killed by Duḥśāsana's son. He also describes the great deeds achieved by Abhimanyu before his death. In a frenzy of grief and rage, Arjuna swears that he will kill Jayadratha, calling down on himself the worst fates if he should fail to do so. Finally, he swears a second oath: that if he does not kill Jayadratha the next day, he will enter fire. Then Kṛṣṇa and Arjuna sound their conches, and the Pāṇḍavas make a mighty noise with musical instruments and lion-roars.*

## THE PROMISE

**[52]** *When Jayadratha hears the cause of the uproar in the Pāṇḍava camp he feels a mixture of sorrow, fear and shame; he does not believe that it will be* *possible to protect him against Arjuna, and so requests leave to quit the battle. Duryodhana encourages him: the mightiest Kaurava warriors will guard his safety. Jayadratha accepts this, but now visits Droṇa and asks him his opinion. Droṇa tells Jayadratha that Arjuna is indeed his superior, but that he will himself protect him by arraying his army in an impenetrable formation; anyway, Jayadratha should not fear, since a heroic death confers the highest blessings on a Kṣatriya.*

[53] *Kṛṣṇa remonstrates with Arjuna for the rashness of his vow. He has learnt from spies of the discussions in the Kaurava camp: Jayadratha will be protected by six great Kaurava warriors and will be guarded by a special array. But Arjuna is dismissive; the combined strength of the Kaurava warriors does not equal half his own, and he will start by attacking Jayadratha's protector Droṇa. In fulfilling his vow to kill Jayadratha he will slaughter thousands. Kṛṣṇa must have his chariot ready at dawn.*

[54] *Neither Arjuna nor Kṛṣṇa sleeps. Knowing that Nara and Nārāyaṇa are angry, the very gods are afraid, and there are fearful portents. Arjuna requests Kṛṣṇa to go and comfort Subhadrā and Abhimanyu's wife Uttarā. He does so: they should not grieve, for Abhimanyu has achieved a hero's greatest desire; and tomorrow they will hear good news, when Arjuna slays Jayadratha.* [55] *Subhadrā grieves for her son; Draupadī and Uttarā join in her lamentations. Again Kṛṣṇa speaks words of consolation: Abhimanyu achieved great deeds.*

[56] *Kṛṣṇa and Arjuna perform the night-time rituals, and Kṛṣṇa withdraws to his own camp. None of the Pāṇḍava warriors sleeps that night, for they are engaged in discussing Arjuna's vow and praying for him to fulfil it. Kṛṣṇa speaks to Dāruka, his own charioteer, and tells him that he will fight fiercely the next day to help Arjuna carry out his word, for Arjuna is very dear to him.*

[57] *Arjuna now sleeps. In his dream he is visited by Kṛṣṇa, who advises him against grief. Arjuna tells him that he is worried in case he fails to fulfil his vow; Kṛṣṇa answers by reminding him of the Pāśupata Weapon, with which Śiva destroyed the Daitya demons. Arjuna should worship Śiva to obtain it, for with it he will be able to kill Jayadratha. Now Arjuna dreams that he and Kṛṣṇa travel together to heaven, where they come before Śiva and worship him. Arjuna tells Śiva that he wishes to obtain the Weapon, and he directs the two men to a lake of* amṛta *nectar where he keeps his weapons. When they arrive there they are confronted by two fierce snakes; they sing the Vedic Śatarudriya hymn to Śiva, and the snakes turn into a bow and arrow, which they take back*

*to Śiva. Śiva takes them, and with the proper* mantras *and in the proper manner he shoots the arrow back into the lake, and returns the bow there also. Arjuna observes everything, and mentally makes his request; Śiva grants it, and the two warriors return to their camp in great joy.*

[58] *As Kṛṣṇa and Dāruka converse, dawn arrives. Yudhiṣṭhira is awoken by musicians and dancers; then, once bathed, anointed and clothed, he performs the morning ritual, gives presents to learned Brahmins, and sits on his jewelled throne, clad in costly garments. Kṛṣṇa is announced, and Yudhiṣṭhira welcomes him.* [59] *He is followed by many of the other leading Pāṇḍava warriors. When they have all arrived, Yudhiṣṭhira addresses Kṛṣṇa and implores his aid, and in particular that Arjuna should fulfil his vow to kill Jayadratha. Kṛṣṇa replies that he will act to ensure that this happens.* [60] *Arjuna now arrives, and relates the story of his dream-meeting with Śiva, to applause. Then the warriors prepare for battle. Arjuna tells Sātyaki that he intends to seek out Jayadratha: Sātyaki himself should protect Yudhiṣṭhira.*

## THE KILLING OF JAYADRATHA

[61] — *Dhṛtarāṣṭra asks Saṃjaya to continue his narration: he can no longer hear the sounds of music and merrymaking in Duryodhana's camp, and wishes to know what has happened. He recalls attempting to dissuade Duryodhana from his actions against the Pāṇḍavas, to no avail; now he fears that the Kauravas will prove no match for their Pāṇḍava enemies, especially the griefstricken Arjuna.* [62] *Saṃjaya replies by cataloguing Dhṛtarāṣṭra's faults: he has repeatedly acted in such a way as to bring this calamity on himself, and he should not cast aspersions on the Kaurava warriors, who are doing everything they can in the battle.*

[63] — *Saṃjaya resumes his narration.* — *At daybreak on the fourteenth day Droṇa arrays his forces, and his warriors show off their martial skills and shout challenges to the Pāṇḍavas. Duryodhana speaks to Jayadratha: he is to take up position far from Droṇa, surrounded by great numbers of warriors; there he will be safe from Pāṇḍava attacks. Droṇa's troops are arrayed in an enormous Wheeled Cart formation, behind which is a Lotus formation containing a Needle formation within it.*

[64] *Arjuna now appears, accompanied by carrion creatures and terrible*

*portents. Durmarṣaṇa, stationed at the head of the Kaurava forces, vows to do battle single-handed against him and the rest of the Pāṇḍavas. Arjuna likewise places his chariot at the head of the Pāṇḍava forces, and he and Kṛṣṇa blow their conches: the sound brings terror to the Kauravas, until their own conches and musical instruments are sounded to encourage them. Arjuna instructs Kṛṣṇa to drive up to Durmarṣaṇa, as he intends to penetrate the Kaurava array; then he attacks fiercely, severing heads at such a rate that his enemies begin to think the world consists of nothing but Arjuna. No one can stand against him, and he inflicts such slaughter that the battlefield resembles doomsday. The Kauravas are routed.* **[65]** *Duḥśāsana responds by attacking Arjuna with an elephant-force. Arjuna wipes it out, killing elephants and the warriors they carry, and smashing chariots. Duḥśāsana retreats into the Cart.*

**[66]** *After his success against Duḥśāsana, Arjuna approaches Droṇa at the head of his array, and requests his blessing in the coming battle against Jayadratha. Droṇa tells him with a smile that defeat of Jayadratha will be impossible without defeat of Droṇa, and showers arrows upon him. A prolonged exchange of arrows takes place, until Kṛṣṇa warns Arjuna not to waste time, but to proceed against Jayadratha. Arjuna agrees to this; when Droṇa asks him if he is really leaving without defeating his enemy, he replies, 'You are my Teacher, not my enemy,' and continues into battle against the Kaurava warriors who now oppose him.* **[67]** *Droṇa pursues him, and he does battle against Droṇa and the assembled Kauravas together. After fighting Kṛtavarman, who separates him from Yudhāmanyu and Uttamaujas, the two guardians of his wheels, he is attacked by Śrutāyudha, who had obtained from his father Varuṇa a wonderful club that conferred invulnerability so long as it was not used against a non-combatant. But Śrutāyudha hurls it at Kṛṣṇa, and it returns against him and kills him. Next, Arjuna is attacked by Sudakṣiṇa prince of Kāmboja; he kills him, and the Kauravas flee.*

**[68]** *Arjuna now comes under attack from the warriors Śrutāyus and Acyutāyus, who hurt him badly with their spears. Kṛṣṇa encourages him, and he makes use of the Weapon of Indra to overwhelm them with arrows and kill them; when their two sons seek to engage him in combat he at once kills both of them also. Then he turns his arrows against the enemy warriors and kills so many of them that a river of blood flows on the battlefield. Śrutāyus of Ambaṣṭha attacks him and hurts Kṛṣṇa with his club: Arjuna slays him too.*

**[69]** *Seeing the destruction caused by Arjuna, Duryodhana goes in distress to*

*Droṇa and accuses him of favouring the Pāṇḍavas; he appeals to him to protect Jayadratha. Droṇa replies that he is no longer capable of keeping up with the speed of Arjuna's chariot, and that he is anyway sworn to capture Yudhiṣṭhira; Duryodhana himself should attack Arjuna. When Duryodhana objects that he stands no chance against Arjuna, Droṇa fastens Duryodhana's armour in such a way as to render him invulnerable, repeating the* mantras *which Śiva had used to grant Indra invulnerability against Vṛtra.*

[70] *Duryodhana sets off in pursuit of Arjuna. Meanwhile a battle begins between the Pāṇḍava forces led by Dhṛṣṭadyumna and Droṇa's Kaurava troops. Dhṛṣṭadyumna attacks so fiercely that the Kauravas are split into three; Droṇa responds with an equally violent onslaught on the Pāṇḍavas, and numerous single combats also take place. All this while, Jayadratha remains at the rear, under the protection of Aśvatthāman, Karṇa, Kṛpa and other great warriors.* [71] *There are many further single combats between Kaurava and Pāṇḍava warriors. Nakula and Sahadeva attack Śakuni and force him to flee, and Ghaṭotkaca does battle with the Rākṣasa Alāyudha.*

[72] *The Pāṇḍavas battle against the three sections into which the Kaurava army has been split: Bhīma against Jalasaṃdha, Yudhiṣṭhira against Kṛtavarman, and Dhṛṣṭadyumna against Droṇa himself. The conflict between these last two is terrible, and causes great loss of life. Dhṛṣṭadyumna now mounts Droṇa's chariot, and at first Droṇa is unable to strike him. However, he is soon able to destroy his shield and sword with his arrows, and to slay his horses and charioteers. Droṇa is on the point of shooting a deadly arrow at Dhṛṣṭadyumna himself when Sātyaki intervenes, cutting it down with his own arrows and piercing Droṇa himself as he rescues Dhṛṣṭadyumna.* [73] *Droṇa and Sātyaki now fight: so terrific is their battle that the other warriors on both sides stop fighting and watch in silence, as do the gods themselves. Sātyaki severs Droṇa's bow; when Droṇa takes up another he severs that too, and this happens repeatedly. Droṇa is impressed. He prepares to shoot the Fire Weapon, and Dhṛṣṭadyumna counteracts it with the Weapon of Varuṇa. As the sun begins to sink in the sky, Yudhiṣṭhira and the other Pāṇḍavas come to Sātyaki's aid, while Duḥśāsana leads the Kauravas to Droṇa's assistance.*

[74] *Meanwhile, Arjuna and Kṛṣṇa drive towards Jayadratha, Arjuna clearing the way for the chariot with his arrows, and Kṛṣṇa driving so fast that the chariot catches up with the arrows as they strike their targets. The brothers Vinda and Anuvinda of Avanti attack them; after a fierce exchange of arrows, Arjuna kills*

*first Vinda, then Anuvinda. Then, to give Kṛṣṇa an opportunity to remove the arrows that have pierced their horses, he dismounts and faces the vast throng of his enemies on foot, warding off their arrows with his own and covering them with dense showers of arrows. In the midst of the conflict, Kṛṣṇa tells him that the horses need water, and he shoots an arrow into the earth to create a wonderful lake, to which he then adds a dwelling formed entirely from arrows.* **[75]** *Now Kṛṣṇa releases the horses from their harness and tends them, while Arjuna, fighting on foot, continues to withstand the onslaught of all his foes. Once the horses are recovered, Kṛṣṇa yokes them once more to the chariot, to the dismay of the Kauravas, who fear for Jayadratha. Kṛṣṇa drives on into the enemy ranks, travelling now so fast that Arjuna's arrows fall behind the chariot. Many Kaurava warriors, including Duryodhana, pursue Arjuna as he seeks Jayadratha while the sun sinks westwards.*

**[76]** *Kṛṣṇa and Arjuna succeed in passing through the ranks of Droṇa's force and out the other side: Kaurava hopes for Jayadratha fade. Seeing Jayadratha, they rush at him; but Duryodhana, wearing his invulnerable armour, overtakes them and turns to face them.* **[77]** *Kṛṣṇa urges Arjuna to fight Duryodhana, and he agrees. Duryodhana challenges them, and they joyfully accept the challenge, blowing their conches, while the Kauravas despair of Duryodhana's life.* **[78]** *Duryodhana shoots arrows at Kṛṣṇa and at Arjuna, who replies in kind; but Arjuna's arrows have no effect against the armour fastened on Duryodhana by Droṇa. Kṛṣṇa comments on this, and Arjuna answers that Duryodhana must indeed be wearing the armour of invulnerability known only to Droṇa; but he does not know how the wearer of such armour should act, and is wearing it like a woman. Arjuna consecrates arrows with special* mantras *and is about to shoot them when Aśvatthāman cuts them down with his own arrow; Arjuna tells Kṛṣṇa that he cannot use this weapon a second time, for it would kill his own forces. Duryodhana now shoots many arrows at him. Unable to find a chink in Duryodhana's armour, he responds by killing his horses and charioteers, and destroying his chariot; then he shoots him through the palms of both hands. Great numbers of Kauravas rush up to support Duryodhana; Arjuna slaughters them before they can even come near, while Kṛṣṇa sounds his conch. The warriors protecting Jayadratha now join in the attack.*

**[79]** *Arjuna comes under attack from Bhūriśravas, Śala, Karṇa, Vṛṣasena, Jayadratha, Kṛpa, Śalya and Aśvatthāman; other warriors too join in. Kṛṣṇa and Arjuna sound their conches; their enemies cannot bear the sound. Duryodhana* *and his eight warriors continue their attack, and they exchange great numbers of arrows with Arjuna.*

**[80]** — *Dhṛtarāṣṭra asks Saṃjaya to describe the standards of the warriors on both sides, and Saṃjaya does so, adding that many men lost their lives to Arjuna's bow Gāṇḍīva, and that this was through Dhṛtarāṣṭra's fault.*

**[81]** — *Meanwhile, the Pāṇḍava forces are doing battle with the forces of Droṇa in a large number of single combats. Yudhiṣṭhira faces Droṇa himself, and the two of them exchange enormous numbers of arrows. Yudhiṣṭhira attacks Droṇa with a spear that can rend mountains; Droṇa uses the Weapon of Brahmā to destroy it, and Yudhiṣṭhira likewise uses the Weapon of Brahmā against Droṇa's Weapon. Droṇa's arrows kill Yudhiṣṭhira's horses and sever his standard and his bow, but Yudhiṣṭhira escapes in Sahadeva's chariot.* **[82]** *Further single combats take place, in which the Pāṇḍavas are victorious. Sātyaki slays Vyāghradatta, prince of Magadha; he is then attacked by great numbers of Vyāghradatta's followers, but overcomes them easily. Furious, Droṇa rushes at him.*

**[83]** *Meanwhile the sons of Draupadī do battle against Somadatta's son and kill him. Bhīma does battle against the Rākṣasa Alambusa: the two of them exchange great numbers of arrows, until Alambusa, recalling that Bhīma had killed his brother Baka, assumes numerous different forms and begins to slaughter the Pāṇḍava forces so fiercely that a river of blood flows. Bhīma responds with the Weapon of Tvaṣṭṛ, which releases thousands of arrows; the Kauravas flee, and Alambusa retreats to Droṇa's army.* **[84]** *Ghaṭotkaca now attacks Alambusa, and the two Rākṣasas battle against each other using their illusory powers. Seeing Alambusa's skill at fighting, Bhīma leads the Pāṇḍavas in a new assault against him. They pierce him with many arrows, and then Ghaṭotkaca seizes him and kills him by smashing him on the ground like a pot.*

**[85]** *Battle rages between Droṇa and Sātyaki, until Sātyaki is overwhelmed by his enemy's arrows. Yudhiṣṭhira now sends Dhṛṣṭadyumna to his aid and follows behind with his own forces; but no one can withstand Droṇa's arrows, which are like the sun's burning rays. Yudhiṣṭhira now hears Arjuna's conch being sounded, and, fearful for his brother's safety, urges Sātyaki to go to his aid.* **[86]** *Sātyaki answers that he is prepared to fight to the death to save Arjuna; however, he is under orders from Arjuna himself to protect Yudhiṣṭhira against Droṇa, and he cannot leave unless that duty is entrusted to some other warrior. Yudhiṣṭhira assures him that he will be protected by all those who are fighting on his side, and especially by Dhṛṣṭadyumna; Sātyaki must go to Arjuna's* *assistance.* **[87]** *Sātyaki is torn between his two conflicting duties, but agrees to do as Yudhiṣṭhira wishes. He describes the awesome forces pitted against him, but declares that he will destroy them, and he requests that his chariot be equipped with five times the normal weaponry and drawn by the very best horses. Yudhiṣṭhira gives the command for this to be done, and Sātyaki, after bathing and performing the other proper rites, prepares to set off. Bhīma proposes to accompany him, but at Sātyaki's request he returns to protect Yudhiṣṭhira. Now Sātyaki attacks the Kaurava forces.*

**[88]** *Dhṛṣṭadyumna orders his warriors to fight in support of Sātyaki, who inflicts heavy casualties on the Kauravas. Droṇa attacks him, and he and Sātyaki exchange many arrows, but Sātyaki refuses to be drawn into a decisive battle against Droṇa as his main task is to reach Arjuna, and he instructs his charioteer to drive him to where Karṇa's troops are stationed. Kṛtavarman confronts him, and a fierce fight takes place between them. Sātyaki slays Kṛtavarman's charioteer, but Kṛtavarman brings the horses under control himself; in the meantime Sātyaki moves on to the forces of the Kāmbojas, pursued by Droṇa. Kṛtavarman attacks Bhīma's warriors, who fight back resolutely.*

**[89]** — *Dhṛtarāṣṭra speaks of the Kaurava army: it is great, it is disposed in the proper formations, it is composed of excellent soldiers and led by the finest generals. For such an army to suffer such slaughter can only be the work of fate.*[1] *The successes of Arjuna and Sātyaki must be causing grief to Duryodhana and his brothers.* **[90]** *Saṃjaya answers that the fault lies entirely with Dhṛtarāṣṭra, and resumes his narration. — Kṛtavarman fights with amazing valour: pierced with arrows by all the great Pāṇḍava heroes, he replies in kind, engaging in a fierce exchange of arrows, first with Bhīma and then with all of them together. The encounter becomes restricted to Kṛtavarman and Śikhaṇḍin, who shower each other with arrows until Śikhaṇḍin sinks down unconscious and is borne away by his charioteer. The Pāṇḍavas flee before the triumphant Kṛtavarman.*

**[91]** *When Sātyaki becomes aware of this turn of events, he attacks Kṛtavarman and rapidly overcomes him. Then he instructs his charioteer to take him to the elephant force of the Trigartas, and slaughters it. Furious, Jalasaṃdha attacks him, and a fierce battle takes place between the two, at the end of which Sātyaki severs first his opponent's arms and then his head: Jalasaṃdha's elephant runs wild, crushing the troops on its own side.* **[92]** *Droṇa and many Kaurava warriors*

1 The first part of this chapter is closely similar to 6.72.

*now shower arrows upon Sātyaki, piercing him repeatedly, but in answer he pierces each of them with his own arrows. A fierce battle develops between him and Duryodhana; seeing their brother under heavy attack the other Dhārtarāṣṭras shoot great numbers of arrows at Sātyaki, but are pierced by his arrows. Sātyaki kills Duryodhana's horses and charioteer, and Duryodhana flees, to the dismay of the Kauravas. Kṛtavarman attacks Sātyaki, but is overcome by him. Sātyaki, anxious to reach Arjuna, passes on through the midst of Kṛtavarman's troops.* **[93]** *Droṇa resumes his attack on Sātyaki, and the two warriors exchange enormous numbers of arrows. When Droṇa severs Sātyaki's bow, Sātyaki hurls a club at him, takes up another bow and continues the fight; when Droṇa's arrows render his charioteer unconscious, Sātyaki takes up the reins and fights and drives simultaneously. Felling Droṇa's own charioteer, he puts his horses to flight, and Droṇa's chariot is dragged all over the battlefield. The Kauravas rush to seize the fleeing horses, and their formation is broken.*

**[94]** *The Kauravas are unable to withstand Sātyaki's onslaught. The warrior Sudarśana attacks him, but Sātyaki's arrows sever both his charioteer's head and his own, and Sātyaki continues on his way towards Arjuna, slaughtering enemies with his arrows as he goes.* **[95]** *Confident from his successes, and convinced he is nearing Arjuna, he instructs his charioteer to drive him to where Duryodhana has a mighty force of Kāmbojas and other barbarians waiting to do battle against him: he will slay them in their thousands. The charioteer does as he is bidden, and Sātyaki sets about making good his word, until the earth is covered with bodies and the few survivors flee.*

**[96]** *Sātyaki continues on his way, passing through the midst of the enemy army. Many Kaurava warriors rush at him, but they are killed by his arrows, not one of which is shot in vain; not even Arjuna could match the slaughter he causes. Various of the leading Kauravas pierce him with arrows, but he replies in kind, finally killing Duryodhana's charioteer; the chariot is drawn away rapidly by its horses, and the Kauravas flee.*

**[97]** *— Dhṛtarāṣṭra remarks that Sātyaki's extraordinary achievements indicate that fate must be hostile to the Kauravas, but Saṃjaya once again assures him that the fault is his own, and continues the story of the battle. — Huge numbers of Kaurava warriors rally to attack Sātyaki, but he slays them. Duḥśāsana urges a force of mountain-men to fight against Sātyaki with stones, since this way of fighting is unknown to him; they do so, but Sātyaki cuts the flying stones to pieces with his arrows, and many warriors are killed by the hurtling* *fragments, while horses, elephants and other warriors flee. Droṇa hears the uproar and understands what has happened, and at that moment Sātyaki reappears, killing many chariot-fighters as they flee towards Droṇa's ranks.* **[98]** *Droṇa sees Duḥśāsana in flight from Sātyaki, and remonstrates with him: having caused so much hostility between the Kauravas and the Pāṇḍavas, why is he now running away? If he flees from Sātyaki, how much worse will it be when he encounters Bhīma or Arjuna? Duḥśāsana returns to do battle against Sātyaki with a large force of barbarians, and Droṇa himself launches a powerful assault on the Pāṇḍavas and Pāñcālas. Several Pāñcāla princes fight against him, but all are slain. Furious, Dhṛṣṭadyumna attacks him fiercely, piercing him with so many arrows that he loses consciousness. At this, Dhṛṣṭadyumna takes up a sword and climbs into Droṇa's own chariot, intent on cutting off his head; but Droṇa comes to and shoots many arrows at him, whereupon Dhṛṣṭadyumna returns to his own chariot and the terrible battle between them resumes. Droṇa kills Dhṛṣṭadyumna's charioteer, and his horses bear him away from the triumphant Droṇa.* **[99]** *Meanwhile, Duḥśāsana attacks Sātyaki and showers him with arrows; in response, Sātyaki shoots so many arrows at Duḥśāsana that he becomes invisible. Alarmed, Duryodhana sends a force of Trigartas to his brother's aid, but Sātyaki slaughters them. Duḥśāsana continues his attack, and the two warriors exchange many arrows; Sātyaki slays Duḥśāsana's horses and charioteer, and Duḥśāsana is taken up into the chariot of the Trigarta general. Remembering Bhīma's vow to kill the Dhārtarāṣṭras, Sātyaki lets him live, and continues on his way towards Arjuna.*

**[100]** *The battle rages on. The Pāṇḍavas urge their supporters to the attack, to give Arjuna and Sātyaki the best chance of success, and the Kauravas fight back fiercely. Duryodhana showers arrows on the Pāṇḍava heroes; Yudhiṣṭhira severs his bow and pierces him. The Pāñcālas advance against him as he takes up another bow and challenges Yudhiṣṭhira again, but Droṇa comes to his rescue.*

**[101]** *Droṇa does battle against the Kekaya warrior Bṛhatkṣatra. After an exchange of arrows, Droṇa prepares to make use of the Weapon of Brahmā, but Bṛhatkṣatra uses his own Weapon of Brahmā against Droṇa's Weapon. However, a further exchange of arrows leads to Bṛhatkṣatra's death. Seeing this, Śiśupāla's son Dhṛṣṭaketu furiously attacks Droṇa; he too exchanges many arrows with him, and he too is killed. Droṇa now launches a powerful assault on the Pāṇḍavas and Pāñcālas, killing Dhṛṣṭadyumna's son Kṣatradharman and overcoming Cekitāna the Vṛṣṇi. Though in his eighties, Droṇa fights like a* *sixteen-year-old.* [**102**] *Dismayed by Droṇa's successes and by the lack of news concerning Arjuna and Sātyaki, Yudhiṣṭhira resolves to send Bhīma to their support. He tells Bhīma that he has heard Kṛṣṇa's conch Pāñcajanya sounding, suggesting that Arjuna has been killed and Kṛṣṇa himself has now joined in the battle, and he asks Bhīma to go after the endangered Pāṇḍava heroes. Bhīma agrees, but first instructs Dhṛṣṭadyumna to protect Yudhiṣṭhira against Droṇa; then he sets off to the beat of a drum and the blast of his conch, followed by the Pāñcālas and Somakas. Nineteen of the Dhārtarāṣṭra brothers surround him and attack him together with their followers, but he gets past them and rushes at Droṇa's troops, dispersing the elephant-force in the van with his arrows. Droṇa expects him to pay his respects, but instead he declares himself Droṇa's enemy and hurls his club at him. Droṇa leaps down from his chariot, which is utterly destroyed by Bhīma's club. Again the Dhārtarāṣṭras surround Bhīma, while Droṇa takes to another chariot, but Bhīma slays many of them and puts the rest to flight.*

[**103**] *Bhīma kills many warriors with his club. Then Droṇa, with a terrifying roar, attacks him, showering many arrows on him; Bhīma, ignoring them, leaps down from his chariot, runs towards Droṇa's chariot, seizes it, and overthrows it; again Droṇa takes to another, and retreats. Back in his own chariot, Bhīma now rushes at his enemies, overcoming and passing through host after host of them. Soon he sees Arjuna, and roars; hearing this, Arjuna and Kṛṣṇa roar back. Yudhiṣṭhira hears the sound, and is filled with joy.*

[**104**] — *Dhṛtarāṣṭra requests Saṃjaya to tell him which Kaurava warriors fought against Bhīma, and Saṃjaya proceeds to do so. — Karṇa rushes at Bhīma, whose roar terrifies all creatures. The two warriors exchange great numbers of arrows; finally Bhīma kills Karṇa's charioteer and his horses, and Karṇa takes refuge in Vṛṣasena's chariot. Hearing Bhīma's roar of victory, all the Pāṇḍavas sound their conches.*

[**105**] *Meanwhile, Duryodhana approaches Droṇa and asks him how it is that the Pāṇḍava heroes are achieving such successes, and what should be done to protect Jayadratha. Droṇa answers that Kṛṣṇa and Arjuna present the greatest danger, and that the protection of Jayadratha must be the first task of the Kauravas. This battle is the continuation of the gambling match, and Jayadratha is the stake. Duryodhana should go to protect those who are protecting him; Droṇa will send others to help, and will keep back the Pāṇḍavas and their supporters. Duryodhana does as Droṇa says, and comes upon the two guardians of Arjuna's*

*wheels, Yudhāmanyu and Uttamaujas, who had been separated from Arjuna by Kṛtavarman. He engages them in a battle which ends with all three of them chariotless; he then climbs into Śalya's chariot, while his two enemies climb into another chariot and continue on their way towards Arjuna.*

**[106]** — *Dhṛtarāṣṭra asks to hear details of the battle between Bhīma and Karṇa, and Saṃjaya gives them.* — *As Bhīma sets out to join Arjuna and Kṛṣṇa, Karṇa resumes his battle against him, showering him with arrows and challenging him to fight, and the two warriors exchange many arrows. Bhīma is struck by so many arrows that he resembles a porcupine, but once again he slays Karṇa's horses and charioteer, and again Karṇa takes to another chariot.* **[107]** *The battle continues. Bhīma recalls all the wrongs that the Pāṇḍavas have suffered, and fights without regard for his life. So many arrows are exchanged that they appear like birds flying in the sky; as they fall they kill elephants, horses and men in great numbers.*

**[108]** — *Dhṛtarāṣṭra is appalled to hear that so great a warrior as Karṇa has been repeatedly vanquished by Bhīma, who is spurred on by thoughts of the evil that Duryodhana has done to the Pāṇḍavas. Saṃjaya continues his narration.* — *Karṇa and Bhīma continue to shoot numerous arrows at each other, and each continues to cut down the other's arrows with his own. They are like competing bulls, tigers, or elephants, as each seeks to find a weak spot in the other. Yet again Bhīma severs Karṇa's bow and kills his horses. Duryodhana, seeing Karṇa in difficulties, sends his brother Durjaya to attack Bhīma; Bhīma slays him. Karṇa respectfully circumambulates the fallen warrior, while Bhīma continues to shoot arrows at him.* **[109]** *Once again Karṇa takes to another chariot and resumes the exchange of arrows with Bhīma, until Bhīma hurls a club which kills Karṇa's horses, and shoots two arrows which sever his standard and slay his charioteer. Duryodhana sends his brother Durmukha to provide Karṇa with a chariot; Bhīma kills him. Karṇa circumambulates the body, while Bhīma shoots at him again. There is another brief exchange, after which Karṇa flees, overcome.*

**[110]** — *Dhṛtarāṣṭra laments the supremacy of fate over human effort: even the mighty Karṇa is defeated, and Bhīma appears invincible. Saṃjaya tells him that he is himself the cause of all the destruction, and takes up the story again.* — *Five Dhārtarāṣṭra brothers, Durmarṣaṇa, Duḥsaha, Durmada, Durdhara and Jaya, rush at Bhīma, showering him with arrows, and seeing this Karṇa too returns to the attack. But Bhīma slays all five of them. He and Karṇa stare at each other.* **[111]** *Karṇa is now without regard for his life, and believes himself* *to blame for the death of Dhṛtarāṣṭra's sons. He shoots more arrows at Bhīma, who kills his horses and charioteer, laughs a great laugh, and severs his bow. The battle continues with Karṇa on foot, until Karṇa retreats under Bhīma's assault. Duryodhana tells six of his brothers to go to Karṇa's aid; they are slain by Bhīma. Karṇa, weeping, takes to a new chariot, and the battle between the two warriors resumes. Bhīma appears like a rain-cloud flashing with lightning; the sound of his bowstring is like thunder as he showers arrows on Karṇa as if showering rain on a mountain.*

[**112**] *Karṇa briefly withdraws from the range of Bhīma's arrows, observes the Dhārtarāṣṭras lying killed by Bhīma, then returns to the fight in fury, showering Bhīma with dense masses of arrows. Bhīma replies in kind, and Duryodhana, anxious for Karṇa's safety, sends seven of his brothers to his assistance. They shoot many arrows at Bhīma; he slays them with one arrow apiece and roars a lion-roar. Yudhiṣṭhira hears this with joy; Duryodhana, seeing thirty-one of his brothers slain, reflects that Vidura's words have come true. — Now Saṃjaya tells Dhṛtarāṣṭra that what is happening is the consequence of the Kauravas' wrongdoing: this is why Vikarṇa, Citrasena and so many others of his sons lie dead.* [**113**] *Dhṛtarāṣṭra accepts that he is to blame, and asks Saṃjaya to continue his narration. Saṃjaya does so. — Bhīma and Karṇa continue to shoot great numbers of arrows at each other: many warriors are killed, and others flee to watch the conflict from a distance. A river of blood flows on the battlefield; the earth is covered with the detritus of war.*

[**114**] *The battle between Karṇa and Bhīma rages on, each shooting inconceivable numbers of arrows at the other. After a prolonged exchange, Karṇa succeeds in killing Bhīma's horses, wounding his charioteer and severing his bow. Bhīma hurls a spear, but Karṇa cuts it in pieces with his arrows; Bhīma hurls a sword which severs Karṇa's bow, but Karṇa takes up a new one. Bhīma leaps into the sky and endeavours to seize Karṇa from his chariot, as Garuḍa might seize a snake; Karṇa, alarmed, hides and eludes him. The terrible combat resumes. Bhīma, on foot, seeks to impede the passage of Karṇa's chariot by getting amongst the great elephants slain by Arjuna; he picks up an elephant and brandishes it, but Karṇa cuts it to pieces with his arrows; he hurls severed limbs of elephants, chariot-wheels and horses at Karṇa, but Karṇa cuts them all down. However, Karṇa will not kill the unarmed Bhīma. Instead he touches him with the tip of his bow and insults him. Arjuna, hearing this, shoots many arrows at Karṇa, forcing him away from Bhīma, who now climbs into Sātyaki's*

*chariot. Arjuna aims a deadly shaft at Karṇa; Aśvatthāman cuts it down with an arrow. Furious, Arjuna pierces him with sixty-four arrows and pursues him into the Kaurava host, which he proceeds to slaughter.*

[115] *Sātyaki is attacked by the great king Alambusa, and the two warriors exchange many arrows; Sātyaki kills Alambusa's horses and charioteer, and then severs Alambusa's head with an arrow. He is attacked by the Dhārtarāṣṭras under Duḥśāsana, but swiftly checks them and kills Duḥśāsana's horses.* [116] *Then he is attacked by a force of Trigarta archers, but defeats five hundred of them single-handed. He appears to be everywhere, moving as if dancing, like a hundred warriors. He does battle with the Śūrasenas, then with the Kaliṅgas; at last he comes up to Arjuna, like a tired swimmer reaching the shore. Kṛṣṇa speaks to Arjuna in Sātyaki's praise, but Arjuna is displeased: Sātyaki was to have remained with Yudhiṣṭhira to protect him. Now Bhūriśravas is preparing to attack Sātyaki, and Arjuna has much to do: he must find out whether Yudhiṣṭhira is safe, he must protect the weary Sātyaki, and he must kill Jayadratha; and the sun is sinking.*

Saṃjaya spoke:
[117] When Bhūriśravas saw the Sātvata warrior Sātyaki descending upon him mad for battle, swiftly and furiously he rushed to attack him, O king. Then the strong-armed Kaurava hero said to Śini's bull-like heir, 'Today by good fortune you have come within my sight! Today I shall achieve a long-felt desire in battle, for you will not escape me alive unless you quit the fight. Today in battle I shall kill you, the Daśārha prince who is always so proud of his courage, and so bring joy to Duryodhana king of the Kurus. Today in battle the heroes Kṛṣṇa and Arjuna will see you fallen to the ground, consumed by the fire of my arrows. Today King Yudhiṣṭhira, son of Dharma, will hear that I have slain you, and will at once fall prey to shame at having made you come here. Today Kuntī's son, wealth-winner Arjuna, will recognize my valour when you lie slain on the earth, doused in blood, for I have long desired today's encounter with you, as Indra desired to encounter Bali in the war of the gods and demons long ago. Today I shall engage you in the most dreadful battle, Sātvata warrior; today you will learn the truth about my heroism, my strength and my manly resolve. Today you will go to the dwelling of Yama, slain by me in battle, like Rāvaṇa's

son, killed in battle by Lakṣmaṇa, the younger brother of Rāma. Today Kṛṣṇa, and Kuntī's son Arjuna, and Yudhiṣṭhira lord of *dharma*, will lose the will to fight when you are slain, Sātyaki, and will surely abandon the battle. Today, O Sātyaki, I shall pay you back with my sharp arrows, and bring joy to the women whose menfolk you have killed in battle. Now you have come within my sight you will not escape, like a fawn that has come within range of a lion!'

Laughingly, O king, Sātyaki answered him: 'Fear in battle is outside
my experience, O Kaurava. The man who can render me weaponless 15
may kill me in battle; and the man who can kill me in battle may kill whoever he wishes for all time. What is the use of so many vain words? Act to make them real! But your words bear no fruit, like the thunder of an autumn cloud; when I hear its roar, O hero, I am reduced to laughter. O Kaurava, let the battle so long desired in this world take place today, for my heart is in haste, and you, my son, are eager to do battle. Today I shall not return without killing you, basest of men!'

Then those two bull-like heroes, after lashing each other with words, struck out in the most furious combat, each longing to kill the other.
Those tiger-like, virile warriors met and contended in battle like two 20
rutting elephants fighting furiously for a female. Bhūriśravas and Sātyaki, foe-tamers both, poured terrible showers of arrows upon one another, like clouds pouring rain. Somadatta's son Bhūriśravas covered Sātyaki with his swift-flying arrows and pierced him with his sharp darts in an effort to kill him, best heir of Bharata; he pierced him with ten darts, and then shot further sharp arrows at Śini's bull-like heir in an effort to kill him. But, lord of the peoples, Sātyaki consumed those sharp arrows in mid-air with his own magic weapons before they could reach
their target. Thus those two most well-born heroes, one a credit to the 25
Kurus, the other to the Vṛṣṇis, poured showers of arrows upon one another. Like tigers with their claws, or mighty elephants with their tusks, they wounded each other with their lances and their arrows; piercing each other's limbs, and flowing with blood, they checked one another, gamblers wagering their lives. Thus the two warriors of unmatched deeds, one a credit to the Kurus, the other to the Vṛṣṇis, battled against each other like two rival elephant lords.

Ready to enter Brahmā's heaven at once, and eager to gain the highest place, they struck at one another; Sātyaki and Somadatta's son covered each other with a shower of arrows before the delighted eyes of the Dhārtarāṣṭras. People there watched the two warrior lords as they fought like two elephant lords battling over a female. They slew one another's horses, severed one another's bows; then, chariotless, they met in a mighty combat to fight each other with swords. Wielding huge, beautiful shields of bull-hide and unsheathing their swords, they strode over the battlefield; the two foe-crushers manoeuvred this way and that, sometimes circling, as they repeatedly struck at one another in fury. Bearing swords and bright shields, neck-chains, armlets and other ornaments, mad for battle, they harried each other, O king; then, lord of kings, after harrying each other for a while before the eyes of all the soldiers, the two heroes paused for breath.

When they had cut each other's huge, beautiful shields and arrow-shields to pieces with their swords, the two tiger-like heroes began to wrestle one another. Both broad of chest and long of arm, both skilled at close combat, they fought each other with their arms like iron bars: their smashes, arm-locks and neck-locks, executed with skill and strength, delighted all the warriors. The sound made by those two excellent warriors as they battled, O king, was as loud and as fearsome as a thunderbolt striking a mountain; like elephants with their pointed tusks, or mighty bulls with their horns, those two noble bull-like men, the Kuru and the Sātvata, fought each other.

Then as Sātyaki fought on, his weapons destroyed, Kṛṣṇa Vāsudeva addressed Arjuna: 'See him fighting chariotless in battle, the foremost of all bowmen! He entered the army of the Bhāratas behind you, son of Pāṇḍu; and he has fought with all the great Bhārata heroes, O heir of Bharata! Now weary, this best of warriors has encountered Bhūriśravas, so generous to Brahmins, approaching him seeking battle. This is not fair, Arjuna!' At this point, O king, the furious Bhūriśravas made ready and struck down the battle-crazed Sātyaki, like one rutting elephant striking another, before the eyes of Kṛṣṇa Keśava and Arjuna, best and most furious of warriors, waiting in their chariot in that battle. Strong-armed Kṛṣṇa again spoke to Arjuna: 'See, the tiger of the Vṛṣṇis and Andhakas is overpowered by Somadatta's son; weary after performing difficult feats, your brave disciple Sātyaki stands on the ground – protect him, Arjuna! Act swiftly, tiger-like hero, lest that excellent enemy-slayer is overcome by Bhūriśravas the sacrificer on your account!'

Joyful in heart, wealth-winner Arjuna answered Vāsudeva: 'See the 50
bull-like Kuru sporting with the Vṛṣṇi hero, like a lion-lord sporting
in the forest with a mighty rutting elephant!' But then there came a
great uproar among the soldiers, O bull-like heir of Bharata, as strong-
armed Bhūriśravas made ready and struck down Sātyaki to the ground.
Bhūriśravas, best of Kurus, so generous to Brahmins, was resplendent
in that battle as he dragged the Sātvata hero like a lion dragging an
elephant; then he drew his sword from its sheath, seized him by the
hair, and kicked him in the chest.

When Kṛṣṇa Vāsudeva saw the Sātvata being dragged about in battle
in this way, he spoke once again to Arjuna, O king: 'See, strong-armed 55
hero, your disciple Sātyaki, your equal with the bow, the tiger of the
Vṛṣṇis and Andhakas, is overpowered by Somadatta's son; O son of
Kuntī, if the Vṛṣṇi Sātyaki of true valour is overcome in battle by
Bhūriśravas, that valour of his becomes untrue!' Pāṇḍu's strong-armed
son Arjuna heard Vāsudeva's words, and he mentally paid honour to
Bhūriśravas in that battle: 'By dragging Sātyaki, best of the Sātvatas,
in battle, as if sporting with him, Bhūriśravas increases both my joy
and the Kurus' glory; for instead of killing that foremost Vṛṣṇi hero
he drags him like a lion dragging a mighty elephant in a forest!' Then 60
after mentally honouring the Kaurava, Kuntī's strong-armed son gave
his reply to Kṛṣṇa Vāsudeva, O king: 'Heir of Madhu, my eyes were
fixed on Jayadratha of Sindhu, so I did not notice Sātyaki; but now I
shall undertake a difficult feat for the sake of that Yādava hero.' And
with these words, Pāṇḍu's son Arjuna, acting on Kṛṣṇa's instruction,
severed with an arrow the arm, complete with sword, of the sacrificer
Bhūriśravas.

[**118**] That arm, complete with sword and beautiful armlets, fell to the ground, and Bhūriśravas, greatest of men, experienced the greatest dismay. His arm, severed by the unseen Arjuna as it was about to strike, fell swiftly to the ground like a five-headed snake. When the Kaurava saw that Kuntī's son had finished him as a warrior, he was furious; abandoning Sātyaki, he censured the Pāṇḍava: 'This is a cruel deed that you have done, son of Kuntī, to sever my arm when I could not see you

5 and was not engaged in combat with you! What will you say to King
Yudhiṣṭhira, son of Dharma, when he asks how you killed Bhūriśravas
in battle? Did noble Indra in person teach you this way with weapons,
son of Kuntī, or was it Śiva, or Droṇa or Kṛpa? You know your *dharma*
better than anyone else in this world, so how did you strike a warrior
who was not engaged in combat with you? The wise do not strike at a
warrior who is distracted or frightened, chariotless or pleading, or one
who is overcome by misfortune; such a base deed would be practised
only by the wicked. Why have you done such a hard thing, son of
10 Kuntī? For they say that a noble deed is one that is easy for a noble
man to do, O wealth-winner Arjuna, and an ignoble deed one that is
very hard for a noble man. A man quickly takes on the characteristics
of those with whom he associates, son of Kuntī, as we see in your case:
for how else can it be that one of royal line – indeed, a Kuru – should
have abandoned the Kṣatriya *dharma*, when you were once a virtuous
upholder of duty? This vile act that you have carried out for the sake of
Sātyaki the Vṛṣṇi was obviously Kṛṣṇa's idea, and is uncharacteristic of
you; for who except a friend of Kṛṣṇa's would inflict such a catastrophe
15 on one who was distracted, engaged in fighting another? The Vṛṣṇis
and Andhakas are debased, unable to tell good from evil, natural objects
of censure; how have you taken them for your standard?'

With these words strong-armed Bhūriśravas of great renown, he
whose banner was the sacrificial stake, abandoned Sātyaki and sat down
upon the battlefield, preparing to die. With his left hand he scattered
arrows like grass at a sacrifice; then that virtuous man, seeking to reach
Brahmā's heaven, made an offering of his own life's breath. He fixed
his eye upon the sun and his tranquil mind upon water; meditating on
the Great Upaniṣad and absorbed in Yoga, he fell silent. Then everyone
in the whole army began to censure Kṛṣṇa and Arjuna, and to praise
20 that bull-like hero. Though censured, Kṛṣṇa and Arjuna spoke no harsh
word; though praised, the hero whose banner was the sacrificial stake
experienced no joy.

But wealth-winner Arjuna could not bear in his heart that your sons
should speak thus, nor could he bear what they and Bhūriśravas said.
With a mind devoid of anger, O heir of Bharata, Pāṇḍu's son Arjuna
spoke defiantly to remind them. 'Every king here knows my great oath,

that no ally of mine may be slain within bowshot of me. Bearing this
in mind, Bhūriśravas, you ought not to censure me, for it is not proper
to censure another without knowing his *dharma*. My severing your arm 25
when you had raised your weapon in battle to kill Sātyaki the Vṛṣṇi
was not prohibited by *dharma*; but what righteous man would applaud
the killing of Abhimanyu, a child, disarmed, chariotless and without
armour?'[1]

When Kuntī's son spoke these words, Bhūriśravas touched the earth
with his head, and with his left hand he held out his right hand to
Arjuna; that most radiant hero, whose banner was the sacrificial stake,
heard what Arjuna had to say, great king, and he remained silent, looking
at the ground. Then Arjuna addressed him once more: 'The love I bear
Yudhiṣṭhira lord of *dharma*, and Bhīma best of those who speak, and
Nakula and Sahadeva, that same love I bear towards you too, O elder
brother of Śala. Now, with my leave and that of the noble Kṛṣṇa, go 30
forth like Uśīnara's son Śibi to the realms of the virtuous!'

At this point, Sātyaki heir of Śini rose to his feet. Freed by Somadatta's
son, he now took up his sword to sever that noble man's head: though
Bhūriśravas, so generous to Brahmins, sat distracted and dying at the
hands of Pāṇḍu's son Arjuna, his arm severed like an elephant's severed
trunk,[2] the wicked Sātyaki intended to kill Śala's sinless elder brother.
The whole army called out its censure, and Kṛṣṇa and Kuntī's noble
son Arjuna sought to stop him, as did Bhīma, and the two guardians of
Arjuna's wheels, and Aśvatthāman, Kṛpa, Karṇa, Vṛṣasena and Jayadratha 35
of Sindhu. But though the whole army called out against him, he slew
Bhūriśravas, keeper of his word; Sātyaki struck off with his sword the
head of that Kaurava prince as he sat on the battlefield preparing to die,
his arm severed by Arjuna.

Bhūriśravas's troops did not applaud Sātyaki for his act in killing that
Kaurava who was already slain by Arjuna. Siddhas, Cāraṇas, mortals and

**1** I have here adopted the 'easier' reading *ko nu pūjayet*. The text of the critical edition in fact reads *ko na pūjayet* 'Who would *not* applaud it?' One possible way to make sense of this reading is to interpret *sākṣepam* in verse 22, which I have translated 'defiantly', as meaning 'ironically'.

**2** Play on words: *hasta* 'trunk' also means 'hand'.

gods all saw Bhūriśravas, Indra's equal in might, killed on the battlefield
as he sat preparing to die, and they honoured him, astonished by his
40 feats. Many of his warriors too expressed their opinions. Some said,
'Sātyaki the Vṛṣṇi is not at fault: it was fated to happen so, and therefore
you should not be angry. Anger brings grief to mankind. There is no
room for debate: he was destined to be killed by the brave Sātyaki, for
the creator ordained Sātyaki to slay him in battle.' Now Sātyaki himself
spoke: 'If you are telling me that I should never have killed him, then
you are deeply wicked men, using virtuous words to assume a virtuous
guise. Where was that virtue of yours when you killed Subhadrā's son
Abhimanyu in battle, a child who had been disarmed? I, on the other
hand, had vowed that any enemy living who abused me disrespectfully
in battle, and struck me angrily with his foot, would earn death at
45 my hands, even if he were a great sage. As I struggled to overcome
Bhūriśravas, you – though you had eyes to see – reckoned that I was
as good as dead – though I had arms to fight. This was foolishness on
your part! I did overcome him, and I did so properly, O bull-like Kurus!
But I have been cheated because Kuntī's son Arjuna, out of love for me
and to maintain his vow, severed his arm complete with sword. That
which is destined will happen; it is fate which makes us act; and so this
man has been slain in this conflict. What is immoral in such an deed?
Remember too the verse sung long ago by Vālmīki: "Whatever causes
pain to one's enemies *must* be done!"'

Great king, when Sātyaki had finished speaking, not one of the
Kauravas and Pāṇḍavas spoke a word, though mentally they honoured
50 him. No one present would applaud the killing of a man rendered pure
by *mantras* at great sacrifices, a famous donor of many thousands who
lived like a forest-dwelling sage. The head of that heroic granter of
boons, with its black hair and its eyes as red as a dove's, appeared like the
severed head of a sacrificial horse lying next to the vessel of the oblation.
His vital energy destroyed by a weapon, Bhūriśravas, the pure and most
worthy granter of boons, quit his body on the great field of battle and
rose aloft, filling heaven and earth with the excellence of his *dharma*.

[119] — *Dhṛtarāṣṭra asks how it happened that Sātyaki, having triumphed over so many great warriors, was thrown down by Bhūriśravas. Saṃjaya ex-*

*plains that in days gone by a great battle had taken place at the princess Devakī's* svayaṃvara *between Sātyaki's grandfather Śini and Bhūriśravas's father Somadatta. Śini had thrown Somadatta down in the presence of the thousands of kings who were attending, and had drawn his sword, seized him by the hair and kicked him in the chest. Somadatta had obtained a boon from Śiva that his son would do the same to Śini's son, and so it has come about.*

[**120**] — *Saṃjaya resumes his narration. — Arjuna now tells Kṛṣṇa to drive him swiftly up to Jayadratha, as the sun is close to setting, and Kṛṣṇa does so. Duryodhana urges Karṇa to protect Jayadratha: if Arjuna fails to fulfil his vow before the day ends he will enter fire, and the Pāṇḍavas will be destroyed. Despite his wounds, Karṇa assents. Then Duryodhana, Karṇa and other leading Kaurava warriors surround Arjuna as he slaughters his enemies and draws close to Jayadratha. With their backs to Jayadratha, and longing for sunset, they attack Arjuna, but Arjuna cannot be overcome; slaying most of the force opposing him, he approaches Jayadratha. Karṇa opposes him, and a mighty battle takes place between the two heroes. Arjuna kills Karṇa's horses and his charioteer, but Aśvatthāman takes Karṇa up into his own chariot, while Arjuna continues fighting and killing.*

Saṃjaya spoke:
[**121**] Wealth-winner Arjuna, Kuntī's handsome son, ranged over the
battlefield displaying his splendid weapons simultaneously in every
direction. No one could look at the noble Pāṇḍava blazing like the
midday sun in the sky; but we saw the hosts of arrows shot from his
bow Gāṇḍīva, flying over the battlefield like rows of geese crossing the
sky. He countered all the weapons of the Kaurava heroes with his own
weapons, and showed himself a grim man settled on a fierce task. O king, 5
in his longing to slay Jayadratha, Arjuna passed through those excellent
chariot-fighters, dumbfounding them with his iron arrows; shooting
arrows in every direction, the handsome wealth-winner ranged swiftly
over the battlefield with Kṛṣṇa for his charioteer. The hosts of arrows
of that noble hero seemed to spin around the sky in their hundreds and
thousands, and we could not tell when the Pāṇḍava hero, Kuntī's son,
took up his bow, when he fixed an arrow to it, and when he shot. So,
O king, the son of Kuntī overwhelmed the entire horizon and all the

chariot-fighters, as he rushed to attack Jayadratha and pierced him with sixty-four straight arrows.

10 But the king of Sindhu with his standard of a boar, finding himself thus pierced with arrows by the bearer of Gāṇḍīva, would not tolerate it; furious as an elephant tormented by the goad, he swiftly shot sharp arrows at ambidextrous Arjuna, vulture-feathered, straight-flying, polished by the smith, resembling venomous snakes. He pierced Gāṇḍīva with three iron arrows, and Arjuna himself with six, his horses with eight and his standard with a single arrow. But Arjuna scattered the sharp arrows shot at him by the king of Sindhu, and with two arrows of his own simultaneously severed both the head of Jayadratha's charioteer and his highly ornamented standard; torn by arrows, its staff severed, the huge boar of the king of Sindhu fell to earth like a blazing arrow.

15 Now at that moment, as the sun sped on, Kṛṣṇa the stirrer of men spoke hastily to Pāṇḍu's son. 'Wealth-winner Arjuna, sever the head of the wicked king of Sindhu! The sun will soon set behind the excellent western mountain, so listen to what I have to say about the killing of Jayadratha! The king of Sindhu's father, Vṛddhakṣatra, is famous throughout the earth; he waited long for the birth of his son Jayadratha, slayer of his enemies. At that time an invisible voice addressed the king, sounding like thunder or drums: "This son of yours, lord, will be virtuous among men. By lineage, character and self-control he will prove worthy of both his families; he will ever be honoured by heroes
20 as one of the world's leading Kṣatriyas. But as with his bow he fights against his enemies in battle, one enemy, known throughout the earth, will sever his head in fury."

'When Vṛddhakṣatra king of Sindhu heard this, O foe-tamer, he thought long. Then, afflicted by love for his son, he addressed all his kinsmen: "The man who causes my son's head to fall upon the ground as he bears his great burden by fighting in battle, that man's own head will burst into a hundred pieces, make no doubt!" When he had spoken, Vṛddhakṣatra settled the kingship upon Jayadratha, and retired to the forest to practise austerities; full of mighty ardour, he is undertaking incomparably severe austerities beyond this region of Samantapañcaka.
25 So, O foe-slayer, when you sever Jayadratha's head in the great battle with your wonderful, terrible celestial weapon, you must cause it to fall

at once, still decked with earrings, into the lap of Vṛddhakṣatra lord of
Sindhu. If you cause his head to fall upon the ground, your own head
will burst into a hundred pieces, make no doubt! Best of Kurus, use
your celestial weapon in such a way that Vṛddhakṣatra king of Sindhu
does not know what you have done. Son of Indra, there is nothing in all
the three worlds that you cannot accomplish, nothing you cannot do!'

When Arjuna heard these words appointing him to kill Jayadratha, 30
he licked the corners of his mouth and swiftly shot an arrow. Hard as
Indra's thunderbolt, consecrated with divine *mantras*, always honoured
with perfumes and garlands, it was capable of carrying out any task.
Released from the bow Gāṇḍīva, that arrow sped and carried off the head
of Jayadratha of Sindhu like a hawk carrying off a bird from a treetop.
Moreover, the wealth-winner dismayed his enemies and delighted his
friends by carrying that head aloft with his arrows; with his clustered
arrows Pāṇḍu's son bore it away beyond Samantapañcaka.

Now at that moment King Vṛddhakṣatra of mighty ardour – your 35
kinsman, sir – was seated performing the twilight prayers. As he sat there,
Arjuna caused the head of his son the king of Sindhu, black-haired,
still decked with earrings, to fall into his lap. That head with its lovely
earrings fell unnoticed into King Vṛddhakṣatra's lap, O foe-tamer; then
when wise Vṛddhakṣatra arose after completing his prayers, it fell at
once upon the ground. Foe-tamer, when his son's head landed on the
ground, King Vṛddhakṣatra's own head broke into a hundred pieces.

All creatures were utterly amazed, and Kṛṣṇa Vāsudeva praised the 40
mighty chariot-fighter Arjuna; but on seeing Jayadratha king of Sindhu
slain many tears of grief fell from your sons' eyes. As for Bhīma, he stood
on the battlefield and filled heaven and earth with his mighty lion-roar,
as if to pass the news to the Pāṇḍava lord; and when Yudhiṣṭhira son of
Dharma heard that great roar he knew the noble Arjuna had killed the
king of Sindhu. Then, encouraging his soldiers with the sound of musical
instruments, he attacked Bharadvāja's son Droṇa on the battlefield in
his eagerness for the fight. And so, O king, as the sun sank westwards, a 45
hair-raising battle took place between Droṇa and the Somakas. For now
that Jayadratha of Sindhu was dead, those great chariot-fighters battled
with all their might to kill Bharadvāja's son; the Pāṇḍavas, having gained
a victory by slaying the king of Sindhu, engaged Droṇa in battle on all

sides, drunk with their triumph. Arjuna too, great king, now that he had killed Jayadratha, battled against the best of your chariot-fighters on the field. The heroic wearer of the diadem had carried out the oath he swore before; now he meted out destruction on all sides, like Indra, the gods' king, destroying their enemies, or the sun destroying darkness.

## THE KILLING OF GHAṬOTKACA

[**122**] *Arjuna is now attacked by Kṛpa and Aśvatthāman; out of respect for them he responds mildly, but even so Kṛpa is overcome and his charioteer bears him away; Aśvatthāman follows. Seeing Kṛpa's plight Arjuna laments and berates himself for having struck his teacher. At this point Karṇa attacks Sātyaki, who is still without a chariot; but Kṛṣṇa, foreseeing what would happen, had instructed his charioteer Dāruka to have his chariot ready, and at a blast from Kṛṣṇa's conch he drives it up. Sātyaki mounts and rushes at Karṇa. A terrific battle takes place. Then Sātyaki kills Karṇa's charioteer and his horses, to the dismay of the Kauravas; he also deprives the Dhārtarāṣṭras of their chariots, but does not kill them because of Bhīma's vow to do so. Dāruka's younger brother now brings a fresh chariot for Sātyaki, and Karṇa too is provided with a new one.*

[**123**] *Meanwhile Bhīma complains to Arjuna of the insults that Karṇa directed at him when he deprived him of his chariot. Arjuna goes up to Karṇa and reproaches him for this and for Abhimanyu's death, and he vows in return to kill Karṇa's son Vṛṣasena before his eyes. The sun now sets. Kṛṣṇa congratulates Arjuna on his achievements, which Arjuna ascribes to Kṛṣṇa's own grace; then he describes the battlefield to him.* [**124**] *Yudhiṣṭhira now greets Kṛṣṇa and Arjuna and congratulates them on the killing of Jayadratha; the Pāṇḍavas are sure to achieve victory through the grace of Kṛṣṇa, source of all that is good. Kṛṣṇa and Arjuna reply that the slaughter of the Kauravas is a consequence of the anger of Yudhiṣṭhira himself, whose very gaze can kill. Bhīma and Sātyaki too greet Yudhiṣṭhira, who congratulates them on their triumphs.*

[**125**] *Duryodhana, by contrast, is in despair: it appears to him that Arjuna is invincible. He goes to see Droṇa, and laments the deaths of so many of his followers, for which he blames himself, though he also once again accuses Droṇa of partiality towards Arjuna. He proposes to die fighting and thus rejoin those who have died for him, and he asks Droṇa's permission for this.* [**126**] *Stung*

*by Duryodhana's words, Droṇa answers that, as he has repeatedly said, Arjuna cannot be defeated. The dice which Śakuni played against the Kauravas were not dice but deadly arrows; by ignoring Vidura's advice Duryodhana has brought the entire disaster on himself. None the less, Droṇa pledges to continue to fight on his behalf. Telling Duryodhana to look after the army, since in their fury their enemies will fight even at night, he sets off to attack the Pāṇḍavas.* [**127**] *Duryodhana now takes his complaints of Droṇa's partiality towards Arjuna to Karṇa, but Karṇa tells him not to blame Droṇa: it is fate that is thwarting all their efforts.*

*At this point the Pāṇḍava forces attack the Kauravas.* [**128**] *There is a great battle. Duryodhana, intent on death in battle and grieving at the fall of Jayadratha, forces his way into the Pāṇḍava army. He slays great numbers with his arrows, and pierces many of the greatest heroes, but Yudhiṣṭhira severs his bow and pierces him so severely that he sinks down in his chariot. Droṇa comes to the rescue, and Duryodhana recovers. The battle resumes.*

[**129**] *The five Pāṇḍava brothers together with their chief allies attack Droṇa as terrible darkness falls. The battle is like a storm, with gold-adorned elephants and chariots for its lightning-flashing clouds, the beat of drums for its thunder, swords, spears and clubs for its thunderbolts, and arrows for its rain. The Pāṇḍava forces attack Droṇa, but are forced back or killed.*

Dhṛtarāṣṭra spoke:

[**130**] When Droṇa, unconquerable and boundlessly powerful, unfor-
bearing and furious, penetrated the Sṛñjaya force, what did you all
think? When that immeasurably great warrior spoke as he did to Dur-
yodhana, my undisciplined son, and penetrated the enemy ranks, what
counter-measures were taken by Kuntī's son Arjuna? When the brave
king of Sindhu was slain, and Bhūriśravas too, and undefeated Droṇa of
great ardour attacked the Pāñcālas, what did the unconquerable Pāṇḍava
hero think? When Droṇa penetrated his enemies to afflict them, what
course of action did Duryodhana think would suit the hour? Who 5
followed that hero, granter of boons, truest among Brahmins? Which
heroes formed the rearguard as he fought? Who fought in the van as he
slew his enemies in battle? I am sure that the Pāṇḍavas were all afflicted
by the arrows of Bharadvāja's son Droṇa, and that they trembled like
lean cattle in winter, sir. When Droṇa, great bowman and foe-crusher,
had penetrated the Pāñcālas, how did that tiger-like hero meet his

death? When all the Pāṇḍava warriors together, and all their assembled chariot-fighters of various ranks, were being harassed at night, which of you wise ones were there at that time? You say that in the battles my soldiers were killed, that they cowered together and were defeated, that my chariot-fighters were made chariotless. How could you distinguish at night between the unretreating Pāṇḍavas and the Kurus?

Saṃjaya spoke:
O king, while that terrible night-time battle continued, the Pāṇḍavas with their troops rushed against Droṇa. Droṇa dispatched the Kekayas and all Dhṛṣṭadyumna's sons to the world of death with his swift-flying arrows; all the mighty chariot-fighters who faced him he dispatched to the other world, O heir of Bharata. Then Śibi of great energy furiously attacked Bharadvāja's son, O king, as that heroic chariot-fighter ravaged his foes. When Droṇa saw the mighty Pāṇḍava chariot-fighter descending upon him, he pierced him with ten arrows of pure iron; in return, Śibi pierced him with thirty sharp arrows, and smilingly felled his charioteer with a broad shaft. But Droṇa slew that noble warrior's horses and his charioteer, and then severed his helmeted head from his body.

Now the son of the king of Kaliṅga, furious at his father's earlier death,[1] rushed to attack Bhīma on the battlefield with a force of men of Kaliṅga: he pierced Bhīma with five arrows, then pierced him again with seven; with three he struck his charioteer Viśoka, and with one his standard. Enraged, wolf-belly Bhīma leapt from his chariot to the chariot of the enraged Kaliṅga hero, and struck him with his fist; the mighty Pāṇḍava's punch killed him, and all his bones at once fell separately on the battlefield. Karṇa and the Kaliṅga prince's brothers, great chariot-fighters, would not tolerate this, and they struck Bhīma with iron arrows like venomous snakes; but Bhīma left his enemy's chariot for the chariot of his brother Dhruva, and smashed Dhruva with his fist as he ceaselessly shot his arrows, so that he fell, slain by the mighty Pāṇḍava. After killing him, great king, Bhīma of mighty strength came to Jayarāta's chariot, roaring again and again like a lion; as he roared, he dragged Jayarāta out of his chariot with his left hand and slew him with

1 At Bhīma's hands: 6.50.

a slap before the very eyes of Karṇa. Karṇa now threw a golden spear at the Pāṇḍava; with a laugh, the unconquerable wolf-belly seized it and hurled it straight back across the battlefield at Karṇa. But Śakuni cut it down in mid-air with a well-oiled arrow.

Now your sons approached Bhīma's chariot, O king, and covered the wolf-belly with a great shower of arrows. With a laugh, Bhīma dispatched Durmada's charioteer and horses to the realm of Yama with
his arrows; then Durmada leapt on to the chariot of Duṣkarṇa. The two 30
brothers, afflicters of their enemies now mounted on a single chariot, rushed against Bhīma in the forefront of the battle, like the sun and moon attacking Tāraka, greatest of demons: mounted on a single chariot, your sons Durmada and Duṣkarṇa pierced Bhīma with their arrows. Then before the very eyes of Karṇa, Aśvatthāman and Duryodhana, Kṛpa, Somadatta and Bāhlika, the Pāṇḍava foe-tamer forced the chariot of heroic Durmada and Duṣkarṇa into the ground with a stamp of his foot; furiously he struck your sons, the mighty heroes Durmada and
Duṣkarṇa, with his fist, and then crushed them with his foot. At this 35
there was uproar among the troops; the kings looked at Bhīma and said, 'This is the fierce god Rudra pursuing the Dhārtarāṣṭras in Bhīma's form!' With these words all the princes took flight, O heir of Bharata; senseless with fear, they drove on their horses, so that no two men fled together.

After ravaging the enemy force at nightfall, the mighty wolf-belly, his eyes wide open like lotuses, received great honour from all the bull-like kings, and paid his own respects to King Yudhiṣṭhira. Then the twins Nakula and Sahadeva, together with Drupada, Virāṭa and the Kekayas, and Yudhiṣṭhira himself, were filled with the greatest delight, and they honoured the wolf-belly highly, as the gods honoured Śiva after the slaying of Andhaka. As for your sons, who are like the sons of Varuṇa,[1] they were filled with rage. Together with their noble Teacher Droṇa and a force of chariots, footsoldiers and elephants, they surrounded Bhīma,

1 The only explanation I can suggest for this comparison is that the sons of Dhṛtarāṣṭra had learnt their knowledge of weaponry from Droṇa, who was the pupil of Agniveśya (1.121.6), who was the pupil of Agastya (1, App. I, 80.16–18), who was the son of Varuṇa.

40 fiercely eager to fight. Then as that fearful night fell, a most terrible, wonderful battle took place, enveloped in clouds of darkness, between those noble kings, to the joy of jungle crows, wolves and vultures.

[**131**] *Somadatta, the father of Bhūriśravas, furious at the manner of his son's death at the hands of Sātyaki, challenges him to battle: he swears that he will slay him with his sons and brothers unless Arjuna comes to his protection. Sātyaki similarly swears to kill Somadatta and all his family, and the two heroes attack each other with their arrows, while other mighty warriors from both sides draw near to give support. After an exchange of arrows, Somadatta sinks down unconscious and is borne away by his charioteer. Seeing this, Aśvatthāman rushes at Sātyaki, but he is counterattacked by Ghaṭotkaca, riding on an eight-wheeled chariot drawn by huge, unknown beasts, and accompanied by a force of terrifying Rākṣasas hurling stones and weapons. The Kaurava army and the Dhārtarāṣṭras themselves all flee, as does Karṇa; only Aśvatthāman stands his ground. With his arrows he destroys the illusory spectacle Ghaṭotkaca has created, and the two warriors begin to fight. Ghaṭotkaca's son Añjanaparvan attacks Aśvatthāman, but after a fierce exchange he is killed. Ghaṭotkaca himself again makes use of illusion. First he launches a shower of arrows as big as chariot-axles; then he becomes a mountain whose streams pour forth torrents of weapons, then a cloud raining down stones; but Aśvatthāman destroys these illusions one after the other. Now Ghaṭotkaca attacks him with an army of terrible Rākṣasas; Duryodhana is dismayed, but Aśvatthāman promises him that he will triumph, and Duryodhana, reassured, instructs Śakuni to lead a great force against Arjuna. Aśvatthāman and Ghaṭotkaca do battle: Aśvatthāman slays a huge force of Rākṣasas. Ghaṭotkaca hurls a thunderbolt at him; he catches it and hurls it back, and it reduces Ghaṭotkaca's chariot, horses and driver to ashes, and disappears into the earth. Ghaṭotkaca mounts Dhṛṣṭadyumna's chariot, and he and Dhṛṣṭadyumna exchange many arrows with Aśvatthāman. Bhīma arrives in time to see Aśvatthāman kill another great force of Rākṣasas; so great is the slaughter he causes that a river of blood flows on the battlefield. Numbers of Pāṇḍava warriors also die from his arrows. Then he shoots a terrible arrow at Ghaṭotkaca, who sinks down unconscious; Dhṛṣṭadyumna, thinking him dead, bears him away.*

[**132**] *Somadatta attacks Sātyaki once more, but Bhīma joins Sātyaki in his counterattack: struck simultaneously on the head by Bhīma's iron club and*

*in the chest by Sātyaki's arrow, Somadatta falls down unconscious. His father Bāhlika attacks Bhīma; Bhīma slays him with his club. Bhīma is now attacked in turn by ten of Dhṛtarāṣṭra's sons, Karṇa's brother Vṛṣaratha, and a succession of other warriors: he kills them all with his arrows. Yudhiṣṭhira too causes great carnage, and Droṇa shoots at him a sequence of celestial weapons; Yudhiṣṭhira counters them with celestial weapons of his own. Droṇa now turns his attack on the Pāñcālas, who begin to flee, but Bhīma and Arjuna rally them and mount a two-pronged assault on the Kaurava force; Droṇa and Duryodhana are unable to prevent a rout.*

**[133]** *Duryodhana appeals to Karṇa for help, and Karṇa promises that he will overcome Arjuna and the Pāṇḍavas. Kṛpa accuses him of empty boasting: he roars loudly as long as Arjuna is out of sight, but his roars are not heard in Arjuna's presence. Karṇa defends himself: it is the way of heroes to boast, and he will make his boasts good. Kṛpa replies that the Pāṇḍavas are too powerful to be beaten; Karṇa insists that he will do as he has said, and that the Kauravas too are invincibly strong. However, the outcome is dependent on fate.* **[134]** *Aśvatthāman rushes up in fury at Karṇa's insolence towards Kṛpa, his mother's brother, and the two men trade insults with each other. Their quarrel is halted by the arrival of a large Pāṇḍava force eager to do battle against Karṇa. Karṇa takes them on single-handed, and overwhelms them; then Arjuna appears, and Aśvatthāman, Kṛpa, Śalya and Kṛtavarman go to defend Karṇa against him. Arjuna and Karṇa exchange great numbers of arrows; then Arjuna severs Karṇa's bow and kills his horses and his charioteer. Karṇa mounts Kṛpa's chariot, and Duryodhana announces that he will fight Arjuna himself. Kṛpa urges Aśvatthāman to prevent him, and Aśvatthāman asks Duryodhana for permission to fight in his place; Duryodhana expresses his concern that Droṇa and Aśvatthāman are both partial towards the Pāṇḍavas, but he agrees to Aśvatthāman's proposal.*

**[135]** *Aśvatthāman upbraids Duryodhana for his suspicious nature and other faults; none the less, he says, he will take on the Pāṇḍavas and slay great numbers of them. He attacks, and kills ten warriors. Dhṛṣṭadyumna challenges him and pierces him with many arrows; Aśvatthāman showers arrows upon Dhṛṣṭadyumna in return. Dhṛṣṭadyumna insults him, and tells him that before killing him he will kill his father Droṇa, and Aśvatthāman attacks him in fury. The exchange of arrows is extremely fierce, till Aśvatthāman severs Dhṛṣṭadyumna's bow and standard, and kills his charioteers and his horses. Then* *he slays great numbers of Pāñcālas.* **[136]** *The Pāṇḍavas surround Aśvatthāman, and seeing this Duryodhana and Droṇa come to his support. There is a great battle. Yudhiṣṭhira, Bhīma and Arjuna kill hordes of enemies; Droṇa puts the Pāñcālas to flight, but Bhīma and Arjuna rally them and mount a two-pronged assault on the Kaurava force; Droṇa and Duryodhana are unable to prevent a rout.*

**[137]** *Sātyaki attacks Somadatta, and the two warriors exchange many arrows. Bhīma and Ghaṭotkaca join in to support Sātyaki. Finally Sātyaki severs Somadatta's bow, and kills his horses and his charioteer; then he slays him with an arrow through the chest. The Kaurava warriors rush to attack Sātyaki, and seeing this Yudhiṣṭhira attacks them. He and Droṇa exchange many arrows. Yudhiṣṭhira is getting the better of the exchange when Kṛṣṇa advises him to avoid fighting against Droṇa, who is keen to capture him; so he withdraws and joins Bhīma, who is busy killing enemies.*

**[138]** *The battle rages on in darkness and dust; warriors slaughter each other in great numbers, whilst others flee in panic and are killed in flight. Duryodhana orders his soldiers to light lamps, and they do so: brightly illuminated by lamplight, the Kaurava army appears splendid. The Pāṇḍavas now do likewise, and the light reaches the heavens and awakens the immortals; they come to see the battlefield, so that it resembles a second heaven.*

**[139]** *The battle resumes by lamplight. Arjuna scatters and slays his enemies. — Dhṛtarāṣṭra asks to hear details of the encounter, and Saṃjaya gives them. — Duryodhana instructs a number of his brothers, together with Kṛtavarman, Śalya and the surviving Trigartas, to protect Droṇa against Dhṛṣṭadyumna, who he believes is the only Pāṇḍava warrior capable of killing him. Thus protected, Droṇa will slay great numbers of the enemy, after which Aśvatthāman will be able to kill Dhṛṣṭadyumna and Karṇa to kill Arjuna; he himself will kill Bhīma, and so achieve victory. The fighting continues fiercely on both sides.* **[140]** *Yudhiṣṭhira commands his troops to attack Droṇa. As they do so, they are resisted by the Kauravas in numerous single combats. Yudhiṣṭhira himself has to face Kṛtavarman, with whom he has a lengthy exchange of arrows. In the end Kṛtavarman deprives him of horses, charioteer and chariot; when Yudhiṣṭhira takes up sword and shield he cuts them apart with arrows; when Yudhiṣṭhira hurls a lance he cuts it in two; finally he cuts off Yudhiṣṭhira's armour, at which Yudhiṣṭhira retreats.*

**[141]** *Sātyaki faces Bhūri, brother of Bhūriśravas; after an exchange of* *arrows he slays him with a spear. Seeing this, Aśvatthāman attacks him, but is in turn attacked by Ghaṭotkaca. The two heroes battle against each other; Ghaṭotkaca's arrows render Aśvatthāman briefly unconscious, but he recovers and at once shoots at Ghaṭotkaca a terrible arrow that renders him unconscious; Ghaṭotkaca's charioteer bears him away. Bhīma faces Duryodhana, who succeeds in repeatedly severing his bow; when Bhīma hurls a spear, Duryodhana cuts it to pieces. Then Bhīma hurls a club, which kills Duryodhana's horses and charioteer; Duryodhana escapes, but Bhīma believes him slain and roars a lion-roar. Hearing it, the Pāṇḍavas rush to attack Droṇa.*

[**142**] *As Sahadeva advances on Droṇa, he faces Karṇa. After an exchange of arrows Karṇa kills Sahadeva's horses and charioteer; when Sahadeva takes up sword and shield he cuts them to pieces, and the same happens when Sahadeva hurls in turn a club, a spear and a chariot-wheel. Then Karṇa tells Sahadeva that he should fight with his equals, not with distinguished warriors, touches him with the tip of his bow, and lets him go. Sahadeva, downcast, mounts the chariot of the Pāñcāla prince Janamejaya. Virāṭa is attacked by Śalya, who kills his horses and charioteer; when Virāṭa's brother Śatānīka comes to his aid, Śalya slays him. Virāṭa mounts his fallen brother's chariot, but Śalya overwhelms him with arrows and the charioteer bears him away. The Pāṇḍava army begins to flee from Śalya; seeing this, Kṛṣṇa and Arjuna set out to attack him, but are attacked in turn by the Rākṣasa Alambusa*[1] *riding on an eight-wheeled chariot. Arjuna severs his bow and kills his charioteer and horse; Alambusa flees.*

[**143**] *Nakula's son Śatānīka does battle against Citrasena son of Dhṛtarāṣṭra,*[2] *and succeeds in depriving him of armour, bow, horses and charioteer; Citrasena finds refuge in Kṛtavarman's chariot. Karṇa's son Vṛṣasena attacks Drupada and his troops; he overcomes them and sets out towards Yudhiṣṭhira. Duḥśāsana attacks Prativindhya and kills his horses and charioteer; Prativindhya finds refuge in Sutasoma's chariot.* [**144**] *Śakuni attacks Nakula; each showers arrows on the other. An arrow of Śakuni's renders Nakula briefly unconscious, but he recovers and overwhelms Śakuni with arrows, severing his bow and standard and piercing him so badly that he loses consciousness; his charioteer bears him away,*

**1** Alambusa was said to have been killed by Ghaṭotkaca in chapter 84.

**2** Citrasena was said to have been killed by Bhīma in chapter 112. (Both he and his brother Vikarṇa, killed at the same time, were also listed among the brothers whom Duryodhana addressed in chapter 139.)

*and Nakula continues on his way towards Droṇa. Śikhaṇḍin is attacked by Kṛpa. The two warriors exchange many arrows, and Śikhaṇḍin severs Kṛpa's bow; but Kṛpa takes up another, and his arrows render Śikhaṇḍin unconscious. As Śikhaṇḍin withdraws from the battle the Pāñcālas and Somakas come to his support, and similarly the Dhārtarāṣṭras come to support Kṛpa. A fierce nocturnal battle takes place between the two forces.*

[145] *Dhṛṣṭadyumna attacks Droṇa. Droṇa severs his bow, but Dhṛṣṭadyumna takes up another and shoots a lethal arrow at Droṇa. However, it is cut to pieces by Karṇa, who then pierces Dhṛṣṭadyumna with arrows, as do Aśvatthāman, Droṇa, Śalya, Duḥśāsana, Duryodhana and Śakuni. Dhṛṣṭadyumna replies in kind. Drumasena attacks Dhṛṣṭadyumna, who slays him and then severs Karṇa's bow. Karṇa takes up another, and Droṇa's six supporters continue their attack on Dhṛṣṭadyumna. Sātyaki comes to his support, and he and Karṇa begin a fierce but even exchange. The Dhārtarāṣṭras and Karṇa's son Vṛṣasena join in the fray; an arrow of Sātyaki's renders Vṛṣasena unconscious, and Karṇa, thinking him dead, redoubles his attack. But now Karṇa hears the sounds of Arjuna's chariot and his bow Gāṇḍīva, and urges Duryodhana to prevent him from coming to the aid of Dhṛṣṭadyumna and Sātyaki; if these two can be killed, the Kauravas will achieve victory. Duryodhana sends Śakuni at the head of a great force to attack Arjuna and the other Pāṇḍavas, while Karṇa continues his battle against Sātyaki and Droṇa continues his against Dhṛṣṭadyumna.*

[146] *Sātyaki comes under attack from a great force of Kauravas; he slaughters them. Duryodhana rushes at him, and there is a fierce exchange; Sātyaki slays Duryodhana's horses and charioteer, and severs his bow. Duryodhana takes refuge in Kṛtavarman's chariot, and Sātyaki routs the Kaurava army. Meanwhile, Śakuni attacks Arjuna with a mighty force, but Arjuna repulses them, slaying great numbers of warriors. He severs Śakuni's bow and kills his horses, and Śakuni takes refuge in the chariot of his son Ulūka. Arjuna puts the Kaurava force to flight. As for Dhṛṣṭadyumna, he continues his battle against Droṇa, and he too routs the Kauravas who oppose him. The Pāṇḍavas joyfully blow their conches and roar their lion-roars.*

[147] *Seeing his troops slain and fleeing, Duryodhana goes to see Karṇa and Droṇa, and accuses them of failing to keep their vow to defeat the Pāṇḍavas. Stung by his words, they attack the Pāṇḍava army. Droṇa kills great numbers of warriors, and the rest flee; they cast aside their torches, but their flight can be seen by the light of the Kaurava army. Droṇa and Karṇa harry their rear. Kṛṣṇa*

*urges Arjuna to fight the two Kaurava generals to give courage to his troops, and the two of them approach Droṇa and Karṇa to do battle. At this the Pāṇḍava forces return to the fray, and a terrible nocturnal battle takes place.* **[148]** *Karṇa and Dhṛṣṭadyumna exchange many arrows; Karṇa kills Dhṛṣṭadyumna's horses and his charioteer, and severs his bow. Dhṛṣṭadyumna smashes Karṇa's horses with a club, and mounts Sahadeva's chariot. But Karṇa's charioteer yokes new horses to his chariot, and Karṇa assails the Pāñcāla forces, slaying great numbers and putting the rest to flight. Many did not even realize as they fled that their limbs had been severed; others imagined that their fleeing fellow-warriors were Karṇa and fled from them in fear. Yudhiṣṭhira, seeing the rout, asks Arjuna to do what he thinks best suited to bring about Karṇa's death. Arjuna tells Kṛṣṇa that he intends to battle to the death against Karṇa, but Kṛṣṇa tells him that the time is not yet right for this: Ghaṭotkaca should go instead. Ghaṭotkaca is summoned, and both Kṛṣṇa and Arjuna urge him to kill Karṇa. Ghaṭotkaca sets out to do battle.*

**[149]** *Seeing Ghaṭotkaca advancing on Karṇa, Duryodhana orders Duḥśāsana to go with a large force to protect him. At this point Alambala, son of the Rākṣasa Jaṭāsura, approaches and asks permission to avenge his father's death at the hands of the Pāṇḍavas. Duryodhana answers that he requires no help to slay his enemies, and tells Alambala to kill Ghaṭotkaca instead. The two Rākṣasas exchange great numbers of arrows, each scattering the forces of his enemies. Then Ghaṭotkaca reduces Alambala's chariot, his charioteer and all his weapons to fragments the size of sesame seeds, and they begin fighting hand-to-hand, each seeking to smash the other against the ground. Next they battle against each other in a series of illusory forms. Finally Ghaṭotkaca flies up and swoops down on Alambala like a hawk; he raises him up and throws him down, then severs his head with a sword. He takes the head to Duryodhana and throws it into his chariot, telling him that this death will be followed by the deaths of Karṇa and himself.*

**[150]** *Ghaṭotkaca is fearsome to see, with his huge body, red eyes, green beard, pointed ears, and numerous other alarming characteristics; the sound of his bow sets the Kaurava warriors trembling. He and Karṇa shower arrows on each other, but neither gains the upper hand. Karṇa deploys a celestial weapon; Ghaṭotkaca responds with the illusion of a force of Rākṣasas hurling terrible weapons. Karṇa destroys this with his arrows, and he cuts down the discus and the club that Ghaṭotkaca then hurls at him. Ghaṭotkaca flies into the air and* *rains down trees on Karṇa; Karṇa pierces Ghaṭotkaca with so many arrows that there is not two fingers' breadth on his body free. Next, Ghaṭotkaca assumes a bewildering sequence of illusory forms, dismaying the Kauravas and showering arrows and other missiles on Karṇa; but Karṇa dispels the illusions with his arrows and with celestial weapons. Ghaṭotkaca hurls a thunderbolt at Karṇa; Karṇa catches it and hurls it back, and it reduces Ghaṭotkaca's chariot, horses and driver to ashes, and disappears into the earth. Ghaṭotkaca continues with his illusions, but Karṇa destroys them all, and Ghaṭotkaca vanishes, promising Karṇa's death.*

**[151]** *At this point the Rākṣasa Alāyudha comes to Duryodhana and offers to fight the Pāṇḍavas: he wishes to avenge Bhīma's killing of Baka, Kirmīra and Hiḍimba and his seduction of Hiḍimbā. Duryodhana welcomes him and places him at the head of his troops: he is no less fearsome than Ghaṭotkaca.* **[152]** *Duryodhana assigns to Alāyudha the task of killing Ghaṭotkaca before he kills Karṇa, and Alāyudha agrees to this. He rushes at Ghaṭotkaca, and a great battle begins between the two Rākṣasas. Karṇa, released from his fight with Ghaṭotkaca, attacks Bhīma; Bhīma ignores him and attacks Alāyudha; Alāyudha and his followers return Bhīma's attack. Alāyudha fends off Bhīma's weapons, and his followers begin to destroy his force of elephants. Seeing Bhīma in distress, Kṛṣṇa urges Arjuna to protect him. Meanwhile Alāyudha severs Bhīma's bow and slays his horses and charioteer. The two warriors fight with clubs, then with fists.* **[153]** *Now Kṛṣṇa tells Ghaṭotkaca to relieve Bhīma by attacking Alāyudha, and Ghaṭotkaca does so. Nakula, Sahadeva and Sātyaki set about killing Alāyudha's followers, then join Bhīma in an attack on Karṇa, while the two Rākṣasas battle it out with clubs and other weapons, and with their powers of illusion. Finally, Ghaṭotkaca cuts off Alāyudha's head, to the joy of the Pāṇḍavas, and casts it down before Duryodhana. Duryodhana feels that Bhīma's vow to kill him is now as good as fulfilled.*

Saṃjaya spoke:
**[154]** Full of joy at his slaying of Alāyudha, the Rākṣasa Ghaṭotkaca stood at the head of the army and roared many great roars; when they heard that tumultuous sound, great king, that set their elephants trembling, your warriors were filled with a terrible fear.

Now when strong-armed Karṇa saw Bhīma's son Ghaṭotkaca locked in combat with Alāyudha, he rushed to attack the Pāñcālas, and wounded

both Dhṛṣṭadyumna and Śikhaṇḍin with ten strong, straight arrows,
shot from a fully stretched bow; then with his excellent iron arrows 5
he set Yudhāmanyu, Uttamaujas and the noble chariot-fighter Sātyaki trembling. As all these warriors shot back at him from both left and right, their bows could be seen drawn tight in a circle, lord of men, and the sound of their bowstrings against the palm, and the din of their chariot-wheels in the night, were like the roar of thunderclouds at summer's end. Indeed, O king, the battle itself seemed like a storm-cloud, with the sound of bowstrings and chariot-wheels for its thunder, bows for its lightning, round banners for its crests, and torrential showers of arrows for its rain. But Karṇa the Cutter, crusher of enemy hosts, unshakable and strong as a mountain, destroyed that intense shower
of arrows on the battlefield, O lord. Then the noble Cutter, devoted 10
to your son's welfare, forced back his enemies in that battle with his incomparable sharp arrows, falling like thunderbolts, shafts beautiful with gold.

Some had their standards swiftly severed and broken by Karṇa, some had their bodies afflicted and wounded with arrows, some lost their charioteers, and others their horses; finding no refuge on the battlefield, they joined Yudhiṣṭhira's force. Seeing them broken and forced to retreat, Ghaṭotkaca became extremely angry. Mounting his wonderful chariot, splendid with gold and jewels, he roared like a lion, then drove up to Karṇa the Cutter and pierced him with arrows like thunderbolts. The two warriors made the sky resound with their showers of barbed arrows and iron arrows, their reed-arrows, calves-tooth and hogs-ear arrows,
their arrows tipped with horn and arrows edged like razors. Covered 15
with torrents of arrows flying across the battlefield, blazing bright with their shafts of gold, the sky shone as if it were covered with garlands of lovely flowers. Equal in their incomparable strength, they both struck each other with their wonderful weapons; no one could tell which of those two excellent heroes had the better of that battle. The combat between the son of Bhīma and the son of the Sun was an extremely fine sight, tumultuous and dreadful, full of falling weapons, like the violent battle of Sun and Eclipse in the sky.

When Ghaṭotkaca could not get the better of Karṇa, O king, he used his unrivalled knowledge of weapons to create a terrible weapon. First

Hiḍimbā's Rākṣasa son slew Karṇa's horses with that weapon, and his charioteer too, and then he suddenly vanished.

Dhṛtarāṣṭra spoke:
20 When that treacherous Rākṣasa vanished in that manner, what did my warriors do? Tell me, Saṃjaya!

Saṃjaya spoke:
When the Kurus realized that the Rākṣasa had vanished they all cried out, 'What is to prevent this treacherous Rākṣasa from killing Karṇa in battle whilst invisible?' Then Karṇa, fighting with fine weapons and lightness of touch, covered the entire horizon with torrents of arrows. The sky was so dark with arrows that no creatures appeared there. So light was his touch that, while he covered the sky with his arrows, it was impossible to see when the Sūta's son took up his bow, when he fixed an arrow to it, and when he touched his arrow-cases with his fingers. But now we saw an illusion created in the sky by the Rākṣasa, terrible, dreadful, fearful! It was like the flame of a fierce fire, blazing in the midst
25 of red clouds. Flashes of lightning emerged from it, and flaming meteors, O prince of the Kauravas, and also a most dreadful noise of thousands of kettledrums roaring together. Then there fell from it gold-shafted arrows, spears, lances, bludgeons and other weapons, axes and well-oiled swords, javelins, and darts with blazing points, gleaming maces of iron, fine clubs and sharp-bladed pikes, and heavy gold clubs laced with strings. On every side there appeared hundred-slaying weapons, and great rocks fell everywhere, together with thunderbolts by the thousand, while fire-bright discuses with hundreds of blades also made their appearance.

Now for all his torrents of arrows, Karṇa could not destroy that vast, blazing shower of spears, rocks, axes, lances, swords, thunderbolts
30 and hammers; and there arose a great cry of horses falling slain by arrows, elephants falling slain by thunderbolts, and mighty chariot-fighters falling slain by rocks. Duryodhana's army could be seen reeling in affliction as Ghaṭotkaca assailed it on every side with dreadful weapons of every description. There was uproar among the troops as they shifted to and fro and cowered in distress; but the heroes amongst them showed

their true nobility and did not turn their backs at that awful time. However, when your sons saw the Rākṣasa's dreadful shower of mighty weapons, and their own massive forces laid low, great fear entered their hearts. Jackals by the hundred, tongues blazing with fire, began to cry dreadful cries; and the warrior princes were shaken to see hordes of roaring Rākṣasas with blazing tongues and faces, sharp teeth, terrible 35
bodies like mountains, roaming the sky clutching spears in their hands, like clouds pouring down a fierce rain.

Your warriors fell, struck by arrows, spears and pikes, by fierce clubs and blazing bludgeons, by thunderbolts and adamantine tridents, and ravaged by discuses and hundred-slaying weapons. Rams, projectiles, stones, throwing-balls, hundred-slaying weapons and rods of black iron laced with strings, were showered upon your son's army, and a terrible despair took hold of them. Your brave warriors lay there, entrails cast about, heads struck off, limbs broken; your horses were slain, your elephants smashed and your chariots shattered by rocks. Thus those evil beings, most dreadful to see upon earth, Ghaṭotkaca's magic creation, poured forth a great shower of weapons, sparing neither the man who asked for quarter nor the man overpowered by fear. Broken in that 40
dreadful massacre of Kuru heroes, that fateful annihilation of Kṣatriyas, the entire Kaurava army suddenly took flight, crying, 'Flee, Kurus! All is lost! The very gods led by Indra are slaying us to aid the Pāṇḍavas!' Thus the Kaurava forces perished, as if sinking far from dry land.

In the midst of this uproar and tumult, while the army of the Kurus broke and cowered, the distinguishing marks of the different forces became unclear, and one could not tell Kuru from foe. In that dreadful, unruly rout, the entire horizon seemed empty before our gaze: only Karṇa could be seen there, O king, forcing his way chest-first through that shower of weapons. He covered the sky with his arrows, engaging the Rākṣasa's celestial illusion in battle; modestly performing noble feats of great difficulty, the Sūta's son did not lose his senses in that combat. All the warriors of Sindhu and Bāhlika, O king, watched Karṇa in their 45
terror, honouring him for keeping his senses, but observing the Rākṣasa triumph. Now Ghaṭotkaca let fly a hundred-slaying weapon together with a discus. It struck all four of Karṇa's horses together, and they fell to their knees on the ground, lifeless, toothless, eyeless and tongueless.

Leaping down from his chariot, now that its horses were slain, Karṇa reflected. The Kurus were fleeing headlong, and his use of celestial weapons was thwarted by Ghaṭotkaca's illusion, but he did not lose his senses as he considered what would suit the hour.

Now when the Kurus saw Karṇa and the terrible illusion facing him, every one of them cried out, 'Karṇa, today you must swiftly kill the Rākṣasa with your Spear, for the Kurus, Dhṛtarāṣṭra's sons, are dying! What will Bhīma and Kuntī's son Arjuna do to us? You must kill this Rākṣasa as he afflicts us by night; then those of us who survive this
50 terrible conflict will engage Kuntī's sons in battle. So kill this dreadful Rākṣasa! Kill him with the Spear that Indra gave you! The Kauravas themselves are all warriors like Indra; do not allow them to perish by night with their troops, Karṇa!'

Karṇa was losing his night-time battle against the Rākṣasa; he saw that Duryodhana's force was being destroyed, O king, and heard the loud cries of the Kauravas, and he made up his mind to use his Spear. Unforbearing as an angry lion, he could not tolerate Ghaṭotkaca's resistance in battle, and to slay him he took up that best of weapons, the unbearable Spear of victory. O king, that honoured Spear which he had stored for many years in order to kill Arjuna in battle, that best of Spears which Indra gave the Sūta's son in exchange for his earrings[1] – now, as it blazed and seemed to lick its lips, like the night of Yama decked with nooses, like a flaming meteor, like Death's own sister, Karṇa the Cutter hurled it at the Rākṣasa.

55 Ghaṭotkaca saw that most excellent smiter of enemy bodies blazing in the hand of the Sūta's son, and in terror he turned and ran headlong, O king, making his body the size of a foothill of Mount Vindhya. All the sky-creatures cried out, lord of men, when they saw the Spear resting in Karṇa's hand; and wild winds blew, O king, whilst thunderbolts violently struck the earth. The blazing weapon reduced Ghaṭotkaca's illusion to ashes, and tore open the Rākṣasa's heart, then flew aloft, gleaming in the night, to mingle with the constellations. As for Ghaṭotkaca, he had fought with fine weapons, many and varied, against celestial, human and Rākṣasa foes; now, roaring many great and terrible roars, he was

1 See 3.284–94.

stripped of his life by the Spear of Indra. And he performed this last fine and astonishing foe-slaying feat: at the time he was pierced in the heart by the Spear, he appeared, O king, huge as a cloud, or a mountain; then 60
that Rākṣasa prince fell headlong to earth from on high, body torn, limbs stilled, lifeless and speechless, but gigantic in form. Bhīma's son Ghaṭotkaca, doer of fearful deeds, fell with the terrifying, fearful form he had assumed; and thus even in death he smashed one whole section of your army, bringing terror to the Kauravas.

But then the Kurus perceived that the Rākṣasa was killed and his illusion destroyed, and they cried out in joy; then, mingled with lion-roars, there came the roar of kettledrums, conches, hand-drums and tabors. Karṇa was honoured by the Kauravas as was Indra by the gods for the slaying of Vṛtra. He followed your son Duryodhana in mounting his chariot, and returned in joy to his own division.

## THE KILLING OF DROṆA

**[155]** *Seeing Ghaṭotkaca lying dead like a broken mountain, the Pāṇḍavas grieve, but Kṛṣṇa roars with joy, embraces Arjuna and dances. Arjuna remonstrates with him and asks him to explain his behaviour, and Kṛṣṇa does so: Karṇa is now as good as dead, for he has been cheated of his Spear by means of Ghaṭotkaca. With it, he was invincible to the very gods; now he is like a tamed snake or a spent fire. None the less only Arjuna can slay him, and only through a stratagem, by striking when he is in difficulties with his chariot-wheel stuck. Indeed, adds Kṛṣṇa, through such stratagems he has killed a succession of heroes for Arjuna's sake: Jarāsaṃdha, Śiśupāla, Ekalavya, and the Rākṣasas Hiḍimba, Kirmīra and Baka, as well as Alāyudha and now Ghaṭotkaca.* **[156]** *Arjuna asks Kṛṣṇa to explain, and he does so: if Jarāsaṃdha, Śiśupāla and Ekalavya had not been killed they would have sided with Duryodhana and oppressed the earth in his name. They could only be killed through stratagems. Similarly the Rākṣasas were killed because they were over-powerful and destroyers of sacrifices. Ghaṭotkaca was spared for a time for Arjuna's benefit; but if Karṇa had not killed him, Kṛṣṇa himself would have had to do so as part of his mission to establish* dharma. *Arjuna should not worry: he will kill Karṇa, and Bhīma will kill Duryodhana; Kṛṣṇa will explain how.*

**[157]** — *Dhṛtarāṣṭra asks why Karṇa did not use his Spear against Arjuna, which would have given the Kauravas victory; instead, Kṛṣṇa has engineered an outcome highly beneficial to the Pāṇḍavas. Why did Saṃjaya himself not point out the right strategy to Karṇa? Saṃjaya replies that the Kaurava chiefs had discussed this night after night: Karṇa was to slay Arjuna, and if Kṛṣṇa then put one of the other Pāṇḍavas in his place, Kṛṣṇa too should be killed. But when the time came to fight, this resolve was always confounded, and Kṛṣṇa always took care to protect Arjuna. Sātyaki had asked Kṛṣṇa the same question Dhṛtarāṣṭra has asked; Kṛṣṇa answered by describing the firm Kaurava resolve that Karṇa should kill Arjuna, and explaining that he himself sowed confusion in Karṇa's mind to protect Arjuna.*

**[158]** — *Dhṛtarāṣṭra repeats his question, and Saṃjaya repeats his answer, ascribing the blame to fate. Dhṛtarāṣṭra agrees that the Kauravas have been destroyed by fate and by Kṛṣṇa, and asks Saṃjaya to continue his narration. — The Kauravas are overjoyed at Ghaṭotkaca's death, but Yudhiṣṭhira is deeply distressed. He sends Bhīma to do battle against the Kauravas, then confides in Kṛṣṇa: Ghaṭotkaca was very dear to him and had done many hard deeds to help him; and now Droṇa and Karṇa are slaughtering the Pāṇḍava army. They should have been killed sooner, and he intends to do battle himself against Karṇa now, while Bhīma fights Droṇa's army. With these words he sets out, followed by Śikhaṇḍin with a mighty force. Kṛṣṇa tells Arjuna that he should not allow Yudhiṣṭhira to fight Karṇa. Vyāsa appears before Yudhiṣṭhira to tell him of the great benefit conferred by Ghaṭotkaca's death, and to counsel him not to act from anger and grief: in five days the earth will be his.* **[159]** *Yudhiṣṭhira now orders his forces to attack Droṇa, and they do so. A battle commences, but the participants are so weary that some fall asleep on horseback or elephant-back or in their chariots, while others, fighting in their sleep, slay friend and enemy indiscriminately. Arjuna announces a pause in the fighting until moonrise, and the warriors on both sides take the opportunity to rest. But after a while the moon appears, and the battle resumes.*

**[160]** *Duryodhana approaches Droṇa and repeats his complaint that he is favouring the Pāṇḍavas. Furious, Droṇa replies that he is fighting with all his might, that it would be wrong for him, expert in arms, to slay those without such skill, but that he will do whatever Duryodhana wishes, be it good or ill. However, he adds, Arjuna is invincible to mere mortals. Duryodhana, angered in his turn, tells Droṇa that he, together with Duḥśāsana, Karṇa and Śakuni,* *will kill Arjuna. Droṇa laughs at him and calls him a fool, but he none the less urges him to keep his word, in order to spare the Kaurava warriors who will otherwise be slain, and to make good his repeated boasts.*

**[161]** *Day breaks on the continuing battle. Arjuna is attacked by Duryodhana and his comrades, but he replies in kind. The fighting is very fierce; sky, earth and horizon are obscured by dust and arrows, and slain horses, elephants and warriors are everywhere. Droṇa strikes fear into the Pāṇḍava forces; he kills Drupada's three grandsons and overcomes the Cedis, Kekayas, Sṛñjayas and Matsyas; then he slays Drupada and Virāṭa. Seeing this, Dhṛṣṭadyumna in grief and anger swears an oath: may he lose all religious merit if he does not kill Droṇa today. He attacks Droṇa with a Pāñcāla force, but Droṇa is too well protected for them. Now Bhīma goads Dhṛṣṭadyumna to greater exertions, and the two of them penetrate Droṇa's array and launch a terrible attack against their enemies.*

**[162]** *The sun rises on the fifteenth day, but the battle continues without interruption, fierce and tumultuous. Duryodhana and Duḥśāsana fight the twins Nakula and Sahadeva, while Karṇa does battle with Bhīma, and Droṇa with Arjuna. Nakula circles round Duryodhana, showering him with arrows; Duryodhana tries to reply in kind, but Nakula is more than a match for him.* **[163]** *Duḥśāsana attacks Sahadeva, who severs the head of his charioteer with such rapidity that Duḥśāsana does not even know it has happened until his horses run out of control. Karṇa seeks to come to Duḥśāsana's aid, but is attacked by Bhīma; the two heroes fight each other with clubs and with arrows, until Karṇa kills Bhīma's horses and his charioteer, at which Bhīma leaps into Nakula's chariot. Meanwhile, Droṇa and Arjuna are battling against each other. Unable to get the upper hand, Droṇa resorts to numerous celestial weapons, but Arjuna destroys them all; finally Droṇa deploys the Weapon of Brahmā, but Arjuna uses his own Weapon of Brahmā against Droṇa's Weapon. As the two warriors battle it out, the sky is so full of flying arrows that birds can no longer pass through it.*

Saṃjaya spoke:

**[164]** As the slaughter of men and horses and elephants continued, great king, Duḥśāsana engaged Dhṛṣṭadyumna in battle. Dhṛṣṭadyumna in his gold chariot was afflicted by Duḥśāsana's arrows; he would not tolerate it, and showered your son's horses with his own arrows, so

that in a moment his chariot, complete with standard and charioteer,
became invisible under the covering arrows of Pṛṣata's heir, great king;
in his suffering from those torrents of arrows, lord of kings, Duḥśāsana
5 could not remain before the noble Pāñcāla prince. Then after forcing
Duḥśāsana to retreat with his arrows, the heir of Pṛṣata attacked Droṇa
in that battle, showering thousands of arrows upon him. At once
Kṛtavarman, Hṛdika's son, took counter-measures together with three
of his brothers. They all surrounded Dhṛṣṭadyumna; but the twins
Nakula and Sahadeva, bull-like heroes both, were following behind to
protect him as he made his way towards Droṇa, blazing like a fire.

Now those seven great chariot-fighters all began to do battle. Un-
forbearing and mettlesome, keeping death before them, pure in person
and in conduct, and intent on heaven, O king, they fought a noble
10 fight as they sought to defeat one another; those wise lords of men, of
unblemished descent and deed, did battle according to *dharma*, hold-
ing their end in view. They employed no form of warfare contrary to
*dharma* or to the rules of weaponry: no barbed arrows or reed-arrows, no
poison-smeared arrows or poison-injecting arrows, no needle-arrows or
monkey-arrows, no arrows of cow-bone or elephant-bone, no double-
arrows or infected arrows, no crooked-flying arrows.[1] The weapons
they all used were straight and pure, for all desired to gain the world of
heaven, and glory too, through fair fight.

A tumultuous battle, free of any wrongdoing, now took place between
15 your four warriors and the three Pāṇḍava heroes; but when Dhṛṣṭa-
dyumna of swift weapons saw your bull-like chariot-fighters held in
check by the twins, O king, he left them and made his way towards
Droṇa. Your four warriors, held back by those two lion-like her-
oes, fought against them like winds beating against two mountains,
while the twins, bull-like chariot-fighters both, fought back against
two chariot-fighters each. Meanwhile, Dhṛṣṭadyumna attacked Droṇa.
When Duryodhana saw the Pāñcāla prince heading towards Droṇa,
mad for battle, and realized that his own warriors were busy fighting
against the twins, he rushed at once to attack him, great king, showering

1 Very little is known about these weapons, though it is curious that the first two of them are in fact quite frequently referred to as being used in the great battle.

him with blood-drinking arrows; whereupon he was rapidly attacked
by Sātyaki once again. Encountering each other at close quarters, the 20
two tiger-like heroes, the Kuru and the Vṛṣṇi, came together, laughing fearlessly.

The two of them recalled with pleasure all the deeds of their boyhood, and they looked at one another and laughed again and again. Then King Duryodhana spoke to his ever-dear friend Sātyaki, and censured his own actions. 'A curse on anger! A curse on greed, my friend! A curse upon folly, and upon intolerance! Cursed be the way of the Kṣatriyas, and cursed be manly strength, that you should aim at me and I at you, O bull-like heir of Śini! For you are dearer to me than life, and so was I
always to you. I remember all those boyhood deeds we shared; now on 25
this field of battle they have all withered away for us! What reason have I to fight you today, other than anger and greed, O Sātvata?'

When Duryodhana spoke thus, O king, Sātyaki, master of weaponry, brandished his sharp arrows and answered with a laugh, 'This is not the assembly, prince, or our Teacher's house where once we used to meet and play!' But Duryodhana replied, 'Long past in our boyhood we had games, O bull-like heir of Śini, and now we have this mighty war. How insurmountable is fate! What use is wealth to us, or desire for wealth? It is through greed for wealth that we are all assembled here to
fight.' When the king spoke thus, Madhu's heir Sātyaki replied, 'This 30
has always been the Kṣatriya way, to slay even their elders. If I am dear to you, O king, then kill me! Do not delay! On your account I shall attain to the realms of the virtuous, bull-like heir of Bharata. Swiftly display to me all your power and strength, for I have no wish to see my friends overtaken by this great calamity.'

Sātyaki had spoken clearly, and had answered Duryodhana's objections; now, lord of the peoples, calm and disinterested, he continued his rapid advance against him. When your son saw him coming, he made ready to receive him, and showered Śini's heir with arrows, O king;
and then there took place a battle between those lion-like warriors, the 35
Kuru and the Vṛṣṇi, terrible as a furious battle between a lion and an elephant. Duryodhana pierced the battle-crazed Sātvata with ten sharp arrows shot from a fully stretched bow, and in return Sātyaki likewise pierced him with ten arrows in that battle, and then with fifty, then

thirty, and then a further ten. He severed his bow even as Duryodhana
fixed an arrow to it, and then rapidly showered him with arrows; and
Duryodhana, deeply pierced and shaken, great king, took refuge in
another chariot in his suffering from the arrows of the Daśārha prince.
40 Then your son recovered, and advanced once more against Sātyaki,
shooting torrents of arrows at his chariot. And Sātyaki likewise cease-
lessly shot arrows at Duryodhana's chariot, O king; and so the battle
went on.

Now all the arrows that were shot, as they flew in every direction,
caused a mighty noise, like a fire in a great dry forest; and Karṇa,
perceiving that Madhu's heir Sātyaki, best of chariot-fighters, had the
upper hand, came up swiftly to rescue your son. Bhīma of mighty
strength would not tolerate this, and advanced rapidly against Karṇa,
45 shooting many arrows. But Karṇa struck down those sharp arrows with
a laugh, and with his own arrows severed Bhīma's bow and his arrows,
and slew his charioteer. In fury Pāṇḍu's son Bhīma took up his club in
that battle, and smashed his enemy's standard, his bow and his charioteer.
Karṇa would not tolerate this, and battled against Bhīma with torrents
of arrows of every kind, and with other weapons too.

While the battle continued, King Yudhiṣṭhira, son of Dharma, ad-
dressed the tiger-like men of Pāñcāla and the bull-like men of Matsya.
'Those bull-like heroes who are our life, our head, our warriors of
50 mighty strength, are locked in combat with the Dhārtarāṣṭras. Why
do you all stand like senseless fools? Go to where my chariot-fighters
are doing battle! Show your allegiance to the Kṣatriya *dharma*, and cast
off your sickness. Whether you conquer or whether you die, you will
all attain the end you long for: conquering, you will become great
sacrificers, generous to Brahmins; dying, you will join the gods and
attain many heavenly realms!'

Urged on by the king, those mighty chariot-fighters, ready to fight
heroically, formed their force into four divisions and advanced rapidly
against Droṇa. The Pāñcālas assailed him from one side with many
arrows, while the warriors under Bhīma's leadership surrounded him
55 on the other side. Now three straight sons of Pāṇḍu, the great chariot-
fighters Nakula, Sahadeva and Bhīma, were there, and they called out
to wealth-winner Arjuna: 'Hurry here swiftly, Arjuna, and drive away

the Kurus from Droṇa! Once his protectors are slain, the Pāñcālas will kill him.' Then Kuntī's son rushed at once to attack the Kauravas, while Droṇa for his part rushed at the Pāñcālas under Dhṛṣṭadyumna's leadership; Droṇa made great slaughter of the Pāñcālas, as furious Indra long ago destroyed the Dānava demons in battle. Though many of those excellent, mettlesome chariot-fighters were killed by Droṇa's weapons
in that battle, they showed no fear of Droṇa. Though many were slain, 60
great king, the Pāñcālas and Sṛñjayas advanced straight against Droṇa in battle, dumbfounding the mighty chariot-fighter; but as they died on every side, slain by his arrows and spears, they let out a terrible cry.

While noble Droṇa killed the Pāñcālas and cast his weapons in battle, the Pāṇḍavas were seized by fear; they saw enormous throngs of horses and men slaughtered in battle, great king, and then they lost hope of victory. 'Let not Droṇa, master of weaponry, wipe us all out like a well-
fuelled spring fire consuming a dry thicket! There is no one capable of 65
meeting his gaze in battle; not even righteous Arjuna can fight against him!' Now Kṛṣṇa Keśava saw that Kuntī's sons were suffering from Droṇa's arrows and afraid, and in his wisdom and concern for the best outcome he spoke to Arjuna. 'This lord of lords of chariot-fighters cannot possibly be conquered by simply fighting him in battle – not even by Indra slayer of Vṛtra. Therefore we must put aside *dharma* and resort to stratagem to conquer him, if Droṇa of the golden chariot is not to kill you all in battle. If Aśvatthāman were slain, I believe that he would cease to fight; so some person must inform him that his son has been killed on the battlefield.'

Wealth-winner Arjuna, Kuntī's son, could not agree to this, O king; 70
but the others all agreed, though Yudhiṣṭhira only with difficulty. Then strong-armed Bhīma with his club killed a mighty elephant from his own army, O king; that elephant's name was Aśvatthāman. Bhīma approached Droṇa on the battlefield with due modesty, and cried aloud 'Aśvatthāman is slain!' Aśvatthāman was the name of the elephant he had killed, and Bhīma lied by referring to it.

When Droṇa heard Bhīma speak these deeply distressing words, his
heart sank within him, like sand in water; but, wondering whether 75
it might be a lie, and remembering his son's valour, he did not relax his steadfastness on hearing of his death. He regained his composure,

and at once comforted himself with the thought that no enemy could resist his son. Then he rushed against Dhṛṣṭadyumna, Pṛṣata's heir, as if longing to kill his own death,[1] showering him with a thousand sharp stork-feathered arrows. In return twenty thousand bull-like Pāñcāla warriors showered him with arrows from all sides as he ranged over the battlefield. Then unforbearing Droṇa, afflicter of his enemies, brought
80 forth the Weapon of Brahmā to slay those Pāñcāla heroes. Droṇa was resplendent in the great battle as he killed all the Somakas, and lopped off the Pāñcālas' heads and their arms like iron bars, still decked with gold ornaments. Slain in battle by Droṇa son of Bharadvāja, those princes lay scattered on the ground like wind-felled trees; and the earth, muddy with flesh and blood, became impassable with fallen elephants and teams of horses. The killer of twenty thousand Pāñcāla chariot-fighters, Droṇa now stood on the battlefield, blazing like a smokeless fire; then Bharadvāja's son of great energy, filled once again with that same fury,
85 severed Vasudāna's head from his body with a broad arrow. And he slew a further five hundred Matsyas, and six thousand Sṛñjayas, and ten thousand elephants, and ten thousand horses also.

When the seers saw Droṇa standing there dealing out destruction to the Kṣatriyas, they hurried towards him, led by Fire, bearer of the oblation: Viśvāmitra and Jamadagni, Bharadvāja and Gautama, Vasiṣṭha, Kaśyapa and Atri, the Sikatas and Pṛśnis, the descendants of Garga, the Vālakhilyas who drink nothing but moonbeams, the Bhṛgus and Aṅgirases, and other subtle seers all came, intending to conduct him to Brahmā's heaven. And they all addressed Droṇa as he stood resplendent in battle: 'You have fought in breach of *dharma*. Now is the time of
90 your death: cast down your weapons on the battlefield, and accompany us. You should commit no further acts of great cruelty, for this does not become one such as you, especially a Brahmin learned in the Veda and its branches, and devoted to truth and *dharma*. Cast down your unfailing weapons, and step on to the road of eternity, for your time of dwelling in the world of men is completed today.'

Droṇa heard their words, as he had heard those of Bhīma; he saw Dhṛṣṭadyumna on the battlefield; and he became distressed in mind.

1 Dhṛṣṭadyumna was destined to kill Droṇa: 1.155.

Consumed with grief and shaken, Droṇa asked Kuntī's son Yudhiṣṭhira
whether his son had been killed or not, for he was sure that the Pāṇḍava 95
lord would never speak untruth, even to gain sovereignty over the three
worlds. That was why he asked Yudhiṣṭhira in particular, not anybody
else, for from childhood on he had trusted Kuntī's son to speak the
truth. But Kṛṣṇa Govinda realized that the warrior lord Droṇa intended
to wipe the Pāṇḍavas from the face of the earth, and he was troubled,
and spoke to Yudhiṣṭhira lord of *dharma*: 'If Droṇa, full of fury, fights
for so much as half a day, believe me, your army will be destroyed. So
protect us against Droṇa, sir! A lie would be better than truth, and he
that speaks a lie in order to live is not contaminated by it.' Then as the 100
two of them spoke together, Bhīma said, 'As soon as I heard the plan
for slaying noble Droṇa, great king, I attacked and killed in battle an
elephant named Aśvatthāman, as fine as Indra's elephant, belonging to
the Mālava prince Indravarman who was deep within your army. Then I
said to Droṇa, "Withdraw from the battle, O Brahmin, for Aśvatthāman
is slain!" But it was clear that the bull-like hero did not believe what I
said. Therefore you should accept the words of Kṛṣṇa Govinda, if you
wish for victory; tell Droṇa that Kṛpī's son has been killed, O king. If
you say this to him the bull-like Brahmin will surely cease to fight, for
in this world of mortals you are famous as a speaker of the truth, O lord
of men.'

Hearing his speech, great king, and urged on by what Kṛṣṇa had said, 105
and also by fate, Yudhiṣṭhira now made ready to speak. Deeply fearful of
lying, but longing for victory, O king, he spoke to Droṇa. 'Aśvatthāman
is slain,' he said; then, in an undertone, 'the elephant.' Now previously
Yudhiṣṭhira's chariot had always remained four fingers off the ground;
but when he spoke these words his horses came down to earth. As for
the mighty chariot-fighter Droṇa, when he heard what Yudhiṣṭhira said
he lost his desire for life in his grief at the death of his son. Believing
himself to have wronged the noble Pāṇḍavas, and believing the words
of the seers, and hearing of his son's death, he became distracted and 110
deeply distressed; he saw Dhṛṣṭadyumna, but could no longer fight as
before, O foe-tamer.

Dhṛṣṭadyumna, son of the king of Pāñcāla, saw that Droṇa was deeply
distressed and out of his mind with grief, and he rushed towards him.

Born for Droṇa's destruction, he had emerged from the well-fuelled
fire at King Drupada's great sacrifice; now the Pāñcāla prince took
up his terrible victory-granting bow, with its roar like thunderclouds,
strongly strung, unbreakable and celestial. He took up his arrows like
venomous snakes, and to slay Droṇa he fixed to that bow an arrow
115 that blazed like a mighty fire. Framed by the circle of his bow, that
arrow seemed like a radiant sun edged by cloud. When the soldiers saw
that blazing bow in the hand of Pṛṣata's heir, it seemed to them that
the end of the world had come; and when Bharadvāja's son of great
energy saw that arrow fixed to it, it seemed to him his body's final
hour.

Now Droṇa the Teacher made an effort to ward off that shaft, but
that noble warrior's Weapons would not come forth, lord of kings.[1]
Four days and one night had passed while he continued to shoot them,
but now during the third part of the day his arrows came to an end.
120 But though his arrows had ceased, though he was afflicted with grief
for his son, and though his various celestial weapons would no longer
obey him, he wished to battle on despite the urging of the seers; and
so, impelled by his own mighty ardour, he fought a superhuman fight.
He took up another celestial bow, the gift of Aṅgiras, and arrows like
the staff of Brahmā, and engaged Dhṛṣṭadyumna in battle. Then he
covered him with a great shower of arrows; unforbearing and furious,
Droṇa wounded Dhṛṣṭadyumna, and with his own sharp arrows cut his
enemy's terrible arrow into a hundred pieces, and felled his standard,
bow and charioteer.

125 With a laugh, Dhṛṣṭadyumna took up another bow, and in return
pierced him in the breast with a sharp arrow. The mighty bowman Droṇa
seemed troubled to be so severely pierced in battle, and with a broad,
sharp-bladed arrow he severed Dhṛṣṭadyumna's great bow; indeed, the
unconquerable afflicter of his enemies severed every one of his decorated
arrows, and his bows, lord of the peoples, and his club and sword as well;

1 In his translation, K. M. Ganguli notes at this point, 'The celestial weapons were all living agents that appeared at the bidding of him who knew how to invoke them. They abandoned, however, the person whose death was imminent, though invoked with the usual formulae.'

then, enraged, he pierced the enraged Dhṛṣṭadyumna with nine sharp
death-dealing arrows. Now Droṇa, the immeasurably great chariot-
fighter, released the Weapon of Brahmā, and caused Dhṛṣṭadyumna's
chariot-horses to become entangled with his own. Those steeds, swift 130
as the wind, looked very splendid when they were entangled, some
dove-coloured and some red, O bull-like heir of Bharata; great king,
entangled at the forefront of the battle, they shone like lightning-clouds
at the onset of the rains. Then the immeasurably great Brahmin warrior
destroyed the fastenings of Dhṛṣṭadyumna's chariot-pole, and those of
his wheels, and of his chariot itself. Brave Dhṛṣṭadyumna, chariotless,
his bow severed and his horses and charioteer slain, had reached a sorry
pass. He seized a club, but furious Droṇa of true valour struck it down
in mid-air with his sharp arrows.

Seeing his club struck down by Droṇa's arrows, the tiger-like Dhṛṣ- 135
ṭadyumna took up a shining sword and a bright shield adorned with a
hundred moons. It was very clear that, in the circumstances, the Pāñcāla
prince considered the time had come to slay Droṇa, noblest of Teachers.
Standing now on the driver's perch, now on the pole of his chariot,
he brandished his sword and his bright shield adorned with a hundred
moons, for he wished to perform a difficult feat: Dhṛṣṭadyumna the
mighty chariot-fighter intended to cut open the breast of Bharadvāja's
son in battle; and so he stood now on the middle of the yoke, now amidst
its fastenings, now amongst the hindquarters of Droṇa's red horses; and
the soldiers honoured his skill. Whether he stood on the edges of the 140
yoke or among the red horses, Droṇa too could find no weak spot in his
defence, which was a great wonder. His movement as he tried to reach
Droṇa was like that of a swift-flying hawk seeking out a piece of flesh.

But now Droṇa the valiant furiously killed all Dhṛṣṭadyumna's dove-
coloured horses, one after another, with his lance; all his steeds fell slain
to the ground, and Droṇa's red steeds became disentangled from the
chariot-fastenings, lord of the peoples. When Pṛṣata's heir, the great
chariot-fighter Dhṛṣṭadyumna, best of warriors, saw his horses killed by
Droṇa, foremost among Brahmins, he would not tolerate it; chariotless, 145
that excellent swordsman took his sword and fell upon Droṇa, O king,
like Garuḍa falling upon a snake. As he strove to slay Bharadvāja's
son, he looked as splendid as Viṣṇu slaying Hiraṇyakaśipu. Pṛṣata's heir

manoeuvred this way and that, and, bearing sword and shield, displayed the twenty-one methods of fighting: whirling the sword, whirling it aloft, whirling it about oneself; advancing to attack, striking with the point of the sword, striking by feint; striking on both sides, retreating on foot; exchanging blows, and overcoming the enemy.

Then in the press of battle the Brahmin struck down with a thousand arrows Dhṛṣṭadyumna's sword and his shield adorned with a hundred
150 moons. Those arrows were of the type used in close combat to strike a nearby enemy, one hand's span in length; Droṇa possessed them, but no one else except Kṛpa, Kuntī's son Arjuna, Droṇa's son Aśvatthāman, Karṇa the Cutter, Pradyumna, Sātyaki and Abhimanyu. Then the Teacher fixed to his bow a strong, extremely sharp arrow to slay his disciple, dear to him as a son; but Sātyaki, Śini's bull-like heir, cut it down with ten sharp arrows before the very eyes of your son and the noble Karṇa, and rescued Dhṛṣṭadyumna from death at the hands of Droṇa, foremost of teachers. Noble Kṛṣṇa and wealth-winner Arjuna saw Sātyaki of true valour ranging in the path of his enemies' chariots,
155 close to Droṇa, Karṇa and Kṛpa, and they honoured the invincible Vṛṣṇi, crying, 'Bravo! Bravo!' as he struck down all his foes' celestial weapons on the battlefield, and fell upon the Kuru army. The wealth-winner said to Kṛṣṇa, 'See, Keśava, how Madhu's heir sports in the midst of the excellent Kuru warriors and their Teacher! I am filled with great joy by Sātyaki of true valour, and so are Mādrī's twin sons, and Bhīma, and King Yudhiṣṭhira, seeing him range over the battlefield, modest in his skilfulness, increasing the Vṛṣṇis' glory as he sports with mighty chariot-fighters. Siddhas and soldiers alike are filled with amazement and offer him their praise!' And indeed, seeing the unconquerable Sātvata hero on the battlefield, all the warriors on both sides honoured him for his feats: 'Bravo! Bravo!'

[**165**] A savage battle now began amongst those assembled kings, as if a furious Rudra were slaying his victims. O heir of Bharata, hands and heads and bows, discarded royal umbrellas and yak-tail fans, broken-wheeled chariots, huge severed standards, and slain charioteer heroes littered the battlefield ground. And your warriors, O best of Kurus, were cut down by falling arrows; all over the battlefield they could be
5 seen, writhing in their pain. The terrible battle was like that of the gods

and the demons. As it continued, Yudhiṣṭhira lord of *dharma* addressed his Kṣatriyas. 'Make ready, great warriors! Rush now against Droṇa! Pṛṣata's heir, brave Dhṛṣṭadyumna, is battling against him, striving with all his might to slay the son of Bharadvāja. From such things as I have seen on the great battlefield, I believe that Pṛṣata's furious heir will kill Droṇa in battle today; therefore join forces, and attack Bharadvāja's son!

Commanded by Yudhiṣṭhira, the great Sṛñjaya chariot-fighters made ready and rushed against Droṇa to slay him. When the son of Bharadvāja saw them all descending on him, that mighty chariot-fighter swiftly
attacked them, bent on death. But when Droṇa, keeper of his word, 10
advanced, the earth trembled, and violent winds blew, terrifying your army. A great meteor fell; it seemed to fall from the sun; it seemed to burn with heat, and to presage great danger. All Droṇa's weapons blazed, sir; chariots groaned loudly, and their horses shed tears. Bharadvāja's son, great chariot-fighter that he was, seemed to have lost his might. Now he made ready to give up his life in fair fight, remembering what the seers, expounders of the Veda, had told him about passing to heaven. Droṇa was entirely surrounded by Drupada's forces; he ranged over the
battlefield, consuming those companies of Kṣatriyas. The foe-crusher 15
had already killed twenty thousand of them. Now with his sharp, well-pointed arrows he slew a hundred thousand more; standing purposefully on the battlefield like a smokeless fire, he used his Brahmin power to deal out destruction to the Kṣatriyas.

The Pāñcāla prince, noble Dhṛṣṭadyumna, was chariotless and weaponless, but he was not dismayed. Obedient to his brother's command, foe-crusher Bhīma hurried towards him and took the Pāñcāla prince up into his own chariot. Then he looked at where Droṇa, not far away, was shooting his arrows, and said to Dhṛṣṭadyumna, 'There is no man other than you who dares to fight against the Teacher. Make haste to kill
him soon: this burden is laid upon you.' When he heard these words, 20
the strong-armed prince swiftly took up a new and excellent weapon, strong and capable of carrying out any task, and fell upon Droṇa. Furiously shooting arrows, he sought to resist that irresistible warrior, and showered arrows upon the Teacher. Those two fine warriors, splendid on the battlefield in their rage, opposed each other, releasing many celestial weapons of Brahmā. Great king, Pṛṣata's heir struck down all Droṇa's

weapons, and covered Bharadvāja's son with his own mighty weapons in that conflict. The Vasātis and Śibis, the Bāhlikas and Kauravas sought to defend Droṇa in the battle, but invincible Dhṛṣṭadyumna meted out destruction to them; O king, he shone as splendid as the sun with its rays, covering the entire horizon with his torrents of arrows.

Then Droṇa severed his bow and pierced him with his shafts, and further struck his vital organs, inflicting extreme pain. At this point, the ever-wrathful Bhīma grabbed Droṇa's chariot, lord of kings, and softly spoke to Droṇa: 'If self-styled Brahmins, full of learning but dissatisfied with the Brahmin way, stayed out of battle, the Kṣatriyas would not be heading for destruction! Non-violence towards all beings is said to be the most exalted *dharma*, and the Brahmin is its basis. You know the Brahmin way better than anyone else, and yet, Brahmin, for the sake of a single son you have killed many hordes of barbarians and others, who in their foolish ignorance, longing for sons and wives and wealth, abided by their own code, while you broke yours as if *dharma* were unknown to you. As well cook a dog! Are you not ashamed? And that son today lies slain, as Yudhiṣṭhira lord of *dharma* informed you when you asked him. Do not doubt his word!'

When righteous Droṇa heard Bhīma's words, he laid aside his bow and prepared to cast off all his weapons. And he called out, 'O Karṇa, mighty bowman Karṇa! O Kṛpa! O Duryodhana! Strive in the battle! I say this, and say it again: may you be safe from the Pāṇḍavas! I am laying aside my weapons.' Then, great king, he cried aloud for his son Aśvatthāman. He laid aside his weapons, placed them within his chariot, and, absorbed in Yoga, conferred freedom from fear upon all.

Dhṛṣṭadyumna saw his opportunity. He arose, leapt, sword in hand, down from his chariot, and rushed towards Droṇa. All beings, human and non-human, were in uproar to see Droṇa thus fallen into the power of Dhṛṣṭadyumna, and they made a tumultuous roar of 'Woe!' and 'Alas!', while Droṇa, weapons laid aside, sat in perfect equanimity. After speaking, he had absorbed himself in Yoga; now, brilliant and rich in ascetic power, the Teacher was reaching a heavenly realm hard for even the virtuous to reach. As he passed thus it seemed to us that two suns were shining, for the sky seemed filled entirely with lights, and two sun-like beings appeared: the sun itself and Bharadvāja's son. Then in

a moment that light disappeared, and there came a came a shout of joy from joyful heaven-dwellers as Droṇa arrived at Brahmā's realm. Dhṛṣṭadyumna was dumbfounded. Only five of us mortals then saw noble Droṇa, absorbed in Yoga, reach his final state: I, and Kuntī's son wealth-winner Arjuna, and the Brahmin Kṛpa, son of Śaradvat, and Kṛṣṇa Vāsudeva the Vṛṣṇi, and the Pāṇḍava Yudhiṣṭhira, lord of *dharma*. None of the others could see the greatness of Bharadvāja's wise son, great king, as he passed, absorbed in Yoga; mortals did not know that 45
he had reached his final state, for they did not see him, Teacher and foe-tamer, absorbed in Yoga, pass with the mighty bull-like seers to Brahmā's realm.

His body lay, pierced by hundreds of arrows, weapons cast aside, flowing with blood. To curses from all beings, Pṛṣata's heir Dhṛṣṭadyumna laid hands on it; he seized the head of the lifeless man and without a word severed it from the body with his sword. Then, with great joy at the fall of Bharadvāja's son, he roared a lion-roar, whirling his sword on the battlefield.

Grey-haired to the ears, complexion darkened, eighty-five years old, Droṇa had ranged over the battlefield like a boy of sixteen for your sake. Strong-armed wealth-winner Arjuna, Kuntī's son, had said, 'Son 50
of Drupada, bring back the Teacher alive! Do not slay him!' Your soldiers too had cried out, 'Do not kill him, do not kill him!' Arjuna had even hurried towards Dhṛṣṭadyumna with the same cry. But while he and all the other princes cried against it, Dhṛṣṭadyumna slew Droṇa, bull-like warrior, on the seat of his chariot. Then, soaked in blood, the foe-tamer leapt down from his chariot to the ground; red-limbed as the sun, he had become terrible to look upon. Thus the soldiery beheld Droṇa slain in battle. But, O king, the great bowman Dhṛṣṭadyumna took the mighty head of Bharadvāja's son and threw it down in front of your warriors; and seeing the head of Bharadvāja's son, your warriors, 55
full of the will to flee, ran in every direction. As for Droṇa, he came to heaven and entered among the constellations. So it was that at that time I witnessed Droṇa's death, O king; and through the grace of the seer Kṛṣṇa Dvaipāyana Vyāsa, Satyavatī's son, we saw that most radiant hero reaching heaven as he passed, flying like a blazing, smokeless meteor.

After the killing of Droṇa, the Kurus lost the will to fight. The

Pāṇḍavas and Sṛñjayas rushed against them at great speed, and the army was ripped apart. Most of the horses lay slain by sharp arrows in the battle, and when Droṇa was killed your warriors became like dead men.
60 They had tasted defeat and, worse, great fear, and they were unmanned by both, and could summon up no fortitude. Their princes tried to reach the body of Bharadvāja's son, but they could not get through the mass of headless bodies.

The Pāṇḍavas, however, had tasted victory and, better, great fame, and they rattled their arrows and roared resounding lion-roars. Bhīma and Dhṛṣṭadyumna heir of Pṛṣata, O king, danced in the midst of the army, and embraced one another. Then Bhīma spoke to Pṛṣata's heir, afflicter of his enemies: 'I shall embrace you once more for your victory, heir of Pṛṣata, when Karṇa the Sūta's son lies slain in battle, and likewise
65 the wicked son of Dhṛtarāṣṭra!' With these words Pāṇḍu's son Bhīma set the earth trembling in his great joy, with the beating of arm on chest; and your warriors, terrified by that sound, ran headlong on the battlefield, abandoning the Kṣatriya way in their haste to flee. But the Pāṇḍavas were full of joy at the victory they had gained, lord of the peoples; and they had the pleasure of having destroyed their enemy in battle.

*Only Aśvatthāman, unaware of what has happened, continues to resist. When he hears from Kṛpa of the manner of his father's death he is filled with fury.*

## THE WEAPON OF NĀRĀYAṆA

**[166]** — *Dhṛtarāṣṭra asks Saṃjaya to tell him how Aśvatthāman reacted when he learnt that his father had been killed by Dhṛṣṭadyumna in violation of* dharma, *and Saṃjaya describes the scene.* — *Aśvatthāman is gripped by rage and grief. That his father, a warrior, should have died in battle, is no cause for sorrow, but that Dhṛṣṭadyumna should have seized him by the hair is intolerable. Aśvatthāman swears that he will slaughter the Pāṇḍava forces and slay Dhṛṣṭadyumna: he will deploy the Weapon which Droṇa obtained as a boon from Nārāyaṇa. Hearing this the Kauravas rally, and joyfully blow their conches and beat their drums.*

**[167]** *When Aśvatthāman deploys the Weapon of Nārāyaṇa, storms break out in a cloudless sky, the earth trembles, the sea heaves, and rivers flow backwards. Yudhiṣṭhira, seeing that the Kauravas have ceased to flee and are now attacking in force, asks Arjuna who has rallied them. Arjuna answers that it is Aśvatthāman, and that it will prove impossible to protect Dhṛṣṭadyumna from him. He upbraids Yudhiṣṭhira for the wickedness he has committed for the sake of a kingdom: after killing Droṇa in such a fashion, death is preferable to life.* **[168]** *When the Pāṇḍavas hear Arjuna's words they are silent, except for Bhīma, who forcefully reminds him of the Kauravas' wrongdoings: it is to wipe out that wrong that the Pāṇḍavas are fighting this war, and if Arjuna will not fight, Bhīma will continue single-handed. Dhṛṣṭadyumna adds that Droṇa was a false Brahmin and an enemy, and killing of enemies is a Kṣatriya duty: now Droṇa has been killed, Arjuna should fight and triumph.*

**[169]** *The Pāṇḍavas are once again silent when they hear Dhṛṣṭadyumna's words, until Sātyaki bursts out in fury: Dhṛṣṭadyumna deserves death for his wicked deed, and in particular for boasting of it; if he says such a thing again, Sātyaki will strike off his head with his club. Dhṛṣṭadyumna replies that his action in killing Droṇa was blameless, whereas Sātyaki's own slaying of Bhūriśravas when his arm had been severed by Arjuna was an act of extreme wickedness; if Sātyaki is foolish enough to repeat what he has said, he will kill him with his arrows. In fury, Sātyaki rushes at Dhṛṣṭadyumna. At Kṛṣṇa's prompting Bhīma restrains him, while Sahadeva urges forbearance; but Dhṛṣṭadyumna continues to taunt him, and it is with difficulty that Kṛṣṇa and Yudhiṣṭhira are able to calm both heroes down.*

**[170]** *Meanwhile, Aśvatthāman is slaughtering his enemies, piling up a mountain of their bodies. The Weapon of Nārāyaṇa unleashes a torrent of weapons against the Pāṇḍavas: thousands of arrows, iron balls, hundred-slaying weapons and razor-edged discuses fall upon them. Seeing his troops overwhelmed, Yudhiṣṭhira urges them to abandon the battle: now that Droṇa has been killed, he and his brothers will accept death. But Kṛṣṇa prevents the army from fleeing and explains that if they cast down their weapons and descend from their mounts they will be safe from the Weapon, whereas if they fight against it they will die. Bhīma refuses to act on this advice and engages Aśvatthāman in combat, whereupon he is covered with an ever-increasing mass of blazing arrows. Seeing this, the other Pāṇḍava warriors cast down their weapons and dismount.*

**[171]** *Arjuna makes use of the Weapon of Varuṇa to protect Bhīma, and* *he and Kṛṣṇa leap down from their chariot and run, weaponless, to rescue him. At first he resists, and the strength of Aśvatthāman's Weapon increases; but when Kṛṣṇa succeeds in persuading him to dismount and cast aside his weapons, the Weapon is stilled. The sky clears, pleasant breezes blow, and the Pāṇḍava forces revive. Duryodhana asks Aśvatthāman to deploy the Weapon again, but Aśvatthāman explains that it cannot be used more than once. Then he attacks Dhṛṣṭadyumna; after a fierce exchange of arrows he kills his horses and charioteer and puts his followers to flight. Sātyaki attacks Aśvatthāman, but he is overwhelmed; his charioteer bears him away, while Aśvatthāman renews his attack on Dhṛṣṭadyumna. Arjuna and Bhīma counterattack, but Aśvatthāman fends them off and kills their followers. The Pāñcālas flee, while Aśvatthāman showers them with arrows.*

[172] *Arjuna, in his distress at the turn of events, speaks harshly to Aśvatthāman, who, furious, deploys the Fire Weapon. The sun ceases to shine, clouds rain down blood, and the whole universe is scorched; many warriors are slain. The Kauravas rejoice. Arjuna deploys the Weapon of Brahmā to restore light and calm: an entire Pāṇḍava division is revealed to have been wiped out, but when Kṛṣṇa and Arjuna himself are seen unharmed and resplendent in their chariot, the remaining Pāṇḍavas are full of joy, while the Kauravas are dismayed, and Aśvatthāman abandons the fight. Meeting Vyāsa, he asks him why his Weapon failed to kill Arjuna and Kṛṣṇa, and Vyāsa tells him that Nārāyaṇa had once performed great austerities, as a result of which he was able to see the great god Śiva in majesty. He worshipped him and requested boons, and Śiva granted him invincibility and invulnerability. Nara was born as a result of Nārāyaṇa's austerities and is his equal; he is Arjuna. Aśvatthāman is himself a portion of Śiva, and in a former life gained boons from him for his devotion: he should worship Kṛṣṇa, who is greatly loved by Śiva. Hearing this, Aśvatthāman honours both Śiva and Kṛṣṇa, and calls a halt to the day's fighting.*

[173] *Arjuna also encounters Vyāsa, and tells him that wherever he goes in battle he is preceded by a man looking like fire, whose feet do not touch the ground; he does not throw his spear, but from it issue thousands of spears that slay all the warriors that appear to be slain by Arjuna himself. He asks Vyāsa who this is, and Vyāsa answers that he has seen the great god Śiva, whom he praises at length; then he relates the stories of Śiva's disruption of Dakṣa's sacrifice, his destruction of the triple city, and the gods' acceptance of his pre-eminence. It is Śiva who goes before Arjuna killing his enemies, and who gave him his weapons;*

*the man devoted to Śiva obtains his desires. Arjuna should go and fight; with Kṛṣṇa for his counsellor and protector he will not suffer defeat.*

# KARṆA

## THE KILLING OF KARṆA

[1] *After Droṇa's death, Duryodhana and the seniormost Kauravas pass a miserable, sleepless night, full of regret for their offences against Draupadī and the Pāṇḍavas. In the morning Karṇa is appointed as commander in place of Droṇa. A fierce battle takes place against the Pāṇḍavas; it lasts for two days, and then Karṇa is killed by Arjuna.*

*— Saṃjaya arrives to convey this news to Dhṛtarāṣṭra, first expressing the sardonic hope that all is well with him. Dhṛtarāṣṭra demands to hear all that has happened.* [2] *Saṃjaya describes how, when the Kaurava troops saw that Droṇa had been killed, they despaired and their weapons fell from their hands; how Duryodhana extolled Karṇa's valour and appointed him commander; and how Karṇa fought fiercely, causing the Pāṇḍavas much affliction, until he was killed by Arjuna.*

[3] *— Hearing this, Dhṛtarāṣṭra faints with grief, convinced that Duryodhana too must have been killed, and Gāndhārī and the other ladies likewise weep and faint. When he regains his composure, Dhṛtarāṣṭra asks whether Duryodhana is dead; Saṃjaya answers that Karṇa has been killed together with his sons and brothers, and also that Bhīma has slain Duḥśāsana and drunk his blood.*

[4] *— Dhṛtarāṣṭra asks Saṃjaya which warriors on both sides are alive and which dead. Saṃjaya replies that, before his death, Karṇa killed half of the Pāṇḍava forces who had survived the earlier slaughter; then he lists the Kaurava leaders who have met their deaths. He blames this disaster on Dhṛtarāṣṭra himself. Dhṛtarāṣṭra requests the names of the fallen Pāṇḍava warriors, and Saṃjaya supplies them. Finally Dhṛtarāṣṭra asks which of his warriors still survive, and Saṃjaya gives their names. Dhṛtarāṣṭra faints once more.* [5] *When he recovers,*

*he extols Karṇa's incomparable prowess as a warrior and expresses amazement and despair that one so mighty should have been slain. He argues that the power of fate alone can be responsible for Duryodhana's foolishness and the disaster to which it has led, and he demands to hear in detail all the circumstances.*

[6] — *Saṃjaya resumes his narration.* — *After Droṇa's death, Duryodhana rallies his troops and continues the battle till nightfall; then he withdraws to his camp and consults with his allies. Aśvatthāman proposes that Karṇa be appointed commander. Duryodhana approves this suggestion and asks Karṇa to assume the command; Karṇa accepts, and receives honours and blessings from the assembled Kauravas.*

[7] *On the sixteenth day of the battle Duryodhana commands the army to be arrayed, and Karṇa comes out to lead it; at the sight of him, the Kauravas forget their woes. He stations his leading warriors in positions of his choosing. Yudhiṣṭhira now tells Arjuna that Karṇa is the Kauravas' one remaining warrior of true might, and urges him to kill him. Arjuna positions his own chief warriors within the Pāṇḍavas' Half-moon formation, and, with a mighty noise of musical instruments and lion-roars, the two armies prepare to do battle against one another.*

[8] *Fierce fighting commences. Bhīma, riding an elephant and heading a powerful force, advances against the Kauravas. He is attacked by the Kulūta king Kṣemadhūrti, also mounted on an elephant, and the two men fight with lances and arrows. Kṣemadhūrti pierces Bhīma in the chest with a lance; in return Bhīma wounds his elephant with arrows and pursues it as it flees, but Kṣemadhūrti continues his assault and succeeds in killing Bhīma's elephant. Bhīma, who has leapt clear, now crushes Kṣemadhūrti's elephant with his club; when Kṣemadhūrti attacks him on foot he kills him too, and the Kaurava troops flee in dismay.*

[9] *Now Karṇa begins to inflict heavy casualties on the Pāṇḍava army with his arrows. Nakula advances to attack him, while Bhīma attacks Aśvatthāman, and other warriors from both sides pair up to fight one another. Sātyaki and the two Kekaya brothers, Vinda and Anuvinda,*[1] *exchange showers of arrows so dense that they cause darkness. Sātyaki's bow is severed, but he takes up another and cuts off Anuvinda's head with a razor-edged arrow. Vinda fights on, and*

1 Not the two princes of Avanti who bore the same names: these have already been killed by Arjuna (see 7.74).

*he and Sātyaki continue to exchange great numbers of arrows, and then to fight with swords. Finally Vinda is killed by a blow from Sātyaki, who now mounts another chariot and routs the Kekaya troops.*

[**10**] *Arjuna's son Śrutakarman attacks King Citrasena,*[1] *and the two exchange many arrows. Śrutakarman succeeds in overcoming Citrasena; he cuts off his head and puts his followers to flight. Yudhiṣṭhira's son Prativindhya likewise does battle against Citrasena's brother Citra; after a fierce fight he slays him and routs the Kaurava forces. Only Aśvatthāman stands firm, and he attacks Bhīma.* [**11**] *The two warriors shower great numbers of arrows on each other and wound each other repeatedly: sometimes, concealed by the masses of their own flying arrows, they are like the sun and moon hidden by cloud, but then they blaze forth into sight once again. The clash of their mighty weapons illuminates the horizon like doomsday fire, and the Siddhas applaud the two warriors. Eventually both are rendered unconscious by each other's arrows, and their charioteers bear them away.*

[**12**] *Arjuna battles against a force of warriors sworn to kill him;*[2] *warding off their attacks, he slays them in large numbers, winning the praise of the celestials. Seeing this great wonder, Aśvatthāman now challenges Arjuna. Arjuna accepts the challenge, and the two warriors engage in combat. Aśvatthāman's arrows fall on Kṛṣṇa and Arjuna in their millions, but Arjuna breaks every one of them into three pieces, destroying them like a wind dispersing mist. Then whilst continuing to do battle with Aśvatthāman, he resumes his deadly onslaught on the sworn warriors, destroying many of their force. Aśvatthāman keeps up his assault, until at Kṛṣṇa's urging Arjuna attacks him with such vehemence that his horses bear him away; realizing that Kṛṣṇa and Arjuna are invincible, he makes no attempt to resume the fight.*

[**13**] *The Magadha chief Daṇḍadhāra, mounted on his terrible elephant, is causing great carnage in the northern section of the Pāṇḍava army, and Kṛṣṇa drives Arjuna there. Arjuna attacks Daṇḍadhāra, and the two warriors engage in battle; after several exchanges, Arjuna slays the elephant and its rider with his arrows. Daṇḍadhāra's brother Daṇḍa takes up the fight, but Arjuna severs his arms and head, and kills his elephant; then he kills other mighty elephants,*

**1** Not the son of Dhṛtarāṣṭra who bore the same name, and who was killed at 7.112 (and then reappeared at 7.143).

**2** See 7.16.

*until the forces of Magadha are destroyed. The Pāṇḍava troops praise Arjuna for saving them; Arjuna returns to his battle against the sworn warriors.* **[14]** *They attack him in their thousands, but he smashes their chariots, elephants and horses, and dispatches their fighting men to heaven. Kṛṣṇa accuses him of toying with his enemies, instead of destroying them swiftly in order to take up his task of killing Karṇa. In response, Arjuna redoubles his assault. Kṛṣṇa describes the scene on the battlefield at length: there has been so much killing on Duryodhana's account, but Arjuna's deeds are worthy of him, or of Indra himself.*

*Meanwhile the Pāṇḍya king is slaying great numbers of Kaurava warriors.* **[15]** *— Dhṛtarāṣṭra asks to hear in detail of Pāṇḍya's deeds, and Saṃjaya narrates. — Pāṇḍya regards himself as equal to all the mightiest warriors of the Kauravas and Pāṇḍavas. He is causing great slaughter among Karṇa's forces when Aśvatthāman challenges him. Pāṇḍya accepts the challenge, and a fierce battle gets under way between the two men. In the eighth part of a day, Aśvatthāman shoots as many arrows as would be carried in eight carts, each drawn by eight oxen. He overwhelms Pāṇḍya and destroys his chariot, but refrains from slaying him, wishing to prolong the fight. Pāṇḍya now mounts a riderless elephant and resumes his attack, breaking Aśvatthāman's crown; enraged, Aśvatthāman cuts Pāṇḍya's elephant to pieces and severs his arms and head.*

**[16]** *Kṛṣṇa points out to Arjuna that Karṇa is slaying the Sṛñjaya forces, and he hastens to protect Yudhiṣṭhira against this danger. A terrible battle takes place. Karṇa causes great destruction among the forces of the Pāṇḍavas and their allies; he is attacked by the Pāñcāla leaders together with Draupadī's sons, the twins Nakula and Sahadeva, and Sātyaki. The battlefield is covered with the bodies of the fallen.*

**[17]** *Dhṛṣṭadyumna comes under heavy attack, and the Pāṇḍavas and Pāñcālas ride to his rescue. Sātyaki kills the king of Vaṅga, while Sahadeva destroys the elephant of the Puṇḍra king and Nakula slays the Aṅga lord. The elephant-fighters of Aṅga attack him, but his Pāṇḍava and Pāñcāla allies join in the fight and slay them, before turning on Karṇa himself. Meanwhile Duḥśāsana attacks Sahadeva, and the two men join in combat. After a fierce exchange of arrows, Duḥśāsana loses consciousness and is borne away by his charioteer. Now Nakula challenges Karṇa, threatening to kill him; Karṇa derides Nakula but accepts the challenge. The two warriors exchange vast numbers of arrows, until Karṇa kills Nakula's charioteer and horses, and destroys his chariot. Nakula stands brandishing an iron bar, but Karṇa continues his assault until Nakula* *flees in distress. Karṇa catches up with him, hangs his bow round his neck, and advises him not to fight with his seniors; but, remembering his conversation with Kuntī,*[1] *he spares his life and lets him go. Then he launches a savage assault on the Pāṇḍava forces.*

**[18]** *Ulūka attacks Yuyutsu and overcomes him; Dhṛtarāṣṭra's son Śrutakarman does battle with Nakula's son Śatānīka; Śakuni and Sutasoma fight fiercely. Kṛpa attacks Dhṛṣṭadyumna with such might that he is completely overwhelmed; he orders his charioteer to retreat to a safe position near Arjuna or Bhīma, and the charioteer does so while Kṛpa pursues them, still shooting. Śikhaṇḍin and Kṛtavarman shower each other with arrows until Śikhaṇḍin loses consciousness and is borne away by his charioteer, and the Pāṇḍava forces flee.* **[19]** *Arjuna is assailed by a huge Kaurava force, but he kills its leaders and then deploys the Weapon of Indra against the rest, till the mountainous piles of the slain make the earth impassable.*

*Meanwhile Yudhiṣṭhira and Duryodhana are engaged in combat. Yudhiṣṭhira kills Duryodhana's horses and his charioteer, but Karṇa, Aśvatthāman and Kṛpa come to his aid; Yudhiṣṭhira is likewise joined by the other Pāṇḍavas, and a fierce battle takes place. There is great loss of life on both sides as noon passes.* **[20]** *— Dhṛtarāṣṭra asks to hear more about the course of the battle between Yudhiṣṭhira and Duryodhana, and Saṃjaya narrates. — Duryodhana mounts another chariot and resumes his attack on Yudhiṣṭhira. The two kings shower each other with arrows, piercing each other repeatedly. Then as Duryodhana stands on his chariot brandishing a club, Yudhiṣṭhira hurls a terrible spear at him, and he loses consciousness and falls. Kṛtavarman hurries to his rescue, and Bhīma rushes to attack Kṛtavarman.*

**[21]** *Karṇa leads the Kaurava forces in a fierce encounter that leaves many warriors dead. He attacks Sātyaki, but then Arjuna begins an assault on the Kauravas, slaying many. Duryodhana engages him in combat, but Arjuna overwhelms him, Aśvatthāman, Kṛpa, Kṛtavarman and Duḥśāsana, and then attacks Karṇa. Karṇa abandons his attack on Sātyaki and devotes his attention to Kṛṣṇa and Arjuna, whom he pierces with many arrows; he is assailed by all the greatest Pāṇḍava warriors, but overcomes them. Meanwhile Arjuna, warding off Karṇa's arrows, is slaughtering the Kaurava forces. The sun sets; the Kauravas retreat from the field, and the Pāṇḍavas return happily to their camp.*

1 See 5.144.

[**22**] — *Dhṛtarāṣṭra remarks that it is only through Arjuna's choice that anyone survived at all; those who fought against him deserve praise, not blame. He asks to hear what the Kauravas did next; Saṃjaya tells him that they placed their hopes on Karṇa. Dhṛtarāṣṭra replies that Karṇa would not be able to defeat the Pāṇḍavas, and blames fate for the woeful situation he is in. Saṃjaya answers that the blame lies with Dhṛtarāṣṭra himself, but that there is no point in grieving over what is past. He resumes his narration. — In the morning of the seventeenth day of fighting Karṇa approaches Duryodhana and tells him that today either he will kill Arjuna or Arjuna will kill him. He no longer has his mighty Spear,*[1] *so Arjuna will attack him. Karṇa has the better bow, though Arjuna has a divine bowstring and inexhaustible arrow-cases; but Arjuna's advantage is that Kṛṣṇa is his charioteer. Karṇa asks to have Śalya as his own charioteer: in this way he will outmatch Arjuna. Duryodhana gives his agreement.*

[**23**] *Duryodhana approaches Śalya and asks him to act as Karṇa's charioteer. Śalya is furious at this insult: he does not consider Karṇa to be a better warrior, and he will not demean himself, a king, by acting as charioteer to a Sūta. As Śalya prepares to depart for his home, Duryodhana tries to win him round, explaining that he considers neither Karṇa nor himself to be a better warrior. The reason for asking him to act as charioteer is that, just as the world considers Karṇa superior to Arjuna, so it considers Śalya superior to Kṛṣṇa. Mollified, Śalya agrees to act, but adds that he will speak to Karṇa in accordance with a promise he has made.*[2]

[**24**] *Duryodhana now narrates a story to Śalya. — After the defeat of the demons by the gods, the three demons Tārakākṣa, Kamalākṣa and Vidyunmālin perform fierce austerities until Brahmā offers them a boon. They choose invulnerability towards all creatures, but Brahmā replies that that is impossible. They then choose to live separately for a thousand years, each in his own fortress, and for those three fortresses then to be combined into one: whichever god can destroy the triple fortress with a single arrow will kill them. This is granted, and so Tārakākṣa rules a golden fortress in the heavens, Kamalākṣa a silver fortress in the air and Vidyunmālin an iron fortress on the earth. As a reward for his asceticism, Tārakākṣa's son Hari obtains a lake in which fallen demon warriors are returned to life. The demons now lord it over the whole world,*

**1** See 7.154–5.

**2** See 5.8.

*and not even Indra can overcome them. On Brahmā's advice the gods appeal to Śiva; they praise him greatly and ask for his help. Śiva advises them that they will defeat the demons by taking half of his own fiery energy, but they answer that they will be unable to bear it. Instead, he takes half of their energy, and thenceforth becomes known as Mahādeva, the great god. At his request the gods create for him a wonderful chariot and bow consisting of the might of the entire universe. Śiva demands a being superior to himself to be the driver, and Brahmā undertakes the task. The three fortresses become one, and Śiva destroys it with a single arrow. — Duryodhana tells Śalya that in the same way he, though superior to both Kṛṣṇa and Karṇa, should drive Karṇa's chariot in battle. He also reminds Śalya of Rāma son of Jamadagni, who obtained celestial weapons from Śiva as a reward for his devotion and for defeating the demons in battle. Rāma himself taught Karṇa archery and gave him weapons; he would not have done this for a mere Sūta. Mighty Karṇa, who was born with armour and earrings, must be the son of a god born into a Kṣatriya lineage.*

[25] *Duryodhana repeats his request to Śalya to act as charioteer to Karṇa, and he agrees to do so, but adds that he must be pardoned for anything he may say to Karṇa out of a desire for what is good. He also assures Karṇa that he is an excellent charioteer.* [26] *Then he makes ready Karṇa's chariot, and he and Karṇa mount. Duryodhana pronounces a blessing, imploring Karṇa either to kill or capture the Pāṇḍavas, and Karṇa instructs Śalya to drive him into battle so that he may slay Yudhiṣṭhira and his brothers. In reply Śalya tells him not to underestimate the Pāṇḍavas: they are invincible, and even Indra would be afraid of them. But Karṇa ignores him. When the Kaurava forces see Karṇa preparing for battle, they are overjoyed; terrible portents appear indicating their coming destruction, but they take no notice. Karṇa now boasts to Śalya of his great prowess, and orders him to drive where the Pāṇḍavas and their allies are: he will slay them in battle. In particular, he will kill Arjuna, even if the gods themselves come to protect him. In reply, Śalya tells him to stop bragging: Arjuna is a far greater hero than Karṇa, and if Karṇa fights him he will die. Karṇa is furious, but commands Śalya to drive him into battle. He travels forward, slaying enemies as he goes, seeking for Arjuna.*

[27] *To every Pāṇḍava warrior whom he meets, Karṇa promises vast wealth if he will show him where Arjuna is.*

Saṃjaya spoke:
The Kaurava army were delighted as the mighty chariot-fighter Karṇa son of Rādhā, the tormentor of his enemies, boasted of how he would plunge into battle. But Śalya king of Madra laughed at him, and retorted, 'Son of a Sūta, do not proudly give away gold or a team of six bull elephants to any man! Today you shall meet wealth-winner Arjuna. Like a silly child you are handing out riches as though you were Kubera the god of wealth, but today, son of Rādhā, you will not need to exert yourself to meet the wealth-winner! Why do you pointlessly give so much away like a fool? In your folly you are forgetting the evils that arise from giving to those who are unworthy. That wealth of which you speak so much could be used by you to perform many kinds of sacrifices; Sūta, perform them! As for your foolish desire to slay Kṛṣṇa and Arjuna, that is utterly vain – I have never heard of a jackal killing a pair of lions in battle! You desire that which you should not, for you have no friends to hold you back as you rush headlong into fire. You are ignorant of what should be done at what time, and so time has ripened you for picking, make no doubt! For why would any man who aspires to live speak such utter nonsense, unfit for human ears? Your plan of action is like swimming across the ocean with a boulder tied round your neck, or leaping from a mountain-top! If you want to achieve something good, then do not fight with the wealth-winner until you have all your soldiers with you and are protected by their arrayed ranks. I tell you this to benefit Dhṛtarāṣṭra's son, not from any wish to cause harm. If you want to live, believe what I have said!'

'I put my trust in my own valour as I seek out Arjuna on the battlefield,' answered Karṇa. 'But you are an enemy with the face of a friend, trying to frighten me. No one today shall turn me aside from my resolve – not even Indra brandishing his thunderbolt, much less a mere mortal!'

After Karṇa had spoken, Śalya king of Madra made his reply, hoping once more to enrage Karṇa beyond measure: 'When sharp-pointed stork-feathered arrows pursue you, dextrously shot by Arjuna, impelled by his strength and hastened by his bowstring, then you will regret attacking him! When Kuntī's ambidextrous son takes up his celestial bow, its brightness illuminating the whole army, and torments you with

his sharp arrows, then you will repent, son of a Sūta! As a child might
lie in its mother's lap and long to grab the moon, so you in your folly
stand eagerly on your chariot and long to defeat Arjuna today. Karṇa,
by seeking to fight today with Arjuna you are clasping a sharp-bladed
trident to flail all your own limbs, for his deeds are as sharp as blades.
35 For you to challenge Arjuna today, Sūta's son, is as if a spirited but
foolish little fawn should challenge a mighty maned lion standing ready
to spring. Son of a Sūta, do not challenge the heroic prince, like a
well-fed jackal challenging a maned lion in the forest; do not die in an
encounter with Kuntī's son!

'Karṇa, if you challenge Arjuna to battle, you are a hare challenging
a mighty elephant with tusks like plough-shafts, its temporal glands
bursting with rut. If you want to fight the son of Kuntī, you are a silly
child poking with a stick a deadly poisonous king cobra in its hole, its
hood expanded. You are roaring your foolish defiance at Pāṇḍu's lion-
like son, Karṇa, like a jackal roaring defiance at an angry maned lion;
40 you are challenging Kuntī's son the wealth-winner as a sparrow might
challenge spirited Garuḍa, best of birds, to compete at flying. You are
trying to cross the terrible ocean without a boat, while it swirls at high
tide with its waves and its mighty fish. Karṇa, if you challenge Arjuna
to battle, you are a calf challenging a fighting bull with sharp horns and
a neck like a drum. Like a frog croaking at a great thundercloud that
brings the world all the water it wants, so you croak at Arjuna, who
is an Indra in human form. And, Karṇa, like a dog confined at home,
snarling at a tiger in the forest, you snarl at the tiger-like wealth-winner.

45 'The jackal that lives in the forest surrounded by hares considers itself
to be a lion, until it sees a lion; and in the same way you too, son of
Rādhā, want to think yourself a lion, until you see the foe-taming,
tiger-like hero, the wealth-winner Arjuna. You may consider yourself
a tiger until you see Kṛṣṇa and Arjuna standing together on a single
chariot, looking like sun and moon; until you hear the twang of Arjuna's
bow Gāṇḍīva in battle, you may speak as you please, O Karṇa; but once
you see him, roaring like a tiger, filling the horizon with the din of his
50 chariot and the twang of his bow, a jackal is what you will be. You are
for ever a jackal, and the wealth-winner for ever a lion; always you seem
like a jackal, fool, because you detest heroes so. As a mouse is to a cat

in strength, as a dog is to a tiger, as a jackal is to a lion, as a hare is to an elephant, as untruth is to truth, as poison is to nectar, so are you to Kuntī's son; so your deeds proclaim you both.'

*Enraged, Karṇa retorts that he knows Arjuna's abilities and can match them; he will kill Arjuna and Kṛṣṇa, and then Śalya himself. Śalya is a Madra, and the Madras are notorious barbarians, but Karṇa will hold fast to the Kṣatriya* dharma *in fighting for his dear friend Duryodhana; a treacherous Madra cannot prevent him. He commands Śalya to drive him onward.*

**[28]** *In reply, Śalya tells Karṇa a story. A certain crow, grown proud as a result of the indulgence shown to it by the children of a Vaiśya, challenged the leader of a group of geese to a flying contest. When the geese mocked it, the crow insisted that it would demonstrate 101 different ways of flying; the chief goose answered that it knew only one way. The two birds set off, and at first the crow's agility allowed it to outdo the steady flight of the goose. But then the goose began to fly over the ocean, and the crow, finding nowhere to alight, became exhausted and fell into the water; it confessed its error and begged the goose to rescue it, and the goose did so. Śalya tells Karṇa that he is like the crow, looking down on his betters in his pride at Duryodhana's indulgence towards him: he has shown no heroism in the past, and he should realize that Kṛṣṇa and Arjuna are men like lions, whereas he is a man like a dog.*

Saṃjaya spoke:
**[29]** When Adhiratha's son Karṇa heard these unpleasant words spoken by the king of Madra, he was displeased, and he answered Śalya, 'I know what kind of men Arjuna and Kṛṣṇa Vāsudeva are. The might and the great weapons of Kṛṣṇa, who drives the chariot, and of Arjuna son of Pāṇḍu, are known exactly to me here and now, whereas you, Śalya, have no direct knowledge of them. I shall fearlessly engage Kṛṣṇa and Arjuna in battle, though they are unassailable, the best of all who bear arms. But what causes me greater anguish today is the curse laid on me by Rāma Jāmadagnya, and by a noble Brahmin.

'Long ago, disguised as a Brahmin, I lived with Rāma, seeking celestial weapons; it was there, Śalya, that Indra king of the gods frustrated me in order to favour this very Arjuna. Having taken the hideous form of an insect, he came up to my thigh and bored into it, while I, for fear of disturbing my teacher, remained motionless. But when he awoke, that Brahmin saw what had happened, and questioned me. I replied, "Great seer, I am a Sūta," and then he cursed me: "Sūta, since you have obtained this weapon by fraud, it will fail to appear for you when you need it. It will appear save at the time of your death, for *brahman* cannot remain permanently with one who is not a Brahmin."

'The measureless, turbulent mass of water covers the ocean with mountainous waves, seeking to overwhelm all the multitudes of creatures; it is the shore that holds it back. Kuntī's son is the best of all who bend the bow in the world today, shooting volleys of unfailing feathered arrows that pierce the vital organs of heroes and slay them; I am the one who will combat him in battle. So, as the shore resists the ocean, I will forcibly withstand the fierce, unassailable son of Kuntī with his enormous strength and his mighty weapons, as he overwhelms the princes with the torrents of his arrows. No other man who bears a bow may be reckoned his equal in warfare, for he could defeat the very gods and demons. See me do battle against him today! Pāṇḍu's son is exceedingly proud and bellicose, and he will assail me with mighty celestial weapons; but on the battlefield I shall destroy his weapons with my own, and lay low the son of Kuntī with my excellent arrows!

'Though he shines like the sun, blazing in glory with all his rays and driving out darkness, I, like a huge cloud, shall overshadow wealth-winner Arjuna with my arrows! Though he burns like a smoke-crested flame, scorching this world with his fiery energy, I, becoming a cloud, shall extinguish Kuntī's son in battle with the showers of my arrows! Though he buffets and beats like a mighty wind, fierce and shattering, I, like Mount Himālaya, shall bear in battle the force of the furious, merciless wealth-winner!

'He may have great skill in the coursing of chariots; he may always fight in the van, heroic in combat yet detached; he may be the best of all bowmen in the world; but I shall withstand the wealth-winner in battle! No other among men who bear bows is his equal in warfare today; he could vanquish this entire world. I know this, and I am going to fight him! In Khāṇḍavaprastha the ambidextrous warrior defeated all

creatures, including the gods.[1] What other man but me, hoping to save
his own life, would seek to do battle with him?

'I would gladly speak out in an assembly of Kṣatriyas of the manliness
of Arjuna son of Pāṇḍu; but by what right did you, a snarling, dimwitted
fool, speak of it to me? For you are disagreeable, cruel and hard-hearted; 20
an unforgiving man yourself, you utter base slander of those who forgive.
I could slay hundreds like you – but compassion and fate prompt me
to forgive you. You have spoken unpleasant words to me to wound
me and benefit the Pāṇḍava, you wicked fool; but I retain my honesty
while you, with your crooked ways, are cursed as a betrayer of your
friends – for he is a friend who walks with one for seven steps.[2] This is
a time of death, a most terrible time, now that Duryodhana has gone
to war. But because I desire to see him succeed in his aims, I shall
always follow him, whereas you bear him no friendship. What makes
a friend a friend, O bestower of honour, is affection, delight, pleasure,
helpfulness, joy; and all of these I feel towards Duryodhana. What makes
an enemy an enemy is aggression, retribution, sharpness, injuriousness;
and all of these I generally feel towards you. So to please Duryodhana 25
and displease you, and for the sake of glory, and myself, and my god, I
shall do battle with all my effort against Kṛṣṇa Vāsudeva and the son of
Pāṇḍu: see me perform this feat today!

'See today my excellent weapons, both human and celestial, including
Weapons of Brahmā! I shall attack Arjuna of fierce valour, like one rutting
elephant attacking another. Concentrating my mind, I shall hurl my
matchless, invincible Weapon of Brahmā at the son of Kuntī to defeat
him. He will not escape from that, so long as the wheel of my chariot
does not become stuck in rough ground in the course of battle.

'I have no fear of Yama with his staff, Varuṇa with his noose, Kubera
with his club, Indra with his thunderbolt, or any other being bent on
killing me; so understand, Śalya, that I do not fear, that I am fearless.
Thus I am not afraid of Kuntī's son or of Kṛṣṇa the stirrer of men, 30
and in this conflict I shall do battle against them. But a Brahmin once
cursed me: "When you are fighting in battle, and encounter danger

1 See 1.214 ff.

2 Cf. 3.281.22.

in a hard place, may your wheel fall into a fissure in the ground!" Of those words of a Brahmin I am mightily afraid, for they are the lords of Soma, who rule over happiness and unhappiness. By accident I had killed the calf of his oblation cow[1] as it grazed in the wild, Śalya, far from that ascetic Brahmin. I presented him 700 elephants with tusks like plough-shafts, and hundreds of slaves and slave-girls, but that lord of the
35 twice-born did not pardon me. I brought him 14,000 black cows, each with a white calf, but I did not obtain pardon from the most excellent Brahmin. A rich dwelling filled with everything he could desire, and whatever wealth I have: all this I offered to him with due honour, but he did not want it. Then as I continued to beg forgiveness for my crime, he spoke again: "Sūta, what I have said will come to be; it cannot happen otherwise. An untrue speech would kill creatures and so incur sin; therefore to preserve my *dharma* I dare not speak untruth. You must not harm my position as a Brahmin. As for the atonement you have performed, no one in this world can make my words false, so you must stop it now."

40 'I have told you this out of friendship, Śalya, though you have insulted me, and I know you still blame me. Now remain silent, and hear my answer to you.'

**[30]** *Karṇa now insists that Śalya will not succeed in frightening him. He goes on to discourse at length on the immorality of the Madra and Bāhlika peoples; Śalya replies that there are good and bad people everywhere. Karṇa orders him to drive forward.* **[31]** *Then he arrays his forces against Dhṛṣṭadyumna's army, and attacks Yudhiṣṭhira. — Dhṛtarāṣṭra asks Saṃjaya to tell him more about Karṇa's array and how the battle proceeded, and Saṃjaya proceeds to do so. — The Kaurava army is vast; Karṇa is in the centre at its head. Seeing it, Yudhiṣṭhira assigns to each of his closest supporters a particular enemy to fight: Arjuna is to take on Karṇa. Seeing his chariot advancing towards them, Śalya points out to Karṇa the many portents of destruction and warns him that his men will die in their thousands. All the Pāṇḍavas are as mighty as Arjuna, and all are ready to fight.*

**[32]** *Arjuna does battle with a force of warriors sworn to kill him, slaying them*

1 A cow kept by Brahmins to give milk for their oblations.

*in huge numbers. Other encounters take place between Kaurava and Pāṇḍava heroes. Karṇa attacks the Pāñcālas, killing many of them; his two younger sons, Suṣeṇa and Satyasena, act as guardians of his wheels, and his eldest son Vṛṣasena protects his rear. He is attacked in turn by Dhṛṣṭadyumna and many of the foremost Pāṇḍava warriors. Bhīma slays Satyasena, and he and Nakula and Sātyaki attack Karṇa and his remaining sons, but Vṛṣasena fights them off fiercely. Karṇa comes under attack from a number of Pāṇḍava warriors; in response, he shoots arrows so fast that they appear to cover earth, air and sky in all directions. Forcing his enemies to give way, he then penetrates Yudhiṣṭhira's force and attacks him.*

**[33]** *Karṇa slays many thousands of Pāṇḍava warriors as he seeks to reach Yudhiṣṭhira; finally he is checked by the Pāṇḍavas, Pāñcālas and Kekayas, and he and Yudhiṣṭhira fight. There is a fierce exchange of arrows, and then a group of leading Pāṇḍava warriors joins in to protect Yudhiṣṭhira. Karṇa deploys the Weapon of Brahmā against them and continues his assault on Yudhiṣṭhira, severing his bow, cutting off his armour and reducing his chariot to fragments. When Yudhiṣṭhira flees, Karṇa mocks him for his failure to behave like a Kṣatriya, but lets him go. Karṇa attacks Yudhiṣṭhira's supporters, and they retreat with him; but Yudhiṣṭhira mounts another chariot and urges them back into the fray. There is a violent battle, and the Kaurava forces flee before the Pāṇḍava onslaught.*

**[34]** *Karṇa rides to attack Bhīma. Seeing Karṇa coming, Bhīma tells Sātyaki and Dhṛṣṭadyumna to protect Yudhiṣṭhira while he engages with him: one of them will kill the other. Śalya tells Karṇa that Bhīma appears even more furious than when Abhimanyu and Ghaṭotkaca were killed, but Karṇa laughs. He says that Śalya is right, but that if he succeeds in battle against Bhīma he will find himself facing Arjuna, which is his great desire. Śalya now drives him to where Bhīma is attacking the Kaurava forces, and the two warriors exchange many arrows. Eventually one of Bhīma's arrows renders Karṇa unconscious, and Śalya bears him away.*

**[35]** *— Dhṛtarāṣṭra asks Saṃjaya how Duryodhana reacted to Karṇa's defeat, and Saṃjaya narrates. — Duryodhana commands various of his brothers to go to Karṇa's aid, and they rush towards Bhīma like moths towards a flame. They surround him and shower him with arrows, but he slays one after another, till the rest flee. Seeing this, Karṇa returns to attack Bhīma a second time, and soon deprives him of his chariot; Bhīma leaps down club in hand, and* *destroys hundreds of elephants, chariots, footsoldiers, chariot-fighters and horses. Then he mounts another chariot to resume his battle with Karṇa. Karṇa attacks first Yudhiṣṭhira, then Bhīma once again. Seeing Karṇa and their other leaders engaging with the enemy, the Kaurava forces rally, and the terrible battle between the two sides resumes.*

**[36]** *The battle rages on. Elephants tear at each other with their tusks; others lie slain on the battlefield, and yet others run amok. Horses too run hither and thither, or lie writhing in pain. Fallen men cry out, and running men call to each other; severed arms twist on the ground like snakes. Rivers of blood flow, and carrion creatures come to feed on the dead. Meanwhile great warriors fight on, and the Kaurava army begins to sink like a holed ship.*

**[37]** *Arjuna is attacked by a force of warriors sworn to kill him, and by Suśarman, king of Trigarta. One of Suśarman's arrows pierces Arjuna's banner with its emblem of a great monkey; the monkey roars, and the Kaurava army swoons at the sound. When they recover, they surround Arjuna's chariot and attempt to seize him and Kṛṣṇa, but Arjuna hurls them down and slays many of them with short-range arrows. He and Kṛṣṇa both blow their conches, terrifying their attackers. Then he deploys the Serpent Weapon, which binds his enemies' legs, allowing him to kill many more of them. Suśarman replies with the Eagle Weapon, causing eagles to devour the snakes binding the legs of his men. He also shoots an arrow which renders Arjuna briefly unconscious; however, Arjuna recovers and deploys the Weapon of Indra, releasing arrows which slay the Kaurava forces in thousands.*

**[38]** *Duryodhana and his leading allies attempt to rally their forces. Kṛpa does battle with Śikhaṇḍin, while other Kauravas engage in combat with the chief Pāṇḍava warriors. Suketu observes that Śikhaṇḍin is being overcome by Kṛpa, and attacks the latter himself, allowing Śikhaṇḍin to withdraw from the fight. After a brief but fierce exchange of arrows, Kṛpa beheads Suketu with a single broad shaft. Dhṛṣṭadyumna and Kṛtavarman likewise shower arrows upon each other, till Dhṛṣṭadyumna kills Kṛtavarman's charioteer.* **[39]** *Aśvatthāman attacks Yudhiṣṭhira, performing amazing feats of archery. Sātyaki and the sons of Draupadī, who are guarding Yudhiṣṭhira, counterattack. Aśvatthāman continues to battle against them and against Yudhiṣṭhira himself; he slays Sātyaki's charioteer, and inflicts great casualties on the Pāṇḍava forces. Yudhiṣṭhira reviles him for his behaviour, which resembles that of a Kṣatriya rather than a Brahmin, but Aśvatthāman does not answer him.*

[**40**] *Karṇa and Bhīma fight, then separate to attack the Pāñcālas and Kauravas respectively. Duryodhana does battle with Nakula and Sahadeva; Dhṛṣṭadyumna sees that the twins are in imminent danger of death, and intervenes. He and Duryodhana exchange many arrows, till Dhṛṣṭadyumna destroys Duryodhana's horses, charioteer, weapons and chariot. His brothers bear him away from the battle. Meanwhile Karṇa causes great carnage among the Pāñcālas; he attacks Yudhiṣṭhira, and is then counterattacked by Dhṛṣṭadyumna with other leading Pāṇḍavas, but he continues to fight fiercely. Bhīma too continues to battle against the Kauravas, killing thousands of warriors. Arjuna, seeing Karṇa's activities, asks Kṛṣṇa to drive him towards him, and begins to slaughter the Kauravas. In response, Duryodhana once again sends thousands of sworn warriors against him, but Arjuna destroys them. Now Aśvatthāman attacks Arjuna with such vehemence that Arjuna is overwhelmed; furious, Kṛṣṇa urges him back into action, and Arjuna shoots fourteen broad arrows at Aśvatthāman, destroying his weapons and rendering him unconscious; his charioteer bears him away.*

[**41**] *Kṛṣṇa describes the battle scene to Arjuna: Karṇa is rallying the fleeing Kauravas, while Dhṛṣṭadyumna and Aśvatthāman do battle.* [**42**] *Now Dhṛṣṭadyumna leads an attack on Karṇa, and he and Karṇa exchange many arrows; then Droṇa's son Aśvatthāman attacks Dhṛṣṭadyumna, swearing to kill him in revenge for the death of Droṇa. He showers Dhṛṣṭadyumna with enormous numbers of arrows, and Dhṛṣṭadyumna replies in kind, severing Aśvatthāman's bow. Aśvatthāman takes up another bow and destroys Dhṛṣṭadyumna's weapons, horses, charioteer and chariot; Dhṛṣṭadyumna seizes a sword and shield, but Aśvatthāman destroys these also. Then he rushes at Dhṛṣṭadyumna. Kṛṣṇa sees Dhṛṣṭadyumna's danger and drives the chariot towards him, urging Arjuna to rescue him; Arjuna pierces Aśvatthāman with many arrows while Sahadeva bears Dhṛṣṭadyumna away. Aśvatthāman too is rendered unconscious by one of Arjuna's shafts, and is borne away by his charioteer, to the joy of the Pāṇḍavas' allies.*

[**43**] *Again Kṛṣṇa describes the events of the battle to Arjuna. Yudhiṣṭhira is in mortal danger from Duryodhana and Karṇa. Karṇa is causing great carnage among the Pāṇḍava forces; he is eyeing Arjuna and will soon attack him, like a moth flying into a flame. Meanwhile Bhīma is slaughtering the Kaurava forces. Seeing Bhīma's deeds, Arjuna too slays the Kauravas with his arrows.* [**44**] *Karṇa and Śikhaṇḍin do battle, till Śikhaṇḍin is overwhelmed*

*by Karṇa's arrows and has to retreat. Duḥśāsana withstands Dhṛṣṭadyumna's attack; Nakula gets the better of Vṛṣasena; Sahadeva overcomes Ulūka. Sātyaki kills Śakuni's horses and his charioteer, and Śakuni is borne away from the battle by Ulūka. Duryodhana has to retreat from Bhīma, Yudhāmanyu from Kṛpa, and Uttamaujas from Kṛtavarman.*

**[45]** *Arjuna and Aśvatthāman battle fiercely against each other, till Arjuna strikes down Aśvatthāman's charioteer with a broad arrow. Aśvatthāman now drives and fights simultaneously, but Arjuna severs his reins, and his horses bolt. Seeing this, the joyful Pāṇḍavas put the Kaurava army to rout. Duryodhana appeals to Karṇa to rally the troops, and Karṇa deploys the Weapon of Bhṛgu, which causes millions of arrows to descend on the Pāṇḍava army. So many slain warriors fall to the ground that the earth shakes, while others flee. Kṛṣṇa takes Arjuna in search of Yudhiṣṭhira, who has been wounded, but they cannot find him. Arjuna asks Bhīma for news of Yudhiṣṭhira, and Bhīma answers that he has left the battlefield after being badly wounded by Karṇa's arrows. Leaving Bhīma to do battle against the sworn warriors, Arjuna and Kṛṣṇa go to see Yudhiṣṭhira. Seeing them approach, Yudhiṣṭhira concludes that they must have killed Karṇa, and he is filled with joy.*

**[46]** *Yudhiṣṭhira congratulates Kṛṣṇa and Arjuna on having slain so mighty a warrior as Karṇa, and he describes how Karṇa had earlier defeated and humiliated him. Again and again he asks Arjuna whether he has indeed killed the enemy whom he fears and hates so much.* **[47]** *In reply, Arjuna describes how he had battled fiercely with Aśvatthāman, who finally took refuge among Karṇa's army. Then, though challenged by Karṇa himself, he had come to see Yudhiṣṭhira. Now he will do battle against Karṇa, who is slaying so many of the Pāṇḍava forces; if he does not kill him, may he suffer the fate of those who break their word.* **[48]** *Yudhiṣṭhira is furious to learn that Karṇa is still unharmed. He upbraids Arjuna fiercely, telling him that it would have been better if he had given his bow Gāṇḍīva to Kṛṣṇa and served as his driver, or if Kuntī had aborted him.*

**[49]** *Arjuna is so enraged by Yudhiṣṭhira's words that he draws his sword to kill him, for he has vowed to slay anyone who tells him to give Gāṇḍīva to another person. But Kṛṣṇa rebukes Arjuna for his lack of wisdom, adding that a wise person may acquire merit even through violence, as did Balāka, whilst a foolish and ignorant person may incur sin even when striving for* dharma, *as did Kauśika.*

*At Arjuna's request, Kṛṣṇa relates these stories.*[1] *Balāka was a hunter who used to hunt, not from desire, but to support his wife and sons and blind parents. One day he had come upon a sightless creature unlike any he had seen before. He slew it, and was carried straight to heaven, for the creature had been an ascetic planning the death of all beings. Kauśika, on the other hand, was a priest who had sworn a vow of truthfulness. Some men had fled from robbers into the forest; when the robbers approached Kauśika and demanded to know where they had gone, he told them, and they found and killed the men. For this, Kauśika entered a terrible hell.*

*Kṛṣṇa now asks Arjuna whether he still believes that he should kill Yudhiṣṭhira. Arjuna reminds him of his vow, and asks Kṛṣṇa to advise him: how may he preserve the vow without killing his brother? Kṛṣṇa's advice is that Yudhiṣṭhira spoke when weary and wounded, and so does not deserve to die: instead, Arjuna should address him without using the normal forms of respect,*[2] *for to an elder lack of respect is tantamount to death. Arjuna does so, rebuking Yudhiṣṭhira for scolding him when far from the battle himself. Bhīma, who is fighting so valiantly, has the right to scold him, but not Yudhiṣṭhira, for whose sake the battle is being fought, yet who has brought about the family's disaster himself. After speaking in this manner, Arjuna is filled with remorse and proposes to take his own life; Kṛṣṇa tells him instead to proclaim his own virtues to Yudhiṣṭhira. Arjuna does so, then takes leave of Yudhiṣṭhira so that he may go to do battle against Karṇa. But now Yudhiṣṭhira announces that he has done wrong: he cannot bear the harsh words that Arjuna has spoken, and will go into exile in the forest, leaving Bhīma to become king. Kṛṣṇa explains why Arjuna spoke as he did, and promises that Karṇa will die today. Yudhiṣṭhira thanks Kṛṣṇa for saving them from calamity.*

[50] *Arjuna is distressed to have addressed Yudhiṣṭhira in such a way, and at Kṛṣṇa's suggestion he asks for forgiveness. The two brothers are reconciled, and Arjuna vows to kill Karṇa that very day. His chariot is prepared, and he sets out towards Karṇa amongst auspicious portents. Kṛṣṇa, observing that he is anxious, praises him highly; he says that Karṇa is a great warrior whom no one but Arjuna can slay, and urges him to his task.*

[51] *Kṛṣṇa points out to Arjuna that today, on the seventeenth day of the*

1 The stories seem to be variants of those told at 3.197–206.

2 Using 'thou' instead of 'your honour'.

*battle, the Kaurava forces are greatly reduced from their original vast numbers. Arjuna himself has killed great numbers of enemies. The deaths of the mighty Kaurava leaders Bhīṣma and Droṇa were due to Arjuna, and now they are gone the Kauravas are reduced to only five great warriors: Aśvatthāman, Kṛtavarman, Karṇa, Śalya and Kṛpa. Arjuna may have reservations about killing four of these, but he should not hesitate to slay Karṇa. Karṇa has always been the Pāṇḍavas' bitterest enemy, and Arjuna should take joy in killing him.* **[52]** *Encouraged by Kṛṣṇa's words, Arjuna vows to slay Karṇa that very day, destroying the Kauravas' hopes and avenging the insults suffered by the Pāṇḍavas.*

**[53]** *The battle is raging, and heroes on both sides are engaged in combat against one another. Uttamaujas beheads Karṇa's son Suṣeṇa and destroys Kṛpa's horses and chariot; Śikhaṇḍin sees Kṛpa chariotless, but declines to attack him.* **[54]** *Meanwhile Bhīma continues to fight alone. He is attacked by a large Kaurava force, but routs it; however, he remains deeply concerned at Arjuna's continued absence. At this point he observes the ranks of the enemy fleeing in panic, and realizes that Arjuna has returned to the battle. Viśoka, his charioteer, confirms this, and Bhīma rewards him richly for announcing such welcome news.*

**[55]** *At Arjuna's command, Kṛṣṇa drives towards Bhīma. Arjuna is attacked by many Kaurava warriors, but he overwhelms them single-handed; then he penetrates the enemy army. Again he comes under attack, but he scatters his attackers like a wind dispersing clouds, and kills them in their thousands. The survivors flee, and Arjuna faces Karṇa's array. Bhīma is delighted to hear the sound of his approach, and renews his assault on the Kauravas. Duryodhana commands his men to kill him, and they strive to do so, but Bhīma slaughters them in vast numbers, causing a river of blood to flow. Now Duryodhana urges Śakuni to overcome Bhīma, and the two men engage in combat. After a fierce exchange, Bhīma succeeds in killing Śakuni's horses and charioteer and leaves him almost lifeless on the ground. Bhīma continues his rout of the demoralized Kaurava warriors, who flee; but then their retreat brings them to where Karṇa stands, and the sight of him restores their spirits.*

**[56]** *— Dhṛtarāṣṭra asks to hear how Karṇa and the other Kaurava leaders responded to Bhīma's onslaught against the Kaurava army, and Saṃjaya narrates. — Seeing Bhīma crushing the Dhārtarāṣṭra forces, Karṇa commands Śalya to drive him to the Pāñcālas, where he proceeds to slay great numbers of the Pāṇḍava troops. He is surrounded and attacked by Śikhaṇḍin, Bhīma, Dhṛṣṭadyumna, Nakula, Sahadeva, Sātyaki and the sons of Draupadī, but he overcomes them* *all and forces them to retreat; then he returns to his assault on the Pāṇḍava army, which he ravages like a lion attacking a herd of deer. The other senior Kauravas likewise slaughter the Pāṇḍavas in great numbers, while the Pāṇḍava heroes slaughter the Kauravas.*

**[57]** *Arjuna sees the various heroes fighting one another, and asks Kṛṣṇa to drive him towards Karṇa; Kṛṣṇa does so. Śalya sees him approaching and urges Karṇa to do battle against him, assuring him that he is the only warrior capable of matching Arjuna. Karṇa notes that Śalya is once again behaving agreeably towards him. Next he discourses at length on Arjuna's might and his heroic achievements; either he will kill Arjuna and Kṛṣṇa today, or they will kill him. He then asks a number of leading Kauravas to engage Arjuna in combat so as to weary him. They do so, but Arjuna is too much for them, and he overcomes them all.*

**[58]** *Now Arjuna sets about rescuing Bhīma, who is beginning to sink under the Kaurava attack. The earth is soon covered with the bodies of warriors, horses and elephants, and with broken chariots. The Kauravas flee, and Arjuna meets Bhīma and tells him that the arrows have now been removed from Yudhiṣṭhira's body. Then he does battle with ten of Dhṛtarāṣṭra's sons, and slays them.*

**[59]** *As Kṛṣṇa drives him towards Karṇa's chariot, Arjuna is attacked by ninety sworn warriors; he kills them all. Then another large body of Kauravas assails him with a great shower of arrows, but he disperses them with his own arrows. Next comes a barbarian force riding elephants; these too are slain. Bhīma observes that Arjuna is surrounded, and comes to his rescue, killing with his club those who have survived Arjuna's own attack. The two Pāṇḍava brothers continue to afflict the Kaurava forces, who flee from them. The despairing Dhārtarāṣṭras approach Karṇa; he tells them not to fear, and continues his deadly attack on the Pāñcālas.*

Saṃjaya spoke:
**[60]** Then, O king, as the Kurus were routed by the chariot-fighter Arjuna with his white horses, Karṇa the Sūta's son slaughtered the sons of the Pāñcālas with his mighty arrows, like a wind dispersing a mass of clouds. With his *añjalika* weapon he struck Janamejaya's[1] driver down

1 This refers to a Pāñcāla prince, not the Janamejaya to whom Vaiśaṃpāyana relates the *Mahābhārata*.

from his chariot and slew his horses; then he poured showers of broad arrows upon Śatānīka and Sutasoma, severing their bows. Next in that battle the Sūta's son pierced Dhṛṣṭadyumna with six arrows, and slew his rightmost horse; slaying Sātyaki's horses too, he then killed Viśoka, son of the Kekaya king. Upon the death of the prince, the Kekaya general Ugradhanvan attacked Karṇa and struck his son Suṣeṇa,[1] piercing him
5 deeply with his fiercely speeding arrows. But with three half-moon arrows Karṇa violently severed his arms and his head, and he fell lifeless from his chariot to the earth like a *śāla* tree felled with axes. Now that Sātyaki, the heroic heir of Śini, was horseless, Karṇa's son Suṣeṇa covered him with sharp, speeding arrows, seeming to dance as he did so; then he himself fell, slain by Sātyaki's arrows.

Seeing his son killed, Karṇa, his mind full of fury, longed to slay the bull of the Śinis; crying, 'Sātyaki, you are dead!' he shot at him an enemy-vanquishing arrow. But Śikhaṇḍin cut off Karṇa's arrow with three arrows, and with three more he struck Karṇa himself. Fierce Karṇa severed Śikhaṇḍin's bow and his standard with two arrows, and struck noble Śikhaṇḍin himself, piercing him with six; then, full of self-control, the noble son of Adhiratha severed the head of Dhṛṣṭadyumna's son, and pierced Sutasoma with a sharp arrow.

10 Now as the tumultuous battle proceeded, Kṛṣṇa, observing that the son of Dhṛṣṭadyumna had been killed, addressed Arjuna, O lion-like king: 'The Pāñcālas are being wiped out! Advance, son of Kuntī! Slay Karṇa!' Then with a laugh that strong-armed hero travelled in his chariot towards the chariot of Karṇa, hoping to rescue the Pāñcālas in the danger they faced from that leading chariot-fighter, who was slaughtering them. He stretched his fierce-roaring bow Gāṇḍīva, and snapped the bowstring hard against his palm. Then in an instant he created darkness with his arrows as he destroyed chariots and slew elephants, horses and men. Bhīma followed him in his chariot to protect the solitary Pāṇḍava hero from the rear; the two princes hastened in their chariots towards Karṇa, while their enemies kept out of their way.

Meanwhile the Sūta's son was fighting a great battle and crushing the Somakas. He destroyed chariots, horses and elephants in throngs and

1 Suṣeṇa was earlier said to have been killed by Uttamaujas: see 8.53.

covered the horizon with his arrows. Uttamaujas, Janamejaya and the 15
furious Yudhāmanyu and Śikhaṇḍin, together with Dhṛṣṭadyumna heir of Pṛṣata, roared loudly as together they attacked him with their arrows. The five heroic Pāñcāla chariot-fighters rushed at Karṇa the Cutter, but they could no more tip him from his chariot than sensual temptations can cause a disciplined man to fall from steadfastness. Karṇa roared like a lion as he destroyed with his shafts their bows, standards, horses, drivers, arrow-cases and banners, and struck each of them with five arrows. As he shot and slew, his hand busy with arrows and bowstring, people began to fear that the earth itself, with all its mountains and trees, was being split open by the sound of his bow. Shooting arrows with a fully stretched bow that looked like the bow of Indra,[1] the son of Adhiratha shone in battle like the sun with its corona, encircled by blazing rays.

He pierced Śikhaṇḍin with twelve sharp shafts, and Uttamaujas with 20
six; he wounded Yudhāmanyu with three swift arrows, and the Somaka prince Janamejaya and Pṛṣata's heir with three each. Sir, those five mighty foe-crushing chariot-fighters, defeated in that great battle by the Sūta's son, stood enfeebled like sensual temptations overcome by a self-possessed man. Then as they all floundered, like shipwrecked merchants, in the ocean that was Karṇa, the sons of Draupadī rescued their uncles with their well-equipped chariots like ships.

Now Sātyaki, bull of the Śinis, cut down with his sharp shafts the many arrows discharged by Karṇa; he wounded Karṇa with his iron shafts and pierced your eldest son with eight of them. Then Kṛpa, the Bhoja king Kṛtavarman and your son Duryodhana, together with Karṇa himself, struck Sātyaki with their own sharp arrows. He, the best of the Yadus, fought with all four of them like a demon lord fighting with
the four world-guardian gods; bending his roaring bow and stretching 25
it fiercely to shower numberless arrows on his enemies, Sātyaki was as unassailable as the sun in the middle of the autumn sky. The enemy-afflicting Pāñcāla chariot-fighters, once more armed and mounted, combined in that great battle to protect the heroic heir of Śini, as the hosts of the Maruts protect Indra when he subjugates his enemies. Then a most terrible battle took place between your opponents and your

1 The rainbow.

soldiers, resulting in the destruction of chariots, horses and elephants, like the battle of the gods and demons long ago. Chariots, elephants, horses and footsoldiers reeled hither and thither, covered with weapons of every kind; struck by one another, they stumbled, moaned in distress, and fell lifeless.

At this point your son Duḥśāsana, younger brother of the king, advanced fearlessly against Bhīma, showering him with arrows. Wolf-belly Bhīma rushed straight at him like a lion falling upon a large *ruru*
30 deer; then the two of them engaged in a superhuman battle as they gambled with one another in a wager for life, each enraged with the other, like mighty Indra and Śambara.[1] They struck each other fiercely with well-pointed, death-dealing arrows, like two mighty elephants, both in rut and both lusting for the same female. The wolf-belly rapidly cut off your son's bow and his standard with two razor-edged arrows, and pierced his forehead with a feathered shaft; then he severed his driver's head from his body. Prince Duḥśāsana took up another bow and pierced the wolf-belly with twelve arrows. Then, driving the chariot himself, he covered Bhīma with shower upon shower of straight-flying shafts.

[**61**] Then, as he fought in that tumultuous battle, the prince Duḥśāsana did a hard deed: he severed Bhīma's bow with a razor-edged arrow, and further pierced his charioteer with six shafts; then the noble hero swiftly wounded Bhīma with many excellent arrows. At this Bhīma, like an elephant flowing with rut, hurled his club at him in the midst of the tumult. The force of Bhīma's blow carried Duḥśāsana ten bow-lengths from his chariot; struck down by that speeding club, the prince fell, quivering. Lord of men, his horses and driver were killed and his chariot reduced to dust by that club as it fell; he writhed in a torment of agony, his armour and ornaments, his garments and garlands in ruins.

5 Then the spirited Bhīma, calling to mind the enmity enacted by your sons, leapt down from his chariot on to the ground, fixing his eye eagerly upon him. Drawing his sharp sword with its excellent blade, and treading upon the throat of the writhing man, he cut open his breast as he lay on the ground, and drank his warm blood. Then, having quaffed

1 Śambara was a demon killed by Indra.

and quaffed again, he looked about him, and in his rage spoke these extravagant words: 'Better than mother's milk, or honey with ghee, better than well-prepared mead, better than a draught of the water of heaven, or milk or curd, or the finest buttermilk, today I consider this draught of the blood of my enemy better than all of these!' With these words he rushed forward once more, bounding on in exhilaration after his drink; and those who saw him then, they too fell down, confounded with fear. And even those men who did not themselves fall, their weapons dropped from their hands, and they howled loudly
in their fear, and closed their eyes so as not to see the scene. Those on 10
all sides who saw Bhīma there, drinking that blood of Duḥśāsana, all fled, overpowered by fear, and they said, 'This is no mortal man!'

Then as the world's heroes stood listening, Bhīma spoke again. 'Here I drink the blood from your throat, basest of men! Now work yourself once more into a frenzy and call out "Cow! Cow!"[1] We were attacked as we slept at Pramāṇakoṭi; we were fed deadly poison; we were horribly bitten by snakes; our house of lac was set on fire;[2] our kingdom was stolen in a wager; we were exiled to the forest; we have suffered arrows and spears in battle, and many griefs at home. Thanks to the wickedness of Dhṛtarāṣṭra and his son, these woes are all we know – we have never known happiness!'

After uttering these words, great king, the wolf-belly spoke further 15
to Kṛṣṇa and Arjuna, smiling for the victory he had won: 'O heroes, today I have accomplished here all that I swore to do with Duḥśāsana in battle; and today I shall also fulfil my second vow by slaughtering Duryodhana like a sacrificial beast! I shall not find peace until I have trampled his head with my foot before all the Kauravas!' With these words he roared aloud in delight, his limbs all drenched with blood; noble Bhīma of mighty strength danced like thousand-eyed Indra after slaying Vṛtra.

**[62]** *Ten of Duḥśāsana's brothers attack Bhīma; Arjuna kills all of them, and the Kaurava army takes flight. Śalya urges Karṇa to do battle with Arjuna,*

1 Bhīma is referring to Duḥśāsana's jeering words at 2.68.19.

2 See 1.119.29–35, 39–41, 36–8; 1.132–6.

*reminding him that Duryodhana had given him full responsibility for the conduct of the war. Meanwhile, Karṇa's son Vṛṣasena attacks Bhīma, and is then attacked in turn by Nakula. The two heroes fight fiercely. Vṛṣasena kills Nakula's horses, but Nakula continues to fight on foot, leaping about so nimbly that he seems to fly like a bird; then he mounts Bhīma's chariot. The battle rages on. Vṛṣasena attacks the Pāṇḍavas, and Arjuna faces him; Vṛṣasena pierces him with many arrows, but in response Arjuna shoots arrows that penetrate Vṛṣasena's vital organs and sever his bow, his arms and his head. Seeing his son slain, Karṇa immediately advances against Arjuna.*

[**63**] *Arjuna and Karṇa face each other ready to do battle, two glorious, evenly matched warriors. The Dhārtarāṣṭras support Karṇa, the Pāṇḍavas Arjuna; all mortal and immortal beings likewise take sides. Indra requests Brahmā and Śiva to grant victory to Arjuna; they answer that Karṇa will attain heaven, but Arjuna and Kṛṣṇa will attain victory. The two heroes prepare to fight one another. In response to a question from Karṇa, Śalya promises that in the event of Karṇa's death he will kill both Kṛṣṇa and Arjuna; but when Arjuna puts a similar question to Kṛṣṇa, Kṛṣṇa assures him that Karṇa will not be able to slay him. Arjuna vows that soon he will avenge the insult to Draupadī and the death of Abhimanyu by killing Karṇa.*

[**64**] *Arjuna and Karṇa, each surrounded by troops of their supporters, begin to assail one another's forces. Arjuna is attacked by a group of Kauravas led by Duryodhana which he defeats easily, and then by a much larger enemy force which he slaughters, prompting celestial cries of 'Bravo!' and a shower of flowers. Aśvatthāman attempts to persuade Duryodhana to make peace with the Pāṇḍavas, but Duryodhana insists on continuing hostilities, assuring him that Karṇa will kill Arjuna. Then he orders his warriors to fight.*

Saṃjaya spoke:
[**65**] As the din of conches and kettledrums increased, Arjuna and Karṇa the Cutter, the Sūta's son, both foremost of heroes, both with white horses, met in battle, thanks to the evil policy of your son, O king. Like two rutting Himālayan elephants brandishing tusks against each other for a female, the two heroes, wealth-winner Arjuna and the son of Adhiratha, attacked each other with fierce speed. Their meeting, as both poured forth showers of arrows while their bows and chariot-wheels thundered and the bowstrings roared against their palms, was like the

chance collision of two storm-clouds, or two mountains; like the clash of two mighty mountains, teeming with peaks and trees, creepers and herbs, and with the various creatures that dwell on mountains, they struck each other with their mighty weapons. Their encounter was as fierce as that of Indra king of the gods with Virocana's son Bali long ago;[1] the bodies of their charioteers and steeds were mangled with arrows, till a river of acrid blood began to flow. No other warriors could possibly have borne it.

As their two chariots approached one another, each bearing its standard, they seemed like two great lakes lying close together, stirred by the wind, full of red and blue lotuses, fish and turtles, and resounding with the cries of flocks of birds. Both those mighty chariot-fighters resembled great Indra; both were equal to great Indra in valour; they fought each other like great Indra fighting Vṛtra, using arrows like great Indra's thunderbolts. Both armies, with their elephants, footsoldiers, horses and chariots, adorned with ornaments, garments and garlands of wonderful colours, trembled with amazement as they craned to see the battle of Arjuna and Karṇa, and so did the celestials. Passionate onlookers raised their arms and roared like lions when the son of Adhiratha advanced on Arjuna to slay him, like one rutting elephant advancing on another. Then the Somakas cried out to Kuntī's son, 'Make haste, Arjuna, go and pierce Karṇa! Do not delay! Cut off his head and Duryodhana's hopes of kingship!' And in the same way many of our fighters then called out to Karṇa, 'Go, Karṇa, go! Kill Arjuna, Karṇa, and then let Kuntī's sons return in rags for another long stay in the forest!'

It was Karṇa who now first pierced Arjuna with ten great arrows. In return, Arjuna, enraged beyond measure, pierced him in the armpit with ten sharp-pointed shafts. Then the Sūta's son and Arjuna hewed at each other with the keenest of arrows; filled with a dreadful joy, they advanced to seek out each other's weak spots in the battle. As the mighty conflict wore on, noble Bhīma lost patience; angrily beating one hand against the other and biting his lower lip, he looked as though he was dancing to the sound of an instrument. 'How can it be,' he demanded,

1 See 5.128.5 and note.

'that the son of a Sūta was first to pierce you with ten arrows, O wearer
15 of the diadem? You showed great fortitude when you vanquished all beings at Khāṇḍavaprastha to feed the god of Fire; now slay the Sūta's son with that same fortitude, or I shall smash him with my club!'

Then Kṛṣṇa Vāsudeva also addressed Kuntī's son, when he saw that warrior's arrows being struck down by his enemy: 'What is this, wearer of the diadem? Today Karṇa has utterly crushed your weapons with his own! Why are you daydreaming, hero? Are you not aware of these Kurus all roaring with joy for Karṇa, because they have seen your weapons brought down by his? You have shown great fortitude in age after age by destroying the weapons of darkness, and by slaying terrible Rākṣasas and demons in battle, as well as Dambhodbhava and his followers;[1] now slay the Sūta's son with that same fortitude! Violently sever the head of your enemy now with Sudarśana, this razor-edged discus of mine – I give it to you – like Indra beheading his enemy Namuci with his
20 thunderbolt! You showed great fortitude when you satisfied Lord Śiva in his form as a mountain man;[2] now take up that fortitude once again, hero, and slay the Sūta's son and his followers! Then, when all the hosts of your enemies lie dead, present the sea-girdled earth with all its cities and villages and wealth to King Yudhiṣṭhira, and attain matchless glory, son of Kuntī!'

When both Bhīma and Kṛṣṇa the stirrer of men urged him so, Arjuna recalled himself and considered his mettle; and, knowing as he did the reason for noble Kṛṣṇa's presence on earth, he answered him thus: 'For the good of the world and the death of the Sūta's son I shall now bring forth a mighty and fierce Weapon. Let me have your permission, sir, and also that of the gods, and Brahmā and Śiva, and those who know *brahman*.' With these words he brought forth the unbearable Weapon of Brahmā, which has to be deployed with the mind, and with it that hero of mighty ardour covered the entire horizon with arrows, both the cardinal and intermediate points; Bharata's bull-like heir shot swift-flying arrows in hundreds as though shooting a single shaft.

**1** Kṛṣṇa (Nārāyaṇa) is here referring to Arjuna's deeds as his companion Nara. For Dambhodbhava, see 5.94.

**2** See 3.40.

But Karṇa the Cutter likewise let fly hosts of arrows by the thousand 25
in the middle of the battlefield, and these thundered down on Pāṇḍu's
son like torrents of water released by a storm-cloud. Fearful in strength
and more than mortal in deed, Karṇa struck Bhīma and Kṛṣṇa and the
wearer of the diadem with three arrows each; then he roared a terrible
roar. When Kuntī's son was struck by Karṇa's shafts and saw that Bhīma
and the stirrer of men were wounded too, he could not bear it, and
he once again took up eighteen arrows. With one he pierced Suṣeṇa,[1]
with four, Śalya, and with three, Karṇa. Then with ten well-shot shafts
he slew Sabhāpati in his armour of gold, and that prince fell from
the front of his chariot, headless, armless, steedless, driverless, bowless,
bannerless, broken like a *śāla* tree felled with axes. Next he pierced 30
Karṇa with three arrows, then with eight, with two, with four, with
ten. He slew 400 elephants with the warriors who rode them; he slew
800 chariot-fighters, a thousand horses with their drivers, and 8,000
brave footsoldiers.

Onlookers reined in their steeds and remained where they were on
earth or in heaven, watching the fight between those two foremost foe-
slaying heroes, the lords of battle, Karṇa and Kuntī's son. Then the string
of the Pāṇḍava's bow, which he had drawn exceedingly tight, broke
suddenly with a very loud noise. Immediately the Sūta's son covered
the son of Kuntī with a hundred small arrows, and pierced Vāsudeva
with sixty iron arrows like snakes that have sloughed their skins, sharp,
well oiled and speeded by the feathers of birds. At this the Somakas
fled headlong. Swiftly Kuntī's son restrung his bow and scattered the
arrows shot by the son of Adhiratha, enraged as he was at the wounds to
his body from Karṇa's shafts. He joined the Somakas on the battlefield,
where his swift-flying weapons brought a darkness so dense that no birds
flew in the sky. Laughing aloud, Arjuna violently pierced Śalya's armour 35
with ten arrows; then he struck Karṇa with twelve well-shot shafts,
and again with seven more. Wounded badly by the fiercely speeding
feathered arrows swiftly propelled from the bow of Kuntī's son, Karṇa,
his limbs torn, his body doused in blood, appeared like the fierce god

1 See 8.60.4 and note; however, the reference here is probably to a son of Dhṛtarāṣṭra with the same name.

Rudra bending his bow. Then the son of Adhiratha pierced with three arrows wealth-winner Arjuna, who resembled Indra king of the gods. And in an effort to slay invincible Kṛṣṇa, he directed at him five blazing arrows like snakes. Well shot, they penetrated the bright golden armour of the highest lord; then, falling from his body, they swiftly entered the earth, where they bathed in the water of the underworld river before returning to Karṇa. But with five broad arrows, swift and well shot, the wealth-winner cut each one of them into three pieces, and they fell to the ground: they were five mighty snakes that had sided with Takṣaka's son.[1]

40 Then the wearer of the diadem blazed with anger, like fire consuming a dry thicket, and he drew his bow back to the ear to pierce Karṇa's vital organs with blazing, death-dealing arrows. Karṇa staggered with pain, but he stood steadfast, for he was a man of extreme steadfastness. Thanks to the anger of the wealth-winner, the cardinal and intermediate points of the horizon became invisible through his torrents of arrows, and so did the brightness of the sun, and Karṇa's chariot, O king, as if the sky were filled with winter fog. There were 2,000 foe-slaying chariot-fighters, excellent men picked at Duryodhana's own choice to protect the wheels of his chariots and the feet of his elephants, and to serve as his vanguard and rearguard; all these Kuru heroes, together with their chariots and horses and drivers, were dispatched in that battle in a moment, O king, by the solitary hero Arjuna, the ambidextrous bull of the Kurus. At that your sons and the surviving Kurus abandoned Karṇa
and fled, leaving scattered behind them the slain and the wounded,
45 and their grieving sons and fathers. Karṇa looked all about him, and
saw he was alone, deserted by the fear-ravaged Kurus. But he was unperturbed, heir of Bharata, and he rushed straight at Arjuna to attack him.

[**66**] The Kurus, fleeing the fall of Arjuna's arrows, their ranks broken, now halted, and they saw the wealth-winner's weapon darting all over the battlefield, like a lightning-flash. That weapon of Arjuna, swiftly released by Kuntī's furious son to slay Karṇa in the great battle, consumed the Kaurava heroes as the ever-resounding ether consumes all empty

1 At the burning of the Khāṇḍava forest: see 1.218.

space.[1] But Karṇa blew Arjuna's flaming weapon apart with the foe-
destroying magic weapon of mighty power that he had obtained from
Rāma Jāmadagnya, and he struck Kuntī's son with many sharp arrows.
Tremendous then was the battle between Arjuna and Adhiratha's son, O
king, as they attacked each other with arrows like two elephants fighting
with fierce blows of their tusks. In that battle Karṇa fixed a dreadful 5
foe-slaying arrow to his bow, keenly sharpened, snake-headed, blazing,
well oiled and deadly as venom, for it was descended from the serpent
Airāvata. For long years he had saved it for Kuntī's son, always treating
it with honour, keeping it in a golden cylinder amid sandalwood dust;
now he planned to sever Arjuna's head with that blazing arrow in battle.

At this point noble Śalya king of Madra, seeing the Cutter with that arrow fixed to his bow, said to him, 'Karṇa, this arrow of yours will never cut through a neck! Choose some head-severing arrow to fix to your bow!'

Karṇa, his eyes red with rage, answered Śalya as he obstinately aimed
the arrow, 'Śalya, Karṇa does not aim his arrow twice; warriors like me
are never devious!' With these words he released that arrow Balāhaka
that he had honoured for so many years,[2] crying, 'Arjuna, you are dead!'
as he swiftly shot the powerful shaft. But Madhu's heir Kṛṣṇa, mightiest 10
of the mighty, seeing Karṇa aim that serpent-weapon, used all his might
to tread down on the chariot with both feet; the chariot sank into the
ground, till the horses were on their knees, and so that arrow struck
wise Arjuna's diadem. Thus the Sūta's son, for all the furious effort with
which he discharged that powerful weapon, severed with his arrow only
the ornament worn by Arjuna on his head, famous throughout earth,
air, sky and water.

Brilliant as sun, moon or stars, adorned with gold and with clusters of pearls, it had been fashioned with care and austerity for Indra by the self-born Brahmā himself; very costly in appearance, yet an object of

1 The ether (*ākāśa*) is an non-perceptible but all-permeating element, the location of sound.

2 The name Balāhaka is applied to a particular race of serpents, and I take it to be used here as the name of Karṇa's serpent-weapon, identified with Takṣaka's son Aśvasena (see 1.218). Curiously, the word can also mean 'storm-cloud', and the whole phrase could mean 'a storm-cloud honoured by rain-clouds'.

fear to enemies, it was exceedingly lovely to look upon and sweet to smell, and the lord of the gods, pleased with Arjuna's slaughter of the enemies of the gods, had given it to him with his own hand for him
15 to become the diadem-wearer.[1] Not Śiva with his weapon Pināka, not Varuṇa lord of the waters with his noose, not Indra with his thunderbolt, not Kubera the protector of wealth with the finest arrow, not even the greatest gods could harm it, but Karṇa now violently severed it with his serpent-weapon. Destroyed by that excellent arrow with the fire of its venom, blazing with flames, Arjuna's glorious, much-loved diadem fell to the ground as the burning sun falls behind the western mountain at sunset.

So Karṇa's serpent-weapon forcibly struck off from Arjuna's head his gem-studded diadem, like great Indra's thunderbolt striking off a mountain's highest peak, covered with trees bearing blossom and lovely shoots. And just as happens when earth, air, sky and water are rent by storm and wind, heir of Bharata, a mighty noise arose then in all the worlds, while people resolved to stand firm, yet still staggered in distress. But Arjuna stood unperturbed, and tied up his hair with a white cloth, till he resembled the eastern mountain crowned by the rising sun blazing
20 with all its rays. As for that mighty serpent Balāhaka himself, Arjuna's sworn enemy, hurled by the arm of Karṇa and blazing bright as fire or sun, after striking Arjuna's diadem to the ground he rose up high once more and said, 'Kṛṣṇa, you should know that I have been wronged! My enmity arises from the slaying of my mother!'

Then Kṛṣṇa spoke to Kuntī's son on the field of battle, and told him to kill that mighty serpent, his sworn enemy. Hearing the words of Madhu's slayer, Arjuna, bearer of the bow Gāṇḍīva, fierce bowman against his enemies, said, 'Who is this serpent who has chosen to approach me today, as if approaching the mouth of Garuḍa himself?'

'He is one', replied Kṛṣṇa, 'whose body you pierced with your arrows as, bow in hand, you sought to satisfy the god of Fire at Khāṇḍavaprastha. Assuming a different form he took to the air, but you slew his mother.'[2]

Then victorious Arjuna, ignoring everyone else, shot six sharp arrows

1 See 3.170–71.

2 See 1.218.

with excellent blades, and cut down that serpent as it rose slantwise
into the air; its body cut to pieces, it fell to earth. At that instant, 25
Karṇa, glaring at Arjuna, pierced the heroic wealth-winner with ten stone-whetted, peacock-feathered arrows. Arjuna, striking him with twelve sharp arrows shot from a well-stretched bowstring, now released an excellent iron shaft that sped like a venomous snake as he drew it all the way back to his ear. The well-shot shaft tore through Karṇa's bright shield as if to dispel his vital breath. It drank his blood, and then entered the earth, its feathers smeared with his gore. Enraged at the wound from this arrow like a snake that is struck with a stick, he rapidly shot back many deadly shafts, as a poisonous snake would spit deadly venom. He pierced Kṛṣṇa the stirrer of men with twelve shafts, and Arjuna with ninety-nine; then, wounding Pāṇḍu's son with one more terrible arrow, he roared and laughed aloud.

The Pāṇḍava could not tolerate Karṇa's joy; with his expertise in the 30
vital organs of the body and his Indra-like valour, he powerfully pierced Karṇa's vital organs with his feathered arrows, just as Indra used his might to slay Bala. Then Arjuna shot at Karṇa ninety-nine arrows like the staff of Yama, till Karṇa was shaken by intense physical pain, as a mountain is shaken when struck by a thunderbolt; his crown, adorned as it was with wonderful jewels and the finest gold and diamonds, fell to the ground, severed by Arjuna's feathered shafts, and so too did his lovely earrings. His costly, shining armour, lovingly crafted for him over years by the best artisans, was smashed to pieces in a moment by the Pāṇḍava's arrows. Now that he was without armour, the furious Arjuna pierced him with four excellent shafts, till Karṇa, deeply afflicted by his enemy's blows, seemed like a diseased man, suffering from wounds caused by phlegm, bile and wind.[1]

Now Arjuna made haste to hew at Karṇa and pierce his vital organs 35
with all his deadly, sharp arrows, shooting them with care and power, his great bow drawn tight in a circle. Wounded badly by the Pāṇḍava's many fiercely speeding, sharp-bladed shafts, Karṇa looked like a mountain dyed red by its mineral ores, its cliffs flowing with reddened water. Then, heir of Bharata, the wearer of the diadem covered Karṇa, his

1 The three bodily humours of Indian medicine.

horse and his chariot with calves-tooth arrows, exerting himself to
envelop the very horizon with his gold-shafted bolts. Covered with
those calves-tooth arrows, the broad-chested son of Adhiratha appeared
like a mountain covered with blooming *aśoka*, *palāśa* and kapok trees[1]
and quivering sandal trees; struck on the body by so many arrows in
battle, lord of the peoples, he seemed like a mighty mountain with tree-
40 lined summits and caves, covered with lovely Karṇikāra trees. Bloodied,
but still shooting volleys of arrows like beams of light from his bow, he
looked like the disc of the sun with its red rays approaching the western
mountain at sunset; but the blazing shafts like mighty snakes shot from
the arm of Adhiratha's son were attacked and destroyed wherever they
were by sharp-bladed arrows shot from Arjuna's arm.

Then Karṇa's wheel sank into the ground. In the thick of battle
the Sūta's son was distraught to see his chariot keel over through the
Brahmin's curse, and the weapon of Rāma Jāmadagnya lose its lustre.[2]
He could not bear these disasters; he shook his fists and railed at *dharma*.
'Always experts in *dharma* have proclaimed that *dharma* protects those
who honour *dharma*. But my base *dharma* is not protecting me today,
despite my devotion to it. It does not appear to me that *dharma* always
protects!' Even as he spoke, while his horses and charioteer stumbled,
Arjuna's weapons continued to fall and set him reeling. Deluded in his
actions by the wounds to his vital organs, he railed against *dharma* again
45 and again on the battlefield.[3] He pierced Kuntī's son with three terrible
shafts, then pierced him in the hand with seven more; but Arjuna shot
at him seventeen straight-flying arrows, full of fiery energy, dreadful as
Indra's thunderbolt, burning like fire, and these pierced through him
with terrible speed before falling to the surface of the earth.

Though shaken to his very soul, Karṇa displayed his determination: he composed himself with all his strength, and then released the Weapon of Brahmā. But when Arjuna saw it, he countered by invoking the

1 The blossom of all these trees is red.

2 See 8.29.

3 At this point, unexpectedly, the narrative of the battle resumes (in *anuṣṭubh* metre, rather than the *triṣṭubhs* that have been used till now), and we do not return to Karṇa's predicament for another fifteen stanzas. This is presumably the result of two versions of the story being patched together at an early period.

Weapon of Indra; the wealth-winner consecrated with *mantras* his bow
Gāṇḍīva, his bowstring and arrows, and then shot shafts in torrents,
like Indra pouring forth rain. Those shafts issued forth from the chariot 50
of Kuntī's son and appeared, in all their fiery energy and power, in
front of Karṇa's chariot; but Karṇa, mighty chariot-fighter that he was,
thwarted them as they multiplied before him.

Then Kṛṣṇa, hero of the Vṛṣṇis, seeing that Arjuna's weapon had
been destroyed, said, 'Shoot a better weapon, son of Kuntī! Rādhā's son
is consuming all your arrows!' So Arjuna consecrated the Weapon of
Brahmā, and deployed it: he covered Karṇa with arrows, sending him
reeling. But Karṇa, enraged, severed Arjuna's bowstring with his own
well-pointed shafts. Pāṇḍu's son fitted a new string and rubbed it down
before showering Karṇa with blazing arrows in their thousands; so swift 55
was he that Karṇa could not tell when the string broke and when it was
refitted, which was a great wonder. But the son of Rādhā countered
the weapons of the ambidextrous Arjuna with his own, showing even
greater valour than Kuntī's son.

Kṛṣṇa saw that Arjuna was suffering greatly from Karṇa's shafts, and
he told him, 'Keep trying! Use your best weapon!' Then the wealth-
winner consecrated another celestial arrow: forged of iron, it was as
deadly as fire or snake-venom. The wearer of the diadem had taken up
this terrible weapon to shoot, when, in the midst of that mighty battle,
the earth swallowed up the chariot-wheel of Rādhā's son.

Karṇa shed tears of rage to see his wheel stuck, and he said to Arjuna, 60
'Forbear for a moment, O Pāṇḍava! You can see that fate has caused my
wheel to sink up to the axle; abandon your intention to act as only a
coward would do, son of Kuntī! One whose hair is dishevelled[1] or who
has turned away from battle, a Brahmin, one who has joined his hands
together; one who seeks refuge, or who has cast aside his weapons, or
been overtaken by disaster; one whose arrows are spent, or who has
lost his armour, or whose weapons are lost or broken – no hero strikes
at such a man on the battlefield, O Arjuna, nor does any prince do so
to serve his king. And you are a hero, son of Kuntī; therefore forbear
for a moment while I raise this wheel out of the earth! You should not

1 In token of supplication.

slay me, O wealth-winner, for you are mounted on a chariot and I am
standing unready on the ground. I have no fear of Kṛṣṇa Vāsudeva or
65 of you, son of Pāṇḍu, for you are the heir of Kṣatriyas and the scion of
a great lineage. So remember the teachings of *dharma*, O Pāṇḍava, and
forbear for a moment!'

**[67]** Then Kṛṣṇa Vāsudeva spoke from his chariot. 'How fortunate,
son of Rādhā, that you recall *dharma* here! Generally when low people
find themselves sunk in misfortune, they blame fate, but never this or
that misdeed of their own. When, with Duryodhana, Duḥśāsana and
Subala's son Śakuni, you had Draupadī fetched into the assembly though
she was wearing a single garment, this *dharma* of yours did not appear
then! When Śakuni, a skilled gamester, defeated Kuntī's son Yudhiṣṭhira,
who did not know how to play, where did your *dharma* go then? When
you laughed at Draupadī Kṛṣṇā, standing in the assembly in the midst
of her period because Duḥśāsana had her in his power, where did your
5 *dharma* go then? When in your greed for the kingdom you recalled
Pāṇḍu's son to gamble with Śakuni king of Gāndhāra, where did your
*dharma* go then, Karṇa?'

When he heard Vāsudeva speak thus to Karṇa, fierce anger filled
Pāṇḍu's son the wealth-winner as he remembered each episode; so
great was his rage that fiery flames issued forth from his every orifice,
O king, which was a great wonder. When Karṇa saw the wealth-winner
looking so, he used the Weapon of Brahmā to shower him with arrows,
then tried once again to free his wheel. But Kuntī's son the Pāṇḍava
struck down that Weapon with his own, and then released another
10 at Karṇa, his cherished Weapon of Fire, which blazed mightily. Karṇa
extinguished that Fire with his Weapon of Varuṇa,[1] blackening the entire
horizon with rain-clouds; but the heroic son of Pāṇḍu was undaunted,
and before Karṇa's very eyes he blew away those clouds with a Weapon
of Wind.

Now Karṇa's standard bore the device of a splendid elephant-rope gleaming with gold, pearls and diamonds; it had been fashioned by the efforts of the finest artisans, working over years, and it was lovely to see, and intensely bright. Always its admirable beauty invigorated your

1 The god of the waters.

troops and terrified your foes. It was famous throughout the world for its brilliance, which was equal to that of the sun; in fact the standard resembled the sun or the moon, or fire. That glorious standard of Karṇa the mighty chariot-fighter was now destroyed by the noble wearer of the diadem with a razor-edged, gold-shafted arrow that he shot with the greatest of care; and with the fall of that standard there fell too the Kurus' fame and *dharma*, and their hopes of victory, sir, and all that they held dear, and their very hearts. There was a great roar of grief.

Then Kuntī's son the Pāṇḍava made haste to slay Karṇa. He drew from his arrow-case his *añjalika* weapon that appeared like Indra's thunderbolt, or the staff of the god of Fire, or the most brilliant ray of the thousand-rayed sun. It was smeared with blood and flesh from piercing the vital organs of warriors, a costly weapon resembling fire or the sun; dealing death to men, horses and elephants, the fierce-speeding shaft was three cubits long, and bore six feathers. Its fiery energy equalled Indra's thunderbolt; it was as unendurable as a flesh-eating ghoul, as terrifying as Śiva's Pināka or Viṣṇu's discus, and a slayer of living beings. This was the mighty, paramount weapon that Arjuna, expert in *mantras*, fixed to his bow; then he drew Gāṇḍīva and spoke in a sonorous voice: 'Let this arrow, this unequalled weapon I hold, cleave my enemy's body and take his life! I have performed austerities and satisfied my elders; whatever my friends have desired, that I have sworn to do. By this truth may this my arrow, well aimed and undefeated, slay my enemy Karṇa!'

With these words the wealth-winner let fly that terrible arrow for the killing of Karṇa, fierce as an Atharvaveda rite,[1] blazing, unendurable even to Death himself; and as he did so he said, in great exultation, 'May this arrow bring me victory! Mighty as sun or fire as it seeks to slay, may it take Karṇa to his dissolution and to the realm of Yama!' Full of joy, the wearer of the diadem, bent on killing his foe while he was busy with his chariot-wheel, strove to slay him with that excellent victory-granting arrow, brilliant as sun or moon. And the head of the Kaurava commander, radiant as the rising sun or the sun in the middle of the autumn sky, fell to earth like the red disc of the sun falling behind the western mountain at sunset.

1 Many of the hymns of the Atharvaveda consist of spells to do good or harm to others.

25 Like a man of great wealth leaving the house he owns and loves, it was
a mighty hardship for Karṇa's spirit to quit the body in which he had
always enjoyed such happiness and which so perfectly embodied a man
of his noble deeds. His armour was gone; his tall body, mangled with
arrows and lifeless, fell, streaming blood from his wounds. He seemed
like the summit of a mountain smashed by a thunderbolt, flowing with
water dyed red by its mineral ores. From Karṇa's slain body a blazing
fiery energy swiftly pervaded the sky. All the warriors and other men
saw that marvel, O king, when Karṇa was killed.

When they saw him lying slain, the Somakas were filled with delight,
and let out a great roar along with the rest of the troops; overjoyed,
some sounded trumpets and waved their arms and their garments, while
other mighty warriors danced, embraced one another and roared. And
30 they said, 'Drenched in torrents of blood, and with every limb covered
by arrows, Karṇa's body is like the sun with its rays! He has scorched
the army of his foes with the blazing beams of his arrows, but now the
sun that was Karṇa has been made to set by mighty fate in the form of
Arjuna. And as the sun takes its brightness with it when it sets behind
the western mountain, so Arjuna's arrow has taken away Karṇa's life. It
was in the afternoon of his second day as commander that the lofty head
of the Sūta's son was severed on the battlefield by the *añjalika* weapon,
and fell to the ground: his enemy's arrow swiftly carried off the lofty
head of Karṇa, who stood over and above all his warriors.'

35 Śalya king of the Madras saw brave Karṇa lying fallen on the earth,
covered with arrows, his limbs smeared with blood. Then he drove away
on the chariot with its severed standard. As for the Kauravas, they had
suffered deep wounds in the battle, and when Karṇa was killed they
fled headlong in terror, their eyes constantly drawn to Arjuna's great
standard that blazed with such beauty. Karṇa's deeds matched those of
thousand-eyed Indra, the beauty of his face that of a thousand-petalled
lotus; his head fell to the ground like the thousand-rayed sun at the end
of day.

**[68]** *Śalya approaches Duryodhana and tells him that the disaster that has befallen his army is due to fate, which favours the Pāṇḍavas. He describes the scene of devastation on the battlefield. Duryodhana weeps for Karṇa, and he* *and his followers return grieving to their camp. Karṇa, who in death appeared as glorious as in life, the hero of unbounded generosity, goes to heaven, taking with him the Kauravas' hopes of victory. Rivers cease flowing, the setting sun is stained, and other terrible portents appear. But Arjuna and Kṛṣṇa blow their conches in triumph on the battlefield.* [**69**] *Kṛṣṇa congratulates Arjuna on his deed and takes him to inform Yudhiṣṭhira of Karṇa's death. Yudhiṣṭhira applauds the feat that Arjuna has achieved with Kṛṣṇa's aid; he mounts his chariot and returns to the battlefield to see Karṇa and his sons lying slain. He and the other Pāṇḍavas rejoice at their great victory. — Saṃjaya concludes by telling Dhṛtarāṣṭra that he is to blame for all this dreadful destruction. Dhṛtarāṣṭra and Gāndhārī both fall in a faint.*

# ŚALYA

## THE KILLING OF ŚALYA

[1] *Karṇa's death plunges Duryodhana into grief, but he remains determined to fight; he appoints Śalya as his commander, and sets off with those kings who still survive, but after a fierce battle Śalya is killed by Yudhiṣṭhira. Duryodhana, desperate, takes refuge in a lake, but Bhīma challenges him to fight and slays him, after which the three surviving Kaurava warriors attack the Pāṇḍavas at night and slaughter them. — Saṃjaya arrives to bring Dhṛtarāṣṭra the news that Duryodhana and his supporters are dead, and so are almost all their enemies. On the Pāṇḍava side there are seven survivors, the five brothers along with Kṛṣṇa and Sātyaki; on the Kaurava side there are three, Kṛpa, Kṛtavarman and Aśvatthāman. Dhṛtarāṣṭra faints at these tidings, as do Vidura, Gāndhārī and all the royal ladies. When he recovers he sends the ladies away, and remains with Vidura and Saṃjaya.*

[2] *Dhṛtarāṣṭra grieves for the death of all his sons, in particular Duryodhana. He recalls how Duryodhana had often boasted of the coming defeat of the Pāṇḍavas, and how he himself had believed him. Now all his sons and their supporters are dead. Dhṛtarāṣṭra maintains that nothing but fate can be held responsible for this catastrophe, and announces that he intends to retire to the forest. Then, after lamenting long, he asks Saṃjaya to tell him exactly what happened,* [3] *and Saṃjaya takes up the narrative once more.*

*— Duryodhana and his warriors are stunned by the killing of Karṇa and the losses that have been inflicted on them. Kṛpa approaches Duryodhana and offers him advice. He begins by insisting that the Kṣatriya* dharma *is to fight, and that it is better to die than to flee; but then he turns his attention to the disastrous situation facing the Kauravas, which he blames on Duryodhana's own*

*wicked deeds. He urges Duryodhana to make peace with the Pāṇḍavas; if he does so he will be able to retain his own kingship, whereas there is nothing to be gained from defeat and loss of sovereignty.*

**[4]** *Duryodhana acknowledges that Kṛpa has spoken as a friend and ally, but he cannot accept his proposal. The Pāṇḍavas have suffered so much at the hands of the Kauravas that peace is no longer possible, and Duryodhana himself could not endure losing his sovereignty. It is better to fight, and to attain heaven through a glorious death in battle. These words raise the Kauravas' spirits, and they prepare to do battle once more.*

**[5]** *In their camp, Duryodhana's remaining allies request him to appoint a new commander for the army, and Duryodhana asks Aśvatthāman to advise him who to appoint. Aśvatthāman proposes Śalya, to the delight of the kings. Duryodhana requests Śalya to accept the appointment, and Śalya agrees, vowing to dedicate his life and all he possesses to help Duryodhana,* **[6]** *and assuring him that he will defeat the Pāṇḍavas. Duryodhana consecrates him as commander. The Kauravas rejoice, considering their enemies as good as slain, and they retire to a peaceful sleep. Meanwhile Yudhiṣṭhira hears their rejoicing, and understands that Śalya has been appointed commander. He asks Kṛṣṇa for advice, and Kṛṣṇa answers that Śalya is a very great warrior, and that the only man capable of matching him in battle is Yudhiṣṭhira himself. The Pāṇḍavas sleep well, still delighting at the death of Karṇa.*

**[7]** *In the morning of the eighteenth day, the Kauravas arrange themselves in divisions behind Śalya, vowing always to support one another in battle and to avoid single combat. The Pāṇḍavas likewise enter battle formation and advance towards the Kauravas. The dreadful conflict begins once more.* **[8]** *Warriors do battle against one another till the earth is covered with severed limbs and with the bodies of elephants and horses. A river of blood flows on the battlefield. Arjuna and Bhīma overwhelm the Kauravas and blow their conches in triumph; hearing the sound, Dhṛṣṭadyumna and Śikhaṇḍin follow Yudhiṣṭhira in an attack on Śalya, while Nakula and Sahadeva join in the assault against Duryodhana's forces. The Kaurava army is routed.*

**[9]** *Seeing the rout of his troops, Śalya commands his charioteer to drive him to where Yudhiṣṭhira is. Single-handed, he withstands the mighty Pāṇḍava army, and the Kauravas, seeing this, return to do battle once more. Nakula and Karṇa's son Citrasena engage in combat; Citrasena severs Nakula's bow and kills his horses and charioteer, but Nakula climbs on to Citrasena's chariot and beheads* *him with his sword. The dead man's brothers Suṣeṇa and Satyasena attack Nakula fiercely, but he fights back from a new chariot with a new bow and succeeds in slaying both of them. At this the Kaurava army takes flight once again, but again Śalya rallies them. The battle continues, with great slaughter on both sides.*

[10] *The dreadful carnage continues, but the Pāṇḍavas have the upper hand; Śalya attacks them, while portents of doom appear. He inflicts heavy casualties, but then comes under severe attack himself. The leading Kauravas come to his rescue. Kṛtavarman kills Bhīma's horses; Bhīma, fighting on foot, uses his terrible club to kill the horses of Śalya. Śalya pierces Bhīma with a lance, but Bhīma pulls the weapon from his body and uses it to slay Śalya's charioteer.*

[11] *Bhīma and Śalya now attack one another fiercely with their clubs; they injure each other so badly that both men fall to the ground simultaneously. Kṛpa bears Śalya away in his chariot, but Bhīma, though still groggy from his wounds, leaps up club in hand and challenges him again. However, at this point Duryodhana leads an attack on the Pāṇḍavas, slaying Cekitāna. The battle between the two sides is terrible; the wind raises so much dust that onlookers cannot see what is happening, but then the blood that is shed lays that dust and restores visibility. Śalya and Yudhiṣṭhira exchange many arrows; Yudhiṣṭhira succeeds in severing Śalya's standard, but this merely enrages Śalya further, and he redoubles his attack on Yudhiṣṭhira and his supporters.*

[12] *Sātyaki, Bhīma, Nakula and Sahadeva come to Yudhiṣṭhira's aid. The five warriors repeatedly attack Śalya together, but he fights back against all of them, piercing them many times and defeating their weapons with his arrows. The fierceness with which he fights brings encouragement to Duryodhana and fills Yudhiṣṭhira with concern. The air seems full of nothing but Śalya's arrows, and the Pāṇḍavas are unable to make any progress against him.*

[13] *Arjuna, meanwhile, is doing battle with Aśvatthāman and his followers; they shoot so many arrows at him that his chariot is completely enveloped. Arjuna responds with so many arrows that his route is marked by heaps of broken chariots and severed limbs, and the earth becomes an impassable quagmire of blood. Two thousand chariots are destroyed. Then Arjuna and Aśvatthāman engage in a long and even combat, exchanging great numbers of arrows; eventually Arjuna kills Aśvatthāman's horses, and then cuts down with his arrows the two clubs that Aśvatthāman hurls at him. The Pāñcāla warrior Suratha joins in the attack on Aśvatthāman, but Aśvatthāman slays him and mounts his chariot to continue the battle with Arjuna.*

[**14**] *Dhṛṣṭadyumna engages Duryodhana in an exchange of arrows; Duryodhana has to be rescued by his brothers. Śikhaṇḍin fights Kṛtavarman and Kṛpa simultaneously. Meanwhile Yudhiṣṭhira and the other Pāṇḍavas together with Sātyaki continue their battle against Śalya, but he is a match for all of them at once.*

[**15**] *The Kaurava assault causes many of the Pāṇḍava troops to flee, but the Pāṇḍavas themselves continue to resist, along with Śikhaṇḍin and the sons of Draupadī.*

Saṃjaya spoke:
Yudhiṣṭhira lord of *dharma* was enraged to see Śalya king of the Madras slaughtering his troops. Exerting his own manly strength, Pāṇḍu's son attacked the Madra king, his mind resolved on victory or death. The great chariot-fighter summoned all his brothers, and Kṛṣṇa heir of Madhu, and he said, 'Bhīṣma, Droṇa, Karṇa and all the other princes who fought for the Kaurava cause have met their deaths in battle. You have performed many manly deeds, acting resolutely in the tasks allotted you; now this one task remains, and it is mine: Śalya the mighty chariot-fighter! So today I wish to defeat the king of the Madras in battle, and I tell you now everything that I have in mind to bring that about.

'The two brave sons of Mādrī here shall be the guardians of my wheels, for they are renowned as heroes whom not even Indra could defeat. Indeed, for me they shall fight their mother's brother in battle, for they are honourable men, true to their word, who follow the Kṣatriya *dharma.* Either Śalya shall slay me on the battlefield, or I will slay him: know these words for truth, world-heroes, and blessings on you! I shall myself fight Mādrī's brother today in keeping with the Kṣatriya *dharma,* O princes, vowing to triumph or to die. So let the harnessers swiftly harness my chariot for battle in the approved manner, with a great amount of weaponry and all other kinds of gear! Sātyaki heir of Śini is to guard my right wheel, and Dhṛṣṭadyumna my left; today let Kuntī's son the wealth-winner Arjuna be my rearguard, and let Bhīma, best of all bearers of arms, be my vanguard. In this way I shall outmatch Śalya in the great battle!'

On receiving his orders, all the king's well-wishers did as he bade

them. Then all his troops were filled with joy once more, O king – especially the Pāñcālas, Somakas and Matsyas – as they set about fulfilling the lord of *dharma*'s vow in battle. The Pāñcālas sounded conches, kettledrums and *puṣkara* drums in hundreds, and roared their lion-roars; in fury the spirited, bull-like Kurus rushed to attack the
30 Madra king with a mighty roar of pure joy, making the earth resound with the clang of their elephant-bells, the din of their conches and the loud braying of their trumpets.

Your son Duryodhana and the heroic king of the Madras received them, as the eastern and western mountains receive advancing massive thunderclouds. Battle-boasting Śalya poured showers of arrows upon the foe-taming lord of *dharma*, as bountiful Indra pours down rain. Yudhiṣṭhira, the high-minded Kuru king, likewise took up his splendid bow and demonstrated all the many kinds of accomplishments taught him by Droṇa; he poured forth showers of arrows with elegance, swiftness and skill, and as he ranged over the battlefield no one could
35 perceive any weak point in him. These two hewed at each other with arrows of every type, like two tigers attacking one another in a battle over a kill.

As for Bhīma, he encountered your battle-crazed son, while the Pāñcāla prince Dhṛṣṭadyumna, with Sātyaki and Mādrī's twin sons, resisted Śakuni's heroic troops on every side. Now once again, O king, thanks to your evil policy, a tumultuous battle took place between your warriors and their enemies, all of them bent on victory. In that battle Duryodhana with a straight arrow took aim at Bhīma's gold-decked standard, and severed it; and Bhīma's beautiful lion-emblem, adorned
40 with a great cluster of tinkling bells, fell with a dreadful roar. Next King Duryodhana took up a sharp, razor-edged arrow, and with it he severed Bhīma's bow, handsome as the trunk of an elephant-lord. Ardent Bhīma, now bowless, attacked your son and pierced him in the breast with a lance, so that he sank down within his chariot; and when he lost consciousness, the wolf-belly further beheaded his driver too with a razor-edged weapon. On the death of the charioteer, heir of Bharata, Duryodhana's horses took flight and bore his chariot in every direction, causing a great uproar. The mighty chariot-fighter Aśvatthāman hurried to his aid, as did Kṛpa and Kṛtavarman, for they wished to rescue him.

Seeing that warrior carried hither and thither, his followers were afraid; whereupon Arjuna stretched his bow Gāṇḍīva and slew them with his arrows.

Meanwhile, unforbearing Yudhiṣṭhira rushed to attack the Madra lord, urging on his horses, white as ivory and swift as thought. Then we beheld a wonder in Kuntī's son Yudhiṣṭhira, for, having formerly always been mild and self-controlled, he now became savage. Trembling with fury, his eyes staring wide, he cut down warriors by hundreds and thousands with his arrows. Whatever force of men he met, the eldest son of Pāṇḍu felled it with arrows, king, like mountains felled by thunderbolts; alone he sported, cutting down hosts of chariot-fighters with their horses, charioteers, standards and chariots, like a mighty wind dispersing clouds. In his battle rage he slaughtered horses with their riders and footsoldiers in their thousands, like Rudra slaying his victims; then, having emptied the battlefield by showering arrows in every direction, he rushed at the lord of the Madras, calling out, 'Stand! Stand!'

Your warriors were all terrified to see him achieve this feat, and the fearful deeds he accomplished in battle. But Śalya confronted him, and the two enraged warriors, blowing their conches and challenging and reviling one another, then met in combat. Śalya covered Yudhiṣṭhira with a shower of arrows, and Kuntī's son covered the Madra king with showers of arrows. At that time, king, those two heroes, the Madra lord and Yudhiṣṭhira, could be seen on the battlefield, covered with stork-feathered arrows, blood gushing forth; blazing with brilliance and mad for battle even at the cost of their lives, those two noble men appeared like a kapok and a *kiṃśuka* tree blooming in a forest. Seeing them, the troops on all sides could not determine which of them would triumph. 'Will Kuntī's son slay the king of the Madras and rule over the earth today? Or will Śalya kill the Pāṇḍava and award the earth to Duryodhana?' Heir of Bharata, the fighters could not resolve these questions; but all respectfully circumambulated the lord of *dharma*.

Śalya now swiftly shot a hundred arrows at Yudhiṣṭhira, and severed his bow with a keen-pointed shaft; whereupon Yudhiṣṭhira took up another bow and pierced Śalya with 300 arrows, and severed his bow with a razor-sharp shaft. With his straight arrows he killed his four horses,

and with two further keen-pointed shafts slew his paired charioteers;
then with a blazing, sharp, broad arrow of steel he cut off Śalya's standard
at the head of Duryodhana's army. At this, foe-tamer, that army broke.
65 Seeing the Madra king in such a state, Droṇa's son Aśvatthāman
hurried to his aid; he took him up into his own chariot and bore him
rapidly away. For a while they drove on, while Yudhiṣṭhira roared in
triumph; then the lord of the Madras halted, and mounted another
splendid chariot. It was equipped with all the proper gear and apparatus,
and with its mighty cloud-like thunder it made enemies' hair stand
on end. [**16**] Now the Madra lord took up another powerful bow,
swifter than the first, and with a roar he pierced Yudhiṣṭhira with his
arrows. Then that bull-like Kṣatriya of immeasurable greatness covered
his Kṣatriya enemies with a shower of arrows, like the god of rain in
spate. He pierced Sātyaki with ten arrows and Bhīma and Sahadeva with
three each, and he wounded Yudhiṣṭhira also. Śalya, best of chariot-
fighters, destroyed many other mighty bowmen together with their
horses and chariots and elephants; he destroyed elephants and elephant-
5 riders, horses and horse-riders, chariots and chariot-fighters. He severed
banners and weapon-bearing arms till the earth seemed like an altar
strewn with *kuśa* grass.

While he was thus slaying the forces of his enemies like Death
the destroyer himself, the Pāṇḍavas, Pāñcālas and Somakas surrounded
him, full of terrible rage. Bhīma and Śini's grandson Sātyaki, together
with Mādrī's heroic twin sons, came up to him as he fought with King
Yudhiṣṭhira of terrible might, and they urged each other on. When those
heroes reached King Śalya, lord of the Madras, best of warriors, on the
battlefield, they checked him and struck him with fiercely speeding
feathered arrows. Now King Yudhiṣṭhira son of Dharma, protected by
Bhīma, and by Mādrī's sons and Kṛṣṇa heir of Madhu, pierced the Madra
10 king in the centre of his chest with his fiercely speeding arrows. Then
on that battlefield the massed chariot-fighters of your force, perceiving
that the lord of the Madras had been wounded by arrows, encircled him
bravely on every side, in accordance with Duryodhana's wishes. The
Madra king now swiftly pierced Yudhiṣṭhira in battle with seven arrows;
whereupon, in the midst of the tumult, Kuntī's noble son pierced him
with nine shafts, O king.

Now the two mighty chariot-fighters, the Madra lord and Yudhiṣṭhira, covered one another on the battlefield with their well-oiled arrows, shooting them from bows stretched all the way back to the ear; mighty and unassailable by enemies, watching each other's weak points, in that battle the two great kings swiftly and fiercely pierced one another with arrows. The twang of the bowstring against their palms was as loud as the roar of Indra's thunderbolt, as the noble Madra king and Pāṇḍava
hero showered each other with hosts of arrows. They ranged about the 15
battlefield like young tigers in dense forest vying with each other over a kill; full of pride in battle, they hewed at each other like two mighty elephants with their tusks.

Then the noble king of the Madras violently and rapidly pierced heroic Yudhiṣṭhira of terrible might in the breast with an arrow that blazed bright as fire or sun; at which the bull of the Kurus, noble Yudhiṣṭhira, though badly wounded, struck the Madra lord with a well-shot arrow, O king, and rejoiced at the deed. Śalya, lord among princes, recovered consciousness after a moment; eyes red with anger, equal in might to thousand-eyed Indra, he swiftly struck Kuntī's son with a hundred shafts. Then Dharma's noble son, enraged, rapidly pierced Śalya's breast with nine arrows, and struck his gold shield with six more.
Now the king of the Madras, filled with joy, drew his bow and shot 20
his shafts; and with two razor-sharp arrows he succeeded in severing the bow of the bull-like Kuru, King Yudhiṣṭhira. But as the battle continued, the noble king took up another bow, new and more terrible than the first, and he pierced Śalya on all sides with keen-pointed shafts, as great Indra did with Namuci. Noble Śalya in turn cut off with nine arrows the strong gold armour of Bhīma and King Yudhiṣṭhira, and wounded them both in the arms. Next he took up another razor-sharp shaft with the fiery energy of the blazing sun, and with it he destroyed King Yudhiṣṭhira's bow; then Kṛpa killed his charioteer with six shafts, so that he fell down in front of the chariot. With four arrows the Madra lord slew Yudhiṣṭhira's horses; and having slain his horses, noble Śalya set about destroying the warriors of King Yudhiṣṭhira, son of Dharma.

Seeing the king reduced to this state, noble Bhīma now quickly 25
severed the Madra king's bow with a swift arrow, and pierced the lord of men fiercely with two more; with another he severed the driver's

head from his armour-cased body; and he swiftly slew the four horses in the fierceness of his rage. Now Bhīma, foremost of all those who bear arms, showered a hundred arrows upon Śalya as he ranged rapidly over the battlefield, and Sahadeva son of Mādrī did likewise. Then, as he saw Śalya fainting from those shafts, Bhīma used further arrows to cut off his armour.

Finding his armour cut off by Bhīma, the lord of the Madras seized a
shield adorned with a thousand stars, and a sword. Then the noble man
leapt down from his chariot, and rushed to confront Kuntī's son. He
30 severed Nakula's chariot-pole, and then attacked Yudhiṣṭhira. Seeing
King Śalya descending rapidly upon them like furious Death, Dhṛṣṭa-
dyumna, the sons of Draupadī, Śikhaṇḍin and Śini's grandson Sātyaki
quickly surrounded him. Then noble Bhīma severed his matchless shield
with ten shafts, and with broad arrows he cut off his sword at the hilt,
while he roared with joy in the midst of your army. All the finest massed
chariot-fighters of the Pāṇḍavas rejoiced to see Bhīma's deed; they
roared, and laughed aloud, and blew their moon-white conches. Your
troops suffered to hear that terrible sound; joyless, they were drenched
in sweat and bathed in blood, almost swooning in their dejection.

The Madra king, though violently battered by the foremost Pāṇḍava
warriors led by Bhīma, advanced swiftly towards Yudhiṣṭhira like a
35 lion stalking a deer. When the lord of *dharma* saw the lord of the
Madras hastening towards him, his horses and charioteer slain, blazing
like a fire in his fury, he rushed to attack his enemy with might.
Suddenly recalling the words of Kṛṣṇa Govinda,[1] he set his mind on
the destruction of Śalya, and, though standing on a horseless and
driverless chariot, he longed to take up his spear. Observing Śalya's
feats, and considering that his own allotted task remained to be done,
he fixed his mind with discipline on killing Śalya, as Indra's younger
brother[2] had said. The lord of *dharma* took up a gold-bright spear with
a handle of jewelled gold; opening suddenly wide his blazing eyes,
he gazed with furious heart upon the Madra king. Lord of men, it

1 See 9.6.

2 i.e. Kṛṣṇa, incarnation of Viṣṇu, who, as the youngest of the group of gods known as the Ādityas, is junior to Indra, the principal member of the group.

amazes me that when the king of the Madras felt the gaze of King Yudhiṣṭhira, utterly pure of heart and freed from sin, he was not reduced to ashes!

Then noble Yudhiṣṭhira, best of the Kurus, hurled fiercely and swiftly 40
at the Madra lord that spear with its beautiful, terrible shaft, flaring and sparkling with jewels and coral. All the Kurus together watched it as it violently flew with great force, blazing with sparks like a mighty doomsday comet. The weapon that the lord of *dharma* released with such care in that battle, unfailing as a Brahmin's curse, was like the Night of Death, noose in hand, or Yama's wet-nurse, terrible to behold. Pāṇḍu's sons had always taken care to honour it with perfumes, garlands and the finest seats and food and drink;[1] it blazed as bright as doomsday fire, and was as fierce as an Atharvaveda rite. Tvaṣṭṛ the divine craftsman had created it for Lord Śiva to consume the lives and bodies of foes, for it could deal out violent death to all beings, even the earth and
the sky and the oceans. Decked with bells and banners, jewels and 45
diamonds, bright with beryl, its shaft made of gold, it had been cast by Tvaṣṭṛ with care and with observances as an unfailing destroyer of all who hate *brahman*. Having increased its speed by means of might and effort, having consecrated it with terrible *mantras*, Yudhiṣṭhira released it then along the best course for the killing of the king of the Madras. Roaring, 'You there! You are slain!', the lord of *dharma* hurled that spear, stretching forth his firm arm with its fair hand and seeming to dance with fury, just as Rudra had released his arrow to slay Andhaka.

That spear of irresistible might was dispatched by Yudhiṣṭhira with all his power. Śalya roared aloud as he received it, like a fire receiving a well-poured oblation of ghee. Tearing through his vital organs, his fair, broad chest and his armour, the spear entered the earth unimpeded as if
it were water, burning up King Śalya's renown and glory. His body was 50
drenched with the blood from his wound that flowed from his nose, eyes, ears and mouth, so that he resembled mighty Mount Krauñca split open by Skanda the god of war.[2] Mighty as Indra's elephant, noble Śalya

1 That is, treating it like a revered human guest.

2 See 9.45.

fell from his chariot to the earth,[1] stretching forth both his arms, his
armour rent asunder by Kuru's heir.

Stretching forth both his arms, King Śalya fell to the earth before the
lord of *dharma* like a toppled Pole of Indra. The earth herself seemed to
rise to greet with affection that bull-like hero, wounded in every limb
as he was, and doused in blood, like a dear wife greeting her beloved
as he fell upon her breast. Long had King Śalya enjoyed the earth like
a dear wife, and now he seemed to fall asleep with her, embracing her
55 with every limb. Slain in a war of *dharma* by Dharma's righteous son,
he was like a sacrificial fire that has received a well-poured oblation and
made a good sacrifice, and now lies extinguished. His breast was cloven,
his weapons and standard cast asunder, yet royal glory did not desert the
lord of the Madras, though he now lay lifeless.

Yudhiṣṭhira now took up his bow as fair as the bow of Indra, and he
scattered his enemies on the battlefield, as Garuḍa, king of birds, scatters
snakes. In an instant he destroyed the bodies and lives of his enemies
with his sharp, broad arrows. Kuntī's son covered your warriors with
torrents of arrows till they began to slay one another in their distress;
casting away the armour from their bodies, they lost their weapons and
their lives.

After Śalya's fall, the Madra king's junior brother, a young chariot-
fighter who was his brother's equal in all respects, advanced against
60 Pāṇḍu's son. That best of men rapidly pierced Yudhiṣṭhira with many
iron arrows, for he was mad for battle and wished to avenge his slain
brother. The lord of *dharma* in turn rapidly pierced him with six swift
shafts, and severed his bow and his standard with two razor-sharp arrows;
then with a sharp, broad arrow, blazing and strong, he severed his head
as the young man fought before him. I beheld that head, still decked
with earrings, falling from the chariot like a celestial falling from heaven
upon the exhaustion of his merits.

Seeing his headless body too fall from the chariot, every limb drenched
65 with blood, your army broke. On the death of the Madra king's younger
brother with his splendid armour, the Kurus fled headlong, making a
great uproar; seeing him slain, your warriors, who had been willing to

1 In fact he had already left his chariot: see verse 29 above.

sacrifice their lives for you, now became enveloped in the dust of their flight, terrified of the son of Pāṇḍu. Then as the Kauravas fled thus in terror, O bull-like heir of Bharata, Śini's grandson Sātyaki attacked them, showering them with arrows. But Hṛdika's son Kṛtavarman, O king, seemingly unafraid, hastened to resist that mighty, invincible, irresistible bowman as he advanced. Those two noble, undefeated Vṛṣṇis, Hṛdika's son and Sātyaki, met in battle like two crazed lions. Both bright as the 70
sun, they covered each other with arrows as bright as sunbeams; we saw the shafts that the two lion-like Vṛṣṇis powerfully shot up from their bows flying through the sky like swift-moving insects. The son of Hṛdika pierced Sātyaki with ten arrows and his horse with three; then he severed his bow with a single straight shaft. Casting aside his excellent bow, now severed, Śini's bull-like heir swiftly took up another weapon, swifter than the first, and having taken up that excellent bow, the best of bowmen pierced Hṛdika's son in return with ten arrows in the centre of his chest. Then with well-aimed broad arrows he destroyed his chariot 75
and its pole, and killed his horses and his paired charioteers.

Now that the king of the Madras was slain and Kṛtavarman was chariotless, all Duryodhana's troops once more turned their backs on the battle. Their enemies could not see it, for the army was shrouded in dust, but in fact the greater part of the force was slain as it turned from the battle; then moments later they saw that dust which had risen from the earth laid by all the many streams of blood, O bull-like hero.

Duryodhana was close at hand. When he saw his army broken, he himself, fighting alone, warded off all the Pāṇḍavas as they swooped down on his force. When he saw the sons of Pāṇḍu, and Dhṛṣṭadyumna 80
heir of Pṛṣata, and the unconquerable man of Ānarta, Sātyaki, he showered them with sharp arrows; and his enemies did not attack him in return, for they felt like mortals confronted by Death.

Meanwhile Hṛdika's son Kṛtavarman had mounted another chariot and returned to the fray. But the mighty chariot-fighter King Yudhiṣṭhira swiftly slew his horses with four feathered arrows, and pierced Kṛpa heir of Gotama with six well-pointed shafts. Then when Hṛdika's son had been made horseless and chariotless by the king, Aśvatthāman bore him away from Yudhiṣṭhira in his own chariot; and Kṛpa son of Śaradvat pierced Yudhiṣṭhira with eight arrows in return, and also pierced his

85 horses with eight sharp shafts. Thus, great king, the last remains of the war took place, thanks to the evil policy of yourself and your son. Now that Śalya, best of mighty bowmen, lay slaughtered by the bull-like Kuru in the midst of the battlefield, Kuntī's sons were all filled with the highest joy, and they blew their conches at the sight of his dead body. They lauded Yudhiṣṭhira there on the field of battle, as formerly the gods lauded Indra for killing Vṛtra; and they played many kinds of musical instruments till the earth resounded on every side.

## DURYODHANA ENTERS THE LAKE

[17] *Śalya's followers the Madras now attack Yudhiṣṭhira, though forbidden to do so by Duryodhana; they are slaughtered by the sons of Draupadī. Śakuni asks Duryodhana why he is standing by while his troops are dying; when Duryodhana explains that they had disobeyed his command, Śakuni counters that in the heat of battle heroes do not heed commands, and urges Duryodhana to go to their rescue. Duryodhana sets out with a large force, but as they advance the Pāṇḍavas wipe out the remainder of the Madras, and at this sight his men flee once more.*

[18] *The rout of the Kauravas continues; the Pāṇḍavas maintain their attack on the fleeing enemy, and acclaim their victory, which they attribute to Kṛṣṇa. Duryodhana is convinced that he can still rally his forces by fighting on; he is supported by 21,000 chariotless warriors who are prepared to fight to the death for him. But Bhīma slays all 21,000 with his club. The Pāṇḍava forces now turn their attack on Duryodhana himself, but they are unable to overcome him; he urges his remaining supporters to fight on for victory or a glorious death, and they return to the battle.*

[19] *Now Śālva, the king of the barbarians, begins an assault on the Pāṇḍava troops. Mounted on a fearsome elephant he causes great loss of life, and his enemies flee from him. Dhṛṣṭadyumna attacks him, but has to leap from his chariot, club in hand, as the great beast crushes it. Bhīma, Śikhaṇḍin and Sātyaki are able to check its advance with their arrows, and Dhṛṣṭadyumna succeeds in clubbing it to death while Sātyaki beheads Śālva with a broad arrow.*

[20] *Kṛtavarman manages to rally the Kauravas, and the battle resumes. Kṛtavarman does battle with Sātyaki; the two exchange many arrows, until*

*Kṛtavarman is rendered chariotless and is borne away by Kṛpa. Once again Duryodhana's forces take flight and he is left to face his enemies alone. But he attacks them all fearlessly.* [**21**] *His arrows fly so thick and fast that not a man in the entire Pāṇḍava army remains unwounded. He strikes the leading Pāṇḍava warriors with numerous shafts; they reply in kind, but Duryodhana fights on without faltering. His supporters return to the fray and engage the Pāṇḍavas in combat, and the terrible battle rages on once more.*

[**22**] *Duryodhana sends 700 chariot-fighters against Yudhiṣṭhira; they are all slain by the Pāṇḍava warriors. Terrible portents appear. The Kaurava troops take to flight once more as the arrows of the Pāṇḍavas kill many of Duryodhana's men, but Śakuni is able to rally his force of 10,000 men of Gāndhāra, and he attacks the Pāṇḍavas from the rear. Yudhiṣṭhira commands Sahadeva and the sons of Draupadī to proceed against Śakuni with a powerful body of men. He does so, and a terrible battle takes place from which both sides eventually retreat after suffering severe casualties. But no sooner has Sahadeva withdrawn than Śakuni attacks once again, and the fierce conflict between him and the Pāṇḍava warriors resumes.*

[**23**] *Śakuni seeks out Duryodhana. He tells him of his own success against the Pāṇḍavas' cavalry and urges him now to attack their chariot-fighters; after this they will be able to slay their elephants, infantry and other troops. The Kauravas rush once more to the attack. Arjuna instructs Kṛṣṇa to drive through the mass of warriors so that he may bring the eighteen-day war to an end. He reflects at length on Duryodhana's obduracy and foolishness, and vows to wipe out Duryodhana's army before his very eyes. Kṛṣṇa does as he is bidden, and soon Arjuna's arrows are everywhere, each one finding its mark.* [**24**] *The Kaurava warriors flee before his onslaught, but while some quit the battlefield, others return to fight again. Now Dhṛṣṭadyumna, Śikhaṇḍin and Nakula's son Śatānīka launch a fierce assault on the Kaurava chariot-fighters. Duryodhana attacks Dhṛṣṭadyumna, but Dhṛṣṭadyumna kills his charioteer, and Duryodhana mounts a horse and rides to join Śakuni. Having destroyed the Kauravas' chariot-fighters, the five Pāṇḍava brothers find themselves surrounded by their elephants; but Arjuna slaughters them with his arrows and Bhīma with his club, while Yudhiṣṭhira and the twins shoot the warriors riding them. Now Dhṛṣṭadyumna joins them. Aśvatthāman, Kṛpa and Kṛtavarman go in search of Duryodhana while Dhṛṣṭadyumna and the Pāṇḍavas continue their destruction of the Kaurava army.*

[**25**] *Though Duryodhana himself cannot be found, his surviving Dhārtarāṣṭra*

*brothers join forces to attack Bhīma, but Bhīma slays them one after another: soon Durmarṣaṇa, Śrutānta, Jayatsena, Jaitra, Bhūribala, Ravi, Durvimocana, Duṣpradharṣa, Sujāta and Durviṣaha all lie dead. Only Śrutārvan survives, and he fights fiercely against Bhīma, but in the end he too is slain. The remaining Kaurava warriors surround Bhīma, but he slaughters them, destroying 500 chariots, 700 elephants, 10,000 footsoldiers and 800 horses, till there is little left of the Dhārtarāṣṭra army.*

**[26]** *Now of the Dhārtarāṣṭras only Duryodhana and Sudarśa survive. Sighting Duryodhana in the midst of his cavalry, Kṛṣṇa urges Arjuna to kill him: when Duryodhana sees his weary forces suffering heavy casualties he is bound to enter the fray, and this will lead to his destruction. Arjuna agrees: Duryodhana's force is now reduced to 500 horses belonging to Śakuni, 200 chariots, a hundred elephants and 3,000 infantry, together with Aśvatthāman, Kṛpa, Ulūka and Kṛtavarman. Arjuna himself will kill all of these unless they flee the battle. Now Bhīma, Arjuna and Sahadeva attack. Arjuna destroys the cavalry, then turns on the chariot-fighters of Trigarta; he slays Satyakarman and Satyeṣu, then does battle against Suśarman, king of Trigarta, and slays him too, along with his sons and followers. Bhīma likewise kills Sudarśa and all his followers.*

**[27]** *Sahadeva does battle with Śakuni, Bhīma with Ulūka. The two Pāṇḍava heroes cause so much carnage that the earth is covered with severed limbs. Śakuni's troops flee, but Duryodhana calls them back, urging them to seek death and glory in battle. After further exchanges, Sahadeva cuts off Ulūka's head with a broad arrow. Śakuni now attacks Sahadeva, who severs his bow. Śakuni resorts in turn to sword and spear, but Sahadeva cuts them to pieces, and he and his supporters flee. Sahadeva pursues him and beheads him. The Kauravas take flight once more; the Pāṇḍavas rejoice.*

**[28]** *Śakuni's remaining followers attack Sahadeva, and Bhīma and Arjuna come to his aid, inflicting heavy casualties. Seeing this, Duryodhana assembles his surviving fighters and commands them to attack the Pāṇḍavas. They do so, but are swiftly slain. Duryodhana decides to retreat.*

*— Dhṛtarāṣṭra asks how much was left of the Pāṇḍava army, and what Duryodhana did next. Saṃjaya continues his narration. — The Pāṇḍavas still have 2,000 chariots, 700 elephants, 5,000 horses and 10,000 infantry under Dhṛṣṭadyumna's charge, whereas when Duryodhana looks he sees not a single supporter left on the battlefield. Club in hand, he sets off on foot for a nearby*

*lake, reflecting that Vidura's predictions of disaster had been correct. Aside from Duryodhana, the only Kaurava survivors are Aśvatthāman, Kṛtavarman and Kṛpa. Saṃjaya himself has also survived; Sātyaki is about to slay him when Vyāsa appears and insists he be allowed to go free. Saṃjaya leaves the battlefield and meets Duryodhana, who enters the lake, solidifying its water. Aśvatthāman, Kṛtavarman and Kṛpa arrive, and together with Saṃjaya they return to the Kaurava camp, where there is terrible grief at the disaster that has befallen the Dhārtarāṣṭras. Meanwhile Yuyutsu, realizing that he is the last surviving son of Dhṛtarāṣṭra, obtains permission from Yudhiṣṭhira to return to Hāstinapura with the ladies of Duryodhana's household.*

## THE PILGRIMAGE

**[29]** — *Dhṛtarāṣṭra asks what Kṛtavarman, Kṛpa and Aśvatthāman did next, and also what Duryodhana did. Saṃjaya narrates. — Yudhiṣṭhira and the other Pāṇḍavas search for Duryodhana to kill him, but eventually they give up and return to their camp. Meanwhile the three surviving Kaurava warriors go to the lake where Duryodhana is hiding. They urge him to return to the battlefield and fight for victory or death; he argues in favour of resting for one night, but Aśvatthāman swears that he will slay all his foes before dawn comes. Their debate is overheard by hunters who are engaged in carrying Bhīma's enormous daily supply of meat to him; they return to the Pāṇḍava camp and inform Bhīma of Duryodhana's whereabouts. The Pāṇḍavas and their followers rejoice to hear the news, and they set off for the lake. Hearing their joyful arrival, the three surviving Kaurava warriors withdraw, while Duryodhana waits within the lake.*

**[30]** *Yudhiṣṭhira remarks to Kṛṣṇa that Duryodhana is using the power of illusion to hide within the lake. Kṛṣṇa replies that those who make use of illusion should be slain by means of illusion, and cites numerous precedents. Yudhiṣṭhira addresses Duryodhana: he appeals to his honour as a Kṣatriya to leave his hiding-place and fight. First Duryodhana answers that he will indeed do so, but that first he must rest; then when Yudhiṣṭhira repeats his challenge he announces a plan to retire to the forest, leaving Yudhiṣṭhira to enjoy the fruits of his triumph. But Yudhiṣṭhira does not want sovereignty under these terms, and continues to insist that Duryodhana must leave the lake and fight.*

**[31]** — *Dhṛtarāṣṭra asks how Duryodhana, so angry and proud by nature,* *responded to the taunts of his victorious enemy, and Saṃjaya continues his narration. — Duryodhana is stung into accepting Yudhiṣṭhira's challenge, but he points out that he is chariotless and weaponless, and adds that it is not proper for many to fight against one; he will fight the Pāṇḍavas one by one. In reply, Yudhiṣṭhira congratulates him on rediscovering his Kṣatriya* dharma, *and makes him an offer: he can fight a single Pāṇḍava with a weapon of his choice, while the rest watch, and if he wins he will regain his kingdom. Duryodhana opts to fight with a club, and Yudhiṣṭhira tells him to come forth from the lake. He does so, and repeats that he will fight the Pāṇḍavas one at a time, since it is not proper for many to fight against one, especially one without armour and exhausted by fighting. Yudhiṣṭhira asks him how this knowledge deserted him when he participated in the killing of Abhimanyu. None the less he tells him to choose a single adversary; if he can slay him, he will be king once more. Duryodhana retorts that he is a match for any of the Pāṇḍavas: he will fight whoever is willing to fight him.*

[32] *Kṛṣṇa reprimands Yudhiṣṭhira for his rashness. Of the Pāṇḍavas, only Bhīma has the strength for a fight with clubs against Duryodhana, and in a fair fight even he is likely to lose to Duryodhana's cunning. Bhīma insists that he will kill Duryodhana, and Kṛṣṇa praises him but warns him to fight with care. Vowing to avenge the wrongs he has done the Pāṇḍavas, Bhīma challenges Duryodhana; he reminds him of his misdeeds, and of the many deaths he has caused, and assures him that today he will meet his death. Duryodhana tells him to stop boasting: not even Indra could defeat him in a fair fight. The two heroes make ready for battle.*

[33] *At this point Balarāma appears. He has been away for forty-two days,*[1] *but has now returned on hearing that his two pupils are about to join battle.*[2] *He is greeted with great respect, and settles down to watch the fight.*

[34] *—Janamejaya interrupts Vaiśaṃpāyana's account of the battle as narrated by Saṃjaya; he asks to hear about Balarāma's journey, and Vaiśaṃpāyana obliges. —After the failure of Kṛṣṇa's peace mission,*[3] *when preparations for war are under*

1 See 5.154.

2 When Balarāma left at 5.154 he similarly referred to Bhīma and Duryodhana as his pupils. Bhīma is said to have been taught arms by Balarāma in an Appendix passage: 1, App. I, 80.7–10. I have not found any evidence that Duryodhana was Balarāma's pupil.

3 See 5.70–137.

*way,*[1] *Balarāma determines on a pilgrimage along the river Sarasvatī. He travels along the river to Kurukṣetra, making munificent gifts in the hermitages on the way. — Janamejaya asks to hear in detail about every hermitage; Vaiśaṃpāyana narrates. — First Balarāma arrives at the bathing-place named Prabhāsa, where the Moon was cured of consumption. The Moon had married the twenty-seven constellations, Dakṣa's daughters, but favoured Rohiṇī and neglected all the others, persisting in this behaviour despite warnings from Dakṣa. At last Dakṣa therefore afflicted him with consumption. As the Moon wasted away day after day, plants lost their goodness, and in turn living creatures perished. The gods were concerned; learning from the Moon of Dakṣa's curse they appealed to him to show mercy. Dakṣa conceded that, provided the Moon henceforth favoured all his wives equally, he might reverse his decline by bathing at Prabhāsa ('Radiant brightness'); by doing so once a month he would wax and wane fortnightly.*

*Next Balarāma visits the bathing-place called Camasodbheda, then Udapāna,* **[35]** *which was established by the glorious Trita. Gautama's three sons Ekata, Dvita and Trita attained great merit through their austerities. When their father died, the kings who had been his sacrificial patrons transferred their reverence to the three brothers, but it is Trita who was held in highest regard. Ekata and Dvita plotted together to gain both wealth and sacrificial merit by visiting all their patrons with Trita, thus acquiring many cattle and drinking much Soma. The plan was carried out; when they had accumulated a large herd of cattle, Ekata and Dvita determined to abandon Trita and deprive him of his share. That night Trita, fleeing from a wolf, fell into a deep well; his brothers heard his cries but travelled on, leaving him to his fate. Trita feared death as he had not yet drunk Soma: he mentally performed a Soma sacrifice at the bottom of the well, and the gods became aware of this and came to receive their shares in the sacrifice. They then granted him boons; he chose to be released from the well, and for anyone who bathed in its waters to attain the status of a Soma-drinker. Later, meeting his brothers, he cursed them and their descendants to become fierce wild animals.*

*Now Balarāma moves on to Vinaśana ('Disappearance'),* **[36]** *so named because there the river Sarasvatī disappears. Balarāma bathes there and moves on in turn to the lovely Subhūmika; the bathing-place of the Gandharvas; Gargasrotas; Śaṅkha; Dvaitavana; Nāgadhanvan. At each place he visits, he*

1 See 5.149–52.

*gives away great wealth. Next he travels eastwards to the place where the Sarasvatī turned in an easterly direction for the benefit of the seers of the Naimiṣa forest. Long ago in the Kṛta Age, so many Naimiṣa ascetics performed their sacrificial rituals on the banks of the Sarasvatī that there was no room left for the later arrivals; the river took compassion on them and changed direction towards the East for a while before resuming her normal westerly flow.*

*Now Balarāma travels on to the lovely bathing-place known as Saptasārasvata ('Place of the seven Sarasvatīs'), where the great ascetic Maṅkaṇaka performed his austerities.* **[37]** *There are indeed seven forms of the Sarasvatī, which have appeared when summoned by powerful beings. The form known as Suprabhā was invoked at Puṣkara, by Brahmā when he was performing a great sacrifice there; Kāñcanākṣī in the Naimiṣa forest, by the Naimiṣa sages; Viśālā in the land of Gaya, by the king of the same name; Manohradā in North Kosala, by King Auddālaka; Suveṇu at Ṛṣabhadvīpa, by Kuru; Oghavatī at Kurukṣetra, by Vasiṣṭha; and Vimalodā at Gaṅgādvāra, by Dakṣa. All these seven Sarasvatīs flow together at the celebrated bathing-place of Saptasārasvata.*

*As for Maṅkaṇaka: as a young man in a state of holy celibacy he was once bathing in the river when he saw a beautiful woman in the water naked. His seed gushed forth; he caught it in a jar, and from it were born seven seers, the fathers of the Maruts. On another occasion Maṅkaṇaka cut himself; the wound produced not blood but sap. Seeing this, he danced for joy, and the whole of creation joined in his dance. Gods and seers appealed to Śiva to stop the dancing, and Śiva appeared to Maṅkaṇaka; he cut his own thumb, which bled ash. Maṅkaṇaka worshipped him, and Śiva announced that henceforth anyone worshipping him at Saptasārasvata would gain his desire.*

**[38]** *Next Balarāma visits the bathing-place of Śukra Uśanas,*[1] *which is also known as Kapālamocana ('Skull-releaser'). During his stay in the Daṇḍaka forest,*[2] *Rāma had once beheaded a Rākṣasa; the severed head became attached to the leg of a Brahmin named Mahodara, and he was unable to rid himself of it until he bathed at this bathing-place.*

*From here Balarāma goes on to the hermitage of Ruṣaṅgu, who gave up his body there and announced that anyone doing likewise would be freed from further deaths. Then he visits the bathing-place where various Kṣatriyas in ancient*

**1** The household priest of the demons.

**2** See 3.261.

*times had succeeded in becoming Brahmins.* **[39]** *In the Kṛta Age Ārṣṭiṣeṇa had achieved mastery of the Vedas in that bathing-place after much unsuccessful effort, and he had pronounced on it the blessing that there even small efforts would achieve great rewards. There Sindhudvīpa and Devāpi had become Brahmins. Likewise King Viśvāmitra had performed great austerities there, and received from Brahmā the boon of becoming a Brahmin.*

*Now Balarāma travels to the hermitage of Dālbhya Baka.* **[40]** *Dālbhya had once requested Dhṛtarāṣṭra for some cattle; Dhṛtarāṣṭra had angrily given him the bodies of some dead animals. Furious, Dālbhya offered up Dhṛtarāṣṭra's kingdom in a sacrifice with their flesh. The kingdom began to fail, and Dhṛtarāṣṭra was unable to rescue it. Eventually, on the advice of soothsayers, he had gone to the Sarasvatī to make his peace with Dālbhya, and the seer had accepted many cattle from him and sacrificed to restore the welfare of the kingdom.*

*Next Balarāma visits the bathing-place where Yayāti gained heaven through sacrifice, and then the fast-flowing bathing-place of Vasiṣṭha.* **[41]** *Viśvāmitra and Vasiṣṭha occupied bathing-places on opposite banks of the Sarasvatī; they competed fiercely with each other in the matter of asceticism. Viśvāmitra had commanded the river to carry Vasiṣṭha to him so that he might kill him. Fearing a curse from both seers, Sarasvatī had informed Vasiṣṭha of Viśvāmitra's plan; he had advised her to save herself by carrying out the command. Won over by Vasiṣṭha's compassion, she determined to help him. She swept him across to Viśvāmitra's hermitage, but then swept him back again; the furious Viśvāmitra cursed her to flow with blood for the pleasure of Rākṣasas.*

**[42]** *After some time a group of ascetic seers came to visit the bathing-places of the Sarasvatī; seeing her flowing with blood and being drunk by Rākṣasas, they asked the river the reason, and she told them what had happened. They then caused her waters to become pure once again. The Rākṣasas asked for the seers' compassion, and at their urging the Sarasvatī produced a new form of herself called Aruṇā ('Reddish'); the Rākṣasas bathed in it and attained heaven.*

*Indra too bathed there to free himself of the sin of Brahminicide; he had sworn to the demon Namuci that he would not kill him with anything wet or dry, by day or by night; then he used a piece of foam to behead him in the middle of a mist.*

*Now Balarāma too bathes there, before progressing to the bathing-place where the Moon had performed the sacrifice of the royal consecration, after which a great battle took place in which the forces of the gods were led by Skanda.*

**[43]** — *Janamejaya asks to hear all about the installation of Skanda as commander of the gods and his battle against the demons. Vaiśaṃpāyana narrates.* — *Śiva's seed gushes forth, and falls into Fire. Fire cannot bear it, and places it in the Gaṅgā; Gaṅgā in turn places it on Mount Himālaya, where the mighty child begins to grow. The Kṛttikās*[1] *see him and want to nurse him; he forms six mouths with which to suck from all six of them. He comes to be known as Kumāra and Kārttikeya, adored and honoured by all. Seeing Śiva seated with Pārvatī, accompanied by all his* bhūtas,[2] *he approaches him; understanding that Śiva, Pārvatī, Gaṅgā and Fire all hope he will honour them first, he assumes four different forms, approaching Śiva as Skanda, Pārvatī as Viśākha, Fire as Śākha and Gaṅgā as Naigameṣa. The four deities request Brahmā to bestow some form of sovereignty on him, and Brahmā bestows the status of military commander. All the gods go to Samantapañcaka on the bank of the Sarasvatī for the installation ceremony.*

**[44]** *Kārttikeya's installation takes place in the presence of all the gods and other celestials, who give him great numbers of followers.* **[45]** *A large band of divine Mothers*[3] *also attend on him, and the gods present him with wonderful gifts, including a terrible spear given by Indra. As commander of the vast celestial army, Kārttikeya swears to slay the enemies of the gods. Then he advances against the demons and Rākṣasas, who flee in terror. With his spear he slays the demon leaders Tāraka, Tripāda and Hradodara, as well as vast numbers of their followers. The demon leader Bāṇa takes refuge in Mount Krauñca, but Kārttikeya splits it apart with his spear and kills him and his warriors. The celestials celebrate his great victory.*

— *This is the bathing-place where Kārttikeya was installed as commander; before that, under the name Aujasa, it was the place where Varuṇa was installed as lord of the waters. Balarāma bathes and passes the night there.* **[46]** *Then he moves on to the bathing-place of the Fire god. Fearing Bhṛgu's curse, Fire had hidden within the* śamī *tree;*[4] *the gods, anxious at his absence, had searched for him, and it was here that they found him.*

1 The six stars of the Pleiades.

2 Śiva's ghostly followers.

3 Female beings embodying the power of the various gods.

4 For the curse, see 1.5–6. Fire was thought to reside within *śamī* wood, which was one of the two woods used for the firesticks with which the sacrificial fire was kindled.

*After bathing there, Balarāma travels to the bathing-place of Kubera, and then to the one known as Badarapācana ('the jujube-cooking place').* **[47]** *Here Bharadvāja's daughter Srucāvatī had performed austerities to become the wife of Indra. Indra had appeared to her in Vasiṣṭha's form, and she had promised him whatever he asked save for her own hand, which was for Indra alone. In response, Indra assured her that she would gain her desire, and gave her five jujube fruits to cook. She cooked them for a long time, but they did not soften, and her supply of logs ran out; so she put her own feet on the fire and burnt them as fuel. Indra now returned and told her that she would abandon her body and dwell with him in heaven; her hermitage would be famous as Badarapācana. He also told her how, in this same place, Śiva had asked Vasiṣṭha's wife Arundhatī for alms during a time of drought; she had offered him jujubes, and he had commanded her to cook them. For twelve years she had cooked the jujubes and listened to his words; pleased with her devotion, he had granted her the boon that anyone fasting for three days at this place would gain the reward for a twelve-year fast. After telling Srucāvatī this story, Indra granted her an even greater boon: that anyone who passed a single night here would attain highest heaven.*

*Balarāma bathes here and travels on to the bathing-place of Indra.* **[48]** *After bathing there, he proceeds in turn to the bathing-place of Rāma Jāmadagnya and those of the river Yamunā and the Sun; at the bathing-place of the Sun he attains the highest yogic powers.* **[49]** *At this bathing-place there had once lived the seer Asita Devala, who practised austerities while living the life of a householder. He was visited by the great ascetic Jaigīṣavya, who took up residence at his hermitage. He lived there for a long time, but Asita never saw him except when it was time to eat, and he began to resent the fact that Jaigīṣavya never spoke a word to him. One day he travelled to the sea, and saw Jaigīṣavya there before him; when he returned home, there was Jaigīṣavya. After this, wherever he went and however holy the place, Jaigīṣavya was there; finally Asita learnt that Jaigīṣavya had even attained the realm of Brahmā, where Asita himself could not go. He now proposed to abandon his householder's existence in favour of the way of renunciation, but then he heard the ancestors and other creatures lament that now no one would feed them. So he changed his mind, only to hear the plants lament that now he would start cutting them down again. At this he finally resolved on renunciation.*

*After bathing at the bathing-place of the Sun, Balarāma travels to that of the Moon.* [50] *Next he travels to the bathing-place of Sārasvata, who was the son of the seer Dadhīca and the river Sarasvatī. Once a drought had occurred that lasted for twelve years; all the great seers had fled, but Sarasvatī told her son to remain; she fed him with excellent fish throughout the drought. When it was over, the seers returned, but they had lost their Vedic knowledge. Discovering that Sārasvata was expert in the Vedas, they made him their teacher, though he was only a boy.*

*Balarāma bathes at Sārasvata's bathing-place, then proceeds to the bathing-place of the old maid.* [51] *The famous seer Kuṇi Gārgya created a beautiful daughter for himself by the power of his asceticism; then he went to heaven. The girl never wedded, but devoted her life to austerities. Finally, old and infirm, she decided to depart for the other world; but the seer Nārada told her that, as she had never married, she had not won a place in heaven. She therefore offered half her ascetic merit to any seer who would marry her, and Gālava's son accepted on condition that they would spend only one night together. The wedding took place, and that night she became a beautiful young woman. The next morning she left for heaven, announcing that this bathing-place would confer the merit of fifty-eight years of holy celibacy on anyone spending a night there. Soon afterwards her husband, grieved by his loss, followed her.*

*Here Balarāma comes to know about the death of Śalya. From the seers at this bathing-place he also learns the reward for giving up one's life at Kurukṣetra,* [52] *when they explain how Kurukṣetra gained its name ('The field of Kuru'). The mighty seer Kuru had assiduously ploughed this field. Indra asked his purpose, and he replied that those who died there should attain heaven; but Indra merely laughed at him. However, Kuru persevered and the gods became alarmed. Indra then proposed to Kuru that men who willingly gave up their lives there or who died in battle there would reach heaven, and Kuru accepted this. Thus it is that Kurukṣetra, also known as Samantapañcaka, is an extremely holy place that confers great benefits.*

[53] *Balarāma next visits the hermitage where Viṣṇu himself performed austerities, then the bathing-places called Plakṣaprasravaṇa and Kārapacana. Finally he reaches the hermitage of Mitra and Varuṇa, and here he meets Nārada, who tells him what has happened in the battle at Kurukṣetra and advises him to hasten there to see the combat between Duryodhana and Bhīma. Balarāma does so.*

# THE DUEL WITH CLUBS

[54] — *Now Vaiśaṃpāyana resumes his account of the battle as related by Saṃjaya to Dhṛtarāṣṭra.* — *Balarāma proposes that the duel between Bhīma and Duryodhana should take place at Samantapañcaka, since men dying in battle there are assured of heaven. Both sides agree to this, and Duryodhana and the Pāṇḍavas go there. The two warriors face each other, each holding his club.*

[55] — *Dhṛtarāṣṭra laments that his son, once so mighty, should have come to such a pass, and lays the blame on fate. Saṃjaya continues his narration.* — *Duryodhana roars out his challenge to Bhīma; terrible portents appear. Bhīma addresses Yudhiṣṭhira: he swears that he will slay Duryodhana. Then he reminds Duryodhana of his misdeeds, and of the many deaths he has caused, and assures him that today he will meet his death. Duryodhana tells him to stop boasting. The two heroes make ready for battle.*[1] [56] *Duryodhana attacks Bhīma, and the two warriors fight with their clubs for some time, then rest, then fight again, fiercely and with great skill. They strike each other terrible blows, and both men are covered in blood, but each recovers from his enemy's attacks. A blow from Duryodhana's club lays Bhīma low and also rends open his armour, but he gets back to his feet.*

Saṃjaya spoke:
[57] Then Arjuna, who was observing the battle that was under way between the two Kuru chiefs, spoke to Kṛṣṇa Vāsudeva of great renown. 'In the combat between these two heroes, whom do you consider to be superior, and which of them has the greater ability? Tell me, stirrer of men!'

'Both have received equal instruction,' answered Kṛṣṇa, 'but Bhīma is the stronger of the two, while Dhṛtarāṣṭra's son is more practised than the wolf-belly. Now if Bhīma fights according to *dharma*, he will never triumph; but if he fights unfairly he can kill Duryodhana. It is said that the gods defeated the demons by means of deception; Indra used deception to defeat Virocana, my friend, and it was by deception that he dissipated Vṛtra's fiery energy. What is more, at the time of

1 This passage is very similar to the end of 9.32.

the gambling match Bhīma made a vow, O wealth-winner: "I shall
smash Duryodhana's thighs in battle with my club!"[1] The tormentor
of his enemies ought to fulfil that vow and use deception to cut down
deceitful King Duryodhana. If he fights fairly, relying on his strength,
then King Yudhiṣṭhira will be placed in danger.

'I will say more: hear me, Pāṇḍava. It is Yudhiṣṭhira's fault that we
10 find ourselves in danger once again, for, after achieving great deeds and
slaying Bhīṣma and the other Kurus, he had gained victory and utmost
glory, and had requited his enemies' feud against him; and then he
chose to endanger once more the triumph he had thus gained. Son of
Pāṇḍu, this was great foolishness on the part of the lord of *dharma*, to
gamble the outcome of the entire war on this single victory, and it is
brave Duryodhana, who shows such single-minded purpose, who will
benefit!

'Indeed, there is an ancient verse sung by Śukra Uśanas that conveys
the real truth. Listen as I recite: "The last remnants of a broken enemy,
returning in hopes of survival, are greatly to be feared, for they show
single-minded purpose." This Duryodhana was utterly defeated; his
army was slain, and he had hidden in a lake; knowing himself conquered,
he was planning exile in the forest, and had lost all hope of regaining
15 the kingdom. Now who with any wisdom in matters of warfare would
challenge such a man to single combat? We must pray that Duryodhana
does not seize the kingdom that we had won. For thirteen years he
has practised fighting with a club; he is leaping both long and high in
his efforts to slay Bhīma. If that strong-armed hero will not kill him
unfairly, you will have this Kaurava, Dhṛtarāṣṭra's son, for your king!'

When he heard noble Kṛṣṇa Keśava speak these words, wealth-winner
Arjuna, standing in view of Bhīma, struck his own thigh with his hand.
Bhīma understood his sign, and now he began to move to and fro on
the battlefield with his club, executing wonderful circles, and double
20 circles too. Sometimes the Pāṇḍava circled to the right, sometimes to
the left, and sometimes he zigzagged, all to bewilder his enemy. And
in just the same way, your son too nimbly executed wonderful moves
in his efforts to slay Bhīma, for he was expert at club manoeuvres.

1 See 2.63.14.

Whirling their terrible clubs that were perfumed with sandal and aloe, both men sought to bring their feud to its conclusion on the battlefield, like two furious Deaths; the two bull-like heroes, each seeking to kill the other, fought like two Garuḍas seeking the flesh of a single snake. As King Duryodhana and Bhīma executed wonderful circles, the clash of their clubs produced sparks of fire; the mighty heroes struck 25
equally at each other on the battlefield, like two oceans whipped up by the wind, O king. And as they struck equally at each other, like two elephants in rut, the blows of their clubs produced a sound like thunder.

In the course of that dreadful, intensely violent combat, both foe-tamers became weary as they fought; both those afflicters of their enemies paused a moment for breath, but then they took up their great clubs once more and furiously attacked one another, engaging in a terrible, unconstrained battle as they hewed at each other with blows of their clubs, lord of kings. Exerting themselves to attack, the two 30
bull-eyed, spirited heroes struck one another like two buffaloes fighting in mud; bathed in blood, with every limb wounded, they looked like blossoming *kiṃśuka* trees on Mount Himālaya. Then, glimpsing a weak spot presented by Duryodhana, Kuntī's son smiled to himself and suddenly lunged forward; wise in matters of warfare, mighty Bhīma saw his enemy come too close and instantly swung his club at him. But your son saw the blow, lord of the peoples, and sidestepped so that it fell uselessly on the earth. Then, having avoided that blow, the truest of 35
Kurus hastened to strike Bhīma with his club.

Because of the blood that flowed from the wound, and the violence of the blow, Bhīma of boundless power came close to losing consciousness. Duryodhana knew that he had hurt Pāṇḍu's son on the battlefield. But Bhīma, despite his terrible pain, kept himself upright, so that your son believed he was standing firm, ready to strike, and did not deal him a second blow. Then, after pausing a moment for breath, O king, Bhīma of mighty energy rushed swiftly at Duryodhana as he stood by. Seeing 40
Bhīma of boundless power descending rapidly upon him, and thinking to thwart his blow, O bull-like heir of Bharata, your high-minded son resolved to hold his ground, and to leap up high to deceive the wolf-belly. But Bhīma understood the king's intention. He rushed like a lion

to the attack, and as Duryodhana feinted and made to leap up once more, Pāṇḍu's son swiftly brought down his club on his two thighs, O king.

Bhīma of fearful deeds brought down that club with an impact like that of a thunderbolt, and it smashed Duryodhana's two handsome thighs.
45 Lord of the earth, your tiger-like son, his thighs smashed by Bhīma, fell, and the earth resounded with his fall. Now violent winds began to blow, and dust rained down from the sky; the earth trembled, with all her trees and shrubs and mountains. At the fall of King Duryodhana, the heroic lord of all kings, a great blazing meteor fell with a thunderous roar, bringing terror to all; and Indra rained down blood and dust, heir of Bharata, when your son was laid low. The sky was filled with loud
50 cries of Yakṣas, Rākṣasas and Piśācas, and this dreadful sound caused beasts and birds on every side to utter terrible cries. The horses and elephants and men that remained of the army cried aloud when your son was laid low; a mighty sound of kettledrums, conches and tabors was heard within the earth when your son was laid low. O king, in every direction there appeared headless creatures of dreadful form, with many feet and many arms, dancing a terrifying dance. Men armed with throwing weapons and cutting weapons, men bearing standards,
55 all began to tremble, king, when your son was laid low. Lakes and wells spewed blood, truest of kings, and fast-flowing rivers flowed backwards; women took on the appearance of men, and men that of women, O king, when your son Duryodhana fell. Observing these extraordinary portents, the Pāñcālas and Pāṇḍavas were all troubled in mind, bull-like heir of Bharata. Gods, Gandharvas and Apsarases set out on their various ways, talking of the wonderful battle between your two sons; similarly Siddhas, Vātikas and Cāraṇas praised those two lion-like heroes as they returned whence they had come, lord of kings.

**[58]** Seeing Duryodhana felled like a mighty *śāla* tree, all the Pāṇḍavas rejoiced in their hearts; the Somakas too, seeing him laid low like a rutting elephant by a lion, all felt the hair rise on their bodies. Then Bhīma of mighty energy approached the Kaurava prince whom he had cut down, and spoke these words: 'Evil-minded fool! Long ago you laughed to see Draupadī in your assembly wearing a single garment,

and you addressed me as "Cow! Cow!"[1] Receive today the reward for
your mirth!' With these words he placed his left foot on the lion-like 5
king's head and pushed it roughly about. Then that destroyer of enemy
armies, his eyes red with rage, spoke again: hear what he said, lord of
men. 'Those who danced about before us saying, "Cow! Cow!" shall
now see us dance about and utter those same words. But we have no
trickery, no fire, no gambling match, no deception; we use the might
of our own arms to harm our enemies!'

The wolf-belly had brought the feud to its conclusion; now with a
soft laugh he said to Yudhiṣṭhira, Kṛṣṇa, the Sṛñjayas, wealth-winner
Arjuna and Mādrī's twin sons, 'Those who brought Draupadī before 10
them in the midst of her period, who stripped her clothes from her in
the assembly – behold those sons of Dhṛtarāṣṭra slain by Pāṇḍu's sons
on the battlefield, thanks to Draupadī's austerities! The cruel sons of
King Dhṛtarāṣṭra, who formerly called us sterile sesame seeds, now lie
slain with their forces and followers, and we are free to go to heaven or
to hell!' Then, eyeing the club resting on his shoulder, he once more
trampled the fallen king's head with his left foot, and addressed him the
single word, 'Cheat!'

O king, the righteous-minded Somaka leaders were not happy to see
joyful Bhīma mean-mindedly placing his foot on the head of the Kuru
king. Yudhiṣṭhira lord of *dharma* spoke to the wolf-belly as he boasted
and danced about after striking down your son: 'Do not trample his 15
head with your foot, do not let your great *dharma* fail! He is a king
and a kinsman, and he lies fallen; sinless Bhīma, it is not right for
you to behave thus. He is destroyed; his ministers and brothers and
sons are all slain; no one survives to perform his funeral offerings; he
is our brother. It is not right for you to behave thus. People used to
call you "Righteous Bhīma" – so why, Bhīma, are you trampling the
king?' Then Kuntī's son King Yudhiṣṭhira, seeing Duryodhana reduced
to this state, addressed him with eyes filled with tears. 'This must have
been ordained by the all-powerful, noble creator, that we should seek
to kill you, and you us, truest of Kurus. For this great calamity that 20
you have suffered results from your own wrongdoing, thanks to your

1 See 2.68.19; in fact it was Duḥśāsana who used these words.

greed and arrogance and childish folly. You have caused the deaths of friends and brothers, fathers, sons, grandsons and teachers, and so now you have reached your own death. Because of your wrongdoing we have slain those mighty chariot-fighters your brothers, and many other kinsmen; I am sure this was due to insurmountable fate. But the wives of Dhṛtarāṣṭra's sons and grandsons, now widows, distraught and racked with grief, are bound to revile us.' With these words King Yudhiṣṭhira, son of Dharma, sighed and lamented long in the torment of his sorrow.

Dhṛtarāṣṭra spoke:
**[59]** When mighty Balarāma, best of Madhu's heirs, saw that the king had been slain unrighteously, what did he then say, O Sūta? Rohiṇī's son is skilled at club-fighting and knows all about it: tell me what he did, O Saṃjaya.

Saṃjaya spoke:
When mighty Balarāma, the best of fighting men, saw Bhīma kick your
son in the head, he was furiously angry; raising his hand in the midst
of all the lords of men, the plough-bearer spoke in a tone of terrible
5 distress: 'A curse upon you, Bhīma, a curse upon you for striking a
warrior of blameless valour below the navel! What the wolf-belly has
done is something never before seen in a battle with clubs: the learned
texts are clear that no blow should be struck below the navel, but Bhīma,
this unlearned fool, acts however he wishes!' As he spoke these words
great anger filled him, and he raised his plough and rushed to attack
Bhīma.
As he stood with arm upraised the noble hero appeared like mighty
Mount Śveta dyed red by its mineral ores. But when powerful Kṛṣṇa
Keśava saw him leap forward, he seized hold of him strongly but
carefully with his stout, well-muscled arms, head humbly bowed the
10 while. Those two best of Yadus, the dark and the fair, looked supremely
lovely together, O king, like sun and moon appearing together in the
sky at the close of day. To calm Balarāma's passion, Keśava said to him,
'One may experience six kinds of gain: one's own gain, one's friend's
gain, one's friend's friend's gain, and the three equivalent kinds of loss
among one's enemies. When a loss occurs for oneself or one's friends,

one should understand the mental distress it causes, and make haste to assuage it. The Pāṇḍavas are our natural friends; they are men of blameless valour; they are the sons of our father's sister, and they have been grievously cheated by their enemies. You know that the *dharma* of a Kṣatriya is to carry out what he has sworn to do. Now Bhīma, speaking on the floor of the assembly, swore long ago that he would
break Duryodhana's thighs with his club in a great battle; and the 15
mighty seer Maitreya also cursed Duryodhana that Bhīma would break his thighs with a club.[1] Therefore I do not see that Bhīma has done anything wrong: do not be angry with him, slayer of Pralamba! We are tied to the Pāṇḍavas by ties of birth and affection. Their gain is our gain; do not be angry, bull-like hero!'

'*Dharma* is properly practised by the virtuous,' answered Balarāma, 'but two things cause it to fail: the pursuit of wealth by those who desire it too strongly, and the pursuit of pleasure by those who are addicted to it.[2] The person who pursues *dharma*, wealth and pleasure, all three, without suppressing two of them, whether *dharma* and wealth, or *dharma* and pleasure, or pleasure and wealth, he is the one that finds the greatest happiness. But Kṛṣṇa Govinda, Bhīma has disordered everything by suppressing *dharma*. You have spoken to me only of what favours your own case!'

'You are famed in this world,' said Kṛṣṇa, 'as one who is void of 20
anger, and righteous by nature and temperament. So be calm, do not be angry! Consider that the Age of Kali is upon us;[3] remember too the oath that Pāṇḍu's son had sworn. Allow him to free himself from both feud and oath!'

But, lord of the peoples, not even Keśava's sophistry could placate Balarāma, and in the midst of the assembly he proclaimed, 'For killing righteous King Duryodhana unrighteously, Pāṇḍu's son shall be known in this world as a crooked fighter; but the son of Dhṛtarāṣṭra, righteous King Duryodhana, whom he has slain, shall go the eternal way of the fair

**1** See 2.63.14, 3.11.

**2** See 1.56.16 and note.

**3** See 5.140. Kṛṣṇa is arguing that in the new age of barbarism breaches of *dharma* are to be expected.

25 fighter! Having undergone initiation on the battlefield for the sacrifice
of war, having performed the sacrifice itself, having offered himself as an
oblation into the fire of his enemies, he has attained the final ritual bath
of glory!' With these words Rohiṇī's son, Balarāma of mighty energy,
fair as the crest of a white cloud, mounted his chariot and set off for
Dvārakā.

Balarāma's departure for Dvārakā, lord of the peoples, left the Pāṇḍ-
avas, Pāñcālas and Vṛṣṇis despondent. Then as Yudhiṣṭhira stood down-
cast, anxious and irresolute in his grief, Kṛṣṇa Vāsudeva addressed him:
'Lord of *dharma*, why do you give your approval to an act of *adharma*?
30 Bhīma has trampled with his foot the head of Duryodhana, a fallen,
unconscious warrior, one whose kin have all been slain; O king, how
can you as lord of *dharma* connive at this?'

'Kṛṣṇa, it does not please me,' replied Yudhiṣṭhira, 'that the wolf-belly
should have touched the king's head with his foot in his fury, any more
than I rejoice at the destruction of the Kuru lineage. But always we
have been cheated by the trickery of Dhṛtarāṣṭra's sons, who insulted
us repeatedly and exiled us to the forest. Bhīma's grief weighs heavy on
his heart, and so, lord of the Vṛṣṇis, I overlooked his act. He has slain a
man without wisdom, a greedy man in thrall to his desires, so now let
the Pāṇḍava have his own desire, whether what he did was *dharma* or
*adharma*.'

35 Hearing what the lord of *dharma* had to say, the Yadu prince Kṛṣṇa
Vāsudeva spoke the following words, though with difficulty: 'Let it
indeed be so.'

Now that Yudhiṣṭhira had obtained the agreement of Vāsudeva, who
wished Bhīma well, he announced his approval of everything that Bhīma
had done in the battle. Then unforbearing Bhīma left your son on the
battlefield and stood joyfully before Yudhiṣṭhira, hands joined together
to pay his respects. Lord of the peoples, that warrior of great ardour, his
eyes opened wide in joy, triumphantly proclaimed to Yudhiṣṭhira lord of
*dharma*, 'O king, today the earth is yours, secure and empty of enemies!
40 Rule it, mighty lord, according to your *dharma*. As for the deceiver who
initiated this feud with his trickery, here he lies slain on the ground,
lord of the earth. The enemies who insulted you, Duḥśāsana, Karṇa son
of Rādhā, Śakuni and the rest, have all been killed. And so, great king,

this jewel-filled earth with all her forests and mountains comes to you for her protection, for all your foes lie slain!'

'The feud has reached its end,' replied Yudhiṣṭhira, 'and King Duryodhana has been cut down; following Kṛṣṇa's advice, we have conquered the earth. I felicitate you on discharging the debts you owed, to your mother and your anger! I felicitate you on your victory, and on the downfall of your enemy!'

Dhṛtarāṣṭra spoke:
[**60**] When they saw Duryodhana cut down in battle by Bhīma, O Saṃjaya, what did the Pāṇḍavas and Sṛñjayas do?

Saṃjaya spoke:
When they saw Duryodhana cut down in battle by Bhīma, like a rutting wild elephant slain in the forest by a lion, great king, the Pāṇḍavas and Kṛṣṇa rejoiced in their hearts; when the heir of Kuru was laid low, the Pāñcālas and Sṛñjayas waved their garments and roared their lion-roars till the very earth could scarcely support the celebrating warriors. Some drew their bows, others twanged their bowstrings; some blew great conches, others beat drums; yet others of your enemies capered about and laughed. And again and again those heroes addressed Bhīma: 'Sir, you have achieved a supremely difficult task in today's battle by striking down the Kaurava prince with your club, for he had trained extremely hard! We all thought your slaying of your enemy here was like Indra's slaying of Vṛtra in that greatest of battles. Who but the wolf-belly could have cut down heroic Duryodhana here, as he executed all his many manoeuvres and circles? You have brought the feud to its conclusion, something which would have been exceedingly difficult for anyone else – no one else could have achieved such an outcome as this! We felicitate you, O hero, on having trampled Duryodhana's head with your foot like a rutting elephant in the thick of battle! We felicitate you, sinless one, on having drunk the blood of Duḥśāsana after fighting a wonderful battle, like a lion drinking a buffalo's blood! We felicitate you on having crushed underfoot through your deeds those who had acted against righteous Yudhiṣṭhira! We felicitate you, Bhīma, on overcoming your enemies and slaying Duryodhana! Your mighty fame has spread

15 throughout the earth. We know that bards cheered Indra after he slew Vṛtra; in just the same way we now cheer you for slaying your enemies! Indeed, heir of Bharata, you should know that, of the hairs that rose on our bodies when we learnt of the slaying of Duryodhana, every one remains erect even now!' Such was the praise that the assembled Vātikas showered on Bhīma there.

Hearing the joyful, tiger-like Pāñcālas and Pāṇḍavas speaking in this manner, Kṛṣṇa the slayer of Madhu interrupted them. 'Lords of men, it is not right,' he said, 'for an enemy who lies slain to be slain a second time with repeated cruel comments. For this fool is slain; this shameless, wicked man was slain from the moment he refused in his greed to grant
20 the Pāṇḍavas their rightful share in the kingdom, preferring his wicked companions to the advice of his true friends, and ignoring the many protestations of Vidura, Droṇa, Kṛpa, Bhīṣma and Saṃjaya. This basest of men is no longer fit to be an enemy or a friend; why waste words on one who is no more animate than a log of wood? Mount your chariots swiftly, lords of the earth, and let us leave! It is a blessing that this wicked man lies slain, with all his ministers, his kinsmen and his friends.'

When he heard this abuse from Kṛṣṇa, King Duryodhana was enraged, and began to lift himself from the ground: propping himself in a seated
25 position with his two arms, he glared at Vāsudeva. At that time the king, his body half raised from the ground, looked like an angry snake whose tail has been severed, heir of Bharata. Ignoring the dreadful pain that was killing him, Duryodhana lashed Vāsudeva with cruel words. 'Son of Kaṃsa's slave,[1] have you no shame that I have been brought down unfairly in a battle with clubs, because you deceitfully reminded Bhīma, "Break his thighs!"? How could I not be aware of what you said to Arjuna? Have you no shame, no self-disgust, that you employed so many crooked stratagems to slay thousands of kings who fought fairly?
30 Slaughtering heroes day after day, you caused the death of grandfather Bhīṣma by bringing Śikhaṇḍin forward.[2] You killed an elephant sharing

1 Kaṃsa was the cousin of Kṛṣṇa's mother Devakī, and was ultimately killed by Kṛṣṇa. The reference here is probably to the fact that he imprisoned Devakī and Kṛṣṇa's father Vasudeva.

2 See 6.103, 6.114.

Aśvatthāman's name, you evil-minded man, to slay Droṇa the Teacher:
how could I not know of this?[1] And as cruel Dhṛṣṭadyumna cut down
that hero, you saw, and you did not stop him. The Spear that Karṇa
had requested from Indra for the purpose of killing Pāṇḍu's son Arjuna
was diverted by you on to Ghaṭotkaca: who is there more wicked than
you?[2] In the same way, mighty Bhūriśravas, his sword-arm severed, was
seated preparing to die, when he was killed by Sātyaki heir of Śini at
your instigation.[3] Karṇa was performing wonderful feats to triumph 35
over Arjuna son of Kuntī, but you brought about his ruin and defeat
when his wheel had sunk into the earth, by diverting Aśvasena, son of
the serpent king Takṣaka; you caused the death of Karṇa, foremost of
men, when he was distracted over his wheel.[4] If you had fought fairly
in battle against me and Karṇa and Bhīṣma and Droṇa, be assured that
you would not have gained the victory! But I and the other princes
who were abiding by our *dharma* have been slain thanks to you and your
ignoble, crooked ways.'

'You have been slain, son of Gāndhārī,' answered Kṛṣṇa, 'together
with your brothers and sons and kinsmen and friends and troops, because
you were pursuing a path of wickedness. Heroic Bhīṣma and Droṇa 40
were cut down because of your own misdeeds; Karṇa was killed in
battle because his character matched yours. When I asked you to grant
the Pāṇḍavas their rightful share of half the kingdom, you were not
willing to do so, thanks to your own greed and Śakuni's plans, you fool!
You tried to poison Bhīma, you evil-minded man, and to burn all the
Pāṇḍavas with their mother in the house of lac.[5] During the gambling
match you dragged Draupadī into the assembly when she was in the
midst of her period: wicked and shameless, you merited death from that
moment. Yudhiṣṭhira understands *dharma*, not dicing; you defeated him
by trickery with the help of Śakuni, an expert gambler; therefore you
have been slain on the battlefield. Draupadī was molested in the forest, 45

1 See 7.164–5.

2 See 3.293–4, 7.154; also 7.155–6.

3 See 7.117–18.

4 See 8.66–7.

5 See 1.119.39–41, 1.132–6.

in the hermitage of Tṛṇabindu, by the wicked Jayadratha when her husbands had gone out hunting; and Abhimanyu, a child and fighting alone, was slain by many in battle because of your misdeeds.[1] Therefore you have been slain on the battlefield, you wicked man!'

But Duryodhana retorted, 'I have studied, I have given gifts in the
proper manner, I have ruled the earth with all her oceans, I have stood
over the heads of my enemies. Who is more blessed than me? The
death that is desired by all who call themselves Kṣatriyas and abide by
their *dharma*, that death I have now attained. Who is more blessed than
me? I have experienced human pleasures worthy of the gods, beyond
the reach of other kings, and I have known supreme sovereignty. Who
50 is more blessed than me? Invincible one, I am to go with my friends
and my followers to heaven. All of you shall remain here grieving, your
purposes frustrated!'

At the conclusion of the Kuru king's speech, heir of Bharata, a great
shower of sweet-scented flowers fell from heaven. Gandharvas played
musical instruments, Apsarases sang in groups, and Siddhas cried, 'Bravo!
Bravo!' A fragrant breeze blew, sweet-scented, gentle and pleasant, and
the sky shone pure blue as beryl.

Seeing these most wonderful happenings, and the honour paid to
55 Duryodhana, the Pāṇḍavas felt ashamed; they grieved mightily to hear
it said that Bhīṣma, Droṇa, Karṇa and Bhūriśravas had been killed
unfairly. But Kṛṣṇa, seeing them anxious and downcast, proclaimed in
a voice sounding like thunder or drums, 'Duryodhana here with his
swift weapons, and those other valiant chariot-fighters, could not have
been slain by you on the battlefield in fair fight. That is why I devised
these stratagems, lords of men – otherwise the victory of the Pāṇḍavas
could never have happened. For not even the world-guardian gods
themselves could have killed by fair means those four noble warriors,
60 famed throughout the world. As for Dhṛtarāṣṭra's son here, not even
staff-wielding Death could kill him fairly if he stood club in hand and
free from weariness. You should not take it to heart that this king has
been slain, for, when enemies become too numerous and powerful,
they should be slain by deceit and stratagems. This is the path formerly

1 See 3.248–56, 7.32–51.

trodden by the gods to slay the demons; and a path trodden by the virtuous may be trodden by all. We have achieved success. Now it is evening, and we should enjoy sleep. Lords of men, let us rest, with our horses and elephants and chariots.'

Then the Pāñcālas and Pāṇḍavas, hearing Kṛṣṇa's words, were greatly
cheered, and they roared like a throng of lions. They blew their conches, 65
and Madhu's heir blew his conch Pāñcajanya, for all those bull-like heroes rejoiced to see Duryodhana cut down.

**[61]** *The Pāṇḍavas and their chief allies now enter Duryodhana's deserted camp. Kṛṣṇa tells Arjuna to dismount from his chariot, then dismounts himself; at once the chariot is consumed by flames. Kṛṣṇa explains that it had already been burnt by various weapons, including the Weapon of Brahmā, and that only his presence had prevented it from falling to pieces. He then congratulates Yudhiṣṭhira on his triumph, and Yudhiṣṭhira acknowledges that that triumph is due to Kṛṣṇa himself. The Pāṇḍavas now appropriate the treasure of the Dhārtarāṣṭras; as an auspicious act they spend the night outside the camp.*

*Next day Kṛṣṇa prepares to ride to Hāstinapura; the Pāṇḍavas urge him to comfort Gāndhārī, who had lost all her sons.* **[62]** *— Janamejaya asks why it was necessary for Kṛṣṇa to go to Hāstinapura, and Vaiśaṃpāyana promises to explain. — Yudhiṣṭhira fears that on hearing the manner of Duryodhana's death Gāndhārī will use her ascetic power to destroy the Pāṇḍavas; he therefore asks Kṛṣṇa to allay her anger. Kṛṣṇa rides to Hāstinapura, where he meets Dhṛtarāṣṭra. He reminds him that the calamity was caused by his own actions, and tells him not to lay blame on the Pāṇḍavas, who will now be his only sons. Then he meets Gāndhārī, and points out that what has happened has borne out the warnings she herself issued to Duryodhana,*[1] *which he had ignored. He implores her not to resolve on the destruction of the Pāṇḍavas, though she is certainly capable of it. Gāndhārī agrees. Kṛṣṇa now leaves hurriedly, having come to know that Aśvatthāman is planning a night-raid against the Pāṇḍavas.*

**[63]** *Meanwhile, Duryodhana laments his condition to Saṃjaya. He wishes his surviving followers, Aśvatthāman, Kṛtavarman and Kṛpa, to be told that he was killed unfairly by Bhīma, and that Yudhiṣṭhira should not be trusted. His parents, Dhṛtarāṣṭra and Gāndhārī, understand the Kṣatriya* dharma*: they*

1 See 5.127.

*should be told that he achieved great things in life and died honourably. Finally, Duryodhana dispatches messengers to tell Aśvatthāman of his fate.*

**[64]** *Hearing what has happened to Duryodhana, Aśvatthāman, Kṛtavarman and Kṛpa hasten to where he lies, writhing and bloody, on the battlefield. Aśvatthāman laments this terrible reversal of fortune. Duryodhana replies that death is fated for everyone, and that he has died honourably: his three surviving friends should not grieve for him. But Aśvatthāman is filled with rage. First his father was killed through deceit, and now he finds his king in this state. He swears to slay all the Pāñcālas before Kṛṣṇa's eyes if Duryodhana will permit it. In reply, Duryodhana commands Kṛpa to bring water and to consecrate Aśvatthāman as commander.*

# THE NIGHT-RAID

## THE NIGHT-RAID

[1] — *Saṃjaya continues his narrative. — Kṛpa, Kṛtavarman and Aśvatthāman move away from the battlefield. Wounded and griefstricken, they rest for a while. Then the three warriors see a dense forest, containing a huge banyan tree.*

Saṃjaya spoke:
As fearful nightfall came, Kṛpa, Kṛtavarman and Droṇa's son Aśvatthāman sat down together, overwhelmed with their misery and grief; and as they sat there round the banyan, grieving over the destruction that had overtaken both Kauravas and Pāṇḍavas, their limbs were seized 30
with weariness, and they lay down upon the ground, for they were fatigued and wounded with many arrows. Wearied, those two mighty chariot-fighters, Kṛpa and the Bhoja Kṛtavarman, both accustomed to comfort and undeserving of hardship, now lay on the earth; yielding to exhaustion and grief, great king, they slept.

But Droṇa's son, heir of Bharata, ruled as he was by fury and resentment, could not sleep. Hissing like a snake, burning with savage anger, he lay unsleeping, and gazed out at the terrifying forest. And as he gazed at that forest tract, thronged by many different kinds of creatures, the strong-armed hero noticed a second banyan tree that was full of crows. Crows in their thousands were passing the night there, 35
king of the Kurus, sleeping peacefully, each on its separate perch. As those crows slept, secure on every side, the son of Droṇa saw an owl approaching. It was dreadful to behold: huge, yellow-eyed and tawny, with a penetrating cry and a long beak and claws, swift-flying as Garuḍa.

Softening its cry, heir of Bharata, the great bird headed for a branch of the banyan tree, as if to settle; but as it alighted on the banyan branch, that owl attacked and killed crows by the score as they slept, for owls are crow-slayers. From some it ripped the wings; it severed the heads of others, or broke their legs with its own fierce claws. In an instant the mighty creature slew every bird that it could see, lord of the peoples, till the foot of the banyan tree was covered all round with their bodies and severed limbs. Then, having slaughtered all those crows, the owl appeared as happy as a foe-slaying hero who has fully avenged himself on his foes.

Droṇa's son Aśvatthāman watched that owl carry out its guileful attack at night. The bird's behaviour filled him with new resolve, and he said to himself, 'This bird has given me good advice in warfare! I think the proper time has come for wiping out my enemies. At present the triumphant Pāṇḍavas cannot be slain by me, for they are strong and determined warriors, and their aim is true. Yet in the presence of King Duryodhana I have sworn their death; I have undertaken an act of self-destruction, like a moth flying into a flame, and in a fair fight I would certainly lose my life. But through guile I may meet with success, and cause great destruction to my enemies! Certainty is much preferred over uncertainty by those who are expert in political science; and though this act may be reviled and blamed throughout the world, it must none the less be carried out to maintain the Kṣatriya *dharma*. Time after time the Pāṇḍavas, knowing no self-control, have committed acts of guile that merit blame and condemnation!

'There are two verses on this topic, sung long ago by men who, pondering *dharma* and reflecting on right and wrong, had come to a true understanding: "The army of the foe should be attacked by its enemies whether exhausted, or routed, or occupied in eating, or riding forth, or retiring to camp; it should be attacked if it is overcome by weariness at dead of night, or leaderless, or broken, or if its arrays become separated!"'

*Aśvatthāman wakes Kṛpa and Kṛtavarman and tells them of his plan; when they do not answer, he reminds them of the terrible reversal of fate that has befallen them all, and demands to know what is to be done about it.*

[2] *Kṛpa explains that there are two forces, fate and human effort, and that everything that is accomplished results from the two acting together. The wise man engages in effort, but that effort should have the approval of the gods and the elders. Duryodhana's exertions were undertaken against the advice of those who wished him well, and led to disaster. Kṛpa's view is that the three warriors should consult Dhṛtarāṣṭra, Gāndhārī and Vidura on the best course of action.*

[3] *Aśvatthāman rejects Kṛpa's reasoning: all men favour their own judgements and condemn those of others, and all men act according to their own judgements. Aśvatthāman, though a Brahmin, has always followed the Kṣatriya* dharma, *and now that the death of his father Droṇa has to be avenged he cannot adopt any other. He will attack the Pāñcālas and Pāṇḍavas as they sleep peacefully at night, and destroy them like a fire burning dry grass.*

[4] *Kṛpa approves Aśvatthāman's determination to take revenge on his enemies, and proposes that he and Kṛtavarman should accompany him in an attack the next day; but first they should rest. Aśvatthāman insists that he cannot rest while his heart burns with so much rage. He will slaughter his enemies now, while they sleep; then he will rest easy.*

[5] *Kṛpa emphasizes the importance of taking the advice of friends and elders, and counsels Aśvatthāman against pursuing his plan: it is against* dharma *to attack a sleeping enemy. Aśvatthāman retorts that the Pāṇḍavas have already violated* dharma *in many ways – why does Kṛpa not censure them? Aśvatthāman will avenge his father even if it results in his being reborn as a worm or an insect. He yokes horses to his chariot and sets off towards the enemy. Kṛpa and Kṛtavarman ask him where he is going; when he tells them of his determination to avenge Droṇa, they follow him to the enemy camp.*

[6] *At the entrance to the camp Aśvatthāman is confronted by a colossal, terrifying figure wearing a tiger-skin and with a snake for its sacred thread. Flames issue from its mouth, nose, ears and thousands of eyes, and from the flames there issue hundreds and thousands of Kṛṣṇas. Aśvatthāman attacks it with weapon after weapon; none has the slightest effect. Now Kṛṣṇas densely pack the sky. Aśvatthāman reflects that Kṛpa's observations on the wisdom of accepting good advice have been shown to be correct, and that fate is more powerful than human effort. He determines to seek the aid of the great god Śiva.*

[7] *Aśvatthāman prays for Śiva's protection: he worships the god, and offers himself to him as a sacrificial victim. A golden altar appears, along with great numbers of extraordinary beings, the hosts of Śiva's followers. Many have the*

*faces of animals, many bear weapons of various kinds; they caper and leap about, and are terrible to see. They approach Aśvatthāman; he dedicates himself as a sacrificial offering, and ascends the altar. Śiva now addresses him directly, and explains that thus far he has protected the Pāñcālas to honour Kṛṣṇa, but that now their time has come. He gives Aśvatthāman a sword, and enters his body. Surrounded by Rākṣasas and unseen beings, Aśvatthāman approaches the camp of his enemies.*

Dhṛtarāṣṭra spoke:
**[8]** When the mighty chariot-fighter, Droṇa's son Aśvatthāman, set out for the camp, I trust that Kṛpa and the Bhoja Kṛtavarman did not turn back in fear? and that they were not arrested by the minions of the Pāṇḍavas, or observed by the guards? I trust the two great warriors did not retreat, thinking their task impossible? I trust they laid waste to the camp, and killed the Somakas and the Pāṇḍavas, and followed Duryodhana's matchless path in battle? I trust they were not slain by the Pāñcālas, to sleep upon the earth? I trust that they achieved some feats? Tell me this, Saṃjaya!

Saṃjaya spoke:
5 When Droṇa's noble son Aśvatthāman set out for the camp, Kṛpa and
Kṛtavarman remained stationed at the camp gate. Aśvatthāman was glad
to see that the two mighty chariot-fighters were ready for the fray,
O king, and in a whisper he told them, 'When you two are intent
on combat you can annihilate the entire Kṣatriya line, never mind the
remnant of an army, and fast asleep at that! I shall enter the camp, and
range about it like Death himself. My order is that you must both ensure
that not one man escapes from me alive!'

With these words Droṇa's son entered the camp of the sons of Kuntī,
10 fearlessly leaping the wall rather than using the gate. Once he had
entered, the strong-armed hero, knowing the way,[1] went silently to
Dhṛṣṭadyumna's sleeping-quarters, while Dhṛṣṭadyumna's guards, who
were mightily fatigued by the great deeds they had done in battle, lay

1 Aśvatthāman would hardly know his way around the camp of his enemies; presumably he is guided by Śiva, who has entered him.

trustfully fast asleep, surrounded by their troops. The son of Droṇa entered Dhṛṣṭadyumna's quarters, heir of Bharata, and there before him he beheld the prince of the Pāñcālas, lying asleep on a great bed of purest linen, covered with rich drapes, strewn with the finest garlands, perfumed with incense and with powders.

The noble man lay sleeping on his bed, free from all doubt and fear.
Lord of the earth, Aśvatthāman woke him with a kick. Dhṛṣṭadyumna 15
of immeasurable greatness, that warrior mad for battle, feeling the kick, raised himself up, and recognized the great chariot-fighter, Droṇa's son. As he arose from his bed, mighty Aśvatthāman lifted him with both hands by the hair of his head, and dashed him to the ground. Forcibly hurled down, and frightened, heir of Bharata, and barely awake, the prince of the Pāñcālas could not so much as move. Then, treading on him, one foot on his chest, one on his throat, while he bellowed and writhed, O king, Aśvatthāman prepared to slaughter him like a sacrificial beast. Clawing him with his nails, Dhṛṣṭadyumna spoke faintly to Droṇa's son. 'Son of my Teacher, slay me with a sword – do not delay! Let me attain the realms of the virtuous through your deed, O best of men!'

Hearing his faint request, Droṇa's son spoke. 'Such realms are not 20
for those who slay their Teachers, defiler of your lineage; therefore you do not merit death by the sword, you evil-minded man!'[1] And as he spoke, he trampled him in his rage, crushing his vital organs with appalling blows from his feet, like a lion mauling a rutting elephant. The hero's cries as he was murdered in his quarters awoke his women and his guards, great king; but when they saw Aśvatthāman, a massive being of superhuman strength, they thought him an evil ghost, and in their fear they could not utter a sound.

This was how Aśvatthāman of mighty ardour dispatched Dhṛṣṭadyumna to the realm of Yama. Then he took the prince's lovely chariot

1 In addition to denying Dhṛṣṭadyumna access to the warrior's heaven, Aśvatthāman is explicitly enacting an animal sacrifice. The victim in such a sacrifice was killed by suffocation or strangulation: no blood was to flow and no sound to be made. Aśvatthāman similarly kills the first several of his victims without weapons, though he insultingly uses his feet rather than his hands. Only when he has dispatched the Pāñcāla leaders and begins to attack 'the common soldiery' (verse 37 below) does he do them the honour of using a sword to slay them.

25 and mounted it, filling the horizon with its roar as he left the royal
quarters. Now the mighty hero set forth by chariot for the rest of the
camp, bent on slaying his enemies.

When Droṇa's son, the mighty chariot-fighter, had left, the women-
folk then wailed aloud, and so did all the guards; when they saw their
king slain, all Dhṛṣṭadyumna's Kṣatriya wives gave way to utter grief
and lamentation, heir of Bharata. Hearing their cries close by, bull-like
Kṣatriyas swiftly tied on their armour and asked what the matter was.
The women, terrified at the sight of Aśvatthāman heir of Bharadvāja,
30 replied in downcast tones, 'Hurry to attack him! We do not know
whether he is a Rākṣasa or a man, but he has killed the king of the
Pāñcālas and now is riding on his chariot!' At this those warrior chiefs
rapidly surrounded Droṇa's son; but as they descended on him, he
smashed them all with a Weapon of Rudra.

After killing Dhṛṣṭadyumna and his followers, he saw, not far away,
Uttamaujas sleeping on a bed. Him too he attacked with might, one foot
on his throat and one upon his chest, and slew the bellowing foe-tamer
as before. Yudhāmanyu now arrived; supposing that a Rākṣasa had killed
his brother, he swiftly took up a club and struck Droṇa's son in the
35 chest. Aśvatthāman rushed at him, seized him and hurled him to the
ground; then, while he writhed, he slew him also like a sacrificial beast.
And having killed him in that manner, the hero now attacked other
mighty chariot-fighters, lord of kings, wherever they lay sleeping, and
slew them as they writhed and trembled, like a sacrificial slaughterman.

Then he took up a sword and began to slay the others, the com-
mon soldiery, manoeuvring this way and that, for he was expert at
sword-fighting. So when he came on troopers sleeping in their troops,
exhausted and weaponless, he slew them all in a moment: with his
excellent sword he cut down soldiers and horses and elephants, till, his
every limb doused in blood, he seemed like Death himself, unloosed
40 by fate; for the death-throes of his enemies, and his brandishing of
his sword, and the sword-stroke itself, drenched Droṇa's son in gore
in three different ways. His mien as he fought, blood-soaked, sword
blazing, seemed inhuman and utterly terrifying, and those in the camp
who were wakened by the din, king of the Kurus, and gazed bewildered
at each other, quaked at the sight of Droṇa's son; when those Kṣatriyas,

tormentors of their enemies, saw his appearance, they thought him a
Rākṣasa, and closed their eyes.

Ranging about the camp like Death in this dreadful form, his eye
now fell on the sons of Draupadī and the surviving Somakas. Alarmed 45
by all the noise, bows in their hands, Draupadī's sons knew of the death
of Dhṛṣṭadyumna, and the mighty chariot-fighters boldly showered
Bharadvāja's heir with hosts of arrows. The noise awoke Śikhaṇḍin
and the Prabhadrakas, and they too tormented Droṇa's son with their
shafts. But when Bharadvāja's heir saw them pouring forth torrents of
arrows, he roared a powerful roar in his longing to slay those invincible
heroes. Enraged beyond measure as he recalled the death of his father, he
dismounted from his chariot and rushed at speed to the attack. Wielding
his huge shield that was decked with a thousand moons, and his great
gold-embellished celestial sword, the mighty hero attacked the sons of
Draupadī, manoeuvring in battle with his sword.

The tiger-like hero smote Prativindhya son of Yudhiṣṭhira in the 50
belly, O king, and he fell slain to the ground. Bhīma's son, Sutasoma of
great energy, pierced the son of Droṇa with a lance, and then attacked
him, brandishing his sword; but the bull-like hero severed Sutasoma's
arm, sword and all, and struck him in the ribs; he fell, his breast cloven.
Heroic Śatānīka, Nakula's son, snatched up a chariot-wheel in his two
arms and smote Aśvatthāman in the chest with it; but as soon as he
had done so, the Brahmin returned the blow, and he fell in distress to
the ground, where Aśvatthāman struck off his head. Śrutakarman son 55
of Arjuna took up a club, then rushed at Droṇa's son and smote him
fiercely on the left shoulder; but he struck Śrutakarman in the mouth
with his excellent sword, so that he fell to the ground, senseless in
death, his face mangled. At that, brave Śrutakīrti with his mighty bow
approached Aśvatthāman and showered him with torrents of arrows;
but Droṇa's son with his shield warded off his arrows too, and struck
his head, still decked with earrings, from his body. Then the slayer of
Bhīṣma, Śikhaṇḍin, followed by all the Prabhadrakas, attacked the hero
from every side with every kind of weapon, and smote him with a
shaft between the eyebrows; but Droṇa's mighty son, still full of rage, 60
confronted him and split him from head to toe with his sword. And
when the afflicter of his enemies had slain Śikhaṇḍin in his rage, he

rushed at speed against all the hosts of the Prabhadrakas, and also attacked Virāṭa's surviving troops.

The mighty hero made dreadful slaughter of Drupada's sons, grandsons and allies, slaying every one he saw; attacking man after man, the son of Droṇa cut them down with his sword, for he was expert at sword manoeuvres. And now they beheld the Night of Death: a black-skinned woman with a single tuft of hair, her mouth and eyes red, her garlands and unguents red, her garments red, standing alone, noose in hand, and smiling as she bound men and horses and elephants with her terrible nooses and took them away, carrying off all manner of hairless departed beings, all bound. Those foremost warriors had seen her on other nights as they slept, leading sleeping men away, and they had seen Droṇa's son, too, constantly slaying; ever since the beginning of the battle between the Kaurava and Pāṇḍava armies, they had seen that dread goddess and the son of Droṇa in their dreams. First fate afflicted them, and then Droṇa's son slew them as he terrified all creatures with the frightful roars he roared; and now those heroes, remembering the visions they had seen before, realized that those dreams had come true, for they were under fate's oppression.

The din awoke hundreds and thousands of bowmen in the Pāṇḍava camp. Aśvatthāman cut off the feet of one and the buttocks of another; some he split open in the ribs, for he was like Death himself, unloosed by fate. Others lay scattered over the earth, O lord, savagely crushed, moaning in terrible pain, trampled by horses and elephants. Men cried out, 'What's this? Who's this? What's that sound? What's happening?' and as they spoke the son of Droṇa became their Death; Aśvatthāman, the best of fighting men, dispatched to the realm of death all the Pāṇḍavas and Sṛñjayas, weaponless and armourless, panic-stricken. Terrified of his weapon, leaping up from their beds in fear, blind with sleep and senseless, they perished where they stood; their thighs seized by paralysis, their strength killed by despair, moaning in utter terror, they trampled one another.

Now Droṇa's son took once more to his dreadfully roaring chariot; bow in hand, he used his arrows to dispatch more men to the realm of Yama. Some other heroes leapt from their beds while he was yet far off, and rushed to the attack: these best of men he delivered to the Night of

Death. And he careered about, crushing his enemies with his chariot or
showering torrents of arrows of every kind upon them. Then again he 80
ranged about on foot, with his sky-bright sword and his lovely shield
decked with a hundred moons. In this way the son of Droṇa, mad for
battle, reduced his enemies' camp to chaos, like an elephant churning
up a pond.

O king, the noise caused many warriors to leap from their beds.
Confused, and troubled by both sleep and fear, they ran aimlessly
about, while others shrieked or babbled incoherently, leaving their
weapons and their clothes untouched. Some, hair dishevelled, could
not recognize each other; others, leaping up in terror, wandered about
the camp; yet others pissed and shat themselves. Horses and elephants 85
broke their tethers, lord of kings, and rushed about together, causing
great confusion. Some men threw themselves to the ground in their
fear, and elephants and horses crushed them where they lay. In the midst
of all this, bull-like hero, Rākṣasas glutted themselves and roared with
loud joy, and the joyful shouts of throngs of evil ghosts filled the horizon
and the sky, O king.

Horses and elephants, frightened by the cries of the afflicted, broke
loose and ran about the camp, crushing its occupants and making the 90
darkness of the night doubly dark with the dust raised by their running
feet. Bewildered in the universal darkness, fathers could not recognize
their sons, nor brothers their brothers, while riderless elephants and
horses broke free from their teams, striking and injuring and crushing
all whom they encountered. Routed warriors, rushing headlong, struck
each other down, felled one another, and trampled the fallen. Senseless,
sleep-befuddled and plunged in darkness, men in the camp succumbed
to fate and even slew their kin. Gatekeepers abandoned their gates, 95
troopers their troops, and all ran headlong as best they could, but
senselessly, at random; and those who fled no longer recognized each
other, and shouted, 'Father?' and 'My son?', for fate had deprived them
of their senses. Fleeing in every direction, abandoning their own kin,
some called out to each other by family name, while others simply lay
on the ground and howled. But Droṇa's battle-crazed son knew all of
them, and slaughtered all of them.

Some Kṣatriyas, out of their minds with terror at the ceaseless carnage,

100 burst out from the camp; but as they did so, fearfully hoping to escape
the camp alive, Kṛpa and Kṛtavarman cut them down at the gate.
They had no weapons, no gear, no armour; hair dishevelled, hands
joined together, they trembled in fear on the ground, but the two
Kauravas spared none of them: not one man who emerged outside the
camp escaped from Kṛpa and Hṛdika's evil-minded son. Then the two
Kauravas, wishing to please the son of Droṇa further, fired the camp in
three places.

Now Aśvatthāman, Droṇa's joy, ranged about the blazing camp, great
105 king, showing his expertise with the sword. Some brave men attacked
him, others ran headlong from him, but that best of Brahmins with his
sword sundered them all from their lives. In his rage, Droṇa's heroic son
felled some warriors by cutting them in two like sesame stalks, till the
earth was strewn with the fallen, heir of Bharata: the finest men and
elephants and horses, wailing in agony. So many thousands of men were
falling slain that often corpses, struck by one newly dead, would rise
up, and, having risen, fall again.

Aśvatthāman cut off arms, still bearing weapons and armlets; he cut
off heads, and thighs like elephants' trunks, and hands and feet, O heir
110 of Bharata. In encounter after encounter Droṇa's son broke the backs
of some, the heads of others and the ribs of others, while there were yet
others whom he reduced to flight. Some he cut open at the waist, others
through the ears; some men he cut open at the shoulder, and forced
their heads down within their bodies. Thus Aśvatthāman ranged about,
slaying so many men, through the dreadful night, the ghastly darkness.
The earth presented a grim appearance, strewn with thousands of dying
and dead men and with hosts of elephants, horses and chariots, and
haunted by Yakṣas and Rākṣasas; and on that earth fell ever more men,
cut down in rage by Droṇa's son.

115 Men called out for their mothers, or their fathers, or their brothers.
Others exclaimed, 'The furious sons of Dhṛtarāṣṭra never once achieved
in battle what cruel Rākṣasas have done to us while we sleep! We are
slaughtered thus because the sons of Kuntī are not here, for no god
or demon, no Gandharva or Yakṣa or Rākṣasa could triumph over
Kuntī's son Arjuna, who has Kṛṣṇa the stirrer of men for his protector.
The wealth-winner is a supporter of Brahmins and a speaker of truth;

self-controlled and compassionate to all, he would not slay a sleeping
or distracted man, or one who had laid down his weapons and sued for
peace, or one fleeing with dishevelled hair! This dreadful thing is done
to us by cruel Rākṣasas.' With such laments many men lay down and
died.

But soon the great uproar of men's roars and groans was stilled; soon 120
the dreadful clouds of dust all vanished, king, laid by the blood that
drenched the earth. In his rage the son of Droṇa had slain men in
their thousands who writhed in pain, or had lost the will to fight, as
Śiva, lord of beasts, destroys beasts;[1] whether they lay clinging to one
another, or fled, or hid, or fought, he had slaughtered all of them.
Indeed, warriors slew one another rather than be burnt by the fire or
killed by Aśvatthāman. By midnight, lord of men, the son of Droṇa had 125
dispatched the mighty army of the Pāṇḍavas to Yama's realm.

That night, so dreadful and destructive of men and elephants and
horses, brought joy to those creatures that come out in the dark. Rākṣasas
could be seen there, and Piśācas of every sort, eating the flesh of men
and drinking their blood. These fearsome, unruly creatures had gaping
mouths, orange skin and teeth of stone; their hair was matted, their legs
long, their bellies huge; they had five feet; their fingers grew backwards
from their hands; ugly and cruel, they uttered fearsome sounds; their
knees bulged like water-pots, their throats were blue; they were dwarfish
and yet terrifying, savage, hideous and pitiless. They had brought their 130
wives and children with them.

Rākṣasas of every shape were to be seen there, gleefully drinking
blood, or dancing in groups, crying out, 'This food is good! This food
is fresh! This food tastes wonderful!' Carrion-eaters and carnivores
gorged on fat, marrow, bone, blood and grease as they consumed
the flesh of others; fearsome corpse-eating Piśācas of many different
forms, all swollen-bellied, ran about sucking up human fat. There
were Rākṣasas in their tens of thousands and millions and hundreds of
millions, fearsome and huge and cruel; joyfully they gorged themselves 135
at the scene of that great slaughter, where many evil ghosts were also
assembled, lord of men.

1 The word *paśu*, 'beast', is also the term for a sacrificial victim.

When dawn broke, Droṇa's son decided to leave the camp. So soaked he was in human blood that his sword-hilt lay glued to his hand as if the two were one. His enemies were utterly destroyed, and now he blazed in the midst of that destruction like the doomsday fire when all beings are reduced to ash. Lord, Aśvatthāman son of Droṇa had carried out the task that he had vowed; he had travelled a path that no one else could travel, and slaked his anguish for his father.

The camp that he had entered had been silent, full of men sleeping at night; now too the bull-like hero left a camp that was soundless from
140 his killing. Emerging from the camp, brave Aśvatthāman rejoined his two companions and told them everything that he had done, O lord, delighting them and delighted for himself; and they too, his well-wishers, told him the glad news of the Pāñcālas and Sṛñjayas that they had cut down in their thousands. Then all three roared aloud for pleasure and clapped their hands.

Thus did that most dreadful of nights bring the destruction of the Somakas, who were sleeping heedlessly. The course of fate is irresistible, make no doubt: those who destroyed us were themselves cut down.

Dhṛtarāṣṭra spoke:
But why did Droṇa's son, that mighty chariot-fighter, not do such a great deed as this sooner? He was resolved that my son should triumph,
145 so why did the great bowman only do this deed after the slaughter of my Kṣatriyas? Please tell me this!

Saṃjaya spoke:
Heir of Kuru, it was clearly through fear of the sons of Kuntī that he did not do it sooner: their absence, and that of wise Kṛṣṇa Keśava and Sātyaki, allowed Droṇa's son to accomplish this task. Not even Indra could have carried out the killing in their presence. Besides, O king, this deed was done against a sleeping foe.

Now the three mighty chariot-fighters, having completed that most evil massacre of the Pāṇḍavas, all congratulated one another. Droṇa's son embraced the other two and received their salutations, and then
150 in joy he uttered these matchless words: 'The Pāñcālas are all slain; so are all the sons of Draupadī; and I have slain every one of the Somakas

and the surviving Matsyas! We have achieved success. Now let us go without delay to where our king lies, if he lives, and tell him the happy news!'

[9] *When they reach Duryodhana they find him still alive, though only just. Kṛpa laments the state to which fate has brought him; Aśvatthāman does the same, and asks Duryodhana to pass on his greetings to the fallen Kaurava warriors when he meets them in heaven. Then he tells him of the massacre of Draupadī's sons and Pāñcālas and Matsyas. Hearing this news, Duryodhana seems to revive slightly. He says that, since Dhṛṣṭadyumna and Śikhaṇḍin have been killed, he now considers himself Indra's equal. He bids farewell to the three warriors, whom he will meet again in heaven. Then he dies.*

*— Saṃjaya has finished his narrative. He tells Dhṛtarāṣṭra that the gift of divine sight that had allowed him to describe the battle has now come to its end. Dhṛtarāṣṭra sighs and is lost in thought.*

## THE REED WEAPON

[10] *— Vaiśaṃpāyana's narration to Janamejaya continues. — In the morning Dhṛṣṭadyumna's charioteer brings news of the massacre to Yudhiṣṭhira, who swoons with grief. Regaining consciousness, he laments that the princes who had survived the battles against Karṇa, Droṇa and Bhīṣma should have perished through sheer heedlessness. He knows how dreadful the news will be for Draupadī, who has lost her brother, her sons and her father; he sends Nakula to fetch her. Then he returns to the battlefield, where he sees the bodies of his sons and friends. He swoons again.*

[11] *Yudhiṣṭhira is comforted by his kinsmen. Now Nakula arrives with Draupadī; she has heard the news, and she too faints from grief. Bhīma comforts her. Then she turns on Yudhiṣṭhira, congratulating him with fierce sarcasm on his attainment of world sovereignty. She tells him that if he does not kill Aśvatthāman and his associates at once, she will fast to death. Yudhiṣṭhira replies that she should not grieve for her sons and brothers, who have died in pursuit of* dharma, *and he points out that Aśvatthāman is now far away: how will Draupadī assure herself that he is dead? She answers that Aśvatthāman was born with a jewel on his head; only if she sees that jewel and places it on Yudhiṣṭhira's*

*head will she be willing to live. Then she approaches Bhīma, reminds him of the many times he has rescued her, and implores him to kill Aśvatthāman. Bhīma, with Nakula as his charioteer, drives off at once in pursuit.*

[**12**] *Kṛṣṇa now addresses Yudhiṣṭhira to warn him that Bhīma is in danger: Aśvatthāman has the Weapon of Brahmā's Head. His father Droṇa had given it to Arjuna; Aśvatthāman, jealous, demanded to have it too, and Droṇa reluctantly gave it to him with an injunction never to use it against human beings. Later he had attempted to exchange it for Kṛṣṇa's own discus, but had found himself unable even to lift that; Kṛṣṇa had reprimanded him for his arrogance. He is a dangerous man, and Bhīma must be protected from him.*

[**13**] *Kṛṣṇa, Yudhiṣṭhira and Arjuna mount Kṛṣṇa's chariot and ride in pursuit of Bhīma; they catch up with him, but he will not slow down. On the bank of the Gaṅgā he sees Kṛṣṇa Dvaipāyana Vyāsa, and near to him Aśvatthāman. He challenges him; Aśvatthāman, panicking, determines to use his Weapon, plucks a reed to be its carrier, and dispatches it for the destruction of the Pāṇḍavas.*

[**14**] *Understanding Aśvatthāman's intention, Kṛṣṇa urges Arjuna to release his own Weapon to check Aśvatthāman's Weapon; Arjuna does so. The sky is filled with sound and flame as the two Weapons threaten the destruction of the three worlds. The seers Nārada and Vyāsa appear and upbraid Aśvatthāman and Arjuna for what they have done.*

Vaiśampāyana spoke:

[**15**] As soon as he saw those two seers, radiant and strong as fire, the tiger-like hero, wealth-winner Arjuna, hastened to withdraw his celestial shaft. Best of all those who speak, he joined his hands together and addressed them both: 'I deployed this Weapon to still another Weapon; once this supreme Weapon has been withdrawn, the wicked son of Droṇa is certain to burn us all to nothingness with his Weapon's fiery energy. Now you two with your godlike powers must restrain it for our sake and the sake of all the three worlds.'

5 With these words the wealth-winner withdrew the Weapon once more. To withdraw such a Weapon in battle would be difficult for the very gods; no one but Pāṇḍu's son, not even Indra in person, could have withdrawn that supreme Weapon once it was released in battle, for it had its origin in Brahmā's own fiery energy. Once released, it

could only be called back by a disciplined man following a vow of holy celibacy; if one not following such a vow should release it and then try to call it back, the Weapon would sever the heads of himself and his followers. Arjuna had obtained the almost unobtainable Weapon while practising that vow, and had never released it even in extreme distress. Pāṇḍu's son was a hero true to his vows, a holy celibate, a respecter of his elders; for this reason he was able to withdraw the Weapon once more.[1]

As for the son of Droṇa, he too beheld the two seers standing before him; but he could not withdraw the dreadful Weapon he had released in battle. Knowing himself incapable of withdrawing that supreme Weapon, O king, Aśvatthāman was downcast in mind, and he said to Kṛṣṇa Dvaipāyana Vyāsa, 'In extreme distress, to save my life, I released this Weapon, O sage, for I feared Bhīma. Blessed lord, Bhīma had behaved improperly: he performed an act of *adharma* in battle in order to slay Dhṛtarāṣṭra's son Duryodhana. So in my indiscipline I released this Weapon, Brahmin, and now I am not capable of withdrawing it again. O sage, I released this irresistible celestial weapon with the words, "For the destruction of the Pāṇḍavas!", consecrating it with the energy of Fire; and since it was invoked to bring about the Pāṇḍavas' death, it must now deprive all Pāṇḍu's sons of their lives. I committed this sin, Brahmin, when my mind was filled with anger, releasing a Weapon in battle in hopes of killing the sons of Kuntī.'

Vyāsa replied, 'Child, Kuntī's son the wealth-winner, knowing the Weapon of Brahmā's Head, released it neither through anger nor to slay you in battle: Arjuna released his Weapon to still your Weapon on the battlefield, and now he has withdrawn it again. Through your father's instruction he had obtained a Weapon of Brahmā, and yet the

1 There are two accounts of Arjuna's acquisition of the Weapon of Brahmā's Head: in the first he receives it from Droṇa as the latter's favourite pupil (1.123), in the second he is awarded it by Śiva (3.40). As Droṇa's student he would indeed have been a 'holy celibate' (*brahmacārin*), but by the time of the great war he has long passed on to being a 'householder' (*gṛhastha*) – a married man and a father. The suggestion here seems to be that his observance of his vow as a young man was so remarkable that its effects remain in place many years later.

strong-armed wealth-winner did not waver from the Kṣatriya *dharma*. So steadfast he is, so virtuous, so expert with all weapons; so why did you try to slay him with his brothers and their kin?

'Where a Weapon of Brahmā's Head is destroyed by another supreme Weapon, Indra does not grant rain to that land for twelve years. For this reason Pāṇḍu's strong-armed son did not strike down this Weapon of yours though he had the power to do so, for he sought the welfare of all beings. The Pāṇḍavas must be protected, and so must you yourself, and this land of ours must always be protected – therefore withdraw this celestial weapon, strong-armed hero! Let your anger cease, let Kuntī's sons be safe, for the royal seer Yudhiṣṭhira son of Pāṇḍu does not wish for victory through *adharma*.[1] And give to them this jewel that you bear upon your head: in return for that, the Pāṇḍavas will grant you your life.'

'This jewel of mine', answered Droṇa's son, 'is more precious than all the gems and other wealth that the Pāṇḍavas and Kauravas have ever owned. The man who ties it on has nothing at all to fear from weapons, sickness or hunger, or from gods, demons or serpents; Rākṣasas do not threaten him, nor robbers. Such is the power of this jewel that I would not give it up for anything; but I must at once do as the blessed one has commanded me. Here is the jewel, and here am I. As for the reed weapon, it will fall into the wombs of the Pāṇḍava women, for it cannot be deployed in vain.'

'Do thus,' said Vyāsa; 'and do not let any other thought enter your mind. Release the Weapon into the wombs of the Pāṇḍavas, then do no more!'

Then Aśvatthāman, suffering grievously, released that supreme Weapon into the Pāṇḍava wombs, as Vyāsa had commanded.

[**16**] Kṛṣṇa lord of the senses knew that Droṇa's wicked son had released his Weapon, and yet it was with joy that he turned on him and said, 'Virāṭa's daughter Uttarā, widow of Abhimanyu, daughter-in-law of Arjuna the bearer of the bow Gāṇḍīva, was once told by a pious Brahmin who saw her at Upaplavya, "When the Kuru lineage fails, a son shall be born to you, and he shall be Parikṣit even

1 i.e. he does not wish to have to instruct Arjuna to use his Weapon after all.

while still in the womb."[1] The words of that virtuous man will indeed come true, and Parikṣit will be the son who re-establishes the Pāṇḍava line!'

Hearing Kṛṣṇa Govinda, best of the Sātvatas, speaking thus, the son of Droṇa was filled with extreme rage, and he retorted, 'Lotus-eyed Keśava, you speak these words through partiality, but they cannot be true: my words cannot be uttered in vain. Kṛṣṇa, this Weapon that I have deployed shall fall into the womb of the daughter of Virāṭa, though you may wish to spare her!'

'That supreme Weapon will not fall in vain,' said Kṛṣṇa Vāsudeva, 'but the child, though stillborn, shall attain long life. Now as for you, all wise men know you for a coward and an evildoer, a man of frequent wickedness, a killer of children. Receive now, therefore, the reward for this evil that you have done. You shall wander this earth for three thousand years, not once speaking to anyone anywhere; without companions, you shall pass your time in uninhabited lands, for you shall have no place in human society, you vile and wicked man. Stinking of pus and blood, exiled to remote wastelands, you shall live a life plagued by every disease.

'But Parikṣit, on attaining to manhood and completing his Vedic studies, shall receive all weapons from Kṛpa son of Śaradvat, as befits a hero; and when he has learnt the greatest Weapons, he shall rule the earth for sixty years, righteously maintaining the Kṣatriya *dharma*. Basest, most evil-minded man! In years to come strong-armed Parikṣit shall become king of the Kurus before your very eyes: behold the power of my austerities and my truth!'

Vyāsa added, 'In that you have committed a dreadful act without regard for us – worse, in that you have acted so despite your Brahmin birth – therefore the matchless words that Devakī's son has spoken shall come true for you, make no doubt! Man of vile deeds, go swiftly hence!'

'Brahmin,' said Aśvatthāman, 'along with you I shall remain long in the world of men. Let the words of blessed Kṛṣṇa here, the highest lord, come true!'

1 His name will be Parikṣit since his birth will occur when the Kuru line has failed (*parikṣīṇa*).

Then Droṇa's son gave the noble Pāṇḍavas his jewel, and before the eyes of all of them he departed sadly for the forest.

The Pāṇḍavas had eliminated all their enemies. Now, with Kṛṣṇa, Vyāsa and the great sage Nārada at their head, they took the jewel with which Droṇa's son had been born, and quickly hurried back to the spirited Draupadī, who was fasting to death. The tiger-like heroes, with their excellent horses swift as the wind, returned once more with Kṛṣṇa prince of Daśārha to their camp. The mighty chariot-fighters leapt down from their chariots; but when they saw the suffering of Draupadī Kṛṣṇā, joyless, overwhelmed with misery and grief, they suffered even more themselves.

With Kṛṣṇa Keśava, the Pāṇḍavas approached her and positioned themselves around her. Then mighty Bhīma, at the king's bidding, presented that celestial jewel to her, and spoke these words: 'Lady, this jewel is yours. He who killed your sons is defeated. Cast aside grief, arise; call to mind the Kṣatriya *dharma*! Timid, dark-eyed lady, when Kṛṣṇa Vāsudeva, the slayer of Madhu, set out on his mission for peace,[1] you spoke these words: "I have no husbands, I have no sons, I have no brothers, I have not even you, Govinda, as long as the king seeks peace!" These were the resolute words that you spoke to the highest lord. They accord with the Kṣatriya *dharma*: please call them to mind now!

'Wicked Duryodhana, our adversary for the kingship, is slain, and I have drunk the blood of Duḥśāsana as he lay writhing on the ground. We have avenged the feud, and no longer shall we blamed by those who like to talk. Droṇa's son has been defeated, but we have freed him in honour of his Brahmin rank, and because of our respect for his father. O queen, his good name has been destroyed, and only his body remains; he has been parted from his jewel, and made to lay his weapons on the earth.'

Draupadī replied, 'My debt is entirely repaid. I treat the son of the Teacher as my elder. Heir of Bharata, let King Yudhiṣṭhira bind this jewel upon his head.'

1 See 5.70 ff. The specific reference is to Draupadī's lament at 5.80, though the words Bhīma quotes do not appear there.

Then the king took it, and he wore it on his head as a relic of the
Teacher, and because Draupadī wished it so. Wearing that celestial jewel 35
on his head, the mighty king shone like a mountain silhouetted by the
moon.

[**17**] *Yudhiṣṭhira now asks Kṛṣṇa how Aśvatthāman could have slain so many great warriors. Kṛṣṇa explains that he had gained the help of the great lord Śiva, to whom the whole world owes its existence. In the beginning, Brahmā had requested Śiva to create living beings. Śiva agreed, but he spent so long performing austerities in the waters that Brahmā created Prajāpati to create beings instead. Once created, they sought in their hunger to eat Prajāpati, who fled to Brahmā; Brahmā gave them plants for their food, and gave the weaker beings as food to the stronger; satisfied, they multiplied. Śiva now emerged from the waters; in his anger at seeing the creation made without him, he cast his* liṅga *into the earth, as its creative power was not now needed; but he stated that both beings and plants would continue to thrive.* [**18**] *Later, the gods planned a sacrifice, but they assigned no share to Śiva. Śiva appeared before them in the guise of a holy celibate but bearing a bow formed from the elements of the sacrifice. The universe was thrown into chaos. Śiva shot an arrow at the gods' sacrifice, which took the form of a deer and fled, as did the Fire; he also assaulted various of the gods. The gods succeeded in placating him: he healed their injuries, and they gave him all the oblations for his share. Kṛṣṇa explains that the whole world's welfare thus depends on Śiva's state of mind; it was because he showed favour to Aśvatthāman that all the Pāṇḍava and Pāñcāla warriors were slain.*

# THE WOMEN

## THE END OF GRIEF

[1] — *Janamejaya asks to hear what Dhṛtarāṣṭra, Yudhiṣṭhira and the three surviving Kauravas did after Duryodhana's death, and Vaiśaṃpāyana narrates.* — *Dhṛtarāṣṭra falls to the ground and grieves for the death of his hundred sons and the rest of his supporters. He regrets not restraining Duryodhana, but continues to blame the disaster on misdeeds in a former birth, or on fate. Saṃjaya retorts that the blame is his, for continuing to humour his bellicose son, and counsels him to stop grieving.* [2] *Vidura too advises an end to grief: life is brief and death inevitable, and the fallen warriors now have everything they could wish for in heaven. The wise man does not indulge in grief.*

[3] *Dhṛtarāṣṭra asks how one may free oneself from the misery that is caused by unwished-for events. Vidura answers that successive constant rebirth, conditioned by deeds in earlier births, is the order of things: grief is pointless, and those who are wise seek to find an end to the sequence.* [4] *At Dhṛtarāṣṭra's request, Vidura goes into further detail. A foetus is formed; he grows, already a prey to suffering; he is born as a human being, subject to woe and disease; enslaved by sensuality and passion, he proceeds towards death like everyone else.* Dharma *and knowledge are the only ways to release.*

[5] *Vidura now tells the story of a Brahmin who, fleeing through a terrible forest filled with savage beasts, falls into a well. As he falls he is caught by creepers and suspended head-down. Menaced by a snake at the bottom of the well, a six-headed elephant at the top, and by rats gnawing at the creepers, he none the less drinks thirstily from a stream of honey produced by a swarm of dreadful bees.* [6] *Vidura expounds this story as an allegory: man is threatened by disease, old age and the passing of time, yet gives himself up to pleasures. Wise men know*

*that the course of rebirth is so, and seek to escape from it.* [7] *After expanding further on his theme, Vidura concludes that a man of good character who exercises self-control, renunciation and vigilance will attain to the world of Brahmā.*

[8] *Dhṛtarāṣṭra swoons with grief for his sons. Comforted by Kṛṣṇa Dvaipāyana Vyāsa, Vidura, Saṃjaya and others, he rails against human existence and the suffering it brings, and proposes to take his life. Vyāsa tells him that the destruction of the Kurus was destined to occur. He himself was present in Indra's world when Viṣṇu promised Earth that her burden would be lightened when Dhṛtarāṣṭra's son Duryodhana caused a great slaughter at Kurukṣetra. Everything that has happened was preordained; Dhṛtarāṣṭra's sons were evil, and there is no reason to grieve for them. He commands Dhṛtarāṣṭra not to take his life; Dhṛtarāṣṭra agrees to this, and promises to try not to grieve.*

## THE WOMEN

[9] *Dhṛtarāṣṭra gives orders for Gāndhārī and the other women to be brought to him. He then sets out from the city with them. Every household is full of women weeping inconsolably: Dhṛtarāṣṭra is surrounded by thousands of them as he makes his way towards the battlefield. Non-Kṣatriya menfolk also follow him.*

[10] *After travelling a mile they encounter Aśvatthāman, Kṛpa and Kṛtavarman. Kṛpa tells Gāndhārī that her sons died heroically, and that they have certainly attained the heavenly realms. Then he describes the massacre of the Pāñcālas and the sons of Draupadī. The three now ask leave to depart, since the Pāṇḍavas will be pursuing them. They go their separate ways.*

Vaiśaṃpāyana spoke:
[11] After all the warriors had been slain, Yudhiṣṭhira lord of *dharma* learnt that the aged Dhṛtarāṣṭra had set forth from Hāstinapura. Great king, Yudhiṣṭhira, afflicted with grief for his sons, travelled to meet Dhṛtarāṣṭra, overwhelmed with grief for his sons. His brothers went with him, and he was followed by noble Kṛṣṇa the heroic prince of Daśārha, and also by Sātyaki and Yuyutsu. Behind them came Draupadī, racked with grief and tormented by sorrow, together with the Pāñcāla women who had gathered there.

5 Along the bank of the Gaṅgā, O truest heir of Bharata, Yudhiṣṭhira
beheld women in throngs, shrieking like stricken ospreys. At once they
surrounded the king in their thousands, weeping, waving their arms
aloft in their distress, speaking without caring whether their words were
soft or harsh. 'How can the king know *dharma* and yet show such cruelty
that he slew fathers, brothers, elders, sons and friends? Strong-armed
hero, what was your state of mind when you ordered the deaths of
Droṇa, and grandfather Bhīṣma, and Jayadratha? What good is your
kingdom to you? You will not see fathers or brothers, or unconquerable
Abhimanyu, or the sons of Draupadī!'

10 Strong-armed Yudhiṣṭhira lord of *dharma* passed by them as they
shrieked like ospreys, and greeted his father Dhṛtarāṣṭra. Then the
Pāṇḍavas, tormentors of their enemies, paid the old man their respects,
announcing their names one by one. But their father Dhṛtarāṣṭra,
afflicted by the killing of his sons, was reluctant in his grief to embrace
the Pāṇḍava who had slain them. He embraced the lord of *dharma*, heir
of Bharata, and spoke kindly to him; but as for Bhīma, he pounced
wickedly on him like a fire eager to consume him – the flames of his
anger, fanned by the wind of his grief, seemed ready to make a forest
fire of Bhīma.

15 Kṛṣṇa understood that he was planning some evil for Bhīma; he
dragged the latter aside with both hands, and gave Dhṛtarāṣṭra a Bhīma
made of iron. In his great wisdom the stirrer of men had read Dhṛtarāṣṭra's
body-language in advance, and had put this arrangement in place. No
sooner had King Dhṛtarāṣṭra got his hands on the iron Bhīma than he
used his might to break it, believing it was the wolf-belly; exerting the
strength of ten thousand elephants, the king smashed that iron Bhīma,
so that his own chest was crushed and blood flowed from his mouth.
Then he fell to the ground, so doused in blood that he looked like a
20 coral tree in blossom. Saṃjaya, the learned Sūta, took hold of him and
gently calmed him, saying, 'Do not act so.' But now that he had released
his anger, the high-minded king, freed from his rage, cried out once
more in grief, 'Alas, alas! Bhīma!'

Understanding that his anger had passed, and that now he was full of
grief at killing Bhīma, the best of men, Kṛṣṇa Vāsudeva, addressed him
thus: 'Do not grieve, Dhṛtarāṣṭra. You have not slain Bhīma. This was

an iron effigy, king, that you laid low. I knew that you were in thrall to anger, bull-like heir of Bharata, and so I pulled Kuntī's son away as he entered the jaws of death. No one is your equal in might, tiger-like king! What man could bear the pressure of your two strong arms? Just as nobody escapes alive from a meeting with Death, so no one would survive the grip of your two arms. Therefore I had an iron effigy of Bhīma made by your son,[1] and placed it here before you.

'The pain of grief for your sons had distracted your mind from *dharma*, and so, lord of kings, you wanted to kill Bhīma. But for you to slay the wolf-belly, king, would not have been right, for it could never bring your sons back to life. So please give your approval to everything that we have done with right in mind; and do not give your heart over to grief.'

[12] Attendants now approached the king to clean his wounds, and when this was done, Kṛṣṇa the slayer of Madhu addressed him once more. 'King, you have studied the Vedas, and many kinds of learned texts; you have heard the ancient tales, and all the rules for kings. Knowing all these, wise heir of Kuru, you did not follow their advice, although you knew the Pāṇḍavas to be superior in might and heroism. The king whose wisdom remains steadfast, and who can see for himself where problems lie, and where and when to act, he fares excellently well. But the one who does not accept advice for his welfare, whether in good times or in bad, that man meets with misfortune, and grieves for his foolish policy. See how your actions differed from this ideal, Bhārata king, for you, lacking all self-control, were controlled by Duryodhana.

'Your pain results from your own wrongdoing. Why then try to slay Bhīma? Contain your anger; think on your misdeeds. As for the base and envious man who brought Draupadī to the assembly,[2] he has been killed by Bhīma to avenge the feud. Recognize your own crimes, afflicter of your enemies, and those of your wicked son: you repudiated the eldest son of Pāṇḍu, though he had done nothing wrong.'

King Dhṛtarāṣtra heard all that Kṛṣṇa so truthfully said, O lord of men,

1 i.e. Yuyutsu.

2 Duryodhana, who caused this to happen, rather than Duḥśāsana, who carried out the order.

and he replied to the son of Devakī, 'Strong-armed heir of Madhu, it is just as you say: love for my son deflected me from steadfastness. What a blessing, righteous Kṛṣṇa, that the tiger-like hero, mighty Bhīma of true valour, had your protection, and did not feel the grip of my two arms! But now my mind is focused; rage and anguish have left me, Kṛṣṇa Keśava, and I wish to embrace heroic Arjuna, Pāṇḍu's middle son. Now all the lords among princes are slain, and all my sons too, my safety and my happiness are to be found with the Pāṇḍavas.' Weeping, he embraced with his arms those strong-armed heroes, Bhīma, wealth-winner Arjuna, and Mādrī's two valiant sons, encouraging each with words of kindness.

**[13]** *Kṛṣṇa and the Pāṇḍavas now approach Gāndhārī. She is on the point of cursing Yudhiṣṭhira when Vyāsa, divining her intention, arrives and urges her to curb her anger. She answers that she does not wish the Pāṇḍavas harm, and that the slaughter of the Kurus was the fault of Duryodhana and his allies. But she remains enraged at Bhīma's low blow in his battle with Duryodhana.* **[14]** *Fearful of her anger, Bhīma seeks to placate her, reminding her of the sufferings and insults Duryodhana had inflicted on the Pāṇḍavas. She then takes him to task for his drinking of Duḥśāsana's blood, but he assures her that he did not actually swallow it. Still Gāndhārī complains that he has not spared a single one of her sons to support the elderly blind couple.*

Vaiśampāyana spoke:
**[15]** Now Gāndhārī asked to see Yudhiṣṭhira. 'Where is that king?' she asked, angry and full of suffering because of the slaughter of her sons and grandsons.

Trembling, with hands joined together, Yudhiṣṭhira lord of kings approached her, and gently said, 'Lady, I am Yudhiṣṭhira, the cruel slayer of your sons. I deserve to be cursed, for I am to blame for this devastation of the earth. Curse me! For I am a friend-betraying fool, and having slain such friends, I have no use for life, or wealth, or kingdom.'

Fearful, he stood close to her as he spoke these words. Gāndhārī did not answer, but could only exhale deeply. Then as he bent down to fall at her feet, the queen, who knew and understood *dharma*, glimpsed through the edge of her blindfold the tips of King Yudhiṣṭhira's fingers,

and his nails, which had always been most fair, were scorched by her
gaze.

When Arjuna saw what had happened, he stood behind Kṛṣṇa
Vāsudeva, and the other Pāṇḍavas too shifted nervously about, heir of
Bharata. But Gāndhārī's anger was now gone,[1] and she spoke words of
comfort to them, as a mother should.

With her leave the broad-chested men then together approached
their own mother Kuntī, the mother of heroes. Seeing her sons after so 10
long, and overwhelmed by anxiety for them, Queen Kuntī shed tears,
and covered her face with her garment. Weeping with her sons, she
gazed at their bodies, wounded repeatedly by torrents of arrows. Then
she embraced them one by one, again and again; and she mourned and
grieved with Draupadī, whose sons were slain, as the Pāñcāla princess
lay weeping on the ground.

'Noble lady,' said Draupadī, 'where have Abhimanyu and all your
other grandsons gone? You are distressed, and it is long since they saw
you, yet today they do not visit you. What good is a kingdom to me?
I have lost my sons!' But wide-eyed Kuntī consoled Drupada's daughter,
and raised her up as she wept, racked with grief. Side by side with her, 15
and followed by her sons, she approached poor, suffering Gāndhārī,
suffering even more herself.

Seeing that lady of high repute with her daughter-in-law, Gāndhārī
spoke: 'Daughter, do not grieve so. See, I too am suffering. I think this
devastation of the world has been brought about by the course of fate;
horrific as it is, it had to be, and happened naturally. What has occurred
here is what wise Vidura said in his great speech after the failure of
Kṛṣṇa's peace mission.[2] So do not grieve for what could not be avoided,
especially now it is past; you should not mourn those who have met
their deaths in battle. I am in just the same state as you; but who will 20
comfort me? For this noble lineage has been destroyed through my
fault.'

**[16]** Thus Gāndhārī spoke of the slaughter of the Kurus; and then,

**1** As with Dhṛtarāṣṭra's attack on Bhīma in chapter 11 above, an act of physical violence (though in this case seemingly unintended) discharges the anger (cf. 11.11.21).

**2** See 5.128.40–52.

whilst remaining where she stood, she beheld it all in a divine vision. That blessed lady, so intent on serving her husband that she practised the vow of sameness,[1] fiercely ascetic, ever a speaker of truth, received this boon from the great seer Kṛṣṇa Dvaipāyana Vyāsa of holy deeds. Equipped now with the power of divine knowledge, she lamented greatly.

Though far off, wise Gāndhārī beheld as if it were before her the field
5 of battle where those heroes had fought: prodigious, horrific, strewn with bones and hair, overflowing with torrents of blood, covered on every side with thousands upon thousands of corpses, littered with the blood-smeared remains of elephants, horses, chariots and warriors, and with headless bodies and bodiless heads, piled high with lifeless elephants, horses and heroic men, swarming with jackals, jungle crows, ravens, storks and crows, the pleasure-ground of man-eating Rākṣasas, the haunt of eagles, echoing with the frightful howls of jackals, teeming with vultures.

Then King Dhṛtarāṣṭra received Vyāsa's leave, and he, with all the
10 sons of Pāṇḍu, Yudhiṣṭhira and the others, set off for the battlefield, led by Kṛṣṇa Vāsudeva and the prince whose kinsmen were all killed,[2] and taking the Kuru women with them. Reaching Kurukṣetra, the widows saw there their sons and brothers, fathers and husbands, lying slain and being devoured by jackals, jungle crows and other carrion-eaters, and by the creatures of the night – Rākṣasas, Piśācas and evil ghosts. The slaughter resembled a pleasure-ground of Rudra, and when they saw it, the women rushed wailing from their costly carriages. Seeing a sight never before seen, the Bhārata ladies were griefstricken. Some stumbled
15 over bodies, others fell to the ground; exhausted and unprotected, the Kuru and Pāñcāla women lost their wits, which was a great woe.

The ghastly battlefield echoed on every side with shrieks of women driven mad by grief. Subala's daughter Gāndhārī surveyed it. Knowing *dharma* well, she addressed lotus-eyed Kṛṣṇa, the highest lord, and, wretched at the sight of the Kurus' slaughter, she said, 'See these women, lotus-eyed heir of Madhu, my widowed daughters-in-law!

1 i.e. she wore a blindfold because her husband was blind; see 1.103.9–13.

2 i.e. Yuyutsu, Dhṛtarāṣṭra's one surviving son.

See them, hair dishevelled, wailing like ospreys! Together they came here, recalling their bull-like lords, but now they run separately about, searching for sons and brothers, fathers and husbands.

'Strong-armed hero, the field of battle here is filled with the mothers of heroes whose sons lie slain, while elsewhere it is thronged with the wives of heroes whose brave lords are dead; it is made bright, as if by blazing fires, by the tiger-like heroes Bhīṣma, Karṇa, Abhimanyu, Droṇa, Drupada and Śalya; it is adorned by the gold armour of noble men, and by their neck-chains and jewels, their armlets and bracelets and garlands; it is covered with weapons launched by the hands of heroes – spears and bludgeons, sharp, bright swords, arrows and bows; here it teems with joyful carrion-eaters standing in groups together, while elsewhere they make merry or sleep after feeding. Behold the field of battle, heroic lord, as I have described it! As I look on it I burn with grief.

'Slayer of Madhu, I never thought that the Pāñcālas and Kurus would be wiped out, as if reduced to the five elements; yet now eagles and vultures in their thousands are gripping their armour to tear at their blood-soaked bodies and devour them. Who could have thought that Jayadratha, Karṇa, Bhīṣma, Droṇa and Abhimanyu would all be destroyed? Those men seemed impossible to kill; yet, slayer of Madhu, I have seen them slain and turned into fodder for vultures, storks, jungle crows, hawks, dogs and jackals.

'See these tiger-like heroes! They were in thrall to anger, they were in thrall to Duryodhana; now they lie extinguished like fires. Accustomed to sleeping in soft beds of spotless linen, now they all lie dead upon the open earth. Bards always used to cheer them, singing their praises on suitable occasions; now they listen to the frightful howls of jackals. Heroes of great renown, who once reclined on beds, bodies anointed with sandal and aloe, now lie among the dust, while vultures, jackals and crows toss their ornaments aside, shrieking horribly again and again.

'They still bear bows and arrows, steel swords and shining clubs, as if yet living and rejoicing in the pride of war. Many fair, handsome, bull-eyed heroes lie, garlanded with gold, while carrion-eaters tear them apart. Some of them, heroes with arms like iron bars, lie holding their clubs before them, as if embracing their beloved wives. Others, bearing armour and bright weapons, are unmolested by the carrion-eaters, who think them still alive, stirrer of men. But the same creatures drag other noble warriors about, so that their lovely garlands of gold lie scattered all around. And here dreadful jackals in thousands toss aside pearl necklaces from the throats of warriors of renown, now lying slain.

'Men whom trained bards would cheer as each night ended with exquisite songs of praise and reverence – now their fine ladies, grief-stricken and suffering dreadful misery, lament them piteously, tiger-like Vṛṣṇi. The faces of all those ladies are fair yet worn, Kṛṣṇa Keśava, like groves of bright but withered red lotuses. The Kuru women have stopped weeping now; they are running to and fro, care-worn and overwhelmed with woe, and their faces, reddened by weeping and by fury, shine like the sun or purest gold. Hearing each other's incoherent lamentations, they cannot understand what each one wails. Here some, sighing long sighs, and shrieking and lamenting, quivering with misery, bravely give themselves up to death. Many shriek and lament to see the bodies; others beat their heads with their soft hands.

'The earth itself seems overspread with fallen heads and hands and other limbs, mingled in heaps. The blameless women see dreadful headless bodies and bodiless heads, and, unaccustomed to such sights, they are struck senseless. Staring distractedly, they join a head to a body, failing in their misery to see that it is another's, and does not belong there; full of woe, they also join up arms and thighs and feet that have been separately severed by arrows, swooning again and again. Some of the Bhārata women see decapitated bodies that the beasts and birds have been devouring, and they do not recognize their own husbands; others beat their heads with their hands, slayer of Madhu, when they see their brothers or fathers, sons or husbands, lying slain by the enemy.

'The earth, muddy with flesh and blood, is almost impassable with arms still grasping swords and heads still wearing earrings. The blameless ladies, never previously accustomed to misery, miserably force their way through the fallen brothers, fathers and sons who litter the earth.

'See, stirrer of men, the many groups of Dhṛtarāṣṭra's daughters-in-law, fair as herds of long-maned fillies. What could be a more wretched sight for me, Keśava, than to see all these women in so many different plights? Keśava, I must have done great ill in former births to see my sons and grandsons and my brothers slain.'

As she suffered and lamented thus, she found herself gazing at her fallen son. [17] When she saw Duryodhana, Gāndhārī, racked with grief, fell instantly to the ground like a severed wild plantain tree. Then, regaining consciousness, she shrieked again and again to see Duryodhana lying there, doused in blood. She embraced him and lamented piteously; beside herself with grief, she wailed, 'Ah, son, my son,' and moistened with her tears his broad, well-muscled chest, still decked with neck-chain and pearl necklace.

Then she spoke to Kṛṣṇa, who was standing next to her. 'Lord of the 5
Vṛṣṇis, as this war approached to wipe out all our kin, this son of mine, this truest of kings, joined his hands together and said to me, "Mother, wish me victory in this war of kinsmen!" Knowing that total disaster was soon to befall us, I answered, "Tiger-like hero, where *dharma* is, there is victory.[1] But by fighting with completely focused mind, my son, you will assuredly attain the realms that can be won with weapons, and dwell there like a god." That is what I said to him earlier. And I do not grieve for him, my lord; I grieve for Dhṛtarāṣṭra, reduced to wretchedness by the slaughter of his kin.

'Heir of Madhu, behold my son – the best of warriors, unforbearing,
expert in arms and mad for battle – now lying on a hero's bed. The 10
afflicter of his enemies used to lead consecrated kings to battle; now he lies in the dust. Behold the turn of fate! Assuredly brave Duryodhana has gone the hardest way, for here he lies before us on this bed of heroes. Lords of the earth used to gather round to entertain him; now he lies on the earth, slain, and vultures gather round him. Women used to fan him with the finest fans; now carrion birds fan him with their wings.

'This mighty, strong-armed hero of true valour was cut down in
battle by Bhīma, like an elephant cut down by a lion. Kṛṣṇa, behold 15
Duryodhana: doused in blood, he lies slain by club-wielding Bhīma, heir of Bharata. The strong-armed hero used to lead eleven armies to war, Keśava; now his foolish policy has led him to his death. Here lies Duryodhana, mighty bowman, mighty chariot-fighter, slain by Bhīma as a lion slays a tiger. The poor fool despised Vidura, and even his own

1 A common saying: see for example 6.2.14. Sometimes it is amplified to 'Where *dharma* is, there is Kṛṣṇa, and where Kṛṣṇa is, there is victory' (e.g. 6.41.55).

father – an immature boy despising his elders – and so he has fallen prey to death. For thirteen years the earth was his, uncontested; now the lord of the earth, my son, lies slain upon the earth. Kṛṣṇa, I saw the earth well stocked with horses, cattle and elephants under Duryodhana's rule; nor was that long ago. But now, strong-armed Vṛṣṇi, I see it empty of horses, cattle and elephants, under the rule of another. Why should I go on living, heir of Madhu?

'And behold what is even more painful than the killing of my son: these women gathered round the fallen heroes on the field of battle. See Lakṣmaṇa's mother, Kṛṣṇa:[1] that lady of fine hips, waist slender as a sacrificial altar of gold, now lies, her hair dishevelled, in Duryodhana's arms. While the strong-armed hero lived, the spirited girl used to take her pleasure in those same handsome arms. (How does this heart of mine not break into a hundred pieces to see my son slain on the battlefield together with his son?) The blameless lady kisses her bloodstained son; the girl with fine thighs caresses Duryodhana with her hand. How can this spirited girl grieve for both her husband and her son? Yet that is her situation. She gazes at her son with her long eyes, and beats her head with her hands; then she falls on the breast of her brave lord, the Kuru king, O heir of Madhu. See her, lovely as a lotus but also pale as a lotus, as the poor girl wipes the face of her son and then her husband.

'If the traditional teachings are true, if the sacred texts themselves are true, this king has assuredly attained the realms that can be won by force of arms.'

**[18]** *Gāndhārī describes her hundred sons, lying dead on the ground while their womenfolk wail in grief. Similarly, she laments the death of Duḥśāsana;* **[19]** *of her sons Vikarṇa, Durmukha, Citrasena, Viviṃśati and Duḥsaha;* **[20]** *of Abhimanyu and Virāṭa;* **[21]** *of Karṇa;* **[22]** *of the lord of Avanti, Bāhlika and Jayadratha;* **[23]** *of Śalya, Bhagadatta, Bhīṣma, who lies on a bed of arrows waiting for the day when he will die, and Droṇa;* **[24]** *of Bhūriśravas and Śakuni;* **[25]** *of Sudakṣiṇa, the king of Kaliṅga, Jayatsena, Bṛhadbala, the five Kekaya brothers, Drupada, Dhṛṣṭaketu, Vinda and Anuvinda.*

*Overwhelmed by grief, Gāndhārī falls to the ground. Then she uses the ascetic*

1 Lakṣmaṇa was Duryodhana's son: he was killed by Abhimanyu (see 7.45).

*merit she has gained through her devotion to her husband to curse Kṛṣṇa for conniving at the slaughter. She announces that, thirty-six years hence, he will cause the death of his own kin and will himself die ignominiously; his womenfolk will grieve as the Bhārata women are grieving now. Kṛṣṇa smiles and replies that no one but himself is capable of destroying the Vṛṣṇis, who will die at one another's hands. The Pāṇḍavas are greatly distressed to hear this.*

## THE OFFERINGS TO THE DEAD

[**26**] *Kṛṣṇa tells Gāndhārī to get up, and not to give way to grief. She herself is to blame for the disaster, because she thought well of her wicked son; the sons of Kṣatriya women are born to be slain. Gāndhārī says nothing.*

*Dhṛtarāṣṭra asks Yudhiṣṭhira the numbers of battle casualties: he reports that 1,660,020,000 men are dead and 24,165 missing. At Dhṛtarāṣṭra's request he outlines the different realms attained by the fallen warriors, depending on the manner of their death.*

Vaiśaṃpāyana spoke:
'Heir of Bharata,' said Dhṛtarāṣṭra, 'some of these men have people to care for them, while others do not; I trust that all their bodies will be burnt in the proper manner? Some have no one to perform the rites for them, others have not installed the sacred fires in their homes. They are so many: for whom should we perform the rituals, son? Eagles and vultures are dragging them to and fro, but through the rituals these men will attain the heavenly realms, Yudhiṣṭhira.'

When wise Yudhiṣṭhira, Kuntī's son, heard these words, he gave orders to Sudharman, Dhaumya, Saṃjaya the Sūta, Vidura of mighty wisdom, Yuyutsu the Kaurava, Indrasena, and all the other servants and Sūtas.[1] 'Gentlemen, have the rites for the departed performed for all these men: let no one's body perish as if not cared for.'

At the command of the lord of *dharma*, Vidura the chamberlain, the Sūta Saṃjaya, Sudharman, Dhaumya, Indrasena and the others collected

1 Sudharman and Dhaumya are the household priests of Duryodhana and the Pāṇḍavas respectively; Indrasena is Yudhiṣṭhira's charioteer.

costly material together: logs of sandal and aloe, both light and dark, and also ghee, oil, perfumes, linen cloth, piles of wood, and broken chariots and weapons of every kind. They built pyres, and then, carefully and with focused minds, they burnt all those kings by the prescribed rite, in order of seniority: King Duryodhana and his hundred brothers; Śalya, Śala the king and his brother Bhūriśravas; King Jayadratha, O heir of Bharata, and Abhimanyu; Duḥśāsana's son, Lakṣmaṇa son of Duryodhana, and King Dhṛṣṭaketu; mighty Somadatta and a hundred Sṛñjayas; King Kṣemadhanvan, and Virāṭa and Drupada; Śikhaṇḍin prince of Pāñcāla, and Pṛṣata's heir Dhṛṣṭadyumna; valiant Yudhāmanyu and Uttamaujas; the king of Kosala, Draupadī's sons and Śakuni son of Subala; Śakuni's brothers Acala and Vṛṣaka, and King Bhagadatta; Karṇa the unforbearing Cutter and his sons; Baka's brother Ghaṭotkaca, lord of Rākṣasas; Alambusa the Rākṣasa king, and King Jalasaṃdha; and other princes too, O king, by hundreds and by thousands.

They burnt them all in fires that blazed with ghee, offered up in streams. Offerings were made to some of the noble dead: their praises were sung with hymns of the Sāmaveda, and they were mourned with other songs. As night fell to the sounds of Sāmaveda and Ṛgveda hymns, and of women weeping, despair overwhelmed all beings. The fires, blazing bright and smokeless, looked like planets shining in an almost cloudless sky.

As for those men with no one to care for them, men who had come from many different lands, Vidura, acting on the command of the lord of *dharma*, had them heaped together in their thousands, and then, with focused mind, he burnt them with many logs ignited with oil.

After having their rites performed, Yudhiṣṭhira, king of the Kurus, followed Dhṛtarāṣṭra towards the Gaṅgā.

## THE WATER OFFERINGS

Vaiśaṃpāyana spoke:

**[27]** They reached the holy Gaṅgā, the river that delights people of virtue, with its pools and banks, and its great floodplains and forests, and there they removed their ornaments, upper garments and belts. Then all the Kuru women, weeping in their terrible misery, made offerings of water to their fathers and grandsons, their brothers and close kin, their sons and elders and husbands. And, understanding *dharma*, they performed the water rite too for fallen friends. While the heroes' wives were offering water to the heroes, the Gaṅgā spread out further to give easy access to her waters; but her banks, though vast like oceans and thronged with the wives of heroes, were joyless, melancholy places.

Then suddenly, great king, Kuntī, racked with grief and weeping, spoke softly to her sons. 'That hero, the lord of lords of chariot-fighters whom Arjuna slew in battle; that mighty bowman, bearing the stamp of heroism, whom you knew as the Sūta's son, the son of Rādhā; the man who shone in the midst of the army like the god Sun himself; who was always a match for you Pāṇḍavas and all your followers; who radiated brilliance as he led Duryodhana's troops; who had no equal for heroism anywhere on earth; the keeper of his word, the hero who never retreated in battle – offer water to him, your tireless brother. For he was your first-born brother, my son by the Sun, born with earrings and armour, a hero bright as the Sun.'

When Pāṇḍu's sons heard their mother say these painful words, they became yet more griefstricken, and they mourned Karṇa. Then Kuntī's son Yudhiṣṭhira, the tiger-like hero, addressed his mother, hissing like a snake: 'No one but wealth-winner Arjuna could withstand the fall of his arrows; how was he your son, lady, by divine conception? All of us were burnt by the fiery energy of his arms; how could you conceal him, like a fire wrapped in cloth? The fearsome might of Karṇa's arms won the honour of Dhṛtarāṣṭra's sons, and none but Arjuna could take it from him. Warrior of warriors, best of all those who bear arms, he was our first-born brother. Lady, how did you come to give birth to Karṇa of marvellous valour?'

'Alas, alas, lady! By concealing this secret you have undone us all, for now we and our kin will suffer torment because of Karṇa's death. The woe that has seized me now is a hundred times more fierce than that caused by the death of Abhimanyu, or the killing of Draupadī's sons, or the destruction of the Pāñcālas, or the downfall of the Kurus. My grief for Karṇa burns me like a fire.

'Nothing would have been beyond our reach, even if it were in heaven; and this appalling slaughter of the Kurus would never have happened.'

Thus Yudhiṣṭhira lord of *dharma* lamented again and again; then, weeping softly, O king, the lord of men made an offering of water to his brother. At that, those who stood round him at the water offering all burst out weeping, men and women both. Then in his love for his brother, wise Yudhiṣṭhira, the lord of the Kurus, had Karṇa's womenfolk brought to him with all their attendants, and with them he at once performed the rites for the departed. Then the righteous king came forth from Gaṅgā's waters, beside himself with grief.

# TRANQUILLITY

## THE *DHARMA* OF KINGS

[1] *After completing the offerings of water, the Pāṇḍavas remain outside the city for a month to purify themselves. Yudhiṣṭhira is visited by great numbers of Brahmins, and the seer Nārada congratulates him on his triumph. But Yudhiṣṭhira is full of grief and guilt over the death of his kinsmen. In particular he mourns Karṇa, whom he now knows to have been his elder brother, and whose sense of honour led him to reject Kuntī's efforts to reconcile him with the Pāṇḍavas.*

*He asks Nārada why Karṇa was cursed to die in the battle,* [2] *and Nārada recounts Karṇa's story. — Brought up as a Sūta, Karṇa is Duryodhana's friend and deeply hostile to the Pāṇḍavas. He requests Droṇa to grant him the Weapon of Brahmā, but Droṇa refuses. He then visits Rāma Jāmadagnya, pretending to be a Brahmin; Rāma accepts him and teaches him weaponry. But he accidentally kills the oblation cow of a Brahmin, who curses him that his wheel will become stuck in battle and he will be killed.*[1] [3] *Rāma is pleased with Karṇa and teaches him the use of the Weapon of Brahmā. However, as Rāma sleeps with his head in Karṇa's lap, an insect bores into Karṇa's thigh;*[2] *Karṇa, fearful of waking his teacher, does not move despite suffering terrible pain. Blood from the wound awakes Rāma, who kills the insect with a glance. At once a Rākṣasa appears: long ago he had been cursed to assume the form of a bloodsucking insect as a punishment for abducting Bhṛgu's wife, and Rāma's action has freed him.*

*After the Rākṣasa leaves, Rāma demands to know who Karṇa really is, as*

1 Cf. 8.29.31–9 and note.

2 Cf. 8.29.4–7, where the insect is said to be a form of Indra, not a Rākṣasa.

*the fortitude he has shown is that of a Kṣatriya, not a Brahmin. Karṇa replies that he is a Sūta, that is, half Brahmin and half Kṣatriya. Rāma curses him that at the time of his death he will not be able to invoke the Weapon of Brahmā.*

*Karṇa returns to Duryodhana.* **[4]** *Duryodhana attends the* svayaṃvara *of the princess of Kaliṅga. Furious when the girl does not choose him for her husband, he abducts her by force and, with the aid of Karṇa who is acting as his charioteer, fights off the other kings and carries her back to Hāstinapura.*

**[5]** *King Jarāsaṃdha of Magadha challenges Karṇa to single combat; Karṇa almost severs the part of his body that had been joined by Jarā.*[1] *Impressed by his fighting skills, Jarāsaṃdha then grants Karṇa the kingdom of Campā to add to that of Aṅga.*[2]

*— Nārada ends his narrative by listing all the reasons which led to Karṇa's death at Arjuna's hands, and tells Yudhiṣṭhira not to grieve for him.* **[6]** *Kuntī too advises Yudhiṣṭhira not to grieve for Karṇa: she and Karṇa's father the Sun had tried to persuade him to side with the Pāṇḍavas, but he had remained hostile.*[3] *But Yudhiṣṭhira remains deeply upset that Kuntī had concealed the truth about Karṇa, and he curses all women to be incapable of keeping secrets.*

**[7]** *Yudhiṣṭhira addresses Arjuna. He rails against the Kṣatriya* dharma *that has caused such a disaster: desire for the kingdom has resulted in so many deaths, and so many parents have lost their sons in the prime of life. He blames Duryodhana and Dhṛtarāṣṭra; then he announces that he will renounce the kingship in favour of Arjuna, and retire to the forest.* **[8]** *Arjuna answers scornfully, accusing Yudhiṣṭhira of feebleness. It is not right for a king to renounce; poverty is bad and wealth is good. Yudhiṣṭhira should now perform the horse sacrifice, as is his duty.* **[9]** *Yudhiṣṭhira insists that he will retire to the forest, and describes the life he will live there, practising austerities and living off alms, freed from all passion.* **[10]** *Bhīma objects strongly to Yudhiṣṭhira's plan. What was the point in exterminating the Kauravas if Yudhiṣṭhira is going to ignore the* dharma *of kings and give up all exertion? He is quitting when the goal is already achieved. Renunciation is appropriate in old age or in times of trouble; it is not at all appropriate in Yudhiṣṭhira's case.*

**[11]** *Arjuna tells Yudhiṣṭhira the story of some foolish Brahmin youths who*

1 See 2.16–17.

2 Duryodhana had made Karṇa king of Aṅga: 1.126.35–6.

3 See 5.142–4.

*set out for the forest for a life of renunciation, eating nothing but others' leavings. Indra, in the form of a gold bird, told them that they were acting wrongly, and explained that the highest form of asceticism is to perform the rituals and duties of the householder, eating the remnants of food served to others. Yudhiṣṭhira should follow this same advice, and rule the earth that he has conquered.* **[12]** *Nakula too maintains that proper performance of ritual and the life of the householder constitute true renunciation, not abandoning one's family in order to retire to the forest. Kings have duties to their subjects, and it is wrong to neglect them. Yudhiṣṭhira has conquered the earth in keeping with the Kṣatriya* dharma*; he has no cause to grieve.* **[13]** *Sahadeva agrees that a king who conquers the earth but fails to enjoy it lives in vain; a forest-dwelling renouncer who has not fully renounced in his heart lives in mortal danger.*

**[14]** *When Yudhiṣṭhira remains silent, Draupadī speaks. She urges him to respond to his brothers, and points out that during their forest exile he had often encouraged them with promises of a better life once their enemies were defeated: he should not disappoint them now. The* dharma *of kings is different from that of Brahmins. Yudhiṣṭhira should make his brothers happy, and raise Draupadī herself from her present misery, by ruling the earth and giving rich gifts to the Brahmins.*

**[15]** *Arjuna speaks again. The king's rod of force is essential for the welfare of the world. No king attains royal glory without killing enemies; indeed, no creature exists that does not harm other creatures. Every act involves both right and wrong. Yudhiṣṭhira should rule, sacrifice, give gifts, kill his enemies and protect his friends.*

**[16]** *Bhīma, restraining his impatience, speaks once more. Yudhiṣṭhira's uncertainty is putting everything in danger. Disease of the body can induce disease of the mind, but disease of the mind also induces disease of the body; Yudhiṣṭhira has fought a fierce battle with his foes, but now he has to fight an equally fierce battle with his own mind. He must win it, and then rule the kingdom and perform a horse sacrifice.* **[17]** *Yudhiṣṭhira tells Bhīma that the reason he longs for Yudhiṣṭhira to rule is because he is full of desires: he should conquer them. Renunciation leads to the highest of states, but it is not possible for kings. One should practise renunciation and cultivate the true understanding that alone leads to oneness with* brahman.

**[18]** *Arjuna tells Yudhiṣṭhira of King Janaka of Videha,*[1] *who abandoned*

1 The father of Sītā (see the story of Rāma, 3.257–75; also 6.25.20).

*his kingdom to become a renouncer, and of the angry words that his wife spoke to him: she accused him of abandoning royal glory, betraying his dependants, and giving up the true renunciation of the householder in favour of the life of ascetics who put on a mere show of* dharma. **[19]** *Yudhiṣṭhira replies that he has a proper understanding of* dharma, *while Arjuna's knowledge is of fighting. He insists that men of true* dharma *practise asceticism.*

**[20]** *The ascetic Devasthāna now joins in to support Arjuna's contention*[1] *that wealth is of the highest importance. The creator created wealth for the purpose of sacrifice, and both gods and men have attained great things through costly sacrifices.* **[21]** *Different people favour different* dharmas; *the true* dharma *is that which does no harm to others. That king attains the highest of states who exercises self-control, protects his subjects, and goes to war to protect cows and Brahmins.*

**[22]** *Arjuna now asks Yudhiṣṭhira why he is grieving. Death in battle is the highest achievement for a Kṣatriya, while asceticism and renunciation are laid down for Brahmins. A Brahmin will not be censured for following the Kṣatriya way, since the Kṣatriya order is based on* brahman, *the spiritual order of the Brahmins. But asceticism and renunciation are not prescribed for Kṣatriyas. Yudhiṣṭhira should cast aside his mental agitation and engage in sacrifice and the giving of gifts.*

**[23]** *Vyāsa agrees with Arjuna: Yudhiṣṭhira should live the life of a householder, not retire to the forest. Renunciation is enjoined upon Brahmins, but Kṣatriyas have quite different duties, chief among them the inflicting of punishment. It was through his use of the rod of force that the royal seer Sudyumna attained perfection.* **[24]** *Yudhiṣṭhira asks to hear this story, and Vyāsa narrates it. Śaṅkha and Likhita were two Brahmin brothers. Once Likhita ate some fruit from a tree belonging to Śaṅkha without first asking permission. When Śaṅkha learnt of this he angrily insisted that Likhita go to King Sudyumna and demand to be punished. Likhita did so, and Sudyumna, after first offering to pardon him, punished him by having his hands cut off. Likhita returned to Śaṅkha, who told him that his breach of* dharma *had been expiated, and caused his hands to reappear through his ascetic power. Sudyumna attained perfection through his act. Vyāsa tells Yudhiṣṭhira that the rod of force, not the shaven head, is the* dharma *of the Kṣatriya.*

1 In chapter 8 above.

[**25**] *Vyāsa tells Yudhiṣṭhira that he should allow his brothers to obtain what they longed for during their forest exile. He should experience* dharma, *the proper making of wealth, and pleasure before retiring to the forest. The king who rules properly does not breach* dharma. [**26**] *Yudhiṣṭhira replies that he feels no joy at the thought of ruling the earth, only grief at the slaughter of the Kurus. Vyāsa counsels him that nothing happens before its due time, and that happiness brings misery, and misery happiness. The king who performs his duties will enjoy happiness in the world of the gods.*

[**27**] *Now Yudhiṣṭhira laments his responsibility for the deaths of Bhīṣma, Droṇa, Karṇa and Abhimanyu. He considers himself a wicked, sinful man, and resolves to fast to death. Vyāsa again tells him to restrain his grief: what has happened was fated, and he should carry out the tasks for which he was created.* [**28**] *Vyāsa cites the advice that the wise Brahmin Aśman gave to King Janaka. The miseries of human existence occur through the action of fate; all that befalls a man does so through the course of time, and in the end death comes to all. Kings should act according to their* dharma. *Vyāsa says that Janaka heeded this advice, stopped grieving and returned home. Yudhiṣṭhira should do likewise.*

[**29**] *Yudhiṣṭhira remains silent, and Arjuna asks Kṛṣṇa to try to dispel his grief. Kṛṣṇa tells Yudhiṣṭhira that the fallen warriors died honourably and have attained heaven: he should not grieve for them. Then he cites Nārada's advice to King Sṛñjaya, who was mourning the death of his young son Suvarṇaṣṭhīvin. Nārada listed glorious king after king of the past, and pointed out that each one of those most excellent men had died; Sṛñjaya should not grieve for his son. Sṛñjaya thanked Nārada for his discourse; then he asked for his son to be brought back to life, and Nārada agreed to this.*

[**30**] *Yudhiṣṭhira asks to hear the story of Suvarṇaṣṭhīvin. Kṛṣṇa explains that Nārada, together with his companion seer Parvata, was himself involved in the events: he will describe them to Yudhiṣṭhira.* [**31**] *At Yudhiṣṭhira's request, Nārada tells how he and Parvata had spent many years as guests of Sṛñjaya; when they were about to leave they had granted him a boon, and he had asked for a mighty, long-lived son, as splendid as Indra. Parvata answered that he would indeed have a son; he would be named Suvarṇaṣṭhīvin,*[1] *because he would spit gold; but he would not live long, because Sṛñjaya's aim was for him to overcome Indra. Nārada had then consoled Sṛñjaya by promising to bring the boy back*

1 'Spitter of gold'.

*to life. Suvarṇaṣṭhīvin was born, and Indra began to look for ways of killing him. When the boy was five years old, Indra made his thunderbolt assume the form of a tiger and slay him; then Nārada had brought him back to life. Nārada concludes by counselling Yudhiṣṭhira to give up his grief.*

**[32]** *Again Yudhiṣṭhira remains silent. Vyāsa tells him that it is the* dharma *of kings to punish all who rebel against their rule; this is what Yudhiṣṭhira has done, and he has no cause to grieve. He should continue to maintain his* dharma, *and abandon thoughts of renunciation: only thus can he perform expiation for any acts of wickedness he may be guilty of.* **[33]** *But Yudhiṣṭhira insists that after causing the deaths of so many men and the bereavement of so many women his only recourse is fierce asceticism, and he asks Vyāsa to recommend some good hermitages.* **[34]** *Vyāsa replies that the fallen warriors died in the performance of their Kṣatriya* dharma, *and it was not Yudhiṣṭhira or any of the Pāṇḍavas who killed them, but Time: fate used Yudhiṣṭhira as its instrument. Now he should perform expiation, which should take the form of a horse sacrifice, and he should rule.*

**[35]** *Yudhiṣṭhira asks what actions require expiation, and what form the expiation must take. Vyāsa lists numerous sins, and also various actions that are not in fact sinful;* **[36]** *then he lists the expiations appropriate to different actions, including the horse sacrifice. He assures Yudhiṣṭhira that he will be freed of all sin.* **[37]** *Yudhiṣṭhira asks Vyāsa what food may and may not be eaten, what gifts may and may not be given, and to whom gifts may and may not be made. Vyāsa cites the views of Manu, who first lays down some general legal principles and then lists specific instances.*

**[38]** *Now Yudhiṣṭhira tells Vyāsa that he wishes to know all about the* dharma *of kings and others, for it appears to him that the practice of* dharma *and kingship are mutually opposed. In reply, Vyāsa praises the learning of Bhīṣma, who is still waiting for the right time to die, and advises Yudhiṣṭhira to consult him. Yudhiṣṭhira objects that, having committed such a great slaughter, and, in particular, having used deceit to bring about Bhīṣma's own death, he cannot approach him. But Kṛṣṇa urges him to give up his grief for the benefit of the world, and Yudhiṣṭhira now agrees to do so. Then with great ceremony he and his followers enter Hāstinapura.*

**[39]** *The Pāṇḍavas are greeted with joy by the citizens, who shower praises upon them. Yudhiṣṭhira enters the palace and worships the gods. A large crowd of Brahmins surrounds him to pronounce blessings and proclaim his triumph.*

*At this point a Rākṣasa named Cārvāka, a friend of Duryodhana disguised as a Brahmin, announces that he speaks for all the assembled Brahmins, and then berates Yudhiṣṭhira for the slaughter of his kin, concluding that he deserves death. Yudhiṣṭhira asks for compassion; the Brahmins assure him that they do not agree with Cārvāka, whom they recognize through their power of insight. They then kill the Rākṣasa by uttering the sound* 'huṃ'.

*Kṛṣṇa tells Yudhiṣṭhira Cārvāka's story. Through asceticism he had acquired from Brahmā the boon of security against all creatures, with the one exception that he must not insult Brahmins. The gods, oppressed by Cārvāka's power, appealed to Brahmā, who told them that the Rākṣasa would soon become the friend of a king named Duryodhana, and as a result of that friendship would insult Brahmins and so die. Kṛṣṇa urges Yudhiṣṭhira to attend to his kingly duties.*

**[40]** *Yudhiṣṭhira, free now of his anguish, sits on a golden throne; his supporters also sit on thrones. His subjects bring the many auspicious objects required for a royal installation. Dhaumya, the Pāṇḍavas' household priest, marks out an altar and makes Yudhiṣṭhira and Draupadī sit on a throne covered by a tiger-skin. Then he pours consecrated water over Yudhiṣṭhira's head, and so in turn do Dhṛtarāṣṭra and all the citizens. Drums are beaten, and Yudhiṣṭhira presents costly gifts to the Brahmins, who pronounce blessings upon him. He has now regained his kingdom.*

**[41]** *Yudhiṣṭhira acknowledges the Brahmins' kind words. He vows to obey Dhṛtarāṣṭra in everything, and asks his followers to do likewise. He appoints Bhīma his heir apparent, and assigns other positions to Vidura, Saṃjaya, Dhaumya and his other brothers.* **[42]** *Then he has the* śrāddha *rites performed for his slain kinsmen.*[1] *Dhṛtarāṣṭra makes generous donations to the Brahmins for the sake of his sons, and Yudhiṣṭhira similarly gives costly gifts for the sake of his fallen elders and allies. He has lodges and watering-stations built and tanks excavated for his subjects; he grants his protection to the women whose menfolk have been slain; he helps the needy with shelter, clothing and food. He enjoys a happy life as king without rivals.* **[43]** *He praises Kṛṣṇa*

1 These rituals, in which offerings of food are made to sustain the deceased person, are performed every month during the first year after death and on particular occasions thereafter. The one referred to here is the first *śrāddha* after the end of the war a month earlier, and is particularly important: the first *śrāddha* grants the deceased person access to the world of the ancestors.

*under a hundred different names, and Kṛṣṇa replies with much praise for him.*

**[44]** *Yudhiṣṭhira now gives leave to his subjects to return to their homes, and tells his brothers to rest. Bhīma takes up residence in Duryodhana's palace, which Yudhiṣṭhira has given him with Dhṛtarāṣṭra's assent. Similarly, Arjuna enters the palace of Duḥśāsana, Nakula that of Durmarṣaṇa, and Sahadeva that of Durmukha. They and Yudhiṣṭhira's other allies all retire for the night.*

**[45]** *— Janamejaya asks what Yudhiṣṭhira did after regaining the kingdom, and Vaiśaṃpāyana narrates. — Yudhiṣṭhira favours many people, great and small, with gifts or honour. One day he approaches Kṛṣṇa to thank him for his part in the restoration of the kingdom. But Kṛṣṇa is deep in meditation and does not answer.* **[46]** *Yudhiṣṭhira expresses his wonder at Kṛṣṇa's stillness and worships him as highest lord. He asks to hear what Kṛṣṇa is meditating on. Kṛṣṇa replies that his mind has been with Bhīṣma, the noble warrior lying on a bed of arrows who knows past, present and future. He urges Yudhiṣṭhira to visit Bhīṣma and ask him about* dharma *and related matters while he still lives. Yudhiṣṭhira agrees readily, and asks Kṛṣṇa to go before him so that Bhīṣma may have a sight of him. Kṛṣṇa commands Sātyaki to have his chariot yoked.*

**[47]** *— Janamejaya asks how Bhīṣma gave up his body. Vaiśaṃpāyana answers that, as soon as the winter solstice passed, Bhīṣma caused his self to enter the universal Self. Surrounded by great seers, he meditated on Kṛṣṇa and praised Kṛṣṇa with a great hymn. Kṛṣṇa granted him knowledge of past, present and future. Now Vaiśaṃpāyana continues the principal narrative.*

*— Kṛṣṇa and Sātyaki travel to see Bhīṣma in one chariot, Yudhiṣṭhira and Arjuna in a second, Bhīma and the twins in a third, and Kṛpa, Yuyutsu and Saṃjaya in a fourth.* **[48]** *As they approach the scene of the battle at Kurukṣetra, Kṛṣṇa points out to Yudhiṣṭhira the five lakes of Rāma Jāmadagnya, and tells him that that is where Rāma annihilated the Kṣatriyas twenty-one times. Yudhiṣṭhira asks how this could have happened.*

**[49]** *Kṛṣṇa relates how King Kuśika performed fierce austerities to obtain a son of great might, till Indra himself became his son Gādhi. Gādhi had a daughter Satyavatī, whom he married to the Bhārgava Brahmin Ṛcīka. He prepared a sacrificial meal for her, to produce an ascetic Brahmin son, and another for her mother, to produce a fierce Kṣatriya warrior who would slay many Kṣatriyas.*

*But the two meals were accidentally switched,*[1] *and Ṛcīka told Satyavatī that her son would be a fierce warrior. At her request, however, he allowed this disgrace to skip a generation and to affect not her son but her grandson. Thus the son she bore was the peaceable Jamadagni, while Gādhi's son Viśvāmitra had all the characteristics of a Brahmin. But Jamadagni's son Rāma was a killer of Kṣatriyas. Meanwhile, the Fire god had requested the mighty Kṣatriya king Arjuna Kārtavīrya to provide him with food, and Arjuna had consigned many lands to the flames. But when he burnt down the hermitage of the seer Vasiṣṭha, Vasiṣṭha cursed him to die at Rāma's hands, and when Arjuna's sons stole the calf of Jamadagni's oblation cow, Rāma killed him. His sons then killed Jamadagni, at which Rāma, enraged, wiped out the entire Kṣatriya order. Thousands of years passed, and the Kṣatriyas re-established themselves;*[2] *again Rāma killed them all, and this was repeated twenty-one times in all. He then handed the earth over to the seer Kaśyapa. But in the absence of Kṣatriya rulers, Vaiśyas and Śūdras began to take Brahmin women, and Earth herself begged Kaśyapa to install Kṣatriyas as kings. Kṛṣṇa adds that the Kṣatriya lineages of the present day are descended from those kings.*

**[50]** *Yudhiṣṭhira expresses his amazement at the story of Rāma Jāmadagnya, and in particular that such a deed was done by a Brahmin. Then he and Kṛṣṇa proceed to where Bhīṣma lies on his bed of arrows. Kṛṣṇa addresses Bhīṣma, hoping that his mind is not confused and that the pain of all the arrows in his limbs is not too severe. He praises him for his great knowledge and his virtues, and requests him to dispel Yudhiṣṭhira's grief.* **[51]** *Bhīṣma reverently praises Kṛṣṇa as supreme lord. Kṛṣṇa assures Bhīṣma that, after the fifty-six remaining days of his life, Bhīṣma will attain the heavenly realms. He points out that Bhīṣma's learning will die with him, and again requests him to dispel Yudhiṣṭhira's grief.*

**[52]** *Bhīṣma answers that the pain of the arrows and the agitated state of his mind prevent him from speaking to Yudhiṣṭhira. In reply, Kṛṣṇa promises that he will feel no pain or hunger or thirst, and that his mind will be clear. All the assembled seers praise Kṛṣṇa, and flowers fall from the sky. The sun sets; Kṛṣṇa and the Pāṇḍavas set off for Hāstinapura; they will return the next day.*

**[53]** *In the morning Kṛṣṇa awakes; he performs various auspicious actions and then sends Sātyaki to find out if Yudhiṣṭhira is ready to see Bhīṣma. Sātyaki*

1 For other versions of the story, see 3.115 and 13.4.

2 From boys not yet born when the massacre occurred.

*tells Yudhiṣṭhira that Kṛṣṇa is awaiting him, and Yudhiṣṭhira commands Arjuna to make his chariot ready; the Pāṇḍavas will go unaccompanied by their usual attendants to hear the great mysteries that Bhīṣma will reveal. Kṛṣṇa and the five brothers now set out across Kurukṣetra to where Bhīṣma lies. They salute the seers who are with him. Yudhiṣṭhira sees Bhīṣma, and feels great fear.*

**[54]** *Nārada says that the time has come to put questions to Bhīṣma, as he is near death; the Pāṇḍavas approach Bhīṣma, but no one speaks. Yudhiṣṭhira asks Kṛṣṇa to question him, and Kṛṣṇa asks the old man if he is now comfortable and clear-minded. Bhīṣma answers that, thanks to Kṛṣṇa, his pain and confusion have left him, and he is ready to expound his knowledge of* dharma*; but first he wants to know why Kṛṣṇa does not teach Yudhiṣṭhira himself. Kṛṣṇa replies that he wishes to enhance Bhīṣma's fame and to ensure that what he says to Yudhiṣṭhira will be remembered for ever.*

**[55]** *Bhīṣma agrees to expound his knowledge, but insists that it must be Yudhiṣṭhira who questions him. Kṛṣṇa explains that Yudhiṣṭhira is filled with shame and fears Bhīṣma's curse, but Bhīṣma insists that the killing even of relatives and elders is in accord with the Kṣatriya* dharma. *Yudhiṣṭhira now approaches Bhīṣma; Bhīṣma welcomes him and bids him put his questions.*

**[56]** *Yudhiṣṭhira requests Bhīṣma to expound to him the* dharma *of kings, and Bhīṣma begins his exposition. He says that kings should act with vigour. Divine destiny alone will not accomplish their purposes; human exertion is also needed. A king should be both mild and fierce. He should protect Brahmins, but punish Brahmin wrongdoers with exile; he should be merciful towards his people, but always maintain his dignity to prevent subordinates treating him disrespectfully.* **[57]** *He should constantly exert himself: he should act against opponents, even if they are relatives or elders. After listing many kingly virtues, Bhīṣma states that protection of their people is the primary duty of kings,* **[58]** *and he lists various ways of achieving it. A king must strive keep the kingdom safe from attack; he needs to behave both honestly and deceitfully.*

*The sun sets, and Yudhiṣṭhira and the others leave, promising to return the next day.*

**[59]** *In the morning the Pāṇḍavas return to Kurukṣetra with Kṛṣṇa and Sātyaki. Yudhiṣṭhira asks Bhīṣma how a king, who does not differ in any way from other men, none the less rules over all other men and is honoured by them like a god. Bhīṣma answers that originally in the Kṛta Age there was no king, and men protected one another. But as men came under the sway of greed, desire* *and passion, the Vedas and* dharma *were lost. The gods appealed in fear to Brahmā, who responded by composing a work of a hundred thousand chapters on* dharma, *the proper making of wealth, and pleasure, detailing the* dharma *of kings; seers made abridged versions for the use of mortals. Then the gods asked Viṣṇu to appoint one mortal to rule over the rest. Viṣṇu created Virajas for this purpose, but he and his son and grandson all preferred the ascetic life. His great-grandson Anaṅga ruled well, but was succeeded by a libertine son, Atibala, and grandson, Vena. The seers killed Vena and produced two men from his body: the ancestor of the wild Niṣāda tribes, and an armed man learned in the Vedas. The latter agreed to rule. Viṣṇu consecrated him as king; then he himself entered into him, so that the world would worship him. Kingship incorporates* dharma, *wealth and glory.*

**[60]** *Yudhiṣṭhira asks Bhīṣma what* dharmas *are common to all for classes of society, and what* dharmas *particular to each class. He also asks what are the* dharmas *of the four stages of life,*[1] *and what are the* dharmas *of kings. In reply, Bhīṣma lists nine general virtues that apply to all four classes, and then describes the* dharmas *of the four classes in turn. Brahmins should be self-controlled and study the Vedas. Kṣatriyas should give gifts, perform sacrifices, protect people and show courage in battle. Vaiśyas should tend cattle. Śūdras should obey the three higher classes. All four classes should offer sacrifices, though there are restrictions on Śūdras.*

**[61]** *Now Bhīṣma addresses the* dharmas *of the four stages of life. Having completed the stage of householder and begotten children, one may pass on to that of forest-dweller, becoming celibate once more. A Brahmin seeking final release may pass directly from the holy celibacy of studentship to living entirely from alms. But a man may also pass from studentship to the difficult stage of householder, where he must be faithful, pious and self-controlled. Lastly Bhīṣma speaks of the life of the celibate student, who must be disciplined, attentive and obedient.*

**[62]** *Bhīṣma says that the four stages of life are prescribed for Brahmins, but that the other three classes follow them also. However, a Brahmin who acts in the manner of any of the other classes is condemned in this world and goes to hell*

1 Normally the four stages, which a Brahmin was expected to pass through in sequence, were listed as those of the celibate student (*brahmacārin*), the householder (*gṛhastha*), the forest-dweller (*vānaprastha*) and the renouncer (*saṃnyāsin*).

*in the next, whereas the Brahmin who performs the* dharma *of Brahmins in every stage of his life attains heaven.* **[63]** *A Brahmin must avoid non-Brahmin behaviour, and should be self-controlled, pure and upright.*

*Bhīṣma specifies the circumstances in which Śūdras, Vaiśyas and Kṣatriyas may follow the sequence of the four stages of life. The Vedas state that the* dharmas *of the non-Kṣatriya classes all depend upon the* dharma *of the king; without the king's rod of force the Vedas would perish, and so would all* dharmas *and the stages of life themselves.* **[64]** *He tells Yudhiṣṭhira the story of Māndhātṛ,*[1] *king during a time of demonic lawlessness, who performed a sacrifice in order to see the god Viṣṇu. Viṣṇu appeared before him in the form of Indra, and told him his desire was impossible, but Māndhātṛ was insistent, saying that he had performed the Kṣatriya* dharma *well and now wanted to learn the* dharma *of Viṣṇu. Indra (Viṣṇu) replied that the Kṣatriya* dharma *was Viṣṇu's first creation; all other* dharmas *followed. Without the Kṣatriya* dharma *there would be no Brahmins, no* dharmas, *no classes of society, no stages of life.* **[65]** *Kings must maintain the Kṣatriya* dharma, *which involves the highest form of renunciation, that of life itself; they must rule over the whole of society, wielding the rod of force. Then the god returned to his heaven. Bhīṣma counsels Yudhiṣṭhira to adhere to the ancient Kṣatriya* dharma.

**[66]** *Yudhiṣṭhira asks Bhīṣma to tell him more about the four stages of life. In reply, Bhīṣma explains that the exercise of every one of a king's duties qualifies him for one or another of the stages, or in some cases for all of them at once. A king shares in the* dharma *of his subjects; by protecting them, he acquires a hundred times more* dharma *than the person who follows the stages of life. Bhīṣma urges Yudhiṣṭhira to carry out his kingly duties: these will bring him the merit of the four stages of life and the four classes of society.*

**[67]** *Next Yudhiṣṭhira asks Bhīṣma what is a country's first task; Bhīṣma answers that it is the consecration of a king. All goes ill in the land with no king. Long ago men asked Brahmā for a king; he gave them Manu, but Manu did not wish to rule, for fear of the cruelty he would have to inflict. His subjects promised him a share in their wealth and their* dharma, *and with their help he stopped men from doing wrong and set them to their proper tasks. Those seeking well-being should first establish a king.*

**[68]** *Yudhiṣṭhira requests Bhīṣma to tell him why kings are referred to as gods,*

**1** See also 3.126.

*and Bhīṣma responds with the story of Vasumanas, king of Kosala. Vasumanas had asked Bṛhaspati the basis for the welfare of subjects. Bṛhaspati had answered that it is the king who prevents all that is evil and promotes all that is good; the king is a great deity in the form of a man, taking on different divine aspects as he performs his different duties. A wise man never opposes his king, who is the heart of his subjects, and who, after ruling well, earns an honoured place in Indra's heaven.*

**[69]** *Now Yudhiṣṭhira asks Bhīṣma about the specific duties of kings. Bhīṣma replies that the king must conquer first himself, then his enemies. Then he speaks about the king's use of spies, his dealings with other kings, and numerous other topics. The king who rules righteously rules long; the one who fails to protect his subjects performs austerities and sacrifices in vain.*

**[70]** *Yudhiṣṭhira's next question to Bhīṣma is about the administration of punishment. Bhīṣma insists on its importance. The king is not a product of his time; he determines it. He creates a Kṛta Age if he enforces punishment in full, a Tretā Age if he abandons a quarter of it, Dvāpara Age if he abandons a half, and a Kali Age if he abandons it completely; after death, he will gain rewards appropriate to the Age he brought into being. The king's highest* dharma *is to administer punishment.* **[71]** *Yudhiṣṭhira asks Bhīṣma how a king should conduct himself to assure happiness in this life and the next. Bhīṣma responds with a list of thirty-six good qualities that a king should have.*

**[72]** *Next Yudhiṣṭhira asks how the king may avoid ensnaring himself in the cycle of rebirth and committing offences against* dharma *as he protects his subjects. Bhīṣma advises him to surround himself with Brahmins and to be moderate in levying tax. Protection of his subjects is the king's highest* dharma*: if he performs it well, he will attain great rewards both on earth and in heaven.*

**[73]** *Bhīṣma goes on to say that a king should appoint a virtuous Brahmin as his household priest, and he cites the dialogue of King Purūravas with the Wind god. Purūravas had asked about the origins of the four classes of society; the Wind replied that the Brahmin arose from Brahmā's mouth, the Kṣatriya from his arms, the Vaiśya from his thighs and the Śūdra from his feet. The Brahmin is the lord of all beings, charged with the protection of* dharma*; the Kṣatriya was created for the protection of the earth and the people with the rod of force; the Vaiśya is to support the three highest classes with agriculture and trade, and the Śūdra is to serve them all. The earth belongs to the Brahmin; but as a woman weds a man's younger brother if she cannot have the man himself, so* *the earth has taken the Kṣatriya for her lord. A king should have a well-born, wise Brahmin as his household priest to guide him.*

**[74]** *Bhīṣma says that when the king's household priest and the king himself both adhere to* dharma, *the subjects flourish. He cites the dialogue of King Purūravas with the seer Kaśyapa. Questioned by Purūravas, Kaśyapa stated that the land where the Brahmin and Kṣatriya orders are opposed to one another comes to grief. The two orders rely on one another; if there is discord between them, evil will follow, and Rudra will appear to kill both the virtuous and the wicked. A king should make a learned Brahmin his household priest, and should honour Brahmins in general, so that the two orders support each other.*

**[75]** *Bhīṣma adds that the country prospers where the subjects' invisible fears are allayed by the Brahmin and their visible fears by the king. He cites the dialogue of King Mucukunda with the god Kubera. Mucukunda had conquered the earth; now he attacked Kubera's realm of Alakā, but Kubera's Rākṣasas slaughtered his men. Mucukunda laid the blame on his household priest, Vasiṣṭha, who performed fierce austerities and slew the Rākṣasas. Kubera revealed himself to Mucukunda and challenged his reliance on brahmanical power, but Mucukunda angrily retorted that kings are supposed to make use of both Brahmin and Kṣatriya powers to protect their subjects. He declined Kubera's offer to give him the earth to rule, preferring to win it by force of arms.*

**[76]** *Yudhiṣṭhira asks Bhīṣma what conduct in a king leads to welfare for his subjects and heaven for himself. Bhīṣma recommends liberality, sacrifice, asceticism and the protection of the subjects. The king who looks after his subjects acquires a quarter of their* dharma; *the one who fails to do so receives a share in the evil that his subjects do. The people depend on their king.*

*At this point Yudhiṣṭhira once again announces that he does not want the kingship and will retire to the forest. Bhīṣma argues that he must abandon his softness if he is to achieve the rewards of his* dharma *of protecting his subjects. The person most assured of heaven is the one on whom people rely and through whom they find security.*

**[77]** *Now Yudhiṣṭhira asks Bhīṣma about the proper and improper occupations of Brahmins. Bhīṣma grades Brahmins from highest to lowest according to occupation: the lowest sorts should be taxed and put to forced labour. The king should never ignore Brahmins who are not performing proper occupations: a Brahmin reduced by poverty to theft should be supported, but if he does not then mend his ways he and his kin should be banished.* **[78]** *Yudhiṣṭhira requests*

*Bhīṣma to tell him whose wealth comes under the king's control. Bhīṣma's answer is: that of non-Brahmins and of Brahmins who are engaged in improper occupations. He recites the song sung by a Kekaya king as a Rākṣasa abducted him, saying that in his kingdom all the classes perform their proper tasks and all are treated well. Impressed, the Rākṣasa let him go. Bhīṣma repeats that the king must protect Brahmins and prevent them from engaging in improper occupations.*

**[79]** *Yudhiṣṭhira points out that in times of trouble a Brahmin may follow the Kṣatriya* dharma*: are there circumstances in which he may follow the Vaiśya* dharma*? Bhīṣma replies that this is allowed, though there are certain items that a Brahmin should never trade in. In answer to further questions, he states that in times of crisis, when the subjects give up their proper occupations and arm themselves, Brahmins should use the power of the Vedas to strengthen the king so that he can restore normality; but in case of attack by barbarians, it is right that all classes should take up arms. If the Kṣatriya order should act against the Brahmins, Brahmins may resort to any means, including weapons, to protect themselves. Circumstances may arise in which it is right for a Brahmin to fight, or for a non-Kṣatriya to rule. But Bhīṣma concludes by repeating once again that both kings and Brahmins should carry out their proper tasks.*

**[80]** *Yudhiṣṭhira asks what kind of men ritual priests should be, and Bhīṣma describes the characteristics they ought to have. Then Yudhiṣṭhira raises the question of the gifts that are to be made to the priests: they take no account of the sacrificer's capacity to pay, and this is dreadful. But Bhīṣma insists that the gifts are crucial to the efficacy of the sacrifice: a single vessel of rice is adequate, so all the three highest classes of society should sacrifice.*

**[81]** *Yudhiṣṭhira next asks about the king's aides: what kind of men should they be, and who should be trusted? Bhīṣma lists various sorts of friends, but states that a king should be cautious with all of them. However, both trust and mistrust are fraught with danger, so the king needs to trust some and mistrust others as appropriate; Bhīṣma lists various specific cases of each kind, and gives other general advice. He concludes by pointing out that kinsmen in particular are both good and bad: one should always act agreeably towards them and act in a trusting manner, while in fact mistrusting them.*

**[82]** *If even kinsmen are not to be trusted, says Yudhiṣṭhira, how should one conduct oneself towards both friends and enemies? In reply, Bhīṣma cites the dialogue of Kṛṣṇa Vāsudeva with the seer Nārada. Kṛṣṇa had complained that he was a slave to his kin and even suffered abuse from them: there was no one* *whom he could think of as a friend. Nārada recognized that Kṛṣṇa's situation was very difficult, and recommended use of 'the weapon not made of iron', which he explained as consisting of mildness, generosity and self-control. He advised Kṛṣṇa to act thus to pacify his kinsmen and avoid destructive conflicts.*

**[83]** *Bhīṣma says that, in addition, a king should protect anyone who acts for his benefit, and he cites the tale of what the sage Kālakavṛkṣīya said to Kṣemadarśin, king of Kosala. Kālakavṛkṣīya kept a crow in a cage and claimed that crows told him all that happened in the past, present and future; he accused many of Kṣemadarśin's men of embezzlement, and they responded by killing his crow. He now went in person to the king and gained his permission to tell him what he knew; then he informed him of the treachery of his men, and advised him how to deal with it. Kṣemadarśin made Kālakavṛkṣīya his household priest, and flourished greatly.*

**[84]** *Bhīṣma goes on to tell Yudhiṣṭhira what qualities his courtiers should have, giving detailed advice on what sort of men to confer with and what sort to avoid.* **[85]** *Then he cites the dialogue of Bṛhaspati with Indra. Indra had asked what single action could secure authority and fame, and Bṛhaspati recommended pleasant speech. Bhīṣma likewise recommends it to Yudhiṣṭhira.*

**[86]** *Yudhiṣṭhira asks how, and with whose help, he should administer justice. The qualities Bhīṣma has earlier specified as desirable are rarely to be found in a single man. Bhīṣma advises him to appoint a panel of four Brahmins, three Śūdras and a Sūta. All cases should be heard in public, and great care must be taken to ensure that justice is done. Punishments should be appropriate: fines for the wealthy, death or imprisonment for the poor, discipline and beatings for the ill-behaved, encouragement and gifts for the educated. The worst offenders should suffer death by torture. The king who wields the rod of force properly acquires not* adharma *but* dharma. *After listing the qualities that are desirable in various royal functionaries, Bhīṣma ends by reiterating that the greatest secret of kingship is lack of trust.*

**[87]** *Questioned by Yudhiṣṭhira about the kind of city a king should live in, Bhīṣma replies that it should be secure, well provisioned and well administered. The king should honour learned ascetics and should entrust them with his wealth and take counsel from them.* **[88]** *For the maintenance of the kingdom, Bhīṣma recommends a hierarchy of officers extending from the man in charge of one village to the man in charge of a thousand. Each city should have a powerful governor. The king should be moderate in levying taxes, but should also impress on the* *people the dangers from which he protects them with the wealth they give him. However, he should take care of cattle-owners and tax them mildly, since they may otherwise leave the kingdom.*

**[89]** *Yudhiṣṭhira asks how an already powerful king may increase his revenue. Bhīṣma advocates a gentle approach that will not harm the subjects: small taxes that increase gradually as the taxpayer prospers. However, drinking dens, whores, pimps and other public nuisances should be suppressed, and so should beggars except in times of trouble. Thieves who enrich themselves at the expense of others should also be kept out.* **[90]** *If a Brahmin proposes to leave the realm because of poverty, the king should take every step to dissuade him. The Kṣatriya order was created in order to slay those who impede the welfare of the people: the king should kill his enemies and protect his subjects. He should reflect on his own weaknesses and use spies to discover how his people regard him. He must be watchful for cases of the mighty preying on the weak; he must be careful not to over-tax merchants or farmers.*

**[91]** *Now Bhīṣma tells Yudhiṣṭhira that he will reveal to him everything that the learned Utathya, descendant of Aṅgiras, said to Māndhātṛ on the subject of the* dharma *of kings. Utathya proclaimed that a king exits to foster* dharma, *not to pursue his own interests: his subjects depend on* dharma, *and* dharma *depends on him. If a king seeks his own highest* dharma *while reigning, he does evil, and* adharma *prevails in his land. The king must restrain the wicked, for he is the embodiment of* dharma, *and he must honour Brahmins, for they are the origin of* dharma. *He should avoid envy and pride; he should not keep low company or have unlawful sexual relationships. When a king neglects his kingdom, great evil results.* **[92]** *The four classes of society each have their own roles; the good king is able to keep each one free from wrong conduct. The king is himself the Age – Kṛta, Tretā, Dvāpara or Kali – and all goes to ruin if he is neglectful. The king is responsible for the welfare of the weak, and should fear the great power of the weak, which will destroy him if he does not care for them. The king should take care to rule well in every respect. Bhīṣma concludes by saying that Māndhātṛ followed Utathya's advice, and that Yudhiṣṭhira should do the same.*

**[93]** *Questioned further by Yudhiṣṭhira on how a king should maintain* dharma, *Bhīṣma cites the advice of the seer Vāmadeva to Vasumanas, king of Kosala. Vāmadeva stated that* dharma *is paramount. The king who treats his subjects harshly will soon be destroyed, whereas the one who rules well will* *be cherished by them.* **[94]** *If the king behaves unjustly, he and his kingdom will not last long, whereas if he acts kindly towards his subjects he will prosper. However, he should be wary of rival rulers and be prepared to slay them in battle. His rule should be kind but cautious.* **[95]** *Victories achieved without fighting are better than those resulting from warfare. A king should only strive to expand his kingdom when his kingship is firmly established and he has the goodwill of his troops and subjects. Bhīṣma recommends Yudhiṣṭhira to follow Vāmadeva's advice, as Vasumanas did.*

**[96]** *Asked by Yudhiṣṭhira about the* dharma *in one Kṣatriya's defeat of another, Bhīṣma describes how a king should proceed in invading another land. Then, at Yudhiṣṭhira's request, he gives rules for battle: one should not attack an unarmed man, one should not use poison-smeared or barbed arrows, and many other precepts. Wounded opponents should receive medical care or be returned home. Manu himself laid down that battles must be fought according to* dharma*: better to die adhering to* dharma *than to triumph through evil deeds.* **[97]** *Victory gained through* adharma *is short-lived, and harms both the king and the land. Bhīṣma gives rules for dealing with defeated enemies and their property. Then he recommends that a triumphant invader should try to win over the conquered people swiftly with pleasant words and gifts; otherwise they will seek his downfall. One should never ill-treat one's enemies.*

**[98]** *Yudhiṣṭhira says that the Kṣatriya* dharma *is more evil than any other because of the many deaths it causes; so how can a king attain heaven? Bhīṣma insists that kings are purified of their sins by curbing the wicked, furthering the virtuous, sacrificing and giving gifts; they make the land they conquer thrive once more, and so attain a heavenly reward. The king who fights on behalf of Brahmins engages in a great sacrifice. However, not all warriors are heroic fighters: some are contemptible cowards. A Kṣatriya should not die uninjured in his bed; he should die of wounds suffered in battle, and so reach Indra's heaven.* **[99]** *Yudhiṣṭhira asks Bhīṣma about the realms that heroic Kṣatriyas attain on their deaths. In reply, Bhīṣma cites the dialogue of King Ambarīṣa with Indra. Arriving in heaven, Ambarīṣa observed Sudeva, the commander of his army, flying above him in a marvellous chariot. He pointed out his own many meritorious deeds to Indra, and asked why Sudeva now outranked him; Indra replied that Sudeva had performed the sacrifice of battle, and at Ambarīṣa's request explained in detail the correspondences between elements of battle and elements of sacrifice.*

**[100]** *Bhīṣma recounts to Yudhiṣṭhira how King Janaka encouraged his troops before battle with visions of the heavens and hells that awaited them. He advises Yudhiṣṭhira on arraying his troops and maintaining their morale, and emphasizes the greatness of the heroic warrior.* **[101]** *Yudhiṣṭhira asks Bhīṣma how best to secure a victory, even at the cost of some slight violation of* dharma. *Bhīṣma replies that the king should be aware of both straight and crooked tactics, but he should not knowingly resort to crookedness, and should seek to thwart it if he encounters it. Then he gives detailed advice on weapons, the proper times of year for an army to march to war, suitable routes and sites for their camps, terrains favouring different varieties of fighter, and the advantages of various differently constituted armies. He lists the types of warriors who must not be attacked, and counsels Yudhiṣṭhira on pay-scales and promotions for distinguished soldiers. Then he speaks of how best to encourage the troops, how best to deploy them,* **[102]** *the fighting styles of warriors from different regions, and the various sounds and appearances that characterize different warriors.*

**[103]** *Yudhiṣṭhira asks Bhīṣma about the signs that portend victory for an army, and Bhīṣma lists these. Then he advises Yudhiṣṭhira that he should assemble a powerful army, but should seek first to achieve his objectives through peaceful means, only resorting to war as a last resort. He speaks of the proper use of conciliation, threats, and the sowing of dissension. He recommends forgiving one's defeated enemies, and winning them over by feigning sorrow over their casualties.*

**[104]** *Yudhiṣṭhira requests Bhīṣma's advice on dealing with enemies of various kinds, and Bhīṣma replies by citing the dialogue of Indra with Bṛhaspati. Indra had asked how to subdue his foes without wiping them out, and Bṛhaspati had counselled him to avoid violence and open hostility: better to feign friendship and dupe enemies into falling under one's sway. Kings should use stratagems against their foes: sowing dissension, giving gifts, and so forth. Bṛhaspati concluded by teaching Indra how to recognize wicked men. Bhīṣma adds that Indra followed Bṛhaspati's advice, and subdued his enemies.*

**[105]** *Yudhiṣṭhira asks how a king should behave once he has lost power; in reply, Bhīṣma tells him of the advice that the sage Kālakavṛkṣīya gave to King Kṣemadarśin when the latter had fallen on hard times:*[1] *he had emphasized the impermanence of the things of this world and recommended the way of*

1 Kālakavṛkṣīya was Kṣemadarśin's household priest: see chapter 83 above.

*renunciation.* **[106]** *Then he had offered Kṣemadarśin a way of regaining his position: he should assume a humble attitude towards his enemy, King Janaka of Videha, and secure employment with him, then surreptitiously work to ruin him in many different ways.* **[107]** *Kṣemadarśin rejected such deceitful strategies, and Kālakavṛkṣīya at once commended him for adhering to a policy of benevolence even in the face of great adversity; he promised to secure him a position as Janaka's minister. Janaka did indeed accept the conquered Kṣemadarśin, and married his daughter. Bhīṣma concludes that the highest* dharma *of kings is to be able to endure both victory and defeat.*

**[108]** *Yudhiṣṭhira, after listing the topics that Bhīṣma has dealt with so far, asks about the kingless communities:*[1] *how may they avoid breaking apart, as they are liable to do? Bhīṣma observes that in such communities, as in noble and royal lineages, it is greed and resentment that lead to dissension and collapse; therefore they should concentrate on promoting communal solidarity, which is what leads to their prosperity. Their leaders should be respected, and knowledge of state secrets should be restricted to them. Mutual disaffection and private initiatives are to be avoided: solidarity is what keeps the community together.*

**[109]** *Now Yudhiṣṭhira asks Bhīṣma which of the many aspects of* dharma *is the most important to ensure a man's acquisition of merit in this world and the next. Bhīṣma answers that it is honouring one's father, mother and teacher. These three are the three worlds, the three stages of life, the three Vedas, the three sacrificial fires;*[2] *the man who treats them with proper honour gains merit, fame, and heavenly realms.* **[110]** *Yudhiṣṭhira asks about truth and untruth. What are they, and when should each be spoken? Bhīṣma replies that it is good to speak truth, but sometimes untruth should be spoken instead, as in the story of Kauśika.*[3] *He gives examples of various cases where good and evil are not simply defined, such as the killing of dishonest folk for whom loss of wealth means more than loss of life: this is no sin. One should act towards each man as he acts towards oneself, whether deceitfully or honestly.* **[111]** *Then he gives a list of*

**1** The Sanskrit word used is *gaṇa*, often used non-technically to refer to a large group of any sort. Here it appears to refer to small states in ancient India that were administered as oligarchic chiefdoms.

**2** Four stages of life are commonly enumerated (see chapters 60–66 above); where three are mentioned, *brahmacarya* (holy celibacy as a student) is omitted. Similarly, the 'three Vedas' omits the Atharvaveda.

**3** See 8.49.

*forms of virtuous behaviour which enable people to overcome the difficulties that they may face.*

**[112]** *Yudhiṣṭhira asks Bhīṣma to advise him on how to distinguish between honourable and dishonourable people. In reply, Bhīṣma cites the dialogue of the tiger with the jackal. A certain evil king was reborn as a jackal; he lived a life of extreme virtue, eating nothing but fallen fruit. A tiger, learning of his virtues, wished to make him his aide; the jackal agreed, but only subject to a number of stipulations, including that he should never be punished. But the tiger's existing servants resented him and the honest regime he instituted. They convinced the tiger that the jackal had stolen his own meat, and the tiger gave orders for the jackal to be killed. The tiger's mother and one honest servant succeeded in persuading the tiger of the jackal's innocence, and he was released; but he upbraided the tiger for violating his trust, and then fasted to death, thus attaining heaven.*

**[113]** *Next Yudhiṣṭhira asks what a king should do to be happy. Bhīṣma answers that he should avoid behaving like the camel whose asceticism won a boon from Brahmā. He chose to have a neck a hundred leagues long, and then became too lazy to go out to graze, using his long neck to feed at will. Once when a storm blew up he sheltered his head in a mountain cave; a pair of jackals also sought shelter there and began to devour the camel's neck, and despite his struggles the beast was killed. Bhīṣma concludes that idleness is to be shunned, and one should act with intelligence.*

**[114]** *Yudhiṣṭhira wants to know how a weak king should face a powerful enemy. Bhīṣma replies by telling how the ocean asked the rivers why, though they carried many uprooted trees to him, they never brought him reeds. The river Gaṅgā explained that trees remain unyielding in a single place till eventually they are forced to leave it, whereas reeds bend with the current. In the same way, says Bhīṣma, the wise man acts in accordance with the known strengths and weaknesses of his enemy.*

**[115]** *Yudhiṣṭhira asks Bhīṣma how a man of learning should respond when abused in public by a fool. Bhīṣma answers that if in such a case the victim avoids becoming angry, he takes the abuser's merit and gives him his own demerit. The abuser should be ignored like a sandpiper uttering a distress call. Then Bhīṣma mentions others who should be shunned: the man who will do or say anything in public; the backbiter; the malicious gossip.*

**[116]** *Now Yudhiṣṭhira asks in general how a king should act to bring* *happiness to his kingdom and his lineage. Specifically, he points out the dangers that arise when a king is swayed by affection into favouring base men, and so loses the benefits that good servants bring; he asks what sort of men a king should have to help him. Bhīṣma lists the virtues that a king's various associates should have, and adds that the king himself should govern well and know the* dharma *of kings if he is to attain merit.* **[117]** *He goes on to cite the story of a holy ascetic who lived in the forest unmolested by the wild beasts. He had as his companion a faithful dog that shared his diet of fruit and roots. One day the dog was threatened by a fierce leopard, and appealed for help; the ascetic turned it into a leopard. The leopard was threatened by a tiger; the ascetic turned it into a tiger, which began to prey on the forest creatures. Further transformations followed, into an elephant and a lion. Finally a ferocious* śarabha[1] *threatened the lion, and the ascetic turned it into a* śarabha; *it terrorized the creatures of the forest, and then determined to kill the ascetic. But the latter discerned its purpose, chided it and turned it back into a dog,* **[118]** *and then expelled it from his hermitage. Bhīṣma draws the conclusion that a king should make sure his servants are of good birth and character. His aides should be men of the best sort, and the king himself should possess excellent qualities and be prepared to use the rod of force. His warriors should be devoted, brave and skilful, and he should never treat them with disrespect.* **[119]** *A king should ensure that his servants are appointed to appropriate positions, and do not achieve status for which they are unfitted, like the ascetic's ungrateful dog. Only men of the best character should be the king's associates; the treasury, in particular, should be entrusted to men of virtue.*

**[120]** *Yudhiṣṭhira asks Bhīṣma to state what the* dharma *of kings consists of, and Bhīṣma answers that its chief component is protection of all creatures. He uses the analogy of a peacock to describe in detail how the king should exercise his duty of protection, then gives advice on many aspects of a king's behaviour.* **[121]** *Next Yudhiṣṭhira asks Bhīṣma to speak further about the rod of force, to which he has ascribed such great importance. In reply, Bhīṣma says that everything depends upon the rod of force and the king's administration of justice. The rod is a great god; it may assume the form of any weapon that inflicts violence. Without it, men would destroy one another. The rod is the administration of justice, which in turn is* dharma. **[122]** *He cites the account of the origin of the rod of force*

1 A *śarabha* is a mythical beast with eight legs, four of them on its back.

*that King Vasuhoma of Aṅga gave to Māndhātṛ. Brahmā was once engaged in a sacrifice; the rod of force vanished because he was happy. Anarchy set in, and Brahmā requested Viṣṇu to restore order; Viṣṇu created himself as the rod of force, and appointed the various deities to their duties. The rod was subsequently passed down to Manu and his sons: it exists to protect.*

**[123]** *Yudhiṣṭhira requests Bhīṣma to tell him about* dharma, *the proper making of wealth, and pleasure. After some generalities, Bhīṣma cites the advice of the seer Kāmanda to King Aṅgāriṣṭha, who had asked him how a king can free himself from sins he has committed. Kāmanda said that a king who abandons* dharma *and the proper making of wealth in favour of pleasure causes evildoing to arise in his kingdom and loses the support of his subjects and the Brahmins. He should eradicate the evil by studying the three Vedas, honouring Brahmins and behaving virtuously: in this way he will free himself from even severe sins.*

**[124]** *Now Yudhiṣṭhira asks Bhīṣma how one may acquire a disposition to* dharma. *In reply, Bhīṣma cites the dialogue of Dhṛtarāṣṭra with Duryodhana following Yudhiṣṭhira's own royal consecration.*[1] *The sight of Yudhiṣṭhira's opulence had made Duryodhana deeply unhappy; Dhṛtarāṣṭra counselled that to acquire similar wealth he should cultivate a virtuous disposition. He told Duryodhana of the demon Prahrāda, whose great virtue allowed him to wrest control of the three worlds from Indra. Indra in the guise of a Brahmin had then sought Prahrāda's advice, and Prahrāda had granted him a boon: Indra chose Prahrāda's own virtuous disposition. Prahrāda's virtue now left him to go to Indra, as did* dharma, *truth, good conduct, strength, and royal glory. At Duryodhana's request, Dhṛtarāṣṭra explained that the way to acquire such a disposition is to practise kindness towards all creatures in thought, speech and action.*

**[125]** *Yudhiṣṭhira observes that he had had great hope that Duryodhana would act with propriety, but Duryodhana had shattered it. He asks Bhīṣma about the mystery of hope. Bhīṣma tells him of the Haihaya king Sumitra, who wounded a deer while hunting; he pursued it, shooting more and more arrows at it, but it led him into a great forest and then disappeared with a laugh. Sumitra now encountered a group of ascetics; he told them of the chase and the dashing of his hopes, and then asked them to teach him about hope, which seems as*

1 The occasion referred to is described at 2.45, though that chapter contains little hint of the kind of advice that Dhṛtarāṣṭra is here said to have given his son.

*vast as the sky.* [**126**] *The seer Ṛṣabha answered Sumitra by telling him of his own meeting with an extremely emaciated ascetic named Tanu. While the two were talking, the mighty king Vīradyumna had passed by in a desperate search for his missing son Bhūridyumna, and had asked Tanu about the enormity of hope. Tanu had in fact had his own hopes shattered by Vīradyumna himself, and had determined to rid himself of all hope; he told Vīradyumna that nothing is more difficult to reduce than hope. The king still pleaded for his son; Tanu produced him. Then he revealed that he was in reality the god Dharma, and went away. Now Bhīṣma tells Yudhiṣṭhira that, on hearing Ṛṣabha's words, Sumitra rid himself of his hope; Yudhiṣṭhira should likewise be as unmoved as Mount Himālaya.*

[**127**] *Yudhiṣṭhira asks to hear more about* dharma*; Bhīṣma responds with a story about the seer Gautama, who performed austerities until Yama appeared before him. He asked Yama how one may discharge one's debt to one's parents and attain the heavenly realms; Yama replied that one should honour one's parents and perform horse sacrifices complete with many gifts to the Brahmins.*

[**128**] *Yudhiṣṭhira now asks Bhīṣma how a king should behave whose rule has fallen into utter ruin. Bhīṣma answers that this is a great mystery, and that Yudhiṣṭhira will have to apply his own judgement to it. Expedients for survival are in accord with* dharma *even when they cannot be approved in absolute terms: there is one* dharma *for the strong, another in times of trouble. Self-preservation takes precedence over everything else, and one in distress may live other than by his regular* dharma. *However, even in famine a king should maintain his treasury, his rod, his army and his allies. Nothing can be achieved without wealth, and a king should use any means to obtain wealth for sacrifice: he will not incur sin. The poor are weak, the rich strong. The man with wealth can achieve anything:* dharma, *pleasure, this world and the next.*

## *DHARMA* IN TIMES OF TROUBLE

[**129**] *Yudhiṣṭhira asks Bhīṣma what a king should do when his rule is in ruins and he is threatened by an enemy. Bhīṣma advises making peace if possible, otherwise flight: a king should avoid capture. Alternatively, the threatened king may attack: he may triumph, or he may attain Indra's heaven.* [**130**] *Next, Yudhiṣṭhira wants to know how a householder Brahmin should behave in evil*

*times. In reply, Bhīṣma emphasizes the importance of good judgement. Common people follow rules without qualification, but the man of intelligence does more. A king should not harm Brahmins: this is the standard by which he should judge whether any given action is good or bad. He should not listen to slanderous gossip: the gods themselves punish wrongdoers. Bhīṣma advises Yudhiṣṭhira to follow the ways established by virtuous kings of old.*

**[131]** *Bhīṣma stresses the importance to a king of maintaining his treasury, which he should do by methods midway between scrupulous purity and harshness. In evil times it is better for a king to break than to bend before anyone. Forest-dwelling barbarians may furnish an army, but he should establish rules for them, and he should never wipe out those who are in his power.* **[132]** *Kṣatriyas should maintain both* dharma *and wealth. The consequences of* dharma *cannot be seen in this world, but without wealth and the strength it confers,* dharma *is impossible. They should free themselves of evil by studying the three Vedas, honouring Brahmins and behaving virtuously.*

**[133]** *Bhīṣma relates the story of Kāpavya, son of a Kṣatriya father and a Niṣāda woman, who maintained the Kṣatriya* dharma, *hunting and caring for his old, blind parents and the Brahmins who lived in the forest. The wicked barbarians made him their leader; he instructed them to live virtuously according to* dharma, *and they abandoned their evil ways.* **[134]** *Next Bhīṣma cites verses sung by Brahmā on how kings should accumulate riches. They should take the wealth of barbarians and non-sacrificers, for wealth not used for sacrifice is pointless; it should be taken from the wicked and given to the good.*

**[135]** *Bhīṣma tells the story of three fish in a pool, one quick-witted, one far-sighted and one procrastinating. When fishermen began to drain the pool, the far-sighted fish fled elsewhere; as the remaining fish were caught and threaded on a string, the quick-witted fish bit the string and pretended to have been caught, later escaping when the fishermen washed their catch in fresh water. But the procrastinating fish was killed. Bhīṣma concludes that the man who plans ahead fares best.*

**[136]** *Yudhiṣṭhira asks Bhīṣma how a king should act when threatened by enemies: how can he tell friend from foe, and how should he behave towards both? Bhīṣma answers that neither friends nor foes are permanent, and that the wise man will sometimes ally himself with his foes and quarrel with his friends. He illustrates his point with the story of a mouse that lived under a banyan tree* *and a cat that lived in its branches. A Caṇḍāla*[1] *hunter used to visit the tree every night to set snares, and one day the cat was caught. At first the mouse rejoiced in his new freedom from danger, but soon he was threatened by a mongoose and an owl. Deciding to try to make common cause with the cat, he offered to free it from its bonds if it would agree to protect him and not kill him. The two creatures very warily entered into an alliance; then as the hunter approached next morning, the mouse severed the bond securing the cat, and they both fled to their usual homes. Later the cat proposed that the mouse should come and join him, but the mouse rejected this: there had been a reason for them to be friends, but now they must be enemies again, since cats eat mice. Bhīṣma concludes by urging Yudhiṣṭhira always to pay close attention to his own interests when dealings with friends and foes.*

**[137]** *Taking up Bhīṣma's theme that a king should be mistrustful, Yudhiṣṭhira objects that it is difficult to achieve anything without trusting someone. Bhīṣma responds with the story of King Brahmadatta and the bird Pūjanī, who lived in Brahmadatta's palace. Bird and king each had a child of the same age. Pūjanī fed her own son and the prince with wonderful, strength-enhancing fruit, but the boy, growing strong, killed the young bird as he played with it. Then Pūjanī, reviling the ways of Kṣatriyas, blinded him with her claws. Brahmadatta repeatedly assured her that her retaliation was fair, and asked her to continue living in the palace, but she insisted that hostility between them would remain, making friendship impossible. After a lengthy debate with the king, she took leave of him and left.*

**[138]** *Yudhiṣṭhira asks how one should behave in times of trouble. In reply, Bhīṣma cites Kaṇiṅka's advice to King Śatruṃtapa. A king should be ready to wield the rod of force; he should be outwardly agreeable, but inwardly mistrustful and intent on his own interests.* **[139]** *Now Yudhiṣṭhira asks how Brahmins and kings should act when calamities befall. Bhīṣma emphasizes the importance of judgement, and tells the story of Viśvāmitra, who was wandering about during a famine caused by severe drought when he saw a piece of dog-meat in the house of a Caṇḍāla. He resolved to steal it, arguing that theft is permitted to preserve life at a time of distress. Entering the house at night, he accidentally awoke the Caṇḍāla, who challenged him. Viśvāmitra told the man who he was and what he intended to do; the Caṇḍāla did his best to dissuade him from eating such forbidden food, but Viśvāmitra insisted, and took the meat. At this moment,*

1 Caṇḍālas were people of the lowest social status, regarded by those of high birth as deeply polluting.

*Indra poured down rain in abundance. Bhīṣma adds that this is how judgements about* dharma *and* adharma *should be made in times of trouble.*

**[140]** *Yudhiṣṭhira professes horror at Bhīṣma's view of* dharma. *Bhīṣma responds that* dharma *is not simply what is taught by tradition: it has many sources, and a king should use them with intelligence. Decrying false expounders of* dharma, *he says that as a Kṣatriya Yudhiṣṭhira was created to be fierce: he should rule his kingdom.*

**[141]** *Yudhiṣṭhira now asks Bhīṣma about the merit that comes from offering refuge to one who seeks it. Bhīṣma replies that this brings great merit, and tells the story of a wicked fowler who used to kill the forest birds for sale. Once he was caught in the forest by a terrible storm. When the sky cleared, he approached a great tree, formally requested it to grant him refuge, and fell asleep at its foot.* **[142]** *In the tree was a dove whose mate had not returned: anxious for her safety, he spoke at length of her great virtues. The female dove had in fact been caught by the fowler; she was happy to hear her mate speak thus of her, but then she counselled him that he must treat the fowler with all respect, as he had come to their dwelling for refuge. The male dove therefore asked the fowler what he desired. The fowler complained of the cold, and the dove brought fire for him. Then the fowler complained of hunger, and the dove, having no other source of food for him, entered the fire. The fowler was shocked, and lamented his ill deeds:* **[143]** *he now determined on a life of asceticism and* dharma. **[144]** *The female dove, grieving bitterly for her mate, entered the fire herself. Then she saw her mate arriving in heaven in a flying chariot, honoured by the hosts of the virtuous, and she joined him there.* **[145]** *The fowler saw the two doves entering heaven and resolved on austerities that would result in heaven for himself. Eating and drinking nothing, he passed by a charming lake and entered a terrible forest where thorns tore his flesh. Seeing a raging forest fire he ran into it; his sins were destroyed, and he found himself in heaven. Bhīṣma adds that this great* dharma *can expiate even the sin of cow-slaughter, but that nothing can expiate the sin of killing one who come for refuge.*

**[146]** *Yudhiṣṭhira asks how someone who commits an unintentional sin can free himself from it. In reply, Bhīṣma tells the story of King Janamejaya, son of Parikṣit.*[1] *Janamejaya had accidentally killed a Brahmin. Ostracized by all,*

1 This name and parentage normally denote the descendant of the Pāṇḍavas at whose snake sacrifice Vaiśaṃpāyana recited the *Mahābhārata* (see 1.1.9, etc.); however, at this point in the narrative neither Janamejaya nor Parikṣit has yet been born.

*he left for the forest, where he attempted to propitiate the great ascetic Indrota Śaunaka. Indrota rebuked him sharply, telling him that he had condemned his ancestors to hell and would suffer endless torments himself.* **[147]** *Janamejaya pleaded with Indrota to help him rescue himself and his lineage; Indrota told him that he would have to perform a rite of expiation and win the support of the Brahmins by repenting of his sin. Janamejaya answered that he did indeed repent, and Indrota made him swear never again to harm Brahmins.* **[148]** *Then he spoke to him of the six different ways of purifying oneself: sacrifice, the giving of gifts, compassion, the Vedas, truthfulness and asceticism. He also recommended visiting holy places, but added that for a king the best way is to conquer heaven and attain purification by means of military might and the distribution of wealth. Finally, says Bhīṣma, Indrota officiated at a horse sacrifice for Janamejaya.*

**[149]** *Next Bhīṣma cites the dialogue of a vulture with a jackal. A family whose son had died in childhood took his body to the burning-ground. As they grieved, a vulture addressed them; he pointed out that death comes to everyone, and advised them to let go of their love for the child and go home. But as they set out, a jackal reproved them for their lack of feeling, and they turned back. Again the vulture spoke of the futility of grief; again the jackal argued for the strength of human feeling and the importance of remaining hopeful. The dispute went on and on, with the vulture seeking to persuade the family to leave before sunset, and the jackal urging them to remain until after sunset, for both creatures were hungry.*[1] *Then Śiva arrived; he granted the mourners the boon of a hundred years of life for their dead son, and he removed the hunger of the vulture and the jackal. Bhīṣma observes that hope, determination and divine grace lead to great rewards.*

**[150]** *Bhīṣma now cites the dialogue of a kapok tree with the Wind. Nārada had once seen a huge and ancient kapok tree that sheltered many birds and other creatures, and had remarked that the mighty Wind had broken none of its branches: he concluded that the Wind must be protecting the tree out of friendship. The tree denied this, claiming that its own strength was much greater than that of the Wind. This angered Nārada, who scolded the tree for belittling the Wind's great might, and told it that he would inform the Wind of the insult.* **[151]** *Then he told the Wind that the kapok tree had insulted him. The Wind went to the tree and told it that the reason he had favoured it was that Brahmā had rested under it during the creation; now he would show himself to the tree in*

1 Vultures feed by day, jackals by night.

*his real form. The tree scoffed, and the Wind promised to show it his might the next day. During the night the tree, knowing its words to Nārada had been false, resolved to use its wits to escape the Wind's anger, and it shed all its branches. The Wind arrived, and derided the kapok tree for doing to itself exactly what he was going to do to it: it had brought itself under the Wind's sway. Bhīṣma tells Yudhiṣṭhira that a weak man should never antagonize a stronger man, nor a fool an intelligent man. He adds that he has now stated the* dharma *of kings and the* dharma *in times of trouble; what else does Yudhiṣṭhira wish to hear?*

**[152]** *Yudhiṣṭhira asks what is the origin of evil. Bhīṣma replies that all evils result from greed. This affects all human beings, but the deluded greed that is never satisfied must be conquered by those who are self-controlled. Even learned men may be in the grip of greed and ignorance, and so may introduce distortions in the forms of* dharma *that they preach. Such men are uncultured boors; they are unlike the truly cultured, who are self-controlled and free from greed, and who deserve Yudhiṣṭhira's favour.* **[153]** *Having learnt about greed, Yudhiṣṭhira asks to learn also about ignorance. Bhīṣma answers that this is the name given to many human passions and failings. Ignorance and greed lead to the same bad results; they are the same thing. Ignorance arises from greed, and grows greater or less with it; greed arises from Time. Bhīṣma counsels Yudhiṣṭhira to free himself from greed.*

**[154]** *Now Yudhiṣṭhira remarks that the road of* dharma *is long and contains many branches, and he asks Bhīṣma what is the fundamental aspect of* dharma *for a pious Brahmin. In reply, Bhīṣma praises self-control as the highest virtue, an aggregate of all other virtues. The man who controls his senses and takes to the forest is ready to become one with* brahman. *The only fault of self-control is that people mistake it for weakness, but its great merit is that it enables one to attain the heavenly realms. Indeed, the self-controlled man does not need a forest to retire to: wherever he is, that is his forest and his hermitage.* **[155]** *Then Bhīṣma speaks of asceticism, which he describes as the basis of all things: the creation of the world, the acquisition of the Vedas, the power of medicines. Asceticism can also expiate even the worst sins, and fasting is its best form.*

**[156]** *Yudhiṣṭhira asks what is truth. Bhīṣma replies that truth is* dharma, *it is asceticism, it is Yoga, it is* brahman. *It underpins everything. Bhīṣma lists the thirteen forms that truth may take: truth itself, equanimity, self-control, selflessness, forbearance, modesty, endurance, lack of envy, renunciation, meditation, nobility, steadfastness and non-violence.*

**[157]** *Yudhiṣṭhira now lists thirteen faults and asks how they originate: anger, desire, grief, delusion, desire for possessions, weariness, pride, greed, envy, spite, contempt, selfishness and lack of pity.*[1] *Bhīṣma describes how each of these comes into being and what brings it to an end.* **[158]** *Yudhiṣṭhira says that he does not understand vicious men, and asks Bhīṣma to elucidate their position with regard to* dharma. *Bhīṣma responds by listing the characteristics of such men and advising Yudhiṣṭhira to avoid them.*

**[159]** *Bhīṣma tells Yudhiṣṭhira that it is right to give gifts to worthy Brahmins, and that if a Brahmin's sacrifice is lacking some element, the king should make good the lack by taking from a person who is not a sacrificer; likewise, a hungry Brahmin may take food for one meal from the store of an irreligious man. He goes on to detail various rules of behaviour regarding Brahmins, followed by the expiations appropriate for a variety of sins.*

**[160]** *Nakula takes advantage of a pause in the talk to ask Bhīṣma about weapons. Most people regard the bow as the finest weapon, but he favours the sword. What is Bhīṣma's view, and what is the origin of the sword? In reply, Bhīṣma describes Brahmā's creation of the universe. The gods followed the* dharma *laid down in the Vedas, but the demons violated it, vying with the gods and practising wickedness. Brahmā performed a great sacrifice which culminated in the appearance of a terrifying creature; Brahmā named it 'Sword', and it assumed the form of a sword, which Rudra used to destroy the demons. Thereafter the sword was passed on through Indra and the world-guardian gods to Manu and the race of men, for the purpose of protecting* dharma. *The bow was created by Pṛthu, son of Vena;*[2] *the sword should be honoured by all warriors.*

**[161]** *Bhīṣma falls silent. Yudhiṣṭhira addresses his brothers and Vidura; he asks them which is the most important out of* dharma, *the proper making of wealth, and pleasure. Vidura argues for* dharma, *Arjuna for the making of wealth, the twins Nakula and Sahadeva for the two in combination; Bhīma speaks in favour of pleasure. But Yudhiṣṭhira wins the applause of all of them when he recommends detachment and final release.*[3]

**1** Reading *akṛpā*. The text in fact reads 'pity' (*kṛpā*) at all three occurrences of the word in this chapter, but in every case the preceding word ends with a vowel which would cause the initial *a* of *akṛpā* to disappear. The decision which word to prefer is thus entirely editorial, and I can see no reason not to prefer the more obvious *akṛpā*.

**2** Apparently the righteous 'armed man' consecrated as king by Viṣṇu at 12.59.

**3** See note to 1.56.16.

*Then Yudhiṣṭhira resumes his questioning of Bhīṣma,* **[162]** *by asking what kind of people make the best friends. Bhīṣma begins by issuing a long list of the sort of people who ought to be avoided, then lists the qualities one should look for in a friend. He remarks that the very worst type of person is the ingrate who hurts his friends, and by way of illustration he tells the story of Gautama, an unlearned Brahmin who settled in a barbarian village. He married a widow and took up barbarian ways, hunting and killing wildfowl in great numbers. One day an old Brahmin friend of his came to that village, recognized him and rebuked him for abandoning Brahmin ways. Gautama resolved to leave the village the next day.* **[163]** *He fell in with a caravan travelling towards the sea, but fled when they were savaged by a wild elephant. Then he wandered in a lovely forest and sat beneath a magnificent banyan tree. As the sun set, the wise and glorious king of the cranes, known as Rājadharman,*[1] *arrived back at that tree after a visit to Brahmā. The hungry Gautama planned to kill him, but the bird welcomed him as a guest;* **[164]** *he treated Gautama with great hospitality, and when he learnt that he was a poor man he directed him to visit his nearby friend Virūpākṣa, the lord of the Rākṣasas. Gautama set off, and soon arrived at the opulent city of Meruvraja. When Virūpākṣa learnt that he had been sent by his friend Rājadharman, he had him brought at once into his presence,* **[165]** *and asked him about himself. Gautama replied truthfully that he lived in a barbarian village and had married a Śūdra widow. Reflecting that his visitor was none the less a Brahmin and the friend of his friend Rājadharman, Virūpākṣa resolved to honour him along with the thousand Brahmins who were due to arrive that day for his annual distribution of food and wealth. The Brahmins came, and were fed and presented with rich gifts. Gautama too received a load of gold; he carried it back with difficulty to the banyan tree, where Rājadharman welcomed him. But Gautama was worried that he would get nothing to eat on his onward journey, and he resolved to kill Rājadharman and carry him with him as a supply of meat.* **[166]** *Rājadharman lit a fire for protection, and by its side he slept; but the ingrate Gautama lay awake waiting for his chance. He killed Rājadharman and roasted his flesh; then he hurried away with his food and his gold. The next day, Virūpākṣa became worried when Rājadharman failed to pay him his normal visit. Fearing that the fallen Brahmin Gautama might have killed him, he sent his son to find out what had happened. The prince*

1 'The *dharma* of kings'.

*set off with some Rākṣasas and discovered the remains of Rājadharman. Then they pursued Gautama, captured him and returned with him to Virūpākṣa's city. Virūpākṣa ordered his Rākṣasas to kill and eat Gautama, but none of them wished to eat the flesh of such an evildoer. At their suggestion Virūpākṣa commanded that he should be given to the barbarians. The Rākṣasas hacked him to pieces and handed him over, but neither the barbarians nor even the carrion creatures would eat him.* **[167]** *Virūpākṣa had Rājadharman's remains cremated, but the celestial cow Surabhi appeared overhead and dropped some milk on to the body, and Rājadharman was restored to life. Indra arrived and explained that what had happened was the result of a curse. At Rājadharman's request Gautama too was brought back to life; he returned with his gold to the barbarian village, where he sired many wicked sons, and the gods cursed him to go to hell. Bhīṣma tells Yudhiṣṭhira that one should never harm one's friends; anyone who does so should be shunned.*

## THE *DHARMA* OF FINAL RELEASE

**[168]** *Now Yudhiṣṭhira asks Bhīṣma to speak of the* dharmas *of those who follow the four stages of life. Bhīṣma's reply is that a wise man should strive for release from this imperfect world. Yudhiṣṭhira responds with a second question: what way of thinking can help a man to dispel the grief caused by a serious loss? In answer, Bhīṣma cites the story of King Senajit and a Brahmin. Senajit was distraught at the death of his son; the Brahmin reproved him for grief, pointing out that Senajit himself and everyone else in the world would also die. Then at Senajit's request he explained how to avoid despair. He counselled Senajit against affection for others, explaining that happiness leads to unhappiness and unhappiness to happiness; only the wisest and the most foolish know true happiness, which arises from passing beyond the pairs of opposites. One should eliminate all desire: the idea of possession leads to nothing but affliction. Bhīṣma adds that, thanks to the Brahmin's words, Senajit experienced great joy.*

**[169]** *Next Bhīṣma cites the dialogue of a father with his wise son. The father recommended begetting sons for the sake of the ancestors,*[1] *and performing*

1 Sons are necessary to perform the *śrāddha* ceremonies for deceased forebears; see note to 12.42.

*sacrifices. The son objected that death is inevitable and can come at any time; one should practise* dharma *from earliest youth, for death may take a man in the midst of his concerns about sons and sacrifices. The non-violent man is not enslaved by his own actions; nothing but truth can overcome death. The son stated that he would shun violence, and that his sacrifice would be that of tranquillity and holiness in thought, word and deed; in this way he would become one with* brahman *and would need no offspring to save him. Bhīṣma says that the father followed his son's advice, and that Yudhiṣṭhira should follow it too.*

**[170]** *Yudhiṣṭhira asks how happiness and unhappiness come about for rich and for poor. In reply Bhīṣma cites the song of Śamyāka, who had attained release: only renunciation can lead to happiness.* **[171]** *After hearing this, Yudhiṣṭhira asks how the man with insufficient wealth can find happiness. Bhīṣma answers that happiness is achieved through equanimity, non-striving, truthfulness, indifference and lack of desire for possessions. He cites the song of Maṅki, whose efforts at gaining wealth were disappointed. When his two newly bought bullocks were lost, he concluded that fate was more powerful than human effort, praised indifference, and resolved to free himself from desire, and Bhīṣma says that he succeeded in this and became one with* brahman. *He also cites the words of King Janaka and the seer Bodhya on indifference.*

**[172]** *Now Bhīṣma cites the dialogue of King Prahrāda with the sage Ājagara. Prahrāda had commented on the sage's tranquillity of mind; Ājagara replied that he had seen how all things come and go, and so was indifferent to everything. Sometimes his life was easy, sometimes hard, but he accepted both equally, for he practised the* ājagara *vow. Bhīṣma says that this vow leads to true happiness.*

**[173]** *Yudhiṣṭhira asks whether kin, ritual, wealth or wisdom provides the best basis for a man; Bhīṣma speaks strongly in favour of wisdom, citing the dialogue of Indra with the Brahmin Kāśyapa. Kāśyapa had been hurt in an accident, and as he lay in pain he resolved to die, saying that a poor man has no purpose in living. Now Indra appeared in the form of a jackal and upbraided him, pointing out that the highest birth is birth as a human, and that Brahmins are the highest humans. All lower creatures long to have hands as humans do; Kāśyapa was very much more fortunate than most other beings, but he should not fall prey to desire, for one desire leads to another, and the best course for a man is to avoid all sensory impressions. The jackal told Kāśyapa to stop thinking of dying and to live a virtuous life, and Kāśyapa, now recognizing him as Indra, worshipped him.*

**[174]** *Bhīṣma says that sinners suffer repeated woes and deaths, while the virtuous enjoy repeated heavenly delights. Atheists go to terrible regions, while believers and other good folk take the auspicious path of the self-possessed. A man's former deeds follow him everywhere, like a shadow; deeds bear their consequences as surely as plants bear flowers and fruit. Only by long asceticism in the forest can men free themselves of sin and obtain what they long for.*

**[175]** *Now Yudhiṣṭhira asks Bhīṣma about the origin of the universe and the creatures who inhabit it: how do they live, and where do they go when they die? In reply, Bhīṣma cites the answer that Bhṛgu gave to Bharadvāja when he asked him the same questions. Bhṛgu said that everything first originated from a primal being named Mānasa;*[1] *he created the lotus from which was born Brahmā, the lord of creation.* **[176]** *He described how Mānasa in his form as Brahmā first created water, and then from water created the other elements;* **[177]** *he stated that all five elements are present in every being, whether immediately obvious or not; the elements also determine the properties of sensory perceptions.* **[178]** *He described the various vital breaths that maintain life, and explained that all of these contain the element fire.* **[179]** *Bharadvāja objected that Bhṛgu's account of the elements had said little about life itself, and he asked what happens to creatures when they die.* **[180]** *Bhṛgu explained that the living being does not perish when the body perishes; like fire that has consumed all its fuel, it continues to exist imperceptibly in the ether.*[2] *Bharadvāja responded with a further question: if the body is simply an assemblage of the five elements, what is the living being itself? If the mind is not applied, one is unaware even of sensory perceptions: what is it that experiences joy, anger, grief, and so forth? Bhṛgu answered that this is the inner self, which is also Mānasa Brahmā, the creator.* **[181]** *He described how Brahmā first created Brahmins, then the major virtues, and then the various orders of beings; the four classes of men were distinguished by colour.*[3] *Bharadvāja observed that the distinctions appeared to have been lost, and all men were now equally subject to desire, anger and other disagreeable emotions. Bhṛgu explained that originally all men were created as Brahmins, but that they had come to be divided into classes on the basis of their behaviour.* **[182]** *He listed the kinds of behaviour associated with each of the four classes, and emphasized that*

**1** 'Mental power'.

**2** See note to 8.66.2.

**3** The word translated as 'class', *varṇa*, has the literal meaning 'colour'.

*the self-controlled Brahmin becomes one with* brahman. **[183]** *He argued for the importance of happiness, which he equated with truth,* dharma *and light.* **[184]** *Bharadvāja requested Bhṛgu to speak about the four stages of life. Bhṛgu described the student's life of holy celibacy, and the lives of the householder,* **[185]** *forest-dweller and mendicant renouncer. Then at Bharadvāja's request he spoke of the heaven-like land to the north of Mount Himālaya, where there is no evildoing; he contrasted it with the ordinary world of men.*

**[186]** *At Yudhiṣṭhira's request, Bhīṣma now lists a large number of rules for good conduct in everyday life.* **[187]** *He speaks of the five elements that the creator placed in all beings, and of the sensory perceptions that derive from them; of mind, intelligence and the self; and of the three Sāṃkhya qualities.*[1] **[188]** *Then he describes Yoga meditation, which leads to the greatest happiness and to release from the cycle of rebirth.*

**[189]** *Yudhiṣṭhira asks Bhīṣma about the practice of reciting Vedic texts in a murmur. Bhīṣma draws a distinction between two forms of religious life, the one engaged in activities, the other disengaged. The murmuring reciter should be disengaged; meditating on* brahman, *and by degrees ceasing even to meditate, he attains freedom from rebirth.* **[190]** *In reply to a question from Yudhiṣṭhira, he adds that those who perform murmuring recitation without the necessary disengagement and discipline go to hell.* **[191]** *Yudhiṣṭhira wants to know more; Bhīṣma explains that the heavenly realms of the gods are hell in comparison with the place of the universal Self, which is beyond all human experience.*

**[192]** *Now Bhīṣma tells the story of a pious Brahmin who performed austerities and recited in a murmur for a thousand years. The goddess Sāvitrī offered him a boon, but all he wanted was to continue to be absorbed in his recitation; she granted this. After a further hundred celestial years, Dharma approached him and urged him to abandon his body and enter the heaven he had earned, but the Brahmin preferred to go on reciting. Yama, Time and Death came to take him, but he simply offered them hospitality. King Ikṣvāku came and asked the Brahmin to give him the reward his recitation had earned; the Brahmin insisted on giving it, even when Ikṣvāku changed his mind and argued against the gift. Eventually Desire and Anger revealed that they, together with Time, Dharma and Death, had been testing the two men, and invited both to go to the worlds they had earned. Bhīṣma explains that a reciter attains whatever*

1 See 3.203.

*he desires; but if he is free from desire, he attains release.* **[193]** *Yudhiṣṭhira asks Bhīṣma what answer the Brahmin and Ikṣvāku gave. Bhīṣma replies that the Brahmin proposed to return to his recitation, and he and Ikṣvāku agreed to share their rewards equally with each other. At this the celestials arrived, musical instruments were played in the heavens, and flowers rained down. The two men entered deep yogic meditation, and Brahmā granted them oneness with himself.*[1] **[194]** *Next Yudhiṣṭhira asks what the rewards are for various religious practices, and how one may come to know the universal Self. In reply, Bhīṣma says that the seer Bṛhaspati had asked similar questions of Manu. Manu answered that whilst the purpose of the way of action is to gain happiness, the purpose of the way of knowledge is to avoid both happiness and unhappiness; only by eliminating desire can one achieve the highest state. The Eternal one from whom all creation sprang is beyond human perception and understanding; only those who know* brahman *behold him.* **[195]** *It is only by withdrawing one's senses from their objects that one may perceive the Eternal one,* brahman, *to be one's own self. The wise man can do this through his inherent knowledge, which is superior to the senses. At death one abandons one's old body to the elements, and enters a new one constituted of those same elements, and one receives back all one's former good and bad deeds.* **[196]** *The senses cannot perceive themselves, but the self, which is omniscient and all-seeing, perceives them. The self cannot be perceived through the senses, but that does not mean it does not exist; it is through knowledge that it can be seen. When separated by death from the body, the self is like the moon on the night of no moon: it cannot be seen, but it exists, and is the same self as before, accompanied by the fruits of all its former deeds.* **[197]** *When the senses are tranquil, one may through knowledge see the self like a reflection in still water, but when they are disturbed one cannot see the self; the mind hankers after sensual enjoyments. Only by ridding oneself of sinful deeds does one gain the knowledge that allows one to perceive the self; one should strive to keep oneself free from sensual attachments.* **[198]** *When the mind is endowed with knowledge, understanding results, and it becomes possible to know* brahman. *But the mind apprehends qualities, and in order to know* brahman, *which is without qualities, the senses must be withdrawn and the mind focused in meditation.* **[199]** *A person may be reborn as any kind of creature as the result of his deeds. Results arise from deeds, which arise from perception, which*

1 i.e. with *brahman*.

*arises from knowledge; but the heavenly knowledge of* brahman *follows from the destruction of all of these. It is the eternal god Viṣṇu, who transcends all other things, that is called the supreme* brahman*; those who reach him attain final release. He cannot be reached by those who are attached to the senses or to qualities, but only by one who has purified his understanding by means of knowledge, his mind by means of understanding, and his senses by means of his mind.*

**[200]** *Yudhiṣṭhira asks Bhīṣma to tell him more about Viṣṇu. Bhīṣma praises Viṣṇu's greatness, and describes how Brahmā was born from a lotus that grew from his navel. Then a demon named Madhu was born from the darkness; Viṣṇu slew him, thus gaining his name Madhusūdana, 'slayer of Madhu'. Brahmā now created seven sons for himself, including Dakṣa, who begat thirteen daughters, and Marīci, who became the father of Kaśyapa. Kaśyapa married Dakṣa's daughters, and from those unions were born the races of animals of all sorts, and the demons, and various of the gods. Now Viṣṇu created the divisions of time, and clouds, and all other moving and stationary things. Next, from his mouth he created Brahmins, from his arms Kṣatriyas, from his thighs Vaiśyas and from his feet Śūdras. He assigned roles to the gods. At that time there was no sexual intercourse: children were produced by an act of will. Procreation through sex came about in the Dvāpara Age, and marriage in the Kali Age. The creator, lotus-eyed Kṛṣṇa Keśava, is no mere man; he is beyond understanding.*

**[201]** *Yudhiṣṭhira wishes to know who were formerly Prajāpatis, lords of creation, and which seers dwell at which points of the compass. Bhīṣma lists the Prajāpatis, and also names the various classes of gods, including the Kṣatriya Ādityas, the Vaiśya Maruts, the Śūdra Aśvins and the Brahmin descendants of Aṅgiras. Then he names the cardinal points at which the various seers dwell.*

**[202]** *Now Yudhiṣṭhira asks to hear more about Kṛṣṇa, and in particular about the time he took on the form of an animal. In reply, Bhīṣma repeats the story as it was told to him by Kaśyapa. Long ago the gods and seers were oppressed by the mighty, warlike demons. The Ādityas approached Brahmā for help, and so Viṣṇu assumed the form of a boar and attacked the demons beneath the earth where they were massing. The demons were unable to withstand the boar, whose roars spread terror throughout the universe. The boar slew the demons; the gods approached Brahmā and asked what creature it was that roared so, and Brahmā revealed that it was the supreme lord, lotus-eyed Kṛṣṇa.*

**[203]** *Yudhiṣṭhira asks Bhīṣma to reveal to him the great Yoga of final* *release. In reply, Bhīṣma cites the dialogue of a* guru *with his pupil. The pupil asked about the origin and destruction of beings and about the applicability of statements made in the Vedas. The* guru *answered that Kṛṣṇa Vāsudeva is supreme* brahman, *and described to the pupil how he creates all beings, together with the* dharmas *regulating them and the Vedas, at the beginning of each cycle of ages, and brings them all to destruction again at its end. At the end of each cycle the Vedas and related matter disappear, but at each new beginning the great seers are permitted to regain them through asceticism, along with knowledge of* brahman, *and the universe is re-formed.* **[204]** *The beginnings and ends of all things are unmanifest; the manifest develops from the unmanifest, as in the case of the mighty tree which exists within the seed; the development follows natural inclination, as when iron runs towards a magnet.* **[205]** *A person seeking release should avoid impure acts; knowledge unfreed from passion is like gold adulterated with iron. Only fools become attached to things of the senses; one should take food as a sick man takes medicine, to take one forward on one's way, not for the sake of taste. The man who seeks tranquillity should restrain his senses, and avoid the faults caused by ignorance and the delusion of the three Sāṃkhya qualities.*[1] *Questioned by his pupil, the* guru *explained that to purify oneself and attain release, one needs to rid oneself of Darkness and Passion, and adhere to Goodness.* **[206]** *Those who betake themselves to Viṣṇu while under the thrall of Darkness and Passion fall victim to his illusory* māyā*; their knowledge fails them and they become subject to desire, which leads in turn to anger, greed, delusion, pride, the sense of 'I', actions, bonds of affection, grief and rebirth. The wise man should avoid women, and should regard children in the same way as he would regard a parasite growing on his body. Sorrow arises from acceptance of birth and increases from the sense of 'I', but it is suppressed by ridding oneself of both; he who knows how to suppress it gains release.* **[207]** *Among all the virtues the highest is* brahmacarya,[2] *which involves shunning all sensory objects. Practised in full this leads to release, practised partially it leads to heaven, practised a little it leads to a good rebirth as a Brahmin. Avoiding all contact with women, freeing oneself from Passion and Darkness, one passes beyond sin and attains the nectar*

**1** See 3.203.

**2** This word normally refers to the first of the four stages of life, the holy celibacy of the young student; here it is being used more generally to refer to a mode of life directed at attaining release and oneness with *brahman*.

*of release.* **[208]** *The intelligent man should be free from attachment to things of the senses, and should strive for release. He should be tranquil and pure. Since one always obtains the fruit of former deeds, it is by practising the virtues that one escapes misery and finds happiness. One should cultivate calmness in thought, word and deed, avoiding acts of Passion and Darkness; by living in solitude, eating little, performing austerities and restraining the senses one attains the highest good, finally reaching* brahman. **[209]** *The man who wishes to practise perfect* brahmacarya *should avoid sleep, since in dreams one is overwhelmed by Passion and Darkness. Dreams arise because the senses are exhausted and the mind unconscious; the imaginings that come to one in sleep are those that come in wakefulness. Of the three Sāṃkhya qualities, Goodness belongs to the gods, the other two to the demons; but* brahman *transcends all three.* **[210]** *The engaged form of religious life leads to rebirth; the disengaged form leads to eternal* brahman. *One who intends to follow the way of disengagement must know both unmanifest nature (*prakṛti*) and individual self (*puruṣa*), as well as that which transcends them both (*brahman*).*[1] *Such a one should practise mental austerities in the form of restraint of mind and speech, and physical austerities in the form of* brahmacarya *and non-violence. He should eat little. Such* yogīs *may follow different practices, but all attain the final release of* brahman.

**[211]** *At Yudhiṣṭhira's request Bhīṣma tells how King Janaka of Videha attained release. He had a hundred spiritual advisers, but was not satisfied with them. To him there came a great sage named Pañcaśikha, who was said to be none other than Kapila himself:*[2] *he had drunk the milk of his* guru*'s wife, who was named Kapilā. His knowledge of* dharma *confounded Janaka's hundred advisers, and the king dismissed them and became his follower. He taught Janaka final release as laid down in Sāṃkhya, and spoke of the sorrows of existence, the futility of ritual, and the various erroneous doctrines taught by others.* **[212]** *Janaka said that, if everything ends in annihilation, he could see no point in distinguishing between knowledge and ignorance, heedfulness and heedlessness, and so forth. Pañcaśikha explained that everything does not end in annihilation: the individual self is eternal, and cannot be destroyed. He praised the way of non-attachment, which leads to freedom from joy and sorrow, and cited the words of an earlier king of Videha on seeing his city of Mithilā in*

**1** Important terms in Sāṃkhya philosophy: cf. 6.35–6.

**2** Kapila was the founder of the Sāṃkhya school.

*flames: 'Not even a grain of chaff of mine is burning here.' Pañcaśikha's teaching brought King Janaka the highest happiness.*

**[213]** *Yudhiṣṭhira asks what way of life leads to happiness and success. In answer Bhīṣma praises the virtue of self-control, which brings great rewards.* **[214]** *Yudhiṣṭhira questions Bhīṣma about fasting Brahmins who consume the oblation at sacrifices; Bhīṣma condemns the practice. Then Yudhiṣṭhira asks whether people are right to regard fasting as a form of asceticism; Bhīṣma replies that true asceticism consists of renunciation and humility; however, one should also practise fasting, celibacy and the other virtues.*

**[215]** *Yudhiṣṭhira wants to know whether man is really the doer of those good and bad deeds whose fruit he receives. In reply, Bhīṣma cites the dialogue of Prahrāda with Indra. Prahrāda had achieved non-attachment, freedom from sin and control over his senses; Indra asked him how it was that he did not grieve for the loss of his freedom and royal glory.*[1] *Prahrāda answered that whatever comes to be or ceases to be is the result of nature, not of human effort; the person who considers himself the doer of deeds, good or bad, is in error. Understanding this, Prahrāda did not grieve, for he felt neither liking nor hatred towards nature or the transformations produced by nature. Indra asked him how this wisdom and tranquillity could be gained; Prahrāda answered that by rectitude, heedfulness, serenity, self-possession and obedience to elders a man could gain much, but that wisdom and tranquillity, like everything else, come from nature.*

**[216]** *Now Yudhiṣṭhira asks Bhīṣma what way of thinking should be adopted by the man who has been overcome by adversity. In reply, Bhīṣma cites the dialogue of Indra with Bali, son of Virocana.*[2] *After defeating the demons, Indra wanted to find the mighty Bali, whose wealth remained undiminished though he gave it away. Acting on Brahmā's advice, he found him living in a deserted dwelling in the form of an ass, and asked him if he grieved for his lost fortune. Bali upbraided Indra for trying to humiliate him.* **[217]** *Indra laughed and repeated his question; Bali answered that, knowing all things to be ephemeral, he did not grieve. A person without this understanding is a slave to Passion and delusion, but by gaining it he rids himself of sin and acquires Goodness and serenity. Men are not the doers of deeds; all creatures are formed from the elements, and Time will reclaim them: what cause is there for anguish in this?*

1 Prahrāda, king of the demons, had been defeated and taken captive by Indra.

2 Virocana was the son of Prahrāda.

*Everything is the work of Time, said Bali; Indra should not brag of his might. Formerly Bali himself used to be very mighty, but he did not now grieve over his loss, for he knew that he was in the power of the ordainer. Neither his nor Indra's present condition was of their own making, for no one is the doer of deeds. Time is an aspect of* brahman*; it is inescapable. Indra should be calm: soon enough his royal glory will pass to another.*

**[218]** *Indra observed the radiant goddess Śrī*[1] *coming forth from Bali's body. At his request she identified herself, but she denied that her leaving Bali was prompted by either Indra or Bali himself; she was governed by Time alone. She had stayed with Bali as long as he had remained truthful and devout, but had abandoned him now that he had become lax and boastful. She announced that she would now stay with Indra himself, but he would have to be vigilant. She told Indra to divide her into four parts, and he assigned a quarter of her each to the earth, water, fire and Brahmins. Bali now predicted that when the sun shone equally in all directions and sunset came at midday, there would be another war between gods and demons, and that this time he would be the victor. Indra told him that such a time would never come, and the two went their separate ways.*

**[219]** *Now Bhīṣma cites the dialogue of Indra with the demon Namuci, who was tranquil though he had lost his freedom and royal glory. Asked by Indra whether he grieved for his loss, Namuci replied that grief was pointless and destructive. All things are ephemeral; what is ordained to happen will happen; the wise man accepts this, while the one who thinks himself to be the doer suffers sorrow. One should cultivate non-attachment and understand that all one's deeds and experiences are preordained.*

**[220]** *Yudhiṣṭhira asks what is best for a man who is sunk in misfortune; Bhīṣma answers that steadfastness is best, and cites another dialogue of Indra with Bali. After the defeat of the demons by the gods, Indra in all his majesty approached Bali, who was living in a cave, and asked him how he managed not to be distressed at his own loss of majesty. Bali rebuked Indra for gloating, and insisted that Indra's rise and his own fall were not due to their own actions, but rather the consequence of Time. All things happen because of Time, for which there is no remedy; sorrow is caused by thinking oneself to be the doer. In age after age, said Bali, thousands of Indras and thousands of demons had passed away thanks to irresistible Time. Indra was foolish to imagine that his royal*

1 Royal glory personified.

*glory would remain with him; Time had destroyed all the mighty demon lords of old. Bali counselled Indra to give up desire and pride, for otherwise he would be overwhelmed by grief when he came to lose his sovereignty. He explained that he did not grieve at his own loss, for grief achieves nothing. Now Indra responded, agreeing that Time rules all things and praising Bali for his wisdom. Joyful and tranquil in mind, he returned to his heaven.*

**[221]** *Next Yudhiṣṭhira wants to know the signs of future success and failure; Bhīṣma answers that it is the mind that reveals these, and cites the dialogue of Indra with Śrī. One morning Nārada and Indra, having bathed together in the Gaṅgā, were honouring the rising sun when they saw Śrī approaching them, brilliant as a second sun. After worshipping her, Indra asked why she had come, and Śrī replied that she used to live with the demons, but now wanted to live with him. The demons had formerly been supremely virtuous, but times had changed, and they were now thoroughly given over to vice. She and her companion goddesses Hope, Faith, Steadfastness, Splendour, Victory, Humility, Forbearance and Good Conduct had therefore left them, and would now live with Indra and the other gods. Nārada, Indra and the other gods welcomed her with great honour, ushering in a time of great happiness and prosperity for men and celestials alike.*

**[222]** *Yudhiṣṭhira asks what kind of person attains oneness with* brahman. *Replying that such a person is abstemious and disciplined, Bhīṣma cites the dialogue of Jaigīṣavya with Asita Devala.*[1] *Questioned by Asita as to how he remained free of both anger and joy, Jaigīṣavya praised tranquillity, and said that* brahman *is attained by those who maintain equanimity under all circumstances.*

**[223]** *Now Yudhiṣṭhira asks Bhīṣma what person is dear to all and possessed of all virtues. In reply, Bhīṣma cites Ugrasena's dialogue with Kṛṣṇa on the subject of Nārada. Ugrasena remarked that everyone liked to speak well of Nārada; Kṛṣṇa answered by listing Nārada's many virtues, and added that such a person would be loved by all.*

**[224]** *Next Yudhiṣṭhira requests Bhīṣma to tell him about the origin, life and end of all beings, expanding on the account he previously gave of Bhṛgu's dialogue with Bharadvāja.*[2] *In reply, Bhīṣma cites the answer that Vyāsa gave to his son Śuka when he asked him the same questions. He said that only*

**1** For an account of these two, see 9.49.

**2** See chapters 175–85 above.

brahman *is without beginning and end, and existed before creation; then he gave an account of the divisions of human time. A human month is one day and night for the ancestors; a human year is one day and night for the gods. The Kṛta Age lasts for four thousand years of the gods, with a dawn and dusk of four hundred years each; each of the three succeeding ages is shorter by a thousand years, and its dawn and dusk are both shorter by a hundred years. In the Kṛta Age,* dharma *is complete, but in each succeeding age it is diminished by a quarter; in the Kṛta Age there is no disease and men live for four hundred years, but in each succeeding age the span of life is reduced by a quarter, as is knowledge of the Veda and the benefits it brings. The paramount* dharma *of the Kṛta Age is asceticism, of the Tretā Age it is knowledge, of the Dvāpara Age sacrifice, and of the Kali Age the giving of gifts. The twelve thousand years of the gods constituting the four ages make up one* yuga;[1] *a thousand* yugas *make up one day of Brahmā, and a further thousand* yugas *one night of Brahmā, who sleeps during the cosmic dissolution.* Brahman *awakes at the end of his night to create the universe: first intelligence, then mind, from which emanate successively the elements ether, wind, fire, water and earth, with their associated sensory properties; from combinations of intelligence, mind, and the elements are formed bodies. The creator Brahmā creates all beings; every time they are re-created they take on the deeds done in their previous creation. Vyāsa spoke further of the Vedas, of the different characteristics of each of the four ages, and of Time, which creates and destroys all creatures. Then he described the dissolution when Brahmā's day comes to an end: seven suns blaze in the sky, and the universe bursts into flame.* **[225]** *Everything on the earth's surface is absorbed into the earth, which is now as bare as the shell of a tortoise. In turn each element yields up its sensory property to the next and dissolves into it: earth gives way to water, water to fire, fire to wind and wind to ether. Ether yields up its property of sound to mind, and in a mysterious process all is finally reabsorbed into* brahman.

**[226]** *Bhīṣma continues Vyāsa's discourse to his son Śuka. Now Vyāsa described the duties of a Brahmin. After completing his studies he should follow the four stages of life until his death. He should teach, study, and perform sacrifices for others and for himself. It is proper for Brahmins to be rewarded with wealth, and many have attained the heavenly realms by making gifts to*

1 *Yuga* is in fact also the word used for each of the four ages; the aggregate of all four is sometimes distinguished as a *mahāyuga* or 'great age'.

*Brahmins.* **[227]** *A Brahmin should study the Veda and practise his* dharma*; he should be disciplined and free from passion, cultivating virtues and ridding himself of sin, and should seek to attain* brahman. *Next Vyāsa spoke again of Time, likening it to a great river bearing all things to their destruction, which only the wise man can cross. Then he returned to the theme of the virtues that should characterize a Brahmin.* **[228]** *He said that knowledge is like a raft for a drowning man; to attain the high knowledge that alone leads to tranquillity, one must exercise self-control. He compared the body of the man who seeks* brahman *to a chariot: properly equipped, it can speed him to the Eternal one. He described seven forms of yogic mental exercise, and spoke of the discipline and equanimity necessary to pass beyond the pairs of opposites and attain* brahman. **[229]** *Repeating his comparison of knowledge to a raft, he listed the benefits that wisdom brings. Dividing and subdividing all creation into categories, he stated that the most excellent beings are those who know the self. The gods have the highest regard for the man who knows the* dharmas *of both engagement and disengagement.* **[230]** *Then he spoke of deeds, asceticism and the Vedas.*

**[231]** *Bhīṣma continues Vyāsa's discourse to his son Śuka. Śuka asked how a pious Brahmin could attain* brahman. *Vyāsa replied that the only ways were knowledge, asceticism, restraining of the senses and renunciation. He described how human beings are formed from the elements, and spoke of the senses, which are under the control of the mind; the mind is under the control of the self. The self cannot be perceived through the senses but can be illuminated by the mind; though unmanifest it is present in every person, and he who perceives it, seeing himself in everything and everything in himself, becomes one with* brahman, *eternal and transcendent.* **[232]** *Having answered Śuka in terms of Sāṃkhya, Vyāsa said that he would now expound the teachings of Yoga. He said that the highest knowledge was the uniting of the intelligence, the mind, the senses and the self. This knowledge can only be attained after ridding oneself of the five impediments: desire, anger, greed, fear, sleep. Disciplined, cultivating virtues and ridding oneself of sin, one should seek to attain* brahman. *One should first restrain the mind, then restrain the organs of sense and fix them on the mind, and finally fix the mind on the self; then one perceives* brahman.

**[233]** *Bhīṣma continues Vyāsa's discourse to his son Śuka. Śuka asked Vyāsa to explain the contradiction that the Vedas enjoin one both to perform deeds and not to do so. Vyāsa spoke of the way of knowledge, disengagement, and the way of deeds, engagement, and said that deeds bind a creature while knowledge frees* *him. Ascetics shun deeds, through which one experiences rebirth, while through knowledge one attains an imperishable state. Deeds lead to the pairs of opposites, such as happiness and unhappiness; knowledge leads to eternal* brahman. **[234]** *Śuka asked Vyāsa to explain further about the contradiction between doing and not doing deeds. Vyāsa recommended* brahmacarya *and an ascetic life in the forest, and insisted that all four stages of life lead to the highest good; in sequence, they form a four-runged ladder leading to* brahman. *He described the life of the* brahmacārin *in detail, and stated that after completing it one should marry and become a householder.* **[235]** *He spoke of the duties of a householder, and said that noble, self-controlled householders attain the heavenly realms; but after completing that stage one should undertake the superior third stage, that of the forest-dweller.* **[236]** *He said that when a householder had wrinkles and grey hair, and his children had had children, he should take himself to the forest. Continuing to maintain the sacred fires, he should live a very abstemious life. Then, when troubled by old age and illness, he should enter the fourth stage by giving up all possessions and companions, and focusing entirely on the self.* **[237]** *Vyāsa described the life of renunciation. One should no longer maintain the fires; homeless, one should beg for one's food, eating little; one should remain silent, experiencing neither anger nor joy, and steadfastly restraining one's senses.*

**[238]** *Bhīṣma continues Vyāsa's discourse to his son Śuka. Vyāsa stated that the self hidden in every being is capable of being seen by those tranquil men who restrain their mind and senses and withdraw from worldly matters; they attain the state of immortality. He told his son that the instruction he had given him was the secret essence of all the Vedas, churned from the ten thousand verses of the Ṛgveda like butter from curd or fire from fuel; it was to be delivered only to those who had completed their* brahmacarya, *and must not be communicated to anyone unworthy.* **[239]** *Then he said that the whole universe consists of the five elements, distributed unevenly by the creator. Sound, the ear and the cavities within the body arise from ether; breath, motion and touch from wind; form, the eye and the digestion from fire; taste, the tongue and affection from water; smell, the nose and the body from earth. The senses are thus five; sixth is the mind, seventh the intelligence, and eighth the self. The senses exist to perceive, the mind to doubt, the intelligence to determine; the self simply witnesses. The three qualities of Passion, Darkness and Goodness cause beings to experience states such as sorrow, bewilderment and pleasure.* **[240]** *The mind produces an idea, the intelligence determines it, the self judges it pleasant or unpleasant; this* *is the threefold impulse to action. The intelligence is central: when it forms an idea it becomes the mind, and when it perceives it becomes the relevant sense organ. It experiences states determined by the three qualities, but it surpasses these. The senses should be conquered; when a man of knowledge, free from both grief and joy, controls them with his mind like a charioteer holding the reins, the self becomes visible to him.* **[241]** *The intelligence transforms the qualities into experienced reality; the self oversees the transformation without being involved in it. Passing beyond happiness and unhappiness, a man should think of the Eternal. Knowledge of the self brings enlightenment and freedom from fear and grief.*

**[242]** *Bhīṣma continues Vyāsa's discourse to his son Śuka. Śuka asked Vyāsa what was the highest* dharma, *and Vyāsa replied that it was to restrain the senses and focus the mind; when he had succeeded in doing so, Śuka would perceive his self to be the Eternal, and would be able to cross the dreadful river of existence that only the wise can cross, and so attain oneness with* brahman. **[243]** *Vedic study and worship does not make one a Brahmin; to attain to* brahman *one must be free of desire and hatred, and not practise evil against other creatures by thought, word or deed. The true knower of the Veda is he who knows the source of real contentment and strength; the true Brahmin is he whose only delight is the self.* **[244]** *Vyāsa said that this instruction should be given to a suitable pupil seeking final release, and briefly summarized what he had already expounded.*

**[245]** *Bhīṣma continues Vyāsa's discourse to his son Śuka. Vyāsa described the abilities of* yogīs, *commenting that even in their dreams they remain free of Passion and maintain their Goodness; in this he contrasted them with ordinary men, who are prey to anger and greed even as they sleep, and whose Passion and Darkness prevent them from perceiving the self.* **[246]** *He likened desire to a tree growing in the heart; its root can only be torn out by the sword of equanimity, which has the form of renunciation and heedfulness. Then he likened the body to a city, with the intelligence as queen, the mind as her adviser, and the senses as citizens; the two greatest dangers they face are Passion and Darkness. When the mind is estranged from the intelligence, it allies itself with Passion and hands the citizens over to it.* **[247]** *Bhīṣma concludes Vyāsa's discourse by listing the properties of each of the five elements, and those of the mind and the intelligence.*

**[248]** *Now Yudhiṣṭhira speaks of all the mighty kings who have died in the great battle, and asks Bhīṣma to tell him about death. In reply, Bhīṣma tells the* *story of Avikampa, a king in the Kṛta Age who was defeated by his enemies in a battle in which his son was killed. Meeting Nārada one day, he related what had happened to him; to allay his grief for his son, Nārada told him how, after creating living beings, Brahmā had lost patience as they multiplied to fill up all space; his anger produced a fire which began to consume the world. Śiva approached him* **[249]** *and appealed to him to stop the burning; Brahmā explained that anger had overcome him when he could think of no way to lighten the burden on the earth. Śiva requested that, instead of outright destruction, creatures should be subject to rebirth. Brahmā stilled the flames, and brought birth and death into being: from his body there appeared a black woman dressed in red, who took her place on his right as the goddess Death. Brahmā commanded her to kill all creatures; at this she wept, but caught the tears in her hands.* **[250]** *She told Brahmā that she did not wish to carry out such a terrible task, and asked permission to take up an ascetic life instead; Brahmā insisted that she do what she was intended to do. But despite his repeated urging, she would not act as he demanded; she went away and performed austerities for many millions of years. Again and again Brahmā came to her and commanded her to do his bidding; again and again she refused. Finally Brahmā told her that the teardrops she still held in her hands would become dreadful diseases that would afflict mankind, and he assured her that by carrying out his word she would acquire not* adharma *but* dharma. *At last she assented; thus, when their time comes, all creatures die.*

**[251]** *Yudhiṣṭhira now asks Bhīṣma to tell him about* dharma. *Bhīṣma answers that* dharma *is the conduct of the virtuous, prescribed in the Vedas and traditional teachings; it is also characterized by the purpose of an act. It governs life in this world, but leads to happiness in both this and the next world. Even sinners deplore the sins of others. Truth is the highest virtue; one should not steal; one should bestow charity; one should not do to others what would be disagreeable if done to oneself; one should apply to others what one would wish for oneself; one should share surplus wealth. Any agreeable deed is* dharma.

**[252]** *Yudhiṣṭhira raises a number of objections.* Dharma *cannot be known by study of texts, since it varies according to circumstance. It cannot be characterized as the conduct of the virtuous, since what characterizes the virtuous is their conduct.* Adharma *sometimes appears under the guise of* dharma, *and* vice versa. *The* dharmas *of different ages of the world are different. The sacred texts contradict one another. There is no course of conduct that is universally beneficial: what benefits one man harms another. Yudhiṣṭhira suggests that what* *was said about* dharma *by the seers of old has come to be accepted as a permanent standard.*

**[253]** *In reply, Bhīṣma cites the dialogue of Tulādhāra with Jājali. Jājali was a Brahmin who performed great austerities, at one point living under the sea, at another remaining still for so long that a pair of birds nested and reared their chicks on his head. He was proud of his yogic accomplishments and boasted of them, at which a voice in the air told him that he was not the equal of Tulādhāra of Vārāṇasī. Jājali travelled to Vārāṇasī, where he met the merchant Tulādhāra,*[1] *who revealed that he already knew who he was and why he had come.* **[254]** *Questioned by Jājali as to how he had acquired such understanding, Tulādhāra answered that he knew* dharma. *He was honest in his business, practised non-violence, regarded all creatures equally, and was free from desire and hatred. He said that the man who practises no evil against other creatures by thought, word or deed attains to* brahman. *The man whom no one fears need fear no one. Many men commit acts of great cruelty against animals in the pursuit of agriculture, and this is sanctioned by custom, but the* dharma *that wins the approval of the wise is to regard equally those who do one harm and those who offer one praise.* **[255]** *Jājali objected that Tulādhāra's version of* dharma *would bar men from gaining heaven and from subsisting; he said that agriculture was needed to live, and accused Tulādhāra of atheism in opposing sacrifice. Tulādhāra countered that true sacrifice did not necessitate the use of animals, and that the earth produced food without the need for cultivation. Formerly men had sacrificed without thought of gain. Those virtuous men who seek release succeed in attaining oneness with* brahman; *they do not desire heaven and they do not perform costly sacrifices, but follow the way of non-violence; by contrast, greedy priests will not officiate for such men, because what they seek is wealth. The products of the cow and rice-cakes are all that is needed for a sacrifice; likewise all rivers are the Sarasvatī, and all mountains are holy. Indeed the self is a sacred place; there is no point in travelling to other lands.* **[256]** *Tulādhāra pointed out to Jājali the birds that had been reared on his head, and told him to call them; when he did so, they answered with heavenly cries. Now Bhīṣma speaks in praise of faith. Prajāpati himself had ruled that the offering of a generous usurer was acceptable, while that of a mean Brahmin was not, because the one was purified by faith, the other destroyed by lack of faith; lack of faith is the greatest sin, while*

1 'The holder of the scales'.

*faith frees one from sin. He adds that Tulādhāra and Jājali both reached the heaven they had earned.* **[257]** *Then he cites the words of King Vicakhnu on seeing a sacrifice at which cattle were to be slaughtered: he declaimed a blessing on all cattle, and spoke strongly against animal sacrifices and other perversions of the Vedic rites.*

**[258]** *Yudhiṣṭhira asks whether it is better to be quick or slow in considering how one should act. Bhīṣma praises those who take time to think, and cites the story of Gautama's son Cirakārin ('Delayer'), who was so named because he always reflected long before acting. When Gautama's wife was unfaithful to him,*[1] *he angrily commanded Cirakārin to kill her. True to his name, Cirakārin thought long about what he should do, for his duty to his father led one way, his duty to his mother another, and he knew that the man she had given herself to had appeared to her in her husband's guise. A long time passed while Cirakārin considered; meanwhile Gautama had repented of his action, reflecting that his wife was not to blame for Indra's deception, and hoping that his son would delay in carrying out his order. When he found that this was indeed so, he was overjoyed; he praised Cirakārin, and spoke in favour of delaying whenever a disagreeable act is in prospect.*

**[259]** *Next Yudhiṣṭhira asks how a king may protect his subjects without harming anyone. In reply, Bhīṣma cites the dialogue of King Dyumatsena with his son Satyavat. Seeing some men being taken for execution, Satyavat said that* dharma *could not sanction such killing; Dyumatsena maintained that if robbers were not executed, normal life would not be possible. Satyavat argued for punishment short of death, and pointed out that to kill an offender also harms his relatives, who are innocent; in the case of a first offence it would even be right to release the offender in return for a promise of good behaviour. Dyumatsena countered that capital punishment was needed to prevent social restraints from breaking down. Formerly when men were more virtuous a mere rebuke had been enough, but with the decline of* dharma *down the ages*[2] *increasingly severe punishment had become necessary. But the king must himself be virtuous and self-controlled, for men imitate their betters.*

**1** The story of Ahalyā's unfaithfulness is a well-known one, and the author of the present narrative seems to take it for granted that it will be familiar to his audience. The main details emerge as the narrative proceeds.

**2** See chapter 224 above.

[**260**] *Yudhiṣṭhira now asks which is superior, the way of the householder or the way of renunciation. In reply, Bhīṣma cites the dialogue of the ascetic Kapila with a cow. Seeing a cow tethered ready to be sacrificed, Kapila voiced a regret that the truth of the Vedas had become weakened. The seer Syūmaraśmi entered the body of the cow and asked him what an ascetic like himself had to say against the holy Vedas. Kapila answered that he did not condemn them, but that they are contradictory, stating both that one should perform deeds and that one should not do so,*[1] *and he asked if Syūmaraśmi knew of any doctrine superior to that of non-violence. Syūmaraśmi replied with a lengthy defence of sacrifices, emphasizing that they lead to heaven.* [**261**] *Kapila argued that those who practise renunciation achieve such felicity that they have no need for the way of the householder. Syūmaraśmi retorted that all other ways of life depend on that of the householder, and condemned renunciation as a false doctrine. Kapila answered that the true Brahmin is the self-controlled ascetic who is one with all creatures; rituals bring only temporary rewards. Now Syūmaraśmi asked Kapila to expound to him what it is that renouncers seek, and Kapila spoke of oneness with the universal Self, pursued as the highest goal through a life of self-control. Syūmaraśmi objected that if release could not be attained through the practices enjoined in the Vedas, people would become atheists and reject the Vedas, and he asked Kapila to teach him further.* [**262**] *Kapila said that the Vedas were the world's authority and could not be rejected, and emphasized the importance of carrying out the duties they prescribe; in former times there had been many pious kings and Brahmins who, performing sacrifices and observing the duties of householders, attained to* brahman. *But the householder can never achieve the joy of the renouncer.*

[**263**] *Yudhiṣṭhira remarks that the Vedas speak of* dharma, *the proper making of wealth, and pleasure, and asks Bhīṣma which profits a man most. In reply, Bhīṣma cites the story of the cloud Kuṇḍadhāra. A certain poor Brahmin, seeking to acquire wealth with which to sacrifice, performed austerities and worshipped the gods, but without success. Seeing the noble Kuṇḍadhāra he offered him worship; Kuṇḍadhāra, pleased, uttered a denunciation of ingratitude and allowed the Brahmin to see a vision. In that vision Kuṇḍadhāra prostrated himself before the gods and asked for the Brahmin to receive their favour, and Maṇibhadra*[2] *agreed to give him immeasurable riches. But Kuṇḍadhāra replied*

**1** See chapter 233 above.

**2** Brother of the god of wealth Kubera.

*that he did not seek wealth for the Brahmin, but rather that he should delight in* dharma. *Maṇibhadra offered the rewards of* dharma, *but Kuṇḍadhāra insisted on* dharma *itself. Awaking, the Brahmin saw costly garments laid out by him, but, filled with indifference towards the things of the world, he set out for a life of asceticism in the forest. After long years of austerities in which he achieved great success, Kuṇḍadhāra reappeared, and gave him another vision: it was of kings sunk in hell. Kuṇḍadhāra explained that it would have been no favour to the Brahmin to allow him to suffer such a fate. The gods fear men and command the vices to keep them out of heaven. The Brahmin thanked Kuṇḍadhāra, who embraced him and vanished. Bhīṣma adds that good men and the celestials honour those who observe* dharma, *not those who follow wealth or pleasure. Wealth gives a little happiness, but the highest happiness comes from* dharma.

[**264**] *Yudhiṣṭhira asks how it is that sacrifice is intended only for* dharma, *not for happiness. In reply, Bhīṣma cites a story told by Nārada of a Brahmin named Satya. Satya was about to perform a sacrifice to attain heaven, against his virtuous wife's inclinations, when a deer addressed him, asking to be sacrificed to make sure the ritual was not incomplete. The goddess Sāvitrī also appealed to him to sacrifice the deer; when he refused, the deer showed him a vision of heaven. Now Satya decided to attain heaven through violence; but the deer, who was really Dharma, saved him from doing so. His thoughts of slaying the deer had already destroyed his great ascetic merit, but now Dharma employed him as priest in his own rite, and through further austerities he came to share his wife's attitude. Bhīṣma adds that non-violence is the whole of* dharma; *violence has no part in sacrifice.*

[**265**] *Now Yudhiṣṭhira asks about sin,* dharma, *indifference to the world and release. Bhīṣma answers that desire for sensual pleasure leads to striving; passion arises, followed by hate, greed and delusion. Overcome by these, the intelligence has no base in* dharma, *but fraudulently feigns* dharma; *this leads to fraudulent acquisition of wealth, after which sins of all kinds increasingly follow, along with the making of similarly wicked friends. Such a man finds no happiness in this world, never mind the next. The man of* dharma, *on the other hand, has the wisdom to recognize such faults in advance; he delights in* dharma *and seeks only wealth that can be acquired through* dharma; *his friends are good. He does not rejoice in the things of the senses, and becomes indifferent to the world, striving for complete renunciation, and ultimately gaining release.*

[**266**] *Yudhiṣṭhira wishes to know the method for attaining release. Bhīṣma*

*says that only one way leads to release. One must free oneself from anger, desire, sleep and other vices; one should cast off hope, material wealth and affection; speech and mind are to be controlled by the intelligence, the intelligence by knowledge, knowledge by the self, and the self by tranquillity. Avoiding the five impediments to Yoga,*[1] *one should practise meditation, study, the giving of gifts, truth, modesty, rectitude, forgiveness, purity of conduct and food, and the control of the senses. This is the path to release: non-delusion, non-attachment, freedom from desire and anger, vigour, lack of pride, imperturbability and steadfastness.*

**[267]** *Bhīṣma cites the dialogue of Nārada with Asita Devala. Questioned by Nārada about the origin and dissolution of the universe, Asita stated that Time creates all beings from the five elements. When any creature is brought into being it arises from them, and when it is destroyed it dissolves into all five of them. The five sensory properties are perceived by the five senses in five different ways, but it is the self, not the senses, that is aware. Asita listed the faculties of cognition and those of action;*[2] *he spoke of sleeping and dreaming, and of the states of Goodness, Passion and Darkness that creatures experience in both wakefulness and dreaming. Whatever creature comes into being dissolves again into the five elements, and enters a new body constituted by its former deeds; but sometimes through knowledge one may destroy one's stock of good and bad actions and attain to* brahman.

**[268]** *Yudhiṣṭhira laments the slaughter of friends and kinsmen that has been carried out for the sake of wealth, and asks how the desire for wealth, which causes such evil, can be checked. In reply, Bhīṣma cites the song sung by the king of Videha to Māṇḍavya. He said that he lived happily because he possessed nothing: if the city of Mithilā were in flames nothing of his would be burnt.*[3] *Wealth brings woe; the happiness brought by satisfying desire on earth and the highest happiness of heaven are not worth even a sixteenth part of the happiness that results from eliminating desire. By passing beyond the pairs of opposites one attains tranquillity. Desire is a fatal disease, and happiness comes from ridding oneself of it.*

**[269]** *Next Yudhiṣṭhira asks how a man should behave to attain oneness with* brahman; *Bhīṣma answers with a list of rules.* **[270]** *Yudhiṣṭhira says that*

**1** See chapter 232 above.

**2** Cf. 6.25.6 and note.

**3** See chapter 212 above.

*all people consider the Pāṇḍavas blessed, but in fact they are the most miserable of men. When will they be able to give up kingship and become renouncers? Bhīṣma assures him that nothing is endless, and in time they will be able; when anyone uses knowledge to rid himself of the darkness born of ignorance,* brahman *is revealed. Then he cites the song of the demon Vṛtra after his defeat: questioned by Śukra Uśanas, he said that he felt neither grief nor joy. Helplessly compelled by Time, creatures undergo rebirth after rebirth, each one conditioned by their former deeds. As for himself, he had gained great majesty through his austerities, and then lost it through his own actions; he did not grieve over this. During his battle with Indra, he had had a sight of Lord Viṣṇu; now he asked Śukra to teach him about the gain and loss of greatness and the way to achieve the highest goal, the Eternal.* [**271**] *Sanatkumāra now arrived and, at Śukra's request, spoke to Vṛtra of the greatness of Viṣṇu. He said that the universe is based wholly on Viṣṇu; it merges into him at the dissolution, and then arises once more from him. Viṣṇu cannot be reached through asceticism or sacrifice, only through restraint of the senses. Sanatkumāra described in detail how a person may attain to* brahman, *and Vṛtra, praising Viṣṇu, was able to give up his life and achieve that state. Now Yudhiṣṭhira asks Bhīṣma whether Kṛṣṇa is that same Viṣṇu; Bhīṣma confirms that he is indeed the eternal creator of all. Yudhiṣṭhira considers Vṛtra's great achievement, and wonders how he and his brothers will fare. Bhīṣma tells him not to fear: after enjoying both the heavenly and earthly realms they will be numbered among the perfected ones.*

[**272**] *Yudhiṣṭhira asks Bhīṣma how it was that Vṛtra, for all his virtue and devotion to Viṣṇu, was defeated by Indra. Bhīṣma describes how Indra was paralysed with fear when he saw the gigantic form of Vṛtra advancing on him, whilst Vṛtra was unperturbed at the sight of Indra. Then the fearsome battle began, watched by all the celestials. Vṛtra used his mighty powers of illusion to stupefy Indra, but Vasiṣṭha revived him, and he resorted to Yoga to dispel Vṛtra's illusions. Bṛhaspati and the great seers appealed to Śiva for help: his fiery energy took the form of a fever and entered Vṛtra, and Viṣṇu entered Indra's thunderbolt. Śiva urged Indra to destroy Vṛtra, who had performed austerities for sixty thousand years and secured great powers as a boon from Brahmā. The fever began to afflict Vṛtra while the gods and seers cheered Indra on.* [**273**] *As the fever tormented Vṛtra, Indra released his thunderbolt at him and slew him, to the joy of the gods. Then there emerged from Vṛtra's body the sin of Brahminicide in*

*the form of a woman of dreadful appearance;*[1] *she seized Indra by the throat, and he could not rid himself of her. He went to Brahmā, who asked Brahminicide to leave Indra; she agreed to do so, but asked for a dwelling of her own. Brahmā now told Agni the Fire god that he was going to divide Brahminicide into pieces, and asked him to take a fourth part.*[2] *Fire asked how he would be freed of her, and Brahmā replied that she would immediately transfer herself to any man who did not offer proper oblations into the Fire; Fire agreed. Next, Brahmā asked plants to receive a fourth part; it would transfer itself to any man who cut them on the day of the moon's change of phase. They agreed, and left. Now Brahmā asked the Apsarases to receive a fourth part; it would transfer itself to any man who lay with a woman in the midst of her period; the Apsarases agreed. Lastly Brahmā requested the waters to receive a fourth part; it would transfer itself to any man who fouled water with phlegm or piss or shit. Rid at last of Brahminicide, Indra purified himself with a horse sacrifice.*

**[274]** *Yudhiṣṭhira wishes to know the origin of the fever that afflicted Vṛtra. Bhīṣma relates how Śiva used to dwell on a peak of Mount Meru, surrounded by gods, seers, and all kinds of celestial beings, as well as by Rākṣasas and Piśācas. Once the Prajāpati Dakṣa was preparing to perform a horse sacrifice, and the gods set out to attend; Śiva's wife Umā asked him why he did not join them, and he explained that the gods had assigned him no share in sacrifices. Umā was deeply unhappy to hear this, and so Śiva went with his dreadful followers and attacked Dakṣa's sacrifice, which took the form of a deer and fled into the sky. As Śiva pursued it in fury, a drop of sweat fell from his forehead on to the earth, where it produced a great fire like the fire of doomsday. From the fire there appeared a fearsome figure of a man: short and dark, with red eyes, he burnt up the sacrifice as if he were himself a fire. The gods fled in terror, and the earth shook. Brahmā appeared; he requested Śiva to calm his rage, and promised that henceforth the other gods would give him a share in sacrifices. Then he added that the creature that had been produced from Śiva's sweat was called Fever; he would range over the earth, but the earth could not support him as a single being: Śiva must re-create him as many beings. Śiva, delighted at receiving his share, did as he was asked, and so now there are many different forms of Fever.*

**1** As the child of the divine craftsman Tvaṣṭṛ, Vṛtra, like the three-headed Viśvarūpa, is simultaneously a demon and a Brahman: cf. 5.9–10.

**2** For the distribution of Indra's sin, cf. 5.13.

**[275]** *Yudhiṣṭhira asks how sorrow and death, which are feared by all beings, may be avoided. In reply, Bhīṣma cites the dialogue of Nārada with Samaṅga. Nārada remarked that Samaṅga appeared to be forever happy; Samaṅga answered that this was because he knew past, present and future, commencements and consequences. He said that wisdom lies in tranquillity of the senses; delusion of the senses prevents wisdom. Pleasure leads to joy, joy to pride, and pride to hell; therefore, he said, he had abandoned wealth and pleasure, desire and delusion, and wandered the earth free from fear of death or of anything else.*

**[276]** *Now Yudhiṣṭhira asks what is most beneficial for an uncertain man who is not familiar with the learned texts. Bhīṣma prescribes reverence for one's* guru, *waiting on elders, and listening to expositions of learning; then he cites the dialogue of Gālava with Nārada. Gālava, confused by the differences found in the learned texts, asked Nārada what was truly most beneficial. Nārada spoke of the four stages of life, of favouring friends and restraining enemies, and of the three aims of life;*[1] *then he discoursed at length on vices to be avoided and virtues to be cultivated.*

**[277]** *Yudhiṣṭhira asks Bhīṣma how a king such as himself can be free from attachment. In reply, Bhīṣma cites the dialogue of Ariṣṭanemi with Sagara. Sagara had asked how he might avoid grief and perturbation; Ariṣṭanemi replied that release is the only true happiness, but that it is known only to those who are unattached; those who are held in the bonds of affection cannot attain it. Once one's children have grown up, one should leave and roam free. The man who sees that the world is subject to death and disease, who is indifferent, who observes the sorrows of family life and the faults of children, he attains release.*

**[278]** *Yudhiṣṭhira wishes to know more about Śukra Uśanas: though a divine seer, why does he favour the demons? How did he come to be Śukra (the planet Venus), and why does he not reach the centre of the sky? Bhīṣma answers that Uśanas was a descendant of Bhṛgu who used his yogic power to enter Kubera, the god of wealth, and rob him. Kubera complained to Śiva; Śiva looked for Uśanas to strike him with his lance, but Uśanas transferred himself to the point of the lance.*[2] *Seeing this, Śiva bent the lance, so that it became his bow Pināka; this brought Uśanas into his hand, and he swallowed him. Within Śiva's belly he gained the benefit of the mighty austerities the great god performed, and grew*

1 *Dharma*, the proper making of wealth, and pleasure.

2 The one safe place.

*brilliant, but he could find no way out. He appealed to Śiva, who told him to leave by way of his penis, for he had closed off every other aperture. Uśanas did so, and thus became Śukra; for the same reason he cannot reach the centre of the sky.*[1] *Śiva, angry at seeing him emerge in his brilliance, was going to kill him, but Umā prevented him, saying that Uśanas had become her son.*

**[279]** *Yudhiṣṭhira asks Bhīṣma what acts secure the highest benefit for a man in this world and the next. In reply, Bhīṣma cites the dialogue of King Janaka with Parāśara. Asked the same question by Janaka, Parāśara emphasized* dharma. *Each being is what it is because of the deeds done in previous lives, though some deny this since they cannot recall those lives. As one acts, by eye, mind, speech and deed, so one receives back.* **[280]** *One should strive to improve one's position with good deeds and avoid damaging it by means of bad deeds. The consequences of sin are terrible, and cannot be avoided; if a man attempts to atone for a sin by practising virtue, he simply reaps the fruit of each separately. However, inadvertent acts of sin bear slighter consequences than deliberate acts; similarly, the best meritorious deeds are those done with full consciousness.* **[281]** *After observing that all creatures act out of self-interest, Parāśara spoke of wealth and gifts. It is good both to give to and to receive from a worthy person, but giving is more meritorious than receiving. Wealth should never be earned by causing harm, and one should give according to one's capacity: Rantideva and Śibi's son attained the highest felicity by making gifts of roots, fruit and leaves. All men are born indebted: one pays one's debt to the gods by sacrifice, to the ancestors by the* śrāddha *ceremony, and so forth. Effort can lead to great results.* **[282]** *Śūdras should serve the three higher social classes: by associating with good people they will themselves take on their qualities. Whatever the circumstances, the wise man will always practise virtue, for even seemingly advantageous acts of* adharma *bring no benefit. Vaiśyas should create wealth, Kṣatriyas should protect it, Brahmins should use it. Śūdras should be honest, and work as cleaners. In this way* dharma *is maintained and the people are happy; if it is otherwise,* dharma *is harmed. Parāśara added that different kinds of gifts yield different rewards to the giver.* **[283]** *When even a little wealth is acquired for a righteous purpose in a manner in keeping with a person's social class, it brings great benefits. A Brahmin in need may follow the* dharma *of the Kṣatriya or Vaiśya without*

1 As well as referring to the planet Venus, the word *śukra* also means 'semen'. Uśanas is prevented from ascending to the highest point of the sky because of his low 'birth'.

*incurring fault, but he must not follow the Śūdra* dharma*; a Śūdra in need may lawfully take to trade, farming or a craft. Acting and the sale of liquor, meat, leather or iron should not be taken up by one who has not formerly practised them; the abandonment of these trades also brings great* dharma. *In former times men held* dharma *in high honour; however, the demons entered them,*[1] *and they became full of pride, anger and delusion, and ceased to respect the gods and Brahmins. But Śiva destroyed the demons and restored men to virtue, and kings began to wield the rod of force. However, the demonic influence did not wholly die out, and foolish men still commit acts of wickedness. The wise man avoids violence and other sins, and adheres to* dharma. **[284]** *Parāśara spoke of asceticism. The householder is prey to states of Passion and Darkness, and to the attachment and desire for possessions that they bring. He is led into greed, and his affection for his children may cause him to acquire wealth in wrong ways; acting for nothing but enjoyment, he is destroyed. But asceticism is the happiness of intelligent men who seek* brahman. *It is available to all, even the lowest; it leads to heaven for those who are disciplined and self-controlled. Celestials and mortals alike have gained great rewards from asceticism, and there is nothing in the three worlds that it cannot confer.* **[285]** *Janaka asked how the distinct classes of society had arisen; since all arose from Brahmā, how is it that all are not Brahmins? Parāśara attributed this to the weakening of asceticism; then he reminded Janaka that Brahmā created Brahmins from his mouth, Kṣatriyas from his arms, Vaiśyas from his thighs and Śūdras from his feet; all other classes have arisen by intermixture of these four. Next, Janaka asked how the different lineages have arisen; Parāśara explained that they are named after the great ascetic seers who established them. Janaka wanted to know the* dharmas *of the four classes, and Parāśara listed those that are particular to each class and those that are held in common.* **[286]** *Then he spoke of kinsfolk, the norms of war, death and rebirth, and various other topics* **[287]** *including attachment and non-attachment, birth and death, and the inescapability of one's own acts.*

**[288]** *Yudhiṣṭhira asks Bhīṣma to speak about the virtues of truth, forbearance, self-control and wisdom. In reply, Bhīṣma cites the dialogue of the Sādhyas with a goose. Brahmā, in the form of a gold goose, approached the Sādhyas, who*

1 Ganguli, following the commentator Nīlakaṇṭha, takes these 'demons' to be metaphorical references to the sins that afflict mankind.

*asked him what is the highest action that leads to release from all bonds. The goose praised self-control, truth and guardedness. He said that one should not speak to wound others; if abused, one should not abuse in return. The man whose speech and mind are guarded and well focused attains the Vedas, asceticism and renunciation; everything done by an man in anger fails. Truth, self-control, rectitude, non-violence, steadfastness, patience, study, non-covetousness, single-mindedness: these lead to heaven.*

**[289]** *Yudhiṣṭhira requests Bhīṣma to explain the distinction between the Sāṃkhya and Yoga schools. Bhīṣma starts by saying that followers of Yoga do not believe that an atheist can attain release, whereas followers of Sāṃkhya maintain that anyone who uses knowledge to free himself from attachment to the things of the senses will find release on leaving the body. The arguments of Yoga are based on evidence, those of Sāṃkhya on learned texts. Both schools have the approval of the learned; both enjoin purity, compassion and observances, but their doctrines differ. Yudhiṣṭhira asks about the differences, and Bhīṣma gives an exposition of Yoga. Through Yoga one can rid oneself of passion, delusion, affection, desire and anger, and attain release; Yoga confers the power to break these bonds. The* yogī *can enter at will into seers and gods; he can replicate himself into thousands of bodies and roam the earth with them; he can certainly attain release. At Yudhiṣṭhira's request, Bhīṣma describes what the* yogī *has to do to acquire this power: his diet must be limited in the extreme, and he must master desire, anger, heat, cold, rain, fear, sleep, breath, sensory pleasures, celibacy, thirst, sensation and weariness. Few can travel this dangerous road; those who can do so attain* brahman, *and can enter at will into gods, ancestors, mountains, oceans, men and women.*

**[290]** *Having heard Bhīṣma's account of Yoga, Yudhiṣṭhira asks him to expound Sāṃkhya. Bhīṣma answers that the followers of Sāṃkhya attain release through knowledge and understanding, and lists numerous essential items of knowledge, with an emphasis on examples of impermanence and decline. He lists the five faults that inhere in the body as desire, anger, fear, sleep and breath, and explains how they may be overcome; then he describes how the Sāṃkhya sage may succeed in crossing the terrible ocean of life and arrive by stages at the universal Self, from which he does not return. Yudhiṣṭhira asks whether those who attain release retain memory and understanding there: this would be a great flaw, and would incline Yudhiṣṭhira to favour the* dharma *of engagement. Bhīṣma replies that when the self first arrives at the universal Self its mind* *and senses remain active, but that soon afterwards it can attain tranquillity. He concludes by praising the Sāṃkhya doctrine.*

**[291]** *Yudhiṣṭhira asks Bhīṣma to teach him the difference between the imperishable, from which one does not return, and the perishable, from which one returns. In reply, Bhīṣma cites the dialogue of the seer Vasiṣṭha with King Karāla Janaka. Asked the same question by Karāla, Vasiṣṭha answered that after the dissolution of the universe, the unmanifest awakes and creates the manifest creator, from whom the new creation proceeds. The formless Self inheres in every creature, taking on all kinds of forms as it unites with Nature and takes on the qualities of Passion, Darkness and Goodness.*[1] **[292]** *Ignorant of its true nature, the self takes on body after body, now high, now low, following this or that course of action, convinced that it is performing deeds. Though uncreated, it thinks it was created; though without existence, it thinks it exists; though imperishable, it thinks it will perish.* **[293]** *Vasiṣṭha compared the self's constant rebirths with the waxing and waning of the moon. Karāla compared the relationship between the imperishable and the perishable with that between woman and man, and suggested that if Self and Nature are so firmly interconnected, there can be no possibility of release. Vasiṣṭha found fault with Karāla's understanding of the Vedic texts to which he had referred, and continued his exposition of Sāṃkhya, which he said was not different from Yoga.* **[294]** *He spoke again of the Yoga whereby one comes to see the self as the eternal universal Self, and of the Sāṃkhya view in which the Self attains freedom on understanding its own nature,* **[295]** *then discoursed further on Sāṃkhya, regretting that, through ignorance, he himself had passed through so many births. Now, however, he was free from the sense of 'I', and could find equanimity.* **[296]** *Vasiṣṭha completed his exposition of Sāṃkhya, which he had learnt from Brahmā himself. Bhīṣma reveals that he himself learnt it from Nārada, to whom Vasiṣṭha taught it: it has rescued Yudhiṣṭhira from the fathomless ocean of ignorance that causes rebirth.*

**[297]** *Bhīṣma tells Yudhiṣṭhira of King Vasumat, who was once out hunting when he encountered a holy Bhārgava seer and asked him what brings the highest benefit in this world and the next. The seer's answer was* dharma, *but he told Vasumat that if he wanted the rewards of* dharma *he would have to seek to*

1 'Self' here is *puruṣa*, the Sāṃkhya term for the passive personal principle. According to Sāṃkhya, each created being results from a separate union of *puruṣa* with *prakṛti* (here 'Nature').

*acquire it, giving up the search for pleasure; he would have to practise virtue and rid himself of sin. He urged him to acquire patience, understanding, tranquillity and wisdom: in this way he would be able to secure the highest benefit in this world and the next. King Vasumat took his advice, and turned from desire to* dharma.

**[298]** *Yudhiṣṭhira asks Bhīṣma to teach him about the imperishable Eternal that transcends* dharma *and* adharma, *birth and death, and good and evil. In reply, Bhīṣma cites the dialogue of the seer Yājñavalkya with King Daivarāti Janaka. Daivarāti asked about Nature, the unmanifest, and* brahman, *and Yājñavalkya discoursed on Sāṃkhya,* **[299]** *and described the divisions of cosmic time and the creation of the universe.*[1] *Then he spoke of the senses, and stated that they do not themselves perceive; it is the mind that perceives through them.*[2] **[300]** *He described the dissolution of the universe,*[3] **[301]** *then listed various component parts of the human being, such as the feet, and for each one named the corresponding capability (such as motion) and presiding deity (Viṣṇu). Then he spoke of the way in which Nature transforms the three qualities of the Self into hundreds and thousands of entities, and listed the characteristics associated with each of those qualities.* **[302]** *Next he described the kinds of rebirth to which the three qualities lead, both singly and in combinations. Daivarāti asked him to discourse further on Sāṃkhya and Yoga.* **[303]** *He spoke of Nature and the Self in the Sāṃkhya system, and stated that a correct understanding of these two leads to freedom;* **[304]** *then, turning to Yoga, he emphasized that, though foolish people consider Sāṃkhya and Yoga to be distinct, in reality they are the same. He described the powers that Yoga confers, and enumerated the practices in which it consists, leading finally to freedom.* **[305]** *Now he listed the heavenly regions to which one goes upon dying: in each case this corresponds to the presiding deity of the part of the body through which the soul passes away. Then he spoke of portents indicating that a person has only a short time to live, and advised how such a person should prepare for death, or else conquer it by attaining the Eternal through Yoga.* **[306]** *Finally he described how he had received the Yajurvedic formulae from the Sun god and used them in a sacrifice for Daivarāti's father, and how he had compiled the*

**1** See chapter 224 above.

**2** Cf. chapter 267 above.

**3** See chapters 224–5 above.

Śatapathabrāhmaṇa.[1] *He also described his exposition of Sāṃkhya to the Gandharva Viśvāvasu, who expounded it in turn to Brahmā and the other celestials, and to the inhabitants of earth and the underworld. Bhīṣma says that after receiving this instruction from Yājñavalkya, Daivarāti took up the Sāṃkhya way. He himself received this knowledge from Daivarāti; he commends it to Yudhiṣṭhira.*

**[307]** *Yudhiṣṭhira asks Bhīṣma how one may escape old age and death. In reply, Bhīṣma cites the dialogue of Pañcaśikha with Janaka.*[2] *Janaka had asked the same question; Pañcaśikha answered that nothing could stop the passage of time. All things are transitory, and it is pointless to rejoice at birth or grieve at death.* **[308]** *Yudhiṣṭhira wishes to know whether it is possible to attain release whilst still a householder. In reply, Bhīṣma cites the dialogue of King Janaka and the female* yogī *Sulabhā. Sulabhā heard it said that the virtuous King Janaka was advanced in the discipline of release even while still ruling, but she did not believe it. She came to Mithilā and met him; he welcomed her and asked her who she was and where she had come from. She then used her yogic power to enter him, and the two of them conversed. Janaka said that Pañcaśikha had taught him the way of release without making him give up the kingship, and he was now free from passion and illusion, and had passed beyond the pairs of opposites. He then rebuked Sulabhā for the impropriety of her action in entering him, and accused her of seeking to score a victory over him and his assembly. Sulabhā answered him: she urged him to listen carefully, then discoursed on Sāṃkhya; next, pointing out that the particles that constitute the human body are in a state of constant change, she observed that it was meaningless to ask her who she was and where she had come from. If he saw himself in others and had passed beyond the pairs of opposites, why did he ask those questions? She detailed many aspects of the life of a king that made the attainment of release impossible. Hearing her words, Janaka abandoned his attempt to combine the two.*

**[309]** *At Yudhiṣṭhira's request, Bhīṣma recounts the advice Vyāsa gave to his son Śuka, urging him to subdue his senses and to practise* dharma *and austerities.* **[310]** *Yudhiṣṭhira asks to hear how Śuka came to be born as Vyāsa's son, and how he attained* brahman *as a mere child. Bhīṣma describes how*

**1** A major Yajurvedic text.

**2** See chapter 211 above.

*Vyāsa performed intense austerities and petitioned Śiva on the peak of Mount Meru for a son; Śiva granted his wish, promising him a son who would be as pure as the elements, and who would win fame for his spiritual accomplishments.* **[311]** *After obtaining this boon, Vyāsa was one day rubbing two firesticks when the Apsaras Ghṛtācī appeared; her beauty aroused uncontrollable desire in him. Taking the form of a female parrot, she approached him as he tried to make fire, and his seed gushed forth and fell on one of the firesticks. As he continued to rub, Śuka was born from that stick,*[1] *blazing bright like a sacrificial fire. Gaṅgā came in her own form to Meru's peak to bathe him; all the celestials came, and Śiva invested him with the sacred thread. The Vedas presented themselves to him as soon as he was born, and he chose Bṛhaspati to be his* guru. *Taking no interest in the first three stages of life, he directed his mind towards release.* **[312]** *He studied Yoga and Sāṃkhya at his father's direction; Vyāsa then sent him to Mithilā to learn from King Janaka about* dharma *and release. Though capable of circling the earth in the sky, he travelled humbly on foot, and finally reached the prosperous land of Videha. Arriving in Mithilā, he was admitted to the royal palace, where he was waited on by women of outstanding loveliness; but, unmoved, he passed the night there in meditation and rest.* **[313]** *The next morning, King Janaka greeted Śuka, the son of his* guru, *with the greatest respect. Presenting him with a jewelled seat to sit on, whilst himself sitting on the ground, he politely asked the reason for his visit. On learning that Vyāsa had commanded Śuka to seek Janaka's instruction on the attainment of release, the king outlined the four stages of life. Śuka queried whether it was necessary to pass through all of these; Janaka answered that if a man attained release in the first stage, there would be no point in pursuing the other three. Then he spoke of the way to attain* brahman*: ridding oneself of desire and hatred, passing beyond the pairs of opposites, equanimity, the restraint of the senses. But, said Janaka, it was clear to him that Śuka knew all this and had already achieved it.* **[314]** *Śuka, happy and tranquil, his aim achieved, returned northward to beautiful Mount Himālaya, where the celestials often visit. It was here that Skanda the god of war once drove his spear into the earth and challenged anyone whose reverence for Brahmins was greater than his to pull it out or shake it; Viṣṇu shook it, shaking the whole earth, but Prahrāda could not move it at*

1 He is Śuka both because Ghṛtācī assumed the form of a female parrot (*śukī*) and because he was produced directly from his father's semen (*śukra*).

*all, and fell in a faint. It was here that Śiva performed his austerities. Śuka returned to his father's hermitage there, travelling through the air, radiant as the sun, and told Vyāsa what Janaka had said. He then joined Vyāsa's four existing disciples.*[1] *Once these five appealed to Vyāsa to take no sixth disciple, and to let the dissemination of the Veda be their task. Vyāsa agreed to this, and gave them instruction on who should and should not be allowed to receive the sacred knowledge.* **[315]** *His four disciples now left the mountain to spread the Veda on earth, performing sacrifices and teaching; Vyāsa remained with his son, meditating in silence. Nārada saw him there; he complained that the sound of the Vedas was no longer heard, and told him he should resume recitation. Vyāsa now recited with his son. One day a terrible wind began to blow, and Vyāsa told his son to stop reciting; he explained that the wind was a portent indicating that the recitation should cease, and he spoke of the different winds that exist, before leaving for the heavenly Gaṅgā.*[2] **[316]** *Nārada visited Śuka and discoursed to him on non-attachment, freedom from desire and hatred, virtue, control of the senses, and equanimity.* **[317]** *He told him of the benefits of knowledge and understanding, and the futility of grief for what is past.* **[318]** *He spoke of the inexorable passage of time that bears away human lives, of the unpredictable vicissitudes of life, of how the wise may fail and the foolish succeed, of the great uncertainty of securing offspring, and of disease and the failure of human effort. He urged Śuka not to fall into delusion over all these woes, but to pass beyond the pairs of opposites. Śuka considered how he might avoid attachment and rebirth, and resolved to make use of Yoga to abandon his body and enter the Sun. Taking leave of Nārada he went to see his father; Vyāsa greeted him affectionately, but, indifferent and freed from the bonds of affection, Śuka could now think only of release, and he went on his way.* **[319]** *He climbed to the peak of Mount Kailāsa and applied himself to Yoga for the sake of release. Achieving great mastery, he returned and took his leave from Nārada; then he resumed his Yoga. He flew up from the mountain-top into the sky; all creatures beheld him travelling towards the Sun with fully focused mind, and the seers and celestials praised him greatly.*

**1** Sumantu, Vaiśampāyana (the narrator of the *Mahābhārata*), Jaimini and Paila. Apart from his authorship of the *Mahābhārata*, Vyāsa is most celebrated for having 'arranged' the Veda into its present form (his name means 'arranger'); these were the pupils to whom he taught it.

**2** The Gaṅgā flows through heaven as well as on earth.

*He requested that if his father came after him calling his name he should receive an answer; the horizon, forests, seas, rivers and mountains all promised to do what he asked.* [**320**] *As he travelled on there were great portents. Before him he saw the huge conjoined double peak of the mountains Meru and Himālaya; unhesitating, he flew straight on and passed through unimpeded, parting the two peaks and earning the congratulations of the celestials. Apsarases, sporting and bathing naked, did not react as they saw him pass, indifference showing in his face. Now Vyāsa followed him: seeing the split mountain peak and hearing from the seers what Śuka had done, he cried out for his son; Śuka, now one with the universe, replied, 'Bhoḥ!' ('Sir!'), and the whole world echoed him; even today, mountain caves and peaks echo every call with Śuka's cry. When the Apsarases saw Vyāsa, they made haste to cover themselves, and he realized that though his son had gained release, he had not; he was both pleased and shamed. Śiva comforted him: his son, as he had requested, had been as mighty as the elements, and had won lasting fame for his great achievement.*

[**321**] *Yudhiṣṭhira asks Bhīṣma what deity one should worship to attain release, and who is the god of the gods and the ancestor of the ancestors. In reply, Bhīṣma cites the dialogue of Nārada with Nārāyaṇa.*[1] *In the Kṛta Age the eternal Nārāyaṇa took birth as the son of Dharma in four forms: Nara, Nārāyaṇa, Hari and Kṛṣṇa. Arriving at the mountain hermitage of Badarī where Nara and Nārāyaṇa were performing austerities, Nārada asked Nārāyaṇa who it was that he, as the eternal unborn creator, was worshipping as god. The blessed lord replied that the object of worship of the gods and ancestors was the inner self of all beings, which is the universal Self.* [**322**] *Nārada took his leave and flew up to the top of Mount Meru. To the north of the ocean of milk he could see the White Island, where men are beyond things of the senses, take no food, remain motionless and smell sweet.*

*Yudhiṣṭhira asks to hear more about these people, as they share the characteristics of those who have found release. Bhīṣma tells him of the virtuous and pious king Vasu Uparicara,*[2] *who was utterly devoted to Nārāyaṇa. The seven*

**1** 'Nārāyaṇa' is in general a name used for the god Viṣṇu. However, chapters 321–39 glorify Nārāyaṇa as highest lord in the manner of the sect known as Pāñcarātra, identifying him with the universal Self and making him the creator of the gods Brahmā and Rudra (Śiva). The passage is therefore known as the *Nārāyaṇīya*. The paired divine seers Nara and Nārāyaṇa are manifestations of this highest lord.

**2** Elsewhere identified as Vyāsa's maternal grandfather: see 1.57.

*seers had composed a learned text on* dharma, *the proper making of wealth, pleasure and release, and Nārāyaṇa had stated that in the course of time King Vasu Uparicara would receive it from Bṛhaspati and would base all his actions upon it, but that after his death it would disappear.* **[323]** *King Vasu became Bṛhaspati's pupil, acquired the seers' learning, and ruled the earth as Indra rules heaven. He held a great horse sacrifice at which Bṛhaspati officiated, and which was attended by Brahmā's sons Ekata, Dvita and Trita, and by many great seers; no animal was slaughtered in it. When Nārāyaṇa took his share of the offering, he showed himself to Vasu but remained invisible to everyone else, and Bṛhaspati became enraged. To pacify him, Ekata, Dvita and Trita explained that they themselves had performed austerities for thousands of years in order to see Nārāyaṇa; the god's voice had then directed them to go to the White Island, where he had revealed himself to his devotees. They had done so, and had seen a brilliant light and heard the islanders praising Nārāyaṇa; but though the god had clearly appeared there they themselves had not seen him, for he can be seen only by those who have devoted themselves solely to him for a great length of time. Bṛhaspati then completed the sacrifice. Later he was cursed by Brahmins to fall from heaven and to be confined beneath the earth, but because of his devotion Nārāyaṇa raised him from there, and he attained* brahman.

**[324]** *Yudhiṣṭhira asks to hear the story, and Bhīṣma tells him of a dispute which once took place between the gods and the seers, the gods maintaining that goats are necessary for sacrifice, the seers that animal slaughter is against* dharma. *They appealed to Vasu for judgement, and he sided with the gods; the seers then angrily cursed him, and he fell from heaven and was swallowed up by the earth. Protected from hunger and thirst by the gods, he continued to offer his adoration to Nārāyaṇa day after day according to the proper rites, till Nārāyaṇa, pleased by his devotion, sent Garuḍa to rescue him.*

**[325]** *Bhīṣma now tells how Nārada reached the White Island, honoured the islanders and was honoured by them in return, and then, desiring to see Nārāyaṇa, sang a hymn of praise to him.* **[326]** *Nārāyaṇa appeared to him in unimaginable bodily form, and offered him a boon; Nārada replied that seeing the god was the greatest boon he could have. Nārāyaṇa identified himself as the self of all beings, the universal Self: it was only through the power of illusion that Nārada could see him. Men who were devoted solely to him and were free from Passion and Darkness would enter him; all the gods were contained within him, as were the Vedas, sacrifices, austerities, oceans, lakes, rivers and the ancestors.*

*He had created Brahmā as his son to oversee the worlds. At the end of a thousand ages he would absorb the world into himself, and later he would create it again. He would repeatedly take incarnate form to protect his creation from harm: as boar, man-lion, dwarf, Rāma Jāmadagnya, Rāma son of Daśaratha, and finally Kṛṣṇa. Brahmā himself had never seen him as Nārada had been able to do. After speaking thus, Nārāyaṇa disappeared from view, and Nārada returned to the hermitage of Badarī.*

*At this point Yudhiṣṭhira asks Bhīṣma how it could be that Brahmā, who is so close to Nārāyaṇa, does not truly know him. Bhīṣma answers that Brahmā creates the universe at the beginning of each cycle of ages, but he knows that Nārāyaṇa is the universal Self, the highest lord and his own creator. Then Bhīṣma describes how the narrative he has just told was disseminated, and explains that it is the essence of all the holy tales Yudhiṣṭhira has heard. After hearing it, Yudhiṣṭhira and his brothers all become devotees of Nārāyaṇa.*

**[327]** — *Janamejaya asks how it is that the same blessed Nārāyaṇa who favours disengagement has also established engagement: the gods themselves, by accepting their shares in the sacrifice, follow the way of engagement. Release, the highest joy, means extinction; why do the gods prefer the transitory rewards of engagement, and to whom do they offer sacrifices themselves? In reply, Vaiśaṃpāyana remarks that once when Vyāsa was teaching him and his four co-pupils the four Vedas with the* Mahābhārata *as the fifth,*[1] *they had asked him the same question. Vyāsa answered with the knowledge of past, present and future that Nārāyaṇa had granted him for the great asceticism he had undertaken. He explained that, after Brahmā had created the deities and divine seers, the question had arisen of the duties that each should do. They had performed long austerities on the northern shore of the ocean of milk; finally, the highest lord spoke. He commanded them to perform sacrifices to him; he would then determine their duties. When they had sacrificed, he announced that from now on they would receive the fruits of engagement through the sacrifices offered to them: each would receive the same share that he had just offered. Then he instructed them to support the worlds, strengthened by their share in sacrifices, and strengthening him in turn. He said that some of them would follow the way of engagement, others of disengagement, and they left to set about their duties. Only Brahmā remained, for he desired to see the blessed lord; Nārāyaṇa revealed himself to him, in a form*

1 See chapter 314 and note above.

*with a great horse's head,*[1] *before sending him to his task of creating and ruling the worlds. Thus Nārāyaṇa receives the first share of sacrifices, but is himself disengaged; he established the way of engagement so that there would be variety in the world. He should be worshipped as highest lord. Now Vaiśaṃpāyana concludes Vyāsa's discourse by saying that to hear it confers great benefits.*

**[328]** *Janamejaya asks Vaiśaṃpāyana to explain the names with which Vyāsa and his disciples had praised Nārāyaṇa. In reply, Vaiśaṃpāyana cites the answer Kṛṣṇa gave to Arjuna when he asked a similar question. — Kṛṣṇa refers to the birth of the creator Brahmā from the lotus in Nārāyaṇa's navel and the birth of the destroyer Rudra from his forehead; he states that Rudra and Nārāyaṇa are one, though in two forms, and says that when a man of wisdom worships Brahmā or Rudra or some other god, it is Kṛṣṇa himself whom he reaches. Then he gives explanations for a number of his names.* **[329]** *He speaks of the first creation and of the innate superiority of Brahmins, then relates a number of mythological narratives,* **[330]** *and gives explanations for more of his names. In doing so he refers to Rudra's battle with Nara and Nārāyaṇa during his attack on Dakṣa's sacrifice,*[2] *and Arjuna asks to hear more about this. Kṛṣṇa replies that the three worlds were terrified, but Brahmā appealed to Rudra to drop his weapons; Rudra did so, and was reconciled with Nārāyaṇa.*

**[331]** — *Janamejaya praises the narrative of Nārāyaṇa, and then asks how long Nārada stayed at the hermitage of Badarī when he returned there from the White Island. In reply, Vaiśaṃpāyana describes how Nārada reached the hermitage, where he saw Nara and Nārāyaṇa engaged in austerities. They greeted Nārada with great respect, and Nārāyaṇa asked him whether he had seen the universal Self in the White Island; he replied that he had, and that in looking at them he saw it still; praising that most blessed one, he said that he intended to remain with them, devoted to the universal Self.* **[332]** *Nara and Nārāyaṇa praised him for having achieved a sight of the highest lord, from whom all things ultimately arise, and into whom those who find release are absorbed. Nārada remained at that hermitage for a thousand years of the gods, worshipping the highest lord.*

**1** In the previous chapter it was said that Brahmā had never seen Nārāyaṇa as Nārada saw him; evidently the reference was to the particular 'unimaginable bodily form' that Nārāyaṇa assumed on that occasion. See further chapter 335 below.

**2** See chapter 274 above.

[333] *Vaiśaṃpāyana says that one day, observing Nārada performing rites for the gods and ancestors, Nara asked him about them. Nārada reminded Nara that he himself had said that worship of the gods was worship of Nārāyaṇa; similarly, in worshipping the ancestors Nārada was worshipping Nārāyaṇa. Then he asked how it was that the ancestors had acquired the name of* piṇḍas,[1] *and the two seers replied that when Viṣṇu had assumed the form of a boar, three balls of mud had fallen from his tusk. The god, who was preparing to bring ancestors into being, declared that the three balls would become the ancestors – father, grandfather and great-grandfather – and that he himself would be present in them. Thus those who worship the ancestors worship Viṣṇu, who is present in all as the universal Self.*

[334] *Vaiśaṃpāyana now says that after a thousand years Nārada returned to his mountain hermitage, while Nara and Nārāyaṇa continued their austerities at Badarī. Then he tells Janamejaya that what he has heard about the highest lord Nārāyaṇa has cleansed him of sin; he has recited it to him as he heard it himself from the great Kṛṣṇa Dvaipāyana Vyāsa. He advises Janamejaya to proceed with his preparations for a horse sacrifice, and Janamejaya does so. Vaiśaṃpāyana concludes with a hymn of praise to Nārāyaṇa.*

[335] *Janamejaya now asks Vaiśaṃpāyana to tell him more about Nārāyaṇa's appearance to Brahmā in his form with a horse's head.[2] Vaiśaṃpāyana replies that Yudhiṣṭhira had made the same request to Vyāsa. Vyāsa began by describing the dissolution of the universe and the beginning of the new creation. Two drops of water lay on the lotus that sprang from Nārāyaṇa's navel; from one arose the demon Madhu, from the other the demon Kaiṭabha. Seeing Brahmā in the act of creating the Vedas, Madhu and Kaiṭabha stole them and fled into the underworld beneath the ocean. Brahmā lamented: without the Vedas he could not continue the creation. Then he sang a hymn of praise to Nārāyaṇa. Nārāyaṇa assumed a cosmic form with the head of a horse, retrieved the Vedas from the underworld and returned them to Brahmā; then he killed the two demons, thus becoming the 'slayer of Madhu',[3] and Brahmā resumed the creation of the worlds.*

[336] *Janamejaya observes that total devotion to Nārāyaṇa leads to the highest*

---

1 The *piṇḍas* are in fact the balls of rice offered to the ancestors in the *śrāddha* ceremony. The extended usage referred to here is not normal.

2 See chapter 327 above.

3 See also chapter 200 above.

*benefit, and asks who has proclaimed this practice. Vaiśaṃpāyana refers him to the* Bhagavadgītā, *preached by Kṛṣṇa to Arjuna as the war at Kurukṣetra was about to begin.*[1] *He explains that Nārāyaṇa himself first established the way of devotion, and describes the manner in which it has been promulgated in creation after creation. Janamejaya asks why not all Brahmins follow it; Vaiśaṃpāyana ascribes this to the influence of Passion and Darkness.* **[337]** *He praises Vyāsa, referring to him as the son of Nārāyaṇa. Janamejaya points out that earlier he had spoken of Vyāsa as Parāśara's son, and requests and explanation. Vaiśaṃpāyana replies that, as one of Vyāsa's five pupils, he had been present when Vyāsa spoke of the matter. He said that on the occasion of the seventh creation,*[2] *when Nārāyaṇa had told Brahmā to create beings, he had not known how to do so; Nārāyaṇa had commanded Intelligence to enter him, and Brahmā had succeeded in the task of creation. Nārāyaṇa now himself created various forms – boar, man-lion, dwarf and other human forms – with which he would be able to slay evildoers. He also created a seer named Apāntaratamas to make the Vedas known. Apāntaratamas divided and distributed the Vedas, and Nārāyaṇa, pleased with his work, told him that he would carry out this task in every successive creation; he also said that at the start of the Kali Age he would be born as the son of Parāśara to become the progenitor of famous princes called Kurus, who would wipe each other out in a family feud. Thus Vyāsa came into being. Vaiśaṃpāyana goes on to list various religious systems: Sāṃkhya, Yoga, the Pāñcarātra sect devoted to Nārāyaṇa, the Vedas, and the Pāśupata sect devoted to Śiva; he states that all of these are agreed that Nārāyaṇa is the highest lord.*

**[338]** *Janamejaya asks whether there are many selves*[3] *or a single self. Vaiśaṃpāyana answers that the followers of Sāṃkhya and Yoga believe in many selves, but that they have a single source which is the universal Self; he will tell Janamejaya what the venerable Vyāsa had said on the topic. Then he cites the dialogue of Brahmā with Rudra on Mount Vaijayanta. Questioned by Rudra, Brahmā said that his mind was focused on the most excellent Self. Rudra replied that Brahmā had created many selves, and asked what this one Self was; Brahmā said that it transcended and was the source of the many; it was universal and*

1 See 6.23–40.

2 The present one.

3 The word is *puruṣa*: see chapters 210 and 291 above, and the notes thereto.

*eternal.* **[339]** *He continued to expound to Rudra on the universal Self, which dwells in all bodies without being affected by them, and which pervades the cosmos. Like fire, or the rays of the sun, or wind, or the waters of the ocean, it is both many and one. It is Nārāyaṇa.*

**[340]** — *Now Yudhiṣṭhira says to Bhīṣma that, having taught him the* dharma *of release, he ought to teach him the* dharmas *that apply to the different stages of life. In reply, Bhīṣma refers to a conversation that once took place between Indra and Nārada. Indra had asked Nārada to recount any wonder he had seen during his travels through the universe. Nārada had responded with a tale: Bhīṣma will now recount it to Yudhiṣṭhira.* **[341]** *Once a certain virtuous householder Brahmin reflected that one* dharma *is declared in the Vedas, another in the learned texts, a third practised by men of eminence; he wondered which would be best for him to follow. When a wise guest visited him, he addressed him on the topic.* **[342]** *The Brahmin told his guest that he wished to undertake the highest* dharma, *to join himself to the universal Self and free himself from repeated births in the world, but he did not know what way to choose. The guest too confessed himself puzzled, since different people follow many different courses;* **[343]** *then he told him of a certain serpent named Padmanābha, who lived by the bank of the river Gomatī. He was highly virtuous and hospitable, and the guest advised the Brahmin to go and put his question to him.* **[344]** *The Brahmin was delighted with the suggestion. He and his guest spent the night happily discussing topics concerning* dharma*; then in the morning he took leave of his family and set off to find the serpent.*

**[345]** *Bhīṣma continues the story of the Brahmin. After travelling through lovely forests, he arrived at the serpent's dwelling and announced himself. He told the serpent's beautiful and virtuous wife that he wished to see her husband; she answered that he was away on service to the Sun god, and would return in fifteen days. The Brahmin said that he would await his return, staying on the nearby riverbank.* **[346]** *The serpent's kinsmen were distressed that the Brahmin continued to live on the riverbank, foodless and practising austerities. On the sixth day they approached him and pleaded to be allowed to perform the duties of hospitality, but he insisted that he would only break his fast if the serpent failed to return in eight days' time.* **[347]** *After completing the term of his service, the serpent returned home; greeted by his wife, he asked her whether she had properly performed her duties towards gods and guests. In reply, she listed the* dharmas *appropriate to people of different social classes and in different stages* *of life, and said that a wife's highest duty was devotion to her husband. She had not failed in her duties towards gods or guests; however, fifteen days ago a Brahmin had arrived for an undisclosed purpose, and was awaiting the serpent's return on the bank of the Gomatī; he had told her to send her husband to him as soon as he arrived.* **[348]** *The serpent wondered whether the Brahmin was in fact some deity – how could a mere mortal seek an audience with him, or give commands? His wife assured him that the visitor was human, and urged him not to incur sin by disappointing him. The serpent thanked her for helping him overcome his natural pride and anger, and said that he would see the Brahmin at once and do what he wanted.*

**[349]** *Bhīṣma continues the story of the Brahmin. The serpent met the Brahmin, and promised to fulfil his wishes. The Brahmin said that he wished to join himself to the universal Self; first, however, he wanted to ask a question.* **[350]** *He asked the serpent to tell him of any wonderful things he had seen during his service to the Sun. The serpent related various wonders, then spoke of the wonder of wonders that he had beheld: a being like a second Sun that approached the Sun, illuminating the worlds with his fiery energy. He and the Sun had saluted one another, and then he had entered the Sun and become one with it. The serpent had asked the Sun who that being was,* **[351]** *and the Sun had answered that it was a Brahmin who had performed the most difficult* uñcha *vow.*[1]

**[352]** *Bhīṣma continues the story of the Brahmin. The Brahmin replied that the serpent's words had shown him the way he must go, and he asked leave to depart. The serpent objected that the Brahmin had not explained his purpose in meeting him: he should not leave like a wandering ascetic after merely setting eyes on him, for each of them formed a part of the other. The Brahmin agreed that he and the serpent and all other beings were present everywhere, but explained that he had had doubts. Now he had attained his purpose: he would undertake the* uñcha *vow. He bade farewell to the serpent.* **[353]** *Bhṛgu's son Cyavana subsequently inducted the Brahmin into the* uñcha *vow.*

*Now Bhīṣma describes how this story came to be known to him; he adds that he has told it to Yudhiṣṭhira in reply to his question as to what constitutes the highest* dharma.

1 This vow consists of living entirely on food obtained by gleaning.

# INSTRUCTION

## THE *DHARMA* OF GIVING

[1] *Yudhiṣṭhira tells Bhīṣma that, for all his teaching on tranquillity, he cannot be tranquil when he sees what he has done to Bhīṣma himself and to so many others. Bhīṣma asks him why he considers himself to be the cause of the slaughter when in fact he is under the control of forces outside himself. Then he cites the story of Gautamī, a tranquil old Brahmin lady who found that a snake had killed her son. A hunter caught the snake, brought it before her, and repeatedly urged her to have him kill it, but she would not agree. The snake spoke, and told the hunter that blame for the killing lay not with himself but with Death, who had instigated it; then Death arrived, and said that he in turn had acted at the instigation of Time; then Time arrived, and said that none of them were to blame: the boy's death was the result of his own former deeds. Gautamī agreed, adding that her loss of her son likewise resulted from her own deeds. Then Time, Death and the snake went their ways; the hunter became free of his anger, and Gautamī became free of her grief. Bhīṣma urges Yudhiṣṭhira to be tranquil: everything results from prior deeds, and it was neither he nor Duryodhana that caused the slaughter at Kurukṣetra, but Time.*

[2] *Yudhiṣṭhira asks whether any householder has ever overcome Death through* dharma. *In reply, Bhīṣma cites the story of Sudarśana, son of the Fire god, and his beautiful wife Oghavatī. Sudarśana had vowed to defeat Death as a householder, and since hospitality is the highest* dharma *for householders, he commanded Oghavatī always to give a guest whatever he asked for, even including herself. Meanwhile Death followed him everywhere, looking for any weak spot. One day while he was out gathering fuel, a Brahmin guest arrived; when Oghavatī asked what he wanted, he told her that he wanted her. Unable to*

*dissuade him, she retired with him in private. Sudarśana returned and called out to his wife, but, considering herself to have been defiled, she did not answer him. However, the Brahmin answered; he told Sudarśana what form of hospitality he had demanded, and asked for his response. Death stood ready to strike Sudarśana, but he replied, 'Enjoy yourself – it is my pleasure!' The Brahmin now came outside and identified himself as Dharma: he had come to test Sudarśana, who had defeated Death through his truth to his vow; Oghavatī's honour had been protected by his virtues and her own. With half her body she would become the river Oghavatī to purify the world, and with half she would accompany Sudarśana to the eternal realms, which they would enter in bodily form.*

[3] *Yudhiṣṭhira lists some of the extraordinary doings of Viśvāmitra,*[1] *and asks how he, as a Kṣatriya, was able to become a Brahmin.* [4] *Bhīṣma tells Yudhiṣṭhira of King Gādhi's daughter Satyavatī, whom the Bhārgava Brahmin Ṛcīka wished to marry. In an effort to block the match, Gādhi demanded as dowry a thousand white horses with one black ear each;*[2] *but Ṛcīka prayed to Varuṇa, and the horses he needed arose from the waters of the Gaṅgā. After the wedding, he granted Satyavatī the boon that both she and her mother would have fine sons: her mother should embrace an* aśvattha *tree and she herself should embrace a fig tree, and they must each eat a particular sacrificial meal. But Satyavatī's mother insisted on switching both trees and meals, and Ṛcīka told Satyavatī that as a result of the substitution her mother would give birth to a great Brahmin and she to a fierce Kṣatriya. She begged for the effect to fall upon her grandson, not her son, and Ṛcīka agreed to this. Satyavatī subsequently bore Jamadagni,*[3] *and her mother bore Viśvāmitra.*

[5] *Yudhiṣṭhira requests Bhīṣma to speak of the virtues of compassion and devotion. In reply, Bhīṣma tells him how once a hunter, attempting to shoot a deer with a poisoned arrow, struck a tree instead. The tree withered and died, but a parrot who had long lived in its hollows would not abandon it: foodless, he too began to wither. Indra, puzzled by his behaviour, descended and told the*

1 See 1.65–6, 1.165–7, 5.104–117, 9.41, 12.139. For other versions of the story of his birth, see 3.115 and 12.49.

2 Later Viśvāmitra himself will make a similar demand of his student Gālava: cf. 5.104–117.

3 Father of Rāma Jāmadagnya: see 12.49.

*bird that he should find a better tree to live in. Sighing long, the parrot answered that the tree had offered him protection all his life; it was wrong to compel him to abandon it. Pleased by his compassion, Indra offered him a boon, and he chose that the tree should be revived.*

[6] *Yudhiṣṭhira asks which is greater, destiny or human exertion. In reply Bhīṣma cites the dialogue of Vasiṣṭha with Brahmā. Vasiṣṭha had asked the same question; Brahmā answered that without human exertion, destiny bears no fruit. To rely on destiny without performing human actions is to strive in vain, like a woman with an impotent husband. Virtuous action protects one against destiny: Brahmā gave many examples of the effectiveness of exertion, including the Pāṇḍavas' regaining of their kingdom.*

[7] *Yudhiṣṭhira now asks Bhīṣma to tell him what the fruits are of good deeds. Bhīṣma says that no deed ever perishes: whatever good or bad deed one does in whatever circumstances, one will receive the reward for it in the same circumstances in subsequent births. He lists numerous forms of virtuous conduct, specifying the benefit that each will bring, and says that one's former actions follow one as surely as a calf picks out its mother among thousands of cows.*

[8] *Next, Yudhiṣṭhira asks which people are deserving of honour; Bhīṣma mentions pious Brahmins and those who give generously to them, and speaks of his own deep devotion to Brahmins, whom Kṣatriyas should protect like sons but revere like elders.*

[9] *Yudhiṣṭhira wants to know what becomes of those who break their promises to give to Brahmins. Bhīṣma replies that all their good deeds and ritual performances from birth to death are destroyed; then he cites the dialogue of a jackal with a monkey. In a former human birth the two had been friends, and now the monkey asked the jackal what ill deed he had done to reduce him to eating rotting bodies in a burning-ground; the jackal answered that he had broken a promise to a Brahmin. Bhīṣma emphasizes the importance of not disappointing Brahmins: a disappointed Brahmin burns like fire, while a satisfied Brahmin brings great welfare.*

[10] *Yudhiṣṭhira asks Bhīṣma whether it is wrong to offer instruction out of friendship to someone of inferior birth. Bhīṣma answers that it is a great fault, and tells the story of a Śūdra who arrived at the hermitage of Brahmā on Mount Himālaya hoping to become a wandering ascetic; the head of the hermitage told him that this was impossible for a Śūdra, so he went away, constructed a hut and an altar, and began living a life of observances and worship. A certain seer*

*began to visit him, and one day at the Śūdra's request he instructed him in how to perform the rite for the ancestors. In the course of time both men died; the Śūdra was reborn in the family of a great king, and the seer in a priestly family, and when the former Śūdra became king he appointed the former seer to be his household priest. But whenever the king saw the priest he smiled; this angered the priest, who finally requested an explanation. The king told him of their former births, and of the fault he had committed by instructing a Śūdra. This accounted for their reversal of fortunes;*[1] *the king smiled when he remembered their former births. At the king's urging the priest took wealth and left; by distributing the wealth to Brahmins he attained purity once more and became revered by the sages in that same hermitage. Bhīṣma concludes that instruction may be given to the twice-born classes of Brahmin, Kṣatriya and Vaiśya, but not to anyone else.*

[11] *Yudhiṣṭhira requests Bhīṣma to tell him in what kinds of men and women Śrī*[2] *dwells. In reply, Bhīṣma says that Kṛṣṇa's wife Rukmiṇī once put this question to Śrī herself, and the goddess had replied that she dwelt in the virtuous, never in the vicious or those unwilling to exert themselves; she also listed other auspicious places that were her dwellings.*

[12] *Yudhiṣṭhira asks whether men or women have greater enjoyment in sexual intercourse. In reply, Bhīṣma cites the story of the enmity between King Bhaṅgāśvana and Indra. Desiring offspring, Bhaṅgāśvana performed the Agniṣṭut sacrifice, which Indra hates,*[3] *and from then on Indra looked for weak spots in Bhaṅgāśvana. Seeing his opportunity when the king went hunting alone on horseback, he caused him to fall into a stupor, and Bhaṅgāśvana wandered in the forest, lost and thirsty. Seeing a beautiful pool, he watered his horse and bathed; the waters turned him into a woman. Mounting his horse with difficulty, he returned home and explained what had happened. He told the hundred sons he had gained through the Agniṣṭut to share the kingdom in amity; then he retired to the forest. There, as a woman, he bore a hundred sons to an ascetic, and took them to join the earlier sons; all the brothers enjoyed the kingdom*

1 The household priest of a king holds a low status among Brahmins because of his association with the Kṣatriya *dharma* and the necessary violence of the king.

2 The goddess of wealth and glory.

3 Ganguli, following the commentator Nīlakaṇṭha, explains that this is '[i]n consequence of the fact that the deity of fire is alone adored in that sacrifice'.

*together. Furious that he seemed to have achieved good rather than harm for Bhaṅgāśvana, Indra sowed dissension among the brothers until they fought and killed one another. Then he visited the lamenting Bhaṅgāśvana and explained the reason for what had befallen him. Bhaṅgāśvana pleaded for forgiveness, and Indra, pleased, granted him a boon: one of his two sets of sons would return to life. To Indra's surprise Bhaṅgāśvana chose the sons he had born as a woman, explaining that women are more loving than men. Indra now told him to choose whether to remain a woman or to become a man once more, and he chose to be a woman, because women have the greater pleasure in sexual intercourse.*

**[13]** *Now Yudhiṣṭhira asks Bhīṣma how one should behave to live a good life. Bhīṣma answers that one should shun the three evils of the body: murder, theft and adultery. One should shun the four evils of speech: wicked gossip, harsh words, slander and falsehood. One should shun the three evils of the mind by not coveting others' property, by practising friendship towards all and by accepting that all acts bear fruit.*

**[14]** *Yudhiṣṭhira requests Bhīṣma to tell him the names of Śiva.*[1] *Bhīṣma responds by asking Kṛṣṇa to recite the thousand names of Śiva that the seer Taṇḍi proclaimed in Brahmā's heaven, so that both Yudhiṣṭhira and the seers may hear them. Kṛṣṇa begins by describing how his wife Jāmbavatī asked him to offer his adorations to Śiva for a son, as he had done to get sons for Rukmiṇī. He had travelled to Himālaya, to the lovely hermitage of Upamanyu. Upamanyu had welcomed him and assured him that he would get a son by propitiating Lord Śiva, who had conferred great boons upon so many; then he had described how he himself had performed long austerities to see the great god. Śiva had appeared before him in Indra's form and had offered him a boon, but he had replied that he only wanted a boon from Śiva. Śiva had then revealed himself to Upamanyu in his own supreme form, accompanied by the other gods, and Upamanyu had praised him greatly. Then Śiva had blessed him.* **[15]** *Kṛṣṇa had performed austerities at Upamanyu's hermitage, and as a result he too had seen Lord Śiva in glory, surrounded by the gods and other great beings. He had offered up praise to the god, who had granted him boons.* **[16]** *Kṛṣṇa had*

1 This request introduces a five-chapter sequence devoted to glorifying Śiva as supreme lord, much as the *Nārāyaṇīya* (12.321–39) glorified Viṣṇu/Nārāyaṇa; significantly, it is Kṛṣṇa, himself an incarnation of Viṣṇu, who proclaims Śiva's greatness. The culmination is a hymn consisting of a thousand names of Śiva; later, chapter 135 will contain a thousand names of Viṣṇu.

*chosen his boons from Śiva, and Umā had then told him that he would have a son named Sāmba, before granting him further boons. Then Śiva and all those with him had disappeared. Upamanyu now told Kṛṣṇa of the seer Taṇḍi, who had offered his adorations to Śiva for ten thousand years. He had praised the great god at length; Śiva, pleased, had granted him a boon, and he had chosen unwavering devotion to his lord. Then he had visited Upamanyu's hermitage and passed on to him the thousand names of Śiva, which Upamanyu would now reveal to Kṛṣṇa.* [17] *Upamanyu told Kṛṣṇa that this great hymn of praise had been composed by Brahmā; it was the most auspicious of all things, capable of freeing one from sin and granting one's desires. Then he recited the thousand names. Afterwards he spoke further of the great benefits conferred by this hymn.*

[18] *One after the other, the great seers who have been listening to Kṛṣṇa's words reveal how they too have benefited from Śiva's favour. Kṛṣṇa concludes by saying that the entire universe has its origin in Śiva, and that the hymn of praise he has recited brings great rewards.*

[19] *Yudhiṣṭhira tells Bhīṣma that he is puzzled by the concept of shared* dharma *for a married couple. How can that apply when one partner dies before the other, and how is it that one is to share one's* dharma *with a woman, when it said in the Vedas that women are false? In reply, Bhīṣma cites the story of ascetic Aṣṭāvakra and Diśā. Aṣṭāvakra asked Vadānya for permission to marry his lovely daughter; Vadānya answered that he could do so once he had travelled north past the land of Kubera and paid reverence to an aged female ascetic he would find there.* [20] *Aṣṭāvakra agreed to this, and set off northwards. Kubera greeted him in person and entertained him with great honour: Apsarases danced for him and Gandharvas played music. After a year as Kubera's guest he took his leave and continued on his way. As he travelled he came upon a palace finer even than Kubera's; he was ushered in by girls of captivating loveliness and shown into the presence of an old woman. The girls left, and Aṣṭāvakra and the old woman lay down on separate beds to sleep, but after a time she came to his bed and tried to persuade him to make love to her, telling him that women take great pleasure in sexual enjoyment. Politely, Aṣṭāvakra declined, but he agreed to remain as her guest. She was so ugly that he thought she must have been the victim of a curse. The next evening, he asked her to fetch him water for washing.* [21] *The old woman, whose name was Diśā, brought oil and massaged him; then she bathed him with her own hands. Aṣṭāvakra found it so pleasant that he did not notice that the night had passed. During the day she brought him*

*excellent food; the next night she once again tried to induce him to lie with her. She insisted that she was dependent on no man, and that he would incur no fault in making love to her. Aṣṭāvakra was astonished that now she appeared young and beautiful, but he maintained his resolve not to deviate from* dharma. **[22]** *She now revealed that she was the Lady of the North: she had tested his resolution and shown him the capricious nature of women at the behest of his future father-in-law. He now returned home and told Vadānya everything that had occurred; Vadānya was delighted, and Aṣṭāvakra was married to his daughter and lived happily with her in his hermitage.*

**[23]** *Yudhiṣṭhira asks Bhīṣma a number of detailed questions, several of them concerning the giving of gifts to Brahmins, and receives answers from Bhīṣma.* **[24]** *Then he asks him the rules governing the performance of* śrāddha *ceremonies and rituals directed at the gods. Bhīṣma specifies the appropriate times of day, the kinds of food that should not be offered as gifts, and the kinds of Brahmins who should and should not be invited to officiate. He adds some details about the performance of particular rituals, and mentions ritual faults to be avoided. At Yudhiṣṭhira's request he lists the kinds of Brahmin recipients to whom gifts should be given to secure the best reward; then he catalogues acts that lead to hell, and acts that lead to heaven.*

**[25]** *Yudhiṣṭhira now asks what acts constitute Brahminicide even though no one is physically harmed. Bhīṣma replies that he had once asked Vyāsa the same question; he had answered that the man who invites a poor Brahmin but gives him nothing is a Brahminicide, and so is the man who takes away a Brahmin's living, or who prevents thirsty cows from drinking, or who ignorantly insults the scriptures, or who refuses to marry his daughter to a suitable man, or who causes terrible grief to Brahmins, or who steals from the disabled, or who sets fire to a hermitage or a forest or a place of human habitation.*

**[26]** *Yudhiṣṭhira asks to hear about the sacred bathing-places. In reply, Bhīṣma cites the answer given by Aṅgiras when Gautama had asked him the same question: he had listed the best bathing-places and specified what the benefit was of bathing in each one.*

**[27]** *As Bhīṣma lies on his bed of arrows attended by Yudhiṣṭhira and his brothers, all the great seers come to see him. They speak to each other about him, and Bhīṣma, hearing their sweet words, feels as if he has reached heaven already. Then they vanish, while the Pāṇḍavas bow and praise them. They are amazed to see the horizon blazing with the power of the seers' austerities, and* *they discuss them with Bhīṣma. Then Yudhiṣṭhira resumes his questioning: he asks which are the holiest places. In reply, Bhīṣma cites the dialogue of an ascetic*[1] *with a perfected seer who had ranged all over the earth more than once. The ascetic had asked the seer the same question; the seer had answered that the holiest places are where the Gaṅgā flows, and he had bestowed the highest of praise upon the river before flying up into the sky. The ascetic now worshipped Gaṅgā and himself attained perfection.*

**[28]** *Yudhiṣṭhira asks how a Kṣatriya, Vaiśya or Śūdra may become a Brahmin. Bhīṣma replies that this can only happen through rebirth, and cites the story of the Brahmin boy Mataṅga. One day his father sent him out in a donkey cart to gather materials for sacrifice; the donkey was young, and carried him towards its mother, despite his beating it. Seeing her son's injuries, the female donkey remarked that the driver was a Caṇḍāla, and that no Brahmin would act thus; questioned by Mataṅga, she told him that he had been begotten on a lustful Brahmin woman by a Śūdra, and had no Brahmin status. He returned home and undertook fierce austerities; Indra offered him a boon, and he asked to become a Brahmin, but Indra told him that that was impossible for one born a Caṇḍāla.* **[29]** *Mataṅga redoubled his austerities; now Indra warned him that what he was doing was* adharma *and would lead to his destruction. An animal that attained human rebirth would be born as a Caṇḍāla; only after a long time might he then attain Śūdra birth, and so by slow stages progress towards becoming a Brahmin.* **[30]** *Mataṅga ignored Indra's counsel and continued his extreme austerities; again Indra tried to dissuade him, and Mataṅga finally requested other boons instead: to be able to assume any form and go anywhere, and to attain undying fame. These Indra granted.*

**[31]** *Yudhiṣṭhira remarks that, though it is very hard to attain brahminhood, Viśvāmitra and King Vītahavya succeeded in doing so, and he asks Bhīṣma to tell him the story of the latter.*[2] *Bhīṣma relates how the sons of the Haihaya king Vītahavya overthrew and killed king Haryaśva of Kāśi, and then likewise overthrew his son Sudeva. Sudeva's son Divodāsa, at Indra's command, built the great city of Vārāṇasī. He too was attacked by the Haihayas; after a great battle he fled and appealed to Bharadvāja for help, as his entire family had been destroyed. Bharadvāja promised him a son with whom he could withstand*

**1** Specifically, one performing the *uñcha* vow: see 12.349–53.

**2** For Viśvāmitra, see chapters 3–4 above.

*Haihayas in their thousands; he performed a sacrifice, and a son Pratardana was born to Divodāsa. No sooner was he born than he grew to be a boy of thirteen, and mastered the Vedas and weaponry. Divodāsa, delighted, appointed him crown prince and ordered him to destroy the Haihayas; he fought them in a great battle, and killed them all. Vītahavya now fled and sought refuge with Bhṛgu, who promised him safety. When Pratardana came to Bhṛgu's hermitage and asked him to hand Vītahavya over, Bhṛgu answered that there were no Kṣatriyas in the hermitage, only Brahmins. As a result of Bhṛgu's words Vītahavya became a Brahmin; from him sprang a lineage of great seers.*

**[32]** *Yudhiṣṭhira asks Bhīṣma which men deserve reverence. In reply, Bhīṣma cites the dialogue of Nārada with Kṛṣṇa Vāsudeva. Seeing Nārada paying reverence to some Brahmins, Kṛṣṇa asked him who they were to merit such great respect from him. Nārada answered that he reverenced those who always reverence the gods, who perform austerities and study the Vedas, and who possess all the brahmanical virtues. He counselled Kṛṣṇa to do likewise.*

**[33]** *Next Yudhiṣṭhira asks Bhīṣma what is a king's most important duty. Bhīṣma replies that it is to honour and protect Brahmins. They are powerful and dangerous: the man they favour becomes a king, the man they hate perishes. One cannot seize the wind in one's fist; one cannot touch the moon with one's hand; one cannot support the earth on one's head; one cannot overcome the Brahmins in this world.* **[34]** *Bhīṣma continues to emphasize the importance of honouring Brahmins, and the power that they wield. He cites the dialogue of Kṛṣṇa with the earth: Kṛṣṇa had asked the earth how a householder could free himself of sin, and the earth counselled him always to serve the Brahmins. Bhīṣma advises Yudhiṣṭhira to do the same.* **[35]** *Brahmins deserve reverence by reason of mere birth. Bhīṣma cites verses about them sung by Brahmā, and warns Yudhiṣṭhira of their power and the need to moderate it by giving them gifts.*

**[36]** *Bhīṣma cites the dialogue of Indra with the demon Śambara. Indra had asked Śambara how he had attained his position of superiority; Śambara replied that he always honoured Brahmins and accepted whatever they said. Indra too now began to reverence Brahmins; that is how he became the chief of the gods.*

**[37]** *Yudhiṣṭhira asks whether a stranger, a friend or a visitor from afar is the most appropriate recipient for gifts; Bhīṣma answers that all are appropriate, provided that the gift does not cause hardship to one's dependants. What matters is whether the recipient possesses the brahmanical virtues.*

**[38]** *Now Yudhiṣṭhira wants to learn about the nature of women, who are* *capricious and the cause of much sin. In reply, Bhīṣma cites the dialogue of Nārada with the Apsaras Pañcacūḍā. Nārada asked Pañcacūḍā to speak about the nature of women. At first she was reluctant to do so, but then she said that women's fault was lack of restraint. Given the opportunity, the wives of excellent husbands betray them; they give themselves to any man who approaches them; if they remain faithful it is only for want of suitors or out of fear. Fire is never sated with fuel, or the ocean with rivers, or death with living beings, or a woman with men.*

**[39]** *Yudhiṣṭhira wonders how it is that men seek the company of women when women are so deceitful and so skilled at deluding men, and he asks Bhīṣma whether it is possible to guard women against wrongdoing.* **[40]** *Bhīṣma replies that Yudhiṣṭhira's view of women is correct: they are like all other dangers combined. Brahmā created them at the request of the gods to prevent men from attaining heaven. Then he tells the story of Vipula. The seer Devaśarman had a beautiful wife named Ruci whom Indra greatly desired. On one occasion when he was about to leave to perform a sacrifice, he instructed his pupil Vipula to guard Ruci, warning him that Indra could assume a great variety of forms. Vipula decided that he would have to use his yogic power to enter Ruci, and this he did, without her being aware of him.* **[41]** *Now Indra assumed a most handsome form and came to Devaśarman's home. Ruci wished to rise to greet him, but Vipula prevented her; she wished to reply to Indra's beguiling words, but instead Vipula made her ask him the reason for his visit. With his divine sight Indra perceived the ascetic within the woman, and he was greatly afraid. Vipula returned to his own body; he chided Indra for his wickedness, and told him to go. Indra vanished, and Devaśarman returned. When Vipula told him that he had successfully protected his wife from Indra, Devaśarman was pleased with him; now freed from his fear of Indra, he gave Vipula leave to go and practise austerities.* **[42]** *Later, however, Devaśarman sent Vipula on an errand. As he was returning, he twice encountered people quarrelling with one another; each time, he heard them utter the same oath, that whichever of them was behaving improperly should suffer Vipula's fate in the next world. Greatly perturbed, he realized that he had done wrong in not telling his* guru *the manner in which he had guarded his wife.* **[43]** *He returned from his errand; Devaśarman revealed that he knew what Vipula had done. The people he had met had been day and night, and the seasons; they always know of any wickedness done in secret. Vipula had done wrong in keeping silent, but his actions in guarding Ruci* *had not been sinful. Devaśarman added that he was pleased with Vipula, who would after all go to heaven, not to hell. Then Devaśarman, Ruci and Vipula all ascended to heaven and lived there happily. Bhīṣma concludes that there are good and bad women; one can tell them apart by physical signs. But all women like to take many lovers, and Vipula is the only man who has ever guarded a woman against wrongdoing.*

**[44]** *Yudhiṣṭhira asks what is the highest* dharma *as regards kin, home, ancestors, gods and guests. Bhīṣma answers that it is to give one's daughter in marriage to a suitable man, and he lists the five forms of marriage: the Brahmin form, in which a bridegroom is chosen for his known merits; the Kṣatriya form, in which dowry is paid; the Gandharva form, in which the father puts aside his own choice and gives his daughter to a man she likes and who likes her; the demonic form, in which the girl is purchased for a high price; and the Rākṣasa form, in which she is seized by force after killing her relatives. Of these the first three follow* dharma*, the last two* adharma*. Bhīṣma says that a Brahmin may take three wives,*[1] *a Kṣatriya two; the senior wife will be of the same class as the man. He states the ages at which girls should be married, and at Yudhiṣṭhira's request gives some further rules governing marriage and dowry.* **[45]** *Yudhiṣṭhira asks on what authority only men inherit wealth. Bhīṣma says that a daughter's son and a son have equal inheritance rights; then he speaks with horror of the practice of selling one's children.* **[46]** *He says that when a girl marries, she should be treated with respect and cherished. The family where women are not treated well comes to grief.*

**[47]** *Yudhiṣṭhira asks how the inheritance of a Brahmin should be shared between the sons of his wives from different social classes. After emphasizing that a Brahmin should not take a Śūdra wife, Bhīṣma answers that the property should be divided into ten shares: the son of a Brahmin wife should inherit four, the son of a Kṣatriya wife three, the son of a Vaiśya wife two. The son of a Śūdra wife should not inherit, but should be given the remaining share out of kindness. At Yudhiṣṭhira's request, Bhīṣma then details the arrangements that apply to inheritance in the other social groups.*

1 Elsewhere, e.g. in chapter 48 below, the number of wives permitted to a Brahmin is said to be four. The discrepancy arises from the practice of marriage between Brahmin men and Śūdra women, which is frowned upon but was evidently common enough for customary regulations to have sprung up: see chapter 47.

**[48]** *Yudhiṣṭhira asks about those of mixed social class. Bhīṣma answers that four wives are permitted to a Brahmin: the children of a Brahmin or Kṣatriya wife are Brahmins, those of a Vaiśya wife are Vaiśyas, but those of a Śūdra wife are of degraded mixed class. The children of a Kṣatriya husband and a Kṣatriya or Vaiśya wife are Kṣatriyas, but those of a Śūdra wife are degraded. The children of a Vaiśya husband and a Vaiśya or Śūdra wife are Vaiśyas. Śūdra men may marry only Śūdra women. Where a son is born from the union of a lower-class man and an upper-class woman, he always belongs to a mixed class: thus the son of a Kṣatriya man and a Brahmin woman is a Sūta, whose job is to be a panegyrist, while the son of a Śūdra man and a Brahmin woman is a Caṇḍāla, who acts as executioner. The children born to a man and woman of the same mixed class belong to that class, but other unions produce children of yet more degraded classes.*

*Yudhiṣṭhira asks how people of such impure origin may be recognized.* **[49]** *Bhīṣma replies that one always inherits the disposition of father or mother or both, and that a person of degraded mixed birth cannot suppress his own nature. However, a senior person of bad disposition deserves no respect, while even a Śūdra merits respect if his conduct is good. He lists the mixed classes to which sons belong when born to various different mixed unions, and states that when a man abandons the son he has conceived, that son belongs to the mother and her husband. Likewise, an adopted son belongs to the one who rears him: he takes on his social class.*

**[50]** *Yudhiṣṭhira asks Bhīṣma to speak about the affection that results from seeing and living with someone, and about the excellence of cattle. In reply, Bhīṣma cites the dialogue of King Nahuṣa with the seer Cyavana, Bhṛgu's son.*[1] *Cyavana undertook the ascetic vow of living in water: he remained immersed at the confluence of the Gaṅgā and Yamunā rivers till the river creatures grew fond of him. One day Niṣāda fishermen came to fish; in their net they caught many fish, but they also landed Cyavana, smeared with river-weeds, his hair and beard dyed green and his body encrusted with shells. In great fear they asked him what they should do with him, and he answered that he did not wish to leave the fish with whom he had dwelt so long: he must die with them or be sold with them. The terrified fishermen told King Nahuṣa what had happened.* **[51]** *Nahuṣa hastened to see Cyavana, and asked what he should do; Cyavana*

1 For the story of Cyavana, see 3.121–5.

*told him that he should buy him from the fishermen. Nahuṣa proposed to pay a thousand, then a hundred thousand, then ten million, then half his kingdom, but each proposal was rejected in turn by Cyavana. Nahuṣa now consulted a forest-dwelling sage named Gavijāta,*[1] *who recommended that he offer a cow as the price. Nahuṣa did so, and Cyavana happily agreed; he praised cows highly. Then the fishermen offered the cow to Cyavana. He accepted it, and told them that they were freed from their sins and would go straight to heaven with their fish, and at once this happened.*

**[52]** *Yudhiṣṭhira asks Bhīṣma to tell him about Rāma Jāmadagnya, his origin and his practice of the Kṣatriya* dharma. *In reply, Bhīṣma cites the story of Cyavana and King Kuśika.*[2] *Cyavana, knowing the evil that was to come to his own lineage, wanted to destroy the lineage of Kuśika; he visited Kuśika and announced that he wished to stay with him. Kuśika and his wife treated him with the highest respect. After eating, Cyavana said that he wished to sleep. He ordered the king and queen not to wake him, but to stay awake and massage his feet as he slept. They did as he had told them, and Cyavana slept on one side without stirring for twenty-one days while they tended him. Then he awoke, and vanished without saying a word. Kuśika collapsed, but soon recovered and began to search for Cyavana.* **[53]** *Unable to find him, the king returned with his wife to the palace, where they saw the seer lying on his other side on the same bed. They resumed their massage, and Cyavana slept for a further twenty-one days. Then he awoke, and ordered an oil rub preparatory to taking a bath; famished and exhausted, the king and queen applied costly oil to his limbs without ceasing, while he spoke not a word to them. Finally, seeing that their equanimity was undisturbed, he got up, went into the regal bathroom, and vanished once more. When he reappeared, he was seated upon the throne; Kuśika had wonderful food served to him, but he caused it to burst into flame before vanishing again. His next demand was that Kuśika should yoke himself and his wife to their chariot and bear him along in it while he distributed their wealth to those who passed by; this too was done, and Cyavana applied the sharp goad until the bodies of the king and queen streamed with blood, but still they remained undisturbed. Releasing them on the bank of the Gaṅgā and healing their wounds, he told*

**1** The name means 'born from a cow'.

**2** For various versions of the story of Rāma's birth, see 3.115, 12.49 (where Kuśika's part in it is referred to) and 13.4.

*them to return there to him the next day: he would grant them a great boon.* [54] *In the morning Kuśika and his wife returned to the place where they had left Cyavana; there they saw a most wonderful palace built entirely of gold in a lovely forest. Kuśika wondered whether he had gone to heaven in bodily form, or whether he was dreaming. He saw Cyavana reclining on a costly bed; the seer vanished, and reappeared in another place in the forest, seated on a mat of* kuśa *grass. Then the forest itself vanished. Kuśika remarked to his wife that Brahmins possess great power, and that it is hard to become a Brahmin. Cyavana now summoned them to him and offered Kuśika a boon. Kuśika answered that his best boon was to have been exposed to Cyavana's fire-like presence and not to have been burnt. Then he asked if the seer would explain something he did not understand.* [55] *With Cyavana's permission, he now asked him why he had acted in such extraordinary ways. Cyavana explained that he knew his own lineage would be tainted because of a descendant of Kuśika, and that he had come to Kuśika with the intention of destroying him and his lineage. He had behaved as he did in hopes of provoking Kuśika to anger and so giving him the opportunity to curse him, but Kuśika had shown no weak spot; indeed he had revealed a desire for brahminhood. Cyavana told him that this desire would be granted: his grandson would become a Brahmin. Kuśika asked him how this would happen.* [56] *Cyavana explained that, though the Bhārgava Brahmins were happy to perform sacrifices for the Kṣatriyas, a rift would come between them: it was fated that the Kṣatriyas would slaughter the Bhārgavas, and that a Bhārgava named Aurva*[1] *would survive, whose rage would form a fire capable of destroying the earth; he would place it in the mouth of a mare beneath the sea. His son Ṛcīka would have a son Jamadagni, who would marry the daughter of Kuśika's son Gādhi. His own son Rāma would follow the Kṣatriya* dharma, *whereas Gādhi's son would become a Brahmin. Now Cyavana once more told Kuśika to choose a boon, and he chose brahminhood for his lineage.*

[57] *Now Yudhiṣṭhira announces that he is consumed with grief at all the kings he has himself slain, and that he intends to pursue a life of fierce asceticism: he asks Bhīṣma for advice. Bhīṣma replies with a list of ascetic and other religious practices, followed by a list of gifts, in each case specifying the rewards that can be obtained. He concludes by saying that the man who falls in battle becomes the companion of Brahmā himself. His words turn Yudhiṣṭhira's inclinations away*

1 Often said to be Cyavana's own son. For another version of his story, see 1.169–72.

*from hermitage life and towards the way of the hero; his decision is applauded by his brothers and Draupadī.*

**[58]** *Yudhiṣṭhira wishes to know what is the best of all gifts, the one that follows the giver.*[1] *Bhīṣma praises granting freedom from fear to all creatures, kindness to those in distress, and fulfilling the wants of needy supplicants; he says that the best gift, the one that follows the giver, is the one that the giver thinks of as already given even as he gives it. Gifts can free a man from sin; the person who hopes for eternal benefit should choose his dearest possessions and give them away to the virtuous. Bhīṣma goes on to praise giving, especially to Brahmins, who are the highest of the high. No one is dearer to him than the Brahmins: not his father, not his father's father, not Yudhiṣṭhira.*

**[59]** *Yudhiṣṭhira asks about two Brahmins who are equal in virtue, learning and birth, one of whom begs for alms while the other does not: to which of them is it better to give? Bhīṣma answers that it is better to give to the one who does not beg, for a steadfast man is more worthy than one who is wretched and lacking in fortitude. Kindness is the highest* dharma, *and so it is good to give to one who begs, but one should also offer gifts to those who are distressed but do not beg. Bhīṣma again emphasizes the importance of giving to Brahmins, and he tells Yudhiṣṭhira that he should practise generous giving three times a day, like a Soma sacrifice; indeed, the sacrifice of giving is the best of all sacrifices.*

**[60]** *Yudhiṣṭhira asks Bhīṣma which brings greater rewards, sacrifice or the giving of gifts; he also asks whether gifts made in the context of a sacrifice or gifts made from compassion are superior. Bhīṣma explains that both sacrifices and gifts are effective for purifying a king of the sinful acts that he has to do, but that, since virtuous people will not accept gifts from sinners, it is best for a king to perform sacrifices at which he gives generously to the Brahmins: this achieves purification and other benefits. Bhīṣma goes on to say that a king must protect his subjects. If he fails to do so, a quarter of their sins are his, but if he does so, he receives a quarter of their merit.*

**[61]** *Yudhiṣṭhira remarks that the Vedas insist on generous giving, and kings give liberally; he asks what is the best gift. Bhīṣma replies that it is the gift of land. Such a gift purifies both the giver and the recipient, so that virtuous people will accept such a gift even from a sinful king; the gift of earth brings the same benefits as a horse sacrifice or a heroic death in battle. Bhīṣma cites the dialogue*

1 i.e. brings him rewards in the next life.

*of Bṛhaspati with Indra: Indra had asked what gift brought one happiness in heaven, and Bṛhaspati answered that the giving of gold, cows and land frees the giver from his sins; he went on to praise the gift of earth very highly. Bhīṣma adds that on hearing Bṛhaspati's words, Indra gave him the earth with all its wealth and jewels.*

**[62]** *Yudhiṣṭhira asks what gifts should be given to virtuous Brahmins, and what rewards they bring. In reply, Bhīṣma cites the answer Nārada gave him when he asked him the same question. Nārada praised gifts of food highly, saying that the merit of such a gift is never lost, even if the recipient is a Caṇḍāla or a dog. The Brahmin is the guest of all mankind, and is entitled to the first fruits; that house prospers where Brahmins regularly come to beg for alms and are treated with honour. Bhīṣma adds that in heaven the givers of food occupy the most wonderful palaces.*

**[63]** *Now Yudhiṣṭhira requests instruction on what gifts should be given when the moon is in conjunction with the various constellations. In reply, Bhīṣma cites the dialogue of Devakī with Nārada. Devakī had asked the same question, and Nārada answered by listing the gifts appropriate to each constellation, and the rewards that each yields for the giver.* **[64]** *Bhīṣma discourses on the merits of various gifts: gold, wells and tanks, ghee, water-vessels, fuel for cooking, umbrellas and carts.* **[65]** *At Yudhiṣṭhira's request, he describes the merits of gifts of sandals, sesame seeds, land, cattle and food.*

**[66]** *Yudhiṣṭhira says that he understands that gifts of food are particularly excellent, and asks about gifts of drink. Bhīṣma says that both are unsurpassed gifts. Food sustains life: in giving food one gives life, and there is no higher gift. But all food requires water to come into being; therefore there is no higher gift than the gift of water, which brings great benefits to the giver.*

**[67]** *Yudhiṣṭhira requests Bhīṣma to tell him more about gifts of sesame seeds, lamps, food and clothing. In reply, Bhīṣma cites the story of a Brahmin's dialogue with Yama. Yama once sent his messenger to fetch a particular Brahmin to him; the messenger brought the wrong Brahmin. When Yama told him to take him back and bring the right man, the Brahmin asked to be allowed to stay. Yama said that that was not possible, and asked what else he might do for him, and the Brahmin asked Yama to tell him the most meritorious acts. Yama spoke in favour of the gift of sesame seeds and water. Then the messenger returned him to his home, where he acted as Yama had said. Now the right Brahmin was bought to Yama, who told him the same, and on his return home he too acted according* *to Yama's words. Bhīṣma adds that Yama also favours the gift of lamps, and that jewels and clothing are also very good gifts.*

**[68]** *Yudhiṣṭhira asks Bhīṣma to tell him more about gifts, especially the gift of land. Bhīṣma answers that there are three gifts that share the same name and are equally efficacious in securing rewards: cattle, earth and learned speech.*[1] *To pass on learning to a pupil is as meritorious as to give cattle or land. Cattle are highly praised: they are the mothers of all creatures, and should be afforded the greatest respect. They should never be given to wicked folk, but the man who gives ten cows to a poor but pious Brahmin secures the highest realms. However, as great as the virtue of giving cattle to a worthy recipient is the sin of taking away a Brahmin's property.* **[69]** *Bhīṣma cites the story of King Nṛga. Once some men seeking to clear a weed-covered well in Dvārakā found a huge lizard trapped within it. Unable to lift it out, they appealed for help to Kṛṣṇa, who raised it from the well and questioned it; the lizard replied that it was King Nṛga. Kṛṣṇa remarked that Nṛga had given enormous numbers of cows to the Brahmins: what had happened to bring him to this state? Nṛga explained that once a cow belonging to a certain Brahmin had been accidentally included in a herd of cattle he had given to a second Brahmin. When the mistake came to light, neither Brahmin had been willing to accept any substitute for the disputed animal. Soon after he had passed away to the world of the ancestors, and Yama had told him that he must undergo punishment for the wrongdoing, but that after a thousand years Kṛṣṇa Vāsudeva would rescue him. Then he took Kṛṣṇa's leave and ascended to heaven.*

**[70]** *Yudhiṣṭhira asks to hear in more detail about the rewards for giving cattle. In reply, Bhīṣma cites the story of the seer Uddālaki and his son Nāciketa. Once Uddālaki sent Nāciketa to fetch some items he had left behind at the river, but they had been washed away. When he returned and told his father he could not see them there, his father, hungry, thirsty and exhausted, cursed him to see Yama. At once Nāciketa fell senseless to the ground, and Uddālaki lamented greatly what he had done. But then Nāciketa returned to life, and explained that he had indeed seen Yama, who had told him that he was not dead; now he had seen him, as his father had demanded, he could go back home. Yama had offered to fulfil a wish for him before he left, and Nāciketa had asked to see the realms of the virtuous. Yama had shown him marvellous palaces, and told him*

1 The word *go*, 'cow', is also used to mean 'earth' and 'speech'.

*that some belonged to those who had given gifts of milk-products, and others to those who had given cattle. He explained that such a gift must only be made to the right person, at the right time and in the right way, and detailed the benefits that could be attained by giving particular kinds of cattle to particular kinds of Brahmins. In the absence of a cow, gifts of ghee, sesame seeds or water could be substituted. Nāciketa rejoiced that he now knew the merits of giving cows.*

[71] *Yudhiṣṭhira wishes to hear more about the realms enjoyed by the givers of cattle. In reply, Bhīṣma cites the dialogue of Indra with Brahmā. Indra had asked about the realms of cattle and how people attained them, sometimes without making gifts of cows.* [72] *Brahmā answered that there were realms unknown to Indra, where there is no time, nor aging, sin, disease, weariness, or anything inauspicious. The cows that live there can roam wherever they want and fulfil every desire. There are beautiful pools, rivers, forests and mountains: no realm is finer. Only the most virtuous of men can go there. Brahmā detailed the merit that arises from making gifts of cattle in various ways, and from treating cows with honour.* [73] *Indra asked what would befall the man who stole a cow or sold one for profit. Brahmā replied that anyone who kills or eats a cow suffers in hell for as many years as the cow has hairs; theft or sale of a cow is equivalent to disrupting a Brahmin's sacrifice. He added that to make gifts of gold to Brahmins in association with the giving of cattle secures the greatest benefits.*

[74] *Now Yudhiṣṭhira asks Bhīṣma to teach him the rewards that come from various virtues, and Bhīṣma does so, focusing particularly on self-control, which is superior even to the giving of gifts. He speaks of heroism, which is of many kinds: one may be a hero in the pursuit of any virtuous endeavour. He speaks of truth, which outweighs a thousand horse sacrifices, and of other virtues and the rewards they bring.*

[75] *Yudhiṣṭhira asks Bhīṣma to tell him the rules for giving cattle. In reply, Bhīṣma cites the details of the ritual as originally stated by Bṛhaspati to Māndhātṛ, along with the rewards that it brings. He lists the famous kings who had attained heaven through the gift of cattle, and urges Yudhiṣṭhira to do likewise; and from then on Yudhiṣṭhira gives gifts of cattle and pays them great respect.*

[76] *Yudhiṣṭhira asks to hear more about the gift of cattle; Bhīṣma mentions various kinds of cow as being suitable or unsuitable for giving, and praises the Kapilā cow in particular. When Yudhiṣṭhira asks why, he explains that when the Prajāpati Dakṣa created beings, they cried for food; he then created the celestial*

*cow Surabhi, and she in turn produced the gold-coloured Kapilā cows who fed all the new creatures. Some of their milk fell on Śiva's head, and in anger he burnt them with the fire of his third eye, so that now there are cows of different colours; but some escaped and retained their original colour. Dakṣa appeased Śiva and gave him some of the cows together with a bull, which he made into his emblem.*

**[77]** *Bhīṣma tells Yudhiṣṭhira of Vasiṣṭha's discourse on cattle to King Saudāsa. He praised cattle greatly, and spoke of the rewards brought by gifts of cows and the respect one should show to them and their products.* **[78]** *He said that in ancient times cows had performed fierce austerities for a hundred thousand years in order to become the best of all gifts to Brahmins and for their dung to be used for purification. Then he listed the rewards arising from the gift of various kinds of cows: the man who delights in giving cows dwells in heaven for as many years as a cow has hairs.* **[79]** *Finally, he praised cattle highly and spoke of the honour they should be shown. Hearing his words, Saudāsa gave generous gifts of cattle and attained heaven.*

**[80]** *Yudhiṣṭhira asks Bhīṣma what is the purest of pure things; Bhīṣma answers that it is cattle, and he goes on to praise them, citing Vyāsa's discourse on the topic to his son Śuka.*

**[81]** *Yudhiṣṭhira asks how it is that the goddess Śrī is said to dwell in cowdung. Bhīṣma describes how Śrī once visited some cows. They asked who she was, and she identified herself and explained that she brought prosperity to those she favoured and ruin to those she turned away from; now she wished to dwell in cows. The cows replied that, because of her fickle nature, they did not want her. Śrī said that their rejection of her would cause her to be looked down on, and she appealed to them to let her live in some part of them; they agreed to let her live in their urine and dung, and she accepted this with great happiness.*

**[82]** *Bhīṣma praises cattle greatly, citing Brahmā's discourse on the topic to Indra. He concludes by saying that the man who is devoted to cattle attains all his desires.*

**[83]** *Yudhiṣṭhira remarks that Bhīṣma has spoken of the effectiveness of gifts of land and cattle in purifying kings of the sins they have to incur; however, the sacred texts also refer to gifts of gold, and even state that it is the best gift to give to Brahmins.*[1] *He asks Bhīṣma to tell him about gold. Bhīṣma replies that after he had performed the* śrāddha *ceremony for his father Śaṃtanu, the ancestors*

1 Bṛhaspati too spoke highly of all three gifts in chapter 61 above.

*had revealed themselves to him in a dream and urged him to make gifts of gold, which are able to save the giver's ancestors and descendants for ten generations. He also speaks of Rāma Jāmadagnya, who sought the most effective purification after his massacre of the Kṣatriyas. Vasiṣṭha advised him that there was no gift better than gold, and told him the story of the origin of gold. When Śiva was about to lie with Umā on his wedding night, the other gods appealed to him, fearful that the child of such a union would be so powerful that he would destroy the world. Śiva therefore retained his semen, at which Umā cursed the other gods to remain childless. However, Agni the Fire god was not present at that time; furthermore, a little of Śiva's semen fell to earth, where it united with Fire. Meanwhile the gods were suffering greatly because of the mighty demon Tāraka, and they went to Brahmā for help.* **[84]** *Brahmā reassured them that the Fire god would use Śiva's semen to beget a son upon Gaṅgā: that son who would slay all their enemies. He told them to seek out Fire, but they could not find him. A frog told them Fire was hiding in the waters; Fire cursed frogs to have no tongues, and went to hide elsewhere; the gods blessed frogs to be able to make all kinds of sounds and to aestivate. An elephant told them Fire was hiding in an* aśvattha *tree; Fire cursed elephants to have their tongues bent backwards,*[1] *and went to hide elsewhere; the gods blessed elephants to be able to carry anything and to trumpet loudly. A parrot told them Fire was hiding in a* śamī *tree; Fire cursed parrots to be speechless; the gods blessed parrots to be able to talk charmingly, like a child or an old man. Then they told Fire what they wanted of him, and he agreed. He united with Gaṅgā, and she conceived, but she could not endure the foetus's fiery energy; she placed him on Mount Meru, and told Fire that he was beautiful and brilliantly coloured.*[2] *The child was nurtured by the Kṛttikās,*[3] *and so came to be called Kārttikeya as well as Skanda.*[4] *That is how gold came into being as the child of Fire: it is the purest and most auspicious of all things.* **[85]** *Next Vasiṣṭha described a mighty sacrifice conducted by Śiva in the form of Varuṇa, lord of the waters. As he was offering oblations on the fire, Brahmā became aroused at the sight of the celestial women who were attending, and his*

**1** In the form of their trunks.

**2** *Jātarūpa* and *suvarṇa*; as nouns, both these words mean 'gold'.

**3** The stars of the Pleiades.

**4** For other accounts of Skanda's birth, see 3.213 and 9.43. Here the fiery brilliance of the as yet unborn war god is identified with gold.

*seed gushed forth; the god Pūṣan gathered it up and offered it like an oblation, and from it came into being all the divine seers. Śiva in Varuṇa's form claimed them as his offspring, and so did Brahmā and Fire; the gods pointed out to Brahmā that all beings were already his children, and asked him allow Varuṇa and Fire to have some of their own. Thus Bhṛgu became Varuṇa's son, and Aṅgiras became the son of Agni god of Fire, whilst Kavi*[1] *remained Brahmā's son. From these three all the lineages of men are derived. Returning to the topic of gold, Vasiṣṭha pointed out to Rāma Jāmadagnya that it is used in rituals as a substitute for fire; by giving gold one attains to the blessed realms. Bhīṣma adds that Rāma now gave gold to the Brahmins, thus freeing himself from his sins. He urges Yudhiṣṭhira to do likewise.*

**[86]** *Yudhiṣṭhira reminds Bhīṣma that he has not said how Tāraka met his death. Bhīṣma takes up the story again: none of the celestials is capable of bearing the embryo of the war god alone, and the six Kṛttikās have difficulty in doing so together, but in the end they simultaneously give birth to him. All the gods came to see him. He had six heads, twelve eyes, and twelve arms attached to powerful shoulders; the gods considered Tāraka as good as dead. As he grew, the demon sought ways to slay him, but he failed, and in the end Skanda slew him and became the commander of the gods' army. Since gold was born from Fire along with Skanda, it is highly auspicious. Bhīṣma urges Yudhiṣṭhira to make gifts of gold.*

**[87]** *Yudhiṣṭhira asks Bhīṣma to tell him all about the* śrāddha *ceremony. Bhīṣma answers that all beings, even celestials and demons, should honour their ancestors. Then he lists the advantages and disadvantages that arise from performing the ceremony on the different days of the lunar month.* **[88]** *Next Yudhiṣṭhira asks what offering should be made to the ancestors. Bhīṣma replies that offerings of sesame seeds, rice, barley, beans, water, roots and fruits will satisfy the ancestors for a month; of fish, for two months; of mutton, for three months; of hare, for four months; of goat meat, for five months; of pork, for six months; of poultry, for seven months; of venison from the spotted antelope, for eight months; of venison from the* ruru *deer, for nine months; of venison from the* gavaya,[2] *for ten months; of buffalo meat, for eleven months; of beef, for a year. Then he mentions various other favoured offerings,* **[89]** *and describes the*

1 Another seer, sometimes said to be the son of Bhṛgu.

2 The gayal, in fact a species of ox, but often considered in India to be a deer.

*benefits that arise from performing the* śrāddha *ceremony when the moon is in conjunction with the various constellations.*

**[90]** *Yudhiṣṭhira asks to which kinds of Brahmins the* śrāddha *offerings should be given. Bhīṣma lists faults to be avoided and virtues to be looked for in Brahmins when a* śrāddha *is to be performed: one should choose carefully, and select only Brahmins who are expert in the Veda, no matter whether one likes them or not.*

**[91]** *Next Yudhiṣṭhira asks about the origin of the* śrāddha, *and the rules for performing it. Bhīṣma describes how in ancient times the seer Nimi, full of grief for the death of his son Śrīmat, conceived the idea of a* śrāddha *ritual: inviting revered Brahmins on the day of the new moon, he gave them food made of* śyāmāka *grain without salt, and offered balls of rice to Śrīmat. He was then struck with remorse for having carried out a new ritual with no traditional legitimacy, but his ancestor Atri appeared to him and reassured him that the* śrāddha *had been instituted by Brahmā himself; he then told him the rules for proper performance of the ritual.* **[92]** *After the ritual had been established in this way, people of all four social classes began making offerings to the ancestors; but the ancestors were unable to digest the food they were given, and so suffered greatly. They appealed to Soma, who sent them to Brahmā; Brahmā told them that the Fire god would help, and Fire said that he and they should eat the offerings together; then they would be able to digest them.*[1] *Therefore at* śrāddha *ceremonies the offering is made first to the Fire god, and then to the ancestors. Bhīṣma concludes by giving further rules governing the performance of the* śrāddha.

**[93]** *Yudhiṣṭhira questions Bhīṣma about fasting Brahmins who consume the oblation at sacrifices;*[2] *Bhīṣma condemns the practice. Then Yudhiṣṭhira asks whether people are right to regard fasting as a form of asceticism; Bhīṣma replies that true asceticism consists of renunciation; however, one should also practise fasting, celibacy and the other virtues.*

**[94]** *Yudhiṣṭhira asks what distinguishes the giver from the receiver when gifts are made to Brahmins. Bhīṣma answers that the receiving Brahmin suffers little harm if the giver is virtuous, but great harm if he is not, and he cites the story of King Vṛṣādarbhi and the seven seers. Vṛṣādarbhi had given his son to the*

1 The process of digestion is considered to be a form of fire.

2 This chapter is almost identical with 12.214.

*seers as a sacrificial gift; now, in a severe drought, the boy died, and the starving seers began to cook his body. Vṛṣādarbhi arrived, and, seeing them in this state, offered them generous gifts of livestock and other goods, but they refused, saying that to accept a king's gift would destroy the merit of their austerities. Then they left to search for food in the forest, abandoning the uncooked body. Vṛṣādarbhi sent his men to them with figs containing hidden gold pieces, but the seers saw through his stratagem and refused to accept them. When Vṛṣādarbhi heard about this he was angry, and to avenge himself he raised from his sacrificial fire a fearful sorceress; he instructed her to find the seers and their companions, and, when she had learnt their names, to slay them.* **[95]** *As the seers wandered, eating fruit and roots, they came upon a wandering ascetic named Śunaḥsakha,*[1] *who appeared well nourished in every limb. They concluded that he must be prospering because, unlike them, he had succeeded in maintaining his Brahmin* dharma *intact. Śunaḥsakha joined them in their search for food, and they all arrived at a beautiful lake; they approached to gather lotus stalks for food, when Vṛṣādarbhi's sorceress appeared. She told them that each of them could gather the stalks after giving her his name. Understanding her purpose, each of them named himself in complex Sanskrit phraseology, and each time she confessed herself unable to learn the name and had to let him pass, until Śunaḥsakha's turn came; when she failed to grasp his name and asked him to repeat it, he struck her on the head with his staff and reduced her to ashes. The seers now gathered lotus stalks into a heap, and then went to perform an offering of water to the ancestors; when they returned, their lotus stalks had disappeared. Each in turn pronounced a solemn imprecation upon the thief, in order to show that he was not the guilty one, until Śunaḥsakha's turn came; he called for the thief to complete his Vedic studies and to marry his daughter to a pious Brahmin. When the seers accused him of the theft, he cheerfully confessed to it, adding that he had done it to test them after protecting them from King Vṛṣādarbhi's sorceress. Revealing that he was in reality Indra, he told them that their lack of greed had won them the eternal realms; they now ascended to heaven with him. Bhīṣma concludes that lack of greed is the highest* dharma.

**[96]** *Now Bhīṣma relates another very similar story. The seers had gone on a pilgrimage accompanied by Indra; after bathing in the Pool of Brahmā they found that their lotus stalks had been stolen; each of them in turn pronounced a solemn*

1 'Friend of a dog'.

*imprecation upon the thief, in order to show that he was not the guilty one, until Indra's turn came; Indra called for the thief to complete his Vedic studies and to marry his daughter to a pious Brahmin. When Agastya demanded the return of the lotus stalks, he explained that his reason for taking them was to prompt the seers into expounding* dharma, *and he begged their pardon.*

**[97]** *Yudhiṣṭhira now asks who established the custom of giving umbrellas and sandals at* śrāddha *ceremonies and other observances. In reply, Bhīṣma cites the dialogue of Jamadagni with the Sun. Jamadagni used to amuse himself by shooting arrows from his bow; his wife Reṇukā would always retrieve them for him. One day she was late in returning; questioned by Jamadagni, she explained that she had had to take shelter because her head and feet had been burnt by the sun. Jamadagni vowed to shoot the sun down from the sky for causing her distress. As he prepared to do so, Sūrya the Sun god approached him in the form of a Brahmin and reminded him of all the benefits the sun brings.* **[98]** *Seeing that Jamadagni was unmoved by his words, he then asked him how he would strike a moving target. Jamadagni answered, 'O Sun, you always remain motionless for a moment after midday; I shall pierce you then!' The Sun now formally sought Jamadagni's protection; granting it, Jamadagni asked him to devise a remedy for the wrong he had done. The Sun presented him with an umbrella and a pair of leather sandals, and told him that from that day forward such gifts would be customary when religious offerings were made.*

**[99]** *Yudhiṣṭhira asks Bhīṣma to tell him the rewards that come from planting gardens and digging ponds. Bhīṣma praises ponds highly and lists the rewards that the owners of ponds experience; he urges Yudhiṣṭhira to make gifts of water, which is the finest of gifts. Then he speaks of the rewards for planting trees, whose flowers and fruit satisfy men in this world, and which, like sons, rescue the planter when he reaches the other world.*

**[100]** *Now Yudhiṣṭhira asks Bhīṣma to teach him the* dharma *of householders, and how they should act in order to prosper. In reply, Bhīṣma cites the dialogue of Kṛṣṇa Vāsudeva with Earth. Kṛṣṇa had asked Earth the same question; Earth had listed the offerings that a householder should make, and emphasized the duty of hospitality towards Brahmins, guests, elders and friends; a householder should also put food out twice daily for dogs, birds and people of the lowest class.*

**[101]** *Yudhiṣṭhira asks about the gift of light*[1] *and the rewards it brings. In*

1 i.e. lamps, another favoured gift (cf. chapter 67 above).

*reply, Bhīṣma cites the dialogue of Manu with the ascetic Suvarṇa. Suvarṇa had asked Manu about offerings of flowers, and Manu in turn had cited the dialogue between Śukra Uśanas and the demon Bali. In reply to a question from Bali about the rewards for making gifts of flowers, incense and lamps, Śukra had discoursed on what kinds of flowers and incense are appropriate for what kinds of recipients; then he had praised the giving of lamps and spoken of the rewards such gifts bring, before specifying the offerings most suitable for making to gods, Yakṣas, serpents and other beings.*

**[102]** *Yudhiṣṭhira asks to hear more about such offerings. In reply, Bhīṣma cites the story of the seers Agastya and Bhṛgu and King Nahuṣa. Nahuṣa's asceticism and virtuous deeds had won him the sovereignty of heaven,*[1] *and at first he continued to honour the gods with offerings and other rites; but then he became arrogant, and began to make great seers draw the chariot in which he rode. One day when Agastya's turn fell due, Bhṛgu visited him and suggested that they should act to bring this insult to an end. Agastya reminded him that Nahuṣa was too powerful to curse, because of a boon from Brahmā that whoever came within his sight would come also within his power. Bhṛgu replied that it was Brahmā who had sent him. Today after yoking Agastya to his chariot, Nahuṣa would kick him; this would enable Bhṛgu to curse him to become a snake. Agastya was delighted with the plan.* **[103]** *When Nahuṣa summoned Agastya, Bhṛgu concealed himself in Agastya's matted hair where Nahuṣa could not see him. Nahuṣa applied the goad, yet Agastya did not give way to anger; but then Nahuṣa kicked Agastya in the head with his left foot, and Bhṛgu cursed him to fall to earth as a snake. Nahuṣa appealed for the curse to have an end, and Bhṛgu answered that in the future there would be a king named Yudhiṣṭhira who would release him from it.*[2] *After this, Indra was reinstalled as king of the gods. Bhīṣma adds that it was only because of his earlier pious deeds that Nahuṣa was restored to heaven, and he recommends Yudhiṣṭhira to make gifts of lamps.*

**[104]** *Yudhiṣṭhira asks what befalls those fools who steal the property of Brahmins. In reply, Bhīṣma cites the dialogue of a Caṇḍāla with a Kṣatriya. The Kṣatriya asked the Caṇḍāla why, when he lived among the dust raised by dogs and asses, he was taking such pains to wash away the dust from some cows. The Caṇḍāla answered that once the dust from a herd of cows stolen from*

**1** See 5.9–18.

**2** For the account of how this happened, see 3.173–8.

*a Brahmin fell on some Soma. The Brahmins who drank it went immediately to hell, as did the king for whom they were sacrificing; so too did all those who consumed any of the milk products of those cows. He himself had been living in that place as a devout Brahmin, but some dust from those cows had fallen on the food he had received as alms, and now he was a Caṇḍāla; he asked the Kṣatriya how he might escape from such a state. The Kṣatriya replied that he should give up his life in battle for the sake of a Brahmin; the Caṇḍāla did so, and attained the eternal realms.*

**[105]** *Yudhiṣṭhira asks whether the virtuous all share the same heaven, or whether there are different heavens. Bhīṣma answers that the virtuous go to different heavens according to their deeds, as the wicked go to different hells, and he cites the dialogue of the sage Gautama with Indra. Gautama had reared an orphaned baby elephant; when it was full-grown, Indra assumed the form of King Dhṛtarāṣṭra and seized it. Gautama told him that he would pursue him to the realm of Yama and force him to return the creature; Dhṛtarāṣṭra retorted that he would not go to that realm. Gautama listed realm after realm, promising to reclaim his elephant there, but Dhṛtarāṣṭra made the same response to each. Finally Gautama recognized Indra. Indra agreed to return the elephant to him, and rewarded him by taking both him and his elephant to heaven.*

**[106]** *Yudhiṣṭhira now asks Bhīṣma about asceticism. Bhīṣma replies that there is no form of asceticism superior to fasting, and he cites the dialogue of Bhagīratha with Brahmā. Seeing that Bhagīratha had attained the very highest realm, beyond those of the gods, seers and cattle, Brahmā asked him how he had done so. Bhagīratha listed the sacrifices he had performed, the gifts he had given and the austerities he had undertaken, but added of each that it was not the reason for his reaching such a realm. Then he said that he had accomplished the excellent observance of fasting, which Indra had hidden but Śukra Uśanas had discovered; it was because of this that he had reached the realm of Brahmā.*

**[107]** *Next Yudhiṣṭhira asks Bhīṣma what brings a long span of life, and what a short one; what brings fame and glory? Bhīṣma answers that it is one's conduct that determines these: those whose conduct is wicked never attain great ages, whereas those whose conduct is good live to be a hundred. Then he gives a long list of injunctions for maintaining good conduct.*

**[108]** *Yudhiṣṭhira wishes to know how elder and younger brothers should behave towards each other. Bhīṣma replies that the eldest brother should behave with dignity and wisdom, for his younger brothers are like his pupils. It is the* *eldest brother who brings the lineage to prosperity or ruin. After giving rules for inheritance, Bhīṣma observes that a father outranks ten teachers and a mother ten fathers; on the father's death the eldest son takes his place, and similarly the eldest daughter, or the eldest son's wife, takes the place of the mother.*

**[109]** *Yudhiṣṭhira asks Bhīṣma to tell him about fasting and the rewards it brings. In reply, Bhīṣma cites the answer Aṅgiras gave him when he asked the same question. Aṅgiras spoke of the lengths of time for which people of the different social classes should fast, and the benefits of fasting at different times in the moon's cycle and during different months of the year. Then he described the rewards for maintaining particular regimes of fasting over long periods of time: to do so is equivalent to performing one of the great sacrifices, and secures long years of sensual pleasure in heaven.*

**[110]** *Yudhiṣṭhira remarks that sacrifices can only be performed by kings and princes, since they require great wealth, and he asks what poor people can do to attain the same rewards. In reply, Bhīṣma once again cites Aṅgiras's teachings on fasting; he describes further regimes, specifying in each case the sacrifice to which the regime is equivalent and the heavenly delights that are its reward.*

**[111]** *Yudhiṣṭhira asks which is the best of the sacred bathing-places, where one may be truly cleansed. Bhīṣma replies that it is each person's inner Lake Mānasa, whose waters consist of truth and steadfastness; bathing in it leads to non-covetousness, gentleness, truthfulness, rectitude, non-violence, kindness, self-control and tranquillity. Those who are freed from the sense of 'I', who have passed beyond the pairs of opposites, who have cleansed themselves of the three Sāṃkhya qualities and are intent on renunciation – those men are the purest bathing-places.*

**[112]** *Yudhiṣṭhira asks Bhīṣma what leads a person to heaven or hell, and who accompanies one beyond death. Bhīṣma points out that Bṛhaspati has arrived, and tells Yudhiṣṭhira to put his question to him. Yudhiṣṭhira does so, and Bṛhaspati answers that one is born alone and dies alone; only* dharma *accompanies one beyond death. The man engaged in* dharma *goes to heaven, the one engaged in* adharma *to hell. Yudhiṣṭhira now asks Bṛhaspati a sequence of further questions about the manner in which one acquires a new body after death, and Bṛhaspati answers him. Finally, Yudhiṣṭhira asks about the basis on which living beings experience happiness and unhappiness. Bṛhaspati explains that this depends on their deeds in their former existence, and then catalogues the* *exact sequences of rebirths that have to be endured as a consequence of committing various sins.*

**[113]** *Yudhiṣṭhira asks Bṛhaspati how a man who has sinned can achieve a good outcome for himself. Bṛhaspati replies that by confessing his wrongdoing with his mind fully focused, a man is freed from it like a snake casting off its old skin. Bṛhaspati adds that this is true even if the sinner does not make gifts, but that one who has done wrong can also return to the way of* dharma *by making appropriate gifts; the best gift is food given to Brahmins.*

**[114]** *Yudhiṣṭhira asks which course confers the highest benefit: non-violence, Vedic ritual, meditation, control of the senses, austerities or obedience to the elders. Bṛhaspati answers that these are all ways to* dharma, *but he reserves particular praise for non-violence. Then he ascends to heaven.*

**[115]** *Yudhiṣṭhira observes to Bhīṣma that seers, Brahmins and gods all praise the way of non-violence, and asks how a man who has done harm to others by thought, word or deed can free himself from misery. Bhīṣma agrees that non-violence is the paramount* dharma; *he particularly condemns the eating of meat.* **[116]** *Yudhiṣṭhira asks him to speak further on the demerit of eating meat and the merit of not doing so. Bhīṣma replies that the seers have debated this, and all of them have concluded that it is good to abstain from meat. He himself once again strongly condemns the consumption of meat; he quotes the seer Mārkaṇḍeya as saying that those who eat any meat other than that consecrated in sacrifice go to hell, and adds that abstention from meat leads to heaven.*

**[117]** *Yudhiṣṭhira comments that those who shun all other food in favour of meat are like Rākṣasas, and asks Bhīṣma to continue his discourse on the topic of meat-eating. Bhīṣma allows that for Kṣatriyas it is not sinful to eat meat acquired through hunting, for wild animals have all been consecrated to the deities of the forest. However, there is nothing better than to practise compassion towards all creatures. Non-violence is the highest* dharma, *the highest self-control, the highest gift, the highest asceticism.*

**[118]** *Yudhiṣṭhira asks Bhīṣma what has become of all those who, willingly or unwillingly, were slain in the great battle. In reply, Bhīṣma cites the dialogue of Vyāsa with a creeping insect on a busy road. He asked it from what it was fleeing in haste, and it answered that a large ox-cart was approaching and might kill it. Vyāsa asked whether death might not be preferable to life as an insect; the insect replied that living creatures love whatever form of life they have. Formerly it had been a wicked Śūdra; the Śūdra had, however, honoured his mother, and* *had once paid due honour to a Brahmin guest, and for this reason the insect had retained memory of its former birth, and had hopes of finding happiness once more; it asked Vyāsa for his advice.* **[119]** *Vyāsa told the insect that he would use his ascetic power to rescue it; he assured it that it would be able to achieve an exalted birth. Hearing this, the insect remained motionless upon the road, and so met its end; several births later it had arrived at Kṣatriya status. The Kṣatriya returned to Vyāsa, paid him due respect, and asked what he should do now; Vyāsa answered that he could now attain brahminhood by giving up his life in battle for the sake of cows or Brahmins.* **[120]** *The Kṣatriya undertook austerities, but Vyāsa advised him that a Kṣatriya's observance was to protect his subjects. The Kṣatriya did so, and not long afterwards he passed away and was reborn as a Brahmin. Bhīṣma assures Yudhiṣṭhira that those Kṣatriyas who died at Kurukṣetra have also attained a happy outcome: he should not grieve for them.*

**[121]** *Yudhiṣṭhira asks Bhīṣma whether learning, asceticism or the giving of gifts is the best course. In reply, Bhīṣma cites the dialogue of Maitreya with Vyāsa. Vyāsa, travelling in disguise, visited Maitreya, who gave him a very fine meal, and Vyāsa told him that by making such a gift he had conquered the blessed realms as surely as if he had performed great sacrifices. He praised the giving of gifts very highly.* **[122]** *Maitreya answered that it is asceticism, Vedic learning and birth that make a Brahmin; there is nothing superior to Brahmins, and by making gifts to them one satisfies the ancestors and gods, and earns a great reward.* **[123]** *Vyāsa agreed with Maitreya that asceticism and Vedic learning are superior even to the giving of gifts; he went on to praise all three. Then the two men parted.*

**[124]** *Yudhiṣṭhira asks Bhīṣma about the conduct of virtuous women. In reply, Bhīṣma cites the dialogue of the Kekaya woman Sumanā with the Brahmin lady Śāṇḍilī in heaven.*[1] *Sumanā asked Śāṇḍilī how she had attained her state of radiant sinlessness in the world of the gods, and Śāṇḍilī replied that it was not through asceticism but through devoted service to her husband.*

**[125]** *Yudhiṣṭhira asks whether conciliation or giving gifts is more effective. Bhīṣma replies that some men respond better to one, some to the other, and to illustrate the effectiveness of conciliation he cites the story of the Brahmin seized*

**1** Śāṇḍilī was mentioned briefly as a powerful ascetic woman at 5.111; elsewhere (1.60.19) she is said to be the mother of the Fire god Agni.

*by a Rākṣasa. The Rākṣasa intended to devour the Brahmin, but told him he would free him if he could he could answer the question, 'Why am I so pale and thin?' The Brahmin answered that the Rākṣasa had been subject to a great many disappointments and frustrations: that was why he was so pale and thin. The Rākṣasa now made the Brahmin his friend and released him.*

**[126]** *Yudhiṣṭhira requests Bhīṣma to tell him about Nārāyaṇa in Nārāyaṇa's own presence.*[1] *In reply, Bhīṣma relates how once the seers came to see Kṛṣṇa, who had undertaken a twelve-year observance. They were amazed to see a fire emerge from his mouth; it consumed the entire summit of a mountain before returning to Kṛṣṇa and respectfully touching his feet. Kṛṣṇa then restored the mountain to its normal state with a glance. When the seers asked him to explain what they had seen, he told them that the austerities he was performing were aimed at getting a son;*[2] *they had caused his inner self to take the form of a fire, and it had gone to visit Brahmā and secured from him the boon of a son formed from half of Śiva's fiery energy. Now Nārada, at the request of the other seers, described the great wonder that they had all formerly beheld on Mount Himālaya.*

**[127]** *Bhīṣma relates Nārada's account of the dialogue of Śiva with Umā. Nārada described how Śiva was seated on lovely Mount Himālaya when Umā, approaching from behind, covered his eyes with her hands. At once the world was plunged into darkness and confusion; but then a third eye flared forth on his forehead, setting the forest ablaze and consuming the mountain. Then, seeing that Umā was unhappy at the sight of her father's distress,*[3] *Śiva restored it to its normal state with a glance, and explained that he had created the blaze to rescue the world from the darkness she had caused. Now Umā asked him about his appearance, and* **[128]** *he explained to her the way in which he came to have four faces and a blue throat. In response to further questions, he also explained why he had a bull for his steed and lived in burning-grounds. Then Umā asked him about the characteristics of* dharma, *about the particular* dharmas *of the four classes of society,* **[129]** *about the* dharma *that applies across all the social classes, about the* dharma *of the seers* **[130]** *and that of various kinds of forest-dwellers,* **[131]** *about which acts lead a person of a higher social class to be reborn in a*

1 i.e. in the presence of Kṛṣṇa.

2 Cf. chapters 15–16 above.

3 Umā (Pārvatī) was the daughter of Himālaya.

*lower one and how members of the three lower classes can attain brahminhood,* **[132]** *about which thoughts, words and deeds lead to bondage and which to liberation, about how people's fortunes differ on the basis of their former deeds,* **[133]** *about which acts lead to heaven, which to wisdom or its absence, and which to ill health and impotence, about which acts incur blame and which do not, and what causes some men to be devout and others impious. Śiva answered all her questions.* **[134]** *Now Śiva asked Umā about the* dharma *of women. Umā proposed to consult Gaṅgā and the other rivers before answering,*[1] *but Gaṅgā demurred and asked her to speak on her own authority; Umā then described the* dharma *of women as consisting of devoted service to their husbands. Śiva paid her honour, then dismissed those who were gathered there.*

**[135]** *Yudhiṣṭhira asks Bhīṣma who is the one god, by praising whom one may attain release from the cycle of rebirth. Bhīṣma names Viṣṇu, and recites a thousand names of the god.*[2] *Then he speaks of the great benefits incurred by reciting this hymn.*

**[136]** *Yudhiṣṭhira asks who is deserving of honour. Bhīṣma replies that Brahmins are always deserving of honour, and praises them highly.* **[137]** *Yudhiṣṭhira asks what are the benefits of honouring Brahmins. In reply, Bhīṣma cites the dialogue of the Wind with King Arjuna Kārtavīrya. Arjuna had obtained as a boon that he should be corrected by virtuous people if he was pursuing a wrong course. Once in his chariot he boasted that no one was his equal; a disembodied voice chided him, telling him that Kṣatriyas are dependent on Brahmins. At this he vowed to defeat all the Brahmins; but the Wind addressed him on behalf of the gods and told him to give up such wickedness and honour the Brahmins. Arjuna asked the Wind to teach him about Brahmins.* **[138]** *The Wind listed some of the mighty feats of Brahmins of old to prove their superiority to Kṣatriyas. Arjuna could find nothing to say,* **[139]** *and the Wind began to recount in greater detail some of the deeds he had mentioned. He described how the Brahmin Kaśyapa had used his yogic power to enter and support the earth when the goddess Earth abandoned it and fled; when, thousands of years later, the goddess returned, she became Kaśyapa's daughter. The Wind asked Arjuna to tell him of any Kṣatriya greater than Kaśyapa; Arjuna remained silent. Then the Wind spoke of Utathya, descendant of Aṅgiras, whose wife was abducted by the lord of the*

1 The rivers are all feminine.

2 Cf. the thousand names of Śiva recited in chapter 17 above.

*waters, Varuṇa; Utathya drank up all the waters and forced Varuṇa to return his wife to him. The Wind asked Arjuna to tell him of any Kṣatriya greater than Utathya,* [**140**] *but Arjuna remained silent. Now the Wind described how, after the demons had defeated the gods, the Brahmin Agastya used his ascetic power to burn them, forcing them out of heaven and confining them to the underworld. The Wind asked Arjuna to tell him of any Kṣatriya greater than Agastya; Arjuna remained silent. Then the Wind told him how the gods were attacked and overwhelmed by the Khalin demons, whose dead returned to life if they were bathed in a nearby lake; they appealed to the Brahmin Vasiṣṭha, who burnt up the demons with his ascetic power and caused the river Gaṅgā to sweep away the lake. The Wind asked Arjuna to tell him of any Kṣatriya greater than Vasiṣṭha,* [**141**] *but Arjuna remained silent. Next the Wind described how, in a battle between the gods and demons, the demon Rāhu*[1] *had extinguished the light of both sun and moon, bringing darkness and imperilling the gods; at the gods' request, the Brahmin Atri became a new sun and moon, and he burnt the demons and helped the gods to victory. The Wind asked Arjuna to tell him of any Kṣatriya greater than Atri; Arjuna remained silent. Then the Wind spoke of the Brahmin Cyavana, who forced Indra and the other gods to share their Soma with the Aśvins by creating a terrifying demon named Mada;*[2] *when the gods acceded to his demand, he recalled Mada and distributed him between dice, hunting, liquor and women. The Wind asked Arjuna to tell him of any Kṣatriya greater than Cyavana,* [**142**] *but Arjuna remained silent. The Wind now recounted how, after their encounter with Mada, the gods lost the earth to Cyavana and heaven to the Kapas.*[3] *Brahmā advised them to approach the Brahmins for help; the Brahmins agreed to bring the Kapas down to earth and defeat them, and they undertook rituals for this purpose. When they learnt of this, the Kapas sent an envoy named Dhanin*[4] *to try to dissuade them, but the Brahmins answered that they were themselves considered gods and were therefore the Kapas' enemies. The Kapas attacked them, but the Brahmins destroyed them with their sacred fires. It was after this that the gods attained immortality*

**1** The demon of the eclipse: see 1.17.

**2** 'Intoxication'.

**3** Nothing seems to be known of this class of demons: they are mentioned nowhere else in the *Mahābhārata*.

**4** 'Wealthy'.

*and honour in the three worlds. Hearing this story, Arjuna Kārtavīrya praised Brahmins and vowed always to honour them.*

**[143]** *Yudhiṣṭhira again asks Bhīṣma the benefits of honouring Brahmins. Bhīṣma replies that Kṛṣṇa will be able to answer him in full; his own strength is failing, and he thinks his death is not far off. He goes on to praise Kṛṣṇa highly as supreme lord.* **[144]** *Yudhiṣṭhira puts his question to Kṛṣṇa. In reply, Kṛṣṇa cites the answer he gave his son Pradyumna when he asked the same question after some Brahmins had angered him. Kṛṣṇa told Pradyumna of the greatness of Brahmins, and warned him never to be angry with them; then he told him of the time the fierce seer Durvāsas had stayed as a guest in his house.*[1] *One day Durvāsas would eat an enormous amount, another day very little; he would laugh or weep without cause, and on one occasion he had burnt the beds, sheets and serving-maids. One day he had demanded* pāyasa;[2] *after eating a little he had instructed Kṛṣṇa to smear his body with the leftover portion, while he himself besmeared Pradyumna's mother Rukmiṇī. He had then yoked Rukmiṇī to a chariot and used the goad on her as she drew him along. However, both Kṛṣṇa and Rukmiṇī had continued to treat him with great respect, and Durvāsas now praised both of them highly and blessed them. In particular, he told Kṛṣṇa that he would be in no danger of death through the limbs that he had smeared with* pāyasa, *though he noted that these did not include the soles of his feet. Kṛṣṇa tells Yudhiṣṭhira always to honour Brahmins.*

**[145]** *Yudhiṣṭhira requests Kṛṣṇa to pass on to him the learning he acquired from Durvāsas, and Kṛṣṇa tells him about the Śatarudrīya hymn*[3] *which he recites on rising every morning. Composed by Brahmā, it praises Śiva's greatness. When Śiva destroyed Dakṣa's sacrifice,*[4] *the gods placated him by reciting it; subsequently he destroyed the triple city of the demons and paralysed Indra's arm. Kṛṣṇa explains that Durvāsas is actually a form of Śiva.* **[146]** *Then he tells Yudhiṣṭhira of Śiva's greatness and his many names.*

**[147]** *Now Yudhiṣṭhira asks Bhīṣma whether direct perception or Vedic authority is the better basis for resolving doubts. Bhīṣma answers that only fools give primacy to direct perception; the single true underlying cause of things can*

**1** Cf. the similar story at 3.245–7; also chapters 52–6 above.

**2** A sweet dish made of rice boiled in milk.

**3** A Vedic hymn to Rudra (Śiva).

**4** See 12.274.

*only be understood through long yogic meditation. He advises Yudhiṣṭhira to take his doubts to those whose understanding is based on the Vedas and who have put aside wealth and pleasure to concentrate on* dharma *alone. Yudhiṣṭhira asks how there can be one* dharma *if the Vedas, direct perception and a person's conduct constitute three different authorities; Bhīṣma replies that all three point to a single way, which consists of non-violence, truth, non-anger and the giving of gifts. He urges Yudhiṣṭhira to pursue the way of the Brahmins and to honour them.*

**[148]** *Yudhiṣṭhira asks the consequences of abjuring and observing* dharma; *Bhīṣma answers that the former leads to hell, the latter to heaven. At Yudhiṣṭhira's request he then describes the behaviour that characterizes the virtuous and the vicious. To conceal sin causes it to increase, so one should rid oneself of any sin by confessing it before virtuous people.*

**[149]** *Yudhiṣṭhira remarks that men never attain anything unless they are due to do so: evildoers may be rich or poor, and so may the learned and the unlearned. Bhīṣma replies that nothing can grow if no seed is sown: one should practise austerities, give gifts, abstain from violence and live virtuously, for this is what will determine one's future condition.* **[150]** *It is Time that brings men good and bad outcomes, but Time can never confer* dharma *on one who has practised* adharma; *indeed, Time protects* dharma *from* adharma.

**[151]** *Yudhiṣṭhira asks Bhīṣma what leads to welfare and freedom from sin. Bhīṣma replies that one should recite the names of the host of gods and seers every dawn and dusk.* **[152]** *Then he falls silent. Vyāsa tells him that Yudhiṣṭhira has now been restored to his own nature, and requests him to give the Pāṇḍavas and Kṛṣṇa leave to return to the city. Bhīṣma does so, blessing Yudhiṣṭhira and asking him to return when the sun resumes its northern course.*[1] *Yudhiṣṭhira promises to do so, and returns with all his followers to Hāstinapura.*

## BHĪṢMA'S ASCENT TO HEAVEN

**[153]** *Yudhiṣṭhira takes up the kingship. Then after fifty nights, seeing that the sun has turned northward, he sets out with a large retinue, carrying with him the materials for Bhīṣma's cremation. He finds Bhīṣma attended by Vyāsa, Nārada*

1 See 6.116.13 and note. Bhīṣma has chosen to defer his death until the winter solstice.

*and Asita Devala, and by those kings who have survived the slaughter. Bhīṣma greets him and confirms that the time of his death is now, at last, at hand. Then he addresses Dhṛtarāṣṭra, telling him that the Pāṇḍavas are like sons to him, and that he should not grieve for his own wicked sons. Next he offers praise to Kṛṣṇa, who gives him leave to die. Finally he takes his leave of the Pāṇḍavas, embraces his friends, and adjures Yudhiṣṭhira always to honour Brahmins.*

**[154]** *Bhīṣma brings his vital breath under yogic control; the onlookers are amazed to observe his body become free from its wounds. Then his life breath emerges from the top of his head and shoots up to heaven like a great comet. The Pāṇḍavas perform the proper rites and cremate Bhīṣma's body; then they go to the bank of the Gaṅgā to make the offering of water to him. The goddess Gaṅgā, Bhīṣma's mother, appears and laments his death, but Kṛṣṇa reminds her that her son's birth as a human was the result of a curse;*[1] *he assures her that he has now attained heaven, and urges her not to grieve. Then he and the other lords of men take their leave and depart.*

1 See 1.91–3.

# THE HORSE SACRIFICE

## THE HORSE SACRIFICE

[1] *Yudhiṣṭhira collapses with grief on the bank of the Gaṅgā, but Dhṛtarāṣṭra tells him not to grieve: there is no reason for him to do so, whereas Dhṛtarāṣṭra himself and Gāndhārī have lost their hundred sons through Dhṛtarāṣṭra's foolishness in ignoring the advice of Vidura.*

[2] *Kṛṣṇa advises Yudhiṣṭhira to give up his grief and take up the Kṣatriya* dharma, *but Yudhiṣṭhira replies that after killing Bhīṣma and Karṇa he can find no peace; he wishes to retire to the forest. Vyāsa too reminds Yudhiṣṭhira that he is well acquainted with all the* dharmas *that apply to him: why does he continue to behave in so deluded a way?* [3] *Vyāsa adds that the sin incurred from evil deeds can be removed by means of sacrifices, austerities and the giving of gifts, and he advises Yudhiṣṭhira to perform great sacrifices, in particular the horse sacrifice. Yudhiṣṭhira agrees that the horse sacrifice would purify the earth itself. However, his war with Duryodhana has destroyed the earth and exhausted his treasury; without wealth he cannot perform such a rite. Vyāsa explains that there is much wealth to be found at Mount Himālaya, left there by Brahmins at the sacrifice of King Marutta.* [4] *Yudhiṣṭhira asks to hear about Marutta, and Vyāsa explains that he was the son of the righteous King Avikṣit in the line of Ikṣvāku, and relates how he came to Mount Meru on the northern side of Himālaya and performed a great sacrifice there using numerous vessels of gold.*

[5] *At Yudhiṣṭhira's request, Vyāsa tells the story of Marutta in greater detail. — Aṅgiras's two sons Bṛhaspati and Saṃvarta are great rivals. On achieving sovereignty, Indra appoints Bṛhaspati as his household priest, and instructs him not to act as priest for Marutta, who is his own great rival.* [6] *Marutta decides to undertake a sacrifice and approaches Bṛhaspati with a request to act as priest,*

*reminding him that he has inherited this role from his father, but Bṛhaspati refuses. Meeting Nārada, the humiliated king tells him what has happened; Nārada advises him to approach Saṃvarta, who lives in Vārāṇasī in the guise of a madman. He tells Marutta how to win Saṃvarta's favour, and Marutta follows his instructions.*

[7] *Saṃvarta tells Marutta that he should approach his brother Bṛhaspati. When he learns that Bṛhaspati has already refused, he agrees to act as priest for Marutta; however, he warns him that this will greatly anger Indra.*

[8] *On Saṃvarta's instructions, Marutta travels to Muñjavat, one of Mount Himālaya's peaks, where Kubera's attendants guard great deposits of gold; he pays homage to Śiva, and receives gold for the performance of his sacrifice. Bṛhaspati is greatly distressed when he hears this.*

[9] *Indra learns the cause of Bṛhaspati's distress, and sends the Fire god as a messenger to Marutta to tell him that Bṛhaspati will, after all, act as his priest. But Marutta rejects the offer, and Saṃvarta warns Fire that he will burn him with the fire of his terrible eye if he ever brings such a message again. Fire returns to Indra and tells him what has happened; he refuses to carry any further messages.* [10] *Indra now sends a Gandharva named Dhṛtarāṣṭra to Marutta; when Marutta repeats that only Saṃvarta will be his priest, Dhṛtarāṣṭra warns him that Indra will attack him, and a terrifying storm approaches. Marutta asks Saṃvarta to invite Indra to attend his sacrifice, and Saṃvarta does so. Indra arrives, professes himself pleased, and accedes to Saṃvarta's request to direct the conduct of the ritual. The sacrifice takes place with great splendour, and Marutta distributes heaps of gold. — Now Vyāsa tells Yudhiṣṭhira that he should take this gold for his own sacrifice, and Yudhiṣṭhira resolves to do so.*

[11] *Yudhiṣṭhira is still afflicted with grief at the slaughter of his kinsfolk; Kṛṣṇa tells him that he needs to understand the enemy within himself, and describes the battle between Vṛtra and Indra. Vṛtra had entered and pervaded the earth, and had taken over smell, its sensory property,*[1] *so that everything smelt bad. When Indra attacked him with his thunderbolt, he had entered water, then in turn light, air and ether, taking over the sensory property of each. Finally he had entered Indra himself, but Indra had killed the Vṛtra within himself by means of an invisible thunderbolt.*

[12] *Kṛṣṇa tells Yudhiṣṭhira that the time is near for him to fight the battle*

1 See 12.224–5, 12.239.

*with himself, which has to be fought with the mind and without allies. He must triumph, and rule his ancestral kingdom.* **[13]** *Kṛṣṇa speaks of the mortal danger posed by desire, which is very hard to overcome, and urges Yudhiṣṭhira to practise* dharma *by performing a horse sacrifice at which munificent gifts are given to the Brahmins.* **[14]** *Comforted and encouraged by the words of seers and Brahmins, and by his brothers, Yudhiṣṭhira now gives up his grief and begins to rule the earth. Together with Dhṛtarāṣṭra he performs the last rites for the fallen warriors.*

**[15]** *Kṛṣṇa and Arjuna pass much time together in Indraprastha. Kṛṣṇa observes that it is through* dharma *that Yudhiṣṭhira has conquered the earth, regained his kingdom and slain Duryodhana; he adds that now he himself plans to return to Dvārakā.* **[16]** *Arjuna reminds Kṛṣṇa of everything he taught him before the great battle,*[1] *and confesses that he has forgotten it all. Kṛṣṇa answers that he cannot repeat it a second time, but that he will tell Arjuna what was once said to him on the same topic by a Brahmin who came from the heavenly realms, and who cited the instruction that Kāśyapa had received from a certain great ascetic.*

**[17]** *Kṛṣṇa begins his account of the Brahmin's discourse. When a man's good* karma *is exhausted, he begins to indulge in harmful practices that lead to death or even suicide. At death the soul leaves the body, accompanied by its collection of good and bad deeds. This world is the world of deeds, and it is in this world that creatures attain the rewards of their good and bad deeds. But bad deeds also lead to hell, which is very hard to escape from; and though good deeds lead to heaven, once they have been exhausted one falls back to earth again.* **[18]** *One's good and bad deeds cannot be eliminated: they will inevitably bear their fruit. When the soul enters and animates a new body, that person receives the fruit of his former deeds; and as these deeds come to be exhausted, new ones accumulate for as long as he remains ignorant of the Yoga of release. Happiness can be achieved only through virtue, and virtuous people keep the world on the paths of* dharma, *but the* yogī *who attains release is greater than the merely virtuous.* **[19]** *The man who attains release must be free of all passions; his senses conquered, he passes beyond the pairs of opposites. The way to release is through Yoga, through which one attains* brahman. *Kṛṣṇa adds that this great mystery leads to the highest felicity.*

1 In the *Bhagavadgītā* (6.23–40). Chapters 16–50 of the present book are known as the *Anugītā* ('subsidiary *gītā*').

**[20]** *Now Kṛṣṇa cites the dialogue of a Brahmin with his wife. The wife asked her husband what realms awaited her, since he had ceased to perform the sacrificial rituals. He answered that instead of vain rituals he had seen* brahman *within himself. Then he spoke of an internal sacrifice in which the objects of the senses, mind and understanding are sacrificed into flames which are the respective organs, by priests who are the possessors of those organs.* **[21]** *He gave a second symbolic account of sacrifice, and spoke of the relationship between speech and the mind;* **[22]** *a third, and spoke of the relationship between the mind and the senses;* **[23]** *a fourth, and spoke of the relationship between the various vital breaths.* **[24]** *He expounded Nārada's teaching on the vital breaths;* **[25]** *then he gave a fifth symbolic account of sacrifice, in which the objects of the senses are offered up in the sacrifice of Yoga.*

**[26]** *Kṛṣṇa continues the Brahmin's dialogue with his wife. The Brahmin described to his wife how the gods, seers, serpents and demons approached Prajāpati for instruction. To all he proclaimed the sacred syllable 'Om', which is* brahman, *and all went their separate ways to interpret it in the manner of their kind: the serpents as biting, the demons as deceit, the gods as giving and the seers as self-control. As a being acts in the world, so he becomes.* **[27]** *The Brahmin said that he had succeeded in crossing the dangerous badland of this world, and had entered the great and wonderful forest that leads to Brahmā.* **[28]** *He emphasized that he was free from desire and anger, and cited the dialogue of an ascetic with a sacrificial priest about to sacrifice a goat; the ascetic taught the priest the way of final release, and the priest proceeded with his sacrifice freed from delusion.*

**[29]** *Kṛṣṇa continues the Brahmin's dialogue with his wife. The Brahmin told how King Arjuna Kārtavīrya asked the ocean to name a warrior to equal him, and the ocean had named Rāma Jāmadagnya; Arjuna attacked Rāma, but Rāma overcame and slew him. Many of the remaining Kṣatriyas fled; their lineages became debased, and Rāma continued to slaughter them. His ancestors urged him to stop,* **[30]** *and cited the story of King Alarka, who, having subjugated the whole earth by force of arms, proposed to subjugate his organs of sense, mind and intelligence in the same way, but who in the end did so through Yoga. The ancestors had implored Rāma to abandon his violence and undertake austerities, and he had done so.*

**[31]** *Kṛṣṇa continues the Brahmin's dialogue with his wife. The Brahmin listed nine faults and cited the verses sung by King Ambarīṣa, who regarded acquisitiveness as the hardest fault to overcome, but who succeeded in ridding* *himself of it.* **[32]** *Next he cited the dialogue of King Janaka with a certain Brahmin. Janaka had ordered the Brahmin into exile outside his domain; the Brahmin asked him to state the extent of his domain, and Janaka came to understand that both everything and nothing came within it. The Brahmin revealed that he was Dharma, come to test Janaka.*

**[33]** *Kṛṣṇa continues the Brahmin's dialogue with his wife. The Brahmin told his wife that he pervaded the universe, and that she should have no fear for the next world, for it was to himself that she would come.* **[34]** *At his wife's request, he gave her further instruction. Kṛṣṇa concludes his account by explaining that the Brahmin is his own mind, the wife his own intelligence, and that he himself is the self.*

**[35]** *Next Kṛṣṇa cites the dialogue of a teacher with his pupil, in which the teacher expounded Brahmā's teachings before an assembly of great seers. Brahmā stated that the entire universe has its origin in truth, and said that by pursuing the four different stages of life a man would come to understand the creation and destruction of all beings.* **[36]** *He spoke of the three Sāṃkhya qualities, and discoursed on Darkness,* **[37]** *then on Passion,* **[38]** *then on Goodness.* **[39]** *After speaking further of the three qualities, which are all-pervasive, he described how to attain liberation from them.* **[40]** *Next he spoke of the Great Self,* **[41]** *and of the sense of 'I'.*

**[42]** *Kṛṣṇa continues the teachings of Brahmā. Brahmā spoke of the five elements and the organs, objects and presiding deities corresponding to them. He said that the man who overcomes the three qualities and the five elements gains the highest place in heaven.* **[43]** *Next he listed beings that are the foremost in the class to which they belong and the characteristics of various entities; he also spoke further of the elements and the corresponding sense organs and deities.* **[44]** *He gave another list of beings that stand first in their class, and stated that he who rids himself of the sense of 'I' is freed from his sins.* **[45]** *He spoke of life as being like a wheel: the man who knows how to set it in motion and how to stop it attains the highest good. He gave rules for the life of the virtuous householder,* **[46]** *the student's life of holy celibacy and the life of the forest-dweller, the observance of which leads to heaven; then he described the way of the renouncer, which confers final release.*

**[47]** *Kṛṣṇa continues the teachings of Brahmā. Brahmā spoke of* brahman *and how it may be attained,* **[48]** *and of Sāṃkhya doctrine. The seers then asked him to resolve their doubts as to which is the highest* dharma*;* **[49]** *Brahmā* *answered that it is non-violence. Then he continued to expound Sāṃkhya,* [50] *ending by urging the seers to cultivate serenity. Kṛṣṇa tells Arjuna that the teacher whose exposition of Brahmā's teachings he has been citing told his pupil to follow the same advice, and that by doing so the pupil arrived where grief is no more. Questioned by Arjuna, Kṛṣṇa says that he himself is the teacher, and the mind is his pupil. He tells Arjuna to follow the instruction he has given him. Then the two men prepare to travel back to Hāstinapura, so that Kṛṣṇa can take leave of Yudhiṣṭhira and return to Dvārakā.*

[51] *Kṛṣṇa and Arjuna mount Kṛṣṇa's chariot and set out for Hāstinapura; on the way, Arjuna praises Kṛṣṇa highly as the supreme lord. On arrival they pay their respects to Dhṛtarāṣṭra, Gāndhārī, Kuntī, Yudhiṣṭhira and Bhīma. The next day they approach Yudhiṣṭhira, and Arjuna formally asks leave for Kṛṣṇa to depart for Dvārakā to see his father. Yudhiṣṭhira at once grants this request; he bestows wealth on Kṛṣṇa, and asks him to return for the coming horse sacrifice. Kṛṣṇa then sets out for Dvārakā, taking his sister Subhadrā with him and accompanied by Sātyaki.*

[52] *After travelling some distance, Kṛṣṇa encounters the mighty sage Uttaṅka, who is performing austerities in a desert region. Uttaṅka asks Kṛṣṇa whether his efforts to bring about peace between the Kauravas and Pāṇḍavas*[1] *had met with success; when Kṛṣṇa tells him that, on the contrary, almost everyone has been killed, Uttaṅka is enraged and announces that he is going to curse Kṛṣṇa. Concerned that this would destroy Uttaṅka's ascetic merit, Kṛṣṇa asks him first to listen to what he has to say.* [53] *Bidden by Uttaṅka to speak, Kṛṣṇa says that, as the eternal god of gods, he is in all beings and they in him. When he exists as a god he acts as a god, and similarly for all other classes of being. Existing as a man, he had implored the Kauravas to make peace, but despite his efforts they had fallen in battle and gone to heaven, while the Pāṇḍavas had achieved great renown.*

[54] *At Uttaṅka's request Kṛṣṇa shows him his divine form. Then, after resuming his human appearance, he tells Uttaṅka to ask for a boon, and Uttaṅka requests that water may appear wherever he wishes it. Kṛṣṇa answers, 'Whenever you desire it, think of me,' and leaves for Dvārakā. Uttaṅka, desiring water, thinks of Kṛṣṇa. At this a filthy, naked Caṇḍāla appears, urinating profusely; he offers Uttaṅka the urine to drink. When Uttaṅka refuses, he disappears.*

1 As described in Book 5, 'Perseverance'.

*Kṛṣṇa arrives once more, and Uttaṅka remonstrates with him; Kṛṣṇa reveals that the Caṇḍāla was Indra and his urine the nectar of immortality. He tells Uttaṅka that he committed a great wrong in refusing it, but promises as a new boon that whenever he desires water, rain-clouds called the Clouds of Uttaṅka will appear. To this day, clouds that bring rain to the desert are known as the Clouds of Uttaṅka.*

[55] — *Janamejaya asks to hear about Uttaṅka's asceticism, and Vaiśampāyana narrates. Uttaṅka was deeply devoted to his teacher, Gautama, who held him in such great affection that he never granted him leave to depart on completion of his studies. Without realizing it, Uttaṅka became an old man. When he discovered this, he wept, and his tears burnt the hands of Gautama's lovely daughter, who tried to catch them. Learning the reason for Uttaṅka's distress, Gautama immediately gave him leave to go; he refused to accept any gift in fee, changed Uttaṅka into a young man of sixteen, and gave him his daughter in marriage. But when Uttaṅka asked Gautama's wife Ahalyā what gift she desired, she requested the earrings of the wife of Saudāsa the man-eating king, and he left to fetch them. Hearing what Ahalyā had done, Gautama feared that Saudāsa would kill Uttaṅka, and agreed to grant him protection.*

[56] *Uttaṅka met King Saudāsa, who at once announced his intention of eating him. Uttaṅka agreed, on condition that he first receive the gift he was seeking. When Saudāsa learnt what it was, he told Uttaṅka to make the request direct to the queen. Uttaṅka did so; the queen told him that her earrings were so marvellous that the very celestials kept trying to take them from her. She asked Uttaṅka to bring some sign from the king.*

[57] *Uttaṅka received a sign from Saudāsa and presented it to the queen; she gave him the earrings. He then asked Saudāsa whether, as a friend, he would advise him to return to him as had been agreed, and Saudāsa advised against doing so. Uttaṅka now left with the earrings, but on the way they were taken by a serpent while he gathered fruit to eat. His efforts to dig a way into the underworld with his staff were unsuccessful, but Indra arrived and helped him. Once he was inside, the Fire god approached him in the form of a horse; he produced so much smoke from the pores of his body that the underworld was plunged into darkness. The serpents, discovering what the matter was, honoured Uttaṅka and returned the earrings to him, and he went and presented them to Ahalyā.*

[58] — *Kṛṣṇa and Sātyaki continue their journey, finally arriving at Dvārakā, where great festivities are under way on Mount Raivataka. Both men enter their*

*dwellings. Kṛṣṇa greets his parents and answers the questions his father Vasudeva puts to him about the great battle.* **[59]** *He tells Vasudeva how for ten days the Kauravas were led by Bhīṣma and the Pāṇḍavas by Śikhaṇḍin, till finally Bhīṣma fell at the hands of Śikhaṇḍin and Arjuna and lay on a bed of arrows awaiting the time of his death; how the next commanders were Droṇa and Dhṛṣṭadyumna, and how after five days Dhṛṣṭadyumna slew Droṇa; how Karṇa succeeded Droṇa as commander of the Kauravas, only to be killed by Arjuna after two days of fighting; how Śalya then took command, but was slain by Yudhiṣṭhira; how on the collapse of the Kaurava force Duryodhana fled and hid in a lake, but fell in single combat with Bhīma; and how Aśvatthāman massacred the surviving members of the Pāṇḍava army by night. The Vṛṣṇis are filled with grief and joy and pain at his account.*

**[60]** *Kṛṣṇa had omitted the death of Abhimanyu from his narration to avoid causing Vasudeva terrible sorrow, but Subhadrā now demands that he tell the story. She and Vasudeva both fall to the ground in their grief, and Vasudeva insists on hearing how his grandson died; he hopes that he fought bravely. Kṛṣṇa answers that if Abhimanyu had fought one against one he would never have been slain. However, he was surrounded by furious foes when Arjuna was engaged elsewhere; even then he killed many of his enemies before perishing. Kṛṣṇa assures Vasudeva that his grandson has certainly attained heaven; therefore he should not grieve. He describes how the women had lamented after Abhimanyu's fall, and how Kuntī had comforted his pregnant widow Uttarā, urging her not to grieve. Vasudeva too should put an end to his grief.* **[61]** *Now Vasudeva and the other Vṛṣṇis perform* śrāddha *ceremonies for Abhimanyu, and Kṛṣṇa also performs funeral rites for him, with munificent gifts to the Brahmins.*

*In Hāstinapura the Pāṇḍavas too are grieving; Uttarā will not eat, and people worry lest she should lose her baby. But Vyāsa arrives to reassure them that she will give birth to a mighty hero who will rule the earth, as Kṛṣṇa had formerly prophesied.*[1] *He urges Yudhiṣṭhira to perform the horse sacrifice. Then he vanishes.* **[62]** *Yudhiṣṭhira now reminds his brothers of Vyāsa's words concerning the treasure of Marutta,*[2] *and asks Bhīma how it may be obtained. Bhīma agrees that this treasure will allow them to achieve their goal, and suggests that if they offer worship to Śiva, the fierce servants who guard the treasure for*

**1** See 10.16.1–8.

**2** See chapters 3–10 above.

*him will be willing to let them take it. The other brothers concur, and so in due course the Pāṇḍavas set out with an army.*

**[63]** *They travel along in great splendour until they reach the mountains, where the treasure is to be found. There they set up their camp; then Yudhiṣṭhira instructs the Brahmins whom he has brought with him to determine an auspicious day and constellation for his purpose. They answer that that very day is an auspicious one. So both Brahmins and Pāṇḍavas fast, and the Pāṇḍavas spend the night listening to priestly discourses.* **[64]** *In the morning Yudhiṣṭhira, acting on the Brahmins' instructions, has his household priest*[1] *make various kinds of offerings to Śiva and his servants, and to Kubera, Maṇibhadra and the other Yakṣas. Then, preceded by Vyāsa and continuing to make offerings, he travels to the place of the treasure, and orders his men to dig. Vast riches are uncovered and loaded on to thousands of camels, horses, elephants, carts, chariots, asses and men. After offering further worship to Śiva, they slowly return in very short stages to Hāstinapura, weighed down by this massive treasure.*

**[65]** *Meanwhile Kṛṣṇa and a party of Vṛṣṇis travel to Hāstinapura for the coming horse sacrifice. They are greeted by Dhṛtarāṣṭra and Vidura, and take up residence in the city. It is at this time that Uttarā gives birth to Parikṣit; but because of Aśvatthāman's use of the Weapon of Brahmā's Head*[2] *he is stillborn, and the townspeople's great roar of joy is cut short. Kṛṣṇa, hurrying to the women's quarters, is greeted by Kuntī, who implores him to carry out his promise and revive Parikṣit; then she falls to the ground. Kṛṣṇa comforts her.* **[66]** *Subhadrā too laments greatly that the son of her beloved son Abhimanyu should have been born dead. She begs Kṛṣṇa to do what he vowed to do: to thwart Aśvatthāman by reviving Uttarā's son.* **[67]** *To the joy of the womenfolk, Kṛṣṇa agrees. He hastens to the lying-in chamber, which he finds very well equipped. Uttarā greets him, then pours out her grief and implores him to revive the child.*

Vaiśaṃpāyana spoke:

**[68]** Poor Uttarā lamented pitifully; then in her wretchedness she fell to the ground like a mad woman, so great was her longing for her son. It grieved Kuntī to see her lying there after losing all her family and kin,

1 Dhaumya.

2 See 10.13–16.

and she and all the other Bhārata women cried aloud, so that for a time the Pāṇḍavas' dwelling seemed like a place to be shunned, O king, for it resounded with the cries of the afflicted. And for a time, heroic lord of kings, Virāṭa's daughter Uttarā was overwhelmed with despair in her grief at the loss of her son. But then, regaining consciousness, bull-like heir of Bharata, she lifted the child on to her lap and spoke to him.

'You are the son of a man well acquainted with *dharma*, but all you know is *adharma*, for you offer no greeting to this Vṛṣṇi hero! Go to your father, son, and tell him what I say: "How very hard it is, O hero, for living things to die when their time comes; see, here I am today bereft of you my husband and also of this son of mine. I ought to die, for my fortunes have been dashed and I have lost everything I had; and yet I live. It would be better, strong-armed warrior, for me to take my leave of Yudhiṣṭhira lord of *dharma*, and swallow deadly poison or enter fire."

'How hard it is to die, son; see, I am bereft of son and husband, and yet this heart of mine does not shatter into a thousand pieces. My son, arise: behold, here is your father's father's sorrowing mother Kuntī, distraught in her woe and desolation, drowning in a sea of grief. And here is noble Draupadī, princess of Pāñcāla, and here the poor Sātvata lady Subhadrā; and here am I myself, as griefstricken as a doe shot by a hunter. Arise, and look upon the face of the wise lord of the worlds; look upon lotus-eyed Kṛṣṇa as once you would have looked on your restless-eyed father.'

As Uttarā lay on the ground lamenting, the other women all helped her to sit up; then the Matsya king's daughter composed herself once more, joined her hands together and greeted lotus-eyed Kṛṣṇa from where she sat. That bull-like hero had heard her great lament; now he touched water, and then drew out the Weapon of Brahmā from the child.[1] And the pure, invincible prince of Daśārha promised him life, and said, in a voice that resounded through the whole universe, 'Uttarā, my words are never false; this will come to pass. See me bring him to life before the eyes of all. As I have never uttered falsehood, even in a trivial

1 This was the celestial weapon that Aśvatthāman had used to cause Parikṣit to be stillborn: see 10.15.11 ff. Of course it was not a physical weapon, but rather a channelling of divine power.

matter, as I have never turned away in battle, so let this one live! As I love *dharma*, as I greatly love Brahmins, so let this son of Abhimanyu, born dead, now live! As I have never known discord between myself and Arjuna, by this truth let this dead child live! As truth and *dharma* always have their basis in me, so let this dead child of Abhimanyu live! As I slew Kaṃsa and Keśin according to *dharma*, by this truth let this child here live once more!' Great king, when Kṛṣṇa Vāsudeva spoke these words, the child gained consciousness and began little by little to stir.

[**69**] When Kṛṣṇa drew out the Weapon of Brahmā, king, your father's fiery energy lit up the whole dwelling. The waiting Rākṣasas all fled the house and vanished, and a voice in the air said, 'Bravo, Kṛṣṇa Keśava, bravo!' The blazing Weapon returned to Grandfather Brahmā, and your father began to breathe, O lord of men; the child exerted his energy and strength to move his limbs.

Then the Bhārata women rejoiced, O king, and at Kṛṣṇa's direction they asked Brahmins to pronounce blessings. All the joyful womenfolk of the lion-like Bhāratas praised Kṛṣṇa the stirrer of men, like shipwrecked travellers rescued by a boat; Kuntī, Draupadī, Subhadrā, Uttarā and all the other women rejoiced in their hearts. Then wrestlers, actors, prizefighters, storytellers, bedside attendants and throngs of Sūta and Māgadha bards all praised the stirrer of men, O bull-like heir of Bharata, and uttered blessings praising the Kuru lineage. In due time happy Uttarā too arose, and with her son she paid her respects to Yadu's heir; he, pleased, bestowed a wealth of jewels on her, as did the other tiger-like Vṛṣṇis. Lord Kṛṣṇa, keeper of his word, now gave your father his name, great king, saying, 'Since this son of Abhimanyu was born when his lineage had failed (*parikṣīṇa*), let his name be Parikṣit.'

O lord of men, as time went by, your father began to grow, delighting the hearts of all; he was one month old, Bhārata hero, when the Pāṇḍavas arrived with their great treasure. When the bull-like Vṛṣṇi heroes heard of their arrival, they decked the city of Hāstinapura with masses of garlands and lovely banners and numerous standards; the citizens too decked out their dwellings, lord of men. Vidura commanded many forms of worship to be performed in the temples for the benefit of Pāṇḍu's sons. The royal highways were decorated with flowers, and the city resounded with pleasant sounds like the roar of the ocean's swell; dancers danced and singers sang, till Hāstinapura seemed like Kubera's city of Alakā, adorned by thousands of male bards with their women accompanists scattered throughout its secluded spots. The banners waved this way and that in the breeze, as if to show that there were Kurus everywhere, both south and north. And the governor of the city proclaimed a night-long festivity to mark the fetching of the treasure.

**[70]** When Kṛṣṇa Vāsudeva heard of the arrival of the Pāṇḍavas, that tormentor of his enemies set out with his ministers to meet them, for he longed to see them. Then the Pāṇḍavas and Vṛṣṇis together duly entered the city of Hāstinapura, O king; earth, sky and the very heavens were filled with the sound of that mighty army's chariot-wheels and hoofbeats. Bearing the treasure before them, the Pāṇḍavas entered their city with joyful hearts, accompanied by their ministers and surrounded by throngs of friends. First, as was proper, they met Dhṛtarāṣṭra lord of men, announcing their names as they respectfully touched his feet. After Dhṛtarāṣṭra, those truest heirs of Bharata paid honour to Subala's daughter Gāndhārī, then to Kuntī, O tiger-like king, and then to Vidura and Yuyutsu, the son of a Vaiśya woman; receiving honour in return, lord of the peoples, those heroes now sat enthroned in splendour.

Next, the brave Pāṇḍavas heard of that great wonder, that highest marvel, the birth of your father Parikṣit; and when they learnt what Kṛṣṇa Vāsudeva had done, they paid honour to the honourable son of Devakī.

A few days later, Satyavatī's son Vyāsa of mighty ardour arrived in the city of Hāstinapura, the City of the Elephant. The Kurus did him honour as was proper, then waited on him with the tiger-like Vṛṣṇis and Andhakas. Yudhiṣṭhira son of Dharma spoke with him on many kinds of topics, and then he said, 'Blessed sir, it is through your grace that we have brought this treasure home. Now I wish to use it in the great rite of the horse sacrifice. I wish to have your honour's leave to do so, truest of sages, for we all depend upon you, as we do upon noble Kṛṣṇa.'

'I give you leave, O king,' said Vyāsa. 'Let it be done at once! Perform the horse sacrifice in due form, with gifts to all the Brahmins; for the horse sacrifice purifies one of all sins, lord of kings, and after sacrificing with that rite you will be sinless, make no doubt.'

Receiving this reply, the Kuru king, righteous Yudhiṣṭhira, determined to perform the horse sacrifice, O heir of Kuru. Having gained

the assent of Kṛṣṇa Dvaipāyana Vyāsa, the eloquent king now addressed
Kṛṣṇa Vāsudeva, and said, 'Truest of men, strong-armed, invincible
hero, whom Queen Devakī was blessed to have as her son, do as I
ask! The pleasures we enjoy were earned through your might, O heir 20
of Yadu; it was you who conquered this earth with your valour and
cunning. Have yourself initiated to perform this rite yourself! For you
are our greatest elder, and when you sacrifice, righteous lord, I too shall
be freed from sin. You are the sacrifice, the Eternal, the all; you are
*dharma*; you are Prajāpati!'

'Strong-armed foe-tamer,' answered Kṛṣṇa, 'you speak becomingly.
But you are the refuge of all creatures: of this I have no doubt. Amongst
the Kuru heroes, today it is you who shine supreme in *dharma*. We are
all subordinate to you, O king, and we reckon you our elder. Perform
the sacrifice: I give you leave, for you must accomplish this rite. Employ
me in any office you desire, O sinless heir of Bharata; I promise you
truly that I shall do all you ask of me. And when you sacrifice, Bhīma, 25
Arjuna and the sons of Mādrī will also be sacrificers, heir of Bharata.'

**[71]** When he heard Kṛṣṇa's reply, Dharma's intelligent son Yudhi-
ṣṭhira addressed these words to Vyāsa: 'Sir, you have true knowledge of
the proper timing for the horse sacrifice, so have the initiation performed
for me at the right time; my rite depends on you.'

Vyāsa answered, 'You need not doubt that I and Paila and Yājñavalkya
will perform every ritual act at its due time, son of Kuntī! Your initiation
will take place on the full-moon day of the month of Caitra. Let all the
sacrificial materials be assembled for the rite, O bull-like hero; let Sūtas 5
learned in horse-lore and knowledgeable priests choose the sacrificial
horse, so that your rite may succeed; then loose it as the learned texts
prescribe, and let it roam the sea-clad earth to increase your glory and
your fame, O prince!'[1]

The Pāṇḍava lord of the earth gave his word, and he did everything

1 In the horse sacrifice, a horse is released to wander at will for a year, and the sacrificing king claims for himself all the territory over which it travels. This necessarily involves doing battle with the rulers of the lands in question. Arjuna will bring the whole earth under Yudhiṣṭhira's sway; however, most of the battles that are actually described in chapters 73–85 below are with the descendants of former enemies who perished during or before the war at Kurukṣetra.

as Vyāsa, speaker of *brahman*, had bidden him, lord of kings, and
made arrangements for all the sacrificial materials. When they were all
assembled, Dharma's son King Yudhiṣṭhira of immeasurable greatness
then informed Kṛṣṇa Dvaipāyana Vyāsa. Vyāsa of mighty ardour replied
to the son of Dharma, 'The time and conditions are right, and we
10 are ready to perform your initiation. Let the *sphya* and the *kūrca*[1] be
golden, heir of Kuru, and let everything else that may be needed also
be fashioned from gold. And in due order let the horse be loosed on
earth today; let it be well protected as it roams, O Yudhiṣṭhira, as the
learned texts prescribe.'

'When I loose the horse,' answered Yudhiṣṭhira, 'it will roam this
earth at will, O Brahmin; let preparations be made for this. But, O sage,
please tell me: who should protect the horse as it freely wanders the
earth?'

In reply, lord of kings, Kṛṣṇa Dvaipāyana Vyāsa spoke these words:
15 'He who was born after Bhīma, the best of all bowmen, bold and
enduring, victorious Arjuna will protect it; he who destroyed the Nivā-
takavaca demons[2] is capable of conquering the earth. He has celestial
weapons, celestial strength of body and a celestial bow and arrow-
cases; he will follow the horse. He is versed in *dharma* and the proper
making of wealth, and is learned in every lore; he will allow your
horse to roam, best of kings, as the texts prescribe. Abhimanyu's heroic
father, the strong-armed prince, dark-skinned and lotus-eyed, will fol-
low the horse. As for Kuntī's son Bhīma of immeasurable valour, he
is full or ardour: he can protect your kingdom, lord of the peoples,
20 along with Nakula; and, heir of Kuru, intelligent Sahadeva of great
renown will deal with all household concerns in the proper man-
ner.'

The Kuru king Yudhiṣṭhira properly carried out everything he had
been told, and he appointed Arjuna to accompany the horse: 'Come,

**1** The *sphya* is a wooden implement shaped like a sword; the *kūrca* is a bundle of *kuśa* grass. Both are used for various purposes in Vedic rituals. To substitute golden equivalents would violate the rules laid down in the sacred texts, but no doubt Vyāsa had sufficient authority to override these.

**2** See 3.165–9.

brave Arjuna, and let this horse have you for its protector; for you are able to guard it as no other mortal can. When kings oppose you, sinless and strong-armed hero, act to avoid doing battle against them; and tell all princes of this sacrifice of mine, instructing them to attend at the appointed time.' After speaking thus to his brother the ambidextrous warrior Arjuna, righteous Yudhiṣṭhira, with the permission of King Dhṛtarāṣṭra, appointed Bhīma and Nakula to the protection of the city, and Sahadeva the warrior-lord to matters of the household.

**[72]** The time arrived for the rite of initiation, and then those greatest of ritual priests initiated the king in the proper manner for the horse sacrifice. When this had been done, and the sacrificial victims had been bound to their stakes, Pāṇḍu's son of mighty ardour, the lord of *dharma*, sat in splendour among the priests. The sacrificial horse was loosed in the manner prescribed in the learned texts by the speaker of *brahman*, Vyāsa of boundless ardour himself. Once initiated, the king, the son of Dharma, shone like a blazing fire, with a garland of gold at his throat; wrapped in an antelope-skin, bearing a staff, with garments of linen, Dharma's son shone brighter than ever, like Prajāpati at a sacrifice. His ritual priests, lord of the peoples, were all dressed just the same; and Arjuna too resembled a blazing fire.

Lord of the earth, wealth-winner Arjuna, whose horses were white, duly followed that piebald horse at the lord of *dharma*'s command; bending his bow Gāṇḍīva, O king, and wearing finger-guards, he rejoiced to follow the horse. The whole city, down to the very children, turned out at that time, O lord, to see the wealth-winner, the best of Kurus, preparing to set forth. Those who came to see the horse and the follower of the horse were pressed so close that their friction seemed to generate heat; and the cry of those men as they looked on Kuntī's son the wealth-winner filled all the ten regions,[1] great king: 'There goes the son of Kuntī! There goes the splendid horse that the strong-armed hero will follow with his mighty bow!' Noble-minded Arjuna heard the words they spoke, O heir of Bharata: 'Fare you well! Go safely and return!' Prince of men, others said, 'In this great press we cannot see Arjuna himself, but that bow of his is clearly visible, the famed Gāṇḍīva

1 The four cardinal points, the four intermediate points, above and below.

of fearsome roar! May he fare well; may his path be free from dangers; and may we see him once again on his return!' Such were the sweet words that he heard uttered again and again by both men and women, bull-like heir of Bharata.

With Kuntī's son there set out also a disciple of Yājñavalkya, an expert in the Vedas and skilled ritualist, to keep him safe from evil; and many other expert Brahmins followed the noble hero, lord of the earth, as did Kṣatriyas and Vaiśyas too.

The horse began, in the manner prescribed, to roam the earth that the Pāṇḍavas had already conquered with the power of their weapons, truest of kings. I shall tell you, O hero, of the great and wonderful battles that Pāṇḍu's son had to fight. The horse circumambulated the entire earth, and he followed it as it turned from north to east; that most excellent horse wandered slowly from place to place, trampling the kingdoms of many princes, and so did the mighty white-horsed chariot-fighter Arjuna. To count the kings who fought against him, Kṣatriyas whose kinsmen had been slain at Kurukṣetra, would be impossible, great king: they numbered tens of thousands. And numerous mountain men took up arms against him, as well as other barbarians of various races, for they had suffered at his hands in the great war; and many princes of noble birth, mad for battle, leading exultant warriors and steeds, fought against Pāṇḍu's son. So battle after battle took place, lord of the earth, between Arjuna and the kings of so many countries. I shall describe to you those which were fiercely fought on both sides, sinless king.

**[73]** *Arjuna does battle with the men of Trigarta, who have long been his enemies.*[1] *When they learn that the sacrificial horse has arrived, they try to capture it. Arjuna endeavours to persuade them against fighting, as Yudhiṣṭhira has instructed him not to kill those who lost kinsmen at Kurukṣetra, but they persist. Arjuna slays their king Sūryavarman, then his brother Ketuvarman. After a fierce battle between Arjuna and the Trigarta warrior Dhṛtavarman, the Trigartas surrender to Arjuna and accept his authority.*

1 They had formed the 'sworn warriors' who had vowed his death in the great war: see 7.16 ff.

**[74]** *The horse now moves on to Prāgjyotiṣa,*[1] *where Bhagadatta's son Vajradatta attempts to seize it; he is forced to abandon it by the arrows from Arjuna's bow Gāṇḍīva. After retreating to his city to don armour, he returns to the attack mounted on a magnificent elephant, hurling lances and then shooting arrows at Arjuna. But Arjuna's arrows inflict grave wounds on both Vajradatta and his elephant.* **[75]** *The battle continues for three days. On the fourth day Vajradatta, longing to avenge his father, attacks again, but after a sharp exchange Arjuna succeeds in slaying his elephant. However, he spares Vajradatta, citing Yudhiṣṭhira's desire that hostile kings and their warriors should not be killed, but that they should be politely instructed to attend the horse sacrifice. Vajradatta agrees to do so.*

**[76]** *Next Arjuna has to fight the men of Sindhu,*[2] *who launch an attack on him and the sacrificial horse. Surrounding him in their thousands as he stands alone on foot, they overwhelm him with their arrows. Terrible portents appear as he loses consciousness and drops his bow Gāṇḍīva; his enemies redouble their attack. However, the celestials and seers utter prayers for Arjuna's victory, and his energy returns to him; he showers arrows on the men of Sindhu in such vast numbers that they flee,* **[77]** *before rallying and resuming their attack. Remembering Yudhiṣṭhira's wishes, Arjuna announces that he will spare the life of anyone who surrenders, but they continue to battle fiercely against him. Foiling their weapons, Arjuna showers them with arrows, severing many heads and rendering most of the survivors unconscious. Now Duḥśalā*[3] *brings her young grandson to Arjuna in great distress, and explains that the boy's father, her own son Suratha, has died of grief on hearing that the slayer of his father had arrived with a sacrificial horse. She pleads for mercy and compares the dead Suratha's child with Parikṣit, son of the dead Abhimanyu. Arjuna embraces Duḥśalā, and she orders her men to stop fighting.*

*The horse now moves on to Maṇipūra.*[4] **[78]** *Babhruvāhana, king of Maṇipūra*

**1** Bhagadatta, king of Prāgjyotiṣa, had died at Arjuna's hands during the war at Kurukṣetra: see 7.25–8.

**2** For the enmity between Jayadratha king of Sindhu and the Pāṇḍavas, see 3.248 ff. For Jayadratha's death at Arjuna's hands, see 7.61 ff., especially 7.121.

**3** Dhṛtarāṣṭra's daughter, who had been married to Jayadratha of Sindhu (see 1.108).

**4** This is the more normal name for the place that was referred to as Maṇalūra at 1.207–9.

*and Arjuna's son,*[1] *greets him politely with a guest-offering; Arjuna berates him for behaving so towards one who has come to fight. Learning of this, the serpent princess Ulūpī arises through the earth from the underworld, identifies herself to Babhruvāhana as his mother,*[2] *and urges him to fight his father. Babhruvāhana resolves to do so, arms himself, and approaches Arjuna in his chariot, ordering his men to seize the horse. The two men fight. Arjuna, pleased with his son, avoids pressing him too hard; Babhruvāhana sees his father apparently weakening, and in boyish naivety shoots him in the breast with great force. Both men fall to the ground.*

*Citrāṅgadā sees her husband lying slain and her son unconscious, and goes out weeping to the battlefield.* **[79]** *She bitterly rounds on Ulūpī for causing such a disaster; then she addresses the fallen Arjuna, imploring him to arise and follow the horse once more. Finally she turns again to Ulūpī, vowing to fast to death if she does not restore Arjuna's life.* **[80]** *Babhruvāhana regains consciousness to see his mother holding the feet of her dead husband. Overwhelmed with grief, he declares that there is no expiation for the sin he has committed short of wandering for twelve years clad in his father's skin and using his skull as a food-bowl. He too vows that he will fast to death if Arjuna is not restored to life.* **[81]** *Ulūpī now calls to mind the Revivifying Jewel, and it appears. She tells Babhruvāhana that he has not slain Arjuna, who is invincible, and that he has done no wrong; Arjuna wished to test his might as a warrior, and this was why she urged him to fight. She tells him to place the Jewel on Arjuna's breast. Babhruvāhana does so, and Arjuna arises as if from sleep. Indra rains down flowers, and there is the sound of heavenly drums and cries of 'Bravo!' Arjuna wants to know what has happened; Babhruvāhana tells him to ask Ulūpī.*

**[82]** *Questioned by Arjuna, Ulūpī explains that she has acted for his benefit and should not be censured. By killing Bhīṣma with the help of Śikhaṇḍin,*[3] *Arjuna had breached* dharma, *and he had been cursed to go to hell for this deed by the Vasus with Gaṅgā's agreement.*[4] *When she had told her father of this, he had pleaded with the Vasus, and had secured a limit on the curse: it would*

**1** He was the son of Arjuna and the princess Citrāṅgadā: see 1.206–9.

**2** As Ganguli points out, she was in fact his stepmother.

**3** See 6.114.

**4** Bhīṣma was Gaṅgā's son, the only survivor of the eight sons she bore to give the Vasus human births: see 1.91–2.

*come to an end when Arjuna was laid low in battle by his son, the ruler of Maṇipūra. Arjuna is delighted by Ulūpī's revelations. He tells Babhruvāhana to attend Yudhiṣṭhira's horse sacrifice; Babhruvāhana answers that he will do so, and invites Arjuna to enter the city, but Arjuna declines: he must continue to follow the sacrificial horse.*

**[83]** *The horse now arrives at Rājagṛha, capital of Magadha. The young king Meghasaṃdhi, the son of Jarāsaṃdha's son Sahadeva,*[1] *comes forth fully armed in his chariot, and challenges Arjuna as he stands alone on foot. They fight. Meghasaṃdhi showers Arjuna with arrows, which he parries; he then showers arrows on Meghasaṃdhi's chariot and horses, whilst sparing the king and his charioteer. However, Meghasaṃdhi supposes that it is his own valour that is protecting him, and shoots more arrows at Arjuna, wounding him. Arjuna now kills his horses and charioteer, and destroys his bow. Meghasaṃdhi advances against him bearing a club, but Arjuna destroys this too; then he tells the boy that he has done enough to show himself a true Kṣatriya. Meghasaṃdhi pays Arjuna honour and agrees to attend the horse sacrifice.*

*The horse continues its journey round the coast of India, from Bengal to Kerala, and Arjuna defeats numerous barbarian forces along the way.* **[84]** *Then it roams through many lands, in each of which Arjuna defeats and receives honour from the ruler; these include the Cedi king Śarabha, son of Śiśupāla,*[2] *and the Niṣāda king, Ekalavya's son.*[3] *In Dvārakā the horse is attacked by the young men, but King Ugrasena tells them to stop, and together with Vasudeva he pays honour to Arjuna. Then it moves on to Gāndhāra, where Arjuna has to fight the son of Śakuni.*[4] **[85]** *The men of Gāndhāra will not agree to Arjuna's offer of peace, and attack; Arjuna beheads many of them with his razor-sharp arrows. Śakuni's son insists on continuing to fight. Arjuna carries off his helmet with a crescent-shaped arrow, as he had done Jayadratha's head;*[5] *everyone understands that he has deliberately refrained from killing the king. The king and his warriors flee, while Arjuna continues to harry them. Finally the king's mother arrives with a guest-offering for Arjuna, and puts a stop to the fighting. Arjuna rebukes*

**1** See 2.18 ff.

**2** See 2.37 ff.

**3** See 1.123.

**4** See 9.27.

**5** 7.121.30 ff.

*the king for his inimical attitude, and tells him he has spared him only because he is Gāndhārī's nephew. He instructs him to attend the horse sacrifice.*

Vaiśaṃpāyana spoke:

**[86]** Now once more Kuntī's son Arjuna followed the horse as it roamed at will, until it turned in the direction of Hāstinapura. Yudhiṣṭhira was informed by a scout that the horse was now on its way back. His heart was filled with joy to learn that Arjuna was safe and well, and when he heard of his victorious brother's deeds in the region of Gāndhāra, and in all the other lands, the king was well pleased.

Now Yudhiṣṭhira lord of *dharma* realized that the twelfth day had arrived of the bright fortnight of the month of Māgha; and seeing that the moon was also in an auspicious constellation, the high-minded Kuru of mighty ardour convened all three of his other brothers, Bhīma, Nakula and Sahadeva. Then, when the time was right, Yudhiṣṭhira, best upholder of *dharma* and best of all those who speak, addressed Bhīma of terrible valour and pronounced these words: 'Bhīma, your younger brother the wealth-winner is returning with the horse, as I have learnt from those men who are following him. The time has come; the horse is drawing near, and the full-moon day of Māgha is at hand. One month remains,[1] so let learned Brahmins expert in the Vedas be dispatched to seek for the place where the rite shall be performed, so that my horse sacrifice may succeed.'

Thus directed, Bhīma, delighted to learn that the ambidextrous warrior Arjuna was returning, carried out the king's command. Accompanied by wise ritual specialists and led by Brahmins skilled in sacrificial rites, the Kuru set forth and duly marked out a sacrificial enclosure with fences, mounds and pathways; he had three fine shelters constructed in the proper manner, for the sacrificer and his wife and for the sacred fire, and he had them adorned with jewels and with gold. Righteous Bhīma raised pillars bright with gold and lofty gold-decked arches all over the enclosure; he had dwellings properly built in many places for the ladies who would accompany the kings of so many lands;

1 In fact, two months separate the full-moon day of Māgha from that of Caitra, when the sacrifice was due to take place.

and in the same way he ordered the construction of many and various lodges for the Brahmins that were to gather from far and wide.

Next, great king, Bhīma sent out envoys in Yudhiṣṭhira's name to summon all those tireless monarchs, those truest of kings; and they, to please the Kuru lord, came and brought with them many gems and women, horses and weapons.[1] The sound they made as they entered their encampments in thousands seemed to reach to heaven itself like
the ocean's roar. Lotus-eyed King Yudhiṣṭhira commanded food and 20
drink for his guests, as well as heavenly beds; tiger-like hero, the lord of *dharma* also provided many stables for their steeds, well stocked with grain and sugar-cane and milk.

At that great sacrifice of the wise lord of *dharma* there gathered sages, speakers of *brahman*, in numerous throngs, and eminent Brahmins too assembled there, lord of the earth; the Kuru king Yudhiṣṭhira of mighty ardour welcomed them and also their disciples, and without ostentation he accompanied each one in person to the very door of his allotted
dwelling-place. Then the ritual specialists and other craftsmen, O king, 25
informed the lord of *dharma* that they had completed the arrangements for the rite; and invincible King Yudhiṣṭhira rejoiced with his brothers to learn that all was ready, and all perfect.

**[87]** As the sacrifice began, eloquent debaters debated many topics, seeking to refute each other's views. The kings beheld the magnificent arrangements made by Bhīma for the ritual, heir of Kuru, as if the sacrificer were to be Indra lord of the gods himself. There they saw arches of pure gold, and multitudes of jewel-studded beds and chairs and couches; pitchers, pots, pans, jars, dishes – the kings could see nothing
there that was not made of gold. They saw sacrificial stakes made ready 5
in due form and at the due time, fashioned of wood, as specified in the learned texts, but ornamented brilliantly with gold. They saw all the animals that had been brought together there, lord, creatures of the land and of the waters: cattle and buffaloes; aquatic creatures, beasts of prey and birds; viviparous and oviparous things, insects produced from

1 Though the text is silent on the point, these are clearly intended as tribute to their new overlord, Yudhiṣṭhira. Weapons would certainly not have been welcome otherwise.

sweat; and sprouting plants from mountain, riverbank and forest. Seeing the whole enclosure thus gaily teeming with animals, cattle and grain, those kings were utterly amazed.

For the Brahmins and Vaiśyas there was much costly well-cooked food. Whenever a full hundred thousand priests sat down to eat there, a thunderous drum was beaten repeatedly; it sounded several times each day. Thus it was at the sacrifice of the wise lord of *dharma*. O king, the numerous heaps of food to be served were like mountains; there were trenches of curd and lakes of ghee. The whole of Jambūdvīpa[1] with all its different kingdoms could be seen gathered together at king Yudhiṣṭhira's great sacrifice, O king; there were many thousands of races of men who had come from different lands bearing wealth, O bull-like heir of Bharata. Kings wearing garlands and gleaming jewelled earrings waited on the foremost Brahmins assembled there in hundreds and thousands, while their attendants likewise gave the Brahmins food and drink of many kinds, all of it fit for kings.

**[88]** Seeing those kings and those experts in the Veda assembled, King Yudhiṣṭhira now addressed Bhīma: 'Pay honour to the tiger-like lords of the earth who have come here, for kings are worthy of honour.' Thus commanded by the renowned lord of men, Bhīma of great ardour did as instructed, and so did the twins. Next Kṛṣṇa Govinda, best of all those who draw breath, approached Yudhiṣṭhira son of Dharma, together with the Vṛṣṇis headed by Balarāma; with him were Sātyaki, Pradyumna, Gada, Niśaṭha, Sāmba and Kṛtavarman. Those bull-like heroes too received the greatest honour from strong-armed Bhīma, before retiring to their gem-studded lodges.

Now after talking with Yudhiṣṭhira, Kṛṣṇa the slayer of Madhu told him that Arjuna was exhausted by the many battles he had fought. Kuntī's son, the lord of *dharma*, had repeatedly asked foe-taming Kṛṣṇa about his victorious brother, and now the lord of the world told him, 'A trusted agent of mine from Dvārakā came to see me, O king: he had seen that noble Pāṇḍava, and found him exhausted by his many battles. He told me that the strong-armed hero is nearby; so, son of Kuntī, do what needs to be done to bring the horse sacrifice to a successful conclusion.'

1 See note to 6.1.8.

Hearing Kṛṣṇa's words, Yudhiṣṭhira lord of *dharma* replied to him, 'What a blessing that victorious Arjuna is safe, and that he now approaches, heir of Madhu! I wish you to tell me, Yadu lord, what message that foremost Pāṇḍava warrior sent to you.'

At this, tiger-like king, the lord of the Vṛṣṇis and Andhakas, eloquent Kṛṣṇa, then spoke these words to righteous Yudhiṣṭhira: 'Great king, my agent told me what Kuntī's son had said. "Kṛṣṇa, when the time comes, tell Yudhiṣṭhira this. Kings will come before the Kurus from all parts of the earth; honour must be paid to every one of them, for it is right for us to do thus. And, bestower of honour, tell the king from me that nothing untoward must happen when the guest-offerings are presented. King Yudhiṣṭhira must ensure this, and you too must comply, O king, so that the people are not once again slaughtered because of the hatred of kings for one another."[1] Son of Kuntī, my agent said all this, and he said more; listen while I tell you the words of wealth-winner Arjuna, O king. "The king of Maṇipūra will attend our sacrifice. He is my beloved son, Babhruvāhana of mighty ardour. Please honour him duly out of regard for me, lord, for he always shows me devotion and love." '

When he heard these words, Yudhiṣṭhira lord of *dharma* was pleased by them, and he said, **[89]** 'Kṛṣṇa, it is becoming for you to have spoken the pleasing words that I have heard; they gladden my heart, lord, like a draught of nectar. I have heard that victorious Arjuna has battled again and again against kings in many places, O Kṛṣṇa lord of the senses, for Kuntī's wise son the ever-victorious Arjuna is always deprived of happiness on my account, and this pains my heart. Often I have thought of him when I am alone, Vṛṣṇi hero. What undesirable characteristic does he have on his body, home to every auspicious sign, that he should suffer so many hardships? Kuntī's son Arjuna Bībhatsu is ever prey to terrible unhappiness, and yet I do not see upon his limbs any blameworthy feature. Please explain this to me, Kṛṣṇa, if it is something that I may hear.'

The lord of the senses heard these words. Long he thought, and then

1 Arjuna is thinking of the equivalent point in Yudhiṣṭhira's royal consecration, where a dispute arose that led to the killing of Śiśupāla: see 2.33–42.

Viṣṇu, the glory of the Bhoja Kṣatriyas, answered the king. 'Lord of men, I can think of no undesirable feature, save that the lion-like hero's calves are too muscular; it is because of them that tiger-like Arjuna is forever employed in travelling. I can see no other reason why your victorious brother should be prey to unhappiness.'

O lord, Yudhiṣṭhira, best heir of Kuru, heard wise Kṛṣṇa's truthful words, and replied to the tiger-like Vṛṣṇi, 'That is so.' But Draupadī Kṛṣṇā cast an angry glare at Kṛṣṇa, and he, lord of the senses and slayer of Keśin, received it as if he were his friend wealth-winner Arjuna in person, receiving her love for him.

Bhīma and the other Kurus and Yadus rejoiced to hear the wonderful tales of the wealth-winner's deeds, O lord. Even as they were telling one another stories about noble Arjuna, a man arrived, sent by their victorious brother. He approached Yudhiṣṭhira, best heir of Kuru, and wisely paid his respects; then he informed him that Arjuna was now close by. At this the king's eyes filled with tears of joy, and he rewarded the messenger with great wealth for these happy tidings.

Two days later a mighty roar broke out as the tiger-like Pāṇḍava lord arrived. The dust raised by the sacrificial horse as it walked at his side looked like the dust raised by Uccaiḥśravas.[1] Arjuna heard men call out, hoarse with joy, 'What a blessing that you are safe, O son of Kuntī! How fortunate is King Yudhiṣṭhira! For who else but Arjuna could have conquered the whole earth with all its princes, and then returned after making this fine horse roam all over it? We have not heard that such a deed was done even by noble kings of the past such as Sagara; and in the future too no other kings will be capable of the difficult feat that you have accomplished, best heir of the line of Kuru!'

Righteous Arjuna could still hear men speaking such delightful words as he entered the sacrificial area. Then King Yudhiṣṭhira, his ministers, and Kṛṣṇa heir of Yadu, all went forth to greet him, headed by Dhṛtarāṣṭra. He paid his respects at the feet of Dhṛtarāṣṭra his father, then at those of the wise lord of *dharma*; then he honoured Bhīma and the others, and finally embraced Kṛṣṇa Keśava. Thus he greeted them all, received due honour from them, and honoured them duly in return;

1 See 1.15.

and then the righteous hero took his rest, like a mariner who has finally
reached land.

Meanwhile wise King Babhruvāhana with his two mothers[1] arrived 25
among the Kurus. He greeted them all and received their salutations
before setting foot in the wonderful mansion of Kuntī his grandmother.
[**90**] He entered the Pāṇḍavas' dwelling in the proper manner, addressing
his grandmother with gentle and charming speech. Likewise, Queen
Citrāṅgadā and Ulūpī together approached Kuntī and Draupadī with
due politeness, as also Subhadrā and the other Kuru ladies; Kuntī gave
them both jewels of various kinds, and so did Draupadī and Subhadrā
and the others, and the two queens took up their lodging there, among
the costliest beds and seats. Kuntī herself paid them honour, for she
wanted to please Arjuna. 5

As for heroic King Babhruvāhana of mighty ardour, after receiving
honour from Kuntī, he duly attended on Dhṛtarāṣṭra lord of the earth,
then visited King Yudhiṣṭhira, Bhīma and the other Pāṇḍavas, and
greeted them politely. They embraced him lovingly and paid him
proper honour; those mighty chariot-fighters delightedly gave him
gifts of abundant wealth. Next he waited on Kṛṣṇa Govinda, wielder
of discus and club, as humbly as if he were Kṛṣṇa's son Pradyumna; and
Kṛṣṇa gave him a wonderful, costly chariot adorned with gold, yoked to
horses of celestial splendour. Yudhiṣṭhira lord of *dharma*, Bhīma, Arjuna 10
and the twins also each individually paid the highest of honours to that
honourable king.

Three days later the sage Kṛṣṇa Dvaipāyana Vyāsa, son of Satyavatī,
approached Yudhiṣṭhira and eloquently spoke these words: 'Son of
Kuntī, start the sacrifice today: the time is come for you to do so. The
auspicious moment for the rite has arrived, and the sacrificial priests
urge you to begin. Lord of kings, this sacrifice of yours lasts many days
and is rich in complexity; because of the great amount of gold that it
requires, it is known as the Ritual of Much Gold. And so, great king,
you should pay the priests three times the usual fee-gift, so that your rite
may also become three times as powerful; for in such matters it is the
Brahmins who make everything happen. In this way you will achieve 15

1 Citrāṅgadā and Ulūpī: see chapters 77–83 above.

three horse sacrifices, each rich in fee-gifts to the Brahmins, and so will free yourself of the sin caused by the slaughter of your kinsfolk, lord of men. For the final ritual bath that you will take at the conclusion of the horse sacrifice, heir of Kuru, is highly purificatory: it is the purifier of purifiers!'

Thus Vyāsa of boundless ardour addressed ardent Yudhiṣṭhira. The
righteous lord of men underwent initiation for the achievement of the
horse sacrifice, and then performed the mighty rite itself. The sacrificial
priests employed in it were experts in the Veda; O king, they carried out
all the rituals properly as they moved about the enclosure, for they had
been well schooled and knew the learned texts. Not a mistake did they
make; not an oblation went astray; those bull-like priests did everything
20 for the rite correctly and in due sequence. Expert in *dharma*, those
truest of Brahmins duly performed the *pravargya* ceremony; then they
likewise carried out the pressing of the Soma, O king.[1] Once the Soma
was pressed, those truest of Soma-drinkers made offerings of Soma in
due sequence, following the learned texts.

No one attending that rite was wretched, no one poor; no person
was hungry or sad or ill-mannered. To those who wished for food,
ardent Bhīma had food distributed constantly and ceaselessly at the
king's command. Day after day the sacrificial priests, skilled in matters
of sacrifice and observing the precepts laid down in the learned texts,
25 performed all the rituals; there was not one of the Brahmins participating
in wise Yudhiṣṭhira's rite who was not expert in the six branches of
the Veda, not one who fell short of his vows, not one who was not a
teacher, not one who could not argue and debate.

When the time came to erect the sacrificial stakes for the Kuru lord's rite, the ritual priests set up six made of *bilva* wood, O bull-like heir of Bharata, and an equal number made of *khadira* and of *sarvavarṇin*, as well as two stakes of *devadāru* and one of *śleṣmātaka*. And in addition, bull-like hero, Bhīma, acting on the lord of *dharma*'s command, set up further stakes of gold to beautify the enclosure; adorned with cloths, O royal

1 At a Soma sacrifice, in which the pressed juice of the plant is consumed for the religious ecstasy it inspires, the main ritual is preceded by the *pravargya*, in which milk is dropped into boiling ghee, with volcanic results.

seer, they shone like the Seven Seers alongside the gods in heaven.[1]
Bricks of gold had also been prepared for the piling of Yudhiṣṭhira's 30
altar, so that it too shone as brilliantly as that of Prajāpati Dakṣa; four layers high and eighteen cubits long, it was piled up in the form of a mighty bird[2] with wings of gold, but three times greater in size.

Next, the animal victims were bound to their stakes by wise priests in accordance with the learned texts: beasts and birds, each dedicated to its particular god. There were bulls, as specified in the learned texts, and aquatic creatures; the priests made use of all of them in the rite of piling the fire-altar. Three hundred victims were bound to stakes for Kuntī's
son, noble King Yudhiṣṭhira, in addition to that marvellous horse. The 35
splendid rite was thronged with divine seers attending it in person, and made yet more splendid by hosts of Gandharvas and Apsarases; it resounded with the lovely songs of Kiṃpuruṣas and Kiṃnaras, and all around it could be seen the dwellings of priestly Siddhas. Vyāsa's disciples, those most excellent Brahmins, propounders of every branch of learning, experts in sacrificial rites, were always to be found within the enclosure. Nārada was there, and radiant Tumburu; Viśvāvasu and Citrasena were present, along with other expert singers. In the pauses separating sacrificial rituals from one another, the Gandharvas entertained the priests with the singing and dancing at which they were so skilled.

**[91]** Those truest of Brahmins first sacrificed the other victims in the proper manner, then they sacrificed the horse, as the learned texts prescribe; and after duly sacrificing the horse, the bull-like ritual priests caused Drupada's spirited daughter Draupadī to sit with it, O king.[3] The bull-like Brahmins now calmly removed and cooked the horse's

**1** The Seven Seers are the stars forming the Great Bear.

**2** This is the normal shape for the fire altar in Vedic ritual.

**3** Strikingly, three different standard euphemisms are used for 'sacrifice' in the first two verses of this chapter: the priests 'tranquillize' the other victims, then 'lay hold of' the horse; after 'gaining the horse's acquiescence (in its own death)', they send Draupadī to it. Draupadī's part in the ritual too is barely hinted at: the chief queen of the sacrificing monarch was supposed to copulate with the recently throttled stallion, to the accompaniment of an obscene verse dialogue between the officiants and the other queens.

I do not understand the third line of verse 2, and have omitted most of it.

intestinal sac in accordance with the learned texts, O bull-like heir of Bharata; then Yudhiṣṭhira lord of *dharma* and his younger brothers duly smelt the smoke of the cooking sac, the scent of which destroys all sins.
5 As for the remaining limbs of that horse, O lord of men, the sixteen wise ritual priests offered them up together on the fire.

Thus blessed Vyāsa with his disciples brought to its conclusion the rite of King Yudhiṣṭhira, Indra's equal in ardour, after which he glorified that king. Yudhiṣṭhira then presented to the participating priests, as was proper, ten billion gold coins; and to Vyāsa he presented the earth. Receiving the earth, O king, Vyāsa son of Satyavatī replied to righteous Yudhiṣṭhira, best heir of Bharata: 'Truest of kings, let this earth remain in trust with you, and give me an equivalent sum in wealth, for wealth is what Brahmins seek.'

10 But high-minded, wise Yudhiṣṭhira, surrounded by his brothers and the other noble kings, answered those priests. 'It is said that in the great rite of the horse sacrifice the fee-gift is the earth. Arjuna has won it for me, and I have handed it over to the ritual priests. Now I shall enter the forest, O mighty priests; divide this earth four ways between the four chief sacrificial officiants. I do not wish to receive wealth that belongs to Brahmins, O truest of sinless sages; this has been my constant opinion, and that of my brothers too.'

When he had finished speaking, his brothers and Draupadī too all said,
15 'Indeed, it is so,' which made the hair rise on everyone's body; a voice in the air said, 'Bravo, heir of Bharata, bravo!', while the lovely sound was heard of hosts of Brahmin voices raised in praise. But after receiving Yudhiṣṭhira's reply, Kṛṣṇa Dvaipāyana Vyāsa addressed him once more; paying him honour, the sage spoke thus amongst all the priests: 'Sir, you have given me this earth, but I return it to you; let gold be given to these Brahmins, but let the earth be yours.' Next Kṛṣṇa Vāsudeva spoke to Yudhiṣṭhira lord of *dharma*, and told him that he should do as the blessed Vyāsa had said. The Kuru king was delighted to receive this advice, and with his brothers he gave away a hundred thousand billion,
20 three times the fee-gift for the rite. No other king in this world will ever do what the lion-like Kuru did in emulation of Marutta.[1]

1 See chapters 3–10 above.

The lord Kṛṣṇa Dvaipāyana Vyāsa received that wealth; he divided it four ways and gave it to the sacrificial priests, while Yudhiṣṭhira, having given so much gold as a sum equivalent to the value of the Earth, rejoiced with his brothers at having freed himself from sin and conquered the realms of heaven. The sacrificial priests now further divided that limitless store of gold, distributing it amongst the Brahmins according to each's energy and strength; they also, with Yudhiṣṭhira's permission, divided out everything made of gold within the sacrificial enclosure: ornaments, arches, stakes, pitchers, pots and altar-bricks.
After the Brahmins, Kṣatriyas claimed their share of the wealth, and so 25
did throngs of Vaiśyas and Śūdras, as well as other barbarian tribes, so that for a long time people were carrying gold hither and thither.

Then all the Brahmins returned joyfully to their homes, sated with wealth by the noble lord of *dharma*. With the greatest reverence, blessed Vyāsa of mighty radiance gave his share of the great store of gold to Kuntī; Kuntī was happy to receive that loving gift from her father-in-law, and used it to do great good in the world. King Yudhiṣṭhira, freed from his sins by undergoing the final ritual bath, shone like Indra amongst
the deities as he with his brothers received the homage of all; and the 30
Pāṇḍavas too shone amongst the assembled kings surrounding them, great king, like planets shining amongst the hosts of stars. To those kings Yudhiṣṭhira gave jewels of many kinds, and elephants, horses, ornaments, women, garments and gold; as he handed out a limitless tide of riches to the princes of the earth, Kuntī's royal son shone like Kubera god of wealth. He had King Babhruvāhana brought before him; bestowing much wealth upon that hero, he then gave him leave to return to his home; and he lovingly consecrated Duḥśalā's young grandson[1] as king over the realm ruled by his ancestors, O bull-like
prince. Finally Yudhiṣṭhira, king of the Kurus and master of himself, 35
gave leave to depart to all the kings, honouring them greatly in properly defined groups.

Thus occurred the sacrifice of the wise lord of *dharma*, with its floods of food and wealth and jewels, its oceans of intoxicating liquors, its lakes of ghee, its many mountains of food, its trenches of spiced sweet

1 See chapter 77 above.

curd, O bull-like heir of Bharata. Of the preparation and consumption of foodstuffs and sweetmeats, and of the butchering of animals, no end could be seen; and it was lovely to behold young women singing in the
40 joy of intoxication to the sounds of drum and conch. Day and night, unchecked, the cry was 'Give!' then 'Eat!' The press of joyful folk was like a mighty festival, as men in many different lands would later describe.

The king had showered everyone with torrents of wealth, with jewels and riches and other objects of desire. Now, freed from sin, his aims achieved, that best heir of Bharata entered his city.

**[92]** —*Janamejaya asks to hear of any remarkable incident that occurred during Yudhiṣṭhira's horse sacrifice, and Vaiśaṃpāyana relates.* — *When all has been concluded, a huge mongoose appears. Half of his body is gold. He declaims in a thunderous voice that this sacrifice is not equal to the gift of a pound of barley-meal by a resident of Kurukṣetra performing the* uñcha *vow.*[1] *The amazed Brahmins question the mongoose, emphasizing how correctly the sacrifice has been performed, but the mongoose repeats its claim and prepares to explain it.*

**[93]** *The mongoose tells the story of a pious Brahmin who lived at Kurukṣetra with his wife, son and daughter-in-law. They ate once a day the food he obtained by gleaning. Once a terrible famine struck, and the family were without food for days. One day he managed to collect a pound of barley, which they made into barley-meal and divided into four portions. Then a guest arrived. They welcomed him with a guest-offering including one portion of meal, but he remained hungry. One after another, the Brahmin's wife, son and daughter-in-law told him to give their portions to the guest; each time the Brahmin argued against doing so, but finally agreed when they insisted. At last the guest was satisfied. Telling the Brahmin that his gift had won him renown in heaven and saved his ancestors and descendants for generations to come, the guest identified himself as Dharma; at Dharma's word, the entire family ascended to heaven. The mongoose adds that at this point he came up out of his hole; as a result of smelling the scent of the barley-meal and touching the remaining water and grains of barley, half his body had turned to gold. He had come to Yudhiṣṭhira's sacrifice in hopes that the other half would also become gold, but this had not happened; hence his statement that*

1 See 12.349–53.

*the sacrifice was not equal to the gift. — Having narrated this tale, Vaiśaṃpāyana tells Janamejaya that he should not regard sacrifice as wonderful, for millions of seers have attained heaven by simply performing austerities. Non-violence, contentment, good conduct, rectitude, asceticism, self-control, truth and the giving of gifts: these are all the equals of sacrifice.*

**[94]** *Janamejaya speaks in favour of sacrifice, and asks why the mongoose had condemned it. Vaiśaṃpāyana relates how once at a sacrifice of Indra the priests were touched by compassion for the unhappy animal victims, and told Indra that this was not a proper form of sacrifice. Indra did not accept what they said, and a great dispute arose as to whether it is better to sacrifice with animate or inanimate offerings. They consulted King Vasu Uparicara; when he answered that one should sacrifice with whatever is available, he was punished by having to enter the underworld.*[1] *True* dharma *consists of renunciation, giving, compassion and the other related virtues; it is through these that men attain heaven.*

**[95]** *Janamejaya asks how he can be certain in the matter of sacrifices. In reply, Vaiśaṃpāyana cites the story of Agastya's sacrifice. Agastya had embarked on a great twelve-year ritual involving many gifts of food, but Indra sent no rain, endangering the supply of food. Agastya, untroubled, said that if no rain fell for twelve years he would substitute other forms of sacrifice, either purely mental or using seeds as offerings, for it was impossible for his ritual to fail; if necessary he would become Indra himself in order to prevent famine. He commanded wealth, the celestials, heaven and its residents, and Dharma himself to attend his rite, and everything he commanded came about. The sages who were present now decided in favour of non-violent sacrifice, and Indra granted rain.*

**[96]** *Janamejaya asks Vaiśaṃpāyana who the half-gold mongoose was, and Vaiśaṃpāyana narrates. Once the seer Jamadagni milked his cow, intending to use the milk in a* śrāddha *ceremony. To test him, Anger spoilt the milk, but Jamadagni did not become angry. He told Anger to approach the ancestors, since it was they who had been caused to suffer. When Anger did so, the ancestors turned him into a mongoose; he would only be freed from the curse by censuring* dharma. *When he censured Yudhiṣṭhira at the horse sacrifice the curse came to an end, for Yudhiṣṭhira is Dharma.*

1 This is a variant of the story told at 12.324.

# THE HERMITAGE

## THE HERMITAGE

[1] *Having regained their kingdom, the Pāṇḍavas now rule the earth for fifteen years. They treat Dhṛtarāṣṭra with the highest respect and defer to him in everything, while their womenfolk similarly wait upon Gāndhārī. Yudhiṣṭhira instructs his brothers to make sure that Dhṛtarāṣṭra, who has suffered the loss of his sons, experiences no further grief, and they all take care to obey, with the sole exception of Bhīma; he cannot forget everything that happened as a result of the dicing, thanks to Dhṛtarāṣṭra's foolishness.*

[2] *Dhṛtarāṣṭra passes his time pleasantly, honoured by the Pāṇḍavas; Yudhiṣṭhira is happy to allow him control of matters such as grants to Brahmins, and he tells his brothers and ministers that whoever obeys Dhṛtarāṣṭra is his friend, while whoever opposes him is an enemy to be cast out. In particular he permits him to spend as much as he wishes on the* śrāddha *ceremonies for his sons. The Pāṇḍavas take care to mitigate his grief as far as possible, and he treats them as a* guru *might treat his disciples;* [3] *both he and Gāndhārī behave affectionately towards them. Yudhiṣṭhira always seeks to please Dhṛtarāṣṭra, and carries out reverentially whatever commands he and Gāndhārī might give. Pāṇḍu's sons give Dhṛtarāṣṭra a happiness he never gained from his own sons, and Yudhiṣṭhira will not permit any man to speak ill of Dhṛtarāṣṭra or Duryodhana.*

*Gāndhārī and Vidura are both well pleased with Yudhiṣṭhira's demeanour; they are less pleased with Bhīma, who follows Yudhiṣṭhira's deference to Dhṛtarāṣṭra with reluctant ill grace.* [4] *Dhṛtarāṣṭra dislikes Bhīma, and Bhīma constantly performs secret acts of unkindness towards Dhṛtarāṣṭra, such as boasting within his and Gāndhārī's hearing of having killed the blind king's sons. The other Pāṇḍavas are unaware of what is happening, save for the twins Nakula and Sahadeva, who approve of Bhīma's attitude.*

*When fifteen years have passed, Dhṛtarāṣṭra requests his friends to assemble, and addresses them tearfully.* [**5**] *He tells them that he is consumed with remorse for having ignored all the wise advice he received and for having continued to favour his wicked son Duryodhana. He reveals that, in an effort to expiate his sin and unknown to his attendants, he and Gāndhārī eat very little and sleep on the ground. He has lived a pleasant life under Yudhiṣṭhira's protection, and has been able to perform* śrāddha *ceremonies and give gifts; now he seeks Yudhiṣṭhira's leave to retire with Gāndhārī to the forest to live a life of asceticism, as is fitting for descendants of Kuru at the close of their lives when they have handed the kingship over to their sons.*

[**6**] *Yudhiṣṭhira expresses his dismay at Dhṛtarāṣṭra's words: the kingship means nothing to him if Dhṛtarāṣṭra is unhappy. He appeals to Dhṛtarāṣṭra to appoint as king Yuyutsu, or anyone else whom he wishes, or to rule the kingdom himself, so that Yudhiṣṭhira may retire to the forest. What has happened was fated to happen, and Dhṛtarāṣṭra should free himself from his anguish. But Dhṛtarāṣṭra answers by again requesting Yudhiṣṭhira to allow him to retire to the forest. He asks Saṃjaya and Kṛpa to intercede on his behalf, then clutches at Gāndhārī and faints.*

*Yudhiṣṭhira grieves to see the once mighty Dhṛtarāṣṭra reduced to such a state. He gently rubs his breast and face with cold water, and Dhṛtarāṣṭra regains consciousness.* [**7**] *He explains that eight watches of the day have passed since he has eaten; this is why he fainted, but now Yudhiṣṭhira's touch has restored him. He embraces Yudhiṣṭhira closely, while many of the onlookers weep. Once again he requests permission to become an ascetic. Yudhiṣṭhira replies that he will take his decision after Dhṛtarāṣṭra has taken food, and Dhṛtarāṣṭra assents to this.*

*Now Vyāsa arrives.* [**8**] *He urges Yudhiṣṭhira to grant Dhṛtarāṣṭra's wish without delay: he is old, and he should be allowed to follow the way of royal seers of former times. Yudhiṣṭhira answers that Vyāsa is a father to him, and that a son must follow a father's commands. Vyāsa continues to press him not to impede Dhṛtarāṣṭra's desire, and Yudhiṣṭhira gives his agreement, whereupon Vyāsa leaves once more. Yudhiṣṭhira now begs Dhṛtarāṣṭra to eat; afterwards he may leave for the forest.* [**9**] *Dhṛtarāṣṭra returns to his own dwelling, and after performing the morning rituals and giving gifts to the Brahmins he eats, as does everyone else. Then the Pāṇḍavas come to see him.*

*Dhṛtarāṣṭra gives Yudhiṣṭhira instruction on running a kingdom. He tells him to honour, consult and obey men of learning; he advises him on the employment of ministers and spies and the fortification of the city; he describes how he should protect his own person and his womenfolk; he tells him what kind of counsellors he should consult, and how to keep his consultations secret; he urges him to acquaint himself with the virtues and vices of his subjects.* **[10]** *Next he describes how legal proceedings should be conducted; he gives advice on which tasks should be performed at which times of day; he speaks of the importance of keeping the treasury well filled, the identification and destruction of enemies, and the appointment and maintenance of subordinates.* **[11]** *Then he speaks of friends, foes and neutrals, and of prosperity, adversity and stasis; he states when it is appropriate to make war and when to seek peace; he describes how to concede as little as possible in the event of a defeat, but counsels Yudhiṣṭhira not to accept similar concessions from those he has defeated; he favours repressing internal foes and countering powerful external foes by sowing dissension rather than making war openly; he says that in the event of attack by a stronger enemy one should first attempt to reach a settlement, then resort to all-out warfare.* **[12]** *Finally he speaks of war and peace, of the different tactics that a king should adopt in different circumstances, and of the need to consider one's own and one's enemy's strength; he discourses on the various strengths that a king should acquire, on possible disasters, and on marching to war. After various other observations he concludes by saying that the merit that arises from protecting one's subjects is equal to that of a thousand horse sacrifices.*

**[13]** *Yudhiṣṭhira assures Dhṛtarāṣṭra that he will obey the precepts he has given.*

*Dhṛtarāṣṭra decides that, before leaving for the forest, he wishes to make gifts of wealth for the benefit of his dead sons. Then he requests Yudhiṣṭhira to call the subjects together; Yudhiṣṭhira does so, and Dhṛtarāṣṭra addresses them. He tells them of his decision to retire to the forest, and asks for their permission to do so. His announcement causes much weeping.* **[14]** *Dhṛtarāṣṭra reminds the assembled subjects that they have been ruled by Śaṃtanu, Vicitravīrya, Pāṇḍu and himself. Duryodhana too ruled them, and did them no wrong, but a great slaughter of kings occurred through his wickedness and pride and Dhṛtarāṣṭra's own foolish policy. Dhṛtarāṣṭra asks pardon for any faults he may have committed. He asks the subjects to consider his and Gāndhārī's griefs and hardships, and to grant him the permission he seeks; he will leave them with Yudhiṣṭhira as their excellent ruler. The people say nothing, but continue to weep.*

**[15]** *Dhṛtarāṣṭra repeats his request yet again. Still the subjects weep; but after some time they begin to discuss his words amongst themselves, and then they appoint a Brahmin named Sāmba to speak on behalf of all of them. He confirms that what Dhṛtarāṣṭra said is true: none of the Kuru kings has done anything to earn the subjects' displeasure, and that includes Duryodhana. Dhṛtarāṣṭra should do as Vyāsa has said, but they will grieve at his departure.*

*Then Sāmba indicates that he has more to say on the topic of Duryodhana and the slaughter at Kurukṣetra.* **[16]** *He tells Dhṛtarāṣṭra that the destruction of the Kurus was not caused by Duryodhana, or by Dhṛtarāṣṭra himself, or by Karṇa or Śakuni; it was caused by fate, which cannot be overcome by human effort. The subjects pardon Duryodhana of any wrong: let him attain the realms of the heroes. Dhṛtarāṣṭra himself will gain great merit, and Yudhiṣṭhira and the other Pāṇḍavas will protect the people. The assembled subjects applaud Sāmba's words, as does Dhṛtarāṣṭra, who then courteously dismisses the people.*

**[17]** *Next morning, Dhṛtarāṣṭra sends Vidura to Yudhiṣṭhira to announce that a date has been fixed for his departure for the forest, and to request sufficient wealth to allow him to perform* śrāddha *ceremonies for Bhīṣma, Droṇa, Somadatta, Bāhlika, Jayadratha, and his own sons and other allies. Yudhiṣṭhira and Arjuna are both pleased with this plan, but Bhīma reacts angrily, remembering all that Duryodhana did. Arjuna attempts to persuade him to give Dhṛtarāṣṭra what he asks, but Bhīma remains angry. He proposes that the Pāṇḍavas themselves should perform* śrāddhas *for Dhṛtarāṣṭra's allies, and that Kuntī should do so for Karṇa, but he does not want Duryodhana to receive a* śrāddha*; rather, he wants him and the other Dhārtarāṣṭras to go from bad to worse in their posthumous state. He reminds his brothers of all that they suffered for thirteen years, until Yudhiṣṭhira rebukes him and bids him hold his peace.* **[18]** *Arjuna tells Bhīma that it is virtuous to remember only good deeds, not offences, and he instructs Vidura to tell Dhṛtarāṣṭra that he will personally give him as much as he needs for the ceremonies. Yudhiṣṭhira applauds Arjuna's words, but Bhīma continues to glare. Yudhiṣṭhira instructs Vidura to inform Dhṛtarāṣṭra that he and Arjuna will supply the wealth he needs, and to request him to overlook Bhīma's hostility, which springs from all his suffering in the forest.*

**[19]** *Vidura reports to Dhṛtarāṣṭra that both Yudhiṣṭhira and Arjuna gladly pledged to give him whatever he asks, but that Bhīma found it hard to accept his plan; he also reports Yudhiṣṭhira's request that he forgive Bhīma. Dhṛtarāṣṭra is* *happy at the news, and he settles on a date for the distribution of the wealth he has been promised.*

Vaiśampāyana spoke:
[**20**] Hearing what Vidura had to say, Dhṛtarāṣṭra lord of men was
pleased with what King Yudhiṣṭhira and victorious Arjuna had done.
For the sake of Bhīṣma and of his own sons and allies, he selected suitable
Brahmins and excellent seers by the thousand. He ordered food and
drink, carriages, clothes, gold and jewels, slaves, slave-girls and other
gear, fine blankets and antelope-skins, villages, fields, goats and sheep,
ornaments, elephants, horses, the loveliest virgins; Dhṛtarāṣṭra the truest
of kings gave all away to the priests. With each gift he announced the
5 intended beneficiary: he named Droṇa, Bhīṣma, Somadatta and Bāhlika,
King Duryodhana, every one of his other sons, and all his allies, starting
with Jayadratha. That *śrāddha* ceremony grew ever more prodigious, as
Yudhiṣṭhira desired: great wealth in the form of cattle was bestowed
upon the Brahmins, as well as jewels and other riches in torrent after
torrent. On Yudhiṣṭhira's instructions, tellers and reckoners constantly
asked the old king, 'Command us: what are these persons to receive?
It is ready here to give.' And when Dhṛtarāṣṭra had spoken, it became
evident that where he had named a hundred, a thousand was awarded,
and where he had named a thousand, ten thousand, all on the orders of
wise King Yudhiṣṭhira, Kuntī's son.

10 So, like a cloud sating the earth with rain, King Dhṛtarāṣṭra sated
those priests with the torrents of wealth he showered upon them; and
when all was done, that lord of the earth then deluged his guests of
every class with downpours of food and drink. Indeed, the whole world
was deluged by the ocean of Dhṛtarāṣṭra's compassion; its foam was the
garments he gave away, its flood-water the jewels; its thundering roar
was the beating of his drums, its crocodiles and whirlpools the cows and
horses he bestowed; it was full of rich deposits of gems in the shape of
lovely women; grants of land and villages formed the rivers that fed it,
and gold and jewels its massed waters.

In this way, great king, Dhṛtarāṣṭra made the funerary offerings for
15 his sons and grandsons, and for his and Gāndhārī's ancestors. Then
when he grew weary from giving so many gifts, the Kaurava brought

that sacrifice of giving to a close. A great festival of giving had been undertaken by the Kuru king, with actors and male and female dancers, and generous gifts of food and drink; now, after ten days of giving, King Dhṛtarāṣṭra son of Ambikā had discharged his debt towards his sons and grandsons, O bull-like heir of Bharata.

[**21**] The next day, wise King Dhṛtarāṣṭra son of Ambikā summoned the heroic Pāṇḍavas, for he was impatient to leave for the forest. Together with Gāndhārī he greeted them duly; then, after having asked Brahmins who were expert in the Veda to perform the offering proper to the full-moon day of the month of Kārttika, as well as an offering to the Fire god Agni, the king set out from his dwelling, clad in bark garments and antelope-skins, and accompanied by his daughters-in-law. As King Dhṛtarāṣṭra son of Vicitravīrya set out, a great cry went up from all the wives of the Kauravas and Pāṇḍavas, as well as from other women born into the line of Kuru.

Then the old king paid honour to his home with offerings of roasted 5
grain and lovely flowers; he presented gifts of wealth to those who had been his servants, and then he turned away and left. King Yudhiṣṭhira stood with hands joined together; trembling, his voice choked with tears, he lamented loudly, saying, 'Great king and good man, where will you go now?' Then he fell to the ground. Arjuna too was suffering the burning pangs of grief; again and again that foremost heir of Bharata sighed, but, though plunged in despair, he strove to maintain his composure, and cautioned Yudhiṣṭhira to pull himself together. The two heroes wolf-belly Bhīma and Arjuna, along with Mādrī's twin sons, and Vidura, Saṃjaya, Yuyutsu the son of a Vaiśya woman, Kṛpa heir of Gotama, and Dhaumya and the other priests, followed the old king, weeping as they went. Kuntī led the blindfolded Gāndhārī forward, bearing her hand on her shoulder, while King Dhṛtarāṣṭra placed his own hand on the shoulder of Gāndhārī and walked confidently ahead.
Draupadī Kṛṣṇā, and Subhadrā the Yādava princess, and Uttarā of the 10
Kurus, the mother of young Parikṣit, and Citrāṅgadā, and all the other women set out with the old king, and so did his daughters-in-law; the sound of their griefstricken weeping, O king, was as loud as that of ospreys. The wives of the city's Brahmins and Kṣatriyas and Vaiśyas and Śūdras likewise rushed out of their houses on every side, for the townsfolk

in Hāstinapura were as deeply grieved at Dhṛtarāṣṭra's departure as they had formerly been when the Pāṇḍavas had had to leave after the dicing in the Kauravas' assembly hall. Even fair ladies whom neither sun nor moon had ever seen took to the streets in their grief when the lord of men, the lord of the Kauravas, set out for the mighty forest.

[**22**] *Dhṛtarāṣṭra leaves Hāstinapura. Vidura and Saṃjaya are determined to accompany him into the forest, but he orders Kṛpa and Yuyutsu to turn back, entrusting them to Yudhiṣṭhira's protection. Yudhiṣṭhira attempts to persuade Kuntī to return to the city, offering to go with Dhṛtarāṣṭra himself instead, but Kuntī insists that she will accompany Dhṛtarāṣṭra and Gāndhārī. She implores Yudhiṣṭhira to look after Sahadeva, who is so devoted to her*[1] *and to Yudhiṣṭhira himself; she asks him to remember Karṇa, whom she wronged so badly; she tells him to care for Draupadī and the other Pāṇḍavas. Yudhiṣṭhira appeals to her to change her mind: having encouraged him to follow the Kṣatriya way by citing the words of Vidurā,*[2] *how can she abandon him now that he has triumphed? Bhīma too tries to dissuade her from entering the forest. But Kuntī continues on her way, while Draupadī and the Pāṇḍavas follow her.* [**23**] *She acknowledges that she encouraged her sons; however, she did so for the sake of Pāṇḍu's lineage and the Pāṇḍavas' glory, not for her own sake. She does not desire the rewards of kingship; rather, she wishes to practise austerities, and thus to attain the realms won by her husband. She tells Yudhiṣṭhira and the others to return to the city.*

[**24**] *Realizing that they cannot change Kuntī's mind, the Pāṇḍavas bid farewell to Dhṛtarāṣṭra and turn back. But now Dhṛtarāṣṭra himself speaks against Kuntī entering the forest, and he appeals to Gāndhārī to persuade her to return; however, her resolve is firm. While the Pāṇḍavas and their womenfolk return to a joyless Hāstinapura, Dhṛtarāṣṭra travels on to the forest, where he and Gāndhārī and Kuntī pass their first night on the banks of the Gaṅgā, surrounded by pious Brahmins and attended by Vidura and Saṃjaya.* [**25**] *After spending some time there, they move on to Kurukṣetra, where Dhṛtarāṣṭra enters the hermitage of Śatayūpa, a Kekaya ruler who has handed the kingship over to his son in order to enter the forest. Śatayūpa accompanies him to Vyāsa's*

**1** The special affection between Kuntī and Mādrī's son Sahadeva has not been particularly evident till now, but it reappears in chapters 29, 31, 44 and 46 below.

**2** See 5.130–34.

*hermitage, where he is inducted into the life of the forest-dweller. Then he takes up residence in Śatayūpa's hermitage; Śatayūpa gives him instruction in his new way of life. Dhṛtarāṣṭra, Gāndhārī and Kuntī practise austerities there. Vidura and Saṃjaya wait on the king and queen; they also practise asceticism.*

**[26]** *On one occasion Dhṛtarāṣṭra is visited by Nārada, Parvata, Devala, Vyāsa and other wise ascetics. Nārada tells Dhṛtarāṣṭra of many former kings who have attained Indra's realm by taking up austerities and the forest life, and assures him that he and Gāndhārī will also achieve the highest goal: his brother Pāṇḍu, who now lives with Indra, is always thinking of him and will secure his well-being. Kuntī will be reunited with her husband; Vidura will enter into Yudhiṣṭhira,*[1] *and Saṃjaya will attain heaven.* **[27]** *Śatayūpa remarks that, though Nārada has specified that many other kings have attained the realm of Indra, he has not said what realm awaits Dhṛtarāṣṭra. Nārada replies that he has heard Indra himself say that Dhṛtarāṣṭra has three years of life left, after which he and Gāndhārī will travel in a flying chariot to the realm of Kubera. Freed as he is of his sins through asceticism, he will be able to travel through all the celestial regions.*

**[28]** *Meanwhile the Pāṇḍavas grieve for the loss of Dhṛtarāṣṭra and their mother, and the Brahmins and other people of Hāstinapura ask one another how Dhṛtarāṣṭra, Gāndhārī, Kuntī, Vidura and Saṃjaya may be faring in the forest. Nothing lightens the Pāṇḍavas' misery as they think of the five forest-dwellers, and as they remember the massacre at Kurukṣetra and the deaths of young Abhimanyu, Karṇa, Draupadī's sons, and other friends. Only the sight of Uttarā's son Parikṣit sustains them.*

**[29]** *The Pāṇḍavas continue to grieve, neglecting their duties and social responsibilities as they think about their mother, Dhṛtarāṣṭra and Gāndhārī. They determine to visit them in the forest. Sahadeva expresses his happiness that he is to see Kuntī again, and Draupadī echoes his sentiments. Now Yudhiṣṭhira gives the order for a great army to set forth, and for litters and carriages to be prepared for the ladies: they will set out the next day, and any citizen who wishes to do so may accompany them. In the morning they leave the city; they wait five days, guarding the great mass of people who assemble.* **[30]** *Then at Yudhiṣṭhira's command the army sets forth: there are men on horses, on elephants, on camels,*

1 See chapter 33 below. Vidura is the god Dharma incarnate (1.100.22–8); Yudhiṣṭhira is also the son and a partial incarnation of Dharma (1.114.1–7).

*riding in chariots, travelling on foot. The citizens too undertake the journey in many different ways. Kṛpa leads the army, while Yudhiṣṭhira travels in great glory along with his brothers; Yuyutsu and Dhaumya have remained behind to guard the city. Crossing the Yamunā, they see Śatayūpa's hermitage in the distance. Then they enter the forest.*

**[31]** *The Pāṇḍavas now humbly approach the hermitage on foot, followed by the rest of the host accompanying them. The ascetics there tell Yudhiṣṭhira that Dhṛtarāṣṭra has gone to the Yamunā, so he and his companions proceed there on foot, hurrying as they come into view. Sahadeva rushes ahead to fall weeping at Kuntī's feet; she embraces him closely. Then, seeing the other Pāṇḍavas, she hastens towards them; they too fall at her feet, and pay due honour to Dhṛtarāṣṭra and Gāndhārī. Yudhiṣṭhira now presents to Dhṛtarāṣṭra all those who have come to see him, till the old king feels as if he is back home in Hāstinapura. The greetings completed, everyone returns to the hermitage.* **[32]** *The ascetics there wish to know who among their visitors are the Pāṇḍavas and Draupadī. Saṃjaya responds by identifying the five Pāṇḍava brothers, Draupadī and the other wives of the Pāṇḍavas, Abhimanyu's widow Uttarā, and the widows of Dhṛtarāṣṭra's sons. The ascetics now withdraw, the troops move away from the hermitage, and the women, children and old folk sit down. Dhṛtarāṣṭra formally greets Yudhiṣṭhira.*

Vaiśampāyana spoke:
**[33]** 'Strong-armed Yudhiṣṭhira, my son,' said Dhṛtarāṣṭra, 'I trust that
you are well, along with all your brothers and the town and country
people? I trust that your dependants too are in good health, O lord, your
aides and servant-folk and all the elders? I trust you are following in the
ways trodden since days of old by royal sages? and that you maintain
a full treasury, so that your giving of gifts suffers no interruption? and
that you act appropriately towards friends, neutrals and enemies, and
give due thought to the Brahmins, favouring them with grants of land?
5 I trust, O bull-like heir of Bharata, that your disposition causes no
dissatisfaction to enemies or elders, citizens or servants, or to your own
close kin? I trust you offer faithful sacrifices to the ancestors and deities,
lord of kings? and that you honour guests with food and drink, O heir of
Bharata? I trust the priests within your realm delight in the performance
of their duties? and likewise the householders, whether Kṣatriya, Vaiśya

or Śūdra? I trust the women and the children and the old folk suffer no hardship, and want for nothing? and that the womenfolk of your household receive every honour, bull-like hero? I trust, great king, that, with you as ruler, this lineage of royal sages continues to maintain its rightful glory?'

Yudhiṣṭhira too was knowledgeable in matters of propriety and skilled as a speaker; he replied to Dhṛtarāṣṭra's words with his own polite greetings. 'O king, I trust that you perform your austerities without weariness, and that they are successful? I trust my mother here serves you with unwearying obedience? and that her life in the forest will bring its reward? Here is my senior mother, Queen Gāndhārī, exhausted with cold and wind and travel: I trust that as she practises her fierce asceticism she does not fall prey to grief for her slain sons, mighty heroes who were devoted to the Kṣatriya *dharma*? and that she does not constantly blame us as evildoers? But where is Vidura, O king? I do not see him. I trust, though, that Saṃjaya here remains well as he performs his austerities?'

'Vidura is well, son,' answered King Dhṛtarāṣṭra. 'He is engaged in fierce asceticism, taking no food, subsisting on nothing but air; he is grown thin, and his veins stand out. Sometimes the priests catch sight of him here or there in this deserted forest.'

Even as he spoke, the former chamberlain was sighted far off, naked and thin, hair matted, his mouth filled with stones, his body smeared with dirt and covered with dust from the forest. He looked towards the hermitage, saw all the people gathered there, and swiftly turned away. When King Yudhiṣṭhira was informed of this, he ran all alone in pursuit of him, following Vidura as he plunged deeper into the dreadful forest, sometimes in view, sometimes not. And as he ran after him with all his might, the king cried out, 'Vidura, O Vidura, I am your much-loved king Yudhiṣṭhira!' Then Vidura, foremost of the wise, halted in a solitary spot in the depths of the forest and leant against a tree there.

King Yudhiṣṭhira of mighty wisdom recognized Vidura of mighty wisdom from his look, though he was wasted almost completely away. Standing before him, the king said 'I am Yudhiṣṭhira' in his hearing. In answer, wise Vidura gestured with his hand; then, gazing unblinking at the king and deep in meditation, he entered into him, fusing his own sight with his sight, his own limbs with his limbs, his own breath with his breath, his own senses with his senses. Thus Vidura, seeming to blaze with fiery energy, used his yogic power to enter the body of King Yudhiṣṭhira lord of *dharma*. As for his own body, it remained as it was, leaning with staring eyes against the tree. The king saw that it was now lifeless; he also sensed that he himself was now many times more powerful than before. Pāṇḍu's learned son of mighty ardour, the lord of *dharma*, recalled his own entire former history, lord of the peoples, and the way of Yoga, as Vyāsa had described.[1]

30 Now learned Yudhiṣṭhira wished to perform the last rites for Vidura, so he prepared to cremate his body. But then a voice spoke: 'Sir, good king, this body known by the name of Vidura should not be burnt, for it is your body too, and he is eternal *dharma*. The unending realms shall be his, prince, for he held to the way of asceticism; do not grieve for him, O afflicter of your enemies!' At this, the lord of *dharma* returned once more and told King Dhṛtarāṣṭra son of Vicitravīrya all that had happened; that radiant king was utterly astonished, and so were Bhīma and all the others.

35 King Dhṛtarāṣṭra was pleased to hear Yudhiṣṭhira's words, and now he said to the son of Dharma, 'Please accept from me this water, and these roots and fruits, for it is said that a man's guest should eat the same food that he eats himself.' The son of Dharma accepted the king's offer, and he and his brothers fed on the fruits and roots that Dhṛtarāṣṭra gave them; then, having eaten his fruits and roots and drunk his water, they all encamped beneath the trees and passed the night there.

**[34]** *In the morning, Yudhiṣṭhira looks round the hermitage with his family and followers. He sees many sacrificial altars with blazing fires tended by forest sages, and beasts and birds with no fear of man. Then he gives away to the ascetics the vessels of gold and numerous other items he has brought for them. Returning to Dhṛtarāṣṭra, he finds him seated with Gāndhārī while Kuntī stands humbly nearby like a disciple standing before a* guru. *Dhṛtarāṣṭra bids Yudhiṣṭhira and his brothers to sit down, and they do so; then Śatayūpa and the other seers of Kurukṣetra join them. Next Vyāsa arrives with his disciples, and is honoured by all present.* **[35]** *Vyāsa enquires after the welfare of Dhṛtarāṣṭra, Gāndhārī,*

1 See note to chapter 26 above.

*Kuntī, Yudhiṣṭhira and the other Pāṇḍavas. He speaks of Vidura, whom he praises highly; he says that the one who is Dharma is Vidura, and the one who is Vidura is Yudhiṣṭhira, who stands before Dhṛtarāṣṭra like a servant. Then he announces that through the power of his asceticism he will show Dhṛtarāṣṭra some wonderful thing. He asks him to choose what it should be.*

## THE VISION OF THE SONS

**[36]** *—Janamejaya wants to know what wonder Vyāsa revealed; he also asks how long Yudhiṣṭhira and the other Pāṇḍavas lived in the forest, and what food they ate there. Vaiśaṃpāyana answers that they spent a month there enjoying various kinds of food and drink; it was then that Vyāsa and the other great seers arrived. Then he resumes his narrative.*

*— Vyāsa tells Dhṛtarāṣṭra that he is aware of the grief felt by him and by Gāndhārī, Kuntī, Draupadī and Subhadrā. He can grant Dhṛtarāṣṭra a boon: what is it to be? Dhṛtarāṣṭra answers that his only remaining anxiety is to know what befell all the heroes who perished in the slaughter caused by Duryodhana's wickedness; the memory of it torments him night and day.*

**[37]** *Dhṛtarāṣṭra's words renew the grief of Gāndhārī, Kuntī, Draupadī, Subhadrā and the Kaurava widows. Gāndhārī tells Vyāsa that Dhṛtarāṣṭra has grieved for the past sixteen years, unable to sleep at night; let Vyāsa show him his sons. Similarly, Draupadī, Subhadrā and the others who have lost sons and husbands in the great war are all still full of grief; Vyāsa can free them of their grief before they die. After Gāndhārī has spoken Vyāsa asks Kuntī to speak.* **[38]** *She tells Vyāsa the story of Karṇa's birth:*[1] *how she had pleased the irascible ascetic Durvāsas, and he had granted her the boon of being able to command deities to come to her; how one day, in childish innocence, she had used this boon to summon the Sun god, who had appeared before her; how she had asked him to leave once again, but he, unwilling to have been summoned in vain, had impregnated her with a son; how she had given birth to Karṇa, but cast him away in the waters. She says that her neglect of Karṇa torments her, and asks Vyāsa to allay her fears and to grant the king his desire. Vyāsa reassures her that she is not to blame for what happened.*

1 See 1.104.4–13.

**[39]** *Now Vyāsa announces that Gāndhārī and the others whose menfolk died in the slaughter will see them again. He adds that they should not grieve for the dead, since they met their deaths in carrying out their Kṣatriya* dharma*; everything that happened was inevitable, since it was purposed by the gods. Those who died at Kurukṣetra were incarnations of celestial and demonic beings; after completing their work in human form, the gods had returned to heaven once more. Vyāsa says that he will dispel the grief of the bereaved: they are to go to the Gaṅgā, where they will see all those who died on the battlefield.*

*At this everyone shouts for joy, and sets off for the Gaṅgā. They wait there for nightfall, when they will see their dead; the day passes as if it were a century, but finally the sun sets.*

Vaiśampāyana spoke:

**[40]** When night fell, all those who had gathered there completed their evening rituals and then approached Vyāsa. Righteous Dhṛtarāṣṭra sat with the Pāṇḍavas and the seers, pure and with focused mind; the ladies sat with Gāndhārī, and all the people of town and country sat together, grouped by age. That great sage Vyāsa of mighty ardour plunged into the holy water of the Gaṅgā and summoned up all those warrior hosts, fighters for the Pāṇḍavas and fighters for the Kauravas, and noble kings from many different lands.

Then, Janamejaya, a tumultuous roar could be heard within the waters, like the roar of the Kaurava and Pāṇḍava armies in former times; and then in their thousands all those princes arose from the waters, headed by Bhīṣma and Droṇa, and followed by their troops. Virāṭa and Drupada were both there, together with their sons and their warriors; the sons of Draupadī, and Abhimanyu son of Subhadrā, and the Rākṣasa Ghaṭotkaca; both Duryodhana and Karṇa, and the mighty chariot-fighter Śakuni, as well as Duḥśāsana and the other sons of Dhṛtarāṣṭra; Jarāsaṃdha's son Sahadeva; Bhagadatta and Prince Jalasaṃdha; Bhūriśravas, Śala, Śalya, Vṛṣasena son of Karṇa and his younger brother Suṣeṇa; Prince Lakṣmaṇa, Dhṛṣṭadyumna's son Kṣatradharman, and all of Śikhaṇḍin's sons; Dhṛṣṭaketu and his younger brother; Śakuni's brothers Acala and Vṛṣaka, and the Rākṣasa Alāyudha – these and many others too numerous to mention all rose up from the waters with shining bodies.

It could be seen that each of those heroic lords of men was equipped with his own proper dress and standard and chariot; all wore heavenly garments, all had brilliant earrings. Free from enmity and arrogance and anger, they wore heavenly clothes and garlands, while Gandharvas hymned them, bards praised them, and Apsarases thronged about them. Satyavatī's son, the sage Vyāsa, then benevolently made use of his ascetic power to bestow divine sight upon Dhṛtarāṣṭra, O lord of men; and Gāndhārī of high repute likewise received the power of divine knowledge, so that she beheld all her sons and all the others that had been slain upon the battlefield. This amazing, unthinkable vision made the hair rise on everyone's body, and all the people there, astonished, gazed at it with unblinking eyes. The advancing mass of warriors, intermingled with throngs of joyful women and full of festive high spirits, looked like a picture painted upon cloth. As for Dhṛtarāṣṭra, he rejoiced to behold all those heroes with the divine sight graciously granted him by the sage.

[**41**] Now all those best heirs of Bharata met together, free from their anger and jealousy and sin; observing the fair and exalted rules laid down by Brahmin seers, they were all now as cheerful-hearted as the gods in heaven. Son met with father and mother, wife with husband, brother with brother and friend with friend, O king. With joy the Pāṇḍavas met the mighty bowman Karṇa, and also Abhimanyu son of Subhadrā, and all of Draupadī's sons; happy at meeting Karṇa, those lords of the earth entered into friendship with him, and through the seer's grace other Kṣatriyas too, their anger gone for ever, gave up their enmities and made friends.

Thus the tiger-like heroes, both Kurus and men of other lines, all met their kinsmen and their elders and their sons. They passed the whole of that one night in cheerful-hearted enjoyment; in their contentment, the kings felt they were living in heaven. As the warriors met one another, bull-like heir of Bharata, they experienced no grief, no danger, no fear, no ill will, no dishonour; the women too, overjoyed at meeting their fathers, brothers, husbands and sons, cast their grief aside. After passing one night in such enjoyment, the heroes and their women embraced and bade each other farewell. Then they left as they had come; the bull-like sage Vyāsa dismissed the warrior hosts, and in a trice they disappeared before the eyes of all. Plunging into the holy river Gaṅgā with their chariots and standards, the noble heroes returned to their own abodes; some went to the realm of the gods, some to the place of Brahmā; some reached the realm of Varuṇa, others that of Kubera; of the kings, some went to the realm of Yama, while some of the Rākṣasas and Piśācas reached the land of the northern Kurus.[1] Thus all of those noble heroes came, with their steeds and followers, to the wonderful situations they had attained with the gods.

When they had all gone, the great sage righteous Vyāsa of mighty ardour, ever the benefactor of the Kurus, then addressed all the Kṣatriya widows from the water where he stood: 'Those foremost of women amongst you who desire the realms gained by their husbands should not delay, but hasten to plunge into the waters of the Gaṅgā!' Then, hearing his words, those lovely women, full of faith, took leave of their father-in-law Dhṛtarāṣṭra, and entered Gaṅgā's waters. Freed from their mortal bodies, those virtuous women were then all reunited with their husbands, lord of the peoples; in this way all those well-bred, well-born women, entering the water, gained freedom and the realms of their husbands. Like their husbands they acquired a heavenly form, and were adorned with heavenly ornaments and heavenly clothes and garlands; those well-bred, mettlesome women, freed from weariness and Darkness and filled with every virtue, all now went to their own abodes.

At that time, whatever desire any man had, Vyāsa the righteous giver of boons granted it. All men who heard of this reunion of the kings were filled with delight and joy, even those who had passed on to new bodies.

— *Vaiśaṃpāyana says that whoever hears this tale of reunion prospers in this world and the next; whoever recites it gains the highest perfection.* **[42]** *Janamejaya asks how men who had left their bodies could be seen again in embodied form. Vaiśaṃpāyana replies that deeds do not perish, and that bodies and features have their existence as the result of deeds.*

1 See note to 1.102.10.

Vaiśaṃpāyana spoke:
[**43**] King Dhṛtarāṣṭra, who had never seen his sons, gained a sight of them in their own true forms through the seer's grace, heir of Kuru; likewise that best of kings gained knowledge of the *dharma* of kings and of the nature of *brahman*, as well as acquiring intellectual decisiveness. Wise Vidura attained perfection through the power of his asceticism; Dhṛtarāṣṭra did so through his contact with the ascetic Vyāsa.

Janamejaya spoke:
If Vyāsa the giver of boons were to allow me to see my father in his own form and dress, and at his own age, then I would have faith in all that you have told me. That would please me; that would give me fulfilment. I am resolved: may my desire come to fruition through the grace of the seer's son!

The Sūta[1] spoke:
When King Janamejaya had spoken, wise Vyāsa of mighty energy showed him his grace, and brought Parikṣit before him. King Parikṣit came there from heaven in his own form and dress, and at his own age, and Janamejaya beheld his glorious father thus; he also beheld noble Śamīka and his son Śṛṅgin, as well as Parikṣit's ministers.[2] King Janamejaya, who was taking the final ritual bath to conclude his snake sacrifice, was filled with joy, and bathed his father as well as himself; then after bathing that best heir of Bharata addressed Āstīka son of Jaratkāru, born in the line of the Yāyāvara Brahmins:[3] 'Āstīka, it seems to me that this sacrifice has produced marvels of many kinds, for now my father has appeared to me to destroy my grief.'

'Best heir of Kuru's line,' answered Āstīka, 'when a sacrifice is attended by that great ascetic Vyāsa, the ancient seer, the sacrificer conquers both

**1** Ugraśravas, who has been narrating the tale of the *Mahābhārata* as related by Vaiśaṃpāyana to Janamejaya at the latter's snake sacrifice: see 1.53–4. Now both sacrifice and narrative are drawing to a close.

**2** See 1.36–40 for Śṛṅgin's curse and Parikṣit's consequent death; for Janamejaya's decision to avenge his death by means of a snake sacrifice see 1.45–7.

**3** For Āstīka's birth see 1.41–4; for his mission to save the snakes by bringing Janamejaya's sacrifice to a premature end see 1.48–51.

heaven and earth. You have heard a wonderful narrative, heir of Pāṇḍu; you have reduced the snakes to ash; you have followed in your father's footsteps; through your truthfulness, O prince, I have even been able to save Takṣaka;[1] you have honoured all the seers, and seen your noble father's condition. By hearing this sin-destroying narrative you have gained immense merit, and by seeing that noble man you have untied the knots that oppressed your heart. Those who take *dharma*'s side, those who delight in good conduct, those at whose sight sin wanes: these are the men who deserve honour.'

When King Janamejaya heard that excellent Brahmin seer say these words, he did him honour again and again. Then, knowing *dharma* as he did, he asked the invincible seer Kṛṣṇa Dvaipāyana Vyāsa to relate the rest of the story of Dhṛtarāṣṭra's life in the forest, O truest one.

Janamejaya spoke:
**[44]** After seeing his sons and grandsons and their followers in this way, what did King Dhṛtarāṣṭra do? And what did King Yudhiṣṭhira do?

Vaiśampāyana spoke:
When he had experienced the great wonder of seeing his sons once more, Dhṛtarāṣṭra the royal seer, freed from his grief, came back to the hermitage, where he gave leave to all the common people and the great seers to return home as they wished. The noble Pāṇḍavas too, along with their small force of soldiers, followed the noble king and his wife back to the hermitage. Once he arrived there, Dhṛtarāṣṭra was addressed by Satyavatī's son Vyāsa the sage, the wise Brahmin seer honoured by all the world: 'Strong-armed heir of Kuru! Listen to what I say, Dhṛtarāṣṭra. You have heard many different pronouncements made by ancient seers, men of holy deeds who are senior in learning and high birth, expert in the Vedas and their branches, learned expounders of *dharma*. You have heard the mysteries of the gods from Nārada, who knows them well. Do not set your heart on grief! The wise man does not trouble himself over fate. By practising the Kṣatriya *dharma*, your sons have attained that

1 See 1.50–53: Janamejaya was true to his word in giving Āstīka what he sought, even though it was disagreeable to himself.

fair state that the sword makes pure; as you have seen, they pass their time at pleasure. However, wise Yudhiṣṭhira here, together with all his 10
brothers and his wife and friends, now seeks your leave. Let him go, to resume ruling his kingdom, for all of them have spent more than a month living here in the forest. Kingship has to be constantly and carefully guarded, O enemy-afflicting king, and this kingdom certainly has many foes.'

The Kuru king heard what Vyāsa of boundless understanding had said, and he summoned Yudhiṣṭhira, and eloquently spoke these words: 'Bless you, Yudhiṣṭhira Ajātaśatru! Listen with your brothers to what I have to say. Through your grace, lord of the earth, grief no longer torments me; thanks to you, my learned son, I am as happy as I formerly 15
was in Hāstinapura, for I am attended by my lord who occupies himself with pleasing me. From you I have gained the reward that a father gains from a son, and I am highly pleased with you.

'Strong-armed hero, no anger remains with me. Go now, my son; do not delay, for my austerities are being eroded by seeing you; therefore, having seen you, I have once more set my body to asceticism. Your two mothers here share my observances, son, living on fallen leaves; they will not survive long. Thanks to the power of Vyāsa's austerities, and to your arrival here, I have seen Duryodhana and the others, though they have passed to the other world. The purpose of my life 20
was completed long ago, sinless hero, and now I shall devote myself to fierce asceticism; please give me your consent. From today my funeral offerings and good name, and this entire lineage, all depend on you. Go today or tomorrow, my son; do not delay. You have heard much about the conduct proper for kings, O bull-like heir of Bharata, and I do not see what further instruction I can give. Lord, there is no more to say.'

When King Dhṛtarāṣṭra had finished speaking, King Yudhiṣṭhira addressed him: 'It is not right for you who know *dharma* to abandon me when I have done no wrong. By all means let my brothers go, and likewise my attendants; but I shall follow you, sir, and my two vow-observing mothers.'

'Do not speak so,' replied Gāndhārī. 'Son, listen to me. The Kuru 25
lineage depends on you, and so do my father-in-law's funeral offerings.

Go, son: you have paid us honour enough. What the king has said should be done. Son, do your father's bidding.'

At this, Yudhiṣṭhira, wiping the loving tears from his eyes, spoke to Kuntī, who was weeping too. 'The king is sending me away, and so is Gāndhārī of high repute. How am I to bear the pain of leaving when my heart is tied to you? However, I would not dare to impede your asceticism, righteous lady, for there is nothing higher than asceticism, through which one attains great things. I too no longer care for kingship as once I did, O queen; it is asceticism that now completely attracts my mind. This entire earth seems empty now, fair lady, and causes me no pleasure. My kinsmen have been destroyed, and my might is not what it was; the Pāñcālas have been utterly wiped out, and nothing remains but daughters. I do not see anyone who might restore their line, fair lady, for Droṇa reduced them single-handed to ash in battle, and Droṇa's son slew by night those who survived. The same applies to the Cedis and Matsyas, whom once we used to see. Only the Vṛṣṇis remain, thanks to Kṛṣṇa Vāsudeva, to give me the will to continue as I am; and that is for *dharma*'s sake and for no other reason.

'Look kindly on us all, mother. It is not likely that we shall see you again, for the king is going to undertake severe austerities.'

When Sahadeva, the strong-armed warrior lord, heard this, his eyes were flooded with tears, and he spoke these words to Yudhiṣṭhira. 'I cannot bring myself to leave our mother, bull-like prince. You should return home without delay, sir; I, however, shall perform austerities in the forest. Here I shall remain, mortifying my body with asceticism, devoted to serving at the feet of the king and these two mothers of ours.'

But Kuntī, embracing the strong-armed hero, said to him, 'Go, son, and do not speak thus; do my bidding. My sons, may your ways be auspicious. Stay well. If you were to act as you have said, Sahadeva, it would impede my asceticism: bound by the ties of my affection for you, I would fail in my high austerities. So go, son; for there is little life left to me.' With various such speeches Kuntī strengthened the hearts of Sahadeva and, more particularly, King Yudhiṣṭhira, O lord of kings.

Now that all the bull-like Kurus had received leave to depart from their mother and King Dhṛtarāṣṭra, they saluted that best heir of Kuru and began bidding him farewell. 'O king,' said Yudhiṣṭhira, 'with your good

blessing we shall return home; with your leave we shall depart, freed
from all sin.' In answer, the royal seer Dhṛtarāṣṭra returned Yudhiṣṭhira's 45
salutation and gave him leave, with blessings for his triumph. He spoke with kindness to Bhīma, the best of mighty men, and that intelligent hero accepted his words in the proper spirit.[1] Next, the Kuru king embraced Arjuna and the bull-like twins; with many embraces and salutations, he gave them leave to go. They all paid their respects at Gāndhārī's feet, and received her leave also; their mother kissed them and embraced them; then, like calves being separated from the herd, they respectfully circumambulated King Dhṛtarāṣṭra. Again and again they walked around him and gazed at him.

In the same way, virtuous Draupadī and all the Kuru women paid the 50
proper respects to their father-in-law before setting forth; with many embraces and salutations, their mothers-in-law both gave them leave to go, along with much advice on proper conduct. Then they set out with their husbands. Now a great roar went up: charioteers called out, 'Yoke!', camels bellowed and horses whinnied, as King Yudhiṣṭhira with his wife and kin and warriors came back once more to the city of Hāstinapura.

## THE ARRIVAL OF NĀRADA

**[45]** *Two years later, Nārada visits Yudhiṣṭhira. After the formalities have been exchanged, Yudhiṣṭhira asks him if he has seen the forest-dwellers. Nārada replies that he has, and asks Yudhiṣṭhira to listen calmly. After the Pāṇḍavas left Kurukṣetra, he says, Dhṛtarāṣṭra and his companions proceeded to Gaṅgādvāra,*[2] *where they engaged in extreme austerities, living without a home. Saṃjaya was Dhṛtarāṣṭra's guide, while Kuntī guided Gāndhārī. One day the wind whipped up a fierce forest fire. The king and the two women were too weak to escape it. Dhṛtarāṣṭra told Saṃjaya to find safety for himself; he, Gāndhārī and Kuntī*

1 The reference is to Bhīma's simmering hostility towards Dhṛtarāṣṭra: see chapters 1, 3–4, 17–18 above.

2 Modern Haridwar, where the river Gaṅgā enters the plain.

*would allow the fire to end their lives. Saṃjaya's efforts to persuade him not to die in an unsanctified fire were fruitless, so he bade farewell and left; Dhṛtarāṣṭra, Gāndhārī and Kuntī were taken by the fire. Subsequently Saṃjaya left for Mount Himālaya. Many ascetics assembled on hearing of the old king's end, but they did not grieve. Nārada tells Yudhiṣṭhira that he too should refrain from grieving, as all three met a good end.*

*Despite his words, all the Pāṇḍavas and their womenfolk are filled with grief and lament loudly, as do the citizens. Then Yudhiṣṭhira speaks.* **[46]** *He says that the course of human existence is hard to understand: a king as mighty as Dhṛtarāṣṭra has died a wretched death in a forest fire. He feels no grief for Gāndhārī, who has gained the realms won by her husband, but he does grieve for his mother Kuntī, who abandoned her sons' wealth and majesty for life in the forest. He rails against his own sovereignty and the Kṣatriya* dharma*; he rails against the Fire god for burning his mother despite having received help from Arjuna.*[1] *Even worse, this was an unsanctified fire. Yudhiṣṭhira laments to think of the fear Kuntī must have experienced as the fire surrounded her, and not even Sahadeva, her favourite son, came to rescue her.*

Vaiśampāyana spoke:
**[47]** 'Heir of Bharata,' answered Nārada, 'as I learnt there, it was no unsanctified fire that burnt King Dhṛtarāṣṭra son of Vicitravīrya. I shall inform you of what happened. I was told that the wise king, who was subsisting on nothing but air, entered the forest once more after having an offering made. He left his sacred fires behind; but the sacrificial priests abandoned his fires in the deserted forest and went their way, O truest heir of Bharata. It seems that fire then grew and spread in the forest, till the trees themselves were ablaze with it; this is what the ascetics told me.
5 O bull-like heir of Bharata, it was his own fire that the king met with on Gaṅgā's bank, in the manner I described to you before; this is what those sages told me, sinless hero. So King Dhṛtarāṣṭra fell victim to his own sacred fire, lord of the earth. You should not grieve for him, for he has attained the highest state. Your mother too, O son of Pāṇḍu, thanks to her devoted service to her elders, has attained the highest perfection; of this I have no doubt. You should perform the water offerings for

1 See 1.214 ff.

them all, O heir of Kuru, along with all your brothers. Let this be undertaken.'

O bull-like heir of Bharata, King Yudhiṣṭhira the Pāṇḍava lord then 10
set forth with his wife and brothers. The town and country people too, full of devotion for the old king, set out towards the Gaṅgā, each person dressed in a single garment. Then all of the bull-like Kurus plunged into the water and, under the leadership of Yuyutsu,[1] offered water to noble Dhṛtarāṣṭra, Gāndhārī and Kuntī in the proper manner, proclaiming each recipient's name and family. They then returned to Hāstinapura to purify themselves, remaining outside the city.[2]

Yudhiṣṭhira sent his trusted agents, men skilled in rituals, to Gaṅgā-
dvāra where King Dhṛtarāṣṭra, best heir of Kuru, had been burnt; the 15
lord of the earth paid them their due, then ordered them to gather the bones of the deceased at Gaṅgādvāra itself. On the twelfth day, his purification completed, the Pāṇḍava king performed *śrāddha* ceremonies for the dead in the proper manner, complete with many gifts to the Brahmins: in Dhṛtarāṣṭra's name he gave gold, silver, cattle and costly beds, whilst in the names of Gāndhārī and Kuntī the king of mighty ardour gave many different gifts of unprecedented wealth. Whatever a Brahmin desired, and however much, that he received – beds, food,
carriages, jewels and other wealth; the king gave out carriages, clothes, 20
food, slave-girls and maidservants in the names of his two mothers. Then, having performed numbers of *śrāddhas*, the wise lord of the earth once more entered his city of Hāstinapura.

The men who had gone to Gaṅgādvāra at the king's command now returned after gathering the bones of the deceased; they informed King Yudhiṣṭhira that they had honoured the bones properly with many garlands and perfumes, and then released them into the Gaṅgā.

As for Nārada, that highest of seers spoke words of comfort to
righteous King Yudhiṣṭhira and then went his way. But Yudhiṣṭhira 25
himself was cheerless at heart; his kinsmen and close relatives were now all slain, but he continued to maintain his kingship.

1 Dhṛtarāṣṭra's one surviving son.

2 Cf. 12.1.

# THE CLUBS

## THE CLUBS

[1] *Thirty-six years after the end of the war at Kurukṣetra, Yudhiṣṭhira observes inauspicious portents: violent winds blow, birds circle from right to left, rivers flow backwards, and many other such signs. Then he learns of a great slaughter of the Vṛṣṇis in a club battle. He summons his brothers. They are distressed to hear of the destruction of the Vṛṣṇis; they find the news of Kṛṣṇa's death as incredible as the drying-up of the ocean.*

Janamejaya spoke:
[2] Blessed sir, how did it happen that the Andhakas, the Vṛṣṇis and those mighty chariot-fighters the Bhojas were all destroyed before Kṛṣṇa Vāsudeva's very eyes?

Vaiśaṃpāyana spoke:
In the thirty-sixth year after the war a great evil befell the Vṛṣṇis, and, urged on by fate, they slaughtered one another with clubs.

Janamejaya spoke:
Who cursed the Vṛṣṇis, Andhakas and Bhojas, that those heroes went to their destruction? Best of Brahmins, tell me in detail.

Vaiśaṃpāyana spoke:
Viśvāmitra, Kaṇva and Nārada the ascetic once visited Dvārakā, and the Vṛṣṇi heroes headed by Sāraṇa saw them there. Suffering under the rod of destiny, they dressed Sāmba up as a woman, took him before the

visitors, and said, 'This is the wife of Babhru of boundless ardour, who wishes for a son. Foretell it truly: to what will she give birth?'

When the sages heard these words, O king, they were furious at the deception; now hear the reply they gave. 'This Sāmba, Kṛṣṇa Vāsudeva's son, shall give birth to a fearsome iron club that will destroy the Vṛṣṇis and the Andhakas. By means of it you shall wipe out the entire Vṛṣṇi line, save for Balarāma and Kṛṣṇa, for you are men of evil conduct, malicious and prey to anger. As for Balarāma the glorious plough-bearer, he will cast off his body and enter the ocean, while noble Kṛṣṇa will be cut down by Jarā as he lies upon the ground.'[1]

That was what the sages said, O king, when those wicked Vṛṣṇis deceived them. They gazed at each other through eyes that were red with anger; then, after speaking those words, they went to see Kṛṣṇa Keśava. The slayer of Madhu heard what had happened, and then he told the Vṛṣṇis of it. 'It is inevitable,' he said, for he was wise and knew what end was coming. Then he entered his house once more; the lord of the world did not want to change fate.

The next day, Sāmba gave birth to that club that would destroy the Vṛṣṇis and the Andhakas. It was huge, like a Kiṃkara Rākṣasa. King Āhuka was saddened to learn that that dreadful club had been produced, thanks to the curse; he gave orders for it to be pulverized, and then agents acting at his command hurled it into the ocean. And they made this proclamation in the city on Āhuka's instructions: 'From today on, it is forbidden for residents of the city to manufacture liquor in the houses of the Vṛṣṇis and Andhakas. Any man who makes strong drink in any place shall, if we come to know of it, be impaled alive upon a stake for his act, together with his family!' When the men of Dvārakā learnt of noble Āhuka's command they all obeyed it, for they were frightened of the king.

**[3]** Despite the precautions of the Vṛṣṇis and the Andhakas, Time constantly stalked round all their houses, in the form of a fearsome, monstrous man, bald-headed, with black and orange skin; he gazed in at the Vṛṣṇi houses, but nowhere could he be seen. Day after day many

1 As a feminine noun, *jarā* means 'old age'. In this narrative it is used as the name of a (male) hunter.

dreadful gales blew, making everyone's hair stand on end, signalling
the destruction of the Vṛṣṇis and Andhakas. The streets teemed with
huge rats; water-pots broke; in the Vṛṣṇi houses, the cries of shrieking
5 mynah birds were not silenced by day or night. Cranes imitated the
call of owls, and goats howled like jackals; white birds with red feet
appeared at the prompting of fate, and pigeons flew about the Vṛṣṇi
houses. Cows gave birth to asses, mules to elephants, dogs to cats, and
mongooses to rats. The Vṛṣṇis began to sin without shame, showing
hostility to Brahmins, ancestors and gods; apart from Balarāma and
Kṛṣṇa the stirrer of men, they now despised their elders. Wives betrayed
10 husbands, and husbands betrayed wives. Fires blazed towards the left
and emitted flames of differing colours, blue and red and scarlet; the
sun, as it rose and set each day above the city, seemed to be surrounded
by headless bodies.[1] Food that was perfectly prepared in the kitchen
was found to be full of maggots when it came to be eaten, Bhārata
king; when benedictions were pronounced, and when noble people
prayed, the sound of running feet was heard, but no one could be
seen. Everyone saw the constellations and planets collide again and
again with one another, but no man could make out the constellation
15 of his birth. In the Vṛṣṇi and Andhaka houses, the sound of Kṛṣṇa's
conch Pāñcajanya was echoed back on every side by asses braying
horribly.

Kṛṣṇa lord of the senses could see the turn that Time had taken; he
could see that the new-moon night had fallen on the thirteenth day
of the month,[2] and he announced, 'Rāhu[3] has once again made the
thirteenth day of the month into the fifteenth. That happened during
the Bhārata war, and it has happened again today for our destruction.'
The slayer of Keśin, Kṛṣṇa the stirrer of men, deliberated and reflected
on the time, and he realized that the thirty-sixth year had arrived, and
that the curse pronounced by Gāndhārī, distraught with grief for her
20 sons and slain kinsmen, had now come to pass.[4] 'What has befallen now,'

1 These were highly inauspicious clouds associated with eclipses: cf. 6.2.20 and note.

2 Two days early.

3 The demon of the eclipse: see 1.17.

4 See 11.25.

he said, 'is what Yudhiṣṭhira spoke of long ago, when he saw dreadful portents as the armies stood arrayed.'

After speaking these words, Kṛṣṇa Vāsudeva, resolved to make it happen, then ordered a pilgrimage, O foe-tamer; at Keśava's command men proclaimed, 'Bull-like heroes! You must undertake a pilgrimage to the ocean.'

[4] Meanwhile, the city women were robbed in their dreams by a black woman with white teeth who ran about Dvārakā entering houses by night and laughing; and frightful Rākṣasas were seen to steal the men's ornaments and umbrellas, their standards and armour. The iron discus Vajranābha that the Fire god had given to Kṛṣṇa[1] now flew up to heaven before the eyes of the Vṛṣṇis. Before the eyes of Kṛṣṇa's charioteer Dāruka the horses carried off his ready-yoked chariot, splendid as the sun; those four excellent steeds, swift as thought, ran away across the surface of the ocean. The two great standards of Balarāma and Kṛṣṇa 5
that they had so highly reverenced, that of the palm tree and that of Garuḍa,[2] were carried aloft by Apsarases, who cried out day and night, 'You must go on this pilgrimage!'

So the mighty Vṛṣṇi and Andhaka chariot-fighters decided to go; the bull-like heroes and their womenfolk now made ready for the pilgrimage. They prepared foodstuffs of every kind, and drink, and many varieties of meat and liquor, and then those rum-quaffing heroes set out from the city in all their glory, full of fiery energy, travelling by chariot or on horseback or elephant-back. The Yādavas came to Prabhāsa[3] and settled there with their wives and their stocks of food and drink in the dwellings that were assigned to them.

Kṛṣṇa's friend Uddhava, hearing they had arrived at the ocean's 10
edge, went there to bid farewell to those heroes, for he was expert in Yoga and knew the truth of things. As that noble man left with hands joined together, Hari Kṛṣṇa saluted him, knowing the destruction of the Vṛṣṇis was at hand, and with no desire to prevent it. The mighty

**1** See 1.216.

**2** See 2.22.22–3.

**3** The nearby holy site now known as Somnath, on the coast of Saurashtra in modern Gujarat.

Vṛṣṇi and Andhaka chariot-fighters, for whom time had run out, now saw Uddhava travelling away from them, filling heaven and earth with his fiery energy.

But then the noble Vṛṣṇis took the food that had been prepared for the Brahmins, and gave it, newly flavoured with liquor, to the monkeys. Those heroes of fiery energy began a great drinking party at Prabhāsa, to the sound of hundreds of trumpets, while actors acted and dancers danced. In Kṛṣṇa's presence Balarāma began to drink, and so did Kṛtavarman, Sātyaki, Gada and Babhru. Then in the midst of the company, Sātyaki, very drunk, laughed mockingly at Kṛtavarman and said contemptuously, 'Who that considers himself a Kṣatriya would slay men who were sleeping as if already dead? Son of Hṛdika, the Yādavas could never pardon what you did!'[1] Pradyumna applauded Sātyaki's words, for that best of chariot-fighters despised Hṛdika's son.

Now Kṛtavarman, utterly enraged, replied to Sātyaki, pointing at him insultingly with his left hand: 'How could you, as a heroic warrior, cut down Bhūriśravas in battle when his arm had been severed and he was preparing to die? That was a cruel murder!'[2] Kṛṣṇa Keśava, the slayer of enemy heroes, heard what he said, and glared angrily at him; and then Sātyaki reminded the slayer of Madhu of the story of the gem Syamantaka that had belonged to Satrājit,[3] at which Satrājit's daughter, Kṛṣṇa's queen Satyabhāmā, ran weeping to Keśava, furious herself and goading him to fury.

Sātyaki now stood up and angrily said, 'Here I swear truly that I shall follow in the path of Draupadī's five sons, of Dhṛṣṭadyumna and Śikhaṇḍin, and of all those who were slain as they slept during the night-raid by this wicked Kṛtavarman and Droṇa's son Aśvatthāman. Slender-waisted lady Satyabhāmā, today this man's life and his good name have reached their end!' With these words he furiously attacked Kṛtavarman, and in Kṛṣṇa Keśava's presence he cut off his head. Then

1 In the night-raid of Book 10.

2 See 7.117–18.

3 Nothing further is said about this fabulous gem in the *Mahābhārata*, but its complex history, which led to Satrājit's death, is told in later mythological texts.

he began to cut down others all around him, till Kṛṣṇa the lord of the senses rushed up to prevent him.

Great king, the Bhojas and Andhakas, urged on by the evil turn of
Time, all combined to surround Śini's son Sātyaki; Kṛṣṇa of mighty 30
ardour saw them running to attack him in their anger, but, knowing the turn that Time had taken, he did not himself at first grow angry. However, in their drunken rage, they beat Sātyaki with dishes defiled with leftover food. Pradyumna, son of Kṛṣṇa and Rukmiṇī, was enraged to see the son of Śini beaten so, and rushed at once to rescue him. He and Sātyaki battled with the Bhojas and Andhakas, but they were too numerous, and both men were killed before Kṛṣṇa's eyes.

When Yadu's heir Keśava beheld the son of Śini and his own son slain,
he grew angry. Then he plucked a handful of *erakā* grass; it became a 35
dreadful iron club, as hard as adamant, and with that club Kṛṣṇa slew all those who stood before him. At this, the Andhakas, Bhojas, Śaineyas and Vṛṣṇis, urged on by fate, fell to fighting, and killed one another with clubs; for whichever of them angrily plucked a blade of *erakā*, O king, at once that was seen to turn to adamant; prince, you should know that every single blade of grass there became a club, thanks to the curse of those Brahmins. Whenever a man whirled a blade of grass and hurled it, it was seen to become a mighty adamantine club, O king.

Son killed father, and father son, heir of Bharata, as men rushed 40
drunkenly about, smashing each other with clubs. The Kukuras and Andhakas fell, like moths falling into a flame; yet no one thought to flee as the massacre proceeded. Strong-armed Kṛṣṇa the slayer of Madhu, seeing the turn that Time had taken, stood brandishing a club. He saw that Sāmba had been killed, and Cārudeṣṇa, Pradyumna and Aniruddha, O heir of Bharata, and he was filled with anger. Seeing Gada too lying dead, the bearer of bow, discus and club became greatly enraged, and slaughtered those who still lived.

Babhru of mighty ardour, the conqueror of enemy fortresses, saw the 45
prince of Daśārha engaged in his slaughter, and so did Dāruka. Hear what they said to him: 'Blessed lord, invincible one, you have destroyed almost all of them. Now seek the path taken by Balarāma. Let us go to where he is.'

**[5]** Then Dāruka, Keśava and Babhru set out to follow Balarāma's

track. They found that hero of infinite strength in a solitary spot, standing
by a tree deep in thought. Once they had found him, noble-minded
Kṛṣṇa commanded Dāruka, 'Go swiftly to the Kurus, and inform Kuntī's
son of this great slaughter of the Yadus. Arjuna must hasten to come
here when he learns that the Yādavas have died through the curse of
Brahmins.' On receiving this order, Dāruka set out by chariot for the
Kurus, out of his mind with grief.

Once Dāruka had left, Keśava, seeing that Babhru was still at his
side, said, 'Go at once, sir, to protect the womenfolk, lest robbers
5 molest them to steal their wealth.' Babhru, overcome by liquor and by
grief at the death of his kinsmen, set out at Keśava's command. He
had not gone far, hurrying on alone, when he was slain by a huge
club let fly by a hidden hunter, for he too had been cursed by the
Brahmins.

When Kṛṣṇa saw that Babhru had been killed, he said to his elder brother Balarāma, 'Wait for me right here till I have appointed relatives to look after the women.' Then the stirrer of men returned to the city of Dvārakā and said to his father Vasudeva, 'Sir, you must protect all our womenfolk until the arrival of wealth-winner Arjuna. Balarāma is waiting for me in the forest, and I shall rejoin him now. I have seen the deaths of the Yadus here, and, before that, the deaths of the bull-like Kuru kings, and now I cannot bear to see this city of the Yādavas empty of Yādavas. I shall take to the forest with Balarāma and practise asceticism: hear what I say.' With these words Kṛṣṇa touched his head to his father's feet, and left quickly.

10 But now a great hubbub arose from women and children of the
city. Keśava, hearing the cries of wailing women, stopped them from
following him, and said, 'That foremost of heroes the ambidextrous
warrior Arjuna will come to this city to rescue you from your grief.' Then
he went straight to the forest, where he saw Balarāma still standing alone
in that solitary place. He was absorbed in Yoga, and Kṛṣṇa saw a great
serpent issuing from his mouth, white in colour; that noble-minded
creature had a thousand heads with red mouths, and his hood was as
high as a mountain. As Kṛṣṇa watched, he abandoned the body that had
been his, and set off for the ocean; and the ocean received him with
15 honour, as did the celestial serpents and sacred rivers, and King Varuṇa

himself, O king. Advancing to greet him, they made him welcome and honoured him by making the guest-offering and washing his feet.

Now that his brother had passed on, Kṛṣṇa Vāsudeva, who with his divine vision knew all ends, wandered for some time in the deserted forest, deep in thought. Then that most ardent one lay down upon the earth. All this had been known to him before, from the words that Gāndhārī had spoken to him long ago; he remembered too what Durvāsas had said when he had made Kṛṣṇa smear himself with leftover *pāyasa*.[1] Reflecting on the destruction of the Andhakas and Vṛṣṇis, and also on that of the Kurus, the noble-minded one decided that the time had come for him to pass on himself, and he therefore used Yoga to restrain his senses. Kṛṣṇa lay absorbed in highest Yoga, his senses, speech and mind restrained. It was then that the fierce hunter Jarā arrived at that place, hoping to catch deer. Mistaking Kṛṣṇa Keśava, who was lying absorbed 20
in Yoga, for a deer, Jarā the hunter swiftly pierced him with an arrow in the sole of the foot, and then approached to claim his prey. What that hunter beheld was a man with many arms dressed in yellow garments, absorbed in Yoga. Thinking that he had committed a dreadful crime, he touched his head to Kṛṣṇa's feet in distress; but noble Kṛṣṇa reassured him, even as he soared aloft, filling all heaven and earth with his glory.

When Kṛṣṇa reached heaven, Indra came forth to greet him, and so did the Aśvins and Rudras, the Ādityas and Vasus, the All-gods, sages and Siddhas, and the foremost Gandharvas and Apsarases. Then, O king, blessed Nārāyaṇa of fierce ardour, he who is both origin and end, the noble preceptor of Yoga, filling all heaven and earth with his glory, arrived at his own unfathomable realm. There Kṛṣṇa met the gods and seers and Cāraṇas, O king, while the foremost Gandharvas, the fairest Apsarases, and the Siddhas and Sādhyas all bowed and did him honour. The gods bade him welcome, king, and the leading sages worshipped 25
him aloud as lord; the Gandharvas praised him as they attended on him, and Indra too greeted him with joy.

[6] *Dāruka arrives and informs the Kurus of the slaughter at Dvārakā. The Pāṇḍavas are grieved at the news. Arjuna sets out to see Vasudeva; arriving*

1 See 11.25, 13.144.

*with Dāruka, he finds Dvārakā appearing like a widowed woman. When the womenfolk see him they wail; when he sees them he weeps and falls to the ground, and Satyabhāmā and Rukmiṇī fall at his side. The ladies raise him up and seat him on a golden throne; he comforts them with praise of Kṛṣṇa, then goes to see Vasudeva,* [7] *whom he finds lying on the ground in his grief. He embraces Arjuna and weeps as he remembers his brothers, sons, grandsons and friends; he says that he must be one to whom death does not come easily, since he still lives without them. He does not blame Sātyaki or Kṛtavarman or Akrūra or Pradyumna for the slaughter; the curse was the cause. Kṛṣṇa himself, the killer of mighty enemies, the lord of all, had done nothing to prevent it. Vasudeva says that Kṛṣṇa had promised that Arjuna would come, for he said that he and Arjuna were one. Arjuna would provide for the women and children and perform the funeral rites; then after his departure the city would be inundated by the ocean. As for Vasudeva himself, he has given up all food, and he will give up his life.*

Vaiśaṃpāyana spoke:
[8] When Arjuna, afflicter of his enemies, heard his mother's brother
Vasudeva[1] speak thus in his dejection, he answered him dejectedly:
'Uncle, I cannot long bear to look upon this earth, now that it is bereft
of the Vṛṣṇi hero Kṛṣṇa and the others of his line. King Yudhiṣṭhira,
Bhīma, Sahadeva son of Pāṇḍu, Nakula, Draupadī and I are all six of one
mind: the time has certainly arrived for the king to pass on. You should
5 know that this time has come, O best knower of times. However, first
I shall definitely conduct the Vṛṣṇi wives and children and old folk to
Indraprastha, O foe-tamer.'

Then wealth-winner Arjuna said to Dāruka, 'I wish without delay to
see the ministers of the fallen Vṛṣṇi heroes.' With these words the heroic
Arjuna, grieving for those mighty chariot-fighters, entered Sudharmā,
the Yādava assembly hall, where he sat surrounded by counsellors,
Brahmins and merchants, all attending on him. All were downcast,
silent and senseless with grief; yet more downcast himself, Kuntī's son
10 addressed them. 'I shall personally conduct the surviving Vṛṣṇis and
Andhakas to Indraprastha. As for this city, the ocean will engulf it

1 See 1.104.1–3.

completely. Make ready your carriages and all the wealth you can carry! Vajra here[1] will be your king in Indraprastha. On the seventh day from now, as soon as the bright sun has risen, we shall all move out of the city. Make ready; do not delay!'

When the citizens heard these words of Kuntī's tireless son, they hastened to make ready, eager to do the best for themselves. Arjuna spent that night in the dwelling of Kṛṣṇa Keśava, where he was suddenly
overcome by a swoon of violent grief; and in the morning Śūra's son 15
Vasudeva of mighty energy and ardour, absorbed in Yoga, attained his final state. Then a great cry went up in Vasudeva's dwelling, a dreadful sound of women wailing and weeping, their hair dishevelled, their ornaments and garlands cast aside as they all beat their breasts with their hands and lamented piteously. Devakī, Bhadrā, Rohiṇī and Madirā, those best of women, resolved to follow their lord on to the funeral pyre.

Now Kuntī's son had Vasudeva's body carried out on a great bier
swathed in garlands and borne by men, O bull-like heir of Bharata, and 20
every one of the citizens of Dvārakā followed it as it went, struck down by grief and woe. Before the bier went Vasudeva's ritual priests, his sacred fires, and the umbrella from his horse sacrifice; behind followed his queens, now well adorned, attended by their daughters-in-law and other women in their thousands. His body was raised on to its pyre in a spot the noble man had been fond of in life, and the offerings to the dead were made; then his wives, those four fine ladies, joined Śūra's heroic son upon the pyre, and thus attained the realms that he had won.
Now Pāṇḍu's son burnt him and the four women using sandal logs and 25
many other perfumes. All that could be heard were the crackle of the blazing fire, and the sounds of Brahmins chanting Sāmaveda hymns and men weeping. The sons of the Vṛṣṇi heroes, led by Vajra, and also the women, now made the water offerings to noble Vasudeva.

Now that he had had the rites performed according to *dharma*, Arjuna, never negligent in *dharma*, went to the place where the Vṛṣṇis had perished, bull-like heir of Bharata. The Kuru hero grieved greatly to see them where they had fallen in the slaughter; then he set about the

1 Kṛṣṇa's grandson.

30 tasks proper to the time. In order of seniority he performed all the rites
for those killed by clubs sprung from *erakā* grass through the Brahmins'
curse. Then he sought out the bodies of Balarāma and Kṛṣṇa Vāsudeva,
and had them cremated by trustworthy men.

After properly performing the rites for all the departed, the Pāṇḍava
set swiftly out on the seventh day, mounted upon his chariot. Riding
in carriages drawn by horses, oxen, asses and camels, the weeping,
griefstricken widows of the Vṛṣṇi heroes followed Pāṇḍu's noble son
the wealth-winner. At the command of Kuntī's son, the servants of
the Andhakas and Vṛṣṇis, their chariot-fighters and horsemen, their
children and old folk, now leaderless, and all the town and country
35 people encircled the womenfolk as they travelled along. Elephant-
riders, accompanied by reserve troops, made the journey on mountain-
ous elephants flanked by warriors assigned to protect their feet. The
Andhaka and Vṛṣṇi boys faithfully followed Kuntī's son, and so did the
Brahmins, Kṣatriyas, Vaiśyas and well-to-do Śūdras within the caravan:
they travelled behind wise Kṛṣṇa's grandson Vajra and his womenfolk,
who numbered sixteen thousand. Many thousands and millions and
hundreds of millions of Bhoja, Vṛṣṇi and Andhaka widows also set
out on the journey. This Vṛṣṇi throng, vast as the ocean and loaded
with great wealth, was conducted by Kuntī's son Arjuna, the best of
chariot-fighters, the conqueror of enemy fortresses.

40 As soon as the multitude had left, the ocean, the abode of crocodiles,
engulfed the wealthy city of Dvārakā with its waters. Those who
had formerly lived there, beholding this marvel, fled faster than ever,
lamenting the ways of fate.

Now wealth-winner Arjuna led the Vṛṣṇi women forward, encamp-
ing among lovely forests and hills and rivers. Reaching the prosperous
land of the five rivers,[1] wise Arjuna set up camp in a region rich in
cattle and corn. But then robbers observed those widowed women
under the leadership of Kuntī's son alone, O heir of Bharata, and greed
45 overtook them. Crazed with greed, those hideous Ābhīra evildoers
plotted together: 'Here is this solitary warrior, Arjuna, leading children
and old people whose menfolk have been slain. He is trespassing on our

1 Modern Punjab.

lands, and his fighting men have no vigour.' So, armed with sticks, the
plundering robbers attacked the Vṛṣṇi caravan in their thousands; with
their mighty lion-roars they put the common folk to flight, and then,
urged on by the evil turn of Time, they fell upon the caravan to loot it.

At once Kuntī's son turned back with his followers. Laughing a little,
strong-armed Arjuna said, 'Stand off, unrighteous men, if you do not 50
wish to die! Do not suffer the woe of being slain by my piercing arrows!'
Thus spoke heroic Arjuna; but those fools ignored his words and fell
upon the travellers, though he tried again and again to stop them.
So Arjuna prepared to string his heavenly bow, mighty, unbreakable
Gāṇḍīva, but he had the greatest difficulty. Stringing it with an effort
in the midst of the tumult and confusion, he set his thoughts upon his
Weapons, but he could not bring them to mind.[1] Seeing this dreadful
failure of the prowess of his arm in battle and the loss of his Weapons,
he was ashamed.

Meanwhile all the Vṛṣṇi warriors, fighting from chariots or on 55
horseback or elephant-back, could not rescue those whom the robbers
were abducting; the women were too many, and were running hither
and thither. Kuntī's son strove to protect them, but those fine women
were dragged away in all directions before the very eyes of all the
warriors, while those who remained fled wherever they were able.
Alarmed, the wealth-winner with his Vṛṣṇi supporters began to slay
robbers with arrows shot from Gāṇḍīva, but a moment later, king, he ran
out of his straight-flying shafts. Formerly they had been inexhaustible,
but now those blood-drinking arrows were exhausted. Indra's son,[2] 60
finding his arrows at an end, struck down by grief and woe, now used
the end of his bow to strike at the robbers; but before the very eyes of
Kuntī's son the barbarians carried off the Vṛṣṇi and Andhaka women in
all directions, Janamejaya.

The wealth-winner considered what had happened to be the doing of fate. Filled with grief and woe, he could only sigh; the loss of his Weapons, the failure of the prowess of his arm, his bow's recalcitrance, the exhaustion of his arrows, all plunged Kuntī's son into dejection as

1 See note to 7.164.118.

2 Arjuna.

he thought of the working of fate. He turned away, O king, and said,
65 'All is lost!' Then the sagacious hero travelled to Kurukṣetra with the
remaining women, most of whose wealth had been stolen. Thus those
among the Vṛṣṇi women who had escaped abduction were brought
to Kurukṣetra by Kuru's heir wealth-winner Arjuna, and settled in
various places there. Kuntī's son, that most excellent of men, conveyed
Kṛtavarman's son and the remaining women of the Bhoja king to the
city of Mārttikāvata; then he took all the rest of the children, old folk and
women who had lost their menfolk, and settled them in Indraprastha;
finally the righteous hero established Sātyaki's beloved son on the banks
of the river Sarasvatī, along with the old folk and children of his line.

70 Arjuna, the slayer of enemy heroes, awarded the kingship of In-
draprastha to Vajra. Akrūra's wives retired to the forest, though Vajra
tried to dissuade them. Of Kṛṣṇa's honoured wives, Rukmiṇī, Gāndhārī,
Śaibyā, Haimavatī and Queen Jāmbavatī entered fire, while Satyabhāmā
and the other queens entered the forest, O king, resolved on asceticism.
Those men of Dvārakā who had followed Kuntī's victorious son were
handed over by him in suitable groups to Vajra.

Having done all the tasks proper to the time, Arjuna, eyes filled with tears, [9] entered the hermitage of Kṛṣṇa Dvaipāyana Vyāsa, speaker of the truth, and there he saw the sage, the son of Satyavatī, O king, seated in solitude. Approaching righteous Vyāsa of mighty vows, he stood in his presence and paid his respects, saying, 'I am Arjuna.' 'Welcome!' answered Satyavatī's son. Then the great sage, being well disposed, added, 'Be seated.'

Vyāsa could see that Kuntī's son was wretched and dejected at heart,
5 sighing over and over again, and so he asked him, 'Have you been
wounded by some unmanly opponent? Have you killed a Brahmin?
Have you been defeated in battle? You seem to have lost your Kṣatriya
glory, so that I hardly recognize you – what is this, bull-like heir of
Bharata? Please explain it to me, son of Kuntī, if it is something that I
may hear.'

'He whose form was as dark as a cloud,' replied Arjuna, 'glorious Kṛṣṇa with his great lotus-eyes, has, with Balarāma, cast off his body and gone to heaven. In Prabhāsa, through the curse of Brahmins, a horrific massacre of Vṛṣṇi heroes took place in a battle with clubs, and those heroes are no more, for, mighty, noble, brave and proud as lions though they were, the Bhojas and Vṛṣṇis and Andhakas slaughtered one another in combat, O Brahmin. Their arms were like iron bars; they could withstand clubs, iron bars and spears; and now they lie slain by blades of *erakā* grass. Behold the turn of Time! Five hundred thousand strong-armed heroes have met their deaths at one another's hands. As I think again and again of the slaughter of the Yadus of boundless power, and of Kṛṣṇa of great renown, I cannot bear it; I find the death of Kṛṣṇa, bearer of the bow Śārṅga, as hard to credit as though the ocean should dry up, or a mountain be moved, or the sky fall, or fire become cold, and I do not wish to remain in this world without Kṛṣṇa.

'And there is something else even more grievous, O ascetic: hear this. It breaks my heart to think of it, and yet I do so over and over again. O Brahmin, before my very eyes the wives of the Vṛṣṇis were pursued and abducted in their thousands, in an assault by Ābhīras from the land of the five rivers. When that happened I took up my bow, but I was unable to bend it. My arms lost their former prowess, none of my many different Weapons would appear, and my arrows were completely exhausted in a mere moment.

'And Kṛṣṇa with his long lotus-eyes, the measureless hero, the bearer of conch, discus and club, four-armed, with yellow garments and dark complexion, Kṛṣṇa who rode before my chariot in his mighty splendour, burning the armies of his foes, consuming them with his fiery energy so that I could then slaughter them with the arrows I shot from Gāṇḍīva – him I can see no more. And, deprived of the sight of him, I sink into despair; truest of sages, I feel deeply shaken, and my dejected heart can find no peace. I cannot bring myself to live without Kṛṣṇa, the heroic stirrer of men, for as soon as I heard that Viṣṇu had left me, I lost all sense of where I was. Now I run hither and thither, utterly alone, my kinsmen and my prowess destroyed. Truest of sages, please advise me what is best for me.'

'The mighty Vṛṣṇi and Andhaka chariot-fighters have been consumed by the Brahmins' curse,' answered Vyāsa; 'they have perished, tiger-like Kuru; you should not grieve for them. It had to happen so: this is what was destined for those noble heroes, and Kṛṣṇa permitted it, though he had the power to avert it. For Kṛṣṇa could change the entire universe of three worlds, complete with everything that moves and that stands still, never mind a curse uttered by wise Brahmins. He who, because of his love for you, rode before your chariot wielding discus and club, he was the ancient seer, the four-armed Vāsudeva; having relieved the earth of her burden and granted the world release, the wide-eyed one has returned to his own supreme state.

30 'As for you, strong-armed and bull-like hero, with the aid of Bhīma
and the twins you have carried out this great work for the gods. I
consider that you have all completed your tasks and attained perfection,
and that the time has now arrived for you to depart; that is what I believe
is now best for you. Strength and intelligence, energy and achievement
prosper during days of well-being, heir of Bharata, but fail when the
Time turns evil. All that exists is rooted in Time, wealth-winner Arjuna,
for Time is the seed of the universe; but it is Time, too, that reclaims it
all when it chooses to do so. A man grows mighty, then that same man
becomes powerless once more; a man achieves lordship upon earth, and
35 later others order him about. Your Weapons have accomplished what
they had to do, and have now gone back whence they came; they will
return to your hand when the time is right. Now it is time for all of you
to go the highest way. This, bull-like heir of Bharata, is what I believe
is your ultimate good.'

Hearing these words spoken by Vyāsa of boundless ardour, Kuntī's heroic son took his leave and returned to the City of the Elephant, Hāstinapura. He entered, sought out Yudhiṣṭhira, and told him all that had happened to the Vṛṣṇis and the Andhakas.

# THE GREAT JOURNEY

## THE GREAT JOURNEY

Janamejaya spoke:
[1] When they learnt of the battle with clubs that had taken place amongst the Vṛṣṇis and the Andhakas, and that Kṛṣṇa had departed to heaven, what did the Pāṇḍavas do?

Vaiśampāyana spoke:
As soon as the Kuru king Yudhiṣṭhira learnt of the great slaughter of the Vṛṣṇis, he resolved on departure himself. To Arjuna he said, 'All creatures are cooked by Time; no one escapes. I consider that it is Time for us to renounce all our doings. You are sagacious; you too must see this.'

The heroic son of Kuntī heard his elder brother's words; repeating,
'It is Time! It is Time!', he gave them his assent. Likewise, when Bhīma 5
and the twins Nakula and Sahadeva heard Arjuna's opinion, they too
concurred with what the ambidextrous warrior had said.

Now Yudhiṣṭhira summoned Yuyutsu, Dhṛtarāṣṭra's son by a Vaiśya woman. Resolved as he was on departing for *dharma*'s sake, he entrusted the entire state to him; then he consecrated Parikṣit as king over his own kingdom.[1] Griefstricken King Yudhiṣṭhira, Pāṇḍu's eldest son, spoke to Subhadrā: 'This your son's son will be king of the Kurus, and Vajra, last

1 There is a strange discrepancy over Parikṣit's age. It has generally been assumed that Yuyutsu was installed as regent for a youthful Parikṣit. For example, the commentator Nīlakaṇṭha explains that the kingdom was not given to Yuyutsu but merely placed in dependence on him; he adds that the 'evil' against which Yudhiṣṭhira warns Subhadrā in

of the Yadus, has also been made king. Parikṣit will rule in Hāstinapura, and the Yadu king in Indraprastha. Vajra must enjoy your protection; do not think of doing any evil.'

10 When he had finished speaking, the righteous lord of *dharma* hastened
with his brothers to make offerings of water to wise Kṛṣṇa Vāsudeva, to
his mother's aged brother,[1] and to Balarāma and the rest; then for each of
them he performed dedicated *śrāddha* ceremonies in the proper manner,
bestowing jewels, garments, villages, horses, chariots and women upon
the leading Brahmins, as well as cattle in hundreds and thousands. That
truest heir of Bharata also paid reverence to his *guru*, Kṛpa, offering him
both wealth and honour; and he gave Parikṣit to him to be his pupil.

Now the royal seer Yudhiṣṭhira summoned all his subjects and in-
15 formed them of what he intended to do. No sooner had the town and
country people heard his words than they were filled the deepest alarm.
They refused to accept what he said, telling the king, 'You must not act
in this way! No king who understands the *dharma* of evil times has ever
behaved so!'

But righteous Yudhiṣṭhira managed to win the people over, and now
he and his brothers put their minds to the matter of their departure. The
Kuru king, Yudhiṣṭhira son of Dharma, cast off the ornaments from his
body and took up garments of bark; and Bhīma, Arjuna, the twins and
Draupadī of high repute all likewise put on bark garments, lord of men.
20 Next, heir of Bharata, they had their priests perform a final offering
in the proper manner, before casting their sacred fires into the waters.
Then those bull-like heroes all set forth. All the womenfolk wept aloud
to see the five Pāṇḍavas set out with Draupadī, just as they had done
long ago after their defeat at gambling; but, in view of Yudhiṣṭhira's
resolve and the destruction of the Vṛṣṇis, the brothers all regarded their
departure with joy.

---

verse 9 below would consist of failure to protect 'the two boys, Parikṣit and Vajra'. Similarly, in verse 13 below Yudhiṣṭhira makes Parikṣit Kṛpa's pupil (*śiṣya*). However, Parikṣit was the posthumous son of Abhimanyu, who died at Kurukṣetra; he must therefore have been somewhere between 34 and 36 years old at the time of his consecration (see 16.1, 16.2.2).

1 Kṛṣṇa's father Vasudeva.

The king left the City of the Elephant, Hāstinapura, along with his four brothers; Draupadī was sixth, and seventh was a dog that accompanied them. For a long way they were followed by all the citizens and their womenfolk, but no one could persuade them to turn back, and at last the townspeople all turned back themselves.

In Hāstinapura, Yuyutsu was surrounded by Kṛpa and his other 25
counsellors. The serpent princess Ulūpī entered the Gaṅgā, heir of Kuru, and Citrāṅgadā returned to Maṇipūra,[1] but the other Pāṇḍava women remained with Parikṣit to look after him.

As for the noble Pāṇḍavas and Draupadī of high repute, heir of Kuru, after fasting they set out towards the East. Absorbed in Yoga, the noble ones devoted themselves to the *dharma* of renunciation as they visited many lands and rivers and mountains. Yudhiṣṭhira went ahead, and Bhīma followed close behind him; behind Bhīma went Arjuna and the twins, in due order; at the rear, truest heir of Bharata, travelled that best of 30
women, Draupadī Kṛṣṇā of fine hips and lotus-petal eyes; and a solitary dog continued to follow the Pāṇḍavas as they set out for the forest. In the course of time the heroes arrived at the ocean named Lauhitya.[2]

Wealth-winner Arjuna had never given up his heavenly bow Gāṇḍīva or his two mighty and inexhaustible arrow-cases, great king; such is the allure of treasure. Now the Pāṇḍavas beheld the Fire god standing in human form before them, mountainous, blocking their way. The god of seven flames addressed them: 'Good sirs, brave sons of Pāṇḍu, know that I am Fire. Strong-armed Yudhiṣṭhira and enemy-afflicter Bhīma, Arjuna 35
and the two heroic sons of the Aśvins, hear what I say! I am Fire, O best of Kurus, and it was I who burnt the Khāṇḍava forest[3] thanks to the power of Arjuna and Kṛṣṇa Nārāyaṇa. This brother of yours, Arjuna here, should give up the supreme weapon Gāṇḍīva before he enters the forest. He no longer has need of it. The wonderful discus that was in noble Kṛṣṇa's possession left him; it will return to his hand when the time is right.[4]

**1** See 1.207–9, 14.77–83.

**2** Literally, 'Redness'. According to Nīlakaṇṭha, it lies to the side of the eastern mountain behind which the sun rises.

**3** See 1.214 ff.

**4** See 16.4.3, also 16.9.35.

Gāṇḍīva, this best of bows, was acquired long ago by me from Varuṇa for
the sake of Kuntī's son,[1] and it is to Varuṇa that it should now be returned.'

40 Then, at the urging of all his brothers, the wealth-winner cast both his
bow and his two inexhaustible arrow-cases into the water. The Fire god
vanished at once, best heir of Bharata, and the Pāṇḍava heroes travelled
on towards the South. Passing along the ocean's northern shore, they
continued in a south-westerly direction, tiger-like Bhārata, then turned
again due west, and there they saw Dvārakā, engulfed by the ocean.
After this, those truest heirs of Bharata travelled northwards once again,
for in their devotion to Yoga they wished to circumambulate the entire
earth.

**[2]** Disciplined and absorbed in Yoga, they journeyed towards the
North until they beheld mighty Mount Himālaya. Crossing that too,
they then saw a sandy desert and, beyond that, great Mount Meru, the
best of mountains. But even as they speeded onwards in their devotion
to Yoga, Draupadī's Yoga failed, and she fell down on the ground. When
Bhīma of mighty strength saw that she had fallen, he asked Yudhiṣṭhira
5 lord of *dharma*, 'O afflicter of your enemies, the princess Draupadī
Kṛṣṇā never violated *dharma*. For what reason has she fallen to the earth,
O king?'

'She had a particularly strong partiality for wealth-winner Arjuna,'
answered Yudhiṣṭhira, 'and today she has received the fruit of that,
O truest of men.' And with these words King Yudhiṣṭhira son of
Dharma paid her no further notice; wise and righteous, the bull-like
hero once more focused his mind.

Then wise Sahadeva also fell to the ground. When Bhīma saw that
he too had fallen, he asked the king, 'Mādrī's son here always served us
all obediently and humbly. Why has he fallen to the earth?'

10 'Prince Sahadeva thought that no one equalled him for wisdom,'
replied Yudhiṣṭhira; 'it is for that fault that he has fallen.' And having
spoken thus Yudhiṣṭhira son of Kuntī abandoned Sahadeva and travelled
on with his brothers and the dog.

Seeing that both Draupadī and Pāṇḍu's son Sahadeva had fallen,
heroic Nakula, who was fond of his kinsmen, was filled with distress,

1 See 1.216.

and he too fell down. When Nakula, who was brave and handsome, fell, Bhīma once more addressed the king: 'This brother of ours was unfailing in *dharma* and ever obedient; yet Nakula, matchless for beauty in the world, has fallen to the earth.'

Righteous Yudhiṣṭhira, foremost of all wise men, answered Bhīma's question concerning Nakula: 'In beauty he believed that no one equalled him, and considered himself superior to all. Therefore has Nakula fallen. Come, heroic wolf-belly; whatever is ordained for a man, that assuredly he receives.'

Then seeing that all three of them had fallen, Pāṇḍu's son Arjuna, the white-horsed slayer of enemy heroes, was afflicted with grief, and fell down himself. When that unconquerable tiger-like hero, Indra's equal in valour, fell dying, Bhīma asked the king, 'I do not remember that this noble man told any untruth even in trivial matters; so whence comes this evil turn of events, that he should fall to the ground?'

'Arjuna said that he would slay all our enemies in a single day,' replied Yudhiṣṭhira, 'and he did not do so; he was a boaster, and so he has fallen, for he looked down on all other bowmen. The man who hopes to prosper should act as he speaks.'

With these words the king set forth once more; then Bhīma fell down. Lying where he had fallen, he asked Yudhiṣṭhira lord of *dharma*, 'Sir, good king, see: I who am dear to you have fallen. If you know it, tell me the reason for my fall.'

'You ate too much, son of Kuntī,' answered Yudhiṣṭhira, 'and you boasted of your strength while overlooking others. Therefore you have fallen to the ground.' After speaking these words, strong-armed Yudhiṣṭhira went on with not a further glance. His only follower now was the dog that I have mentioned several times to you.

[**3**] Then Indra came to Kuntī's son, making all heaven and earth resound with the roar of his chariot; and he said to him, 'Mount!'

Yudhiṣṭhira lord of *dharma* looked at his brothers lying where they had fallen, and in his grief and affliction he addressed the thousand-eyed god: 'My brothers lie fallen here. Let them come with me, for I do not wish to go to heaven without my brothers, O lord of the gods. And let the delicate princess Draupadī, deserving of happiness, come with us also, O Indra; be pleased to agree to this.'

5 Indra answered him. 'Bull-like heir of Bharata, do not grieve. Your brothers and your sons have gone to the highest heaven before you, along with Draupadī Kṛṣṇā, and you will see them there. They went there after casting off their mortal bodies, Bhārata, whereas you shall go to heaven with this your own body, make no doubt.'

'Lord of past and future,' said Yudhiṣṭhira, 'this dog is constant in his devotion to me. Let him go with me, for I feel a kindness towards him.'

'King,' replied Indra, 'today you have attained immortality, equality with myself, great fame, unbounded glory and the joys of heaven itself. Abandon the dog – there is no unkindness in this.'

'O thousand-eyed god,' said Yudhiṣṭhira, 'O noble one, it is difficult for a noble man to do an ignoble deed. Let me not gain a glory for which I have to abandon a creature devoted to me.'

10 'Dog-owners have no place in heaven,' answered Indra; 'the furious Rākṣasas seize the merit of their sacrifices. So think before acting, lord of *dharma*. Abandon the dog – there is no unkindness in this.'

'Great Indra,' said Yudhiṣṭhira, 'abandoning one who is devoted is considered an extreme sin in the world, equal to that of killing a Brahmin. Therefore for my own well-being today I shall certainly not abandon him.'

'Whatever gift or public sacrifice or offering is seen by a dog,' Indra replied, 'is seized by the furious Rākṣasas. So abandon this one; by doing so you will attain the world of the gods. You abandoned your brothers and your beloved Draupadī Kṛṣṇā to attain the heavenly realms through your own deeds, hero. So why will you not abandon this dog? Why are you so acting so senselessly now, when you have undertaken to renounce everything?'

'It is universally agreed,' said Yudhiṣṭhira, 'that there can be neither friendship nor enmity with the mortal dead; nor was there anything I could do to revive them. That is why I abandoned them, something
15 I never did while they lived. Surrendering to his enemies someone seeking refuge; killing a woman; robbing a Brahmin; harming a friend – these four, and abandoning one who is devoted, I consider equal, O Indra.'

When he heard the lord of *dharma*'s words, the dog, assuming his own form as the blessed god Dharma, delightedly addressed King

Yudhiṣṭhira, praising him in soft tones.[1] 'You are of noble birth, Lord of kings, with your father's intelligence, good conduct and compassion towards all beings. Long ago, my son, I tested you at Dvaitavana,[2] where your valorous brothers all lost their lives for the sake of a drink of water, and where you gave up your own two brothers, Bhīma and Arjuna, asking instead that Nakula might live, because you wished to treat his
mother equally with your own. Now you have given up a chariot to 20
heaven because a mere dog is devoted to you. For this, lord of men, no one in heaven is equal to you. Therefore, best heir of Bharata, the imperishable realms are yours, even in your own body, and you have attained the highest celestial state.'

Then Dharma, Indra, the Maruts, the Aśvins and the other gods and divine seers made Pāṇḍu's son mount the chariot, and all of them set out in their respective flying chariots, perfected beings who could roam at will, immaculate, holy, pure in thought, word and deed. The Kuru king rose rapidly aloft in his chariot, filling heaven and earth with his blazing energy.

Now, from amidst the hosts of gods, the great ascetic and great speaker 25
Nārada, he who knows all worlds, proclaimed aloud, 'The Kuru king has eclipsed the fame of all those royal seers who have come here; he stands supreme, filling the worlds with his glory, his ardour and his excellent conduct.[3] We have not heard of any save for Pāṇḍu's son who reached this place in his own body.'

But when the righteous king heard Nārada's words, he first saluted the gods and the princes who had been his allies, and then said, 'The place I now wish to reach, whether it is good or ill, is that of my brothers. I desire no other realms.'

In response to King Yudhiṣṭhira's words, Indra king of the gods spoke 30
kindly to him: 'Dwell here, lord of kings, in the realm won by your own good deeds. Why do you still burden yourself with human affection?

1 The text does not in fact specify that it is the dog that is transformed into Dharma, merely speaking of 'The blessed one in his own form as Dharma'. However, there can be no doubt that this is what is meant.

2 See 3.296–8.

3 Cf. 1.114.5–7.

You have attained the highest perfection, as no other man has ever done, heir of Kuru, whereas your brothers have failed to reach this place; yet still human emotion touches you, lord of men. This is heaven! Behold here the divine seers and Siddhas for whom the highest heaven is home!'

But even as Indra lord of the gods uttered these words, wise Yudhiṣṭhira
35 once more spoke meaningfully: 'Crusher of demons, I could not bear to dwell here without them. I wish to go where my brothers have gone, and where great Draupadī Kṛṣṇā is, intelligent, virtuous, the best of women, and my beloved.'

# THE ASCENT TO HEAVEN

## THE ASCENT TO HEAVEN

Janamejaya spoke:
[1] After reaching Indra's heaven, what realms did my forefathers, the Pāṇḍavas and Kauravas, obtain? I wish to hear this, and I believe that all is known to you through the grace of Vyāsa, the great seer of wonderful deeds.

Vaiśaṃpāyana spoke:
Hear what your forefathers, Yudhiṣṭhira and the others, did after reaching Indra's heaven. When Yudhiṣṭhira lord of *dharma* reached that heaven, he saw there Duryodhana, seated at his ease upon a throne in royal majesty, blazing in splendour like the sun, full of the glory of a hero, and mingling with resplendent gods and virtuous Sādhyas.

Yudhiṣṭhira could not bear to see Duryodhana there; at the sight of him sitting in royal glory he turned quickly away, addressing the others in a loud voice: 'I have no wish to share the blessed realms with Duryodhana. It was through his shortsightedness and envy that all the kings of earth, and all my friends and kinsmen, met violent deaths at our hands on the battlefield; and this was after our sufferings in the great forest, and the suffering of the Pāñcāla princess Draupadī, our lovely and virtuous wife, in the midst of the assembly in the presence of our elders. Fare you well, O gods, for I do not desire to see Duryodhana; I wish to go where my brothers are.'

'Do not speak so,' Nārada answered him, laughing a little. 'Lord of kings, your dwelling-place is in heaven, and here hostility comes to an end. Strong-armed Yudhiṣṭhira, you really should not talk thus of King Duryodhana! Listen to my words. Here King Duryodhana is honoured, along with the gods and those virtuous mighty kings who dwell in heaven. He gained access to the realms of the heroes by sacrificing his own body on the battlefield; indeed all of you are equal to gods, in that you massed for battle. So he has gained his position here by following the Kṣatriya *dharma*, a king who was never afraid even when danger was great. My son, you should not dwell upon what happened to you as a result of the gambling match. You ought not to brood on Draupadī's torment, and you should forget the other torments you yourselves suffered because of the gambling match, both on the battlefield and elsewhere. Come now and meet King Duryodhana, as is proper! This is heaven; there are no enmities here, lord of men.'

When Nārada had finished speaking, intelligent Yudhiṣṭhira the Kuru king asked about his brothers, saying, 'If Duryodhana has attained the eternal realms of the heroes, though he was unrighteous and sinful, though he harmed his friends, though all the kings of earth were destroyed on his account along with their horses and chariots and elephants, though we burnt with rage as we sought to avenge the feud, then what of my brave and noble brothers, keepers of mighty vows, true to their promises, world heroes, speakers of the truth? What realms are theirs now? I desire to see them, and also Karṇa, Kuntī's noble son, ever true to his word, and Dhṛṣṭadyumna and Sātyaki, and Dhṛṣṭadyumna's sons, and all those princes who found death by the sword by following the Kṣatriya *dharma*. Where are they, Brahmin? I do not see them here, nor Virāṭa, Drupada, or Dhṛṣṭaketu and his followers. Nārada, I desire to see Śikhaṇḍin prince of Pāñcāla, and all the sons of Draupadī, and unconquerable Abhimanyu!

[2] 'O gods, I do not see Rādhā's son Karṇa of boundless power here, nor the two noble brothers Yudhāmanyu and Uttamaujas. Where are those mighty chariot-fighters who sacrificed their bodies in the fire of battle, the kings and sons of kings who were slain for my sake on the battlefield, all of them valiant as tigers, the truest of heroes? I trust that they have also won this realm! If these realms have indeed been attained by all those noble warriors, then, gods, you may know that I shall

remain here with them. But if those kings have not gained this lovely, imperishable realm, then I will not dwell here without my kinsmen and my brothers.

'Ever since I heard my mother instruct me, during the water offerings, to make an offering to Karṇa,[1] I have been consumed with grief at her words; and I grieve incessantly also about this, O gods, that I perceived that the feet of Karṇa of boundless power resembled those of my mother, and yet I did not follow him. Not even Indra himself could have defeated us in battle if Karṇa, the destroyer of enemy armies, had been with us. I desire now to see the son of the Sun, wherever he may be, for while he was yet unknown to me I had him killed by the ambidextrous warrior Arjuna. And I desire to see Bhīma of terrible valour, dearer to me than life itself, and Arjuna who resembled Indra, and the twins who were like Yama. And I desire to see the Pāñcāla princess, virtuous Draupadī. I do not desire to remain here: I tell you this truthfully. For what is heaven to me, O truest of gods, if I am sundered from my brothers? My heaven is where they are: I cannot think of this as heaven.'

'If that is where you long to be,' answered the gods, 'go, son, without delay. We are at your service, to do what pleases you – this is the command of the king of the gods.' And with these words, O afflicter of your enemies, the gods instructed their agent to show Yudhiṣṭhira his friends.

Then Kuntī's son King Yudhiṣṭhira and the agent of the gods set off together, tiger-like king, to find those bull-like heroes. The agent went ahead, while the king followed him behind, along a horrible, difficult path. Wicked creatures thronged there, and a dreadful darkness enveloped the place. Where moss and weeds should have been, there was human hair; where mud, there was human flesh and blood. The smell of stinking evildoers was everywhere, and there were swarms of gnats, flies, mosquitoes and other insects. Everywhere corpses lay about, and bones and hair were strewn around, full of maggots and worms. All was fenced in on every side by blazing flame. Ravens and vultures infested the place, alongside birds with beaks hard as iron or sharp as

1 See 11.27.6–11.

needles. There were gigantic ghosts as big as the Vindhya mountain, and littered everywhere were bodies smeared with fat and blood, arms, thighs and hands severed, bellies cut out and feet cut off.

Deep in thought as he went, the righteous king pursued his way through the stench of corpses along that horrible, hair-raising path. He saw an impassable river full of scalding water, a forest of trees with sword-like leaves sharp as razors, scorching sands, scattered rocks of iron; all round were boiling iron pots of oil. There was also a spiny kapok tree, impossible to touch with its sharp thorns.

Kuntī's son saw evildoers being tortured with all of these, and he smelt the foul odour; then he asked the agent of the gods, 'How far are we to travel along such a road as this? And, please tell me, where are those brothers of mine? I desire, too, to know which region of the gods this is.'

Hearing the lord of *dharma*'s words, the agent turned and said, 'This is as far as you go. I must return, for thus the celestials commanded me. If you are weary, lord of kings, be pleased to come with me.'

Dejected and nearly swooning from the stench, Yudhiṣṭhira decided to go back. He turned around, but even as he turned, sorrowful and grieving, the righteous king heard distressful voices speaking all about him. 'Sir, righteous son of Pāṇḍu, nobly born royal seer, stay for just a moment as a favour to us! At your approach, unconquerable one, a fair breeze has started to blow, carrying your scent; sir, this has brought us pleasure! Bull-like son of Kuntī, truest of kings, for as long as you are here we shall experience the joy of seeing you. So stay a moment longer, strong-armed heir of Bharata! While you remain, O Kuru, the tortures do not hurt us.'

O king, as he stood there Yudhiṣṭhira heard all round him many such wretched utterances spoken by folk in torment, and, hearing them, he felt compassion for those who spoke so in their affliction. 'What dreadful suffering!' he said, and remained where he was.

Though he had heard those voices many times before, the son of Pāṇḍu did not recognize the speakers, exhausted with misery as they were. So, unaware of who was speaking, Yudhiṣṭhira son of Dharma said, 'Who are you, sirs? and why are you in this place?'

Then from all sides the answers came. 'I am Karṇa!' 'I am Bhīma!' 'O lord, I am Arjuna!' 'I am Nakula!' 'I, Sahadeva!' 'I am Dhṛṣṭadyumna!' 'We are Draupadī and her sons!' Thus the voices called out to him.

Lord of men, when King Yudhiṣṭhira heard those voices, as wretched as the place in which they spoke, he asked himself, 'What has fate accomplished here? What sin has been committed by these noble ones, by Karṇa, or the sons of Draupadī, or the slender-waisted princess of Pāñcāla herself, that they should find themselves in this terrible, stinking place? I do not know of any wrong done by any of them; they have always acted virtuously! And what has wicked King Duryodhana son of Dhṛtarāṣṭra done to attain such glory, along with all his followers? He dwells in heaven, enjoying the highest honour, as fortunate as great Indra himself! Whence comes this evil turn of events, that these should go to hell, though all were experts in *dharma*, brave, devoted to truth and the Vedas, wise maintainers of their Kṣatriya vows, sacrificers, and generous to Brahmins? Am I dreaming or awake? Though sentient, I am not in my senses. Have I gone mad? Or am I suffering from brain-fever?'

Thus and much more King Yudhiṣṭhira pondered, full of grief and woe, beside himself with anxious thought. Then in a sudden show of violent anger, the son of Dharma reviled the gods, and even Dharma himself. Suffering though he was from the dreadful stench, he addressed the agent of the gods: 'Go, good sir, back to those who sent you, and tell them that I shall not return to them; I am remaining here, since these my brothers gain comfort from my company.' Commanded so by the wise Pāṇḍava, the agent went back to the king of the gods, Indra of a hundred sacrifices, O lord of men, and informed him of the lord of *dharma*'s intention in full, just as Yudhiṣṭhira had said to him.

[**3**] Kuntī's son Yudhiṣṭhira lord of *dharma* had stayed there but a moment, heir of Kuru, when the gods, with Indra at their head, came to where he was; even Dharma himself came there in human form to see the Kuru king Yudhiṣṭhira. No sooner had the gods of noble birth and deeds arrived in all their brilliance than the darkness melted away, O king; the tortures suffered by evildoers vanished from sight, and so did the hellish river, the spiny kapok tree, and the frightful rocks and iron pots. The mutilated corpses that Kuntī's royal son had seen all round him also disappeared. Then a fair breeze, gentle, sweet-

scented and wonderfully cool, began to blow from the direction of the gods.

In that place where Dharma's son, King Yudhiṣṭhira of mighty ardour, stood, Indra was joined by the Maruts, the Vasus and the Aśvins, the Sādhyas, Rudras and Ādityas, all the Siddhas and the greatest of seers, and all the other celestials. And now the lord of the gods, Indra the most glorious, spoke to Yudhiṣṭhira these words of comfort. 'Strong-armed Yudhiṣṭhira, the hosts of gods are pleased with you. Come, tiger-like hero: it is finished. You have attained perfection, king, and the imperishable realms are yours. Do not be angry; listen to my words.

'All kings have to see hell – this is inescapable, son. One's merits and demerits form two heaps, bull-like hero. He who first enjoys the merit of his good deeds goes afterwards to hell, whereas he who first endures hell goes afterwards to heaven. The man who goes initially to heaven is the one in whom sin preponderates. Therefore, O king, for your own well-being I had you treated in this way. Now, you acted deceitfully towards Droṇa in the matter of his son;[1] therefore, O king, you have yourself been deceived into seeing hell. Bhīma, Arjuna son of Kuntī, the twins and Draupadī Kṛṣṇā have all been deceived into visiting hell, exactly like yourself. Come, tiger-like hero! They have been freed from sin, and so have the princes who were slain in battle as your allies; all of them have gained heaven, so come and see them, bull-like heir of Bharata!

'As for the mighty bowman, best of all those who bear arms, Karṇa for whom you grieve so much: he too has attained the highest perfection. Come, strong-armed lord, and see the tiger-like hero, the son of the Sun, in his own abode. Have done with grief! See too your other brothers, and the princes who were your allies, every one of them now established in his own place. Cast off your mental anguish; having first experienced suffering, heir of Kuru, you shall henceforth pass your days in pleasure with me, freed from all grief and sickness.

'Strong-armed son of Pāṇḍu, enjoy the fruit of your virtuous deeds, your ascetic achievements, and the gifts that you have given. Let gods, Gandharvas and celestial Apsarases in immaculate garments now attend

1 See 7.164.105 ff.

on you agreeably in heaven! Enjoy the heavenly realms that you won with your royal consecration and augmented with your horse sacrifice; these are the great fruit of your asceticism, strong-armed hero. Your realms, Yudhiṣṭhira son of Kuntī, are higher than those of other kings; the realms where you shall pass your days in pleasure rank with those of Hariścandra. Where the royal seer Māndhātṛ dwells, and King Bhagīratha, and Bharata son of Duḥṣanta, that is where you will pass your days.[1]

'Here, lord of kings, is the sacred river of the gods, the heavenly Gaṅgā that purifies the three worlds; bathe in it, and then go to your own place. By bathing here you will cast off your mortality and be freed from grief, weariness and enmity.'

As the lord of the gods finished speaking these words to the Kuru king Yudhiṣṭhira, Dharma, in human form, addressed his son: 'Sir, good king, my most wise child! I am well pleased with your devotion to me, your truthful speech, your forbearance and self-control. This is the third time, son of Kuntī, that I have tested you,[2] and despite all I could do I could not deflect you from your proper nature. You were first tested by me near Dvaitavana in the matter of the Brahmin and his firesticks, and you passed that test. Then when your brothers and Draupadī perished, my son, I assumed the form of a dog to test you again. This has been the third; and since you chose to remain for your brothers' sake, you are now purified, noble king, and happy, and freed from sin.

'Lord of the peoples, your brothers are not in hell: this was an illusion employed by great Indra, the king of the gods. All kings have to see hell – this is inescapable, son, and that is why you suffered this extreme misery for a brief time. Neither Arjuna nor Bhīma merits a long period in hell, O king, and neither do the bull-like twins, or the heroic and truth-speaking Karṇa. The princess Draupadī Kṛṣṇā does not merit hell, Yudhiṣṭhira. So come, best heir of Bharata, and see Gaṅgā as she flows through the three worlds!'

When the royal seer, your ancestor Yudhiṣṭhira, heard these words, he set out with Dharma and all the celestials for the sacred river of the gods, Gaṅgā, the purifier praised by the seers. Plunging in, King

1 For these great figures of the past, see 2.11, 3.126, 3.104–7, 1.69.

2 For the first two tests, see 3.296–8, 17.3.16 ff.

40 Yudhiṣṭhira lord of *dharma* cast off his mortal body; then, with a new, celestial form, freed from enmity and grief by bathing in those waters, the Kuru king, wise Yudhiṣṭhira, set forth with Dharma, surrounded by gods and praised by great seers; [4] honoured by all, he proceeded to the place where the bull-like Kurus were.

There he beheld Kṛṣṇa Govinda in his *brahma*-form,[1] but recognizable because of its similarity to that form already known to Yudhiṣṭhira. He blazed with light from his body, his discus and other terrible celestial weapons stood close to him in human shape, and heroic Arjuna of great radiance waited reverently upon him.

In another spot the heir of Kuru saw Karṇa, best of all those who
5 bear arms, accompanied by the twelve Ādityas;[2] elsewhere he could see mighty Bhīma, with that same radiance of body and accompanied by the Maruts; and in the place belonging to the Aśvins, Kuru's heir saw Nakula and Sahadeva blazing with their own fiery energy.

King Yudhiṣṭhira also beheld the Pāñcāla princess Draupadī, garlanded with pink and blue lotuses, eclipsing heaven itself with the sun-like brilliance of her body, and all at once he wanted to know more about her. Then blessed Indra, the king of the gods, told him, 'This, Yudhiṣṭhira, is Śrī, unborn from any womb, fragrant and loved throughout the world.
10 For your sake she took mortal form as Draupadī; born in the line of Drupada to live in dependence on all you Pāṇḍavas, she was created by staff-wielding Śiva for you all to love. And, O king, these five blessed Gandharvas, bright as fire, are the sons of boundless power whom the five of you begat on Draupadī.

'See this Gandharva king, and know that he is wise Dhṛtarāṣṭra, your father's elder brother. And here is your own eldest brother Karṇa, bright

1 It is not clear exactly what is meant by this. The commentator Nīlakaṇṭha suggests that it is a form worthy of worship by even the god Brahmā, but I do not find this convincing. It is evidently not the 'supreme godly form' revealed by Kṛṣṇa to Arjuna at 6.33.

2 The group of gods known as Ādityas are essentially solar deities, as befits Karṇa, son of the Sun; similarly Bhīma, vehement son of the Wind, is attended by the storm-gods known as Maruts. The twins Nakula and Sahadeva are also found with their divine fathers the twin Aśvin gods, Abhimanyu with his divine father, the Moon, and Bhīṣma with the Vasus, of whom he was originally one. See further 1.61.

as fire, Kuntī's son by the Sun, first-born and seniormost, known as the son of Rādhā. See too the mighty Vṛṣṇi and Andhaka chariot-fighters, lord of kings, and the heroic Bhoja warriors headed by Sātyaki; they are now numbered among the hosts of Sādhyas, gods, Vasus and Maruts.

'Behold here Subhadrā's son, the undefeated bowman Abhimanyu, 15
in company with the Moon, whose radiance he equals. Here is your father, the bowman Pāṇḍu, united with Kuntī and Mādrī; he often visits me in his flying chariot. See Bhīṣma here, Śaṃtanu's royal son, together with the other Vasus; and you should know that the one by Bṛhaspati's side is Droṇa, your Teacher. These, and the other kings and warriors who fought for you, O Pāṇḍava, now mix with the Gandharvas, Yakṣas and Puṇyajanas, while other noble heroes have become Guhyakas. They have all cast off their bodies and won heaven through their virtuous thoughts, words and deeds.'

Janamejaya spoke:
**[5]** Noble Bhīṣma and Droṇa, and Dhṛtarāṣṭra lord of the earth; Virāṭa and Drupada, Śaṅkha and Uttara; Dhṛṣṭaketu, Jayatsena and King Satyajit; the sons of Duryodhana, and Śakuni son of Subala; Karṇa's valiant sons, and King Jayadratha; Ghaṭotkaca and all the others whom you have not so far mentioned; and those kings of blazing form of whom you have spoken already: tell me this also – for how long a time did
they remain in heaven? Do they have an eternal place there, best of 5
Brahmins? If not, what became of those bull-like heroes once their good *karma* was exhausted? O Brahmin, I desire you to proclaim this to me!

The Sūta[1] spoke:
In answer, the Brahmin seer began, with the permission of noble Vyāsa, to expound to the king.

Vaiśampāyana spoke:
Upon the exhaustion of his good deeds, lord of men, every person has to

1 Ugraśravas the Sūta now begins to conclude the narration that Śaunaka requested at 1.53 and that he began at 1.54.

leave heaven. Hear this mystery of the gods, bull-like Bhārata king, as it was told by the ancient sage of mighty energy and ardour, Parāśara's son Vyāsa of divine vision, keeper of mighty vows, unfathomably intelligent, who in his omniscience knows the outcome of all acts.[1]

Radiant Bhīṣma of great ardour became one of the Vasus; thus there are now once more eight Vasus, bull-like heir of Bharata. Droṇa entered Bṛhaspati, the best of the Aṅgirases, and Kṛtavarman son of Hṛdika entered the host of the Maruts. Pradyumna entered Sanatkumāra, from whom he had originated; Dhṛtarāṣṭra attained the realms of Kubera god of wealth, which are hard to come to, and Gāndhārī of high repute accompanied him. Pāṇḍu with his two wives travelled to the dwelling of great Indra.

Virāṭa, Drupada, Prince Dhṛṣṭaketu, Niśaṭha, Akrūra, Sāmba, Bhānu, Kampa, Viḍūratha, Bhūriśravas, Śala, King Bhūri, Ugrasena, Kaṃsa, heroic Vasudeva, and bull-like Uttara with his brother Śaṅkha – those truest of heroes entered into the All-gods.

The Moon's son Varcas[2] of great energy and ardour had become Abhimanyu, son of the lion-like hero Arjuna, who fought like no other man according to the Kṣatriya *dharma*; upon the exhaustion of his good *karma*, that mighty and righteous chariot-fighter entered the Moon.

O bull-like hero, Karṇa entered into his father the Sun, Śakuni into Dvāpara, and Dhṛṣṭadyumna into the Fire god. The sons of Dhṛtarāṣṭra had all been evil Rākṣasas, drunk with their own strength; now, purified by the sword, noble and perfected, they travelled to heaven. The chamberlain Vidura entered Dharma, and so did king Yudhiṣṭhira himself.

The blessed and divine serpent Ananta[3] entered the underworld at the command of Grandfather Brahmā to support the earth through his yogic power. Kṛṣṇa Vāsudeva's harem had consisted of sixteen thousand

1 In what follows, many of the heroes who were in fact incarnations of particular gods (1.61) are said by Vaiśaṃpāyana to have ended their independent existence and become one once more with those gods (to have 'entered' them).

2 Referred to at 1.61.86 as Suvarcas.

3 Another name for Śeṣa, the snake that serves as Viṣṇu's couch and that had become incarnate as Balarāma.

women, and they, O Janamejaya, had drowned themselves in the river Sarasvatī when his time came; now they became Apsarases and returned to Vāsudeva.

Ghaṭotkaca and the other mighty and heroic chariot-fighters who had been slain in the great battle all became gods or Yakṣas. Duryodhana's bull-like allies, who were known to have been Rākṣasas, attained in time, O king, to all the matchless realms, entering the regions of great Indra, wise Kubera, and Varuṇa.

I have now related in detail, radiant heir of Bharata, the tale of the 25
Kauravas and Pāṇḍavas, entire and complete.

The Sūta spoke:
This was the tale that King Janamejaya heard that best of Brahmins tell in intervals during the sacrificial rite, and he was filled with the greatest wonder. Then the ritual priests completed that rite for him, and Āstīka rejoiced that he had saved the snakes from destruction in it. All the Brahmins were delighted with the fee-gifts given by the king; receiving honour from him, they returned to their homes. As for King Janamejaya, after giving the priests leave to depart, he returned from Takṣaśilā to Hāstinapura, the City of the Elephant.

I have now related the entire tale narrated by Vaiśampāyana at Vyāsa's 30
command during the king's snake sacrifice. Known as a history, it is holy and purifying. O priest, this excellent narrative was established by the sage Kṛṣṇa Dvaipāyana Vyāsa, speaker of the truth, omniscient, expert in destiny and in *dharma*, virtuous, who has passed beyond the senses, pure, perfected by austerities, possessor of superhuman powers, learned in Sāṃkhya and Yoga, skilled in many doctrines, who, having seen all with his divine vision, now broadcasts throughout the world the fame of the noble Pāṇḍavas and other Kṣatriyas, rich in ardour as well as
wealth.[1] The man of learning who always recites it at the lunar festivals 35
is washed clean of his sin, conquers the realms of heaven, and becomes

1 As the editor of Book 18, S. K. Belvalkar, points out, a number of verses from here to the end of the *Mahābhārata* unsurprisingly echo verses from near its beginning. For this verse (34), cf. 1.56.26; for verses 35–6, cf. 1.56.28–9; for verse 37, cf. 1.56.30; for verse 38, cf. 1.56.33; for verse 39, cf. 1.56.19; for verse 41, cf. 1.56.32; for verse 52, cf. 1.56.27.

one with *brahman*; and if a man recites as much as a quarter-verse to Brahmins at a *śrāddha* ceremony, food and drink unfailingly reach that man's ancestors. If by day one should do evil with one's senses or one's mind, one is freed from it by narrating this *Mahābhārata* as evening falls.

What is found here concerning *dharma*, the proper making of wealth, pleasure and final release, is to be found elsewhere too, O bull-like heir of Bharata; but what is not found here is to be found nowhere. This history is named the Tale of Victory; it should be heard by him who hopes to prosper, and by kings, the sons of kings, and pregnant
40 women. He whose desire is heaven shall gain heaven; he whose desire is victory shall gain victory; a pregnant woman shall gain a son, or a highly favoured daughter.

Mighty Kṛṣṇa Dvaipāyana Vyāsa composed this formerly unknown *Bhārata* tale in the course of three years for *dharma*'s sake. Nārada recited it to the gods, Asita Devala to the ancestors, and Śuka to the Rākṣasas and Yakṣas; but it was Vaiśaṃpāyana who recited it to mortal men. This history is holy, full of great significance, equal to the Vedas; the man who recites it to the three highest classes of men, putting Brahmins first, is freed from his sins, O Śaunaka, gains renown here on earth, and
45 attains the highest perfection – of this I have no doubt. The man of faith who learns a mere quarter-verse through holy study of this *Bhārata* tale is completely purified of all his sins.

When blessed Vyāsa, the great seer, first compiled this tale, he taught it to Śuka his son, together with these four verses:

Thousands of mothers and fathers, hundreds of sons and wives
come into existence after existence only to pass away, and more will do so.

Thousands of occasions for joy, hundreds of occasions for fear
trouble the fool day after day, but not the learned man.

Here I cry out, arms raised, and no one hears me:
'Both wealth and pleasure spring from *dharma*, so why is *dharma* not followed?'

Not for pleasure, not for fear, not for greed 50
should one ever abandon *dharma* – not even to save one's life.
*Dharma* is eternal; happiness and misery are not eternal.
The living self is eternal; the body through which it lives is not.

He who rises at dawn and recites this *Bhārata* hymn[1] gains the reward due to one who recites the *Bhārata* itself: he attains union with highest *brahman*. The blessed ocean and Mount Himālaya are both considered treasuries of gems, and the *Bhārata* is reckoned so too; he who recites the *Mahābhārata* tale with full attention attains the highest perfection – of this I have no doubt.

This *Bhārata* that emerged from the lips of Kṛṣṇa Dvaipāyana Vyāsa
is without measure;
holy, purifying and auspicious, it drives away sin.
If a man studies it as he hears it recited,
what need has he to bathe in the waters of holy Lake Puṣkara?

1 i.e. the four verses preceding.

# Variant Readings Adopted

In a relatively small number of instances I have found it necessary to adopt a reading other than that printed in the critical edition of the *Mahābhārata*. These cases vary in kind. On the one hand, I have sometimes had to correct what are certainly simple typographic or editorial slips in that edition, as for example with my preference for *yogayuktasya* over the printed *yogamuktasya* at 7.165.44d; all such cases will be more fully documented in the 'General information' file that accompanies the electronic text of the *Mahābhārata* (see Further Reading, paragraph 2). On the other hand, as with my choice of *avadhāya* rather than the printed *avadhamya* at 8.65.34a, I have sometimes simply been compelled to select a reading that made some sense to me. The following is a complete list of all instances where I have translated a reading different from the one found in the critical edition.

| | |
|---|---|
| 1.58.43a: | tām |
| 2.11.67a: | gantāsi tvaṃ |
| 2.35.21c: | hṛṣīkeśaḥ |
| 2.45.20a: | gajayoṣidgavāśvasya |
| 2.52.31c: | tā |
| 2.61.7d: | arhasi |
| 2.62.14c: | 'dharmavelāyāṃ |
| 3.282.17b: | sāvitrī ca yathāvratam |
| 3.294.6b: | nivāpaṃ |
| 4.13.19a: | aśakyarūpaṃ |
| 4.15.37b: | rudantyāviratam |
| 5.75.14a: | nātiprahīṇaraśmiḥ |
| 5.127.49c: | spraṣṭā |
| 6.33.8a: | śakṣyase |
| 6.41.54c: | pratijānāmi |

| | |
|---|---|
| 6.55.121c: | naramedaphenā |
| 6.55.124c: | kākaśālāvṛkagṛdhrakaṅkaiḥ |
| 6.72.10d: | na kulair na parigrahaiḥ |
| 6.72.14c: | pakṣisaṃkāśai |
| 6.73.19b: | niḥśvasan |
| 6.73.31b: | bhārata |
| 6.86.54c: | samatiṣṭhetāṃ |
| 6.102.68c: | kariṣyāmi |
| 7.48.10d: | tryambakāndhakau |
| 7.118.5c: | tvayā |
| 7.118.26d: | nu |
| 7.154.35d: | vṛṣṭim ugrām |
| 7.164.37a: | pratyavidhyat |
| 7.164.87b: | bharadvājo |
| 7.164.88b: | vālakhilyā |
| 7.165.44d: | yogayuktasya |
| 8.60.16a: | pāñcālarathapravīrāḥ |
| 8.65.34a: | avadhāya |
| 8.66.13d: | vibhunā svayaṃbhuvā |
| 8.66.39d: | girīndraḥ |
| 8.67.20b: | tathāśrutam |
| 8.67.20c: | susaṃhitaḥ |
| 8.67.25a: | sukhocitaṃ |
| 9.16.37b: | tam ātmano |
| 9.16.47b: | 'ndhakāyāntakaraṃ |
| 9.16.58d: | vipannāyudhajīvitāḥ |
| 9.16.77b: | sainye ca |
| 9.60.20ab: | viduradroṇakṛpagāṅgeyasaṃjayaiḥ |
| 10.8.8ef: | tathā bhavadbhyāṃ kāryaṃ syād iti me niścitā matiḥ |
| 10.8.27c: | sarvā |
| 11.16.50b: | ghorān aninditāḥ |
| 14.69.24b: | prāpya eṣa kratus tvayā |
| 14.71.6c: | yaśonāmnī |
| 15.33.12b: | śītavātādhvakarśitā |
| 15.44.8b: | diṣṭe na |
| 15.44.39c: | maivaṃ |
| 16.2.19a: | viditaṃ |
| 16.3.17a: | trayodaśī |
| 16.9.12a: | mṛṣyāmi |
| 17.1.11a: | bhrātṛbhiḥ |

# Key to Names and Glossary

Only words and names of some significance are included; for comprehensive information on names, see S. Sörensen, *An Index to the Names in the Mahabharata, with Short Explanations and a Concordance to the Bombay and Calcutta Editions and P. C. Roy's Translation* (London: Williams and Norgate, 1904; reprinted Delhi: Motilal Banarsidass, 1978). Note that many of the names of peoples overlap with one another, so that they may be used as synonyms or partial synonyms; Kṛṣṇa, for example, is referred to at different points as a Daśārha, a Yādava, a Vṛṣṇi and a Sātvata.

**Abhimanyu** son of Arjuna and Subhadrā
***adharma*** opposite of *dharma*
**Adhiratha** adoptive father of Karṇa
**Ādityas** a group of deities, primarily solar in nature
**Agastya** a great seer
**Agni** the Fire god
**Āhuka** Vṛṣṇi king of Dvārakā
**Akrūra** a Vṛṣṇi prince
**Alambusa** a Rākṣasa king, ally of Duryodhana
**All-gods** a group of deities notionally including all the gods
**Ambā**, **Ambikā**, **Ambālikā** three sister princesses of Kāśi abducted by Bhīṣma as brides for Vicitravīrya
**Ananta** (also **Śeṣa**) the great snake that serves as the god Viṣṇu's couch
**Ānarta** the land of the Vṛṣṇis; another name for the city of Dvārakā
**Andhaka** a demon killed by the god Śiva
**Andhakas** a Yādava people closely associated with the Vṛṣṇis and not always separable from them
**Aṅga** an eastern land
**Aṅgiras** a great seer

**Aṅgirases** descendants of Aṅgiras
***Anugītā*** 'subsidiary *gītā*', sermon preached by Kṛṣṇa to Arjuna at 14.16–50
**Anuvinda** a prince of Avanti, brother of Vinda and ally of Duryodhana
**Apsarases** celestial nymphs of great beauty, often associated with the (male) Gandharvas
**Arjuna** Pāṇḍu's third and last son by Kuntī, in fact fathered by Indra
**Arjuna Kārtavīrya** an ancient king, son of Kṛtavīrya, killed by Rāma (2) (Rāma Jāmadagnya)
**Arundhatī** wife of the seer Vasiṣṭha
**Asita Devala** a great seer
**Āstīka** son of the ascetic Jaratkāru and the snake king Vāsuki's sister, also called Jaratkāru; saved the surviving snakes at Janamejaya's snake sacrifice
**Aśvapati** king of Madra, father of Sāvitrī
**Aśvasena** son of the snake king Takṣaka
**Aśvatthāman** a warrior Brahmin, son of Droṇa and ally of Duryodhana
**Aśvins** twin deities celebrated in the Vedas for their beauty and skill at healing
**Atharvaveda** the fourth Veda, not used in the great rituals and consisting largely of spells
**Atri** a great seer
**Avanti** a western land
**Āyus** son of Purūravas and father of Nahuṣa
**Babhru** a Vṛṣṇi hero
**Babhruvāhana** son of Arjuna and the princess Citrāṅgadā
**Bāhlika** a north-western land (known to the Greeks as Bactria); also a king of that land, ally of Duryodhana
**Bāhlikas** people of Bāhlika
**Bāhuka** name adopted by Nala when acting as Ṛtuparṇa's charioteer
**Baka** a Rākṣasa killed by Bhīma
**Balarāma** Kṛṣṇa's elder brother, incarnation of Śeṣa
**Ballava** name adopted by Bhīma when acting as Virāṭa's cook
**Bhagadatta** king of Prāgjyotiṣa and ally of Duryodhana
***Bhagavadgītā*** sermon preached by Kṛṣṇa to Arjuna at 6.23–40
**Bhagīratha** ancient king who brought the Gaṅgā to earth
**Bharadvāja** a great seer, father of Droṇa
**Bharata** (1) son of Duḥṣanta and Śakuntalā, founder of the Bhārata lineage; (2) son of Daśaratha and brother of Rāma (1)
**Bhāratas** descendants of Bharata (includes both the Kauravas and the Pāṇḍavas)
**Bhārgavas** (also **Bhṛgus**) descendants of Bhṛgu

**Bhīma** Pāṇḍu's second son by Kuntī, in fact fathered by the Wind god

**Bhīṣma** Śaṃtanu's son by Gaṅgā; renounced right to kingship and swore eternal celibacy to allow his father's sons by Satyavatī (2) to inherit

**Bhojas** a Yādava people associated with the Vṛṣṇis

**Bhṛgu** a great seer, founder of the Bhārgava lineage of Brahmins

**Bhṛgus** *see* Bhārgavas

**Bhūriśravas** son of Somadatta and ally of Duryodhana

**Brahmā** the creator god

***brahmacarya*** the first stage of life, that of celibate studentship

***brahman*** the absolute, the ultimate reality

**Brahmins** (Sanskrit *brāhmaṇa*) members of the highest of the four primary social classes, serving as priests and scholars

**Bṛhadratha** king of Magadha and father of Jarāsaṃdha

**Bṛhannaḍā** name adopted by Arjuna when acting as Virāṭa's eunuch

**Bṛhaspati** son of Aṅgiras and household priest of the gods

**Caṇḍālas** members of the most degraded mixed social class, carrying out the most defiling tasks; said to spring from the union of a Śūdra man and a Brahmin woman

**Cāraṇas** celestial singers

**Cārudeṣṇa** son of Kṛṣṇa

**Cedi, Cedis** a central land and its people

**Cekitāna** a Vṛṣṇi warrior and ally of Yudhiṣṭhira

**Citrāṅgada** elder of Śaṃtanu's two sons by Satyavatī (2)

**Citrāṅgadā** princess of Maṇalūra/Maṇipūra and mother of Arjuna's son Babhruvāhana

**Citrasena** (1) a Dhārtarāṣṭra; (2) king of the Gandharvas

**Cyavana** a great seer, son of Bhṛgu

**Daityas** a class of demons

**Dakṣa** a Prajāpati, from whose progeny sprang all classes of living beings

**Damayantī** princess of Vidarbha and wife of Nala

**Dānavas** a class of demons

**Dāruka** Kṛṣṇa's charioteer

**Daśaratha** Ikṣvāku king of Ayodhyā and father of Rāma (1)

**Daśārha, Daśārhas** a western land and its Yādava people

**Daśārṇa, Daśārṇas** a south-eastern land and its people

**Devadatta** Arjuna's conch

**Devakī** mother of Kṛṣṇa

**Devala** *see* Asita Devala

**Devavrata** original name of Bhīṣma

***dharma*** right conduct; see introduction, pp. xviii–xxi

**Dhārtarāṣṭras** sons or descendants of Dhṛtarāṣṭra; specifically, the hundred sons borne him by his wife Gāndhārī

**Dhaumya** the Pāṇḍavas' household priest

**Dhṛṣṭadyumna** son of Drupada and ally of Yudhiṣṭhira

**Dhṛṣṭaketu** king of Cedi and ally of Yudhiṣṭhira

**Dhṛtarāṣṭra** posthumous son of Vicitravīrya, in fact fathered on Ambikā by Vyāsa; born blind; father of the hundred Dhārtarāṣṭras

**Draupadī** (also **Kṛṣṇā**) daughter of Drupada and joint wife of all five Pāṇḍava brothers

**Droṇa** a warrior Brahmin, son of Bharadvāja, father of Aśvatthāman and ally of Duryodhana; taught martial skills to both Kauravas and Pāṇḍavas

**Drupada** king of Pāñcāla, father of Dhṛṣṭadyumna, Śikhaṇḍin and Draupadī and ally of Yudhiṣṭhira

**Duḥsaha** a Dhārtarāṣṭra

**Duḥśalā** daughter of Dhṛtarāṣṭra by Gāndhārī

**Duḥṣanta** father of Bharata, the founder of the Bhārata lineage

**Duḥśāsana** second-eldest of the Dhārtarāṣṭras

**Durdhara**, **Durjaya**, **Durmada**, **Durmarṣaṇa**, **Durmukha** Dhārtarāṣṭras

**Durvāsas** a seer famed for his irascible temper

**Durvimocana**, **Durviṣaha** Dhārtarāṣṭras

**Duryodhana** eldest of the Dhārtarāṣṭras, the Pāṇḍavas' sworn enemy

**Duṣkarṇa**, **Duṣpradharṣa** Dhārtarāṣṭras

**Dvaipāyana** *see* Vyāsa

**Dvaitavana** the forest where the Pāṇḍavas start their forest exile; a lake in that forest

**Dvāpara** the second-worst throw in dicing, and the second-worst of the four ages of the world, personified as a powerful evil being

**Dvāpara Age** the third age and second-worst of the four ages of the world

**Dvārakā** the capital city of the Vṛṣṇis, on the western coast of India

**Dyumatsena** father of Satyavat

**Ekalavya** a Niṣāda prince who briefly out-performs Arjuna at archery

**Gada** Kṛṣṇa's younger brother

**Gādhi** son of Kuśika and father of Viśvāmitra

**Gālava** a student of Viśvāmitra

**Gāndhāra**, **Gāndhāras** a north-western land and its people

**Gāndhārī** daughter of Subala king of Gāndhāra, wife of Dhṛtarāṣṭra and mother of the Dhārtarāṣṭas

**Gandharvas** celestial musicians, often associated with the (female) Apsarases

**Gāṇḍīva** Arjuna's bow

**Gaṅgā** the sacred river Ganges; the goddess of the river

**Gaṅgādvāra** modern Haridwar, where the Gaṅgā enters the plain

**Garuḍa** a celestial bird

**Gautama** a great seer

**Ghaṭotkaca** Rākṣasa son of Bhīma by Hiḍimbā

**ghee** clarified butter

**Girikā** wife of Vasu Uparicara

**Gotama** a seer, father of Śaradvat and grandfather of Kṛpa and Kṛpī

**Granthika** name adopted by Nakula when acting as Virāṭa's master of horses

**Guhyakas** celestial beings who attend on the god Kubera

**Hanumān** the monkey god, half-brother to Bhīma (both are sons of the Wind god); plays an important role in the story of Rāma (1)

**Hariścandra** an ancient king

**Hāstinapura** capital of the undivided kingdom of the Kurus

**Hiḍimba** a Rākṣasa, brother of Hiḍimbā; killed by Bhīma

**Hiḍimbā** a female Rākṣasa, sister of Hiḍimba and mother of Bhīma's son Ghaṭotkaca

**Ikṣvāku** founder of the lineage of Kṣatriya kings that bears his name

**Indra** in the Vedas, the chief among the gods, associated with the bringing of rain; by the time of the *Mahābhārata* his significance is diminished by comparison with Viṣṇu/Nārāyaṇa and Śiva

**Indraprastha** Yudhiṣṭhira's capital after the division of the Kuru kingdom

**Irāvat** Arjuna's son by a snake king's widowed daughter

**Jaitra, Jalasaṃdha** Dhārtarāṣṭras

**Jamadagni** a seer, father of the warrior Brahmin Rāma (2) (Rāma Jāmadagnya)

**Janaka** father of Sītā in the story of Rāma (1); a model of royal piety, he is also frequently referred to in Book 12, 'Tranquillity'

**Janamejaya** Kuru king (great-grandson of Arjuna) at whose snake sacrifice the *Mahābhārata* was recited by Vaiśaṃpāyana

**Jarāsaṃdha** wicked king of Magadha who plans to sacrifice 100 kings to Śiva

**Jaratkāru** (1) an ascetic (weds Jaratkāru (2)); (2) sister of the snake king Vāsuki (weds Jaratkāru (1))

**Jaya** a Dhārtarāṣṭra

**Jayadratha** king of Sindhu and ally of Duryodhana

**Jayatsena** a Dhārtarāṣṭra

**Kadrū** wife of the seer Kaśyapa and mother of the snakes

**Kailāsa** a northern mountain frequented by gods, particularly Śiva and Kubera

**Kaiṭabha** a demon killed by Viṣṇu

**Kali** the worst throw in dicing, and the worst of the four ages of the world, personified as a powerful evil being

**Kali Age** the fourth and worst of the four ages of the world

**Kaliṅga**, **Kaliṅgas** an eastern land and its people

**Kāmboja**, **Kāmbojas** a north-western land and its barbarian people

**Kaṃsa** wicked king of Mathurā, killed by Kṛṣṇa

**Kāmyaka** the western forest in which the Pāṇḍavas spend most of their term of exile

**Kaṅka** name adopted by Yudhiṣṭhira when acting as a Brahmin in Virāṭa's court

**Kaṇva** a great seer, adoptive father of Śakuntalā

**Kapila** a great sage, founder of the Sāṃkhya system of religious philosophy

**Karṇa** (also **Vasuseṇa**) Kuntī's son by the Sun god, brought up by the Sūta Adhiratha and his wife Rādhā; a great ally of Duryodhana and a fierce enemy of Arjuna

**Kārtavīrya** *see* Arjuna Kārtavīrya

**Kārttikeya** *see* Skanda

**Kāśi** (also **Vārāṇasī**), **Kāśis** a city (modern Varanasi) and its people

**Kaśyapa** a great seer

**Kāśyapa** family name used for various Brahmins

**Kauravas** literally 'descendants of Kuru', and so applicable to both Dhṛtarāṣṭra's and Pāṇḍu's sons; in practice generally reserved for the former (and, by extension, their allies)

**Kekayas** a warlike people who fight on both sides at the battle of Kurukṣetra

**Keśin** a demon killed by Kṛṣṇa

**Khāṇḍava** a forest destroyed by the Fire god with the assistance of Kṛṣṇa and Arjuna

**Khāṇḍavaprastha** the Khāṇḍava region; the city of Indrapastha that Yudhiṣṭhira built there

**Kīcaka** a Sūta, Virāṭa's general; said to be Sudeṣṇā's brother

**Kīcakas** Sūta kinsmen of Kīcaka

**Kosala** a north-eastern land

**Kṛpa** a Brahmin, grandson of Gotama, son of Śaradvat, brother of Kṛpī and ally of Duryodhana

**Kṛpī** sister of Kṛpa, married to Droṇa

**Kṛṣṇa** a Vṛṣṇi prince, son of Vasudeva and incarnation of the supreme lord Viṣṇu/Nārāyaṇa

**Kṛṣṇā** *see* Draupadī

**Kṛta Age** the first and best of the four ages of the world, named after the winning throw in dicing

**Kṛtavarman** a Bhoja king, son of Hṛdika and ally of Duryodhana

**Kṣatradharman** son of Dhṛṣṭadyumna and ally of Yudhiṣṭhira

**Kṣatriyas** members of the second-highest of the four primary social classes, serving as warriors and rulers

**Kubera** the god of wealth, attended by Yakṣas and Guhyakas

**Kuntī** (also **Pṛthā**) daughter of Śūra, sister of Vasudeva, adopted daughter of Kuntibhoja, first wife of Pāṇḍu and mother of the three eldest Pāṇḍavas

**Kuntibhoja** adoptive father of Kuntī

**Kuru** descendant of Bharata and ancestor of the Kauravas and Pāṇḍavas

**Kurukṣetra** (also **Samantapañcaka**) 'the field of Kuru', the land north of modern Delhi ruled by the Kuru kings of the city of Hāstinapura; specifically, the site of the great battle between the Kauravas and the Pāṇḍavas

**Kurus** descendants of Kuru

**Lakṣmaṇa** (1) son of Daśaratha and brother of Rāma (1); (2) son of Duryodhana

**Lomaśa** a seer who accompanies Yudhiṣṭhira on his pilgrimage to the sacred bathing-places

**Madhu** (1) a demon killed by Viṣṇu; (2) an ancestor of the Vṛṣṇis[1]

**Madra**, **Madras** a north-western land and its barbarian people

**Mādrī** a Madra princess, second wife of Pāṇḍu and mother of the Pāṇḍava twins Nakula and Sahadeva

**Magadha**, **Magadhas** an eastern land and its people

**Maitreya** a great seer

**Mālava**, **Mālavas** a western land and its people

**Maṇalūra**, **Maṇipūra** a coastal city in Kaliṅga

***mantra*** an incantation, a powerful utterance

**Manu** the first man

**Mārkaṇḍeya** a great seer

**Maruts** a group of deities associated with storms

**Mātali** Indra's charioteer

**Mathurā** a major city of the Vṛṣṇis

**Matsya** (1) adopted son of Vasu Uparicara; (2) Matsyas: name of several lands (including the kingdom of Virāṭa) and their peoples

**Maya** the architect of the demons

**Merut** a great mountain to the north of the Himālaya, circled by sun and moon and frequented by the gods

**Mithilā** capital of Videha

1 Since he is both an incarnation of Viṣṇu, killer of Madhu (1), and a descendant of Madhu (2), Kṛṣṇa is regularly referred to as both 'slayer of Madhu' and 'heir of Madhu'.

**Nahuṣa** an ancient king, son of Āyus and father of Yayāti

**Naimiṣa** an eastern forest, where Śaunaka and other seers heard the *Mahābhārata* recited by the Sūta Ugraśravas

**Nakula** one of Pāṇḍu's twin sons by Mādrī, in fact fathered by the twin Aśvin gods

**Nala** king of Niṣadha and husband of Damayantī

**Namuci** a demon killed by Indra

**Nara** a divine seer, associated with Nārāyaṇa

**Nārada** a great seer

**Nārāyaṇa** Viṣṇu as supreme god; a divine seer associated with Nara

***Nārāyaṇīya*** *Mahābhārata* 12.321–39, in which Nārāyaṇa is glorified

**Niṣādas** a barbarian people

**Pāñcajanya** Kṛṣṇa's conch

**Pāñcāla**, **Pāñcālas** a northern land and its people

**Pāṇḍavas** the sons of Pāṇḍu (and, by extension, their allies)

**Pāṇḍu** posthumous son of Vicitravīrya, in fact fathered on Ambālikā by Vyāsa; father of the five Pāṇḍava brothers

**Pāṇḍya**, **Pāṇḍyas** a southern land and its people

**Parāśara** a great seer, grandson of Vasiṣṭha and father of Vyāsa

**Parikṣit** posthumous son of Abhimanyu and father of Janamejaya

**Pārvatī** (also **Umā**) daughter of Himālaya and wife of Śiva

**Pauravas** descendants of Pūru

**Piśācas** flesh-eating ghouls, generally malign

**Prabhāsa** a sacred bathing-place on the coast of Saurashtra in modern Gujarat, the site of present-day Somnath

**Pradyumna** son of Kṛṣṇa by Rukmiṇī

**Prāgjyotiṣa** an eastern city

**Prahlāda**, **Prahrāda** a demon king noted for his virtue

**Prajāpati** 'lord of creatures'; in the singular, the creator god, sometimes identified with Brahmā, sometimes distinct; in the plural, the first ancestral men, often said to be created or begotten by Brahmā to people the world

**Pratīpa** father of Śaṃtanu and grandfather of Bhīṣma

**Prativindhya** Yudhiṣṭhira's son by Draupadī

**Prayāga** place of pilgrimage where the waters of the rivers Gaṅgā and Yamunā (and, it is believed, the subterranean Sarasvatī) join together (modern Allahabad)

**Pṛṣata** father of Drupada

**Pṛthā** *see* Kuntī

**Puṇḍra**, **Puṇḍras** an eastern land and its people

**Purocana** Duryodhana's aide

**Pūru** son of Yayāti and ancestor of Bharata, the founder of the Bhārata lineage

**Purūravas** father of Āyus and grandfather of Nahuṣa

**Puṣkara** a sacred lake in western India (modern Pushkar)

**Rādhā** adoptive mother of Karṇa

**Rāhu** the demon of the eclipse

**Raivata**, **Raivataka** a mountain outside Dvārakā

**Rākṣasas** ogre-like beings who roam at night and can change form at will; generally but not always malign

**Rāma** (1) son of Daśaratha and husband of Sītā; (2) (Rāma Jāmadagnya), a warrior Brahmin, son of Jamadagni, who wiped out the Kṣatriyas twenty-one times

**Rāvaṇa** Rākṣasa king of Laṅkā in the story of Rāma (1)

**Ṛcīka** a Bhārgava Brahmin, father of Jamadagni

**Ṛgveda** one of the four Vedas, used in the sacred ritual by the *hotṛ* priest

**Rohiṇī** (1) the constellation Taurus, favourite wife of the moon; (2) mother of Balarāma

**Ṛśyaśṛṅga** (1) young ascetic with a deer's horn, son of Vibhāṇḍaka; (2) father of the Rākṣasa Alambusa

**Rudra** in the Vedas, a fierce storm god; later identified with Śiva

**Rudras** a group of eight deities associated with Śiva

**Rukmiṇī** sister of the Bhoja king Rukmin, wife of Kṛṣṇa and mother of Pradyumna

**Śacī** wife of Indra

**Sādhyas** a group of celestial beings, sometimes referred to as gods

**Sahadeva** one of Pāṇḍu's twin sons by Mādrī, in fact fathered by the twin Aśvin gods

**Śakuni** son of Subala king of Gāndhāra, brother of Gāndhārī and ally of Duryodhana

**Śakuntalā** daughter of Viśvāmitra, adopted daughter of Kaṇva, wife of Purūravas and mother of Āyus

**Śala** younger brother of Bhūriśravas

**Śālva** (1) king of the city of Saubha, betrothed to Ambā before her abduction by Bhīṣma; (2) demonic lord of the flying city of Saubha, killed by Kṛṣṇa; (3) Śālvas, a central land and its people

**Śalya** king of Madra and brother of Pāṇḍu's second wife Mādrī; ally of Duryodhana

**Samantapañcaka** *see* Kurukṣetra

**Sāmaveda** one of the four Vedas, used in the sacred ritual by the *udgātṛ* priest

**Sāmba** son of Kṛṣṇa

**Saṃjaya** a Sūta, son of Gavalgaṇa and aide to Dhṛtarāṣṭra; narrates events of the great battle to the latter

**Sāṃkhya** a religio-philosophical system founded by the sage Kapila

**Śaṃtanu** son of Pratīpa and father of Bhīṣma

**Sanatkumāra** son of Brahmā

**Śaṅkha** son of Virāṭa and brother of Uttara

**Śaradvat** son of Gotama, father of Kṛpa and Kṛpī

**Sāraṇa** brother of Kṛṣṇa

**Sarasvatī** (1) goddess of learning and eloquence; (2) a sacred river, believed to disappear under the earth and to flow into the Gaṅgā and Yamunā at Prayāga

**Śatānīka** (1) brother of Virāṭa; (2) Nakula's son by Draupadī

**Śatrughna** son of Daśaratha and brother of Rāma (1)

**Sātvatas** a Yādava people

**Satyabhāmā** a wife of Kṛṣṇa

**Sātyaki** a Vṛṣṇi warrior, grandson (sometimes son) of Śini and ally of Yudhiṣṭhira

**Satyasena** son of Karṇa

**Satyavat** husband of Sāvitrī (2)

**Satyavatī** (1) daughter of Gādhi, wife of Ṛcīka and mother of Jamadagni; (2) mother of Vyāsa, Citrāṅgada and Vicitravīrya

**Saubha** (1) city ruled by King Śālva; (2) flying city ruled by the demonic lord Śālva

**Śaunaka** chief of the seers in the Naimiṣa forest to whom Ugraśravas recited the *Mahābhārata*

**Sauvīra**, **Sauvīras** a western land and its people

**Sāvitrī** (1) wife of Brahmā; (2) daughter of Aśvapati king of Madra, and wife of Satyavat

**Śeṣa** *see* Ananta

**Śibi** (1) an ancient king, son of Uśīnara; (2) Śibis: a western land and its people

**Siddhas** 'perfected ones', celestial beings of great sanctity

**Śikhaṇḍin** son of Drupada and ally of Yudhiṣṭhira; initially born as Śikhaṇḍinī

**Śikhaṇḍinī** Ambā reborn as the daughter of Drupada; later becomes Śikhaṇḍin

**Sindhu** the river Indus and the land round it (modern Sindh)

**Śini** grandfather (sometimes father) of Sātyaki

**Śiśupāla** wicked king of Cedi who insults Kṛṣṇa

**Sītā** wife of Rāma (1)

**Śiva** with Viṣṇu, one of the two great gods of the *Mahābhārata*

**Skanda** (also **Kārttikeya**) the god of war

**Soma** sacred drink prepared and consumed during great Vedic rituals, also regarded as a deity

**Somadatta** a Kuru king, father of Bhūriśravas and ally of Duryodhana

**Somakas** a people closely associated with the Pāñcālas

***śrāddha*** ceremony in which offerings of food and water are made to deceased relatives

**Śrī** the goddess of prosperity, wife of Viṣṇu

**Sṛñjayas** a people, strictly a subgroup of the Pāñcālas, but often used to refer to the Pāñcālas as a whole

**Śrutakarman** name sometimes used instead of Śrutakīrti, sometimes instead of Śrutasena

**Śrutakīrti** Arjuna's son by Draupadī

**Śrutānta** a Dhārtarāṣṭra

**Śrutasena** Sahadeva's son by Draupadī

**Subhadrā** sister of Kṛṣṇa and wife of Arjuna

**Sudeṣṇā** a Kekaya princess, wife of Virāṭa; said to be Kīcaka's sister

**Śūdras** members of the lowest of the four primary social classes, serving the needs of the three higher classes

**Sujāta** a Dhārtarāṣṭra

**Śuka** son of Vyāsa

**Śukra** (also **Uśanas**) household priest of the demons

**Śūra** father of Vasudeva and Pṛthā (Kuntī)

**Surabhi** a celestial cow, mother of all cattle

**Śūrasena**, **Śūrasenas** a central land and its people

**Surāṣṭra**, **Surāṣṭras** a western land and its people

**Suśarman** king of Trigarta and ally of Duryodhana

**Suṣeṇa** son of Karṇa

**Sūtas** members of a mixed social class, serving as bards and charioteers; said to spring from the union of a Kṣatriya man and a Brahmin woman

**Sutasoma** Bhīma's son by Draupadī

***svayaṃvara*** ceremony at which a girl chooses her husband from among suitors who come to contend for her

**Takṣaka** a king of the snakes

**Tantipāla** name adopted by Sahadeva when acting as Virāṭa's overseer of cattle

**Tretā Age** the second age and third-worst of the four ages of the world, named after the third-worst throw in dicing

**Trigarta**, **Trigartas** a western land and its people

**Tvaṣṭṛ** the craftsman of the gods, sometimes identified with Viśvakarman

**Ugraśravas** the Sūta bard who recited the *Mahābhārata* to the seers in the Naimiṣa forest

**Ulūka** son of Śakuni

**Ulūpī** a snake princess, wife of Arjuna

**Umā** *see* Pārvatī

**Upaniṣads** speculative religious texts forming the final part of the Vedic corpus

**Upaplavya** capital of Virāṭa's kingdom

**Uparicara** *see* Vasu Uparicara

**Urvaśī** an Apsaras, wife of Purūravas

**Uśanas** *see* Śukra

**Uśīnara** an ancient king, father of Śibi (1)

**Uttamaujas** a Pāñcāla warrior, brother of Yudhāmanyu and ally of Yudhiṣṭhira

**Uttaṅka** an ascetic sage

**Uttara** son of Virāṭa and brother of Śaṅkha

**Uttarā** daughter of Virāṭa, sister of Śaṅkha and Uttara and wife of Abhimanyu

**Vaiśaṃpāyana** pupil of Vyāsa who recited the *Mahābhārata* at Janamejaya's snake sacrifice

**Vaiśyas** members of the third-highest of the four primary social classes, serving as farmers and merchants

**Vajra** grandson of Kṛṣṇa; as a child, survives the massacre of the Vṛṣṇis and the engulfment of Dvārakā, and becomes king of the Yadus in Indraprastha

**Vaṅga**, **Vaṅgas** an eastern land and its people

**Vārāṇasī** *see* Kāśi

**Varuṇa** the god of the waters

**Vasiṣṭha** a great seer, rival of Viśvāmitra

**Vasu Uparicara** an ancient king

**Vasudeva** father of Kṛṣṇa

**Vāsudeva** *see* Kṛṣṇa

**Vāsuki** a king of the snakes

**Vasus** a group of eight deities

**Vasuṣeṇa** *see* Karṇa

**Vedas** ancient sacred texts, used chiefly in connection with brahmanical rituals; 'the Veda' refers to the corpus of these texts as a whole

**Vibhāṇḍaka** an ascetic, father of Ṛśyaśṛṅga (1)

**Vicitravīrya** younger of Śaṃtanu's two sons by Satyavatī (2)

**Videha**, **Videhas** a north-eastern land and its people
**Vidura** son of Vyāsa by Ambikā's maidservant
**Vikarṇa** a Dhārtarāṣṭra
**Vinda** a prince of Avanti, brother of Anuvinda and ally of Duryodhana
**Virāṭa** a Matsya king, father of Uttara and Śaṅkha, in whose court the Pāṇḍavas lived incognito for a year; ally of Yudhiṣṭhira
**Viṣṇu** with Śiva, one of the two great gods of the *Mahābhārata*
**Viśvakarman** the architect of the gods, sometimes identified with Tvaṣṭṛ
**Viśvāmitra** a great seer, father of Śakuntalā and rival of Vasiṣṭha; originally born a Kṣatriya
**Viviṃśati** a Dhārtarāṣṭra
**Vṛṣasena** eldest son of Karṇa
**Vṛṣṇis** a Yādava people
**Vṛtra** a great demon killed by Indra
**Vyāsa** a great seer, son of Parāśara and Satyavatī (2), biological father of Dhṛtarāṣṭra, Pāṇḍu and Vidura; author of the *Mahābhārata*
**Yādavas** (also **Yadus**) descendants of Yadu
**Yadu** an ancient king, son of Yayāti and founder of the Yādava lineage
**Yadus** *see* Yādavas
**Yājñavalkya** a great seer
**Yajurveda** one of the four Vedas, used in the sacred ritual by the *adhvaryu* priest
**Yakṣas** celestial beings who attend on the god Kubera
**Yakṣīs** female Yakṣas
**Yama** the god of the dead
**Yamunā** the sacred river Jumna
**Yayāti** an ancient king, son of Nahuṣa and father of five sons including Yadu and Pūru
**Yoga** a religio-philosophical system closely linked to Sāṃkhya and advocating meditation as the way to release
**Yudhāmanyu** a Pāñcāla warrior, brother of Uttamaujas and ally of Yudhiṣṭhira
**Yudhiṣṭhira** Pāṇḍu's eldest son by Kuntī, in fact fathered by Dharma
**Yuyutsu** son of Dhṛtarāṣṭra by a Vaiśya woman; fought on the Pāṇḍava side at Kurukṣetra

# Further Reading

Considerations of space rule out any possibility of including in this volume anything approaching a comprehensive bibliography of the *Mahābhārata*. Instead I here merely indicate some of the works that I have found myself consulting again and again as I prepared my translation, works that would also be useful to anyone who wished to engage in further study of the text.

The central publication for any serious study of the *Mahābhārata* is the critical edition of the Sanskrit text published in Poona (Pune) over a period spanning a third of the entire twentieth century, a gigantic scholarly labour that seems unlikely ever to be superseded: V. S. Sukthankar *et al.* (eds), *The Mahābhārata, for the first time critically edited* (Poona: Bhandarkar Oriental Research Institute, 1933–66). The text and the major variant readings of this edition are also available in electronic form at <http://bombay.indology.info/mahabharata/statement.html>.

Still important is the so-called Bombay edition (also known as the vulgate), which consists of the text as edited and supplied with a commentary by the seventeenth-century scholar Nīlakantha. This was first published in Bombay in the nineteenth century, and appeared in various forms (sometimes containing little or no bibliographic information). A recent reprint is Paṇḍita Rāmacandra-śāstrī Kiṃjavaḍekara (ed.), *Śrīḥ Mahābhāratam: caturdharavaṃśāvataṃsaśrīman nīlakaṇṭhaviracitabhāratabhāvadīpākhyaṭīkayā sametam*, 2nd edn (New Delhi: Oriental Books Reprint Corporation, 1979).

A complete translation of the *Mahābhārata* into English exists: it is the work of K. M. Ganguli, though in early editions the name appearing on the title-page is that of the publisher, Pratap Chandra Roy. It predates the critical edition, and is based on Ganguli's own choice of what he considered the best readings to be found in the editions available to him; to a large extent he follows the text and interpretations of the commentator Nīlakaṇṭha as found in the Bombay edition. For a specimen of his style of translation see Introduction, pp. liv–lv.

Though first published in fascicles between 1883 and 1896, Ganguli's work is still available in print: *The Mahabharata of Krishna-Dwaipayana Vyasa, translated into English prose from the original Sanskrit text* (Delhi: Munshiram Manoharlal, 1998–2003). It is also available in electronic form at <http://www.sacred-texts.com/hin/maha/index.htm>. Despite the differences between Ganguli's text and the critical edition on which I have based my translation, and despite his tendency to accept Nīlakaṇṭha's interpretations where I might not be inclined to do so, I have found Ganguli enormously helpful, not least because of his admirable grasp of epic Sanskrit idiom. (A second complete translation into English was published by M. N. Dutt; it appears, however, to be highly derivative from Ganguli: *Mahabharata, translated into English from the original Sanskrit text*, reprint (Delhi: Parimal Publications, 1997).)

Another projected complete translation was undertaken by J. A. B. van Buitenen shortly after the completion of the critical edition (on which it is based). Unfortunately van Buitenen died after publishing approximately a third of his planned translation; the project has since been taken over by a team of other scholars, and the first of the 'new' volumes has appeared: J. A. B. van Buitenen, James L. Fitzgerald *et al.*, *The Mahābhārata, translated and edited* (Chicago and London: University of Chicago Press, 1973–8, 2004–). In addition to its considerable worth as a scholarly translation of the now standard scholarly text, the 'Chicago translation' contains much else of value, notably van Buitenen's general introduction to the *Mahābhārata* as a whole, and the various introductions to the specific sections of the text covered thus far. Though I have not always found myself in agreement with the interpretations found in this translation, I have naturally paid very close attention to it as I worked on my own rendering.

Certain classic works of *Mahābhārata*-related scholarship, though now somewhat old, remain required reading. E. Washburn Hopkins, *The Great Epic of India: Its Character and Origin* (New York: Charles Scribner's Sons, and London: Edward Arnold, 1901; reprinted Calcutta: Punthi Pustak, 1978), is a detailed analysis of the work from various perspectives; though inevitably now dated in many respects, it remains extremely valuable. The same applies to the same author's *Epic Mythology* (Strasburg: K. J. Trübner, 1915; reprinted Delhi: Indological Book House, 1968). Equally indispensable is S. Sörensen's *An Index to the Names in the Mahabharata, with Short Explanations and a Concordance to the Bombay and Calcutta Editions and P. C. Roy's Translation* (London: Williams and Norgate, 1904; reprinted Delhi: Motilal Banarsidass, 1978). All three of these works predate the critical edition and therefore have to be used with some caution – but they still have to be used.

Rather more recently, John Brockington has published his study of *The*

*Sanskrit Epics* (Leiden: Brill, 1998). As the title indicates, this covers the *Rāmāyaṇa* as well as the *Mahābhārata.* It gives a thorough, balanced account of the state of scholarship on the two texts; it also provides the comprehensive bibliography lacking here.

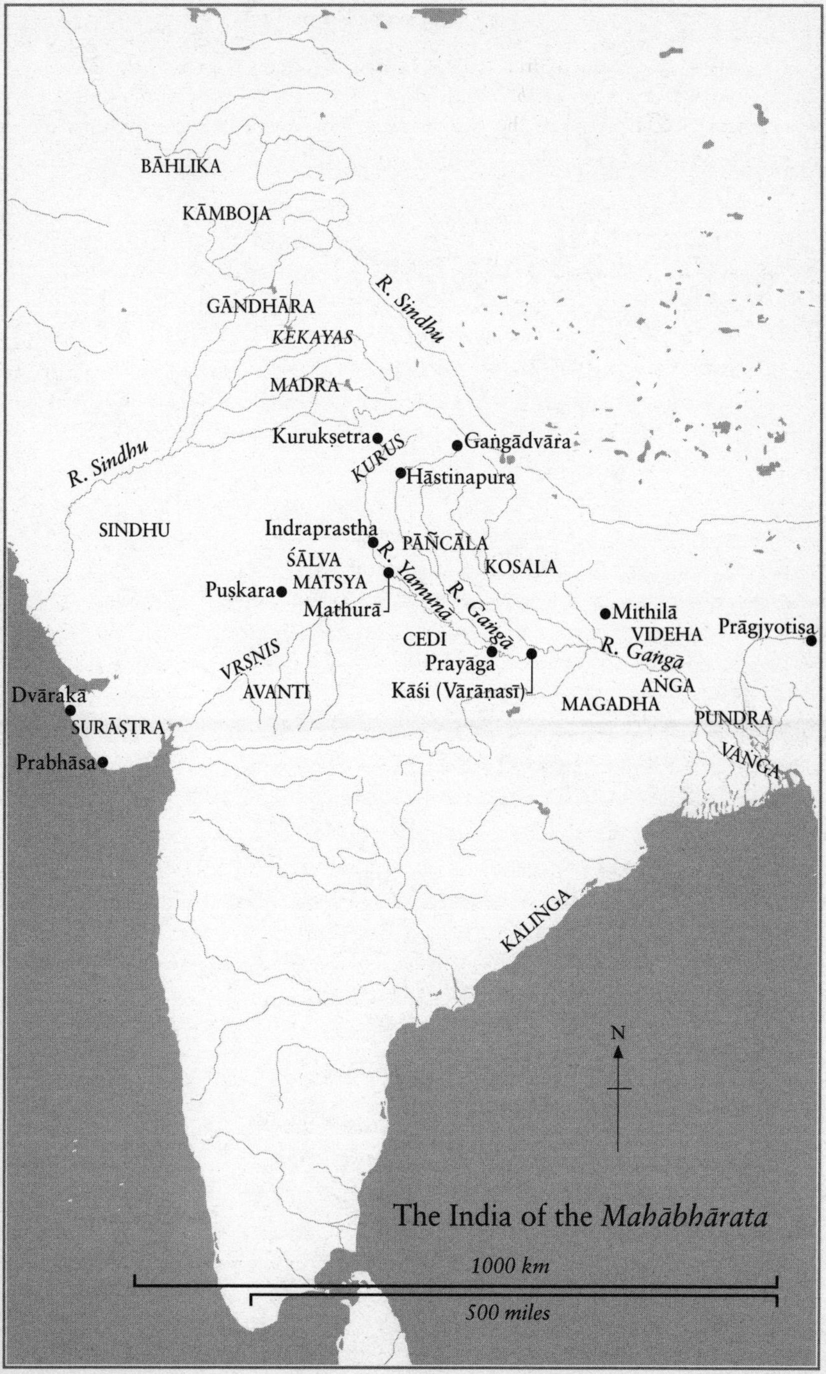


The India of the *Mahābhārata*

# Genealogical Tables

## I. The Line of Śaṃtanu

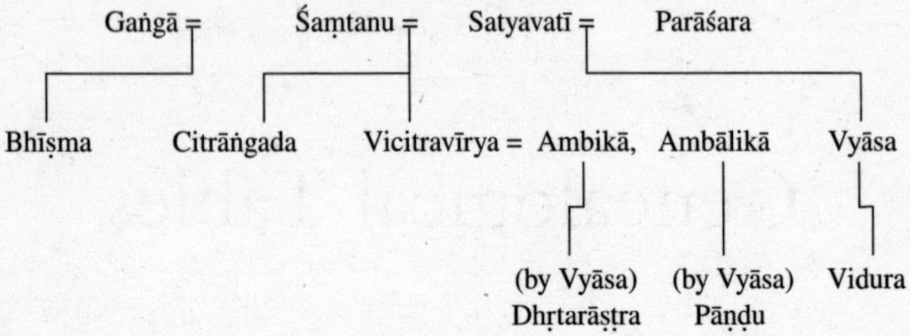


## II. The Kauravas

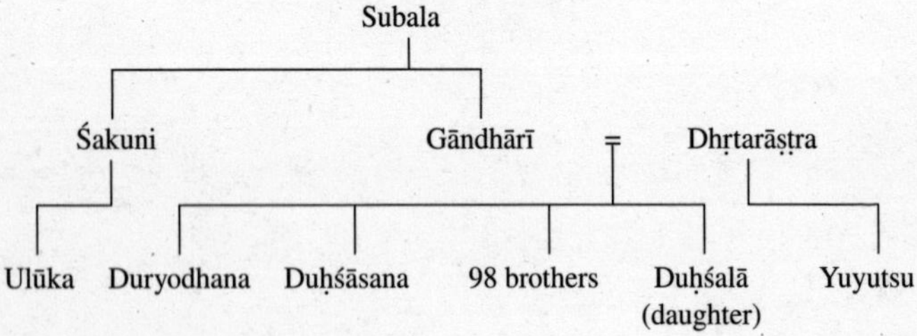


## III. The Pāṇḍavas

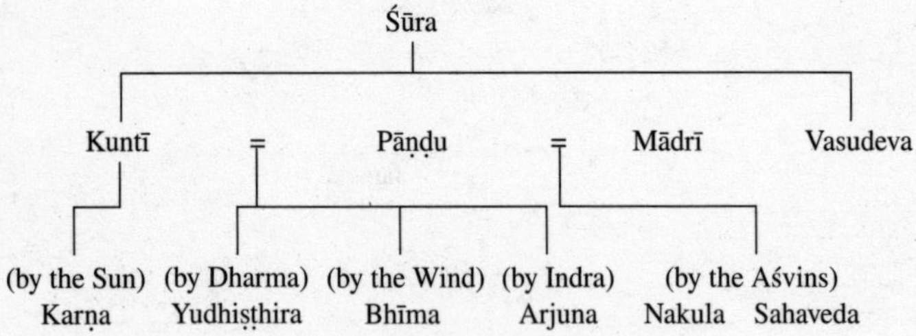

## IV. The Line of Drupada

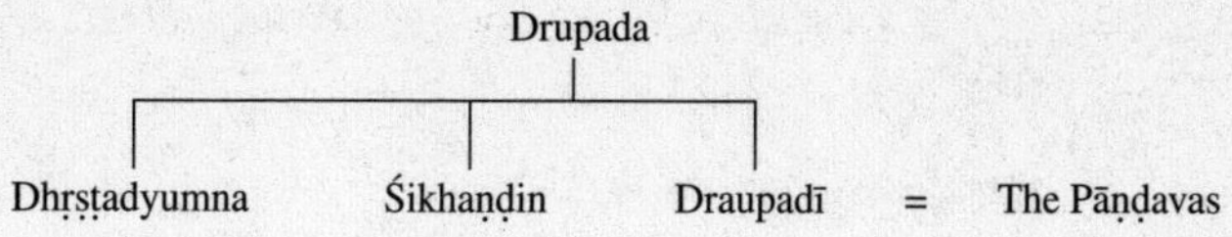


## V. The Ancestry of Janamejaya

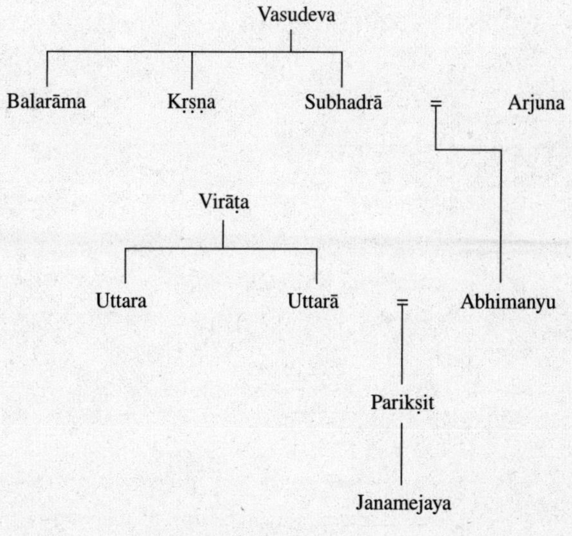


The translator acknowledges his indebtedness to the Genealogical Tables appearing in Chakravarthi V. Narasimhan, *The Mahābhārata: An English Version Based on Selected Verses* (New York and London: Columbia University Press, 1965) which he has modified for this edition.

# Index


Abhimanyu, xvi–xvii
birth of, 81
betrothal of, 290
weds Uttarā, 290–91
battles with Bhīṣma, 373
battles with Lakṣmaṇa, 374, 381
battles with the Kauravas, 387–8, 397, 398, 403, 405, 415, 418–28
battles with Karṇa, 425
death of, 428
lamentation for, 431, 432, 449, 450, 710, 711
*adharma*, 128, 149, 168, 315, 358, 475, 549–50, 556, 577, 578, 612–14, 623, 643, 652, 656, 675, 678, 694, 701, 712, see also *dharma*
Agastya, 177–8, 196, 198, 298, 457, 691–2, 699, 733
Agni, 171, 172, 190, 204–6, 336, 650, 696, 739, see also Fire
Ambā, 37, 343–5
death of, 345
reborn in Drupada's family, 345
Ambālikā, 37–8, 343
death of, 51
Ambikā, 37–8, 343
death of, 51
Andhakas, 69, 81, 112, 134, 166, 291, 294, 330, 336, 337, 448, 714, 756–61, 763, 764, 766, 767
*Anugītā*, 705–8
Arjuna, xv–xviii, xxx
birth of, 22, 48
taught martial skills by Droṇa, 54
excels as warrior, 54
competes against Karṇa, 54–8
wins Draupadī, 70–71
exile in the forest, 80–81
weds Subhadrā, 81
allows Fire to burn the Khāṇḍava forest, 82–3
receives bow Gāṇḍīva, 82
receives celestial weapons, 83, 169, 170, 196, 432–3
receives conch Devadatta, 85, 196, 197
vows to kill Karṇa, 161, 505, 506
meets Śiva, 169–70
visits Indra's world, 170
returns from Indra's world, 196
disguises self as Bṛhannaḍā, liii–liv, 245, 254–5

Arjuna – *comt.*
defeats Kauravas, rescues cattle, 278–81
battles with Droṇa, 280, 397, 434, 471–5
seeks Kṛṣṇa's aid, 294–6
vows to kill Bhīṣma, 342
hears the *Bhagavadgītā* from Kṛṣṇa, 354–66
battles with Bhīṣma, 375, 399–401, 403, 405–7
tends to the fallen Bhīṣma, 409–11
battles with the sworn warriors, 415–31, 490–91, 500, 502, 507
battles with Jayadratha, 435–6, 451–4
battles with Duryodhana, 436–7
severs Bhūriśravas's arm, 446–9
battles with Karṇa, 451, 459, 512–24
kills Karṇa, 523
hears the *Anugītā* from Kṛṣṇa, 705–8
protects the sacrificial horse as it roams, 716–26
meets Babhruvāhana, 720
rescues the survivors at Dvārakā, 763–8
death of, 775
*artha*, see wealth, making of
asceticism, xii, 88, 204, 209, 302, 365, 366, 599, 600, 610, 624, 625, 630, 634–6, 639, 640, 653–4, 689, 693, 695–6, 701, 703, 733, 752
Āstīka, xlviii–xlvix, 4, 5, 9–10, 749, 789
birth of, 8, 9
Aśvatthāman, xvii, xxvii–xxviii
birth of, 21, 53
urges peace, 157, 304, 321, 512
reproves Karṇa, 279
battles with Arjuna, 280, 381, 490, 503, 504, 528
battles with Śikhaṇḍin, 390
battles with Ghaṭotkaca, 396, 458, 461
battles with Dhṛṣṭadyumna, 459–60, 486, 503
swears vengeance for the death of his father Droṇa, 484
deploys Nārāyaṇa Weapon, 485–6
deploys Fire Weapon, 486
vows to kill all his enemies, 541, 562
one of three Kaurava survivors, 561
slaughters his enemies by night, xliv, 563–74
wins Śiva's aid, 565–6
kills Dhṛṣṭadyumna, 567
deploys Weapon of Brahmā's Head, 576
receives the curse of Kṛṣṇa and Vyāsa, 579
austerities, see asceticism

Babhruvāhana, 81, 719–21, 725, 727, 731
Bāhlika, 332, 377, 398
urges peace, 157, 321
death of, 459
Balarāma, 69–73, 81, 188, 293, 295, 341, 542–9, 554–6, 757, 758, 760, 761
birth of, 23, 74
death of, 762
Ballava, see Bhīma

barbarians, 27, 39, 66, 105, 109, 201, 262, 372, 439, 440, 482, 497, 507, 538, 611, 621, 627–8, 718, 721, 731, 767
bathing-places, 80, 176–7, 187–90, 341, 543–8, 674, 694
Bhagadatta, 91, 104, 380, 395–6
  death of, 417–18
*Bhagavadgītā*, xiii–xiv, xvii, xx, xxxvii, 354–66
Bharata, 12, 25, 28, 785
Bhīma, xv–xviii, xxxi–xxxii
  birth of, 22, 47
  hated by Dhṛtarāṣṭra's sons, 51–2
  plotted against by Duryodhana, 52–3
  mocks Karṇa, 57
  rescues family from burning house, 61–2
  kills Hiḍimba, weds Hiḍimbā, 62
  kills Baka, 63–4
  kills Jarāsaṃdha, 100–101
  reproves Yudhiṣṭhira, 145, 171
  vows to kill Duḥśāsana, 147, 161
  vows to kill Duryodhana, 152, 161
  urges war, 168, 171
  sent for flowers by Draupadī, 193–6
  meets Hanumān, 193–4
  disguises self as Ballava, 244, 251
  wrestles for Virāṭa, 257–8
  kills Kīcaka and his kin, 263–70
  urges peace, 306–7
  battles with Duryodhana, 378–80, 388, 461, 530
  slaughters elephant force, 378–80, 397, 417, 539
  battles with Dhṛtarāṣṭra's sons, 384–8, 540
  battles with the Kauravas, 404, 417, 441, 456–7, 489, 506
  battles with Droṇa, 441
  battles with Karṇa, 442–3, 471, 474, 501–3
  kills Duḥśāsana, 510–11
  battles with Śalya, 528, 533–4
  kills Duryodhana, 549–56
  pursues Aśvatthāman, 576
  oversees horse sacrifice, 722–9
  harbours ill will towards Dhṛtarāṣṭra and Gāndhārī, 734–5, 737
  death of, 775
Bhīṣma, xv-xvii, xxii–xxiii
  birth of, 21, 30–32
  naming of, 33–6
  abducts Ambā, Ambikā and Ambālikā, 36–7
  rules over the Kurus, 40
  arranges Dhṛtarāṣṭra's marriage to Gāndhārī, 41–2
  arranges Pāṇḍu's marriage to Mādrī, 43
  appoints Droṇa as teacher of the Kauravas and Pāṇḍavas, 53
  urges peace, 75, 157, 208, 299, 304, 312, 321, 323–4, 339, 381, 411
  favours Kṛṣṇa over Śiśupāla, 112–17
  battles with Arjuna, 280–81, 375, 378, 399–401, 403, 405–7
  despises Karṇa, 303, 304, 342, 347
  intalled as commander, 341
  reviews the Kaurava and Pāṇḍava warriors, 342–3
  explains why he will not kill Śikhaṇḍin, 343–6
  blesses Yudhiṣṭhira, 368–9

Bhīṣma – *cont.*
battles with the Pāṇḍavas, 373, 381, 392–3, 398–401
explains how he may be killed, 401–3
killing of, 404–7
blesses Karṇa, 413
preaches deathbed sermon to Yudhiṣṭhira, lx–lxiii, 606–701
death of, 701–2
Bhojas, 27, 81, 90, 92, 117, 134, 166, 291, 294, 329, 341, 756, 761, 766
Bhṛgu, 4, 187–8, 630–31, 676, 688, 692
Bhūriśravas, 375–7, 392
urges peace, 157
battles with Sātyaki, 381–2, 444–7
death of, 444–9
Brahmā, 4, 7–8, 19–20, 74, 79, 87, 178–9, 200, 202, 211, 380, 493–4, 512, 514, 546, 581, 603, 607–9, 619, 626, 630, 633, 639, 643, 650, 653, 662–5, 670, 685, 687–9, 693, 707–8
*brahmacarya*, 634, 635, 641, see also celibacy, holy
*brahman*, 2, 12, 17, 199, 302, 355–6, 359–60, 365–6, 498, 599, 600, 625, 629, 631–5, 637–42, 644, 646, 648–9, 653, 654, 656–8, 661, 705, 706, 790, 791
Bṛhannaḍā, see Arjuna

Caṇḍālas, 622, 675, 679, 683, 692–3, 708–9
Cedi, Cedis, 12–14, 48, 91, 105, 113, 117, 119, 166, 167, 173, 243, 298, 307, 377, 419, 471, 721, 752
celestial weapons, lvii–lviii, 32, 49, 53–65, 68, 83, 123, 169–70, 176, 196–8, 207, 211, 213–14, 245, 279–81, 344–5, 347, 376–7, 386–7, 391–2, 397, 405, 411, 414, 416–18, 424, 432, 434–5, 437, 440, 452–3, 459, 463–4, 468, 471, 476, 478–81, 484–7, 492, 494, 497–9, 501–2, 504, 514, 520–22, 561, 568, 576–9, 597–8, 711–13, 716, 767, 769, 770, 786
celibacy, holy, 36, 181, 230, 544, 548, 577, 607, 616, 631, 707, see also *brahmacarya*
Citrāṅgada, 36, 343
classes, xviii–xix, 18, 302, 358, 366, 607–9, 611, 613, 630, 652–3, 666, 671, 678–9, 689, 694, 697–8, 790

*daiva*, see fate
Damayantī, 171–5
Darkness, 204, 366, 634–5, 641–2, 648, 653, 655, 661, 665
Daśārha, Daśārhas, 85, 89, 290, 296
*dharma*, xviii–xxi, lxi–lxiii, 2, 11, 12, 18, 128, 144, 148–50, 168, 203, 300, 315–16, 322, 357–8, 429, 448–9, 469, 472, 475–6, 482, 484, 520, 522, 549, 555–6, 565, 584, 585, 601, 607, 619, 626, 646, 647, 651, 661, 701, 707, 712, 720, 733, 790–91, see also *adharma*
in times of trouble, xx, lxi, 49, 300, 611, 613, 620–28, 652

of women, 203, 224, 698
of kings, lxi, 597–620
of final release, lxi, 628–67
of giving, lxi, 668–701
Dhaumya, 68, 74, 107, 163–4, 176, 196, 210, 242, 247, 593, 603, 742
Dhṛṣṭadyumna, xvii
birth of, 22, 65
vows to kill Droṇa, 166, 471
threatens the Kauravas, 304
installed as commander, 341
leads Pāṇḍava forces, 342
arrays Pāṇḍava forces, 373
battles with Droṇa, 374, 387–8, 405, 414, 416, 435, 440, 462, 471–83
battles with the Kauravas, 378–9, 381, 386–8, 393, 435, 462
battles with Duryodhana, 391, 503, 529, 539
battles with Aśvatthāman, 459, 486, 503
battles with Karṇa, 463
battles with Duḥśāsana, 471–2
kills Droṇa, 483
reviled by Sātyaki, 485
reviles Sātyaki, 485
death of, 566–7
Dhṛtarāṣṭra, xv–xvi, xviii, xxiii–xxiv
birth of, 22, 37–8
debarred from kingship through blindness, 41
weds Gāndhārī, 41
birth of 100 sons, 44–6
lures Yudhiṣṭhira to Vāraṇāvata, 59
grieves for the seeming death of the Pāṇḍavas, 62
consults advisers, 75–6, 164–5, 301–4
refuses to act against the Pāṇḍavas, 76
divides the kingdom, 77
agrees to act against the Pāṇḍavas, 126, 128, 157, 207
rejects advice, 127–8, 157, 158, 164, 303
urges peace, 128, 304, 325, 335
offers boons to Draupadī, 153
releases Pāṇḍavas, 155
blames fate, 163, 165, 302, 352, 383, 392, 393, 417, 438, 439, 442, 470, 493, 526, 549
sends Saṃjaya as envoy to the Pāṇḍavas, 299
declines Vyāsa's offer of sight, 350
attempts to kill Bhīma, 584
proposes to retire to the forest, 735
addresses citizens, 736–7
distributes wealth, 738–9
sets out for the forest, 739
visited in the forest by the Pāṇḍavas, 742–53
death of, 753–4
Draupadī, xv–xvi, xxxiii
birth of, 23, 65
*svayaṃvara* of, 68–74
weds all five Pāṇḍavas, xlvi–xlvii, 74–5
bears five sons, 81
queries Yudhiṣṭhira's wager, 142, 145
dragged by Duḥśāsana, 143, 148
stripped by Duḥśāsana, 147–8
frees the Pāṇḍavas, 153
laments to Kṛṣṇa, 166
argues for action against the Kauravas, 168
carried by Ghaṭotkaca, 193

Draupadī – *cont.*
sends Bhīma for flowers, 193–6
conversation with Satyabhāmā, 206
abducted by Jayadratha, 209–10
disguises self as maidservant, 247, 251
taken as maidservant by Sudeṣṇā, 251–3
rejects Kīcaka's advances, 259
insulted by Kīcaka, 260–61
complains to Virāṭa, 261–2
complains to Bhīma, 263
scornful of Yudhiṣṭhira, 263
agrees to meet Kīcaka, 264
rejoices at Kīcaka's death, 267
rescued by Bhīma, 268
urges war, 311
demands death of Aśvatthāman, 575
death of, 774
Droṇa, xv, xvii, xxv
birth of, 21, 53
appointed teacher of the Kauravas and Pāṇḍavas, 53
repudiated by Drupada, 53, 64
and Ekalavya, 54
attacks Drupada, 58, 64
urges peace, 75, 157, 303, 304, 321, 324, 339
agrees to support the Kauravas, 163
battles with Arjuna, 280, 397, 434, 471–5
despises Karṇa, 342
teaches arms to Śikhaṇḍin, 346
blesses Yudhiṣṭhira, 369
explains how he may be killed, 370
battles with Dhṛṣṭadyumna, 374, 387–8, 405, 414, 435, 440, 462, 471–82
battles with Drupada, 386
battles with the Pāṇḍavas, 388, 413–14, 416–17
battles with Virāṭa, 389–90
installed as commander, 413
battles with Yudhiṣṭhira, 415, 437, 460
battles with Sātyaki, 435, 437–9
renders Duryodhana invulnerable, 435
battles with Bhīma, 441
grieved to hear of Aśvatthāman's death, 477
death of, 483
Drupada
birth of, 21
repudiates Droṇa, 53, 64
attacked by Droṇa, seeks revenge, 58, 64
holds *svayaṃvara* for daughter Draupadī, 68
allies self to Pāṇḍavas, 73
sends household priest as envoy to the Kauravas, 293–4
battles with Droṇa, 386–8
battles with the Kauravas, 386
death of, 471
Duḥśalā, 719
birth of, 46
weds Jayadratha, 46
Duḥśāsana, xxvii
drags Draupadī, 143, 148
attempts to strip Draupadī, 147–8
derides the Pāṇḍavas, 161
battles with Arjuna, 403–4, 434
battles with the Pāṇḍavas, 405
battles with Abhimanyu, 424
battles with Sātyaki, 439–40, 444

battles with Dhṛṣṭadyumna, 471–2
battles with Sahadeva, 471, 491
battles with Bhīma, 510–11
death of, 510
Duryodhana, xv–xviii, xxv–xxvii
birth of, 22, 45, 47
plots against Bhīma, 52–3
befriends Karṇa, 55–8
installs Karṇa as king of Aṅga, 56
plots against the Pāṇḍavas, 58–62, 156
urges action against the Pāṇḍavas, 75
humiliated in Yudhiṣṭhira's hall, 121–2
resents the Pāṇḍavas' success, 122–3, 125–6
proposes a gambling match against Yudhiṣṭhira, 126
orders Draupadī to be brought to the assembly, 141, 142
orders Duḥśāsana to bring Draupadī, 143
exposes his thigh to Draupadī, 152
proposes a second gambling match, 156–7
mocks Bhīma, 161
cursed by Maitreya, 165
rescued by the Pāṇḍavas, 207
agrees to a cattle raid, 271
refuses to restore the Pāṇḍavas' kingdom, 279
defeated by Arjuna, 281
prepares for war, 293, 341, 342, 349
seeks Kṛṣṇa's aid, 294–5
gains Śalya as ally, 296
intent on war, 304
walks out of the assembly, 329
blames his commander, 375, 397, 418, 423, 434, 454, 455, 462, 470
battles with Bhīma, 378–80, 388, 417, 461, 530
battles with Dhṛṣṭadyumna, 391, 503, 529, 539
battles with Ghaṭotkaca, 395–6
battles with the Pāṇḍavas, 398, 440, 528
attacks Abhimanyu, 423, 424
rendered invulnerable, 435
battles with Arjuna, 436
battles with Sātyaki, 439, 462, 473–4
battles with Yudhiṣṭhira, 492
abandons the battle, 540
enters lake, 541
accepts Yudhiṣṭhira's challenge, 542
killing of, 549–57
death of, xxxix–xli, 575
Dvaitavana, Lake, 167, 169, 198, 207, 241
Dvāpara, 21, 172
Dvāpara Age, 194, 200, 353, 609, 613, 633, 639
Dvārakā, 78, 81, 84, 89, 93, 94, 117, 120, 166–7, 293, 294, 556, 708, 709, 721, 756–66, 774

Earth, 19–20, 187, 418, 583, 605, 691, 698, 730–31
Ekalavya, 54
epics, xiii, lxv–lxvi
exile, 79–81, 157, 159, 164–292

fate, xli–xlvii, 48, 65, 100, 122–3, 127, 129–31, 134, 152, 158, 162, 163, 165, 168, 181, 223,

fate – *cont.*
302, 303, 310–11, 350, 352, 383, 392–3, 398, 399, 403, 412, 413, 417, 438, 439, 442, 450, 455, 459, 467, 470, 473, 477, 489, 493, 499, 521, 522, 524, 526, 549, 554, 565, 570–71, 574, 575, 582, 583, 587, 591, 601–2, 606, 629, 670, 681, 735, 737, 750, 756–7, 761, 767–9

Fire, 4, 22, 48, 57, 82–3, 105, 123, 205–6, 211, 245, 298, 476, 546, 605, 650, 687–9, 704, 709, 773–4

gambling, 5, 121–63, 172, 174–5, 244, 250, 283, 441

Gāndhāra, Gāndhāras, 41, 162, 418, 428, 539, 721, 722

Gāndhārī, xv, xviii, xxiv–xxv
- birth of, 23
- dons blindfold, 41
- weds Dhṛtarāṣṭra, 41
- gives birth to 100 sons, 44–6
- urges peace, 157–8, 331–3
- promises not to destroy Pāṇḍavas, 561
- angry with Bhīma, 586
- scorches Yudhiṣṭhira's nails, 586–7
- sees vision of the battlefield, 587–92
- sets out for the forest, 739
- visited in the forest by the Pāṇḍavas, 742–53
- death of, 753–4

Gaṅgā, 28–33, 57, 80, 164, 170, 176, 179, 340, 344–5, 546, 584, 594–6, 658, 659, 669, 675, 679, 680, 687, 698–9, 702–3, 720, 740, 746–8, 753–5, 773, 785

Ghaṭotkaca, xvii, 194, 198, 380, 393, 396, 435, 437, 460
- birth of, 62–3
- carries Draupadī, 193
- battles with Duryodhana, 395–6
- battles with Aśvatthāman, 396, 458, 461
- battles with Karṇa, 463–9
- death of, 468

giving, 110, 111, 209, 365, 366, 495, 599, 600, 614, 615, 624, 639, 648, 652, 674, 703, 733, 735, 738–9, 742, see also *dharma*

Goodness, 204, 366, 634–6, 641, 642, 648, 655

Granthika, see Nakula

Hanumān, 212–14
- meets Bhīma, 193–4

Hāstinapura, xv, 24, 32, 34, 36, 41, 43, 51, 53, 76–7, 108, 130, 165, 177, 208, 270, 298, 300, 343, 541, 561, 598, 602, 701, 710–11, 713–14, 722, 740, 755, 770, 772–3, 789

heaven, lxiii–lxiv, 12, 20, 27–8, 99, 112, 168, 170, 199, 201–3, 209, 235, 236, 262, 286, 319–20, 327, 332, 339, 354, 527, 536, 548–9, 593, 601, 608, 610, 614–16, 620, 625, 630–32, 634, 639, 641, 644–7, 653, 654, 656, 661, 677, 683, 686, 692–5, 705, 707, 732–3, 775–7, 779–90

Hiḍimba, 62

Hiḍimbā, 62–3

Himālaya, Mount, 12, 45, 51, 68, 169, 179, 193, 200, 546, 631, 658, 660, 670, 672, 697, 703, 754, 774, 791 human effort, xlii–xliii, 48, 122–3, 168, 302, 310, 336, 442, 565, 606, 629, 670, 737

incarnation, 21–3, 74, 112, 746, 787–9
Indra, 6–7, 9, 12–14, 20, 22, 24, 26–7, 43, 48, 56, 63, 74, 79, 82–3, 85, 87–8, 126, 169–72, 178, 180–81, 186, 189–91, 196–7, 205–6, 234–41, 279–80, 296–8, 317, 367, 512, 547–8, 601–2, 604, 619, 636–8, 645, 649–50, 671–2, 675, 677, 692, 700, 703–4, 709, 733, 763, 775–8, 783–6
Indraprastha, xv, 78–82, 85, 105, 127, 156, 316, 705, 768, 772
Irāvat, 392–5
  death of, 395

Janaka, 191, 210, 356, 599, 601, 615–16, 635–6, 652–3, 657–9, 707
Janamejaya, xlv, xlviii–xlix, 1–5, 8–10, 664, 749–50, 789
Jarā, 757, 763
Jarāsaṃdha, 91–104, 598
Jayadratha, 419, 424–5, 431–6, 441, 444–54
  weds Duryodhana's daughter Duḥśalā, 46
  abducts Draupadī, 209–10
  death of, 453

Kali, 22, 127, 172–4
Kali Age, 194, 200–201, 339, 353, 555, 609, 613, 633, 639, 665
*kāma*, see pleasure
Kaṅka, see Yudhiṣṭhira
*karma*, xiii, 27, 168, 199, 203, 355, 357, 359–61, 366, 582, 630, 632, 635–7, 640–41, 646, 648, 649, 652, 655, 668, 670, 672, 692, 694, 698, 705, 748, 784, 787, 788
Karṇa, xv–xvii, xxviii–xxix
  birth of, 22, 42, 238
  gives Indra his armour and earrings, 43, 234–41
  competes against Arjuna, 54–8
  scorns Pāṇḍavas, 54
  befriended by Duryodhana, 55–8
  matches Arjuna, 55
  installed by Duryodhana as king of Aṅga, 56
  mocked by Bhīma, 57
  battles with Arjuna, 71, 279–80, 451, 459, 512–24
  urges war, 75, 165, 271, 299
  insults Pāṇḍavas, 148, 151, 154
  receives Indra's Spear, 240
  boasts, 278–80, 304, 347, 459, 494, 495
  refuses to fight while Bhīṣma lives, 305, 341, 342
  rejects Kṛṣṇa's offer of the Pāṇḍava kingship, 339
  promises Kuntī not to kill any Pāṇḍava but Arjuna, 340
  rejects Kuntī's offer of the Pāṇḍava kingship, 340
  refuses to change sides, 371
  receives Bhīṣma's blessing, 411–13
  battles with Abhimanyu, 425
  battles with Bhīma, 442–3, 471, 474, 501–3
  battles with Sātyaki, 454, 462, 509
  battles with Sahadeva, insults him, 461

Karṇa – *cont.*
battles with Dhṛṣṭadyumna, 463
battles with Ghaṭotkaca, 463–9
battles with the Pāṇḍavas, 463, 501, 504, 508–9
kills Ghaṭotkaca with Indra's Spear, 468
installed as commander, 488, 489
battles with Nakula, insults him, 491–2
insulted by Śalya, 494–500
kills Śikhaṇḍin, 508
death of, 520–24
Kaśyapa, 5–7, 25, 187, 605, 610, 633, 698
Khāṇḍava forest, 48, 82–3, 245, 273, 274, 773, see also Khāṇḍavaprastha
Khāṇḍavaprastha, 77–8, 273, 323, 498, 514, 518
Kīcaka, Kīcakas, xvi, 258–70
Kṛpa, 53, 56, 278, 392, 459, 492, 537, 740, 742, 772, 773
birth of, 21
battles with Arjuna, 279, 454
urges peace, 304, 321
blesses Yudhiṣṭhira, 370
battles with Śikhaṇḍin, 462, 502
counsels Duryodhana, 526–7
one of three Kaurava survivors, 561
counsels Aśvatthāman, 565
Kṛṣṇa, xvi–xviii, xxxiv–xliv
supreme lord, xxxvi–xxxvii, 2, 112, 115–16, 200, 305, 336–7, 361–6, 380–81, 604, 633–4, 649, 663, 700, 708, see also Nārāyaṇa, Viṣṇu
birth of, 23, 74
recognizes Pāṇḍavas at Draupadī's *svayaṃvara*, 69, 71
counsels Arjuna to abduct his sister Subhadrā, 81
allows Fire to burn the Khāṇḍava forest, 82–3
receives discus, 82
counsels Yudhiṣṭhira to destroy Jarāsaṃdha, 90–94
hints to Bhīma to kill weakened Jarāsaṃdha, 101
insulted by Śiśupāla, 113–14, 116
kills Śiśupāla, 118
kills Śālva, 167
grants Arjuna his aid, Duryodhana his army, 295
envoy to the Kauravas, 305–39
urges peace, 320–23
offers Karṇa the Pāṇḍava kingship, 339
expounds the *Bhagavadgītā* to Arjuna, 354–66
asks Karṇa to change sides, 371
makes to battle with Bhīṣma, 375, 400
urges Arjuna to attack Bhūriśravas, xxxviii–xxxix, 446–7
sends Ghaṭotkaca to be killed by Karṇa's Spear of Indra, 463
advocates devious stratagems, xxxviii, 469, 560–61
rejoices at Ghaṭotkaca's death, xliii–xliv, 469
sows confusion in Karṇa's mind, 470
counsels *adharma* to kill Droṇa, xxxix, 475
urges Yudhiṣṭhira to lie to Droṇa, xliv, 477

counsels *adharma* to kill Duryodhana, xxxix–xli, 549–50
curses Aśvatthāman, 579
cursed by Gāndhārī, 593
urges Yudhiṣṭhira to hear about *dharma* from the dying Bhīṣma, 604
renders Bhīṣma comfortable and clear-minded, 605–6
recites the thousand names of Śiva, 672–3
expounds the *Anugītā* to Arjuna, 705–8
revives Parikṣit, 711–13
death of, 763
Kṛta Age, 18, 39, 194, 200–201, 353, 544, 545, 606, 609, 613, 639, 643, 660
Kṛtavarman
birth of, 22
gives Duryodhana his army, 295
battles with Sātyaki, 438, 537–8
battles with the Pāṇḍavas, 438–9
battles with Śikhaṇḍin, 492
one of three Kaurava survivors, 561
death of, 760
Kubera, 69, 87, 126, 170, 194–6, 211, 213, 298, 346, 610, 651, 673, 711, 741, 788
Kuntī, xv, xviii, xxiii–xxiv, 42
birth of, 23
receives *mantra* from Durvāsas, 42
gives birth to Karṇa, 42, 238
gives birth to the Pāṇḍavas, 44, 46–9
agrees to help Mādrī bear sons, 50
faints to see Karṇa and Arjuna fight, 56
recognizes Karṇa, 58
tells sons to share what they have won, 72–3
stays with Vidura during Pāṇḍavas' exile, 162
visited by Kṛṣṇa, 312, 338–9
offers Karṇa the Pāṇḍava kingship, 339
reunited with her sons, 587
reveals truth about Karṇa to her sons, 595
sets out for the forest, 740
visited in the forest by her sons, 742–53
death of, 753–4
Kuru, xliii, 28, 66, 548
Kurukṣetra, xvii, xliii, 2, 3, 79, 176, 248, 341, 344, 347–562, 583, 588, 604, 606, 740, 744, 768
Kurus, xv, xxii, 10, 23, 39–40, 48, 51, 104, 243, 248, 300, 305, 313, 340, 578–9, 583, 594, 665, 713, 714, 725, 748, 771

Lakṣmaṇa son of Daśaratha, 210–14
Lakṣmaṇa son of Duryodhana, 342, 419
battles with Abhimanyu, 374, 381
death of, 424–5

Mādrī
birth of, 23
weds Pāṇḍu, 43
gives birth to Nakula and Sahadeva, 44, 49–50
death of, 51

Matsya, Matsyas, 92, 105, 243–4, 247, 250, 255–8, 262, 264, 265, 270–72, 276, 278, 281, 289–92, 307, 377, 389, 420, 471, 474, 476, 530, 575, 752
*mokṣa*, see release, final

Nakula, xv, xxix, 193, 249, 461–2, 471, 491, 512, 527–8, 575–6, 626
  birth of, 22, 50
  vows to kill many of Dhṛtarāṣṭra's sons, 162
  disguises self as Granthika, 246, 256
  urges peace, 311
  battles with Karṇa, 491–2
  death of, 774
Nala, li–lii, 171–5
Nara, xxxvii, 1, 5, 82, 85, 143, 166, 170, 193, 303, 316–17, 381, 414, 432, 486, 514, 660, 663–4
Nārada, 69, 79–80, 86–9, 111–12, 163, 171, 176–7, 179, 198, 199, 217–21, 223, 232, 317–18, 320, 337, 345, 411, 548, 576, 580, 597–8, 601–2, 606, 611–12, 624–5, 638, 643, 647–8, 651, 655, 659–64, 666, 676–7, 683, 697, 701, 704, 706, 729, 741, 750, 753–6, 777, 779, 780, 790
Nārāyaṇa (divine seer), xxxvii, 1, 5, 83, 85, 143, 166, 170, 193, 195, 303, 316–17, 381, 414, 432, 484–6, 514, 660–64
Nārāyaṇa (highest god), xxxvii, 20, 23, 74, 112, 200, 240, 660–66, 697, 763, 773, see also Kṛṣṇa, Viṣṇu
*Nārāyaṇīya*, 660–66
Niṣādas, 6, 54, 61, 374, 607, 621, 679, 721

Pāñcāla, Pāñcālas, 28, 53, 58, 64–5, 75, 92, 105, 166, 171, 243, 247, 248, 343, 376, 377, 397, 398, 404, 408, 420, 440–41, 455, 459–60, 462–4, 471, 474–6, 486, 491, 501, 503, 506–9, 528, 530, 532, 552, 556–8, 561, 562, 565, 566, 574–5, 581, 583, 588, 589, 595, 752
Pāṇḍu, xv, xiii
  birth of, 38
  becomes king, 41
  weds Kuntī, 43
  weds Mādrī, 43
  birth of five sons, 44, 46–51
  death of, 51
Parāśara, 16–17, 37, 67–8, 652–3, 665
Parikṣit, xviii, xlviii, 4, 9, 579, 741, 749, 771–3
  death of, 8
  birth of, 578–9, 711–14
Passion, 204, 357, 366, 634–6, 641–2, 648, 653, 655, 661, 665
*pauruṣa*, see human effort
pleasure, 11, 12, 104, 322, 555, 601, 607, 619–20, 626, 646, 647, 651, 661, 701, 790, 791
Pradyumna, 93, 109, 337, 420, 480, 700, 724, 727, 760, 761
  birth of, 23
  battles with Śālva, 167
  death of, 761
Pratīpa, 28–30
Pṛthā, see Kuntī

*rajas*, see Passion
Rāma son of Daśaratha, lii, 194, 210–14, 662
Rāma son of Jamadagni, 17, 21, 33, 37, 49, 53, 64, 90, 91, 187–8, 237, 311, 316–17, 324, 344–5, 353, 494, 497, 517, 520, 547, 597–8, 604–5, 662, 680, 681, 687–8, 706
*Rāmāyaṇa*, xiv, xlvii, lii, lxv–lxvi
Rāvaṇa, 194, 210–14
release, final, lxiii–lxiv, 11, 12, 204, 209, 361, 582, 607, 626, 698, 705–7, 790, see also *dharma*
renouncers, 599, 600, 631, 646, 649, 707
renunciation, xii, 355, 360, 366, 547, 583, 599–600, 602, 608, 616, 625, 629, 636, 640–42, 646–7, 654, 689, 694, 733, 773
rivers of blood, lvi, 280, 377, 393, 396, 398, 415, 416, 430, 434, 437, 443, 458, 502, 506, 513, 527
Ṛśyaśṛṅga, lii, 180–87
Rukmiṇī, 118, 341, 671, 672, 700, 764, 768

Sahadeva, xv, xxix, 392, 539
  birth of, 22, 50
  vows to kill Śakuni, 162
  disguises self as Tantipāla, 246, 253–4
  urges war, 311
  battles with Karṇa, 461
  battles with Duḥśāsana, 471, 491
  kills Śakuni, 540
  special relationship with Kuntī, 740–42, 752, 754
  death of, 774
Śakuni, xvi, xxvii
  birth of, 21
  marries his sister Gāndhārī to Dhṛtarāṣṭra, 41
  attempts to console Duryodhana, 123
  proposes a gambling match against Yudhiṣṭhira, 124, 126, 128
  challenges Yudhiṣṭhira to gamble, 131–2, 159
  gambles with Yudhiṣṭhira, 132–40, 159
  uses powers of illusion on the battlefield, 418
  battles with Nakula, 461
  battles with Arjuna, 462
  battles with Sātyaki, 504
  battles with Bhīma, 506
  battles with the Pāṇḍavas, 539
  death of, 540
Śakuntalā, 24–5, 28
Śalya, xvii
  promises to support Duryodhana, 296
  promises Yudhiṣṭhira to act against Karṇa, 296, 298, 371
  blesses Yudhiṣṭhira, 370–71
  battles with Dhṛṣṭadyumna, 378
  battles with Nakula and Sahadeva, 392
  battles with Abhimanyu, 415, 426
  battles with Bhīma, 415, 528, 533–4
  battles with Virāṭa, 461
  reluctantly agrees to act as Karṇa's charioteer, 493–4
  insults Karṇa, 494–500
  urges Karṇa on, 507, 511
  blames fate, 524
  installed as commander, 527

Śalya – *cont.*
battles with Yudhiṣṭhira, 528–36
death of, 536
Samantapañcaka, see Kurukṣetra
Sāmba, 93, 109, 167, 291, 673, 724, 756–7
gives birth to iron club, 757
death of, 761
Saṃjaya, xlv
blames Dhṛtarāṣṭra, 163, 170, 380, 383–4, 392, 393, 433, 438, 439, 442, 443, 525, 582
envoy to the Pāṇḍavas, 299–300
reports to the Kauravas, 303–5
speaks to Dhṛtarāṣṭra of Kṛṣṇa, 305
urges peace, 321
narrates events of the war to Dhṛtarāṣṭra, 342–575
receives boon of divine sight from Vyāsa, 350
describes the earth to Dhṛtarāṣṭra, 352–3
blames fate, 470
survives war, 541
sets out for the forest, 740
leaves for Mount Himālaya, 754
Sāṃkhya, 204, 355, 365, 631, 634, 635, 640, 654–8, 665, 694, 707–8, 789
Śaṃtanu, 21, 28, 30–36, 53
weds Satyavatī, 35–6
*sattva*, see Goodness
Sātyaki, 93, 298, 390–91, 403, 444, 489–90
birth of, 21
urges war, 188, 311
battles with Bhūriśravas, 381–2, 444–7
battles with Droṇa, 435, 437–9
battles with Kṛtavarman, 438, 537–8
battles with Duḥśāsana, 439–40, 444
battles with Duryodhana, 439, 462, 473–4
battles with the Kauravas, 439–40, 480
kills Bhūriśravas, 449
battles with Karṇa, 454, 462, 509
battles with Somadatta, 458–60
kills Somadatta, 460
reviled by Dhṛṣṭadyumna, 485
reviles Dhṛṣṭadyumna, 485
death of, 760–61
Satyavat, 217–32
Satyavatī
birth of, 15–16
gives birth to Vyāsa, 16–17
weds Śaṃtanu, 35–6
gives birth to Citrāṅgada and Vicitravīrya, 36
arranges for Vyāsa to father heirs to the kingship, 37–8
death of, 51
Śaunaka, 1, 4–7, 9–10, 790
Sāvitrī, lii, 215–33
self, 302, 332, 356–7, 361, 362, 365, 604, 630–32, 635, 640–42, 644, 646, 648, 654–6, 660–67, 707, 791
Śikhaṇḍin
birth of, 22
initially a girl, 346
battles with Aśvatthāman, 390
shields Arjuna against Bhīṣma, 403–7
pierces Bhīṣma, 403, 405
battles with Kṛpa, 462, 502

battles with Kṛtavarman, 492
death of, 508
Śikhaṇḍinī, 346
Śiśupāla, 91, 105, 109, 113–19
insults Kṛṣṇa, 113–14
death of, 116–18
Sītā, 194, 210–14
Śiva, xxviii, xxxvi, 21, 41, 57, 65, 74, 79, 85, 87, 94, 95, 98, 169, 178–9, 196, 206, 208, 210, 267, 345–6, 424, 431–3, 435, 451, 486–7, 494, 512, 514, 535, 544, 546–7, 565–6, 581, 624, 643, 649–53, 658–60, 665, 672–3, 686–8, 697–8, 700, 704, 710–11, 786
thousand names of, 673
Somadatta, 451
urges peace, 157, 321
battles with Sātyaki, 458–60
death of, 460
Somakas, 334, 348–50, 367, 386, 393, 397, 398, 405, 408, 441, 453, 462, 476, 508, 509, 513, 515, 524, 530, 532, 552, 553, 566, 569, 574
*śrāddha* ceremony, 12, 14, 51, 387, 603, 628, 652, 664, 674, 686, 688–9, 691, 710, 733–5, 737–8, 755, 772, 790
Śrī, 5, 23, 74, 205, 637–8, 671, 686, 786
Sṛñjayas, 326, 393, 404–5, 419, 420, 455, 471, 475, 476, 481, 484, 491, 553, 557, 570, 574, 594
stages of life, xix, 27, 607–8, 616, 628, 631, 639, 641, 651, 658, 666, 667
Subhadrā, 708, 771
weds Arjuna, 81
gives birth to Abhimanyu, 81
grieves for Abhimanyu, 432, 710, 711
Sudeṣṇā, 247, 258–60, 263, 269, 270, 291
takes Draupadī as maidservant, 251–3
Śuka, 17, 638–42, 657–60, 686, 790
Śukra, 25–6, 134–6, 550, 649, 651–2, 692–3
Sun, 22, 42–3, 55, 56, 65–6, 87, 164, 175, 234–8, 240, 260–61, 340, 598, 656, 659, 666–7, 691, 745

Takṣaka, 3–4, 8–10, 82, 750
*tamas*, see Darkness
Tantipāla, see Arjuna
Tretā Age, 194, 200, 353, 609, 613, 639
Trigarta, Trigartas, 104, 105, 271, 276, 278, 281–2, 342, 378, 392, 397–8, 407, 415–17, 438, 440, 444, 460, 502, 540, 718

Ugraśravas, xliv–xlv, xlvii–xlix, 1–10, 749–50, 787–91
narrates the Mahābhārata, 3–791
Ulūpī, 80, 720–21, 727, 773
Umā, 69, 87, 650, 652, 673, 687, 697–8
Urvaśī, 25, 180
Uttamaujas, 434, 442, 465, 504, 506, 509, 568, 594
Uttaṅka, 3, 202, 708–9
Uttara, liii–liv, 272–82, 284–9
Uttarā, xvi, 255, 275, 283, 286, 288–90
weds Abhimanyu, 290–91
gives birth to Parikṣit, 711–13

Vaiśampāyana, xlv, xlviii–xlix, 2, 789, 790
narrates the Mahābhārata, 10–789
Vajra, 765, 766, 768, 771–2
Varuṇa, 82, 85, 87, 90, 91, 111, 125, 126, 152, 170–72, 191, 298, 317, 330, 336, 434, 457, 546, 548, 669, 687–8, 699, 762, 774
Vasiṣṭha, 21, 28, 31–3, 46, 66–8, 318, 352, 545, 547, 605, 610, 649, 655, 670, 686–8, 699
Vasu Uparicara, 12–15, 102, 660–61, 733
Vasudeva, 23, 42, 106, 113, 167, 558, 710, 721, 762–5
death of, 765
Vāsudeva, see Kṛṣṇa
Vāsuki, 5, 7–9
Vedas, xi, 2, 9–11, 17–18, 21, 33–4, 40, 50, 51, 53, 56, 78, 87, 106–8, 111, 115, 118, 132, 191, 230, 240, 287, 296, 302, 321, 324, 350, 354, 365, 476, 481, 545, 548, 585, 607–8, 611, 616, 619, 621, 624–6, 634, 639–43, 646, 654, 658–9, 661, 662, 664–6, 673, 676, 682, 689, 701, 718, 722, 724, 728, 739, 750, 783, 790
Vicitravīrya, 36–7, 343
Vidura, xxv
birth of, 22, 38–9
unequalled for knowledge and practice of *dharma*, 40
debarred from kingship through mixed parentage, 41
wedding of, 43
urges Dhṛtarāṣṭra to abandon Duryodhana, 45, 134–6
warns Pāṇḍavas of plot against them, 60
urges peace, 75, 127, 128, 157, 164, 301, 321, 335
envoy to the Pāṇḍavas, 76
counsels Dhṛtarāṣṭra, 301–2, 582–3
sets out for the forest, 740
death of, 743–4
enters Yudhiṣṭhira, 744
Vikarṇa, xxvii, 76, 272, 276, 279–81, 314, 338, 383, 384, 392, 393, 405
argues in favour of Draupadī, 146
urges peace, 157, 321
death of, 443
Virāṭa, xvi, liii
birth of, 22
employs the disguised Pāṇḍavas, 249–51, 253–6
battles with raiders from Trigarta, 271
strikes Yudhiṣṭhira, 284
learns the Pāṇḍavas' identity, 287–8
offers his daughter Uttarā to Arjuna, 289
battles with Droṇa, 389–90
battles with Śalya, 461
death of, 471
Viṣṇu, xvi, xxxvi, 2, 5, 7, 103, 178, 202, 211, 296–7, 317, 363, 427, 583, 607–8, 619, 633–4, 649, 658, 664, 698, 726, 769, see also Kṛṣṇa, Nārāyaṇa
Viśvāmitra, 24, 66, 318–19, 545, 605, 622, 669, 675, 756
Vṛṣṇis, 69, 81, 93, 109, 112, 114, 166–7, 291, 294, 330, 336, 337,

448, 537, 556, 593, 710, 711, 713, 714, 724, 752, 764
destruction of, 756–62
survivors leave with Arjuna, 766–8
Vyāsa, xv, xxiii, 2, 3, 10–12, 44–5, 63, 65, 73–4, 165, 169, 209, 352, 470, 486, 541, 576–80, 583, 586, 588, 600–602, 638–42, 657–60, 662–5, 695–6, 701, 703–4, 710, 714–17, 727–31, 735, 740–41, 744–50, 779, 787–91
birth of, 16–17, 37
fathers Dhṛtarāṣṭra, Pāṇḍu and Vidura, 37–9
offers Dhṛtarāṣṭra divine sight, 350
grants Saṃjaya divine sight, 350–51
curses Aśvatthāman, 579
shows the fallen warriors, 746–8
shows Janamejaya his father Parikṣit, 749
counsels Arjuna, 768–70

wealth, making of, 11–12, 15, 33, 104, 111, 168, 307, 313, 315, 316, 320, 322, 324, 329, 331, 332, 334, 410, 555, 601, 607, 619–21, 626, 629, 646–8, 651–3, 661, 701, 703, 716, 790
Weapons, see celestial weapons
Wind, 22, 24, 47, 74, 175, 609, 624–5, 698–9

Yādavas, 23, 27, 41, 42, 69, 97, 134, 330, 726, 759, 760, 762, 764, 769, 772
Yadu, 14, 25–7
Yadus, see Yādavas
Yājñavalkya, 107, 656–7, 715, 718
Yama, 25, 69, 74, 87, 126, 170–72, 223–7, 232, 298, 620, 631, 683–4
Yayāti, 25–8, 90, 318–20
Yoga, 47, 302, 361–2, 365, 408, 448, 482–3, 625, 631, 633, 640, 648, 649, 654–6, 658–9, 665, 705–6, 744, 759, 762–3, 765, 773–4, 789
Yudhāmanyu, 434, 442, 465, 504, 509, 568, 594
Yudhiṣṭhira, xv–xviii, xxx–xxxii
birth of, 22, 47
declares that all five brothers will wed Draupadī, 73
king in Indraprastha, 78
considers performing royal consecration, 89–90
performs royal consecration, 105–12
attempts to conciliate Śiśupāla, 114
installs Śiśupāla's son as king of Cedi, 119
receives challenge to gamble, 129, 158
gambles with Śakuni, 132–40, 159
stakes his brothers, 138–9
stakes himself, 139–40
stakes Draupadī, 140
argues for *dharma* and forbearance, 168
tours the sacred bathing-places, 176–95
disguises self as Kaṅka, 244, 249–50
struck by Virāṭa, 284
prepares for war, 293, 340, 348–9
pays respects to Bhīṣma, 368–9
pays respects to Droṇa, 369

Yudhiṣṭhira – *cont.*
asks Droṇa how he may be defeated, 370
pays respects to Śalya, 370–71
pays respects to Kṛpa, 370
battles with the Kauravas, 392–3, 415, 460
asks Bhīṣma how he may be defeated, 402
battles with Droṇa, 415, 437, 460
sends Abhimanyu against Droṇa's army, 420
lies to Droṇa, 477
battles with Duryodhana, 492
battles with Karṇa, 501
battles with Śalya, 528–36
kills Śalya, 536
challenges Duryodhana to fight, 541
performs the funeral rites, 593–4
grieved to learn truth about Karṇa, 595–6
overwhelmed with grief, 597–603, 703–5
regains kingdom, 603
hears Bhīṣma's deathbed sermon, 606–701
performs horse sacrifice, 710–32
entered by Vidura, 744
reaches heaven, 777–87
Yuyutsu, xxvii, 314, 338, 492, 583, 593, 735, 740, 742, 755, 771, 773
birth of, 46
wishes Pāṇḍavas well, 53
urges peace, 157
changes sides before battle, 372
last surviving son of Dhṛtarāṣṭra, 541

# PENGUIN CLASSICS

## THE BHAGAVAD GITA

'In death thy glory in heaven, in victory thy glory on earth.
Arise therefore, Arjuna, with thy soul ready to fight'

*The Bhagavad Gita* is an intensely spiritual work that forms the cornerstone of the Hindu faith, and is also one of the masterpieces of Sanskrit poetry. It describes how, at the beginning of a mighty battle between the Pandava and Kaurava armies, the god Krishna gives spiritual enlightenment to the warrior Arjuna, who realizes that the true battle is for his own soul.

Juan Mascaró's translation of *The Bhagavad Gita* captures the extraordinary aural qualities of the original Sanskrit. This edition features a new introduction by Simon Brodbeck, which discusses concepts such as dehin, prakriti and Karma.

'The task of truly translating such a work is indeed formidable. The translator must at least possess three qualities. He must be an artist in words as well as a Sanskrit scholar, and above all, perhaps, he must be deeply sympathetic with the spirit of the original. Mascaró has succeeded so well because he possesses all these'
*The Times Literary Supplement*

Translated by Juan Mascaró with an introduction by Simon Brodbeck

# PENGUIN CLASSICS

## BUDDHIST SCRIPTURES

'Whoever gives something for the good of others, with heart full of sympathy, not heeding his own good, reaps unspoiled fruit'

While Buddhism has no central text such as the Bible or the Koran, there is a powerful body of scripture from across Asia that encompasses the *dharma*, or the teachings of Buddha. This rich anthology brings together works from a broad historical and geographical range, and from languages such as Pali, Sanskrit, Tibetan, Chinese and Japanese. There are tales of the Buddha's past lives, a discussion of the qualities and qualifications of a monk, and an exploration of the many meanings of Enlightenment. Together they provide a vivid picture of the Buddha and of the vast nature of the Buddhist tradition.

This new edition contains many texts presented in English for the first time as well as new translations of some well-known works, and also includes an informative introduction and prefaces to each chapter by scholar of Buddhism Donald S. Lopez Jr, with suggestions for further reading and a glossary.

Edited with an introduction by Donald S. Lopez, Jr